Charlie Chan

FIVE COMPLETE NOVELS

Charlie Chan

FIVE COMPLETE NOVELS

by Earl Derr Biggers

The House Without a Key

The Chinese Parrot

Behind That Curtain

The Black Camel

Keeper of the Keys

AVENEL BOOKS · NEW YORK

This edition is published by Avenel Books,
distributed by Crown Publishers, Inc.,
by arrangement with Leisure Concepts, Inc.

h g f e d c b a

AVENEL 1981 EDITION

Manufactured in the United States of America

Library of Congress Cataloging in Publication Data

Biggers, Earl Derr, 1884-1933.
    Charlie Chan, five complete novels.

    Contents: The house without a key—The Chinese
parrot—Behind that curtain—[etc.]
    1. Detective and mystery stories, American. I. Title.
PS3503.I54A6   1981   813'.52   81-3570
ISBN 0-517-347075   AACR2

CONTENTS

The House Without a Key

To my mother and father

1

Kona Weather

Miss Minerva Winterslip was a Bostonian in good standing, and long past the romantic age. Yet beauty thrilled her still, even the semi-barbaric beauty of a Pacific island. As she walked slowly along the beach she felt the little catch in her throat that sometimes she had known in Symphony Hall, Boston, when her favorite orchestra rose to some new and unexpected height of loveliness.

It was the hour at which she liked Waikiki best, the hour just preceding dinner and the quick tropic darkness. The shadows cast by the tall cocoanut palms lengthened and deepened, the light of the falling sun flamed on Diamond Head and tinted with gold the rollers sweeping in from the coral reef. A few late swimmers, reluctant to depart, dotted those waters whose touch is like the caress of a lover. On the springboard of the nearest float a slim brown girl poised for one delectable instant. What a figure! Miss Minerva, well over fifty herself, felt a mild twinge of envy—youth, youth like an arrow, straight and sure and flying. Like an arrow the slender figure rose, then fell; the perfect dive, silent and clean.

Miss Minerva glanced at the face of the man who walked beside her. But Amos Winterslip was oblivious to beauty, he had made that the first rule of his life. Born in the Islands, he had never known the mainland beyond San Francisco. Yet there could be no doubt about it, he was the New England conscience personified—the New England conscience in a white duck suit.

"Better turn back, Amos," suggested Miss Minerva. "Your dinner's waiting. Thank you so much."

"I'll walk as far as the fence," he said. "When you get tired of Dan and his carryings-on, come to us again. We'll be glad to have you."

"That's kind of you," she answered, in her sharp crisp way. "But I really must go home. Grace is worried about me. Of course, she can't understand. And my conduct *is* scandalous, I admit. I came over to Honolulu for six weeks, and I've been wandering about these islands for ten months."

"As long as that?"

She nodded. "I can't explain it. Every day I make a solemn vow I'll start packing my trunks—to-morrow."

"And to-morrow never comes," said Amos. "You've been taken in by the tropics. Some people are."

"Weak people, I presume you mean," snapped Miss Minerva. "Well, I've never been weak. Ask anybody on Beacon Street."

He smiled wanly. "It's a strain in the Winterslips," he said. "Supposed to be Puritans, but always sort of yearning toward the lazy latitudes."

"I know," answered Miss Minerva, her eyes on that exotic shore line.

"It's what sent so many of them adventuring out of Salem harbor. Those who stayed behind felt that the travelers were seeing things no Winterslip should look at. But they envied them just the same—or maybe for that very reason." She nodded. "A sort of gypsy strain. It's what sent your father over here to set up as a whaler, and got you born so far from home. You know you don't belong here, Amos. You should be living in Milton or Roxbury, carrying a little green bag and popping into a Boston office every morning."

"I've often thought it," he admitted. "And who knows—I might have made something of my life—"

They had come to a barbed-wire fence, an unaccustomed barrier on that friendly shore. It extended well down on to the beach; a wave rushed up and lapped the final post, then receded.

Miss Minerva smiled. "Well, this is where Amos leaves off and Dan begins," she said. "I'll watch my chance and run around the end. Lucky you couldn't build it so it moved with the tide."

"You'll find your luggage in your room at Dan's, I guess," Amos told her. "Remember what I said about—" He broke off suddenly. A stocky, white-clad man had appeared in the garden beyond the barrier, and was moving rapidly toward them. Amos Winterslip stood rigid for a moment, an angry light flaming in his usually dull eyes. "Good-by," he said, and turned.

"Amos!" cried Miss Minerva sharply. He moved on, and she followed. "Amos, what nonsense! How long has it been since you spoke to Dan?"

He paused under an algaroba tree. "Thirty-one years," he said. "Thirty-one years the tenth of last August."

"That's long enough," she told him. "Now, come around that foolish fence of yours, and hold out your hand to him."

"Not me," said Amos. "I guess you don't know Dan, Minerva, and the sort of life he's led. Time and again he's dishonored us all—"

"Why, Dan's regarded as a big man," she protested. "He's respected—"

"And rich," added Amos bitterly. "And I'm poor. Yes, that's the way it often goes in this world. But there's a world to come, and over there I reckon Dan's going to get his."

Hardy soul though she was, Miss Minerva was somewhat frightened by the look of hate on his thin face. She saw the uselessness of further argument. "Good-by, Amos," she said. "I wish I might persuade you to come East some day—" He gave no sign of hearing, but hurried along the white stretch of sand.

When Miss Minerva turned, Dan Winterslip was smiling at her from beyond the fence. "Hello, there," he cried. "Come this side of the wire and enjoy life again. You're mighty welcome."

"How are you, Dan?" She watched her chance with the waves and joined him. He took both her hands in his.

"Glad to see you," he said, and his eyes backed him up. Yes, he did have a way with women. "It's a bit lonely at the old homestead these days. Need a young girl about to brighten things up."

Miss Minerva sniffed. "I've tramped Boston in galoshes too many winters," she reminded him, "to lose my head over talk like that."

"Forget Boston," he urged. "We're all young in Hawaii. Look at me."

She did look at him, wonderingly. He was sixty-three, she knew, but only the mass of wavy white hair overhanging his temples betrayed his age. His face, burned to the deepest bronze by long years of wandering under the Polynesian sun, was without a line or wrinkle. Deep-chested and muscular, he could have passed on the mainland for a man of forty.

"I see my precious brother brought you as far as the dead-line," he remarked as they moved on through the garden. "Sent me his love, I presume?"

"I tried to get him to come round and shake hands," Miss Minerva said.

Dan Winterslip laughed. "Don't deprive poor Amos of his hate for me," he urged. "It's about all he lives for now. Comes over every night and stands under that algaroba tree of his, smoking cigarettes and staring at my house. Know what he's waiting for? He's waiting for the Lord to strike me down for my sins. Well, he's a patient waiter, I'll say that for him."

Miss Minerva did not reply. Dan's great rambling house of many rooms was set in beauty almost too poignant to be borne. She stood, drinking it all in again, the poinciana trees like big crimson umbrellas, the stately golden glow, the gigantic banyans casting purple shadows, her favorite hau tree, seemingly old as time itself, covered with a profusion of yellow blossoms. Loveliest of all were the flowering vines, the bougainvillea burying everything it touched in brick-red splendor. Miss Minerva wondered what her friends who every spring went into sedate ecstasies over the Boston Public Gardens would say if they could see what she saw now. They would be a bit shocked, perhaps, for this was too lurid to be quite respectable. A scarlet background—and a fitting one, no doubt, for Cousin Dan.

They reached the door at the side of the house that led directly into the living-room. Glancing to her right, Miss Minerva caught through the lush foliage glimpses of the iron fence and tall gates that fronted on Kalia Road. Dan opened the door for her, and she stepped inside. Like most apartments of its sort in the Islands, the living-room was walled on but three sides, the fourth was a vast expanse of wire screening. They crossed the polished floor and entered the big hall beyond. Near the front door a Hawaiian woman of uncertain age rose slowly from her chair. She was a huge, high-breasted, dignified specimen of that vanishing race.

"Well, Kamaikui, I'm back," Miss Minerva smiled.

"I make you welcome," the woman said. She was only a servant, but she spoke with the gracious manner of a hostess.

"Same room you had when you first came over, Minerva," Dan Winterslip announced. "Your luggage is there—and a bit of mail that came in on the boat this morning. I didn't trouble to send it up to Amos's. We dine when you're ready."

"I'll not keep you long," she answered, and hurried up the stairs.

Dan Winterslip strolled back to his living-room. He sat down in a rattan chair that had been made especially for him in Hong-Kong, and glanced complacently about at the many evidences of his prosperity. His butler entered, bearing a tray with cocktails.

"Two, Haku?" smiled Winterslip. "The lady is from Boston."

"Yes-s," hissed Haku, and retired soundlessly.

In a moment Miss Minerva came again into the room. She carried a letter in her hand, and she was laughing.

"Dan, this is too absurd," she said.

"What is?"

"I may have told you that they are getting worried about me at home. Because I haven't been able to tear myself away from Honolulu, I mean. Well, they're sending a policeman for me."

"A policeman?" He lifted his bushy eyebrows.

"Yes, it amounts to that. It's not being done openly, of course. Grace writes that John Quincy has six weeks' vacation from the banking house, and has decided to make the trip out here. 'It will give you some one to come home with, my dear,' says Grace. Isn't she subtle?"

"John Quincy Winterslip? That would be Grace's son."

Miss Minerva nodded. "You never met him, did you, Dan? Well, you will, shortly. And he certainly won't approve of you."

"Why not?" Dan Winterslip bristled.

"Because he's proper. He's a dear boy, but oh, so proper. This journey is going to be a great cross for him. He'll start disapproving as he passes Albany, and think of the long weary miles of disapproval he'll have to endure after that."

"Oh, I don't know. He's a Winterslip, isn't he?"

"He is. But the gypsy strain missed him completely. He's all Puritan."

"Poor boy." Dan Winterslip moved toward the tray on which stood the amber-colored drinks. "I suppose he'll stop with Roger in San Francisco. Write him there and tell him I want him to make this house his home while he's in Honolulu."

"That's kind of you, Dan."

"Not at all. I like youth around me—even the Puritan brand. Now that you're going to be apprehended and taken back to civilization, you'd better have one of these cocktails."

"Well," said his guest, "I'm about to exhibit what my brother used to call true Harvard indifference."

"What do you mean?" asked Winterslip.

"I don't mind if I do," twinkled Miss Minerva, lifting a cocktail glass.

Dan Winterslip beamed upon her. "You're a good sport, Minerva," he remarked, as he escorted her across the hall.

"When in Rome," she answered, "I make it a point not to do as the Bostonians do. I fear it would prove a rather thorny path to popularity."

"Precisely."

"Besides, I shall be back in Boston soon. Tramping about to art exhibits and Lowell Lectures, and gradually congealing into senility."

But she was not in Boston now, she reflected, as she sat down at the gleaming table in the dining-room. Before her, properly iced, was a generous slice of papaia, golden yellow and inviting. Somewhere beyond the foliage outside the screens, the ocean murmured restlessly. The dinner would be perfect, she knew, the Island beef dry and stringy, perhaps, but the fruits and the salad more than atoning.

"Do you expect Barbara soon?" she inquired presently.

Dan Winterslip's face lighted like the beach at sunrise. "Yes, Barbara has graduated. She'll be along any day now. Nice if she and your perfect nephew should hit on the same boat."

"Nice for John Quincy, at any rate," Miss Minerva replied. "We thought Barbara a lively charming girl when she visited us in the East."

"She's all of that," he agreed proudly. His daughter was his dearest possession. "I tell you, I've missed her. I've been mighty lonesome."

Miss Minerva gave him a shrewd look. "Yes, I've heard rumors," she remarked, "about how lonesome you've been."

He flushed under his tan. "Amos, I suppose?"

"Oh, not only Amos. A great deal of talk, Dan. Really, at your age—"

"What do you mean, my age? I told you we're all young out here." He ate in silence for a moment. "You're a good sport—I said it and I meant it. You must understand that here in the Islands a man may behave a—a bit differently than he would in the Back Bay."

"At that," she smiled, "all men in the Back Bay are not to be trusted. I'm not presuming to rebuke you, Dan. But—for Barbara's sake—why not select as the object of your devotion a woman you could marry?"

"I could marry this one—if we're talking about the same woman."

"The one I refer to," Miss Minerva replied, "is known, rather widely, as the Widow of Waikiki."

"This place is a hotbed of gossip. Arlene Compton is perfectly respectable."

"A former chorus girl, I believe."

"Not precisely. An actress—small parts—before she married Lieutenant Compton."

"And a self-made widow."

"Just what do you mean by that?" he flared. His gray eyes glittered.

"I understand that when her husband's aeroplane crashed on Diamond Head, it was because he preferred it that way. She had driven him to it."

"Lies, all lies!" Dan Winterslip cried. "Pardon me, Minerva, but you mustn't believe all you hear on the beach." He was silent for a moment. "What would you say if I told you I proposed to marry this woman?"

"I'm afraid I'd become rather bromidic," she answered gently, "and remind you that there's no fool like an old fool." He did not speak. "Forgive me, Dan. I'm your first cousin, but a distant relative for all that. It's really none of my business. I wouldn't care—but I like you. And I'm thinking of Barbara—"

He bowed his head. "I know," he said, "Barbara. Well, there's no need to get excited. I haven't said anything to Arlene about marriage. Not yet."

Miss Minerva smiled. "You know, as I get on in years," she remarked, "so many wise old saws begin to strike me as utter nonsense. Particularly that one I just quoted." He looked at her, his eyes friendly again. "This is the best avocado I ever tasted," she added. "But tell me, Dan, are you sure the mango is a food? Seems more like a spring tonic to me."

By the time they finished dinner the topic of Arlene Compton was forgotten and Dan had completely regained his good nature. They had coffee on his veranda—or, in Island parlance, lanai—which opened off one end of the living-room. This was of generous size, screened on three sides and stretching far down on to the white beach. Outside the brief tropic dusk dimmed the bright colors of Waikiki.

"No breeze stirring," said Miss Minerva.

"The trades have died," Dan answered. He referred to the beneficent winds which—save at rare, uncomfortable intervals—blow across the Islands out of the cool northeast. "I'm afraid we're in for a stretch of Kona weather."

"I hope not," Miss Minerva said.

"It saps the life right out of me nowadays," he told her, and sank into a chair. "That about being young, Minerva—it's a little bluff I'm fond of."

She smiled gently. "Even youth finds the Kona hard to endure," she comforted. "I remember when I was here before—in the 'eighties. I was only nineteen, but the memory of the sick wind lingers still."

"I missed you then, Minerva."

"Yes. You were off somewhere in the South Seas."

"But I heard about you when I came back. That you were tall and blonde and lovely, and nowhere near so prim as they feared you were going to be. A wonderful figure, they said—but you've got that yet."

She flushed, but smiled still. "Hush, Dan. We don't talk that way where I come from."

"The 'eighties," he sighed. "Hawaii was Hawaii then. Unspoiled, a land of opera bouffe, with old Kalakaua sitting on his golden throne."

"I remember him," Miss Minerva said. "Grand parties at the palace. And the afternoons when he sat with his disreputable friends on the royal lanai, and the Royal Hawaiian Band played at his feet, and he haughtily tossed them royal pennies. It was such a colorful, naive spot then, Dan."

"It's been ruined," he complained sadly. "Too much aping of the mainland. Too much of your damned mechanical civilization—automobiles, phonographs, radios—bah! And yet—and yet, Minerva—away down underneath there are deep dark waters flowing still."

She nodded, and they sat for a moment busy with their memories. Presently Dan Winterslip snapped on a small reading light at his side. "I'll just glance at the evening paper, if you don't mind."

"Oh, do," urged Miss Minerva.

She was glad of a moment without talk. For this, after all, was the time she loved Waikiki best. So brief, this tropic dusk, so quick the coming of the soft alluring night. The carpet of the waters, apple-green by day, crimson and gold at sunset, was a deep purple now. On top of that extinct volcano called Diamond Head a yellow eye was winking, as though to hint there might still be fire beneath. Three miles down, the harbor lights began to twinkle, and out toward the reef the lanterns of Japanese sampans glowed intermittently. Beyond, in the roadstead, loomed the battered hulk of an old brig slowly moving toward the channel entrance. Always, out there, a ship or two, in from the East with a cargo of spice or tea or ivory, or eastward bound with a load of tractor salesmen. Ships of all sorts, the spic and span liner and the rakish tramp, ships from Melbourne and Seattle, New York and Yokohama, Tahiti and Rio, any port on the seven seas. For this was Honolulu, the Crossroads of the Pacific—the glamorous crosswords where, they said, in time all paths crossed again. Miss Minerva sighed.

She was conscious of a quick movement on Dan's part. She turned and looked at him. He had laid the paper on his knee, and was staring straight ahead. That bluff about being young—no good now. For his face was old, old.

"Why, Dan—" she said.

"I—I'm wondering, Minerva," he began slowly. "Tell me again about that nephew of yours."

She was surprised, but hid it. "John Quincy?" she said. "He's just the usual thing, for Boston. Conventional. His whole life has been planned for him, from the cradle to the grave. So far he's walked the line. The inevitable preparatory school, Harvard, the proper clubs, the family banking house—even gone and got himself engaged to the very girl his mother would have picked for him. There have been times when I hoped he might kick over—the war—but no, he came back and got meekly into the old rut."

"Then he's reliable—steady?"

Miss Minerva smiled. "Dan, compared with that boy, Gibraltar wobbles occasionally."

"Discreet, I take it?"

"He invented discretion. That's what I'm telling you. I love him—but a little bit of recklessness now and then—However, I'm afraid it's too late now. John Quincy is nearly thirty."

Dan Winterslip was on his feet, his manner that of a man who had made an important decision. Beyond the bamboo curtain that hung in the door leading to the living-room a light appeared. "Haku!" Winterslip called. The Japanese servant came swiftly.

"Haku, tell the chauffeur—quick—the big car! I must get to the dock before the *President Tyler* sails for San Francisco. Wikiwiki!"

The servant disappeared into the living-room, and Winterslip followed. Somewhat puzzled, Miss Minerva sat for a moment, then rose and pushed aside the curtain. "Are you sailing, Dan?" she asked.

He was seated at his desk, writing hurriedly. "No, no—just a note—I must get it off on that boat—"

There was an air of suppressed excitement about him. Miss Minerva stepped over the threshold into the living-room. In another moment Haku appeared with an announcement that was unnecessary, for the engine of an automobile was humming in the drive. Dan Winterslip took his hat from Haku. "Make yourself at home, Minerva—I'll be back shortly," he cried, and rushed out.

Some business matter, no doubt. Miss Minerva strolled aimlessly about the big airy room, pausing finally before the portrait of Jedediah Winterslip, the father of Dan and Amos, and her uncle. Dan had had it painted from a photograph after the old man's death; it was the work of an artist whose forte was reputed to be landscapes—oh, it must assuredly have been landscapes, Miss Minerva thought. But even so there was no mistaking the power and personality of this New Englander who had set up in Honolulu as a whaler. The only time she had seen him, in the 'eighties, he had been broken and old, mourning his lost fortune, which had gone with his ships in an Arctic disaster a short time before.

Well, Dan had brought the family back, Miss Minerva reflected. Won again that lost fortune and much more. There were queer rumors about his methods—but so there were about the methods of Bostonians who had never strayed from home. A charming fellow, whatever his past. Miss Minerva sat down at the grand piano and played a few old familiar bars—*The Beautiful Blue Danube*. Her thoughts went back to the 'eighties.

Dan Winterslip was thinking of the 'eighties too as his car sped townward along Kalakaua Avenue. But it was the present that concerned him when they reached the dock and he ran, panting a little, through a dim pier-shed toward the gangplank of the *President Tyler*. He had no time to spare, the ship was on the point of sailing. Since it was a through boat from the Orient it left without the ceremonies that attend the departure of a liner plying only between Honolulu and the mainland. Even so, there were cries of "Aloha," some hearty and some tremulous, most of the travelers were bedecked with leis, and a confused little crowd milled about the foot of the plank.

Dan Winterslip pushed his way forward and ran up the sharp incline. As he reached the dock he encountered an old acquaintance, Hepworth, the second officer.

"You're the man I'm looking for," he cried.

"How are you, sir," Hepworth said. "I didn't see your name on the list."

"No, I'm not sailing. I'm here to ask a favor."

"Glad to oblige, Mr. Winterslip."

Winterslip thrust a letter into his hand. "You know my cousin Roger in 'Frisco. Please give him that—him and no one else—as soon after you land as you possibly can. I'm too late for the mail—and I prefer this way anyhow. I'll be mighty grateful."

"Don't mention it—you've been very kind to me and I'll be only too happy—I'm afraid you'll have to go ashore, sir. Just a minute, there—" He took Winterslip's arm and gently urged him back on to the plank. The instant Dan's feet touched the dock, the plank was drawn up behind him.

For a moment he stood, held by the fascination an Islander always feels at sight of a ship outward bound. Then he turned and walked slowly through the pier-shed. Ahead of him he caught a glimpse of a slender lithe figure which he recognized at once as that of Dick Kaohla, the grandson of Kamaikui. He quickened his pace and joined the boy.

"Hello, Dick," he said.

"Hello." The brown face was sullen, unfriendly.

"You haven't been to see me for a long time," Dan Winterslip said. "Everything all right?"

"Sure," replied Kaohla. "Sure it's all right." They reached the street, and the boy turned quickly away. "Good night," he muttered.

Dan Winterslip stood for a moment, thoughtfully looking after him. Then he got into the car. "No hurry now," he remarked to the chauffeur.

When he reappeared in his living-room, Miss Minerva glanced up from the book she was reading. "Were you in time, Dan?" she asked.

"Just made it," he told her.

"Good," she said, rising. "I'll take my book and go up-stairs. Pleasant dreams."

He waited until she reached the door before he spoke. "Ah—Minerva—don't trouble to write your nephew about stopping here."

"No, Dan?" she said, puzzled again.

"No. I've attended to the invitation myself. Good night."

"Oh—good night," she answered, and left him.

Alone in the great room, he paced restlessly back and forth over the polished floor. In a moment he went out on to the lanai, and found the newspaper he had been reading earlier in the evening. He brought it back to the living-room and tried to finish it, but something seemed to trouble him. His eyes kept straying—straying—with a sharp exclamation he tore one corner from the shipping page, savagely ripped the fragment to bits.

Again he got up and wandered about. He had intended paying a call down the beach, but that quiet presence in the room above—Boston in its more tolerant guise but Boston still—gave him pause.

He returned to the lanai. There, under a mosquito netting, was the cot where he preferred to sleep; his dressing-room was near at hand. However, it was too early for bed. He stepped through the door on to the beach. Unmistakable, the soft treacherous breath of the Kona fanned his cheek—the "sick wind" that would pile the breakers high along the coast and blight temporarily this Island paradise. There was no moon, the stars that usually seemed so friendly and so close were now obscured. The black water rolled in like a threat. He stood staring out into the dark—out there to the cross-roads where paths always crossed again. If you gave them time—if you only gave them time—

As he turned back, his eyes went to the algaroba tree beyond the wire, and he saw the yellow flare of a match. His brother Amos. He had a sudden friendly feeling for Amos, he wanted to go over and talk to him, talk of the far days when they played together on this beach. No use, he knew. He sighed, and the screen door of the lanai banged behind him—the screen door without a lock in a land where locks are few.

Tired, he sat in the dark to think. His face was turned toward the curtain of bamboo between him and the living-room. On that curtain a shadow appeared, was motionless a second, then vanished. He caught his breath—again the shadow. "Who's there?" he called

A huge brown arm was thrust through the bamboo. A friendly brown face was framed there.

"Your fruit I put on the table," said Kamaikui. "I go to bed now."

"Of course. Go ahead. Good night."

The woman withdrew. Dan Winterslip was furious with himself. What was the matter with him, anyhow? He who had fought his way through unspeakable terrors in the early days—nervous—on edge—

"Getting old," he muttered. "No, by heaven—it's the Kona. That's it. The Kona. I'll be all right when the trades blow again."

When the trades blew again! He wondered. Here at the crossroads one could not be sure.

2

The High Hat

John Quincy Winterslip walked aboard the ferry at Oakland feeling rather limp and weary. For more than six days he had been marooned on sleepers—his pause at Chicago had been but a flitting from one train to another—and he was fed up. Seeing America first—that was what he had been doing. And what an appalling lot of it there was! He felt that for an eternity he had been staring at endless plains, dotted here and there by unesthetic houses the inmates of which had unquestionably never heard a symphony concert.

Ahead of him ambled a porter, bearing his two suitcases, his golf clubs and his hat-box. One of the man's hands was gone—chewed off, no doubt, in some amiable frontier scuffle. In its place he wore a steel hook. Well, no one could question the value of a steel hook to a man in the porter's profession. But how quaint—and western!

The boy indicated a spot by the rail on the forward deck, and the porter began to unload. Carefully selecting the man's good hand, John Quincy dropped into it a tip so generous as to result in a touching of hook to cap in a weird salute. The object of this attention sank down amid his elaborate trappings, removed the straw hat from his perspiring head, and tried to figure out just what had happened to him.

Three thousand miles from Beacon Street, and two thousand miles still to go! Why, he inquired sourly of his usually pleasant self, had he ever agreed to make this absurd expedition into heathen country? Here it was late June, Boston was at its best. Tennis at Longwood, long mild evenings in a single shell on the Charles, weekends and golf with Agatha Parker at Magnolia. And if one must travel, there was Paris. He hadn't seen Paris in two years and had been rather planning a quick run over, when his mother had put this preposterous notion into his head.

Preposterous—it was all of that. Traveling five thousand miles just as a gentle hint to Aunt Minerva to return to her calm, well-ordered life behind purple window-panes on Beacon Street. And was there any chance that his strong-minded relative would take the hint? Not one in a thousand. Aunt Minerva was accustomed to do as she pleased—he had an uncomfortable, shocked recollection of one occasion when she had said she would do as she damn well pleased.

John Quincy wished he was back. He wished he was crossing Boston Common to his office on State Street, there to put out a new issue of bonds. He was not yet a member of the firm—that was an honor accorded only to Winterslips who were bald and a little stooped—but his heart was in his work. He put out a bond issue with loving apprehension, waiting for the verdict as a playwright waits behind the scenes on a first night. Would those First Mortgage Sixes go over big, or would they flop at his feet?

The hoarse boom of a ferry whistle recalled John Quincy to his present unbelievable location on the map. The boat began to move. He was dimly conscious of a young person of feminine gender who came and sat at his side. Away from the slip and out into the harbor the ferry carried John Quincy, and he suddenly sat up and took notice, for he was never blind to beauty, no matter where he encountered it.

And he was encountering beauty now. The morning air was keen and dry and bright. Spread out before him was that harbor which is like a tired navigator's dream come true. They passed Goat Island, and he heard the faint echo of a bugle, he saw Tamalpias lifting its proud head toward the sparkling sky, he turned, and there was San Francisco scattered blithely over its many hills.

The ferry plowed on, and John Quincy sat very still. A forest of masts and steam funnels—here was the water front that had supplied the atmosphere for those romantic tales that held him spellbound when he was a boy at school—a quiet young Winterslip whom the gypsy strain had missed. Now he could distinguish a bark from Antwerp, a great liner from the Orient, a five-masted schooner that was reminiscent of those supposedly forgotten stories. Ships from the Treaty Ports, ships from cocoanut islands in southern seas. A picture as intriguing and colorful as a back drop in a theater—but far more real.

Suddenly John Quincy stood up. A puzzled look had come into his calm gray eyes. "I—I don't understand," he murmured.

He was startled by the sound of his own voice. He hadn't intended to speak aloud. In order not to appear too utterly silly, he looked around for some one to whom he might pretend he had addressed that remark. There was no one about—except the young person who was obviously feminine and therefore not to be informally accosted.

John Quincy looked down at her. Spanish or something like that, blue-black hair, dark eyes that were alight now with the amusement she was striving to hide, a delicate oval face tanned a deep brown. He looked again at the harbor—beauty all about the boat, and beauty on it. Much better than traveling on trains!

The girl looked up at John Quincy. She saw a big, broad-shouldered young man with a face as innocent as a child's. A bit of friendliness, she decided instantly, would not be misunderstood.

"I beg your pardon," she said.

"Oh—I—I'm sorry," he stammered. "I didn't mean—I spoke without intending—I said I didn't understand—"

"You didn't understand what?"

"A most amazing thing has happened," he continued. He sat down, and waved his hand toward the harbor. "I've been here before."

She looked perplexed. "Lots of people have," she admitted.

"But—you see—I mean—I've never been here before."

She moved away from him. "Lots of people haven't." She admitted that, too.

John Quincy took a deep breath. What was this discussion he had got into, anyhow? He had a quick impulse to lift his hat gallantly and walk away, letting the whole matter drop. But no, he came of a race that sees things through.

"I'm from Boston," he said.

"Oh," said the girl. That explained everything.

"And what I'm trying to make clear—although of course there's no reason why I should have dragged you into it—"

"None whatever," she smiled. "But go on."

"Until a few days ago I was never west of New York, never in my whole life, you understand. Been about New England a bit, and abroad a few times, but the West—"

"I know. It didn't interest you."

"I wouldn't say that," protested John Quincy with careful politeness. "But there was such a lot of it—exploring it seemed a hopeless undertaking. And then—the family thought I ought to go, you see—so I rode and rode on trains and was—you'll pardon me—a bit bored. Now—I come into this harbor, I look around me, and I get the oddest feeling. I feel that I've been here before."

The girl's face was sympathetic. "Other people have had that experience," she told him. "Choice souls, they are. You've been a long time coming, but you're home at last." She held out a slim brown hand. "Welcome to your city," she said.

John Quincy solemnly shook hands. "Oh, no," he corrected gently. "Boston's my city. I belong there, naturally. But this—this is familiar." He glanced northward at the low hills sheltering the Valley of the Moon, then back at San Francisco. "Yes, I seem to have known my way about here once. Astonishing, isn't it?"

"Perhaps—some of your ancestors—"

"That's true. My grandfather came out here when he was a young man. He went home again—but his brothers stayed. It's the son of one of them I'm going to visit in Honolulu."

"Oh—you're going on to Honolulu?"

"To-morrow morning. Have you ever been there?"

"Ye-es," Her dark eyes were serious. "See—there are the locks—that's where the East begins. The real East. And Telegraph Hill—" she pointed; no one in Boston ever points, but she was so lovely John Quincy overlooked it—"and Russian Hill, and the Fairmont on Nob Hill."

"Life must be full of ups and downs," he ventured lightly. "Tell me about Honolulu. Sort of a wild place, I imagine?"

She laughed. "I'll let you discover for yourself how wild it is," she told him. "Practically all the leading families came originally from your beloved New England. 'Puritans with a touch of sun,' my father calls them. He's clever, my father," she added, in an odd childish tone that was wistful and at the same time challenging.

"I'm sure of it," said John Quincy heartily. They were approaching the Ferry Building and other passengers crowded about them. "I'd help you with that suitcase of yours, but I've got all this truck. If we could find a porter—"

"Don't bother," she answered. "I can manage very well." She was staring down at John Quincy's hat box. "I—I suppose there's a silk hat in there?" she inquired.

"Naturally," replied John Quincy.

She laughed—a rich, deep-throated laugh. John Quincy stiffened slightly. "Oh, forgive me," she cried. "But—a silk hat in Hawaii!"

John Quincy stood erect. The girl had laughed at a Winterslip. He filled his lungs with the air sweeping in from the open spaces, the broad open spaces where men are men. A weird reckless feeling came over him. He stooped, picked up the hat box, and tossed it calmly over the rail. It bobbed indignantly away. The crowd closed in, not wishing to miss any further exhibition of madness.

"That's that," said John Quincy quietly.

"Oh," gasped the girl, "you shouldn't have done it."

And indeed, he shouldn't. The box was an expensive one, the gift of his admiring mother at Christmas. And the topper inside, worn in the gloaming along the water side of Beacon Street, had been known to add a touch of distinction even to that distinguished scene.

"Why not?" asked John Quincy. "The confounded thing's been a nuisance ever since I left home. And besides—we do look ridiculous at times, don't we? We easterners? A silk hat in the tropics! I might have been mistaken for a missionary." He began to gather up his luggage. "Shan't need a porter any more," he announced gaily. "I say—it was awfully kind of you—letting me talk to you like that."

"It was fun," she told him. "I hope you're going to like us out here. We're so eager to be liked, you know. It's almost pathetic."

"Well," smiled John Quincy, "I've met only one Californian to date. But—"

"Yes?"

"So far, so good!"

"Oh, thank you." She moved away.

"Please—just a moment," called John Quincy. "I hope—I mean, I wish—"

But the crowd surged between them. He saw her dark eyes smiling at him and then, irrevocably as the hat, she drifted from his sight.

3

Midnight on Russian Hill

A few moments later John Quincy stepped ashore in San Francisco. He had taken not more than three steps across the floor of the Ferry Building when a dapper Japanese chauffeur pushed through the crowd and singling out the easterner with what seemed uncanny perspicacity, took complete charge of him.

Roger Winterslip, the chauffeur announced, was too busy to meet ferries, but had sent word that the boy was to go up to the house and after establishing himself comfortably there, join his host for lunch down-town. Gratified to feel solid ground once more beneath his feet, John Quincy followed the chauffeur to the street. San Francisco glittered under the morning sun.

"I always thought this was a foggy town," John Quincy said.

The Japanese grinned. "Maybe fog will come, maybe it will not. Just now one time maybe it will not. Please." He held open the car door.

Through bright streets where life appeared to flow with a pleasant rhythm, they bowled along. Beside the curbs stood the colorful carts of the flower venders, unnecessarily painting the lily of existence. Weary traveler though he was, John Quincy took in with every breath a fresh supply of energy. New ambitions stirred within him, bigger, better bond issues than ever before seemed ridiculously easy of attainment.

Roger Winterslip had not been among those lured to suburban life down the peninsula; he resided in bachelor solitude on Nob Hill. It was an ancient, battered house viewed from without, but within, John Quincy found, were all known comforts. A bent old Chinese man showed him his room and his heart leaped up when he beheld, at last, a veritable bath.

At one o'clock he sought out the office where his relative carried on, with conspicuous success, his business as an engineer and builder. Roger proved a short florid man in his late fifties.

"Hello, son," he cried cordially. "How's Boston?"

"Every one is quite well," said John Quincy. "You're being extremely kind—"

"Nonsense. It's a pleasure to see you. Come along."

He took John Quincy to a famous club for lunch. In the grill he pointed out several well-known writers. The boy was not unduly impressed, for Longfellow, Whittier and Lowell were not among them. Nevertheless it was a pleasant place, the service perfect, the food of an excellence rare on the codfish coast.

"And what," asked Roger presently, "do you think of San Francisco?"

"I like it," John Quincy said simply.

"No? Do you really mean that?" Roger beamed. "Well, it's the sort of place that ought to appeal to a New Englander. It's had a history, brief, but believe me, my boy, one crowded hour of glorious life. It's sophisticated, knowing, subtle. Contrast it with other cities—for instance, take Los Angeles—"

He was off on a favorite topic and he talked well.

"Writers," he said at last, "are for ever comparing cities to women. San Francisco is the woman you don't tell the folks at home an awful lot about. Not that she wasn't perfectly proper—I don't mean that—but her stockings were just a little thinner and her laugh a little gayer—people might misunderstand. Besides, the memory is too precious to talk about. Hello."

A tall, lean, handsome Englishman was crossing the grill on his way out. "Cope! Cope, my dear fellow!" Roger sped after him and dragged him back. "I knew you at once," he was saying, "though it must be more than forty years since I last saw you."

The Britisher dropped into a chair. He smiled a wry smile. "My dear old chap," he said. "Not so literal, if you don't mind."

"Rot!" protested Roger. "What do years matter? This is a young cousin of mine, John Quincy Winterslip, of Boston. Ah—er—just what is your title now?"

"Captain. I'm in the Admiralty."

"Really? Captain Arthur Temple Cope, John Quincy." Roger turned to the Englishman. "You were a midshipman, I believe, when we met in Honolulu. I was talking to Dan about you not a year ago—"

An expression of intense dislike crossed the captain's face. "Ah, yes, Dan. Alive and prospering, I presume?"

"Oh, yes," answered Roger.

"Isn't it damnable," remarked Cope, "how the wicked thrive?"

An uncomfortable silence fell. John Quincy was familiar with the frankness of Englishmen, but he was none the less annoyed by this open display of hostility toward his prospective host. After all, Dan's last name was Winterslip.

"Ah—er—have a cigarette," suggested Roger.

"Thank you—have one of mine," said Cope, taking out a silver case. "Virginia tobacco, though they are put up in Piccadilly. No? And you, sir—" He held the case before John Quincy, who refused a bit stiffly.

The captain nonchalantly lighted up. "I beg your pardon—what I said about your cousin," he began. "But really, you know—"

"No matter," said Roger cordially. "Tell me what you're doing here."

"On my way to Hawaii," explained the captain. "Sailing at three to-day on the Australian boat. A bit of a job for the Admiralty. From Honoluly I drop down to the Fanning Group—a little flock of islands that belongs to us," he added with a fine paternal air.

"A possible coaling station," smiled Roger.

"My dear fellow—the precise nature of my mission is, of course, a secret." Captain Cope looked suddenly at John Quincy. "By the way, I once knew a very charming girl from Boston. A relative of yours, no doubt."

"A—a girl," repeated John Quincy, puzzled.

"Minerva Winterslip."

"Why," said John Quincy, amazed, "you mean my Aunt Minerva."

The captain smiled. "She was no one's aunt in those days," he said. "Nothing auntish about her. But that was in Honolulu in the 'eighties—we'd put in there on the old wooden *Reliance*—the poor unlucky ship was limping home crippled from Samoa. Your aunt was visiting at that port—there were dances at the palace, swimming parties—ah, me, to be young again."

"Minerva's in Honolulu now," Roger told him.

"No—really?"

"Yes. She's stopping with Dan."

"With Dan." The captain was silent for a moment. "Her husband—"

"Minerva never married," Roger explained.

"Amazing," said the captain. He blew a ring of smoke toward the paneled ceiling. "The more shame to the men of Boston. My time is hardly my own, but I shall hope to look in on her." He rose. "This was a bit of luck—meeting you again, old chap. I'm due aboard the boat very shortly—you understand, of course." He bowed to them both, and departed.

"Fine fellow," Roger said, staring after him. "Frank and British, but a splendid chap."

"I wasn't especially pleased," John Quincy admitted, "by the way he spoke of Cousin Dan."

Roger laughed. "Better get used to it," he advised. "Dan is not passionately beloved. He's climbed high, you know, and he's trampled down a few on his way up. By the way, he wants you to do an errand for him here in San Francisco."

"Me!" cried John Quincy. "An errand?"

"Yes. You ought to feel flattered. Dan doesn't trust everybody. However, it's something that must wait until dark."

"Until dark," repeated the puzzled young man from Boston.

"Precisely. In the meantime I propose to show you about town."

"But—you're busy. I couldn't think of taking you away—"

Roger laid his hand on John Quincy's shoulder. "My boy, no westerner is ever too busy to show a man from the East about his city. I've been looking forward to this chance for weeks. And since you insist on sailing to-morrow at ten, we must make the most of our time."

Roger proved an adept at making the most of one's time in San Francisco. After an exhilarating afternoon of motoring over the town and the surrounding country, he brought John Quincy back to the house at six, urging him to dress quickly for a dinner of which he apparently had great hopes.

The boy's trunk was in his room, and as he put on a dinner coat he looked forward with lively anticipation to a bit of San Francisco night life in Roger's company. When he came down-stairs his host was waiting, a distinguished figure in his dinner clothes, and they set out blithely through the gathering dusk.

"Little place I want you to try," Roger explained as they sat down at a table in a restaurant that was outwardly of no special note. "Afterward we'll look in on that musical show at the Columbia."

The restaurant more than justified Roger's hopes of it. John Quincy began to glow with a warm friendly feeling for all the world, particularly this city by the western gate. He did not think of himself as a stranger here. He wasn't a stranger, anyhow. The sensation he had first experienced in the harbor returned to him. He had been here before, he was treading old familiar ground. In far, forgotten, happy times he had known the life of this city's streets. Strange, but true. He spoke to Roger about it.

Roger smiled. "A Winterslip, after all," he said. "And they told me you were just a sort of—of Puritan survival. My father used to know that sensation you speak of, only he felt it whenever he entered a new town. Might be something in reincarnation, after all."

"Nonsense," said John Quincy.

"Probably. Just the blood of the roaming Winterslips in your veins." He leaned across the table. "How would you like to come to San Francisco to live?"

"Wha-what?" asked John Quincy, startled.

"I'm getting along in years, and I'm all alone. Lots of financial details in my office—take you in there and let you look after them. Make it worth your while.

"No, no, thank you," said John Quincy firmly. "I belong back east. Besides, I could never persuade Agatha to come out here."

"Agatha who?"

"Agatha Parker—the girl I'm engaged to—in a way. Been sort of understood between us for several years. No," he added, "I guess I'd better stay where I belong."

Roger Winterslip looked his disappointment. "Probably had," he admitted. "I fancy no girl with that name would follow you here. Though a girl worth having will follow her man anywhere—but no matter." He studied John Quincy keenly for a moment. "I must have been wrong about you, anyhow."

John Quincy felt a sudden resentment. "Just what do you mean by that?" he inquired.

"In the old days," Roger said, "Winterslips were the stuff of which pioneers are made. They didn't cling to the apron-strings of civilization. They got up some fine morning and nonchalantly strolled off beyond the horizon. They lived—but there, you're of another generation. You can't understand."

"Why can't I?" demanded John Quincy.

"Because the same old rut has evidently been good enough for you. You've never known a thrill. Or have you? Have you ever forgot to go to bed because of some utterly silly reason—because, for example, you were young and the moon was shining on a beach lapped by southern seas? Have you ever lied like a gentleman to protect a woman not worth the trouble? Ever made love to the wrong girl?"

"Of course not," said John Quincy stiffly.

"Ever run for your life through crooked streets in the rowdy quarter of a strange town? Ever fought with a ship's officer—the old-fashioned kind with fists like flying hams? Ever gone out on a man hunt and when you got your quarry cornered, leaped upon him with no weapon but your bare hands? Have you ever—"

"The type of person you describe," John Quincy cut in, "is hardly admirable."

"Probably not," Roger agreed. "And yet—those are incidents from my own past, my boy." He regarded John Quincy sadly. "Yes, I must have been wrong about you. A Puritan survival, after all."

John Quincy deigned no reply. There was an odd light in the older man's eyes—was Roger secretly laughing at him? He appeared to be, and the boy resented it.

But he forgot to be resentful at the revue, which proved to be witty and gay, and Roger and he emerged from the theater at eleven the best of friends again. As they stepped into Roger's car, the older man gave the chauffeur an address on Russian Hill.

"Dan's San Francisco house," he explained, as he climbed in after John

Quincy. "He comes over about two months each year, and keeps a place here. Got more money than I have."

Dan's San Francisco house? "Oh," said John Quincy, "the errand you mentioned?"

Roger nodded. "Yes." He snapped on a light in the top of the limousine, and took an envelope from his pocket. "Read this letter. It was delivered to me two days ago by the Second Officer of the *President Tyler*."

John Quincy removed a sheet of note paper from the envelope. The message appeared to be rather hastily scrawled.

"Dear Roger," he read. "You can do me a great service—you and that discreet lad from Boston who is to stop over with you on his way out here. First of all, give John Quincy my regards and tell him that he must make my house his home while he is in the Islands. I'll be delighted to have him.

"About the errand. You have a key to my house on Russian Hill. Go up there—better go at night when the caretaker's not likely to be around. The lights are off, but you'll find candles in the pantry. In the store room on the top floor is an old brown trunk. Locked, probably—smash the lock if it is. In the lower section you'll find a battered strong box made of ohia wood and bound with copper. Initials on it—T.M.B.

"Wrap it up and take it away. It's rather an armful, but you can manage it. Have John Quincy conceal it in his luggage and some dark night when the ship's about half-way over, I want him to take it on deck and quietly drop it overboard. Tell him to be sure nobody sees him. That's all. But send me a guarded cable when you get the box, and tell him to send me a radio when the Pacific has it at last. I'll sleep better then.

"Not a word, Roger. Not a word to any one. You'll understand. Sometimes the dead past needs a bit of help in burying its dead.

"YOUR COUSIN DAN."

Solemnly John Quincy handed the letter back into Roger's keeping. The older man thoughtfully tore it to bits and tossed them through the car window open beside him. "Well," said John Quincy. "Well—" A fitting comment eluded him.

"Simple enough," smiled Roger. "If we can help poor old Dan to sleep better as easily as that, we must do it, eh?"

"I—I suppose so," John Quincy agreed.

They had climbed Russian Hill, and were speeding along a deserted avenue lined by imposing mansions. Roger leaned forward. "Go on to the corner," he said to the chauffeur. "We can walk back," he explained to John Quincy. "Best not to leave the car before the house. Might excite suspicion."

Still John Quincy had no comment to make. They alighted at the corner and walked slowly back along the avenue. In front of a big stone house, Roger paused. He looked carefully in all directions, then ran with surprising speed up the steps. "Come on," he called softly.

John Quincy came. Roger unlocked the door and they stepped into a dark vestibule. Beyond that, darker still, was a huge hall, the dim suggestion of a grand staircase. Here and there an article of furniture, shrouded in white, stood like a ghost, marooned but patient. Roger took out a box of matches.

"Meant to bring a flashlight," he said, "but I clean forgot. Wait here—I'll hunt those candles in the pantry."

He went off into the dark. John Quincy took a few cautious steps. He was about to sit down on a chair—but it was like sitting on the lap of a ghost. He changed his mind, stood in the middle of the floor, waited. Quiet, deathly quiet. The black had swallowed Roger, with not so much as a gurgle.

After what seemed an age, Roger returned, bearing two lighted candles. One each, he explained. John Quincy took his, held it high. The flickering yellow flame accentuated the shadows, was really of small help.

Roger led the way up the grand staircase, then up a narrower flight. At the foot of still another flight, in a stuffy passage on the third floor, he halted.

"Here we are," he said. "This leads to the storage room under the roof. By gad, I'm getting too old for this sort of thing. I meant to bring a chisel to use on that lock. I know where the tools are—I'll be gone only a minute. You go on up and locate the trunk."

"All—all right," answered John Quincy.

Again Roger left him. John Quincy hesitated. Something about a deserted house at midnight to dismay the stoutest heart—but nonsense! He was a grown man. He smiled, and started up the narrow stair. High above his head the yellow light of the candle flickered on the brown rafters of the unfinished store room.

He reached the top of the stairs, and paused. Gloom, gloom everywhere. Odd how floor boards will creak even when no one is moving over them. One was creaking back of him now.

He was about to turn when a hand reached from behind and knocked the candle out of his grasp. It rolled on the floor, extinguished.

This was downright rude! "See here," cried John Quincy, "wh—who are you?"

A bit of moonlight struggled in through a far window, and suddenly between John Quincy and that distant light there loomed the determined figure of a man. Something told the boy he had better get ready, but where he came from one had a moment or two for preparation. He had none here. A fist shot out and found his face, and John Quincy Winterslip of Boston went down amid the rubbish of a San Francisco attic. He heard, for a second, the crash of planets in collision, and then the clatter of large feet on the stairs. After that, he was alone with the debris.

He got up, thoroughly angry, and began brushing off the dinner coat that had been his tailor's pride. Roger arrived. "Who was that?" he demanded breathlessly. "Somebody went down the back stairs to the kitchen. Who was it?"

"How should I know?" inquired John Quincy with pardonable peevishness. "He didn't introduce himself to me." His cheek was stinging; he put his handkerchief to it and noted in the light of Roger's candle that it was red when it came away. "He wore a ring," added John Quincy. "Damned bad taste!"

"Hit you, eh?" inquired Roger.

"I'll say he did."

"Look!" Roger cried. He pointed. "The trunk-lock smashed." He went over to investigate. "And the box is gone. Poor old Dan!"

John Quincy continued to brush himself off. Poor old Dan's plight gave him a vast pain, a pain which had nothing to do with his throbbing jaw. A fine nerve poor old Dan had to ask a complete stranger to offer his face for punishment in a dusty attic at midnight. What was it all about, anyhow?

Roger continued his search. "No use," he announced. "The box is gone, that's plain. Come on, we'll go down-stairs and look about. There's your candle on the floor."

John Quincy picked up the candle and relighted it from Roger's flame. Silently they went below. The outer door of the kitchen stood open. "Left that way," said Roger. "And see"—he pointed to a window with a broken pane—"that's where he came in."

"How about the police?" suggested John Quincy.

Roger stated at him. "The police? I should say not! Where's your discretion, my boy? This is not a police matter. I'll have a new glass put in that window to-morrow. Come on—we might as well go home. We've failed."

The note of reproof in his voice angered John Quincy anew. They left the extinguished candles on a table in the hall, and returned to the street.

"Well, I'll have to cable Dan," Roger said, as they walked toward the corner. "I'm afraid he'll be terribly upset by this. It won't tend to endear you to him, either."

"I can struggle along," said John Quincy, "without his affection."

"If you could only have held that fellow till I came—"

"Look here," said John Quincy, "I was taken unawares. How could I know that I was going up against the heavyweight champion in that attic? He came at me out of the dark—and I'm not in condition—"

"No offense, my boy," Roger put in.

"I see my mistake," went on John Quincy. "I should have trained for this trip out here. A stiff course in a gymnasium. But don't worry. The next lad that makes a pass at me will find a different target. I'll do a daily three dozen and I'll take boxing lessons. From now on until I get home, I'll be expecting the worst."

Roger laughed. "That's a nasty cut on your cheek," he remarked. "We'd better stop at this drug store and have it dressed."

A solicitous drug clerk ministered to John Quincy with iodine, cotton and court plaster, and he reentered the limousine bearing honorably the scar of battle. The drive to Nob Hill was devoid of light chatter.

Just inside the door of Roger's house, a whirlwind in a gay gown descended upon them. "Barbara!" Roger said. "Where did you come from?"

"Hello, old dear," she cried, kissing him. "I motored up from Burlingame. Spending the night with you—I'm sailing on the *President Tyler* in the morning. Is this John Quincy?"

"Cousin John," smiled Roger. "He deserves a kiss, too. He's had a bad evening."

The girl moved swiftly toward the defenseless John Quincy. Again he was unprepared, and this time it was his other cheek that suffered, though not unpleasantly. "Just by way of welcome," Barbara laughed. She was blonde and slender. John Quincy thought he had never seen so much energy imprisoned in so slight a form. "I hear you're bound for the Islands?" she said.

"To-morrow," John Quincy answered. "On your boat."

"Splendid!" she cried. "When did you get in?"

"John Quincy came this morning," Roger told her.

"And he's had a bad evening?" the girl said. "How lucky I came along. Where are you taking us, Roger?"

John Quincy stared. Taking them? At this hour?

"I'll be getting along up-stairs," he ventured.

"Why, it's just after twelve," said Barbara. "Lots of places open. You dance, don't you? Let me show you San Francisco. Roger's a dear old thing—we'll let him pay the checks."

"Well—I—I—" stammered John Quincy. His cheek was throbbing and he thought longingly of that bed in the room up-stairs. What a place, this West!

"Come along!" The girl was humming a gay little tune. All vivacity, all life. Rather pleasant sort at that. John Quincy took up his hat.

Roger's chauffeur had lingered a moment before the house to inspect his engine. When he saw them coming down the steps, he looked as though he rather wished he hadn't. But escape was impossible; he climbed to his place behind the wheel.

"Where to, Barbara?" Roger asked. "Tait's?"

"Not Tait's," she answered. "I've just come from there."

"What! I thought you motored in from Burlingame?"

"So I did—at five. I've traveled a bit since then. How about some chop-suey for this Boston boy?"

Good lord, John Quincy thought. Was there anything in the world he wanted less? No matter. Barbara took him among the Chinese.

He didn't give a hang about the Chinese. Nor the Mexicans, whose restaurants interested the girl next. At the moment, he was unsympathetic toward Italy. And even toward France, But he struggled on the international round, affronting his digestion with queer dishes, and dancing thousands of miles with the slim Barbara in his arms. After scrambled eggs at a place called Pete's Fashion, she consented to call it an evening.

As John Quincy staggered into Roger's house, the great clock in the hall was striking three. The girl was still alert and sparkling. John Quincy hastily concealed a yawn.

"All wrong to come home so early," she cried. "But we'll have a dance or two on the boat. By the way, I've been wanting to ask. What does it mean? The injured cheek?"

"Why—er—I—" John Quincy remarked. Over the girl's shoulder he saw Roger violently shaking his head. "Oh, that," said John Quincy, lightly touching the wound. "That's where the West begins. Good night. I've had a bully time." And at last he got up-stairs.

He stood for a moment at his bedroom window, gazing down at the torchlight procession on the streets through this amazing city. He was a little dazed. That soft warm presence close by his side in the car—pleasant, very pleasant. Remarkable girls out here. Different!

Beyond shone the harbor lights. That other girl—wonderful eyes she had. Just because she had laughed at him his treasured hat box floated now forlorn on those dark waters. He yawned again. Better be careful. Mustn't be so easily influenced. No telling where it would end.

4

A Friend of Tim's

It was another of those mornings on which the fog maybe did not come. Roger and his guests were in the limousine again; it seemed to John Quincy that they had left it only a few minutes before. So it must have seemed to the chauffeur too as, sleepy-eyed, he hurried them toward the water-front.

"By the way, John Quincy," Roger said, "you'll want to change your money before you go aboard."

John Quincy gathered his wandering thoughts. "Oh, yes, of course," he answered.

Roger smiled. "Just what sort of money would you like to change it for?" he inquired.

"Why—" began John Quincy. He stopped. "Why, I always thought—"

"Don't pay any attention to Roger," Barbara laughed. "He's spoofing you." She was fresh and blooming, a little matter like three A.M. made no difference to her. "Only about one person out of a thousand in this country knows that Hawaii is a part of the United States, and the fact annoys us deeply over in the Islands. Dear old Roger was trying to get you in wrong with me by enrolling you among the nine hundred and ninety-nine."

"Almost did it, too," chuckled Roger.

"Nonsense," said Barbara. "John Quincy is too intelligent. He's not like that congressman who wrote a letter to 'the American Consul at Honolulu.'"

"Did one of them do that?" smiled John Quincy.

"He certainly did. We almost gave up the struggle after that. Then there was the senator who came out on a junket, and began a speech with: 'When I get home to my country—' Some one in the audience shouted: 'You're there now, you big stiff!' It wasn't elegant, of course, but it expressed our feeling perfectly. Oh, we're touchy, John Quincy."

"Don't blame you a bit," he told her. "I'll be very careful what I say."

They had reached the Embarcadero, and the car halted before one of the piers. The chauffeur descended and began to gather up the baggage. Roger and John Quincy took a share of it, and they traversed the pier-shed to the gangplank.

"Get along to your office, Roger," Barbara said.

"No hurry," he answered. "I'll go aboard with you, of course."

Amid the confusion of the deck, a party of girls swept down on Barbara, pretty lively girls of the California brand. John Quincy learned with some regret that they were there only to see Barbara off. A big broad-shouldered man in white pushed his way through the crowd.

"Hello there!" he called to Barbara.

"Hello, Harry," she answered. "You know Roger, don't you? John Quincy, this is an old friend of mine, Harry Jennison."

Mr. Jennison was extremely good-looking, his face was deeply tanned by the Island sun, his hair blond and wavy, his gray eyes amused and cynical. Altogether, he was the type of man women look at twice and never forget; John Quincy felt himself at once supplanted in the eyes of Barbara's friends.

Jennison seized the boy's hand in a firm grip. "Sailing too, Mr. Winterslip?" he inquired. "That's good. Between us we ought to be able to keep this young woman entertained."

The shore call sounded, and the confusion increased. Along the deck came a little old lady, followed by a Chinese woman servant. They walked briskly, and the crowd gave way before them.

"Hello—this is luck," cried Roger. "Madame Maynard—just a moment. I want you to meet a cousin of mine from Boston." He introduced John Quincy. "I give him into your charge. Couldn't find a better guide, philosopher and friend for him if I combed the Islands."

The old lady glanced at John Quincy. Her black eyes snapped. "Another Winterslip, eh?" she said. "Hawaii's all cluttered up with 'em now. Well, the more the merrier. I know your aunt."

"Stick close to her, John Quincy," Roger admonished.

She shook her head. "I'm a million years old," she protested. "The boys don't stick so close any more. They like 'em younger. However, I'll keep my eye on him. My good eye. Well, Roger, run over some time." And she moved away.

"A grand soul," said Roger, smiling after her. "You'll like her. Old missionary family, and her word's law over there."

"Who's this Jennison?" asked John Quincy.

"Him?" Roger glanced over to where Mr. Jennison stood, the center of an admiring feminine group. "Oh, he's Dan's lawyer. One of the leading citizens of Honolulu, I believe. John J. Adonis himself, isn't he?" An officer appeared, herding the reluctant throng toward the gangplank. "I'll have to leave you, John Quincy. A pleasant journey. When you come through on your way home, give me a few more days to try to convince you on my San Francisco offer."

John Quincy laughed. "You've been mighty kind."

"Not at all." Roger shook his hand warmly. "Take care of yourself over there. Hawaii's a little too much like Heaven to be altogether safe. So long, my boy, so long."

He moved away. John Quincy saw him kiss Barbara affectionately and with her friends join the slow procession ashore.

The young man from Boston stepped to the rail. Several hundred voices were calling admonitions, promises, farewells. With that holiday spirit so alien to John Quincy's experience, those ashore were throwing confetti. The streamers grew in number, making a tangle of color, a last frail bond with the land. The gangplank was taken up, clumsily the *President Tyler* began to draw away from the pier. On the topmost deck a band was playing—*Aloha-oe*, the sweetest, most melancholy song of good-by ever written. John Quincy was amazed to feel a lump rising in his throat.

The frail, gay-colored bond was breaking now. A thin veined hand at John Quincy's side waved a handkerchief. He turned to find Mrs. Maynard. There were tears on her cheeks.

"Silly old woman," she said. "Sailed away from this town a hundred and twenty-eight times. Actual count—I keep a diary. Cried every time. What about? I don't know."

The ship was well out in the harbor now. Barbara came along, Jennison trailing her. The girl's eyes were wet.

"An emotional lot, we Islanders," said the old lady. She put her arm about the girl's slim waist. "Here's another one of 'em. Living way off the way we do, any good-by at all—it saddens us." She and Barbara moved on down the deck.

Jennison stopped. His eyes were quite dry. "First trip out?" he inquired.

"Oh, yes," replied John Quincy.

"Hope you'll like us," Jennison said. "Not Massachusetts, of course, but we'll do our best to make you feel at home. It's a way we have with strangers."

"I'm sure I shall have a bully time," John Quincy remarked. But he felt somewhat depressed. Three thousand miles from Beacon Street—and moving on! He waved to some one he fancied might be Roger on the dock, and went to find his stateroom.

He learned that he was to share his cabin with two missionaries. One was a tall, gloomy old man with a lemon-colored face—an honored veteran of the foreign field named Upton. The other was a ruddy-cheeked boy whose martyrdom was still before him. John Quincy suggested drawing lots for a choice of berths, but even this mild form of gambling appeared distasteful to those emissaries of the church.

"You boys take the berths," said Upton. "Leave me the couch. I don't sleep well anyhow." His tone was that of one who prefers to suffer.

John Quincy politely objected. After further discussion it was settled that he was to have the upper berth, the old man the lower, and the boy the couch. The Reverend Mr. Upton seemed disappointed. He had played the role of martyr so long he resented seeing any one else in the part.

The Pacific was behaving in a most unfriendly manner, tossing the great ship about as though it were a piece of driftwood. John Quincy decided no dispense with lunch, and spent the afternoon reading in his berth. By evening he felt better, and under the watchful and somewhat disapproving eyes of the missionaries, arrayed himself carefully for dinner.

His name being Winterslip, he had been invited to sit at the captain's table. He found Madame Maynard, serene and twinkling, at the captain's right, Barbara at his left, and Jennison at Barbara's side. It appeared that oddly enough there was an aristocracy of the Islands, and John Quincy, while he thought it quaint there should be such distinctions in an outpost like Hawaii, took his proper place as a matter of course.

Mrs. Maynard chatted brightly of her many trips over this route. Suddenly she turned to Barbara. "How does it happen, my dear," she asked, "that you're not on the college boat?"

"All booked up," Barbara explained.

"Nonsense," said the frank old lady. "*You* could have got on. But then"—she looked meaningly toward Jennison—"I presume this ship was not without its attractions."

The girl flushed slightly and made no reply.

"What," John Quincy inquired, "is the college boat?"

"So many children from Hawaii at school on the mainland," the old lady explained, "that every June around this time they practically fill a ship. We call it the college boat. This year it's the *Matsonia*. She left San Francisco to-day at noon."

"I've got a lot of friends aboard her," Barbara said. "I do wish we could beat her in. Captain, what are the chances?"

"Well, that depends," replied the captain cautiously.

"She isn't due until Tuesday morning," Barbara persisted. "Wouldn't it be a lark if you could land us the night before? As a favor to me, Captain."

"When you look at me like that," smiled the officer, "I can only say that I'll make a supreme effort. I'm just as eager as you to make port on Monday—it would mean I could get off to the Orient that much sooner."

"Then it's settled," Barbara beamed.

"It's settled that we'll try," he said. "Of course, if I speed up there's always the chance I may arrive off Honolulu after sundown, and be compelled to lay by until morning. That would be torture for you."

"I'll risk it," Barbara smiled. "Wouldn't dear old dad be pleased if I should burst upon his vision Monday evening?"

"My dear girl," the captain said gallantly, "any man would be pleased to have you burst upon his vision any time."

There was, John Quincy reflected, much in what the captain said. Up to that moment there had been little of the romantic in his relations with girls; he was accustomed to look upon them merely as tennis or golf opponents or a fourth at bridge. Barbara would demand a different classification. There was an enticing gleam in her blue eyes, a hint of the eternal feminine in everything she did or said, and John Quincy was no wooden man. He was glad that when he left the dinner table, she accompanied him.

They went on deck and stood by the rail. Night had fallen, there was no moon, and it seemed to John Quincy that the Pacific was the blackest, angriest ocean he had ever seen. He stood gazing at it gloomily.

"Homesick, John Quincy?" Barbara asked. One of his hands was resting on the rail. She laid her own upon it.

He nodded. "It's a funny thing. I've been abroad a lot, but I never felt like this. When the ship left port this morning, I nearly wept."

"It's not so very funny," she said gently. "This is an alien world you're entering now. Not Boston, John Quincy, nor any other old, civilized place. Not the kind of place where the mind rules. Out here it's the heart that charts our course. People you're fond of do the wildest, most unreasonable things, simply because their minds are sleeping and their hearts are beating fast. Just—just remember, please, John Quincy."

There was an odd note of wistfulness in her voice. Suddenly at their side appeared the white-clad figure of Harry Jennison.

"Coming for a stroll, Barbara?" he inquired.

For a moment she did not reply. Then she nodded. "Yes," she said. And called over her shoulder as she went: "Cheer up, John Quincy."

He watched her go, reluctantly. She might have stayed to assuage his loneliness. But there she walked along the dim deck, close to Jennison's side.

After a time, he sought the smoking-room. It was deserted, but on one of the tables lay a copy of the *Boston Transcript*. Delighted, John Quincy pounced upon it, as Robinson Crusoe might have pounced on news from home.

The issue was ten days old, but no matter. He turned at once to the financial pages. There it was, like the face of a well-beloved friend, the record of one day's trading on the Stock Exchange. And up in one corner, the advertisement of his own banking house, offering an issue of preferred stock in a Berkshire cotton mill. He read eagerly, but with an odd detached feeling. He was gone, gone from that world, away out here on a black ocean bound for picture-book islands. Islands where, not so long ago, brown tribes had battled, brown kings ruled. There seemed no link with that world back home, those gay-colored streamers of confetti breaking so readily had been a symbol. He was adrift. What sort of port would claim him in the end?

He threw the paper down. The Reverend Mr. Upton entered the smoking-room.

"I left my newspaper here," he explained. "Ah—did you care to look at it?"

"Thank you, I have," John Quincy told him.

The old man picked it up in a great bony hand. "I always buy a *Transcript* when I get the chance," he said. "It carries me back. You know, I was born in Salem, over seventy years ago."

John Quincy stared at him. "You've been a long time out here?" he asked.

"More than fifty years in the foreign field," answered the old man. "I was one of the first to go to the South Seas. One of the first to carry the torch down there—and a dim torch it was, I'm afraid. Afterward I was transferred to China." John Quincy regarded him with a new interest. "By the way, sir," the missionary continued, "I once met another gentleman named Winterslip. Mr. Daniel Winterslip."

"Really?" said John Quincy. "He's a cousin of mine. I'm to visit to Honolulu."

"Yes? I heard he had returned to Hawaii, and prospered. I met him just once—in the 'eighties, it was, on a lonely island in the Gilbert group. It was—rather a turning point in his life, and I have never forgotten." John

Quincy waited to hear more, but the old missionary moved away. "I'll go and enjoy my *Transcript*," he smiled. "The church news is very competently handled."

John Quincy rose and went aimlessly outside. A dreary scene, the swish of turbulent waters, dim figures aimless as himself, an occasional ship's officer hurrying by. His stateroom opened directly on the deck, and he sank into a steamer chair just outside the door.

In the distance he saw his room steward, weaving his way in and out of the cabins under his care. The man was busy with his last duties for the night, refilling water carafes, laying out towels, putting things generally to rights.

"Evening, sir," he said as he entered John Quincy's room. Presently he came and stood in the door, the cabin light at his back. He was a small man with gold-rimmed eye-glasses and a fierce gray pompadour.

"Everything O. K., Mr. Winterslip?" he inquired.

"Yes, Bowker," smiled John Quincy. "Everything's fine."

"That's good," said Bowker. He switched off the cabin light and stepped out on to the deck. "I aim to take particular care of you, sir. Saw your home town on the sailing list. I'm an old Boston man myself."

"Is that so?" said John Quincy cordially. Evidently the pacific was a Boston suburb.

"Not born there, I don't mean," the man went on. "But a newspaper man there for ten years. It was just after I left the University."

John Quincy started through the dark. "Harvard?" he asked.

"Dublin," said the steward. "Yes, sir—" He laughed an embarrassed little laugh. "You might not think it now, but the University of Dublin, Class of 1901. And after that, for ten years, working in Boston on the *Gazette*—reporting, copy desk, managing editor for a time. Maybe I bumped into you there—at the Adams House bar, say, on a night before a football game."

"Quite possible," admitted John Quincy. "One bumped into so many people on such occasions."

"Don't I know it?" Mr. Bowker leaned on the rail, in reminiscent mood. "Great times, sir. Those were the good old days when a newspaper man who wasn't tanked up was a reproach to a grand profession. The *Gazette* was edited mostly from a place called the Arch Inn. We'd bring our copy to the city editor there—he had a regular table—a bit sloppy on top, but his desk. If we had a good story, maybe he'd stand us a cocktail."

John Quincy laughed.

"Happy days," continued the Dublin graduate, with a sign. "I knew every bartender in Boston well enough to borrow money. Were you ever in that place in the alley back of the Tremont Theater—?"

"Tim's place," suggested John Quincy, recalling an incident of college days.

"Yeah, bo. Now you're talking. I wonder what became of Tim. Say, and there was that place on Boylston—but they're all gone now, of course. An old pal I met in 'Frisco was telling me it would break your heart to see the cobwebs on the mirrors back in Beantown. Gone to the devil, just like my profession. The newspapers go on consolidating, doubling up, combining the best features of both, and an army of good men go on the town. Good men and true, moaning about the vanished days and maybe landing in jobs like this one of mine." He was silent for a moment. "Well, sir, anything I can do for you—as a mutual friend of Tim's—"

"As a friend of Tim's," smiled John Quincy, "I'll not hesitate to mention it."

Sadly Bowker went on down the deck. John Quincy sat lonely again. A couple passed, walking close, talking in low tones. He recognized Jennison and his cousin. "Between us we ought to be able to keep this young woman entertained," Jennison had said. Well, John Quincy reflected, his portion of the entertainment promised to be small.

5

The Blood of the Winterslips

The days that followed proved that he was right. He seldom had a moment alone with Barbara; when he did, Jennison seemed always to be hovering near by, and he did not long delay making the group a threesome. At first John Quincy resented this, but gradually he began to feel that it didn't matter.

Nothing appeared to matter any more. A great calm had settled over the waters and over John Quincy's soul. The Pacific was one vast sheet of glass, growing a deeper blue with every passing hour. They seemed to be floating in space in a world where nothing ever happened, nothing could happen. Quiet restful days gave way to long brilliant nights. A little walk, a little talk, and that was life.

Sometimes John Quincy chatted with Madame Maynard on the deck. She who had known the Islands so many years had fascinating tales to tell, tales of the monarchy and the missionaries. The boy liked her immensely, she was a New Englander at heart despite her glamourous lifetime in Hawaii.

Bowker, too, he found excellent company. The steward was that rarity even among college graduates, an educated man; there was no topic upon which he could not discourse at length and brilliantly. In John Quincy's steamer trunk were a number of huge imposing volumes—books he had been meaning to tackle long ago, but it was Bowker who read them, not John Quincy.

As the days slipped by, the blue of the water deepened to ultramarine, the air grew heavier and warmer. Underfoot throbbed the engines that were doing their best for Barbara and an early landing. The captain was optimistic, he predicted they would make port late Monday afternoon. But Sunday night a fierce sudden storm swept down upon them, and lashed the ship with a wet fury until dawn. When the captain appeared at luncheon Monday noon, worn by a night on the bridge, he shook his head.

"We've lost our bet, Miss Barbara," he said. "I can't possibly arrive off Honolulu before midnight."

Barbara frowned. "But ships sail at any hour," she reminded him. "I don't see why—if we sent radios ahead—"

"No use," he told her. "The Quarantine people keep early hours. No, I'll have to lay by near the channel entrance until official sunrise—about six. We'll get in ahead of the *Matsonia* in the morning. That's the best I can offer you."

"You're a dear, anyhow," Barbara smiled. "That old storm wasn't your fault. We'll drown our sorrow to-night with one last glorious dance—a costume party." She turned to Jennison. "I've got the loveliest fancy dress—Marie Antoinette—I wore it at college. What do you say, Harry?"

"Fine!" Jennison answered. "We can all dig up some sort of costume. Let's go."

Barbara hurried off to spread the news. After dinner that evening she appeared, a blonde vision straight from the French Court, avid for dancing. Jennison had rigged up an impromptu pirate dress, and was a striking figure. Most of the other passengers had donned weird outfits; on the Pacific boats a fancy dress party is warmly welcomed and amusingly carried out.

John Quincy took small part in the gaiety, for he still suffered from New England inhibitions. At a little past eleven he drifted into the main saloon and found Madame Maynard seated there alone.

"Hello," she said. "Come to keep me company? I've sworn not to go to bed until I see the light on Diamond Head."

"I'm with you," John Quincy smiled.

"But you ought to be dancing, boy. And you're not in costume."

"No," admitted John Quincy. He paused, seeking an explanation. "A—a fellow can't make a fool of himself in front of a lot of strangers."

"I understand," nodded the old lady. "It's a fine delicacy, too. But rather rare, particularly out this way."

Barbara entered, flushed and vibrant. "Harry's gone to get me a drink," she panted. She sat down beside Mrs. Maynard. "I've been looking for you, my dear. You know, you haven't read my palm since I was a child. She's simply wonderful—" this to John Quincy. "Can tell you the most amazing things."

Mrs. Maynard vehemently shook her head. "I don't read 'em any more," she said. "Gave it up. As I've grown older, I've come to understand how foolish it is to peer into the future. To-day—that's enough for me. That's all I care to think about."

"Oh, please," the girl pouted.

The old woman took Barbara's slim hand in hers, and studied the palm for a moment. John Quincy thought he saw a shadow cross her face. Again she shook her head.

"*Carpe diem*," she said. "Which my nephew once translated as 'grab the day.' Dance and be happy to-night, and let's not try to look behind the curtain. It doesn't pay, my dear. Take an old woman's word for that."

Harry Jennison appeared in the door. "Oh, here you are," he said. "I've got your drink waiting in the smoking-room."

"I'm coming," the girl said, and went. The old woman stared after her. "Poor Barbara," she murmured. "Her mother's life was none too happy, either—"

"You saw something in her hand—" John Quincy suggested.

"No matter," the old lady snapped. "There's trouble waiting for us all, if we look far enough ahead. Now, let's go on deck. It's getting on toward midnight."

She led him out to the starboard rail. A solitary light, like a star, gleamed in the distance. Land, land at last. "Diamond Head?" John Quincy asked.

"No," she said. "That's the beacon on Makapuu Point. We shall have to round Koko Head before we sight Honolulu." She stood for a moment by the rail, one frail hand resting upon it. "But that's Oahu," she said gently. "That's home. A sweet land, boy. Too sweet, I often think. I hope you'll like it."

"I'm sure I shall," replied John Quincy gallantly.

"Let's sit down here." They found deck chairs. "Yes, a dear land," she went on. "But we're all sorts, in Hawaii—just as it is the whole world over—honest folks and rascals. From the four corners of the globe men

come to us—often because they were no longer welcome at home. We offer
them a paradise, and some repay us by becoming good citizens, while others
rot away. I often think it will take a lot of stamina to make good in
Heaven—and Hawaii is the same."

The tall emaciated figure of the Reverend Mr. Upton appeared before
them. He bowed. "Good evening, Madame. You're nearly home."

"Yes," she said. "Glad of it, too."

He turned to John Quincy. "You'll be seeing Dan Winterslip in the
morning, young man."

"I expect I shall," John Quincy replied.

"Just ask him if he recalls that day on Apiang Island in the 'eighties. The
Reverend Frank Upton."

"Of course," replied John Quincy. "But you haven't told me much about
it, you know."

"No, I haven't." The missionary dropped into a chair. "I don't like to
reveal any secrets about a man's past," he said. "However, I understand
that the story of Dan Winterslip's early life has always been known in
Honolulu." He glanced toward Madame Maynard.

"Dan was no saint," she remarked. "We all know that."

He crossed his thin legs. "As a matter of fact, I'm very proud of my
meeting with Dan Winterslip," he went on. "I feel that in my humble way
I persuaded him to change his course—for the better."

"Humph," said the old lady. She was dubious, evidently.

John Quincy was not altogether pleased at the turn the conversation had
taken. He did not care to have the name of a Winterslip thus bandied
about. But to his annoyance, the Reverend Mr. Upton was continuing.

"It was in the 'eighties, as I told you," said the missionary. "I had a lonely
station on Apiang, in the Gilbert group. One morning a brig anchored just
beyond the reef, and a boat came ashore. Of course, I joined the procession
of natives down to the beach to meet it. I saw few enough men of my own
race.

"There was a ruffianly crew aboard, in charge of a dapper, rather handsome young white man. And I saw, even before they beached her, midway
in the boat, a long pine box.

"The white man introduced himself. He said he was First Officer Winterslip, of the brig *Maid of Shiloh*. And when he mentioned the name of the
ship, of course I knew at once. Knew her unsavory trade and history. He
hurried on to say that their captain had died the day before, and they had
brought him ashore to bury him on land. It had been the man's last wish.

"Well." The Reverend Mr. Upton stared at the distant shore line of Oahu.
"I looked over at that rough pine box—four Malay sailors were carrying
it ashore. 'So Tom Brade's in there,' I said. Young Winterslip nodded. 'He's
in there, right enough,' he answered. And I knew I was looking on at the
final scene in the career of a famous character of the South Seas, a callous
brute who knew no law, a pirate and adventurer, the master of the notorious
Maid of Shiloh. Tom Brade, the blackbirder."

"Blackbirder?" queried John Quincy.

The missionary smiled. "Ah, yes—you come from Boston. A blackbirder,
my boy, is a shipping-master who furnishes contract labor to the plantations
at so much a head. It's pretty well wiped out now, but in the 'eighties! A
horrible business—the curse of God was on it. Sometimes the laborers came
willingly. Sometimes. But mostly they came at the point of a knife or the
muzzle of a gun. A bloody, brutal business.

"Winterslip and his men went up the beach and began to dig a grave
under a cocoanut palm. I followed. I offered to say a prayer. Winterslip

laughed—not much use, he said. But there on that bright morning under the palm I consigned to God the soul of a man who had so much to answer for. Winterslip agreed to come to my house for lunch. He told me that save for a recruiting agent who had remained aboard the brig, he was now the only white man on the ship.

"During lunch, I talked to him. He was so young—I discovered this was his first trip. 'It's no trade for you,' I told him. And after a time, he agreed with me. He said he had two hundred blacks under the hatches that he must deliver to a plantation over in the Kingsmill group, and that after he'd done that, he was through. 'I'll take the *Maid* back to Sydney, Dominie,' he promised, 'and turn her over. Then I'm pau. I'm going home to Honolulu.' "

The Reverend Mr. Upton rose slowly. "I learned later that he kept his word," he finished. "Yes, Dan Winterslip went home, and the South Seas saw him no more. I've always been a little proud of my part in that decision. I've had few rewards. It's not everywhere that the missionaries have prospered in a worldly way—as they did in Hawaii." He glanced at Madame Maynard. "But I've had satisfactions. And one of them arose from that meeting on the shore of Apiang. It's long past my bed hour—I must say good night."

He moved away. John Quincy sat turning this horror over and over in his mind. A Winterslip in the blackbirding business! That was pretty. He wished he was back on Beacon Street.

"Sweet little dig for me," the old lady was muttering indignantly. "That about the missionaries in Hawaii. And he needn't be so cocky. If Dan Winterslip dropped blackbirding, it was only because he'd found something more profitable, I fancy." She stood up suddenly. "At last," she said.

John Quincy rose and stood beside her. Far away a faint yellow eye was winking. For a moment the old lady did not speak.

"Well, that's that," she said finally, in a low voice. "I've seen Diamond Head again. Good night, my boy."

"Good night," John Quincy answered.

He stood alone by the rail. The pace of the *President Tyler* was slowing perceptibly. The moon came from behind a cloud, crept back again. A sort of unholy calm was settling over the hot, airless, deep blue world. The boy felt a strange restlessness in his heart.

He ascended to the boat deck, seeking a breath of air. There, in a secluded spot, he came upon Barbara and Jennison—and stopped, shocked. His cousin was in the man's arms, and their bizarre costumes added a weird touch to the scene. They did not see John Quincy, for in their world at that moment there were only two. Their lips were crushed together, fiercely—

John Quincy fled. Good lord! He had kissed a girl or two himself, but it had been nothing like that.

He went to the rail outside his stateroom. Well, what of it? Barbara was nothing to him, a cousin, yes, but one who seemed to belong to an alien race. He had sensed that she was in love with Jennison; this was no surprise. Why did he feel that frustrated pang deep in his heart? He was engaged to Agatha Parker.

He gripped the rail, and sought to see again Agatha's aristocratic face. But it was blurred, indistinct. All Boston was blurred in his memory. The blood of the roaming Winterslips, the blood that led on to blackbirding and hot breathless kisses in the tropic night—was it flowing in his veins too? Oh, lord—he should have stayed at home where he belonged.

Bowker, the steward, came along. "Well, here we are," he said. "We'll anchor in twelve fathoms and wait for the pilot and the doctor in the morning. I heard they'd been having Kona weather out this way, but I imagine this is the tail end of it. There'll be a moon shortly, and by dawn the old trades will be on the job again, God bless them."

John Quincy did not speak. "I've returned all your books, sir," the steward went on, "except that one by Adams on *Revolutionary New England.* It's a mighty interesting work. I intend to finish it to-night, so I can give it to you before you go ashore."

"Oh, that's all right," John Quincy said. He pointed to dim harbor lights in the distance. "Honolulu's over there, I take it."

"Yeah—several miles away. A dead town, sir. They roll up the sidewalks at nine. And let me give you a tip. Keep away from the okolehau."

"The what?" asked John Quincy.

"The okolehau. A drink they sell out here."

"What's it made of?"

"There," said Bowker, "you have the plot for a big mystery story. What *is* it made of? Judging by the smell, of nothing very lovely. A few gulps, and you hit the ceiling of eternity. But oh, boy—when you drop! Keep off it, sir. I'm speaking as one who knows."

"I'll keep off it," John Quincy promised.

Bowker disappeared. John Quincy remained by the rail, that restless feeling growing momentarily. The moon was hidden still, the ship crept along through the muggy darkness. He peered across the black waters toward the strange land that awaited him.

Somewhere over there, Dan Winterslip waited for him too. Dan Winterslip, blood relative of the Boston Winterslips, and ex-blackbirder. For the first time, the boy wished he had struck first in that dark attic in San Francisco, wished he had got that strong box and cast it overboard in the night. Who could say what new scandal, what fresh blot on the honored name of Winterslip, might have been averted had he been quicker with his fists?

As John Quincy turned and entered his cabin, he made a firm resolution. He would linger but briefly at this, his journey's end. A few days to get his breath, perhaps, and then he would set out again for Boston. And Aunt Minerva would go with him, whether she wanted to or not.

6

Beyond the Bamboo Curtain

Had John Quincy been able to see his Aunt Minerva at that moment, he would not have been so sure that he could persuade her to fall in with his plans. He would, indeed, have been profoundly shocked at the picture presented by his supposedly staid and dignified relative.

For Miss Minerva was sitting on a grass mat in a fragrant garden in the Hawaiian quarter of Honolulu. Pale golden Chinese lanterns, inscribed with scarlet letters, hung above her head. Her neck was garlanded with ropes of buff ginger blossoms twined with maile. The sleepy, sensuous music of ukulele and steel guitar rose on the midnight air and before her, in a cleared space under the date palms, Hawaiian boys and girls were performing a dance she would not be able to describe in great detail when she got back to Beacon Street.

Miss Minerva was, in her quiet way, very happy. One of the ambitions of her life had been realized, and she was present at a luau, or native Hawaiian feast. Few white people are privileged to attend this intimate ceremony, but Honolulu friends had been invited on this occasion, and had asked her to go with them. At first she had thought she must refuse, for Dan was expecting Barbara and John Quincy on Monday afternoon. When on Monday evening he had informed her that the *President Tyler* would not land its passengers until the next day, she had hastened to the telephone and asked to reconsider her refusal.

And she was glad she had. Before her, on another mat, lay the remnants of a dinner unique in her experience. Dan had called her a good sport, and she had this evening proved him to be correct. Without a qualm she had faced the queer food wrapped in brown bundles, she had tasted everything, poi served in individual calabashes, chicken stewed in cocoanut milk, squid and shrimps, limu, or sea-weed, even raw fish. She would dream to-night!

Now the feasting had given way to the dance. The moonlight was tracing lacy patterns on the lawn, the plaintive wail of the music rose ever louder, the Hawaiian young people, bashful at first in the presence of strangers, were bashful no longer. Miss Minerva closed her eyes and leaned back against the trunk of a tall palm. Even in Hawaiian love songs there is a note of hopeless melancholy, it touched her emotions as no symphony ever could. A curtain was lifted and she was looking into the past, the primitive, barbaric past of these Islands in the days before the white men came.

A long, heart-breaking crescendo, and the music stopped, the swaying bodies of the dancers were momentarily still. It seemed to Miss Minerva's friends an opportune moment to depart. They entered the house and in the stuffy little parlor, took leave of their brown, smiling host and hostess. The baby whose arrival in the world was the inspiration for the luau awoke for a second and smiled at them too. Outside in the narrow street their car was waiting.

Through silent, deserted Honolulu they motored toward Waikiki. As they passed the Judiciary Building on King Street the clock in the tower struck the hour of one. She had not been out so late, Miss Minerva reflected, since that night when a visiting company sang *Parsifal* at the Boston Opera House.

The iron gates that guarded the drive at Dan's house were closed. Leaving the car at the curb, Miss Minerva bade her friends good night and started up the walk toward the front door. The evening had thrilled her, and she moved with the long confident stride of youth. Dan's scarlet garden was shrouded in darkness, for the moon, which had been playing an in-and-out game with the fast-moving clouds all evening, was again obscured. Exotic odors assailed her nostrils, she heard all about her the soft intriguing noises of the tropic night. She really should get to bed, she knew, but with a happy truant feeling she turned from the front walk and went to the side of the house for a last look at the breakers.

She stood there under a poinciana tree near the door leading into Dan's living-room. For nearly two weeks the Kona wind had prevailed, but now on her cheek, she thought she felt the first kindly breath of the trades. Very wide awake, she stared out at the dim foaming lines of surf between the shore and the coral reef. Her mind strayed back to the Honolulu she had known in Kalakaua's day, to that era when the Islands were so naive, so colorful—unspoiled. Ruined now, Dan had said, ruined by a damned mechanical civilization. "But away down underneath, Minerva, there are deep dark waters flowing still."

The moon came out, touching with silver the waters at the crossroads, then was lost again under fleecy clouds. With a little sigh that was perhaps for her lost youth and the 'eighties, Miss Minerva pushed open the unlocked door leading into the great living-room, and closed it gently so as not to waken Dan.

An intense darkness engulfed her. But she knew her way across the polished floor and set out confidently, walking on tiptoe. She had gone half-way to the hall door when she stopped, her heart in her mouth. For not five feet away she saw the luminous dial of a watch, and as she stared at it with frightened eyes, it moved.

Not for nothing had Miss Minerva studied restraint through more than fifty years. Many women would have screamed and fainted, Miss Minerva's heart pounded madly, but that was all. Standing very still, she studied that phosphorescent dial. Its movement had been slight, it was now at rest again. A watch worn on some one's wrist. Some one who had been on the point of action, but had now assumed an attitude of cautious waiting.

Well, Miss Minerva grimly asked herself, what was she going to do about it? Should she cry out a sharp: "Who's there?" She was a brave woman, but the foolhardiness of such a course was apparent. She had a vision of that dial flashing nearer, a blow, perhaps strong hands at her throat.

She took a tentative step, and then another. Now, surely, the dial would stir again. But it remained motionless, steady, as though the arm that wore it were rigid at the intruder's side.

Suddenly Miss Minerva realized the situation. The wearer of the watch had forgotten the tell-tale numerals on his wrist, he thought himself hidden in the dark. He was waiting for her to go on through the room. If she made no sound, gave no sign of alarm, she might be safe. Once beyond that bamboo curtain leading into the hall, she could rouse the household.

She was a woman of great will power, but it took all she had to move serenely on her way. She shut her lips tightly and accomplished it, veering a bit from that circle of light that menaced her, looking back at it over her shoulder as she went. After what seemed an eternity the bamboo curtain received her, she was through it, she was on the stairs. But it seemed to her that never again would she be able to look at a watch or a clock and find that the hour was anything save twenty minutes past one!

When she was half-way up the stairs, she recalled that it had been her intention to snap on the lights in the lower hall. She did not turn back, nor did she search for the switch at the head of the stairs. Instead, she went hastily on into her room, and just as though she had been an ordinary woman she closed her door and dropped down, trembling a little, on a chair.

But she was no ordinary woman, and in two seconds she was up and had reopened her door. Her sudden terror was evaporating; she felt her heart beat in a strong regular rhythm again. Action was required of her now, calm confident action; she was a Winterslip and she was ready.

The servants' quarters were in a wing over the kitchen, she went there at once and knocked on the first door she came to. She knocked once, then again, and finally the head of a very sleepy Japanese man appeared.

"Haku," said Miss Minera, "there is some one in the living-room. You must go down and investigate at once."

He stared at her, seeming unable to comprehend.

"We must go down," amended Miss Minerva. "Wikiwiki!"

He disappeared, and Miss Minerva waited impatiently. Where was her nerve, she wondered, why hadn't she seen this through alone? At home, no doubt, she could have managed it, but here there was something strange and terrifying in the very air. The moonlight poured in through a small window beside her, forming a bright square at her feet. Haku reappeared, wearing a gaudy kimono that he often sported on the beach.

Another door opened suddenly, and Miss Minerva started. Bah! What ailed her, anyhow, she wondered. It was only Kamaikui, standing there a massive figure in the dim doorway, a bronze statue clad in a holoku.

"Some one in the living-room," Miss Minerva explained again. "I saw him as I came through."

Kamaikui made no reply, but joined the odd little procession. In the upper hall Haku switched on the lights, both up-stairs and down. At the head of the stairs there was a brief pause—then Miss Minerva took her rightful place at the head of the line. She descended with a firm step, courageous and competent, Boston at its best. After her followed a stolid little Japanese man in a kimono gay with passionate poppies, and a Polynesian woman who wore the fearful Mother Hubbard of the missionaries as though it were a robe of state.

In the lower hall Miss Minerva did not hesitate. She pushed on through the bamboo curtain and her hand—it trembled ever so slightly—found the electric switch and flooded the living-room with light. She heard the crackle of Bamboo behind her as her strange companions followed where she led. She stood looking curiously about her.

There was no one in sight, no sign of any disturbance, and it suddenly occurred to Miss Minerva that perhaps she was behaving in a rather silly fashion. After all, she had neither seen nor heard a living thing. The illuminated dial of a watch that moved a little—might it not have been a figment of her imagination? She had experienced a stirring evening. Then, too, she remembered, there had been that small glass of okolehau. A potent concoction.

Kamaikui and Haku were looking at her with the inquiring eyes of little children. Had she roused them for a fool's errand? Her cheeks flushed slightly. Certainly in this big brilliant room, furnished with magnificent native woods and green with many potted ferns, everything seemed proper and in order.

"I—I may have been mistaken," she said in a low voice. "I was quite sure—but there's no sign of anything wrong. Mr. Winterslip has not been resting well of late. If he should be asleep we won't waken him."

She went to the door leading on to the lanai and pushed aside the curtain. Bright moonlight outside revealed most of the veranda's furnishings, and here, too, all seemed well. "Dan," Miss Minerva called softly. "Dan. Are you awake?"

No answer. Miss Minerva was certain now that she was making a mountain out of a molehill. She was about to turn back into the living-room when her eyes, grown more accustomed to the semi-darkness, noted a rather startling fact.

Day and night, over Dan's cot in one corner of the lanai, hung a white mosquito netting. It was not there now.

"Come, Haku," Miss Minerva said. "Turn on the light out here."

Haku came, and the green-shaded lamp glowed under his touch. The little lamp by which Dan had been reading his evening paper that night when he had seemed suddenly so disturbed, and rushed off to send a letter to Roger in San Francisco. Miss Minerva stood recalling that incident, she recalled others, because she was very reluctant to turn toward that cot in the corner. She was conscious of Kamaikui brushing by her, and then she heard a low, half-savage moan of fear and sorrow.

Miss Minerva stepped to the cot. The mosquito netting had been torn down as though in some terrific struggle and there, entangled in the meshes of it, she saw Dan Winterslip. He was lying on his left side, and as she stared down at him, one of the harmless little Island lizards ran up his chest and over his shoulder—and left a crimson trail on his white pajamas.

7

Enter Charlie Chan

Miss Minerva leaned far over, her keen eyes seeking Dan's face. It was turned toward the wall, half buried in the pillow. "Dan," she said brokenly. She put her hand on his cheek. The night air was warm and muggy, but she shivered a little as she drew the hand quickly away. Steady! She must be steady now.

She hurried through the living-room to the hall; the telephone was in a closet under the front stairs. Her fingers were trembling again as she fumbled with the numerals on the dial. She got her number, heard finally an answering voice.

"Amos? Is that you, Amos? This is Minerva. Come over here to Dan's as quickly as you can."

The voice muttered in protest. Miss Minerva cut in on it sharply.

"For God's sake, Amos, forget your silly feud. Your brother is dead."

"Dead?" he repeated dully.

"Murdered, Amos. Will you come now?"

A long silence. What thoughts, Miss Minerva wondered, were passing through the mind of that stern unbending Puritan?

"I'll come," a strange voice said at last. And then, a voice more like that of the Amos she knew: "The police! I'll notify them, and then I'll come right over."

Returning to the hall, Miss Minerva saw that the big front door was closed. Amos would enter that way, she knew, so she went over and opened it. There was, she noted, an imposing lock, but the key had long since been lost and forgotten. Indeed, in all Dan's great house, she could not recall ever having seen a key. In these friendly trusting islands, locked doors were obsolete.

She reentered the living-room. Should she summon a doctor? But no, it was too late, she knew that only too well. And the police—didn't they bring some sort of doctor with them? Suddenly she began to wonder about the police. During all her time in Honolulu she had never given them a thought before. Away off here at the end of the world—did they have policemen? She couldn't remember ever having seen one. Oh, yes—there was that handsome, brown-skinned Hawaiian who stood on a box at the corner of Fort and Kint Streets, directing traffic with an air that would have become Kamehameha himself. She heard the scrape of a chair being moved on the lanai, and went to the door.

"Nothing is to be touched out here," she said. "Leave it just as it was. You'd better go up-stairs and dress, both of you."

The two frightened servants came into the living-room, and stood there regarding her. They seemed to feel that this terrible affair called for discussion. But what was there to be said? Even in the event of murder, a Winterslip must maintain a certain well-bred aloofness in dealing with servants. Miss Minerva's feeling for them was kindly. She sympathized with their evident grief, but there was, she felt, nothing to discuss.

"After you've dressed," she ordered, "stay within reach. You'll both be wanted."

They went out, Haku in his absurd costume, Kamaikui moaning and muttering in a way that sent shivers up and down Miss Minerva's spine. They left her there alone—with Dan—and she who had always thought herself equal to anything still hesitated about going out on the lanai.

She sat down in a huge chair in the living-room and gazed about her at the trappings of wealth and position that Dan had left for ever now. Poor Dan. Despite all the whispering against him, she had liked him immensely. It is said of many—usually with small reason—that their lives would make an interesting book. It had been said of Dan, and in his case it was true. What a book his life would have made—and how promptly it would have been barred for all time from the shelves of the Boston Public Library! For Dan had lived life to the full, made his own laws, fought his battles without mercy, prospered and had his way. Dallied often along forbidden paths, they said, but his smile had been so friendly and his voice so full of cheer—always until these last two weeks.

Ever since that night he sent the letter to Roger, he had seemed a different man. There were lines for the first time in his face, a weary apprehensive look in his gray eyes. And how furious he had been when, last Wednesday, he received a cable from Roger. What was in that message, Miss Minerva wondered; what were those few typewritten words that had caused him to fly into such a rage and set him to pacing the floor with tigerish step?

She thought of him as she had seen him last—he had seemed rather pathetic to her then. When the news came that the *President Tyler* could not dock until morning, and that Barbara—

Miss Minerva stopped. For the first time she thought of Barbara. She thought of a sprightly, vivacious girl as yet untouched by sorrow—and of the morning's homecoming. Tears came into her eyes, and it was through a mist she saw the bamboo curtain that led into the hall pushed aside, and the thin white face of Amos framed here.

Amos entered, walking gingerly, for he was treading ground he had sworn his feet should never touch. He paused before Miss Minerva.

"What's this?" he said. "What's all this?"

She nodded toward the lanai, and he went out there. After what seemed a long time, he reappeared. His shoulders drooped wearily and his watery eyes were staring.

"Stabbed through the heart," he muttered. He stood for a moment regarding his father's picture on the wall. "The wages of sin is death," he added, as though to old Jedediah Winterslip.

"Yes, Amos," said Miss Minerva sharply. "I expected we should hear that from you. And there's another one you may have heard—judge not that ye be not judged. Further than that, we'll waste no time moralizing. Dan is dead, and I for one am sorry."

"Sorry!" repeated Amos drearily. "How about me? My brother—my young brother—I taught him to walk on this very beach—"

"Yes." Miss Minerva looked at him keenly. "I wonder. Well, Dan's gone. Some one has killed him. He was one of us—a Winterslip. What are we going to do about it?"

"I've notified the police," said Amos.

"Then why aren't they here? In Boston by this time—but then, I know this isn't Boston, Stabbed, you say. Was there any sign of a weapon?"

"None whatever, that I could see."

"How about that Malay kris on the table out there? The one Dan used as a paper cutter?"

"I didn't notice," Amos replied. "This is a strange house to me, Minerva."

"So it is." Miss Minerva rose and started for the lanai. She was her old competent self again. At that moment a loud knock sounded on the screen door at the front of the house. Presently there were voices in the hall, and Haku ushered three men into the living-room. Though evidently police, they were all in plain clothes. One of them, a tall, angular Yankee with the look of a sailing master about him, stepped forward.

"I'm Hallet," he said. "Captain of Detectives. You're Mr. Amos Winterslip, I believe?"

"I am," Amos answered. He introduced Miss Minerva. Captain Hallet gave her a casual nod; this was man's business and he disliked having a woman involved.

"Dan Winterslip, you said," he remarked, turning back to Amos. "That's a great pity. Where is he?"

Amos indicated the lanai. "Come, Doctor," Hallet said, and went through the curtain, followed by the smaller of the two men.

As they went out, the third man stepped farther into the room, and Miss Minerva gave a little gasp of astonishment as she looked at him. In those warm islands thin men were the rule, but here was a striking exception. He was very fat indeed, yet he walked with the light dainty step of a woman. His cheeks were as chubby as a baby's, his skin ivory tinted, his black hair close-cropped, his amber eyes slanting. As he passed Miss Minerva he bowed with a courtesy encountered all too rarely in a work-a-day world, then moved on after Hallet.

"Amos!" cried Miss Minerva. "That man—why he—"

"Charlie Chan," Amos explained. "I'm glad they brought him. He's the best detective on the force."

"But—he's Chinese!"

"Of course."

Miss Minerva sank into a chair. Ah, yes, they had policemen out here, after all.

In a few moments Hallet came briskly back into the living-room. "Look here," he said. "The doctor tells me Mr. Winterslip has been dead a very short while. I don't want your evidence just yet—but if either of you can give me some idea as to the hour when this thing happened—"

"I can give you a rather definite idea," said Miss Minerva calmly. "It happened just previous to twenty minutes past one. Say about one fifteen."

Hallet stared at her. "You're sure of that?"

"I ought to be. I got the time from the wrist watch of the person who committed the murder."

"What! You saw him!"

"I didn't say that. I said I saw his wrist watch."

Hallet frowned. "I'll get that straight later," he said. "Just now I propose to comb this part of town. Where's the telephone?"

Miss Minerva pointed it out to him, and heard him in earnest conversation with a man at headquarters named Tom. Tom's job, it seemed, was to muster all available men and search Honolulu, particularly the Waikiki district, rounding up any suspicious characters. He was also to have on hand, awaiting his chief's return, the passenger lists of all ships that had made port at Honolulu during the past week.

Hallet returned to the living-room. He took a stand directly in front of Miss Minerva. "Now," he began, "you didn't see the murderer, but you saw his wrist watch. I'm a great believer in taking things in an orderly fashion. You're a stranger here. From Boston, I believe?"

"I am," snapped Miss Minerva.

"Stopping in this house?"

"Precisely."

"Anybody here besides you and Mr. Winterslip?"

Miss Minerva's eyes flashed. "The servants," she said. "And I would like to call your attention to the fact that I am Dan Winterslip's first cousin."

"Oh, sure—no offense. He has a daughter, hasn't he?"

"Miss Barbara is on her way home from college. Her ship will dock in the morning."

"I see. Just you and Winterslip. You're going to be an important witness."

"It will be a novel experience, at any rate," she remarked.

"I dare say. Now, go back—" Miss Minerva glared at him—it was a glare that had frightened guards on the Cambridge subway. He brushed it aside. "You understand that I haven't time for please, Miss Winterslip. Go back and describe last evening in this house."

"I was here only until eight-thirty," she told him, "when I went to a luau with some friends. Previous to that, Mr. Winterslip dined at his usual hour and we chatted for a time on the lanai."

"Did he seem to have anything on his mind?"

"Well, he has appeared a bit upset—"

"Wait a minute!" The captain took out a note-book. "Want to put down some of this. Been upset, has he? For how long?"

"For the past two weeks. Let me think—just two weeks ago to-night—or rather, last night—he and I were sitting on the lanai, and he was reading the evening paper. Something in it seemed to disturb him. He got up, wrote a note to his cousin Roger in San Francisco, and took it down for a friend aboard the *President Tyler* to deliver. From that moment he appeared restless and unhappy."

"Go on. This may be important."

"Last Wednesday morning he received a cable from Roger that infuriated him."

"A cable. What was in it?"

"It was not addressed to me," said Miss Minerva haughtily.

"Well, that's all right. We'll dig it up. Now, about last night. Did he act more upset than ever?"

"He did. But that may have been due to the fact he had hoped his daughter's ship would dock yesterday afternoon, and had learned it could not land its passengers until this morning."

"I see. You said you was only here until eight-thirty?"

"I did not," replied Miss Minerva coldly. "I said I was here only until eighty-thirty."

"Same thing."

"Well, hardly."

"I'm not here to talk grammar," Hallet said sharply. "Did anything occur—anything out of the ordinary—before you left?"

"No. Wait a moment. Some one called Mr. Winterslip on the telephone while he was at dinner. I couldn't help overhearing the conversation."

"Good for you!" She glared at him again. "Repeat it."

"I heard Mr. Winterslip say: 'Hello, Egan. What—you're not coming over? Oh, yes you are. I want to see you. I insist on it. Come about eleven. I want to see you.' That was, at least, the import of his remarks."

"Did he seem excited?"

"He raised his voice above the ordinary tone."

"Ah, yes." The captain stared at his note-book. "Must have been Jim Egan, who runs this God-forsaken Reef and Palm Hotel down the beach." He turned to Amos. "Was Egan a friend of your brother?"

"I don't know," said Amos.

"You see, Amos was not a friend of his brother, either," explained Miss Minerva. "There was an old feud between them. Speaking for myself, I never heard Dan mention Egan, and he certainly never came to the house while I was here."

Hallet nodded. "Well, you left at eight-thirty. Now tell us where you went and when you got back. And all about the wrist watch."

Miss Minerva rapidly sketched her evening at the luau. She described her return to Dan's living-room, her adventure in the dark—the luminous dial that waited for her to pass.

"I wish you'd seen more," Hallet complained. "Too many people wear wrist watches."

"Probably not many," said Miss Minerva, "wear a wrist watch like that one."

"Oh. It had some distinguishing mark?"

"It certainly did. The numerals were illuminated, and stood out clearly—with an exception. The figure 2 was very dim—practically obliterated."

He looked at her admiringly. "Well, you certainly had your wits about you."

"That's a habit I formed early in life," replied Miss Minerva. "And old habits are hard to break."

He smiled, and asked her to continue. She told of rousing the two servants and, finally, of the gruesome discovery on the lanai.

"But it was Mr. Amos," Hallet said, "who called the station."

"Yes. I telephoned him at once, and he offered to attend to that."

Hallet turned to Amos. "How long did it take you to reach here, Mr. Winterslip?" he inquired.

"Not more than ten minutes," said Amos

"You could dress and get here in that time?"

Amos hesitated. "I—I did not need to dress," he explained. "I hadn't gone to bed."

Hallet regarded him with a new interest. "Half past one—and you were still up?"

"I—I don't sleep very well," said Amos. "I'm up till all hours."

"I see. You weren't on friendly terms with your brother? And old quarrel between you?"

"No particular quarrel. I didn't approve of his manner of living, and we went separate ways."

"And stopped speaking to each other, eh?"

"Yes. That was the situation," Amos admitted.

"Humph." For a moment the captain stared at Amos, and Miss Minerva stared at him too. Amos! It flashed through her mind that Amos had been a long time alone out there on the lanai before the arival of the police.

"Those two servants who came down-stairs with you, Miss Winterslip," Hallet said. "I'll see them now. The others can go over until morning."

Haku and Kamaikui appeared, frightened and wide-eyed. Haku had nothing to tell, he had been sleeping soundly from nine until the moment Miss Minerva knocked on his door. He swore it. But Kamaikui had something to contribute.

"I come here with fruit." She pointed to a basket on the table. "On lanai out there are talking—Mr. Dan, a man, a woman. Oh, very much angry."

"What time was that?" Hallet asked.

"Ten o'clock I think."

"Did you recognize any voice except your master's?"

Miss Minerva thought the woman hesitated a second. "No. I do not."

"Anything else?"

"Yes. Maybe eleven o'clock. I am sitting close to window up-stairs. More talking on lanai. Mr. Dan and other man. Not so much angry this time."

"At eleven, eh? Do you know Mr. Jim Egan?"

"I have seen him."

"Could you say if it was his voice?"

"I could not say."

"All right. You two can go now." He turned to Miss Minerva and Amos. "We'll see what Charlie has dug up out here," he said, and led the way to the lanai.

The huge Chinese man knelt, a grotesque figure, by a table. He rose laboriously as they entered.

"Find the knife, Charlie?" the captain asked.

Chan shook his head. "No knife are present in neighborhood of crime," he announced.

"On that table," Miss Minerva began, "there was a Malay kris, used as a paper cutter—"

The Chinese man nodded, and lifted the kris from the desk. "Same remains here still," he said, "untouched, unsullied. Person who killed carried individual weapon."

"How about finger-prints?" asked Hallet

"Considering from recent discovery," Chan replied, "search for finger-prints are hopeless one." He held out a pudgy hand, in the palm of which lay a small pearl button. "Torn from kid's glove," he elucidated. "Aged trick of criminal mind. No finger-prints."

"Is that all you've got?" asked his chief.

"Most sincere endeavors," said Chan, "have revealed not much. However, I might mention this." He took up a leather-bound book from the table. "Here are written names of visitors who have enjoyed hospitality of the house. A guest book is, I believe, the term. You will find that one of the earlier pages has been ruthlessly torn out. When I make discovery the volume are lying open at that locality."

Captain Hallet took the book in his thin hand. "All right, Charlie," he said. "This is your case."

The slant eyes blinked with pleasure. "Most interesting," murmured Chan.

Hallet tapped the note-book in his pocket. "I've got a few facts here for you—we'll run over them later." He stood for a moment, staring about the lanai. "I must say we seem a little shy on clues. A button torn from a glove, a page ripped from a guest book. And a wrist watch with an illuminated dial on which the figure 2 was damaged." Chan's little eyes widened at mention of that. "Not much, Charlie, so far."

"Maybe more to come," suggested Chan. "Who knows it?"

"We'll go along now," Hallet continued. He turned to Miss Minerva and Amos. "I guess you folks would like a little rest. We'll have to trouble you again to-morrow."

Miss Minerva faced Chan. "The person who did this must be apprehended," she said firmly.

He looked at her sleepily. "What is to be, will be," he replied in a high, sing-song voice.

"I know—that's your Confucius," she snapped. "But it's a do-nothing doctrine, and I don't approve of it."

A faint smile flickered over Chan's face. "Do not fear," he said. "The fates are busy, and man may do much to assist. I promise you there will be no do-nothing here." He came closer. "Humbly asking pardon to mention it. I detect in your eyes slight flame of hostility. Quench it, if you will be so kind. Friendly cooperation are essential between us." Despite his girth, he managed a deep bow. "Wishing you good morning," he added, and followed Hallet.

Miss Minerva turned weakly to Amos. "Well, of all things—"

"Don't you worry about Charlie," Amos said. "He has a reputation for getting his man. Now you go to bed. I'll stay here and notify the—the proper people."

"Well, I will lie down for a little while," Miss Minerva said. "I shall have to go early to the dock. Poor Barbara! And there's John Quincy coming too." A grim smile crossed her face. "I'm afraid John Quincy won't approve of this."

She saw from her bedroom window that the night was breaking, the rakish cocoanut palms and the hau tree were wrapped in a gray mist. Changing her dress for a kimono, she lay down under the mosquito netting on the bed. She slept but briefly, however, and presently was at her window again. Day had come, the mist had lifted, and it was a rose and emerald world that sparkled before her tired eyes.

The freshness of that scene revivified her. The trades were blowing now—poor Dan, he had so longed for their return. The night, she saw, had worked its magic on the blossoms of the hau tree, transformed them from yellow to a rich mahogany, through the morning they would drop one by one upon the sand. In a distant algaroba a flock of myna birds screamed at the new day. A party of swimmers appeared from a neighboring cottage and plunged gaily into the surf.

A gentle knock sounded on the door, and Kamaikui entered. She placed a small object in Miss Minerva's hand.

Miss Minerva looked down. She saw a quaint old piece of jewelry, a brooch. Against a background of onyx stood the outline of a tree, with emeralds forming the leaves, rubies the fruit, and a frost of diamonds over all.

"What is this, Kamaikui?" she asked.

"Many, many years Mr. Dan have that. One month ago he gives it to a woman down the beach."

Miss Minerva's eyes narrowed. "To the woman they call the Widow of Waikiki?"

"To her, yes."

"How do you happen to have it, Kamaikui?"

"I pick it up from floor of lanai. Before policemen come."

"Very good." Miss Minerva nodded. "Say nothing of this, Kamaikui. I will attend to the matter."

"Yes. Of course." The woman went out.

Miss Minerva sat very still, staring down at that odd bit of jewelry in her hand. It must date back to the 'eighties, at least.

Close above the house sounded the loud whir of an aeroplane. Miss Minerva turned again to the window. A young lieutenant in the air service, in love with a sweet girl on the beach, was accustomed to serenade her thus every morning at dawn. His thoughtfulness was not appreciated by many innocent bystanders, but Miss Minerva's eyes were sympathetic as she watched him sweep exultantly out, far out, over the harbor.

Youth and love, the beginning of life. And on that cot down on the lanai, Dan—and the end.

8

Steamer Day

Out in the harbor, by the channel entrance, the *President Tyler* stood motionless as Diamond Head, and from his post near the rail outside his stateroom, John Quincy Winterslip took his first look at Honolulu. He had no feeling of having been here before; this was an alien land. Several miles away he saw the line of piers and unlovely warehouses that marked the water-front; beyond that lay a vast expanse of brilliant green pierced here and there by the top of a modest skyscraper. Back of the city a range of mountains stood on guard, peaks of crystal blue against the azure sky.

A trim little launch from Quarantine chugged importantly up to the big liner's side, and a doctor in a khaki uniform ran briskly up the accommodation ladder to the deck not far from where the boy stood. John Quincy wondered at the man's vitality. He felt like a spent force himself. The air was moist and heavy, the breeze the ship had stirred in moving gone for ever. The flood of energy that had swept over him in San Francisco was but a happy memory now. He leaned wearily on the rail, staring at the bright tropical landscape before him—and not seeing it at all.

He saw instead a quiet, well-furnished Boston office where at this very moment the typewriters were clicking amiably and the stock ticker was busily writing the story of another day. In a few hours—there was a considerable difference of time—the market would close and the men he knew would be piling into automobiles and heading for the nearest country club. A round of golf, then a calm, perfectly served dinner, and after that a quiet evening with a book. life running along as it was meant to go, without rude interruption or disturbing incident; life devoid of ohia wood boxes, attic encounters, unwillingly witnessed love scenes, cousins with blackbirding pasts. Suddenly John Quincy remembered, this was the morning when he must look Dan Winterslip in the eye and tell him he had been a bit dilatory with his fists. Oh, well—he straightened resolutely—the sooner that was done, the better.

Harry Jennison came along the deck, smiling and vigorous, clad in spotless white from head to foot. "Here we are," he cried. "On the threshold of paradise!"

"Think so?" said John Quincy.

"Know it," Jennison answered. "Only place in the world, these islands. You remember what Mark Twain said—"

"Ever visited Boston?" John Quincy cut in.

"Once," replied Jennison briefly. "That's Punch Bowl Hill back of the town—and Tantalus beyond. Take you up to the summit some day—wonderful view. See that tallest building? The Van Patten Trust Company—my office is on the top floor. Only drawback about getting home—I'll have to go to work again."

"I don't see how any one can work in this climate," John Quincy said.

"Oh, well, we take it easy. Can't manage the pace of you mainland people. Every now and then some go-getter from the States comes out here and tries to hustle us." He laughed. "He dies of disgust and we bury him in a leisurely way. Been down to breakfast?"

John Quincy accompanied him to the dining saloon. Madame Maynard and Barara were at the table. The old lady's cheeks were flushed and her eyes sparkled; Barbara, too, was in her gayest mood. The excitement of coming home had made her very happy—or was her happiness all due to that? John Quincy noted her smile of greeting for Jennison, and rather wished he knew less than he did.

"Prepare for a thrill, John Quincy," the girl said. "Landing in Hawaii is like landing nowhere else on the globe. Of course, this is a through boat, and it isn't welcomed as the Matson liners are. But there'll be a crowd waiting for the *Matsonia* this morning, and we'll steal a little of her aloha."

"A little of her what?" inquired John Quincy.

"Aloha—meaning loving welcome. You shall have all my leis, John Quincy. Just to show you how glad Honolulu is you've come at last."

The boy turned to Madame Maynard. "I suppose this is an old story to you?"

"Bless you, my boy," she said. "It's always new. A hundred and twenty-eight times—yet I'm as thrilled as though I were coming home from college." She sighed. "A hundred and twenty-eight times. So many of those who once hung leis about my neck are gone for ever now. They'll not be waiting for me—not on this dock."

"None of that," Barbara chided. "Only happy thoughts this morning. It's steamer day."

Nobody seemed hungry, and breakfast was a sketchy affair. John Quincy returned to his cabin to find Bowker strapping up his luggage.

"I guess you're all ready, sir," said the steward. "I finished that book last night, and you'll find it in your suit-case. We'll be moving on to the dock shortly. All good luck to you—and don't forget about the okolehau."

"It's graven on my memory," smiled John Quincy. "Here—this is for you."

Bowker glanced at the bank-note and pocketed it. "You're mighty kind, sir," he remarked feelingly. "That will sort of balance up the dollar each I'll get from those two missionaries when we reach China—if I'm lucky. Of course, it's rather distasteful to me to accept anything. From a friend of Tim's, you know."

"Oh, that's for value received," said John Quincy, and followed Bowker on deck.

"There she is," announced Bowker, pausing by the rail. "Honolulu. The South Seas with a collar on, driving a Ford car. Polynesia with a private still and all the other benefits of the white man's civilization. We'll go out at eight to-night, thank heaven."

"Paradise doesn't appeal to you," suggested John Quincy.

"No. Nor any other of these bright-colored lands my poor old feet must tread. I'm getting fed up, sir." He came closer. "I want to buy a little newspaper in some country town and starve to death on the proceeds of running it. What a happy finish! Well, maybe I can manage it, before long."

"I hope so," said John Quincy.

"I hope so, too," said Bowker. "Here's wishing you a happy time in Honolulu. And one other word of warning—don't linger there."

"I don't intend to," John Quincy assured him.

"That's the talk. It's one of those places—you know—dangerous. Lotus on the menu every day. The first thing you know, you've forgot where you put your trunk. So long, sir."

With a wave of the hand, Tim's friend disappeared down the deck. Amid much confusion, John Quincy took his place in line for the doctor's inspection, passed the careful scrutiny of an immigration official who finally admitted that maybe Boston was in the Union, and was then left to his own devices and his long, long thoughts.

The *President Tyler* was moving slowly toward the shore. Excited figures scurried about her decks, pausing now and then to stare through lifted glasses at the land. John Quincy perceived that early though the hour was, the pier toward which they were heading was alive with people. Barbara came and stood by his side.

"Poor old dad," she said, "he's been struggling along without me for nine months. This will be a big morning in his life. You'll like dad, John Quincy."

"I'm sure I shall," he answered heartily.

"Dad's one of the finest—" Jennison joined them. "Harry, I meant to tell the steward to take my luggage ashore when we land."

"I told him," Jennison said. "I tipped him, too."

"Thanks," the girl replied. "I was so excited, I forgot."

She leaned eagerly over the rail, peering at the dock. Her eyes were shining. "I don't see him yet," she said. They were near enough now to hear the voices of those ashore, gay voices calling flippant greetings. The big ship edged gingerly closer.

"There's Aunt Minerva," cried John Quincy suddenly. That little touch of home in the throng was very pleasant. "Is that your father with her?" He indicated a tall anemic man at Minerva's side.

"I don't see—where—" Barbara began. "Oh—that—why, that's Uncle Amos!"

"Oh, is that Amos?" remarked John Quincy, without interest. But Barbara had gripped his arm, and as he turned he saw a wild alarm in her eyes.

"What do you suppose that means?" she cried. "I don't see dad. I don't see him anywhere—"

"Oh, he's in that crowd somewhere—"

"No, no—you don't understand! Uncle Amos! I'm—I'm frightened."

John Quincy didn't gather what it was all about, and there was no time to find out. Jennison was pushing ahead through the crowd, making a path for Barbara, and the boy meekly brought up the rear. They were among the first down the plank. Miss Minerva and Amos were waiting at the foot.

"My dear." Miss Minerva put her arms about the girl and kissed her gently. She turned to John Quincy. "Well, here you are—"

There was something lacking in this welcome. John Quincy sensed it at once.

"Where's dad?" Barbara cried.

"I'll explain in the car—" Miss Minerva began.

"No, now! Now! I must know now!"

The crowd was surging about them, calling happy greetings, the Royal Hawaiian Band was playing a gay tune, carnival was in the air.

"Your father is dead, my dear," said Miss Minerva.

John Quincy saw the girl's slim figure sway gently, but it was Harry Jennison's strong arm that caught her.

For a moment she stood, with Jennison's arm about her. "All right," she said. "I'm ready to go home." And walked like a true Winterslip toward the street.

Amos melted away into the crowd, but Jennison accompanied them to the car. "I'll go out with you," he said to Barbara. She did not seem to hear. The four of them entered the limousine, and in another moment the happy clamor of steamer day was left behind.

No one spoke. The curtains of the car were drawn, but a warm streak of sunlight fell across John Quincy's knees. He was a little dazed. Shocking, this news about Cousin Dan. Must have died suddenly—but no doubt that was how things always happened out this way. He glanced at the white stricken face of the girl beside him, and because of her his heart was heavy.

She laid her cold hand on his. "It's not the welcome I promised you, John Quincy," she said softly.

"Why, my dear girl, I don't matter now."

No other word was spoken on the journey, and when they reached Dan's house, Barbara and Miss Minerva went immediately up-stairs. Jennison disappeared through a doorway at the left; evidently he knew his way about. Haku volunteered to show John Quincy his quarters, so he followed the Haku to the second floor.

When his bags were unpacked, John Quincy went down-stairs again. Miss Minerva was waiting for him in the living-room. From beyond the bamboo curtain leading to the lanai came the sound of men's voices, mumbling and indistinct.

"Well," said John Quincy, "how have you been?"

"Never better," his aunt assured him.

"Mother's been rather worried about you. She'd begun to think you were never coming home."

"I've begun to think it myself," Miss Minerva replied.

He stared at her. "Some of those bonds you left with me have matured. I haven't known just what you wanted me to do about them."

"What," inquired Miss Minerva, "is a bond?"

That sort of wild reckless talk never did make a hit with John Quincy. "It's about time somebody came out here and brought you to your senses," he remarked.

"Think so?" said his aunt.

A sound up-stairs recalled John Quincy to the situation. "This was rather sudden—Cousin Dan's death?" he inquired.

"Amazingly so."

"Well, it seems to me that it would be rather an intrusion—our staying on here now. We ought to go home in a few days. I'd better see about reservations—"

"You needn't trouble," snapped Miss Minerva. "I'll not stir from here until I see the person who did this brought to justice."

"The person who did what?" asked John Quincy.

"The person who murdered Cousin Dan," said Miss Minerva.

John Quincy's jaw dropped. His face registered a wide variety of emotions. "Good lord!" he gasped.

"Oh, you needn't be so shocked," said his aunt. "The Winterslip family will still go on."

"Well, I'm not surprised," remarked John Quincy, "when I stop to think. The things I've learned about Cousin Dan. It's a wonder to me—"

"That will do," said Miss Minerva. "You're talking like Amos, and that's no compliment. You didn't know Dan. I did—and I liked him. I'm going to stay here and do all I can to help run down the murderer. And so are you."

"Pardon me. I am not."

"Don't contradict. I intend you shall take an active part in the investigation. The police are rather informal in a small place like this. They'll welcome your help."

"My help! I'm no detective. What's happened to you, anyhow? Why should you want me to go round hobnobbing with policemen—"

"For the simple reason that if we're not careful some rather unpleasant scandal may come out of this. If you're on the ground you may be able to avert needless publicity. For Barbara's sake."

"No, thank you," said John Quincy. "I'm leaving for Boston in three days, and so are you. Pack your trunks."

Miss Minerva laughed. "I've heard your father talk like that," she told him. "But I never knew him to gain anything by it in the end. Come out on the lanai and I'll introduce you to a few policemen."

John Quincy received this invitation with the contemptuous silence he thought it deserved. But while he was lavishing on it his best contempt, the bamboo curtain parted and the policemen came to him. Jennison was with them.

"Good morning, Captain Hallet," siad Miss Minnerva brightly. "May I present my newphew, Mr. John Quincy Winterslip, of Boston."

"I'm very anxious to meet Mr. John Quincy Winterslip," the captain replied.

"How do you do," said John Quincy. His heart sank. They'd drag him into this affair if they could.

"And this, John Quincy," went on Miss Minerva, "is Mr. Charles Chan, of the Honolulu detective force."

John Quincy had thought himself prepared for anything, but—"Mr.—Mr. Chan," he gasped.

"Mere words," said Chan, "can not express my unlimitable delight in meeting a representative of the ancient civilization of Boston."

Harry Jennison spoke. "This is an appalling business, Miss Winterslip," he said. "As perhaps you know, I was your cousin's lawyer. I was also his friend. Therefore I hope you won't think I am intruding if I show a keen interest in what is going forward here."

"Not at all," Miss Minerva assured him. "We shall need all the help we can get."

Captain Hallet had taken a paper from his pocket. He faced John Quincy.

"Young man," he began, "I said I wanted to meet you. Last night Miss Winterslip told me of a cablegram received by the dead man about a week ago, which she said angered him greatly. I happen to have a copy of that message, turned over to me by the cable people. I'll read it to you:

"JOHN QUINCY SAILING ON PRESIDENT TYLER STOP OWING TO UNFORTUNATE ACCIDENT HE LEAVES HERE WITH EMPTY HANDS. SIGNED ROGER WINTERSLIP."

"Yes?" said John Quincy haughtily.

"Explain that, if you will."

John Quincy stiffened. "The matter was strictly private," he said. "A family affair."

Captain Hallet glared at him. "You're mistaken," he replied. "Nothing that concerns Mr. Dan Winterslip is private now. Tell me what that cable meant, and be quick about it. I'm busy this morning."

John Quincy glared back. The man didn't seem to realize to whom he was talking. "I've already said—" he began.

"John Quincy," snapped Miss Minerva. "Do as you're told!"

Oh, well, if she wanted family secrets aired in public! Reluctantly John Quincy explained about Dan Winterslip's letter, and the misadventure in the attic of Dan's San Francisco house.

"An ohia wood box bound with copper," repeated the captain. "Initials on it, T.M.B. Got that, Charlie?"

"It is written in the book," said Chan.

"Any idea what was in that box?" asked Hallet.

"Not the slightest," John Quincy told him.

Hallet turned to Miss Minerva. "You knew nothing about this?" She assured him she did not. "Well," he continued, "one thing more and we'll go along. We've been making a thorough search of the premises by daylight—without much success, I'm sorry to say. However, by the cement walk just outside that door"—he pointed to the screen door leading from the living-room into the garden—"Charlie made a discovery."

Chan stepped forward, holding a small white object in the palm of his hand.

"One-half cigarette, incompletely consumed," he announced. "Very recent, not weather stained. It are of the brand denominated Corsican, assembled in London and smoked habitually by Englishmen."

Hallet again addressed Miss Minerva: "Did Dan Winterslip smoke cigarettes?"

"You were the only other person living here."

"I haven't acquired the cigarette habit," snapped Miss Minerva. "Though undoubtedly it's not too late yet."

"The servants, perhaps?" went on Hallet.

"Some of the servants may smoke cigarettés, but hardly of this quality. I take it these are not on sale in Honolulu?"

"They're not," said the captain. "But Charlie tells me they're put up in air-tight tins and shipped to Englishmen the world over. Well, stow that away, Charlie." The Chinese man tenderly placed the half cigarette, incompletely consumed, in his pocketbook. "I'm going on down the beach now to have a little talk with Mr. Jim Egan," the captain added.

"I'll go with you," Jennison offered. "I may be able to supply a link or two there."

"Sure, come along," Hallet replied cordially.

"Captain Hallet," put in Miss Minerva, "it is my wish that some member of the family keep in touch with what you are doing, in order that we may give you all the aid we can. My nephew would like to accompany you—"

"Pardon me," said John Quincy coldly, "you're quite wrong. I have no intention of joining the police force."

"Well, just as you say," remarked Hallet. He turned to Miss Minerva. "I'm relying on you, at any rate. You've got a good mind. Anybody can see that."

"Thank you," she said.

"As good as a man's," he added.

"Oh, now you've spoiled it. Good morning."

The three men went through the screen door into the bright sunshine of the garden. John Quincy was aware that he was not in high favor with his aunt.

"I'll go up and change," he said uncomfortably. "We'll talk things over later—"

He went into the hall. At the foot of the stairs he paused.

From above came a low, heart-breaking moan of anguish. Barbara. Poor Barbara, who had been so happy less than an hour ago.

John Quincy felt his head go hot, the blood pound in his temples. How dare any one strike down a Winterslip! How dare any one inflict this grief on his Cousin Barbara! He clenched his fists and stood for a moment, feeling that he, too, could kill.

Action—he must have action! He rushed through the living-room, past the astonished Miss Minerva. In the drive stood a car, the three men were already in it.

"Wait a minute," called John Quincy. "I'm going with you."

"Hop in," said Captain Hallet.

The car rolled down the drive and out on to the hot asphalt of Kalia Road. John Quincy sat erect, his eyes flashing, by the side of a huge grinning Chinese man.

9

At the Reef and Palm

They reached Kalakua Avenue and swerving sharply to the right, Captain Hallet stepped on the gas. Since the car was without a top, John Quincy was getting an unrestricted view of this land that lay at his journey's end. As a small boy squirming about on the hard pew in the First Unitarian Church, he had heard much of Heaven, and his youthful imagination had pictured it as something like this. A warm, rather languid country, freshly painted in the gaudiest colors available.

Creamy white clouds wrapped the tops of the distant mountains, and their slopes were bright with tropical foliage. John Quincy heard near at hand the low monotone of breakers lapping the shore. Occasionally he caught a glimpse of apple-green water and a dazzling white stretch of sand. "Oh, Waikiki! Oh, scene of peace—" What was the rest of that poem his Aunt Minerva had quoted in her last letter—the one in which she had announced that she was staying on indefinitely. "And looking down from tum-tum skies, the angels smile on Waikiki." Sentimental, but sentiment was one of Hawaii's cheif exports. One had only to look at the place to understand and forgive.

John Quincy had not delayed for a hat, and the sun was beating down fiercely on his brown head. Charlie Chan glanced at him.

"Humbly begging pardon," he remarked, "would say it is unadvisable to venture forth without headgear. Especially since you are a malihini."

"A what?"

"The term carries no offense. Malihini—stranger, newcomer."

"Oh." John Quincy looked at him curiously. "Are you a malihini?"

"Not in the least," grinned Chan. "I am kamaaina—old-timer. Pursuing the truth further, I have been twenty-five years in the Islands."

They passed a huge hotel, and presently John Quincy saw Diamond Head standing an impressive guardian at the far end of that lovely curving beach. A little farther along the captain drew up to the curb and the four men alighted. On the other side of a dilapidated fence was a garden that might have been Eden at its best.

Entering past a gate that hung sorrowfully on one hinge they walked up a dirt path and in a moment a ramshackle old building came into view. They were approaching it on an angle, and John Quincy saw that the greater part of it extended out over the water. The tottering structure was of two stories, with double-decked balconies on both sides and the rear. It had rather an air about it; once, no doubt, it had been worthy to stand in this setting. Flowering vines clambered over it in a friendly endeavor to hide its imperfections from the world.

"Some day," announced Charlie Chan solemnly, "those rafters underneath will disintegrate and the Reef and Palm Hotel will descend into the sea with a most horrid gurgle."

As they drew nearer, it seemed to John Quincy that Chan's prophecy might come true at any moment. They paused at the foot of a crumbling stair that led to the front door, and as they did so a man emerged hurriedly from the Reef and Palm. His once white clothes were yellowed, his face lined, his eyes tired and disillusioned. But about him, as about the hotel, hung the suggestion of a distinguished past.

"Mr. Egan," said Captain Hallet promptly.

"Oh—how are you?" the man replied, with an accent that recalled to John Quincy's mind his meeting with Captain Arthur Temple Cope.

"We want to talk to you," announced Hallet brusquely.

A shadow crossed Egan's face. "I'm frightfully sorry," he said, "but I have a most important engagement, and I'm late as it is. Some other time—"

"Now!" cut in Hallet. The word shot through the morning like a rocket. He started up the steps.

"Impossible," said Egan. He did not raise his voice. "Nothing on earth could keep me from the dock this morning—"

The captain of detectives seized his arm. "Come inside!" he ordered.

Egan's face flushed. "Take your hand off me, damn you! By what right—"

"You watch your step, Egan," advised Hallet angrily. "You know why I'm here."

"I do not."

Hallet stared into the man's face. "Dan Winterslip was murdered last night," he said.

Jim Egan removed his hat, and looked helplessly out toward Kalakaua Avenue. "So I read in the morning paper," he replied. "What has his death to do with me?"

"You were the last person to see him alive," Hallet answered. "Now quit bluffing and come inside."

Egan cast one final baffled glance at the street, where a trolley bound for the city three miles away was rattling swiftly by. Then he bowed his head and led the way into the hotel.

They entered a huge, poorly furnished public room, deserted save for a woman tourist writing post-cards at a table, and a shabby Japanese clerk lolling behind the desk. "This way," Egan said, and they followed him past the desk and into a small private office. Here all was confusion, dusty piles of magazines and newspapers were everywhere, battered old ledgers lay upon the floor. On the wall hung a portrait of Queen Victoria; many pictures cut from the London illustrated weeklies were tacked up haphazardly. Jennison spread a newspaper carefully over the window-sill and sat down there. Egan cleared chairs for Hallet, Chan and John Quincy, and himself took his place before an ancient roll-top desk.

"If you will be brief, Captain," he suggested, "I might still have time—" He glanced at a clock above the desk.

"Forget that," advised Hallet sharply. His manner was considerably different from that he employed in the house of a leading citizen like Dan Winterslip. "Let's get to business." He turned to Chan. "Got your book, Charlie?"

"Preparations are complete," replied Chan, his pencil poised.

"All right." Hallet drew his chair closer to the desk. "Now Egan, you come through and come clean. I know that last night about seven-thirty you called up Dan Winterslip and tried to slide out of an appointment you had made with him. I know that he refused to let you off, and insisted on seeing you at eleven. About that time, you went to his house. You and he had a rather excited talk. At one-twenty-five Winterslip was found dead. Murdered, Egan! Now give me your end of it."

Jim Egan ran his fingers through his curly, close-cropped hair—straw-colored once, but now mostly gray. "That's all quite true," he said. "Do—do you mind if I smoke?" He took out a silver case and removed a cigarette. His hand trembled slightly as he applied the match. "I did make an appointment with Winterslip for last night," he continued. "During the course of the day I—I changed my mind. When I called up to tell him so, he insisted on seeing me. He urged me to come at eleven, and I went."

"Who let you in?" Hallet asked.

"Winterslip was waiting in the garden when I came. We went inside—"

Hallet glanced at the cigarette in Egan's hand. "By the door leading directly into the living-room?" he asked.

"No," said Egan. "By the big door at the front of the house. Winterslip took me out on his lanai, and we had a bit of a chat regarding the—the business that had brought me. About half an hour later, I came away. When I left Winterslip was alive and well—in good spirits, too. Smiling, as a matter of fact."

"I see." Hallet looked at him thoughtfully for a moment. "You went back later, perhaps."

"I did not," said Egan promptly. "I came directly here and went to bed."

"Who saw you?"

"No one. My clerk goes off duty at eleven. The hotel is open, but there is no one in charge. My patronage is—not large."

"You came here at eleven-thirty and went to bed," Hallet said. "But no one saw you. Tell me, were you well acquainted with Dan Winterslip?"

Egan shook his head. "In the twenty-three years I've been in Honolulu, I had never spoken to him until I called him on the telephone yesterday morning."

"Humph." Hallet leaned back in his chair and spoke in a more amiable tone. "As a younger man, I believe you traveled a lot?"

"I drifted about a bit," Egan admitted. "I was just eighteen when I left England—"

"At your family's suggestion," smiled the captain.

"What's that to you?" Egan flared.

"Where did you go?"

"Australia. I ranched it for a time—and later I worked in Melbourne."
"What doing?" persisted Hallet.
"In—in a bank."
"A bank, eh? And then—"
"The South Seas. Just—wandering about—I was restless—"
"Beach-combing, eh?"
Egan flushed. "I may have been on my uppers at times, but damn it—"
"Wait a minute," Hallet cut in. "What I want to know is—those years you were drifting about—did you by any chance run into Dan Winterslip?"
"I—I might have."
"What sort of an answer is that! Yes or no?"
"Well, as a matter of fact, I did," Egan admitted. "Just once—in Melbourne. But it was quite unimportant meeting. So unimportant Winterslip had completely forgotten it."
"But you hadn't. And yesterday morning, after twenty-three years' silence between you, you called him on the telephone. On rather sudden business."
"I did."
Hallet came closer. "All right, Egan. We've reached the important part of your story. What was that business?"
A tense silence fell in the little office as they awaited Egan's answer. The Englishman looked Hallet calmly in the eye. "I can't tell you that," he said.
Hallet's face reddened. "Oh, yes, you can. And you're going to."
"Never," answered Egan, without raising his voice.
The captain glared at him. "You don't seem to realize your position."
"I realize it perfectly."
"If you and I were alone—"
"I won't tell you under any circumstances, Hallet."
"Maybe you'll tell the prosecutor—"
"Look here," cried Egan wearily. "Why must I say it over and over? I'll tell nobody my business with Winterslip. Nobody, understand!" He crushed the half-smoked cigarette savagely down on to a tray at his side.
John Quincy saw Hallet nod to Chan. He saw Chan's pudgy little hand go out and seize the remnant of cigarette. A happy grin spread over the Oriental's fat face. He handed the stub to his chief.
"Corsican brand!" he cried triumphantly.
"Ah, yes," said Hallet. "This your usual smoke?"
A startled look crossed Egan's tired face. "No, it's not," he said.
"It's a make that's not on sale in the Islands, I believe?"
"No, I fancy it isn't."
Captain Hallet held out his hand. "Give me your cigarette case, Egan." The Englishman passed it over, and Hallet opened it. "Humph," he said. "You've managed to get hold of a few, haven't you?"
"Yes. They were—given me."
"Is that so? Who gave them to you?"
Egan considered. "I'm afraid I can't tell you that, either," he said.
Hallet's eyes glittered angrily. "Let me give you a few facts," he began. "You called on Dan Winterslip last night, you entered and left by the front door, and you didn't go back. Yet just outside the door leading directly into the living-room, we have found a partly smoked cigarette of this unusual brand. Now will you tell me who gave you these Corsicans?"
"No," said Egan, "I won't."
Hallet slipped the silver cigarette case into his pocket, and stood up. "Very well," he remarked. "I've wasted all the time I intend to here. The district court prosecutor will want to talk to you—"

"Of course," agreed Egan, "I'll come and see him—this afternoon—"

Hallet glared at him. "Quit kidding yourself and get your hat!"

Egan rose too. "Look here," he cried, "I don't like your manner. It's true there are certain matters in connection with Winterslip I can't discuss, and that's unfortunate. But surely you don't think I killed the man. What motive would I have—"

Jennison rose quickly from his seat on the window-ledge and stepped forward. "Hallet," he said, "there's something I ought to tell you. Two or three years ago Dan Winterslip and I were walking along King Street, and we passed Mr. Egan here. Winterslip nodded toward him. 'I'm afraid of that man, Harry.' Just that, and nothing further."

"It's enough," remarked Hallet grimly. "Egan, you're going with me."

Egan's eyes flashed. "Of course," he cried bitterly. "Of course I'm going with you. You're all against me, the whole town is against me, I've been sneered at and belittled for twenty years. Because I was poor. An outcast, my daughter humiliated, not good enough to associate with these New England blue-bloods—these thin-lipped Puritans with a touch of sun—"

At sound of that familiar phrase, John Quincy sat up. Where, where—oh, yes, on the Oakland ferry—

"Never mind that," Hallet was saying. "I'll give you one last chance. Will you tell me what I want to know?"

"I will not," cried Egan.

"All right. Then come along."

"Am I under arrest?" asked Egan.

"I didn't say that," replied Hallet, suddenly cautious. "The investigation is young yet. You are withholding much needed information, and I believe that after you've spent a few hours at the station, you'll change your mind and talk. In fact, I'm sure of it. I haven't any warrant, but your position will be a lot more dignified if you come willingly without one."

Egan considered a moment. "I fancy you're right," he said. "I have certain orders to give the servants, if you don't mind—"

Hallet nodded. "Make it snappy. Charlie will go with you."

Egan and Chan disappeared. The captain, John Quincy and Jennison went out and sat down in the public room. Five minutes passed, ten, fifteen—

Jennison glanced at his watch. "See here, Hallet," he said. "The man's making a monkey of you—"

Hallet reddened, and stood up. At that instant Egan and Chan came down the big open stairway at one side of the room. Hallet went up to the Englishman.

"Say, Egan—what are you doing? Playing for time?"

Egan smiled. "That's precisely what I'm doing," he replied. "My daughter's coming in this morning on the *Mastonia*—the boat ought to be at the dock now. She's been at school on the mainland, and I haven't seen her for nine months. You've done me out of the pleasure of meeting her, but in a few minutes—"

"Nothing doing," cried Hallet. "Now you get your hat. I'm pau."

Egan hesitated a moment, then slowly took his battered old straw hat from the desk. The five men walked through the blooming garden toward Hallet's car. As they emerged into the street, a taxi drew up to the curb. Egan ran forward, and the girl John Quincy had last seen at the gateway to San Francisco leaped out into the Englishman's arms.

"Dad—where were you?" she cried.

"Cary, darling," he said. "I was so frightfully sorry—I meant to be at the dock but I was detained. How are you, my dear?"

"I'm fine, dad—but—where are you going?" She looked at Hallet; John Quincy remained discreetly in the background.

"I've—I've a little business in the city, my dear," Egan said. "I'll be home presently, I fancy. If—if I shouldn't be, I leave you in charge."

"Why, dad—"

"Don't worry," he added pleadingly. "That's all I can say now, Cary. Don't worry, my dear." He turned to Hallet. "Shall we go, Captain?"

The two policemen, Jennison and Egan entered the car. John Quincy stepped forward. The girl's big perplexed eyes met his.

"You?" she cried.

"Coming, Mr. Winterslip?" inquired Hallet.

John Quincy smiled at the girl. "You were quite right," he said. "I haven't needed that hat."

She looked up at him. "But you're not wearing any at all. That's hardly wise—"

"Mr. Winterslip!" barked Hallet.

John Quincy turned. "Oh, pardon me, Captain," he said. "I forgot to mention it, but I'm leaving you here. Good-by."

Hallet grunted and started his car. While the girl paid for her taxi out of a tiny purse, John Quincy picked up her suit-case.

"This time," he said, "I insist on carrying it." They stepped through the gateway into the garden that might have been Eden on one of its better days. "You didn't tell me we might meet in Honolulu," the boy remarked.

"I wasn't sure we would." She glanced at the shabby old hotel. "You see, I'm not exactly a social favorite out here." John Quincy could think of no reply, and they mounted the crumbling steps. The public room was quite deserted. "And why *have* we met?" the girl continued. "I'm fearfully puzzled. What was dad's business with those men? One of them was Captain Hallet—a policeman—"

John Quincy frowned. "I'm not so sure your father wants you to know."

"But I've got to know, that's obvious. Please tell me."

John Quincy relinquished the suit-case, and brought forward a chair. The girl sat down.

"It's this way," he began. "My Cousin Dan was murdered in the night."

Her eyes were tragic. "Oh—poor Barbara!" she cried. That's right, he mustn't forget Barbara! "But dad—oh, go on please—"

"Your father visited Cousin Dan last night at eleven, and he refuses to say why. There are other things he refused to tell."

She looked up at him, her eyes filled with sudden tears. "I was so happy on the boat," she said. "I knew it couldn't last."

He sat down. "Nonsense. Everything will come out all right. Your father is probably shielding some one—"

She nodded. "Of course. But if he's made up his mind not to talk, he just simply won't talk. He's odd that way. They may keep him down there, and I shall be all alone—"

"Not quite alone," John Quincy told her.

"No, no," she said. "I've warned you. We're not the sort the best people care to know—"

"The more fools they," cut in the boy. "I'm John Quincy Winterslip, of Boston. And you—"

"Carlota Maria Egan," she answered. "You see, my mother was half Portuguese. The other half was Scotch-Irish—my father's English. This is the melting pot out here, you know." She was silent for a moment. "My mother was very beautiful," she added wistfully. "So they tell me—I never knew."

John Quincy was touched. "I thought how beautiful she must have been," he said gently. "That day I met you on the ferry."

The girl dabbed at her eyes with an absurd little handkerchief, and stood up. "Well," she remarked, "this is just another thing that has to be faced. Another call for courage—I must meet it." She smiled. "The lady manager of the Reef and Palm. Can I show you a room?"

"I say, it'll be a rather stiff job, won't it?" John Quincy rose too.

"Oh, I shan't mind. I've helped dad before. Only one thing troubles me—bills and all that. I've no head for arithmetic."

"That's all right—I have," replied John Quincy. He stopped. Wasn't he getting in a little deep?

"How wonderful," the girl said.

"Why, not at all," John Quincy protested. "It's my line, at home." Home! Yes, he had a home, he recalled. "Bonds and interest and all that sort of thing. I'll drop in later in the day to see how you're getting on." He moved away in a mild panic. "I'd better be going now," he added.

"Of course." She followed him to the door. "You're altogether too kind. Shall you be in Honolulu long?"

"That depends," John Quincy said. "I've made up my mind to one thing. I shan't stir from here until this mystery about Cousin Dan is solved. And I'm going to do everything in my power to help in solving it."

"I'm sure you're very clever, too," she told him.

He shook his head. "I wouldn't say that. But I intend to make the effort of my life. I've got a lot of incentives for seeing this affair through." Something else trembled on his tongue. Better not say it. Oh, lord, he was saying it. "You're one of them," he added, and clattered down the stairs.

"Do be careful," called the girl. "Those steps are even worse than they were when I left. Just another thing to be repaired—some day—when our ship comes in."

He left her smiling wistfully in the doorway and hurrying through the garden, stepped out on Kalakaua Avenue. The blazing sun beat down on his defenseless head. Gorgeous trees flaunted scarlet banners along his path, tall cocoanut palms swayed above him at the touch of the friendly trades, not far away rainbow-tinted waters lapped a snowy beach. A sweet land—all of that.

Did he wish that Agatha Parker were there to see it with him? Pursuing the truth further, as Charlie Chan would put it, he did not.

10

A Newspaper Ripped in Anger

When John Quincy got back to the living-room he found Miss Minerva pacing up and down with the light of battle in her eyes. He selected a large, comfortable looking chair and sank into it.

"Anything the matter?" he inquired. "You seem disturbed."

"I've just been having a lot of pilikia," she announced.

"What's that—another native drink?" he said with interest. "Could I have some too?"

"Pilikia means trouble," she translated. "Several reporters have been here, and you'd hardly credit the questions they asked."

"About Cousin Dan, eh?" John Quincy nodded. "I can imagine."

"However, they got nothing out of me. I took good care of that."

"Go easy," advised John Quincy. "A fellow back home who had a divorce case in his family was telling me that if you're not polite to the newspaper boys they just plain break your heart."

"Don't worry," said Miss Minerva. "I was diplomatic, of course. I think I handled them rather well, under the circumstances. They were the first reporters I'd ever met—though I've had the pleasure of talking with gentlemen from the *Transcript*. What happened at the Reef and Palm Hotel?"

John Quincy told her—in part.

"Well, I shouldn't be surprised if Egan turned out to be guilty," she commented. "I've made a few inquiries about him this morning, and he doesn't appear to amount to much. A sort of glorified beach-comber."

"Nonsense," objected John Quincy. "Egan's a gentleman. Just because he doesn't happen to have prospered is no reason for condemning him without a hearing."

"He's had a hearing," snapped Miss Minerva. "And it seems he's been mixed up in something he's not precisely proud of. There, I've gone and ended a sentence with a preposition. Profitably all this has upset me more than I realize."

John Quincy smiled. "Cousin Dan," he reminded her, "was also mixed up in a few affairs he could hardly have looked back on with pride. No, Aunt Minerva, I feel Hallet is on the wrong trail there. It's just as Egan's daughter said—"

She glanced at him quickly. "Oh—so Egan has a daughter?"

"Yes, and a mighty attractive girl. It's a confounded shame to put this thing on her."

"Humph," said Miss Minerva.

John Quincy glanced at his watch. "Good lord—it's only ten o'clock!" A great calm had settled over the house, there was no sound save the soft lapping of waves on the beach outside. "What, in heaven's name, do you do out here?"

"Oh, you'll become accustomed to it shortly," Miss Minerva answered. "At first, you just sit and think. After a time, you just sit."

"Sounds fascinating," said John Quincy sarcastically.

"That's the odd part of it," his aunt replied, "it is. One of the things you think about, at first, is going home. When you stop thinking, that naturally slips your mind."

"We gathered that," John Quincy told her.

"You'll meet a man on the beach," said Miss Minerva, "who stopped over between boats to have his laundry done. That was twenty years ago, and he's still here."

"Probably they haven't finished his laundry," suggested John Quincy, yawning openly. "Ho, hum. I'm going up to my room to change, and after that I believe I'll write a few letters." He rose with an effort and went to the door. "How's Barbara?" he asked.

Miss Minerva shook her head. "Dan was all the poor child had," she said. "She's taken it rather hard. You won't see her for some time, and when you do—the least said about all this, the better."

"Why, naturally," agreed John Quincy, and went up-stairs.

After he had bathed and put on his whitest, thinnest clothes, he explored the desk that stood near his bed and found it well supplied with note paper. Languidly laying out a sheet, he began to write.

"Dear Agatha:
Here I am in Honolulu and outside my window I can
hear the lazy swish of waters lapping the famous beach
of—"

Lazy, indeed. John Quincy had a feeling for words. He stopped and
stared at an agile little cloud flitting swiftly through the sky—got up from
his chair to watch it disappear over Diamond Head. On his way back to the
desk he had to pass the bed. What inviting beds they had out here! He
lifted the mosquito netting and dropped down for a moment—

Haku hammered on the door at one o'clock, and that was how John
Quincy happened to be present at lunch. His aunt was already at the table
when he staggered in.

"Cheer up," she smiled. "You'll become acclimated soon. Of course, even
then you'll want your nap just after lunch every day."

"I will not," he answered, but there was no conviction in his tone.

"Barbara asked me to tell you how sorry she is not to be with you. She's
a sweet girl, John Quincy."

"She's all of that. Give her my love, won't you?"

"Your love?" His aunt looked at him. "Do you mean that? Barbara's only
a second cousin—"

He laughed. "Don't waste your time match-making, Aunt Minerva. Some
one has already spoken for Barbara."

"Really? Who?"

"Jennison. He seems like a fine fellow, too."

"Handsome, at any rate," Miss Minerva admitted. They ate in silence for
a time. "The coroner and his friends were here this morning," said Miss
Minerva presently.

"That so?" replied John Quincy. "Any verdict?"

"Not yet. I believe they're to settle on that later. By the way, I'm going
down-town immediately after lunch to do some shopping for Barbara. Care
to come along?"

"No, thanks," John Quincy said. "I must go up-stairs and finish my
letters."

But when he left the luncheon table, he decided the letters could wait.
He took a heavy volume with a South Sea title from Dan's library, and went
out on to the lanai. Presently Miss Minerva appeared, smartly dressed in
white linen.

"I'll return as soon as I'm pau," she announced.

"What is this pau?" John Quincy inquired.

"Pau means finished—through."

"Good lord," John Quincy said. "Aren't there enough words in the English language for you?"

"Oh, I don't know," she answered, "a little Hawaiian sprinkled in makes
a pleasant change. And when one reaches my age, John Quincy, one is
eager for a change. Good-by."

She left him to his book and the somnolent atmosphere of Dan's lanai.
Sometimes he read, colorful tales of other islands farther south. Sometimes
he sat and thought. Sometimes he just sat. The blazing afternoon wore on;
presently the beach beyond Dan's garden was gay with bathers, sunburned
men and girls, pretty girls in brief and alluring costumes. Their cries as
they dared the surf were exultant, happy. John Quincy was keen to try
these notable waters, but it didn't seem quite the thing—not just yet, with
Dan Winterslip lying in that room up-stairs.

Miss Minerva reappeared about five, flushed and—though she well knew it was not the thing for one of her standing in the Back Bay—perspiring. She carried an evening paper in her hand.

"Any news?" inquired John Quincy.

She sat down. "Nothing but the coroner's verdict. The usual thing—person or persons unknown. But as I was reading the paper in the car, I had a sudden inspiration."

"Good for you. What was it?"

Haku appeared at the door leading to the living-room. "You ring, miss?" he said.

"I did. Haku, what becomes of the old newspapers in this house?"

"Take and put in a closet beside kitchen," the man told her.

"See if you can find me—no, never mind. I'll look myself."

She followed Haku into the living-room. In a few minutes she returned alone, a newspaper in her hand.

"I have it," she announced triumphantly. "The evening paper of Monday, June sixteenth—the one Dan was reading the night he wrote that letter to Roger. And look, John Quincy—one corner has been torn from the shipping page!"

"Might have been accidental," suggested John Quincy languidly.

"Nonsense!" she said sharply. "It's a clue, that's what it is. The item that disturbed Dan was on that missing corner of the page."

"Might have been, at that," he admitted. "What are you going to do—"

"You're the one that's going to do it," she cut in. "Pull yourself together and go into town. It's two hours until dinner. Give this paper to Captain Hallet—or better still, to Charlie Chan. I am impressed by Mr. Chan's intelligence."

John Quincy laughed. "Damned clever, these Chinese!" he quoted. "You don't mean to say you've fallen for that bunk. They seem clever because they're so different."

"We'll see about that. The chauffeur's gone on an errand for Barbara, but there's a roadster in the garage—"

"Trolley's good enough for me," said John Quincy. "Here, give me the paper."

She explained to him how he was to reach the city, and he got his hat and went. Presently he was on a trolley-car surrounded by representatives of a dozen different races. The melting pot of the Pacific, Carlota Egan had called Honolulu, and the appellation seemed to be correct. John Quincy began to feel a fresh energy, a new interest in life.

The trolley swept over the low swampy land between Waikiki and Honolulu, past rice fields where bent figures toiled patiently in water to their knees, past taro patches, and finally turned on to King Street. Every few moments it paused to take aboard immigrants, Japanese, Chinese, Hawaiians, Portuguese, Philippinos, Koreans, all colors and all creeds. On it went. John Quincy saw great houses set in blooming groves, a Japanese theater flaunting weird posters not far from a Ford service station, then a huge building he recognized as the palace of the monarchy. Finally it entered a district of modern office buildings.

Mr. Kipling was wrong, the boy reflected, East and West could meet. They had.

This impression was confirmed when he left the car at Fort Street and for a moment walked about, a stranger in a strange land. A dusky policeman was directing traffic on the corner, officers of the United States army and navy in spotless duck strolled by, and on the shady side of the street Chinese girls, slim and immaculate in freshly laundered trousers and jackets, were window shopping in the cool of the evening.

"I'm looking for the police station," John Quincy informed a big American with a friendly face.

"Get back on to King Street," the man said. "Go to your right until you come to Bethel, then turn makai—"

"Turn what?"

The man smiled. "A malihini, I take it. Makai means toward the sea. The other direction is mauka—toward the mountains. The police station is at the foot of Bethel, in Kalakaua Hale."

John Quincy thanked him and went on his way. He passed the post-office and was amazed to see that all the lock boxes opened on the street. After a time, he reached the station. A sergeant lounging behind the desk told him that Charlie Chan was at dinner. He suggested the Alexander Young Hotel or possibly the All American Restaurant on King Street.

The hotel sounded easiest, so John Quincy went there first. In the dim lobby a Chinese house boy wandered aimlessly about with broom and dust pan, a few guests were writing the inevitable post-cards, a Chinese clerk was on duty at the desk. But there was no sign of Chan, either in the lobby or in the dining-room at the left. As John Quincy turned from an inspection of the latter, the elevator door opened and a Britisher in mufti came hurriedly forth. He was followed by a Cockney servant carrying luggage.

"Captain Cope," called John Quincy.

The captain paused. "Hello," he said. "Oh—Mr. Winterslip—how are you?" He turned to the servant. "Buy me an evening paper and an armful of the less offensive-looking magazines." The man hurried off, and Cope again addressed John Quincy. "Delighted to see you, but I'm in a frightful rush. Off to the Fanning Islands in twenty minutes."

"When did you get in?" inquired John Quincy. Not that he really cared.

"Yesterday at noon," said Captain Cope. "Been on the wing ever since. I trust you are enjoying your stop here—but I was forgetting. Fearful news about Dan Winterslip."

"Yes," said John Quincy coolly. Judging by the conversation in that San Francisco club, the blow had not been a severe one for Captain Cope. The servant returned.

"Sorry to run," continued the captain. "But I must be off. The service is a stern taskmaster. My regards to your aunt. Best of luck, my boy."

He disappeared through the wide door, followed by his man. John Quincy reached the street in time to see him rolling off in a big car toward the docks.

Noting the cable office near by, the boy entered and sent two messages, one to his mother and the other to Agatha Parker. He addressed them to Boston, Mass. U.S.A., and was accorded a withering look by the young woman in charge as she crossed out the last three letters. There were only two words in each message, but he returned to the street with the comfortable feeling that his correspondence was now attended to for some time to come.

A few moments later he encountered the All American Restaurant and going inside, found himself the only American in the place. Charlie Chan was seated alone at a table, and as John Quincy approached, he rose and bowed.

"A very great honor," said Chan. "Is it possible that I can prevail upon you to accept some of this terrible provision?"

"No, thanks," answered John Quincy. "I'm to dine later at the house. I'll sit down for a moment, if I may."

"Quite overwhelmed," bobbed Charlie. He resumed his seat and scowled at something on the plate before him. "Waiter," he said. "Be kind enough to summon the proprietor of this establishment."

The proprietor, a suave little Japanese man, came gliding. He bowed from the waist.

"Is it that you serve here insanitary food?" inquired Chan.

"Please deign to state your complaint," said the Jap.

"This piece of pie is covered with finger-marks," rebuked Chan. "The sight is most disgusting. Kindly remove it and bring me a more hygienic sector."

The Japanese man picked up the offending pastry and carried it away.

"Japanese," remarked Chan, spreading his hands in an eloquent gesture. "Is it proper for me to infer that you come on business connected with the homicide?"

John Quincy smiled. "I do," he said. He took the newspaper from his pocket, pointed out the date and the missing corner. "My aunt felt it might be important," he explained.

"The woman has a brain," said Chan. "I will procure an unmutilated specimen of this issue and compare. The import may be vast."

"You know," remarked John Quincy, "I'd like to work with you on this case, if you'll let me."

"I have only delight," Chan answered. "You arrive from Boston, a city most cultivated, where much more English words are put to employment than are accustomed here. I thrill when you speak. Greatest privilege for me, I would say."

"Have you formed any theory about the crime?" John Quincy asked. Chan shook his head. "Too early now."

"You have no finger-prints to go on, you said."

Chan shrugged his shoulders. "Does not matter. Finger-prints and other mechanics good in books, in real life not so much so. My experience tell me to think deep about human people. Human passions. Back of murder what, always? Hate, revenge, need to make silent the slain one. Greed for money, maybe. Study human people at all times."

"Sounds reasonable," admitted John Quincy.

"Mostly so," Chan averred. "Enumerate with me the clues we must consider. A guest book devoid of one page. A glove button. A message on the cable. Story of Egan, partly told. Fragment of Corsican cigarette. This newspaper ripped maybe in anger. Watch on living wrist, numeral 2 undistinct."

"Quite a little collection," commented John Quincy.

"Most interesting," admitted Chan. "One by one, we explore. Some cause us to arrive at nowhere. One, maybe two, will not be so unkind. I am believer in Scotland Yard method—follow only essential clue. But it are not the method here. I must follow all, entire."

"The essential clue," repeated John Quincy.

"Sure." Chan scowled at the waiter, for his more hygienic sector had not appeared. "Too early to say here. But I have fondness for the guest book with page omitted. Watch also claims my attention. Odd enough, when we enumerate clues this morning, we pass over watch. Foolish. Very good-looking clue. One large fault, we do not possess it. However, my eyes are sharp to apprehend it."

"I understand," John Quincy said, "that you've been rather successful as a detective."

Chan grinned broadly. "You are educated, maybe you know," he said. "Chinese most psychic people in the world. Sensitives, like film in camera. A look, a laugh, a gesture perhaps. Something go click."

John Quincy was aware of a sudden disturbance at the door of the All American Restaurant. Bowker, the steward, gloriously drunk, was making a noisy entrance. He plunged into the room, followed by a dark, anxious-looking youth.

Embarrassed, John Quincy turned away his face, but to no avail. Bowker was bearing down upon him, waving his arms.

"Well, well, well, well!" he bellowed. "My o' college chum. See you through the window." He leaned heavily on the table. "How you been, o' fellow?"

"I'm all right, thanks," John Quincy said.

The dark young man came up. He was, from his dress, a shore acquaintance of Bowker's. "Look here, Ted," he said. "You've got to be getting along—"

"Jush a minute," cried Bowker. "I want y' to meet Mr. Quincy from Boston. One best fellows God ever made. Mushual friend o' Tim's—you've heard me speak of Tim—"

"Yes—come along," urged the dark young man.

"Not yet. Gotta buy thish boy a lil' drink. What you having, Quincy, o' man?"

"Not a thing," smiled John Quincy. "You warned me against these Island drinks yourself."

"Who—me?" Bowker was hurt. "You're wrong that time, o' man. Don' like to conter—conterdict, but it mush have been somebody else. Not me. Never said a word—"

The young man took his arm. "Come on—you're due on the ship—"

Bowker wrenched away. "Don' paw me," he cried. "Keep your hands off. I'm my own mashter, ain't I? I can speak to an o' friend, can't I? Now, Quincy, o' man—what's yours?"

"I'm sorry," said John Quincy. "Some other time."

Bowker's companion took his arm in a firmer grasp. "You can't buy anything here," he said. "This is a restaurant. You come with me—I know a place—"

"Awright," agreed Bowker. "Now you're talking. Quincy, o' man, you come along—"

"Some other time," John Quincy repeated.

Bowker assumed a look of offended dignity. "Jush as you say," he replied. "Some other time. In Boston, hey? At Tim's place. Only Tim's place is gone." A great grief assailed him. "Tim's gone—dropped out—as though the earth swallowed him up—"

"Yes, yes," said the young man soothingly. "That's too bad. But you come with me."

Submitting at last, Bowker permitted his companion to pilot him to the street. John Quincy looked across at Chan.

"My steward on the *President Tyler*," he explained. "The worse for wear, isn't he?"

The waiter set a fresh piece of pie before the Chinaman.

"Ah," remarked Chan, "this has a more perfect appearance." He tasted it. "Appearance," he added with a grimace, "are a hellish liar. If you are quite ready to depart—"

In the street Chan halted. "Excuse abrupt departure," he said. "Most honored to work with you. The results will be fascinating, I am sure. For now, good evening."

John Quincy was alone again in that strange town. A sudden homesickness engulfed him. Walking along, he came to a news-cart that was as well supplied with literature as his club reading room. A brisk young man in a cap was in charge.

"Have you the latest *Atlantic?*" inquired John Quincy.

The young man put a dark brown periodical into his hand. "No," said John Quincy. "This is the June issue. I've seen it."

"July ain't in. I'll save you one, if you say so."

"I wish you would," John Quincy replied. "The name is Winterslip."

He went on to the corner, regretting that July wasn't in. A copy of the *Atlantic* would have been a sort of link with home, a reminder that Boston still stood. And he felt the need of a link, a reminder.

A trolley-car marked "Waikiki" was approaching. John Quincy hailed it and hopped aboard. Three giggling Japanese girls in bright kimonos drew in their tiny sandaled feet and he slipped past them to a seat.

11
The Tree of Jewels

Two hours later, John Quincy rose from the table where he and his aunt had dined together.

"Just to show you how quick I am to learn a new language," he remarked, "I'm quite pau. Now I'm going makai to sit on the lanai, there to forget the pilikia of the day."

Miss Minerva smiled and rose too. "I expect Amos shortly," she said as they crossed the hall. "A family conference seemed advisable, so I've asked him to come over."

"Strange you had to send for him," said John Quincy, lighting a cigarette.

"Not at all," she answered. She explained about the long feud between the brothers.

"Didn't think old Amos had that much fire in him," commented John Quincy, as they found chairs on the lanai. "A rather anemic specimen, judging by the look I had at him this morning. But then, the Winterslips always were good haters."

For a moment they sat in silence. Outside the darkness was deepening rapidly, the tropic darkness that had brought tragedy the night before. John Quincy pointed to a small lizard on the screen.

"Pleasant little beast," he hc said.

"Oh, they're quite harmless," Miss Minerva told him. "And they eat the mosquitos."

"They do, eh?" The boy slapped his ankle savagely. "Well, there's no accounting for tastes."

Amos arrived presently, looking unusually pale in the half-light. "You asked me to come over, Minerva," he said, as he sat down gingerly on one of Dan Winterslip's Hong-Kong chairs.

"I did. Smoke if you like." Amos lighted a cigarette, which seeme oddly out of place between his thin lips. "I'm sure," Miss Minerva continued, "that we are all determined to bring to justice the person who did this ghastly thing."

"Naturally," said Amos.

"The only drawback," she went on, "is that in the course of the investigation some rather unpleasant facts about Dan's past are likely to be revealed."

"They're bound to be," remarked Amos coldly.

"For Barbara's sake," Miss Minerva said, "I'm intent on seeing that nothing is revealed that is not absolutely essential to the discovery of the murderer. For that reason, I haven't taken the police completely into my confidence."

"What!" cried Amos.

John Quincy stood up. "Now look here, Aunt Minerva—"

"Sit down," snapped his aunt. "Amos, to go back to a talk we had at your house when I was there, Dan was somewhat involved with this woman down the beach. Arlene Compton, I believe she calls herself."

Amos nodded. "Yes, and a worthless lot she is. But Dan wouldn't see it, though I understand his friends pointed it out to him. He talked of marrying her."

"You knew a good deal about Dan, even if you never spoke to him," Miss Minerva went on. "Just what was his status with this woman at the time of his murder—only last night, but it seems ages ago."

"I can't quite tell you that," Amos replied. "I do know that for the past month a malihini named Leather-bee—the black sheep of a good family in Philadelphia, they tell me—has been hanging around the Compton woman, and that Dan resented his presence."

"Humph." Miss Minerva handed to Amos an odd old brooch, a tree of jewels against an onyx background. "Ever see that before, Amos?"

He took it, and nodded. "It's part of a little collection of jewelry Dan brought back from the South Seas in the 'eighties. There were ear-rings and a bracelet, too. He acted rather queerly about those trinkets—never let Barbara's mother or any one else wear them. But he must have got over that idea recently. For I saw this only a few weeks ago."

"Where?" asked Miss Minerva.

"Our office has the renting of the cottage down the beach occupied at present by the Compton woman. She came in not long ago to pay her rent, and she was wearing this brooch." He looked suddenly at Miss Minerva. "Where did you get it?" he demanded.

"Kamaikui gave it to me early this morning," Miss Minerva explained. "She picked it up from the floor of the lanai before the police came."

John Quincy leaped to his feet. "You're all wrong, Aunt Minerva," he cried. "You can't do this sort of thing. You ask the help of the police, and you aren't on the level with them. I'm ashamed of you—"

"Please wait a moment," said his aunt.

"Wait nothing!" he answered. "Give me that brooch. I'm going to turn it over to Chan at once. I couldn't look him in the eye if I didn't."

"We'll turn it over to Chan," said Miss Minerva calmly, "if it seems important. But there is no reason in the world why we should not investigate a bit ourselves before we do so. The woman may have a perfectly logical explanation—"

"Rot!" interrupted John Quincy. "The trouble with you is, you think you're Sherlock Holmes."

"What is your opinion, Amos?" inquired Miss Minerva.

"I'm inclined to agree with John Quincy," Amos said. "You are hardly fair to Captain Hallet. And as for keeping anything dark on account of Barbara—or on anybody's account—that won't be possible, I'm afraid. No getting round it, Minerva, Dan's indiscretions are going to be dragged into the open at last."

She caught the note of satisfaction in his tone, and was nettled by it. "Perhaps. At the same time, it isn't going to do any harm for some member of the family to have a talk with this woman before we consult the police. If she should have a perfectly sincere and genuine explanation—"

"Oh, yes," cut in John Quincy. "She wouldn't have any other kind."

"It won't be so much what she says," persisted Miss Minerva. "It will be the manner in which she says it. Any intelligent person can see through deceit and falsehood. The only question is, which of us is the intelligent person best fitted to examine her."

"Count me out," said Amos promptly.

"John Quincy?"

The boy considered. He had asked for the privilege of working with Chan, and here, perhaps, was an opportunity to win this respect. But this sounded rather like a woman who would be too much for him.

"No, thanks," he said.

"Very good," replied Miss Minerva, rising. "I'll go myself."

"Oh, no," cried John Quincy, shocked.

"Why not? If none of the men in the family are up to it. As a matter of fact, I welcome the opportunity—"

Amos shook his head. "She'll twist you round her little finger," he predicted.

Miss Minerva smiled grimly. "I should like to see her do it. Will you wait here?"

John Quincy went over and took the brooch from Amos's hand. "Sit down, Aunt Minerva," he said. "I'll see this woman. But I warn you that immediately afterward I shall send for Chan."

"That," his aunt told him, "will be decided at another conference. I'm not so sure, John Quincy, that you are the proper person to go. After all, what experience have you had with women of this type?"

John Quincy was offended. He was a man, and he felt that he could meet and outwit a woman of any type. He said as much.

Amos described the woman's house as a small cottage several hundred yards down the beach, and directed the boy how to get there. John Quincy set out.

Night had fallen over the Island when he reached Kalia Road, a bright silvery night, for the Kona weather was over and the moon traveled a cloudless sky. The scent of plumaria and ginger stole out to him through hedges of flaming hibiscus; the trade winds, blowing across a thousand miles of warm water, still managed a cool touch on his cheek. As he approached what he judged must be the neighborhood of the woman's house, a flock of Indian myna birds in a spreading algaroba screamed loudly, their harsh voices the only note of discord in that peaceful scene.

He had some difficulty locating the cottage, which was almost completely hidden under masses of flowering alamander, its blossoms pale yellow in the moonlight. Before the door, a dark fragrant spot under a heavily laden trellis, he paused uncertainly. A rather delicate errand, this was. But he summoned his courage and knocked.

Only the myna birds replied. John Quincy stood there, growing momentarily more hostile to the Widow of Waikiki. Some huge coarse creature, no doubt, a man's woman, a good fellow at a party—that kind. Then the door opened and the boy got a shock. For the figure outlined against the light was young and slender, and the face, dimly seen, suggested fragile loveliness.

"Is this Mrs. Compton?" he inquired.

"Yeah—I'm Mrs. Compton. What do you want?" John Quincy was sorry she had spoken. For she was, obviously, one of those beauties so prevalent nowadays, the sort whom speech betrays. Her voice recalled the myna birds.

"My name is John Quincy Winterslip." He saw her start. "May I speak with you for a moment?"

"Sure you can. Come in." She led the way along a low narrow passage into a tiny living-room. A pasty-faced young man with stooped shoulders stood by a table, fondling a cocktail shaker.

"Steve," said the woman, "this is Mr. Winterslip. Mr. Leatherbee."

Mr. Leatherbee grunted. "Just in time for a little snifter," he remarked.

"No, thanks," John Quincy said. He saw Mrs. Compton take a smoking cigarette from an ash tray, start to convey it to her lips, then, evidently thinking better of it, crush it on the tray.

"Well," said Mr. Leatherbee, "your poison's ready, Arlene." He proferred a glass.

She shook her head, slightly annoyed. "No."

"No?" Mr. Leatherbee grinned. "The more for little Stevie." He lifted a glass. "Here's looking at you, Mr. Winterslip."

"Say, I guess you're Dan's cousin from Boston," Mrs. Compton remarked. "He was telling me about you." She lowered her voice. "I've been meaning to get over to your place all day. But it was such a shock—it knocked me flat."

"I understand," John Quincy replied. He glanced at Mr. Leatherbee, who seemed not to have heard of prohibition. "My business with you, Mrs. Compton, is private."

Leatherbee stiffened belligerently. But the woman said: "That's all right. Steve was just going."

Steve hesitated a moment, then went. His hostess accompanied him. John Quincy heard the low monotone of their voices in the distance. There was a combined odor of gin and cheap perfume in the air; the boy wondered what his mother would say if she could see him now. A door slammed, and the woman returned.

"Well?" she said. John Quincy perceived that her eyes were hard and knowing, like her voice. He waited for her to sit down, then took a chair facing her.

"You knew my Cousin Dan rather intimately," he suggested.

"I was engaged to him," she answered. John Quincy glanced at her left hand. "He hadn't come across—I mean, he hadn't given me a ring, but it was—you know—understood between us."

"Then his death is a good deal of a blow to you?"

She managed a baby stare, full of pathos. "I'll say it is. Mr. Winterslip was kind to me—he believed in me and trusted me. A lone woman way out here don't get any too much char—kindness."

"When did you see Mr. Winterslip last?"

"Three or four days ago—last Friday evening, I guess it was."

John Quincy frowned. "Wasn't that rather a long stretch?"

She nodded. "I'll tell you the truth. We had a little—misunderstanding. Just a lover's quarrel, you know. Dan sort of objected to Steve hanging around. Not that he'd any reason to—Steve's nothing to me—just a weak kid I used to know when I was trouping. I was on the stage—maybe you heard that."

"Yes," said John Quincy. "You hadn't seen Mr. Winterslip since last Friday. You didn't go to his house last evening?"

"I should say not. I got my reputation to think of—you've no idea how people talk in a place like this—"

John Quincy laid the brooch down upon the table. It sparkled in the lamplight—a reading lamp, though the atmosphere was not in the least literary. The baby stare was startled now. "You recognize that, don't you?" he asked.

"Why—yes—it's—I—"

"Just stick to the truth," said John Quincy, not unkindly. "It's an old piece of jewelry that Mr. Winterslip gave you, I believe."

"Well—"

"You've been seen wearing it, you know."

"Yes, he did give it to me," she admitted. "The only present I ever got from him. I guess from the look of it Mrs. Noah wore it on the Ark. Kinda pretty, though."

"You didn't visit Mr. Winterslip last night," persisted John Quincy. "Yet, strangely enough, this brooch was found on the floor not far from his dead body."

She drew in her breath sharply. "Say—what are you? A cop?" she asked.

"Hardly," John Quincy smiled. "I am here simply to save you, if possible, from the hands of the—er—the cops. If you have any real explanation of this matter, it may not be necessary to call it to the attention of the police."

"Oh!" She smiled. "Say, that's decent of you. Now I will tell you the truth. That's about not seeing Dan Winterslip since Friday was bunk. I saw him last night."

"Ah—you did? Where?"

"Right here. Mr. Winterslip gave me that thing about a month ago. Two weeks ago he came to me in a sort of excited way and said he must have it back. It was the only living thing he ever give me and I liked it and those emeralds are valuable—so—well, I stalled a while. I said I was having a new clasp put on it. He kept asking for it, and last night he showed up here and said he just had to have it. Said he'd buy me anything in the stores in place of it. I must say he was pretty het up. So I finally turned it over to him and he took it and went away."

"What time was that?"

"About nine-thirty. He was happy and pleasant and he said I could go to a jewelry store this morning and take my pick of the stock." She looked pleadingly at John Quincy. "That's the last I ever saw of him. It's the truth, so help me."

"I wonder," mused John Quincy.

She moved nearer. "Say, you're a nice kid," she said. "The kind I used to meet in Boston when we played there. The kind that's got some consideration for a woman. You ain't going to drag me into this. Think what it would mean—to me."

John Quincy did not speak. He saw there were tears in her eyes. "You've probably heard things about me," she went on, "but they ain't true. You don't know what I been up against out here. An unprotected woman don't have much chance anywhere, but on this beach, where men come drifting in from all over the world—I been friendly, that's my only trouble. I was homesick—oh, God, wasn't I homesick! I was having a good time back there, and then I fell for Bill Compton and came out here with him, and sometimes in the night I'd wake up and remember Broadway was five thousand miles away, and I'd cry so hard I'd wake him. And that made him sore—"

She paused. John Quincy was impressed by the note of true nostalgia in her voice. He was, suddenly, rather sorry for her.

"Then Bill's plane crashed on Diamond Head," she continued, "and I was all alone. And these black sheep along the beach, they knew I was alone—and broke. And I was homesick for Forty-second Street, for the old boarding-house and the old gang and the Automat and the chewing-gum sign, and try-outs at New Haven. So I gave a few parties just to forget, and people began to talk."

"You might have gone back," John Quincy suggested.

"I know—why didn't I? I been intending to, right along, but every day out here is just like any other day, and somehow you don't get round to picking one out—I been drifting—but honest to God if you keep me out of this I'll go home on the first boat. I'll get me a job, and—and— If you'll only keep me out of it. You got a chance now to wreck my life—it's all up to you—but I know you ain't going to—"

She seized John Quincy's hand in both of hers, and gazed at him pleadingly through her tears. It was the most uncomfortable moment of his life. He looked wildly about the little room, so different from any in the house on Beacon Street. He pulled his hand away.

"I'll—I'll see," he said, rising hastily. "I'll think it over."

"But I can't sleep to-night if I don't know," she told him.

"I'll have to think it over," he repeated. He turned toward the table in time to see the woman's slim hand reach out and seize the bit of jewelry. "I'll take the brooch," he added.

She looked up at him. Suddenly John Quincy knew that she had been acting, that his emotions had been falsely played upon, and he felt again that hot rush of blood to the head, that quick surge of anger, he had experienced in Dan Winterslip's hall. Aunt Minerva had predicted he couldn't handle a woman of this type. Well, he'd show her—he'd show the world. "Give me that brooch," he said coldly.

"It's mine," answered the woman stubbornly.

John Quincy wasted no words; he seized the woman's wrist. She screamed. A door opened behind them.

"What's going on here?" inquired Mr. Leatherbee.

"Oh, I thought you'd left us," said John Quincy.

"Steve! Don't let him have it," cried the woman. Steve moved militantly nearer, but there was a trace of caution in his attitude.

John Quincy laughed. "You stay where you are, Steve," he advised. "Or I'll smash that sallow face of yours." Strange talk for a Winterslip. "Your friend here is trying to hang on to an important bit of evidence in the murder up the beach, and with the utmost reluctance I am forced to use strong-arm methods." The brooch dropped to the floor, he stooped and picked it up. "Well, I guess that's about all," he added. "I'm sorry if you've been homesick, Mrs. Compton, but speaking as a Bostonian, I don't believe Broadway is as glamorous as you picture it: Distance has lent enchantment. Good night."

He let himself out, and found his way to Kalakaua Avenue. He had settled one thing to his own satisfaction; Chan must know about the brooch, and at once. Mrs. Compton's story might be true or not, it certainly needed further investigation by some responsible person.

John Quincy had approached the cottage by way of Kalia Road, he was planning to return to Dan's house along the better lighted avenue. Having reached that broad expanse of asphalt, however, he realized that the Reef and Palm Hotel was near at hand. There was his promise to Carlota Egan—he had said he would look in on her again to-day. As for Chan, he could telephone him from the hotel. He turned in the direction of the Reef and Palm.

Stumbling through the dark garden, he saw finally the gaunt old hulk of the hotel. Lights of low candle power burned at infrequent intervals on the double-decked veranda. In the huge lobby a few rather shabby-looking guests took their ease. Behind the desk stood—nobody but the Japanese clerk.

John Quincy was directed to a telephone booth, and his keen Bostonian mind required Nipponese aid in mastering the dial system favored by the Honolulu telephone company. At length he got the police station. Chan was out, but the answering voice promised that he would be told to get in touch with Mr. Winterslip immediately on his return.

"How much do I owe you?" inquired John Quincy of the clerk.

"Not a penny," said a voice, and he turned to find Carlota Egan at his elbow. He smiled. This was more like it.

"But I say—you know—I've used your telephone—"

"It's free," she said. "Too many things are free out here. That's why we don't get rich. It was so kind of you to come again."

"Not at all," he protested. He looked about the room. "Your father—"

She glanced at the clerk, and led the way out to the lanai at the side. They went to the far end of it, where they could see the light on Diamond Head, and the silvery waters of the Pacific sweeping in to disappear at last beneath the old Reef and Palm.

"I'm afraid poor dad's having a bad time of it," she said, and her voice broke slightly. "I haven't been able to see him. They're holding him down there—as a witness, I believe. There was some talk of bail, but I didn't listen. We haven't any money—at least, I didn't think we had."

"You didn't think—" he began, puzzled.

She produced a small bit of paper, and put it in his hand. "I want to ask your advice. I've been cleaning up dad's office, and just before you came I ran across that in his desk."

John Quincy stared down at the little pink slip she had given him. By the light of one of the small lamps he saw that it was a check for five thousand dollars, made out to "Bearer" and signed by Dan Winterslip. The date was that of the day before.

"I say, that looks important, doesn't it?" John Quincy said. He handed it back to her, and thought a moment. "By gad—it is important. It seems to me it's pretty conclusive evidence of your father's innocence. If he had that, his business with Cousin Dan must have come to a successful end, and it isn't likely he would—er—do away with the man who signed it and complicate the cashing of it."

The girl's eyes shone. "Just the way I reasoned. But I don't know what to do with it."

"Your father has engaged a lawyer, of course."

"Yes, but a rather poor one. The only kind we can afford. Should I turn this over to him?"

"No—wait a minute. Any chance of seeing your father soon?"

"Yes. It's been arranged I'm to visit him in the morning."

John Quincy nodded. "Better talk with him before you do anything," he advised. He had a sudden recollection of Egan's face when he refused to explain his business with Dan Winterslip. "Take his check with you and ask your father what he wants done with it. Point out to him that it's vital evidence in his favor."

"Yes, I guess that's the best plan," the girl agreed. "Will—will you sit down a moment?"

"Well." John Quincy recalled Miss Minerva waiting impatiently for news. "Just a moment. I want to know how you're getting on. Any big arithmetical problems come up yet?"

She shook her head. "Not yet. It really isn't so bad, the work. We haven't many guests, you know. I could be quite happy—if it weren't for poor dad." She sighed. "Ever since I can remember," she added, "My happiness has had an if in it."

He led her on to speak about herself, there in the calm night by that romantic beach. Through her talk flashed little pictures of her motherless childhood on this exotic shore, of a wearing fight against poverty and her father's bitter struggle to send her to school on the mainland, to give her what he considered her proper place in the world. Here was a girl far different from any he had met on Beacon Street, and John Quincy found pleasure in her talk.

Finally he forced himself to leave. As they walked along the balcony they encountered one of the guests, a meek little man with stooped shoulders. Even at that late hour he wore a bathing suit.

"Any luck, Mr. Saladine?" the girl inquired.

"Luck ith againth me," he lisped, and passed hastily on.

Carlota Egan laughed softly. "Oh, I really shouldn't," she repented at once. "The poor man."

"What's his trouble?" asked John Quincy.

"He's a tourist—a business man," she said. "Des Moines, or some place like that. And he's had the most appalling accident. He's lost his teeth."

"His teeth!" repeated John Quincy.

"Yes. Like so many things in this world, they were false. He got into a battle with a roller out by the second raft, and they disappeared. Since then he spends all his time out there, peering down into the water by day, and diving down and feeling about by night. One of the tragic figures of history," she added.

John Quincy laughed.

"That's the most tragic part of it," the girl continued. "He's the joke of the beach. But he goes on hunting, so serious. Of course, it is serious for him."

They passed through the public room to the front door. Mr. Saladine's tragedy slipped at once from John Quincy's mind.

"Good night," he said. "Don't forget about the check, when you see your father to-morrow. I'll look in on you during the day."

"It was so good of you to come," she said. Her hand was in his. "It has helped me along—tremendously."

"Don't you worry. Happy days are not far off. Happy days without an if. Hold the thought!"

"I'll hold it," she promised.

"We'll both hold it." It came to him that he was also holding her hand. He dropped it hastily. "Good night," he repeated, and fled through the garden.

In the living-room of Dan's house he was surprised to find Miss Minerva and Charlie Chan sitting together, solemnly staring at each other. Chan rose hurriedly at his entrance.

"Hello," said John Quincy. "I see you have a caller."

"Where in the world have you been?" snapped Miss Minerva. Evidently entertaining Chan had got a bit on her nerves.

"Well—I—" John Quincy hesitated.

"Speak out," said Miss Minerva. "Mr. Chan knows everything."

"Most flattering," grinned Chan. "Some things are not entirely well know to me. But about your call on Widow of Waikiki I learn soon after door receives you."

"The devil you did," said John Quincy.

"Simple enough," Chan went on. "Study human people, as I relate to you. Compton lady was friend to Mr. Dan Winterslip. Mr. Leatherbee rival friend. Enter jealous feelings. Since morning both of these people are under watchful regard of Honolulu police. Into the scene, you walk. I am notified and fly to beach."

"Ah—does he also know—" began John Quincy.

"About the brooch?" finished Miss Minerva. "Yes—I've confessed everything. And he's been kind enough to forgive me."

"But not nice thing to do," added Chan. "Humbly begging pardon to mention it. All cards should repose on table when police are called upon."

"Yes," said Miss Minerva, "he forgave me, but I have been gently chided. I have been made to feel, as he puts it, most naughty."

"So sorry," bowed Chan.

"Well, as a matter of fact," said John Quincy, "I was going to tell Mr. Chan the whole story at once." He turned to him. "I've already tried to reach you by telephone at the station. When I left the woman's cottage—"

"Police affairs forbid utmost courtesy," interrupted Chan. "I cut in to remark from the beginning, if you will please do so."

"Oh, yes," smiled John Quincy. "Well, the woman herself let me in, and showed me into her little living-room. When I got there this fellow Leatherbee was mixing cocktails by the table—"

Haku appeared at the door. "Mr. Charlie Chan wanted by telephone," he announced.

Chan apologized and hastened out.

"I intend to tell everything," John Quincy warned his aunt.

"I shan't interfere," she answered. "He has been sitting here looking at me more in sorrow than in anger for the better part of an hour, and I've made up my mind to one thing. I shall have no more secrets from the police."

Chan reentered the room. "As I was saying," John Quincy began, "this fellow Leatherbee was standing by the table, and—"

"Most sorry," said Chan, "but the remainder of that interesting recital is to be told at the station-house."

"At the station-house!" cried John Quincy.

"Precisely the fact. I am presuming you do me the great honor to come with me to that spot. The man Leatherbee is apprehended aboard boat *Niagara* on verge of sailing to Australia. Woman are also apprehended in act of tearful farewell. Both now relax at police station."

"I thought so," said John Quincy.

"One more amazing fact comes into light," added Chan. "In pocket of Leatherbee is the page ruthlessly extracted from guest book. Kindly procure your hat. Outside I have waiting for me one Ford automobile."

12

Tom Brade the Blackbirder

In Hallet's room at headquarters they found the Captain of Detectives seated grimly behind his desk staring at two reluctant visitors. One of the visitors, Mr. Stephen Leatherbee, stared back with a look of sullen defiance. Mrs. Arlene Compton, late of Broadway and the Automat, was dabbing at her eyes with a tiny handkerchief. John Quincy perceived that she had carelessly allowed tears to play havoc with her make-up.

"Hello, Charlie," said Hallet. "Mr. Winterslip, I'm glad you came along. As you may have heard, we've just pulled this young man off the *Niagara*. He seemed inclined to leave us. We found this in his pocket."

He put into Chan's hand a time-yellowed page obviously from Dan Winterslip's guest book. John Quincy and Chan bent over it together. The inscription was written in an old-fashioned hand, and the ink was fading fast. It ran:

"In Hawaii all things are perfect, none more so than the hospitality I have enjoyed in this house.—Joseph E. Gleason, 124 Little Bourke Street, Melbourne, Victoria."

John Quincy turned away, shocked. No wonder that page had been ripped out! Evidently Mr. Gleason had not enjoyed the privilege of studying A. S. Hill's book on the principles of rhetoric. How could one thing be more perfect than another?

"Before I take a statement from these people," Hallet was saying, "what's all this about a brooch?"

John Quincy laid the piece of jewelry on the captain's desk. He explained that it had been given Mrs. Compton by Dan Winterslip, and told of its being discovered on the floor of the lanai.

"When was it found?" demanded the captain, glaring his disapproval.

"Most regrettable misunderstanding," put in Chan hastily. "Now completely wiped out. The littlest said, sooner repairs are made. Mr. Winterslip has already tonight examined this woman—"

"Oh, he has, has he!" Hallet turned angrily on John Quincy. "Just who is conducting this case?"

"Well," began John Quincy uncomfortably, "it seemed best to the family—"

"Damn the family!" Hallet exploded. "This affair is in my hands—"

"Please," broke in Chan soothingly. "Waste of time to winnow that out. Already I have boldness to offer suitable rebukes."

"Well, you talked with the woman, then," said Hallet. "What did you get out of her?"

"Say, listen," put in Mrs. Compton. "I want to take back anything I told this bright-eyed boy."

"Lied to him, eh?" said Hallet.

"Why not? What right did he have to question me?" Her voice became wheedling. "I wouldn't lie to a cop," she added.

"You bet your life you wouldn't," Hallet remarked. "Not if you know what's good for you. However, I want to hear what you told this amateur detective. Sometimes lies are significant. Go on, Winterslip."

John Quincy was deeply annoyed. What was this mix-up he had let himself in for, anyhow? He had a notion to rise, and with a cold bow, leave the room. Something told him, however, that he couldn't get away with it.

Very much on his dignity, he repeated the woman's story to him. Winterslip had come to her cottage the night before to make a final appeal for the brooch. On his promise to replace it with something else, she had given it up. He had taken it and left her at nine-thirty.

"That was the last she saw of him," finished John Quincy.

Hallet smiled grimly. "So she told you, at any rate. But she admits she was lying. If you'd had the sense to leave this sort of thing to the proper people—" He wheeled on the woman. "You were lying, weren't you?"

She nodded nonchalantly. "In a way. Dan did leave my cottage at nine-thirty—or a little later. But I went with him—to his house. Oh, it was perfectly proper. Steve went along."

"Oh, yes—Steve." Hallet glanced at Mr. Leatherbee, who did not appear quite the ideal chaperon. "Now, young woman, go back to the beginning. Nothing but the truth."

"So help me," said Mrs. Compton. She attempted a devastating smile. "I wouldn't lie to you, Captain—you know I wouldn't. I realize you're a big man out here, and—"

"Give me your story," cut in Hallet coldly.

"Sure. Dan dropped into my place for a chat last night about nine, and he found Mr. Leatherbee there. He was jealous as sin, Dan was—honest to God, I don't know why. Me and Steve are just pals—eh, Steve?"

"Pals, that's all," said Steve.

"But anyhow, Dan flew off the handle, and we had one grand blow-up. I tried to explain Steve was just stopping over on his way to Australia, and Dan wants to know what's detaining him. So Steve tells about how he lost all his money at bridge on the boat coming out here. 'Will you move on,' says Dan, 'if I pay your passage?' And Steve answers he will, like a shot. Am I getting this straight, Steve?"

"Absolutely," approved Mr. Leatherbee. "It's just as she says, Captain. Winterslip offered to give—loan me passage money. It was only a loan. And I agreed to sail on the *Niagara* to-night. He said he had a little cash in his safe at the house, and invited Arlene and me to go back with him—"

"Which we did," said Arlene. "Dan opened the safe and took out a roll of bills. He peeled off three hundred dollars. You didn't often seem him in that frame of mind—but as I was saying, he give the money to Steve. Then Steve begins to beef a little—yes, you did, Steve—and wants to know what he's going to do in Australia. Says he don't know a soul down there and he'll just plain starve. Dan was sore at first, then he laughs a nasty little laugh and goes over and tears that there page out of the guest book and gives it to Steve. 'Look him up and tell him you're a friend of mine,' he says. 'Maybe he'll give you a job. The name is Gleason. I've disliked him for twenty years, though he don't know that!'"

"A dirty dig at me," Leatherbee explained. "I took the loan and this Gleason's address and we started to go. Winterslip said he wanted to talk to Arlene, so I came away alone. That was about ten o'clock."

"Where did you go?" Hallet asked.

"I went back to my hotel down-town. I had to pack."

"Back to your hotel, eh? Can you prove it?"

Leatherbee considered. "I don't know. The boy at the desk may remember when I came in, though I didn't stop there for my key—I had it with me. Anyhow, I didn't see Winterslip after that. I just went ahead with my preparations to sail on the *Niagara,* and I must say you've got your nerve—"

"Never mind that!" Hallet turned to the woman. "And after Leatherbee left—what happened then?"

"Well, Dan started in on that brooch again," she said. "It made me sore, too—I never did like a tight-wad. Besides, my nerves was all on edge, I'm funny that way, rows get me all upset. I like everybody pleasant around me. He went on arguing, so finally I ripped off the brooch and threw it at him, and it rolled away under the table somewhere. Then he said he was sorry, and that was when he offered to replace it with something more up-to-date. The best money could buy—that was what he promised. Pretty soon we was friends again—just as good friends as ever when I came away, about ten-fifteen. His last words was that we'd look round the jewelry stores this morning. I ask you, Captain, is it reasonable to think I'd have anything to do with murdering a man who was in a buying mood like that?"

Hallet laughed. "So you left him at ten-fifteen—and went home alone?"

"I did. And when I saw him last he was alive and well—I'll swear to that on a stack of Bibles as high as the Times Building. Gee, don't I wish I was safe on Broadway to-night!"

Hallet thought for a moment. "Well, we'll look into all this. You can both go—I'm not going to hold you at present. But I expect you both to remain in Honolulu until this affair is cleared up, and I advise you not to try any funny business. You've seen to-night what chance you've got to get away."

"Oh, that's all right." The woman stood, looking her relief. "We've got no reason to beat it, have we, Steve?"

"None in the world," agreed Steve. His facetious manner returned. "Speaking for myself," he added, "innocent is my middle name."

"Good night, all," said Mrs. Compton, and they went out.

Hallet sat staring at the brooch. "A pretty straight story," he remarked, looking at Chan.

"Nice and neat," grinned the Chinese man.

"If true." Hallet shrugged his shoulders. "Well, for the present, I'm willing to believe it." He turned to John Quincy. "Now, Mr. Winterslip," he said severely, "I want it understood that any other evidence your family digs up—"

"Oh, that's all right," interrupted the boy. "We'll turn it over at once. I've already given to Chan the newspaper my cousin was reading that night he wrote the letter to Roger Winterslip."

Chan took the paper from his pocket. "Such a busy evening," he explained, "the journal was obscure in my mind. Thanks for the recollection." He called to his chief's attention the mutilated corner.

"Look into that," said Hallet.

"Before sleeping," promised Chan. "Mr. Winterslip, we pursue similar paths. The honor of your company in my humble vehicle would pleasure me deeply." Once in the car on the deserted street, he spoke again. "The page ripped from guest book, the brooch lying silent on floor. Both are now followed into presence of immovable stone wall. We sway about, looking for other path."

"Then you think those two were telling the truth?" John Quincy asked.

"As to that, I do not venture to remark," Chan replied.

"How about those psychic powers?" inquired John Quincy.

Chan smiled. "Psychic powers somewhat drowsy just now," he admitted. "Need prodding into wakefulness."

"Look here," said John Quincy, "there's no need for you to take me out to Waikiki. Just drop me on King Street, and I'll get a trolley."

"Making humble suggestion," Chan replied, "is it not possible you will accompany me to newspaper rooms, where we set out on different path?"

John Quincy looked at his watch; it was ten minutes past eleven. "I'll be glad to, Charlie," he said.

Chan beamed with pleasure. "Greatly honored by your friendly manner," he remarked. He turned into a side street. "Newspaper of this nature burst out at evening, very quiet now. Somebody may loiter in rooms, if we have happy luck."

They had just that, for the building of the evening journal was open, and in the city room an elderly man with a green shade over his eyes hammered on a typewriter.

"Hello, Charlie," he said cordially.

"Hello, Pete. Mr. Winterslip of Boston, I have all the honor to present this Pete Mayberry. For many years he explore water-front ferreting for whatever news are hiding there."

The elderly man rose and removed his eye-shade, revealing a pleasant twinkle. He was evidently interested to meet a Winterslip.

"We pursue," continued Chan, "one copy of paper marked June sixteen, present year. If you have no inclination for objecting."

Mayberry laughed. "Go to it, Charlie. You know where the files are."

Chan bowed and disappeared. "Your first appearance out here, Mr. Winterslip?" inquired the newspaper man.

John Quincy nodded. "I've only just got here," he said, "but I can see it's a rather intriguing place."

"You've said it," smiled Mayberry. "Forty-six years ago I came out from Portsmouth, New Hampshire, to visit relatives. I've been in the newspaper game here ever since—most of the time on the water-front. There's a life-work for you!"

"You must have seen some changes," remarked John Quincy inanely.

Mayberry nodded. "For the worse. I knew Honolulu in the glamourous days of its isolation, and I've watched it fade into an eighth carbon copy of Babbittville, U. S. A. The water-front's just a water-front now—but once, my boy! Once it oozed romance at every pore."

Chan returned, carrying a paper. "Much to be thankful for," he said to Mayberry. "Your kindness are quite overwhelming—"

"Anything doing?" asked Mayberry eagerly.

Chan shook his head. "Presently speaking, no. Our motions just now must be blackly clouded in secrecy."

"Well," said the reporter, "when it comes time to roll them clouds away, don't forget me."

"Impossibility," protested Chan. "Good night."

They left Mayberry bending over his typewriter, and at Chan's suggestion went to the All American Restaurant, where he ordered two cups of "your inspeakable coffee." While they waited to be served, he spread out on the table his complete copy of the newspaper, and laying the torn page on its counterpart, carefully removed the upper right-hand corner.

"The missing fragment," he explained. For a time he studied it thoughtfully, and finally shook his head. "I apprehend nothing to startle," he admitted. He handed it across the table. "If you will condescend greatly—"

John Quincy took the bit of newspaper. On one side was the advertisement of a Japanese dealer in shirtings who wrote his own publicity. Any one might carry off, he said, six yards for the price of five. John Quincy laughed aloud.

"Ah," said Chan, "you are by rights mirthful. Kikuchi, purveyor of shirting cloth, seize on grand English language and make it into a jumble. On that side are nothing to detain us. But humbly hinting you reverse the fragment—"

John Quincy reversed it. The other side was a part of the shipping page. He read it carefully, news of sailings and arrivals, there would be places for five passengers to the Orient on the *Shinyo Maru*, leaving Wednesday, the *Wilhelmina* was six hundred and forty miles east of Makupuu Point, the brig *Mary Jane* from the Treaty Ports—

John Quincy started, and caught his breath. A small item in tiny print had met his eye.

"Among the passengers who will arrive here on the *Sonoma* from Australia a week from Saturday are: Mr. and Mrs. Thomas Macan Brade, of Calcutta—"

John Quincy sat staring at the unwashed window of the All American Restaurant. His mind went back to the deck of the *President Tyler*, to a lean old missionary telling a tale of a bright morning on Apiang, a grave under a palm tree. "Mr. and Mrs. Thomas Macan Brade, of Calcutta." He heard again the missionary's high-pitched voice. "A callous brute, a pirate and adventurer. Tom Brade, the blackbirder."

But Brade had been buried in a long pine box on Apiang. Even at the Crossroads of the Pacific, his path and that of Dan Winterslip could hardly have crossed again.

The waiter brought the coffee. Chan said nothing, watching John Quincy closely. Finally he spoke: "You have much to tell me."

John Quincy looked around quickly, he had forgotten Chan's presence.

His dilemma was acute. Must he here in this soiled restaurant in a far town reveal to this man that ancient blot on the Winterslip name? What would Aunt Minerva say? Well, only a short time ago she had remarked that she was resolved to have no more secrets from the police. However, there was family pride—

John Quincy's eye fell on the Japanese waiter. What were those lines from *The Mikado*? "But family pride must be denied and mortified and set aside."

The boy smiled. "Yes, Charlie," he admitted, "I have much to tell you." And over the inspeakable coffee of the All American Restaurant he repeated to the detective the story the Reverend Frank Upton had told on the *President Tyler*.

Chan beamed. "Now," he cried, "we arrive in the neighborhood of something! Brade the blackbirder, master *Maid of Shiloh* boat, on which Mr. Dan Winterslip are first officer—"

"But Brade was buried on Apiang," protested John Quincy.

"Yes, indeed. And who saw him, pardon me? Was it then an unsealed box? Oh, no!" Chan's eyes were dancing. "Please recollect something more. The strong box of ohia wood. Initials on it are T.M.B. Mysteries yet, but we move, we advance!"

"I guess we do," admitted John Quincy.

"This much we grasp," Chan continued. "Dan Winterslip repose for quiet hour on lanai, in peaceful reading. This news assault his eye. He now leaps up, paces about, flees to dock to send letter requesting, please the ohia wood box must be buried deep in Pacific. Why?" Fumbling in his pocket, Chan took out a sheaf of papers, evidently lists of steamer arrivals. "On Saturday just gone by, the *Sonoma* make this port. Among passengers—yes—yes—Thomas Macan Brade and honorable wife, Calcutta. It is here inscribed they arrive to stay, not being present when *Sonoma* persist on journey. On the night of Monday, Mr. Dan Winterslip are foully slain."

"Which makes Mr. Brade an important person to locate," said John Quincy.

"How very true. But the hurry are not intense. No boats sailing now. Before sleeping, I will investigate down-town hotels, Waikiki to-morrow. Where are you, Mr. Brade?" Chan seized the check. "No—pardon me—the honor of paying for this poison-tasting beverage must be mine."

Out in the street, he indicated an approaching trolley. "It bears imprint of your destination," he pointed out. "You will require sleep. We meet to-morrow. Congratulations on most fruitful evening."

Once more John Quincy was on a Waikiki car. Weary but thrilled, he took out his pipe and filling it, lighted up. What a day! He seemed to have lived a lifetime since he landed that very morning. He perceived that his smoke was blowing in the face of a tired little Japanese woman beside him. "Pardon me," he remarked, and knocking the pipe against the side rail, put it in his pocket. The woman stared at him in meek startled wonder; no one had ever asked her pardon before.

On the seat behind John Quincy a group of Hawaiian boys with yellow leis about their necks twanged on steel guitars and sang a plaintive love song. The trolley rattled on through the fragrant night; above the clatter of the wheels the music rose with a sweet intensity. John Quincy leaned back and closed his eyes.

A clock struck the hour of midnight. Another day—Wednesday—it flashed through his mind that to-day his firm in Boston would offer that preferred stock for the shoe people in Lynn. Would the issue be over-subscribed? No matter.

Here he was, out in the middle of the Pacific on a trolley-car. Behind him brown-skinned boys were singing a melancholy love song of long ago, and the moon was shining on crimson poinciana trees. And somewhere on this tiny island a man named Thomas Macan Brade slept under a mosquito netting. Or lay awake, perhaps, thinking of Dan Winterslip.

13

The Luggage in Room Nineteen

John Quincy emerged from sleep the next morning with a great effort, and dragged his watch from under the pillow. Eight-thirty! Good lord, he was due at the office at nine! A quick bath and shave, a brief pause at the breakfast table, a run past the Public Gardens and the Common and down to School Street—

He sat up in bed. Why was he imprisoned under mosquito netting? What was the meaning of the little lizard that sported idly outside the cloth? Oh, yes—Honolulu. He was in Hawaii, and he'd never reach his office by nine. It was five thousand miles away.

The low murmur of breakers on the beach confirmed him in this dis-covery and stepping to his window, he gazed out at the calm sparkling morning. Yes, he was in Honolulu entangled in a murder mystery, con-sorting with Chinese detectives and Waikiki Widows, following clues. The new day held interesting promise. He must hurry to find what it would bring forth.

Haku informed him that his aunt and Barbara had already breakfasted, and set before him a reddish sort of cantaloupe which was, he explained in answer to the boy's question, a papaia. When he had eaten, John Quincy went out on the lanai. Barbara stood there, staring at the beach. A new Barbara, with the old vivacity, the old joy of living, submerged; a pale girl with sorrow in her eyes.

John Quincy put his arm about her shoulder; she was a Winterslip and the family was the family. Again he felt in his heart that flare of anger against the "person or persons unknown" who had brought this grief upon her. The guilty must pay—Egan or whoever, Brade or Leatherbee or the chorus girl. Pay and pay dearly—he was resolved on that.

"My dear girl," he began. "What can I say to you—"

"You've said it all, without speaking," she answered. "See, John Quincy, this is my beach. When I was only five I swam alone to that first float. He—he was so proud of me."

"It's a lovely spot, Barbara," he told her.

"I knew you'd think so. One of these days we'll swim together out to the reef, and I'll teach you to ride a surf-board. I want your visit to be a happy one."

He shook his head. "It can't be that," he said, "because of you. But because of you, I'm mighty glad I came."

She pressed his hand. "I'm going out to sit by the water. Will you come?"

The bamboo curtain parted, and Miss Minerva joined them. "Well, John Quincy," she said sharply, "this is a pretty hour for you to appear. If you're going to rescue me from lotus land, you'll have to be immune yourself."

He smiled. "Just getting acclimated," he explained. "I'll follow you in a moment, Barbara," he added, and held open the door for her.

"I waited up," Miss Minerva began, when the girl had gone, "until eleven-thirty. But I'd had very little sleep the night before, and that was my limit. I make no secret of it—I'm very curious to know what happened at the police station."

He repeated to her the story told by Mrs. Compton and Leatherbee. "I wish I'd been present," she said. "A pretty woman can fool all the men in Christendom. Lies, probably."

"Maybe," admitted John Quincy. "But wait a minute. Later on, Chan and I followed up your newspaper clue. And it led us to a startling discovery."

"Of course it did," she beamed. "What was it?"

"Well," he said, "first of all, I met a missionary on the boat." He told her the Reverend Frank Upton's tale of that morning on Apiang, and added the news that a man named Thomas Macan Brade was now in Honolulu.

She was silent for a time. "So Dan was a blackbirder," she remarked at last. "How charming! Such a pleasant man, too. But then, I learned that lesson early in life—the brighter the smile, the darker the past. All this will make delightful reading in the Boston papers, John Quincy."

"Oh, they'll never get it," her nephew said.

"Don't deceive yourself. Newspapers will go to the ends of the earth for a good murder. I once wrote letters to all the editors in Boston urging them to print no more details about homicides. It hadn't the slightest effect—though I did get an acknowledgment of my favor from the *Herald*."

John Quincy glanced at his watch. "Perhaps I should go down to the station. Anything in the morning paper?"

"A very hazy interview with Captain Hallet. The police have unearthed important clues, and promise early results. You know—the sort of thing they always give one just after a murder."

The boy looked at her keenly. "Ah," he said, "then you read newspaper accounts of the kind you tried to suppress?"

"Certainly I do," snapped his aunt. "There's little enough excitement in my life. But I gladly gave up my port wine because I felt intoxicants were bad for the lower classes, and—"

Haku interrupted with the news that John Quincy was wanted on the telephone. When the boy returned to the lanai, there was a brisk air of business about him.

"That was Charlie," he announced. "The day's work is about to get under way. They've located Mr. and Mrs. Brade at the Reef and Palm Hotel, and I'm to meet Charlie there in fifteen minutes."

"The Reef and Palm," repeated Miss Minerva. "You see, it keeps coming back to Egan. I'd wager a set of Browning against a modern novel that he's the man who did it."

"You'd lose your Browning, and then where would you be when the lecture season started?" laughed John Quincy. "I never knew you to be so stupid before." His face became serious. "By the way, will you explain to Barbara that I can't join her, after all?"

Miss Minerva nodded. "Go along," she said. "I envy you all this. First time in my life I ever wished I were a man."

John Quincy approached the Reef and Palm by way of the beach. The scene was one of bright serenity. A few languid tourists lolled upon the sand; others, more ambitious, were making picture post-card history out where the surf began. A great white steamer puffed blackly into port. Standing in water up to their necks, a group of Hawaiian women paused in their search for luncheon delicacies to enjoy a moment's gossip.

John Quincy passed Arlene Compton's cottage and entered the grounds of the Reef and Palm. On the beach not far from the hotel, an elderly Englishwoman sat on a camp stool with an easel and canvas before her. She was seeking to capture something of that exotic scene—vainly seeking, for John Quincy, glancing over her shoulder, perceived that her work was terrible. She turned and looked at him, a weary look of protest against his intrusion, and he was sorry she had caught him in the act of smiling at her inept canvas.

Chan had not yet arrived at the hotel, and the clerk informed John Quincy that Miss Carlota had gone to the city. For that interview with her father, no doubt. He hoped that the evidence of the check would bring about Egan's release. It seemed to him that the man was being held on a rather flimsy pretext, anyhow.

He sat down on the lanai at the side, where he could see both the path that led in from the street and the restless waters of the Pacific. On the beach near by a man in a purple bathing suit reclined dejectedly, and John Quincy smiled in recollection. Mr. Saladine, alone with his tragedy, peering out at the waters that had robbed him—waiting, no doubt, for the tide to yield up its loot.

Some fifteen or twenty minutes passed, and then John Quincy heard voices in the garden. He saw that Hallet and Chan were coming up the walk and went to meet them at the front door.

"Splendid morning," said Chan. "Nice day to set out on new path leading unevitably to important discovery."

John Quincy accompanied them to the desk. The Japanese clerk regarded them with sullen unfriendliness; he had not forgotten the events of the day before. Information had to be dragged from him bit by bit. Yes, there was a Mr. and Mrs. Brade stopping there. They arrived last Saturday, on the steamship *Sonoma*. Mr. Brade was not about at the moment. Mrs. Brade was on the beach painting pretty pictures.

"Good," said Hallet, "I'll have a look around their room before I question them. Take us there."

The clerk hesitated. "Boy!" he called. It was only a bluff; the Reef and Palm had no bell-boys. Finally, with an air of injured dignity, he led the way down a long corridor on the same floor as the office and unlocked the door of nineteen, the last room on the right. Hallet strode in and went to the window.

"Here—wait a minute," he called to the clerk. He pointed to the elderly woman painting on the beach. "That Mrs. Brade?"

"Yes-s," hissed the clerk.

"All right—go along." The clerk went out. "Mr. Winterslip, I'll ask you to sit here in the window and keep an eye on the lady. If she starts to come in, let me know." He stared eagerly about the poorly furnished bedroom. "Now, Mr. Brade, I wonder what you've got?"

John Quincy took the post assigned him, feeling decidedly uncomfortable. This didn't seem quite honorable to him. However, he probably wouldn't be called upon to do any searching himself, and if policemen were forced to do disagreeable things—well, they should have thought of that before they became policemen. Not that either Hallet or Chan appeared to be embarrassed by the task before them.

There was a great deal of luggage in the room—English luggage, which is usually large and impressive. John Quincy noted a trunk, two enormous bags, and a smaller case. All were plastered with labels of the *Sonoma,* and beneath were the worn fragments of earlier labels, telling a broken story of other ships and far hotels.

Hallet and Chan were old hands at this game; they went through Brade's trunk rapidly and thoroughly, but without finding anything of note. The captain turned his attention to the small traveling case. With every evidence of delight he drew forth a packet of letters, and sat down with them at a table. John Quincy was shocked. Reading other people's mail was, in his eyes, something that simply wasn't done.

It was done by Hallet, however. In a moment the captain spoke. "Seems to have been in the British civil service in Calcutta, but he's resigned," he announced to Chan. "Here's a letter from his superior in London referring to Brade's thirty-six years on the job, and saying he's sorry to lose him." Hallet took up another letter, his face brightened as he read. "Say—this is more like it!" He handed the typewritten page to Chan. Chan looked at it, and his eyes sparkled. "Most interesting," he cried, and turned it over to John Quincy.

The boy hesitated. The standards of a lifetime are not easily abandoned. But the others had read it first, so he put aside his scruples. The letter was several months old, and was addressed to Brade in Calcutta.

> "Dear Sir:
>   In reply to your inquiry of the sixth instant, would say that Mr. Daniel Winterslip is alive and is a resident of this city. His address is 3947 Kalia Road, Waikiki, Honolulu, T. H."

The signature was that of the British consul at Honolulu. John Quincy returned the epistle to Hallet, who put it in his pocket. At that instant Chan, who had been exploring one of the larger bags, emitted a little grunt of satisfaction.

"What is it, Charlie?" Hallet asked.

Chan set out on the table before his chief a small tin box, and removed the lid. It was filled with cigarettes. "Corsican brand," he announced cheerfully.

"Good," said Hallet. "It begins to look as though Mr. Thomas Macan Brade would have a lot to explain."

They continued their researches, while John Quincy sat silent by the window. Presently Carlota Egan appeared outside. She walked slowly to a chair on the lanai, and sat down. For a moment she stared at the breakers, then she began to weep.

John Quincy turned uncomfortably away. It came to him that here in this so-called paradise sorrow was altogether too rampant. The only girls he knew were given to frequent tears, and not without reason.

"If you'll excuse me—" he said. Hallet and Chan, searching avidly, made no reply, and climbing over the sill, he stepped on to the lanai. The girl looked up as he approached.

"Oh," she said, "I thought I was alone."

"You'd like to be, perhaps," he answered. "But it might help if you told me what has happened. Did you speak to your father about that check?"

She nodded. "Yes, I showed it to him. And what do you think he did? He snatched it out of my hand and tore it into a hundred pieces. He gave me the pieces to—to throw away. And he said I was never to mention it to a soul."

"I don't understand that," frowned John Quincy.

"Neither do I. He was simply furious—not like himself at all. And when I told him you knew about it, he lost his temper again."

"But you can rely on me. I shan't tell any one."

"I know that. But of course father wasn't so sure of you as—as I am. Poor dad—he's having a horrible time of it. They don't give him a moment's rest—keep after him constantly—trying to make him tell. But all the policemen in the world couldn't—Oh, poor old dad!"

She was weeping again, and John Quincy felt toward her as he had felt toward Barbara. He wanted to put his arm about her, just by way of comfort and cheer. But alas, Carlota Maria Egan was not a Winterslip.

"Now, now," he said, "that won't do a bit of good."

She looked at him through her tears. "Won't it? I—I don't know. It seems to help a little. But" she dried her eyes—"I really haven't time for it now. I must go in and see about lunch."

She rose, and John Quincy walked with her along the balcony. "I wouldn't worry if I were you," he said. "The police are on an entirely new trail this morning."

"Really?" she answered eagerly.

"Yes. There's a man named Brade stopping at your hotel. You know him, I suppose?"

She shook her head. "No, I don't."

"What! Why, he's a guest here."

"He was. But he isn't here now."

"Wait a minute!" John Quincy laid his hand on her arm, and they stopped. "This is interesting. Brade's gone, you say?"

"Yes. I understand from the clerk that Mr. and Mrs. Brade arrived her last Saturday. But early Tuesday morning, before my boat got in, Mr. Brade disappeared and he hasn't been seen since."

"Mr. Brade gets better all the time," John Quincy said. "Hallet and Chan are in his room now, and they've unearthed some rather intriguing facts. You'd better go in and tell Hallet what you've just told me."

They entered the lobby by a side door. As they did so, a slim young Hawaiian boy was coming in through the big door at the front. Something in his manner caught the attention of John Quincy, and he stopped. At that instant a purple bathing suit slipped by him, and Mr. Saladine also approached the desk. Carlota Egan went on down the corridor toward room nineteen, but John Quincy remained in the lobby.

The Hawaiian boy moved rather diffidently toward the clerk. "Excuse me, please," he said. "I come to see Mr. Brade. Mr. Thomas Brade."

"Mr. Brade not here," replied the clerk.

"Then I will wait till he comes."

The clerk frowned. "No good. Mr. Brade not in Honolulu now."

"Not in Honolulu!" The Hawaiian seemed startled by the news.

"Mrs. Brade outside on the beach," continued the clerk.

"Oh, then Mr. Brade returns," said the boy with evident relief. "I call again."

He turned away, moving rapidly now. The clerk addressed Mr. Saladine, who was hovering near the cigar case. "Yes, sir, please?"

"Thigarettes," said the bereft Mr. Saladine.

The clerk evidently knew the brand desired, and handed over a box.

"Juth put it on my bill," said Saladine. He stood for a moment staring after the Hawaiian, who was disappearing through the front door. As he swung round his eyes encountered those of John Quincy. He looked quickly away and hurried out.

The two policemen and the girl entered from the corridor. "Well, Mr. Winterslip," said Hallet, "the bird has flown."

"So I understand," John Quincy answered.

"But we'll find him," continued Hallet. "I'll go over these islands with a drag-net. First of all, I want a talk with his wife." He turned to Carlota Egan. "Get her in here," he ordered. The girl looked at him. "Please," he added.

She motioned to the clerk, who went out the door.

"By the way," remarked John Quincy, "someone was just here asking for Brade."

"What's that!" Hallet was interested.

"A young Hawaiian, about twenty, I should say. Tall and slim. If you go to the door, you may catch a glimpse of him."

Hallet hurried over and glanced out into the garden. In a second he returned. "Humph," he said. "I know him. Did he say he'd come again?"

"He did."

Hallet considered. "I've changed my mind," he announced. "I won't question Mrs. Brade, after all. For the present, I don't want her to know we're looking for her husband. I'll trust you to fix that up with your clerk," he added to the girl. She nodded. "Lucky we left things as we found them in nineteen," he went on. "Unless she misses that letter and the cigarettes, which isn't likely, we're all right. Now, Miss Egan, we three will go into your father's office there behind the desk, and leave the door open. When Mrs. Brade comes in, I want you to question her about her husband's absence. Get all you can out of her. I'll be listening."

"I understand," the girl said.

Hallet, Chan and John Quincy went into Jim Egan's sanctum. "You found nothing else in the room?" the latter inquired of the Chinese man.

Chan shook his head. "Even so, fates are in smiling mood. What we have now are plentiful."

"Sh!" warned Hallet.

"Mrs. Brade, a young man was just here inquiring for your husband." It was Carlota Egan's voice.

"Really?" The accent was unmistakably British.

"He wanted to know where he could find him. We couldn't say."

"No—of course not."

"Your husband has left town, Mrs. Brade?"

"Yes. I fancy he has."

"You know when he will return, perhaps?"

"I really couldn't say. Is the mail in?"

"Not yet. We expect it about one."

"Thank you so much."

"Go to the door," Hallet directed John Quincy.

"She's gone to her room," announced the boy.

The three of them emerged from Egan's office.

"Oh, Captain," said the girl, "I'm afraid I wasn't very successful."

"That's all right," replied Hallet. "I didn't think you would be." The clerk was again at his post behind the desk. Hallet turned to him. "Look here," he said. "I understand some one was here a minute ago asking for Brade. It was Dick Kaohla, wasn't it?"

"Yes-s," answered the clerk.

"Had he been here before to see Brade?"

"Yes-s. Sunday night. Mr. Brade and him have long talk on the beach."

Hallet nodded grimly. "Come on, Charlie," he said. "We've got our work cut out for us. Wherever Brade is, we must find him."

John Quincy stepped forward. "Pardon me, Captain," he remarked. "But if you don't mind—just who is Dick Kaohla?"

Hallet hesitated. "Kaohla's father—he's dead now—was a sort of confidential servant to Dan Winterslip. The boy's just plain no good. And oh, yes—he's the grandson of that woman who's over at your place now. Kamaikui—is that her name?"

14
What Kaohla Carried

Several days slipped by so rapidly John Quincy scarcely noted their passing. Dan Winterslip was sleeping now under the royal palms of the lovely island where he had been born. Sun and moon shone brightly in turn on his last dwelling place, but those who sought the person he had encountered that Monday night on his lanai were still groping in the dark.

Hallet had kept his word, he was combing the Islands for Brade. But Brade was nowhere. Ships paused at the crossroads and sailed again; the name of Thomas Macan Brade was on no sailing list. Through far settlements that were called villages but were nothing save clusters of Japanese huts, in lonely coves where the surf moaned dismally, over pineapple and sugar plantations, the emissaries of Hallet pursued their quest. Their efforts came to nothing.

John Quincy drifted idly with the days. He knew now the glamour of Waikiki waters; he had felt their warm embrace. Every afternoon he experimented with a board in the malihini surf, and he was eager for the moment when he could dare the big rollers farther out. Boston seemed like a tale that is told, State Street and Beacon memories of another more active existence now abandoned. No longer was he at a loss to understand his aunt's reluctance to depart these friendly shores.

Early Friday afternoon Miss Minerva found him reading a book on the lanai. Something in the nonchalance of his manner irritated her. She had always been for action, and the urge was on her even in Hawaii.

"Have you seen Mr. Chan lately?" she inquired.

"Talked with him this morning. They're doing their best to find Brade."

"Humph," sniffed Miss Minerva. "Their best is none too good. I'd like to have a few Boston detectives on this case."

"Oh, give them time," yawned John Quincy.

"They've had three days," she snapped. "Time enough. Brade never left this island of Oahu, that's certain. And when you consider that you can drive across it in a motor in two hours, and around it in around six, Mr. Hallet's brilliance does not impress. I'll have to end by solving this thing myself."

John Quincy laughed. "Yes, maybe you will."

"Well, I've given them the two best clues they have. If they'd keep their eyes open the way I do—"

"Charlie's eyes were open," protested John Quincy.

"Think so? They look pretty sleepy to me."

Barbara appeared on the lanai, dressed for a drive. Her eyes were somewhat happier; a bit of color had come back to her cheeks. "What are you reading, John Quincy?" she asked.

He held up the book. *"The City by the Golden Gate,"* he told her.

"Oh, really? If you're interested, I believe dad had quite a library on San Francisco. I remember there was a history of the stock exchange—he wanted me to read it, but I couldn't."

"You missed a good one," John Quincy informed her. "I finished it this morning. I've read five other books on San Francisco since I came."

His aunt stared at him. "What for?" she asked.

"Well—" He hesitated. "I've taken sort of a fancy to the town. I don't know—sometimes I think I'd rather like to live there."

Miss Minerva smiled grimly. "And they sent you out to take me back to Boston," she remarked.

"Boston's all right," said her nephew hastily. "It's Winterslip headquarters—but its hold has never been strong enough to prevent an occasional Winterslip from hitting the trail. You know, when I came into San Francisco harbor, I had the oddest feeling." He told them about it. "And the more I saw of the city, the better I liked it. There's a snap and sparkle in the air, and the people seem to know how to get the most out of life."

Barbara smiled on him approvingly. "Follow that impulse, John Quincy," she advised.

"Maybe I will. All this reminds me—I must write a letter." He rose and left the lanai.

"Does he really intend to desert Boston?" Barbara asked.

Miss Minerva shook her head. "Just a moment's madness," she explained. "I'm glad he's going through it—he'll be more human in the future. But as for leaving Boston! John Quincy! As well expect Bunker Hill Monument to emigrate to England."

In his room up-stairs, however, John Quincy's madness was persisting. He had never completed that letter to Agatha Parker, but he now plunged into his task with enthusiasm. San Francisco was his topic, and he wrote well. He pictured the city in words that glowed with life, and he wondered—just a suggestion—how she'd like to live there.

Agatha was now, he recalled, on a ranch in Wyoming—her first encounter with the West—and that was providential. She had felt for herself the lure of the wide open spaces. Well, the farther you went the wider and opener they got. In California life was all color and light. Just a suggestion, of course.

As he sealed the flap of the envelope, he seemed to glimpse Agatha's thin patrician face, and his heart sank. Her gray eyes were cool, so different from Barbara's, so very different from those of Carlota Maria Egan.

On Saturday afternoon John Quincy had an engagement to play golf with Harry Jennison. He drove up Nuuanu Valley in Barbara's roadster—for Dan Winterslip's will had been read and everything he possessed was Barbara's now. In that sheltered spot a brisk rain was falling, as is usually the case, though the sun was shining brightly. John Quincy had grown accustomed to this phenomenon; "liquid sunshine" the people of Hawaii call such rain, and pay no attention to it. Half a dozen different rainbows added to the beauty of the Country Club links.

Jennison was waiting on the veranda, a striking figure in white. He appeared genuinely glad to see his guest, and they set out on a round of golf that John Quincy would long remember. Never before had he played amid such beauty. The low hills stood on guard, their slopes bright with tropical colors—the yellow of kukui trees, the gray of ferns, the emerald of ohia and banana trees, here and there a splotch of brick-red earth. The course was a green velvet carpet beneath their feet, the showers came and went. Jennison was a proficient driver, but the boy was his superior on approaches, and at the end of the match John Quincy was four up. They putted through a rainbow and returned to the locker room.

In the roadster going home, Jennison brought up the subject of Dan Winterslip's murder. John Quincy was interested to get the reaction of a lawyer to the evidence.

"I've kept more or less in touch with the case," Jennison said. "Egan is still my choice."

Somehow, John Quincy resented this. A picture of Carlota Egan's lovely but unhappy face flashed through his mind. "How about Leatherbee and the Compton woman?" he asked.

"Well, of course, I wasn't present when they told their story," Jennison replied. "But Hallet claims it sounded perfectly plausible. And it doesn't seem likely that if he'd had anything to do with the murder, Leatherbee would have been fool enough to keep that page from the guest book."

"There's Brade, too," John Quincy suggested.

"Yes—Brade complicates things. But when they run him down—if they do—I imagine the result will be nil."

"You know that Kamaikui's grandson is mixed up somehow with Brade?"

"So I understand. It's a matter that wants looking into. But mark my words, when all these trails are followed to the end, everything will come back to Jim Egan."

"What have you against Egan?" inquired John Quincy, swerving to avoid another car.

"I have nothing against Egan," Jennison replied. "But I can't forget the look on Dan Winterslip's face that day he told me he was afraid of the man. Then there is the stub of the Corsican cigarette. Most important of all, Egan's silence regarding his business with Winterslip. Men who are facing a charge of murder, my boy, talk, and talk fast. Unless it so happens that what they have to say would further incriminate them."

They drove on in silence into the heart of the city. "Hallet tells me you're doing a little detective work yourself," smiled Jennison.

"I've tried, but I'm a duffer," John Quincy admitted. "Just at present my efforts consist of a still hunt for that watch Aunt Minerva saw on the murderer's wrist. Whenever I see a wrist watch I get as close to it as I can, and stare. But as most of my sleuthing is done in the day time, it isn't so easy to determine whether the numeral two is bright or dim."

"Persistence," urged Jennison. "That's the secret of a good detective. Stick to the job and you may succeed yet."

The lawyer was to dine with the family at Waikiki. John Quincy set him down at his office, where he had a few letters to sign, and then drove him out to the beach. Barbara was gowned in white; she was slim and wistful and beautiful, and considering the events of the immediate past, the dinner was a cheerful one.

They had coffee on the lanai. Presently Jennison rose and stood by Barbara's chair. "We've something to tell you," he announced. He looked down at the girl. "Is that right, my dear?"

Barbara nodded.

"Your cousin and I"—the lawyer turned to the two from Boston—"have been fond of each other for a long time. We shall be married very quietly in a week or so—"

"Oh, Harry—not a week," said Barbara.

"Well, as you wish. But very soon,"

"Very, very soon," she repeated.

"And leave Honolulu for a time," Jennison continued. "Naturally, Barbara feels she can not stay here for the present—so many memories—you both understand. She has authorized me to put his house up for sale—"

"But, Harry," Barbara protested, "you make me sound so inhospitable. Telling my guests that the house is for sale and I am leaving—"

"Nonsense, my dear," said Aunt Minerva. "John Quincy and I understand, quite. I sympathize with your desire to get away." She rose.

"I'm sorry," said Jennison. "I did sound a little abrupt. But I'm naturally eager to take care of her now."

"Of course," John Quincy agreed.

Miss Minerva bent over and kissed the girl. "If your mother were here, dear child," she said, "she couldn't wish for your happiness any more keenly than I do." Barbara reached up impulsively and put her arms about the older woman.

John Quincy shook Jennison's hand. "You're mighty lucky."

"I think so," Jennison answered.

The boy went over to Barbara. "All—all good wishes," he said. She nodded, but did not reply. He saw there were tears in her eyes.

Presently Miss Minerva withdrew to the livingroom, and John Quincy, feeling like a fifth wheel, made haste to leave the two together. He went out on the beach. The pale moon rode high amid the golden stars, romance whispered through the cocoanut palms. He thought of the scene he had witnessed that breathless night on the *President Tyler*—only two in the world, love quick and overwhelming—well, this was the setting for it. Here on this beach they had walked two and two since the beginning of time, whispering the same vows, making the same promises, whatever their color and creed. Suddenly the boy felt lonely.

Barbara was a Winterslip, and not for him. Why then did he feel again that frustrated pang in his heart? She had chosen and her choice was fitting, what affair was it of his?

He found himself moving slowly toward the Reef and Palm Hotel. For a chat with Carlota Egan? But why should he want to talk with this girl, whose outlook was so different from that of the world he knew? The girls at home were on a level with the men in brains—often, indeed, they were superior, seemed to be looking down from a great height. They discussed that article in the latest *Atlantic*, Shaw's grim philosophy, the new Sargent at the Art Gallery. Wasn't that the sort of talk he should be seeking here? Or was it? Under these palms on this romantic beach, with the moon riding high over Diamond Head?

Carlota Egan was seated behind the desk in the deserted lobby of the Reef and Palm, a worried frown on her face.

"You've come at the psychological moment," she cried, and smiled. "I'm having the most awful struggle."

"Arithmetic?" John Quincy inquired.

"Compound fractions, it seems to me. I'm making out the Brades' bill."

He came round the desk and stood at her side. "Let me help you."

"It's so fearfully involved." She looked up at him, and he wished they could do their sums on the beach. "Mr. Brade has been away since Tuesday morning, and we don't charge for any absence of more than three days. So that comes out of it. Maybe you can figure it—I can't."

"Charge him anyhow," suggested John Quincy.

"I'd like to—that would simply everything. But it's not dad's way."

John Quincy took up a pencil. "What rate are they paying?" he inquired. She told him, and he began to figure. It wasn't a simple matter, even for a bond expert. John Quincy frowned too.

Some one entered the front door of the Reef and Palm. Looking up, John Quincy beheld the Hawaiian boy, Dick Kaohla. He carried a bulky object, wrapped in newspapers.

"Mr. Brade here now?" he asked.

Carlota Egan shook her head. "No, he hasn't returned."

"I will wait," said the boy.

"But we don't know where he is, or when he will come back," the girl protested.

"He will be here soon," the Hawaiian replied. "I wait on the lanai." He went out the side door, still carrying his clumsy burden. John Quincy and the girl stared at each other.

" 'We move, we advance!' " John Quincy quoted in a low voice. "Brade will be here soon! Would you mind going out on the lanai and telling me where Kaohla is now?"

Quickly the girl complied. She returned in a few seconds. "He's taken a chair at the far end."

"Out of earshot?"

"Quite. You want the telephone—"

But John Quincy was already in the booth. Charlie Chan's voice came back over the wire.

"Most warm congratulations. You are number one detective yourself. Should my self-starter not indulge in stubborn spasm, I will make immediate connection with you."

John Quincy returned to the desk, smiling. "Charlie's flying to us in his Ford. Begins to look as though we were getting somewhere now. But about this bill. Mrs. Brade's board and room I make sixteen dollars. The charge against Mr. Brade—one week's board and room minus four days' board—totals nine dollars and sixty-two cents."

"How can I ever thank you?" said the girl.

"By telling me again about your childhood on this beach." A shadow crossed her face. "Oh, I'm sorry I've made you unhappy."

"Oh, no—you couldn't." She shook her head. "I've never been—so very happy. Always an 'if' in it, as I told you before. That morning on the ferry I think I was nearest to real happiness. I seemed to have escaped from life for a moment."

"I remember how you laughed at my hat."

"Oh—I hope you've forgiven me."

"Nonsense. I'm mighty glad I was able to make you laugh like that." Her great eyes stared into the future, and John Quincy pitied her. He had known others like her, others who loved their fathers, built high hopes for them, then saw them drift into a baffled old age. One of the girl's slender,

tanned hands lay on the desk, John Quincy put his own upon it. "Don't be
unhappy," he urged. "It's such a wonderful night. The moon—you're a
what-you-may-call-it—a kamaaina, I know, but I'll bet you never saw the
moon looking so well before. It's like a thousand-dollar gold piece, pale
but negotiable. Shall we go out and spend it?"

Gently she drew her hand away. "There were seven bottles of charged
water sent to the room. Thirty-five cents each—"

"What? Oh, the Brades' bill. Yes, that means two forty-five more. I'd like
to mention the stars too. Isn't it odd how close the stars seem in the
tropics—"

She smiled. "We mustn't forget the trunks and bags. Three dollars for
bringing them up from the dock."

"Say—that's rather steep. Well, it goes down on the record. Have I ever
told you that all this natural beauty out here has left its imprint on your
face? In the midst of so much loveliness, one couldn't be anything but—"

"Mrs. Brade had three trays to the room. That's seventy-five cents more."

"Extravagant lady! Brade will be sorry he came back, for more reasons
than one. Well, I've got that. Anything else?"

"Just the laundry. Ninety-seven cents."

"Fair enough. Adding it all up, I get thirty-two dollars and sixty-nine
cents. Let's call it an even thirty-three."

She laughed. "Oh, no. We can't do that."

Mrs. Brade came slowly into the lobby from the lanai. She paused at the
desk. "Has there been a message?" she inquired.

"No, Mrs. Brade," the girl answered. She handed over the slip of paper.
"Your bill."

"Ah, yes. Mr. Brade will attend to this the moment he returns."

"You expect him soon?"

"I really can't say." The Englishwoman moved on into the corridor leading to nineteen.

"Full of information, as usual," smiled John Quincy. "Why, here's Charlie
now."

Chan came briskly to the desk, followed by another policeman, also in
plain clothes.

"Automobile act noble," he announced, "having fondly feeling for night
air." He nodded toward his companion. "Introducing Mr. Spencer. Now,
what are the situation? Humbly hinting you speak fast."

John Quincy told him Kaohla was waiting on the lanai, and mentioned
the unwieldy package carried by the boy. Chan nodded.

"Events are turning over rapidly," he said. He addressed the girl. "Please
kindly relate to this Kaohla that Brade has arrived and would wish to
encounter him here." She hesitated. "No, no," added Chan hastily, "I forget
nice heathen delicacy. It is not pretty I should ask a lady to scatter false lies
from ruby lips. I humbly demand forgiveness. Content yourself with a
veiled pretext bringing him here."

The girl smiled and went out. "Mr. Spencer," said Chan, "I make bold
to suggest you interrogate this Hawaiian. My reckless wanderings among
words of unlimitable English language often fail to penetrate sort of skulls
plentiful round here."

Spencer nodded and went to the side door, standing where he would
not be seen by any one entering there. In a moment Kaohla appeared,
followed by the girl. The Hawaiian came in quickly but seeing Chan,
stopped, and a frightened look crossed his face. Spencer startled him further by seizing his arm.

"Come over here," said the detective. "We want to talk to you." He led the boy to a far corner of the room. Chan and John Quincy followed. "Sit down—here, I'll take that." He removed the heavy package from under the boy's arm. For a moment the Hawaiian seemed about to protest, but evidently he thought better of it. Spencer placed the package on a table and stood over Kaohla.

"Want to see Brade, eh?" he began in a threatening tone.

"Yes."

"What for?"

"Business is private."

"Well, I'm telling you to come across. You're in bad. Better change your mind and talk."

"No."

"All right. We'll see about that. What have you got in that package?" The boy's eyes went to the table, but he made no answer.

Chan took out a pocket knife. "Simple matter to discover," he said. He cut the rough twine, unwound several layers of newspapers. John Quincy pressed close, he felt that something important was about to be divulged.

The last layer of paper came off. "Hot dog!" cried Chan. He turned quickly to John Quincy. "Oh, I am so sorry—I pick up atrocious phrase like that from my cousin Mr. Willie Chan, Captain of All Chinese baseball team—"

But John Quincy did not hear, his eyes were glued to the object that lay on the table. An ohia wood box, bound with copper—the initials T.M.B.

"We will unlatch it," said Chan. He made an examination. "No, locked most strongly. We will crash into it at police station, where you and I and this silent Hawaiian will now hasten. Mr. Spencer, you will remain on spot here. Should Brade appear, you know your duty."

"I do," said Spencer.

"Mr. Kaohla, do me the honor to accompany," continued Chan. "At police headquarters much talk will be extracted out of you."

They turned toward the door. As they did so, Carlota Egan came up. "May I speak to you a moment?" she said to John Quincy.

"Surely." He walked with her to the desk.

"I went to the lanai just now," she whispered breathlessly. "Some one was crouching outside the window near where you were talking. I went closer and it was—Mr. Saladine!"

"Aha," said John Quincy. "Mr. Saladine had better drop that sort of thing, or he'll get himself in trouble."

"Should we tell Chan?"

"Not yet. You and I will do a little investigating ourselves first. Chan has other things to think about. And we don't want any of our guests to leave unless it's absolutely necessary."

"We certainly don't," she smiled. "I'm glad you've got the interests of the house at heart."

"That's just where I've got them—" John Quincy began, but Chan cut in.

"Humbly begging pardon," he said, "we must speed. Captain Hallet will have high delight to encounter this Kaohla, to say nothing of ohia wood box."

In the doorway, Kaohla crowded close to John Quincy, and the latter was startled by the look of hate he saw in the boy's stormy eyes. "You did this," muttered the Hawaiian. "I don't forget."

15

The Man from India

They clattered along Kalakaua Avenue in Chan's car. John Quincy sat alone on the rear seat; at the detective's request he held the ohia wood box on his knees.

He rested his hands upon it. Once it had eluded him, but he had it now. His mind went back to that night in the attic two thousand miles away, the shadow against the moonlit window, the sting of a jewel cutting across his cheek. Roger's heartfelt cry of "Poor old Dan!" Did they hold at last, in this ohia wood box, the answer to the mystery of Dan's death?

Hallet was waiting in his room. With him was a keen-eyed, efficient looking man evidently in his late thirties.

"Hello, boys," said the captain. "Mr. Winterslip, meet Mr. Greene, our district court prosecutor."

Greene shook hands cordially. "I've been wanting to meet you, sir," he said. "I know your city rather well. Spent three years at your Harvard Law School."

"Really?" replied John Quincy with enthusiasm.

"Yes. I went there after I got through at New Haven. I'm a Yale man, you know."

"Oh," remarked John Quincy, without any enthusiasm at all. But Greene seemed a pleasant fellow, despite his choice of college.

Chan had set the box on the table before Hallet, and was explaining how they had come upon it. The captain's thin face had brightened perceptibly. He inspected the treasure. "Locked, eh?" he remarked. "You got the key, Kaohla?"

The Hawaiian shook his head sullenly. "No."

"Watch your step, boy," warned Hallet. "Go over him, Charlie."

Chan went over him, rapidly and thoroughly. He found a key ring, but none of the keys fitted the lock on the box. He also brought to light a fat roll of bills.

"Where'd you get all that money, Dick?" Hallet inquired.

"I got it," glowered the boy.

But Hallet was more interested in the box. He tapped it lovingly. "This is important, Mr. Greene. We may find the solution of our puzzle in here." He took a small chisel from his desk, and after a brief struggle, pried open the lid.

John Quincy, Chan and the prosecutor pressed close, their eyes staring eagerly as the captain lifted the lid. The box was empty.

"Filled with nothing," murmured Chan. "Another dream go smash against stone wall."

The disappointment angered Hallet. He turned on Kaohla. "Now, my lad," he said. "I want to hear from you. You've been in touch with Brade, you talked with him last Sunday night, you've heard he's returning to-night. You've got some deal on with him. Come across and be quick about it."

"Nothing to tell," said the Hawaiian stubbornly.

Hallet leaped to his feet. "Oh, yes you have. And by heaven, you're going to tell it. I'm not any too patient to-night and I warn you if you don't talk

and talk quick I'm likely to get rough." He stopped suddenly and turned
to Chan. "Charlie, that Inter-Island boat is due from Maui about now. Get
down to the dock and watch for Brade. You've got his description?"

"Sure," answered Chan. "Thin pale face, one shoulder descended below
other, gray mustaches that droop in saddened mood."

"That's right. Keep a sharp lookout. And leave this lad to us. He won't
have any secrets when we get through with him, eh, Mr. Greene?"

The proscutor, more discreet, merely smiled.

"Mr. Winterslip," said Chan. "The night is delicious. A little stroll to
moonly dock—"

"I'm with you," John Quincy replied. He looked back over his shoulder
as he went, and reflected that he wouldn't care to be in Kaohla's shoes.

The pier-shed was dimly lighted and a small but diversified group awaited
the incoming boat. Chan and John Quincy walked to the far end and there,
seated on a packing-case, they found the water-boat reporter of the evening
paper.

"Hello, Charlie," cried Mr. Mayberry. "What you doing here?"

"Maybe friend arrive on boat," grinned Chan.

"Is that so?" responded Mayberry. "You boys over at the station have
certainly become pretty mysterious all of a sudden. What's doing, Charlie?"

"All pronouncements come from captain," advised Chan.

"Yeah, we've heard his pronouncements," sneered Mayberry. "The police
have unearthed clues and are working on them. Nothing to report at
present. It's sickening. Well, sit down, Charlie. Oh—Mr. Winterslip—good
evening. I didn't recognize you at first."

"How are you," said John Quincy. He and Chan also found packing-
cases. There was a penetrating odor of sugar in the air. Through a wide
opening in the pier-shed they gazed along the water-front and out upon
the moonlit harbor. A rather exotic and intriguing scene, John Quincy
reflected, and he said as much.

"Think so?" answered Mayberry. "Well, I don't. To me it's just like Seattle
or Galveston or any of those stereotyped ports. But you see—I knew it
when—"

"I think you mentioned that before," John Quincy smiled.

"I'm likely to mention it at any moment. As far as I'm concerned, the
harbor of Honolulu has lost its romance. Once this was the most picturesque
water-front in the world, my boy. And now look at the damned thing!"
The reporter relighted his pipe. "Charlie can tell you—he remembers. The
old ramshackle, low-lying wharves. Old Naval Row with its sailing ships.
The wooden-hulled steamers with a mast or two—not too proud to use
God's good winds occasionally. The bright little row-boats, the *Aloha*, the
Manu, the *Emma*. Eh, Chan?"

"All extinct," agreed Chan.

"You wouldn't see a Rotary Club gang like this on a pier in those days,"
Mayberry continued. "Just Hawaiian stevedores with leis on their hats and
ukuleles in their hands. Fishermen with their nets, and maybe a breezy old-
time purser—a glad-hander and not a mere machine." He puffed a moment
in sad silence. "Those were the days, Mr. Winterslip, the days of Hawaii's
isolation, and her charm. The cable and the radio hadn't linked us up with
the so-called civilization of the mainland. Every boat that came in we'd
scamper over it, hunting a newspaper with the very latest news of the
outside world. Remember those steamer days, Charlie, when everybody
went down to the wharf in the good old hacks of yesteryear, when the
women wore holokus and lauhala hats, and Berger was there with his band,

and maybe a prince or two—"

"And the nights," suggested Charlie.

"Yeah, old-timer, I was coming to the nights. The soft nights when the serenaders drifted about the harbor in row-boats, and the lanterns speared long paths on the water—"

He seemed about to weep. John Quincy's mind went back to books he had read in his boyhood.

"And occasionally," he said, "I presume somebody went aboard a ship against his will?"

"I'll say he did," replied Mr. Mayberry, brightening at the thought. "Why, it was only in the 'nineties I was sitting one night on a dock a few yards down, when I saw a scuffle near the landing, and one of my best friends shouted to me: 'Good-by, Pete!' I was up and off in a minute, and I got him away from them—I was younger in those days. He was a good fellow, a sailorman, and he wasn't intending to take the journey that bunch had planned for him. They'd got him into a saloon and drugged him, but he pulled out of it just in time—oh, well, those days are gone for ever now. Just like Galveston or Seattle. Yes, sir, this harbor of Honolulu has lost its romance."

The little Inter-Island boat was drawing up to the pier, and they watched it come. As the gangplank went down, Chan rose.

"Who you expecting, Charlie?" asked Mayberry.

"We grope about," said Chan. "Maybe on this boat are Mr. Brade."

"Brade!" Mayberry leaped to his feet.

"Not so sure," warned Chan. "Only a matter we suppose. If correct, humbly suggest you follow to the station. You might capture news."

John Quincy and Chan moved up to the gangplank as the passengers descended. There were not many aboard. A few Island business men, a scattering of tourists, a party of Japanese in western clothes, ceremoniously received by friends ashore—a quaint little group all bowing from the waist. John Quincy was watching them with interest when Chan touched his arm.

A tall stooped Englishman was coming down the plank. Thomas Macan Brade would have been easily spotted in any crowd. His mustache was patterned after that of the Earl of Pawtucket, and to make identification even simpler, he wore a white pith helmet. Pith helmets are not necessary under the kindly skies of Hawaii; this was evidently a relic of Indian days.

Chan stepped forward. "Mr. Brade?"

The man had a tired look in his eyes. He started nervously. "Y—yes," he hesitated.

"I am Detective-Sergeant Chan. Honolulu police. You will do me the great honor to accompany me to the station, if you please."

Brade stared at him, then shook his head. "It's quite impossible," he said.

"Pardon me, please," answered Chan. "It are unevitable."

"I—I have just returned from a journey," protested the man. "My wife may be worried regarding me. I must have a talk with her, and after that—"

"Regret," purred Chan, "are scorching me. But duty remains duty. Chief's words are law. Humbly suggest we squander valuable time."

"Am I to understand that I'm under arrest?" flared Brade.

"The idea is preposterous," Chan assured him. "But the captain waits eager for statement from you. You will walk this way, I am sure. A moment's pardon. I introduce my fine friend, Mr. John Quincy Winterslip, of Boston."

At mention of the name, Brade turned and regarded John Quincy with deep interest. "Very good," he said. "I'll go with you."

They went out to the street, Brade carrying a small hand-bag. The flurry of arrival was dying fast. Honolulu would shortly return to its accustomed evening calm.

When they reached the police station, Hallet and the prosecutor seemed in high good humor. Kaohla sat in a corner, hopeless and defeated; John Quincy saw at a glance that the boy's secret was his no longer.

"Introducing Mr. Brade," said Chan.

"Ah," cried Hallet, "we're glad to see you, Mr. Brade. We'd been getting pretty worried about you."

"Really, sir," said Brade, "I am completely at a loss—"

"Sit down," ordered Hallet. The man sank into a chair. He too had a hopeless, defeated air. No one can appear more humble and beaten than a British civil servant, and this man had known thirty-six years of baking under the Indian sun, looked down on by the military, respected by none. Not only his mustache but his whole figure drooped "in saddened mood." Yet now and then, John Quincy noted, he flashed into life, a moment of self-assertion and defiance.

"Where have you been, Mr. Brade?" Hallet inquired.

"I have visited one of the other islands. Maui."

"You went last Tuesday morning?"

"Yes. On the same steamer that brought me back."

"Your name was not on the sailing list," Hallet said.

"No. I went under another name. I had—reasons."

"Indeed?"

The flash of life. "Just why am I here, sir?" He turned to the prosecutor. "Perhaps you will tell me that?"

Greene nodded toward the detective. "Captain Hallet will enlighten you," he said.

"You bet I will," Hallet announced. "As perhaps you know, Mr. Brade, Mr. Dan Winterslip has been murdered."

"Brade's washed-out eyes turned to John Quincy. "Yes," he said. "I read about it in a Hilo newspaper."

"You didn't know it when you left last Tuesday morning?" Hallet asked.

"I did not. I sailed without seeing a paper here."

"Ah, yes. When did you see Mr. Dan Winterslip last?"

"I never saw him."

"What! Be careful, sir."

"I never saw Dan Winterslip in my life."

"All right. Where were you last Tuesday morning at twenty minutes past one?"

"I was asleep in my room at the Reef and Palm Hotel. I'd retired at nine-thirty, as I had to rise early in order to board my boat. My wife can verify that."

"A wife's testimony, Mr. Brade, is not of great value—"

Brade leaped to his feet. "Look here, sir! Do you mean to insinuate—"

"Take it easy," said Hallet smoothly. "I have a few matters to call to your attention, Mr. Brade. Mr. Dan Winterslip was murdered at one-twenty or thereabouts last Tuesday morning. We happen to know that in his youth he served as first officer aboard the *Maid of Shiloh*, a blackbirder. The master of that vessel had the same name as yourself. An investigation of your room at the Reef and Palm—"

"How dare you!" cried Brade. "By what right—"

"I am hunting the murderer of Dan Winterslip," broke in Hallet coolly. "And I follow the trail wherever it leads. In your room I found a letter

from the British Consul here addressed to you, and informing you that
Winterslip was alive and in Honolulu. I also found this tin of Corsican
cigarettes. Just outside the living-room door of Winterslip's house, we
picked up the stub of a Corsican cigarette. It's a brand not on sale in
Honolulu."

Brade had dropped back into his chair, and was staring in a dazed way
at the tin box in Hallet's hand. Hallet indicated the Hawaiian boy in the
corner. "Ever see this lad before, Mr. Brade?" Brade nodded.

"You had a talk with him last Sunday night on the beach?"

"Yes."

"The boy's told us all about it. He read in the paper that you were coming
to Honolulu. His father was a confidential servant in Dan Winterslip's
employ and he himself was brought up in the Winterslip household. He
could make a pretty good guess at your business with Winterslip, and he
figured you'd be pleased to lay hands on this ohia wood box. In his boyhood
he'd seen it in a trunk in the attic of Winterslip's San Francisco house. He
went down to the *President Tyler* and arranged with a friend aboard that
boat, the quartermaster, to break into the house and steal the box. When
he saw you last Sunday night he told you he'd have the box as soon as the
President Tyler got in, and he arranged to sell it to you for a good sum. Am
I right so far, Mr. Brade?"

"You are quite right," said Brade.

"The initials on the box are T.M.B." Hallet persisted. "They are your
initials, are they not?"

"They happen to be," said Brade. "But they were also the initials of my
father. My father died aboard ship in the South Seas many years ago, and
that box was stolen from his cabin after his death. It was stolen by the first
officer of the *Maid of Shiloh*—by Mr. Dan Winterslip."

For a moment no one spoke. A cold shiver ran down the spine of John
Quincy Winterslip and a hot flush suffused his cheek. Why, oh, why, had
he strayed so far from home? In Boston he traveled in a rut, perhaps, but
ruts were safe, secure. There no one had ever brought a charge such as
this against a Winterslip, no whisper of scandal had ever sullied the name.
But here Winterslips had run amuck, and there was no telling what would
next be dragged into the light.

"I think, Mr. Brade," said the prosecutor slowly, "you had better make
a full statement."

Brade nodded. "I intend to do so. My case against Winterslip is not
complete and I should have preferred to remain silent for a time. But
under the circumstances, of course I must speak out. I'll smoke, if you
don't mind." He took a cigarette from his case and lighted it. "I'm a bit
puzzled just how to begin. My father disappeared from England in the
'seventies, leaving my mother and me to shift for ourselves. For a time we
heard nothing of him, then letters began to arrive from various points in
Australia and the South Seas. Letters with money in them, money we badly
needed. I have since learned that he had gone into the blackbirding trade;
it is nothing to be proud of, God knows, but I like to recall in his favor that
he did not entirely abandon his wife and boy.

"In the 'eighties we got word of his death. He died aboard the *Maid of
Shiloh* and was buried on the island of Apiang in the Gilbert Group—buried
by Dan Winterslip, his first officer. We accepted the fact of his death, the
fact of no more letters with remittances, and took up our struggle again.
Six months later we received, from a friend of my father in Sydney, a
brother captain, a most amazing letter.

"This letter said that, to the writer's certain knowledge, my father had carried a great deal of money in his cabin on the *Maid of Shiloh*. He had done no business with banks, instead he had had this strong box made of ohia wood. The man who wrote us said that he had seen the inside of it, and that it contained jewelry and a large quantity of gold. My father had also shown him several bags of green hide, containing gold coins from many countries. He estimated that there must have been close to twenty thousand pounds, in all. Dan Winterslip, the letter said, had brought the *Maid of Shiloh* back to Sydney and turned over to the proper authorities my father's clothing and personal effects, and a scant ten pounds in money. He had made no mention of anything further. He and the only other white man aboard the *Maid*, an Irishman named Hagin, had left at once for Hawaii. My father's friend suggested that we start an immediate investigation.

"Well, gentlemen"—Brade looked about the circle of interested faces—"what could we do? We were in pitiful circumstances, my mother and I. We had no money to employ lawyers, to fight a case thousands of miles away. We did make a few inquiries through a relative in Sydney, but nothing came of them. There was talk for a time, but the talk died out, and the matter was dropped. But I—I have never forgotten.

"Dan Winterslip returned here, and prospered. He built on the foundation of the money he found in my father's cabin a fortune that inspired the admiration of Honolulu. And while he prospered, we were close to starvation. My mother died, but I carried on. For years it has been my dream to make him pay. I have not been particularly successful, but I have saved, scrimped. I have the money now to fight this case.

"Four months ago I resigned my post in India and set out for Honolulu. I stopped over in Sydney—my father's friend is dead, but I have his letter. I have the depositions of others who knew about that money—about the ohia wood box. I came on here, ready to face Dan Winterslip at last. But I never faced him. As you know, gentlemen"—Brade's hand trembled slightly as he put down his cigarette—"some one robbed me of that privilege. Some unknown hand removed from my path the man I have hated for more than forty years."

"You arrived last Saturday—a week ago," said Hallet, after a pause. "On Sunday evening Kaohla here called on you. He offered you the strong box?"

"He did," Brade replied. "He'd had a cable from his friend, and expected to have the box by Tuesday. I promised him five thousand dollars for it—a sum I intended Winterslip should pay. Kaohla also told me that Hagin was living on a ranch in a remote part of the Island of Maui. That explains my journey there—I took another name, as I didn't want Winterslip to follow my movements. I had no doubt he was watching me."

"You didn't tell Kaohla you were going, either?"

"No, I didn't think it advisable to take him completely into my confidence. I found Hagin, but could get nothing out of him. Evidently Winterslip had bought his silence long ago. I realized the box was of great importance to me, and I cabled Kaohla to bring it to me immediately on my return. It was then that the news of Winterslip's death came through. It was a deep disappointment, but it will not deter me." He turned to John Quincy. "Winterslip's heirs must pay. I am determined they shall make my old age secure."

John Quincy's face flushed again. A spirit of rebellion, of family pride outraged, stirred within him. "We'll see about that, Mr. Brade," he said.

"You have unearthed the box, but so far as any proof about valuables—money—"

"One moment," cut in Greene, the prosecutor. "Mr. Brade, have you a description of any article of value taken from your father?"

Brade nodded. "Yes. In my father's last letter to us—I was looking through it only the other day—he spoke of a brooch he had picked up in Sydney. A tree of emeralds, rubies and diamonds against an onyx background. He said he was sending it to my mother—but it never came."

The prosecutor looked at John Quincy. John Quincy looked away. "I'm not one of Dan Winterslip's heirs, Mr. Brade," he explained. "As a matter of fact, he was a rather distant relative of mine. I can't presume to speak for his daughter, but I'm reasonably sure that when she knows your story, this matter can be settled out of court. You'll wait of course?"

"I'll wait," agreed Brade. "And now, Captain—"

Hallet raised his hand. "Just a minute. You didn't call on Winterslip? You didn't go near his house?"

"I did not," said Brade.

"Yet just outside the door of his living-room we found, as I told you, the stub of a Corsican cigarette. It's a matter still to be cleared up."

Brade considered briefly. "I don't want to get any one into trouble," he said. "But the man is nothing to me, and I must clear my own name. In the course of a chat with the proprietor of the Reef and Palm Hotel, I offered him a cigarette. He was delighted when he recognized the brand—said it had been years he'd seen one. So I gave him a handful, and he filled his case."

"You're speaking of Jim Egan," suggested Hallet delightedly.

"Of Mr. James Egan, yes," Brade replied.

"That's all I want to know," said Hallet. "Well, Mr. Greene—"

The prosecutor addressed Brade. "For the present, we can't permit you to leave Honolulu," he said. "But you are free to go to your hotel. This box will remain here until we can settle its final disposition."

"Naturally." Brade rose.

John Quincy faced him. "I'll call on you very soon," he promised.

"What? Oh, yes—yes, of course." The man stared nervously about him. "If you'll pardon me, gentlemen, I must run—I really must—"

He went out. The prosecutor looked at his watch. "Well, that's that. I'll have a conference with you in the morning, Hallet. My wife's waiting for me at the Country Club. Good night, Mr. Winterslip." He saw the look on John Quincy's face, and smiled. "Don't take those revelations about your cousin too seriously. The 'eighties are ancient history, you know."

As Greene disappeared, Hallet turned to John Quincy. "What about this Kaohla?" he inquired. "It will be a pretty complicated job to prosecute him and his housebreaking friend on the *President Tyler*, but it can be done—"

A uniformed policeman appeared at the door, summoning Chan outside.

"Oh, no," said John Quincy. "Let the boy go. We don't want any publicity about this. I'll ask you, Captain, to keep Brade's story out of the papers."

"I'll try," Hallet replied. He turned to the Hawaiian. "Come here!" The boy rose. "You heard what this gentleman said. You ought to be sent up for this, but we've got more important things to attend to now. Run along—beat it—"

Chan came in just in time to hear the last. At his heels followed a sly little Japanese man and a young Chinese boy. The latter was attired in the extreme of college-cut clothes; he was an American and he emphasized the fact.

"Only one moment," Chan cried. "New and interesting fact emerge into light. Gentlemen, my Cousin Willie Chan, captain All Chinese baseball team and demon back-stopper of the Pacific!"

"Pleased to meetchu," said Willie Chan.

"Also Okamoto, who have auto stand on Kalakaua Avenue, not far from Winterslip household—"

"I know Okamoto," said Hallet. "He sells okolehau on the side."

"No, indeed," protested Okamoto. "Auto stand, that is what."

"Willie do small investigating to help out crowded hours," went on Chan. "He have dug up strange event out of this Okamoto here. On early morning of Tuesday, July first, Okamoto is roused from slumber by fierce knocks on door of room. He go to door—"

"Let him tell it," suggested Hallet. "What time was this?"

"Two of the morning," said Okamoto. "Knocks were as described. I rouse and look at watch, run to door. Mr. Dick Kaohla here is waiting. Demand I drive him to home over in Iwilei district. I done so."

"All right," said Hallet. "Anything else? No? Charlie—take them out and thank them—that's your specialty." He waited until the Orientals had left the room, then turned fiercely on Kaohla. "Well, here you are back in the limelight," he cried. "Now, come across. What were you doing out near Winterslip's house the night of the murder?"

"Nothing," said the Hawaiian.

"Nothing! A little late to be up doing nothing, wasn't it? Look here, my boy, I'm beginning to get you. For years Dan Winterslip gave you money, supported you, until he finally decided you were no good. So he stopped the funds and you and he had a big row. Now, didn't you?"

"Yes," admitted Dick Kaohla.

"On Sunday night Brade offered you five thousand for the box. You thought it wasn't enough. The idea struck you that maybe Dan Winterslip would pay more. You were a little afraid of him, but you screwed up your courage and went to his house—"

"No, no," the boy cried. "I did not go there."

"I say you did. You'd made up your mind to doublecross Brade. You and Dan Winterslip had another big scrap, you drew a knife—"

"Lies, all lies," the boy shouted, terrified.

"Don't tell me I lie! You killed Winterslip and I'll get it out of you! I got the other and I'll get this." Hallet rose threateningly from his chair.

Chan suddenly reentered the room, and handed Hallet a note. "Arrive this moment by special messenger," he explained.

Hallet ripped open the envelope and read. His expression altered. He turned disgustedly to Kaohla. "Beat it!" he scowled.

The boy fled gratefully. John Quincy and Chan looked wonderingly at the captain. Hallet sat down at his desk. "It all comes back to Egan," he said. "I've known it from the first."

"Wait a minute," cried John Quincy. "What about that boy?"

Hallet crumpled the letter in his hand. "Kaohla? Oh, he's out of it now."

"Why?"

"That's all I can tell you. He's out of it."

"That's not enough," John Quincy said. "I demand to know—"

Hallet glared at him. "You know all you're going to," he answered angrily. "I say Kaohla's out, and that settles it. Egan killed Winterslip, and before I get through with him—"

"Permit me to say," interrupted John Quincy, "that you have the most trusting nature I ever met. Everybody's story goes with you. The Compton woman and that rat Leatherbee come in here and spin a yarn, and you bow them out. And Brade! What about Brade! In bed at one-twenty last Tuesday morning, eh? Who says so? He does. Who can prove it? His wife can. What was to prevent his stepping out on the balcony of the Reef and Palm and walking along the beach to my cousin's house? Answer me that!"

Hallet shook his head. "It's Egan. That cigarette—"

"Yes—that cigarette. Has it occurred to you that Brade may have given him those cigarettes purposely—"

"Egan did it," cut in Hallet stubbornly. "All I need now is his story; I'll get it. I have ways and means—"

"I congratulate you on your magnificent stupidity," cried John Quincy. "Good night, sir."

He walked along Bethel Street, Chan at his side.

"You are partly consumed by anger," said the Chinaman. "Humbly suggest you cool. Calm heads needed."

"But what was in that note? Why wouldn't he tell us?"

"In good time, we know. Captain honest man. Be patient."

"But we're all at sea again," protested John Quincy. "Who killed Cousin Dan? We get nowhere."

"So very true," agreed Chan. "More clues lead us into presence of immovable stone wall. We sway about, seeking still other path."

"I'll say we do," answered John Quincy. "There comes my car. Good night!"

Not until the trolley was half-way to Waikiki did he remember Mr. Saladine. Saladine crouching outside that window at the Reef and Palm. What did that mean? But Saladine was a comic figure, a lisping searcher after bridge-work in the limpid waters of Waikiki. Even so, perhaps his humble activities should be investigated.

16

The Return of Captain Cope

After breakfast on Sunday morning, John Quincy followed Miss Minerva to the lanai. It was a neat world that lay outside the screen, for Dan Winterslip's yard boy had been busy until a late hour the night before, sweeping the lawn with the same loving thoroughness a housewife might display on a precious Oriental rug.

Barbara had not come down to breakfast, and John Quincy had seized the opportunity to tell his aunt of Brade's return, and repeat the man's story of Dan Winterslip's theft on board the *Maid of Shiloh*. Now he lighted a cigarette and sat staring seriously out at the distant water.

"Cheer up," said Miss Minerva. "You look like a judge. I presume you're thinking of poor Dan."

"I am."

"Forgive and forget. None of us ever suspected Dan of being a saint."

"A saint! Far from it! He was just a plain—"

"Never mind," put in his aunt sharply. "Remember, John Quincy, man is a creature of environment. And the temptation must have been great. Picture Dan on that ship in these easy-going latitudes, wealth at his feet and not a soul in sight to claim it. Ill-gotten wealth, at that. Even you—"

"Even I," said John Quincy sternly, "would have recalled I am a Winterslip. I never dreamed I'd live to hear you offering apologies for that sort of conduct."

She laughed. "You know what they say about white women who go to the tropics. They lose first their conplexion, then their teeth, and finally their moral sense." She hesitated. "I've had to visit the dentist a good deal of late," she added.

John Quincy was shocked. "My advice to you is to hurry home," he said. "When are you going?"

"Oh, soon—soon."

"That's what we all say. Returning to Boston, I suppose?"

"Of course."

"How about San Francisco?"

"Oh, that's off. I did suggest it to Agatha, but I'm certain she won't hear of it. And I'm beginning to think she'd be quite right." His aunt rose. "You'd better go to church," said John Quincy severely.

"That's just where I am going," she smiled. "By the way, Amos is coming to dinner to-night, and he'd best hear the Brade story from us, rather than in some garbled form. Barbara must hear it too. If it proves to be true, the family ought to do something for Mr. Brade."

"Oh, the family will do something for him, all right," John Quincy remarked. "Whether it wants to or not."

"Well, I'll let you tell Barbara about him," Miss Minerva promised.

"Thank you so much," replied her nephew sarcastically.

"Not at all. Are you coming to church?"

"No," he said. "I don't need it the way you do."

She left him there to face a lazy uneventful day. By five in the afternoon Waikiki was alive with its usual Sunday crowd—not the unsavory holiday throng seen on a mainland beach, but a scattering of good-looking people whose tanned straight bodies would have delighted the heart of a physical culture enthusiast. John Quincy summoned sufficient energy to don a bathing suit and plunge in.

There was something soothing in the warm touch of the water, and he was becoming more at home there every day. With long powerful strokes he drew away from the malihini breakers to dare the great rollers beyond. Surf-board riders flashed by him; now and then he had to alter his course to avoid an outrigger canoe.

On the farthest float of all he saw Carlota Egan. She sat there, a slender lovely figure vibrant with life, and awaited his coming. As he climbed up beside her and looked into her eyes he was—perhaps from his exertion in the water—a little breathless.

"I rather hoped I'd find you," he panted.

"Did you?" She smiled faintly. "I hoped it too. You see, I need a lot of cheering up."

"On a perfect day like this!"

"I'd pinned such hopes on Mr. Brade," she explained. "Perhaps you know he's back—and from what I can gather, his return hasn't meant a thing so far as dad's concerned. Not a thing."

"Well, I'm afraid it hasn't," John Quincy admitted. "But we mustn't get discouraged. As Chan puts it, we sway about, seeking a new path. You and I have a bit of swaying to do. How about Mr. Saladine?"

"I've been thinking about Mr. Saladine. But I can't get excited about him, somehow. He's so ridiculous."

"We mustn't pass him up on that account," admonished John Quincy. "I caught a glimpse of his purple bathing suit on the first float. Come on—we'll just casually drop in on him. I'll race you there."

She smiled again, and leaped to her feet. For a second she stood poised, then dived in a way that John Quincy could never hope to emulate. He slipped off in pursuit, and though he put forth every effort, she reached Saladine's side five seconds before he did.

"Hello, Mr. Saladine," she said. "This is Mr. Winterslip, of Boston."

"Ah, yeth," responded Mr. Saladine, gloomily. "Mr. Winterthlip." He regarded the young man with interest.

"Any luck, sir?" inquired John Quincy sympathetically.

"Oh—you heard about my accident?"

"I did, sir, and I'm sorry."

"I am, too," said Mr. Saladine feelingly. "Not a thrath of them tho far. And I muth go home in a few dath."

"I believe Miss Egan said you lived in Des Moines?"

"Yeth. Deth—Deth—I can't thay it."

"In business there?" inquired John Quincy nonchalantly.

"Yeth. Wholethale grothery buthineth," answered Mr. Saladine, slowly but not very successfully.

John Quincy turned away to hide a smile. "Shall we go along?" he said to the girl. "Good luck to you, sir." He dove off, and as they swam toward the shore, he reflected that they were on a false trail there—a trail as spurious as the teeth. That little business man was too conventional a figure to have any connection with the murder of Dan Winterslip. He kept these thoughts to himself, however.

Half-way to the beach, they encountered an enormous figure floating languidly on the water. Just beyond the great stomach John Quincy perceived the serene face of Charlie Chan.

"Hello, Charlie," he cried. "It's a small ocean, after all! Got your Ford with you?"

Chan righted himself and grinned. "Little pleasant recreation," he explained. "Forget detective worries out here floating idle like leaf on stream."

"Please float ashore," suggested John Quincy. "I have something to tell you."

"Only too happy," agreed Chan.

He followed them in and they sat, an odd trio, on the white sand. John Quincy told the detective about Saladine's activities outside the window the night before, and repeated the conversation he had just had with the middle westerner. "Of course, the man seems almost too foolish to mean anything," he added.

Chan shook his head. "Begging most humble pardon," he said, "that are wrong attitude completely. Detective business made up of unsignificant trifles. One after other our clues go burst in our countenance. Wise to pursue matter of Mr. Saladine."

"What do you suggest?" John Quincy asked.

"To-night I visit city for night work to drive off my piled tasks," Chan replied. "After evening meal, suggest you join with me at capble office. We despatch message to postmaster of this Des Moines, inquiring what are present locality of Mr. Saladine, expert in wholeselling provisions. Your name will be signed to message, much better than police meddling."

"All right," John Quincy agreed, "I'll meet you there at eight-thirty."

Carlota Egan rose. "I must get back to the Reef and Palm. You've no idea all I have to do—"

John Quincy stood beside her. "If I can help, you know—"

"I know," she smiled. "I'm thinking of making you assistant manager. They'd be so proud of you—in Boston."

She moved off toward the water for her homeward swim, and John Quincy dropped down beside Chan. Chan's amber eyes followed the girl. "Endeavoring to make English language my slave," he said, "I pursue poetry. Who were the great poet who said—'She walks in beauty like the night?' "

"Why, that was—er—who was it?" remarked John Quincy helpfully.

"Name is slippery," went on Chan. "But no matter. Lines pop into brain whenever I see this Miss Egan. Beauty like the night, Hawaiian night maybe, lovely as purest jade. Most especially on this beach. Spot of heartbreaking charm, this beach."

"Surely is," agreed John Quincy, amused at Chan's obviously sentimental mood.

"Here on gleaming sand I first regard my future wife," continued Chan. "Slender as the bamboo is slender, beautiful as blossom of the plum—"

"Your wife," repeated John Quincy. The idea was a new one.

"Yes, indeed." Chan rose. "Recalls I must hasten home where she attends the children who are now, by actual count, nine in number." He looked down at John Quincy thoughtfully. "Are you well-fitted with the armor of preparation?" he said. "Consider. Some night the moon has splendor in this neighborhood, the cocoa-palms bow lowly and turn away their heads so they do not see. And the white man kisses without intending to do so."

"Oh, don't worry about me," John Quincy laughed. "I'm from Boston, and immune."

"Immune," repeated Chan. "Ah, yes, I grasp meaning. In my home I have idol brought from China with insides of solid stone. He would think he is—immune. But even so I would not entrust him on this beach. As my cousin Willie Chan say with vulgarity, see you later."

John Quincy sat for a time on the sand, then rose and strolled toward home. His path lay close to the lanai of Arlene Compton's cottage, and he was surprised to hear his name called from behind the screen. He stepped to the door and looked in. The woman was sitting there alone.

"Come in a minute, Mr. Winterslip," she said.

John Quincy hesitated. He did not care to make any social calls on this lady, but he did not have it in him to be rude. He went inside and sat down gingerly, poised for flight. "Got to hurry back for dinner," he explained.

"Dinner? You'll want a cocktail."

"No, thanks. I'm—I'm on the wagon."

"You'll find it hard to stick out here," she said a little bitterly. "I won't keep you long. I just want to know—are those boneheads down at the station getting anywhere, or ain't they?"

"The police," smiled John Quincy. "They seem to be making progress. But it's slow. It's very slow."

"I'll tell the world it's slow. And I got to stick here till they pin it on somebody. Pleasant outlook, ain't it?"

"Is Mr. Leatherbee still with you?" inquired John Quincy.

"What do you mean is he still with me?" she flared.

"Pardon me. Is he still in town?"

"Of course he's in town. They won't let him go, either. But I ain't worrying about him. I got troubles of my own. I want to go home." She nodded toward a newspaper on the table. "I just got hold of an old *Variety* and seen about a show opening in Atlantic City. A lot of the gang is in it, working like dogs, rehearsing night and day, worrying themselves sick over how long the thing will last. Gee, don't I envy them. I was near to bawling when you came along."

"You'll get back all right," comforted John Quincy.

"Say—if I ever do! I'll stop everybody I meet on Broadway and promise never to leave 'em again." John Quincy rose. "You tell that guy Hallet to get a move on," she urged.

"I'll tell him," he agreed.

"And drop in to see me now and then," she added wistfully. "Us easterners ought to stick together out here."

"That's right, we should," John Quincy answered. "Good-by."

As he walked along the beach, he thought of her with pity. The story she and Leatherbee had told might be entirely false; even so, she was a human and appealing figure and her homesickness touched his heart.

Later that evening when John Quincy came downstairs faultlessly attired for dinner, he encountered Amos Winterslip in the living-room. Cousin Amos's lean face was whiter than ever; his manner listless. He had been robbed of his hate; his evenings beneath the algaroba tree had lost their savor; life was devoid of spice.

Dinner was not a particularly jolly affair. Barbara seemed intent on knowing now the details of the search the police were conducting, and it fell to John Quincy to enlighten her. Reluctantly he came at last to the story of Brade. She listened in silence. After dinner she and John Quincy went out into the garden and sat on a bench under the hau tree, facing the water.

"I'm terribly sorry I had to tell you that about Brade," John Quincy said gently. "But it seemed necessary."

"Of course," she agreed. "Poor dad! He was weak—weak—"

"Forgive and forget," John Quincy suggested. "Man is a creature of environment." He wondered dimly where he had heard that before. "Your father was not entirely to blame—"

"You're terribly kind, John Quincy," she told him.

"No—but I mean it," he protested. "Just picture the scene to yourself. That lonely ocean, wealth at his feet for the taking, no one to see or know."

She shook her head. "Oh, but it was wrong, wrong. Poor Mr. Brade. I must make things right with him as nearly as I can. I shall ask Harry to talk with him to-morrow—"

"Just a suggestion," interposed John Quincy. "Whatever you agree to do for Brade must not be done until the man who killed your father is found."

She stared at him. "What! You don't think that Brade—"

"I don't know. Nobody knows. Brade is unable to prove where he was early last Tuesday morning."

They sat silent for a moment; then the girl suddenly collapsed and buried her face in her hands. Her slim shoulders trembled convulsively and John Quincy, deeply sympathetic, moved closer. He put his arm about her. The moonlight shone on her bright hair, the trades whispered in the hau tree, the breakers murmured on the beach. She lifted her face, and he kissed her. A cousinly kiss he had meant it to be, but somehow it wasn't—it was a kiss he would never have been up to on Beacon Street.

"Miss Minerva said I'd find you here," remarked a voice behind them.

John Quincy leaped to his feet and found himself staring into the cynical eyes of Harry Jennison. Even though you are the girl's cousin, it is a bit embarrassing to have a man find you kissing his fiancée. Particularly if the kiss wasn't at all cousinly—John Quincy wondered if Jennison had noticed that.

"Come in—I mean, sit down," stammered John Quincy. "I was just going."

"Good-by," said Jennison coldly.

John Quincy went hastily through the living-room, where Miss Minerva sat with Amos. "Got an appointment down-town," he explained, and picking up his hat in the hall, fled into the night.

He had intended taking the roadster, but to reach the garage he would have to pass that bench under the hau tree. Oh, well, the colorful atmosphere of a trolley was more interesting, anyhow.

In the cable office on the ground floor of the Alexander Young Hotel, Chan was waiting, and they sent off their inquiry to the postmaster at Des Moines, signing John Quincy's name and address. That attended to, they returned to the street. In the park across the way an unseen group of young men strummed steel guitars and sang in soft haunting voices; it was the only sign of life in Honolulu.

"Kindly deign to enter hotel lobby with me," suggested Chan. "It is my custom to regard names in register from time to time."

At the cigar stand just inside the door, the boy paused to light his pipe, while Chan went on to the desk. As John Quincy turned he saw a man seated alone in the lobby, a handsome, distinguished man who wore immaculate evening clothes that bore the stamp of Bond Street. An old acquaintance, Captain Arthur Temple Cope.

At sight of John Quincy, Cope leaped to his feet and came forward. "Hello, I'm glad to see you," he cried, with a cordiality that had not been evident at former meetings. "Come over and sit down."

John Quincy followed him. "Aren't you back rather soon?" he inquired.

"Sooner than I expected," Cope rejoined. "Not sorry, either."

"Then you didn't care for your little flock of islands?"

"My boy, you should visit there. Thirty-five white men, two hundred and fifty natives, and a cable station. Jolly place of an evening, what?"

Chan came up, and John Quincy presented him. Captain Cope was the perfect host. "Sit down, both of you," he urged. "Have a cigarette." He extended a silver case.

"Thanks, I'll stick to the pipe," John Quincy said. Chan gravely accepted a cigarette and lighted it.

"Tell me, my boy," Cope said when they were seated, "is there anything new on the Winterslip murder? Haven't run down the guilty man, by any chance."

"No, not yet," John Quincy replied.

"That's a great pity. I—er—understand the police are holding a chap named Egan?"

"Yes—Jim Egan, of the Reef and Palm Hotel."

"Just what evidence have they against Egan, Mr. Winterslip?"

John Quincy was suddenly aware of Chan looking at him in a peculiar way. "Oh, they've dug up several things," he answered vaguely.

"Mr. Chan, you are a member of the police force," Captain Cope went on. "Perhaps you can tell me?"

Chan's little eyes narrowed. "Such matters are not yet presented to public," he replied.

"Ah, yes, naturally." Captain Cope's tone suggested disappointment.

"You have interest in this murder, I think?" Chan said.

"Why, yes—every one out this way is puzzling about it, I fancy. The thing has so many angles."

"Is it possible that you were an acquaintance with Mr. Dan Winterslip?" the detective persisted.

"I—I knew him slightly. But that was many years ago."

Chan stood. "Humbly begging pardon to be so abrupt," he said. He turned to John Quincy. "The moment of our appointment is eminent—"

"Of course," agreed John Quincy. "See you again, Captain." Perplexed, he followed Chan to the street. "What appointment—" he began, and stopped. Chan was carefully extinguishing the light of the cigarette against the stone façade of the hotel. That done, he dropped the stub into his pocket.

"You will see," he promised. "First we visit police station. As we journey, kindly relate all known facts concerning this Captain Cope."

John Quincy told of his first meeting with Cope in the San Francisco club, and repeated the conversation as he recalled it.

"Evidence of warm dislike for Dan Winterslip were not to be concealed?" inquired Chan.

"Oh, quite plain, Charlie. He certainly had no love for Cousin Dan. But what—"

"Immediately he was leaving for Hawaii—pardon the interrupt. Does it happily chance you know his date of arrival here?"

"I do. I saw him in the Alexander Young Hotel last Tuesday evening when I was looking for you. He was rushing off to the Fanning Islands, and he told me he had got in the previous day at noon—"

"Monday noon to put it lucidly."

"Yes—Monday noon. But Charlie—what are you trying to get at?"

"Groping about," Chan smiled. "Seeking to seize truth in my hot hands."

They walked on in silence to the station, where Chan led the way into the deserted room of Captain Hallet. He went directly to the safe and opened it. From a drawer he removed several small objects, which he carried over to the captain's table.

"Property Mr. Jim Egan," he announced, and laid a case of tarnished silver before John Quincy. "Open it—what do you find now? Corsican cigarettes." He set down another exhibit. "Tin box found in room of Mr. Brade. Open that, also. You find more Corsican cigarettes."

He removed an envelope from his pocket and taking out a charred stub, laid that too on the table. "Fragment found by walk outside door of Dan Winterslip's mansion," he elucidated. "Also Corsican brand."

Frowning deeply, he removed a second charred stub from his pocket and laid it some distance from the other exhibits. "Cigarette offered just now with winning air of hospitality by Captain Arthur Temple Cope. Lean close and perceive. More Corsican brand!"

"Good lord!" John Quincy cried.

"Can it be you are familiar with these Corsicans?" inquired Chan.

"Not at all."

"I am more happily located. This afternoon before the swim I pause at public library for listless reading. In Australian newspaper I encounter advertising talk of Corsican cigarette. It are assembled in two distinct fashions, one, labeled on tin 222, holds Turkish tobacco. Note 222 on tin of Brade. Other labeled 444 made up from Virginia weeds. Is it that you are clever to know difference bewtween Turkish and Virginia tobacco?"

"Well, I think so—" began John Quincy.

"Same with me, but thinking are not enough now. The moment are serious. We will interrogate expert opinion. Honor me by a journey to smoking emporium."

He took a cigarette from Brade's tin, put it in an envelope and wrote something on the outside, then did the same with one from Egan's case.

The two stubs were similarly classified.

They went in silence to the street. John Quincy, amazed by this new turn of events, told himself the idea was absurd. But Chan's face was grave, his eyes awake and eager.

John Quincy was vastly more amazed when they emerged from the tobacco shop after a brisk interview with the young man in charge. Chan was jubilant now.

"Again we advance! You hear what he tells us. Cigarette from Brade's tin and little brother from Egan's case are of identical contents, both being of Turkish tobacco. Stub found near walk are of Virginia stuff. So also are remnant received by me from the cordial hand of Captain Arthur Temple Cope!"

"It's beyond me," replied John Quincy. "By gad—that lets Egan out. Great news for Carlota. I'll hurry to the Reef and Palm and tell her—"

"Oh, no, no," protested Chan. "Please to let that happy moment wait. For the present, indulge only in silence. Before asking Captain Cope for statement we spy over his every move. Much may be revealed by the unsuspecting. I go to station to make arrangements—"

"But the man's a gentleman," John Quincy cried. "A captain in the British Admiralty. What you suggest is impossible."

Chan shook his head. "Impossible in Rear Bay at Boston," he said, "but here at moonly crossroads of Pacific, not so much so. Twenty-five years of my life are consumed in Hawaii, and I have many times been witness when the impossible roused itself and occured."

17

Night Life in Honolulu

Monday brought no new developments, and John Quincy spent a restless day. Several times he called Chan at the police station, but the detective was always out.

Honolulu, according to the evening paper, was agog. This was not, as John Quincy learned to his surprise, a reference to the Winterslip case. An American fleet had just left the harbor of San Pedro bound for Hawaii. This was the annual cruise of the graduating class at Annapolis; the warships were overflowing with future captains and admirals. They would linger at the port of Honolulu for several days and a gay round of social events impended—dinners, dances, moonlight swimming parties.

John Quincy had not seen Barbara all day; the girl had not appeared at breakfast and had lunched with a friend down the beach. They met at dinner, however, and it seemed to him that she looked more tired and wan than ever. She spoke about the coming of the warships.

"It's always such a happy time," she said wistfully. "The town simply blooms with handsome boys in uniform. I don't like to have you miss all the parties, John Quincy. You're not seeing Honolulu at its best."

"Why—that's all right," John Quincy assured her.

She shook her head. "Not with me. You know, we're not such slaves to convention out here. If I should get you a few invitations—what do you think, Cousin Minerva?"

"I'm an old woman," said Miss Minerva. "According to the standards of your generation, I suppose it would be quite the thing. But it's not the sort of conduct I can view approvingly. Now, in my day—"

"Don't you worry, Barbara," John Quincy broke in. "Parties mean nothing to me. Speaking of old women, I'm an old man myself—thirty my next birthday. Just my pipe and slippers by the fire—or the electric fan—that's all I ask of life now."

She smiled and dropped the matter. After dinner, she followed John Quincy to the lanai. "I want you to do something for me," she began.

"Anything you say."

"Have a talk with Mr. Brade, and tell me what he wants."

"Why, I thought that Jennison—" said John Quincy.

"No, I didn't ask him to do it," she replied. For a long moment she was silent. "I ought to tell you—I'm not going to marry Mr. Jennison, after all."

A shiver of apprehension ran down John Quincy's spine. Good lord—that kiss! Had she misunderstood? And he hadn't meant a thing by it. Just a cousinly salute—at least, that was what it had started out to be. Barbara was a sweet girl, yes, but a relative, a Winterslip, and relatives shouldn't marry, no matter how distant the connection. Then, too, there was Agatha. He was bound to Agatha by all the ties of honor. What had he got himself into, anyhow?

"I'm awfully sorry to hear that," he said. "I'm afraid I'm to blame—"

"Oh, no," she protested.

"But surely Mr. Jennison understood. He knows we're related, and that what he saw last night meant—nothing." He was rather proud of himself. Pretty neat the way he'd got that over.

"If you don't mind," Barbara said, "I'd rather not talk about it any more. Harry and I will not be married—not at present, at any rate. And if you'll see Mr. Brade for me—"

"I certainly will," John Quincy promised. "I'll see him at once." He was glad to get away, for the moon was rising on that "spot of heart-breaking charm."

A fellow ought to be more careful, he reflected as he walked along the beach. Fit upon himself the armor of preparation, as Chan had said. Strange impulses came to one here in this far tropic land; to yield to them was weak. Complications would follow, as the night the day. Here was one now, Barbara and Jennison estranged, and the cause was clear. Well, he was certainly going to watch his step hereafter.

On the far end of the Reef and Palm's first floor balcony, Brade and his wife sat together in the dusk. John Quincy went up to them.

"May I speak with you, Mr. Brade?" he said.

The man looked up out of a deep reverie. "Ah, yes—of course—"

"I'm John Quincy Winterslip. We've met before."

"Oh, surely, surely sir." Brade rose and shook hands. "My dear—" he turned to his wife, but with one burning glance at John Quincy, the woman had fled. The boy tingled—in Boston a Winterslip was never snubbed. Well, Dan Winterslip had arranged it otherwise in Hawaii.

"Sit down, sir," said Brade, somewhat embarrassed by his wife's action. "I've been expecting some one of your name."

"Naturally. Will you have a cigarette, sir." John Quincy proffered his case, and when the cigarettes were lighted, seated himself at the man's side. "I'm here, of course, in regard to that story you told Saturday night."

"Story?" flashed Brade.

John Quincy smiled. "Don't misunderstand me. I'm not questioning the truth of it. But I do want to say this, Mr. Brade—you must be aware that you will have considerable difficulty establishing your claim in a court of law. The 'eighties are a long time back."

"What you say may be true," Brade agreed. "I'm relying more on the fact that a trial would result in some rather unpleasant publicity for the Winterslip family."

"Precisely," nodded John Quincy. "I am here at the request of Miss Barbara Winterslip, who is Dan Winterslip's sole heir. She's a very fine girl, sir—"

"I don't question that," cut in Brade impatiently.

"And if your demands are not unreasonable—" John Quincy paused, and leaned closer. "Just what do you want, Mr. Brade?"

Brade stroked those gray mustaches that drooped "in saddened mood." "No money," he said, "can make good the wrong Dan Winterslip did. But I'm an old man, and it would be something to feel financially secure for the rest of my life. I'm not inclined to be grasping—particularly since Dan Winterslip has passed beyond my reach. There were twenty thousand pounds involved. I'll say nothing about interest for more than forty years. A settlement of one hundred thousand dollars would be acceptable."

John Quincy considered. "I can't speak definitely for my cousin," he said, "but to me that sounds fair enough. I have no doubt Barbara will agree to give you that sum"—he saw the man's tired old eyes brighten in the semi-darkness—"the moment the murderer of Dan Winterslip is found," he added quickly.

"What's that you say?" Brade leaped to his feet.

"I say she'll very likely pay you when this mystery is cleared up. Surely you don't expect her to do so before that time?" John Quincy rose too.

"I certainly do!" Brade cried. "Why, look here, this thing may drag on indefinitely. I want England again—the Strand, Piccadilly—it's twenty-five years since I saw London. Wait! Damn it, why should I wait! What's this murder to me—by gad, sir—" He came close, erect, flaming, the son of Tom Brade, the blackbirder, now. "Do you mean to insinuate that I—"

John Quincy faced him calmly. "I know you can't prove where you were early last Tuesday morning," he said evenly. "I don't say that incriminates you, but I shall certainly advise my cousin to wait. I'd not care to see her in the position of having rewarded the man who killed her father."

"I'll fight," cried Brade. "I'll take it to the courts—"

"Go ahead," John Quincy said. "But it will cost you every penny you've saved, and you may lose in the end. Good night, sir."

"Good night!" Brade answered, standing as his father might have stood on the *Maid of Shiloh's* deck.

John Quincy had gone half-way down the balcony when he heard quick footsteps behind him. He turned. It was Brade, Brade the civil servant, the man who had labored thirty-six years in the oven of India, a beaten, helpless figure.

"You've got me," he said, laying a hand on John Quincy's arm. "I can't fight. I'm too tired, too old—I've worked too hard. I'll take whatever your cousin wants to give me—when she's ready to give it."

"That's a wise decision, sir," John Quincy answered. A sudden feeling of pity gripped his heart. He felt toward Brade as he had felt toward that other exile, Arlene Compton. "I hope you see London very soon," he added, and held out his hand.

Brade took it. "Thank you, my boy. You're a gentleman, even if your name is Winterslip."

Which, John Quincy reflected as he entered the lobby of the Reef and Palm, was a compliment not without its flaw.

He didn't worry over that long, however, for Carlota Egan was behind the desk. She looked up and smiled, and it occurred to John Quincy that her eyes were happier than he had seen them since that day on the Oakland ferry.

"Hello," he said. "Got a job for a good bookkeeper?"

She shook her head. "Not with business the way it is now. I was just figuring my pay-roll. You know, we've no undertow at Waikiki, but all my life I've had to worry about the overhead."

He laughed. "You talk like a brother Kiwanian. By the way, has anything happened? You seem considerably cheered."

"I am," she replied. "I went to see poor dad this morning in that horrible place—and when I left some one else was going in to visit him. A stranger."

"A stranger?"

"Yes—and the handsomest thing you ever saw—tall, gray, capable-looking. He had such a friendly air, too—I felt better the moment I saw him."

"Who was he?" John Quincy inquired, with sudden interest.

"I'd never seen him before, but one of the men told me he was Captain Cope of the British Admiralty."

"Why should Captain Cope want to see your father?"

"I haven't a notion. Do you know him?"

"Yes—I've met him," John Quincy told her.

"Don't you think he's wonderful-looking?" Her dark eyes glowed.

"Oh, he's all right," replied John Quincy without enthusiasm. "You know, I can't help feeling that things are looking up for you."

"I feel that too," she said.

"What do you say we celebrate?" he suggested. "Go out among 'em and get a little taste of night life. I'm a bit fed up on the police station. What do people do here in the evening? The movies?"

"Just at present," the girl told him, "everybody visits Punahou to see the night-blooming cereus. It's the season now, you know."

"Sounds like a big evening," John Quincy laughed. "Go and look at the flowers. Well, I'm for it. Will you come?"

"Of course." She gave a few directions to the clerk, then joined him by the door. "I can run down and get the roadster," he offered.

"Oh, no," she smiled. "I'm sure I'll never own a motor-car, and it might make me discontented to ride in one. The trolley's my carriage—and it's lots of fun. One meets so many interesting people."

On the stone walls surrounding the campus of Oahu College, the strange flower that blooms only on a summer night was heaped in snowy splendor. John Quincy had been a bit lukewarm regarding the expedition when they set out, but he saw his error now. For here was beauty, breath-taking and rare. Before the walls paraded a throng of sight-seers; they joined the procession. The girl was a charming companion, her spirits had revived and she chatted vivaciously. Not about Shaw and the art galleries, true enough, but bright human talk that John Quincy liked to hear.

He persuaded her to go to the city for a maidenly ice-cream soda, and it was ten o'clock when they returned to the beach. They left the trolley at a stop some distance down the avenue from the Reef and Palm, and strolled slowly toward the hotel. The sidewalk was lined at their right by dense foliage, almost impenetrable. The night was calm; the street lamps shone brightly; the paved street gleamed white in the moonlight. John Quincy was talking of Boston.

"I think you'd like it there. It's old and settled, but—"

From the foliage beside them came the flash of a pistol, and John Quincy heard a bullet sing close to his head. Another flash, another bullet. The girl gave a startled little cry.

John Quincy circled round her and plunged into the bushes. Angry branches stung his cheek. He stopped; he couldn't leave the girl alone. He returned to her side.

"What did that mean?" he asked, amazed. He stared in wonder at the peaceful scene before him.

"I—I don't know." She took his arm. "Come—hurry!"

"Don't be afraid," he said reassuringly.

"Not for myself," she answered.

They went on to the hotel, greatly puzzled. But when they entered the lobby, they had something else to think about. Captain Arthur Temple Cope was standing by the desk, and he came at once to meet them.

"This is Miss Egan, I believe. Ah, Winterslip, how are you?" He turned again to the girl. "I've taken a room here, if you don't mind."

"Why, not at all," she gasped.

"I talked with your father this morning. I didn't know about his trouble until I had boarded a ship for the Fanning Islands. I came back as quickly as I could."

"You came back—" She stared at him.

"Yes. I came back to help him."

"That's very kind of you," the girl said. "But I'm afraid I don't understand—"

"Oh, no, you don't understand. Naturally." The captain smiled down at her. "You see, Jim's my young brother. You're my niece, and your name is Carlota Maria Cope. I fancy I've persuaded old Jim to own up to us at last."

The girl's dark eyes were wide. "I—I think you're a very nice uncle," she said at last.

"Do you really?" The captain bowed. "I aim to be," he added.

John Quincy stepped forward. "Pardon me," he said. "I'm afraid I'm intruding. Good night, Captain."

"Good night, my boy," Cope answered.

The girl went with John Quincy to the balcony. "I—I don't know what to make of it," she said.

"Things are coming rather fast," John Quincy admitted. He remembered the Corsican cigarette. "I wouldn't trust him too far," he admonished.

"But he's so wonderful—"

"Oh, he's all right, probably. But looks are often deceptive. I'll go along now and let you talk with him."

She laid one slim tanned hand on his white-clad arm. "Do be careful!"

"Oh, I'm all right," he told her.

"But some one shot at you."

"Yes, and a very poor aim he had, too. Don't worry about me." She was very close, her eyes glowing in the dark. "You said you weren't afraid for yourself," he added. "Did you mean—"

"I meant—I was afraid—for you."

The moon, of course, was shining. The cocoa-palms turned their heads away at the suggestion of the trades. The warm waters of Waikiki murmured near by. John Quincy Winterslip, from Boston and immune, drew the girl to him and kissed her. Not a cousinly kiss, either—but why should it have been? She wasn't his cousin.

"Thank you, my dear," he said. He seemed to be floating dizzily in space. It came to him that he might reach out and pluck her a handful of stars.

It came to him a second later that, despite his firm resolve, he had done it again. Kissed another girl. Three—that made three with whom he was sort of entangled.

"Good night," he said huskily, and leaping over the rail, fled hastily through the garden.

Three girls now—but he hadn't a single regret. He was living at last. As he hurried through the dark along the beach, his heart was light. Once he fancied he was being followed, but he gave it little thought. What of it?

On the bureau in his room he found an envelope with his name typewritten on the outside. The note within was typewritten too. He read:

> "You are too busy out here. Hawaii can manage her affairs without the interference of a malihini. Boats sail almost daily. If you are still here forty-eight hours after you get this—look out! To-night's shots were fired into the air. The aim will quickly improve!"

Delighted, John Quincy tossed the note aside. Threatening him, eh? His activities as a detective were bearing fruit. He recalled the glowering face of Kaohla when he said: "You did this. I don't forget." And a remark of Dan Winterslip's his aunt had quoted: "Civilized—yes. But far underneath there are deep dark waters flowing still."

Boats were sailing almost daily, were they? Well, let them sail. He would be on one some day—but not until he had brought Dan Winterslip's murderer to justice.

Life had a new glamour now. Look out? He'd be looking—and enjoying it, too. He smiled happily to himself as he took off his coat. This was better than selling bonds in Boston.

18

A Cable from the Mainland

John Quincy awoke at nine the following morning and slipped from under his mosquito netting eager to face the responsibilities of a new day. On the floor near his bureau lay the letter designed to speed the parting guest. He picked it up and read it again with manifest enjoyment.

When he reached the dining-room Haku informed him that Miss Minerva and Barbara had breakfasted early and gone to the city on a shopping tour.

"Look here, Haku," the boy said. "A letter came for me late last night?"

"Yes-s," admitted Haku.

"Who delivered it?"

"Can not say. It were found on floor of hall close by big front door."

"Who found it?"

"Kamaikui."

"Oh, yes—Kamaikui."

"I tell her to put in your sleeping room."

"Did Kamaikui see the person who brought it?"

"Nobody see him. Nobody on place."

"All right," John Quincy said.

He spent a leisurely hour on the lanai with his pipe and the morning paper. At about half past ten he got out the roadster and drove to the police station.

Hallet and Chan, he was told, were in a conference with the prosecutor. He sat down to wait, and in a few moments word came for him to join them. Entering Greene's office, he saw the three men seated gloomily about the prosecutor's desk.

"Well, I guess I'm some detective," he announced.

Greene looked up quickly. "Found anything new?"

"Not precisely," John Quincy admitted. "But last night when I was walking along Kalakaua Avenue with a young woman, somebody took a couple of wild shots at me from the bushes. And when I got home I found this letter waiting."

He handed the epistle to Hallet, who read it with evident disgust, then passed it on to the prosecutor. "That doesn't get us anywhere," the captain said.

"It may get me somewhere, if I'm not careful," John Quincy replied. "However, I'm rather proud of it. Sort of goes to show that my detective work is hitting home."

"Maybe," answered Hallet, carelessly.

Greene laid the letter on his desk. "My advice to you," he said, "is to carry a gun. That's unofficial, of course."

"Nonsense, I'm not afraid," John Quincy told him. "I've got a pretty good idea who sent this thing."

"You have?" Green said.

"Yes. He's a friend of Captain Hallet's. Dick Kaohla."

"What do you mean he's a friend of mine?" flared Hallet.

"Well, you certainly treated him pretty tenderly the other night."

"I knew what I was doing," said Hallet grouchily.

"I hope you did. But if he puts a bullet in me some lovely evening, I'm going to be pretty annoyed with you."

"Oh, you're in no danger," Hallet answered. "Only a coward writes anonymous letters."

"Yes, and only a coward shoots from ambush. But that isn't saying he can't take a good aim."

Hallet picked up the letter. "I'll keep this. It may prove to be evidence."

"Surely," agreed John Quincy. "And you haven't got any too much evidence, as I see it."

"Is that so?" growled Hallet. "We've made a rather important discovery about that Corsican cigarette."

"Oh, I'm not saying Charlie isn't good," smiled John Quincy. "I was with him when he worked that out."

A uniformed man appeared at the door. "Egan and his daughter and Captain Cope," he announced to Greene. "Want to see them now, sir?"

"Send them in," ordered the prosecutor.

"I'd like to stay, if you don't mind," John Quincy suggested.

"Oh, by all means," Greene answered. "We couldn't get along without you."

The policeman brought Egan to the door, and the proprietor of the Reef and Palm came into the room. His face was haggard and pale; his long siege with the authorities had begun to tell. But a stubborn light still flamed in his eyes. After him came Carlota Egan, fresh and beautiful, and with a new air of confidence about her. Captain Cope followed, tall, haughty, a man of evident power and determination.

"This is the prosecutor, I believe?" he said. "Ah, Mr. Winterslip, I find you everywhere I go."

"You don't mind my staying?" inquired John Quincy.

"Not in the least, my boy. Our business here will take but a moment." He turned to Greene. "Just as a preliminary," he continued, "I am Captain Arthur Temple Cope of the British Admiralty, and this gentleman"—he nodded toward the proprietor of the Reef and Palm—"is my brother."

"Really?" said Greene. "His name is Egan, as I understand it."

"His name is James Egan Cope," the captain replied. "He dropped the Cope many years ago for reasons that do not concern us now. I am here simply to say, sir, that you are holding my brother on the flimsiest pretext I have ever encountered in the course of my rather extensive travels. If necessary, I propose to engage the best lawyer in Honolulu and have him free by night. But I'm giving you this last chance to release him and avoid a somewhat painful expose of the sort of nonsense you go in for."

John Quincy glanced at Carlota Egan. Her eyes were shining but not on him. They were on her uncle.

Greene flushed slightly. "A good bluff, Captain, is always worth trying," he said.

"Oh, then you admit you've been bluffing," said Cope quickly.

"I was referring to your attitude, sir," Greene replied.

"Oh, I see," Cope said. "I'll sit down, if you don't mind. As I understand it, you have two things against old Jim here. One is that he visited Dan Winterslip on the night of the murder, and now refuses to divulge the nature of that call. The other is the stub of a Corsican cigarette which was found by the walk outside the door of Winterslip's living-room."

Greene shook his head. "Only the first," he responded. "The Corsican cigarette is no longer evidence against Egan." He leaned suddenly across his desk. "It is, my dear Captain Cope, evidence against you."

Cope met his look unflinchingly. "Really?" he remarked.

John Quincy noted a flash of startled bewilderment in Carlota Egan's eyes.

"That's what I said," Greene continued. "I'm very glad you dropped in this morning, sir. I've been wanting to talk to you. I've been told that you were heard to express a strong dislike for Dan Winterslip."

"I may have. I certainly felt it."

"Why?"

"As a midshipman on a British war-ship, I was familiar with Australian gossip in the 'eighties. Mr. Dan Winterslip had an unsavory reputation. It was rumored on good authority that he rifled the sea chest of his dead captain on the *Maid of Shiloh.* Perhaps we're a bit squeamish, but that is the sort of thing we sailors can not forgive. There were other quaint deeds in connection with his blackbirding activities. Yes, my dear sir, I heartily disliked Dan Winterslip, and if I haven't said so before, I say it now."

"You arrived in Honolulu a week ago yesterday," Greene continued. "At noon—Monday noon. You left the following day. Did you, by any chance, call on Dan Winterslip during that period?"

"I did not."

"Ah, yes. I may tell you, sir, that the Corsican cigarettes found in Egan's case were of Turkish tobacco. The stub found near the scene of Dan Winterslip's murder was of Virginia tobacco. So also, my dear Captain Cope, was the Corsican cigarette you gave our man Charlie Chan in the lobby of the Alexander Young Hotel last Sunday night."

Cope looked at Chan, and smiled. "Always the detective, eh?" he said.

"Never mind that!" Greene cried. "I'm asking for an explanation."

"The explanation is very simple," Cope replied. "I was about to give it to you when you launched into this silly cross-examination. The Corsican cigarette found by Dan Winterslip's door was, naturally, of Virginia tobacco. I never smoke any other kind."

"What!"

"There can be no question about it, sir. I dropped that cigarette there myself."

"But you just told me you didn't call on Dan Winterslip."

"That was true. I didn't. I called on Miss Minerva Winterslip, of Boston, who is a guest in the house. As a matter of fact, I had tea with her last Monday at five o'clock. You may verify that by telephoning the lady."

Greene glanced at Hallet, who glanced at the telephone, then turned angrily to John Quincy. "Why the devil didn't she tell me that?" he demanded.

John Quincy smiled. "I don't know, sir. Possibly because she never thought of Captain Cope in connection with the murder."

"She'd hardly be likely to," Cope said. "Miss Winterslip and I had tea in the living-room, then went out and sat on a bench in the garden, chatting over old times. When I returned to the house I was smoking a cigarette. I dropped it just outside the living-room door. Whether Miss Winterslip noted my action or not, I don't know. She probably didn't, it isn't the sort of thing one remembers. You may call her on the telephone if you wish, sir."

Again Greene looked at Hallet, who shook his head. "I'll talk with her later," announced the Captain of Detectives. Evidently Miss Minerva had an unpleasant interview ahead.

"At any rate," Cope continued to the prosecutor, "you had yourself disposed of the cigarette as evidence against old Jim. That leaves only the fact of his silence—"

"His silence, yes," Green cut in, "and the fact that Winterslip had been heard to express a fear of Jim Egan."

Cope frowned. "Had he, really?" He considered a moment. "Well, what of it? Winterslip had good reason to fear a great many honest men. No, my dear sir, you have nothing save my brother's silence against him, and that is not enough. I demand—"

Greene raised his hand. "Just a minute. I said you were bluffing, and I still think so. Any other assumption would be an insult to your intelligence. Surely you know enough about the law to understand that your brother's refusal to tell me his business with Winterslip, added to the fact that he was presumably the last person to see Winterslip alive, is suffient excuse for holding him. I can hold him on those grounds, I am holding him, and, my dear captain, I shall continue to hold him until hell freezes over."

"Very good," said Cope, rising. "I shall engage a capable lawyer—"

"That is, of course, your privilege," snapped Greene. "Good morning."

Cope hesitated. He turned to Egan. "It means more publicity, Jim," he said. "Delay, too. More unhappiness for Carlota here. And since everything you did was done for her—"

"How did you know that?" asked Egan quickly.

"I've guessed it. I can put two and two together, Jim. Carlota was to return with me for a bit of schooling in England. You said you had the money, but you hadn't. That was your pride again, Jim. It's got you into a lifetime of trouble. You cast about for the funds, and you remembered Winterslip. I'm beginning to see it all now. You had something on Dan Winterslip, and you went to his house that night to—er—"

"To blackmail him," suggested Greene.

"It wasn't a pretty thing to do, Jim," Cope went on. "But you weren't doing it for yourself. Carlota and I know you would have died first. You did it for your girl, and we both forgive you." He turned to Carlota. "Don't we, my dear?"

The girl's eyes were wet. She rose and kissed her father. "Dear old dad," she said.

"Come on, Jim," pleaded Captain Cope. "Forget your pride for once. Speak up, and we'll take you home with us. I'm sure the prosecutor will keep the thing from the newspapers—"

"We've promised him that a thousand times," Greene said.

Egan lifted his head. "I don't care anything about the newspapers," he explained. "It's you, Arthur—you and Cary—I didn't want you to know. But since you've guessed, and Cary knows too—I may as well tell everything."

John Quincy stood up. "Mr. Egan," he said. "I'll leave the room, if you wish."

"Sit down, my boy," Egan replied. "Cary's told me of your kindness to her. Besides, you saw the check—"

"What check was that?" cried Hallet. He leaped to his feet and stood over John Quincy.

"I was honor bound not to tell," explained the boy gently.

"You don't say so!" Hallet bellowed. "You're a fine pair, you and that aunt of yours—"

"One minute, Hallet," cut in Greene. "Now, Egan, or Cope, or whatever your name happens to be—I'm waiting to hear from you."

Egan nodded. "Back in the 'eighties I was teller in a bank in Melbourne, Australia," he said. "One day a young man came to my window—Williams or some such name he called himself. He had a green hide bag full of gold pieces—Mexican, Spanish and English coins, some of them crusted with dirt—and he wanted to exchange them for bank-notes. I made the exchange for him. He appeared several times with similar bags, and the transaction was repeated. I thought little of it at the time, though the fact that he tried to give me a large tip did rather rouse my suspicion.

"A year later, when I had left the bank and gone to Sydney, I heard rumors of what Dan Winterslip had done on the *Maid of Shiloh*. It occurred to me that Williams and Winterslip were probably the same man. But no one seemed to be prosecuting the case. The general feeling was that it was blood money anyhow, that Tom Brade had not come by it honestly himself. So I said nothing.

"Twelve years later I came to Hawaii, and Dan Winterslip was pointed out to me. He was Williams, right enough. And he knew me, too. But I'm not a blackmailer—I've been in some tight places, Arthur, but I've always played fair—so I let the matter drop. For more than twenty years nothing happened.

"Then, a few months ago, my family located me at last, and Arthur here wrote me that he was coming to Honolulu and would look me up. I'd always felt that I'd not done the right thing by my girl—that she was not taking the place in the world to which she was entitled. I wanted her to visit my old mother and get a bit of English training. I wrote to Arthur and it was arranged. But I couldn't let her go as a charity child—I couldn't admit I'd failed and was unable to do anything for her—I said I'd pay her way. And I—I didn't have a cent.

"And then Brade came. It seemed providential. I might have sold my information to him, but when I talked with him I found he had very little money, and I felt that Winterslip would beat him in the end. No, Winterslip was my man—Winterslip with his rotten wealth. I don't know just what happened—I was quite mad, I fancy—the world owed me that, I figured, just for my girl, not for me. I called Winterslip up and made an appointment for that Monday night.

"But somehow—the standards of a lifetime—it's difficult to change. The moment I had called him, I regretted it. I tried to slip out of it—I told myself there must be some other way—perhaps I could sell the Reef and Palm—anyhow, I called him again and said I wasn't coming. But he insisted, and I went.

"I didn't have to tell him what I wanted. He knew. He had a check ready for me—a check for five thousand dollars. It was Cary's happiness, her chance. I took it, and came away—but I was ashamed. I'm not trying to excuse my action; however, I don't believe I would ever have cashed it. When Cary found it in my desk and brought it to me, I tore it up. That's all." He turned his tired eyes toward his daughter. "I did it for you, Cary, but I didn't want you to know." She went over and put her arm about his shoulder, and stood smiling down at him through her tears.

"If you'd told us that in the first place," said Greene, "you could have saved everybody a lot of trouble, yourself included."

Cope stood up. "Well, Mr. Prosecutor, there you are. You're not going to hold him now?"

Greene rose briskly. "No. I'll arrange for his release at once." He and Egan went out together, then Hallet and Cope. John Quincy held out his hand to Carlota Egan—for by that name he thought of her still.

"I'm mighty glad for you," he said.

"You'll come and see me soon?" she asked. "You'll find a very different girl. More like the one you met on the Oakland ferry."

"She was very charming," John Quincy replied. "But then, she was bound to be—she had your eyes." He suddenly remembered Agatha Parker. "However, you've got your father now," he added. "You won't need me."

She looked up at him and smiled. "I wonder," she said, and went out.

John Quincy turned to Chan. "Well, that's that," he remarked. "Where are we now?"

"Speaking personally for myself," grinned Chan, "I am static in same place as usual. Never did have fondly feeling for Egan theory."

"But Hallet did," John Quincy answered. "A black morning for him."

In the small anteroom they encountered the Captain of Detectives. He appeared disgruntled.

"We were just remarking," said John Quincy pleasantly, "that there goes your little old Egan theory. What have you left?"

"Oh, I've got plenty," growled Hallet.

"Yes, you have. One by one your clues have gone up in smoke. The page from the guest book, the brooch, the torn newspaper, the ohia wood box, and now Egan and the Corsican cigarette."

"Oh, Egan isn't out of it. We may not be able to hold him, but I'm not forgetting Mr. Egan."

"Nonsense," smiled John Quincy. "I asked what you had left. A little button from a glove—useless. The glove was destroyed long ago. A wrist watch with an illuminated dial and a damaged numeral two—"

Chan's amber eyes narrowed. "Essential clue," he murmured. "Remember how I said it."

Hallet banged his fist on a table. "That's it—the wrist watch! If the person who wore it knows any one saw it, it's probably where we'll never find it now. But we've kept it pretty dark—perhaps he doesn't know. That's our only chance." He turned to Chan. "I've combed these islands once hunting that watch," he cried, "now I'm going to start all over again. The jewelry stores, the pawn shops, every nook and corner. You go out, Charlie, and start the ball rolling."

Chan moved with alacrity despite his weight. "I will give it one powerful push," he promised, and disappeared.

"Well, good luck," said John Quincy, moving on.

Hallet grunted. "You tell that aunt of yours I'm pretty sore," he remarked. He was not in the mood for elegance of diction.

John Quincy's opportunity to deliver the message did not come at lunch, for Miss Minerva remained with Barbara in the city. After dinner that evening he led his aunt out to sit on the bench under the hau tree.

"By the way," he said, "Captain Hallet is very much annoyed with you."

"I'm very much annoyed with Captain Hallet," she replied, "so that makes us even. What's his particular grievance now?"

"He believes you knew all the time the name of the man who dropped that Corsican cigarette."

She was silent for a moment. "Not all the time," she said at length. "What has happened?"

John Quincy sketched briefly the events of the morning at the police station. When he had finished he looked at her inquiringly.

"In the first excitement I didn't remember, or I should have spoken," she explained. "It was several days before the thing came to me. I saw it clearly then—Arthur—Captain Cope—tossing that cigarette aside as we reentered the house. But I said nothing about it."

"Why?"

"Well, I thought it would be a good test for the police. Let them discover it for themselves."

"That's a pretty weak explanation," remarked John Quincy severely. "You've been responsible for a lot of wasted time."

"It—it wasn't my only reason," said Miss Minerva softly.

"Oh—I'm glad to hear that. Go on."

"Somehow, I couldn't bring myself to link up that call of Captain Cope's with—a murder mystery."

Another silence. And suddenly—he was never dense—John Quincy understood.

"He told me you were very beautiful in the 'eighties," said the boy gently. "The captain, I mean. When I met him in that San Francisco club."

Miss Minerva laid her own hand on the boy's. When she spoke her voice, which he had always thought firm and sharp, trembled a little. "On this beach in my girlhood," she said, "happiness was within my grasp. I had only to reach out and take it. But somehow—Boston—Boston held me back. I let my happiness slip away."

"Not too late yet," suggested John Quincy.

She shook her head. "So he tried to tell me that Monday afternoon. But there was something in his tone—I may be in Hawaii, but I'm not quite mad. Youth, John Quincy, youth doesn't return, whatever they may say out here." She pressed his hand, and stood. "If your chance comes, dear boy," she added, "don't be such a fool."

She moved hastily away through the garden, and John Quincy looked after her with a new affection in his eyes.

Presently he saw the yellow glare of a match beyond the wire. Amos again, still loitering under his algaroba tree. John Quincy rose and strolled over to him.

"Hello, Cousin Amos," he said. "When are you going to take down this fence?"

"Oh, I'll get round to it some time," Amos answered. "By the way, I wanted to ask you. Any new developments?"

"Several," John Quincy told him. "But nothing that gets us anywhere. So far as I can see, the case has blown up completely."

"Well, I've been thinking it over," Amos said. "Maybe that would be the best outcome, after all. Suppose they do discover who did for Dan—it may only reveal a new scandal, worse than any of the others."

"I'll take a chance on that," replied John Quincy. "For my part, I intend to see this thing through—"

Haku came briskly through the garden. "Cable message for Mr. John Quincy Winterslip. Boy say collect. Requests money."

John Quincy followed quickly to the front door. A bored small boy awaited him. He paid the sum due and tore open the cable. It was signed by the postmaster at Des Moines, and it read:

"No one named Saladine ever heard of here."

John Quincy dashed to the telephone. Some one on duty at the station informed him that Chan had gone home, and gave him an address on Punchbowl Hill. He got out the roadster, and in five minutes more was speeding toward the city.

19

"Good-By, Pete!"

Charlie Chan lived in a bungalow that clung precariously to the side of Punchbowl Hill. Pausing a moment at the gate, John Quincy looked down on Honolulu, one great gorgeous garden set in an amphitheater of mountains. A beautiful picture, but he had no time for beauty now. He hurried up the brief walk that lay in the shadow of the palm trees.

A Chinese woman—a servant, she seemed—ushered him into Chan's dimly-lighted living-room. The detective was seated at a table playing chess; he rose with dignity when he saw his visitor. In this, his hour of ease, he wore a long loose robe of dark purple silk, which fitted closely at the neck and had wide sleeves. Beneath it showed wide trousers of the same material, and on his feet were shoes of silk, with thick felt soles. He was all Oriental now, suave and ingratiating but remote, and for the first time John Quincy was really conscious of the great gulf across which he and Chan shook hands.

"You do my lowly house immese honor," Charlie said. "This proud moment are made still more proud by opportunity to introduce my eldest son." He motioned for his opponent at chess to step forward, a slim sallow boy with amber eyes—Chan himself before he put on weight. "Mr. John Quincy Winterslip, of Boston, kindly condescend to notice Henry Chan.

When you appear I am giving him lesson at chess so he may play in such manner as not to tarnish honored name."

The boy bowed low; evidently he was one member of the younger generation who had a deep respect for his elders. John Quincy also bowed. "Your father is my very good friend," he said. "And from now on, you are too."

Chan beamed with pleasure. "Condescend to sit on this atrocious chair. Is it possible you bring news?"

"It certainly is," smiled John Quincy. He handed over the message from the postmaster at Des Moines.

"Most interesting," said Chan. "Do I hear impressive chug of rich automobile engine in street?"

"Yes, I came in the car," John Quincy replied.

"Good. We will hasten at once to home of Captain Hallet, not far away. I beg of you to pardon my disappearance while I don more appropriate costume."

Left alone with the boy, John Quincy sought a topic of conversation. "Play baseball?" he asked.

The boy's eyes glowed. "Not very good, but I hope to improve. My cousin Willie Chan is great expert at that game. He has promised to teach me."

John Quincy glanced about the room. On the back wall hung a scroll with felicitations, the gift of some friend of the family at New Year's. Opposite him, on another wall, was a single picture, painted on silk, representing a bird on an apple bough. Charmed by its simplicity, he went over to examine it. "That's beautiful," he said.

"Quoting old Chinese saying, a picture is a voiceless poem," replied the boy.

Beneath the picture stood a square table, flanked by straight, low-backed armchairs. On other elaborately carved teakwood stands distributed about the room were blue and white vases, porcelain wine jars, dwarfed trees. Pale golden lanterns hung from the ceiling; a soft-toned rug lay on the floor. John Quincy felt again the gulf between himself and Charlie Chan.

But when the detective returned, he wore the conventional garb of Los Angeles or Detroit, and the gulf did not seem so wide. They went out together and entering the roadster, drove to Hallet's house on Iolani Avenue.

The captain lolled in pajamas on his lanai. He greeted his callers with interest.

"You boys are out late," he said. "Something doing?"

"Certainly is," replied John Quincy, taking a proffered chair. "There's a man named Saladine—"

At metion of the name, Hallet looked at him keenly. John Quincy went on to tell what he knew of Saladine, his alleged place of residence, his business, the tragedy of the lost teeth.

"Some time ago we got on to the fact that every time Kaohla figured in the investigation, Saladine was interested. He managed to be at the desk of the Reef and Palm the day Kaohla inquired for Brade. On the night Kaohla was questioned by your men, Miss Egan saw Mr. Saladine crouching outside the window. So Charlie and I thought it a good scheme to send a cable of inquiry to the postmaster at Des Moines, where Saladine claimed to be in the wholesale grocery business." He handed an envelope to Hallet. "That answer arrived to-night," he added.

An odd smile had appeared on Hallet's usually solemn face. He took the cable and read it, then slowly tore it into bits.

"Forget it, boys," he said calmly.

"Wha—what!" gasped John Quincy.

"I said forget it. I like your enterprise, but you're on the wrong trail there."

John Quincy was greatly annoyed. "I demand an explanation," he cried.

"I can't give it to you," Hallet answered. "You'll have to take my word for it."

"I've taken your word for a good many things," said John Quincy hotly. "This begins to look rather suspicious to me. Are you trying to shield somebody?"

Hallet rose and laid his hand on John Quincy's shoulder. "I've had a hard day," he remarked, "and I'm not going to get angry with you. I'm not trying to shield anybody. I'm as anxious as you are to discover who killed Dan Winterslip. More anxious, perhaps."

"Yet when we bring you evidence you tear it up—"

"Bring me the right evidence," said Hallet. "Bring me that wrist watch. I can promise you action then."

John Quincy was impressed by the sincerity in his tone. But he was sadly puzzled, too. "All right," he said, "that's that. I'm sorry if we've troubled you with this trivial matter—"

"Don't talk like that," Hallet broke in. "I'm glad of your help. But as far as Mr. Saladine is concerned—" he looked at Chan—"let him alone."

Chan bowed. "You are undisputable chief," he replied.

They went back to Punchbowl Hill in the roadster, both rather dejected. As Chan alighted at his gate, John Quincy spoke: "Well, I'm pau. Saladine was my last hope."

Chan stared for a moment at the moonlit Pacific that lay beyond the water-front lamps. "Stone wall surround us," he said dreamily. "But we circle about, seeking loophole. Moment of discovery will come."

"I wish I thought so," replied John Quincy.

Chan smiled. "Patience are a very lovely virtue," he remarked. "Seem that way to me. But maybe that are my Oriental mind. Your race, I perceive, regard patience with ever-swelling disfavor."

It was with swelling disfavor that John Quincy regarded it as he drove back to Waikiki. Yet he had great need of patience in the days immediately following. For nothing happened.

The forty-eight-hour period given him to leave Hawaii expired, but the writer of that threatening letter failed to come forward and relieve the tedium. Thursday arrived, a calm day like the others; Thursday night, peaceful and serene.

On Friday afternoon Agatha Parker broke the monotony by a cable sent from the Wyoming ranch.

"You must be quite mad. I find the West crude and impossible."

John Quincy smiled; he could picture her as she wrote it, proud, haughty, unyielding. She must have been popular with the man who transmitted the message. Or was he, too, an exile from the East?

And perhaps the girl was right. Perhaps he was mad, after all. He sat on Dan Winterslip's lanai, trying to think things out. Boston, the office, the art gallery, the theaters. The Common on a winter's day, with the air bracing and full of life. The thrill of a new issue of bonds, like the thrill of a theatrical first night—would it get over big or flop at his feet? Tennis at Longwood, long evenings on the Charles, golf with people of his own kind at Magnolia. Tea out of exquisite cups in dim old drawing-rooms. Wasn't he mad to think of giving up all that? But what had Miss Minerva said? "If your chance ever comes—"

The problem was a big one, and big problems were annoying out here where the lotus grew. He yawned, and went aimlessly down-town. Drifting into the public library, he saw Charlie Chan hunched over a table that held an enormous volume. John Quincy went closer. The book was made up of back numbers of the Honolulu morning paper, and it was open at a time-yellowed sporting page.

"Hello, Chan. What are you up to?"

Chan gave him a smile of greeting. "Hello. Little bit of careless reading while I gallop about seeking loophole." He closed the big volume casually. "You seem in the best of health."

"Oh, I'm all right."

"No more fierce shots out of bushes?"

"Not a trigger pulled. I imagine that was a big bluff—nothing more."

"What do you say—bluff?"

"I mean the fellow's a coward, after all."

Chan shook his head solemnly. "Pardon humble suggestion—do not lose carefulness. Hot heads plenty in hot climate."

"I'll look before I leap," John Quincy promised. "But I'm afraid I interrupted you."

"Ridiculous thought," protested Chan.

"I'll go along. Let me know if anything breaks."

"Most certainly. Up to present, everything are intact."

John Quincy paused at the door of the reference room. Charlie Chan had promptly opened the big book, and was again bending over it with every show of interest.

Returning to Waikiki, John Quincy faced a dull evening. Barbara had gone to the island of Kauai for a visit with old friends of the family. He had not been sorry when she went, for he didn't feel quite at ease in her presence. The estrangement between the girl and Jennison continued; the lawyer had not been at the dock to see her off. Yes, John Quincy had parted from her gladly, but her absence case a pall of loneliness over the house on Kalia Road.

After dinner, he sat with his pipe on the lanai. Down the beach at the Reef and Palm pleasant company was available—but he hesitated. He had seen Carlota Egan several times by day, on the beach or in the water. She was very happy now, though somewhat appalled at thought of her approaching visit to England. They'd had several talks about that—daylight talks. John Quincy was a bit afraid to entrust himself—as Chan had said in speaking of his stone idol—of an evening. After all, there was Agatha, there was Boston. There was Barbara, too. Being entangled with three girls at once was a rather wearing experience. He rose, and went down-town to the movies.

On Saturday morning he was awakened early by the whir of aeroplanes above the house. The American fleet was in the offing, and the little brothers of the air service hastened out to hover overhead in friendly welcome. That day a spirit of carnival prevailed in Honolulu, flags floated from every masthead, and the streets bloomed, as Barbara had predicted, with handsome boys in spotless uniforms. They were everywhere, swarming in the souvenir stores, besieging the soda fountains, skylarking on the trolley-cars. Evening brought a great ball at the beach hotel, and John Quincy, out for a walk, saw that every spic and span uniform moved toward Waikiki, accompanied by a fair young thing who was only too happy to serve as sweetheart in that particular port.

John Quincy felt, suddenly, rather out of things. Each pretty girl he saw recalled Carlota Egan. He turned his wandering footsteps toward the Reef and Palm, and oddly enough, his pace quickened at once.

The proprietor himself was behind the desk, his eyes calm and untroubled now.

"Good evening, Mr. Egan—or should I say Mr. Cope," remarked John Quincy.

"Oh, we'll stick to the Egan, I guess," the man replied. "Sort of got out of the hang of the other. Mr. Winterslip, I'm happy to see you. Cary will be down in a moment."

John Quincy gazed about the big public room. It was a scene of confusion, spattered ladders, buckets of paint, rolls of new wall-paper. "What's going on?" he inquired.

"Freshening things up a bit," Egan answered. "You know, we're in society now." He laughed. "Yes, sir, the old Reef and Palm has been standing here a long time without so much as a glance from the better element of Honolulu. But now they know I'm related to the British Admiralty, they've suddenly discovered it's a quaint and interesting place. They're dropping in for tea. Just fancy. But that's Honolulu."

"That's Boston, too," John Quincy assured him.

"Yes—and precisely the sort of thing I ran away from England to escape, a good many years ago. I'd tell them all to go to the devil—but there's Cary. Somehow, women feel differently about those things. It will warm her heart a bit to have these dowagers smile upon her. And they're smiling—you know, they've even dug up the fact that my Cousin George has been knighted for making a particularly efficient brand of soap." He grimaced. "It's nothing I'd have mentioned myself—a family skeleton, as I see it. But society has odd standards. And I mustn't be hard on poor old George. As Arthur says, making soap is good clean fun."

"Is your brother still with you?"

"No. He's gone back to finish his job in the Fanning Group. When he returns, I'm sending Cary to England for a long stop. Yes, that's right—*I'm* sending her," he added quickly. "I'm paying for these repairs, too. You see, I've been able to add a second mortgage to the one already on the poor tottering Reef and Palm. That's another outcome of my new-found connection with the British Admiralty and the silly old soap business. Here's Cary now."

John Quincy turned. And he was glad he had, for he would not willingly have missed the picture of Carlota on the stairs. Carlota in an evening gown of some shimmering material, her dark hair dressed in a new amazingly effective way, her white shoulders gleaming, her eyes happy at last. As she came quickly toward him he caught his breath, never had he seen her look so beautiful. She must have heard his voice in the office, he reflected, and with surprising speed arrayed herself thus to greet him. He was deeply grateful as he took her hand.

"Stranger," she rebuked. "We thought you'd deserted us."

"I'd never do that," he answered. "But I've been rather busy—"

A step sounded behind him. He turned, and there stood one of those ubiquitous navy boys, a tall, blond Adonis who held his cap in his hand and smiled in a devastating way.

"Hello, Johnnie," Carlota said. "Mr. Winterslip, of Boston, this is Lieutenant Booth, of Richmond, Virginia."

"How are you," nodded the boy, without removing his eyes from the girl's face. Just one of the guests, this Winterslip, no account at all—such was obviously the lieutenant's idea. "All ready, Cary? The car's outside."

"I'm frightfully sorry, Mr. Winterslip," said the girl, "but we're off to the dance. This week-end belongs to the navy, you know. You'll come again, won't you?"

"Of course," John Quincy replied. "Don't let me keep you."

She smiled at him and fled with Johnnie at her side. Looking after them, John Quincy felt his heart sink to his boots, an unaccountable sensation of age and helplessness. Youth, youth was going through that door, and he was left behind.

"A great pity she had to run," said Egan in a kindly voice.

"Why, that's all right," John Quincy assured him. "Old friend of the family, this Lieutenant Booth?"

"Not at all. Just a lad Cary met at parties in San Fancisco. Won't you sit down and have a smoke with me?"

"Some other time, thanks," John Quincy said wearily. "I must hurry back to the house."

He wanted to escape, to get out into the calm lovely night, the night that was ruined for him now. He walked along the beach, savagely kicking his toes into the white sand. "Johnnie!" She had called him Johnnie. And the way she had looked at him, too! Again John Quincy felt that sharp pang in his heart. Foolish, foolish; better go back to Boston and forget. Peaceful old Boston, that was where he belonged. He was an old man out here—thirty, nearly. Better go away and leave these children to love and the moonlit beach.

Miss Minerva had gone in the big car to call on friends, and the house was quiet as the tomb, John Quincy wandered aimlessly about the rooms, gloomy and bereft. Down at the Moana an Hawaiian orchestra was playing and Lieutenant Booth, of Richmond, was holding Carlota close in the intimate manner affected these days by the young. Bah! If he hadn't been ordered to leave Hawaii, by gad, he'd go to-morrow.

The telephone rang. None of the servants appeared to answer it, so John Quincy went himself.

"Charlie Chan speaking," said a voice. "That is you, Mr. Winterslip? Good. Big events will come to pass very quick. Meet me drug and grocery emporium of Liu Yin, number 927 River Street, soon as you can do so. You savvy locality?"

"I'll find it," cried John Quincy, delighted.

"By bank of stream. I will await. Good-by."

Action—action at last! John Quincy's heart beat fast. Action was what he wanted to-night. As usually happens in a crisis, there was no automobile available; the roadster was at a garage undergoing repairs, and the other car was in use. He hastened over to Kalakaua Avenue intending to rent a machine, but a trolley approaching at the moment altered his plans and he swung aboard.

Never had a trolley moved at so reluctant a pace. When they reached the corner of Fort Street in the center of the city, he left it and proceeded on foot. The hour was still fairly early, but the scene was one of somnolent calm. A couple of tourists drifted aimlessly by. About the bright doorway of a shooting gallery loitered a group of soldiers from the fort, with a sprinkling of enlisted navy men. John Quincy hurried on down King Street, past Chinese noodle cafés and pawn shops, and turned presently off into River Street.

On his left was the river, on his right an array of shabby stores. He paused at the door of number 927, the establishment of Liu Yin. Inside, seated behind a screen that revealed only their heads, a number of Chinese were engrossed in a friendly little game. John Quincy opened the door; a bell tinkled, and he stepped into an odor of must and decay. Curious sights met his quick eye, dried roots and herbs, jars of sea-horse skeletons, dejected ducks flattened out and varnished to tempt the palate, gobbets of pork. An old Chinese man rose and came forward.

"I'm looking for Mr. Charlie Chan," said John Quincy.

The old man nodded and led the way to a red curtain across the rear of the shop. He lifted it, and indicated that John Quincy was to pass. The boy did so, and came into a bare room furnished with a cot, a table on which an oil lamp burned dimly behind a smoky chimney, and a couple of chairs. A man who had been sitting on one of the chairs rose suddenly; a huge red-haired man with the smell of the sea about him.

"Hello," he said.

"Is Mr. Chan here?" John Quincy inquired.

The Chinese man withdrew. "Sit down," said the man. John Quincy obeyed; the sailor sat too. One of his eyelids drooped wickedly; he rested his hands on the table—enormous hairy hands. "Charlie'll be here pretty quick," he said. "Then I got a little story to tell the two of you."

"Yes?" John Quincy replied. He glanced about the little vile-smelling room. There was a door, a closed door, at the back. He looked again at the red-haired man. He wondered how he was going to get out of there.

For he knew now that Charlie Chan had not called him on the telephone. It came to him belatedly that the voice was never Charlie's. "You savvy locality?" the voice had said. A clumsy attempt at Chan's style, but Chan was a student of English; he dragged his words painfully from the poets; he was careful to use nothing that savored of "pidgin." No, the detective had not telephoned; he was no doubt at home now bending over his chessboard, and here was John Quincy shut up in a little room on the fringe of the River District with a husky sailorman who leered at him knowingly.

The old Chinese man returned with two small glasses into which the liquor had already been poured. He set them on the table. The red-haired man lifted one of them. "Your health, sir," he said.

John Quincy took up the other glass and raised it to his lips. There was a suspicious eagerness in the sailor's one good eye. John Quincy put the glass back on the table. "I'm sorry," he said. "I don't want a drink, thank you."

The great face with its stubble of red beard leaned close to his. "Y'mean you won't drink with me?" said the red-haired man belligerently.

"That's just what I mean," John Quincy answered. Might as well get it over with, he felt; anything was better than this suspense. He stood up. "I'll be going along," he announced.

He took a step toward the red curtain. The sailor, evidently a fellow of few words, rose and got in his way. John Quincy, himself feeling the futility of talk, said nothing, but struck the man in the face. The sailor struck back with efficiency and promptness. In another second the room was full of battle, and John Quincy saw red everywhere, red curtain, red hair, red lamp flame, great red hairy hands cunningly seeking his face. What was it Roger had said? "Ever fought with a ship's officer—the old-fashioned kind with fists like flying hams?" No, he hadn't up to then, but that sweet experience was his now, and it came to John Quincy pleasantly that he was doing rather well at his new trade.

This was better than the attic; here he was prepared and had a chance. Time and again he got his hands on the red curtain, only to be dragged back and subjected to a new attack. The sailor was seeking to knock him out, and though many of his blows went home, that happy result—from the standpoint of the red-haired man—was unaccountably delayed. John Quincy had a similar aim in life; they lunged noisily about the room, while the surprising Orientals in the front of the shop continued their quiet game.

John Quincy felt himself growing weary; his breath came painfully; he realized that his adversary had not yet begun to fight. Standing with his back to the table in an idle moment while the red-haired man made plans for the future, the boy hit on a plan of his own. He overturned the table; the lamp crashed down; darkness fell over the world. In the final glimmer of light he saw the big man coming for him and dropping to his knees he tackled in the approved manner of Soldiers' Field, Cambridge, Massachusetts. Culture prevailed; the sailor went on his head with a resounding thump; John Quincy let go of him and sought the nearest exit. It happened to be the door at the rear, and it was unlocked.

He passed hurriedly through a cluttered back yard and climbing a fence, found himself in the neighborhood known as the River District. There in crazy alleys that have no names, no sidewalks, no beggining and no end, five races live together in the dark. Some houses were above the walk level, some below, all were out of alignment. John Quincy felt he had wandered into a futurist drawing. As he paused he heard the whine and clatter of Chinese music, the clicking of a typewriter, the rasp of a cheap phonograph playing American jazz, the distant scream of an auto horn, a child wailing Japanese lamentations. Footsteps in the yard beyond the fence roused him, and he fled.

He must get out of this mystic maze of mean alleys, and at once. Odd painted faces loomed in the dusk; pasty-white faces with just a suggestion of queer costumes beneath. A babel of tongues, queer eyes that glittered, once a lean hand on his arm. A group of moon-faced Chinese children under a lamp who scattered at his approach. And when he paused again, out of breath, the patter of many feet, bare feet, sandaled feet, the clatter of wooden clogs, the squeak of cheap shoes made in his own Massachusetts. Then suddenly the thump of large feet such as might belong to a husky sailor. He moved on.

Presently he came into the comparative quiet of River Street, and realized that he had traveled in a circle, for there was Liu Yin's shop again. As he hurried on toward King Street, he saw, over his shoulder, that the red-haired man still followed. A big touring car, with curtains drawn, waited by the curb. John Quincy leaped in beside the driver.

"Get out of here, quick!" he panted.

A sleepy Japanese face looked at him through the gloom. "Busy now."

"I don't care if you are—" began John Quincy, and glanced down at one of the man's arms resting on the wheel. His heart stood still. In the dusk he saw a wrist watch with an illuminated dial, and the numeral two was very dim.

Even as he looked, strong hands seized him by the collar and dragged him into the dark tonneau. At the same instant, the red-haired man arrived.

"Got him, Mike? Say, that's luck!" He leaped into the rear of the car. Quick able work went forward, John Quincy's hands were bound behind his back, a vile-tasting gag was put in his mouth. "Damned if this bird didn't land me one in the eye," said the red-haired man. "I'll pay him for it when we get aboard. Hey you—Pier 78. Show us some speed!"

The car leaped forward. John Quincy lay on the dusty floor, bound and helpless. To the docks? But he wasn't thinking of that, he was thinking of the watch on the driver's wrist.

A brief run, and they halted in the shadow of a pier-shed. John Quincy was lifted and propelled none too gently from the car. His cheek was jammed against one of the buttons holding the side curtain, and he had sufficient presence of mind to catch the gang on it and loosen it. As they left the car he tried to get a glimpse of its license plate, but he was able to ascertain only the first two figures—33—before it sped away.

His two huge chaperons hurried him along the dock. Some distance off he saw a little group of men, three in white uniforms, one in a darker garb. The latter was smoking a pipe. John Quincy's heart leaped. He maneuvered the loosened gag with his teeth, so that it dropped about his collar. "Good-by, Pete!" he shouted at the top of his lungs, and launched at once into a terrific struggle to break away from his startled captors.

There was a moment's delay, and then the clatter of feet along the dock. A stocky boy in a white uniform began an enthusiastic debate with Mike, and the other two were prompt to claim the attention of the red-haired man. Pete Mayberry was at John Quincy's back, cutting the rope on his wrists.

"Well, I'll be damned, Mr. Winterslip," he cried.

"Same here," laughed John Quincy. "Shanghaied in another minute but for you." He leaped forward to join the battle, but the red-haired man and his friend had already succumbed to youth and superior forces, and were in full retreat. John Quincy followed joyously along the dock, and planted his fist back of his old adversary's ear. The sailor staggered, but regained his balance and went on.

John Quincy returned to his rescuers. "The last blow is the sweetest," he remarked.

"I can place those guys," said Mayberry. "They're off that tramp steamer that's been lying out in the harbor the past week. An opium runner, I'll gamble on it. You go to the police station right away—"

"Yes," said John Quincy, "I must. But I want to thank you, Mr. Mayberry. And"—he turned to the white uniforms—"you fellows too."

The stocky lad was picking up his cup. "Why, that's all right," he said. "A real pleasure, if you ask me. But look here, old timer," he added, addressing Mayberry, "how about your Honolulu water-front and its lost romance? You go tell that to the marines."

As John Quincy hurried away Pete Mayberry was busily explaining that the thing was unheared of—not in twenty years—maybe more than that—his voice died in the distance.

Hallet was in his room, and John Quincy detailed his evening's adventure. The captain was incredulous, but when the boy came to the wrist watch on the driver of the car, he sat up and took notice.

"Now you're talking," he cried. "I'll start the force after the car to-night. First two figures 33, you say. I'll send somebody aboard that tramp, too. They can't get away with stuff like that around here."

"Oh, never mind them," said John Quincy magnanimously. "Concentrate on the watch."

Back in the quiet town he walked with his head up, his heart full of the joy of battle. And while he thought of it, he stepped into the cable office. The message he sent was addressed to Agatha Parker on that Wyoming ranch. "San Francisco or nothing," was all it said.

As he walked down the deserted street on his way to the corner to wait for his trolley, he heard quick footsteps on his trail again. Who now? He was sore and weary, a bit fed up on fighting for one evening. He quickened his pace. The steps quickened too. He went even faster. So did his pursuer. Oh, well, might as well stop and face him.

John Quincy turned. A young man rushed up, a lean young man in a cap.

"Mr. Winterslip, ain't it?" He thrust a dark brown object into John Quincy's hand. "Your July *Atlantic*, sir. Came in on the *Maui* this morning."

"Oh," said John Quincy limply. "Well, I'll take it. My aunt might like to look at it. Keep the change."

"Thank you, sir," said the newsman, touching his cap.

John Quincy rode out to Waikiki on the last seat of the car. His face was swollen and cut, every muscle ached. Under his arm, clasped tightly, he held the July *Atlantic*. But he didn't so much as look at the table of contents. "We move, we advance," he told himself exultantly. For he had seen the watch with the illuminated dial—the dial on which the numeral two was very dim.

20

The Story of Lau Ho

Early Sunday morning John Quincy was awakened by a sharp knock on his door. Rising sleepily and donning dressing-gown and slippers, he opened it to admit his Aunt Minerva. She had a worried air.

"Are you all right, John Quincy?" she inquired.

"Surely. That is, I would be if I hadn't been dragged out of bed a full hour before I intended to get up."

"I'm sorry, but I had to have a look at you." She took a newspaper from under her arm and handed it to him. "What's all this?"

An eight-column head on the first page caught even John Quincy's sleepy eye. "Boston Man has Strange Adventure on Water-Front." Smaller heads announced that Mr. John Quincy Winterslip had been rescued from an unwelcome trip to China, "in the nick of time" by three midshipmen from the *Oregon*. Poor Pete Mayberry! He had been the real hero of the affair, but his own paper would not come out again until Monday evening, and rivals had beaten him to the story.

John Quincy yawned. "All true, my dear," he said. "I was on the verge of leaving you when the navy saved me. Life, you perceive, has become a musical comedy."

"But why should any one want to shanghai you?" cried Miss Minerva.

"Ah, I hoped you'd ask me that. It happens that your nephew has a brain. His keen analytical work as a detective is getting some one's goat. He admitted as much in a letter he sent me the night he took a few shots at my head."

"Some one shot at you!" gasped Miss Minerva.

"I'll say so. You rather fancy yourself as a sleuth, but is anybody taking aim at you from behind bushes? Answer me that."

Miss Minerva sat down weakly on a chair. "You're going home on the next boat," she announced.

He laughed. "About two weeks ago I made that suggestion to you. And what was your reply? Ah, my dear, the tables are turned. I'm not going home on the next boat. I may never go home. This gay, care-free, sudden country begins to appeal to me. Let me read about myself."

He returned to the paper. "The clock was turned back thirty years on the Honolulu water-front last night," began the somewhat imaginative account. It closed with the news that the tramp steamer *Mary S. Allison* had left port before the police could board her. Evidently she'd had steam up and papers ready, and was only awaiting the return of the red-haired man and his victim. John Quincy handed the newspaper back to his aunt.

"Too bad," he remarked. "They slipped through Hallet's fingers."

"Of course they did," she snapped. "Everybody does. I'd like a talk with Captain Hallet. If I could only tell him what I think of him, I'd feel better."

"Save that paper," John Quincy said. "I want to send it to mother."

She stared at him. "Are you mad? Poor Grace—she'd have a nervous breakdown. I only hope she doesn't hear of this until you're back in Boston safe and sound."

"Oh, yes—Boston," laughed John Quincy. Quaint old town, they tell me. I must visit there some day. Now if you'll leave me a minute, I'll prepare to join you at breakfast and relate the story of my adventurous life."

"Very well," agreed Miss Minerva, rising. She paused at the door. "A little witch-hazel might help your face."

"The scars of honorable battle," said her nephew. "Why remove them?"

"Honorable fiddlesticks," Miss Minerva answered. "After all, the Back Bay has its good points." But in the hall outside she smiled a delighted little smile.

When John Quincy and his aunt were leaving the dining-room after breakfast Kamaikui, stiff and dignified in a freshly-laundered holoku, approached the boy.

"So very happy to see you safe this morning," she announced.

"Why, thank you, Kamaikui," he answered. He wondered. Was Kaohla responsible for his troubles, and if so, did this huge silent woman know of her grandson's activities?

"Poor thing," Miss Minerva said as they entered the living-room. "She's been quite downcast since Dan went. I'm sorry for her. I've always liked her."

"Naturally," smiled John Quincy. "There's a bond between you."

"What's that?"

"Two vanishing races, yours and hers. The Boston Brahman and the pure Hawaiian."

Later in the morning Carlota Egan telephoned him, greatly excited. She had just seen the Sunday paper.

"All true," he admitted. "While you were dancing your heart out, I was struggling to sidestep a Cook's tour of the Orient."

"I shouldn't have had a happy moment if I'd known."

"Then I'm glad you didn't. Big party, I suppose?"

"Yes. You know, I've been terribly worried about you ever since that night on the avenue. I want to talk with you. Will you come to see me?"

"Will I? I'm on my way already."

He hung up the receiver and hastened down the beach. Carlota was sitting on the white sand not far from the Reef and Palm, all in white herself. A serious wide-eyed Carlota quite different from the gay girl who had been hurrying to a party the night before.

John Quincy dropped down beside her, and for a time they talked of the dance and of his adventure. Suddenly she turned to him.

"I have no right to ask it, I know, but—I want you to do something for me."

"It will make me very happy—anything you ask."

"Go back to Boston."

"What! Not that. I was wrong—that wouldn't make me happy."

"Yes, it would. You don't think so now, perhaps. You're dazzled by the sun out here, but this isn't your kind of place. We're not your kind of people. You think you like us, but you'd soon forget. Back among your own sort—the sort who are interested in the things that interest you. Please go."

"It would be retreating under fire," he objected.

"But you proved your courage, last night. I'm afraid for you. Some one out here has a terrible grudge against you. I'd never forgive Hawaii if—if anything happened to you."

"That's sweet of you." He moved closer. But—confound it—there was Agatha. Bound to Agatha by all the ties of honor. He edged away again. "I'll think about it," he agreed.

"I'm leaving Honolulu too, you know," she reminded him.

"I know. You'll have a wonderful time in England."

She shook her head. "Oh, I dread the whole idea. Dad's heart is set on it, and I shall go to please him. But I shan't enjoy it. I'm not up to England."

"Nonsense."

"No, I'm not. I'm unsophisticated—crude, really—just a girl of the Islands."

"But you wouldn't care to stay here all your life?"

"No, indeed. It's a beautiful spot—to loll about in. But I've too much northern blood to be satisfied with that. One of these days I want dad to sell and we'll go to the mainland. I could get some sort of work—"

"Any particular place on the mainland?"

"Well, I haven't been about much, of course. But all the time I was at school I kept thinking I'd rather live in San Francisco than anywhere else in the world—"

"Good," John Quincy cried. "That's my choice too. You remember that morning on the ferry, how you held out your hand to me and said: 'Welcome to your city—'"

"But you corrected me at once. You said you belonged in Boston."

"I see my error now."

She shook her head. "A moment's madness, but you'll recover. You're an easterner, and you could never be happy anywhere else."

"Oh, yes, I could," he assured her. "I'm a Winterslip, a wandering Winterslip. Any old place we hang our hats—" This time he did lean rather close. "I could be happy anywhere—" he began. He wanted to add "with you." But Agatha's slim patrician hand was on his shoulder. "Anywhere," he repeated, with a different inflection. A gong sounded from the Reef and Palm.

Carlota rose. "That's lunch." John Quincy stood too. "It's beside the point—where you go," she went on. "I asked you to do something for me."

"I know. If you'd asked anything else in the world, I'd be up to my neck in it now. But what you suggest would take a bit of doing. To leave Hawaii—and say good-by to you—"

"I meant to be very firm about it," she broke in.

"But I must have a little time to consider. Will you wait?"

She smiled up at him. "You're so much wiser than I am," she said. "Yes—I'll wait."

He went slowly along the beach. Unsophisticated, yes—and charming. "You're so much wiser than I am." Where on the mainland could one encounter a girl nowadays who'd say that? He had quite forgotten that she smiled when she said it.

In the afternoon, John Quincy visited the police station. Hallet was in his room in rather a grouchy mood. Chan was out somewhere hunting the watch. No, they hadn't found it yet.

John Quincy was mildly reproving. "Well, you saw it, didn't you?" growled Hallet. "Why in Sam Hill didn't you grab it?"

"Because they tied my hands," John Quincy reminded him. "I've narrowed the search down for you to the taxi drivers of Honolulu."

"Hundreds of them, my boy."

"More than that, I've given you the first two numbers on the license plate of the car. If you're any good at all, you ought to be able to land that watch now."

"Oh, we'll land it," Hallet said. "Give us time."

Time was just what John Quincy had to give them. Monday came and went. Miss Minerva was bitterly sarcastic.

"Patience are a very lovely virtue," John Quincy told her. "I got that from Charlie."

"At any rate," she snapped, "it are a virtue very much needed with Captain Hallet in charge."

In another direction, too, John Quincy was called upon to exercise patience. Agatha Parker was unaccountably silent regarding that short peremptory cable he had sent on his big night in town. Was she offended? The Parkers were notoriously not a family who accepted dictation. But in such a vital matter as this, a girl should be willing to listen to reason.

Late Tuesday afternoon Chan telephoned from the station-house—unquestionably Chan this time. Would John Quincy do him the great honor to join him for an early dinner at the Alexander Young café?

"Something doing, Charlie?" cried the boy eagerly.

"Maybe it might be," answered Chan, "and maybe also not. At six o'clock in hotel lobby, if you will so far condescend."

"I'll be there," John Quincy promised, and he was.

He greeted Chan with anxious, inquiring eyes, but Chan was suave and entirely non-committal. He led John Quincy to the dining-room and carefully selected a table by a front window.

"Do me the great favor to recline," he suggested.

John Quincy reclined. "Charlie, don't keep me in suspense," he pleaded.

Chan smiled. "Let us not shade the feast with gloomy murder talk," he replied. "This are social meeting. Is it that you are in the mood to dry up plate of soup?"

"Why, yes, of course," John Quincy answered. Politeness, he saw, dictated that he hide his curiosity.

"Two of the soup," ordered Chan of a white-jacketed waitier. A car drew up to the door of the Alexander Young. Chan half rose, staring at it keenly. He dropped back to his seat. "It is my high delight to entertain you thus humbly before you are restored to Boston. Converse at some length of Boston. I feel interested."

"Really?" smiled the boy.

"Undubitably. Gentleman I meet once say Boston are like China. The future of both, he say, lies in graveyards where repose useless bodies of honored guests on high. I am fogged as to meaning."

"He meant both places live in the past," John Quincy explained. "And he was right, in a way. Boston, like China, boasts a glorious history. But that's not saying the Boston of to-day isn't progressive. Why, do you know—"

He talked eloquently of his native city. Chan listened, rapt.

"Always," he sighed, when John Quincy finished, "I have unlimited yearning for travel." He paused to watch another car draw up before the hotel. "But it are unavailable. I am policeman on small remuneration. In my youth, rambling on evening hillside or by moonly ocean, I dream of more lofty position. Not so now. But that other American citizen, my eldest son, he are dreaming too. Maybe for him dreams eventuate. Perhaps he become second Baby Ruth, home run emperor, applause of thousands making him deaf. Who knows it?"

The dinner passed, unshaded by gloomy talk, and they went outside. Chan proffered a cigar of which he spoke in the most belittling fashion. He suggested that they stand for a time before the hotel door.

"Waiting for somebody?" inquired John Quincy, unable longer to dissemble.

"Precisely the fact. Barely dare to mention it, however. Great disappointment may drive up here any minute now."

An open car stopped before the hotel entrance. John Quincy's eyes sought the license plate, and he got an immediate thrill. The first two figures were 33.

A party of tourists, a man and two women, alighted. The doorman ran forward and busied himself with luggage. Chan casually strolled across the walk, and as the Japanese driver shifted his gears preparatory to driving away, put a restraining hand on the car door.

"One moment, please." The driver turned, fright in his eyes. "You were Okuda, from auto stand across way?"

"Yes-s," hissed the driver.

"You are now returned from exploring island with party of tourists? You leave this spot early Sunday morning?"

"Yes-s."

"Is it possible that you wear wrist watch, please?"

"Yes-s."

"Deign to reveal face of same."

The Jap hesitated. Chan leaned far over into the car and thrust aside the man's coat sleeve. He came back, a pleased light in his eyes, and held open the rear door. "Kindly embark into tonneau, Mr. Winterslip." Obediently John Quincy got in. Chan took his place by the driver's side. "The police station, if you will be so kind." The car leaped forward.

The essential clue! They had it at last. John Quincy's heart beat fast there in the rear of the car where, only a few nights before, he had been bound and gagged.

Captain Hallet's grim face relaxed into happy lines when he met them at the door of his room. "You got him, eh? Good work." He glanced at the prisoner's wrist. "Rip that watch off him, Charlie."

Charlie obeyed. He examined the watch for a moment, then handed it to his chief.

"Inexpensive time-piece of noted brand," he announced. "Numeral two faint and far away. One other fact emerge into light. This Japanese man have small wrist. Yet worn place on strap convey impression of being worn by man with wrist of vastly larger circumference."

Hallet nodded. "Yes, that's right. Some other man has owned this watch. He had a big wrist—but most men in Honolulu have, you know. Sit down,

Okuda. I want to hear from you. You understand what it means to lie to me?"

"I do not lie, sir."

"No, you bet your sweet life you don't. First, tell me who engaged your car last Saturday night."

"Saturday night?"

"That's what I said!"

"Ah, yes. Two sailors from ship. Engage for evening paying large cash at once. I drive to shop on River Street, wait long time. Then off we go to dock with extra passenger in back."

"Know the names of those sailors?"

"Could not say."

"What ship were they from?"

"How can I know? Not told."

"All right. I'm coming to the important thing. Understand? The truth—that's what I want! Where did you get this watch?"

Chan and John Quincy leaned forward eagerly. "I buy him," said the Jap.

"You bought him? Where?"

"At jewel store of Chinese Lau Ho on Maunakea Street."

Hallet turned to Chan. "Know the place, Charlie?"

Chan nodded. "Yes, indeed."

"Open now?"

"Open until hour of ten, maybe more."

"Good," said Hallet. "Come along, Okuda. You can drive us there."

Lau Ho, a little wizened Chinese man, sat back of his work bench with a microscope screwed into one dim old eye. The four men who entered his tiny store filled it to overflowing, but he gave them barely a glance.

"Come on, Ho—wake up," Hallet cried. "I want to talk to you."

With the utmost deliberation Lau Ho descended from his stool and approached the counter. He regarded Hallet with a hostile eye. The captain laid the wrist watch on top of a showcase in which reposed many trays of jade.

"Ever see that before?" he inquired.

Lau Ho regarded it causally. Slowly he raised his eyes. "Maybe so. Can not say," he replied in a high squeaky voice.

Hallet reddened. "Nonsense. You had it here in the store, and you sold it to this fellow. Now, didn't you?"

Lau Ho dreamily regarded the taxi driver. "Maybe so. Can not say."

"Damn it!" cried Hallet. "You know who I am?"

"Policeman, maybe."

"Policeman maybe yes! And I want you to tell me about this watch. Now wake up and come across or by the Lord Harry—"

Chan laid a deferential hand on his chief's arm. "Humbly suggest I attempt this," he said.

Hallet nodded. "All right, he's your meat, Charlie." He drew back.

Chan bowed with a great show of politeness. He launched into a long story in Chinese. Lau Ho looked at him with slight interest. Presently he squeaked a brief reply. Chan resumed his flow of talk. Occasionally he paused, and Lau Ho spoke. In a few moments Chan turned beaming.

"Story are now completely extracted like aching tooth," he said. "Wrist watch was brought to Lau Ho on Thursday, same week as murder. Offered him on sale by young man darkly colored with small knife scar marring cheek. Lau Ho buy and repair watch, interior works being in injured state.

Saturday morning he sell at seemly profit to Japanese, presumably this Okuda here but Lau Ho will not swear. Saturday night dark young man appear much overwhelmed with excitement and demand watch again, please. Lau Ho say it is sold to Japanese. Which Japanese? Lau Ho is not aware of name, and can not describe, all Japanese faces being uninteresting outlook for him. Dark young man curse and fly. Appear frequently demanding any news, but Lau Ho is unable to oblige. Such are story of this jewel merchant here."

They went out on the street. Hallet scowled at the Japanese man. "All right—run along. I'll keep the watch."

"Very thankful," said the taxi driver, and leaped into his car.

Hallet turned to Chan. "A dark young man with a scar?" he queried.

"Clear enough to me," Chan answered. "Same are the Spaniard José Cabrera, careless man about town with reputation not so savory. Mr. Winterslip, is it that you have forgotten him?"

John Quincy started. "Me? Did I ever see him?"

"Recall," said Chan. "It are the night following murder. You and I linger in All American Restaurant engaged in debate regarding hygiene of pie. Door open, admitting Bowker, steward on *President Tyler,* joyously full of okolehau. With him are dark young man—this José Cabrera himself."

"Oh, I remember now," John Quincy answered.

"Well, the Spaniard's easy to pick up," said Hallet. "I'll have him inside an hour—"

"One moment, please," interposed Chan. "To-morrow morning at nine o'clock the *President Tyler* return from Orient. No gambler myself but will wager increditable sum Spaniard waits on dock for Mr. Bowker. If you present no fierce objection, I have a yearning to arrest him at that very moment."

"Why, of course," agreed Hallet. He looked keenly at Charlie Chan. "Charlie, you old rascal, you've got the scent at last."

"Who—me?" grinned Chan. "With your gracious permission I would alter the picture. Stone walls are crumbling now like dust. Through many loopholes light stream in like rosy streaks of dawn."

21

The Stone Walls Crumble

The stone walls were crumbling and the light streaming through—but only for Chan. John Quincy was still groping in the dark, and his reflections were a little bitter as he returned to the house at Waikiki. Chan and he had worked together, but now that they approached the crisis of their efforts, the detective evidently preferred to push on alone, leaving his fellow-worker to follow if he could. Well, so be it—but John Quincy's pride was touched.

He had suddenly a keen desire to show Chan that he could not be left behind like that. If only he could, by some inspirational flash of deductive reasoning, arrive at the solution of the mystery simultaneously with the detective. For the honor of Boston and the Winterslips.

Frowning deeply, he considered all the old discarded clues again. The people who had been under suspicion and then dropped—Egan, the Compton woman, Brade, Kaohla, Leatherbee, Saladine, Cope. He even considered several the investigation had not touched. Presently he came to Bowker. What did Bowker's reappearance mean?

For the first time in two weeks he thought of the little man with the fierce pompadour and the gold-rimmed eye-glasses. Bowker with his sorrowful talk of vanished bar-rooms and lost friends behind the bar. How was the steward on the *President Tyler* connected with the murder of Dan Winterslip? He had not done it himself, that was obvious, but in some way he was linked up with the crime. John Quincy spent a long and painful period seeking to join Bowker up with one or another of the suspects. It couldn't be done.

All through that Tuesday evening the boy puzzled, so silent and distrait that Miss Minerva finally gave him up and retired to her room with a book. He awoke on Wednesday morning with the problem no nearer solution.

Barbara was due to arrive at ten o'clock from Kauai, and taking the small car, John Quincy went down-town to meet her. Pausing at the bank to cash a check, he encountered his old shipmate on the *President Tyler*, the sprightly Madame Maynard.

"I really shouldn't speak to you," she said. "You never come to see me."

"I know," he answered. "But I've been so very busy."

"So I hear. Running round with policemen and their victims. I have no doubt you'll go back to Boston and report we're all criminals and cutthroats out here."

"Oh, hardly that."

"Yes, you will. You're getting a very biased view of Honolulu. Why not stoop to associate with a respectable person now and then?"

"I'd enjoy it—if they're all like you."

"Like me? They're much more intelligent and charming than I am. Some of them are dropping in at my house to-night for an informal little party. A bit of a chat, and then a moonlight swim. Won't you come too?"

"I want to, of course," John Quincy replied. "But there's Cousin Dan—"

Her eyes flashed. "I'll say it, even if he was your relative. Ten minutes of mourning for Cousin Dan is ample. I'll be looking for you."

John Quincy laughed. "I'll come."

"Do," she answered. "And bring your Aunt Minerva. Tell her I said she might as well be dead as hog-tied by convention."

John Quincy went out to the corner of Fort and King Streets, near which he had parked the car. As he was about to climb into it, he paused. A familiar figure was jauntily crossing the street. The figure of Bowker, the steward, and with him was Willie Chan, demon back-stopper of the Pacific.

"Hello, Bowker," John Quincy called.

Mr. Bowker came blithely to join him. "Well, well, well. My old friend Mr. Winterslip. Shake hands with William Chan, the local Ty Cobb."

"Mr. Chan and I have met before," John Quincy told him.

"Know all the celebrities, eh? That's good. Well, we missed you on the *President Tyler*."

Bowker was evidently quite sober. "Just got in, I take it," John Quincy remarked.

"A few minutes ago. How about joining us?" He came closer and lowered his voice. "This intelligent young man tells me he knows a taxi-stand out near the beach where one may obtain a superior brand of fusel oil with a very pretty label on the bottle."

"Sorry," John Quincy answered. "My cousin's coming in shortly on an

Inter-island boat, and I'm elected to meet her."

"I'm sorry, too," said the graduate of Dublin University. "If my strength holds out I'm aiming to stage quite a little party, and I'd like to have you in on it. Yes, a rather large affair—in memory of Tim, and as a last long lingering farewell to the seven seas."

"What? You're pau?"

"Pau it is. When I sail out of here to-night at nine on the old *P. T.* I'm through for ever. You don't happen to know a good country newspaper that can be bought for—well, say ten grand."

"This is rather sudden, isn't it?" John Quincy inquired.

"This is sudden country out here, sir. Well, we must roll along. Sorry you can't join us. If the going's not too rough and I can find a nice smooth table top, I intend to turn down an empty glass. For poor old Tim. So long, sir—and happy days."

He nodded to Willie Chan, and they went on down the street. John Quincy stood staring after them, a puzzled expression on his face.

Barbara seemed paler and thinner than ever, but she announced that her visit had been an enjoyable one, and on the ride to the beach appeared to be making a distinct effort to be gay and sprightly. When they reached the house, John Quincy repeated to his aunt Mrs. Maynard's invitation.

"Better come along," he urged.

"Perhaps I will," she answered. "I'll see."

The day passed quietly, and it was not until evening that the monotony was broken. Leaving the dining-room with his aunt and Barbara. John Quincy was handed a cablegram. He hastily opened it. It had been sent from Boston; evidently Agatha Parker, overwhelmed by the crude impossibility of the West, had fled home again, and John Quincy's brief "San Francisco or nothing" had followed her there. Hence the delay.

The cablegram said simply: "Nothing. Agatha." John Quincy crushed it in his hand; he tried to suffer a little, but it was no use. He was a mighty happy man. The end of a romance—no. There had never been any nonsense of that kind between them—just an affectionate regard too slight to stand the strain of parting. Agatha was younger than he, she would marry some nice proper boy who had no desire to roam. And John Quincy Winterslip would read of her wedding—in the San Francisco papers.

He found Miss Minerva alone in the living-room. "It's none of my business," she said, "but I'm wondering what was in your cablegram."

"Nothing," he answered truthfully.

"All the same, you were very pleased to get it."

He nodded. "Yes. I imagine nobody was ever so happy over nothing before."

"Good heavens," she cried. "Have you given up grammar, too?"

"I'm thinking of it. How about going down the beach with me?"

She shook her head. "Some one is coming to look at the house—a leading lawyer, I believe he is. He's thinking of buying, and I feel I should be here to show him about. Barbara appears so listless and disinterested. Tell Sally Maynard I may drop in later."

At a quarter to eight, John Quincy took his bathing suit and wandered down Kalia Road. It was another of those nights; a bright moon was riding high; from a bungalow buried under purple alamander came the soft croon of Hawaiian music. Through the hedges of flaming hibiscus he caught again the exquisite odors of this exotic island.

Mrs. Maynard's big house was a particularly unlovely type of New England architecture, but a hundred flowering vines did much to conceal that fact. John Quincy found his hostess enthroned in her great airy drawing-room, surrounded by a handsome laughing group of the best people. Pleasant people, too; as she introduced him he began to wonder if he hadn't been missing a great deal of congenial companionship.

"I dragged him here against his will," the old lady explained. "I felt I owed it to Hawaii. He's been associating with the riff-raff long enough."

They insisted that he take an enormous chair, pressed cigarettes upon him, showered him with hospitable attentions. As he sat down and the chatter was resumed, he reflected that here was as civilized a company as Boston itself could offer. And why not? Most of these families came originally from New England, and had kept in their exile the old ideals of culture and caste.

"It might interest Beacon Street to know," Mrs. Maynard said, "that long before the days of 'forty-nine the people of California were sending their children over here to be educated in the missionary schools. And importing their wheat from here, too."

"Go on, tell him the other one, Aunt Sally," laughed a pretty girl in blue. "That about the first printing press in San Francisco being brought over from Honolulu."

Madame Maynard shrugged her shoulders. "Oh, what's the use? We're so far away, New England will never get us straight."

John Quincy looked up to see Carlota Egan in the doorway. A moment later Lieutenant Booth, of Richmond, appeared at her side. It occurred to the young man from Boston that the fleet was rather overdoing its stop at Honolulu.

Mrs. Maynard rose to greet the girl. "Come in, my dear. You know most of these people." She turned to the others. "This is Miss Egan, a neighbor of mine on the beach."

It was amusing to note that most of these people knew Carlota too. John Quincy smiled—the British Admiralty and the soap business. It must have been rather an ordeal for the girl, but she saw it through with a sweet graciousness that led John Quincy to reflect that she would be at home in England—if she went there.

Carlota sat down on a sofa, and while Lieutenant Booth was busily arranging a cushion at her back, John Quincy dropped down beside her. The sofa was, fortunately, too small for three.

"I rather expected to see you," he said in a low voice. "I was brought here to meet the best people of Honolulu, and the way I see it, you're the best of all."

She smiled at him, and again the chatter of small talk filled the room. Presently the voice of a tall young man with glasses rose above the general hubbub.

"They got a cable from Joe Clark out at the Country Club this afternoon," he announced.

The din ceased, and every one listened with interest. "Clark's our professional," explained the young man to John Quincy. "He went over a month ago to play in the British Open."

"Did he win?" asked the girl in blue.

"He was put out by Hagen in the semi-finals," the young man said. "But he had the distinction of driving the longest ball ever seen on the St. Andrews course."

"Why shouldn't he?" asked an older man. "He's got the strongest wrists I ever saw on anybody?"

John Quincy sat up, suddenly interested. "How do you account for that?" he asked.

The older man smiled. "We've all got pretty big wrists out here," he answered. "Surf-boarding—that's what does it. Joe Clark was a champion at one time—body-surfing and board-surfing too. He used to disappear for hours in the rollers out by the reef. The result was a marvelous wrist development. I've seen him drive a golf ball three hundred and eighty yards. Yes, sir, I'll bet he made those Englishmen sit up and take notice."

While John Quincy was thinking this over, some one suggested thtat it was time for the swim, and confusion reigned. A Chinese servant led the way to the dressing-rooms, which opened off the lanai, and the young people trouped joyously after him.

"I'll be waiting for you on the beach," John Quincy said to Carlota Egan.

"I came with Johnnie, you know," she reminded him.

"I know all about it," he answered. "But it was the week-end you promised to the navy. People who try to stretch their week-end through the following Wednesday night deserve all they get."

She laughed. "I'll look for you," she agreed.

He donned his bathing suit hastily in a room filled with flying clothes and great waving brown arms. Lieutenant Booth, he noted with satisfaction, was proceeding at a leisurely pace. Hurrying through a door that opened directly on the beach, he waited under a near-by hau tree. Presently Carlota came, slender and fragile-looking in the moonlight.

"Ah, here you are," John Quincy cried. "The farthest float."

"The farthest float it is," she answered.

They dashed into the warm silvery water and swam gaily off. Five minutes later they sat on the float together. The light on Diamond Head was winking; the lanterns of sampans twinkled out beyond the reef; the shore line of Honolulu was outlined by a procession of blinking stars controlled by dynamos. In the bright heavens hung a lunar rainbow, one colorful end in the Pacific and the other tumbling into the foliage ashore.

A gorgeous setting in which to be young and in love, and free to speak at last. John Quincy moved closer to the girl's side.

"Great night, isn't it?" he said.

"Wonderful," she answered softly.

"Cary, I want to tell you something, and that's why I brought you out here away from the others—"

"Somehow," she interrupted, "it doesn't seem quite fair to Johnnie."

"Never mind him. Has it ever occurred to you that my name's Johnnie, too."

She laughed. "Oh, but it couldn't be."

"What do you mean?"

"I mean I simply couldn't call you that. You're too dignified and—and remote. John Quincy—I believe I could call you John Quincy—"

"Well, make up your mind. You'll have to call me something, because I'm going to be hanging round pretty constantly in the future. Yes, my dear, I'll probably turn out to be about the least remote person in the world. That is, if I can make you see the future the way I see it. Cary dearest—"

A gurgle sounded behind them, and they turned around. Lieutenant Booth was climbing on to the raft. "Swam the last fifty yards under water to surprise you," he sputtered.

"Well, you succeeded," said John Quincy without enthusiasm.

The lieutenant sat down with the manner of one booked to remain indefinitely. "I'll tell the world it's some night," he offered.

"Speaking of the world, when do you fellows leave Honolulu?" asked John Quincy.

"I don't know. To-morrow, I guess. Me, I don't care if we never go.

Hawaii's not so easy to leave. Is it, Cary?"

She shook her head. "Hardest place I know of, Johnnie. I shall have to be sailing presently, and I know what a wrench it will be. Perhaps I'll follow the example of Waioli the swimmer, and leave the boat when it passes Waikiki."

They lolled for a moment in silence. Suddenly John Quincy sat up. "What was that you said?" he asked.

"About Waioli? Didn't I ever tell you? He was one of our best swimmers, and for years they tried to get him to go to the mainland to take part in athletic meets, like Duke Kahanamoku. But he was a sentimentalist—he couldn't bring himself to leave Hawaii. Finally they persuaded him, and one sunny morning he sailed on the *Matsonia*, with a very sad face. When the ship was opposite Waikiki he slipped overboard and swam ashore. And that was that. He never got on a ship again. You see—"

John Quincy was on his feet. "What time was it when we left the beach?" he asked in a low tense voice.

"About eight-thirty," said Both.

John Quincy talked very fast. "That means I've got just thirty minutes to get ashore, dress, and reach the dock before the *President Tyler* sails. I'm sorry to go, but it's vital—vital. Cary, I'd started to tell you something. I don't know when I'll get back, but I must see you when I do, either at Mrs. Maynard's or the hotel. Will you wait up for me?"

She was startled by the seriousness of his tone. "Yes, I'll be waiting," she told him.

"That's great." He hesitated a moment; it is a risky business to leave the girl you love on a float in the moonlight with a handsome naval officer. But it had to be done. "I'm off," he said, and dove.

When he came up he heard the lieutenant's voice. "Say, old man, that dive was all wrong. You let me show you—"

"Go to the devil," muttered John Quincy wetly, and swam with long powerful strokes toward the shore. Mad with haste, he plunged into the dressing-room, donned his clothes, then dashed out again. No time for apologies to his hostess. He ran along the beach to the Winterslip house. Haku was dozing in the hall.

"Wikiwiki," shouted John Quincy. "Tell the chauffeur to get the roadster into the drive and start the engine. Wake up! Travel! Where's Miss Barbara?"

"Last seen on beach—" began the startled Haku.

On the bench under the hau tree he found Barbara sitting alone. He stood panting before her.

"My dear," he said. "I know at last who killed your father—"

She was on her feet. "You do?"

"Yes—shall tell you?"

"No," she said. "No—I can't bear to hear. It's too horrible."

"Then you've suspected?"

"Yes—just suspicion—a feeling—intuition. I couldn't believe it—I didn't want to believe it. I went away to get it out of my mind. It's all too terrible—"

He put his hand on her shoulder. "Poor Barbara. Don't you worry. You won't appear in this in any way. I'll keep you out of it."

"What—what has happened?"

"Can't stop now. Tell you later." He ran toward the drive. Miss Minerva appeared from the house. "Haven't time to talk," he cried, leaping into the roadster.

"But John Quincy—a curious thing has happened—that lawyer who was here to look at the house—he said that Dan, just a week before he died, spoke to him about a new will—"

"That's good! That's evidence!" John Quincy cried.

"But why a new will? Surely Barbara was all he had—"

"Listen to me," cut in John Quincy. "You've delayed me already. Get the big car and go to the station—tell that to Hallet. Tell him too that I'm on the *President Tyler* and to send Chan there at once."

He stepped on the gas. By the clock in the automobile he had just seventeen minutes to reach the dock before the *President Tyler* would sail. He shot like a madman through the brilliant Hawaiian night. Kalakaua Avenue, smooth and deserted, proved a glorious speedway. It took him just eight minutes to travel the three miles to the dock. A bit of Traffic and an angry policeman in the center of the city caused the delay.

A scattering of people in the dim pier-shed waited for the imminent sailing of the liner. John Quincy dashed through them and up the gangplank. The second officer, Hepworth, stood at the top.

"Hello, Mr. Winterslip," he said. "You sailing?"

"No. But let me aboard!"

"I'm sorry. We're about to draw in the plank."

"No, no—you mustn't. This is life and death. Hold off just a few minutes. There's a steward named Bowker—I must find him at once. Life and death, I tell you."

Hepworth stood aside. "Oh, well, in that case. But, please hurry, sir—"

"I will." John Quincy passed him on the run. He was on his way to the cabins presided over by Bowker when a tall figure caught his eye. A man in a long green ulster and a battered green hat—a hat John Quincy had last seen on the links of the Oahu Country Club.

The tall figure moved on up a stairway to the topmost deck. John Quincy followed. He saw the ulster disappear into one of the de luxe cabins. Still he followed, and pushed open the cabin door. The man in the ulster was back to, but he swung round suddenly.

"Ah, Mr. Jennison," John Quincy cried. "Were you thinking of sailing on this boat?"

For an instant Jennison stared at him. "I was," he said quietly.

"Forget it," John Quincy answered. "You're going ashore with me."

"Really? What is your authority?"

"No authority whatever," said the boy grimly. "I'm taking you, that's all."

Jennison smiled, but there was a gleam of hate behind it. And in John Quincy's heart, usually so gentle and civilized, there was hate too as he faced this man. He thought of Dan Winterslip, dead on his cot. He thought of Jennison walking down the gangplank with them that morning they landed, Jennison putting his arm about poor Barbara when she faltered under the blow. He thought of the shots fired at him from the bush, of the red-haired man battering him in that red room. Well, he must fight again. No way out of it. The siren of the *President Tyler* sounded a sharp warning.

"You get out of here," said Jennison through his teeth. "I'll go with you to the gangplank—"

He stopped, as the disadvantages of that plan came home to him. His right hand went swiftly to his pocket. Inspired, John Quincy seized a filled water bottle and hurled it at the man's head. Jennison dodged; the bottle crashed through one of the windows. The clatter of glass rang through the night, but no one appeared. John Quincy saw Jennison leap toward him, something gleaming in his hand. Stepping aside, he threw himself on the man's back and forced him to his knees. He seized the wrist of Jennison's right hand, which held the automatic, in a firm grip. They kept that posture for a moment, and then Jennison began slowly to rise to his feet. The hand that held the pistol began to tear away. John Quincy shut his teeth and sought to maintain his grip. But he was up against a more powerful antagonist than the red-haired sailor, he was outclassed, and the realization of it crept over him with a sickening force.

Jennison was on his feet now, the right hand nearly free. Another moment—what then, John Quincy wondered? This man had no intention of letting him go ashore; he had changed that plan the moment he put it into words. A muffled shot, and later in the night when the ship was well out on the Pacific— John Quincy thought of Boston, his mother. He thought of Carlota waiting his return. He summoned his strength for one last desperate effort to renew his grip.

A serene, ivory-colored face appeared suddenly at the broken window. An arm with a weapon was extended through the jagged opening.

"Relinquish the firearms, Mr. Jennison," commanded Charlie Chan, "or I am forced to make fatal insertion in vital organ belonging to you."

Jennison's pistol dropped to the floor, and John Quincy staggered back against the berth. At that instant the door opened and Hallet, followed by the detective, Spencer, came in.

"Hello, Winterslip, what are you doing here?" the captain said. He thrust a paper into one of the pockets of the green ulster. "Come along, Jennison," he said. "We want you."

Limply John Quincy followed them from the stateroom. Outside they were joined by Chan. At the top of the gangplank Hallet paused. "We'll wait a minute for Hepworth," he said.

John Quincy put his hand on Chan's shoulder. "Charlie, how can I ever thank you? You saved my life."

Chan bowed. "My own pleasure is not to be worded. I have saved a life here and there, but never before one that had beginning in cultured city of Boston. Always a happy item on the golden scroll of memory."

Hepworth came up. "It's all right," he said. "The captain has agreed to delay our sailing one hour. I'll go to the station with you."

On the way down the gangplank, Chan turned to John Quincy. "Speaking heartily for myself, I congratulate your bravery. It is clear you leaped upon this Jennison with vigorous and triumphant mood of heart. But he would have pushed you down. He would have conquered. And why? The answer is, such powerful wrists."

"A great surf-boarder, eh?" John Quincy said.

Chan looked at him keenly. "You are no person's fool. Ten years ago this Harry Jennison are champion swimmer in all Hawaii. I extract that news from ancient sporting pages of Honolulu journal. But he have not been in the water much here lately. Pursuing the truth further, not since the night he killed Dan Winterslip."

22

The Light Streams Through

They moved on through the pier-shed to the street, where Hepworth, Jennison and the three policemen got into Hallet's car. The captain turned to John Quincy.

"You coming, Mr. Winterslip?" he inquired.

"I've got my own car," the boy explained. "I'll follow you in that."

The roadster was not performing at its best, and he reached the station house a good five minutes after the policemen. He noted Dan Winterslip's big limousine parked in the street outside.

In Hallet's room he found the captain and Chan closeted with a third man. It took a second glance at the latter to identify him as Mr. Saladine, for the little man of the lost teeth now appeared a great deal younger than John Quincy had thought him.

"Ah, Mr. Winterslip," remarked Hallet. He turned to Saladine. "Say, Larry, you've got me into a heap of trouble with this boy. He accused me of trying to shield you. I wish you'd loosen up for him."

Saladine smiled "Why, I don't mind. My job out here is about finished. Of course, Mr. Winterslip will keep what I tell him under his hat?"

"Naturally," replied John Quincy. He noticed that the man spoke with no trace of a lisp. "I perceive you've found your teeth," he added.

"Oh, yes—I found them in my trunk, where I put them the day I arrived at Waikiki," answered Saladine. "When my teeth were knocked out twenty years ago in a football game, I was broken-hearted, but the loss has been a great help to me in my work. A man hunting his bridge work in the water is a figure of ridicule and mirth. No one ever thinks of connecting him with serious affairs. He can prowl about a beach to his heart's content. Mr. Winterslip, I am a special agent of the Treasury Department sent out here to break up the opium ring. My name, of course, is not Saladine."

"Oh," said John Quincy, "I understand at last."

"I'm glad you do," remarked Hallet. "I don't know whether you're familiar with the way our opium smugglers work. The dope is brought in from the Orient on tramp steamers—the *Mary S. Allison*, for example. When they arrive off Waikiki they knock together a few small rafts and load 'em with tins of the stuff. A fleet of little boats, supposedly out there for the fishing, pick up these rafts and bring the dope ashore. It's taken downtown and hidden on ships bound for 'Frisco—usually those that ply only between here and the mainland, because they're not so closely watched at the other end. But it just happened that the quartermaster of the *President Tyler* is one of their go-betweens. We searched his cabin this evening and found it packed with the stuff."

"The quartermaster of the *President Tyler*," repeated John Quincy. "That's Dick Kaohla's friend."

"Yeah—I'm coming to Dick. He's been in charge of the pick-up fleet here. He was out on that business the night of the murder. Saladine saw him and told me all about it in that note, which was my reason for letting the boy go."

"I owe you an apology," John Quincy said.

"Oh, that's all right." Hallet was in great good humor. "Larry here has got some of the higher-ups, too. For instance, he's discovered that Jennison is the lawyer for the ring, defending any of them who are caught and brought before the commissioner. The fact has no bearing on Dan Winterslip's murder—unless Winterslip knew about it, and that was one of the reasons he didn't want Jennison to marry his girl."

Saladine stood up. "I'll turn the quartermaster over to you," he said. "In view of this other charge, you can of course have Jennison too. That's all for me. I'll go along."

"See you to-morrow, Larry," Hallet answered. Saladine went out, and the captain turned to John Quincy. "Well, my boy, this is our big night. I don't know what you were doing in Jennison's cabin, but if you'd picked him for the murderer, I'll say you're good."

"That's just what I'd done," John Quincy told him. "By the way, have you seen my aunt? She's got hold of a rather interesting bit of information—"

"I've seen her," Hallet said. "She's with the prosecutor now, telling it to him. By the way, Greene's waiting for us. Come along."

They went into the prosecutor's office. Greene was alert and eager, a stenographer was at his elbow, and Miss Minerva sat near his desk.

"Hello, Mr. Winterslip," he said. "What do you think of our police force now? Pretty good, eh, pretty good. Sit down, won't you?" He glanced through some papers on his desk while John Quincy, Hallet and Chan found chairs. "I don't mind telling you, this thing has knocked me all in a heap. Harry Jennison and I are old friends; I had lunch with him at the club only yesterday. I'm going to proceed a little differently than I would with an ordinary criminal."

John Quincy half rose from his chair. "Don't get excited," Greene smiled. "Jennison will get all that's coming to him, friendship or no friendship. What I mean is that if I can save the territory the expense of a long trial by dragging a confession out of him at once, I intend to do it. He's coming in here in a moment, and I propose to reveal my whole hand to him, from start to finish. That may seem foolish, but it isn't. For I hold aces, all aces, and he'll know it as quickly as any one."

The door opened. Spencer ushered Jennison into the room, and then withdrew. The accused man stood there, proud, haughty, defiant, a viking of the tropics, a blond giant at bay but unafraid.

"Hello, Jennison," Greene said. "I'm mighty sorry about this—"

"You ought to be," Jennison replied. "You're making an awful fool of yourself. What is this damned nonsense, anyhow—"

"Sit down," said the prosecutor sharply. He indicated a chair on the opposite side of the desk. He had already turned the shade on his desk lamp so the light would shine full in the face of any one sitting there. "That lamp bother you, Harry?" he asked.

"Why should it?" Jennison demanded.

"Good," smiled Greene. "I believe Captain Hallet served you with a warrant on the boat. Have you looked at it, by any chance?"

"I have."

The prosecutor leaned across the desk. "Murder, Jennison!"

Jennison's expression did not change. "Damned nonsense, as I told you. Why should I murder any one?"

"Ah, the motive," Greene replied. "You're quite right, we should begin with that. Do you wish to be represented here by counsel?"

Jennison shook his head. "I guess I'm lawyer enough to puncture this silly business," he replied.

"Very well." Greene turned to his stenographer. "Get this." The man nodded, and the prosecutor addressed Miss Minerva. "Miss Winterslip, we'll start with you."

Miss Minerva leaned forward. "Mr. Dan Winterslip's house on the beach has, as I told you, been offered for sale by his daughter. After dinner this evening a gentleman came to look at it—a prominent lawyer named Hailey. As we went over the house, Mr. Hailey mentioned that he had met Dan Winterslip on the street a week before his death, and that my cousin had spoken to him about coming in shortly to draw up a new will. He did not say what the provisions of the will were to be, nor did he ever carry out his intention."

"Ah yes," said Greene. "But Mr. Jennison here was your cousin's lawyer?"

"He was."

"If he wanted to draw a new will, he wouldn't ordinarily have gone to a stranger for that purpose."

"Not ordinarily. Unless he had some good reason."

"Precisely. Unless, for instance, the will had some connection with Harry Jennison."

"I object," Jennison cried. "This is mere conjecture."

"So it is," Greene answered. "But we're not in court. We can conjecture if we like. Suppose, Miss Winterslip, the will was concerned with Jennison in some way. What do you imagine the connection to have been?"

"I don't have to imagine," replied Miss Minerva. "I know."

"Ah, that's good. You know. Go on."

"Before I came down here to-night, I had a talk with my niece. She admitted that her father knew she and Jennison were in love, and that he had bitterly opposed the match. He had even gone so far as to say he would disinherit her if she went through with it."

"Then the new will Dan Winterslip intended to make would probably have been to the effect that in the event his daughter married Jennison, she was not to inherit a penny of his money?"

"There isn't any doubt of it," said Miss Minerva firmly.

"You asked for a motive, Jennison," Green said. "That's motive enough for me. Everybody knows you're money mad. You wanted to marry Winterslip's daughter, the richest girl in the Islands. He said you couldn't have her—not with the money too. But you're not the sort to make a penniless marriage. You were determined to get both Barbara Winterslip and her father's property. Only one person stood in your way—Dan Winterslip. And that's how you happened to be on his lanai that Monday night—"

"Wait a minute," Jennison protested. "I wasn't on his lanai. I was on board the *President Tyler*, and everybody knows that ship didn't land its passengers until nine the following morning—"

"I'm coming to that," Greene told him. "Just now—by the way, what time is it?"

Jennison took from his pocket a watch on the end of a slender chain. "It's a quarter past nine."

"Ah, yes. Is that the watch you usually carry?"

"It is."

"Ever wear a wrist watch?"

Jennison hesitated. "Occasionally."

"Only occasionally." The prosecutor rose and came round his desk. "Let me see your left wrist, please."

Jennison held out his arm. It was tanned a deep brown, but on the wrist was etched in white the outline of a watch and its encircling strap.

Greene smiled. "Yes, you have worn a wrist watch—and you've worn it pretty constantly, from the look of things." He took a small object from his pocket and held it in front of Jennison. "This watch, perhaps?" Jennison regarded it stonily. "Ever see it before?" Greene asked. "No? Well, suppose we try it on, anyhow." He put the watch in position and fastened it. "I can't help noting, Harry," he continued, "that it fits rather neatly over that white outline on your wrist. And the prong of the buckle falls naturally into the most worn of the holes on the strap."

"What of that?" asked Jennison.

"Oh, coincidence, probably. You have abnormally large wrists, however. Surf-boarding, swimming, eh? But that's something else I'll speak of later." He turned to Miss Minerva. "Will you please come over here, Miss Winterslip."

She came, and as she reached his side, the prosecutor suddenly bent over and switched off the light on his desk. Save for a faint glimmer through a transom, the room was in darkness. Miss Minerva was conscious of dim huddled figures, a circle of white faces, a tense silence. The prosecutor was lifting something slowly toward her startled eyes. A watch, worn on a human wrist—a watch with an illuminated dial on which the figure two was almost obliterated.

"Look at that and tell me," came the prosecutor's voice. "You have seen it before?"

"I have," she answered firmly.

"Where?"

"In the dark in Dan Winterslip's living-room just after midnight the thirtieth of June."

Greene flashed on the light. "Thank you, Miss Winterslip." He retired behind his desk and pressed a button. "You identify it by some distinguishing mark, I presume?"

"I do. The numeral two, which is pretty well obscured."

Spencer appeared at the door. "Send the Spaniard in," Greene ordered. "That is all for the present, Miss Winterslip."

Cabrera entered, and his eyes were frightened as they looked at Jennison. At a nod from the prosecutor, Chan removed the wrist watch and handed it to the Spaniard.

"You know that watch, José?" Green asked.

"I—I—yes," answered the boy.

"Don't be afraid," Greene urged. "Nobody's going to hurt you. I want you to repeat the story you told me this afternoon. You have no regular job. You're a sort of confidential errand boy for Mr. Jennison here."

"I was."

"Yes—that's all over now. You can speak out. On the morning of Wednesday, July second, you were in Mr. Jennison's office. He gave you this wrist watch and told you to take it out and get it repaired. Something was the matter with it. It wasn't running. You took it to a big jewelry store. What happened?"

"The man said it is very badly hurt. To fix it would cost more than a new watch. I go back and tell Mr. Jennison. He laugh and say it is mine as a gift."

"Precisely." Greene referred to a paper on his desk. "Late in the afternoon of Thursday, July third, you sold the watch. To whom?"

"To Lau Ho, Chinese jeweler in Maunakea Street. On Saturday evening maybe six o'clock Mr. Jennison telephone my home, much excited. Must have watch again, and will pay any price. I speed to Lau Ho's store. Watch is sold once more, now to unknown Japanese. Late at night I see Mr.

Jennison and he curse me with anger. Get the watch, he says. I have been hunting, but I could not find it."

Greene turned to Jennison. "You were a little careless with that watch, Harry. But no doubt you figured you were pretty safe—you had your alibi. Then, too, when Hallet detailed the clues to you on Winterslip's lanai the morning after the crime, he forgot to mention that some one had seen the watch. It was one of those happy accidents that are all we have to count on in this work. By Saturday night you realized your danger—just how you discovered it I don't know—"

"I do," John Quincy interrupted.

"What! What's that?" said Greene.

"On Saturday afternoon," John Quincy told him, "I played golf with Mr. Jennison. On our way back to town, we talked over the clues in this case, and I happened to mention the wrist watch. I can see now it was the first he had heard of it. He was to dine with us at the beach, but he asked to be put down at his office to sign a few letters. I waited below. It must have been then that he called up this young man in an effort to locate the watch."

"Great stuff," said Greene enthusiastically. "That finishes the watch, Jennison. I'm surprised you wore it, but you probably knew that it would be vital to you to keep track of the time, and you figured, rightly, that it would not be immediately affected by the salt water—"

"What the devil are you talking about?" demanded Jennison.

Again Greene pressed a button on his desk. Spencer appeared at once. "Take this Spaniard," the prosecutor directed, "and bring in Hepworth and the quartermaster." He turned again to Jennison. "I'll show you what I'm talking about in just a minute. On the night of June thirtieth you were a passenger on the *President Tyler*, which was lying by until dawn out near the channel entrance?"

"I was."

"No passengers were landed from that ship until the following morning?"

"That's a matter of record."

"Very well." The second officer of the *President Tyler* came in, followed by a big hulking sailorman John Quincy recognized as the quartermaster of that vessel. He was interested to note a ring on the man's right hand, and his mind went back to that encounter in the San Francisco attic.

"Mr. Hepworth," the prosecutor began, "on the night of June thirtieth your ship reached this port too late to dock. You anchored off Waikiki. On such an occasion, who is on deck—say, from midnight on?"

"The second officer," Hepworth told him. "In this case, myself. Also the quartermaster."

"The accommodation ladder is let down the night before?"

"Usually, yes. It was let down that night."

"Who is stationed near it?"

"The quartermaster."

"Ah, yes. You were in charge then on the night of June thirtieth. Did you notice anything unusual on that occasion?"

Hepworth nodded. "I did. The quartermaster appeared to be under the influence of liquor. At three o'clock I found him dozing near the accommodation ladder. I roused him. When I came back from checking up the anchor bearings before turning in at dawn—about four-thirty—he was dead to the world. I put him in his cabin, and the following morning I of course reported him."

"You noticed nothing else out of the ordinary?"

"Nothing, sir," Hepworth replied.

"Thank you very much. Now, you—" Greene turned to the quarter-master. "You were drunk on duty the night of June Thirtieth. Where did you get the booze?" The man hesitated. "Before you say anything, let me give you a bit of advice. The truth, my man. You're in pretty bad already. I'm not making any promises, but if you talk straight here it may help you in that other matter. If you lie, it will go that much harder with you."

"I ain't going to lie," promised the quartermaster.

"All right. Where did you get your liquor?"

The man nodded toward Jennison. "He gave it to me."

"He did, eh? Tell me all about it."

"I met him on deck just after midnight—we was still moving. I knew him before—him and me—"

"In the opium game, both of you. I understand that. You met him on deck—"

"I did, and he says, you're on watch to-night, eh, and I says I am. So he slips me a little bottle an' says, this will help you pass the time. I ain't a drinking man, so help me I ain't, an' I took just a nip, but there was something in that whiskey, I'll swear to it. My head was all funny like, an' the next I knew I was waked up in my cabin with the bad news I was wanted above."

"What became of that bottle?"

"I dropped it overboard on my way to see the captain. I didn't want nobody to find it."

"Did you see anything the night of June thirtieth? Anything peculiar?"

"I seen plenty, sir—but it was that drink. Nothing you would want to hear about."

"All right." The prosecutor turned to Jennison. "Well, Harry—you drugged him, didn't you? Why? Because you were going ashore, eh? Because you knew he'd be on duty at the ladder when you returned, and you didn't want him to see you. So you dropped something into that whiskey—"

"Guess work," cut in Jennison, stiff unruffled. "I used to have some respect for you as a lawyer, but it's all gone now. If this is the best you can offer—"

"But it isn't," said Greene pleasantly. Again he pushed the button. "I've something much better, Harry, if you'll only wait." He turned to Hepworth. "There's a steward on your ship named Bowker," he began, and John Quincy thought that Jennison stiffened. "How has he been behaving lately?"

"Well, he got pretty drunk in Hong-kong," Hepworth answered. "But that, of course, was the money."

"What money?"

"It's this way. The last time we sailed out of Honolulu harbor for the Orient, over two weeks ago, I was in the purser's office. It was just as we were passing Diamond Head. Bowker came in, and he had a big fat en-velope that he wanted to deposit in the purser's safe. He said it contained a lot of money. The purser wouldn't be responsible for it without seeing it, so Bowker slit the envelope—and there were ten one hundred dollar bills. The purser made another package of it and put it in the safe. He told me Bowker took out a couple of the bills when we reached Hong-kong."

"Where would a man like Bowker get all that money?"

"I can't imagine. He said he'd put over a business deal in Honolulu but—well, we knew Bowker."

The door opened. Evidently Spencer guessed who was wanted this time, for he pushed Bowker into the room. The steward of the *President Tyler* was bedraggled and bleary.

"Hello, Bowker," said the prosecutor. "Sober now, aren't you?"

"I'll tell the world I am," replied Bowker. "They've walked me to San Francisco and back. Can—can I sit down?"

"Of course," Greene smiled. "This afternoon, while you were still drunk, you told a story to Willie Chan, out at Okamoto's auto stand on Kalakaua Avenue. Later on, early this evening, you repeated it to Captain Hallet and me. I'll have to ask you to go over it again."

Bowker glanced toward Jennison, then quickly looked away. "Always ready to oblige," he answered.

"You're a steward on the *President Tyler*," Greene continued. "On your last trip over here from the mainland Mr. Jennison occupied one of your rooms—number 97. He was alone in it, I believe?"

"All alone. He paid extra for the privilege, I hear. Always traveled that way."

"Room 97 was on the main deck, not far from the accommodation ladder?"

"Yes, that's right."

"Tell us what happened after you anchored off Waikiki the night of June thirtieth."

Bowker adjusted his gold-rimmed glasses with the gesture of a man about to make an after-dinner speech. "Well, I was up pretty late that night. Mr. Winterslip here had loaned me some books—there was one I was particularly interested in. I want to finish it so I could give it to him to take ashore in the morning. It was nearly two o'clock when I finally got through it, and I was feeling stuffy, so I went on deck for a breath of air."

"You stopped not far from the accommodation ladder?"

"Yes sir, I did."

"Did you notice the quartermaster?"

"Yes—he was sound asleep in a deck chair. I went over and leaned on the rail, the ladder was just beneath me. I'd been standing there a few minutes when suddenly somebody came up out of the water and put his hands on the lowest rung. I drew back quickly and stood in a shadow.

"Well, pretty soon this man comes creeping up the ladder to the deck. He was barefooted, and all in black—black pants and shirt. I watched him. He went over and bent above the quartermaster, then started toward me down the deck. He was walking on tiptoe, but even then I didn't get wise to the fact anything was wrong.

"I stepped out of the shadow. 'Fine night for a swim, Mr. Jennison,' I said. And I saw at once that I'd made a social error. He gave one jump in my direction and his hands closed on my throat. I thought my time had come."

"He was wet, wasn't he?" Greene asked.

"Dripping. He left a trail of water on the deck."

"Did you notice a watch on his wrist?"

"Yes, but you can bet I didn't make any study of it. I had other things to think about just then. I managed to sort of ooze out of his grip, and I told him to cut it out or I'd yell. 'Look here,' he says, 'you and I can talk business, I guess. Come into my cabin.'

"But I wasn't wanting any tête-à-tête with him in any cabin, I said I'd see him in the morning, and after I'd promised to say nothing to anybody, he let me go. I went to bed, pretty much puzzled.

"The next morning, when I went into his cabin, there he was all fresh and rosy and smiling. If I'd had so much as a whiff of booze the night before, I'd have thought I never saw what I did. I went in there thinking

I might get a hundred dollars out of the affair, but the minute he spoke I began to smell important money. He said no one must know about his swim the night before. How much did I want? Well, I held my breath and said ten thousand dollars. And I nearly dropped dead when he answered I could have it."

Bowker turned to John Quincy. "I don't know what you'll think of me. I don't know what Tim would think. I'm not a crook by nature. But I was fed up and choking over that steward job. I wanted a little newspaper of my own, and up to that minute I couldn't see myself getting it. And you must remember that I didn't know then what was in the air—murder. Later, when I did find out, I was scared to breathe. I didn't know what they could do to me." He turned to Greene. "That's all fixed," he said.

"I've promised you immunity," the prosecutor answered. "I'll keep my word. Go on—you agreed to accept the ten thousand?"

"I did. I went to his office at twelve. One of the conditions was that I could stay on the *President Tyler* until she got back to San Francisco, and after that I was never to show my face out this way again. It suited me. Mr. Jennison introduced me to this Cabrera, who was to chaperon me the rest of that day. I'll say he did. When I went aboard the ship, he handed me a thousand dollars in an envelope.

"When I came back this time, I was to spend the day with Cabrera and get the other nine grand when I sailed. This morning when we tied up I saw the Spaniard on the dock, but by the time I'd landed he had disappeared. I met this Willie Chan and we had a large day. This fusel oil they sell out here loosened my tongue, but I'm not sorry. Of course, the rosy dream has faded, and it's my flat feet on the deck from now to the end of time. But the shore isn't so much any more, with all the bar-rooms under cover, and this sea life keeps a man out in the open air. As I say, I'm not sorry I talked. I can look any man in the eye again and tell him to go to—" He glanced at Miss Minerva. "Madam, I will not name the precise locality."

Greene stood. "Well, Jennison, there's my case. I've tipped it all off to you, but I wanted you to see for yourself how air-tight it is. There are two courses open to you—you can let this go to trial with a plea of not guilty. A long humiliating ordeal for you. Or you can confess here and now and throw yourself on the mercy of the court. If you're the sensible man I think you are, that's what you'll do."

Jennison did not answer, did not even look at the prosecutor. "It was a very neat idea," Greene went on. "I'll grant you that. Only one thing puzzles me—did it come as the inspiration of the moment, or did you plan it all out in advance? You've been over to the mainland rather often of late—were you waiting your chance? Anyhow, it came, didn't it—it came at last. And for a swimmer like you, child's play. You didn't need that ladder when you left the vessel—perhaps you went overboard while the *President Tyler* was still moving. A quick silent dive, a little way under water in case any one was watching from the deck, and then a long but easy swim ashore. And there you were, on the beach at Waikiki. Not far away Dan Winterslip was asleep on his lanai, with not so much as a locked door between you. Dan Winterslip, who stood between you and what you wanted. A little struggle—a quick thrust of your knife. Come on, Jennison, don't be a fool. It's the best way out for you now. A full confession."

Jennison leaped to his feet, his eyes flashing. "I'll see you in hell first!" he cried.

"Very well—if you feel that way about it—" Greene turned his back upon him and began a low-toned conversation with Hallet. Jennison and Charlie

Chan were together on one side of the desk. Chan took out a pencil and accidentally dropped it on the floor. He stooped to pick it up.

John Quincy saw that the butt of a pistol carried in Chan's hip pocket protruded from under his coat. He saw Jennison spring forward and snatch the gun. With a cry John Quincy moved nearer, but Greene seized his arm and held him. Charlie Chan seemed unaccountably oblivious to what was going on.

Jennison put the muzzle of the pistol to his forehead and pulled the trigger. A sharp click—and that was all. The pistol fell from his hand.

"That's it!" cried Greene triumphantly. "That's my confession, and not a word spoken. I've witnesses, Jennison—they all saw you—you couldn't stand the disgrace—a man in your position—you tried to kill yourself. With an empty gun." He went over and patted Chan on the shoulder. "A great idea, Charlie," he said. "Chan thought of it," he added to Jennison. "The Oriental mind, Harry. Rather subtle, isn't it?"

But Jennison had dropped back into his chair and buried his face in his hands.

"I'm sorry," said Greene gently. "But we've got you. Maybe you'll talk now."

Jennison looked up slowly. The defiance was gone from his face; it was lined and old.

"Maybe I will," he said hoarsely.

23

Moonlight at the Crossroads

They filed out, leaving Jennison with Greene and the stenographer. In the anteroom Chan approached John Quincy.

"You go home decked in the shining garments of success," he said. "One thought is tantalizing me. At simultaneous moment you arrive at same conclusion we do. To reach there you must have leaped across considerable cavity."

John Quincy laughed. "I'll say I did. It came to me to-night. First, some one mentioned a golf professional with big wrists who drove a long ball. I had a quick flash of Jennison on the links here, and his terrific drives. Big wrists, they told me, meant that a man was proficient in the water. Then some one else—a young woman—spoke of a champion swimmer who left a ship off Waikiki. That was the first time the idea of such a thing had occurred to me. I was pretty warm then, and I felt Bowker was the man who could verify my suspicion. When I rushed aboard the *President Tyler* to find him, I saw Jennison about to sail, and that confirmed my theory. I went after him."

"A brave performance," commented Chan.

"But as you can see, Charlie, I didn't have an iota of real evidence. Just guesswork. You were the one who furnished the proof."

"Proof are essential in this business," Chan replied.

"I'm tantalized too, Charlie. I remember you in the library. You were on the track long before I was. How come?"

Chan grinned. "Seated at our ease in All American Restaurant that first

night, you will recall I spoke of Chinese people as sensitive, like camera
film. A look, a laugh, a gesture, something go click. Bowker enters and
hovering above, says with alcoholic accent; 'I'm my own mashter, ain't I?'
In my mind, the click. He is not own master. I follow to dock, behold when
Spaniard present envelope. But for days I am fogged. I can only learn
Cabrera and Jennison are very close. Clues continue to burst in our countenance. The occasion remains suspensive. At the library I read of Jennison
the fine swimmer. After that, the watch, and triumph."

Miss Minerva moved on toward the door. "May I have great honor to
accompany you to car?" asked Chan.

Outside, John Quincy directed the chauffeur to return alone to Waikiki
with the limousine. "You're riding out with me," he told his aunt. "I want
to talk with you."

She turned to Charlie Chan. "I congratulate you. You've got brains, and
they count."

He bowed low. "From you that compliment glows rosy red. At this moment of parting, my heart droops. My final wish—the snowy chilling days
of winter and the scorching windless days of summer—may they all be the
springtime for you."

"You're very kind," she said softly.

John Quincy took his hand. "It's been great fun knowing you, Charlie,"
he remarked.

"You will go again to the mainland," Chan said. "The angry ocean rolling
between us. Still I shall carry the memory of your friendship like a flower
in my heart." John Quincy climbed into the car. "And the parting may not
be eternal," Chan added cheerfully. "The joy of travel may yet be mine.
I shall look forward to the day when I may call upon you in your home
and shake a healthy hand."

John Quincy started the car and slipping away, they left Charlie Chan
standing like a great Buddha on the curb.

"Poor Barbara," said Miss Minerva presently. "I dread to face her with
this news. But then, it's not altogether news at that. She told me she'd been
conscious of something wrong between her and Jennison ever since they
landed. She didn't think he killed her father, but she believed he was
involved in it somehow. She is planning to settle with Brade to-morrow and
leave the next day, probably for ever. I've persuaded her to come to Boston
for a long visit. You'll see her there."

John Quincy shook his head. "No, I shan't. But thanks for reminding
me. I must go to the cable office at once."

When he emerged from the office and again entered the car, he was
smiling happily.

"In San Francisco," he explained, "Roger accused me of being a Puritan
survival. He ran over a little list of adventures he said had never happened
to me. Well, most of them have happened now, and I cabled to tell him
so. I also said I'd take that job with him."

Miss Minerva frowned. "Think it over carefully," she warned. "San Francisco isn't Boston. The cultural standard is, I fancy, much lower. You'll be
lonely there—"

"Oh, no, I shan't. Some one will be there with me. At least, I hope she
will."

"Agatha?"

"No, not Agatha. The cultural standard was too low for her. She's broken
our engagement."

"Barbara, then?"

"Not Barbara, either."

"But I have sometimes thought—"

"You thought Barbara sent Jennison packing because of me. Jennison thought so too—it's all clear now. That was why he tried to frighten me into leaving Honolulu, and set his opium running friends on me when I wouldn't go. But Barbara is not in love with me. We understand now why she broke her engagement."

"Neither Agatha nor Barbara," repeated Miss Minerva. "Then who—"

"You haven't met her yet, but that happy privilege will be yours before you sleep. The sweetest girl in the Islands—or in the world. The daughter of Jim Egan, whom you have been heard to refer to as a glorified beachcomber."

Again Miss Minerva frowned. "It's a great risk, John Quincy. She hasn't our background—"

"No, and that's a pleasant change. She's the niece of your old friend—you knew that?"

"I did," answered Miss Minerva softly.

"Your dear friend of the 'eighties. What was it you said to me? If your chance ever comes—"

"I hope you will be very happy," his aunt said. "When you write it to your mother, be sure and mention Captain Cope of the British Admiralty. Poor Grace! That will be all she'll have to cling to—after the wreck."

"What wreck?"

"The wreck of all her hopes for you."

"Nonsense. Mother will understand. She knows I'm a roaming Winterslip, and when we roam, we roam."

They found Madame Maynard seated in her living-room with a few of her more elderly guests. From the beach came the sound of youthful revelry.

"Well, my boy," the old woman cried, "it appears you couldn't stay away from your policemen friends one single evening, after all. I give you up."

John Quincy laughed. "I'm pau now. By the way, Carlota Egan—is she—"

"They're all out there somewhere," the hostess said. "They came in for a bit of supper—by the way, there are sandwiches in the dining-room and—"

"Not just now," said John Quincy. "Thank you so much. I'll see you again, of course—"

He dashed out on the sand. A group of young people under the hau tree informed him that Carlota Egan was on the farthest float. Alone? Well, no—that naval lieutenant—

He was, he reflected as he hurried on toward the water, a bit fed up with the navy. That was hardly the attitude he should have taken, considering all the navy had done for him. But it was human. And John Quincy was human at last.

For an instant he stood at the water's edge. His bathing suit was in the dressing-room, but he never gave it a thought. He kicked off his shoes, tossed aside his coat, and plunged into the breakers. The blood of the wandering Winterslips was racing through his veins; hot blood that tropical waters had ever been powerless to cool.

Sure enough, Carlota Egan and Lieutenant Booth were together on the float. John Quincy climbed up beside them.

"Well, I'm back," he announced.

"I'll tell the world you're back," said the lieutenant. "And all wet, too."

They sat there. Across a thousand miles of warm water the trade winds came to fan their checks. Just above the horizon hung the Southern Cross; the Island lights trembled along the shore; the yellow eye on Diamond Head was winking. A gorgeous setting. Only one thing was wrong with it. It seemed rather crowded.

John Quincy had an inspiration. "Just as I hit the water," he remarked. "I thought I heard you say something about my dive. Didn't you like it?"

"It was rotten," replied the lieutenant amiably.

"You offered to show me what was wrong with it, I believe?"

"Sure. If you want me to."

"By all means," said John Quincy. "Learn one thing every day. That's my motto."

Lieutenant Booth went to the end of the springboard. "In the first place, always keep your ankles close together—like this."

"I've got you," answered John Quincy.

"And hold your arms tight against your ears."

"The tighter the better, as far as I'm concerned."

"Then double up like a jackknife," continued the instructor. He doubled up like a jackknife and rose into the air.

At the same instant John Quincy seized the girl's hands. "Listen to me. I can't wait another second. I want to tell you that I love you—"

"You're mad," she cried.

"Mad about you. Ever since that day on the ferry—"

"But your people?"

"What about my people? It's just you and I—we'll live in San Francisco—that is, if you love me—"

"Well, I—"

"In heaven's name, be quick. That human submarine is floating around here under us. You love me, don't you? You'll marry me?"

"Yes."

He took her in his arms and kissed her. Only the wandering Winterslips could kiss like that. The stay-at-homes had always secretly begrudged them the accomplishment.

The girl broke away at last, breathless. "Johnnie!" she cried.

A sputter beside them, and Lieutenant Booth climbed on to the float, moist and panting. "Wha's that?" he gurgled.

"She was speaking to me," cried John Quincy triumphantly.

The Chinese Parrot

1

The Phillimore Pearls

Alexander Eden stepped from the misty street into the great, marble-pillared room where the firm of Meek and Eden offered its wares. Immediately, behind show-cases gorgeous with precious stones or bright with silver, platinum and gold, forty resplendent clerks stood at attention. Their morning coats were impeccable, lacking the slightest suspicion of a wrinkle, and in the left lapel of each was a pink carnation, as fresh and perfect as though it had grown there.

Eden nodded affably to right and left and went on his way, his heels clicking cheerily on the spotless tile floor. He was a small man, gray-haired and immaculate, with a quick keen eye and the imperious manner that so well became his position. For the clan of Meek, having duly inherited the earth, had relinquished that inheritance and passed to the great beyond, leaving Alexander Eden the sole owner of the best-known jewelry store west of the Rockies.

Arriving at the rear of the shop, he ascended a brief stairway to the luxurious suite of offices on the mezzanine floor where he spent his days. In the anteroom of the suite he encountered his secretary.

"Ah, good morning, Miss Chase," he said.

The girl answered with a smile. Eden's eye for beauty, developed by long experience in the jewel trade, had not failed him when he picked Miss Chase. She was an ash blonde with violet eyes; her manners were exquisite; so was her gown. Bob Eden, reluctant hair to the business, had been heard to remark that entering his father's office was like arriving for tea in a very exclusive drawingroom.

Alexander Eden glanced at his watch. "In about ten minutes," he announced, "I expect a caller—an old friend of mine—Madame Jordan, of Honolulu. When she arrives, show her in at once."

"Yes, Mr. Eden," replied the girl.

He passed on into his own room, where he hung up his hat, coat and stick. On his broad, gleaming desk lay the morning mail; he glanced at it idly, but his mind was elsewhere. In a moment he strolled to one of the windows and stood there gazing at the façade of the building across the way.

The day was not far advanced, and the fog that had blanketed San Francisco the night before still lingered in the streets. Staring into that dull gray mist Eden saw a picture, a picture that was incongruously all color and light and life. His thoughts had traveled back down the long corridor of the years, and in that imagined scene outside the window he himself moved, a slim dark boy of seventeen.

Forty years ago—a night in Honolulu, the gay happy Honolulu of the monarchy. Behind a bank of ferns in one corner of the great Phillimore living-room Berger's band was playing, and over the polished floor young Alec Eden and Sally Phillimore danced together. The boy stumbled now and then, for the dance was a new-fangled one called the two-step, lately introduced into Hawaii by a young ensign from the *Nipsic*. But perhaps it was not entirely his unfamiliarity with the two-step that muddled him, for he knew that in his arms he held the darling of the islands.

Some few are favored by fortune out of all reason, and Sally Phillimore was one of these. Above and beyond her beauty, which would have been sufficient in itself, she seemed, in that simple Honolulu society, the heiress of all the ages. The Phillimore fortunes were at their peak, Phillimore ships sailed the seven seas, on thousands of Phillimore acres the sugar-cane ripened toward a sweet, golden harvest. Looking down, Alec Eden saw hanging about the girl's white throat, a symbol of her place and wealth, the famous pearl necklace Marc Phillimore had brought home from London, and for which he had paid a price that made all Honolulu gasp.

Eden, of Meek and Eden, continued to stare into the fog. It was pleasant to relive that night in Hawaii, a night filled with magic and the scent of exotic blossoms, to hear again the giddy laughter, the distant murmur of the surf, the soft croon of island music. Dimly he recalled Sally's blue eyes shining up at him. More vividly—for he was nearly sixty now, and a business man—he saw again the big lustrous pearls that lay on her breast, reflecting the light with a warm glow—

Oh, well—he shrugged his shoulders. All that was forty years ago, and much had happened since. Sally's married to Fred Jordan, for example, and then, a few years later, the birth of her only child, of Victor. Eden smiled grimly. How ill-advised she had been when she named that foolish, wayward boy.

He went over to his desk and sat down. No doubt it was some escapade of Victor's, he reflected, that was responsible for the scene shortly to be enacted here in this office on Post Street. Yes, of course, that was it. Victor, lurking in the wings, was about to ring down the final curtain on the drama of the Phillimore pearls.

He was deep in his mail when, a few moments later, his secretary opened the door and announced: "Madame Jordan is calling."

Eden rose. Sally Jordan was coming toward him over the Chinese rug. Gay and sprightly as ever—how valiantly she had battled with the years! "Alec—my dear old friend—"

He took both her fragile hands in his. "Sally! I'm mighty glad to see you. Here." He drew a big leather chair close to his desk. "The post of honor for you. Always."

Smiling, she sat down. Eden went to his accustomed place behind his desk. He took up a paper-knife and balanced it; for a man of his poise he appeared rather ill at ease. "Ah—er—how long have you been in town?"

"Two weeks—I think—yes, two weeks last Monday."

"You're not living up to your promise, Sally. You didn't let me know."

"But I've had such a gay round," she protested. "Victor is always so good to me."

"Ah, yes—Victor—he's well, I hope." Eden looked away, out the window. "Fog's lifting, isn't it? A fine day, after all—"

"Dear old Alec." She shook her head. "No good beating round the bush. Never did believe in it. Get down to business—that's my motto. It's as I told you the other day over the telephone. I've made up my mind to sell the Phillimore pearls."

He nodded. "And why not? What good are they, anyhow?"

"No, no," she objected. "It's perfectly true—they're no good to me. I'm a great believer in what's fitting—and those gorgeous pearls were meant for youth. However, that's not the reason I'm selling. I'd hang on to them if I could. But I can't. I—I'm broke, Alec."

He looked out the window again.

"Sounds absurd, doesn't it?" she went on. "All the Phillimore ships—the Phillimore acres—vanished into thin air. The big house on the beach—mortgaged to the hilt. You see—Victor—he's made some unfortunate investments—"

"I see," said Eden softly.

"Oh, I know what you're thinking, Alec. Victor's a bad, bad boy. Foolish and careless and—and worse, perhaps. But he's all I've got, since Fred went. And I'm sticking by him."

"Like the good sport you are," he smiled. "No, I wasn't thinking unkindly of Victor, Sally. I—I have a son myself."

"Forgive me," she said. "I should have asked before. How's Bob?"

"Why, he's all right, I guess. He may come in before you leave—if he happens to have had an early breakfast."

"Is he with you in the business?"

Eden shrugged. "Not precisely. Bob's been out of college three years now. One of those years was spent in the South Seas, another in Europe, and the third—from what I can gather—in the card-room of his club. However, his career does seem to be worrying him a bit. The last I heard he was thinking of the newspaper game. He has friends on the papers." The jeweler waved his hand about the office. "This sort of thing, Sally—this thing I've given my life to—it's a great bore to Bob."

"Poor Alec," said Sally Jordan softly. "The new generation is so hard to understand. But—it's my own troubles I came to talk about. Broke, as I told you. Those pearls are all I have in the world."

"Well—they're a good deal," Eden told her.

"Enough to help Victor out of the hole he's in. Enough for the few years left me, perhaps. Father paid ninety thousand for them. It was a fortune at that time—but to-day—"

"To-day," Eden repeated. "You don't seem to realize, Sally. Like everything else, pearls have greatly appreciated since the 'eighties. To-day that string is worth three hundred thousand if it's worth a cent."

She gasped. "Why, it can't be. Are you sure? You've never seen the necklace—"

"Ah—I was wondering if you'd remember," he chided. "I see you don't. Just before you came in I was thinking back—back to a night forty years ago, when I was visiting my uncle in the islands. Seventeen—that's all I was—but I came to your dance, and you taught me the two-step. The pearls were about your throat. One of the memorable nights of my life."

"And of mine," she nodded. "I remember now. Father had just brought the necklace from London, and it was the first time I'd worn it. Forty years ago—ah, Alec, let's hurry back to the present. Memories—sometimes they hurt." She was silent for a moment. "Three hundred thousand, you say—"

"I don't guarantee I can get that much," he told her. "I said the necklace was worth it. But it isn't always easy to find a buyer who will meet your terms. The man I have in mind—"

"Oh—you've found some one—"

"Well—yes—I have. But he refused to go above two hundred and twenty thousand. Of course, if you're in a hurry to sell—"

"I am," she answered. "Who is this Midas?"

"Madden," he said. "P. J. Madden."

"Not the big Wall Street man?" The Plunger?"

"Yes. You know him?"

"Only through the newspapers. He's famous, of course, but I've never seen him."

Eden frowned. "That's curious," he said. "He appeared to know you. I had heard he was in town, and when you telephoned me the other day, I went at once to his hotel. He admitted he was on the lookout for a string as a present for his daughter, but he was pretty cold at first. However, when I mentioned the Phillimore pearls, he laughed. 'Sally Phillimore's pearls,' he said. 'I'll take them.' 'Three hundred thousand,' I said. 'Two hundred and twenty and not a penny more,' he answered. And looked at me with those eyes of his—as well try to bargain with this fellow here." He indicated a small bronze Buddha on his desk.

Sally Jordan seemed puzzled. "But Alec—he couldn't know me. I don't understand. However, he's offering a fortune, and I want it, badly. Please hurry and close with him before he leaves town."

Again the door opened at the secretary's touch. "Mr. Madden, of New York," said the girl.

"Yes," said Eden. "We'll see him at once." He turned to his old friend. "I asked him to come here this morning and meet you. Now take my advice and don't be too eager. We may be able to boost him a bit, though I doubt it. He's a hard man, Sally, a hard man. The newspaper stories about him are only too true."

He broke off suddenly, for the hard man he spoke of stood upon his rug. P. J. himself, the great Madden, the hero of a thousand Wall Street battles, six feet and over and looming like a tower of granite in the gray clothes he always affected. His cold blue eyes swept the room like an Arctic blast.

"Ah, Mr. Madden, come in," said Eden, rising. Madden advanced farther into the room, and after him came a tall languid girl in expensive furs and a lean, precise-looking man in a dark blue suit.

"Madame Jordan, this is Mr. Madden, of whom we have just been speaking," Eden said.

"Madame Jordan," repeated Madden, bowing slightly. He had dealt so much in steel it had got somehow into his voice. "I've brought along my daughter Evelyn, and my secretary, Martin Thorn."

"Charmed, I'm sure," Eden answered. He stood for a moment gazing at this interesting group that had invaded his quiet office—the famous financier, cool, competent, conscious of his power, the slender haughty girl upon whom, it was reported, Madden lavished all the affection of his later years, the thin intense secretary, subserviently in the background but for some reason not so negligible as he might have been. "Won't you all sit down, please?" the jeweler continued. He arranged chairs. Madden drew his close to the desk; the air seemed charged with his presence; he dwarfed them all.

"No need of any preamble," said the millionaire. "We've come to see those pearls."

Eden started. "My dear sir—I'm afraid I gave you the wrong impression. The pearls are not in San Francisco at present."

Madden stared at him. "But when you told me to come here and meet the owner—"

"I'm so sorry—I meant just that."

Sally Jordan helped him out. "You see, Mr. Madden, I had no intention of selling the necklace when I came here from Honolulu. I was moved to that decision by events after I reached here. But I have sent for it—"

The girl spoke. She had thrown back the fur about her neck, and she was beautiful in her way, but cold and hard like her father—and just now, evidently, unutterably bored. "I thought of course the pearls were here," she said, "or I should not have come."

"Well, it isn't going to hurt you," her father snapped. "Mrs. Jordan, you say you've sent for the necklace?"

"Yes. It will leave Honolulu to-night, if all goes well. It should be here in six days."

"No good," said Madden. "My daughter's starting tonight for Denver. I go south in the morning, and in a week I expect to join her in Colorado and we'll travel east together. No good, you see."

"I will agree to deliver the necklace anywhere you say," suggested Eden.

"Yes—I guess you will." Madden considered. He turned to Madame Jordan. "This is the identical string of pearls you were wearing at the old Palace Hotel in 1889?" he asked.

She looked at him in surprise. "The same string," she answered.

"And even more beautiful than it was then, I'll wager," Eden smiled. "You know, Mr. Madden, there is an old superstition in the jewelry trade that pearls assume the personality of their wearer and become somber or bright, according to the mood of the one they adorn. If that is true, this string has grown more lively through the years."

"Bunk," said Madden rudely. "Oh, excuse me—I don't mean that the lady isn't charming. But I have no sympathy with the silly superstitions of your trade—or of any other trade. Well, I'm a busy man. I'll take the string—at the price I named."

Eden shook his head. "It's worth at least three hundred thousand, as I told you."

"Not to me. Two hundred and twenty—twenty now to bind it and the balance within thirty days after the delivery of the string. Take it or leave it."

He rose and stared down at the jeweler. Eden was an adept at bargaining, but somehow all his cunning left him as he faced this Gibraltar of a man. He looked helplessly toward his old friend.

"It's all right, Alec," Madame Jordan said. "I accept."

"Very good," Eden sighed. "But you are getting a great bargain, Mr. Madden."

"I always get a great bargain," replied Madden. "Or I don't buy." He took out his check-book. "Twenty thousand now, as I agreed."

For the first time the secretary spoke; his voice was thin and cold and disturbingly polite. "You say the pearls will arrive in six days?"

"Six days or thereabouts," Madame Jordan answered.

"Ah, yes." An ingratiating note crept in. "They are coming by—"

"By a private messenger," said Eden sharply. He was taking a belated survey of Martin Thorn. A pale high forehead, pale green eyes that now and then popped disconcertingly, long, pale, grasping hands. Not the jolliest sort of playmate to have around, he reflected. "A private messenger," he repeated firmly.

"Of course," said Thorn. Madden had written the check and laid it on the jeweler's desk. "I was thinking, Chief—just a suggestion," Thorn went on. "If Miss Evelyn is to return and spend the balance of the winter in Pasadena, she will want to wear the necklace there. We'll still be in that neighborhood six days from now, and it seems to me—"

"Who's buying this necklace?" cut in Madden. "I'm not going to have the thing carried back and forth across the country. It's too risky in these days when every other man is a crook."

"But father," said the girl, "it's quite true that I'd like to wear it this winter—"

She stopped. P. J. Madden's crimson face had gone purple, and he was tossing his great head. It was a quaint habit he had when opposed, the newspapers said. "The necklace will be delivered to me in New York," he remarked to Eden, ignoring his daughter and Thorn. "I'll be in the south for some time—got a place in Pasadena and a ranch on the desert, four miles from Eldorado. Haven't been down there for quite a while, and unless you look in on these caretakers occasionally, they get slack. As soon as I'm back in New York I'll wire you, and you can deliver the necklace at my office. You'll have my check for the balance within thirty days."

"That's perfectly agreeable to me," Eden said. "If you'll wait just a moment I'll have a bill of sale drawn, outlining the terms. Business is business—as you of all men understand."

"Of course," nodded Madden. The jeweler went out.

Evelyn Madden rose. "I'll meet you down-stairs, father. I want to look over their stock of jade." She turned to Madame Jordan. "You know, one finds better jade in San Francisco than anywhere else."

"Yes, indeed," smiled the older woman. She rose and took the girl's hands. "Such a lovely throat, my dear—I was saying just before you came—the Phillimore pearls need youth. Well, they're to have it at last. I hope you will wear them through many happy years."

"Why—why, thank you," said the girl, and went.

Madden glanced at his secretary. "Wait for me in the car," he ordered. Alone with Madame Jordan, he looked at her grimly. "You never saw me before, did you?" he inquired.

"I'm so sorry. Have I?"

"No—I suppose not. But I saw you. Oh, we're well along in years now, and it does no harm to speak of these things. I want you to know it will be a great satisfaction to me to own that necklace. A deep wound and an old one is healed this morning."

She stared at him. "I don't understand."

"No, of course you don't. But in the 'eighties you used to come from the islands with your family and stop at the Palace Hotel. And I—I was a bell-hop at that same hotel. I often saw you there—I saw you once when you were wearing that famous necklace. I thought you were the most beautiful girl in the world—oh, why not—we're both—er—"

"We're both old now," she said softly.

"Yes—that's what I mean. I worshiped you, but I—I was a bell-hop—you looked through me—you never saw me. A bit of furniture, that's all I was to you. Oh, I tell you, it hurt my pride—a deep wound, as I said. I swore I'd get on—I knew it, even then. I'd marry you. We can both smile at that now. It didn't work out—even some of *my* schemes never worked out. But to-day I own your pearls—they'll hang about my daughter's neck. It's the next best thing. I've bought you out. A deep wound in my pride, but healed at last."

She looked at him, and shook her head. Once she might have resented this, but not now. "You're a strange man," she said.

"I am what I am," he answered. "I had to tell you. Otherwise the triumph would not have been complete."

Eden came in. "Here you are, Mr. Madden. If you'll sign this—thank you."

"You'll get a wire," said Madden. "In New York, remember, and nowhere else. Good day." He turned to Madame Jordan and held out his hand.

She took it, smiling. "Good-by. I'm not looking through you now. I see you at last."

"And what do you see?"

"A terribly vain man. But a likable one."

"Thank you. I'll remember that. Good-by."

He left them. Eden sank wearily into a chair. "Well, that's that. He rather wears one out. I wanted to stick for a higher figure, but it looked hopeless. Somehow, I knew he always wins."

"Yes," said Madame Jordan, "he always wins."

"By the way, Sally, I didn't want you to tell that secretary who was bringing the pearls. But you'd better tell me."

"Why, of course. Charlie's bringing them."

"Charlie?"

"Detective-Sergeant Chan, of the Honolulu police. Long ago, in the big house on the beach, he was our number-one boy."

"Chan. A Chinese?"

"Yes. Charlie left us to join the police force, and he's made a fine record there. He's always wanted to come to the mainland, so I've had it all arranged—his leave of absence, his status as a citizen, everything. And he's coming with the pearls. Where could I have found a better messenger? Why—I'd trust Charlie with my life—no, that isn't very precious any more. I'd trust him with the life of the one I loved dearest in the world."

"He's leaving to-night, you said."

"Yes—on the *President Pierce*. It's due late next Thursday afternoon."

The door opened, and a good-looking young man stood on the threshold. His face was lean and tanned, his manner poised and confident, and his smile had just left Miss Chase day-dreaming in the outer office. "Oh, I'm sorry, dad—if you're busy. Why—look who's here!"

"Bob," cried Madame Jordan. "You rascal—I was hoping to see you. How are you?"

"Just waking into glorious life," he told her. "How are you, and all the other young folks out your way?"

"Fine, thanks. By the way, you dawdled too long over breakfast. Just missed meeting a very pretty girl."

"No, I didn't. Not if you mean Evelyn Madden. Saw her down-stairs as I came in—she was talking to one of those exiled grand dukes we employ to wait on the customers. I didn't linger—she's an old story now. Been seeing her everywhere I went for the past week."

"I thought her very charming," Madame Jordan said.

"But an iceberg," objected the boy. "B-r-r—how the wintry winds do blow in her vicinity. However, I guess she comes by it honestly. I passed the great P. J. himself on the stairs."

"Nonsense. Have you ever tried that smile of yours on her?"

"In a way. Nothing special—just the old trade smile. But look here—I'm on to you. You want to interest me in the obsolete institution of marriage."

"It's what you need. It's what all young men need."

"What for?"

"As an incentive. Something to spur you on to get the most out of life."

Bob Eden laughed. "Listen, my dear. When the fog begins to drift in through the Gate, and the lights begin to twinkle on O'Farrell Street—well, I don't want to be hampered by no incentive, lady. Besides, the girls aren't what they were when you were breaking hearts."

"Rot," she answered. "They're very much nicer. The young men are growing silly. Alec, I'll go along."

"I'll get in touch with you next Thursday," the elder Eden said. "By the way—I'm sorry it wasn't more, for your sake."

"It was an amazing lot," she replied. "I'm very happy." Her eyes filled. "Dear dad—he's taking care of me still," she added, and went quickly out.

Eden turned to his son. "I judge you haven't taken a newspaper job yet?"

"Not yet." The boy lighted a cigarette. "Of course, the editors are all after me. But I've been fighting them off."

"Well, fight them off a little longer. I want you to be free for the next two or three weeks. I've a little job for you myself."

"Why of course, dad." He tossed a match into a priceless Kang-Hsi vase. "What sort of job? What do I do?"

"First of all, you meet the *President Pierce* late next Thursday afternoon."

"Sounds promising. I presume a young woman, heavily veiled, comes ashore—"

"No. A Chinese comes ashore."

"A what?"

"A Chinese detective from Honolulu, carrying in his pocket a pearl necklace worth over a quarter of a million dollars."

Bob Eden nodded. "Yes. And after that—"

"After that," said Alexander Eden thoughtfully, "who can say? That may be only the beginning."

2

The Detective From Hawaii

At six o'clock on the following Thursday evening, Alexander Eden drove to the Stewart Hotel. All day a February rain had spattered over the town, bringing an early dusk. For a moment Eden stood in the doorway of the hotel, staring at the parade of bobbing umbrellas and at the lights along Geary Street, glowing a dim yellow in the dripping mist. In San Francisco age does not matter—much, and he felt like a boy again as he rode up in the elevator to Sally Jordan's suite.

She was waiting for him in the doorway of her sitting-room, lovely as a girl in a soft clinging dinner gown of gray. Caste tells, particularly when one has reached the sixties, Eden thought as he took her hand.

"Ah, Alec," she smiled. "Come in. You remember Victor."

Victor stepped forward eagerly, and Eden looked at him with interest. He had not seen Sally Jordan's son for some years and he noted that, at thirty-five, Victor began to show the strain of his giddy career as man about town. His brown eyes were tired, as though they had looked at the bright lights too long, his face a bit puffy, his waistline far too generous. But his attire was perfection; evidently his tailor had yet to hear of the failing Phillimore fortunes.

"Come in, come in," said Victor gaily. His heart was light, for he saw important money in the offing. "As I understand it, to-night's the night."

"And I'm glad it is," Sally Jorden added. "I shall be happy to get that necklace off my mind. Too great a burden at my age."

Eden sat down. "Bob's gone to the dock to meet the *President Pierce*," he remarked. "I told him to come here at once with your Chinese friend."

"Ah, yes," said Sally Jordan.

"Have a cocktail," suggested Victor.

"No, thanks," Eden replied. Abruptly he rose and strode about the room. Mrs. Jordan regarded him with concern. "Has anything happened?" she inquired.

The jeweler returned to his chair. "Well, yes—something has happened," he admitted. "Something—well, something rather odd."

"About the necklace, you mean?" asked Victor with interest.

"Yes," said Eden. He turned to Sally Jordan. "You remember what Madden told us, Sally? Almost his last words. 'New York, and nowhere else.' "

"Why, yes—I remember," she replied.

"Well, he's changed his mind," frowned the jeweler. "Somehow, it doesn't seem like Madden. He called me up this morning from his ranch down on the desert, and he wants the necklace delivered there."

"On the desert?" she repeated, amazed.

"Precisely. Naturally, I was surprised. But his instructions were emphatic, and you know the sort of man he is. One doesn't argue with him. I listened to what he had to say, and agreed. But after he had rung off, I got to thinking. What he had said that morning at my office, you know. I asked myself—was it really Madden talking? The voice had an authentic ring—but even so—well, I determined to take no chances."

"Quite right, too," nodded Sally Jordan.

"So I called him back. I had a devil of a time finding his number, but I finally got it from a business associate of his here in town. Eldorado 76. I asked for P. J. Madden and I got him. Oh, it was Madden right enough."

"And what did he say?"

"He commended me for my caution, but his order were even more emphatic than before. He said he had heard certain things that made him think it risky to take the necklace to New York at this time. He didn't explain what he meant by that. But he added that he'd come to the conclusion that the desert was an ideal place for a transaction of this sort. The last place in the world any one would come looking for a chance to steal a quarter of a million dollar necklace. Of course he didn't say all that over the wire, but that was what I gathered."

"He's absolutely right, too," said Victor.

"Well, yes—in a way, he is. I've spent a lot of time on the desert myself. In spite of the story writers, it's the most law-abiding place in America today. Nobody ever locks a door, or so much as thinks of thieves. Ask the average rancher about police protection, and he'll look surprised and murmur something about a sheriff several hundred miles away. But for all that—"

Eden got up again and walked anxiously about the room. "For all that—or rather, for those very reasons, I don't like the idea at all. Suppose somebody did want to play a crooked game—what a setting for it! Away out there on that ocean of sand, with only the Joshua trees for neighbors. Suppose I send Bob down there with your necklace, and he walks into a trap. Madden may not be at that lonely ranch. He may have gone east. He may even, by the time Bob gets there, have gone west—as they said in the war. Lying out on the desert, with a bullet in him—"

Victor laughed derisively. "Look here, your imagination is running away with you," he cried.

Eden smiled. "Maybe it is," he admitted. "Begins to look as though I were growing old, eh, Sally?" He took out his watch. "But where's Bob?

Ought to be here by now. If you don't mind, I'll use your telephone."

He called the dock, and came away from the phone with a still more worried look. "The *President Pierce* got in a full forty-five minutes ago," he announced. "Half an hour should bring them here."

"Traffic's rather thick at this hour," Victor reminded him.

"Yes—that's right, too," Eden agreed. "Well, Sally, I've told you the situation. What do you think?"

"What should she think?" Victor cut in. "Madden's bought the necklace and wants it delivered on the desert. It isn't up to us to question his orders. If we do, he may get annoyed and call the whole deal off. No, our job is to deliver the pearls, get his receipt, and wait for his check." His puffy white hands twitched eagerly.

Eden turned to his old friend. "Is that your opinion, Sally?"

"Why, yes, Alec," she said. "I fancy Victor is right." She looked at her son proudly. Eden also looked at him, but with a vastly different expression.

"Very good," he answered. "Then there is no time to be lost. Madden is in a great hurry, as he wants to start for New York very soon. I shall send Bob with the necklace at eleven o'clock to-night—but I absolutely refuse to send him alone."

"I'll go along," Victor offered.

Eden shook his head. "No," he objected, "I prefer a policeman, even though he does belong to a force as far away as Honolulu. This Charlie Chan—do you think, Sally, that you could persuade him to go with Bob?"

She nodded. "I'm sure of it. Charlie would do anything for me."

"All right—that's settled. But where the devil are they? I tell you, I'm worried—"

The telephone interrupted him, and Madame Jordan went to answer it. "Oh—hello, Charlie," she said. "Come right up. We're on the fourth floor—number 482. Yes. Are you alone?" She hung up the receiver and turned back into the room. "He says he is alone," she announced.

"Alone," repeated Eden. "Why—I don't understand that—" He sank weakly into a chair.

A moment later he looked up with interest at the chubby little man his hostess and her son were greeting warmly at the door. The detective from Honolulu stepped farther into the room, an undistinguished figure in his Western clothes. He had round fat cheeks, an ivory skin, but the thing about him that caught Eden's attention was the expression in his eyes, a look of keen brightness that made the pupils gleam like black buttons in the yellow light.

"Alec," said Sally Jordan. "this is my old friend, Charlie Chan. Charlie—Mr. Eden."

Chan bowed low. "Honors crowd close on this mainland," he said. "First I am Miss Sally's old friend, and now I meet Mr. Eden."

Eden rose. "How do you do," he said.

"Have a good crossing, Charlie?" Victor asked.

Chan shrugged. "All time big Pacific Ocean suffer sharp pain down below, and toss about to prove it. Maybe from sympathy, I am in same fix."

Eden came forward. "Pardon me if I'm a little abrupt—but my son—he was to meet your ship—"

"So sorry," Chan said, regarding him gravely. "The fault must indubitably be mine. Kindly overlook my stupidity, but there was no meeting at dock."

"I can't understand it," Eden complained again.

"For some few minutes I linger round gang-board," Chan continued. "No one ventures to approach out of rainy night. Therefore I engage taxi and hurry to this spot."

"You've got the necklace?" Victor demanded.

"Beyond any question," Chan replied. "Already I have procured room in this hotel, partly disrobing to remove same from money-belt about waist." He tossed an innocent-looking string of beads down upon the table. "Regard the Phillimore pearls at journey's end," he grinned. "And now a great burden drops from my shoulders with a most delectable thud."

Eden, the jeweler, stepped forward and lifted the string in his hands. "Beautiful," he murmured, "beautiful. Sally, we should never have let Madden have them at the price. They're perfectly matched—I don't know that I ever saw—" He stared for a moment into the rosy glow of the pearls, then laid them again on the table. "But Bob—where is Bob?"

"Oh, he'll be along," remarked Victor, taking up the necklace. "Just a case of missing each other."

"I am the faulty one," insisted Chan. "Shamed by my blunder—"

"Maybe," said Eden. "But—now that you have the pearls, Sally, I'll tell you something else. I didn't want to worry you before. This afternoon at four o'clock some one called me—Madden again, he said. But something in his voice—anyhow, I was wary. Pearls were coming on the *President Pierce*, were they? Yes. And the name of the messenger? Why should I tell him that, I inquired. Well, he had just got hold of some inside facts that made him feel the string was in danger, and he didn't want anything to happen. He was in a position to help in the matter. He insisted, so I finally said: 'Very good, Mr. Madden. Hang up your receiver and I'll call you back in ten minutes with the information you want.' There was a pause, then I heard him hang up. But I didn't phone the desert. Instead I had that call traced, and I found it came from a pay-station in a cigar store at the corner of Sutter and Kearny Streets."

Eden paused. He saw Charlie Chan regarding him with deep interest.

"Can you wonder I'm worried about Bob?" the jeweler continued. "There's some funny business going on, and I tell you I don't like it—"

A knock sounded on the door, and Eden himself opened it. His son stepped into the room, debonair and smiling. At sight of him, as so often happens in such a situation, the anxious father's worry gave way to a deep rage.

"You're a hell of a business man," he cried.

"Now, father—no compliments," laughed Bob Eden. "And me wandering all over San Francisco in your service."

"I suppose so. That's about what you would be doing, when it was your job to meet Mr. Chan at the dock."

"Just a moment, dad." Bob Eden removed a glistening rain coat. "Hello, Victor. Madame Jordan. And this, I imagine, is Mr. Chan."

"So sorry to miss meeting at dock," murmured Chan. "All my fault, I am sure—"

"Nonsense," cried the jeweler. "His fault, as usual. When, in heaven's name, are you going to show a sense of responsibility?"

"Now, dad. And a sense of responsibility just what I've only this minute stopped showing nothing else but."

"Good lord—what language is that? You didn't meet Mr. Chan, did you?"

"Well, in a way, I didn't—"

"In a way? In a way!"

"Precisely. It's a long story, and I'll tell it if you'll stop interrupting with these unwarranged attacks on my character. I'll sit down, if I may. I've been about a bit, and I'm tired."

He lighted a cigarette. "When I came out of the club about five to go to the dock, there was nothing in sight but a battered old taxi that had seen better days. I jumped in. When I got down on the Embarcadero I noticed that the driver was a pretty disreputable lad with a scar on one cheek and a cauliflower ear. He said he'd wait for me, and he said it with a lot of enthusiasm. I went into the pier-shed. There was the *President Pierce* out in the harbor, fumbling round trying to dock. In a few minutes I noticed a man standing near me—a thin chilly-looking lad with an overcoat, the collar up about his ears, and a pair of black spectacles. I guess I'm psychic—he didn't look good to me. I couldn't tell, but somehow he seemed to be looking at me from back of those smoked windows. I moved to the other side of the shed. So did he. I went to the street. He followed. Well, I drifted back to the gang-plank, and old Chilly Bill came along."

Bob Eden paused, smiling genially about him. "Right then and there I came to a quick decision. I'm remarkable that way. I didn't have the pearls, but Mr. Chan did. Why tip off the world to Mr. Chan? So I just stood there staring hopefully at the crowd landing from the old *P. P.* Presently I saw the man I took to be Mr. Chan come down the plank, but I never stirred. I watched him while he looked about, then I saw him go out to the street. Still the mysterious gent behind the windows stuck closer than a bill collector. After everybody was ashore, I went back to my taxi and paid off the driver. 'Was you expecting somebody on the ship?' he asked. 'Yes,' I told him. 'I came down to meet the Dowager Empress of China, but they tell me she's dead.' He gave me a dirty look. As I hurried away the man with the black glasses came up. 'Taxi, Mister,' said Cauliflower Ear. And old Glasses got in. I had to meander through the rain all the way to the S. P. station before I could find another cab. Just as I drove away from the station along came Cauliflower Ear in his splendid equipage. He followed along behind, down Third, up Market to Powell, and finally to the St. Francis. I went in the front door of the hotel and out the side, on to Post. And there was Cauliflower Ear and his fare, drifting by our store. As I went in the front door of the club, my dear old friends drew up across the street. I escaped by way of the kitchen, and slipped over here. I fancy they're still in front of the club—they loved me like a brother." He paused. "And that, dad, is the long but thrilling story of why I did not meet Mr. Chan."

Eden smiled. "By jove, you've got more brains than I thought. You were perfectly right. But look here, Sally—I like this less than ever. That necklace of yours isn't a well-known string. It's been in Honolulu for years. Easy as the devil to dispose of it, once it's stolen. If you'll take my advice, you'll certainly not send it off to the desert—"

"Why not?" broke in Victor. "The desert's the very place to send it. Certainly this town doesn't look any too good."

"Alec," said Sally Jordan, "we need the money. If Mr. Madden is down at Eldorado, and asks for the necklace there, then let's send it to him immediately and get his receipt. After that—well, it's his lookout. His worry. Certainly I want it off my hands as soon as may be."

Eden sighed. "All right. It's for you to decide. Bob will take it at eleven, as we planned. Provided—well, provided you make the arrangement you promised—provided he doesn't go alone." He looked toward Charlie Chan who was standing at the window watching, fascinated, the noisy life of Geary Street far below.

"Charlie," said Sally Jordan.

"Yes, Miss Sally." He turned, smiling, to face her.

"What was that you said about the burden dropping from your shoulders? The delectable thud?"

"Now vacation begins," he said. "All my life I have unlimited yearning to face the wonders of this mainland. Moment are now at hand. Care-free and happy, not like crossing on ship. There all time pearls rest heavy on stomach, most undigestible, like sour rice. Not so now."

Madame Jordan shook her head. "I'm sorry, Charlie," she said. "I'm going to ask you to eat one more bowl of sour rice. For me—for auld lang syne."

"I do not quite grasp meaning," he told her.

She outlined the plan to send him with Bob Eden to the desert. His expression did not change.

"I will go," he promised gravely.

"Thank you, Charlie," said Sally Jordan softly.

"In my youth," he continued, "I am house-boy in the Philimore mansion. Still in my heart like old-time garden bloom memories of kindness never to be repaid." He saw Sally Jordan's eyes bright and shining with tears. "Life would be dreary waste," he finished, "if there was no thing called loyalty."

Very flowery, thought Alexander Eden. He sought to introduce a more practical note. "All your expenses will be paid, of course. And that vacation is just postponed for a few days. You'd better carry the pearls—you have the best, and besides, no one knows your connection with the affair. Thank heaven for that."

"I will carry them," Chan agreed. He took up the string from the table. "Miss Sally, toss all worry out of mind. When this young man and I encounter proper person, pearls will be delivered. Until then, I guard them well."

"I'm sure you will," smiled Madame Jordan.

"Well, that's settled," said Eden. "Mr. Chan, you and my son will take the eleven o'clock ferry to Richmond, which connects with the train to Barstow. There you'll have to change to another train for Eldorado, but you should reach Madden's ranch to-morrow evening. If he is there and everything seems in order—"

"Why should everything be in order?" broke in Victor. "If he's there—that's enough."

"Well, of course, we don't want to take any undue risk," Eden went on. "But you two will know what to do when you reach there. If Madden's at the ranch, give him the string and get his receipt. That lets us out. Mr. Chan we will pick you up here at ten-thirty. Until then, you are free to follow your own inclination."

"Present inclination," smiled Chan, "means tub filled with water, steaming hot. At ten-thirty in entrance hall of hotel I will be waiting, undigestible pearls on stomach, as before. Good-by. Good-by." He bobbed to each in turn and went out.

"I've been in the business thirty-five years," said Eden, "but I never employed a messenger quite like him before."

"Dear Charlie," said Sally Jordan. "He'll protect those pearls with his life."

Bob Eden laughed. "I hope it doesn't go as far as that," he remarked. "I've got a life, too, and I'd like to hang on to it."

"Won't you both stay to dinner?" suggested Sally Jordan.

"Some other time, thanks," Alexander Eden answered. "I don't think it wise we should keep together to-night. Bob and I will go home—he has a bag to pack, I imagine. I don't intend to let him out of my sight until train time."

"One last word," said Victor. "Don't be too squeamish when you get down on that ranch. If Madden's in danger, that's no affair of ours. Put those pearls in his hand and get his receipt. That's all."

Eden shook his head. "I don't like the look of this, Sally. I don't like this thing at all."

"Don't worry," she smiled. "I have every confidence in Charlie—and in Bob."

"Such popularity must be deserved," said Bob Eden. "I promise I'll do my best. Only I hope that lad in the overcoat doesn't decide to come down to the desert and warm up. Somehow, I'm not so sure I'd be a match for him—once he warmed up."

3
At Chan Kee Lim's

An hour later Charlie Chan rode down in the elevator to the bright lobby of his hotel. A feeling of heavy responsibility again weighed upon him, for he had restored to the money-belt about his bulging waist the pearls that alone remained of all the Phillimore fortune. After a quick glance about the lobby, he went out into Geary Street.

The rain no longer fell and for a moment he stood on the curb, a little, wistful, wide-eyed stranger, gazing at a world as new and strange to him as though he had wakened to find himself on Mars. The sidewalk was crowded with theater-goers; taxis honked in the narrow street; at intervals sounded the flippant warning of cable-car bells, which is a tune heard only in San Francisco, a city with a voice and a gesture all its own.

Unexplored country to Charlie Chan, this mainland, and he was thrilled by the electric gaiety of the scene before him. Old-timers would have told him that what he saw was only a dim imitation of the night life of other days, but he had no memories of the past, and hence nothing to mourn. Seated on a stool at a lunch-counter he ate his evening meal—a stool and a lunch-counter, but it was adventure enough for one who had never known Billy Bogan's Louvre Café, on the site of which now stands the Bank of Italy—adventure enough for one who had no happy recollections of Delmonico's on O'Farrell Street or of the Odeon or the Pup or the Black Cat, bright spots blotted out forever now. He partook heartily of the white man's cooking, and drank three cups of steaming tea.

A young man, from his appearance perhaps a clerk was eating a modest dinner at Chan's side. After a few words concerned with the sugar bowl, Chan ventured to address him further.

"Please pardon the abrupt advance of a newcomer," he said. "For three hours I am free to wander the damp but interesting streets of your city. Kindly mention what I ought to see."

"Why—I don't know," said the young man, surprised. "Not much doing any more. San Francisco's not what it used to be."

"The Barbary Coast, maybe," suggested Chan.

The young man snorted. "Gone forever. The Thalia, the Elko, the Midway—say, they're just memories now. Spider Kelley is over in Arizona, dealing in land. Yes, sir—all those old dance-halls are just garages to-day—or maybe ten cent flop-houses. But look here—this is New Year's Eve in Chinatown. However—" He laughed. "I guess I don't need to tell you that."

Chan nodded. "Ah yes—the twelfth of February. New Year's Eve."

Presently he was back on the sidewalk, his keen eyes sparkling with excitement. He thought of the somnolent thoroughfares of Honolulu by night—Honolulu, where every one goes home at six, and stays there. How different here in this mainland city. The driver of a sightseeing bus approached him and also spoke of Chinatown. "Show you the old opium dens and the fan-tan joints," he promised, but after a closer look moved off and said no more of his spurious wares.

At a little after eight, the detective from the islands left the friendly glow of Union Square and, drifting down into the darker stretches of Post Street, came presently to Grant Avenue. A loiterer on the corner directed him to the left, and he strolled on. In a few moments he came to a row of shops displaying cheap Oriental goods for the tourist eye. His pace quickened; he passed the church on the crest of the hill and moved on down into the real Chinatown.

Here a spirit of carnival filled the air. The façade of every Tong House, outlined by hundreds of glowing incandescent lamps, shone in yellow splendor through the misty night. Throngs milled on the narrow sidewalks—white sightseers, dapper young Chinese lads in college-cut clothes escorting slant-eyed flappers attired in their best, older Chinese shuffling along on felt-clad feet, each secure in the knowledge that his debts were paid, his house scoured and scrubbed, the new year auspiciously begun.

At Washington Street Chan turned up the hill. Across the way loomed an impressive building—four gaudy stories of light and cheer. Gilt letters in the transom over the door proclaimed it the home of the Chan Family Society. For a moment the detective stood, family pride uppermost in his thoughts.

A moment later he was walking down the dim, almost deserted pavement of Waverly Place. A bright-eyed boy of his own race offered him a copy of the Chinese Daily Times. He bought it and moved one, his gaze intent on dim house numbers above darkened doorways.

Presently he found the number he sought, and climbed a shadowy stair. At a landing where crimson and gold-lettered strips of paper served as a warning to evil spirits he paused, and knocked loudly at a door. It was opened, and against the light from within stood the figure of a Chinese, tall, with a gray meager beard and a loose-fitting, embroidered blouse of black satin.

For a moment neither spoke. Then Chan smiled. "Good evening, illustrious Chan Kee Lim," he said in pure Cantonese. "Is it that you do not know your unworthy counsin from the islands?"

A light shone in the narrow eyes of Kee Lim. "For a moment, no," he replied. "Since you come in the garb of a foreign devil, and knock on my door with the knuckles, as rude foreign devils do. A thousand welcomes. Deign to enter my contemptible house."

Still smiling, the little detective went inside. The room was anything but contemptible, as he saw at once. It was rich with tapestries of Hang-chiu silk, the furniture was of teakwood, elaborately carved. Fresh flowers bloomed before the ancestral shrine, and everywhere were Chinese lilies, the pale, pungent sui-sin-fah, a symbol of the dawning year. On the mantel, beside a tiny Buddha of Ningpo wood, an American alarm clock ticked noisily.

"Please sit in this wretched chair," Kee Lim said. "You arrive unexpectedly as August rain. But I am happy to see you." He clapped his hands and a woman entered. "My wife, Chan So," the host explained. "Bring rice cakes, and my Dew of Roses wine," he ordered.

He sat down opposite Charlie Chan, and regarded him across a teakwood table on which were sprays of fresh almond blossoms. "There was no news of your coming," he remarked.

Chan shrugged. "No. It was better so. I come on a mission. On business," he added, in his best Rotary Club manner.

Kee Lim's eyes narrowed. "Yes—I have heard of your business," he said.

The detective was slightly uncomfortable. "You do not approve?" he ventured.

"It is too much to say that I do not approve," Kee Lim returned. "But I do not quite understand. The foreign devil police—what has a Chinese in common with them?"

Charlie smiled. "There are times, honorable cousin," he admitted, "when I do not quite understand myself."

The reed curtains at the rear parted, and a girl came into the room. Her eyes were dark and bright; her face pretty as a doll's. To-night, in deference to the holiday, she wore the silken trousers and embroidered jacket of her people, but her hair was bobbed and her walk, her gestures, her whole manner all too obviously copied from her American sisters. She carried a tray piled high with New Year delicacies.

"My daughter, Rose," Kee Lim announced. "Behold, our famous cousin from Hawaii." He turned to Charlie Chan. "She, too, would be an American, insolent as the daughters of the foolish white men."

The girl laughed. "Why not? I was born here. I went to American grammar schools. And now I work American fashion."

"Work?" repeated Charlie, with interest.

"The Classics of Girlhood are forgotten," explained Kee Lim. "All day she sits in the Chinatown telephone exchange, shamelessly talking to a wall of teakwood that flashes red and yellow eyes."

"Is that so terrible?" asked the girl, with a laughing glance at her cousin.

"A most interesting labor," surmised Charlie.

"I'll tell the world it is," answered the girl in English, and went out. A moment later she returned with a battered old wine jug. Into Swatow bowls she poured two hot libations—then, taking a seat on the far side of the room, she gazed curiously at this notable relative from across the seas. Once she had read of his exploits in the San Francisco papers.

For an hour or more Chan sat, talking with his cousin of the distant days when they were children in China. Finally he glanced toward the mantel. "Does that clock speak the truth?" he asked.

Kee Lim shrugged. "It is a foreign devil clock," he said. "And therefore a great liar."

Chan consulted his watch. "With the keenest regret," he announced, "I find I must walk my way. To-night my business carries me far from here—to the desert that lies in the south. I have had the presumption, honest and industrious cousin, to direct my wife to send to your house any letters of importance addressed to me. Should a message arrive in my absence, you will be good enough to hold it here awaiting my return. In a few days, at most, I will walk this way again. Meanwhile I go beyond the reach of messengers."

The girl rose and came forward. "Even on the desert," she said, "there are telephones."

Charlie looked at her with sudden interest. "On the desert," he repeated.

"Most assuredly. Only two days ago I had a long distance call for a ranch near Eldorado. A ranch named—but I do not remember."

"Perhaps—the ranch of Madden," said Chan hopefully.

She nodded. "Yes—that was the name. It was a most unusual call."

"And it came from Chinatown?"

"Of course. From the bowl shop of Wong Ching, in Jackson Street. He desired to speak to his relative, Louie Wong, caretaker on Madden's Ranch. The number. Eldorado 76."

Chan dissembled his eagerness, but his heart was beating faster. He was of the foreign devil police now. "Perhaps you heard what was said?"

"Louie Wong must come to San Francisco at once. Much money and a fine position awaited him here—"

"Haie!" cut in Kee Lim. "It is not fitting that you reveal thus the secrets of your white devil profession. Even to one of the family of Chan."

"You are right, ever wise cousin," Charlie agreed. He turned to the girl. "You and I, little blossom, will meet again. Even though the desert has telephones, I am beyond reach there. Now, to my great regret, I must go."

Kee Lim followed him to the door. He stood there on the reed mat, stroking his thin beard and blinking. "Farewell, notable cousin. On that long journey of yours upon which you now set out—walk slowly."

"Farewell," Charlie answered. "All my good wishes for happiness in the new year." Suddenly he found himself speaking English. "See you later," he called, and hurried down the stairs.

Once in the street, however, he obeyed his cousin's parting injunction, and walked slowly indeed. A startling bit of news, this, from Rose, the telephone operator. Louie Wong was wanted in San Francisco—wanted by his relative Wong Ching, the bowl merchant. Why?

An old Chinese on a corner directed him to Jackson Street, and he climbed its steep sidewalk until he reached the shop of Wong Ching. The brightly lighted window was filled with Swatow cups and bowls, a rather beautiful display, but evidently during this holiday season the place was not open for business, for the curtains on the door were drawn. Chan rattled the latch for a full minute, but no one came.

He crossed the street, and took up a post in a dark doorway opposite. Sooner or later his summons would be answered. On a near-by balcony a Chinese orchestra was playing, the whanging flute, the shrill plink of the moon-kwan, the rasping cymbals and the drums filled the night with a blissful dissonance. Presently the musicians ceased, the din died away, and Chan heard only the click of American heels and the stealthy swish of felt slippers passing his hiding-place.

In about ten minutes the door of Wong Ching's shop opened and a man came out. He stood looking cautiously up and down the dim street. A thin man in an overcoat which was buttoned close about him—a chilly-seeming man. His hat was low over his eyes, and as a further means of deceit he wore dark spectacles. Charlie Chan permitted a faint flash of interest to cross his chubby face.

The chilly man walked briskly down the hill, and stepping quickly from the doorway, Chan followed at a distance. They emerged into Grant Avenue; the dark-spectacled one turned to the right. Still Chan followed; this was child's play for him. One block, two, three. They came to a cheap hotel, the Killarney, on one of Grant Avenue's corners, and the man in the overcoat went inside.

Glancing at his watch, Chan decided to let his quarry escape, and turned in the direction of Union Square. His mind was troubled. "This much even a fool could grasp," he thought. "We move toward a trap. But with eyes open—with eyes keenly open."

Back in his tiny hotel room, he restored to his inexpensive suit-case the few articles he had previously removed. Returning to the desk, he found that his trunk had reached the hotel, but had not yet been taken upstairs. He arranged for its storage until his return, paid his bill, and sitting down in a great leather chair in the lobby, with his suit-case at his feet, he waited patiently.

At precisely ten-thirty Bob Eden stepped inside the door of the hotel and beckoned. Following the young man to the street, Chan saw a big limousine drawn up to the curb.

"Jump in, Mr. Chan," said the boy, taking his bag. As the detective entered the darkened interior, Alexander Eden greeted him from the gloom. "Tell Michael to drive slowly—I want to talk," called the older man to his son. Bob Eden spoke to the chauffeur, then leaped into the car and it moved off down Geary Street.

"Mr. Chan," said the jeweler in a low voice, "I am very much disturbed."

"More events have taken place?" suggested Chan.

"Decidedly," Eden replied. "You were not in the room this afternoon when I spoke of a telephone call I had received from a pay-station at Sutter and Kearny Street." He repeated the details. "This evening I called into consultation Al Draycott, head of the Gale Detective Agency, with which I have affiliations. I asked him to investigate and, if possible, find that man in the overcoat Bob saw at the dock. An hour ago he reported that he had located our man with no great difficulty. He has discovered him—"

"At the Killarney Hotel, perhaps, on Grants Avenue," suggested Chan, dissembling a deep triumph.

"Good lord," gasped Even. "You found him, too. Why—that's amazing—"

"Amazing luck," said Chan. "Please pardon rude interruption. Will not occur again."

"Well, Draycott located this fellow, and reports that he is Shaky Phil Maydorf, one of the Maydorf brothers, as slick a pair of crooks as ever left New York for their health. The fellow suffers from malaria, I believe, but otherwise he is in good form and, it seems, very much interested in our little affairs. But Mr. Chan—your own story—how in the world did you find him too?"

Chan shrugged. "Successful detective," he said, "is plenty often man on whom luck turns smiling face. This evening I bask in most heart-warming grin." He told of his visit to Chan Kee Lim, of the telephone call to the desert from Wong's bowl shop, and of his seeing the man in the overcoat leaving the shop. "After that, simple matter to hound him to hotel," he finished.

"Well, I'm more disturbed than ever," Eden said. "They have called the caretaker away from Madden's ranch. Why? I tell you I don't like this business—"

"Nonsense, father," Bob Eden protested. "It's rather interesting."

"Not to me. I don't welcome the attention of these Maydorfs—and where, by the way, is the other one? They are not the modern type of crook—the moron brand that relies entirely on a gun. They are men of brains—old-fashioned outlaws who are regarded with respect by the police whom they have fought for many years. I called Sally Jordan and tried to abandon the whole proceeding—but this son of hers. He's itching to get the money, and he's urging her to go ahead. So what can I do? If it was any one else I'd certainly drop out of the deal—but Sally Jordan—well, she's an old friend. And as you said this afternoon, Mr. Chan, there is such a thing as loyalty in the world. But I tell you I'm sending you two down there with the deepest reluctance."

"Don't you worry, dad. It's going to be great fun, I'm sure. All my life I've wanted to be mixed up in a good exciting murder. As a spectator, of course."

"What are you talking about?" the father demanded.

"Why, Mr. Chan here is a detective, isn't he? A detective on a vacation. If you've ever read a mystery story you know that a detective never works so hard as when he's on a vacation. He's like the postman who goes for a long walk on his day off. Here we are, all set. We've got our bright and shining mark, our millionaire—P. J. Madden, one of the most famous financiers in America. I tell you, poor P. J. is doomed. Ten to one Mr. Chan and I will walk into that ranch house and find him dead on the first rug we come to."

"This is no joking matter," Eden rebuked severely. "Mr. Chan—you seem to be a man of considerable ability. Have you anything to suggest?"

Charlie smiled in the dark car. "Flattery sounds sweet to any ear," he remarked. "I have, it is true, inclination for making humble suggestion."

"Then, for heaven's sake, make it," Eden said.

"Pray give the future a thought. Young Mr. Eden and I walk hand in hand, like brothers, on to desert ranch. What will spectator say? Aha, they bring pearls. If not, why come together for strength?"

"Absolutely true," Eden agreed.

"Then why travel side by side?" Charlie continued. "It is my humble hint that Mr. Bob Eden arrive alone at ranch. Answering all inquiries he says no, he does not carry pearls. So many dark clouds shade the scene, he is sent by honorable father to learn if all is well. When he is sure of that, he will telegraph necklace be sent at once, please."

"A good idea," Eden said. "Meanwhile—"

"At somewhat same hour," Chan went on, "there stumble on to ranch weary old Chinese, seeking employment. One whose clothes are of a notable shabbiness, a wanderer over sand, a what you call—a desert rat. Who would dream that on the stomach of such a one repose those valuable Phillimore pearls?"

"Say—that's immense," cried Bob Eden enthusiastically.

"Might be," admitted Chan. "Both you and old Chinese look carefully about. If all is well, together you approach this Madden and hand over necklace. Even then, others need not know."

"Fine," said the boy. "We'll separate when we board the train. If you're in doubt at any time, just keep your eye on me, and tag along. We're due in Barstow to-morrow at one-fifteen, and there's a train to Eldorado at three-twenty, which arrives about six. I'm taking it, and you'd better do the same. One of my newspaper friends here has given me a letter to a fellow named Will Holley, who's editor of a little paper at Eldorado. I'm going to invite him to have dinner with me, then I'll drive out to Madden's. You, of course, will get out some other way. As somebody may be watching us, we won't speak on our journey. Friends once, but strangers now. That's the idea, isn't it?"

"Precisely the notion," agreed Chan.

The car had stopped before the ferry building. "I have your tickets here," Alexander Eden said, handing over a couple of envelopes. "You have lower berths, in the same car, but at different ends. You'll find a little money there for expenses, Mr. Chan. I may say that I think your plan is excellent—but for heaven's sake, be careful, both of you. Bob, my boy—you're all I've got. I may have spoken harshly to you, but I—I—take care of yourself."

"Don't you worry, dad," Bob Eden said. "Though you'll never believe it, I'm grown up. And I've got a good man with me."

"Mr. Chan," Eden said. "Good luck. And thank you a thousand times."

"Don't talk about it," smiled Charlie. "Happiest walk of postman's life is on his holiday. I will serve you well. Good-by."

He followed Bob Eden through the gates and on to the ferryboat. A moment later they had slipped out upon the black waters of the harbor. The rain was gone, the sky spattered with stars, but a chill wind blew through the Gate. Charlie stood alone by the rail; the dream of his life had come true; he knew the great mainland at last. The flaming ball atop the Ferry Building receded; the yellow lamps of the city marched up the hills and down again. He thought of the tiny island that was his home, of the house on Punchbowl Hill where his wife and children patiently awaited his return. Suddenly he was appalled at the distance he had come.

Bob Eden joined him there in the dark, and waved his hand toward the glow in the sky above Grant Avenue. "A big night in Chinatown," he said.

"Very large night," agreed Chan. "And why not? To-morrow is the first day of the new year. Of the year 4869."

"Great Scott," smiled Eden. "How time flies. A Happy New Year to you."

"Similar one to you," said Chan.

The boat plowed on. From the prison island of Alcatraz a cruel, relentless searchlight swept at intervals the inky waters. The wind was bitter now.

"I'm going inside," shivered Bob Eden. "This is good-by, I guess."

"Better so," admitted Charlie. "When you are finally at Madden's ranch, look about for that desert rat."

Alone, he continued to stare at the lamps of the city, cold and distant now, like the stars.

"A desert rat," he repeated softly, "with no fondly feeling for a trap."

4

The Oasis Special

Dusk was falling in the desert town of Eldorado when, on Friday evening, Bob Eden alighted from the train at a station that looked like a little red schoolhouse gone wrong. His journey down from San Francisco to Barstow had been quite without incident. At that town, however, a rather disquieting thing had happened. He had lost all trace of Charlie Chan.

It was in the Barstow lunch-room that he had last seen the detective from the islands, busy with a cup of steaming tea. The hour of three-twenty and the Eldorado train being some distance off, he had gone for a stroll through the town. Returning about three, he had looked in vain for the little Chinese policeman. Alone he had boarded the train and now, as he stared up and down the dreary railroad tracks, he perceived that he had been the only passenger to alight at this unpromising spot.

Thinking of the fortune in "undigestible" pearls on the detective's person, he was vaguely alarmed. Had Chan met with some unfortunate accident? Or perhaps—who could say? What did they really know about this Charlie Chan? Every man is said to have his price, and this was an overwhelming temptation to put in the way of an underpaid detective from Honolulu. But no—Bob Eden recalled the look in Chan's eyes when he had promised Sally Jordan to guard those pearls well. The Jordans no doubt had good reason for their faith in an old friend. But suppose Shaky Phil Maydorf was no longer in San Francisco—

Resolutely Bob Eden put these thoughts aside and, rounding the station, entered a narrow strip of ground which was, rather pathetically, intended for a park. February had done its worst, and up above the chill evening wind from the desert blew through the stark branches of Carolina poplars and cottonwoods. Crossing a gravel path almost hidden by a mass of yellow leaves, he stood on the curb of the only pavement in Eldorado.

Against the background of bare brown hills, he saw practically the entire town at a glance. Across the way a row of scraggly buildings proclaimed yet another Main Street—a bank, a picture theater, the Spot Cash Store, the News Bureau, the post-office, and towering above the rest, a two-story building that announced itself as the Desert Edge Hotel. Eden crossed the street, and threading his way between dusty automobiles parked head-on at the curb, approached the door of the latter. On the double seat of a shoe-shining stand two ranchers lolled at ease, and stared at him with mild interest as he went inside.

An electric lamp of modest candle-power burned above the desk of the Desert Edge, and a kindly old man read a Los Angeles paper in its dim company.

"Good evening," said Bob Eden.

"Evenin'," answered the old man.

"I wonder if I might leave this suit-case in your check-room for a while?" the boy inquired.

"Check-room, hell," replied the old man. "Just throw her down anywhere. Ain't lookin' fer a room, I suppose. Make you a special rate."

"No," said Eden. "I'm sorry."

" 'Sall right," answered the proprietor. "Not many are."

"I'd like to find the office of the *Eldorado Times*," Eden informed him.

"Round corner on First," murmured the old man, deep in his pink newspaper again.

Bob Eden went to the corner, and turned off. His feet at once left Eldorado's solitary sidewalk for soft crunching sand. He passed a few buildings even meaner than those on Main Street, a plumber's shop, a grocer's, and came to a little yellow shack which bore on its window the fading legend: "The Eldorado Times. Job Printing Neatly Done." There was no light inside, and crossing a narrow, dilapidated porch, he saw a placard on the door. Straining his eyes in the dusk, he read:

Back in an hour—
God knows why.
WILL HOLLEY.

Smiling, Eden returned to the Desert Edge. "How about dinner?" he inquired.

"Wonderin' about it myself," admitted the old man. "We don't serve meals here. Lose a little less that way."

"But there must be a restaurant—"

"Sure there is. This is an up-to-date town." He nodded over his shoulder. "Down beyond the bank—the Oasis Café."

Thanking him, Bob Eden departed. Behind unwashed windows he found the Oasis dispensing its dubious cheer. A long high counter and a soiled mirror running the length of it suggested that in other days this had been an oasis indeed.

The boy climbed on to one of the perilously high stools. At his right, too close for comfort, sat a man in overalls and jumper, with a week's growth of beard on his lean hard face. At his left, equally close but somehow not so much in the way, was a trim girl in khaki riding breeches and blouse.

A youth made up to resemble a motion-picture sheik demanded his order, and from a soiled menu he chose the Oasis Special—"steak and onions, French fries, bread and butter and coffee. Eighty cents." The sheik departed languidly.

Awaiting the special, Bob Eden glanced into the smoky mirror at the face of the girl beside him. Not so bad, even in that dim reflection. Corn yellow hair curling from under the brim of a felt hat; a complexion that no beauty parlor had originated. He held his left elbow close so that she might have more room for the business that engrossed her.

His dinner arrived, a plenteous platter of food—but no plate. He glanced at his neighbors. Evidently plates were an affectation frowned upon in the Oasis. Taking up a tarnished knife and fork, he pushed aside the underbrush of onions and came face to face with his steak.

First impressions are important, and Bob Eden knew at once that this was no meek, complacent opponent that confronted him. The steak looked back at him with an air of defiance that was amply justified by what followed. After a few moments of unsuccessful battling, he summoned the sheik. "How about a steel knife?" he inquired.

"Only got three and they're all in use," the waiter replied.

Bob Eden resumed the battle, his elbows held close, his muscles swelling. With set teeth and grim face he bore down and cut deep. There was a terrific screech as his knife skidded along the platter, and to his horror he saw the steak rise from its bed of gravy and onions and fly from him. It traveled the grimy counter for a second, then dropped on to the knees of the girl and thence to the floor.

Eden turned to meet her blue eyes filled with laugher. "Oh, I'm so sorry," he said. "I thought it was a steak, and it seems to be a lap dog."

"And I hadn't any lap," she cried. She looked down at her riding breeches. "Can you ever forgive me? I might have caught it for you. It only goes to show—women should be womanly."

"I wouldn't have you any different," Bob Eden responded gallantly. He turned to the sheik. "Bring me something a little less ferocious," he ordered.

"How about the pot roast?" asked the youth.

"Well, how about it?" Eden repeated. "Fetch it along and I'll fight another round. I claim a foul on that one. And say—bring this young woman a napkin."

"A what? A napkin. We ain't got any. I'll bring her a towel."

"Oh, no—please don't," cried the girl. "I'm all right, really."

The sheik departed.

"Somehow," she added to Eden. "I think it wiser not to introduce an Oasis towel into this affair."

"You're probably right," he nodded. "I'll pay for the damage, of course."

She was still smiling. "Nonsense. I ought to pay for the steak. It wasn't your fault. One needs long practise to eat in the crowded arena of the Oasis."

He looked at her, his interest growing every minute. "You've had long practise?" he inquired.

"Oh, yes. My work often brings me this way."

"Your—er—your work?"

"Yes. Since your steak seems to have introduced us, I may tell you I'm with the moving pictures."

Of course, thought Eden. The desert was filled with movie people these days. "Ah—have I ever seen you in the films?" he ventured.

She shrugged. "You have not—and you never will. I'm not an actress. My job's much more interesting. I'm a location finder."

Bob Eden's pot roast arrived, mercifully cut into small pieces by some blunt instrument behind the scenes. "A location finder. I ought to know what that is."

"You certainly ought to. It's just what it sounds like. I travel about hunting backgrounds. By the Vandeventer Trail to Piñon Flat, down to the Salton Sea or up to the Morongos—all the time trying to find something new, something the dear old public will mistake for Algeria, Araby, the South Seas."

"Sounds mighty interesting."

"It is, indeed. Particularly when one loves this country as I do."

"You were born here, perhaps?"

"Oh, no. I came out with dad to Doctor Whitcomb's—it's five miles from here, just beyond the Madden ranch—some years ago. When—when dad left me I had to get a job, and—but look here, I'm telling you the story of my life."

"Why not?" asked Eden. "Women and children always confide in me. I've got such a fatherly face. By the way, this coffee is terrible."

"Yes, isn't it?" she agreed. "What will you have for dessert? There are two kinds of pie—apple, and the other's out. Make your selection."

"I've made it," he replied. "I'm taking the one that's out." He demanded his check. "Now, if you'll let me pay for your dinner—"

"Nothing of the sort," she protested.

"But after the way my steak attacked you."

"Forget it. I've an expense account, you know. If you say any more, I'll pay your check."

Ignoring the jar of toothpicks hospitably offered by a friendly cashier, Bob Eden followed her to the street. Night had fallen; the sidewalk was deserted. On the false front of a long low building with sides of corrugated tin, a sad little string of electric lights proclaimed that gaiety was afoot.

"Whither away?" Bob Eden said. "The movies?"

"Heavens, no. I remember that one. It took ten years off my young life. Tell me, what are you doing here? People confide in me, too. Stranger, you don't belong."

"No, I'm afraid I don't," Eden admitted. "It's a complicated story but I'll inflict it on you anyhow, some day. Just at present I'm looking for the editor of the *Eldorado Times*. I've got a letter to him in my pocket."

"Will Holley?"

"Yes. You know him?"

"Everybody knows him. Come with me. He ought to be in his office now."

They turned down First Street. Bob Eden was pleasantly conscious of the slim lithe figure walking at his side. He had never before met a girl so modestly confident, so aware of life and unafraid of it. These desert towns were delightful.

A light was burning in the newspaper office, and under it a frail figure sat hunched over a typewriter. As they entered Will Holley rose, removing a green shade from his eyes. He was a thin tall man of thirty-five or so, with prematurely gray hair and wistful eyes.

"Hello, Paula," he said.

"Hello, Will. See what *I* found at the Oasis Café."

Holley smiled. "You would find him," he said. "You're the only one I know who can discover anything worth while in Eldorado. My boy, I don't know who you are, but run away before this desert gets you."

"I've a letter to you, Mr. Holley," Eden said. He took it from his pocket. "It's from an old friend of yours—Harry Fladgate."

"Harry Fladgate," repeated Holley softly. He read the letter through. "A voice from the past," he said. "The past when we were boys together on the old *Sun,* in New York. Say—that was a newspaper!" He was silent for a moment, staring out at the desert night. "Harry says you're here on business of some sort," he added.

"Why, yes," Eden replied. "I'll tell you about it later. Just at present I want to hire a car to take me out to the Madden ranch."

"You want to see P. J. himself?"

"Yes, just as soon as possible. He's out there, isn't he?"

Holley nodded. "Yes—he's supposed to be. However, I haven't seen him. It's rumored he came by motor the other day from Barstow. This young woman can tell you more about him than I can. By the way, have you two met each other, or are you just taking a stroll together in the moonlight?"

"Well, the fact is—" smiled Eden. "Miss—er—she just let a steak of mine get away from her in the Oasis. I had to credit her with an error in the infield, but she made a splendid try. However, as to names—and all that—"

"So I perceive," said Holley. "Miss Paula Wendell, may I present Mr. Bob Eden. Let us not forget our book of etiquette, even here in the devil's garden."

"Thanks, old man," remarked Eden. "No one has ever done me a greater kindness. Now that we've been introduced, Miss Wendell, and I can speak to you at last, tell me—do you know Mr. Madden?"

"Not exactly," she replied. "It isn't given such humble folk to know the great Madden. But several years ago my company took some pictures at his ranch—he has rather a handsome house there, with a darling patio. The other day we got hold of a script that fairly screamed for the Madden patio. I wrote him, asking permission to use his place, and he answered—from San Francisco—that he was coming down and would be glad to grant our request. His letter was really most kind."

The girl sat down on the edge of Holley's typewriter table. "I got to Eldorado two nights ago, and drove out to Madden's at once. And—well, it was rather queer—what happened. Do you want to hear all this?"

"I certainly do," Bob Eden assured her.

"The gate was open, and I drove into the yard. The lights of my car flashed suddenly on the barn door, and I saw a bent old man with a black beard and a pack on his back—evidently an old-time prospector such as one meets occasionally, even to-day, in this desert country. It was his expression that startled me. He stood like a frightened rabbit in the spotlight, then darted away. I knocked at the ranch house door. There was a long delay, then finally a man came, a pale, excited-looking man—Madden's secretary, Thorn, he said he was. I give you my word—Will's heard this before—he was trembling all over. I told him my business with Madden, and he was very rude. He informed me that I positively could not see the great P. J. 'Come back in a week,' he said, over and over. I argued and pleaded—and he shut the door in my face."

"You couldn't see Madden," repeated Bob Eden slowly. "Anything else?"

"Not much. I drove back to town. A short distance down the road my lights picked up the little old prospector again. But when I got to where I thought he was, he'd disappeared utterly. I didn't investigate—I just stepped on the gas. My love for the desert isn't so keen after dark."

Bob Eden took out a cigarette. "I'm awfully obliged," he said. "Mr. Holley, I must get out to Madden's at once. If you'll direct me to a garage—"

"I'll do nothing of the sort," Holley replied. "An old flivver that answered to the name of Horace Greeley happens to be among my possessions at the moment, and I'm going to drive you out."

"I couldn't think of taking you away from your work."

"Oh, don't joke like that. You're breaking my heart. My work! Here I am, trying to string one good day's work along over all eternity, and you drift in and start to kid me—"

"I'm sorry," said Eden. "Come to think of it, I did see your placard on the door."

Holley shrugged. "I suppose that was just cheap cynicism. I try to steer clear of it. But sometimes—sometimes—"

They went together out of the office, and Holley locked the door. The deserted, sad little street stretched off to nowhere in each direction. The editor waved his hand at the somnolent picture.

"You'll find us all about out here," he said, "the exiles of the world. Of course, the desert is grand, and we love it—but once let a doctor say 'you can go' and you couldn't see us for the dust. I don't mind the daytime so much—the hot friendly day—but the nights—the cold lonely nights."

"Oh, it isn't so bad, Will," said the girl gently.

"Oh no, it isn't so bad," he admitted. "Not since the radio—and the pictures. Night after night I sit over there in that movie theater, and sometimes, in a newsreel or perhaps in a feature, I see Fifth Avenue again, Fifth Avenue at Forty-second, with the motors, and the lions in front of the library, and the women in furs. But I never see Park Row." The three of them walked along in silence through the sand. "If you love me, Paula," added Will Holley softly, "there's a location you'll find. A story about Park Row, with the crowds under the El, and the wagons backed up to the rear door of the post-office, and Perry's Drug Store and the gold dome of the World. Give me a film of that, and I'll sit in the Strand watching it over and over until these old eyes go blind."

"I'd like to," said the girl. "But those crowds under the Elevated wouldn't care for it. What they want is the desert—the broad open spaces away from the roar of the town."

Holley nodded. "I know. It's a feeling that's spread over America these past few years like some dread epidemic. I must write an editorial about it. The French have a proverb that describes it—'Wherever one is not, that is where the heart is.' "

The girl held out her hand. "Mr. Eden, I'm leaving you here—leaving you for a happy night at the Desert Edge Hotel."

"But I'll see you again," Bob Eden said quickly. "I must."

"You surely will. I'm coming out to Madden's ranch to-morrow. I have that letter of his, and this time I'll see him—you bet I'll see him—if he's there."

"If he's there," repeated Bob Eden thoughtfully. "Good night. But before you go—how do you like your steaks?"

"Rare," she laughed.

"Yes—I guess one was enough. However, I'm very grateful to that one."

"It was a lovely steak," she said. "Good night."

Will Holley led the way to an aged car parked before the hotel. "Jump in," he said. "It's only a short run."

"Just a moment—I must get my bag," Eden replied. He entered the hotel and returned in a moment with his suit-case, which he tossed into the tonneau. "Horace Greeley's ready," Holley said. "Come west, young man."

Eden climbed in and the little car clattered down Main Street. "This is mighty kind of you," the boy said.

"It's a lot of fun," Holley answered. "You know, I've been thinking. Old P. J. never gives an interview, but you can't tell—I might be able to persuade him. These famous men sometimes let down a little when they get out here. It would be a big feather in my cap. They'd hear of me on Park Row again."

"I'll do all I can to help," Bob Eden promised.

"That's good of you," Holley answered. The faint yellow lights of Eldorado grew even fainter behind them. They ascended a rough road between two small hills—barren, unlovely piles of badly assorted rocks. "Well, I'm going to try it," the editor added. "But I hope I have more luck than the last time."

"Oh—then you've seen Madden before?" Eden asked with interest.

"Just once," Holley replied. "Twelve years ago, when I was a reporter in New York. I'd managed to get into a gambling house on Forty-fourth Street, a few doors east of Delmonico's. It didn't have a very good reputation, that joint, but there was the great P. J. Madden himself, all dolled up in evening clothes, betting his head off. They said that after he'd gambled all day in Wall Street, he couldn't let it alone—hung round the roulette wheels in that house every night."

"And you tried to interview him?"

"I did. I was a fool kid, with lots of nerve. He had a big railroad merger in the air at the time, and I decided to ask him about it. So I went up to him during a lull in the betting. I told him I was on a newspaper—and that was as far as I got. 'Get the hell out of here,' he roared. 'You know I never give interviews.'" Holley laughed. "That was my first and only meeting with P. J. Madden. It wasn't a very propitious beginning, but what I started that night on Forty-fourth Street I'm going to try to finish out here to-night."

They reached the top of the grade, the rocky hills dropped behind them, and they were in a mammoth doorway leading to a strange new world. Up amid the platinum stars a thin slice of moon rode high, and far below in that meager light lay the great gray desert, lonely and mysterious.

5

Madden's Ranch

Carefully Will Holley guided his car down the steep, rock-strewn grade. "Go easy, Horace," he murmured. Presently they were on the floor of the desert, the road but a pair of faint wheel tracks amid the creosote brush and mesquite. Once their head-lights caught a jack-rabbit, sitting firmly on the right of way; the next instant he was gone forever.

Bob Eden saw a brief stretch of palm trees back of a barbed-wire fence, and down the lane between the trees the glow of a lonely window.

"Alfalfa ranch," Will Holley explained.

"Why, in heaven's name, do people live out here?" Eden asked.

"Some of them because they can't live anywhere else," the editor answered. "And at that—well, you know it isn't a bad place to ranch it. Apples, lemons, pears—"

"But how about water?"

"It's only a desert because not many people have taken the trouble to bore for water. Just go down a ways, and you strike it. Some go down a couple of hundred feet—Madden only had to go thirty odd. But that was Madden luck. He's near the bed of an underground river."

They came to another fence; above it were painted signs and flags fluttering yellow in the moonlight.

"Don't tell me that's a subdivision," Eden said.

Holley laughed. "Date City," he announced. "Here in California the subdivider, like the poor, is always with us. Date City where, if you believe all you're told, every dime is a baby dollar. No one lives there yet—but who knows? We're a growing community—see my editorial in last week's issue."

The car plowed on. It staggered a bit now, but Holley's hands were firm on the wheel. Here and there a Joshua tree stretched out hungry black arms as though to seize these travelers by night, and over that gray waste a dismal wind moaned constantly, chill and keen and biting. Bob Eden turned up the collar of his top coat.

"I can't help thinking of that old song," he said. "You know—about the lad who guaranteed to love somebody 'until the sands of the desert grow cold.' "

"It wasn't much of a promise," agreed Holley. "Either he was a great kidder, or he'd never been on the desert at night. But look here—is this your first experience with this country? What kind of a Californian are you?"

"Golden Gate brand," smiled Eden. "Yes, it's true, I've never been down here before. Something tells me I've missed a lot."

"You sure have. I hope you won't rush off in a hurry. By the way, how long do you expect to be here?"

"I don't know," replied Eden. He was silent for a moment; his friend at home had told him that Holley could be trusted, but he really did not need that assurance. One look into the editor's friendly gray eyes was sufficient. "Holley, I may as well tell you why I've come," he continued. "But I rely on your discretion. This isn't an interview."

"Suit yourself," Holley answered. "I can keep a secret if I have to. But tell me or not, just as you prefer."

"I prefer to tell you," Eden said. He recounted Madden's purchase of the Phillimore pearls, his request for their delivery in New York, and then his sudden unexpected switch to the desert. "That, in itself, was rather disturbing," he added.

"Odd, yes," agreed Holley.

"But that wasn't all," Bob Eden went on. Omitting only Charlie Chan's connection with the affair, he told the whole story—the telephone call from the cigar store in San Francisco, the loving solicitude at the dock and after of the man with the dark glasses, the subsequent discovery that this was Shaky Phil Maydorf, a guest at the Killarney Hotel, and last of all, the fact that Louie Wong had been summoned from the Madden ranch by his relative in Chinatown. As he related all this out there on that lonesome desert, it began to take on a new and ominous aspect, the future loomed dark and thrilling. Had that great opening between the hills been, in reality, the gateway to adventure? Certainly it looked the part. "What do you think?" he finished.

"Me?" said Holley. "I think I'm not going to get that interview."

"You don't believe Madden is at the ranch?"

"I certainly don't. Look at Paula's experience the other night. Why couldn't she see him? Why didn't he hear her at the door and come to find out what the row was about? Because he wasn't there. My lad, I'm glad you didn't venture out here alone. Particularly if you've brought the pearls—as I presume you have."

"Well, in a way, I've got them. About this Louie Wong? You know him, I suppose?"

"Yes. And I saw him at the station the other morning. Look at to-morrow's *Eldorado Times* and you'll find the big story, under the personals. 'Our respected fellow townsman, Mr. Louie Wong, went to San Francisco on business last Wednesday.' "

"Wednesday, eh? What sort of lad is Louie?"

"Why—he's just a Chinaman. Been in these parts a long time. For the past five years he's stayed at Madden's ranch the year round, as caretaker. I don't know a great deal about him. He's never talked much to any one round here—except the parrot."

"The parrot? What parrot?"

"His only companion on the ranch. A little gray Australian bird that some sea captain gave Madden several years ago. Madden brought the bird—its name is Tony—here to be company for the old caretaker. A rough party, Tony—used to hang out in a barroom on an Australian boat. Some of his language when he first came was far from pretty. But they're clever, those Australian parrots. You know, from associating with Louie, this one has learned to speak Chinese."

"Amazing," said Bob Eden.

"Oh, not so amazing as it sounds. A bird of that sort will repeat anything it hears. So Tony rattles along in two languages. A regular linguist. The ranchers round here call him the Chinese parrot." They had reached a little group of cottonwoods and pepper trees sheltering a handsome adobe ranch house—an oasis on the bare plain. "Here we are at Madden's," Holley said. "By the way—have you got a gun?"

"Why, no," Bob Eden replied. "I didn't bring any. I thought that Charlie—"

"What's that?"

"No matter. I'm unarmed."

"So am I. Walk softly, son. By the way, you might open that gate, if you will."

Bob Eden got out and, unlatching the gate, swung it open. When Holley had steered Horace Greeley inside the yard, Eden shut the gate behind him. The editor brought his car to a stop twenty feet away, and alighted.

The ranch house was a one-story structure, eloquent of the old Spanish days in California before Iowa came. Across the front ran a long low veranda, the roof of which sheltered four windows that were glowing warmly in the chill night. Holley and the boy crossed the tile floor of the porch, and came to a big front door, strong and forbidding.

Eden knocked loudly. There was a long wait. Finally the door opened a scant foot, and a pale face looked out. "What is it? What do you want?" inquired a querulous voice. From inside the room came the gay lilt of a fox-trot.

"I want to see Mr. Madden," Bob Eden said. "Mr. P. J. Madden."

"Who are you?"

"Never mind. I'll tell Madden who I am. Is he here?"

The door went shut a few inches. "He's here, but he isn't seeing any one."

"He'll see me, Thorn," said Eden sharply. "You're Thorn, I take it. Please tell Madden that a messenger from Post Street, San Francisco, is waiting."

The door swung instantly open, and Martin Thorn was as near to beaming as his meager face permitted.

"Oh, pardon me. Come in at once. We've been expecting you. Come in—ah—er—gentlemen." His face clouded as he saw Holley. "Excuse me just a moment."

The secretary disappeared through a door at the rear, and left the two callers standing in the great living-room of the ranch house. To step from the desert into a room like this was a revelation. Its walls were of paneled oak; rare etchings hung upon them; there were softly shaded lamps standing by tables on which lay the latest magazines—even a recent edition of a New York Sunday newspaper. At one end, in a huge fireplace, a pile of logs was blazing, and in a distant corner a radio ground out dance music from some far orchestra.

"Say, this is home, sweet home," Bob Eden remarked. He nodded to the wall at the opposite end of the room from the fireplace. "And speaking of being unarmed—"

"That's Madden's collection of guns," Holley explained. "Wong showed it to me once. They're loaded. If you have to back away, go in that direction." He looked dubiously about. "You know, that sleek lad didn't say he was going for Madden."

"I know he didn't," Eden replied. He studied the room thoughtfully. One great question worried him—where was Charlie Chan?

They stood there, waiting. A tall clock at the rear of the room struck the hour of nine, slowly, deliberately. The fire sputtered; the metallic tinkle of jazz flowed on.

Suddenly the door through which Thorn had gone opened suddenly behind them, and they swung quickly about. In the doorway, standing like a tower of granite in the gray clothes he always affected, was the man Bob Eden had last seen on the stairs descending from his father's office, Madden, the great financier—P. J. himself.

Bob Eden's first reaction was one of intense relief, as of a burden dropping from his shoulders with a "most delectable thud." But almost immediately after came a feeling of disappointment. He was young, and he craved excitement. Here was the big desert mystery crashing about his ears, Madden alive and well, and all their fears and premonitions proving groundless. Just a tame handing over of the pearls—when Charlie came—and then back to the old rut again. He saw Will Holley smiling.

"Good evening, gentlemen," Madden was saying. "I'm very glad to see you. Martin," he added to his secretary, who had followed him in, "turn off that confounded racket. An orchestra, gentlemen—an orchestra in the ballroom of a hotel in Denver. Who says the day of miracles is past?" Thorn silenced the jazz; it died with a gurgle of protest. "Now," inquired Madden, "which of you comes from Post Street?"

The boy stepped forward. "I am Bob Eden, Mr. Madden. Alexander Eden is my father. This is my friend, a neighbor of yours, Mr. Will Holley of the *Eldorado Times*. He very kindly drove me out here."

"Ah, yes." Madden's manner was genial. He shook hands. "Draw up to the fire, both of you. Thorn—cigars, please." With his own celebrated hands he placed chairs before the fireplace.

"I'll sit down just a moment," Holley said. "I'm not stopping. I realize that Mr. Eden has some business with you, and I'll not intrude. But before I go, Mr. Madden—"

"Yes," said Madden sharply, biting the end from a cigar.

"I—I don't suppose you remember me," Holley continued.

Madden's big hand poised with the lighted match. "I never forget a face. I've seen yours before. Was it in Eldorado?"

Holley shook his head. "No—it was twelve years ago—on Forty-fourth Street, New York. At"—Madden was watching him closely—"at a gambling house just east of Delmonico's. One winter's night—"

"Wait a minute," cut in the millionaire. "Some people say I'm getting old—but listen to this. You came to me as a newspaper reporter, asking an interview. And I told you to get the hell out of there."

"Splendid," laughed Holley.

"Oh, the old memory isn't so bad, eh? I remember perfectly. I used to spend many evenings in that place—until I discovered the game was fixed. Yes, I dropped a lot of spare change there. Why didn't you tell me it was a crooked joint?"

Holley shrugged. "Well, your manner didn't encourage confidences. But what I'm getting at, Mr. Madden—I'm still in the newspaper game, and an interview from you—"

"I never give 'em," snapped the millionaire.

"I'm sorry," said Holley. "An old friend of mine runs a news bureau in New York, and it would be a big triumph for me if I could wire him something from you. On the financial outlook, for example. The first interview from P. J. Madden."

"Impossible," answered Madden.

"I'm sorry to hear you say that, Mr. Madden," Bob Eden remarked. "Holley here has been very kind to me, and I was hoping with all my heart you would overlook your rule this once."

Madden leaned back, and blew a ring of smoke toward the paneled ceiling. "Well," he said, and his voice was somehow gentler, "you've taken a lot of trouble for me, Mr. Eden, and I'd like to oblige you." He turned to Holley. "Look here—nothing much, you know. Just a few words about business prospects for the coming year."

"That would be extremely kind of you, Mr. Madden."

"Oh, it's all right. I'm away out here, and I feel a bit differently about the newspapers than I do at home. I'll dictate something to Thorn—suppose you run out here to-morrow about noon."

"I certainly will," said Holley, rising. "You don't know what this means to me, sir. I must hurry back to town." He shook hands with the millionaire, then with Bob Eden. His eyes as he looked at the latter said; "Well, everything's all right, after all. I'm glad." He paused at the door. "Good-by—until to-morrow," he added. Thorn let him out.

The door had barely closed behind the editor when Madden leaned forward eagerly. His manner had changed; suddenly, like an electric shock, the boy felt the force of this famous personality. "Now, Mr. Eden," he began briskly, "you've got the pearls, of course?"

Eden felt extremely silly. All their fears seemed so futile here in this bright, home-like room. "Well, as a matter of fact—" he stammered.

A glass door at the rear of the room opened, and some one entered. Eden did not look round; he waited. Presently the newcomer stepped between him and the fire. He saw a plump little Chinese servant, with worn trousers and velvet slippers, and a loose jacket of Canton crêpe. In his arms he carried a couple of logs. "Maybe you wantee catch 'um moah fiah, hey, boss?" he said in a dull voice. His face was quite expressionless. He threw the logs into the fireplace and as he turned, gave Bob Eden a quick look. His eyes were momentarily sharp and bright—like black buttons in the yellow light. The eyes of Charlie Chan.

The little servant went noiselessly out. "The pearls," insisted Madden quickly. "What about the pearls?" Martin Thorn came closer.

"I haven't got them," said Bob Eden slowly.

"What! You didn't bring them?"

"I did not."

The huge red face of Madden purpled suddenly, and he tossed his great head—the old gesture of annoyance of which the newspapers often spoke. "In heaven's name, what's the matter with you fellows, anyhow?" he cried. "Those pearls are mine—I've bought them, haven't I? I've asked for them here—I want them."

"Call your servant." The words were on the tip of Bob Eden's tongue. But something in that look Charlie Chan had given him moved him to hesitate. No, he must first have a word with the little detective.

"Your final instructions to my father were that the pearls must be delivered to New York," he reminded Madden.

"Well, what if they were? I can change my mind, can't I?"

"Nevertheless, my father felt that the whole affair called for caution. One or two things happened—"

"What things?"

Eden paused. Why go over all that? It would sound silly, perhaps—in any case, was it wise to make a confidant of this cold, hard man who was glaring at him with such evident disgust? "It is enough to say, Mr. Madden, that my father refused to send that necklace down here into what might be a well-laid trap."

"Your father's a fool," cried Madden.

Bob Eden rose, his face flushed. "Very well—if you want to call the deal off—"

"No, no. I'm sorry. I spoke too quickly. I apologize. Sit down." The boy resumed his chair. "But I'm very much annoyed. So your father sent you here to reconnoiter?"

"He did. He felt something might have happened to you."

"Nothing ever happens to me unless I want it to," returned Madden, and the remark had the ring of truth. "Well, you're here now. You see everything's all right. What do you propose to do?"

"I shall call my father on the telephone in the morning, and tell him to send the string at once. If I may, I'd like to stay here until it comes."

Again Madden tossed his head. "Delay—delay—I don't like it. I must hurry back east. I'd planned to leave here for Pasadena early in the morning, put the pearls in a vault there, and then take a train to New York."

"Ah," said Eden. "Then you never intended to give that interview to Holley?"

Madden's eyes narrowed. "What if I didn't? He's of no importance, is he?" Bruskly he stood up. "Well, if you haven't got the pearls, you haven't got them. You can stay here, of course. But you're going to call your father in the morning—early—I warn you I won't stand for any more delay."

"I agree to that," replied Eden. "And now, if you don't mind—I've had a hard day—"

Madden went to the door, and called. Charlie Chan came in.

"Ah Kim," said Madden, "this gentleman has the bedroom at the end of the left wing. Over here." He pointed. "Take his suit-case."

"Allight, boss," replied the newly christened Ah Kim. He picked up Eden's bag.

"Good night," said Madden. "If you want anything, this boy will look after you. He's new here, but I guess he knows the ropes. You can reach your room from the patio. I trust you'll sleep well."

"I know I shall," said Eden. "Thank you so much. Good night."

He crossed the patio behind the shuffling figure of the Chinese. Above, white and cool, hung the desert stars. The wind blew keener than ever. As he entered the room assigned him he was glad to see that a fire had been laid. He stooped to light it.

"Humbly begging pardon," said Chan. "That are my work."

Eden glanced toward the closed door. "What became of you? I lost you at Barstow."

"Thinking deep about the matter," said Chan softly, "I decide not to await train. On auto truck belonging to one of my countrymen, among many other vegetables, I ride out of Barstow. Much better I arrive on ranch in warm daylight. Not so shady look to it. I am Ah Kim, the cook. How fortunate I mastered that art in far-away youth."

"You're darned good," laughed Eden.

Chan shrugged. "All my life," he complained, "I study to speak fine English words. Now I must strangle all such in my throat, lest suspicion rouse up. Not a happy situation for me."

"Well, it won't last long," replied Eden. "Everything's all right, evidently."

Again Chan shrugged, and did not answer.

"It is all right, isn't it?" Eden asked with sudden interest.

"Humbly offering my own poor opinion," said Chan, "it are not so right as I would be pleased to have it."

Eden stared at him. "Why—what have you found out?"

"I have found nothing whatever."

"Well, then—"

"Pardon me," Chan broke in. "Maybe you know—Chinese are very psychic people. Can not say in ringing words what is wrong here. But deep down in heart—"

"Oh, forget that," cut in Eden. "We can't go by instinct now. We came to deliver a string of pearls to Madden, if he proved to be here, and get his receipt. He's here, and our course is simple. For my part, I'm not taking any chances. I'm going to give him those pearls now."

Chan looked distressed. "No, no, please! Speaking humbly for myself—"

"Now, see here, Charlie—if I may call you that?"

"Greatly honored, to be sure."

"Let's not be foolish, just because we're far from home on a desert. Chinese may be psychic people, as you say. But I see myself trying to explain that to Victor Jordan—and to dad. All we were to find out was whether Madden was here or not. He is. Please go to Madden at once and tell him I want to see him in his bedroom in twenty minutes. When I go in you wait outside his door, and when I call you—come. We'll hand over our burden then and there."

"An appalling mistake," objected Chan.

"Why? Can you give me one definite reason?"

"Not in words, which are difficult. But—"

"Then I'm very sorry, but I'll have to use my own judgment. I'll take the full responsibility. Now, really, I think you'd better go—"

Reluctantly, Charlie went, Bob Eden lighted a cigarette and sat down before the fire. Silence had closed down like a curtain of fog over the house, over the desert, over the world. An uncanny silence that nothing, seemingly, would ever break.

Eden thought deeply. What had Charlie Chan been talking about, anyhow? Rot and nonsense. They loved to dramatize things, these Chinese. Loved to dramatize themselves. Here was Chan playing a novel rôle, and his complaint against it was not sincere. He wanted to go on playing it, to spy around and imagine vain things. Well, that wasn't the American way. It wasn't Bob Eden's way.

The boy looked at his watch. Ten minutes since Charlie had left him; in ten minutes more he would go to Madden's room and get those pearls off his hands forever. He rose and walked about. From his window opposite the patio he looked out across the dim gray desert to the black bulk of distant hills. Ye gods, what a country. Not for him, he thought. Rather street lamps shining on the pavements, the clamor of cable-cars, crowds, crowds of people. Confusion and—noise. Something terrible about this silence. This lonely silence—

A horrible cry shattered the night. Bob Eden stood, frozen. Again the cry, and then a queer, choked voice: "Help! Help! Murder!" The cry. "Help! Put down that gun! Help! Help!"

Bob Eden ran out into the patio. As he did so, he saw Thorn and Charlie Chan coming from the other side. Madden—where was Madden? But again his suspicion proved incorrect—Madden emerged from the living-room and joined them.

Again came the cry. And now Bob Eden saw, on a perch ten feet away, the source of the weird outburst. A little gray Australian parrot was hanging there uncertainly, screeching its head off.

"That damn bird," cried Madden angrily. "I'm sorry, Mr. Eden—I forgot to tell you about him. It's only Tony, and he's had a wild past, as you may imagine."

The parrot stopped screaming and blinked solemnly at the little group before him. "One at a time, gentlemen, please," he squawked.

Madden laughed. "That goes back to his barroom days," he said. "Picked it up from some bartender, I suppose."

"One at a time, gentlemen, please."

"It's all right, Tony," Madden continued. "We're not lined up for drinks. And you keep quiet. I hope you weren't unduly alarmed, Mr. Eden. There seems to have been a killing or two in those barrooms where Tony used to hang out. Martin,"—he turned to his secretary—"take him to the barn and lock him up."

Thorn came forward. Bob Eden thought that the secretary's face was even paler than usual in the moonlight. He held out his hands to the parrot, Did Eden imagine it, or were the hands really trembling? "Here, Tony," said Thorn. "Nice Tony. You come with me." Gingerly he unfastened the chain from Tony's leg.

"You wanted to see me, didn't you?" Madden said. He led the way to his bedroom, and closed the door behind them. "Waht is it? Have you got those pearls, after all?"

The door opened, and the Chinese shuffled into the room.

"What the devil do you want?" cried Madden.

"You allight, boss?"

"Of course, I'm all right. Getout of here."

"Tomallah," said Charlie Chan in his role of Ah Kim, and a glance that was full of meaning passed between him and Bob Eden. "Tomallah nice day, you bet. See you tomallah, gentlemen."

He departed, leaving the door open. Eden saw him moving across the patio in silent feet. He was not waiting outside Madden's door.

"What was it you wanted?" Madden persisted.

Bob Eden thought quickly. "I wanted to see you alone for just a moment. This Thorn—you can trust him, can't you?"

Madden snorted. "You give me a pain," he said. "Any one would think you were bringing me the Bank of England. Of course, Thorn's all right. He's been with me for fifteen years."

"I just wanted to be sure," Eden answered. "I'll get hold of dad early in the morning. Good night."

He returned to the patio. The secretary was hurrying in from his unwelcome errand. "Good night, Mr. Thorn," Eden said.

"Oh—er—good night, Mr. Eden," answered the man. He passed furtively from sight.

Back in his room, Eden began to undress. He was both puzzled and disturbed. Was this adventure to be as tame as it looked? Still in his ears rang the unearthly scream of the parrot. After all, had it been in a barroom that Tony picked up that hideous cry for help?

6

Tony's Happy New Year

Forgetting the promise he had made to rise and telephone his father early in the morning, Bob Eden lingered on in the pleasant company of his couch. The magnificent desert sunrise, famous wherever books are sold, came and went without the seal of his approval, and a haze of heat spread over the barren world. It was nine o'clock when he awoke from a most satisfactory sleep and sat up in bed.

Staring about the room, he gradually located himself on the map of California. One by one the events of the night before came back to him. First of all the scene at the Oasis—that agile steak eluding him with diabolic cunning—the girl whose charming presence made the dreary café an oasis indeed. The ride over the desert with Will Holley, the bright and cheery living-room of the ranch house, the fox-trot from a Denver orchestra. Madden, leaning close and breathing hard, demanding the Phillimore pearls. Chan in his velvet slippers, whispering of psychic fears and dark premonitions. And then the shrill cry of the parrot out of the desert night.

Now, however, the tense troubled feeling with which he had gone to bed was melting away in the yellow sunshine of the morning. The boy began to suspect that he had made rather a fool of himself in listening to the little detective from the islands. Chan was an Oriental, also a policeman. Such a combination was bound to look at almost any situation with a jaundiced eye. After all he, Bob Eden, was here as the representative of Meek and Eden, and he must act as he saw fit. Was Chan in charge of this expedition, or was he?

The door opened, and on the threshold stood Ah Kim, in the person of Charlie Chan.

"You come 'long, boss," said his confederate loudly. "You ac' lazy bimeby you no catch 'um bleckfast."

Having said which, Charlie gently closed the door and came in, grimacing as one who felt a keen distaste.

"Silly talk like that hard business for me," he complained. "Chinese without accustomed dignity is like man without clothes, naked, and ashamed. You enjoy long, restful sleep, I think."

Eden yawned. "Compared to me last night, Rip Van Winkle had insomnia."

"That's good. Humbly suggest you tear yourself out of that bed now. The great Madden indulges in nervous fit on living-room rug."

Eden laughed. "Suffering, is he? Well, we'll have to stop that." He tossed aside the covers.

Chan was busy at the curtains. "Favor me by taking a look from windows," he remarked. "On every side desert stretches off like floor of eternity. Plenty acres of unlimitable sand."

Bob Eden glanced out. "Yes, it's the desert, and there's plenty of it, that's a fact. But look here—we ought to talk fast while we have the chance. Last night you made a sudden change in our plans."

"Presuming greatly—yes."

"Why?"

Chan stared at him. "Why not? You yourself hear parrot scream out of the dark. 'Murder. Help. Help. Put down gun.' "

Eden nodded. "I know. But that probably meant nothing."

Charlie Chan shrugged. "You understand parrot does not invent talk. Merely repeats what others have remarked."

"Of course," Eden agreed. "And Tony was no doubt repeating something he heard in Australia, or on a boat. I happen to know that all Madden said of the bird's past was the truth. And I may as well tell you, Charlie, that looking at things in the bright light of the morning, I feel we acted rather foolishly last night. I'm going to give those pearls to Madden before breakfast."

Chan was silent for a moment. "If I might presume again, I would speak a few hearty words in praise of patience. Youth, pardon me, is too hot around the head. Take my advice, please, and wait."

"Wait. Wait for what?"

"Wait until I have snatched more conversation out of Tony. Tony very smart bird—he speaks Chinese. I am not so smart—but so do I."

"And what do you think Tony would tell you?"

"Tony might reveal just what is wrong on this ranch," suggested Chan.

"I don't believe anything's wrong," objected Eden.

Chan shook his head. "Not very happy position for me," he said, "that I must argue with bright boy like you are."

"But listen, Charlie," Eden protested. "I promised to call my father this morning. And Madden isn't an easy man to handle."

"Hoo malimali," responded Chan.

"No doubt you're right," Eden said. "But I don't understand Chinese."

"You have made natural error," Chan answered. "Pardon me while I correct you. That are not Chinese. It are Hawaiian talk. Well known in islands—hoo malimali—make Madden feel good by a little harmless deception. As my cousin Willie Chan, captain of All-Chinese baseball team, translate with his vulgarity, kid him along."

"Easier said than done," replied Eden.

"But you are clever boy. You could perfect it. Just a few hours, while I have talk with the smart Tony."

Eden considered. Paula Wendell was coming out this morning. Too bad to rush off without seeing her again. "Tell you what I'll do," he said. "I'll wait until two o'clock. But when the clock strikes two, if nothing has happened in the interval, we hand over those pearls. Is that understood?"

"Maybe," nodded Chan.

"You mean maybe it's understood?"

"Not precisely. I mean maybe we hand over pearls." Eden looked into the stubborn eyes of the Chinese, and felt rather helpless. "However," Chan added, "accept my glowing thanks. You are pretty good. Now proceed toward the miserable breakfast I have prepared."

"Tell Madden I'll be there very soon."

Chan grimaced. "With your kind permission, I will alter that message slightly, losing the word very. In memory of old times, there remains little I would not do for Miss Sally. My life, perhaps—but by the bones of my honorable ancestors, I will not say 'velly.' " He went out.

On his perch in the patio, opposite Eden's window, Tony was busy with his own breakfast. The boy saw Chan approach the bird, and pause. "Hoo la ma," cried the detective.

Tony looked up, and cocked his head on one side. "Hoo la ma," he replied, in a shrill, harsh voice.

Chan went nearer, and began to talk rapidly in Chinese. Now and then he paused, and the bird replied amazingly with some phrase out of Chan's speech. It was, Bob Eden reflected, as good as a show.

Suddenly from a door on the other side of the patio the man Thorn emerged. His pale face was clouded with anger.

"Here," he cried loudly. "What the devil are you doing?"

"Solly, boss," said the Chinese. "Tony nice litta fellah. Maybe I take 'um to cook house."

"You keep away from him," Thorn ordered. "Get me—keep away from that bird."

Chan shuffled off. For a long moment Thorn stood staring after him, anger and apprehension mingled in his look. As Bob Eden turned away, he was deep in thought. Was there something in Chan's attitude, after all?

He hurried into the bath, which lay between his room and the vacant bedroom beyond. When he finally joined Madden, he thought he preceived the afterglow of that nervous fit still on the millionaire's face.

"I'm sorry to be late," he apologized. "But this desert air—"

"I know," said Madden. "It's all right—we haven't lost any time. I've already put in that call for your father."

"Good idea," replied the boy, without any enthusiasm. "Called his office, I suppose?"

"Naturally."

Suddenly Eden remembered. This was Saturday morning, and unless it was raining in San Francisco, Alexander Eden was by now well on his way to the golf links at Burlingame. There he would remain until late to-night at least—perhaps over Sunday. Oh, for a bright day in the north!

Thorn came in, sedate and solemn in his blue serge suit, and looked with hungry eyes toward the table standing before the fire. They sat down to the breakfast prepared by the new servant, Ah Kim. A good breakfast it was, for Charlie Chan had not forgotten his early training in the Phillimore household. As it progressed, Madden mellowed a bit.

"I hope you weren't alarmed last night by Tony's screeching," he said presently.

"Well—for a minute," admitted Eden. "Of course, as soon as I found out the source of the racket, I felt better."

Madden nodded. "Tony's a colorless little beast, but he's had a scarlet past," he remarked.

"Like some of the rest of us," Eden suggested.

Madden looked at him keenly. "The bird was given me by a sea captain in the Australian trade. I brought him here to be company for my caretaker, Louie Wong."

"I thought your boy's name was Ah Kim," said Eden, innocently.

"Oh—this one. This isn't Wong. Louie was called suddenly to San Francisco the other day. This Ah Kim just happened to drift in most opportunely yesterday. He's merely a stop-gap until Louie comes back."

"You're lucky," Eden remarked. "Such good cooks as Ah Kim are rare."

"Oh, he'll do," Madden admitted. "When I come west to stay, I bring a staff with me. This is a rather unexpected visit."

"Your real headquarters out here are in Pasadena, I believe?" Eden inquired.

"Yes—I've got a house there, on Orange Grove Avenue. I just keep this place for an occasional week-end—when my asthma threatens. And it's good to get away from the mob, now and then." The millionaire pushed back from the table, and looked at his watch. "Ought to hear from San Francisco any minute now," he added hopefully.

Eden glanced toward the telephone in a far corner. "Did you put the call in for my father, or just for the office?" he asked.

"Just for the office," Madden replied. "I figured that if he was out, we could leave a message."

Thorn came forward. "Chief, how about this interview for Holley?" he inquired.

"Oh, the devil!" Madden said. "Why did I let myself in for that?"

"I could bring the typewriter in here," began the secretary.

"No—we'll go to your room. Mr. Eden, if the telephone rings, please answer it."

The two went out. Ah Kim arrived on noiseless feet to clear away the breakfast. Eden lighted a cigarette, and dropped into a chair before the fire, which the blazing sun outside made rather superfluous.

Twenty minutes later, the telephone rang. Eden leaped to it, but before he reached the table where it stood, Madden was at his side. He had hoped to be alone for this ordeal, and sighed wearily. At the other end of the wire he was relieved to hear the cool, melodious voice of his father's well-chosen secretary.

"Hello," he said. "This is Bob Eden, at Madden's ranch down on the desert. And how are you this bright and shining morning?"

"What makes you think it's a bright and shining morning up here?" asked the girl.

Eden's heart sank. "Don't tell me it isn't. I'd be broken-hearted."

"Why?"

"Why! Because, while you're beautiful at any time, I like to think of you with the sunlight on your hair—"

Madden laid a heavy hand on his shoulder. "What the blazes do you think you're doing—making a date with a chorus girl? Get down to business."

"Excuse it, please," said Eden. "Miss Chase, is my father there?"

"No. This is Saturday, you know. Golf."

"Oh yes—of course. Then it *is* a nice day. Well, tell him to call me here if he comes in. Eldorado 76."

"Where is he?" demanded Madden eagerly.

"Out playing golf," the boy answered.

"Where? What links?"

Bob sighed. "I suppose he's at Burlingame," he said over the wire.

Then—oh, excellent young woman, thought the boy—the secretary answered: "Not to-day. He went with some friends to another links. He didn't say which."

"Thank you so much," Eden said. "Just leave the message on his desk, please." He hung up.

"Too bad," he remarked cheerfully. "Gone off to play golf somewhere, and nobody knows where."

Madden swore. "The old simpleton. Why doesn't he attend to his business—"

"Look here, Mr. Madden," Eden began.

"Golf, golf, golf," stormed Madden. "It's ruined more good men than whisky. I tell you, if I'd fooled round on golf links, I wouldn't be where I am to-day. If your father had any sense—"

"I've heard about enough," said Eden, rising.

Madden's manner changed suddenly. "I'm sorry," he said. "But this is annoying, you must admit. I wanted that necklace to start to-day."

"The day's young," Eden reminded him. "It may get off yet."

"I hope so," Madden frowned. "I'm not accustomed to this sort of dilly-dallying, I can tell you that."

His great head was tossing angrily as he went out. Bob Eden looked after him, thoughtfully. Madden, master of many millions, was putting what seemed an undue emphasis on a little pearl necklace. The boy wondered. His father was getting on in years—he was far from the New York markets. Had he made some glaring mistake in setting a value on that necklace? Was it, perhaps, worth a great deal more than he had asked, and was Madden fuming to get hold of it before the jeweler learned his error and perhaps called off the deal? Of course, Alexander Eden had given his word, but even so, Madden might fear a slip-up.

The boy strolled idly out into the patio. The chill night wind had vanished and he saw the desert of song and story, baking under a relentless sun. In the sandy little yard of the ranch house, life was humming along. Plump chickens and haughty turkeys strutted back of wire enclosures. He paused for a moment to stare with interest at a bed of strawberries, red and tempting. Up above, on the bare branches of the cottonwoods, he saw unmistakable buds, mute promise of a grateful shade not far away.

Odd how things live and grew, here in this desolate country. He took a turn about the grounds. In one corner was a great reservoir half filled with water—a pleasant sight that must be on an August afternoon. Coming back to the patio, he stopped to speak to Tony, who was sitting rather dejectedly on his perch.

"Hoo la ma," he said.

Tony perked up. "Sung kai yat bo," he remarked.

"Yes, and a great pity, too," replied Eden facetiously.

"Gee fung low hop," added Tony, somewhat feebly.

"Perhaps, but I heard different," said Eden, and moved on. He wondered what Chan was doing. Evidently the detective thought it best to obey Thorn's command that he keep away from the bird. This was not surprising, for the windows of the secretary's room looked out on Tony's perch.

Back in the living-room, Eden took up a book. At a few minutes before twelve he heard the asthmatic cough of Horace Greeley in the yard and rising, he admitted Will Holley. The editor was smiling and alert.

"Hello," Eden said. "Madden's in there with Thorn, getting out the interview. Sit down." He came close. "And please remember that I haven't brought those pearls. My business with Madden is still unfinished."

Holley looked at him with sudden interest. "I get you. But I thought last night that everything was lovely. Do you mean—"

"Tell you later," interrupted Eden. "I may be in town this afternoon." He spoke in a louder tone. "I'm glad you came along. I was finding the desert a bit flat when you flivvered in."

Holley smiled. "Cheer up. I've got something for you. A veritable storehouse of wit and wisdom." He handed over a paper. "This week's issue of the *Eldorado Times,* damp from the presses. Read about Louie Wong's big trip to San Francisco. All the news to fit the print."

Eden took the proffered paper—eight small pages of mingled news and advertisements. He sank into a chair. "Well," he said, "it seems that the Ladies' Aid Supper last Tuesday night was notably successful. Not only that, but the ladies responsible for the affair labored assiduously and deserve much credit."

"Yes, but the real excitement's inside," remarked Holley. "On page three. There you'll learn that coyotes are getting pretty bad in the valley. A number of people are putting out traps."

"Under those circumstances," Eden said, "how fortunate that Henry Gratton is caring for Mr. Dickey's chickens during the latter's absence in Los Angeles."

Holley rose, and stared for a moment down at his tiny newspaper. "And once I worked with Mitchell on the *New York Sun*," he misquoted sadly. "Don't let Harry Fladgate see that, will you? When Harry knew me I was a newspaper man." He moved off across the room. "By the way, has Madden shown you his collection of firearms?"

Bob Eden rose, and followed. "Why no—he hasn't."

"It's rather interesting. But dusty—say, I guess Louie was afraid to touch them. Nearly every one of these guns has a history. See—there's a typewritten card above each one. 'Presented to P. J. Madden by Til Taylor'—Taylor was one of the best sheriffs Oregon ever had. And here—look at this one—it's a beauty. Given to Madden by Bill Tilghman. That gun, my boy, saw action on Front Street in the old Dodge City days."

"What's the one with all the notches?" Eden asked.

"Used to belong to Billy the Kid," said Holley. "Ask them about Billy over in New Mexico. And here's one Bat Masterson used to tote. But the star of the collection"—Holley's eyes ran over the wall—"the beauty of the lot—" He turned to Eden. "It isn't there," he said.

"There's a gun missing?" inquired Eden slowly.

"Seems to be. One of the first Colts made—a forty-five—it was presented to Madden by Bill Hart, who's staged a lot of pictures round here." He pointed to an open space on the wall. "There's where it used to be," he added, and was moving away.

Eden caught his coat sleeve. "Wait a minute," he said in a low, tense voice. "Let me get this. A gun missing. And the card's gone, too. You can see where the tacks held it in place."

"Well, what's all the excitement—" began Holley surprised.

Eden ran his finger over the wall. "There's no dust where that card should be. What does that mean? That Bill Hart's gun has been removed within the last few days."

"My boy," said Holley. "What are you talking about—"

"Hush," warned Eden. The door opened and Madden, followed by Thorn, entered the room. For a moment the millionaire stood, regarding them intently.

"Good morning, Mr. Holley," he said. "I've got your interview here. You're wiring it to New York, you say?"

"Yes. I've queried my friend there about it this morning. I know he'll want it."

"Well, it's nothing startling. I hope you'll mention in the course of it where you got it. That will help to soothe the feelings of the boys I've turned down so often in New York. And you won't change what I've said?"

"Not a comma," smiled Holley. "I must hurry back to town now. Thank you again, Mr. Madden."

"That's all right," said Madden. "Glad to help you out."

Eden followed Holley to the yard. Out of earshot of the house, the editor stopped.

"You seemed a little het up about that gun. What's doing?"

"Oh, nothing, I suppose," said Eden. "On the other hand—"

"What?"

"Well, Holley, it strikes me that something queer may have happened lately on this ranch."

Holley stared. "It doesn't sound possible. However, don't keep me in suspense."

"I've got to. It's a long story, and Madden mustn't see us getting too chummy. I'll come in this afternoon, as I promised."

Holley climbed into his car. "All right," he said. "I can wait, I guess. See you later, then."

Eden was sorry to watch Horace Greeley stagger down the dusty road. Somehow the newspaper man brought a warm, human atmosphere to the ranch, an atmosphere that was needed there. But a moment later he was sorry no longer, for a little speck of brown in the distance became a smart roadster, and at its wheel he saw the girl of the Oasis, Paula Wendell.

He held open the gate, and with a cheery wave of her hand the girl drove past him into the yard.

"Hello," he said, as she alighted. "I was beginning to fear you weren't coming."

"I overslept," she explained. "Always do, in this desert country. Have you noticed the air? People who are in a position to know tell me it's like wine."

"Had a merry breakfast, I suppose?"

"I certainly did. At the Oasis."

"You poor child. That coffee."

"I didn't mind. Will Holley says that Madden's here."

"Madden? That's right—you do want to see Madden, don't you? Well, come along inside."

Thorn was alone in the living-room. He regarded the girl with a fishy eye. Not many men could have managed that, but Thorn was different.

"Thorn," said Eden. "Here's a young woman who wants to see Mr. Madden."

"I have a letter from him," the girl explained, "offering me the use of the ranch to take some pictures. You may remember—I was here Wednesday night."

"I remember," said Thorn sourly. "And I regret very much that Mr. Madden can not see you. He also asks me to say that unfortunately he must withdraw the permission he gave you in his letter."

"I'll accept that word from no one but Mr. Madden himself," returned the girl, and a steely light flamed suddenly in her eyes.

"I repeat—he will not see you," persisted Thorn.

The girl sat down. "Tell Mr. Madden his ranch is charming," she said. "Tell him I am seated in a chair in his living-room and that I shall certainly continue to sit here until he comes and speaks to me himself."

Thorn hesitated a moment, glaring angrily. Then he went out.

"I say—you're all right," Eden laughed.

"I aim to be," the girl answered, "and I've been on my own too long to take any nonsense from a mere secretary."

Madden blustered in. "What is all this—"

"Mr. Madden," the girl said, rising and smiling with amazing sweetness, "I was sure you'd see me. I have here a letter you wrote me from San Francisco. You recall it, of course."

Madden took the letter and glanced at it. "Yes, yes—of course. I'm very sorry, Miss Wendell, but since I wrote that certain matters have come up—I have a business deal on—" He glanced at Eden. "In short, it would be most inconvenient for me to have the ranch overrun with picture people at this time. I can't tell you how I regret it."

The girl's smile vanished. "Very well," she said, "but it means a black mark against me with the company. The people I work for don't accept excuses—only results. I have told them everything was arranged."

"Well, you were a little premature, weren't you?"

"I don't see why. I had the word of P. J. Madden. I believed—foolishly, perhaps—the old rumor that the word of Madden was never broken."

The millionaire looked decidedly uncomfortable. "Well—I—er—of course I never break my word. When did you want to bring your people here?"

"It's all arranged for Monday," said the girl.

"Out of the question," replied Madden. "But if you could postpone it a few days—say, until Thursday." Once more he looked at Eden. "Our business should be settled by Thursday," he added.

"Unquestionably," agreed Eden, glad to help.

"Very well," said Madden. He looked at the girl, and his eyes were kindly. He was no Thorn. "Make it Thursday, and the place is yours. I may not be here then myself, but I'll leave word to that effect."

"Mr. Madden, you're a dear," she told him. "I knew I could rely on you." With a disgusted look at his employer's back, Thorn went out.

"You bet you can," said Madden, smiling pleasantly. He was melting fast. "And the record of P. J. Madden is intact. His word is as good as his bond—isn't that so?"

"If any one doubts it, let him ask me," replied the girl.

"It's nearly lunch time," Madden said. "You'll stay?"

"Well—I—really, Mr. Madden—"

"Of course she'll stay," Bob Eden broke in. "She's eating at a place in Eldorado called the Oasis, and if she doesn't stay, then she's just gone and lost her mind."

The girl laughed. "You're all so good to me," she said.

"Why not?" inquired Madden. "Then it's settled. We need some one like you around to brighten things up. Ah Kim," he added, as the Chinese entered, "another place for lunch. In about ten minutes, Miss Wendell."

He went out. The girl looked at Bob Eden. "Well, that's that. I knew it would be all right, if only he would see me."

"Naturally," said Eden. "Everything in this world would be all right, if every man in it could only see you."

"Sounds like a compliment," she smiled.

"Meant to be," replied the boy. "But what makes it sound so cumbersome? I must brush up on my social chatter."

"Oh—then it was only chatter?"

"Please—don't look too closely at what I say. I may tell you I've got a lot on my mind just now. I'm trying to be a business man, and it's some strain."

"Then you're not a real business man?"

"Not a real anything. Just sort of drifting. You know, you made me think, last night."

"I'm proud of that."

"Now—don't spoof me. I got to thinking—here you are, earning your living—luxurious pot roasts at the Oasis and all that—while I'm just father's little boy. I shouldn't be surprised if you inspired me to turn over a new leaf."

"Then I shan't have lived in vain." She nodded toward the far side of the room. "What in the word is the meaning of that arsenal?"

"Oh—that's gentle old Madden's collection of firearms. A hobby of his. Come on over and I'll teach you to call each one by name."

Presently Madden and Thorn returned, and Ah Kim served a perfect lunch. At the table Thorn said nothing, but his employer, under the spell of the girl's bright eyes, talked volubly and well. As they finished coffee, Bob Eden suddenly awoke to the fact that the big clock near the patio windows marked the hour as five minutes of two. At two o'clock! There was that arrangement with Chan regarding two o'clock. What were they to do? The impassive face of the Oriental as he served lunch had told the boy nothing.

Madden was in the midst of a long story about his early struggle toward wealth, when the Chinese came suddenly into the room. He stood there, and though he did not speak, his manner halted the millionaire as effectively as a pistol shot.

"Well, well, what is it?" Madden demanded.

"Death," said Ah Kim solemnly in his high-pitched voice. "Death unevitable end. No wolly. No solly."

"What in Sam Hill are you talking about?" Madden inquired. Thorn's pale green eyes were popping.

"Poah litta Tony," went on Ah Kim.

"What about Tony?"

"Poah litta Tony enjoy happly noo yeah in Hadesland," finished Ah Kim.

Madden was instantly on his feet, and led the way to the patio. On the stone floor beneath his perch lay the lifeless body of the Chinese parrot.

The millionaire stooped and picked up the bird. "Why—poor old Tony," he said. "He's gone west. He's dead."

Eden's eyes were on Thorn. For the first time since he met that gentleman he thought he detected the ghost of a smile on the secretary's pale face.

"Well, Tony was old," continued Madden. "A very old boy. And as Ah Kim says, death is inevitable—" He stopped, and looked keenly at the expressionless face of the Chinese. "I've been expecting this," he added. "Tony hasn't seemed very well of late. Here, Ah Kim"—he handed over all that was mortal of Tony—"you take and bury him somewhere."

"I take 'um," said Ah Kim, and did so.

In the big living-room the clock struck twice, loud and clear. Ah Kim, in the person of Charlie Chan, was moving slowly away, the bird in his arms. He was muttering glibly in Chinese. Suddenly he looked back over his shoulder.

"Hoo malimali," he said clearly.

Bob Eden remembered his Hawaiian.

7

The Postman Sets Out

The three men and the girl returned to the living-room, but Madden's flow of small talk was stilled, and the sparkle was gone from his luncheon party.

"Poor Tony," the millionaire said when they had sat down. "It's like the passing of an old friend. Five years ago he came to me." He was silent for a long time, staring into space.

Presently the girl rose. "I really must be getting back to town," she announced. "It was thoughtful of you to invite me to lunch, Mr. Madden, and I appreciate it. I can count on Thursday, then?"

"Yes—if nothing new comes up. In that case, where could I reach you?"

"I'll be at the Desert Edge—but nothing must come up. I'm relying on the word of P. J. Madden."

"Nothing will, I'm sure. Sorry you have to go."

Bob Eden came forward. "I think I'll take a little fling at city life myself," he said. "If you don't mind, I'd like to ride into Eldorado with you."

"Delighted," she smiled. "But I'm not sure I can bring you back."

"Oh no—I don't want you to. I'll walk back."

"You needn't do that," said Madden. "It seems that Ah Kim can drive a flivver—a rather remarkable boy, Ah Kim." He was thoughtfully silent for a moment. "I'm sending him to town later in the afternoon for supplies. Our larder's rather low. He'll pick you up." The Chinese entered to clear away. "Ah Kim, you're to bring Mr. Eden back with you this evening."

"Allight. I bling 'um," said Ah Kim, without interest.

"I'll meet you in front of the hotel any time you say," suggested Eden.

Ah Kim regarded him sourly. "Maybe flive 'clock," he said.

"Fine. At five then."

"You late, you no catch 'um lide," warned the Chinese.

"I'll be there," the boy promised. He went to his room and got a cap. When he returned, Madden was waiting.

"In case your father calls this afternoon, I'll tell him you want that matter rushed through," he said.

Eden's heart sank. He hadn't thought of that. Suppose his father returned to the office unexpectedly—but no, that was unlikely. And it wouldn't do to show alarm and change his plans now.

"Surely," he remarked carelessly. "If he isn't satisfied without a word from me, tell him to call again about six."

When he stepped into the yard, the girl was skilfully turning her car about. He officiated at the gate, and joined her in the sandy road.

The car moved off and Eden got his first unimpeded look at this queer world Holley had called the devil's garden. "Plenty acres of unlimitable sand," Chan had said, and that about summed it up. Far in the distance was a touch of beauty—a cobalt sky above snow-capped mountains. But elsewhere he saw only desert, a great gray interminable blanket spattered with creosote brush. All the trees, all the bushes, were barbed and cruel and menacing—a biznaga, pointing like a finger of scorn toward the sky, an unkempt palo verde, the eternal Joshua trees, like charred stumps that had stood in the path of a fire. Over this vast waste played odd tricks of light and shade, and up above hung the sun, a living flame, merciless, ineffably pure, and somehow terrible.

"Well, what do you think of it?" asked the girl.

Eden shrugged. "Hell's burnt out and left the embers," he remarked.

She smiled. "The desert is an acquired taste," she explained. "No one likes it at first. I remember the night, long ago, when I got off the train at Eldorado with poor dad. A little girl from a Philadelphia suburb—a place that was old and settled and civilized. And there I stood in the midst of this savage-looking world. My heart broke."

"Poor kid," said Eden. "But you like it now?"

"Yes—after a while—well, there's a sort of weird beauty in this sun-drenched country. You waken to it in the course of time. And in the spring, after the rains—I'd like to take you over round Palm Springs then. The verbena is like a carpet of old rose, and the ugliest trees put forth the most delicate and lovely blossoms. And at any time of the year there's always the desert nights, with the pale stars overhead, and the air full of peace and calm and rest."

"Oh, no doubt it's a great place to rest," Eden agreed. "But as it happens, I wasn't very tired."

"Who knows?" she said. "Perhaps before we say goodby I can initiate you into the Very Ancient Order of Lovers of the Desert. The requirements for membership are very strict. A sensitive soul, a quick eye for beauty—oh, a very select group, you may be sure. No riff-raff on our rolls."

A blatant sign hung before them. "Stop! Have you bought your lot in Date City?" From the steps of a tiny real estate office a rather shabby young man leaped to life. He came into the road and held up his hand. Obligingly the girl stopped her car.

"Howdy, folks," said the young man. "Here's the big opportunity of your life—don't pass it by. Let me show you a lot in Date City, the future metropolis of the desert."

Bob Eden stared at the dreary landscape. "Not interested," he said.

"Yeah. Think of the poor devils who once said that about the corner of Spring and Sixth, Los Angeles. Not interested—and they could have bought it for a song. Look ahead. Can you picture this street ten years hence?"

"I think I can," Eden replied. "It looks just the way it does to-day."

"Blind!" rebuked the young man. "Blind! This won't be the desert forever. Look!" He pointed to a small lead pipe surrounded by a circle of rocks and trying to act like a fountain. From its top gurgled an anemic stream. "What's that! Water, my boy, water, the pure, life-giving elixir, gushing madly from the sandy soil. What does that mean? I see a great city rising on this spot, skyscrapers and movie palaces, land five thousand a front foot—land you can buy to-day for a paltry two dollars."

"I'll take a dollar's worth," remarked Eden.

"I appeal to the young lady," continued the real-estate man. "If that ring on the third finger of her left hand means anything, it means a wedding." Startled, Bob Eden looked, and saw a big emerald set in platinum. "You, miss—you have vision. Suppose you two bought a lot to-day and held it for your—er—for future generations. Wealth, wealth untold—I'm right, ain't I, miss?"

The girl looked away. "Perhaps you are," she admitted. "But you've made a mistake. This gentleman is not my fiancé."

"Oh," said the youth, deflating.

"I'm only a stranger, passing through," Eden told him.

The salesman pulled himself together for a new attack. "That's it—you're a stranger. You don't understand. You can't realize that Los Angeles looked like this once."

"It still does—to some people," suggested Bob Eden gently.

The young man gave him a hard look. "Oh—I get you," he said. "You're from San Francisco." He turned to the girl. "So this ain't your fiancé, eh, lady? Well—hearty congratulations."

Eden laughed. "Sorry," he said.

"I'm sorry, too," returned the salesman. "Sorry for you, when I think of what you're passing up. However, you may see the light yet, and if you ever do, don't forget me. I'm here Saturdays and Sundays, and we have an office in Eldorado. Opportunity's knocking, but of course if you're from Frisco, you're doing the same. Glad to have met you, anyhow."

They left him by his weak little fountain, a sad but hopeful figure.

"Poor fellow," the girl remarked, as she stepped on the gas. "The pioneer has a hard time of it."

Eden did not speak for a moment. "I'm an observing little chap, aren't I?" he said at last.

"What do you mean?"

"That ring. I never noticed it. Engaged, I suppose?"

"It looks that way, doesn't it?"

"Don't tell me you're going to marry some movie actor who carries a vanity case."

"You should know me better than that."

"I do, of course. But describe this lucky lad. What's he like?"

"He likes me."

"Naturally." Eden lapsed into silence.

"Not angry, are you?" asked the girl.

"Not angry," he grinned, "but terribly, terribly hurt. I perceive you don't want to talk about the matter."

"Well—some incidents in my life I really should keep to myself. On such short acquaintance."

"As you wish," agreed Eden. The car sped on. "Lady," he said presently, "I've known this desert country, man and boy, going on twenty-four hours. And believe me when I tell you, miss, it's a cruel land—a cruel land."

They climbed the road that lay between the two piles of brown rock pretending to be mountains, and before them lay Eldorado, huddled about the little red station. The town looked tiny and helpless and forlorn. As they alighted before the Desert Edge Hotel, Eden said:

"When shall I see you again?"

"Thursday, perhaps."

"Nonsense. I shall probably be gone by then, I must see you soon."

"I'll be out your way in the morning. If you like, I'll pick you up."

"That's kind of you—but morning's a long way off," he said. "I'll think of you to-night, eating at the Oasis. Give my love to that steak, if you see it. Until to-morrow, then—and can't I buy you an alarm clock?"

"I shan't oversleep—much," she laughed. "Good-by."

"Good-by," answered Eden. "Thanks for the buggy ride."

He crossed the street to the railroad station, which was also the telegraph office. In the little cubby-hole occupied by the agent, Will Holley stood, a sheaf of copy paper in his hand.

"Hello," he said. "Just getting that interview on the wire. Were you looking for me?"

"Yes, I was," Eden replied. "But first I want to send a wire of my own."

The agent, a husky youth with sandy hair, looked up. "Say, Mister, no can do. Mr. Holley here's tied up things forever."

Holley laughed. "That's all right. You can cut in with Mr. Eden's message, and then go back."

Frowning, Eden considered the wording of his rather difficult telegram. How to let his father know the situation without revealing it to the world? Finally he wrote:

> BUYER HERE, BUT CERTAIN CONDITIONS MAKE IT ADVIS-
> ABLE WE TREAT HIM TO A LITTLE HOO MALIMALI. MRS. JOR-
> DAN WILL TRANSLATE. WHEN I TALK WITH YOU OVER
> TELEPHONE PROMISE TO SEND VALUABLE PACKAGE AT ONCE
> THEN FORGET IT. ANY CONFIDENTIAL MESSAGE FOR ME CARE
> WILL HOLLEY, ELDORADO TIMES. THEY HAVE NICE DESERT
> DOWN HERE BUT TOO FULL OF MYSTERY FOR FRANK AND
> OPEN YOUNG BUSINESS MAN LIKE YOUR LOVING SON. BOB.

He turned the yellow slip over to the worried telegrapher, with instructions to send it to his father's office, and in duplicate to his house. "How much?" he asked.

After some fumbling with a book, the agent named a sum, which Eden paid. He added a tip, upsetting the boy still further.

"Say, this is some day here," announced the telegrapher. "Always wanted a little excitement in my life, but now it's come I guess I ain't ready for it. Yes, sir—I'll send it twice—I know—I get you—"

Holley gave the boy a few directions about the Madden interview, and returned with Bob Eden to Main Street.

"Let's drop over to the office," the editor said. "Nobody there now, and I'm keen to know what's doing out at Madden's."

In the bare little home of the *Eldorado Times*, Eden took a chair that was already partly filled with exchanges, close to the editor's desk. Holley removed his hat and replaced it with an eye-shade. He dropped down beside his typewriter.

"My friend in New York grabbed at that story," he said. "It was good of Madden to let me have it. I understand they're going to allow me to sign it, too—the name of Will Holley back in the big papers again. But look here—I was surprised by what you hinted out at the ranch this morning. It seemed to me last night that everything was O.K. You didn't say whether you had that necklace with you or not, but I gathered you had—"

"I haven't," cut in Eden.

"Oh—it's still in San Francisco?"

"No. My confederate has it."

"Your what?"

"Holley, I know that if Harry Fladgate says you're all right, you are. So I'm going the whole way in the matter of trusting you."

"That's flattering—but suit yourself."

"Something tells me we'll need your help," Eden remarked. With a glance round the deserted office, he explained the real identity of the servant, Ah Kim.

Holley grinned. "Well, that's amusing, isn't it? But go on. I get the impression that although you arrived at the ranch last night to find Madden there and everything, on the surface, serene, such was not the case. What happened?"

"First of all, Charlie thought something was wrong. He sensed it. You know the Chinese are a very psychic race."

Holley laughed. "Is that so? Surely you didn't fall for that guff. Oh, pardon me—I presume you had some better reason for delay?"

"I'll admit is sounded like guff to me—at the start. I laughed at Chan and prepared to hand over the pearls at once. Suddenly out of the night came the weirdest cry for help I ever expect to hear."

"What! Really? From whom?"

"From your friend, the Chinese parrot. From Tony."

"Oh—of course," said Holley. "I'd forgotten him. Well, that probably meant nothing."

"But a parrot doesn't invent," Eden reminded him. "It merely repeats. I may have acted like a fool, but I hesitated to produce those pearls." He went on to tell how, in the morning, he had agreed to wait until two o'clock while Chan had further talk with Tony, and ended with the death of the bird just after lunch. "And there the matter rests," he finished.

"Are you asking my advice?" said Holley. "I hope you are, because I've simply got to give it to you."

"Shoot," Eden replied.

Holley smiled at him in a fatherly way. "Don't think for a moment I wouldn't like to believe there's some big melodrama afoot at Madden's ranch. Heaven knows little enough happens round here, and a thing like that would be manna from above. But as I look at it, my boy, you've let a jumpy Chinese lead you astray into a bad case of nerves."

"Charlie's absolutely sincere," protested Eden.

"No doubt of that," agreed Holley. "But he's an Oriental, and a detective, and he's simply got to detect. There's nothing wrong at Madden's ranch. True, Tony lets out weird cries in the night—but he always has."

"You've heard him, then?"

"Well, I never heard him say anything about help and murder, but when he first came I was living out at Doctor Whitcomb's, and I used to hang round the Madden ranch a good deal. Tony had some strange words in his small head. He'd spent his days amid violence and crime. It's nothing to wonder at that he screamed as he did last night. The setting on the desert, the dark, Charlie's psychic talk—all that combined to make a mountain out of a molehill, in your eyes."

"And Tony's sudden death this noon?"

"Just as Madden said. Tony was as old as the hills—even a parrot doesn't live forever. A coincidence, yes—but I'm afraid your father won't be pleased with you, my boy. First thing you know P. J. Madden, who is hot and impetuous, will kick you out and call the transaction off. And I can see you back home explaining that you didn't close the deal because a parrot on the place dropped dead. My boy, my boy—I trust your father is a gentle soul. Otherwise he's liable to annihilate you."

Eden considered. "How about that missing gun?"

Holley shrugged. "You can find something queer almost anywhere, if you look for it. The gun was gone—yes. What of it? Madden may have sold it, given it away, taken it to his room."

Bob Eden leaned back in his chair. "I guess you're right, at that. Yes, the more I think about it, here in the bright light of afternoon, the more foolish I feel." Through a side window he saw a flivver swing up before the grocery store next door, and Charlie Chan alight. He went out on to the porch.

"Ah Kim," he called.

The plump little Chinese detective approached and, without a word, entered the office.

"Charlie," said Bob Eden, "this is a friend of mine, Mr. Will Holley. Holley, meet Detective-Sergeant Chan, of the Honolulu Police."

At mention of his name, Chan's eyes narrowed. "How do you do," he said coldly.

"It's all right," Eden assured him. "Mr. Holley can be trusted—absolutely. I've told him everything."

"I am far away in strange land," returned Chan. "Maybe I would choose to trust no one—but that, no doubt, are my heathen churlishness. Mr. Holley will pardon, I am sure."

"Don't worry," said Holley. "I give you my word, I'll tell no one."

Chan made no reply, in his mind, perhaps, the memory of other white men who had given their word.

"It doesn't matter, anyhow," Eden remarked. "Charlie, I've come to the decision that we're chasing ghosts. I've talked things over with Mr. Holley, and from what he says, I see that there's really nothing wrong out at the ranch. When we go back this evening we'll hand over those pearls and head for home." Chan's face fell. "Cheer up," added the boy. "You, your-self, must admit that we've been acting like a couple of old women."

An expression of deeply offended dignity appeared on the little round face. "Just one moment. Permit this old woman more nonsense. Some hours ago parrot drops from perch into vast eternity. Dead, like Caesar."

"What of it?" said Eden wearily. "He died of old age. Don't let's argue about it, Charlie—"

"Who argues?" asked Chan. "I myself enjoy keen distaste for that pastime. Old woman though I am, I now deal with facts—undubitable facts." He spread a white sheet of paper on Holley's desk, and removing an envelope from his pocket, poured its contents on to the paper. "Examine," he directed. "What you see here are partial contents of food basin beside the perch of Tony. Kindly tell me what you look at."

"Hemp seed," said Eden. "A parrot's natural food."

"Ah, yes," agreed Chan. "Seed of the hemp. But that other—the fine, grayish-white powder that seem so plentiful."

"By gad," cried Holley.

"No argument here," continued Chan. "Before seeking grocer I pause at drug emporium on corner. Wise man about powders make most careful test for me. And what does he say?"

"Arsenic," suggested Holley.

"Arsenic, indeed. Much sold to ranchers hereabouts as rat killer. Parrot killer, too."

Eden and Holley looked at each other in amazement.

"Poor Tony very sick before he go on long journey." Chan continued. "Very silent and very sick. In my time I am on track of many murders, but I must come to this peculiar mainland to ferret out parrot murder. Ah, well—all my life I hear about wonders on this mainland."

"They poisoned him," Bob Eden cried. "Why?"

"Why not?" shrugged Chan. "Very true rumor says 'dead men tell no tales'! Dead parrots are in same fix, I think. Tony speaks Chinese like me. Tony and me never speak together again."

Eden put his head in his hands. "Well, I'm getting dizzy," he said. "What, in heaven's name, is it all about?"

"Reflect," urged Chan. "As I have said before, parrot not able to perpetrate original remarks. He repeats. When Tony cry out in night 'help, murder, put down gun' even old woman might be pardoned to think he repeats something recently heard. He repeats because words are recalled to him by—what?"

"Go on, Charlie," Eden said.

"Recalled by event, just preceding cry. What event? I think deep—how is this? Recalled, maybe, by sudden flashing on of lights in bedroom occupied by Martin Thorn, the secretary."

"Charlie, what more do you know?" Eden asked.

"This morning I am about my old woman duties in bedroom of Thorn. I see on wall stained outline same size and shape as handsome picture of desert scene near by. I investigate. Picture has been moved, I note, and not so long ago. Why was picture moved? I lift it in my hands and underneath I see little hole that could only be made by flying bullet."

Eden gasped. "A bullet?"

"Precisely the fact. A bullet embedded deep in wall. One bullet that has gone astray and not found resting place in body of that unhappy man Tony heard cry for help some recent night."

Again Eden and Holley looked at each other. "Well," said the editor, "there was that gun, you know. Bill Hart's gun—the one that's gone from the living-room. We must tell Mr. Chan about that."

Chan shrugged. "Spare yourself trouble," he advised. "Already last night I have noted empty locality deserted by that weapon. I also found this, in waste-basket." He took a small crumpled card from his pocket, a typewritten card, which read: "Presented to P. J. Madden by William S. Hart. September 29, 1923." Will Holley nodded and handed it back. "All day," continued Chan, "I search for missing movie pistol. Without success—so far."

Will Holley rose, and warmly shook Chan's hand. "Mr. Chan," he said, "permit me to go on record here and now to the effect that you're all right." He turned to Bob Eden. "Don't ever come to me for advice again. You follow Mr. Chan."

Eden nodded. "I think I will," he said.

"Think more deeply," suggested Chan. "To follow an old woman. Where is the honor there?"

Eden laughed. "Oh, forget it, Charlie. I apologize with all my heart."

Chan beamed. "Thanks warmly. Then all is settled? We do not hand over pearls to-night, I think?"

"No, of course we don't," agreed Eden. "We're on the trail of something—heaven knows what. It's all up to you, Charlie, from now on. I follow where you lead."

"You were number one prophet, after all," said Chan. "Postman on vacation goes for long walk. Here on broad desert I can not forget profession. We return to Madden's ranch and find what we shall find. Some might say, Madden is there, give him necklace. Our duty as splendid American citizens does not permit. If we deliver necklace, we go away, truth is strangled, guilty escape. Necklace deal falls now into second place." He gathered up the evidence in the matter of Tony and restored it to his pocket. "Poor Tony. Only this morning he tell me I talk too much. Now like boom—boomerang, remark returns and smites him. It is my pressing duty to negotiate with food merchant. Meet me in fifteen minutes before hotel door."

When he had gone out, Holley and Eden were silent for a moment. "Well," said the editor at last, "I was wrong—all wrong. There's something doing out at Madden's ranch."

Eden nodded. "Sure there is. But what?"

"All day," continued Holley, "I've been wondering about that interview Madden gave me. For no apparent reason, he broke one of the strictest rules of his life. Why?"

"If you're asking me, save your breath," advised Eden.

"I'm not asking you—I've got my own solution. Quoting Charlie, I think deep about matter—how is this? Madden knows that at any moment something may break and this thing that has happened at his ranch be spread all over the newspapers. Looking ahead, he sees he may need friends among the reporters. So he's come down from his high horse at last. Am I right?"

"Oh, it sounds logical," agreed Eden. "I'm glad something does. You know, I told dad before I left San Francisco that I was keen to get mixed up in a murder mystery. But this—this is more than I bargained for. No dead body, no weapon, no motive, no murder. Nothing. Why, we can't even prove anybody has been killed." He stood up. "Well, I'd better be moving back to the ranch. The ranch and—what? Whither am I drifting?"

"You stick to your Chinese pal," advised Holley. "The boy's good. Something tells me he'll see you through."

"I hope so," Eden replied.

"Keep your eyes open," added Holley. "And take no chances. If you need help out there, don't forget Will Holley."

"You bet I won't," Bob Eden answered. "So long. Maybe I'll see you tomorrow."

He went out and stood on the curb before the Desert Edge Hotel. It was Saturday evening, and Eldorado was crowded with ranchers, lean, bronzed, work-stained men in khaki riding breeches and gaudy lumber-jack blouses—simple men to whom this was the city. Through the window of the combined barber shop and pool room he saw a group of them shaking dice. Others leaned against the trunks of the cottonwoods, talking of the roads, of crops, of politics. Bob Eden felt like a visitor from Mars.

Presently Chan passed, swung round in the street, and halted the little touring car opposite the boy. As Eden climbed in, he saw the detective's keen eyes fixed on the hotel doorway. Seating himself, he followed Chan's gaze.

A man had emerged from the Desert Edge Hotel—a man who looked strangely out of place among the roughly-clad ranchers. He wore an overcoat buttoned tightly about his throat, and a felt hat was low over his eyes, which were hidden by dark spectacles.

"See who's here," said Eden.

"Yes, indeed," answered Chan, as they moved down the street. "I think the Killarney Hotel has lost one very important guest. Their loss our gain—maybe."

They left the all-too-brief pavement of Main Street, and a look of satisfaction spread slowly over Charlie Chan's face.

"Much work to do," he said. "Deep mysteries to solve. How sweet, though far from home, to feel myself in company of old friend."

Surprised, Bob Eden looked at him. "An old friend," he repeated.

"Chan smiled. "In garage on Punchbowl Hill lonesome car like this awaits my return. With flivver shuddering beneath me I can think myself on familiar Honolulu streets again."

They climbed between the mountains, and before them lay the soft glory of a desert sunset. Ignoring the rough road, Chan threw the throttle wide.

"Wow, Charlie," cried Eden, as his head nearly pierced the top. "What's the idea?"

"Pardon, please," said Chan, slowing a bit. "No good, I guess. For a minute I think maybe this little car can bounce the homesick feeling from my heart."

8

A Friendly Little Game

For a time the little brother of the car on Punch-bowl Hill plowed valiantly on, and neither the detective nor Bob Eden spoke. The yellow glare of the sun was cooling on the gray livery of the desert; the shadows cast by the occasional trees grew steadily longer. The far-off mountains purpled and the wind bestirred itself.

"Charlie," said Bob Eden. "What do you think of this country?"

"This desert land?" asked Charlie.

Eden nodded.

"Happy to have seen it. All my time I yearn to encounter change. Certainly have encountered that here."

"Yes, I guess you have. Not much like Hawaii, is it?"

"I will say so. Hawaii lie like handful of Phillimore pearls on heaving breast of ocean. Oahu little island with very wet neighborhood all about. Moisture hangs in air all time, rain called liquid sunshine, breath of ocean pretty damp. Here I climb round to other side of picture. Air is dry like last year's newspaper."

"They tell me you can love this country if you try."

Chan shrugged. "For my part, I reserve my efforts in that line for other locality. Very much impressed by desert, thank you, but will move on at earliest opportunity."

"Here, too," Eden laughed. "Comes the night, and I long for lights about me that are bright. A little restaurant on O'Farrell Street, a few good fellows, a bottle of mineral water on the table. Human companionship, if it's not asking too much."

"Natural you feel that way," Chan agreed. "Youth is in your heart like a song. Because of you I am hoping we can soon leave Madden's ranch."

"Well, what do you think? What are we going to do now?"

"Watch and wait. Youth, I am thinking, does not like that business. But it must be. Speaking personally for myself, I am not having one happy fine time either. Act of cooking food not precisely my idea of merry vacation."

"Well, Charlie, I can stick it if you can," Eden said.

"Plenty fine sport you are," Chan replied. "Problems that we face are not without interest, for that matter. Most peculiar situation. At home I am called to look at crime, clear-cut like heathen idol's face. Somebody killed, maybe. Clues are plenty, I push little car down one path, I sway about, seeking another. Not so here. Starting forth to solve big mystery I must first ask msyelf, just what are this big mystery I am starting forth to solve?"

"You've said it," Eden laughed.

"Yet one big fact gleams clear like snow on distant mountain. On recent night, at Madden's ranch, unknown person was murdered. Who unknown was, why he was killed, and who officiated at the homicide—these are simple little matters remaining to be cleared."

"And what have we to go on?" Eden asked helplessly.

"A parrot's cry at night. The rude removal of that unhappy bird. A bullet hole hiding back of picture recently changed about. An aged pistol gone from dusty wall. All the more honor for us if we unravel from such puny clues."

"One thing I can't figure out—among others," said Eden. "What about Madden? Does he know? Or is that sly little Thorn pulling something off alone?"

"Important questions," Chan agreed. "In time we learn the answers, maybe. Meanwhile best to make no friend of Madden. You have told him nothing about San Francisco, I hope. Shaky Phil Maydorf and his queer behavior."

"No, oddly enough, I haven't. I was wondering whether I hadn't better, now that Maydorf has shown up in Eldorado."

"Why? Pearls are in no danger. Did I hear you say in newspaper office you would greatly honor by following me?"

"You certainly did."

"Then, for Madden, more of the hoo malimali. Nothing to be gained by other course, much maybe lost. You tell him of Maydorf, and he might answer, deal is off here, bring pearls to New York. What then? You go away, he does away, I go away. Mystery of recent event at ranch house never solved."

"I guess you're right," said Eden. They sped on through the gathering rusk, past the little office of the Date City optimist, deserted now. "By the way," added the boy, "this thing you think has happened at the ranch—it may have occurred last Wednesday night?"

"You have fondly feeling for Wednesday night?" asked Chan. "Why?"

Briefly Bob Eden related Paula Wendell's story of that night—Thorn's obvious excitement when he met her at the door, his insistence that Madden could not speak to her, and most important of all, the little prospector with the black beard whom the girl saw in the yard. Chan listened with interest.

"Now you talk," he commented. "Here is one fine new clue for us. He may be most important, that black-bearded one. A desert rat, I think. The young woman goes much about this country? Am I correct?"

"Yes, she does."

"She can retain secrets, maybe?"

"You bet—this girl can."

"Don't trust her. We talk all over place we may get sorry, after while. However, venture so far as to ask please that she keep her pretty eyes open for that black-bearded rat. Who knows. Maybe he is vital link in our chain." They were approaching the little oasis Madden had set on the desert's dusty face. "Go in now," Chan continued, "and act innocent like very new baby. When you talk with father over telephone, you will find he is prepared. I have sent him telegraph."

"You have?" said Eden. "So did I. I sent him a couple of them."

"Then he is all prepared. Among other matters, I presumed to remind him voice coming over wire is often grasped by others in room as well as him who reclines at telephone."

"Say—that's a good idea. I guess you think of everything, Charlie."

The gate was open, and Chan turned the car into the yard. "Guess I do," he sighed. "Now, with depressing reluctance, I must think of dinner. Recall, we watch and wait. And when we meet alone, the greatest care. No one must pierce my identity. Only this noon I could well have applied to myself resounding kick. That word unevitable too luxurious for poor old Ah Kim. In future I must pick over words like lettuce for salad. Good-by, and splendid luck."

In the living-room a fire was already blazing in the huge fireplace. Madden sat at a broad, flat-topped desk, signing letters. He looked up as Bob Eden entered.

"Hello," he said. "Have a pleasant afternoon?"

"Quite," the boy replied. "I trust you had the same."

"I did not," Madden answered. "Even here I can't get away from business. Been catching up with a three days' accumulation of mail. There you are, Martin," he added, as the secretary entered. "I believe you'll have time to take them in to the post-office before dinner. And here are the telegrams—get them off, too. Take the little car—it'll make better speed over these roads."

Thorn gathered up the letters, and with expert hands began folding them and placing them in envelopes. Madden rose, stretched, and came over to the fire. "Ah Kim brought you back?" he inquired.

"He did," Bob Eden answered.

"Knows how to drive a car all right?" persisted Madden.

"Perfectly."

"An unusual boy, Ah Kim."

"Oh, not very,' Eden said carelessly. "He told me he used to drive a vegetable truck in Los Angeles. I got that much out of him, but that's about all."

"Silent, eh?"

Eden nodded. "Silent as a lawyer from Northampton, Massachusetts," he remarked.

Madden laughed. "By the way," he said, as Thorn went out. "Your father didn't call."

"No? Well, he isn't likely to get home until evening. I'll try the house to-night, if you want me to."

"I wish you would," Madden said. "I don't want to seem inhospitable, my boy, but I'm very anxious to get away from here. Certain matters in the mail to-day—you understand—"

"Of course," Bob Eden answered. "I'll do all I can to help."

"That's mighty good of you," Madden told him, and the boy felt a bit guilty. "I think I'll take a nap before dinner. I find, nowadays, it's a great aid to digestion." The famous millionaire was more human that Bob Eden had yet seen him. He stood looking down at the boy, wistfully. "A matter you can't grasp, just yet," he added. "You're so damned young—I envy you."

He went out, leaving Bob Eden to a Los Angeles paper he had picked up in Eldorado. From time to time, as the boy read, the quaint little figure of Ah Kim passed noiselessly. He was setting the table for dinner.

An hour later, there on the lonely desert, they again sat down to Ah Kim's cooking. Very different from the restaurant of which Bob Eden thought with longing, but if the company was far from lively, the food was excellent, for the Chinese had negotiated well. When the servant came in with coffee, Madden said:

"Light the fire in the patio, Ah Kim. We'll sit out there a while."

The Chinese went to comply with this order, and Eden saw Madden regarding him expectantly. He smiled and rose.

"Well, dad ought to be struggling in from his hard day on the links any minute now," he said. "I'll put in that call."

Madden leaped up. "Let me do it," he suggested. "Just tell me the number."

The boy told him, and Madden spoke over the telephone in a voice to command respect.

"By the way," he said, when he had finished, "Last night you intimated that certain things happened in San Francisco—things that made your father cautious. What—if you don't mind telling me?"

Bob Eden thought rapidly. "Oh, it may all have been a detective's pipe dream. I'm inclined to think now that it was. You see—"

"Detective? What detective?"

"Well, naturally dad has a tie-up with various private detective agencies. An operative of one of them reported that a famous crook had arrived in town and was showing an undue interest in our store. Of course, it may have meant nothing—"

"A famous crook, eh? Who?"

Never a good liar, Bob Eden hesitated. "I—I don't know that I remember the name. English, I believe—the Liverpool Kid, or something like that," he invented lamely.

Madden shrugged. "Well, if anything's leaked out about those pearls, it came from your side of the deal," he said. "My daughter, Thorn and I have certainly been discretion itself. However, I'm inclined to think it's all a pipe dream, as you say."

"Probably is," agreed Eden.

"Come outside," the millionaire invited. He led the way through the glass doors to the patio. There a huge fire roared in the outdoor fireplace, glowing red on the stone floor and on wicker chairs. "Sit down," suggested Madden. "A cigar—no, you prefer your cigarette, eh?" He lighted up, and leaning back in his chair, stared at the dark roof above—the far-off roof of the sky. "I like it out here best," he went on. "A bit chilly, maybe, but you get close to the desert. Ever notice how white the stars are in this country?"

Eden looked at him with surprise. "Sure—I've noticed," he said. "But I never dreamed you had, old boy," he added to himself.

Inside, Thorn was busy at the radio. A horrible medley of bedtime stories, violin solos, and lectures on health and beauty drifted out to them. And then the shrill voice of a woman, urging sinners to repent.

"Get Denver," Madden called loudly.

"I'm trying, Chief," answered Thorn.

"If I must listen to the confounded thing," Madden added to the boy, "I want what I hear to come from far away. Over the mountains and the plains—there's romance in that." The radio swept suddenly into a brisk band tune. "That's it," nodded Madden. "The orchestra at the Brown Palace in Denver—perhaps my girl is dancing to that very music at this moment. Poor kid—she'll wonder what's become of me. I promised to be there two days ago. Thorn!"

The secretary appeared at the door. "Yes, Chief?"

"Remind me to send Evelyn a wire in the morning."

"I'll do that, Chief," said Thorn, and vanished.

"And the band played on," remarked Madden. "All the way from Denver, mile high amid the Rockies. I tell you, man's getting too clever. He's riding for a fall. Probably a sign of age, Mr. Eden, but I find myself longing for the older, simpler days. When I was a boy on the farm, winter mornings, the little schoolhouse in the valley. That sled I wanted—hard times, yes, but times that made men. Oh well, I mustn't get started on that."

They listened on in silence, but presently a bedtime story brought a bellow of rage from the millionaire and Thorn, getting his cue, shut off the machine.

Madden stirred restlessly in his chair. "We haven't enough for bridge," he remarked. "How about a little poker to pass the time, my boy?"

"Why—that would be fine," Eden replied. "I'm afraid you're pretty speedy company for me, however."

"Oh, that's all right—we'll put a limit on it."

Madden was on his feet, eager for action. "Come along."

They went into the living-room and closed the doors. A few moments later the three of them sat about a big round table under a brilliant light.

"Jacks or better," Madden said. "Quarter limit, eh?"

"Well—" replied Eden, dubiously.

He had good reason to be dubious, for he was instantly plunged into the poker game of his life. He had played at college, and was even able to take care of himself in newspaper circles in San Francisco, but all that was child's play by comparison. Madden was no longer the man who noticed how white the stars were. He noticed how red, white and blue the chips were, and he caressed them with loving hands. He was Madden, the plunger, the gambler with railroads and steel mills and the fortunes of little nations abroad, the Madden who, after he had played all day in Wall Street, was wont to seek the roulette wheels on Forty-fourth Street at night.

"Aces," he cried. "Three of them. What have you got, Eden?"

"Apoplexy," remarked Eden, tossing aside his hand. "Right here and now I offer to sell my chances in this game for a canceled postage stamp, or what have you?"

"Good experience for you," Madden replied. "Martin—it's your deal."

A knock sounded suddenly on the door, loud and clear. Bob Eden felt a strange sinking of the heart. Out of the desert dark, out of the vast uninhabited wastes of the world, some one spoke and demanded to come in.

"Who can that be?" Madden frowned.

"Police," suggested Eden, hopefully. "The joint is pinched." No such luck, he reflected.

Thorn was dealing, and Madden himself went to the door and swung it open. From where he sat Eden had a clear view of the dark desert—and of the man who stood in the light. A thin man in an overcoat, a man he had seen first in a San Francisco pier-shed, and later in front of the Desert Edge Hotel. Shaky Phil Maydorf himself, but now without the dark glasses hiding his eyes.

"Good evening," said Maydorf, and his voice, too, was thin and cold. "This is Mr. Madden's ranch, I believe?"

"I'm Madden. What can I do for you?"

"I'm looking for an old friend of mine—your secretary, Martin Thorn."

Thorn rose and came round the table. "Oh, hello," he said, with slight enthusiasm.

"You remember me, don't you?" said the thin man. "McCallum—Henry McCallum. I met you at a dinner in New York a year ago."

"Yes, of course," answered Thorn. "Come in, won't you? This is Mr. Madden."

"A great honor," said Shaky Phil.

"And Mr. Eden, of San Francisco."

Eden rose, and faced Shaky Phil Maydorf. The man's eyes without the glasses were barbed and cruel, like the desert foliage. For a long moment he stared insolently at the boy. Did he realize, Eden wondered, that his movements on the dock at San Francisco had not gone unnoticed? If he did, his nerve was excellent.

"Glad to know you, Mr. Eden," he said.

"Mr. McCallum," returned the boy gravely.

Maydorf turned again to Madden. "I hope I'm not intruding," he remarked with a wan smile. "Fact is, I'm stopping down the road at Doctor Whitcomb's—bronchitis, that's my trouble. It's lonesome as the devil round here, and when I heard Mr. Thorn was in the neighborhood, I couldn't resist the temptation to drop in."

"Glad you did," Madden said, but his tone belied the words.

"Don't let me interrupt your game," Maydorf went on. "Poker, eh? Is this a private scrap, or can anybody get into it?"

"Take off your coat," Madden responded sourly, "and sit up. Martin, give the gentleman a stack of chips."

"This is living again," said the newcomer, accepting briskly. "Well, and how have you been, Thorn, old man?"

Thorn, with his usual lack of warmth, admitted that he had been pretty good, and the game was resumed. If Bob Eden had feared for his immediate future before, he now gave up all hope. Sitting in a poker game with Shaky Phil—well, he was certainly traveling and seeing the world.

"Gimme four cards," said Mr. Maydorf, through his teeth.

If it had been a bitter, brutal struggle before, it now became a battle to the death. New talent had come in—more than talent, positive genius. Maydorf held the cards close against his chest; his face was carved in stone. As though he realized what he was up against, Madden grew wary, but determined. These two fought it out, while Thorn and the boy trailed along, like noncombatants involved in a battle of the giants.

Presently Ah Kim entered with logs for the fire, and if the amazing picture on which his keen eyes lighted startled him, he gave no sign. Madden ordered him to bring highballs, and as he set the glasses on the table, Bob Eden noted with a secret thrill that the stomach of the detective was less than twelve inches from the long capable hands of Shaky Phil. If the redoubtable Mr. Maydorf only knew—

But Maydorf's thoughts were elsewhere than on the Phillimore pearls. "Dealer—one card," he demanded.

The telephone rang out sharply in the room. Bob Eden's heart missed a beat. He had forgotten that—and now— After the long wait he was finally to speak with his father—while Shaky Phil Maydorf sat only a few feet away! He saw Madden staring at him, and he rose.

"For me, I guess," he said carelessly. He tossed his cards on the table. "I'm out of it, anyhow." Crossing the room to the telephone, he took down the receiver. "Hello. Hello, dad. Is that you?"

"Aces and trays," said Maydorf. "All mine?" Madden laid down a hand without looking at his opponent's, and Shaky Phil gathered in another pot.

"Yes, dad—this is Bob," Eden was saying. "I arrived all right—stopping with Mr. Madden for a few days. Just wanted you to know where I was. Yes—that's all. Everything. I may call you in the morning. Have a good game? Too bad. Good-by!"

Madden was on his feet, his face purple. "Wait a minute," he cried.

"Just wanted dad to know where I am," Eden said brightly. He dropped back into his chair. "Whose deal is it, anyhow?"

Madden strangled a sentence in his throat, and once more the game was on. Eden was chuckling inwardly. More delay—and not his fault this time. The joke was on P. J. Madden.

His third stack was melting rapidly away, and he reflected with apprehension that the night was young, and time of no importance on the desert anyhow. "One more hand and I drop out," he said firmly.

"One more hand and we all drop out," barked Madden. Something seemed to have annoyed him.

"Let's make it a good one, then," said Maydorf. "The limit's off, gentlemen."

It was a good one, unexpectedly a contest between Maydorf and Bob Eden. Drawing with the faint hope of completing two pairs, the boy was thrilled to encounter four nines in his hand. Perhaps he should have noted that Maydorf was dealing, but he didn't—he bet heavily, and was finally called. Laying down his hand, he saw an evil smile on Shaky Phil's face.

"Four queens," remarked Maydorf, spreading them out with an expert gesture. "Always was lucky with the ladies. I think you gentlemen pay me."

They did. Bob Eden contributed forty-seven dollars, reluctantly. All on the expense account, however, he reflected.

Mr. Maydorf was in a not unaccountable good humor. "A very pleasant evening," he remarked, as he put on his overcoat. "I'll drop in again, if I may."

"Good night," snapped Madden.

Thorn took a flashlight from the desk. "I'll see you to the gate," he announced. Bob Eden smiled. A flashlight—with a bright moon overhead.

"Mighty good of you," the outsider said. "Good night, gentlemen, and thank you very much." He was smiling grimly as he followed the secretary out.

Madden snatched up a cigar, and savagely bit the end from it. "Well?" he cried.

"Well," said Eden calmly.

"You made a lot of progress with your father, didn't you?"

The boy smiled. "What did you expect me to do? Spill the whole thing in front of that bird?"

"No—but you needn't have rung off so quick. I was going to get him out of the room. Now you can go over there and call your father again."

"Nothing of the sort," answered Eden. "He's gone to bed, and I won't disturb him till morning."

Madden's face purpled. "I insist. And my orders are usually obeyed."

"Is that so?" remarked Eden. "Well, this is one that won't be."

Madden glared at him. "You young—you—er—young—"

"I know," Eden said. "But this was all your fault. If you will insist on cluttering up the ranch with strangers, you must take the consequences."

"Who cluttered up the ranch?" Madden demanded. "I didn't invite that poor fool here. Where the devil did Thorn pick him up, anyhow? You know, the secretary of a man like me is always besieged by a lot of four-flushers—tip hunters and the like. And Thorn's an idiot, sometimes." The secretary entered and laid the flashlight on the desk. His employer regarded him with keen distaste. "Well, your little playmate certainly queered things," he said.

Thorn shrugged. "I know. I'm sorry, Chief. But I couldn't help it. You saw how he horned in."

"Your fault for knowing him. Who is he, anyhow?"

"Oh, he's a broker, or something like that. I give you my word, Chief, I never encouraged him. You know how those fellows are."

"Well, you go out to-morrow and tie a can to him. Tell him I'm busy here and don't want any visitors. Tell him for me that if he calls here again, I'll throw him out."

"All right. I'll go down to the doctor's in the morning and let him know—in a diplomatic way."

"Diplomatic nothing," snorted Madden. "Don't waste diplomacy on a man like that. I won't, if I see him again."

"Well, gentlemen, I think I'll turn in," Eden remarked.

"Good night," said Madden, and the boy went out.

In his bedroom he found Ah Kim engaged in lighting the fire. He closed the door carefully behind him.

"Well, Charlie, I've just been in a poker game."

"A fact already noted by me," smiled Chan.

"Shaky Phil has made a start on us, anyhow. He got forty-seven precious iron men this quiet evening."

"Humbly suggest you be careful," advised Chan.

"Humbly believe you're right," laughed Eden. "I was hoping you were in the offing when Thorn and our friend went to the gate."

"Indeed I was," remarked Chan. "But moonlight so fierce, near approach was not possible."

"Well, I'm pretty sure of one thing, after to-night," Eden told him. "P. J. Madden never saw Shaky Phil before. Either that, or he's the finest actor since Edwin Booth."

"Thorn, however—"

"Oh, Thorn knew him all right. But he wasn't the least bit glad to see him. You know, Thorn's whole manner suggested to me that Shaky Phil has something on him."

"That might be possible," agreed Chan. "Especially come to think of my latest discovery."

"You're found something new, Charlie? What?"

"This evening, when Thorn haste to town in little car and I hear noisome snores of Madden who sleep on bed, I make explicit search in secretary's room."

"Yes—go on—quick. We might be interrupted."

"Under mountain of white shirts in Thorn's bureau reposes—what? Missing forty-five we call Bill Hart's gun."

"Good work! Thorn—the little rat—"

"Undubitably. Two chambers of that gun are quite unoccupied. Reflect on that."

"I'm reflecting. Two empty chambers."

"Humbly suggest you sleep now, gathering strength for what may be most excited to-morrow." The little detective paused at the door. "Two bullets gone who knows where," he said, in a low voice. "Answer is, we know where one went. Went crazy, landing in wall at spot now covered by desert picture."

"And the other?" said Bob Eden thoughtfully.

"Other hit mark, I think. What mark? We watch and wait, and maybe we discover. Good night, with plenty happy dreams."

9

A Ride in the Dark

On Sunday Morning Bob Eden rose at what was, for him, an amazingly early hour. Various factors conspired to induce this strange phenomenon—the desert sun, an extremely capable planet, filling his room with light, the roosters of P. J. Madden, loudly vocal in the dawn. At eight o'clock he was standing in the ranch house yard, ready for whatever the day might bring forth.

Whatever it brought, the day was superb. Now the desert was at its best, the chill of night still lingering in the magic air. He looked out over an opal sea, at changing colors of sand and cloud and mountaintop that shamed by their brilliance those glittering show-cases in the jewelry shop of Meek and Eden. Though it was the fashion of his age to pretend otherwise, he was not oblivious to beauty, and he set out for a stroll about the ranch with a feeling of awe in his heart.

Turning a rear corner of the barn, he came unexpectedly upon a jarring picture. Martin Thorn was busy beside a basket, digging a deep hole in the sand. In his dark clothes, with his pale face glistening from his unaccustomed exertion, he looked not unlike some prominent mortician.

"Hello," said Eden. "Who are you burying this fine morning?"

Thorn stopped. Beads of perspiration gleamed on his high white forehead.

"Somebody has to do it," he compalined. "That new boy's too lazy. And if you let this refuse accumulate the place begins to look like a deserted picnic grounds."

He nodded toward the basket, filled with old tin cans.

"Wanted, private secretary to bury rubbish back of barn," smiled Eden. "A new sidelight on your profession, Thorn. Good idea to get them out of the way, at that," he added, leaning over and taking up a can. "Especially this one, which I perceive lately held arsenic."

"Arsenic?" repeated Thorn. He passed a dark coat sleeve across his brow. "Oh yes—we use a lot of that. Rats, you know."

"Rats," remarked Eden, with an odd inflection, restoring the can to its place.

Thorn emptied the contents of the basket into the hole, and began to fill it in. Eden, playing well his rôle of innocent bystander, watched him idly.

"There—that's better," said the secretary, smoothing the sand over the recent excavation. "You know—I've always had a passion for neatness." He picked up the basket. "By the way," he added, "if you don't mind, I'd like to give you a little advice."

"Glad to have it," Eden replied, walking along beside him.

"I don't know how anxious you people are to sell that necklace. But I've been with the chief fifteen years, and I can tell you he's not the sort of man you can keep waiting with impunity. The first thing you know, young man, that deal for the pearls will be off."

"I'm doing my best," Eden told him. "Besides, Madden's getting a big bargain, and he must know it—if he stops to think—"

"Once P. J. Madden loses his temper," said Thorn, "he doesn't stop to think. I'm warning you, that's all."

"Mighty kind of you," answered Eden carelessly. Thorn dropped his spade and basket by the cookhouse, from which came the pleasant odor of bacon on the stocks. Walking slowly, the secretary moved on toward the patio. Ah Kim emerged from his work-room, his cheeks flushed from close juxtaposition to a cook-stove.

"Hello, boss," he said. "You takee look-see at sunlise thisee mawnin'?"

"Up pretty early, but not as early as that," the boy replied. He saw the secretary vanish into the house. "Just been watching our dear friend Thorn bury some rubbish back of the barn," he added. "Among other items, a can that lately contained arsenic."

Chan dropped the role of Ah Kim. "Mr. Thorn plenty busy man," he said. "Maybe he get more busy as time goes by. One wrong deed leads on to other wrong deeds, like unending chain. Chinese have saying that applies: 'He who rides on tiger can not dismount.' "

Madden appeared in the patio, full of pep and power. "Hey, Eden," he called. "Your father's on the wire."

"Dad's up early," remarked Eden, hurrying to join him.

"I called him," said Madden. "I've had enough delay."

Reaching the telephone, Bob Eden took up the receiver. "Hello, dad, I can talk freely this morning. I want to tell you everything's all right down here. Mr. Madden? Yes—he's fine—standing right beside me now. And he's in a tearing hurry for that necklace."

"Very well—we'll get it to him at once," the elder Eden said. Bob Eden sighed with relief. His telegram had arrived.

"Ask him to get it off to-day," Madden commanded.

"Mr. Madden wants to know if it can start to-day," the boy said.

"Impossible," replied the jeweler. "I haven't got it."

"Not to-day," Bob Eden said to Madden. "He hasn't got—"

"I heard him," roared Madden. "Here—give me that phone. Look here, Eden—what do you mean you haven't got it?"

Bob Eden could hear his father's replies. "Ah—Mr. Madden—how are you? The pearls were in a quite disreputable condition—I couldn't possibly let them go as they were. So I'm having them cleaned—they're with another firm—"

"Just a minute, Eden," bellowed the millionaire. "I want to ask you something—can you understand the English language, or can't you? Keep still—I'll talk. I told you I wanted the pearls now—at once—pronto—what the devil language do you speak? I don't give a hang about having them cleaned. Good lord, I thought you understood."

"So sorry," responded Bob Eden's gentle father. "I'll get them in the morning, and they'll star to-morrow night."

"Yeah—that means Tuesday evening at the ranch. Eden, you make me sick. I've a good mind to call the whole thing off—" Madden paused, and Bob Eden held his breath. "However, if you promise the pearls will start to-morrow sure—"

"I give you my word," said the jeweler. "They will start to-morrow, at the very latest."

"All right. I'll have to wait, I suppose. But this is the last time I deal with you, my friend. I'll be on the look-out for your man on Tuesday. Good-by."

In a towering rage, Madden hung up. His ill-humor continued through breakfast, and Eden's gay attempts at conversation fell on barren ground.

After the meal was finished, Thorn took the little car and disappeared down the road. Bob Eden loafed expectantly about the front yard.

Much sooner than he had dared to hope, his vigil was ended. Paula Wendell, fresh and lovely as the California morning, drove up in her smart roadster and waited outside the barbed-wire fence.

"Hello," she said. "Jump in. You act as though you were glad to see me."

"Glad! Lady, you're a life-saver. Relations are sort of strained this morning at the old homestead. You'll find it hard to believe, but P. J. Madden doesn't love me."

She stepped on the gas. "The man's mad," she laughed.

"I'll say he's mad. Ever eat breakfast with a rattlesnake that's had bad news?"

"Not yet. The company at the Oasis is mixed, but not so mixed as that. Well, what do you think of the view this morning? Ever see such coloring before?"

"Never. And it's not out of a drug store, either."

"I'm talking about the desert. Look at those snow-capped peaks."

"Lovely. But if you don't mind, I prefer to look closer. No doubt he's told you you're beautiful."

"Who?"

"Wilbur, your fiancé."

"His name is Jack. Don't jump on a good man when he's down."

"Of course he's a good man, or you wouldn't have picked him." They plowed along the sandy road. "But even so—look here, lady. Listen to a man of the world. Marriage is the last resort of feeble minds."

"Think so?"

"I know it. Oh, I've given the matter some thought. I've had to. There's my own case. Now and then I've met a girl whose eyes said, 'Well, I might.' But I've been cautious. Hold fast, my lad—that's my motto."

"And you've held fast?"

"You bet. Glad of it, too. I'm free. I'm having a swell time. When evening comes, and the air's full of zip and zowie, and the lights flicker round Union Square, I just reach for my hat. And who says, in a gentle patient voice, 'Where are you going, my dear? I'll go with you.' "

"Nobody."

"Not a living soul. It's grand. And you—your case is just like mine. Of course there are millions of girls who have nothing better to do than marriage. All right for them. But you—why—you've got a wonderful job. The desert, the hills, the cañons—and you're willing to give all that up for a gas-range in the rear room of an apartment."

"Perhaps we can afford a maid."

"Lots of people can—but where to get one nowadays? I'm warning you—think it over well. You're having a great time now—that will end with marriage. Mending Wilbur's socks—"

"I tell you his name is Jack."

"What of it? He'll be just as hard on the socks. I hate to think of a girl like you, tied down somewhere—"

"There's a lot in what you say," Paula Wendell admitted.

"I've only scratched the surface," Eden assured her.

The girl steered her car off the road through an open gate. Eden saw a huge, rambling ranch house surrounded by a group of tiny cottages. "Here we are at Doctor Whitcomb's," remarked Paula Wendell. "Wonderful person, the doctor. I want you two to meet."

She led the way through a screen door into a large living-room, not so beautifully furnished as Madden's, but bespeaking even greater comfort. A gray-haired woman was rocking contentedly near a window. Her face was kindly, her eyes calm and comforting. "Hello, Doctor," said the girl. "I've brought some one to call on you."

The woman rose, and her smile seemed to fill the room. "Hello, young man," she said, and took Bob Eden's hand.

"You—you're the doctor," he stammered.

"Sure am," the woman replied. "But you don't need me. You're all right."

"So are you," he answered. "I can see that."

"Fifty-five years old," returned the doctor, "but I can still get a kick out of that kind of talk from a nice young man. Sit down. The place is yours. Where are you staying?"

"I'm down the road, at Madden's."

"Oh yes—I heard he was here. Not much of a neighbor, this P. J. Madden. I've called on him occasionally, but he's never come to see me. Stand-offish—and that sort of thing doesn't go on the desert. We're all friends here."

"You've been a friend to a good many," said Paula Wendell.

"Why not?" shrugged Doctor Whitcomb. "What's life for, if not to help one another? I've done my best—I only wish it had been more."

Bob Eden felt suddenly humble in this woman's presence.

"Come on—I'll show you round my place," invited the doctor. "I've made the desert bloom—put that on my tombstone. You should have seen this neighborhood when I came. Just a rifle and a cat—that's all I had at first. And the cat wouldn't stay. My first house here I built with my own hands. Five miles to Eldorado—I walked in and back every day. Mr. Ford hadn't been heard of then."

She led the way into the yard, in and out among the little cottages. Tired faces brightened at her approach, weary eyes gleamed with sudden hope.

"They've come to her from all over the country," Paula Wendell said. "Broken-hearted, sick, discouraged. And she's given them new life—"

"Nonsense," cried the doctor. "I've just been friendly. It's a pretty hard world. Being friendly—that works wonders."

In the doorway of one of the cottages they came upon Martin Thorn, deep in conversation with Shaky Phil Maydorf. Even Maydorf mellowed during a few words with the doctor.

Finally, when they reluctantly left, Doctor Whitcomb followed them to the gate. "Come often," she said. "You will, won't you?"

"I hope to," answered Bob Eden. He held her great rough hand a moment. "You know—I'm beginning to sense the beauty of the desert," he added.

The doctor smiled. "The desert is old and weary and wise," she said. "There's beauty in that, if you can see it. Not everybody can. The latch-string's always out at Doctor Whitcomb's. Remember, boy."

Paula Wendell swung the car about, and in silence they headed home.

"I feel as though I'd been out to old Aunt Mary's," said Eden presently. "I sort of expected her to give me a cookie when I left."

"She's a wonderful woman," said the girl softly. "I ought to know. It was the light in her window I saw my first night on the desert. And the light in her eyes—I shall never forget. All the great people are not in the cities."

They rode on. About them the desert blazed stark and empty in the midday heat; a thin haze cloaked the distant dunes and the far-away slopes of the hills. Bob Eden's mind returned to the strange problems that confronted him. "You've never asked me why I'm here," he remarked.

"I know," the girl answered. "I felt that pretty soon you'd realize we're all friends on the desert— and tell me."

"I want to—some day. Just at present—well, I can't. But going back to that night you first visited Madden's ranch—you felt that something was wrong there?"

"I did."

"Well, I can tell you this much—you were probably right." She glanced at him quickly. "And it's my job to find out if you were. That old prospector—I'd give a good deal to meet him. Isn't there a chance that you may run across him again?"

"Just a chance," she replied.

"Well, if you do, would you mind getting in touch with me at once. If it's not asking too much—"

"Not at all," she told him. "I'll be glad to. Of course, the old man may be clear over in Arizona by now. When I last saw him he was moving fast!"

"All the more reason for wanting to find him," Eden said. "I—I wish I could explain. It isn't that I don't trust you, you know. But—It's not altogether my secret."

She nodded. "I understand. I don't want to know."

"You grow more wonderful every minute," he told her.

The minutes passed. After a time the car halted before Madden's ranch, and Bob Eden alighted. He stood looking into the girl's eyes—somehow they were like the eyes of Doctor Whitcomb—restful and comforting and kind. He smiled.

"You know," he said, "I may as well confess it—I've been sort of disliking Wilbur. And now it comes to me suddenly—if I really mean all that about loving my freedom—then Wilbur has done me the greatest service possible. I ought not to dislike him any more. I ought to thank him from the bottom of my heart."

"What in the world are you talking about?"

"Don't you understand? I've just realized that I'm up against the big temptation of my life. But I don't have to fight it. Wilbur has saved me. Good old Wilbur. Give him my love when next you write."

She threw her car into gear. "Don't you worry," she advised. "Even if there hadn't been a Wilbur, your freedom wouldn't have been in the slightest danger. I would have seen to that."

"Somehow, I don't care for that remark," Eden said. "It ought to reassure me, but as a matter of fact, I don't like it at all. Well, I owe you for another buggy ride. Sorry to see you go—it looks like a dull Sunday out here. Would you mind if I drifted into town this afternoon?"

"I probably wouldn't even know it," said the girl. "Good-by."

Bob Eden's prediction about Sunday proved true—it was long and dull. At four in the afternoon he could stand it no longer. The blazing heat was dying, a restless wind had risen, and with the permission of Madden, who was still ill-humored and evidently restless too, he took the little car and sped toward the excitement of Eldorado.

Not much diversion there. In the window of the Desert Edge Hotel the proprietor waded grimly through an interminable Sunday paper. Main Street was hot and deserted. Leaving the car before the hotel, the boy went to Holley's office.

The editor came to the door to meet him. "Hello," he said. "I was hoping you'd come along. Kind of lonesome in the great open spaces this afternoon. By the way, there's a telegram here for you."

Eden took the yellow envelope and hurriedly tore it open. The message was from his father:

I don't understand what it's all about but I am most disturbed. For the present I will follow your instructions. I am trusting you two utterly but I must remind you that it would be most embarrassing for me if sale fell through. Jordans are eager to consummate deal and Victor threatens to come down there any moment. Keep me advised.

"Huh," said Bob Eden. "That would be fine."

"What would?" asked Holley.

"Victor threatens to come—the son of the woman who owns the pearls. All we need here to wreck the works is that amiable bonehead and his spats."

"What's new?" asked Holley, as they sat down.

"Several things," Bob Eden replied. "To start with the big tragedy, I'm out forty-seven dollars." He told of the poker game. "In addition, Mr. Thorn has been observed burying a can that once held arsenic. Furthermore, Charlie has found that missing pistol in Thorn's bureau—with two chambers empty."

Holley whistled. "Has he really? You know, I believe your friend Chan is going to put Thorn back of the bars before he's through."

"Perhaps," admitted Eden. "Got a long way to go, though. You can't convict a man of murder without a body to show for it."

"Oh—Chan will dig that up."

Eden shrugged. "Well, if he does, he can have all the credit. And do all the digging. Somehow, it's not the sort of thing that appeals to me. I like excitement, but I like it nice and neat. Heard from your interview?"

"Yes. It's to be released in New York to-morrow." The tired eyes of Will Holley brightened. "I was sitting here getting a thrill out of the idea when you came in." He pointed to a big scrap-book on his desk. "Some of the stories I wrote on the old *Sun*," he explained. "Not bad, if I do say it myself."

Bob Eden picked up the book, and turned the pages with interest. "I've been thinking of getting a job on a newspaper myself," he said.

Holley looked at him quickly. "Think twice," he advised. "You, with a good business waiting for you—what has the newspaper game to offer you? Great while you're young, maybe—great even now when the old order is changing and the picture paper is making a monkey out of a grand profession. But when you're old—" He got up and laid a hand on the boy's shoulder. "When you're old—and you're old at forty—then what? The copy desk, and some day the owner comes in, and sees a streak of gray in your hair, and he says, 'Throw that doddering fool out. I want young men here.' No, my boy—not the newspaper game. You and I must have a long talk."

They had it. It was five by the little clock on Holley's desk when the editor finally stood up, and closed his scrap-book. "Come on," he said. "I'm taking you to the Oasis for dinner."

Eden went gladly. At one of the tables opposite the narrow counter, Paula Wendell sat alone.

"Hello," she greeted them. "Come over here. I felt in an expansive mood to-night—had to have the prestige of a table."

They sat down opposite her. "Did you find the day as dull as you expected?" inquired the girl of Eden.

"Very dull by contrast, after you left me," he answered.

"Try the chicken," she advised. "Born and raised right here at home, and the desert hen is no weak sister. Not so bad, however."

They accepted her suggestion. When the generously filled platters were placed before them, Bob Eden squared away.

"Take to the lifeboats," he said. "I'm about to carve, and when I carve, it's a case of women and children first."

Holley stared down at his dinner. "Looks like the same old chicken," he sighed. "What wouldn't I give for a little home cooking."

"Ought to get married," smiled the girl. "Am I right, Mr. Eden?"

Eden shrugged. "I've known several poor fellows who got married hoping to enjoy a bit of home cooking. Now they're back in the restaurants, and the only difference is they've got the little woman along. Double the check and half the pleasure."

"Why all this cynicism?" asked Holley.

"Oh, Mr. Eden is very much opposed to marriage," the girl said. "He was telling me to-day."

"Just trying to save her," Eden explained. "By the way, do you know this Wilbur who's won her innocent, trusting heart?"

"Wilbur?" asked Holley blankly.

"He will persist in calling Jack out of his name," the girl said. "It's his disrespectful way of referring to my fiancé."

Holley glanced at the ring. "No, I don't know him," he announced. "I certainly congratulate him, though."

"So do I," Eden returned. "On his nerve. However, I oughtn't to knock Wilbur. As I was saying only this noon—"

"Never mind," put in the girl. "Wake up, Will. What are you thinking about?"

Holley started. "I was thinking of a dinner I had once at Mouquin's," he replied. "Closed up, now, I hear. Gone—like all the other old landmarks—the happy stations on the five o'clock cocktail route. You know, I wonder sometimes if I'd like New York to-day—"

He talked on of the old Manhattan he had known. In what seemed to Bob Eden no time at all, the dinner hour had passed. As they were standing at the cashier's desk, the boy noted for the first time a stranger lighting a cigar near by. He was, from his dress, no native—a small, studious-looking man with piercing eyes.

"Good evening, neighbor," Holley said.

"How are you," answered the stranger.

"Come down to look us over?" the editor asked, thinking of his next issue.

"Dropped in for a call on the kangaroo-rat," replied the man. "I understand there's a local variety whose tail measures three millimeters longer than any hitherto recorded."

"Oh," returned Holley. "One of those fellows, eh? We get them all—beetle men and butterfly men, mouse and gopher men. Drop round to the office of the *Times* some day and we'll have a chat."

"Delighted," said the little naturalist.

"Well, look who's here," cried Holley suddenly. Bob Eden turned, and saw entering the door of the Oasis a thin little Chinese who seemed as old as the desert. His face was the color of a beloved meerschaum pipe, his eyes beady and bright. "Louie Wong," Holley explained. "Back from San Francisco, eh, Louie?"

"Hello, boss," said Louie, in a high shrill voice. "My come back."

"Didn't you like it up there?" Holley persisted.

"San Flancisco no good," answered Louie. "All time lain dlop on nose. My like 'um heah."

"Going back to Madden's, eh?" Holley inquired. Louie nodded. "Well, here's a bit of luck for you, Louie. Mr. Eden is going out to the ranch presently, and you can ride with him."

"Of course," assented Eden.

"Catch 'um hot tea. You wait jus' litta time, boss," said Louie, sitting up to the counter.

"We'll be down in front of the hotel," Holley told him. The three of them went out. The little naturalist followed, and slipped by them, disappearing in the night.

Neither Holley nor Eden spoke. When they reached the hotel they stopped.

"I'm leaving you now," Paula Wendell said. "I have some letters to write."

"Ah, yes," Eden remarked. "Well—don't forget. My love to Wilbur."

"These are business letters," she answered, severely. "Good night."

The girl went inside. "So Louie's back," Eden said. "That makes a pretty situation."

"What's the matter?" Holley said. "Louie may have a lot to tell."

"Perhaps. But when he shows up at his old job—what about Charlie? He'll be kicked out, and I'll be alone on the big scene. Somehow, I don't feel I know my lines."

"I never thought of that," replied the editor. "However, there's plenty of work for two boys out there when Madden's in residence. I imagine he'll keep them both. And what a chance for Charlie to pump old Louie dry. You and I could ask him questions from now until doomsday and never learn a thing. But Charlie—that's another matter."

They waited, and presently Louie Wong came shuffling down the street, a cheap little suit-case in one hand and a full paper bag in the other.

"What you got there, Louie?" Holley asked. He examined the bag. "Bananas, eh?"

"Tony like 'um banana," the old man explained. "Pleasant foah Tony."

Eden and Holley looked at each other. "Louie," said the editor gently, "poor Tony's dead."

Any one who believes the Chinese face is always expressionless should have seen Louie's then. A look of mingled pain and anger contorted it, and he burst at once into a flood of language that needed no translator. It was profane and terrifying.

"Poor old Louie," Holley said. "He's reviling the street, as they say in China."

"Do you suppose he knows?" asked Eden. "That Tony was murdered, I mean."

"Search me," answered Holley. "It certainly looks that way, doesn't it?" Still loudly vocal, Louie Wong climbed on to the back seat of the flivver, and Bob Eden took his place at the wheel. "Watch your step, boy," advised Holley. "See you soon. Good night."

Bob Eden started the car, and with old Louie Wong set out on the strangest ride of his life.

The moon had not yet risen; the stars, wan and far-off and unfriendly, were devoid of light. They climbed between the mountains, and that mammoth doorway led seemingly to a black and threatening inferno that Eden could sense but could not see. Down the rocky road and on to the sandy floor of the desert they crept along: out of the dark beside the way gleamed little yellow eyes, flashing hatefully for a moment, then vanishing forever. Like the ugly ghosts of trees that had died the Joshuas writhed in agony, casting deformed, appealing arms aloft. And constantly as they rode on, muttered the weird voice of the old Chinese on the back seat, mourning the passing of his friend, the death of Tony.

Bob Eden's nerves were steady, but he was glad when the lights of Madden's ranch shone with a friendly glow ahead. He left the car in the road and went to open the gate. A stray twig was caught in the latch, but finally he got it open, and returning to the car, swung it into the yard. With a feeling of deep relief he swept up before the barn. Charlie Chan was waiting in the glow of the headlights.

"Hello, Ah Kim," Eden called. "Got a little playmate for you in the back seat. Louie Wong has come back to his desert." He leaped to the ground. All was silence in the rear of the car. "Come on, Louie," he cried. "Here we are."

He stopped, a sudden thrill of horror in his heart. In the dim light he saw that Louie had slipped to his knees, and that his head hung limply over the door at the left.

"My God!" cried Eden.

"Wait," said Charlie Chan. "I get flashlight."

He went, while Bob Eden stood fixed and frightened in his tracks. Quickly the efficient Charlie returned, and made a hasty examination with the light. Bob Eden saw a gash in the side of Louie's old coat—a gash that was bordered with something wet and dark.

"Stabbed in the side," said Charlie calmly. "Dead—like Tony."

"Dead—when?" gasped Eden. "In the minute I left the car at the gate. Why—it's impossible—"

Out of the shadows came Martin Thorn, his pale face gleaming in the dusk. "What's all this?" he asked. "Why—it's Louie. What's happened to Louie?"

He bent over the door of the car, and the busy flashlight in the hand of Charlie Chan shone for a moment on his back. Across the dark coat was a long tear—a tear such as might have been made in the coat of one climbing hurriedly through a barbed-wire fence.

"This is terrible," Thorn said. "Just a minute—I must get Mr. Madden."

He ran to the house, and Bob Eden stood with Charlie Chan by the body of Louie Wong.

"Charlie," whispered the boy huskily, "you saw that rip in Thorn's coat?"

"Most certainly," answered Chan. "I observed it. What did I quote to you this morning? Old saying of Chinese. 'He who rides a tiger can not dismount.'"

10

Bliss of the Homicide Squad

In another moment Madden was with them there by the car, and they felt rather than saw a quivering, suppressed fury in every inch of the millionaire's huge frame. With an oath he snatched the flashlight from the hand of Charlie Chan and bent over the silent form in the back of the flivver. The glow from the lamp illuminated faintly his big red face, his searching eyes, and Bob Eden watched him with interest.

There in that dusty car lay the lifeless shape of one who had served Madden faithfully for many years. Yet no sign either of compassion or regret was apparent in the millionaire's face—nothing save a constantly growing anger. Yes, Bob Eden reflected, those who had reported Madden lacked a heart spoke nothing but the truth.

Madden straightened, and flashed the light into the pale face of the secretary.

"Fine business!" he snarled.

"Well, what are you staring at me for?" cried Thorn, his voice trembling.

"I'll stare at you if I choose—though God knows I'm sick of the sight of your silly face—"

"I've had about enough from you," warned Thorn, and the tremor in his voice was rage. For a moment they regarded each other while Bob Eden watched them, amazed. For the first time he realized that under the mask of their daily relations these two were anything but friends.

Suddenly Madden turned the light on Charlie Chan. "Look here, Ah Kim—this was Louie Wong—the boy you replaced here—savvy? You've got to stay on the ranch now—after I've gone, too—how about it?"

"I think I stay, boss."

"Good. You're the only bit of luck I've had since I came to this accursed place. Bring Louie into the living-room—on the couch. I'll call Eldorado."

He stalked off through the patio to the house, and after a moment's hesitation Chan and the secretary picked up the frail body of Louie Wong. Slowly Bob Eden followed that odd procession. In the living-room, Madden was talking briskly on the telephone. Presently he hung up the receiver.

"Nothing to do but wait," he said. "There's a sort of constable in town—he'll be along pretty soon with the coroner. Oh, it's fine business. They'll overrun the place—and I came here for a rest."

"I suppose you want to know what happened," Eden began. "I met Louie Wong in town, at the Oasis Café. Mr. Holley pointed him out to me, and—"

Madden waved a great hand. "Oh, save all that for some half-witted cop. Fine business, this is."

He took to pacing the floor like a lion with the toothache. Eden dropped into a chair before the fire. Chan had gone out, and Thorn was sitting silently near by. Madden continued to pace. Bob Eden stared at the blazing logs. What sort of affair had he got into, anyhow? What desperate game was afoot here on Madden's ranch, far out on the lonely desert? He began to wish himself out of it, back in town where the lights were bright and there was no constant undercurrent of hatred and suspicion and mystery.

He was still thinking in this vein when the clatter of a car sounded in the yard. Madden himself opened the door, and two of Eldorado's prominent citizens entered.

"Come in, gentlemen," Madden said, amiable with an effort. "Had a little accident out here."

One of the two, a lean man with a brown, weather-beaten face, stepped forward.

"Howdy, Mr. Madden, I know you, but you don't know me. I'm Constable Brackett, and this is our coroner, Doctor Simms. A murder, you said on the phone."

"Well," replied Madden, "I suppose you could call it that. But fortunately no one was hurt. No white man, I mean. Just my old Chink, Louie Wong."

Ah Kim had entered in time to hear this speech, and his eyes blazed for a moment as they rested on the callous face of the millionaire.

"Louie?" said the constable. He went over to the couch. "Why, poor old Louie. Harmless as they come, he was. Can't figure who'd have anything against old Louie."

The coroner, a brisk young man, also went to the couch and began an examination. Constable Brackett turned to Madden. "Now, we'll make just as little trouble as we can, Mr. Madden," he promised. Evidently he was much in awe of this great man. "But I don't like this. It reflects on me. I got to ask a few questions. You see that, don't you?"

"Of course," answered Madden. "Fire away. I'm sorry, but I can't tell you a thing. I was in my room when my secretary"—he indicated Thorn—"came in and said that Mr. Eden here had just driven into the yard with the dead body of Louie in the car."

The constable turned with interest to Eden. "Where'd you find him?" he inquired.

"He was perfectly all right when I picked him up," Eden explained. He launched into his story—the meeting with Louie at the Oasis, the ride across the desert, the stop at the gate, and finally the gruesome discovery in the yard. The constable shook his head.

"All sounds mighty mysterious to me," he admitted. "You say you think he was killed while you was openin' the gate. What makes you think so?"

"He was talking practically all the way out here," Eden replied. "Muttering to himself there in the back seat. I heard him when I got out to unfasten the gate."

"What was he sayin'?"

"He was talking in Chinese. I'm sorry, but I'm no sinologue."

"I ain't accused you of anything, Have I?"

"A sinologue is a man who understands the Chinese language," Bob Eden smiled.

"Oh." The constable scratched his head. "This here secretary, now—"

Thorn came forward. He had been in his room, he said, when he heard a disturbance in the yard, and went outside. Absolutely nothing to offer. Bob Eden's glance fell on the tear across the back of Thorn's coat. He looked at Charlie Chan, but the detective shook his head. Say nothing, his eyes directed.

The constable turned to Madden. "Who else is on the place?" he wanted to know.

"Nobody but Ah Kim here. He's all right."

The officer shook his head. "Can't always tell," he averred. "All these tong wars, you know." He raised his voice to a terrific bellow. "Come here, you," he cried.

Ah Kim, lately Detective-Sergeant Chan of the Honolulu Police, came with expressionless face and stood before the constable. How often he had played the opposite rôle in such a scene—played it far better than this mainland officer ever would.

"Ever see this Louie Wong before?" thundered the constable.

"Me, boss? No, boss, I no see 'um."

"New round here, ain't you?"

"Come las' Fliday, boss."

"Where did you work before this?"

"All place, boss. Big town, litta town."

"I mean where'd you work last?"

"Lailload, I think, boss. Santa Fe lailload. Lay sticks on glound."

"Ah—er—well, doggone." The constable had run out of questions. "Ain't had much practise at this sort of thing," he apologized. "Been so busy confiscatin' licker these last few years I sort of lost the knack for police work. This is sheriff's stuff. I called him before we come out, an' he's sendin' Captain Bliss of the Homicide Squad down to-morrow mornin'. So we won't bother you no more to-night, Mr. Madden."

The coroner came forward. "We'll take the body in town, Mr. Madden," he said. "I'll have the inquest in there, but I may want to bring my jurors out here sometime to-morrow."

"Oh, sure," replied Madden. "Just attend to anything that comes up, and send all the bills to me. Believe me, I'm sorry this thing has happened."

"So am I," said the constable. "Louie was a good old scout."

"Yes—and—well, I don't like it. It's annoying."

"All mighty mysterious to me," the constable admitted again. "My wife told me I never ought to take this job. Well, so long, Mr. Madden—great pleasure to meet a man like you."

When Bob Eden retired to his room, Madden and Thorn were facing each other on the hearth. Something in the expression of each made him wish he could overhear the scene about to be enacted in that room.

Ah Kim was waiting beside a crackling fire. "I make 'um burn, boss," he said. Eden closed the door and sank into a chair.

"Charlie, in heaven's name, what's going on here?" he inquired helplessly.

Chan shrugged. "Plenty goes on," he said. "Two nights now gone since in this room I hint to you Chinese are psychic people. On your face then I see well-bred sneer."

"I apologize," Eden returned. "No sneering after this, even the well-bred kind. But I'm certainly stumped. This thing to-night—"

"Most unfortunate, this thing to-night," said Chan thoughtfully. "Humbly suggest you be very careful, or everything spoils. Local police come thumping on to scene, not dreaming in their slight brains that murder of Louie are of no importance in the least."

"Not important, you say?"

"No, indeed, Not when compared to other matters."

"Well, it was pretty important to Louie, I guess," said Eden.

"Guess so, too. But murder of Louie just like death of parrot—one more dark deed covering up very black deed occurring here before we arrive on mysterious scene. Before parrot go, before Louie make unexpected exit, unknown person dies screaming unanswered cries for help. Who? Maybe in time we learn."

"Then you think Louie was killed because he knew too much?"

"Just like Tony, yes. Poor Louie very foolish, does not stay in San Francisco when summoned there. Comes with sad blunder back to desert. Most bitterly unwelcome here. One thing puzzles me."

"Only one thing?" asked Eden.

"One at present. Other puzzles put aside for moment. Louie goes on Wednesday morning, probably before black deed was done. How then does he know? Did act have echo in San Francisco? I am most sad not to have talk with im. But there are other paths to follow."

"I hope so," sighed Bob Eden. "But I don't see them. This is too much for me."

"Plenty for me, too," agreed Chan. "Pretty quick I go home, lifelong yearning for travel forever quenched. Keep in mind, much better police do not find who killed Louie Wong. If they do, our fruit may be picked when not yet ripe. We should handle case. Officers of law must be encouraged off of ranch at earliest possible time, having found nothing."

"Well, the constable was easy enough," smiled Eden.

"All looked plenty mysterious to him," answered Chan, smiling, too.

"I sympathized with him in that," Eden admitted. "But this Captain Bliss probably won't be so simple. You watch your step, Charlie, or they'll lock you up."

Chan nodded. "New experiences crowd close on this mainland," he said. "Detective-Sergeant Chan a murder suspect. Maybe I laugh at that, when I get home again. Just now, laugh won't come. A warm good night—"

"Wait a minute," interrupted Eden. "How about Tuesday afternoon? Madden's expecting the messenger with the pearls then, and somehow, I haven't a stall left in me."

Chan shrugged. "Two days yet. Stop the worry. Much may manage to occur before Tuesday afternoon." He went out softly.

Just as they finished breakfast on Monday morning, a knock sounded on the door of the ranch house, and Thorn admitted Will Holley.

"Oh," said Madden sourly. His manner had not improved overnight. "So you're here again."

"Naturally," replied Holley. "Being a good newspaper man, I'm not overlooking the first murder we've had round here in years." He handed a newspaper to the millionaire. "By the way, here's a Los Angeles morning paper. Our interview is on the front page."

Madden took it without much interest. Over his shoulder Bob Eden caught a glimpse of the head-lines:

ERA OF PROSPERITY DUE, SAYS FAMED MAGNATE
P. J. Madden, Interviewed on Desert
Ranch, Predicts Business Boom

Madden glanced idly through the story. When he had finished, he said: "In the New York papers, I suppose?"

"Of course," Holley answered. "All over the country this morning. You and I are famous, Mr. Madden. But what's this about poor old Louie?"

"Don't ask me," frowned Madden. "Some fool bumped him off. Your friend Eden can tell you more than I can." He got up and strode from the room.

Eden and Holley stared at each other for a moment, then went together into the yard.

"Pretty raw stuff," remarked Holley. "It makes me hot. Louie was a kindly old soul. Killed in the car, I understand."

Eden related what had happened. They moved farther away from the house.

"Well, who do you think?" Holley inquired.

"I think Thorn," Eden answered. "However, Charlie says Louie's passing was just a minor incident, and it will be better all round if his murderer isn't found just at present. Of course he's right."

"Of course he is. And there isn't much danger they'll catch the guilty man, at that. The constable is a helpless old fellow."

"How about this Captain Bliss?"

"Oh, he's a big noisy bluff with a fatal facility for getting the wrong man. The sheriff's a regular fellow, with brains, but he may not come round. Let's stroll out and look over the ground where you left the car last night. I've got something to slip you, a telegram—from your father, I imagine."

As they went through the gate, the telegram changed hands. Holding it so it could not be seen from the house, Bob Eden read it through.

"Well, dad says he's going to put up the bluff to Madden that's he's sending Draycott with the pearls tonight."

"Draycott?" asked Holley.

"He's a private detective dad uses in San Francisco. As good a name as any, I suppose. When Draycott fails to arrive, dad's going to be very much upset." The boy considered for a moment. "I guess it's about the best he can do—but I hate all this deception. And I certainly don't like the job of keeping Madden cool. However, something may happen before then."

They examined the ground where Bob Eden had halted the car while he opened the gate the night before. The tracks of many cars passing in the road were evident—but no sign of any footsteps. "Even my footprints are gone," remarked Eden. "Do you suppose it was the wind, drifting the sand—"

Holley shrugged. "No," he said. "It was not. Somebody has been out here with a broom, my boy, and obliterated every trace of footsteps about that car."

Eden nodded. "You're right. Somebody—but who? Our old friend Thorn, of course."

They stepped aside as an automobile swung by them and entered Madden's yard.

"There's Bliss, now, with the constable," Holley remarked. "Well, they get no help from us, eh?"

"Not a bit," replied Eden. "Encourage them off the ranch at earliest possible moment. That's Charlie's suggestion."

They returned to the yard and waited. Inside the living-room they heard Thorn and Madden talking with the two officers. After a time, Bliss came out, followed by the millionaire and Constable Brackett. He greeted Holley as an old friend, and the editor introduced Bob Eden.

"Oh, yes, Mr. Eden," said the captain. "Want to talk to you. What's your version of this funny business?"

Bob Eden looked at him with distaste. He was a big, flat-footed policeman of the usual type, and no great intelligence shone in his eyes. The boy gave him a carefully edited story of the night before.

"Humph," said Bliss. "Sounds queer to me."

"Yes?" smiled Eden. "To me, too. But it happens to be the truth."

"Well, I'll have a look at the ground out there," remarked Bliss.

"You'll find nothing," said Holley. "Except the footprints of this young man and myself. We've just been taking a squint around."

"Oh, you have, have you?" replied Bliss grimly. He strode through the gate, the constable tagging after him. After a perfunctory examination the two returned.

"This is sure some puzzle," said Constable Brackett.

"Is that so?" Bliss sneered. "Well, get on to yourself. How about this Chink, Ah Kim? Had a good job here, didn't he? Louie Wong comes back. What does that mean? Ah Kim loses his job."

"Nonsense," protested Madden.

"Think so, do you?" remarked Bliss. "Well, I don't. I tell you I know these Chinks. They think nothing of sticking knives in each other. Nothing at all." Ah Kim emerged from around the side of the house. "Hey, you," cried Captain Bliss. Bob Eden began to worry.

Ah Kim came up. "You want'um me, boss?"

"You bet I want you. Going to lock you up."

"Why foah, boss?"

"For knifing Louie Wong. You can't get away with that stuff round here."

The Chinese regarded this crude practitioner of his own arts with a lifeless eye. "You clazy, boss," he said.

"Is that so?" Bliss's face hardened. "I'll show you just how crazy I am. Better tell me the whole story now. It'll go a lot easier with you if you do."

"What stoahy, boss?"

"How you sneaked out and put a knife in Louie last night."

"Maybe you catch 'um knife, hey, boss?" asked Ah Kim, maliciously.

"Never mind about that!"

"Poah old Ah Kim's fingah plints on knife, hey, boss?"

"Oh, shut up," said Bliss.

"Maybe you takee look-see, find velvet slippah plints in sand, hey, boss?" Bliss glared at him in silence. "What I tell you—you clazy cop, hey, boss?"

Holley and Eden looked at each other with keen enjoyment. Madden broke in, "Oh, come now, Captain, you haven't got a thing against him, and you know it. You take my cook away from me without any evidence, and I'll make you sweat for it."

"Well—I—" Bliss hesitated. "I know he did it, and I'll prove it later." His eyes lighted. "How'd you get into this country?" he demanded.

"Melican citizen, boss. Boahn San Flancisco. Foahty-flive yeah old now."

"Born here, eh? Is that so? Then you've got your chock-gee, I suppose. Let me see it."

Bob Eden's heart sank to his boots. Though many Chinese were without chock-gee, he knew that the lack of one would be sufficient excuse for this stupid police-man to arrest Chan at once. Another moment, and they'd all be done for—

"Come on," bellowed Bliss.

"What you say, boss?" parried Ah Kim.

"You know what I said. Your chock-gee—certificate—hand it over or by heaven I'll lock you up so quick—"

"Oh, boss—ce'tiflicate—allight, boss." And before Eden's startled gaze the Chinese took from his blouse a worn slip of paper about the size of a bank-note, and handed it to Bliss.

The Captain read it sourly and handed it back. "All right—but I ain't through with you yet," he said.

"Thanks, boss," returned Ah Kim, brightening. "You plenty clazy, boss. Thasaw. Goo'by." And he shuffled away.

"I told you it looked terrible mysterious to me," commented the constable.

"Oh, for Pete's sake, shut up," cried Bliss. "Mr. Madden, I'll have to admit I'm stumped for the time being. But that condition don't last long with me. I'll get to the bottom of this yet. You'll see me again."

"Run out any time," Madden invited with deep insincerity. "If I happen on anything, I'll call Constable Brackett."

Bliss and the constable got into their car and rode away. Madden returned to the house.

"Oh, excellent Chan," said Will Holley softly. "Where in Sam Hill did he get that chock-gee?"

"It looked as though we were done for," Eden admitted. "But good old Charlie thinks of everything."

Holley climbed into his car. "Well, I guess Madden isn't going to invite me to lunch. I'll go along. You know, I'm keener than ever to get the answer to this puzzle. Louie was my friend. It's a rotten shame."

"I don't know where we're going, but we're on our way," Eden answered. "I'd feel pretty helpless if I didn't have Charlie with me."

"Oh, you've got a few brains, too." Holley assured him.

"You're clazy, boss," Eden laughed, as the editor drove away.

Returning to his room, he found Ah Kim clamly making the bed.

"Charlie, you're a peach," said the boy, closing the door. "I thought we were sunk without warning. Whose chock-gee did you have, anyhow?"

"Ah Kim's chock-gee, to be sure," smiled Chan.

"Who's Ah Kim?"

"Ah Kim humble vegetable merchant who drive me admist other garden truck from Barstow to Eldorado. I make simple arrangement to rent chockgee short while. Happy to note long wear in pockets make photograph look like image of anybody. Came to me in bright flash Madden might ask for identification certificate before engaging me for honorable tasks. Madden did not do so, but thing fit plenty neat all the same."

"It certainly did," Eden agreed. "You're a brick to do all this for the Jordans—and for Dad. I hope they pay you handsomely."

Chan shook his head. "What you say in car riding to ferry? Postman on holiday itches to try long stretch of road. All this sincere pleasure for me. When I untie knots and find answer that will be fine reward." He bowed and departed.

Some hours later, while they waited for lunch, Bob Eden and Madden sat talking in the big living-room. The millionaire was reiterating his desire to return east at the earliest possible moment. He was sitting facing the door. Suddenly on his big red face appeared a look of displeasure so intense it startled the boy. Turning about, Eden saw standing in the doorway the slight figure of a man, a stooped, studious-looking man who carried a suitcase in one hand. The little naturalist of the Oasis Café.

"Mr. Madden?" inquired the newcomer.

"I'm Madden," said the millionaire. "What is it?"

"Ah, yes." The stranger came into the room, and set down his bag. "My name, sir, is Gamble, Thaddeus Gamble, and I am keenly interested in certain fauna surrounding your desert home. I have here a letter from an old friend of yours, the president of a college that has received many benefactions at your hands. If you will be so kind as to look it over—"

He offered the letter and Madden took it, glaring at him in a most unfriendly manner. When the millionaire had read the brief epistle, he tore it into bits and, rising, tossed them into the fireplace.

"You want to stop here a few days?" he said.

"It would be most convenient if I could," answered Gamble. "Of course, I should like to pay for my accommodations—"

Madden waved his hand. Ah Kim came in, headed for the luncheon table. "Another place, Ah Kim," ordered Madden. "And show Mr. Gamble to the room in the left wing—the one next to Mr. Eden's."

"Very kind of you, I'm sure," remarked Gamble suavely. "I shall try to make as little trouble as may be. Luncheon impends, I take it. Not unwelcome, either. This—er—this desert air, sir—er—I'll return in a moment."

He followed Ah Kim out. Madden glared after him, his face purple. Bob Eden realized that a new puzzle had arrived.

"The devil with him," cried Madden. "But I had to be polite. That letter." He shrugged. "Gad, I hope I get out of here soon."

Bob Eden continued to wonder. Who was Mr. Gamble? What did he want at Madden's ranch?

11

Thorn Goes on a Mission

Whatever Mr. Gamble's mission at the ranch, Bob Eden reflected during lunch, it was obviously a peaceful one. Seldom had he encountered a more mild-mannered little chap. All through the meal the new-comer talked volubly and well, with a gentle, cultivated accent of a scholar. Madden was sour and unresponsive; evidently he still resented the intrusion of this stranger. Thorn as usual sat silent and aloof, a depressing figure in the black suit he had to-day donned to replace the one torn so mysteriously the night before. It fell to Bob Eden to come to Mr. Gamble's aid and keep the conversation going.

The luncheon over, Gamble rose and went to the door. For a moment he stood staring out across the blazing sand toward the cool white tops of the mountains, far away.

"Magnificent," he commented. "I wonder, Mr. Madden, if you realize the true grandeur of this setting for your ranch house? The desert, the broad lonely desert, that has from time immemorial cast its weird spell on the souls of men. Some find it bleak and disquieting, but as for myself—"

"Be here long?" cut in Madden.

"Ah, that depends. I sincerely hope so. I want to see this country after the spring rains—the verbena and the primroses in bloom. The thought enchants me. What says the prophet Isaiah? 'And the desert shall rejoice and blossom as the rose. And the parched ground shall become a pool, and the thirsty land springs of water.' You know Isaiah, Mr. Madden?"

"No, I don't. I know too many people now," responded Madden grimly.

"I believe you said you were interested in the fauna round here, Professor?" Bob Eden remarked.

Gamble looked at him quickly. "You give me my title," he said. "You are an observant young man. Yes, there are certain researches I intend to pursue—the tail of the kangaroo-rat, which attains here a phenomenal length. The maxillary arch in the short-nosed pocket-mouse, I understand, has also reached in this neighborhood an eccentric development."

The telephone rang, and Madden himself answered it. Listening carefully, Bob Eden heard: "Telegram for Mr. Madden." At this point the millionaire pressed the receiver close to his ear, and the rest of the message was an indistinct blur.

Eden was sorry for that, for he perceived that as Madden listened an expression of keen distress came over his face. When finally he put the receiver slowly back on to hits hook, he sat for a long time looking straight before him, obviously very much perplexed.

"What do you grow here in this sandy soil, Mr. Madden?" Professor Gamble inquired.

"Er—er—" Madden came gradually back to the scene. "What do I grow? A lot of things. You'd be surprised, and so would Isaiah." Gamble was smiling at him in a kindly way, and the millionaire warmed a bit. "Come out, since you're interested, and I'll show you round."

"Very good of you, sir," replied Gamble, and meekly followed into the patio. Thorn rose and joined them. Quickly Eden went to the telephone and got Will Holley on the wire.

"Look here," he said in a low voice, "Madden has just taken a telegram over the phone, and it seemed to worry him considerably. I couldn't make out what it was, but I'd like to know at once. Do you stand well enough with the operator to find out—without rousing suspicion, of course?"

"Sure," Holley replied. "That kid will tell me anything. Are you alone there? Can I call you back in a few minutes?"

"I'm alone just now," Eden responded. "If I shouldn't be when you call back, I'll pretend you want Madden and turn you over to him. You can fake something to say. But if you hurry, that may not be necessary. Speed, brother, speed!"

As he turned away, Ah Kim came in to gather up the luncheon things.

"Well, Charlie," Eden remarked. "Another guest at our little hotel, eh?"

Chan shrugged. "Such news comes plenty quick to cookhouse," he said.

Eden smiled. "You're the one who wanted to watch and wait," he reminded the detective. "If you're threatened with housemaid's knee, don't blame me."

"This Gamble," mused Chan. "Seems harmless like May morning, I think."

"Oh, very. A Bible student. And it strikes me there's a fair opening for a good Bible student round here."

"Undangerous and mild," continued Chan. "Yet hidden in his scant luggage is one pretty new pistol completely loaded."

"Going to shoot the tails off the rats, most likely," Eden smiled. "Now, don't get suspicious of him, Charlie. He's probably just a tenderfoot who believes the movies and so came to this wild country armed to defend himself. By the way, Madden just got a telegram over the phone, and it was, judging by appearances, another bit of unwelcome news for our dear old friend. Holley's looking it up for me. If the telephone rings, go into the patio and be ready to tip me off in case any one is coming."

Silently Ah Kim resumed his work at the table. In a few moments, loud and clear, came the ring of Holley on the wire. Running to the telephone, Eden put his hand over the bell, muffling it. Chan stepped into the patio.

"Hello, Holley," said the boy softly. "Yes. Yes. O.K. Shoot. Um. . . . Say, that's interesting, isn't it? Coming to-night, eh? Thanks, old man."

He hung up, and Charlie returned. "A bit of news," said Eden, rising. "That telegram was from Miss Evelyn Madden. Got tired of waiting in Denver, I guess. The message was sent from Barstow. The lady arrives to-night at Eldorado on the six-forty. Looks as though I may have to give up my room and check out."

"Miss Evelyn Madden?" repeated Chan.

"That's right—you don't know, do you? She's Madden's only child. A proud beauty, too—I met her in San Francisco. Well, it's no wonder Madden was perplexed, is it?"

"Certainly not," agreed Chan. "Murderous ranch like this no place for refined young woman."

Eden sighed. "Just one more complication," he said. "Things move, but we don't seem to get anywhere."

"Once more," returned Chan, "I call to your attention that much unused virtue, patience. Aspect will be brighter here now. A woman's touch—"

"This woman's touch means frost-bite," smiled Eden. "Charlie, I'll bet you a million—not even the desert will thaw out Evelyn Madden."

Chan departed to his duties in the cookhouse. Madden and Thorn drifted in after a time; Gamble, it appeared, had retired to his room. The long hot afternoon dragged by, baking hours of deathly calm during which the desert lived up to its reputaiton. Madden disappeared and presently his "noisome" snores filled the air. A good idea, Bob Eden decided.

In a recumbent position on his bed, he found that time passed more swiftly. In fact, he didn't know it was passing. Toward evening he awoke, hot and muddled of mind, but a cold shower made him feel human again.

At six o'clock he crossed the patio to the living-room. In the yard before the barn he saw Madden's big car standing ready for action, and remembered. The millionaire was no doubt about to meet his daughter in town, and the haughty Evelyn was not to be affronted with the flivver.

But when he reached the living-room, Eden saw that it was evidently Thorn who had been selected for the trip to Eldorado. The secretary stood there in his gloomy clothes, a black slouch hat accentuating the paleness of his face. As Eden entered, what was obviously a serious conversation between Thorn and the millionaire came to a sudden halt.

"Ah, good evening," said Eden. "Not leaving us, Mr. Thorn?"

"Business in town," returned Thorn. "Well, Chief, I'll go along."

Again the telephone rang. Madden leaped to it. For a moment he listened and history repeated itself on his face. "Bad news all the time," Eden thought.

Madden put his great hand over the mouthpiece, and spoke to his secretary. "It's that old bore down the road, Doctor Whitcomb," he announced, and Eden felt a flash of hot resentment at this characterization. "She wants to see me this evening—says she has something very important to tell me."

"Say you're busy," suggested Thorn.

"I'm sorry, Doctor," Madden began over the phone, "but I am very much occupied—"

He stopped, evidently interrupted by a flood of conversation. Again he put his hand over the transmitter. "She insists, confound it," he complained.

"Well, you'll have to see her then," said Thorn.

"All right, Doctor," Madden capitulated. "Come about eight."

Thorn went out, and the big car roared off toward the road and Evelyn Madden's train. Mr. Gamble entered, refreshed and ready with a few apt quotations. Eden amused himself with the radio.

At the usual hour, much to Eden's surprise, they dined. Thorn's chair was empty and there was, oddly enough, no place for Evelyn; nor did the millionaire make any arrangements regarding a room for his daughter. Strange, Eden thought.

After dinner, Madden led them to the patio. Again he had arranged for a fire out there, and the blaze glowed red on the stone floor, on the adobe walls of the house, and on the near-by perch of Tony, now empty and forlorn.

"This is living," remarked Gamble, when they had sat down and he had lighted one of Madden's cigars. "The poor fools cooped up in cities—they don't know what they're missing. I could stay here forever."

His final sentence made no hit with the host, and silence fell. At a little past eight they heard the sound of a car entering the yard. Thorn and the girl, perhaps—but evidently Madden didn't think so, for he said:

"That's the doctor. Ah Kim!" The servant appeared. "Show the lady out here."

"Wel, she doesn't want to see me," Gamble said, getting up. "I'll go in and find a book."

Madden looked at Bob Eden, but the boy remained where he was. "The doctor's a friend of mine," he explained.

"Is that so?" growled Madden.

"Yes—I met her yesterday morning. A wonderful woman."

Doctor Whitcomb appeared. "Well, Mr. Madden?" She shook hands. It's a great pleasure to have you with us again."

"Thanks," said Madden coolly. "You know Mr. Eden, I believe?"

"Oh, hello," smiled the woman. "Glad to see you. Not very pleased with you, however. You didn't drop in to-day."

"Rather busy," Eden replied. "Won't you sit down, please."

He brought forward a chair; it seemed that Madden needed a hint or two on hospitality. The guest sank into it. Madden, his manner very haughty and aloof, sat down some distance away, and waited.

"Mr. Madden," said Doctor Whitcomb. "I'm sorry if I seem to intrude—I know that you are here to rest, and that you don't welcome visitors. But this is not a social call. I came here about—about this terrible thing that has happened on your place."

For a moment Madden did not reply. "You—mean—" he said slowly.

"I mean the murder of poor Louie Wong," the woman answered.

"Oh." Was there relief in Madden's voice? "Yes—of course."

"Louie was my friend—he often came to see me. I was so sorry, when I heard. And you—he served you faithfully, Mr. Madden. Naturally you're doing everything possible to run down his murderer."

"Everything," replied Madden carelessly.

"Whether what I have to tell has any connection with the killing of Louie—that's for policemen to decide," went on the doctor. "You can hand my story on to them—if you will."

"Gladly," replied Madden. "What is your story, Doctor?"

"On Saturday evening a man arrived at my place who said his name was McCallum, Henry McCallum," began Doctor Whitcomb, "and that he came from New York. He told me he suffered from bronchitis, though I must say I saw no symptoms of it. He took one of my cabins and settled down for a stay—so I thought."

"Yes," nodded Madden. "Go on."

"At dark Sunday night—a short time before the hour when poor Louie was killed—some one drove up in a big car before my place and blew the horn. One of my boys went out, and the stranger asked for McCallum. McCallum came, talked with the man in the car for a moment, then got in and rode off with him—in this direction. That was the last I've seen of Mr. McCallum. He left a suit-case filled with clothes in his cabin, but he has not returned."

"And you think he killed Louie?" asked Madden, with a note of polite incredulity in his voice.

"I don't think anything about it. How should I know? I simply regard it as a matter that should be called to the attention of the police. As you are much closer to the investigation than I am, I'm asking you tell them about it. They can come down and examine McCallum's property, if they wish."

"All right," said Madden, rising pointedly. "I'll tell them. Though if you're asking my opinion, I don't think—"

"Thank you," smiled the doctor. "I wasn't asking your opinion, Mr. Madden." She too stood. "Our interview, I see, is ended. I'm sorry if I've intruded—"

"Why, you didn't intrude," protested Madden. "That's all right. Maybe your information is valuable. Who knows?"

"Very good of you to say so," returned the doctor, with gentle sarcasm. She glanced toward the parrot's perch. "How's Tony? He, at least, must miss Louie a lot."

"Tony's dead," said Madden bruskly.

"What! Tony, too!" The doctor was silent for a moment. "A rather memorable visit, this one of yours," she said slowly. "Please give my regards to your daughter. She is not with you?"

"No," returned Madden. "She is not with me." That was all.

"A great pity," Doctor Whitcomb replied. "I thought her a charming girl."

"Thank you," Madden said. "Just a moment. My boy will show you to your car."

"Don't trouble," put in Bob Eden. "I'll attend to that." He led the way through the bright living-room, past Mr. Gamble deep in a huge book. In the yard the doctor turned to him.

"What a man!" she said. "As hard as granite. I don't believe the death of Louie means a thing to him."

"Very little, I'm afraid," Eden agreed.

"Well, I rely on you. If he doesn't repeat my story to the sheriff, you must."

The boy hesitated. "I'll tell you something—in confidence," he said. "Everything possible is being done to find the murderer of Louie. Not by Madden—but by—others."

The doctor sat silent for a moment in the dark car under the dark, star-spangled sky. "I think I understand," she said softly. "With all my heart, I wish you luck, my boy."

Eden took her hand. "If I shouldn't see you again, Doctor—I want you to know. Just meeting you has been a privilege."

"I'll remember that," she answered. "Good night."

The boy watched her back the car through the open gate. When he returned to the living-room, Madden and Gamble were together there. "Confounded old busy-body," Madden said.

"Wait a minute," Eden said hotly. "That woman with just her two hands has done more good in the world than you with all your money. And don't you forget it."

"Does that give her a license to butt into my affairs?" demanded Madden.

Further warm words were on the tip of the boy's tongue, but he restrained himself. However, he reflected that he was about fed up with this arrogant, callous millionaire.

He looked toward the clock. A quarter to nine, and still no sign of Thorn and Evelyn Madden. Was the girl's train late? Hardly likely.

Though he did not feel particularly welcome in the room, he waited on. He would see this latest development through. At ten o'clock Mr. Gamble rose, and commenting favorably on the desert air, went to his room.

At five minutes past ten the roar of the big car in the yard broke the intense stillness. Bob Eden sat erect, his eager eyes straying from one door to another. Presently the glass doors leading to the patio opened. Martin Thorn came in alone.

Without a word to his chief, the secretary threw down his hat and dropped wearily into a chair. The silence became oppressive.

"Got your business attended to, eh?" suggested Eden cheerfully.

"Yes," said Thorn—no more. Eden rose.

"Well, I guess I'll turn in," he said, and went to his room. As he entered he heard the splash of Mr. Gamble in the bath that lay between his apartment and that occupied by the professor. His seclusion was ended. Have to be more careful in the future.

Shortly after his lights were on, Ah Kim appeared at the door. Eden, finger on lips, indicated the bath. The Chinese nodded. They stepped to the far side of the bedroom and spoke in low tones.

"Well, where's little Evelyn?" asked the boy.

Chan shrugged. "More mystery," he whispered.

"Just what has our friend Thorn been doing for the past four hours?" Eden wondered.

"Enjoying moonlit ride on desert, I think," Chan returned. "When big car go out, I note speedometer. Twelve thousand eight hundred and forty miles. Four miles necessary to travel to town, and four to return with. But when big car arrives home, speedometer announces quietly twelve thousand eight hundred and seventy-nine miles."

"Charlie, you think of everything," Eden said admiringly.

"Strange place this Thorn has been," Charlie added. "Much red clay on ground." He exhibited a fragment of earth. "Scraped off on accelerator," he explained. "Maybe you have seen such place round here?"

"Nothing like it," replied Eden. "You don't suppose he's harmed the gal—but no, Madden seems to be in on it, and she's his darling."

"Just one more little problem rising up," said Chan.

Eden nodded. "Lord, I haven't met so many problems since I gave up Algebra. And by the way, to-morrow's Tuesday. The pearls are coming, hurrah, hurrah. At least, old P. J. thinks they are. He's going to be hard to handle to-morrow."

A faint knock sounded on the door to the patio, and Chan had just time to get to the fireplace and busy himself there when it was opened and Madden, oddly noiseless for him, entered.

"Why, hello—" began Eden.

"Hush!" said Madden. He looked toward the bathroom. "Go easy, will you, Ah Kim, get out of here."

"Allight, boss," said Ah Kim, and went.

Madden stepped to the bathroom door and listened. He tried it gently; it opened at his touch. He went in, locked the door leading into the room occupied by Gamble, and returned, shutting the door behind him.

"Now," he began. "I want to see you. Keep your voice down. I've finally got hold of your father on the telephone, and he tells me a man named Draycott will arrive with the pearls at Barstow to-morrow noon."

Eden's heart sank. "Ah—er—that ought to bring him here to-morrow night—"

Madden leaned close, and spoke in a hoarse undertone. "Whatever happens," he said, "I don't want that fellow to come to the ranch."

Eden stared at him in amazement. "Well, Mr. Madden, I'll be—"

"Hush! Leave my name out of it."

"But after all our preparation—"

"I tell you I've changed my mind. I don't want the pearls brought to the ranch at all. I want you to go to Barstow to-morrow, meet this Draycott, and order him to go on to Pasadena. I'm going down there on Wednesday. Tell him to meet me at the door of the Garfield National Bank in Pasadena at noon, sharp, Wednesday. I'll take the pearls then—and I'll put them where they'll be safe."

Bob Eden smiled. "All right," he agreed. "You're the boss."

"Good," said Madden. "I'll have Ah Kim drive you into town in the morning, and you can catch the Barstow train. But remember—this is between you and me. Not a word to anybody. Not to Gamble—of course. Not even to Thorn."

"I get you," Eden answered.

"Fine! Then it's set. Good night."

Madden went softly out. For a long time Eden stared after him, more puzzled than ever.

"Well, anyhow," he said at last, "it means another day of grace. For this relief, much thanks."

12

The Trolley on the Desert

A new day dawned, and over the stunted, bizarre shapes of that land of drought the sun resumed its merciless vigil. Bob Eden was early abroad; it was getting to be a habit with him. Before breakfast was served he had a full hour for reflection, and it could not be denied that he had much upon which to reflect. One by one he recalled the queer things that had happened since he came to the ranch. Foremost in his thoughts was the problem of Evelyn Madden. Where was that haughty lady now? No morning mists on the landscape here, but in his mind a constantly increasing fog. If only something definite would occur, something they could understand.

After breakfast he rose from the table and lighted a cigarette. He knew that Madden was eagerly waiting for him to speak.

"Mr. Madden," he said, "I find that I must go to Barstow this morning on rather important business. It's an imposition, I know. But if Ah Kim could drive me to town in time for the ten-fifteen train—"

Thorn's green eyes popped with sudden interest. Madden looked at the boy with ill-concealed approval.

"Why, that's all right," he replied. "I'll be glad to arrange it for you. Ah Kim—you drive Mr. Eden in town in half an hour. Savvy?"

"All time moah job," complained Ah Kim. "Gettum up sunlise woik woik till sun him dlop. You want 'um taxi dliver why you no say so?"

"What's that?" cried Madden.

Ah Kim shrugged. "Allight, boss. I dlive 'um."

When, later on, Eden sat in the car beside the Chinese and the ranch was well behind them, Chan regarded him questioningly.

"Now you produce big mystery," he said. "Barstow on business has somewhat unexpected sound to me."

Eden laughed. "Orders from the big chief," he replied. "I'm to go down there and meet Al Draycott—and the pearls."

For a moment Chan's free hand rested on his waist and the "undigestible" burden that still lay there.

"Madden changes fickle mind again?" he inquired.

"That's just what he's done." Eden related the purport of the millionaire's call on him the night before.

"What you know concerning that!" exclaimed Chan wonderingly.

"Well, I know this much," Eden answered. "It gives us one more day for the good old hoo malimali. Outside of that, it's just another problem for us to puzzle over. By the way, I didn't tell you why Doctor Whitcomb came to see us last night."

"No necessity," Chan replied. "I am loafing idle inside door close by and hear it all."

"Oh, you were? Then you know it may have been Shaky Phil, and not Thorn, who killed Louie?"

"Shaky Phil—or maybe stranger in car who drive up and call him into road. Must admit that stranger interests me very deep. Who was he? Was it maybe him who carried news of Louie's approach out on to dreary desert?"

"Well, if you're starting to ask me questions," replied Eden, "then the big mystery is over and we may as well wash up and go home. For I haven't got an answer in me." Eldorado lay before them, its roofs gleaming under the morning sun. "By the way, let's drop in and see Holley. The train isn't due yet—I suppose I'd better take it, somebody might be watching. In the interval, Holley may have news."

The editor was busy at his desk. "Hello, you're up and around pretty early this morning," he said. He pushed aside his typewriter. "Just dashing off poor old Louie's obit. What's new out at Mystery Ranch?"

Bob Eden told him of Doctor Whitcomb's call, also of Madden's latest switch regarding the pearls, and his own imminent wild goose chase to Barstow.

Holley smiled. "Cheer up—a little travel will broaden you," he remarked. "What did you think of Miss Evelyn? But then, I believe you had met her before."

"Think of Miss Evelyn? What do you mean?" asked Eden, surprised.

"Why, she came last night, didn't she?"

"Not so anybody could notice it. No sign of her at the ranch."

Holley rose and walked up and down for a moment. "That's odd. That's very odd. She certainly arrived on the six-forty train."

"You're sure of that?" Eden asked.

"Of course I am. I saw her." Holley sat down again. "I wasn't very much occupied last night—it was one of my free nights—I have three hundred and sixty-five of them every year. So I strolled over to the station and met the six-forty. Thorn was there, too. A tall handsome girl got off the train, and I heard Thorn address her as Miss Evelyn. 'How's dad?' she asked. 'Get in,' said Thorn, 'and I'll tell you about him. He wasn't able to come to meet you himself.' The girl entered the car, and they drove away. Naturally, I thought she was brightening your life long before this."

Eden shook his head. "Funny business," he commented. "Thorn got back to the ranch a little after ten, and when he came he was alone. Charlie here discovered, with his usual acumen, that the car had traveled some thirty-nine miles."

"Also clinging to accelerator, as though scraped off from shoe of Thorn, small fragment of red clay," added Chan. "You are accustomed round here, Mr. Holley. Maybe you can mention home of red clay."

"Not off hand," replied Holley. "There are several places— But say, this thing gets deeper and deeper. Oh—I was forgetting—there's a letter here for you, Eden."

He handed over a neat missive addressed in an old-fashioned hand. Eden inspected it with interest. It was from Madame Jordan, a rather touching appeal not to let the deal for the pearls fall through. He went back and began to read it aloud. Mrs. Jordan could not understand. Madden was there, he had bought the pearls—why the delay? The loss of that money would be serious for her.

When he had finished, Eden looked accusingly at Chan, then tore the letter to bits and threw them into a waste-paper basket. "I'm about through," he said. "That woman is one of the dearest old souls that ever lived, and it strikes me we're treating her shamefully. After all, what's happening out at Madden's ranch is none of our business. Our duty to Madame Jordan—"

"Pardon me," broke in Chan, "but coming to that, I have sense of duty most acute myself. Loyalty blooms in my heart forever—"

"Well, and what do you think we ought to do?" demanded Eden.

"Watch and wait."

"But good lord—we've done that. I was thinking about it this morning. One inexplicable event after another, and never anything definite, anything we can get out teeth into. Such a state of affairs may go on forever. I tell you, I'm fed up."

"Patience," said Chan, "are a very lonely virtue. Through long centuries Chinese cultivate patience like kind gardener tending flowers. White men leap about similar to bug in bottle. Which are better method, I inquire?"

"But listen, Charlie. All this stuff we've discovered out at the ranch—that's for the police."

"For stupid Captain Bliss, maybe. He with the feet of large extensiveness."

"I can't help the size of his feet. What's that got to do with it? No, sir—I can't see why we don't give Madden the pearls, get his receipt, and then send for the sheriff and tell him the whole story. After that, he can worry about who was killed at Madden's ranch."

"He would solve the problem," scoffed Chan. "Great mind, no doubt, like Captain Bliss. Your thought has, from me, nothing but hot opposition."

"Well, but I'm considering Madame Jordan. I've got her interests at heart."

Chan patted him on the back. "Who can question that? You fine young fellow, loyal and kind. But listen now to older heads. Mr. Holley, you have inclination to intrude your oar?"

"I certainly have," smiled Holley. "I'm all on the side of Chan, Eden. It would be a pity to drop this thing now. The sheriff's a good sort, but all this would be too deep for him. No, wait just a little while—"

"All right," sighed Eden. "I'll wait. Provided you tell me one thing. What are we waiting for?"

"Madden goes to Pasadena to-morrow," Chan suggested. "No doubt Thorn will accompany, and we quench this Gamble somehow. Great time for us. All our search at ranch up to now hasty and breathless, like man pursuing trolley-car. To-morrow we dig deep."

"You can do it," replied Eden. "I'm not eager to dig for the sort of prize you want." He paused. "At that, I must admit I'm pretty curious myself. Charlie, you're an old friend of the Jordans, and you can take the responsibility for this delay."

"Right here on shoulders," Chan agreed, "responsibility reclines. Same way necklace reposes on stomach. Seem to coddle there now, those Phillimore pearls, happy and content. Humbly suggest you take this aimless journey to Barstow."

Eden looked at his watch. "I suppose I might as well. Bit of city life never did anybody any harm. But I warn you that when I come back, I want a little light. If any more dark, mysterious things happen at that ranch, I certainly will run right out into the middle of the desert and scream."

Taking the train proved an excellent plan, for on the station platform he met Paula Wendell, who evidently had the same idea. She was trim and charming in riding togs, and her eyes sparkled with life.

"Hello," she said. "Where are you bound?"

"Going to Barstow, on business," Eden explained.

"Is it important?"

"Naturally. Wouldn't squander my vast talents on any other kind."

A dinky little train wandered in, and they found a seat together in one of its two cars.

"Sorry to hear you're needed in Barstow," remarked the girl. "I'm getting off a few stations down. Going to rent a horse and take a long ride up into Lonely Cañon. It wouldn't have been so lonely if you could have come along."

Eden smiled happily. Certainly one had few opportunities to look into eyes like hers. "What station do we get off at?" he inquired.

"We? I thought you said—"

"The truth isn't in me, these days. Barstow doesn't need my presence any more than you need a beauty doctor. Lonely Cañon, after to-day, will have to change its name."

"Good," she answered. "We get off at Seven Palms. The old rancher who rents me a horse will find one for you, I'm sure."

"I'm not precisely dressed for the rôle," admitted Eden. "But I trust it will be all the same to the horse."

The horse didn't appear to mind. His rather dejected manner suggested that he had expected something like this. They left the tiny settlement known as Seven Palms and cantered off across the desert.

"For to admire and for to see, for to behold this world so wide," said Eden. "Never realized how very wide it was until I came down here."

"Beginning to like the desert?" the girl inquired.

"Well, there's something about it," he admitted. "It grows on you, that's a fact. I don't know that I could put the feeling into words."

"I'm sure I can't," she answered. "Oh, I envy you, coming here for the first time. If only I could look at this country again with a fresh, disinterested eye. But it's just location to me. I see all about me the cowboys, the cavalcades, the caballeros of Hollywood. Tragedies and feats of daring, rescues and escapes. I tell you, these dunes and cañons have seen more movies than Will Hays."

"Hunting locations to-day?" Eden asked.

"Always hunting," she sighed. "They've just sent me a new script—as new as those mountains over there. All about the rough cowpuncher and the millionaire's dainty daughter from the East—you know."

"I certainly do. Girl's fed up on those society orgies, isn't she?"

"Who wouldn't be? However, the orgies are given in full, with the swimming pool working overtime, as always. But that part doesn't concern me. It's after she comes out here, sort of hungering to meet a real man, that I must start worrying. Need I add, she meets him? Her horse runs away over the desert, and tosses her off amid the sage-brush. In the nick of time, the cow-puncher finds her. Despite their different stations, love blossoms here in the waste land. Sometimes I'm almost glad that mine is beginning to be an obsolete profession."

"Is it? How come?"

"Oh, the movies move. A few years back the location finder was a rather important person. To-day most of this country has been explored and charted, and every studio is equipped with big albums full of pictures. So every time a new efficiency expert comes along—which is about once a week—and starts lopping off heads, it's the people in my line who are the first to go. In a little while we'll be as extinct as the dodo."

"You may be extinct," Eden answered. "But there the similarity between you and the dodo will stop abruptly."

The girl halted her horse. "Just a minute. I want to take a few pictures here. It looks to me like a bit of desert we haven't used yet. Just the sort of thing to thrill the shopgirls and the bookkeepers back there where the East hangs out." When she had swung again into the saddle, she added: "It isn't strange they love it, those tired people in the cities. Each one thinks—oh, if only I could go there."

"Yes, and if they got here once, they'd die of loneliness the first night," Bob Eden said. "Just pass out in agony moaning for the subway and the comics in the evening paper."

"I know they would," the girl replied. "But fortunately they'll never come."

They rode on, and the girl began to point out the various unfriendly-looking plants of the desert, naming them one by one. Arrow-weed, bitter-brush, mesquite, desert plantain, catclaw, thistle-sage.

"That's a cholla," she announced. "Another variety of cactus. There are seventeen thousand in all."

"All right," Eden replied. "I'll take your word for it. You needn't name them." His head was beginning to ache with all this learning.

Presently sumac and Canterbury bell proclaimed their nearness to the cañon, and they cantered out of the desert heat into the cathedral-like coolness of the hills. In and out over almost hidden trails the horses went. Wild plum glowed on the slopes, and far below under native palms a narrow stream tinkled invitingly.

Life seemed very simple and pleasant there in Lonely Cañon, and Bob Eden felt suddenly close indeed to this lively girl with the eager eyes. All a lie that there were crowded cities. The world was new, unsullied and unspoiled, and they were alone in it.

They descended by way of a rather treacherous path and in the shelter of the palms that fringed the tiny stream, dismounted for a lunch which Paula Wendell claimed to have concealed in her knapsack.

"Wonderfully restful here," Bob Eden said.

"But you said the other day you weren't tired," the girl reminded him.

"Well, I'm not. But somehow I like this anyhow. However, I guess it isn't all a matter of geography. It's not so much the place you're in—it's who you're with. After which highly original remark, I hasten to add that I really can't eat a thing."

"You were right," she laughed. "The truth isn't in you. I know what you're thinking—I didn't bring enough for two. But these Oasis sandwiches are meant for ranchers, and one is my limit. There are four of them—I must have had a premonition. We'll divide the milk equally."

"But look here,—it's your lunch. I should have thought to get something at Seven Palms."

"There's a roast beef sandwich. Try that, and maybe you won't feel so talkative."

"Well, I—um—gumph—"

"What did I tell you? Oh, the Oasis aims to fill. Milk?"

"Ashamed of myself," mumbled Eden. But he was easily persuaded.

"You haven't eaten a thing," he said finally.

"Oh, yes I have. More than I usually do. I'm one of those dainty eaters."

"Good news for Wilbur," replied Eden. "The upkeep won't be high. Though if he has any sense, he'll know that whatever the upkeep on a girl like you, it will be worth it."

"I sent him your love," said the girl.

"Is that so? Well, I'm sorry you did, in a way. I'm no hypocrite, and try as I may, I can't discover any lurking fondness for Wilbur. Oddly enough, the boy begins to annoy me."

"But you said—"

"I know. But isn't it just possible that I've overrated this freedom stuff? I'm young, and the young are often mistaken. Stop me if you've heard this one, but the more I see of you—"

"Stop. I've heard it."

"I'll bet you have. Many times."

"And my suggestion is that we get back to business. If we don't that horse of yours is going to eat too much Bermuda grass."

Through the long afternoon, amid the hot yellow dunes, the wind-blown foothills of that sandy waste, they rode back to Seven Palms by a roundabout route. The sun was sinking, the rose and gold wonder of the skies reflected on snow and glistening sand, when finally they headed for the village.

"If only I could find a novel setting for the final love scene," sighed the girl.

"Whose final love scene?"

"The cowpuncher's and the poor little rich girl's. So many times they've just wandered off into the sunset, hand in hand. Really need a little more kick in it than that."

Eden heard a clank as of a horse's hoofs on steel. His mount stumbled, and he reined it in sharply.

"What in Sam Hill's that?" he asked.

"Oh—that! It's one of the half-buried rails of the old branch road—a memento of a dream that never came true. Years ago they started to build a town over there under those cottonwoods, and the railroad laid down fifteen miles of track from the main line. A busy metropolis of the desert—that's what they meant it to be—and there's just one little old ruined house standing to-day. But that was the time of Great Expectations. They brought out crowds of people, and sold six hundred lots one hectic afternoon."

"And the railroad?"

"Ran just one train—and stopped. All they had was an engine and two old street-cars brought down from San Francisco. One of the cars has been demolished and the timber carried away, but the wreck of the other is still standing not far from here."

Presently they mounted a ride, and Bob Eden cried, "What do you know about that?"

There before them on the lonely desert, partly buried in the drifting sand, stood the remnant of a trolley-car. It was tilted rakishly to one side, its windows were yellow with dust, but on the front, faintly decipherable still, was the legend "Market Street."

At that familiar sight, Bob Eden felt a keen pang of nostalgia. He reined in his horse and sat staring at this symbol of the desert's triumph over the proud schemes of man. Man had thought he could conquer, he had come with his engines and his dreams, and now an old battered trolley stood alone as a warning and a threat.

"There's your setting," he said. "They drive out together and sit there on the steps, your lovers. What a background—a car that once trundled from Twin Peaks to the Ferry, standing lonely and forlorn amid the cactus plants."

"Fine," the girl answered. "I'm going to hire you to help me after this."

They rode close to the car and dismounted. The girl unlimbered her camera and held it steady. "Don't you want me in the picture?" Eden asked. "Just as a sample lover, you know."

"No samples needed," she laughed. The camera clicked. As it did so the two young people stood rooted to the desert in amazement. An old man had stepped suddenly from the interior of the car—a bent told man with a coal-black beard.

Eden's eyes sought those of the girl. "Last Wednesday night at Madden's?" he inquired in a low voice.

She nodded. "The old prospector," she replied.

The black-bearded one did not speak, but stood with a startled air on the front platform of that lost trolley under the caption "Market Street."

14

What Mr. Cherry Saw

Bob Eden stepped forward. "Good evening," he said. "I hope we haven't disturbed you."

Moving with some difficulty, the old man descended from the platform to the sandy floor of the desert. "How do," he said gravely, shaking hands. He also shook hands with Paula Wendell. "How do, miss. No, you didn't disturb me none. But takin' my forty winks—I ain't so spry as I used to be."

"We happened to be passing—" Eden began.

"Ain't many pass this way," returned the old man. "Cherry's my name—William I. Cherry. Make yourselves to home. Parlor chairs is kind o' scarce, miss."

"Of course," said the girl.

"We'll stop a minute, if we may," suggested Eden.

"It's comin' on supper time," the old man replied hospitably. "How about grub? There's a can o' beans, an' a mite o' bacon—"

"Couldn't think of it," Eden told him. "You're mighty kind, but we'll be back in Seven Palms shortly." Paula Wendell sat down on the car steps, and Eden took a seat on the warm sand. The old man went to the rear of the trolley and returned with an empty soap-box. After an unsuccessful attempt to persuade Eden to accept it as a chair, he put it to that use himself.

"Pretty nice home you've picked out for yourself," Eden remarked.

"Home?" The old man surveyed the trolley-car critically. "Home, boy? I ain't had no home these thirty years. Temporary quarters, you might say."

"Been here long?" asked Eden.

"Three, four days. Rheumatism's been actin' up. But I'm movin' on to-morrey."

"Moving on? Where?"

"Why—over yonder."

"Just where is that?" Eden smiled.

"Where it's allus been. Over yonder. Somewhere else."

"Just looking, eh?"

"Jest lookin'. You've hit it. Goin' on over yonder an' jest lookin'." His tired old eyes were on the mountaintops.

"What do you expect to find?" inquired Paula Wendell.

"Struck a vein o' copper once, miss," Mr. Cherry said. "But they got her away from me. Howsomever, I'm lookin' still."

"Been on the desert a long time?" Eden asked.

"Twenty, twenty-five years. One desert or another."

"And before that?"

"Prospected in West Australia from Hannans to Hall's Creek—through the Territory into Queensland. Drove cattle from the gulf country into New South Wales. Then I worked in the stoke hole on ocean liners."

"Born in Australia, eh?" Eden suggested.

"Who—me?" Mr. Cherry shook his head. "Born in South Africa—English descent. Been all up and down the Congo an' Zambesi—all through British Central Africa."

"How in the world did you get to Australia?" Eden wondered.

"Oh, I don't know, boy. I was filibusterin' down along the South American continent fer a while, an' then I drifted into a Mexican campaign. Seems like there was somethin' I wanted in Australia—anyhow, I got there. Jest the way I got here. It was over yonder, an' I went."

Eden shook his head. "Ye gods, I'll bet you've seen a lot!"

"I guess I have, boy. Doctor over in Redlands was tellin' me t'other day—you need spectacles, he says. 'Hell, Doc,' I says, 'what fer? I've seen everything,' I says, and I come away.

Silence fell. Bob Eden wasn't exactly sure how to go about this business; he wished he had Chan at his elbow. But his duty was clear.

"You—er—you've been here for three or four days, you say?"

" 'Bout that, I reckon."

"Do you happen to recall where you were last Wednesday night?"

The old man's eyes were keen enough as he glanced sharply at the boy. "What if I do?"

"I was only going to say that if you don't, I can refresh your memory. You were at Madden's ranch house, over near Eldorado."

Slowly Mr. Cherry removed his slouch hat. With gnarled bent fingers he extracted a toothpick from the band. He stuck it defiantly in his mouth. "Maybe I was. What then?"

"Well—I'd like to have a little talk with you about that night."

Cherry surveyed him closely. "You're a new one on me," he said. "An' I thought I knew every sheriff an' deputy west o' the Rockies."

"Then you'll admit something happened at Madden's that might interest a sheriff?" returned Eden quickly.

"I ain't admittin' nothin'," answered the old prospector.

"You have information regarding last Wednesday night at Madden's," Eden persisted. "Vital information. I must have it."

"Nothin' to say," replied Cherry stubbornly.

Eden took another tack. "Just what was your business at Madden's ranch?"

Mr. Cherry rolled the aged toothpick in his mouth. "No business at all. I jest dropped in. Been wanderin' the desert a long time, like I said, an' now an' ag'in I drifted in at Madden's. Me an' the old caretaker, Louie Wong, was friends. When I'd come along he'd stake me to a bit o' grub, an' a bed in the barn. Sort o' company fer him, I was. He was lonesome-like at the ranch—only a Chink, but lonesome-like, same as if he'd been white."

"A kindly old soul, Louie," suggested Eden.

"One o' the best, boy, an' that's no lie."

Eden spoke slowly. "Louie Wong has been murdered," he said.

"What's that?"

"Stabbed in the side last Sunday night near the ranch gate. Stabbed—by some unknown person."

"Some dirty dog," said Mr. Cherry indignantly.

"That's just how I feel about it. I'm not a policeman, but I'm doing my best to find the guilty man. The thing you saw that night at the ranch, Mr. Cherry, no doubt has a decided bearing on the killing of Louie. I need your help. Now, will you talk?"

"Mr. Cherry removed the toothpick from his mouth and, holding it before him, regarded it thoughtfully. "Yes," he said, "I will. I was hopin' to keep out o' this. Judges an' courts an' all that truck ain't fer me. I give 'em a wide berth. But I'm a decent man, an' I ain't got nothin' to hide. I'll talk, but I don't hardly know how to begin."

"I'll help you," Eden answered, delighted. "The other night when you were at Madden's ranch perhaps you heard a man cry, 'Help! Help! Murder! Put down that gun. Help.' Something like that, eh?"

"I ain't got nothin' to hide. That's jest what I heard."

Eden's heart leaped. "And after that—you saw something—"

The old man nodded. "I saw plenty, boy. Louie Wong wasn't the first to be killed at Madden's ranch. I saw murder done."

Eden gasped inwardly. He saw Paula Wendell's eyes wide and startled. "Of course you did," he said. "Now go on and tell me all about it."

Mr. Cherry restored the toothpick to its predestined place in his mouth, but it interfered in no way with his speech.

"Life's funny," he began. "Full o' queer twists an' turns. I thought this was jest one more secret fer me an' the desert together. Nobody knows about you, I says. Nobody ain't goin' to question you. But I was wrong, I see, an' I might as well speak up. It's nothin' to me, one way or t'other, though I would like to keep out o' courtrooms—"

"Well, maybe I can help you," Eden suggested. "Go on. You say you saw murder—"

"Jest hold yer horses, boy," Mr. Cherry advised. "As I was sayin', last Wednesday night after dark I drifts in at Madden's as usual. But the minute I comes into the yard, I see there's something doin' there. The boss has come. Lights in most o' the windows, an' a big car in the barn, longside Louie's old flivver. Howsomever, I'm tired, an' I figures I'll jest wait round fer Louie, keepin' out o' sight o' the big fellow. A little supper an' a bed, maybe, kin be negotiated without gettin' too conspicuous.

"So I puts my pack down in the barn, an' steps over to the cookhouse. Louie ain't there. Jest as I'm comin' out o' the place, I hears a cry from the house—a man's voice, loud an' clear. 'Help,' he says. 'Put down that gun. I know your game. Help. Help.' Jest as you said. Well, I ain't lookin' fer no trouble, an' I stands there a minute, uncertain. An' then the cry comes again, almost the same words—but not the man this time. It's Tony, the Chinese parrot, on his perch in the patio, an' from him the words is shrill an' piercin'—more terrible, somehow. An' then I hears a sharp report—the gun is workin'. The racket seems to come from a lighted room in one ell—a window is open. I creeps closer, an' there goes the gun ag'in. There's a sort of groan. It's hit, sure enough. I goes up to the window an' looks in."

He paused. "Then what?" Bob Eden asked breathlessly.

"Well, it's a bedroom, an' he's standin' there with the smokin' gun in his hand, lookin' fierce but frightened-like. An' there's somebody on the floor, t'other side o' the bed—all I kin see is his shoes. He turns toward the window, the gun still in his hand—"

"Who?" cried Bob Eden. "Who was it with the gun in his hand? You're talking about Martin Thorn?"

"Thorn? You mean that little sneakin' secretary? No—I ain't speakin' o' Thorn. I'm speakin' o' him—"

"Who?"

"The big boss. Madden. P. J. Madden himself."

There was a moment of tense silence. "Good lord," gasped Eden. "Madden? You mean to say that Madden— Why, it's impossible. How did you know? Are you sure?"

"O' course I'm sure. I know Madden well enough. I seen him three years ago at the ranch. A big man, red-faced, thin gray hair—I couldn't make no mistake about Madden. There he was standin', the gun in his hand, an' he looked toward the window. I ducks back. An' at that minute this Thorn you're speakin' of—he comes tearin' into the room. 'What have you done now?' he says. 'I've killed him,' says Madden, 'that's what I've done.' 'You poor fool,' says Thorn. 'It wasn't necessary.' Madden throws down the gun. 'Why not?' he wants to know. 'I was afraid of him.' Thorn sneers. 'You was always afraid o' him,' he says. 'You dirty coward. That time in New York—' Madden gives him a look. 'Shut up,' he says. 'Shut up an' fergit it. I was afraid o' him an' I killed him. Now git busy an' think what we better do.' "

The old prospector paused, and regarded his wide-eyed audience. "Well, mister," he continued. "An' miss—I come away. What else was there to be done? It was no affair o' mine, an' I wasn't hungerin' fer no court-room an' all that. Jest slip away into the night, I tells myself, the good old night that's been yer friend these many years. Slip away an' let others worry. I runs to the barn an' gits my pack, an' when I comes out, a car is drivin' into the yard. I crawls through the fence an' moseys down the road. I thought I was out o' it an' safe, an' how you got on to me is a mystery. But I'm decent, an' I ain't hidin' anything. That's my story—the truth, s'help me."

Bob Eden rose and paced the sand. "Man alive," he said, "this is serious business."

"Think so?" inquired the old prospector.

"Think so! You know who Madden is, don't you? One of the biggest men in America—"

"Sure he is. An' what does that mean? You'll never git him fer what he done. He'll slide out o' it some way. Self-defense—"

"Oh, no, he won't. Not if you tell your story. You've got to go back with me to Eldorado—"

"Wait a minute," cut in Cherry. "That's something I don't aim to do—go an' stifle in no city. Leastways, not till it's absolutely necessary. I've told my story, an' I'll tell it ag'in, any time I'm asked. But I ain't goin' back to Eldorado—bank on that, boy."

"But listen—"

"Listen to me. How much more information you got? Know who that man was, layin' behind the bed? Found his body yet?"

"No, we haven't, but—"

"I thought so. Well, you're jest startin' on this job. What's my word ag'in' the word o' P. J. Madden—an' no other evidence to show? You got to dig some up."

"Well, perhaps you're right."

"Sure I am. I've gone you a favor—now you do one fer me. Take this here information an' go back an' make the most o' it. Leave me out entirely if you kin. If you can't—well, I'll keep in touch. Be down round Needles in about a week—goin' to make a stop there with my old friend, Slim Jones. Porter J. Jones, Real Estate—you kin git me there. I'm makin' you a fair proposition—don't you say so, miss?"

The girl smiled at him. "Seems fair to me," she admitted.

"It's hardly according to Hoyle," said Eden. "But you have been mighty kind. I don't want to see you stifle in a city—though I find it hard to believe you and I are talking about the same Eldorado. However, we're going to part friends, Mr. Cherry. I'll take your suggestion—I'll go back with what you've told me—it's certainly very enlightening. And I'll keep you out of it—if I can."

The old man got painfully to his feet. "Shake," he said. "You're a white man, an' no mistake. I ain't tryin' to save Madden—I'll go on the stand if I have to. But with what I've told you, maybe you can land him without me figurin' in it."

"We'll have to go along," Eden told him. He laughed. "I don't care what the book of etiquette says—Mr. Cherry, I'm very pleased to have met you."

"Same here," returned Cherry. "Like a talk now an' then with a good listener. An' the chance to look at a pretty gal—well, say, I don't need no specs to enjoy that."

They said good-by, and left the lonely old man standing by the trolley-car there on the barren desert. For a long moment they rode in silence.

"Well," said Eden finally, "you've heard something, lady."

"I certainly have. Something I find it difficult to believe."

"Perhaps you won't find it so difficult if I go back and tell you a few things. You've been drawn into the big mystery at Madden's at last, and there's no reason why you shouldn't know as much as I do about it. So I'm going to talk."

"I'm keen to hear," she admitted.

"Naturally, after to-day. Well, I came down here to transact a bit of business with P. J.—I needn't go into that, it has no particular bearing. The first night I was on the ranch—" He proceeded to detail one by one the mysterious sequence of events that began with the scream of the parrot from the dark. "Now you know. Some one had been killed, that was evident. Some one before Louie. But who? We don't know yet. And by whom? To-day gave us that answer, anyhow."

"It seems incredible."

"You don't believe Cherry's story?" he suggested.

"Well—these old boys who wander the desert get queer sometimes. And there was that about his eyes—the doctor at Redlands, you know—"

"I know. But all the same, I think Cherry told the truth. After a few days with Madden, I consider him capable of anything. He's a hard man, and if any one stood in his way—good night. Some poor devil stood there—but not for long. Who? We'll find out. We must."

"We?"

"Yes—you're in on this thing, too. Have to be, after this, whether you like it or not."

"I think I'm going to like it," Paula Wendell said.

They returned their tired horses to the stable at Seven Palms, and after a sketchy dinner at the local hotel, caught the Eldorado train. When they alighted, Charlie and Will Holley were waiting.

"Hello," said the editor. "Why, hello, Paula—where you been? Eden, here's Ah Kim. Madden sent him in for you."

"Hello, gentlemen," cried Eden gaily. "Before Ah Kim and I head for the ranch, we're all going over to the office of that grand old sheet, the *Eldorado Times*. I have something to impart."

When they reached the newspaper office—which Ah Kim entered with obvious reluctance—Eden closed the door and faced them. "Well, folks," he announced, "the clouds are breaking. I've finally got hold of something definite. But before I go any further—Miss Wendell, may I present Ah

Kim? So we sometimes call him, after our quaint fashion. In reality, you are now enjoying the priceless opportunity of meeting Detective-Sergeant Charlie Chan, of the Honolulu police."

Chan bowed. "I'm so glad to know you, Sergeant," said the girl, and took up her favorite perch on Holley's typewriter table.

"Don't look at me like that, Charlie," laughed Eden. "You're breaking my heart. We can rely on Miss Wendell, absolutely. And you can't freeze her out any longer because she now knows more about your case than you do. As they say on the stage—won't you—sit down?"

Puzzled and wondering, Chan and Will Holley found chairs. "I said this morning I wanted a little light," Eden continued. "I've got it already—how's that for service? Aimless trip to Barstow, Charlie, proved to be all aim. Miss Wendell and I turned aside for a canter over the desert, and we have met and interviewed that little black-bearded one—our desert rat."

"Boy—now you're talking," cried Holley.

Chan's eyes lighted.

"Chinese are psychic people, Charlie," Eden went on. "I'll tell the world. You were right. Before we arrived at Madden's ranch, some one staged a little murder there. And I know who did it."

"Thorn," suggested Holley.

"Thorn nothing! No piker like Thorn. No, gentlemen, it was the big chief—Madden himself—the great P. J. Last Wednesday night at his ranch Madden killed a man. Add favorite pastimes of big millionaires."

"Nonsense," objected Holley.

"You think so, eh? Listen." Eden repeated the story Cherry had told.

Chan and Holley heard him out in amazed silence.

"And what are present whereabouts of old prospector?" inquired Chan when he had finished.

"I know, Charlie," answered Eden. "That's the flaw in my armor. I let him go. He's on his way—over yonder. But I know where he's going and we can get hold of him when we need him. We've got other matters to look after first."

"We certainly have," agreed Holley. "Madden! I can hardly believe it."

Chan considered. "Most peculiar case ever shoved on my attention," he admitted. "It marches now, but look how it marches backwards. Mostly murder means dead body on the rug, and from clues surrounding. I must find who did it. Not so here. I sense something wrong, after long pause light breaks and I hear name of guilty man who killed. But who was killed? The reason, please? There is work to be done—much work."

"You don't think," suggested Eden, "that we ought to call in the sheriff—"

"What then?" frowned Chan. "Captain Bliss arrives on extensive feet, committing blunder with every step. Sheriff faces strange situation, all unprepared. Madden awes them with greatness, and escapes Scotch-free. None of the sheriff, please—unless maybe you lose faith in Detective-Sergeant Chan."

"Never for a minute, Charlie," Eden answered. "Wipe out that suggestion. The case is yours."

Chan bowed. "You're pretty good, thanks. Such a tipsy-turvy puzzle rouses professional pride. I will get to bottom of it or lose entire face. Be good enough to watch me."

"I'll be watching," Eden answered. "Well, shall we go along?"

In front of the Desert Edge Hotel Bob Eden held out his hand to the girl. "The end of a perfect day," he said. "Except for one thing."

"Yes? What thing?"

"Wilbur. I'm beginning to find the thought of him intolerable."

"Poor Jack. You're so hard on him. Good night—and—"

"And what?"

"Be careful, won't you? Out at the ranch, I mean."

"Always careful—on ranches—everywhere. Good night."

As they sped over the dark road to Madden's, Chan was thoughtfully silent. He and Eden parted in the yard. When the boy entered the patio, he saw Madden sitting alone, wrapped in an overcoat, before a dying fire.

The millionaire leaped to his feet. "Hello," he said. "Well?"

"Well?" replied Eden. He had completely forgotten his mission to Barstow.

"You saw Draycott?" Madden whispered.

"Oh!" The boy remembered with a start. More deception—would it ever end? "To-morrow at the door of the bank in Pasadena," he said softly. "Noon sharp."

"Good," answered Madden. "I'll be off before you're up. Not turning in already?"

"I think I will," responded Eden. "I've had a busy day."

"Is that so?" said Madden carelessly, and strode into the living-room. Bob Eden stood staring after the big broad shoulders, the huge frame of this powerful man. A man who seemed to have the world in his grasp, but who had killed because he was afraid.

14

The Third Man

As soon as he was fully awake the following morning, Bob Eden's active brain returned to the problem with which it had been concerned when he dropped off to sleep. Madden had killed a man. Cool, confident and self-possessed though he always seemed, the millionaire had lost his head for once. Ignoring the possible effect of such an act on his fame, his high position, he had with murderous intent pulled the trigger on the gun Bill Hard had given him. His plight must have been desperate indeed.

Whom had he killed? That was something yet to be discovered. Why had he done it? By his own confession, because he was afraid. Madden, whose very name struck terror to many and into whose presence lesser men came with awe and trembling, had himself known the emotion of fear. Ridiculous, but "you were always afraid of him," Thorn had said.

Some hidden door in the millionaire's past must be found and opened. First of all, the identity of the man who had gone west last Wednesday night on this lonely ranch must be ascertained. Well, at least the mystery was beginning to clear, the long sequence of inexplicable, maddening events since they came to the desert was broken for a moment by a tangible bit of explanation. Here was a start, something into which they could get their teeth. From this they must push on to—what?

Chan was waiting in the patio when Bob Eden came out. His face was decorated with a broad grin.

"Breakfast reposes on table," he announced. "Consume it speedily. Before us stretches splendid day for investigation with no prying eyes."

"What's that?" asked Eden. "Nobody here? How about Gamble?"

Chan led the way to the living-room, and held Bob Eden's chair. "Oh, cut that, Charlie," the boy said. "You're not Ah Kim to-day. Do you mean to say that Gamble has also left us?"

Chan nodded. "Gamble develops keen yearning to visit Pasadena," he replied. "On which journey he is welcome as one of his long-tailed rats."

Eden quaffed his orange juice. "Madden didn't want him, eh?"

"Not much," Chan answered. "I rise before day breaks and prepare breakfast, which are last night's orders. Madden and Thorn arrive, brushing persistent sleep out of eyes. Suddenly enters this Professor Gamble, plentifully awake and singing happy praise for desert sunrise. 'You are up early,' says Madden, growling like dissatisfied dog. 'Decided to take little journey to Pasadena along with you,' announces Gamble. Madden purples like distant hills when evening comes, but regards me and quenches his reply. When he and Thorn enter big car, behold Mr. Gamble climbing into rear seat. If looks could assassinate Madden would then and there have rendered him extinct, but such are not the case. Car rolls off on to sunny road with Professor Gamble smiling pleasantly in back. Welcome as long-tailed rat but not going to worry about it, thank you."

Eden chuckled. "Well, it's a good thing from our standpoint, Charlie. I was wondering what we were going to do with Gamble nosing round. Big load off our shoulders right away."

"Very true," agreed Chan. "Alone here, we relax all over place and find what is to find. How you like oatmeal, boy? Not so lumpy, if I may be permitted the immodesty."

"Charlie, the world lost a great chef when you became a policeman. But—the devil! Who's that driving in?"

Chan went to the door. "No alarm necessary," he remarked. "Only Mr. Holley."

The editor appeared. "Here I am, up with the lark and ready for action," he announced. "Want to be in on the big hunt, if you don't mind."

"Certainly don't," said Eden. "Glad to have you. We've had a bit of luck already." He explained about Gamble's departure.

Holley nodded wisely. "Of course Gamble went to Pasadena," he remarked. "He's not going to let Madden out of his sight. You know, I've had some flashes of inspiration about this matter out here."

"Good for you," replied Eden. "For instance—"

"Oh, just wait a while. I'll dazzle you with them at the proper moment. You see, I used to do a lot of police reporting. Little bright eyes, I was often called."

"Pretty name," laughed Eden.

"Little bright eyes is here to look about," Holley continued. "First of all, we ought to decide what we're looking for."

"I guess we know that, don't we?" Eden asked.

"Oh, in a general way, but let's be explicit. To go back and start at the beginning—that's the proper method, isn't it, Chan?"

Charlie shrugged. "Always done—in books," he said. "In real life, not so much so."

Holley smiled. "That's right—dampen my young enthusiasm. However, I am now going to recall a few facts. We needn't stress the side issues at present—the pearls, the activities of Shaky Phil in San Francisco, the murder of Louie, the disappearance of Madden's daughter—all these will be explained when we get the big answer. We are concerned to-day chiefly with the story of the old prospector."

"Who may have been lying, or mistaken," Eden suggested.

"Yes—his tale seems unbelievable, I admit. Without any evidence to back it up, I wouldn't pay much attention to it. However, we have that evidence. Don't forget Tony's impassioned remarks, and his subsequent taking off. More important still, there is Bill Hart's gun, with two empty chambers. Also the bullet hole in the wall. What more do you want?"

"Oh, it seems to be well substantiated," Eden agreed.

"It is. No doubt about it—somebody was shot at this place Wednesday night. We thought at first Thorn was the killer, now we switch to Madden. Madden lured somebody to Thorn's room, or cornered him there, and killed him. Why? Because he was afraid of him? We think hard about Wednesday night—and what do we want to know? We want to know—who was the third man?"

"The third man?" Eden repeated.

"Precisely. Ignore the prospector—who was at the ranch? Madden and Thorn—yes. And one other. A man who, seeing his life in danger, called loudly for help. A man who, a moment later, lay on the floor beyond the bed, and whose shoes alone were visible from where the prospector stood. Who was he? Where did he come from? When did he arrive? What was his business? Why was Madden afraid of him? These are the questions to which we must now seek answers. Am I right, Sergeant Chan?"

"Undubitably," Charlie replied. "And how shall we find those answers? By searching, perhaps. Humbly suggest we search."

"Every nook and corner of this ranch," agreed Holley. "We'll begin with Madden's desk. Some stray bit of correspondence may throw unexpected light. It's locked, of course. But I've brought along a pocketful of old keys—got them from a locksmith in town."

"You act like number one detective," Chan remarked.

"Thanks," answered Holley. He went over to the big flat-topped desk belonging to the millionaire and began to experiment with various keys. In a few moments he found the proper one and all the drawers stood open.

"Splendid work," said Chan.

"Not much here, though," Holley declared. He removed the papers from the top left-hand drawer and laid them on the blotting pad. Bob Eden lighted a cigarette and strolled away. Somehow this idea of inspecting Madden's mail did not appeal to him.

The representatives of the police and the press, however, were not so delicately minded. For more than half an hour Chan and the editor studied the contents of Madden's desk. They found nothing, save harmless and understandable data of business deals, not a solitary scrap that could by the widest stretch of the imagination throw any light on the identity or meaning of the third man. Finally, perspiring and baffled, they gave up and the drawers were relocked.

"Well," said Holley, "not so good, eh? Mark the desk off our list and let's move on."

"With your permission," Chan remarked, "we divide the labors. For you gentlemen the inside of the house. I myself have fondly feeling for outdoors." He disappeared.

One by one, Holley and Eden searched the rooms. In the bedroom occupied by the secretary they saw for themselves the bullet hole in the wall. An investigation of the bureau, however, revealed the fact that Bill Hart's pistol was no longer there. This was their sole discovery of any interest.

"We're up against it," admitted Holley, his cheerful manner waning.

"Madden's a clever man, and he didn't leave a warm trail, of course. But somehow—somewhere—"

They returned to the living-room. Chan, hot and puffing, appeared suddenly at the door. He dropped into a chair.

"What luck, Charlie?" Eden inquired.

"None whatever," admitted Chan gloomily. "Heavy disappointment causes my heart to sag. No gambler myself, but would have offered huge wager something buried on this ranch. When Madden, having shot, remarked, 'Shut up and forget. I was afraid and I killed. Now think quick what we had better do,' I would expect first thought is—burial. How else to dispose of dead? So just now I have examined every inch of ground, with highest hope. No good. If burial made, it was not here. I see by your faces you have similar bafflement to report."

"Haven't found a thing," Eden replied.

Chan sighed. "I drag the announcement forth in pain," he said. "But I now gaze solemnly at stone wall."

They sat in helpless silence. "Well, let's not give up yet," Bob Eden remarked. He leaned back in his chair and blew a ring of smoke toward the paneled ceiling. "By the way, has it ever occurred to you that there must be some sort of attic above this room?"

Chan was instantly on his feet. "Clever suggestion," he cried. "Attic, yes, but how to ascend?" He stood staring at the ceiling a moment, then went quickly to a large closet in the rear of the room. "Somewhat humiliated situation for me," he announced. Crowding close beside him in the dim closet, the other two looked aloft at an unmistakable trap-door.

Bob Eden was selected for the climb, and with the aid of a stepladder Chan brought from the barn, he managed it easily. Holley and the detective waited below. For a moment Eden stood in the attic, his head bent low, cob-webs caressing his face, while he sought to accustom his eyes to the faint light.

"Nothing here, I'm afraid," he called. "Oh, yes, there is. Wait a minute."

They heard him walking gingerly above, and clouds of dust descended on their heads. Presently he was lowering a bulky object through the narrow trap—a battered old Gladstone bag.

"Seems to be something in it," Eden announced.

They took it with eager hands, and set it on the desk in the sunny living-room. Bob Eden joined them.

"By gad," the boy said, "not much dust on it, is there? Must have been put there recently. Holley, here's where your keys come in handy."

It proved a simple matter for Holley to master the lock. The three men crowded close.

Chan lifted out a cheap toilet case, with the usual articles—a comb and brush, razors, shaving cream, tooth paste, then a few shirts, socks and handkerchiefs. He examined the laundry mark.

"D—thirty-four," he announced.

"Meaning nothing," Eden said.

Chan was lifting a brown suit of clothes from the bottom of the bag.

"Made to order by tailor in New York," he said, after an inspection of the inner coat pocket. "Name of purchaser, however, is blotted out by too much wearing." He took from the side pockets a box of matches and a half-empty packet of inexpensive cigarettes. "Finishing the coat," he added.

He turned his attention to the vest and luck smiled upon him. From the lower right-hand pocket he removed an old-fashioned watch, attached to a heavy chain. The timepiece was silent; evidently it had been unwound for some time. Quickly he pried open the back case, and a little grunt of satisfaction escaped him. He passed the watch to Bob Eden.

"Presented to Jerry Delancy by his Old Friend, Honest Jack McGuire," read Eden in a voice of triumph. "And the date—August twenty-sixth, 1913."

"Jerry Delaney!" cried Holley. "By Heaven, we're getting on now. The name of the third man was Jerry Delaney."

"Yet to be proved he was the third man," Chan cautioned. "This, however, may help."

He produced a soiled bit of colored paper—a passenger's receipt for a Pullman compartment. "Compartment B—car 198," he read. "Chicago to Barstow." He turned it over. "Date when used, February eighth, present year."

Bob Eden turned to a calendar. "Great stuff," he cried. "Jerry Delaney left Chicago on February eighth—a week ago Sunday night. That got him into Barstow last Wednesday morning, February eleventh—the morning of the day he was killed. Some detectives, we are."

Chan was still busy with the vest. He brought forth a key ring with a few keys, then a worn newspaper clipping. The letter he handed to Eden. "Read it, please?" he suggested.

Bob Eden read:

> "Theater-goers of Los Angeles will be delighted to know that in the cast of *One Night in June,* the musical comedy opening at the Mason next Monday night, will be Miss Norma Fitzgerald. She has the rôle of Marcia, which calls for a rich soprano voice, and her vast army of admirers hereabouts know in advance how well she will acquit herself in such a part. Miss Fitzgerald has been on the stage twenty years—she went on as a mere child—and has appeared in such productions as *The Love Cure.*"

Eden paused. "There's a long list." He resumed reading:

> "Matinées of *One Night in June* will be on Wednesdays and Saturdays, and for this engagement a special scale of prices has been inaugurated."

Eden put the clipping down on the table. "Well, that's one more fact about Jerry Delaney. He was interested in a soprano. So many men are—but still, it may lead somewhere."

"Poor Jerry," said Holley, looking down at the rather pitiful pile of the man's possessions. "He won't need a hair-brush, or a razor, or a gold watch where he's gone." He took up the watch and regarded it thoughtfully. Honest Jack McGuire. I seem to have heard that name somewhere."

Chan was investigating the trousers pockets. He turned them out one by one, but found nothing.

"Search is now complete," he announced. "Humbly suggest we put all back as we found it. We have made delightful progress."

"I'll say we have," cried Eden, with enthusiasm. "More progress than I ever thought possible. Last night we knew only that Madden had killed a man. To-day we know the name of the man." He paused. "I don't suppose there can be any doubt about it?" he inquired.

"Hardly," Holley replied. "A man doesn't part with such personal possessions as a hair-brush and a razor as long as he has any further use for them. If he's through with them, he's through with life. Poor devil!"

"Let's go over it all again before we put these things away," said Eden. "We've learned that the man Madden feared, the man he killed, was Jerry Delaney. What do we know of Delaney? He was not in very affluent circumstances, though he did have his clothes made by a tailor. Not a smart tailor, judging by the address. He smoked Corsican cigarettes. Honest Jack McGuire, whoever he may be, was an old friend of his, and thought so highly of him he gave Jerry a watch. What else? Delaney was interested in an actress named Norma Fitzgerald. A week ago last Sunday he left Chicago at eight P.M.—the Limited—for Barstow, riding in Compartment B, car 198. And that, I guess, about sums up what we know of Jerry Delaney."

Charlie Chan smiled. "Very good," he said. "A splendid list, rich with promise. But one fact you have missed complete."

"What's that?" inquired Eden.

"One very easy fact," continued Chan. "Take this vest once on Jerry Delaney. Examine close—what do you discover?"

Carefully Eden looked over the vest, then with a puzzled air handed it to Holley, who did the same. Holley shook his head.

"Nothing?" asked Chan, laughing silently. "Can it be you are not such able detectives as I thought? Here—place hand in pocket—"

Bob Eden thrust his finger sinto the pocket indicated by Chan. "It's chamois-lined," he said. "The watch pocket, that's all."

"True enough," answered Chan. "And on the left, I presume."

Eden looked foolish. "Oh," he admitted, "I get you. The watch pocket is on the right."

"And why," persisted Charlie. "With coat buttoned, certain man can not reach watch easily when it reposes at left. Therefore he instructs tailor, make pocket for watch on right, please." He began to fold up the clothes in order to return them to the bag. "One other fact we know about Jerry Delaney, and it may be used in tracing his movements the day he came to this ranch. Jerry Delaney had peculiarity to be left-handed."

"Great Scott!" cried Holley suddenly. They turned to him. He had picked up the watch again and was staring at it. "Honest Jack McGuire—I remember now."

"You know this McGuire?" inquired Chan quickly.

"I met him, long ago," Holley replied. "The first night I brought Mr. Eden out here to the ranch, he asked me if I'd ever seen P. J. Madden before. I said that twelve years ago I saw Madden in a gambling house on East Forty-fourth Street, New York, dolled up like a prince and betting his head off. Madden himself remembered the occasion when I spoke to him about it."

"But McGuire?" Chan wanted to know.

"I recall now that the name of the man who ran that gambling house was Jack McGuire. Honest Jack, he had the nerve to call himself. It was a queer joint—that was later proved. But Jack McGuire was Delaney's old friend—he gave Jerry a watch as a token of their friendship. Gentlemen, this is interesting. McGuire's gambling house on Forty-fourth Street comes back into the life of P. J. Madden."

15
Will Holley's Theory

When the bag was completely repacked and again securely locked, Bob Eden climbed with it to the dusty attic. He reappeared, the trap-door was closed and the stepladder removed. The three men faced one another, pleased with their morning's work.

"It's after twelve," said Holley. "I must hurry back to town."

"About to make heartfelt suggestion you remain at lunch," remarked Chan.

Holley shook his head. "That's kind of you, Charlie, but I wouldn't think of it. You must be about fed-up on this cooking proposition, and I won't spoil your first chance for a little vacation. You take my advice, and make Eden rustle his own grub to-day."

Chan nodded. "True enough that I was planning a modest repast," he returned. "Cooking business begins to get tiresome like the company of a Japanese. However, fitting punishment for a postman who walks another man's beat. If Mr. Eden will pardon, I relax to the extent of sandwiches and tea this noon."

"Sure," said Eden. "We'll dig up something together. Holley, you'd better change your mind."

"No," replied Holley. "I'm going to town and make a few inquiries. Just by way of substantiating what we found here to-day. If Jerry Delaney came out here last Wednesday, he must have left some sort of trail through the town. Some one may have seen him. Was he alone? I'll speak to the boys at the gas station, the hotel proprietor—"

"Humbly suggest utmost discretion," said Chan.

"Oh, I understand the need of that. But there's really no danger. Madden has no connection whatever with the life of the town. He won't hear of it. Just the same, I'll be discretion itself. Trust me. I'll come out here again later in the day."

When he had gone, Chan and Eden ate a cold lunch in the cookhouse, and resumed their search. Nothing of any moment rewarded their efforts, however. At four that afternoon Holley drove into the yard. With him was a lean, sad-looking youth whom Eden recognized as the real-estate salesman of Date City.

As they entered the room, Chan withdrew, leaving Eden to greet them. Holley introduced the youth as Mr. DeLisle.

"I've met DeLisle," smiled Bob Eden. "He tried to sell me a corner lot on the desert."

"Yeah," said Mr. DeLisle. "And some day, when the United Cigar Stores and Woolworth are fighting for that stuff, you'll kick yourself up and down every hill in Frisco. However, that's your funeral."

"I brought Mr. DeLisle along," explained Holley, "because I want you to hear the story he's just told me. About Last Wednesday night."

"Mr. DeLisle understands that this is confidential—" began Eden.

"Oh, sure," said the young man. "Will's explained all that. You needn't worry. Madden and I ain't exactly pals—not after the way he talked to me."

"You saw him last Wednesday night?" Eden suggested.

"No, not that night. It was somebody else I saw then. I was out here at the development until after dark, waiting for a prospect—he never showed up, the lowlife. Anyhow, along about seven o'clock, just as I was closing up the office, a big sedan stopped out in front. I went out. There was a little guy driving and another man in the back seat. 'Good evening,' said the little fellow. 'Can you tell me, please, if we're on the road to Madden's ranch?' I said sure, to keep right on straight. The man in the back spoke up. 'How far is it?' he wants to know. 'Shut up, Jerry,' says the little guy. 'I'll attend to this.' He shifted the gears, and then he got kind of literary. 'And an highway shall be there and a way,' he says. 'Not any too clearly defined, Isaiah.' And he drove off. Now why do you suppose he called me Isaiah?"

Eden smiled. "Did you get a good look at him?"

"Pretty good, considering the dark. A thin pale man with sort of grayish lips—no color in them at all. Talked kind of slow and precise—awful neat English, like he was a professor or something."

"And the man in the back seat?"

"Couldn't see him very well."

"Ah, yes. And when did you meet Madden?"

"I'll come to that. After I got home I began to think—Madden was out at the ranch, it seemed. And I got a big idea. Things ain't been going so well here lately—Florida's been nabbing all the easy—all the good prospects—and I said to myself, how about Madden? There's big money. Why not try and interest Madden in Date City? Get him behind it. Worth a shot anyhow. So bright and early Thursday morning, I came out to the ranch."

"About what time?"

"Oh, it must have been a little after eight. I'm full of pep at that hour of the day, and I knew I'd need it. I knocked at the front door, but nobody answered. I tried it—it was locked. I came around to the back and the place was deserted. Not a soul in sight."

"Nobody here," repeated Eden, wonderingly.

"Not a living thing but the chickens and the turkeys. And the Chinese parrot, Tony. He was sitting on his perch. 'Hello, Tony,' I said. 'You're a damn crook,' he answers. Now I ask you, is that any way to greet a hard-working, honest real-estate man? Wait a minute—don't try to be funny."

"I won't," Eden laughed. "But Madden—"

"Well, just then Madden drove into the yard with that secretary of his. I knew the old man right away from his pictures. He looked tired and ugly, and he needed a shave. 'What are you doing here?' he wanted to know. 'Mr. Madden,' I said, 'have you ever stopped to consider the possibilities of this land round here?' And I waltzed right into my selling talk. But I didn't get far. He stopped me, and then he started. Say—the things he called me. I'm not used to that sort of thing—abuse by an expert, and that's what it was. I saw his psychology was all wrong, so I walked out on him. That's the best way—when the old psychology ain't working."

"And that's all?" Eden inquired.

"That's my story, and I'll stick to it," replied Mr. DeLisle.

"I'm very much obliged," Eden said. "Of course, this is all between ourselves. And I may add that if I ever do decide to buy a lot on the desert—"

"You'll consider my stuff, won't you?"

"I certainly will. Just at present, the desert doesn't look very good to me."

Mr. DeLisle leaned close. "Whisper it not in Eldorado," he said. "I sometimes wish I was back in good old Chi myself. If I ever hit the Loop again, I'm going to nail msyelf down there."

"If you'll wait outside a few minutes, DeLisle—" Holley began.

"I get you. I'll just mosey down to the development and see if the fountain's working. You can pick me up there."

The young man went out. Chan came quickly from behind a near-by door.

"Get all that, Charlie?" Eden inquired.

"Yes, indeed. Most interesting."

"We move right on," said Holley. "Jerry Delaney came out to the ranch about seven o'clock Wednesday night, and he didn't come alone. For the first time a fourth man enters the picture. Who? Sounded to me very much like Professor Gamble."

"No doubt about that," replied Eden. "He's an old friend of the prophet Isaiah's—he admitted it here Monday after lunch."

"Fine," commented Holley. "We begin to place Mr. Gamble. Here's another thing—some one drove up to the doctor's Sunday night and carried Shaky Phil away. Couldn't that have been Gamble, too? What do you say, Charlie?"

Chan nodded. "Possible. That person knew of Louie's return. If we could only discover—"

"By George," Eden cried. "Gamble was at the desk of the Oasis when Louie came in. You remember, Holley?"

The editor smiled. "All fits in very neatly. Gamble sped out here like some sinister version of Paul Revere with the news of Louie's arrival. He and Shaky Phil were at the gate when you drove up."

"But Thorn. That tear in Thorn's coat?"

"We must have been on the wrong trail there. This new theory sounds too good. What else have we learned from DeLisle? After the misadventure with Delaney, Madden and Thorn were out all night. Where?"

Chan sighed. "Not such good news, that. Body of Delaney was carried far from this spot."

"I'm afraid it was," admitted Holley. "We'll never find it without help from somebody who knows. There are a hundred lonely cañons round here where poor Delaney could have been tossed aside and nobody any the wiser. We'll have to go ahead and perfect our case without the vital bit of evidence—the body of Delaney. But there are a lot of people in on this, and before we get through, somebody is going to squeal."

Chan was sitting at Madden's desk, idly toying with the big blotting pad that lay on top. Suddenly his eyes lighted, and he began to separate the sheets of blotting paper.

"What is this?" he said.

They looked, and saw in the detective's pudgy hand a large sheet of paper, partly filled with writing. Chan perused the missive carefully, and handed it to Eden. The letter was written in a man's strong hand. "It's dated last Wednesday night," Eden remarked to Holley. He read:

> "Dear Evelyn:
> "I want you to know of certain developments here at the ranch. As I've told you before, Martin Thorn and I have been on very bad terms for the past year. This afternoon the big blow-off finally arrived, and I dismissed him from my service. To-morrow morning I'm going with him to Pasadena, and when we get there, we part for all time. Of course he knows a lot of things I wish he didn't—otherwise I'd have scrapped him a year ago. He may make trouble,

and I am warning you in case he shows up in Denver. I'm
going to take this letter in town myself and mail it to-night,
as I don't want Thorn to know anything about it—"

The letter stopped abruptly at that point.

"Better and better," said Holley. "Another sidelight on what happened
here last Wednesday night. We can picture the scene for ourselves. Madden
is sitting at his desk, writing that letter to his daughter. The door
opens—some one comes in. Say it's Delaney—Delaney, the man P. J.'s
feared for years. Madden hastily slips the letter between the leaves of the
blotter. He gets to his feet, knowing that he's in for it now. A quarrel
ensues, and by the time it's over, they've got into Thorn's room somehow
and Delaney is dead on the floor. Then—the problem of what to do with
the body, not solved until morning. Madden comes back to the ranch tired
and worn, realizing that he can't dismiss Thorn now. He must make his
peace with the secretary. Thorn knows too much. How about it, Charlie?"

"It has plenty logic," Chan admitted.

"I said this morning I had some ideas on this affair out here," the editor
continued, "and everything that has happened to-day has tended to confirm
them. I'm ready to spring my theory now—that is, if you care to listen."

"Shoot," said Eden.

"To me, it's all as clear as a desert sunrise," Holley went on. "Just let me
go over it for you. Reconstruct it, as the French do. To begin with, Madden
is afraid of Delaney. Why? Why is a rich man afraid of anybody? Blackmail,
of course. Delaney has something on him—maybe something that dates
back to that gambling house in New York. Thorn can't be depended
on—they've been rowing and he hates his employer. Perhaps he has even
gone so far as to link up with Delaney and his friends. Madden buys the
pearls, and the gang hears of it and decides to spring. What better place
than way out here on the desert? Shaky Phil goes to San Francisco; Delaney
and the professor come south. Louie, the faithful old retainer, is lured
away by Shaky Phil. The stage is set. Delaney arrives with his threat. He
demands the pearls, money, both. An argument follows, and in the end
Delaney, the blackmailer, is killed by Madden. Am I right so far?"

"Sounds plausible," Eden admitted.

"Well, imagine what followed. When Madden killed Delaney, he probably
thought Jerry had come alone. Now he discovers there are others in the
gang. They have not only the information with which Delaney was threatening him, but they have something else on him too. Murder! The pack
is on him—he must buy them off. They clamor for money—and the pearls.
They force Madden to call up and order the Phillimore necklace sent down
here at once. When did he do that, Eden?"

"Last Thursday morning," Eden replied.

"See—what did I tell you? Last Thursday morning, when he got back
from his grisly midnight trip. They were on him then—they were blackmailing him to the limit. That's the answer to our puzzle. They're blackmailing him now. At first Madden was just as eager as they were for the
necklace—he wanted to settle the thing and get away. It isn't pleasant to
linger round the spot where you've done murder. The past few days his
courage has begun to return, he's temporizing, seeking a way out. I'm a
little sorry for him, I really am." Holley paused. "Well, that's my idea. What
do you think, Charlie? Am I right?"

Chan sat turning Madden's unfinished letter slowly in his hand.

"Sounds good," admitted the detective. "However, here and there objections arise."

"For example?" Holley demanded.

"Madden is big man. Delaney and these others nobody much. He could announce he killed blackmailer in self-defense."

"So he could—if Thorn were friendly and would back him up. But the secretary is hostile and might threaten to tell a different story. Besides, remember it isn't only the killing of Delaney they have against him. There's the information Delaney has been holding over his head."

Chan nodded. "So very true. One other fact, and then I cease my brutal faultfinding. Louie, long in confidence of Chinese parrot, is killed. Yet Louie depart for San Francisco on Wednesday morning, twelve hours before tragic night. Is not his murder then a useless gesturing?"

Holley considered. "Well, that is a point. But he was Madden's friend, which was a pretty good reason for not wanting him here. They preferred their victim alone and helpless. A rather weak explanation, perhaps. Otherwise I'm strong for my theory. You're not so keen on it."

Chan shook his head. "For one reason only. Long experience has taught fatal consequence may follow if I get too addicted to a theory. Then I try and see, can I make everything fit. I can, and first thing I know theory explodes in my countenance with loud bang. Much better I have found to keep mind free and open."

"Then you haven't any idea on all this to set up against mine?" Holley asked.

"No solitary one. Frankly speaking, I am completely in the dark." He glanced at the letter in his hand. "Or nearly so," he added. "We watch and wait, and maybe I clutch something soon."

"That's all right," said Eden, "but I have a feeling we don't watch and wait much longer at Madden's ranch. Remember, I promised that Draycott would meet him today in Pasadena. He'll be back soon, asking how come?"

"Unfortunate incident," shrugged Chan. "Draycott and he have failed to connect. Many times that has happened when two strangers make appointment. It can happen again."

Eden sighed. "I suppose so. But I hope P. J. Madden's feeling good-natured when he comes home from Pasadena to-night. There's a chance that he's toting Bill Hart's gun again, and I don't like the idea of lying behind a bed with nothing showing but my shoes. I haven't had a shine for a week."

16

"The Movies Are in Town"

The sun set behind far peaks of snow; the desert purpled under a sprinkling of stars. In the thermometer that hung on a patio wall the mercury began its quick relentless fall, a sharp wind swept over the desolate waste, and loneliness settled on the world.

"Warm food needed now," remarked Chan. "With your permission I will open numerous cans."

"Anything but the arsenic," Eden told him. He departed for the cook-house.

Holley had long since gone, and Bob Eden sat alone by the window, looking out at a vast silence. Lots of room left in America yet, he reflected.

Did they think that, those throngs of people packed into subways at this hour, seeking tables in noisy restaurants, waiting at jammed corners for the traffic signal, climbing weary and worn at last to the pigeon-holes they called home? Elbow room on the desert; room to expand the chest. But a feeling of disquiet, too, a haunting realization of one man's ridiculous unimportance in the scheme of things.

Chan entered with a tray on which the dishes were piled high. He set down on the table two steaming plates of soup.

"Deign to join me," he suggested. "First course is now served with the kind assistance of the can-opener."

"Aged in the tin, eh, Charlie?" smiled Eden, drawing up. "Well, I'll bet it's good, at that. You're a bit of a magician in the kitchen." They began to eat. "Charlie, I've been thinking," the boy continued. "I know now why I have this sense of unrest on the desert. It's because I feel so blamed small. Look at me, and then look out the window, and tell me where I get off to strut like a somebody through the world."

"Not bad feeling for the white man to experience," Chan assured him. "Chinese has it all time. Chinese knows he is one minute grain of sand on seashore of eternity. With what result? He is calm and quiet and humble. No nerves, like hopping, skipping Caucasian. Life for him not so much ordeal."

"Yes, and he's happier, too," said Eden.

"Sure," replied Chan. He produced a platter of canned salmon. "All time in San Francisco I behold white men hot and excited. Life like a fever, always getting worse. What for? Where does it end? Same place as Chinese life, I think."

When they had finished Eden attempted to help with the dishes, but was politely restrained. He sat down and turned on the radio. The strong voice of a leather-lunged announcer rang out in the quiet room.

"Now, folks, we got a reat treat for you this balmy, typical California evening. Miss Norma Fitzgerald, of the *One Night in June* company now playing at the Mason, is going to sing—er—what are you going to sing, Norma? Norma says wait and find out."

At mention of the girl's name, Bob Eden called to the detective, who entered and stood expectantly. "Hello, folks," came Miss Fitzgerald's greeting. "I certainly am glad to be back in good old L. A."

"Hello, Norma," Eden said, "never mind the songs. Two gentlemen out on the desert would like a word with you. Tell us about Jerry Delaney."

She couldn't have heard him, for she began to sing in a clear, beautiful soprano voice. Chan and the boy listened in silence.

"More of the white man's mysteries," Charlie remarked when she had finished. "So near to her, and yet so far away. Seems to me that we must visit this lady soon."

"Ah yes—but how?" inquired Eden.

"It will be arranged," Chan said, and vanished.

Eden tried a book. An hour later he was interrupted by the peal of the telephone bell, and a cheery voice answered his hello.

"Still pining for the bright lights?"

"I sure am," he replied.

"Well, the movies are in town," said Paula Wendell. "Come on in."

He hurried to his room. Chan had built a fire in the patio, and was sitting before it, the warm light flickering on his chubby impassive face. When Eden returned with his hat, he paused beside the detective.

"Getting some new ideas?" he asked.

"About our puzzle?" Chan shook his head. "No. At this moment I am far from Madden's ranch. I am in Honolulu where nights are soft and sweet, not like chilly desert dark. Must admit my heart is weighed a little with homesick qualms. I picture my humble house on Punch-bowl Hill, where lanterns glow and my ten children are gathered round."

"Ten!" cried Eden. "Great Scott—you *are* a father."

"Very proud one," assented Chan. "You are going from here?"

"I'm running in town for a while. Miss Wendell called up—it seems the picture people have arrived. By the way, I just remembered—to-morrow is the day Madden promised they could come out here. I bet the old man's clean forgot it."

"Most likely. Better not to tell him, he might refuse permission. I have unlimited yearning to see movies in throes of being born. Should I go home and report that experience to my eldest daughter, who is all time sunk in movie magazines, ancestor worship breaks out plenty strong at my house."

Eden laughed. "Well then, let's hope you get the chance. I'll be back early."

A few minutes later he was again in the flivver, under the platinum stars. He thought fleetingly of Louie Wong, buried now in the bleak little grave-yard back of Eldorado, but his mind turned quickly to happier things. With a lively feeling of anticipation he climbed between the twin hills at the gateway, and the yellow lights of the desert town were winking at him.

The moment he crossed the threshold of the Desert Edge Hotel, he knew this was no ordinary night in Eldorado. From the parlor at the left came the strains of giddy, inharmonious music, laughter, and a medley of voices. Paula Wendell met him and led him in.

The stuffy little room, dated by heavy mission furniture and bits of broken plaster hanging crazily from the ceiling, was renewing its youth in pleasant company. Bob Eden met the movies in their hours of ease, child-like, happy people, seemingly without a care in the world. A very pretty girl gave him a hand which recalled his father's jewelry shop, and then restored it to the ukulele she was playing. A tall young man designated as Rannie, whose clothes were perfection and whose collar and shirt shamed the blue of California's sky, desisted briefly from his torture of a saxophone.

"Hello, old-timer," he remarked. "I hope you brought your harp." And instantly ran amuck on the saxophone again.

A middle-aged actor with a bronzed, rather hard face was officiating at the piano. In a far corner a grand dame and an old man with snow-white hair sat apart from the crowd, and Eden dropped down beside them.

"What was the name?" asked the old man, his hand behind his ear. "Ah, yes, I'm glad to meet any friend of Paula's. We're a little clamorous here to-night, Mr. Eden. It's like the early days when I was trouping—how we used to skylark on station platforms! We were happy then—no movies. Eh, my dear?" he added to the woman.

She bent a bit. "Yes—but I never trouped much. Thank heaven I was usually able to steer clear of those terrible towns where Main Street is up-stairs. Mr. Belasco rarely asked me to leave New York." She turned to Eden. "I was in Belasco companies fifteen years," she explained.

"Wonderful experience, no doubt," the boy replied.

"Greatest school in the world," she said. "Mr. Belasco thought very highly of my work. I remember once at a dress rehearsal he told me he could never have put on the piece without me, and he gave me a big red apple. You know that was Mr. Belasco's way of—"

The din had momentarily stopped, and the leading man cried:

"Suffering cats! She's telling him about the apple, and the poor guy only just got here. Go on, Fanny, spring the one about the time you played Portia. What Charlie Frohman said—as soon as he came to, I mean."

"Humph," shrugged Fanny. "If you young people in this profession had a few traditions like us, the pictures wouldn't be such a joke. I thank my stars—"

"Hush, everybody," put in Paula Wendell. "Introducing Miss Diane Day on Hollywood's favorite instrument, the ukulele."

The girl she referred to smiled and, amid a sudden silence, launched into a London music-hall song. Like most of its genre, its import was not such as to recommend it for a church social, but she did it well, with a note of haunting sweetness in her voice. After another of the same sort she switched suddenly into *Way Down upon the Suwanee River* and there were tears in her voice now, a poignant sadness in the room. It was too solemn for Rannie.

"Mr. Eddie Boston at the piano, Mr. Randolph Renault handling the saxophone," he shouted, "will now offer for your approval that touching ballad, *So's Your Old Mandarin*. Let her go, Professor."

"Don't think they're always like this," Paula Wendell said to Eden above the racket. "It's only when they have a hotel to themselves, as they usually have here."

They had it indeed to themselves, save for the lads of the village, who suddenly found pressing business in the lobby, and passed and repassed the parlor door, open-mouthed with wonder.

The approval shown the instrumental duet was scant indeed, due, Mr. Renault suggested, to professional jealousy.

"The next number on our very generous program," he announced. "will follow immediately. "It's called *Let's Talk about My Sweetie Now*. On your mark—Eddie."

"Nothing doing," cried the girl known as Diane. "I haven't had my Charleston lesson to-day, and it's getting late. Eddie—kindly oblige."

Eddie obliged. In another moment every one save the two old people in the corner had leaped into action. The framed, autographed portraits that other film celebrities had bestowed on the proprietor of the Desert Edge rattled on the walls. The windows shook. Suddenly in the doorway appeared a bald man with a gloomy eye.

"Good lord," he shouted. "How do you expect me to get my rest?"

"Hello, Mike," said Rannie. "What is it you want to rest from?"

"You direct a gang like this for a while, and you'll know," replied Mike sourly. "It's ten o'clock. If you'll take my advice for once, you'll turn in. Everybody's to report in costume here in the lobby to-morrow morning at eight-thirty."

This news was greeted with chorus of low moans. "Nine-thirty, you say?" Rannie inquired.

"Eight-thirty. You heard me. And anybody who's late pays a good stiff fine. Now please go to bed and let decent people sleep."

"Decent people?" repeated Rannie softly, as the director vanished. "He's flattering himself again." But the party was over, and the company moved reluctantly up the stairs to the second floor. Mr. Renault returned the saxophone to the desk.

"Say, landlord, there's a sour note in this thing," he complained. "Have it fixed before I come again."

"Sure will, Mr. Renault," promised the proprietor.

"Too early for bed, no matter what Mike says," remarked Eden, piloting Paula Wendell to the street. "Let's take a walk. Eldorado doesn't look much like Union Square, but night air is night air wherever you find it."

"Lucky for me it isn't Union Square," said the girl. "I wouldn't be tagging along, if it was."

"Is that so?"

They strolled down Main Street, white and empty in the moonlight. In a lighted window of the Spot Cash Store hung a brilliant patchwork quilt.

"To be raffled off by the ladies of the Orange Blossom Club for the benefit of the Orphans' Home," Eden read. "Think I'll take a chance on that to-morrow."

"Better not get mixed up with any Orange Blossom Club," suggested Paula Wendell.

"Oh, I can take care of myself. And it's the orphans I'm thinking of, you know."

"That's your kind heart," she answered. They climbed a narrow sandy road. Yellow lamplight in the front window of a bungalow was suddenly blotted out.

"Look at that moon," said Eden. "Like a slice of honeydew melon just off the ice."

"Fond of food, aren't you," remarked the girl. "I'll always think of you wrestling with that steak."

"A man must eat. And if it hadn't been for the steak, we might never have met."

"What if we hadn't?" she asked.

"Pretty lonesome for me down here in that event." They turned about in silence. "You know, I've been thinking," Eden continued. "We're bound to come to the end of things at the ranch presently. And I'll have to go back—"

"Back to your freedom. That will be nice."

"You bet it will. All the same, I don't want you to forget me after I've gone. I want to go on being your—er—your friend. Or what have you?"

"Splendid. One always needs friends."

"Write to me occasionally. I'll want to know how Wilbur is. You never can tell—is he careful crossing the streets?"

"Wilbur will always be fine, I'm sure." They stopped before the hotel. "Good night," said the girl.

"Just a minute. If there hadn't been a Wilbur—"

"But there was. Don't commit yourself. I'm afraid it's the moon, looking so much like a slice of melon—"

"It's not the moon. It's you."

The proprietor of the Desert Edge came to the door. Dim lights burned in the interior of the hotel.

"Lord, Miss Wendell," he said. "I nearly locked you out."

"I'm coming," returned the girl. "See you at the ranch to-morrow, Mr. Eden."

"Fine," answered Eden. He nodded to the landlord, and the front door of the hotel banged shut in his face.

As he drove out across the lonely desert, he began to wonder what he was going to say to the restless P. J. Madden when he reached the ranch. The millionaire would be home from Pasadena now; he had expected to meet Draycott there. And Draycott was in San Francisco, little dreaming of the part his name was playing in the drama of the Phillimore pearls. P. J. would be furious; he would demand an explanation.

But nothing like that happened. The ranch house was in darkness and only Ah Kim was in evidence about the place.

"Madden and others in bed now," explained the Chinese. "Came home tired and very much dusted and at once retired to rooms."

"Well, I've got it on good authority that to-morrow is another day," replied Eden. "I'll turn in, too."

When he reached the breakfast table on Thursday morning, the three men were there before him. "Everything run off smoothly in Pasadena yesterday?" he inquired brightly.

Thorn and Gamble stared at him, and Madden frowned. "Yes, yes, of course," he said. He added a look which clearly meant: "Shut up."

After breakfast Madden joined the boy in the yard. "Keep that matter of Draycott to yourself," he ordered.

"You saw him, I suppose?" Eden inquired.

"I did not."

"What! Why, that's too bad. But not knowing each other I suppose—"

"No sign of anybody that looked like your man to me. You know, I'm beginning to wonder about you—"

"But Mr. Madden. I told him to be there."

"Well, as a matter of fact, I didn't care especially. Things didn't work out as I expected. I think now you'd better get hold of him and tell him to come to Eldorado. Did he call you up?"

"He may have. I was in town last night. At any rate, he's sure to call soon."

"Well, if he doesn't, you'd better go over to Pasadena and get hold of him—"

A truck filled with motion-picture camera men, props, and actors in weird costumes stopped before the ranch. Two other cars followed. Some one alighted to open the gate.

"What's this?" cried Madden.

"This is Thursday," answered Eden. "Have you forgotten—"

"Forgot it completely," said Madden. "Thorn! Where's Thorn?"

The secretary emerged from the house. "It's the movies, Chief. This was the day—"

"Damnation!" growled Madden. "Well, we'll have to go through with it. Martin, you look after things." He went inside.

The movies were all business this morning, in contrast to the careless gaiety of the night before. The cameras were set up in the open end of the patio. The actors, in Spanish costume, stood ready. Bob Eden went over to Paula Wendell.

"Good morning," she said. "I came along in case Madden tried to renig on his promise. You see, I know so much about him now—"

The director passed. "This will be O. K.," he remarked to the girl.

"Pleased him for once," she smiled to Eden. "That ought to get into the papers."

The script was a story of old California, and presently they were grinding away at a big scene in the patio.

"No, no, no," wailed the director. "What ails you this morning, Rannie? You're saying good-by to the girl—you love her, love her, love her. You'll probably never see her again."

"The hell I won't," replied the actor. "Then the thing's a flop right now."

"You know what I mean—you think you'll never see her again. Her father has just kicked you out of the house forever. A bit of a critic, the father. But come on—this is the big farewell. Your heart is broken. Broken, my boy—what are you grinning about?"

"Come on, Diane," said the actor. "I'm never going to see you again, and I'm supposed to be sorry about it. Ye gods, the things these script-writers imagine. However, here goes. My art's equal to anything."

Eden strolled over to where the white-haired patriarch and Eddie Boston were sitting together on a pile of lumber beside the barn. Near at hand, Ah Kim hovered, all eyes for these queer antics of the white men.

Boston leaned back and lighted a pipe. "Speaking of Madden," he remarked, "makes me think of Jerry Delaney. Ever know Jerry, Pop?"

Startled, Eden moved nearer. The old man put his hand behind his ear. "Who's that?" he inquired.

"Delaney," shouted Boston. Chan also edged closer. "Jerry Delaney. There was one smooth worker in his line, pop. I hope I get a chance—I'm going to ask Madden if he remembers—"

A loud outcry for Mr. Boston arose in the patio, and he laid down his pipe and fled. Chan and Bob Eden looked at each other.

The company worked steadily until the lunch hour arrived. Then, scattered about the yard and the patio, they busied themselves with the generous sandwiches of the Oasis and with coffee served from thermos bottles. Suddenly Madden appeared in the doorway of the living-room. He was in a genial mood.

"Just a word of welcome," he said. "Make yourselves at home." He shook hands with the director and, moving about, spoke a few moments with each member of the company in turn. The girl named Diane held his attention for some time.

Presently he came to Eddie Boston. Casually Eden managed it so that he was near by during that interview.

"Boston's the name," said the actor. His hard face lighted. "I was hoping to meet you, Mr. Madden. I wanted to ask if you remember an old friend of mine—Jerry Delaney, of New York?"

Madden's eyes narrowed, but the poker face triumphed.

"Delaney?" he repeated, vacantly.

"Yes—Jerry Delaney, who used to hang out at Jack McGuire's place on Forty-fourth Street," Boston persisted. "You know, he—"

"I don't recall him," said Madden. He was moving away. "I meet so many people."

"Maybe you don't want to recall him," said Boston, and there was an odd note in his voice. "I can't say I blame you either, sir. No, I guess you wouldn't care much for Delaney. It was a crime what he did to you—"

Madden looked anxiously about. "What do you know about Delaney?" he asked in a low tone.

"I know a lot about him," Boston replied. He came close, and Bob Eden could barely distinguish the words. "I know all about Delaney, Mr. Madden."

For a moment they stood staring at each other.

"Come inside, Mr. Boston," Madden suggested, and Eden watched them disappear through the door into the living-room.

Ah Kim came into the patio with a tray on which were cigars and cigarettes, the offering of the host. As he paused before the director, that gentleman looked at him keenly. "By gad, here's a type," he cried. "Say, John—how'd you like to act in the pictures?"

"You clazy, boss," grinned Ah Kim.

"No, I'm not. We could use you in Hollywood."

"Him lookee like you make 'um big joke."

"Nothing of the kind. You think it over. Here." He wrote on a card. "You change your mind, you come and see me. Savvy?"

"Maybe nuddah day, boss. Plenty happily heah now." He moved along with his tray.

Bob Eden sat down beside Paula Wendell. He was, for all his outward calm, in a very perturbed state of mind.

"Look here," he began, "something has happened, and you can help us again." He explained about Jerry Delaney, and repeated the conversation he had just overheard between Madden and Eddie Boston. The girl's eyes were wide. "It wouldn't do for Chan or me to make any inquiries," he added. "What sort of fellow is this Boston?"

"Rather unpleasant person," she said. "I've never liked him."

"Well, suppose you ask him a few questions, the first chance you have. I presume that won't come until you get back to town. Find out all he knows about Jerry Delaney, but do it in a way that won't rouse his suspicions, if you can."

"I'll certainly try," she answered. "I'm not very clever—"

"Who says you're not? You're mighty clever—and kind, too. Call me up as soon as you've talked with him, and I'll hurry in town."

The director was on his feet. "Come on—let's get this thing finished. Is everybody here? Eddie! Where's Eddie?"

Mr. Boston emerged from the living-room, his face a mask, telling nothing. Not going to be an easy matter, Bob Eden reflected, to pump Eddie Boston.

An hour later the movies vanished down the road in a cloud of dust, with Paula Wendell's roadster trailing. Bob Eden sought out Charlie Chan. In the seclusion behind the cookhouse, he again went over Boston's surprising remarks to Madden. The detective's little black eyes shone.

"We march again," he said. "Eddie Boston becomes with sudden flash our one best wager. He must be made to talk. But how?"

"Paula Wendell's going to have a try at it," Eden replied.

Chan nodded. "Fine idea, I think. In presence of pretty girl, what man keeps silent? We pin our eager hopes on that."

17

In Madden's Footsteps

An hour later Bob Eden answered a ring on the telephone. Happily the living-room was deserted. Paula Wendell was on the wire.

"What luck?" asked the boy in a low voice.

"Not so good," she answered. "Eddie was in a terrific rush when we got back to town. He packed his things, paid his bill, and was running out of the hotel when I caught him. 'Listen, Eddie—I want to ask you—' I began, but that was as far as I got. He pointed to the station. 'Can't talk now, Paula,' he said. 'Catching the Los Angeles train.' And managed to swing aboard it just as it was pulling out."

Eden was silent for a moment. "That's odd. He'd naturally have gone back with the company, wouldn't he? By automobile?"

"Of course. He came that way. Well, I'm awfully sorry, Chief. I've fallen down on the job. I guess there's nothing for me to do but turn in my shield and nightstick—"

"Nothing of the sort. You did your best."

"But it wasn't good enough. I'm sorry. I'm forced to start for Hollywood in my car in about an hour. Shall you be here when I come back?"

Eden sighed. "Me? It begins to look as though I'd be here forever."

"How terrible."

"What sort of speech is that?"

"For you, I mean."

"Oh! Well, thank you very much. I'll hope to see you soon."

He hung up and went into the yard. Ah Kim was loitering near the cookhouse. Together they strolled into the barn.

"We pinned our eager hopes on empty air," said Eden. He repeated his conversation with Paula Wendell.

Chan nodded, unperturbed. "I would have made fat wager same would happen. Eddie Boston knows all about Delaney, and admits the fact to Madden. What the use we try to see Boston then? Madden has seen him first."

Bob Eden dropped down on a battered old settee that had been exiled from the house. He put his head in his hands.

"Well, I'm discouraged," he admitted. "We're up against a stone wall, Charlie."

"Many times in my life I find myself in that precise locality," returned the detective. "What happens? I batter old head until it feels sore, and then a splendid idea assails me. I go around."

"What do you suggest?"

"Possibilities of ranch now exhausted and drooping. We must look elsewhere. Names of three cities gallop into mind—Pasadena, Los Angeles, Hollywood."

"All very fine—but how to get there? By gad—I think I can manage it at that. Madden was saying this morning I ought to go to Pasadena and look up Draycott. It seems that for some strange reason they didn't meet yesterday."

Chan smiled. "Did he display peevish feeling as result?"

"No, oddly enough, he didn't. I don't think he wanted to meet Draycott, with the professor tagging along. Paula Wendell's going over that way shortly in her car. If I hurry, I may be able to ride with her."

"Which, to my thinking, would be joyful traveling," agreed Chan. "Hasten along. We have more talk when I act part of taxi-driver and carry you to Eldorado."

Bob Eden went at once to Madden's bedroom. The door was open and he saw the huge figure of the millionaire stretched on the bed, his snores shattering the calm afternoon. He hammered loudly on the panel of the door.

Madden leaped from the bed with startling suddenness, his eyes instantly wide and staring. He seemed like one expecting trouble. For a moment, Eden pitied the great man. Beyond all question Madden was caught in some inexplicable net; he was harassed and worn, but fighting still. Not a happy figure, for all his millions.

"I'm awfully sorry to disturb you, sir," Eden said. "But the fact is I have a chance to ride over to Pasadena with some of the movie people, and I think I'd better go. Draycott hasn't called, and—"

"Hush," said Madden sharply. He closed the door. "The matter of Draycott is between you and me. I suppose you wonder what it's all about, but

I can't tell you—except to say that this fellow Gamble doesn't strike me as being what he pretends, And—"

"Yes, sir," said Eden hopefully, as the millionaire paused.

"Well, I won't go into that. You locate Draycott and tell him to come to Eldorado. Tell him to put up at the Desert Edge and keep his mouth shut. I'll get in touch with him shortly. Until I do he's to lie low. Is that understood?"

"Perfectly, Mr. Madden. I'm sorry this thing has dragged out as it has—"

"Oh, that's all right. You go and tell Ah Kim I said he was to drive you to Eldorado—unless your movie friends are coming out here for you."

"No—I shall have to enlist Ah Kim again. Thank you, sir. I'll be back soon."

"Good luck," answered Madden.

Hastily Eden threw a few things into his suit-case, and waited in the yard for Ah Kim and the flivver. Gamble appeared.

"Not leaving us, Mr. Eden?" he inquired in his mild way.

"No such luck—for you," the boy replied. "Just a short trip."

"On business, perhaps?" persisted the professor gently.

"Perhaps," smiled Eden, and the car with its Chinese chauffeur appearing at that moment, he leaped in.

Again he and Chan were abroad in the yellow glory of a desert sunset. "Well, Charlie," Eden said, "I'm a little new at this detective business. What am I to do first?"

"Toss all worry out of mind. I shall hover round your elbow, doing prompt work."

"You? How are you going to get away?"

"Easy thing. To-morrow morning I announce I take day off to visit sick brother in Los Angeles. Very ancient plea of all Chinese servants. Madden will be angry, but he will not suspect. Train leaves Eldorado at seven in the morning, going to Pasadena. I am aboard, reaching there at eleven. You will, I hope, condescend to meet me at station?"

"With the greatest pleasure. We take Pasadena first, eh?"

"So I would plan it. We ascertain Madden's movements there on Wednesday. What happened at bank? Did he visit home? Then Hollywood, and maybe Eddie Boston. After that, we ask the lady soprano to desist from singing and talk a little time."

"All right, but we're going to be a fine pair," Eden replied, "with no authority to question anybody. You may be a policeman in Honolulu, but that isn't likely to go very big in Southern California."

Chan shrugged. "Ways will open. Paths will clear."

"I hope so," the boy answered. "And here's another thing. Aren't we taking a big chance? Suppose Madden hears of our antics? Risky, isn't it?"

"Risky pretty good word for it," agreed Chan. "But we are desperate now. We take long gambles."

"I'll say we're desperate," sighed Eden. "Me, I'm getting desperater every minute. I may as well tell you that if we come back from this trip with no definite light on things, I'll be strongly tempted to lift a big burden from your stomach—and my mind."

"Patience very nice virtue," smiled Chan.

"Well, you ought to know," Eden said. "You've got a bigger supply on hand than any man I ever met."

When they reached the Desert Edge Hotel, Eden was relieved to see Paula Wendell's car parked in front. They waited by the little roadster, and while they did so, Will Holley came along. They told him of their plans.

"I can help you a bit," said the editor. "Madden has a caretaker at his

Pasadena house—a fine old chap named Peter Fogg. He's been down here several times, and I know him rather well." He wrote on a card. "Give him that, and tell him I sent you."

"Thanks," said Eden. "We'll need it, or I'm much mistaken."

Paula Wendell appeared.

"Great news for you," Eden announced. "I'm riding with you as far as Pasadena."

"Fine," she replied. "Jump in."

Eden climbed into the roadster. "See you boys later," he called, and the car started.

"You ought to get a regular taxi, with a meter," Eden suggested.

"Nonsense. I'm glad to have you."

"Are you really?"

"Certainly am. Your weight will help to keep the car on the road."

"Lady, you surely can flatter," he told her. "I'll drive, if you like."

"No, thanks—I guess I'd better. I know the roads."

"You're always so efficient, you make me nervous," he commented.

"I wasn't so efficient when it came to Eddie Boston. I'm sorry about that."

"Don't you worry. Eddie's a tough bird. Chan and I will try him presently."

"Where does the big mystery stand now?" asked the girl.

"It stands there leering at us," the boy replied. "Just as it always has." For a time they speculated on Madden's unexplained murder of Delaney. Meanwhile they were climbing between the hills, while the night gathered about them. Presently they dropped down into a green fertile valley, fragrant with the scent of blossoms.

"Um," sighed Eden, breathing deep. "Smells pretty. What is it?"

The girl glanced at him. "You poor, benighted soul. Orange blossoms."

"Oh! Well, naturally I couldn't be expected to know that."

"Of course not."

"The condemned man gets a rather pleasant whiff in his last moments, doesn't he? I suppose it acts like ether—and when he comes to, he's married." A reckless driver raced toward them on the wrong side of the road. "Look out!"

"I saw him coming," said the girl. "You're safe with me. How many times must I tell you that?"

They had dinner and a dance or two at an inn in Riverside, and all too soon, it seemed to Eden, arrived at Pasadena. The girl drove up before the Maryland Hotel, prepared to drop him.

"But look here," he protested. "I'll see you safely to Hollywood, of course."

"No need of that," she smiled. "I'm like you. I can take care of myself."

"Is that so?"

"Want to see me to-morrow?"

"Always want to see you to-morrow. Chan and I are coming over your way. Where can we find you?"

She told him she would be at the picture studio at one o'clock, and with a gay good-by, disappeared down the brightly lighted stretch of Colorado Street. Eden went in to a quiet night at the hotel.

After breakfast in the morning he recalled that an old college friend named Spike Bristol was reported in the class histories as living now in Pasadena. The telephone directory furnished Bristol's address, and Eden set out to find him. His friend turned out to be one of the more decorative features of a bond office.

"Bond salesman, eh?" said Eden, when the greetings were over.

"Yes—it was either that or real estate," replied Bristol. "I was undecided for some time. Finally I picked this."

"Of course," laughed Eden. "As any class history proves, gentlemen prefer bonds. How are you getting on?"

"Fine. All my old friends are buying from me."

"Ah, now I know why you were so glad to see me."

"Sure was. We have some very pretty first mortgage sixes—"

"I'll bet you have—and you can keep them. I'm here on business, Spike—private business. Keep what I say under your hat."

"Never wear one," answered Spike brightly. "That's the beauty of this climate—"

"You can't sell me the climate, either. Spike, you know P. J. Madden, don't you?"

"Well—we're not very chummy. He hasn't asked me to dinner. But of course all us big financiers are acquainted. As for Madden, I did him a service only a couple of days ago."

"Elucidate."

"This is just between us. Madden came in here Wednesday morning with a hundred and ten thousand dollars' worth of negotiable bonds—mostly Liberties—and we sold them for him the same day. Paid him in cash, too."

"Precisely what I wanted to know. Spike, I'd like to talk with somebody at Madden's bank about his actions there Wednesday."

"Who are you—Sherlock Holmes?"

"Well—" Eden thought of Chan. "I am connected with the police, temporarily." Spike whistled. "I may go so far as to say—and for heaven's sake keep it to yourself—that Madden is in trouble. At the present moment I'm stopping at his ranch on the desert, and I have every reason to believe he's being blackmailed."

Spike looked at him. "What if he is? That ought to be his business."

"It ought to be, but it isn't. A certain transaction with my father is involved. Do you know anybody at the Garfield Bank?"

"One of my best friends is cashier there. But you know these bankers—hard-boiled eggs. However, we'll have a try."

They went together to the marble precincts of the Garfield Bank. Spike held a long and earnest conversation with his friend. Presently he called Eden over and introduced him.

"How do you do," said the banker. "You realize that what Spike here suggests is quite irregular. But if he vouches for you, I suppose— What is it you want to know?"

"Madden was here on Wednesday. Just what happened?"

"Yes, Mr. Madden came in on Wednesday. We hadn't seen him for two years, and his coming caused quite a stir. He visited the safe deposit vaults and spent some time going through his box."

"Was he alone?"

"No, he wasn't," the banker replied. "His secretary, Thorn, who is well known to us, was with him. Also a little, middle-aged man whom I don't recall very clearly."

"Ah, yes. He examined his safety deposit box. Was that all?"

The banker hesitated. "No. He had wired his office in New York to deposit a rather large sum of money to our credit with the Federal Reserve Bank—but I'd really rather not say any more."

"You paid over to him that large sum of money?"

"I'm not saying we did. I'm afraid I've said too much already."

"You've been very kind," Eden replied. "I promise you won't regret it. Thank you very much."

He and Bristol returned to the street. "Thanks for your help, Spike," Eden remarked. "I'm leaving you here."

"Cast off like an old coat," complained Bristol. "How about lunch?"

"Sorry. Some other time. I must run along now. The station's down here, isn't it? I leave you to your climate."

"Sour grapes," returned Spike. "Don't go home and get lost in the fog. So long."

From the eleven o'clock train a quite different Charlie Chan alighted. He was dressed as Eden had seen him in San Francisco.

"Hello, Dapper Dan," the boy said.

"Chan smiled. "Feel respected again," he explained. "Visited Barstow and rescued proper clothes. No cooking to-day, which makes life very pretty."

"Madden put up a fight when you left?"

"How could he do so? I leave before his awakening, dropping quaintly worded note at door. No doubt now his heart is heavy, thinking I have deserted forever. Happy surprise for him when Ah Kim returns to home nest."

"Well, Charlie, I've been busy," said Eden. He went over his activities of the morning. "When the old boy came back to the ranch the other night, he must have been oozing cash at every pore. I tell you, Holley's right. He's being blackmailed."

"Seems that way," agreed Chan. "Here is another thought. Madden has killed a man, and fears discovery. He gets huge sum together so if necessity arouses he can flee with plenty cash until affair blows overhead. How is that?"

"By George—it's possible," admitted Eden.

"To be considered," replied Chan. "Suggest now we visit caretaker at local home."

A yellow taxi carried them to Orange Grove Avenue. Chan's black eyes sparkled as they drove through the cheerful handsome city. When they turned off under the shade of the pepper trees lining the favorite street of the millionaires, the detective regarded the big houses with awe.

"Impressive sight for one born in thatched hut by side of muddy river," he announced. "Rich men here live like emperors. Does it bring content?"

"Charlie," said Eden, "I'm worried about this caretaker business. Suppose he reports our call to Madden. We're sunk."

"Without bubble showing. But what did I say—we accept long chance and hope for happy luck."

"Is it really necessary to see him?"

"Important to see everybody knowing Madden. This caretaker may turn out useful find."

"What shall we say to him?"

"The thing that appears to be true. Madden in much trouble—blackmail. We are police on trail of crime."

"Fine. And how can you prove that?"

"Quick flash of Honolulu badge, which I have pinned to vest. All police badges much alike, unless person has suspicion to read close."

"Well, you're the doctor, Charlie. I follow on."

The taxi halted before the largest house on the street—or in the world, it seemed. Chan and Eden walked up the broad driveway to find a man engaged in training roses on a pergola. He was a scholarly-looking man even in his overalls, with keen eyes and a pleasant smile.

"Mr. Fogg?" inquired Eden.

"That's my name," the man said. Bob Eden offered Holley's card, and Fogg's smile broadened.

"Glad to meet any friend of Holley's," he remarked. "Come over to the side veranda and sit down. What can I do for you?"

"We're going to ask a few questions, Mr. Fogg," Eden began. "They may seem odd—you can answer them or not, as you prefer. In the first place, Mr. Madden was in Pasadena last Wednesday?"

"Why yes—of course he was."

"You saw him then?"

"For a few minutes—yes. He drove up to the door in the Requa car he uses out here. That was about six o'clock. I talked with him for a while, but he didn't get out of the car."

"What did he say?"

"Just asked me if everything was all right, and added that he might be back shortly for a brief stay here—with his daughter."

"With his daughter, eh?"

"Yes."

"Did you make any inquiries about the daughter?"

"Why, yes—the usual polite hope that she was well. He said she was quite well, and anxious to get here."

"Was Madden alone in the car?"

"No. Thorn was with him—as always. And another man whom I had never seen before."

"They didn't go into the house?"

"No. I had the feeling Mr. Madden intended to, but changed his mind."

Bob Eden looked at Charlie Chan, "Mr. Fogg—did you notice anything about Madden's manner? Was he just as always?"

Fogg's brow wrinkled. "Well, I got to thinking about it after he left. He did act extremely nervous and sort of—er—harassed."

"I'm going to tell you something, Mr. Fogg, and I rely entirely on your discretion. You know that if we weren't all right, Will Holley would not have sent us. Mr. Madden is nervous—he is harassed. We have every reason to believe that he is the victim of a gang of blackmailers. Mr. Chan—" Chan opened his coat for a brief second, and the celebrated California sun flashed on a silver badge.

Peter Fogg nodded. "I'm not surprised," he said seriously. "But I'm sorry to hear it, just the same. I've always liked Madden. Not many people do—but he has certainly been a friend to me. As you may imagine, this work I'm doing here is hardly in my line. I was a lawyer back east. Then my health broke, and I had to come out here. It was a case of taking anything I could get. Yes sir, Madden has been kind to me, and I'll help you any way I can."

"You say you're not surprised. Have you any reason for that statement?"

"No particular reason—but a man as famous as Madden—and as rich—well, it seems to me inevitable."

For the first time Charlie Chan spoke. "One more question, sir. Is it possible you have idea why Mr. Madden should fear a certain man. A man named—Jerry Delaney."

Fogg looked at him quickly, but did not speak.

"Jerry Delaney," repeated Bob Eden. "You've heard that name, Mr. Fogg?"

"I can tell you this," answered Fogg. "The chief is rather friendly at times. Some years ago he had this house gone over and a complete set of burglar-alarms installed. I met him in the hall while the men were busy at the windows. 'I guess that'll give us plenty of notice if anybody tried to break in,' he said. 'I imagine a big man like you has plenty of enemies, Chief,' said I. He looked at me kind of funny. 'There's only one man in the world I'm afraid of, Fogg,' he answered. 'Just one.' I got sort of nervy. 'Who's that, Chief?' I asked. 'His name is Jerry Delaney,' he said. 'Remember that, if anything happens.' I told him I would. He was moving off. 'And why are you afraid of this Delaney, Chief?' I asked him. It was a cheeky thing to say, and he didn't answer at first."

"But he did answer?" suggested Bob Eden.

"Yes. He looked at me for a minute, and he said: 'Jerry Delaney follows one of the queer professions, Fogg. And he's too damn good at it.' Then he walked away into the library, and I knew better than to ask him anything more."

18

The Barstow Train

A few moments later they left Peter Fogg standing on the neatly manicured lawn beside P. J. Madden's empty palace. In silence they rode down the avenue, then turned toward the more lively business district.

"Well, what did we get out of that?" Bob Eden wanted to know. "Not much, if you ask me."

Chan shrugged. "Trifles, mostly. But trifles sometimes blossom big. Detective business consist of one unsignificant detail placed beside other of the same. Then with sudden dazzle, light begins to dawn."

"Bring on your dazzle," said Eden. "We've learned that Madden visited his house here on Wednesday, but did not go inside. When questioned about his daughter, he replied that she was well and would be along soon. What else? A thing we knew before—that Madden was afraid of Delaney."

"Also that Delaney followed queer profession."

"What profession? Be more explicit."

Chan frowned. "If only I could boast expert knowledge of mainland ways. How about you? Please do a little speculating."

Eden shook his head. "Promised my father I'd never speculate. Just as well, too, for in this case I'd get nowhere. My brain—fi you'll pardon the mention of one more insignificant detail—is numb. Too many puzzles make Jack a dull boy."

The taxi landed them at the station whence hourly buses ran to Hollywood, and they were just in time to connect with the twelve o'clock run. Back up the hill and over the bridge spanning the Arroyo they sped. A cheery world lay about them, tiny stucco bungalows tinted pink or green, or gleaming white, innumerable service stations. In time they came to the outskirts of the film city, where gaily colored mansions perched tipsily on miniature hills. Then down a long street that seemed to stretch off into eternity, into the maelstrom of Hollywood's business district.

Expensive cars honked deliriously about the corner where they alighted, and on the sidewalk milled a busy throng, most of them living examples of what the well-dressed man or woman will wear if not carefully watched. They crossed the street.

"Watch your step, Charlie," Eden advised. "You're in the auto salesman's paradise." He gazed curiously about him. "The most picturesque factory town in the world. Everything is here except the smoking chimneys."

Paula Wendell was waiting for them in the reception room of the studio with which she was connected. "Come along," she said. "I'll take you to lunch at the cafeteria, and then perhaps you'd like to look around a bit."

Chan's eyes sparkled as she led them across the lot and down a street lined with the false fronts of imaginary dwellings. "My oldest girl would exchange the favor of the gods to be on this spot with me," he remarked. "I shall have much to relate when I return to Punchbowl Hill."

They lunched among the film players, grotesque in make-up and odd costumes. "No postman before," said Chan, over his chicken pie, "ever encountered such interesting walk on his holiday. Pardon, please, if I eat with unashamed enjoyment and too much gusto. New experience for me to encounter food I have not perspired over myself in person."

"They're taking a picture on Stage Twelve," the girl explained when lunch was finished. "It's against the rules, but if you're not too boisterous I can get you in for a look."

They passed out of the dazzling sunshine into the dim interior of a great building that looked like a warehouse. Another moment, and they reached the set, built to represent a smart foreign restaurant. Rich hangings were in the background, beautiful carpets on the floor. Along the walls were many tables with pink-shaded lights, and resplendent head-waiter stood haughtily at the entrance.

The sequence being shot at the moment involved, evidently, the use of many extras, and a huge crowd stood about, waiting patiently. The faces of most of them were vital and alive, unforgettable. Here were people who had known life—and not too juch happiness—in many odd corners of the world. Nearly all the men were in uniform—a war picture, no doubt. Bob Eden heard snatches of French, German, Spanish; he saw in the eyes about him a hundred stories more real and tragic than any these people would ever act on the silver screen.

"Leading men and women are standardized, more or less," said Paula Wendell, "but the extras—they're different. If you talked with some of them, you'd be amazed. Brains and refinement—remarkable pasts—and on the bargain counter now at five dollars a day."

A call sounded, and the extras filed on to the set and took their allotted stations at the various tables. Chan watched fascinated; evidently he could stay here forever. But Bob Eden, sadly lacking in that lovely virtue, patience, became restless.

"This is all very well," he said. "But we have work to do. How about Eddie Boston?"

"I have his address for you," the girl replied. "I doubt whether you'll find him in at this hour, but you can try."

An old man appeared in the shadowy space behind the cameras. Eden recognized the veteran player who had been yesterday at Madden's ranch—the actor known as "Pop."

"Hello," cried Paula Wendell. "Maybe Pop can help you." She hailed him. "Know where we can find Eddie Boston?" she inquired.

As Pop joined them, Charlie Chan stepped back into a dark corner.

"Why—how are you, Mr. Eden?" the old man said. "You want to see Eddie Boston, you say?"

"I'd like to—yes."

"That's too bad. You won't find him in Hollywood."

"Why not? Where is he?"

"On his way to San Francisco by this time," Pop answered. "At least, that was where he was going when I saw him late last night."

"San Francisco? What's he going there for?" asked Eden, amazed.

"One grand outbreak, to hear him tell it. You know, it looks to me like Eddie's come into a bit of money."

"He has, has he?" Eden's eyes narrowed.

"I met him on the street last night when we got in from the desert. He'd come by train, and I asked him why. 'Had some rush business to attend to, Pop,' he says. 'I'm off to Frisco in the morning. Things are looking up. Now the picture's finished I aim to take a little jaunt for my health.' Said he hadn't been in Frisco since the 'nineties and was hungry to see it again."

Eden nodded. "Well, thank you very much," With Paula Wendell he moved toward the door, and Chan, his hat low over his eyes, followed.

At the foot of the runway in the bright world outside, Eden paused. "That's that," he said. "One more disappointment. Will we ever get to the end of this? Well, Charlie—Boston's beat it. Our bird has flown."

"Why not?" said Chan. "Madden pays him to go, of course. Did Boston not say he knew all about Delaney?"

"Which must mean he knows Delaney's dead. But how could he? Was he on the desert that Wednesday night? Ye gods!" The boy put his hand to his forehead. "You haven't any smelling salts, have you?" he added to Paula Wendell.

She laughed. "Never use 'em."

They moved out to the street.

"Well, we must push on," said Eden. "The night is dark and we are far from home." He turned to the girl. "When do you go back to Eldorado?"

"This afternoon," she replied. "I'm working on another script—one that calls for a ghost city this time."

"A ghost city?"

"Yes—you know. A deserted mining town. So it's me for the Petticoat Mine again."

"Where's that?"

"Up in the hills about seventeen miles from Eldorado. Petticoat Mine had three thousand citizens ten years ago, but there's not a living soul there to-day. Just ruins, like Pompeii. I'll have to show it to you—it's mighty interesting."

"That's a promise," Eden returned. "We'll see you back on your dear old desert."

"Warmest thanks for permitting close inspection of picture factory," Chan remarked. "Always a glowing item on the scroll of memory."

"It was fun for me," answered the girl. "Sorry you must go."

On the trolley bound for Los Angeles, Eden turned to the Chinese. "Don't you ever get discouraged, Charlie?" he inquired.

"Not while work remains to do," the detective replied. "This Miss Fitzgerald. Songbird, perhaps, but she will not have flown."

"You'd better talk with her—" Eden began.

But Chan shook his head.

"No, I will not accompany on that errand. Easy to see my presence brings embarrassed pause. I am hard to explain, like black eye."

"Well, I shouldn't have called you that," smiled the boy.

"Go alone to see this woman. Inquire all she knows about the dead man, Delaney."

Eden sighed. "I'll do my best. But my once proud faith in myself is ebbing fast."

At the stage door of the deserted theater Eden slipped a dollar into the hand of the doorman, and was permitted to step inside and examine the call-board. As he expected, the local addresses of the troupe were posted up, and he located Miss Fitzgerald at the Wynnwood Hotel.

"You have aspect of experienced person," ventured Chan.

Eden laughed. "Oh, I've known a few chorus-girls in my time. Regular man of the world, I am."

Chan took up his post on a bench in Pershing Square, while the boy went on alone to the Wynnwood Hotel. He sent up his name, and after a long wait in the cheap lobby, the actress joined him. She was at least thirty, probably more, but her eyes were young and sparkling. At sight of Bob Eden she adopted a rather coquettish manner.

"You Mr. Eden?" she said. "I'm glad to see you, though why I see you's a mystery to me."

"Well, just so long as it's a pleasant mystery—" Eden smiled.

"I'll say it is—so far. You in the profession?"

"Not precisely. First of all, I want to say that I heard you sing over the radio the other night, and I was enchanted. You've a wonderful voice."

She beamed. "Say, I like to hear you talk like that. But I had a cold—I've had one ever since I struck this town. You ought to hear me when I'm going good."

"You were going good enough for me. With a voice like yours, you ought to be in grand opera."

"I know—that's what all my friends say. And it ain't that I haven't had the chance. But I love the theater. Been on the stage since I was a teeny-weeny girl."

"Only yesterday, that must have been."

"Say, boy—you're good," she told him. "You don't happen to be scouting for the Metropolitan, do you?"

"No—I wish I were." Eden paused. "Miss Fitzgerald, I'm an old pal of a friend of yours."

"Which friend? I've got so many."

"I'll bet you have. I'm speaking of Jerry Delaney. You know Jerry?"

"Do I? I've known him for years." She frowned suddenly. "Have you any news of Jerry?"

"No, I haven't," Eden answered. "That's why I've come to you. I'm terribly anxious to locate him, and I thought maybe you could help."

She was suddenly cautious. "Old pal of his, you say?"

"Sure. Used to work with him at Jack McGuire's place on Forty-fourth Street."

"Did you really?" The caution vanished. "Well, you know just as much about Jerry's whereabouts as I do. Two weeks ago he wrote me from Chicago—I got it in Seattle. He was kind of mysterious. Said he hoped to see me out this way before long."

"He didn't tell you about the deal he had on?"

"What deal?"

"Well, if you don't know—Jerry was about to pick up a nice little bit of change."

"Is that so? I'm glad to hear it. Things ain't been any too jake with Jerry since those old days at McGuire's."

"That's true enough, I guess. By the way, did Jerry ever talk to you about the men he met at McGuire's? The swells. You know, we used to get some pretty big trade there."

"No, he never talked about it much. Why?"

"I was wondering whether he ever mentioned to you the name of P. J. Madden."

She turned upon the boy a baby stare, wide-eyed and innocent. "Who's P. J. Madden?" she inquired.

"Why, he's one of the biggest financiers in the country. If you ever read the papers—"

"But I don't. My work takes so much time. You've no idea the long hours I put in—"

"I can imagine it. But look here—the question is, where's Jerry now? I may say I'm worried about him."

"Worried? Why?"

"Oh—there's risk in Jerry's business, you know."

"I don't know anything of the sort. Why should there be?"

"We won't go into that. The fact remains that Jerry Delaney arrived at Barstow a week ago last Wednesday morning, and shortly afterward he disappeared off the face of the earth."

A startled look came into the woman's eyes. "You don't think he's had an—an accident?"

"I'm very much afraid he has. You know the sort Jerry was. Reckless—"

The woman was silent for a moment. "I know," she nodded. "Such a temper. These red-headed Irishmen—"

"Precisely," said Eden, a little too soon.

The green eyes of Miss Norma Fitzgerald narrowed. "Knew Jerry at McGuire's, you say."

"Of course."

She stood up. "And since when has he had red hair?" Her friendly manner was gone. "I was thinking only last night—I saw a cop at the corner of Sixth and Hill—such a handsome boy. You certainly got fine-looking fellows on your force out here."

"What are you talking about?" demanded Eden.

"Go peddle your papers," advised Miss Fitzgerald. "If Jerry Delaney's in trouble, I don't hold with it, but I'm not tipping anything off. A friend's a friend."

"You've got me all wrong," protested Eden.

"Oh, no, I haven't. I've got you all right—and you can find Jerry without any help from me. As a matter of fact, I haven't any idea where he is, and that's the truth. Now run along."

Eden stood up. "Anyhow, I did enjoy your singing," he smiled.

"Yeah. Such nice cops—and so gallant. Well, listen in any time—the radio's open to all."

Bob Eden went glumly back to Pershing Square. He dropped down on the bench beside Chan.

"Luck was poor," remarked the detective. "I see it in your face."

"You don't know the half of it," returned the boy. He related what had happened. "I certainly made a bloomer of it," he finished. "She called me a cop, but she flattered me. The kindergarten class of rookies would disown me."

"Stop the worry," advised Chan. "Woman a little too smart, that is all."

"That's enough," Eden answered. "After this, you officiate. As a detective, I'm a great little jeweler."

They dined at a hotel, and took the five-thirty train to Barstow. As they sped on through the gathering dusk, Bob Eden looked at his companion.

"Well, it's over, Charlie," he said. "The day from which we hoped for so much. And what have we gained? Nothing. Am I right?"

"Pretty close to right," admitted Chan.

"I tell you, Charlie, we can't go on. Our position is hopeless. We'll have to go to the sheriff—"

"With what? Pardon that I interrupt. But realize, please, that all our evidence is hazy, like flowers seen in a pool. Madden is big man, his word law to many."The train paused at a station. "We go to sheriff with queer talk—a dead parrot, tale of a desert rat, half-blind and maybe crazy, suit-case in attic filled with old clothes. Can we prove famous man guilty of murder on such foolish grounds? Where is body? Few policemen alive who would not laugh at us—"

Chan broke off suddenly, and Eden followed his gaze. In the aisle of the car stood Captain Bliss of the Homicide Squad, staring at them.

Eden's heart sank. The captain's little eyes slowly took in every detail of Chan's attire, then were turned for a moment on the boy. Without a sign, he turned about and went down the aisle and into the car behind.

"Good night!" said Eden.

Chan shrugged. "Fret no longer," he remarked. "We need not go to sheriff—sheriff will come to us. Our time is brief at Madden's ranch. Poor old Ah Kim may yet be arrested for the murder of Louie Wong."

19

The Voice on the Air

They arrived at Barstow at half past ten, and Bob Eden announced his intention of stopping for the night at the station hotel. After a brief talk with the man at the ticket-window, Chan rejoined him.

"I take room that neighbors the one occupied by you," he said. "Next train for Eldorado leaves at five o'clock in the morning. I am on her when she goes. Much better you await subsequent train at eleven-ten. Not so good if we return to ranch like Siamese twins. Soon enough thatblundering Bliss will reveal our connection."

"Suit yourself, Charlie," returned Eden. "If you've got the strength of character to get up and take a five o'clock train, you'll have my best wishes. And those wishes, I may add, will be extended in my sleep."

Chan got his suit-case from the parcel-room and they went up-stairs. But Eden did not at once prepare for bed. Instead he sat down, his head in his hands, and tried to think.

The door between the two rooms opened suddenly, and Chan stood on the threshold. He held in his hand a luminous string of pearls.

"Just to reassure," he smiled. "The Phillimore fortune is still safe."

He laid the pearls on the table, under a brilliant light. Bob Eden reached over, and thoughtfully ran them through his fingers.

"Lovely, aren't they?" he said. "Look here, Charlie—you and I must have a frank talk." Chan nodded. "Tell me, and tell me the truth—have you got the faintest glimmering as to what's doing out at Madden's ranch?"

"One recent day," said Chan, "I thought—"

"Yes?"

"But I was wrong."

"Precisely. I know it's a tough thing for a detective to admit, but you're absolutely stumped, aren't you?"

"You have stumped feeling yourself, maybe—"

"All right—I'll answer the question for you. You are. You're up against it, and we can't go on. To-morrow afternoon I come back to the ranch. I'm supposed to have seen Draycott—more lies, more deception. I'm sick of it, and besides, something tells me it won't work any longer. No, Charlie—we're at the zero hour. We've got to give up the pearls."

Chan's face saddened. "Please do not say so," he pleaded. "At any moment—"

"I know—you want more time. Your professional pride is touched. I can understand, and I'm sorry."

"Just a few hours," suggested Chan.

Eden looked for a long moment at the kindly face of the Chinese. He shook his head. "It's not only me—it's Bliss. Bliss will come thumping in presently. We're at the end of our rope. I'll make one last concession—I'll give you until eight o'clock to-morrow night. That's provided Bliss doesn't show up in the interval. Do you agree?"

"I must," said Chan.

"Very good. You'll have all day to-morrow. When I come back, I won't bother with that bunk about Draycott. I'll simply say: 'Mr. Madden, the pearls will be here at eight o'clock.' At that hour, if nothing has happened, we'll hand them over and go. On our way home we'll put our story before the sheriff, and if he laughs at us, we've at least done our duty." Eden sighed with relief. He stood up. "Thank heaven, that's settled."

Gloomily Chan picked up the pearls. "Not happy position for me," he said, "that I must come to this mainland and be sunk in bafflement." His face brightened. "But another day. Much may happen."

Eden patted his broad back. "Lord knows I wish you luck," he said. "Good night."

When Eden awakened to consciousness the following morning, the sun was gleaming on the tracks outside his window. He took the train for Eldorado and dropped in at Holley's office.

"Hello," said the editor. "Back at last, eh? Your little pal is keener on the job than you are. He went through here early this morning."

"Oh, Chan's ambitious," Eden replied. "You saw him, did you?"

"Yes." Holley nodded toward a suit-cast in the corner. "He left his regular clothes with me. Expects to put 'em on in a day or two, I gather."

"Probably going to wear them to jail," replied Eden glumly. "I suppose he told you about Bliss."

"He did. And I'm afraid it means trouble."

"I'm sure it does. As you probably know, we dug up very little down the valley."

Holley nodded. "Yes—and what you did dig up was mostly in support of my blackmail theory. Something has happened here, too, that goes to confirm my suspicions."

"What's that?"

"Madden's New York office has arranged to send him another fifty thousand, through the bank here. I was just talking to the president. He doesn't think he can produce all that in cash before to-morrow, and Madden has agreed to wait."

Eden considered. "No doubt your theory's the right one. The old boy's being blackmailed. Though Chan has made a rather good suggestion—he thinks Madden may be getting this money together—"

"I know—he told me. But that doesn't explain Shaky Phil and the professor. No, I prefer my version. Though I must admit it's the most appalling puzzle—"

"I'll say it is," Eden replied. "And to my mind we've done all that's humanly possible to solve it. I'm handing over the pearls to-night. I presume Chan told you that?"

Holley nodded. "Yes—you're breaking his heart. But from your viewpoint, you're absolutely right. There's a limit to everything, and you seem to have reached it. However, I'm praying something happens before to-night."

"So am I," said Eden. "If it doesn't, I don't see how I can bring myself to—but doggone it! There's Madame Jordan. It's nothing to her that Madden's killed a man."

"It's been a difficult position for you, my boy," Holley replied. "You've handled it well. I'll pray my hardest—and I did hear once of a newspaper man whose prayers were answered. But that was years ago."

Eden stood up. "I must get back to the ranch. Seen Paula Wendell to-day?"

"Saw her at breakfast down at the Oasis. She was on the point of starting for the Petticoat Mine." Holley smiled. "But don't worry—I'll take you out to Madden's."

"No, you won't. I'll hire a car—"

"Forget it. Paper's off the press now, and I'm at an even looser end than usual. Come along."

Once more Horace Greeley carried them up the rough road between the hills. As they rattled down to the blazing floor of the desert, the editor jawned.

"I didn't sleep much last night," he explained.

"Thinking about Jerry Delaney?" asked the boy.

Holley shook his head. "No—something has happened—something that concerns me alone. That interview with Madden has inspired my old friend in New York to offer me a job there—a mighty good job. Yesterday afternoon I had a doctor in Eldorado look me over—and he told me I could go."

"That's great!" Eden cried. "I'm mighty happy for your sake."

An odd look had come into Holley's eyes. "Yes," he said, "the prison door swings open, after all these years. I've dreamed of this moment, longed for it—and now—"

"What?"

"The prisoner hesitates. He's frightened at the thought of leaving his nice quiet cell. New York! Not the old New York I knew. Could I tackle it again, and win? I wonder."

"Nonsense," Eden answered. "Of course you could."

A determined look passed over Holley's face. "I'll try it," he said. "I'll go. Why the devil should I throw my life away out here? Yes—I'll tackle Park Row again."

He left Eden at the ranch. The boy went at once to his room, and as soon as he had freshed up a bit, stepped into the patio. Ah Kim passed.

"Anything new?" whispered Eden.

"Thorn and Gamble away all day in big car," the Chinese replied. "Nothing more." It was obvious he was still sunk in bafflement.

In the living-room Eden found the millionaire sitting aimless and lonely. Madden perked up at the boy's arrival. "Back safe, eh?" he said. "Did you find Draycott? You can speak out. We're alone here."

Eden dropped into a chair. "It's all set, sir. I'll give you the Phillimore pearls at eight o'clock to-night."

"Where?"

"Here at the ranch."

Madden frowned. "I'd rather it had been at Eldorado. You mean Draycott's coming here—"

"No, I don't. I'll have the pearls at eight o'clock, and I'll give them to you. If you want the transaction kept private, that can be arranged."

"Good." Madden looked at him. "Maybe you've got them now?" he suggested.

"No. But I'll have them at eight."

"Well, I'm certainly glad to hear it," Madden replied. "But I want to tell you right here that if you're stalling again—"

"What do you mean—stalling?"

"You heard me. Do you think I'm a fool. Ever since you came you've been stalling about that necklace. Haven't you?"

Eden hesitated. The moment had come for a fit of frankness, it seemed. "I have," he admitted.

"Why?"

"Because, Mr. Madden, I thought there was something wrong here."

"Why did you think that?"

"Before I tell you—what made you change your mind in the first place? In San Francisco you wanted the necklace delivered in New York. Why did you switch to Southern California?"

"A simple reason," Madden replied. "I thought up there that my daughter was going east with me. Her plans are altered—she's going at once to Pasadena for the balance of the season. And I propose to put the necklace in safety deposit there for her use when she wants it."

"I met your daughter in San Francisco," Eden said. "She's a very charming girl."

Madden looked at him keenly. "You think so, do you?"

"I do. I presume she is still in Denver?"

For a moment Madden was silent, regarding him. "No," he admitted finally, "she is not in Denver now."

"Indeed. If you don't mind telling me—"

"She is in Los Angeles, visiting friends."

At this surprising information, Eden's eyes opened wide.

"How long has she been there?" he inquired.

"Since last Tuesday," Madden answered. "I think it was Tuesday—I got a wire saying she was coming here. I didn't want her here, for certain reasons, so I sent Thorn in to meet her, with instructions to take her back to Barstow and put her on the Los Angeles train."

Eden thought fast. Barstow was about the proper distance away to account for the mileage on the big car. But where was the red clay on station platforms hereabouts?

"You're certain she reached Los Angeles safely?" he asked.

"Of course. I saw her there on Wednesday. Now, I've answered all your questions. It's your turn. Why did you think something was wrong here?"

"What has become of Shaky Phil Maydorf?" countered Eden.

"Who?"

"Shaky Phil—the lad who called himself McCallum, and who won forty-seven dollars from me at poker here the other night?"

"You mean his name was really Maydorf?" inquired Madden with interest.

"I certainly do. I had some experience with Maydorf in San Francisco."

"In what way?"

"He acted as though he was trying to annex the Phillimore pearls."

Madden's face was purple again. "Is that so? Would you mind telling me about it?"

"Not at all," replied Eden. He narrated Maydorf's activities at the pier, but failed to mantion the connection with Louie Wong.

"Why didn't you tell me sooner?" demanded Madden.

"Because I thought you knew it. I still think so."

"You're crazy."

"Maybe. We won't go into that. But when I saw Maydorf down here, it was natural to suspect something was wrong. I'm not convinced yet that it isn't. Why not go back to the original plan and deliver the pearls in New York?"

Madden shook his head. "No. I've set out to get them here, and I'll go through with it. Anybody will tell you I'm no quitter."

"Then at least tell me what the trouble is."

"There is no trouble," Madden replied. "At least, none that I can't handle myself. It's my own affair. I've bought the pearls and I want them. I give you my word that you'll be paid, which is all that need concern you."

"Mr. Madden," said the boy, "I'm not blind. You're in a jam of some sort, and I'd like to help you."

Madden turned, and his tired harassed face was ample proof of Eden's statement. "I'll get out of it," he said. "I've got out of worse holes. I thank you for your kind intentions, but don't you worry about me. At eight o'clock then—I'm relying on you. Now if you'll excuse me, I think I'l lie down. I anticipate a rather busy evening."

He went from the room, and Bob Eden stared after him, perplexed and at sea. Had he gone too far with the millionaire—told him too much? And how about this news of Evelyn Madden? Could it be true? Was she really in Los Angeles? It sounded plausible enough, and her father's manner when he spoke of her seemed frankness itself.

Oh, well—the heat on the desert was now a tangible thing, wave on wave of filmy haze. Eden was weary with his many problems. He followed Madden's example, and slept the afternoon away.

When he rose, the sun was sinking and the cool night coming on. He heard Gamble in the bathroom. Gamble—who was Gamble? Why was he allowed to remain on Madden's ranch?

In the patio, the boy had a few whispered words with Ah Kim, telling him the news about Evelyn Madden.

"Thorn and professor home now," the detective said. "I notice mileage—thirty-nine, as before. And bits of red clay on floor of cab."

Eden shook his head. "Time is passing," he remarked.

Chan shrugged. "If I could arrest it, I would do so," he replied.

At the dinner table, Professor Gamble was amiability personified.

"Well, well, Mr. Eden, we're glad to have you back with us. Sorry to have you miss any of this desert air. Your business—if I may presume—your business prospered?"

"Sure did," smiled Eden. "And how does yours go?"

The professor looked at him quickly. "I—er—I am happy to say I have had a most gratifying day. I found the very rat I was looking for."

"Fine for you, but hard on the rat," said Eden, and the dinner proceeded in silence.

When they rose from the table, Madden lighted a cigar and dropped into his favorite chair before the fire. Gamble sat down with a magazine beside a lamp. Eden took out a packet of cigarettes, lighted one, wandered about. Thorn also selected a magazine. The big clock struck the hour of seven, and then an air of almost intolerable quiet settled over the room.

Eden paused at the radio. "Never could see the sense of these things until I came down here," he explained to Madden. "I realize now there are times when even a lecture on the habits of the hookworm may seem enchanting. How about a bedtime story for the kiddies?"

He tuned in. Ah Kim entered and busied himself at the table. The sharp voice of an announcer in Los Angeles filled the room:

"—next number on our program—Miss Norma Fitzgerald, who is appearing in the musical show at the Mason, will sing a couple of selections—"

Madden leaned forward and tapped the ash from his cigar. Thorn and Gamble looked up with languid interest.

"Hello, folks," came the voice of the woman Bob Eden had talked with the day before. "Here I am again. And right at the start I want to thank all you good friends for the loads and loads of letters I've had since I went on the air out here. I found a lovely bunch at the studio tonight. I haven't had time to read them all, but I want to tell Sadie French, if she's listening in, that I was glad to know she's in Santa Monica, and Ill sure call her up. Another letter that brought me happiness was from my old pal, Jerry Delaney—"

Eden's heart stopped beating. Madden leaned forward, Thorn's mouth opened and stayed that way, and the eyes of the professor narrowed. Ah Kim, at the table, worked without a sound.

"Ive been a little worried about Jerry," the woman went on, "and it was great to know that he's alive and well. I'm looking forward to seeing him soon. Now I must go on with my program, because I'm due at the theater in half an hour. I hope you good people will all come and see us, for we've certainly got a dandy little show, and—"

"Oh, shut the confounded thing off," said Madden. "Advertising, nine-tenths of these radio programs. Makes me sick."

Norma Fitzgerald had burst into song, and Bob Eden shut the counfounded thing off. A long look passed between him and Ah Kim. A voice had come to the desert, come over the bare brown hills and the dreary miles of sage-brush and sand—a voice that said Jerry Delaney was alive and well. Alive and well—and all their fine theories came crashing down.

The man Madden killed was not Jerry Delaney! Then whose was the voice calling for help that tragic night at the ranch? Who uttered the cry that was heard and echoed by Tony, the Chinese parrot?

20

Petticoat Mine

Ah Kim, carrying a heavy tray of dishes, left the room. Madden leaned back at ease in his chair, his eyes closed, and blew thick rings of smoke toward the ceiling. The professor and Thorn resumed their placid reading, one on each side of the lamp. A touching scene of domestic peace.

But Bob Eden did not share that peace. His heart was beating fast—his mind was dazed. He rose and slipped quietly outdoors. In the cookhouse Ah Kim was at the sink, busily washing dishes. To look at the impassive face of the Chinese no one would have guessed that this was not his regular employment.

"Charlie," said Eden softly.

Chan hastily dried his hands and came to the door. "Humbly begging pardon, do not come in here." He led the way to the shadows beside the barn. "What are trouble now?" he asked gently.

"Trouble!" said Eden. "You heard, didn't you? We've been on the wrong track entirely. Jerry Delaney is alive and well."

"Most interesting, to be sure," admitted Chan.

"Interesting! Say—what are you made of, anyhow?" Chan's calm was a bit disturbing. "Our theory blows up completely, and you—"

"Old habit of theories," said Chan. "Not the first to shatter in my countenance. Pardon me if I fail to experience thrill like you."

"But what shall we do now?"

"What should we do? We hand over pearls. You have made foolish promise, which I heartily rebuked. Nothing to do but carry out."

"And go away without learning what happened here! I don't see how I can—"

"What is to be, will be. The words of the infinitely wise Kong Fu Tse—"

"But listen, Charlie—have you thought of this? Perhaps nothing happened. Maybe we've been on a false trail from the start—"

A little car came tearing down the road, and they heard it stop with a wild shriek of the brakes before the ranch. They hurried round the house. The moon was low and the scene in semi-darkness. A familiar figure alighted and without pausing to open the gate, leaped over it. Eden ran forward.

"Hello, Holley," he said.

Holley turned suddenly.

"Good lord—you scared me. But you're the man I'm looking for." He was panting, obviously excited.

"What's wrong?" Eden asked.

"I don't know. But I'm worried. Paula Wendell—"

Eden's heart sank. "What about Paula Wendell?"

"You haven't heard from her—or seen her?"

"No, of course not."

"Well, she never came back from the Petticoat Mine. It's only a short run up there, and she left just after breakfast. She should have been back long ago. She promised to have dinner with me, and we were going to see the picture at the theater to-night. It's one she's particularly interested in."

Eden was moving toward the road. "Come along—in heaven's name—hurry—".

Chan stepped forward. Something gleamed in his hand. "My automatic," he explained. "I rescued it from suit-case this morning. Take it with you—"

"I won't need that," said Eden. "Keep it. You may have use for it—"

"I humbly beg of you—"

"Thanks, Charlie I don't want it. All right, Holley—"

"The pearls," suggested Chan.

"Oh, I'll be back by eight. This is more important—"

As he climbed into the flivver by Holley's side, Eden saw the front door of the ranch house open, and the huge figure of Madden framed in the doorway.

"Hey!" cried the millionaire.

"Hey yourself," muttered Eden. The editor was backing his car, and with amazing speed he swung it round. They were off down the road, the throttle wide open.

"What could have happened?" Eden asked.

"I don't know. It's a dangerous place, that old mine. Shafts sunk all over—the mouths of some of them hidden by underbrush. Shafts several hundred feet deep—"

"Faster," pleaded Eden.

"Going the limit now," Holley replied. "Madden seemed interested in your departure, didn't he? I take it you haven't given him the pearls."

"No. Something new broke to-night." Eden told of the voice over the radio. "Ever strike you that we may have been cuckoo from the start? No one even slightly damaged at the ranch, after all?"

"Quite possible," the editor admitted.

"Well, that can wait. It's Paula Wendell now."

Another car was coming toward them with reckless speed. Holley swung out, and the two cars grazed in passing.

"Who was that?" wondered Eden.

"A taxi from the station," Holley returned. "I recognized the driver. There was some one in the back seat."

"I know," said Eden. "Some one headed for Madden's ranch, perhaps."

"Perhaps," agreed Holley. He turned off the main road into the perilous, half-obliterated highway that led to the long-abandoned mine. "Have to go slower, I'm afraid," he said.

"Oh, hit it up," urged Eden. "You can't hurt old Horace Greeley." Holley again threw the throttle wide, and the front wheel on the left coming at that moment in violent contact with a rock, their heads nearly pierced the top of the car.

"It's all wrong, Holley," remarked Eden with feeling.

"What's all wrong?"

"A pretty, charming girl like Paula Wendell running about alone in this desert country. Why in heaven's name doesn't somebody marry her and take her away from it?"

"Not a chance," replied Holley. "She hasn't any use for marriage. 'The last resort of feeble minds' is what she calls it."

"Is that so?"

"Never coop her up in a kitchenette, she told me, after the life of freedom she's enjoyed."

"Then why did she go and get engaged to this guy?"

"What guy?"

"Wilbur—or whatever his name is. The lad who gave her the ring."

Holley laughed—then was silent for a minute. "I don't suppose she'll like it," he said at last, "but I'm going to tell you anyhow. It would be a pity if you didn't find out. That emerald is an old one that belonged to her mother. She's had it put in a more modern setting, and she wears it as a sort of protection."

"Protection?"

"Yes. So every mush-head she meets won't pester her to marry him."

"Oh," said Eden. A long silence. "Is that the way she characterizes me?" asked the boy finally.

"How?"

"As a mush-head."

"Oh, no. She said you had the same ideas on marriage that she had. Refreshing to meet a sensible man like you, is the way she put it." Another long silence. "What's on your mind?" asked the editor.

"Plenty," said Eden grimly. "I suppose, at my age, it's still possible to make over a wasted life?"

"It ought to be," Holley assured him.

"I've been acting like a fool. Going to give good old dad the surprise of his life when I get home. Take over the business, like he's wanted me to, and work hard. So far, I haven't known what I wanted. Been as weak and vacillating as a—a woman."

"Some simile," replied Holley. "I don't know that I ever heard a worse one. Show me the woman who doesn't know what she wants—and knowing, fails to go after it."

"Oh, well—you get what I mean. How much farther is it?"

"We're getting there. Five miles more."

"Gad—I hope nothing's happened to her."

They rattled on, closer and closer to the low hills, brick red under the rays of the slowly rising moon. The road entered a narrow cañon, it almost disappeared, but like a homing thing Horace Greeley followed it intuitively.

"Got a flashlight?" Eden inquired.

"Yes. Why?"

"Stop a minute, and let me have it. I've an idea."

He descended with the light, and carefully examined the road ahead. "She's been along here," he announced. "That's the tread of her tires—I'd know it anywhere—I changed one of them for her. She's—she's up there somewhere, too. The car has been this way but once."

He leaped back beside Holley, and the flivver sped on, round hairpin turns, and along the edge of a precipice. Presently it turned a final corner, and before them, nestled in the hills, was the ghost city of Petticoat Mine.

Bob Eden caught his breath. Under the friendly moon lay the remnants of a town, here a chimney and there a wall, street after street of houses crumbled now to dust. Once the mine had boomed and the crowd had come, they had built their homes here where the shafts sank deep, silver had fallen in price and the crowd had gone, leaving Petticoat Mine to the most deadly bombardment of all, the patient silent bombardment of the empty years.

They rode down Main Street, weaving in and out among black gaping holes that might have been made by bursting shells. Between the cracks of the sidewalks, thronged once on a Saturday night, grew patches of pale green basket grass. Of the "business blocks" but two remained, and one of these was listing with the wind.

"Cheery sight," remarked Eden.

"The building that's on the verge of toppling is the old Silver Star Saloon," said Holley. "The other one—it never will topple. They built it of stone—built it to stand—and they needed it, too, I guess. That's the old jail."

"The jail," Eden repeated.

Holley's voice grew cautious. "Is that a light in the Silver Star?"

"Seems to be," Eden answered. "Look here—we're at rather a disadvantage—unarmed, you know. I'll just stow away in the tonneau, and appear when needed. The element of surprise may make up for our lack of a weapon."

"Good idea," agreed Holley, and Eden climbed into the rear of the car and hid himself. They stopped before the Silver Star. A tall man appeared suddenly in the doorway, and walked briskly up to the flivver.

"Well, what do you want?" he asked, and Bob Eden thrilled to hear again the thin high voice of Shaky Phil Maydorf.

"Hello, stranger," said Holley. "This is a surprise. I thought old Petticoat was deserted."

"Company's thinking of opening up the mine soon," returned Maydorf. "I'm here to do a little assaying."

"Find anything?" inquired Holley casually.

"The silver's pretty well worked out. But there's copper in those hills to the left. You're a long way off the main road."

"I know that. I'm looking for a young woman who came up here this morning. Maybe you saw her."

"There hasn't been any one here for a week, except me."

"Really? Well, you may be mistaken. If you don't mind, I'll have a look round—"

"And if I do mind?" snarled Shaky Phil.

"Why should you—"

"I do. I'm alone here and I'm not taking any chances. You swing that car of yours around—"

"Now, wait a minute," said Holley. "Put away that gun. I come as a friend—"

"Yeah. Well, as a friend, you turn and beat it. Understand." He was close to the car. "I tell you there's nobody here—"

He stopped as a figure rose suddenly from the tonneau and fell upon him. The gun exploded, but harmlessly into the road, for Bob Eden was bearing down upon it, hard.

For a brief moment, there on that deserted street before the Silver Star, the two struggled desperately. Shaky Phil was no longer young, but he offered a spirited resistance. However, it was not prolonged, and by the time Holley had alighted, Bob Eden was on top and held Maydorf's weapon in his hand.

"Get up," the boy directed. "And lead the way. Give me your keys. There's a brand-new lock on that jail door, and we have a yearning to see what's inside." Shaky Phil rose to his feet and looked helplessly about. "Hurry!" cried Eden. "I've been longing to meet you again, and I don't feel any too gentle. There's that forty-seven dollars—to say nothing of all the trouble you put me to the night the *President Pierce* docked in San Francisco."

"There's nothing in the jail," said Maydorf. "I haven't got the key—"

"Go through him, Holley," suggested the boy.

A quick search produced a bunch of keys, and Eden, taking them, handed Holley the gun. "I give old Shaky Phil into your keeping. If he tries to run, shoot him down like a rabbit."

He took the flashlight from the car and, going over, unlocked the outer door of the jail. Stepping inside, he found himself in what had once been a sort of office. The moonlight pouring in from the street fell upon a dusty desk and chair, an old safe, and a shelf with a few tattered books. On the desk lay a newspaper. He flashed his light on the date—only a week old.

At the rear were two heavy doors, both with new locks. Searching among his keys, he unlocked the one at the left. In a small, cell-like room with high barred windows his flashlight revealed the tall figure of a girl. With no great surprise he recognized Evelyn Madden. She came toward him swiftly. "Bob Eden!" she cried, and then, her old haughtiness gone, she burst into tears.

"There—there," said Eden. "You're all right now." Another girl appeared suddenly in the doorway—Paula Wendell, bright and smiling.

"Hello," she remarked calmly. "I rather thought you'd come along."

"Thanks for the ad," replied Eden. "Say, you might get hurt running about like this. What happened, anyhow?"

"Nothing much. I came up to look round and he"—she nodded to Shaky Phil in the moonlit street—"told me I couldn't. I argued it with him, and ended up in here. He said I'd have to stay overnight. He was polite, but firm."

"Lucky for him he was polite," remarked Eden grimly. He took the arm of Evelyn Madden. "Come along," he said gently. "I guess we're through here—"

He stopped. Some one was hammering on the inside of the second door. Amazed, the boy looked toward Paula Wendell.

She nodded. "Unlock it," she told him.

He unfastened the door and swinging it open, peered inside. In the semi-darkness he saw the dim figure of a man.

Eden gasped, and fell back against the desk for support.

"Ghost city!" he cried. "Well, that's what it is, all right."

21

End of the Postman's Journey

If Bob Eden had known the identity of the passenger in the taxi that he and Holley passed on their way to the mine, it is possible that, despite his concern for Paula Wendell, he would have turned back to Madden's ranch. But he drove on unknowing; nor did the passenger, though he stared with interest at the passing flivver, recognize Eden. The car from the Eldorado station went on its appointed way, and finally drew up before the ranch house.

The driver alighted and was fumbling with the gate, when his fare leaped to the ground.

"Never mind that," he said. "I'll leave you here. How much do I owe you?" He was a plump little man, about thirty-five years old, attired in the height of fashion and with a pompous manner. The driver named a sum and, paying him off, the passenger entered the yard. Walking importantly up to the front door of the house, he knocked loudly.

Madden, talking with Thorn and Gamble by the fire, looked up in annoyance. "Now who the devil—" he began. Thorn went over and opened the door. The plump little man at once pushed his way inside.

"I'm looking for Mr. P. J. Madden," he announced.

The millionaire rose. "All right—I'm Madden. What do you want?"

The stranger shook hands. "Glad to meet you, Mr. Madden. My name is Victor Jordan, and I'm one of the owners of those pearls you bought in San Francisco."

A delighted smile spread over Madden's face. "Oh—I'm glad to see you," he said. "Mr. Eden told me you were coming—"

"How could he?" demanded Victor. "He didn't know it himself."

"Well, he didn't mention you. But he informed me the pearls would be here at eight o'clock—"

Victor stared. "Be here at eight o'clock?" he repeated. "Say, just what has Bob Eden been up to down here, anyhow? The pearls left San Francisco a week ago, when Eden did."

"What!" Purple again in Madden's face. "He had them all the time! Why, the young scoundrel! I'll break him in two for this. I'll wring his neck—" He stopped. "But he's gone. I just saw him driving away."

"Really?" returned Victor. "Well, that may not be so serious as it looks. When I say the pearls left San Francisco with Eden, I don't mean he was carrying them. Charlie had them."

"Charlie who?"

"Why, Charlie Chan, of the Honolulu Police. The man who brought them from Hawaii."

Madden was thoughtful. "Chan—a Chinaman?"

"Of course. He's here, too, isn't he? I understood he was."

A wicked light came into Madden's eyes. "Yes, he's here. You think he still has the pearls?"

"I'm sure he has. In a money-belt about his waist. Get him here and I'll order him to hand them over at once."

"Fine—fine!" chuckled Madden. "If you'll step into this room for a moment, Mr. Jordan, I'll call you presently."

"Yes, sir—of course," agreed Victor, who was always polite to the rich. Madden led him by the inside passage to his bedroom. When the millionaire returned, his spirits were high.

"Bit of luck, this is," he remarked. "And to think that blooming cook—" He went to the door leading on to the patio, and called loudly, "Ah Kim!"

The Chinese shuffled in. He looked at Madden blankly. "Wha's matta, boss?" he inquired.

"I want to have a little talk with you." Madden's manner was genial, even kindly. "Where did you work before you came here?"

"Get 'um woik all place, boss. Maybe lay sticks on gloun' foah lailload—"

"What town—what town did you work in last?"

"No got 'um town, boss. Jus' outdoahs no place, laying sticks—"

"You mean you were laying ties for the railroad on the desert?"

"Yes, boss. You light now."

Madden leaned back, and put his thumbs in the armholes of his vest. "Ah Kim—you're a damned liar," he said.

"Wha's matta, boss?"

"I'll show you what's the matter. I don't know what your game here has been, but it's all over now." Madden rose and stepped to the door. "Come in, sir," he called, and Victor Jordan strode into the room. Chan's eyes narrowed.

"Charlie, what is all this nonsense?" demanded Victor. "What are you doing in that melodramatic outfit?"

Chan did not answer. Madden laughed. "All over, as I told you, Charlie—if that's your name. This is Mr. Jordan, one of the owners of those pearls you're carrying in your money-belt."

Chan chrugged. "Mr. Jordan juggles truth," he replied, dropping his dialect with a sigh of relief. "He has no claim on pearls. They are property of his mother, to whom I give promise I would guard them with life."

"See here, Charlie," cried Victor angrily, "don't tell me I lie. I'm sick and tired of this delay down here, and I've come with my mother's authority to put an end to it. If you don't believe me, read that."

He handed over a brief note in Madame Jordan's old-fashioned script. Chan read it. "One only answer," he remarked. "I must release the pearls." He glanced toward the clock, ticking busily by the patio window. "Though I am much preferring to wait Mr. Eden's come back—"

"Never mind Eden," said Victor. "Produce that necklace."

Chan bowed and turning, fumbled for a moment at his waist. The Phillimore necklace was in his hand.

Madden took it eagerly. "At last," he said.

Gamble was staring over his shoulder. "Beautiful," murmured the professor.

"One minute," said Chan. "A receipt, if you will be so kind."

Madden nodded, and sat at his desk. "I got one ready this afternoon.

Just have to sign it." He laid the pearls on the blotter, and took a typewritten sheet from the top drawer. Slowly he wrote his name. "Mr. Jordan," he was saying, "I'm deeply grateful to you for coming down here and ending this. Now that it's settled, I'm leaving at once—" He offered the receipt to Chan.

A strange look had come into the usually impassive eyes of Charlie Chan. He reached out toward the sheet of paper offered him, then with the speed of a tiger, he snatched for the pearls. Madden snatched, too, but he was a little late. The necklace disappeared into Chan's voluminous sleeve.

"What's this?" bellowed Madden, on his feet. "Why, you crazy—"

"Hush," said Chan. "I will retain the pearls."

"You will, will you?" Madden whipped out a pistol. "We'll see about that—"

There was a loud report, and a flash of fire—but it did not come from Madden's gun. It came from the silken sleeve of Charlie Chan. Madden's weapon clattered to the floor, and there was blood on his hand.

"Do not stoop!" warned Chan, and his voice was suddenly high and shrill. "Postman has been on such long walk, but now at last he has reached journey's end. Do not stoop, or I put bullet in somewhat valuable head!"

"Charlie—are you mad?" cried Victor.

"Not very," smiled Chan. "Kindly favor me by backing away, Mr. Madden." He picked up the pistol from the floor—Bill Hart's present, it seemed to be. "Very nice gun, I use it now." Swinging Madden round, he searched him, then placed a chair in the center of the room. "Be seated here, if you will so far condescend—" he said.

"The hell I will," cried Madden.

"Recline!" said Chan.

The great Madden looked at him a second, then dropped sullenly down upon the chair. "Mr. Gamble," called Chan. He ran over the slim person of the professor. "You have left pretty little weapon in room. That is good. This will be your chair. And not to forget Mr. Thorn, also unarmed. Comfortable chair for you, too." He backed away, facing them. "Victor, I make humble suggestion that you add yourself to group. You are plenty foolish boy, always. I remember—in Honolulu—" His tone hardened. "Sit quickly, or I puncture you and lift big load from mother's mind!"

He drew up a chair between them and the exhibition of guns on the wall. "I also will venture to recline," he announced. He glanced at the clock. "Our wait may be a long one. Mr. Thorn, another suggestion occurs. Take handkerchief and bind up wounded hand of chief."

Thorn produced a handkerchief and Madden held out his hand. "What the devil are we waiting for?" snarled the millionaire.

"We await come back of Mr. Bob Eden," replied Chan. "I am having much to impart when he arrives."

Thorn completed his act of mercy, and slunk back to his chair. The tall clock by the patio windows ticked on. With the patience characteristic of his race Chan sat, staring at his odd assortment of captives. Fifteen minutes passed, a half-hour, the minute hand began its slow advance toward the hour of nine.

Victor Jordan shifted uneasily in his chair. Such disrespect to a man worth millions! "You're clear out of your mind, Charlie," he protested.

"Maybe," admitted Chan. "We wait and see."

Presently a car rattled into the yard. Chan nodded. "Long wait nearly over," he announced. "Now Mr. Eden comes."

His expression altered as a knock sounded on the door. It was pushed open and a man strode bruskly in. A stocky, red-faced, determined man—Captain Bliss of the Homicide Squad. After him came another, a lean wiry individual in a two-quart hat. They stood amazed at the scene before them.

Madden leaped to his feet. "Captain Bliss. By gad, I'm delighted to see you. You're just in time."

"What's all this?" inquired the lean man.

"Mr. Madden," said Bliss, "I've brought along Harley Cox, Sheriff of the County. I guess you need us here."

"We sure do," replied Madden. "This Chinaman has gone crazy. Take that gun away from him and put him under arrest."

The sheriff stepped up to Charlie Chan. "Give me the firearms, John," he ordered. "You know what that means—a Chinaman with a gun in California. Deportation. Good lord—he's got two of them."

"Sheriff," said Charlie with dignity. "Permit me the honor that I introduce myself. I am Detective-Sergeant Chan, of the Honolulu Police."

The sheriff laughed. "You don't say. Well, I'm the Queen of Sheba. Are you going to give me that other gun, or do your want a charge of resisting an officer?"

"I do not resist," said Chan. He gave up his own weapon. "I only call to your attention I am fellow policeman, and I yearn to save you from an error you will have bitter cause to regret."

"I'll take the chance. Now, what's going on here?" The sheriff turned to Madden. "We came about that Louie Wong killing. Bliss saw this Chinaman on a train last night with the fellow named Eden, all dolled up in regular clothes and as chummy as a brother."

"You're on the right trail now, Sheriff," Madden assured him. "There's no doubt he killed Louie. And just at present he has somewhere about him a string of pearls belonging to me. Please take them away from him."

"Sure, Mr. Madden," replied the sheriff. He advanced to make a search, but Chan forestalled him. He handed him the necklace.

"I give it to your keeping," he said. "You are officer of law and responsible. Attend your step."

Cox regarded the pearls. "Some string, ain't it? Kinda pretty, Mr. Madden. You say it belongs to you?"

"It certainly does—"

"Sheriff," pleaded Charlie, with a glance at the clock, "if I may make humble suggestion, go slow. You will kick yourself angrily over vast expanse of desert should you make blunder now."

"But if Mr. Madden says these pearls are his—"

"They are," said Madden. "I bought them from a jeweler named Eden in San Francisco ten days ago. They belonged to the mother of Mr. Jordan here."

"That's quite correct," admitted Victor.

"It's enough for me," remarked the sheriff.

"I tell you I am of the Honolulu Police—" protested Chan.

"Maybe so, but do you think I'd take your word against that of a man like P. J. Madden? Mr. Madden, here are your pearls—"

"One moment," cried Chan. "This Madden says he is the same who bought the necklace at San Francisco jeweler's. Ask him, please, location of jeweler's store."

"On Post Street," said Madden.

"What part Post Street? Famous building across way. What building?"

"Officer," objected Madden, "Must I submit to this from a Chinese cook?

I refuse to answer. The pearls are mine—"

Victor Jordan's eyes were open wide. "Hold on," he said. "Let me in this. Mr. Madden, my mother told me of the time when you first saw her. You were employed then—where—in what position?"

Madden's face purpled. "That's my affair."

The sheriff removed his ample hat and scratched his head. "Well, maybe I better keep this trinket for a minute," he reflected. "Look here, John—or—er—Sergeant Chan, if that's your name—what the devil are you driving at, anyhow?"

He turned suddenly at a cry from Madden. The man had edged his way to the array of guns on the wall, and stood there now, with one of them in his bandaged hand.

"Come on," he cried. "I've had enough of this. Up with your hands—Sheriff, that means you! Gamble—get that necklace! Thorn—get the bag in my room!"

With a magnificent disregard for his own safety, Chan leaped upon him and seized the arm holding the pistol. He gave it a sharp twist, and the weapon fell to the floor.

"Only thing I am ever able to learn from Japanese," he said. "Captain Bliss, prove yourself real policeman by putting handcuffs on Thorn and the professor. If the sheriff will so kindly return my personal automatic, which I employ as detective in Hawaii, I will be responsible for this Madden here."

"Sure, I'll return it," said Cox. "And I want to congratulate you. I don't know as I ever saw a finer exhibition of courage—"

Chan grinned. "Pardon me if I make slight correction. One recent morning at dawn I have busy time removing all cartridges from this splendid collection of old-time pistols on the wall. Long dusty job, but I am glad I did it." He turned suddenly to the big man beside him. "Put up the hands, Delaney," he cried.

"Delaney?" repeated the sheriff.

"Undubitably," replied Chan. "You have questioned value of my speech against word of P. J. Madden. Happy to say that situation does not arise. This is not P. J. Madden. His name is Jerry Delaney."

Bob Eden had entered quietly from the patio. "Good work, Charlie," he said. "You've got it now. But how in Sam Hill did you know?"

"Not long ago," answered Chan, "I shoot gun from his grasp. Observe the bandage on his hand, and note it is the left. Once in this room I told you Delaney was left-handed."

Through the open door behind Eden came a huge, powerful, but weary-looking man. One of his arms was in a sling, and his face was pale beneath a ten days' growth of beard. But there was about him an air of authority and poise; he loomed like a tower of granite, though the gray suit was sadly rumpled now. He stared grimly at Delaney.

"Well, Jerry," he said, "you're pretty good. But they always told me you were—the men who ran across you at Jack McGuire's. Yes—very good, indeed. Standing in my house, wearing my clothes, you look more like me than I do myself."

22

The Road to Eldorado

The man at the door came farther into the room and looked inquiringly about him. His eyes fell on Thorn.

"Hello, Martin," he said. "I warned you it wouldn't work. Which of you gentlemen is the sheriff?"

Cox came forward. "Right here, sir. I suppose you're P. J. Madden?"

Madden nodded. "I suppose so. I've always thought I was. We telephoned the constable from a ranch down the road, and he told us you were here. So we've brought along another little item to add to your collection." He indicated the patio door, through which Holley came at that moment leading Shaky Phil by the arm. Maydorf's hands were tied behind him. Paula Wendell and Evelyn Madden also entered.

"You'd better handcuff this newcomer to Delaney, Sheriff," suggested Madden. "And then I'll run over a little list of charges against the crowd that I think will hold them for a while."

"Sure, Mr. Madden," agreed the sheriff. As he stepped forward, Chan halted him.

"Just one minute. You have string of pearls—"

"Oh, yes—that's right," replied the sheriff. He held out the Phillimore necklace. Chan took it and placed it in the hand of P. J. Madden.

"Fully aware you wanted it in New York," he remarked, "but you will perform vast kindess to accept it here. I have carried it to outside limit of present endurance. Receipt at your convenience, thank you."

Madden smiled. "All right, I'll take it." He put the necklace in his pocket. "You're Mr. Chan, I imagine. Mr. Eden was telling me about you on the way down from the mine. I'm mighty glad you've been here."

"Happy to serve," bowed Chan.

The sheriff turned. "There you are, sir. The charge, I guess, is attempted theft—"

"And a lot of other things," Madden added, "including assault with intent to kill." He indicated his limp arm. "I'll run over my story as quickly as I can—but I'll do it sitting down." He went to his desk. "I'm a little weak—I've been having a rough time of it. You know in a general way what has happened, but you don't know the background, the history, of this affair. I'll have to go back—back to a gambling house on Forty-fourth Street, New York. Are you familiar with New York gamblers and their ways, Sheriff?"

"Been to New York just once," said the sheriff. "Didn't like it."

"No, I don't imagine you would," replied Madden. He looked about. "Where are my cigars? Ah—here. Thanks, Delaney—you left me a couple, didn't you? Well, Sheriff, in order that you may understand what's been going on here, I must tell you about a favorite stunt of shady gamblers and confidence men in New York—a stunt that was flourishing there twelve or fifteen years ago. It was a well-known fact at the time that in the richly furnished houses where they lay in wait for trusting out-of-town suckers, certain members of the ring were assigned to impersonate widely-known millionaires, such as Frank Gould, Cornelius Vanderbilt, Mr. Astor—myself. The greatest care was exercised—photographs of these men were studied;

wherever possible they themselves were closely observed in every feature of height, build, carriage, dress. The way they brushed their hair, the kind of glasses they wore, their peculiar mannerisms—no detail was too insignificant to escape attention. The intended dupe must be utterly taken in, so he might feel that he was among the best people, and that the game was honest."

Madden paused a moment. "Of course, some of these impersonations were rather flimsy, but it was my bad luck that Dr. Delaney here, who had been an actor, was more or less of an artist. Starting with a rather superficial resemblance to me, he built up an impersonation that got better and better as time went on. I began to hear rumors that I was seen nightly at the gambling house of one Jack McGuire, in Forty-fourth Street. I sent my secretary, Martin Thorn, to investigate. He reported that Delaney was making a good job of it—not, of course, so good that he could deceive any one really close to me, but good enough to fool people who knew me only from photographs. I put my lawyer on the matter, and he came back and said that Delaney had agreed to desist, on threat of arrest.

"And I imagine he did drop it—in the gambling houses. What happened afterward I can only conjecture, but I guess I can hit it pretty close. These two Maydorf boys, Shaky Phil and"—he nodded at Gamble—"his brother who is known to the police as the professor, were the brains of the particular gang at McGuire's. They must long ago have conceived the plan of having Delaney impersonate me some where, some time. They could do nothing without the aid of my secretary, Thorn, but they evidently found him willing. Finally they hit on the desert as the proper locale for the enterprise. It was an excellent selection. I come here rarely; meet few people when I do come. Once they could get me here alone, without my family, it was a simple matter. All they had to do was put me out of the way, and then P. J. Madden appears with his secretary, who is better known locally than he is—no one is going to dream of questioning his identity, particularly as he looks just like his pictures."

Madden puffed thoughtfully on his cigar. "I've been expecting some such move for years. I feared no man in the world—except Delaney. The possibilities of the harm he might do me were enormous. Once I saw him in a restaurant, studying me. Well—they had a long wait, but their kind is patient. Two weeks ago I came here with Thorn, and the minute I got here I sensed there was something in the air. A week ago last Wednesday night I was sitting here writing a letter to my daughter Evelyn—it's probably still between the leaves of this blotter where I put it when I heard Thorn cry out sharply from his bedroom. 'Come quick, Chief,' he called. He was typing letters for me, and I couldn't imagine what had happened. I rose and went to his room—and there he was, with an old gun of mine—a gun Bill Hart had given me—in his fist. 'Put up your hands,' he said. Some one entered from the patio. It was Delaney.

" 'Now, don't get excited, Chief,' said Thorn, and I saw the little rat was in on the game. 'We're going to take you for a ride to a place where you can have a nice little rest. I'll go and pack a few things for you. Here, Jerry—you watch him.' And he handed Delaney the gun.

"There we stood, Delaney and I, and I saw that Jerry was nervous—the game was a little rich for his blood. Thorn was busy in my room. I began to call for help at the top of my voice—why? Who would come? I didn't know, but a friend might hear—Louie might have got home—some one might be passing in the road. Delaney told me to shut up. His hand trembled like a leaf. In the patio outside I heard an answering voice—but it was only

Tony, the parrot. I knew well enough what was afoot, and I decided to take a chance. I started for Delaney; he fired and missed. He fired again, and I felt a sort of sting in my shoulder, and fell.

"I must have been unconscious for a second, but when I came to, Thorn was in the room, and I heard Delaney say he'd killed me. In a minute, of course, they discovered I was alive, and my good friend Jerry was all for finishing the job. But Thorn wouldn't let him—he insisted on going through with the original plan. He saved my life—I'll have to admit it—the contemptible little traitor. Cowardice, I imagine, but he saved me. Well, they put me in a car, and drove me up to the jail at Petticoat Mine. In the morning they left—all except the professor, who had joined our happy party. He stayed behind, dressed my wound, fed me after a fashion. On Sunday afternoon he went away and came back late at night with Shaky Phil. Monday morning the professor left, and Shaky Phil was my jailer after that. Not so kind as his brother.

"What was going on at the ranch, you gentlemen know better than I do. On Tuesday my daughter wired that she was coming, and of course the game was up if she reached here. So Thorn met her in Eldorado, told her I was injured and up at the mine, and took her there. Naturally, she trusted him. Since then she has been there with me, and we'd be there now if Mr. Eden and Mr. Holley had not come up to-night, searching for this other young woman who had, unfortunately for her, stumbled on the affair early in the day."

Madden rose. "That's my story, Sheriff. Do you wonder that I want to see this gang behind the bars? I'll sleep better then."

"Well, I reckon it's easy arranged," returned the sheriff. "I'll take 'em along and we can fix the warrants later. Guess I'll see 'em safe in the jail at the county-seat—Eldorado can't offer 'em all the comforts of a first-class cell."

"One thing," said Madden. "Thorn, I heard you say the other night to Delaney, 'You were always afraid of him—that time in New York—' What did that mean? You tried this thing before?"

Thorn looked up with stricken face, which had been hidden in his hands. "Chief, I'm sorry about this. I'll talk. We had it all set to pull it once at the office in New York, when you were away on a hunting trip. But if you were afraid of Delaney, he was a lot more afraid of you. He got cold feet—backed out at the last minute—"

"And why wouldn't I back out?" snarled Delaney. "I couldn't trust any of you. A bunch of yellow dogs—"

"Is that so?" cried Shaky Phil. "Are you talking about me?"

"Sure I'm talking about you. I suppose you didn't try to cop the pearls in Frisco when we sent you up there to draw Louie Wong away? Oh, I know all about that—"

"Why wouldn't I try to cop them?" demanded Shaky Phil. "You been trying to cop them, haven't you? When you thought Draycott was bringing them, what did you try to pull? Oh, brother Henry's been on to you—"

"I sure have," put in the professor. "Trying to sneak off and meet Draycott alone. If you thought I wasn't wise, you must be a fool. But of course that's what you are—a poor fool that writes letters to actresses—"

"Shut up!" bellowed Delaney. "Who had a better right to those pearls? What could you have done if it hadn't been for me? A lot of help you were—mooning round with your tall talk. And you"—he turned back to Shaky Phil—"you pulled some brilliant stuff. Putting a knife in Louie Wong right on the door-step—"

"Who put a knife in Louie Wong?" cried Shaky Phil.

"You did," shouted Thorn. "I was with you and I saw you. I'll swear to that—"

"An accessory, eh?" grinned the sheriff. "By gad, just let this gang loose at one another, and they'll hang themselves."

"Boys, boys," said the professor gently. "Cut it out. We'll never get anywhere that way. Sheriff, we are ready—"

"One moment," said Charlie Chan. He disappeared briefly, and returned with a small black bag, which he set before Madden. "I have pleasure calling your attention to this," he announced. "You will find inside vast crowds of currency. Money from sale of bonds, money sent from New York office. Pretty much intact—but not quite. I ask Delaney."

"It's all there," Delaney growled.

Chan shook his head. "I grieve to differ even with rascal like you are. But there was Eddie Boston—"

"Yes," replied Delaney. "It's true—I gave Boston five thousand dollars. He recognized me the other day in the yard. Go after him and get it back—the dirty crook!"

The sheriff laughed. "Speaking of crooks," he said, "that sounds to me like your cue, boys. We'd better be getting along, Bliss. We can swear in a deputy or two in Eldorado. Mr. Madden, I'll see you to-morrow."

Bob Eden went up to Delaney. "Well, Jerry," he smiled. "I'm afraid this is good-by. You've been my host down here, and my mother told me I must always say I've had a very nice time—"

"Oh, go to the devil," said Delaney.

The sheriff and Bliss herded their captives out into the desert night, and Eden went over to Paula Wendell.

"Exit the Delaney quartet," he remarked. "I guess my stalling days at the ranch are ended. I'm taking the ten-thirty train to Barstow, and—"

"Better call up for a taxi," she suggested.

"Not while you and the roadster are on the job. If you'll wait while I pack—I want a word with you anyhow. About Wilbur."

"One happy thought runs through my mind," Will Holley was saying. "I'm the author of a famous interview with you, Mr. Madden. One you never gave."

"Really?" replied Madden. "Well, don't worry. I'll stand behind you."

"Thanks," answered the editor. "I wonder why they gave out that story," he mused.

"Simple to guess," said Chan. "They are wiring New York office money be sent, please. How better to establish fact Madden is at desert ranch than to blaze same forth in newspapers. Printed word has ring of convincing truth."

"I imagine you're right," nodded Holley. "By the way, Charlie, we thought we'd have a big surprise for you when we got back from the mine. But you beat us to it, after all."

"By a hair's width," replied Chan. "Now that I have leisure I bow my head and do considerable blushing. Must admit I was plenty slow to grasp apparent fact. Only to-night light shone. To please this Victor, I hand over pearls. Madden is signing receipt—he writes slow and painful. Suddenly I think—he does all things slow and painful with that right hand. Why? I recall Delaney's vest, built for left-handed man. Inwardly, out of sight, I gasp. To make a test, I snatch at pearls. Madden, to call him that, snatches, too. But guard is down—he snatches with left hand. He rips out pistol—left hand again. The fact is proved. I know."

"Well, that was quick thinking," Holley said.

Chan sadly shook his head. "Why not? Poor old brain must have been plenty rested. Not at work for many days. When I arrange these dishonest ones in chairs to wait for you, I have much time for bitter self-incriminations. Why have I experienced this stupid sinking spell? All time it was clear as desert morning. A man writes important letter, hides in blotter, goes away. Returning, he never touches same. Why? He did not return. Other easy clues—Madden, calling him so again, receives Doctor Whitcomb in dusk of patio. Why? She has seen him before. He talks with caretaker in Pasadena—when? Six o'clock, when dark has fallen. Also he fears to alight from car. Oh, as I sit here I give myself many resounding mental kicks. Why have I been so thick? I blame this climate of South California. Plenty quick I hurry back to Honolulu, where I belong."

"You're too hard on yourself," said P. J. Madden. "If it hadn't been for you, Mr. Eden tells me, the necklace would have been delivered long ago, and this crowd off to the Orient or somewhere else far away. I owe you a lot, and if mere thanks—"

"Stop thanking me," urged Chan. "Thank Tony. If Tony didn't speak that opening night, where would necklace be now? Poor Tony, buried at this moment in rear of barn." He turned to Victor Jordan, who had been lurking modestly in the background. "Victor, before returning north, it is fitting that you place wreath of blossoms on grave of Tony, the Chinese parrot. Tony died, but he lived to splendid purpose. Before he passed, he saved the Phillimore pearls."

Victor nodded. "Anything you say, Charlie. I'll leave a standing order with my florist. I wonder if some one will give me a lift back to town?"

"I'll take you," Holley said. "I want to get this thing on the wire. Charlie—shall I see you again—"

"Leaving on next train," replied Chan. "I am calling at your office to collect more fitting clothes. Do not wait, however. Miss Wendell has kindly offered use of her car."

"I'm waiting for Paula, too," Eden said. "I'll see you at the station." Holley and Victor said their good-bys to Madden and his daughter, and departed. Bob Eden consulted his watch. "Well, the old home week crowd is thinning out. Just one thing more, Charlie. When Mr. Madden here came in to-night, you weren't a bit surprised. Yet, recognizing Delaney, your first thought must have been that Madden had been killed."

Chan laughed noiselessly. "I observe you have ignorance concerning detective customs. Surprised detective might as well put on iron collar and leap from dock. He is finished. Mr. Madden's appearance staggering blow for me, but I am not letting rival policemen know it, thank you. It is apparent we keep Miss Wendell waiting. I have some property in cookhouse—just one moment."

"The cookhouse," cried P. J. Madden. "By the lord Harry, I'm hungry. I haven't had anything but canned food for days."

An apprehensive look flitted over Chan's face. "Such a pity," he said. "Present cook on ranch has resumed former profession. Miss Wendell, I am with you in five seconds." He went hastily out.

Evelyn Madden put her arm about her father. "Cheer up, dad," she advised. "I'll drive you in town and we'll stop at the hotel to-night. You must have a doctor look at your shoulder at once." She turned to Bob Eden. "Of course, there's a restaurant in Eldorado?"

"Of course," smiled Eden. "It's called the Oasis, but it isn't. However, I can heartily recommend the steaks."

P. J. Madden was on his feet, himself again. "All right, Evelyn. Call up the hotel and reserve a suite—five rooms—no, make it a floor. Tell the proprietor I want supper served in my sitting-room—two porterhouse steaks, and everything else they've got. Tell him to have the best doctor in town there when I arrive. Help me find the telegraph blanks. Put in five long distance calls—no, that had better wait until we reach the hotel. Find out if there's anybody in Eldorado who can take dictation. Call up the leading real-estate man and put this place on the market. I never want to see it again. And oh, yes—don't let that Chinese detective get away without seeing me. I'm not through with him. Make a note to call a secretarial bureau in Los Angeles at eight in the morning—"

Bob Eden hurried to his room, and packed his suit-case. When he returned, Chan was standing in Madden's presence, holding crisp bank-notes in his hand.

"Mr. Madden has given receipt for necklace," said the Chinse. "He has also enforced on me this vast sum of money, which I am somewhat loathsome to accept."

"Nonsense," Eden replied. "You take it, Charlie. You've earned it."

"Just what I told him," Madden declared.

Chan put the bank-notes carefully away. "Free to remark the sum represents two and one half years' salary in Honolulu. This mainland climate not so bad, after all."

"Good-by, Mr. Eden," Madden said. "I've thanked Mr. Chan—but what shall I say to you? You've been through a lot down here—"

"Been through some of the happiest moments of my life," Eden replied.

Madden shook his head. "Well, I don't understand that—"

"I think I do," said his daughter. "Good luck, Bob, and thank you a thousand times."

The desert wind was cool and bracing as they went out to the little roadster, waiting patiently in the yard. Paula Wendell climbed in behind the wheel. "Get in, Mr. Chan," she invited. Chan took his place beside her. Bob Eden tossed his suit-case into the luggage compartment at the back, and returned to the car door.

"Squeeze in there, Charlie," he said. "Don't make a fool of the advertisements. This is a three-seater car."

Charlie squeezed. "Moment of gentle embarrassment for me," he remarked. "The vast extensiveness of my area becomes painfully apparent."

They were out on the road. The Joshua trees waved them a weird farewell in the white moonlight.

"Charlie," said Eden, "I suppose you don't dream why you are in this party?"

"Miss Wendell very kind," remarked Chan.

"Kind—and cautious," laughed Eden. "You're here as a Wilbur—a sort of buffer between this young woman and the dread institution of marriage. She doesn't believe in marriage, Charlie. Now where do you suppose she picked up that foolish notion?"

"Plenty foolish," agreed Chan. "She should be argued at."

"She will be argued at. She brought you along because she knows I'm mad about her. She's seen it in my great trusting eyes. She knows that since I've met her, that precious freedom of mine seems a rather stale joke. She realizes that I'll never give up—that I intend to take her away from the desert—but she thought I wouldn't mention it if you were along."

"I begin to feel like skeleton at feast," remarked Chan.

"Cheer up—you certainly don't feel like that to me," Eden assured him. "Yes, she thought I'd fail to speak of the matter—but we'll fool her. I'll speak of it anyhow. Charlie, I love this girl."

"Natural you do," agreed Chan.

"I intend to marry her."

"Imminently fitting purpose," assented Chan. "But she has said no word."

Paula Wendell laughed. "Marriage," she said. "The last resort of feeble minds. I'm having a great time, thanks. I love my freedom. I mean to hang on to it."

"Sorry to hear that," said Chan. "Permit me if I speak a few words in favor of married state. I am one who knows. Where is the better place than a new home? Truly an earthly paradise where cares vanish, where the heavenly melody of wife's voice vibrates everything in a strange symphony."

"Sounds pretty good to me," remarked Eden.

"The ramble hand in hand with wife on evening streets, the stroll by moonly seaside. I recollect the happy spring of my own marriage with unlimited yearning."

"How does it sound to you, Paula?" Eden persisted.

"And this young man," continued Chan. "I am unable to grasp why you resist. To me he is plenty fine fellow. I have for him a great likeness." Paula Wendell said nothing. "A very great likeness," added Chan.

"Well," admitted the girl, "if it comes to that, I have a little likeness for him myself."

Chan dug his elbow deep into Eden's side. They climbed between the dark hills and the lights of Eldorado shone before them. As they drove up to the hotel, Holley and Victor Jordan greeted them.

"Here you are," said the editor. "Your bag is in the office, Charlie. The door's unlocked."

"Many thanks," returned Chan, and fled.

Holley looked up at the white stars. "Sorry you're going, Eden," he said. "It'll be a bit lonesome down here without you."

"But you'll be in New York," suggested Eden.

Holley shook his head and smiled. "Oh, no, I won't. I sent a telegram this evening. A few years ago, perhaps—but not now. I can't go now. Somehow, this desert country—well, it's got me, I guess. I'll have to take my New York in pictures from this on."

Far off across the dreary waste of sand the whistle of the Barstow train broke the desert silence. Charlie came around the corner; the coat and vest of Sergeant Chan had replaced the Canton crêpe blouse of Ah Kim.

"Hoarse voice of railroad proclaims end of our adventure," he remarked. He took Paula Wendell's hand. "Accept last wish from somewhat weary postman. May this be for you beginning of life's greatest adventure. And happiest."

They crossed the empty street. "Good-by," Eden said, as he and the girl paused in the shadow of the station. Something in the warm clasp of her slender strong fingers told him all he wanted to know, and his heart beat faster. He drew her close.

"I'm coming back soon," he promised. He transferred the emerald ring to her right hand. "Just by way of a reminder," he added. "When I return I'll bring a substitute—the glittering pick of the finest stock on the coast. Our stock."

"Our stock?"

"Yes." The branch-line train had clattered in, and Chan was calling to him from the car steps. "You don't know it yet, but for you the dream of every woman's life has come true. You're going to marry a man who owns a jewelry store."

Behind That Curtain

To
The only critic I love—
My wife

1

The Man from Scotland Yard

Bill Rankin sat motionless before his typewriter, grimly seeking a lead for the interview he was about to write. A black shadow shot past his elbow and materialized with a soft thud on his desk. Bill's heart leaped into his throat and choked him.

But it was only Egbert, the office cat. Pretty lonesome round here, seemed to be Egbert's idea. How about a bit of play? Rankin glared at the cat with deep disgust. Absurd to be so upset by a mere Egbert, but when one has been talking with a great man for over an hour and the subject of the talk has been murder, one is apt to be a trifle jumpy.

He reached out and pushed Egbert to the floor. "Go away," he said. "What do you mean, scaring me out of a year's growth? Can't you see I'm busy?"

His dignity offended, Egbert stalked off through the desert of typewriter tables and empty chairs. Bill Rankin watched him disappear at last through the door leading into the hallway. The hour was five thirty; the street ten stories below was filled with homegoing throngs, but up here in the city room of the *Globe* a momentary quiet reigned. Alone of all the green-shaded lamps in the room, the one above Rankin's typewriter was alight, shedding a ghastly radiance on the blank sheet of paper in his machine. Even the copy desk was deserted. In his cubby-hole at the rear sat the *Globe's* city editor, the only other human thing in sight. And he was not, if you believed the young men who worked for him, so very human at that.

Bill Rankin turned back to his interview. For a brief moment he sat wrapped in thought; then his long, capable fingers sought the keys. He wrote:

> The flights of genius and miracles of science which solve most of the crimes in detective stories have no real part in detective work. This is the verdict of Sir Frederic Bruce, former head of the Criminal Investigation Department at Scotland Yard.
>
> Sir Frederic, who is stopping over for two weeks in San Francisco during the course of a trip around the world, is qualified to give an expert opinion. For nearly seventeen years he acted as Deputy-Commissioner at the head of the most famous detective organization in existence, and though he has now retired, his interest in crime detection is as keen as ever. Sir Frederic is a big man, with a kindly twinkle in his gray eyes, but occasionally those eyes have

a steely look that made this reporter nervous. If we had killed the old Earl of Featherstonehaugh on his rare Persian rug, we would not care to have Sir Frederic on our trail. For the great detective is that type of Scotchman who is a stranger to defeat. He would never abandon the scent.

"I read a great deal of detective fiction," Sir Frederic said. "It amuses me, but there is usually nothing for a detective to learn from it. Except for the fingerprint system and work in the chemical laboratory on stains, scientific research has furnished little assistance to crime detection. Murder mysteries and other difficult criminal cases are solved by intelligence, hard work and luck, with little help from the delicate scientific devices so dear to the authors of——"

Suddenly Bill Rankin stopped writing and sat erect in his uncomfortable chair. There was a familiar ring to the ideas he was setting down on paper; he had heard them before, and recently. Opinions identical with these, expressed not in the polished English of Sir Frederic, but in a quite different idiom——Ah yes. He smiled, recalling that pudgy little man he had interviewed three days ago in the lobby of the Stewart Hotel.

The reporter rose from his chair and, lighting a cigarette, began to pace the floor. He spoke aloud: "Of course—and I never thought of it. A corking feature story staring me right in the face, and I was blind—blind. I must be losing my grip." He looked anxiously at the clock, tossed aside his cigarette and resumed his chair. Completing the sentence which he had interrupted midway, he continued:

Sir Frederic was asked what he considered the greatest piece of detective work within his knowledge.

"I cannot answer that because of the important part played by chance," he replied. "As I have just said, most criminal cases are solved by varying proportions of hard work, intelligence and luck, and I am sorry I must add that of these three, luck is the greatest by far.

"Hard, methodical work, however, has brought results in many instances. For example, it unraveled the famous Crippen mystery. The first intimation we had of something wrong in that case came when we heard that the woman treasurer of a music-hall——"

Bill Rankin wrote on, with lightning speed now, for he was eager to finish. The thing he was doing had suddenly become a minor matter. A far better story was running through his head. His fingers flew over the keys; when he paused, at rare intervals, it was to turn an inquiring gaze on the clock.

He ripped the final sheet of paper from his machine, snatched up the story, and hurried toward the city editor's nook. The lone man in charge of the copy desk, just returned from a bitter argument with the composing-room foreman, watched him sourly as he passed, and grimly sharpened a blue pencil.

"Wha's 'at?" inquired the city editor, as Bill Rankin threw the story down before him.

"Interview with Sir Frederic Bruce," Bill reminded him.

"Oh, you found him, did you?"

"We all found him. The room was full of reporters."

"Where was he?"

"He's putting up at Barry Kirk's bungalow. Kirk knew his son in London. I tried the hotels until my feet ached."

The editor snorted. "The more fool you. No Englishman ever stops at a hotel if he can wangle board and room from somebody. You've been sent out to find enough lecturing British authors to know that."

"The interview's blah," said Rankin. "Every paper in town will have it. But while I was writing it, an idea for a feature hit me hard. It'll be a humdinger—if I can only put it over on Sir Frederic. I thought I'd go back up there and see what I can do."

"A feature?" The editor frowned. "If you happen on a bit of news in the course of your literary work, you'll let me know, won't you? Here I am, trying to get out a newspaper, and all I get from you fellows is an avalanche of pretty little essays. I suspect you're all hoping that some day you'll be tapped for the *Atlantic Monthly*."

"But this feature's good," Rankin protested. "I must hurry along——"

"Just a minute. I'm only your editor, of course. I don't want to pry into your plans——"

Rankin laughed. He was an able man, and privileged. "I'm sorry, sir, but I can't stop to explain now. Some one may beat me to it yet. Gleason of the *Herald* was up there to-day and he'll get the same hunch as sure as fate. So if you don't mind——"

The editor shrugged. "All right—go to it. Hurry up to the Kirk Building. And don't let this sudden attack of energy die there. Hurry back, too."

"Yes, sir," agreed the reporter. "Of course, I'll need a bit of dinner——"

"*I* never eat," growled his charming employer.

Bill Rankin sped across the city room. His fellow reporters were drifting in now from their afternoon assignments, and the place was coming to life. Near the door, Egbert, black as the night from pole to pole, crossed Rankin's path with haughty, aloof manner and dignified stride.

Descending to the street, the reporter stood for a moment undecided. The Kirk Building was not far away; he could walk there—but time was precious. Suppose he arrived to be met by the news that Sir Frederic was dressing for dinner. With this famous and correct Englishman, the act would be a sacred rite not to be lightly interrupted by panting pressmen. No, he must reach Sir Frederic before the detective reached for his black pearl studs. He hailed a passing taxi.

As the car drew up to the curb, a red-cheeked boy, one of the *Globe's* younger reporters, emerged from the crowd and with a deep bow, held open the taxi door.

"To the Royal Opera, my good man," he shouted, "and an extra gold sovereign for you if we pass the Duke's car on the way."

Rankin pushed the facetious one aside. "Don't interfere with your betters, my lad," he remarked, and added, to the driver: "The Kirk Building, on California Street."

The taxi swung out into Market Street, followed the intricate car tracks for a few blocks, and turned off into Montgomery. In another moment they were in the financial district of San Francisco, now wrapped in its accustomed evening calm. The huge buildings of trust companies, investment houses and banks stood solemn and solid in the dusk; across the doorways of many forbidding bronze gates were already shut. Gilded signs met Rankin's eye—"The Yokohama Bank"; on another window, "The

Shanghai Trading Company"; one may not forget the Orient in the city by the Gate. Presently the taxi drew up before a twenty-story office building, and Rankin alighted.

The Kirk Building was architecturally perfect, in the excellent taste that had marked the family ever since the first Dawson Kirk had made his millions and gone his way. Now it was the particular hobby of young Barry Kirk, who lived in bachelor splendor in the spacious but breezy bungalow on its roof. Its pure white lobby was immaculate; its elevator girls trim and pretty in neat uniforms; its elevator starter resplendent as an Admiral of the Fleet. At this hour the fever of the day was ended and cleaning women knelt reverently on the marble floor. One elevator was still running, and into this Bill Rankin stepped.

"All the way," he said to the girl.

He alighted at the twentieth floor, the final stop. A narrow stair led to Barry Kirk's bungalow, and the reporter ascended two steps at a time. Pausing before an imposing door, he rang. The door opened and Paradise, Kirk's English butler, stood like a bishop barring Rankin's path.

"Ah—er—I'm back," panted Rankin.

"So I see, sir." Very like a bishop indeed, with that great shock of snow-white hair. His manner was not cordial. Earlier that day he had admitted many reporters, but with misgivings.

"I must see Sir Frederic at once. Is he in?"

"Sir Frederic is in the offices, on the floor below. I fancy he is busy, but I will announce you——"

"No—please don't trouble," said Rankin quickly. Running down to the twentieth floor, he noted a door with Barry Kirk's name on the frosted glass. As he moved toward it, it opened suddenly, and a young woman came out.

Rankin stopped in his tracks. A remarkably pretty young woman—that much was obvious even in the dim light on the twentieth floor. One of those greatly preferred blonds, with a slender figure trim in a green dress of some knitted material. Not precisely tall, but——

What was this? The young woman was weeping. Silently, without fuss, but indubitably weeping. Tears not alone of grief, but, if Rankin was any judge, of anger and exasperation, too. With a startled glance at the reporter, she hastily crossed the hall and disappeared through a door that bore the sign "Calcutta Importers, Inc."

Bill Rankin pushed on into Barry Kirk's office. He entered a sort of reception-room, but a door beyond stood open, and the newspaper man went confidently forward. In the second room, Sir Frederic Bruce, former head of the C. I. D., sat at a big, flat-topped desk. He swung around, and his gray eyes were stern and dangerous.

"Oh," he said. "It's you."

"I must apologize for intruding on you again, Sir Frederic," Bill Rankin began. "But—I—er—may I sit down?"

"Certainly." The great detective slowly gathered up some papers on the desk.

"The fact is——" Rankin's confidence was ebbing. An inner voice told him that this was not the genial gentleman of the afternoon interview in the bungalow up-stairs. Not the gracious visitor to San Francisco, but Sir Frederic Bruce of Scotland Yard, unbending, cold and awe-inspiring. "The fact is," continued the reporter lamely, "an idea has struck me."

"Really?" Those eyes—they looked right through you.

"What you told us this afternoon, Sir Frederic—— Your opinion of the value of scientific devices in the detection of crime, as against luck and hard work——" Rankin paused. He seemed unable to finish his sentences. "I was reminded, when I came to write my story, that oddly enough I had heard that same opinion only a few days ago."

"Yes? Well, I made no claim to originality." Sir Frederic threw his papers into a drawer.

"Oh, I haven't come to complain about it," smiled Rankin, regaining a trace of his jaunty spirit. "Under ordinary conditions, it wouldn't mean anything, but I heard your ideas from the lips of a rather unusual man, Sir Frederic. A humble worker in your own field, a detective who has evolved his theories far from Scotland Yard. I heard them from Detective-Sergeant Charlie Chan, of the Honolulu police."

Sir Frederic's bushy eyebrows rose. "Really? Then I must applaud the judgment of Sergeant Chan—whoever he may be."

"Chan is a detective who has done some good work in the islands. He happens to be in San Francisco at the moment, on his way home. Came to the mainland on a simple errand, which developed into quite a case before he had finished with it. I believe he acquitted himself with credit. He's not very impressive to look at, but——"

Sir Frederic interrupted. "A Chinese, I take it?"

"Yes, sir."

The great man nodded. "And why not? A Chinese should make an excellent detective. The patience of the East, you know."

"Precisely," agreed Bill Rankin. "He's got that. And modesty——"

Sir Frederic shook his head. "Not such a valuable asset, modesty. Self-assurance, a deep faith in one's self—they help. But Sergeant Chan is modest?"

"Is he? 'Falling hurts least those who fly low'—that's the way he put it to me. And Sergeant Chan flies so low he skims the daisies."

Sir Frederic rose and stepped to the window. He gazed down at the spatter of lights flung like a handful of stars over the darkening town. For a moment he said nothing. Then he turned to the reporter.

"A modest detective," he said, with a grim smile. "That's a novelty, at any rate. I should like very much to meet this Sergeant Chan."

Bill Rankin sighed with relief. His task was unbelievably easy, after all.

"That's exactly what I came here to suggest," he said briskly. "I'd like to bring you and Charlie Chan together—hear you go over your methods and experiences—you know, just a real good talk. I was wondering if you would do us the great honor to join Mr. Chan and me at lunch to-morrow?"

The former head of the C.I.D. hesitated. "Thank you very much. But I am more or less in Mr. Kirk's hands. He is giving a dinner to-morrow night, and I believe he said something about luncheon to-morrow, too. Much as I should like to accept at once, decidedly we must consult Mr. Kirk."

"Well, let's find him. Where is he?" Bill Rankin was all business.

"I fancy he is up in the bungalow." Sir Frederic turned and, swinging shut the door of a big wall safe, swiftly twirled the knob.

"You did that just like an American business man, Sir Frederic," Rankin smiled.

The detective nodded. "Mr. Kirk has kindly allowed me to use his office while I am his guest."

"Ah—then you're not altogether on a pleasure trip," said Bill Rankin quickly.

The gray eyes hardened. "Absolutely—a pleasure trip. But there are certain matters—private business—I am writing my *Memoirs*——"

"Ah, yes—of course," apologized the reporter.

The door opened, and a cleaning woman entered. Sir Frederic turned to her. "Good evening," he said. "You understand that no papers on this desk—or in it—are to be interfered with in any way?"

"Oh, yes, sir," the woman answered.

"Very good. Now, Mr.—er—Mr.——"

"Rankin, Sir Frederic."

"Of course. There is a stairs in this rear room leading up to the bungalow. If you will come with me——"

They entered the third and last room of the office suite, and Bill Rankin followed the huge figure of the Englishman aloft. The stairs ended in a dark passageway on the floor above. Throwing open the nearest door, Sir Frederic flooded the place with light, and Bill Rankin stepped into the great living-room of the bungalow. Paradise was alone in the room; he received the reporter with cold disdain. Barry Kirk, it appeared, was dressing for dinner, and the butler went reluctantly to inform him of the newspaper man's unseemly presence.

Kirk appeared at once, in his shirt-sleeves and with the ends of a white tie dangling about his neck. He was a handsome, lean young man in the late twenties, whose manner spoke of sophistication, and spoke true. For he had traveled to the far corners of the earth seeking to discover what the Kirk fortune would purchase there, and life held no surprises for him any more.

"Ah yes—Mr. Rankin of the *Globe*," he said pleasantly. "What can I do for you?"

Paradise hastened forward to officiate with the tie, and over the servant's shoulder Bill Rankin explained his mission. Kirk nodded.

"A bully idea," he remarked. "I have a lot of friends in Honolulu, and I've heard about Charlie Chan. I'd like to meet him myself."

"Very happy to have you join us," said the reporter.

"Can't be done. You must join me."

"But—the suggestion of the lunch was mine—" began Rankin uncomfortably.

Kirk waved a hand in the airy manner of the rich in such a situation. "My dear fellow—I've already arranged a luncheon for to-morrow. Some chap in the district attorney's office wrote me a letter. He's interested in criminology and wants to meet Sir Frederic. As I explained to Sir Frederic, I couldn't very well ignore it. We never know when we'll need a friend in the district attorney's office, these days."

"One of the deputies?" inquired Rankin.

"Yes. A fellow named Morrow—J. V. Morrow. Perhaps you know him?" Rankin nodded. "I do," he said.

"Well, that's the scenario," went on Kirk. "We're to meet this lad at the St. Francis to-morrow at one. The topic of the day will be murder, and I'm sure your friend from Honolulu will fit in admirably. You must pick up Mr. Chan and join us."

"Thank you very much," said Rankin. "You're extremely kind. We'll be there. I—I won't keep you any longer."

Paradise came forward with alacrity to let him out. At the foot of the stairs on the twentieth floor he met his old rival, Gleason of the *Herald*. He chuckled with delight.

"Turn right around," he said. "You're too late. I thought of it first."

"Thought of what?" asked Gleason, with assumed innocence.

".I'm getting Sir Frederic and Charlie Chan together, and the idea's copyrighted. Lay off."

Gloomily Mr. Gleason turned about, and accompanied Bill Rankin to the elevators. As they waited for the car, the girl in the green dress emerged from the office of the Calcutta Importers and joined them. They rode down together. The girl's tears had vanished, and had happily left no trace. Blue eyes—that completed the picture. A charming picture. Mr. Gleason was also showing signs of interest.

In the street Gleason spoke. "I never thought of it until dinner," he said sourly.

"With me, my career comes first," Rankin responded. "Did you finish your dinner?"

"I did, worse luck. Well, I hope you get a whale of a story—a knock-out, a classic."

"Thanks, old man."

"And I hope you can't print one damn word of it."

Rankin did not reply as his friend hurried off into the dusk. He was watching the girl in the green dress disappear up California Street. Why had she left the presence of Sir Frederick Bruce to weep outside that office door? What had Sir Frederic said to her? Might ask Sir Frederic about it to-morrow. He laughed mirthlessly. He saw himself—or any other man—prying into the private affairs of Sir Frederic Bruce.

2

What Happened to Eve Durand?

The next day at one Sir Frederic Bruce stood in the lobby of the St. Francis, a commanding figure in a gray tweed suit. By his side, as immaculate as his guest, stood Barry Kirk, looking out on the busy scene with the amused tolerance befitting a young man of vast leisure and not a care in the world. Kirk hung his stick on his arm, and took a letter from his pocket.

"By the way, I had this note from J. V. Morrow in the morning's mail," he said. "Thanks me very politely for my invitation, and says that I'll know him when he shows up because he'll be wearing a green hat. One of those green plush hats, I suppose. Hardly the sort of thing I'd put on my head if I were a deputy district attorney."

Sir Frederic did not reply. He was watching Bill Rankin approach rapidly across the floor. At the reporter's side walked, surprisingly light of step, an unimpressive little man with a bulging waistband and a very earnest expression on his chubby face.

"Here we are," Rankin said. "Sir Frederic Bruce—may I present Detective-Sergeant Chan, of the Honolulu police?"

Charlie Chan bent quickly like a jack-knife. "The honor," he said, "is unbelievably immense. In Sir Frederic's reflected glory I am happy to bask. The tiger has condescended to the fly."

Somewhat at a loss, the Englishman caressed his mustache and smiled down on the detective from Hawaii. As a keen judge of men, already he saw something in those black restless eyes that held his attention.

"I'm happy to know you, Sergeant Chan," he said. "It seems we think alike on certain important points. We should get on well together."

Rankin introduced Chan to the host, who greeted the little Chinese with obvious approval. "Good of you to come," he said.

"A four-horse chariot could not have dragged me in an opposite direction," Chan assured him.

Kirk looked at his watch. "All here but J. V. Morrow," he remarked. "He wrote me this morning that he's coming in at the Post Street entrance. If you'll excuse me, I'll have a look around."

He strolled down the corridor toward Post Street. Near the door, on a velvet davenport, sat a strikingly attractive young woman. No other seat was available, and with an interested glance at the girl Kirk also dropped down on the davenport. "If you don't mind——" he murmured.

"Not at all," she replied, in a voice that somehow suited her.

They sat in silence. Presently Kirk was aware that she was looking at him. He glanced up, to meet her smile.

"People are always late," he ventured.

"Aren't they?"

"No reason for it, usually. Just too inefficient to make the grade. Nothing annoys me more."

"I feel the same way," the girl nodded.

Another silence. The girl was still smiling at him.

"Go out of your way to invite somebody you don't know to lunch," Kirk continued, "and he isn't even courteous enough to arrive on time."

"Abominable," she agreed. "You have all my sympathy—Mr. Kirk."

He started. "Oh—you know me?"

She nodded. "Somebody once pointed you out to me—at a charity bazaar," she explained.

"Well," he sighed, "their charity didn't extend to me. Nobody pointed you out." He looked at his watch.

"This person you're expecting——" began the girl.

"A lawyer," he answered. "I hate all lawyers. They're always telling you something you'd rather not know."

"Yes—aren't they?"

"Messing around with other people's troubles. What a life."

"Frightful." Another silence. "You say you don't know this lawyer?" A rather unkempt young man came in and hurried past. "How do you expect to recognize him?"

"He wrote me he'd be wearing a green hat. Imagine! Why not a rose behind his ear?"

"A green hat." The girl's smile grew even brighter. Charming, thought Kirk. Suddenly he stared at her in amazement. "Good lord—you're wearing a green hat!" he cried.

"I'm afraid I am."

"Don't tell me——"

"Yes—it's true. I'm the lawyer. And you hate all lawyers. What a pity."

"But I didn't dream——"

"J. V. Morrow," she went on. "The first name is June."

"And I thought it was Jim," he cried. "Please forgive me."

"You'd never have invited me if you'd known—would you?"

"On the contrary—I wouldn't have invited anybody else. But come along. There are a lot of murder experts in the lobby dying to meet you."

They rose, and walked rapidly down the corridor. "You're interested in murder?" Kirk inquired.

"Among other things," she smiled.

"Must take it up myself," Kirk murmured.

Men turned to look at her a second time, he noticed. There was an alertness in her dark eyes that resembled the look in Chan's, her manner was brisk and businesslike, but for all that she was feminine, alluring.

He introduced her to the surprised Sir Frederic, then to Charlie Chan. The expression on the face of the little Chinese did not alter. He bowed low.

"The moment has charm," he remarked.

Kirk turned to Rankin. "And all the time," he accused, "you knew who J. V. Morrow was."

The reporter shrugged. "I thought I'd let you find it out for yourself. Life holds so few pleasant surprises."

"It never held a pleasanter one for me," Kirk answered. They went in to the table he had engaged, which stood in a secluded corner.

When they were seated, the girl turned to her host. "This was so good of you. And of Sir Frederic, too. I know how busy he must be."

The Englishman bowed. "A fortunate moment for me," he smiled, "when I decided I was not too busy to meet J. V. Morrow. I had heard that in the States young women were emancipated——"

"Of course, you don't approve," she said.

"Oh—but I do," he murmured.

"And Mr. Chan. I'm sure Mr. Chan disapproves of me."

Chan regarded her blankly. "Does the elephant disapprove of the butterfly? And who cares?"

"No answer at all," smiled the girl. "You are returning to Honolulu soon, Mr. Chan?"

A delighted expression appeared on the blank face. "To-morrow at noon the *Maui* receives my humble person. We churn over to Hawaii together."

"I see you are eager to go," said the girl.

"The brightest eyes are sometimes blind," replied Chan. "Not true in your case. It is now three weeks since I arrived on the mainland, thinking to taste the joys of holiday. Before I am aware events engulf me, and like the postman who has day of rest I foolishly set out on long, tiresome walk. Happy to say that walk are ended now. With beating heart I turn toward little home on Punchbowl Hill."

"I know how you feel," said Miss Morrow.

"Humbly begging pardon to mention it, you do not. I have hesitation in adding to your ear that one thing calls me home with unbearable force. I am soon to be happy father."

"For the first time?" asked Barry Kirk.

"The eleventh occasion of the kind," Chan answered.

"Must be sort of an old story by now," Bill Rankin suggested.

"That is one story which does not get aged," Chan replied. "You will learn. But my trivial affairs have no place here. We are met to honor a distinguished guest." He looked toward Sir Frederic.

Bill Rankin thought of his coming story. "I was moved to get you two together," he said, "because I found you think alike. Sir Frederic is also scornful of science as an aid to crime detection."

"I have formed that view from my experience," remarked Sir Frederic.

"A great pleasure," Chan beamed, "to hear that huge mind like Sir Frederic's moves in same groove as my poor head-piece. Intricate mechanics good in books, in real life not so much so. My experience tell me to think deep about human people. Human passions. Back of murder what, always? Hate, greed, revenge, need to make silent the slain one. Study human people at all times."

"Precisely," agreed Sir Frederic. "The human element—that is what counts. I have had no luck with scientific devices. Take the dictaphone—it has been a complete washout at the Yard." He talked on, while the luncheon progressed. Finally he turned to Chan. "And what have your methods gained you, Sergeant? You have been successful, I hear."

Chan shrugged. "Luck—always happy luck."

"You're too modest," said Rankin. "That won't get you anywhere."

"The question now arises—where do I want to go?"

"But surely you're ambitious?" Miss Morrow suggested.

Chan turned to her gravely. "Coarse food to eat, water to drink, and the bended arm for a pillow—that is an old definition of happiness in my country. What is ambition? A canker that eats at the heart of the white man, denying him the joys of contentment. Is it also attacking the heart of white woman? I hope not." The girl looked away. "I fear I am victim of crude philosophy from Orient. Man—what is he? Merely one link in a great chain binding the past with the future. All times I remember I am link. Unsignificant link joining those ancestors whose bones repose on far distant hillsides with the ten children—it may now be eleven—in my house on Punchbowl Hill."

"A comforting creed," Barry Kirk commented.

"So, waiting the end, I do my duty as it rises. I tread the path that opens." He turned to Sir Frederic. "On one point, from my reading, I am curious. In your work at Scotland Yard, you follow only one clue. What you call the essential clue."

Sir Frederic nodded, "Such is usually our custom. When we fail, our critics ascribe it to that. They say, for example, that our obsession over the essential clue is the reason why we never solved the famous Ely Place murder."

They all sat up with interest. Bill Rankin beamed. Now things were getting somewhere. "I'm afraid we never heard of the Ely Place murder, Sir Frederic," he hinted.

"I sincerely wish I never had," the Englishman replied. "It was the first serious case that came to me when I took charge of the C. I. D. over sixteen years ago. I am chagrined to say I have never been able to fathom it."

He finished his salad, and pushed away the plate. "Since I have gone so far, I perceive I must go farther. Hilary Galt was the senior partner in the firm of Pennock and Galt, solicitors, with offices in Ely Place, Holborn. The business this firm carried on for more than a generation was unique of its kind. Troubled people in the highest ranks of society went to them for shrewd professional advice, and Mr. Hilary Galt and his father-in-law, Pennock, who died some twenty years ago, were entrusted with more numerous and romantic secrets than any other firm of solicitors in London. They knew the hidden history of every rascal in Europe, and they rescued many persons from the clutches of blackmailers. It was their boast that they never kept records of any sort."

Dessert was brought, and after this interruption, Sir Frederic continued.

"One foggy January night sixteen years ago, a caretaker entered Mr. Hilary Galt's private office, presumably deserted for the day. The gas lights were ablaze, the windows shut and locked; there was no sign of any disturbance. But on the floor lay Hilary Galt, with a bullet in his brain.

"There was just one clue, and over that we puzzled for many weary months at the Yard. Hilary Galt was a meticulous dresser, his attire was perfect, always. It was perfect on this occasion—with one striking exception. His highly polished boots—I presume you call them shoes over here—were removed and standing on a pile of papers on top of his desk. And on his feet he wore a pair of velvet slippers, embellished with a curious design.

"These, of course, seemed to the Yard the essential clue, and we set to work. We traced those slippers to the Chinese Legation in Portland Place. Mr. Galt had been of some trifling service to the Chinese minister, and early on the day of his murder the slippers had arrived as a gift from that gentleman. Galt had shown them to his office staff, and they were last seen wrapped loosely in their covering near his hat and stick. That was as far as we got.

"For sixteen years I have puzzled over those slippers. Why did Mr. Hilary Galt remove his boots, don the slippers, and prepare himself as though for some extraordinary adventure? I don't know to this day. The slippers still haunt me. When I resigned from the Yard, I rescued them from the Black Museum and took them with me as a souvenir of my first case—an unhappy souvenir of failure. I should like to show them to you, Miss Morrow."

"Thrilling," said the girl.

"Annoying," corrected Sir Frederic grimly.

Bill Rankin looked at Charlie Chan. "What's your reaction to that case, Sergeant?" he inquired.

Chan's eyes narrowed in thought. "Humbly begging pardon to inquire," he said, "have you the custom, Sir Frederic, to put yourself in place of murderer?"

"It's a good idea," the Englishman answered, "if you can do it. You mean——"

"A man who has killed—a very clever man—he knows that Scotland Yard has fiercely fixed idea about essential clue. His wits accompany him. He furnishes gladly one essential clue which has no meaning and leads no place at all."

Sir Frederic regarded him keenly. "Excellent," he remarked. "And it has one great virtue—from your point of view. It completely exonerates your countrymen at the Chinese Legation."

"It might do more than that," suggested Barry Kirk.

Sir Frederic thoughtfully ate his dessert. No one spoke for some moments. But Bill Rankin was eager for more material.

"A very interesting case, Sir Frederic," he remarked. "You must have a lot like it up your sleeve. Murders that ended more successfully for Scotland Yard——"

"Hundreds," nodded the detective. "But none that still holds its interest for me like the crime in Ely Place. As a matter of fact, I have never found murder so fascinating as some other things. The murder case came and went and, with a rare exception such as this I have mentioned, was quickly forgotten. But there is one mystery that to me has always been the most exciting in the world."

"And what is that?" asked Rankin, while they waited with deep interest.

"The mystery of the missing," Sir Frederic replied. "The man or woman who steps quietly out of the picture and is never seen again. Hilary Galt, dead in his office, presents a puzzle, of course; still, there is something to get hold of, something tangible, a body on the floor. But if Hilary Galt had disappeared into the fog that gloomy night, leaving no trace—that would have been another story.

"For years I have been enthralled by the stories of the missing," the detective went on. "Even when they were outside my province, I followed many of them. Often the solution was simple, or sordid, but that could never detract from the thrill of the ones that remained unsolved. And of all those unsolved cases, there is one that I have never ceased to think about. Sometimes in the night I wake up and ask myself—what happened to Eve Durand?"

"Eve Durand," repeated Rankin eagerly.

"That was her name. As a matter of fact, I had nothing to do with the case. It happened outside my bailiwick—very far outside. But I followed it with intense interest from the first. There are others, too, who have never forgotten—just before I left England I clipped from a British periodical a brief reference to the matter—I have it here." He removed a bit of paper from his purse. "Miss Morrow—will you be kind enough to read this aloud?"

The girl took the clipping. She began to read, in a low, clear voice:

> "A gay crowd of Anglo-Indians gathered one night fifteen years ago on a hill outside Peshawar to watch the moon rise over that isolated frontier town. Among the company were Captain Eric Durand and his wife, just out 'from home.' Eve Durand was young, pretty and well-born—a Miss Mannering, of Devonshire. Some one proposed a game of hide-and-seek before the ride back to Peshawar. The game was never finished. They are still looking for Eve Durand. Eventually all India was enlisted in the game. Jungle and bazaar, walled city and teak forest, were fine-combed for her. Through all the subterranean channels of that no-white-man's land of native life the search was carried by the famous secret service. After five years her husband retired to a life of seclusion in England, and Eve Durand became a legend—a horror tale to be told by ayahs to naughty children, along with the ghost stories of that north country."

The girl ceased reading, and looked at Sir Frederic, wide-eyed. There followed a moment of tense silence.

Bill Rankin broke the spell. "Some little game of hide-and-seek," he said.

"Can you wonder," asked Sir Frederic, "that for fifteen years the disappearance of Eve Durand, like Hilary Galt's slippers, has haunted me? A notably beautiful woman—a child, really—she was but eighteen that mysterious night at Peshawar. A blonde, blue-eyed, helpless child, lost in the dark of those dangerous hills. Where did she go? What became of her? Was she murdered? What happened to Eve Durand?"

"I'd rather like to know myself," remarked Barry Kirk softly.

"All India, as the clipping says, was enlisted in the game. By telegraph and by messenger, inquiries went forward. Her heart-broken, frantic husband was given leave, and at the risk of his life he scoured that wild country. The secret service did its utmost. Nothing happened. No word ever came back to Peshawar.

"It was like looking for a needle in a haystack, and in time, for most people, the game lost its thrill. The hue and cry died down. All save a few forgot.

"When I retired from the Yard and set out on this trip around the world, India was of course on my itinerary. Though it was far off my track, I resolved to visit Peshawar. I went down to Ripple Court in Devonshire and had a chat with Sir George Mannering, the uncle of Eve Durand. Poor man, he is old before his time. He gave me what information he could—it was pitifully meager. I promised I would try to take up the threads of this old mystery when I reached India."

"And you did?" Rankin inquired.

"I tried—but, my dear fellow, have you ever seen Peshawar? When I reached there the hopelessness of my quest struck me, as Mr. Chan might say, with an unbearable force. The Paris of the Panthans, they call it, and its filthy alleys teem with every race in the East. It isn't a city, it's a caravansary, and its population is constantly shifting. The English garrison is changed frequently, and I could find scarcely any one who was there in the time of Eve Durand.

"As I say, Peshawar appalled me. Anything could happen there. A wicked town—its sins are the sins of opium and hemp and jealousy and intrigue, of battle, murder and sudden death, of gambling and strange intoxications, the lust of revenge. Who can explain the deviltry that gets into men's blood in certain latitudes? I walked the Street of the Story Tellers and wondered in vain over the story of Eve Durand. What a place to bring a woman like that, delicately reared, young, inexperienced."

"You learned nothing?" inquired Barry Kirk.

"What could you expect?" Sir Frederic dropped a small lump of sugar into his coffee. "Fifteen years since that little picnic party rode back to Peshawar, back to the compound of the lonely garrison, leading behind them the riderless pony of Eve Durand. And fifteen years, I may tell you, make a very heavy curtain on India's frontier."

Again Bill Rankin turned to Charlie Chan. "What do you say, Sergeant?" he asked.

Chan considered. "The town named Peshawar stands with great proximity to the Khyber Pass, leading into wilds of Afghanistan," he said.

Sir Frederic nodded. "It does. But every foot of the pass is guarded night and day by British troops, and no European is permitted to leave by that route, save under very special conditions. No, Eve Durand could never have left India by way of the Khyber Pass. The thing would have been impossible. Grant the impossible, and she could not have lived a day among the wild hill men over the border."

Chan gravely regarded the man from Scotland Yard. "It is not to be amazed at," he said, "that you have felt such deep interest. Speaking humbly for myself, I desire with unlimited yearning to look behind that curtain of which you speak."

"That is the curse of our business, Sergeant," Sir Frederic replied. "No matter what our record of successes, there must always remain those curtains behind which we long with unlimited yearning to look—and never do."

Barry Kirk paid the check, and they rose from the table. In the lobby, during the course of the good-bys, the party broke up momentarily into two groups. Rankin, Kirk and the girl went to the door, and after a hurried expression of thanks, the reporter dashed out to the street.

"Mr. Kirk—it was wonderful," Miss Morrow said. "Why are all Englishmen so fascinating? Tell me that."

"Oh—are they?" He shrugged. "You tell me. You girls always fall for them, I notice."

"Well—they have an air about them. An atmosphere. They're not provincial, like a Rotarian who wants to tell you about the water-works. He took us traveling, didn't he? London and Peshawar—I could listen to him for hours. Sorry I have to run."

"Wait. You can do something for me."

"After what you've done for me," she smiled, "anything you ask."

"Good. This Chinese—Chan—he strikes me as a gentleman, and a mighty interesting one. I believe he would go big at my dinner to-night. I'd like to ask him, but that would throw my table out of gear. I need another woman. How about it? Will old man Blackstone let you off for the evening?"

"He might."

"Just a small party—my grandmother, and some people Sir Frederic has asked me to invite. And since you find Englishmen so fascinating, there'll be Colonel John Beetham, the famous Asiatic explorer. He's going to show us some movies he took in Tibet—which is the first intimation I've had that anything ever moved in Tibet."

"That will be splendid. I've seen Colonel Beetham's picture in the papers."

"I know—the women are all crazy about him, too. Even poor grandmother—she's thinking of putting up money for his next expedition to the Gobi Desert. You'll come then? Seven thirty."

"I'd love to—but it does seem presumptuous. After what you said about lawyers——"

"Yes—that was careless of me. I'll have to live it down. Give me a chance. My bungalow—you know where it is——"

She laughed. "Thanks. I'll come. Good-by—until tonight."

Meanwhile Sir Frederic Bruce had led Charlie Chan to a sofa in the lobby. "I was eager to meet you, Sergeant," he said, "for many reasons. Tell me, are you familiar with San Francisco's Chinatown?"

"I have slight acquaintance with same," Chan admitted. "My cousin, Chan Kee Lim, is an honored resident of Waverly Place."

"Have you, by any chance, heard of a Chinese down there—a stranger, a tourist—named Li Gung?"

"No doubt there are many so named. I do not know the one you bring up."

"This man is a guest of relatives on Jackson Street. You could do me a great service, Sergeant."

"It would remain," said Chan, "a golden item on the scroll of memory."

"Li Gung has certain information and I want it. I have tried to interview him myself, but naturally with no success."

"Light begins to dawn."

"If you could strike up an acquaintance with him—get into his confidence——"

"Humbly asking pardon, I do not spy on my own race with no good reason."

"The reasons in this case are excellent."

"Only a fool could doubt it. But what you hint would demand a considerable interval of time. My humble affairs have rightly no interest for you, so you have properly overlooked my situation. To-morrow at noon I hasten to my home."

"You could stay over a week. I would make it greatly worth your while."

A stubborn look came into the little eyes. "One path only is worth my while now. The path to my home on Punchbowl Hill."

"I mean I would pay——"

"Again asking pardon—I have food, I have clothes which cover even the vast area I possess. Beyond that, what is money?"

"Very good. It was only a suggestion."

"I am desolated by acute pain," replied Chan. "But I must refuse."

Barry Kirk joined them. "Mr. Chan, I'm going to ask you to do something for me," he began.

Chan sought to keep concern from his face, and succeeded. But what next, he wondered. "I am eagerly at attention," he said. "You are my host."

"I've just invited Miss Morrow to dinner to-night and I need another man. Will you come?"

"Your requests are high honors, which only an ungrate would refuse. But I am now already in your debt. More is going to embarrass me."

"Never mind that. I'll expect you at seven thirty—my bungalow on the Kirk Building."

"Splendid," said Sir Frederic. "We'll have another talk then, Sergeant. My requests are not precisely honors, but I may yet persuade you."

"The Chinese are funny people," remarked Chan. "They say no, no is what they mean. They say yes, and they are glued to same. With regard to dinner, I say yes, greatly pleased."

"Good," said Barry Kirk.

"Where's that reporter?" Sir Frederic asked.

"He hurried away," Kirk explained. "Anxious to get to his story, I imagine."

"What story?" asked the Englishman blankly.

"Why—the story of our luncheon. Your meeting with Sergeant Chan."

A startled expression crossed the detective's face. "Good lord—you don't mean he's going to put that into print?"

"Why naturally. I supposed you knew——"

"I'm afraid I'm woefully ignorant of American customs. I thought that was merely a social function. I didn't dream——"

"You mean you don't want him to print it?" asked Barry Kirk, surprised.

Sir Frederic turned quickly to Charlie. "Good-by, Sergeant. This has been a real pleasure. I shall see you to-night——"

He hastily shook hands with Chan, and dragged the dazed Barry Kirk to the street. There he motioned for a taxi. "What paper was that young scoundrel representing?" he inquired.

"The *Globe*," Kirk told him.

"The *Globe* office—and quickly, please," Sir Frederic ordered.

The two got in, and for a moment rode in silence.

"You are curious, perhaps," said Sir Frederic at last.

"I hope you won't think it's unnatural of me," smiled Kirk.

"I know I can rely on your discretion, my boy. I told only a small part of the story of Eve Durand at luncheon, but even that must not reach print just yet. Not here—not now——"

"Great Scott. Do you mean——"

"I mean I am near the end of a long trail. Eve Durand was not murdered in India. She ran away. I know why she ran away. I even suspect the peculiar method of her going. More than that——"

"Yes?" cried Kirk eagerly.

"More than that I can not tell you at present." The journey was continued in silence, and presently they drew up before the office of the *Globe*.

In the city editor's cubby-hole, Bill Rankin was talking exultantly to his chief. "It's going to be a corking good feature——" he was saying, when he felt a grip of steel on his arm. Turning, he looked into the face of Sir Frederic Bruce. "Why—why—hello," he stammered.

"There has been a slight mistake," said the detective.

"Let me explain," suggested Barry Kirk. He shook hands with the editor and introduced Sir Frederic, who merely nodded, not relaxing his grip on the reporter's paralyzed arm. "Rankin, this is unfortunate," Kirk continued, "but it can't be helped. Sir Frederic is unfamiliar with the ways of the American press, and he did not understand that you were gathering a story at lunch. He thought it a purely social affair. So we have come to ask that you print nothing of the conversation you heard this noon."

Rankin's face fell. "Not print it? Oh—I say——"

"We appeal to you both," added Kirk to the editor.

"My answer must depend on your reason for making the request," said that gentleman.

"My reason would be respected in England," Sir Frederic told him. "Here, I don't know your custom. But I may tell you that if you print any of that conversation, you will seriously impede the course of justice."

The editor bowed. "Very well. We shall print nothing without your permission, Sir Frederic," he said.

"Thank you," replied the detective, releasing Rankin's arm. "That concludes our business here, I fancy." And wheeling, he went out. Having added his own thanks, Kirk followed.

"Well, of all the rotten luck," cried Rankin, sinking into a chair.

Sir Frederic strode on across the city room. A cat may look at a king, and Egbert stood staring with interest at the former head of the C. I. D. Just in front of the door, the Englishman paused. It was either that or a collision with Egbert, moving slowly like a dark shadow across his path.

3

The Bungalow in the Sky

Barry Kirk stepped from his living-room through French windows leading into the tiny garden that graced his bungalow in the sky—"my front yard," he called it. He moved over to the rail and stood looking out on a view such as few front yards have ever offered. Twenty stories below lay the alternate glare and gloom of the city; far in the distance the lights of the ferry-boats plodded across the harbor like weary fireflies.

The stars were bright and clear and amazingly close above his head, but he heard the tolling of the fog bell over by Belvedere, and he knew that the sea mist was drifting in through the Gate. By midnight it would whirl and eddy about his lofty home, shutting him off from the world like a veil of filmy tulle. He loved the fog. Heavy with the scent of distant gardens, salt with the breath of the Pacific, it was the trade-mark of his town.

He went back inside, closing the window carefully behind him. For a moment he stood looking about his living-room, which wealth and good taste had combined to furnish charmingly. A huge, deep sofa, many comfortable chairs, a half-dozen floor lamps shedding their warm yellow glow, a brisk fire crackling on a wide hearth—no matter how loudly the wind rattled at the casements, here were comfort and good cheer.

Kirk went on into his dining-room. Paradise was lighting the candles on the big table. The flowers, the snowy linen, the old silver, made a perfect picture, forecasting a perfect dinner. Kirk inspected the ten place cards. He smiled.

"Everything seems to be O.K.," he said. "It's got to be to-night. Grandmother's coming, and you know what she thinks about a man who lives alone. To hear her tell it, every home needs a woman's touch."

"We shall disillusion her once again, sir," Paradise remarked.

"Such is my aim. Not that it will do any good. When she's made up her mind, that's that."

The door-bell rang, and Paradise moved off with slow, majestic step to answer it. Entering the living-room, Barry Kirk stood for a moment fascinated by the picture he saw there. The deputy district attorney had paused just inside the door leading from the hallway; she wore a simple, orange-colored dinner gown, her dark eyes were smiling.

"Miss Morrow," Kirk came forward eagerly. "If you don't mind my saying so, you don't look much like a lawyer to-night."

"I presume that's intended for a compliment," she answered. Chan appeared at her back. "Here's Mr. Chan. We rode up together in the elevator. Heavens—don't tell me we're the first."

"When I was a boy," smiled Kirk, "I always started in by eating the frosting off my cake. Which is just to tell you that with me, the best is always first. Good evening, Mr. Chan."

Chan bowed. "I am deeply touched by your kindness. One grand item is added to my mainland memories to-night." He wore a somewhat rusty dinner coat, but his linen gleamed and his manners shone.

Paradise followed with their wraps on his arm, and disappeared through a distant doorway. Another door opened. Sir Frederic Bruce stood on the threshold.

"Good evening, Miss Morrow," he said. "My word—you look charming. And Mr. Chan. This is luck—you're the first. You know I promised to show you a souvenir of my dark past."

He turned and reentered his room. Kirk led his guests over to the blazing fire.

"Sit down—do," he said. "People are always asking how I can endure the famous San Francisco zephyrs up here." He waved a hand toward the fireplace. "This is one of my answers."

Sir Frederic rejoined them, a distinguished figure in his evening clothes. He carried a pair of slippers. Their tops were of cut velvet, dark red like old Burgundy, and each bore as decoration a Chinese character surrounded by a design of pomegranate blossoms. He handed one to the girl, and the other to Charlie Chan.

"Beautiful," cried Miss Morrow. "And what a history! The essential clue."

"Not any too essential, as it turned out," shrugged the great detective.

"You know, I venture to presume, the meaning of the character inscribed on velvet?" Chan inquired.

"Yes," said Sir Frederic. "Not any too appropriate, in this case, I believe. I was told it signifies 'Long life and happiness.'"

"Precisely." Chan turned the slipper slowly in his hand. "There exist one hundred and one varieties of this character—one hundred for the people, one reserved for the Emperor. A charming gift. The footwear of a mandarin, fitting only for one high-placed and wealthy."

"Well, they were on Hilary Galt's feet when we found him, murdered on the floor," Sir Frederic said. " 'Walk softly, my best of friends'—that was what the Chinese minister wrote in the letter he sent with them. Hilary Galt was walking softly that night—but he never walked again." The Englishman took the slippers. "By the way—I hesitate to ask it—but I'd rather you didn't mention this matter to-night at dinner."

"Why, of course," remarked the girl, surprised.

"And that affair of Eve Durand. Ah—er—I fear I was a little indiscreet this noon. Now that I'm no longer at the Yard, I allow myself too much rope. You understand, Sergeant?"

Chan's little eyes were on him with a keenness that made Sir Frederic slightly uncomfortable. "Getting immodest for a minute," the Chinese said, "I am A 1 honor student in school of discretion."

"I'm sure of that," the great man smiled.

"No impulse to mention these matters would assail me, I am certain," Chan went on. "You bright man, Sir Frederic—you know Chinese are psychic people."

"Really?"

"Undubitably. Something has told me——"

"Ah yes—we needn't go into that," Sir Frederic put in hastily. "I have a moment's business in the offices below. If you will excuse me——"

He disappeared with the slippers into his room. Miss Morrow turned in amazement to Kirk.

"What in the world did he mean? Surely Eve Durand——"

"Mr. Chan is psychic," Kirk suggested. "Maybe he can explain it."

Chan grinned. "Sometimes psychic feelings lead positively nowhere," he remarked.

Paradise escorted two more guests through the outer hall into the living-room. A little, birdlike woman was on tiptoe, kissing Barry Kirk.

"Barry, you bad boy. I haven't seen you for ages. Don't tell me you've forgot your poor old grandmother."

"I couldn't do that," he laughed.

"Not while I have my health and strength," she returned. She came toward the fireplace. "How cozy you are——"

"Grandmother—this is Miss Morrow," Kirk said. "Mrs. Dawson Kirk."

The old lady took both the girl's hands. "My dear, I'm happy to know you——"

"Miss Morrow is a lawyer," Kirk added.

"Lawyer fiddlesticks," his grandmother cried. "She couldn't be—and look like this."

"Just what I said," nodded Kirk.

The old lady regarded the girl for a brief moment. "Youth and beauty," she remarked. "If I had those, my child, I wouldn't waste time over musty law books." She turned toward Chan. "And this is——"

"Sergeant Chan, of the Honolulu police," Kirk told her.

The old lady gave Charlie a surprisingly warm handclasp. "Know all about you," she said. "I like you very much."

"Flattered and overwhelmed," gasped Chan.

"Needn't be," she answered.

The woman who had accompanied Mrs. Kirk stood rather neglected in the background. Kirk hurried forward to present her. She was, it seemed, Mrs. Tupper-Brock, Mrs. Kirk's secretary and companion. Her manner was cold and distant. Chan gave her a penetrating look and then bowed low before her.

"Paradise will show you into one of the guest rooms," said Kirk to the women. "You'll find a pair of military brushes and every book on football Walter Camp ever wrote. If there's anything else you want, try and get it."

They followed the butler out. The bell rang, and going to the door himself, Kirk admitted another couple. Mr. Carrick Enderby, who was employed in the San Francisco office of Thomas Cook and Sons, was a big, slow, blond man with a monocle and nothing much behind it. All the family brilliance seemed to be monopolized by his wife, Eileen, a dark, dashing woman of thirty-five or so, who came in breezily. She joined the women, and the three men stood in the ill-at-ease silence that marks a dinner party in its initial stages.

"We're in for a bit of fog, I fancy," Enderby drawled.

"No doubt of it," Kirk answered.

When the women reappeared, Mrs. Dawson Kirk came at once to Chan's side.

"Sally Jordan of Honolulu is an old friend of mine," she told him. "A very good friend. We're both living beyond our time, and there's nothing cements friendship like that. I believe you were once—er—attached——"

Chan bowed. "One of the great honors of my poor life. I was her house-boy, and memories of her kindness will survive while life hangs out."

"Well, she told me how you repaid that kindness recently. A thousand-fold, she put it."

Chan shrugged. "My old employer has only one weakness. She exaggerates stupendously."

"Oh, don't be modest," said Mrs. Kirk. "Gone out of fashion, long ago. These young people will accuse you of something terrible if you try that tune. However, I like you for it."

A diversion at the door interrupted her. Colonel John Beetham entered the living-room. John Beetham the explorer, whose feet had stood in many dark and lonely places, who knew Tibet and Turkestan, Tsaidam and southern Mongolia. He had lived a year in a house-boat on the largest river in the heart of Asia, had survived two heart-breaking, death-strewn retreats across the snowy plateau of Tibet, had walked amid the ruins of ancient desert cities that had flourished long before Christ was born.

For once, here was a man who looked the part. Lean, tall, bronzed, there was a living flame in his gray eyes. But like Charlie Chan, he came of a modest race, and his manner was shy and aloof as he acknowledged the introductions.

"So glad," he muttered. "So glad." A mere formula.

Suddenly Sir Frederic Bruce was again in the room. He seized Colonel Beetham's hand.

"I met you several years ago," he said. "You wouldn't recall it. You were the lion of the hour, and I a humble spectator. I was present at the dinner of the Royal Geographical Society in London when they gave you that enormous gold doodad—the Founders' Medal—wasn't that it?"

"Ah yes—of course. To be sure," murmured Colonel Beetham.

His eyes bright as buttons in the subdued light, Charlie Chan watched Sir Frederic being presented to the ladies—to Mrs. Tupper-Brock and Eileen Enderby. Paradise arrived with something on a tray.

"All here except Miss Garland," Kirk announced. "We'll wait just a moment." The bell rang, and he motioned to his servant that he would go.

When Kirk returned, he was accompanied by a handsome woman whose face was flushed and who carried some burden in her jeweled hands. She hurried to a table, and deposited there a number of loose pearls.

"I had the most ridiculous accident on the stairs," she explained. "The string of my necklace broke, and I simply shed pearls right and left. I do hope I haven't lost any."

One of the pearls rolled to the floor, and Kirk retrieved it. The woman began counting them off into a gold mesh handbag. Finally she stopped.

"Got them all?" Barry Kirk inquired.

"I—I think so. I never can remember the number. And now—you really must forgive my silly entrance. It would be rather effective on the stage, I fancy, but I'm not on the stage now. In real life, I'm afraid it was rather rude."

Paradise took her cloak, and Kirk introduced her. Charlie Chan studied her long and carefully. She was no longer young, but her beauty was still triumphant. It would have to be, for her profession was the stage, and she was well-beloved in the Australian theaters.

At the table, Charlie found himself at Mrs. Kirk's right, with June Morrow on his other side. If he was a bit awed by the company in which he had landed, he gave no sign. He listened to several anecdotes of Sally Jordan's past from Mrs. Kirk, then turned to the girl beside him. Her eyes were shining.

"I'm thrilled to the depths," she whispered. "Sir Frederic and that marvelous Beetham man all in one evening—and you, too."

Chan smiled, "I am pretty lonely fly in this menagerie of lions," he admitted.

"Tell me—that about being psychic. You don't really think Sir Frederic has found Eve Durand?"

Chan shrugged. "For one word a man may be adjudged wise, and for one word he may be adjudged foolish."

"Oh, please don't be so Oriental. Just think—Eve Durand may be at this table to-night."

"Strange events permit themselves the luxury of occurring," Chan conceded. His eyes traveled slowly about the board, they rested on Mrs. Tupper-Brock, silent and aloof, on the vivacious Eileen Enderby, longest of all on the handsome Gloria Garland, now completely recovered from her excitement over the scattered pearls.

"Tell me, Sir Frederic," remarked Mrs. Kirk. "How are you making out here in Barry's womanless Eden?"

"Splendidly," smiled the detective. "Mr. Kirk has been very kind. I not only have the run of this charming bungalow, but he has also installed me in the offices below. He looked at Kirk. "Which reminds me—I'm afraid I quite forgot to close the safe downstairs."

"Paradise can attend to it," suggested Kirk.

"Oh, no," said Sir Frederic. "Please don't trouble. It doesn't matter—as far as I am concerned."

Carrick Enderby spoke in a loud, booming voice. "I say, Colonel Beetham. I've just read your book, you know."

"Ah, yes—er—which one?" inquired Beetham blandly.

"Don't be a fool, Carry," said Eileen Enderby rather warmly. "Colonel Beetham has written many books. And he's not going to be impressed by the fact that, knowing you were to meet him here to-night, you hastily ran through one of them."

"But it wasn't hastily," protested Enderby. "I gave it my best attention. The *Life*, I mean, you know. All your adventures—and by jove, they were thrilling. Of course, I can't understand you, sir. For me, the cheery old whisky and soda in the comfortable chair by the warm fire. But you—how you do yearn for the desolate places, my word."

Beetham smiled. "It's the white spots—the white spots on the map. They call to me. I—I long to walk there, where no man has walked before. It is an odd idea, isn't it?"

"Well, of course, getting home must be exciting," Enderby admitted. "The Kings and the Presidents pinning decorations on you, and the great dinners, and the eulogies——"

"Quite the most terrible part of it, I assure you," said Beetham.

"Nevertheless, I'd take it in preference to your jolly old deserts," continued Enderby. "That time you were lost on the—er—the——"

"The desert of Takla-makan," finished Beetham. "I was in a bit of a jam, wasn't I? But I wasn't lost, my dear fellow. I had simply embarked on the crossing with insufficient water and supplies."

Mrs. Kirk spoke. "I was enthralled by that entry you quoted from your diary. What you thought was the last entry you would ever make. I know it by heart. 'Halted on a high dune, where the camels fell exhausted. We examined the East through the fieldglasses; mountains of sand in all directions; not a straw, no life. All, men as well as camels, are extremely weak. God help us.' "

"But it wasn't my last entry, you know," Beetham reminded her. "The next night, in a dying condition, I crept along on my hands and knees until I reached a forest, the bed of a dry river—a pool. Water. I came out much better than I deserved."

"Pardon me if I make slight inquiry," said Charlie Chan. "What of old superstition, Colonel? Mention was made of it by Marco Polo six hundred fifty years ago. When a traveler is moving across desert by night, he hears strange voices calling his name. In bewitched state, he follows ghostly voices to his early doom."

"It is quite obvious," returned Beetham, "that I followed no voices. In fact, I heard none."

Eileen Enderby shuddered. "Well, I never could do it," she said. "I'm frightfully afraid of the dark. It drives me almost insane with fear."

Sir Frederic Bruce looked at her keenly. For the first time in some moments he spoke. "I fancy many women are like that," he said. He turned suddenly to Mrs. Kirk's companion. "What has been your experience, Mrs. Tupper-Brock?"

"I do not mind the dark," said that lady, in a cool, even tone.

"Miss Garland?" His piercing eyes turned on the actress.

She seemed a little embarrassed. "Why—I—really, I much prefer the spotlight. No, I can't say I fancy darkness."

"Nonsense," said Mrs. Dawson Kirk. "Things are the same in the dark as in the light. I never minded it."

Beetham spoke slowly. "Why not ask the gentlemen, Sir Frederic? Fear of the dark is not alone a woman's weakness. Were you to ask me, I should have to make a confession."

Sir Frederic turned on him in amazement. "You, Colonel?"

Beetham nodded. "When I was a little shaver, my life was made miserable by my horror of the dark. Every evening when I was left alone in my room, I died a thousand deaths."

"By jove," cried Enderby. "And yet you grew up to spend your life in the dark places of the world."

"You conquered that early fear, no doubt?" Sir Frederic suggested.

Beetham shrugged. "Does one ever quite conquer a thing like that? But really—there is too much about me. Mr. Kirk has asked me to let you see, after dinner, some pictures I took last year in Tibet. I fear I shall bore you by becoming, as you Americans say, the whole show."

Again they chatted by two and two. Miss Morrow leaned over to Chan.

"Imagine," she said, "that picture of the great explorer, as a little boy, frightened of the dark. It's quite the most charming and human thing I ever heard."

He nodded gravely, his eyes on Eileen Enderby. "The dark drives me almost insane with fear," she had said. How dark it must have been that night in the hills outside Peshawar.

After he had served coffee in the living-room, Paradise appeared with a white, glittering screen which, under the Colonel's direction, he stood on a low table against a Flemish tapestry. Barry Kirk helped Beetham carry in from the hallway a heavy motion-picture projector and several boxes of films.

"Lucky we didn't overlook this," the young man laughed. "A rather embarrassing thing for you if you had to go home without being invited to perform. Like the man who tried to slip away from an evening party with a harp that he hadn't been asked to play."

The machine was finally ready, and the company took their places in comfortable chairs facing the screen.

"We shall want, of course, complete darkness," Beetham said. "Mr. Kirk, if you will be so kind——"

"Surely." Barry Kirk turned off the lights, and drew thick curtains over doors and windows. "Is it all right now?"

"The light in the hallway," Beetham suggested.

Kirk also extinguished that. There was a moment of tense silence.

"Heavens—this is creepy," spoke Eileen Enderby out of the blackness. There was a slight note of hysteria in her voice.

Beetham was placing a roll of film in the machine. "On the expedition I am about to describe," he began, "we sat out from Darjeeling. As you no doubt know, Darjeeling is a little hill station on the extreme northern frontier of India——"

Sir Frederic interrupted. "You have been in India a great deal, Colonel?"

"Frequently—between journeys——"

"Ah yes—pardon me for breaking in——"

"Not at all." The film began to unwind. "These first pictures are of Darjeeling, where I engaged my men, rounded up supplies, and——" The Colonel was off on his interesting but rather lengthy story.

Time passed, and his voice droned on in the intense darkness. The air was thick with the smoke of cigarettes; now and then there was the stir of some one moving, walking about in the rear, occasionally a curtain parted at a window. But Colonel Beetham gave no heed. He was living again on the high plateau of Tibet; the old fervor to go on had returned; he trekked through snowy passes, leaving men and mules dead in the wasteland, fighting like a fanatic on toward his goal.

A weird feeling of oppression settled down over Charlie Chan, a feeling he attributed to the thick atmosphere of the room. He rose and dodged guiltily out into the roof-top garden. Barry Kirk was standing there, a dim figure in the mist, smoking a cigarette. For it was misty now, the fog bell was tolling its warning, and the roof was wrapped in clouds.

"Hello," said Kirk, in a low voice. "Want a bit of air, too, eh? I hope he's not boring my poor guests to death. Exploring's a big business now, and he's trying to persuade grandmother to put up a lot of money for a little picnic he's planning. An interesting man, isn't he?"

"Most interesting," Chan admitted.

"But a hard one," added Kirk. "He leaves the dead behind with never so much as a look over his shoulder. I suppose that's the scientific type of mind—what's a few dead men when you're wiping out one of those white spots on the map? However, it's not my style. That's my silly American sentimentality."

"It is undubitably the style of Colonel Beetham," Chan returned. "I read same in his eyes."

He went back into the big living-room, and walked about in the rear. A slight sound in the hallway interested him, and he went out there. A man had just entered by the door that led to the floor below. Before he closed it the light outside fell on the blond hair of Carrick Enderby.

"Just having a cigarette on the stairs," he explained in a hoarse whisper. "Didn't want to add any more smoke to the air in there. A bit thick, what?"

He stole back into the living-room, and Chan, following, found a chair. A clatter of dishes sounded from the distant pantry, competing with the noise of the unwinding film and the steady stream of Beetham's story. The tireless man was starting on a new reel.

"Voice is getting a bit weary," the Colonel admitted. "I'll just run this one off without comment. It requires none." He fell back from the dim light by the machine, into the shadows.

In ten minutes the reel had unwound its length, and the indomitable Beetham was on hand. He was preparing to start on what he announced as the final reel, when the curtains over one of the French windows parted suddenly, and the white figure of a woman came into the room. She stood there like a wraith in the misty light at her back.

"Oh, stop it!" she cried. "Stop it and turn up the lights. Quickly! Quickly—please!" There was a real hysteria in Eileen Enderby's voice now.

Barry Kirk leaped to the light switch, and flooded the room. Mrs. Enderby stood, pale and swaying slightly, clutching at her throat. "What is it?" Kirk asked. "What's the trouble?"

"A man," she panted. "I couldn't stand the dark—it was driving me mad—I stepped out into the garden. I was standing close to the railing when I saw a man leap from a lighted window on the floor below, out on to the fire-escape. He ran down it into the fog."

"My offices are below," Kirk said quietly. "We had better look into this. Sir Frederic——" His eyes turned from one to the other. "Why—where is Sir Frederic?" he asked.

Paradise had entered from the pantry. "I beg your pardon, sir," he said. "Sir Frederic went down to the offices some ten minutes ago."

"Down to the offices? Why?"

"The burglar alarm by your bed was buzzing, sir. The one connected up down-stairs. Just as I discovered it, Sir Frederic entered your room. 'I will investigate this, Paradise,' he said. 'Don't disturb the others.' "

Kirk turned to Charlie Chan. "Sergeant, will you come with me, please?"

Silently Charlie followed him to the stairs, and together they went below. The offices were ablaze with light. The rear room, into which the stairs led, was quite empty. They advanced into the middle room.

A window was open as far as it would go, and in the mist outside Chan noted the iron gratings of a fire-escape. This room too seemed empty. But beyond the desk Barry Kirk, in advance, gave a little cry and dropped to his knees.

Chan stepped around the desk. He was not surprised by what he saw, but he was genuinely sorry. Sir Frederic Bruce lay on the floor, shot cleanly through the heart. By his side lay a thin little volume, bound in bright yellow cloth.

Kirk stood up, dazed. "In my office," he said slowly, as though that were important. "It's—it's horrible. Good God—look!"

He pointed to Sir Frederic. On the detective's feet were black silk stockings—and nothing else. He wore no shoes.

Paradise had followed. He stood for a moment staring at the dead man on the floor, and then turned to Barry Kirk.

"When Sir Frederic came down-stairs," he said, "he was wearing a pair of velvet slippers. Sort of heathen-looking slippers they were, sir."

4

The Reckoning of Heaven

Barry Kirk stood looking about his office; he found it difficult to believe that into this common-place, familiar room, tragedy had found its way. Yet there was that silent figure on the floor, a few moments before so full of life and energy.

"Poor Sir Frederic," he said. "Only to-day he told me he was near the end of a long trail. Nearer than he dreamed, it appears." He stopped. "A long trail, Sergeant,—only a few of us know how far back into the past this thing must reach."

Chan nodded. He had been consulting a huge gold watch; now he snapped shut the case and restored it to his pocket. "Death is the reckoning of heaven," he remarked. "On this occasion, a most complicated reckoning."

"Well, what shall we do?" Kirk asked helplessly. "The police, I suppose. But good lord—this is a case beyond any policeman I ever met. Any uniformed man, I mean." He paused, and a grim smile flashed across his face. "It looks very much to me, Mr. Chan, as though you would have to take charge and——"

A stubborn light leaped into the little black eyes. "Miss Morrow is above," said Chan. "What a happy chance, since she is from the district attorney's office. If I may humbly suggest——"

"Oh, I never thought of that." Kirk turned to his servant. "Paradise, ask Miss Morrow to come here. Make my excuses to my guests, and ask them to wait."

"Very good, sir," replied Paradise, and departed.

Kirk walked slowly about the room. The drawers of the big desk were open and their contents jumbled. "Somebody's been on a frantic search here," he said. He paused before the safe; its door was slightly ajar.

"Safe stands open," suggested Chan.

"Odd about that," said Kirk. "This afternoon Sir Frederic asked me to take out anything of value and move it up-stairs. I did so. He didn't explain."

"Of course," nodded Chan. "And at the dinner table he makes uncalled-for reference to fact that he has not locked safe. The matter struck me at the time. One thing becomes clear—Sir Frederic desired to set a trap. A safe unlocked to tempt marauders." He nodded to the small volume that lay at the dead man's side. "We must disturb nothing. Do not touch, but kindly regard book and tell me where last reposing."

Kirk leaned over. "That? Why, it's the year-book of the Cosmopolitan Club. It was usually in that revolving case on which the telephone stands. It can't mean anything."

"Maybe not. Maybe"—Chan's little eyes narrowed—"a hint from beyond the unknown."

"I wonder," mused Kirk.

"Sir Frederic was guest of Cosmopolitan Club?"

"Yes—I gave him a two weeks' card. He wrote a lot of his letters there. But—but—I can't see——"

"He was clever man. Even in moment of passing, his dying hand would seek to leave behind essential clue."

"Speaking of that," said Kirk, "how about those velvet slippers? Where are they?"

Chan shrugged. "Slippers were essential clue in one case, long ago. What did they lead to? Positively nothing. If I am suiting my own taste, this time I look elsewhere."

Miss Morrow entered the room. Her face was usually full of color—an authentic color that is the gift of the fog to San Francisco's daughters. Now it was deathly pale. Without speaking, she stepped beyond the desk and looked down. For a moment she swayed, and Barry Kirk leaped forward.

"No, no," cried the girl.

"But I thought——" he began.

"You thought I was going to faint. Absurd. This is my work—it has come to me and I shall do it. You believe I can't——"

"Not at all," protested Kirk.

"Oh, yes you do. Everybody will. I'll show them. You've called the police, of course."

"Not yet," Kirk answered.

She sat down resolutely at the desk, and took up the telephone. "Davenport 20," she said. "The Hall of Justice? . . . Captain Flannery, please . . . Hello—Captain? Miss Morrow of the district attorney's office speaking. There has been a murder in Mr. Kirk's office on the top floor of the Kirk Building. You had better come yourself. . . . Thank you. . . . Yes—I'll attend to that."

She got up, and, going round the desk, bent over Sir Frederic. She noted the book, and her eyes strayed wonderingly to the stocking feet. Inquiringly she turned to Chan.

"The slippers of Hilary Galt," he nodded. "Souvenir of that unhappy case, they adorned his feet when he came down. Here is Paradise—he will explain to you."

The butler had returned, and Miss Morrow faced him. "Tell us what you know, please," she said.

"I was busy in the pantry," Paradise said. "I thought I heard the buzz of the burglar alarm by Mr. Kirk's bed—the one connected with the windows and safe in this room. I hastened to make sure, but Sir Frederic was just behind. It was almost as though he had been expecting it. I don't know how I got that impression— I'm odd that way——"

"Go on," said the girl. "Sir Frederic followed you into Mr. Kirk's room?"

"Yes, Miss. 'There's some one below, sir,' I said. 'Some one who doesn't belong there.' Sir Frederic looked back into the pitch dark living-room. 'I fancy so, Paradise,' he said. He was smiling. 'I will attend to it. No need to disturb Mr. Kirk or his guests.' I followed him into his room. He tossed off his patent leather pumps. 'The stairs are a bit soiled, I fear, sir,' I reminded him. He laughed. 'Ah, yes,' he said. 'But I have the very thing.' The velvet slippers were lying near his bed. He put them on. 'I shall walk softly in these, Paradise,' he told me. At the head of the stairs, I stopped him. A sort of fear was in my heart— I am given to that—to have premonitions——"

"You stopped him," Kirk cut in.

"I did, sir. Respectfully, of course. 'Are you armed, Sir Frederic?' I made bold to inquire. He shook his head. 'No need, Paradise,' he answered. 'I fancy our visitor is of the weaker sex.' And then he went down, sir—to his death."

They were silent for a moment, pondering the servant's story.

"We had better go," said the girl, "and tell the others. Some one must stay here. If it's not asking too much, Mr. Chan——"

"I am torn with grief to disagree," Chan answered. "Please pardon me. But for myself, I have keen eagerness to note how this news is taken in the room above."

"Ah, yes. Naturally."

"I shall be glad to stay, Miss," Paradise said.

"Very well," the girl answered. "Please let me know as soon as Captain Flannery arrives." She led the way above, and Kirk and the little detective from Honolulu followed.

Barry Kirk's guests were seated, silent and expectant, in the now brightly lighted living-room. They looked up inquiringly as the three from below entered. Kirk faced them, at a loss how to begin.

"I have dreadful news for you," he said. "An accident—a terrible accident." Chan's eyes moved rapidly about the group and, making their choice, rested finally on the white, drawn face of Eileen Enderby. "Sir Frederic Bruce has been murdered in my office," Kirk finished.

There was a moment's breathless silence, and then Mrs. Enderby got to her feet. "It's the dark," she cried in a harsh, shrill voice. "I knew it. I knew something would happen when the lights were turned off. I knew it, I tell you——"

Her husband stepped to her side to quiet her, and Chan stood staring not at her, but at Colonel John Beetham. For one brief instant he thought the mask had dropped from those weary, disillusioned eyes. For one instant only.

They all began to speak at once. Gradually Miss Morrow made herself heard above the din. "We must take this coolly," she said, and Barry Kirk admired her composure. "Naturally, we are all under suspicion. We——"

"What? I like that!" Mrs. Dawson Kirk was speaking. "Under suspicion, indeed——"

"The room was in complete darkness," Miss Morrow went on. "There was considerable moving about. I don't like to stress my official position here, but perhaps you would prefer my methods to those of a police captain. How many of you left this room during the showing of Colonel Beetham's pictures?"

An embarrassed silence fell. Mrs. Kirk broke it. "I thought the pictures intensely interesting," she said. "True, I did step into the kitchen for a moment——"

"Just to keep an eye on my domestic arrangements," suggested Barry Kirk.

"Nothing of the sort. My throat was dry. I wanted a glass of water."

"You saw nothing wrong?" inquired Miss Morrow.

"Aside from the very wasteful methods that seemed to be in vogue in the kitchen—nothing," replied Mrs. Kirk firmly.

"Mrs. Tupper-Brock?" said Miss Morrow.

"I was on the sofa with Miss Garland," replied that lady. "Neither of us moved from there at any time." Her voice was cool and steady.

"That's quite true," the actress added.

Another silence. Kirk spoke up. "I'm sure none of us intended a discourtesy to the Colonel," he said. "The entertainment he gave us was delightful, and it was gracious of him to honor us. I myself—er—I was in the room constantly—except for one brief moment in the garden. I saw no one there—save——"

Chan stepped forward. "Speaking for myself, I found huge delight in the pictures. A moment I wish to be alone, in order that I may digest great events flashed before me on silvery screen. So I also invade the garden, and meet Mr. Kirk. For a time we marvel at the distinguished Colonel

Beetham—his indomitable courage, his deep resource, his service to humanity. Then we rush back, that we may miss no more." He paused. "Before I again recline in sitting posture, noise in hallway offend me. I hurry out there in shushing mood, and behold——"

"Ah—er—the pictures were marvelous," said Carrick Enderby. "I enjoyed them immensely. True enough, I stepped out on the stairs for a cigarette——"

"Carry, you fool," his wife cried. "You would do that."

"But I say—why not? I saw nothing. There was nothing to see. The floor below was quite deserted." He turned to Miss Morrow. "Whoever did this horrible thing left by way of the fire-escape. You've already learned that——"

"Ah, yes," cut in Chan. "We have learned it indeed—from your wife." He glanced at Miss Morrow and their eyes met.

"From my wife—yes," repeated Enderby. "Look here—what do you mean by that? I——"

"No matter," put in Miss Morrow. "Colonel Beetham—you were occupied at the picture machine. Except for one interval of about ten minutes, when you allowed it to run itself."

"Ah, yes," said the Colonel evenly. "I did not leave the room, Miss Morrow."

Eileen Enderby rose. "Mr. Kirk—we really must be going. Your dinner was charming—how terrible to have it end in such a tragic way. I——"

"Just a moment," said June Morrow. "I can not let you go until the captain of police releases you."

"What's that?" the woman cried. "Outrageous. You mean we are prisoners here——"

"Oh—but, Eileen——" protested her husband.

"I'm very sorry," said the girl. "I shall protect you as much as possible from the annoyance of further questioning. But you really must wait."

Mrs. Enderby flung angrily away, and a filmy scarf she was wearing dropped from one shoulder and trailed after her. Chan reached out to rescue it. The woman took another step, and he stood with the scarf in his hand. She swung about. The detective's little eyes, she noticed, were fixed with keen interest on the front of her pale blue gown, and following his gaze, she looked down.

"So sorry," said Chan. "So very sorry. I trust your beautiful garment is not a complete ruin."

"Give me that scarf," she cried, and snatched it rudely from him.

Paradise appeared in the doorway. "Miss Morrow, please," he said. "Captain Flannery is below."

"You will kindly wait here," said the girl. "All of you. I shall arrange for your release at the earliest possible moment."

With Kirk and Charlie Chan, she returned to the twentieth floor. In the central room they found Captain Flannery, a gray-haired, energetic policeman of about fifty. With him were two patrolmen and a police doctor.

"Hello, Miss Morrow," said the Captain. "This is a he—I mean, a terrible thing. Sir Frederic Bruce of Scotland Yard—we're up against it now. If we don't make good quick we'll have the whole Yard on our necks."

"I'm afraid we shall," admitted Miss Morrow. "Captain Flannery—this is Mr. Kirk. And this—Detective-Sergeant Charlie Chan, of Honolulu."

The Captain looked his fellow detective over slowly. "How are you, Sergeant? I've been reading about you in the paper. You got on this job mighty quick."

Chan shrugged. "Not my job, thank you," he replied. "All yours, and very welcome. I am here in society role, as guest of kind Mr. Kirk."

"Is that so?" The Captain appeared relieved. "Now, Miss Morrow, what have you found out?"

"Very little. Mr. Kirk was giving a dinner up-stairs." She ran over the list of the guests, the showing of the pictures in the dark, and the butler's story of Sir Frederic's descent to the floor below, wearing the velvet slippers. "There are other aspects of the affair that I will take up with you later," she added.

"All right. I guess the D. A. will want to get busy on this himself."

The girl flushed. "Perhaps. He is out of town tonight. I hope he will leave the matter in my hands——"

"Great Scott, Miss Morrow—this is important," said the Captain, oblivious of his rudeness. "You're holding those people up-stairs?"

"Naturally."

"Good. I'll look 'em over later. I ordered the night-watchman to lock the front door and bring everybody in the building here. Now, we better fix the time of this. How long's he been dead, Doctor?"

"Not more than half an hour," replied the doctor.

"Humbly begging pardon to intrude," said Chan. "The homicide occurred presumably at ten twenty."

"Sure of that?"

"I have not the habit of light speaking. At ten twenty-five we find body, just five minutes after lady on floor above rush in with news of man escaping from this room by fire-escape."

"Huh. The room seems to have been searched." Flannery turned to Barry Kirk. "Anything missing?"

"I haven't had time to investigate," said Kirk. "If anything has been taken, I fancy it was Sir Frederic's property."

"This is your office, isn't it?"

"Yes. But I had made room here for Sir Frederic. He had various papers and that sort of thing."

"Papers? What was he doing? I thought he'd retired."

"It seems he was still interested in certain cases, Captain," Miss Morrow said. "That is one of the points I shall take up with you later."

"Again interfering with regret," remarked Chan, "if we do not know what was taken, all same we know what was hunted."

"You don't say." Flannery looked at Chan coldly. "What was that?"

"Sir Frederic English detective, and great one. All English detectives make exhausting records of every case. No question that records of certain case, in which murderer was hotly interested, were sought here."

"Maybe," admitted the Captain. "We'll go over the room later." He turned to the patrolmen. "You boys take a look at the fire-escape." They climbed out into the fog. At that moment the door leading from the reception-room into the hallway opened, and an odd little group came in. A stout, middle-aged man led the procession; he was Mr. Cuttle, the night-watch-man.

"Here they are, Captain," he said. "I've rounded up everybody in the building, except a few cleaning women who have nothing to do with this floor. You can see 'em later, if you like. This is Mrs. Dyke, who takes care of the two top floors."

Mrs. Dyke, very frightened, said that she had finished with Kirk's office at seven and gone out, leaving the burglar alarm in working order, as was her custom. She had not been back since. She had seen no one about the building whom she did not recognize.

"And who is this?" inquired the Captain, turning to a pale, sandy-haired young man who appeared extremely nervous.

"I am employed by Brace and Davis, Certified Public Accountants, on the second floor," said the young man. "My name is Samuel Smith. I was working to-night to catch up—I have been ill—when Mr. Cuttle informed me I was wanted up here. I know nothing of this horrible affair."

Flannery turned to the fourth and last member of the party, a young woman whose uniform marked her as an operator of one of the elevators. "What's your name?" he asked.

"Grace Lane, sir," she told him.

"Run the elevator, eh?"

"Yes, sir. Mr. Kirk had sent word that one of us must work overtime to-night. On account of the party."

"How many people have you brought up since the close of business?"

"I didn't keep count. Quite a few—ladies and gentlemen—Mr. Kirk's guests, of course."

"Don't remember anybody who looked like an outsider?"

"No, sir."

"This is a big building," said Flannery. "There must have been others working here to-night besides this fellow Smith. Remember anybody?"

The girl hesitated. "There—there was one other, sir."

"Yes? Who was that?"

"A girl who is employed in the office of the Calcutta Importers, on this floor. Her name is Miss Lila Barr."

"Working here to-night, eh? On this floor. She's not here now?"

"No, sir. She left some time ago."

"How long ago?"

"I can't say exactly, sir. Half an hour—perhaps a little more than that."

"Humph." The Captain took down their names and addresses, and dismissed them. As they went out, the two patrolmen entered from the fire-escape, and, leaving them in charge, Flannery asked to be directed up-stairs.

The dinner guests were sitting with rather weary patience in a semicircle in the living-room. Into their midst strode the Captain, with an air of confidence he was far from feeling. He stood looking them over.

"I guess you know what I'm doing here," he said. "Miss Morrow tells me she's had a talk with you, and I won't double back over her tracks. However, I want the name and address of every one of you." He turned to Mrs. Kirk. "I'll start with you."

She stiffened at his tone. "You're very flattering, I'm sure. I'm Mrs. Dawson Kirk." She added her address. Flannery turned to the explorer.

"Colonel John Beetham. I am a visitor in the city, stopping at the Fairmont."

Flannery went on down the list. When he had finished, he added:

"Any one got any light to throw on this affair? If you have, better give it to me now. Things'll be a lot pleasanter all round than if I dig it up for myself later." No one spoke. "Some lady saw a man running down the fire escape," he prompted.

"Oh—I did," said Eileen Enderby. "I've been all over that with Miss Morrow. I had gone out into the garden——" Again she related her experience.

"What'd this man look like?" demanded Flannery.

"I couldn't say. A very dim figure in the fog."

"All right. You can all go now. I may want to see some of you later."

Flannery strode past them into the garden.

One by one they said their strained farewells and departed—Mrs. Kirk and her companion, Miss Gloria Garland, then the Enderbys, and finally the explorer. Charlie Chan also got his hat and coat, while Miss Morrow watched him inquiringly.

"Until dark deed shaded the feast," said Chan, "the evening was an unquestioned joy. Mr. Kirk——"

"Oh, but you're not leaving," cried Miss Morrow. "Please. I want to have a talk with you."

"To-morrow I am sea-going man," Chan reminded her. "The experience weakens me considerably. I have need of sleep, and relaxing——"

"I'll keep you only a moment," she pleaded, and Chan nodded.

Captain Flannery appeared from the garden. "Dark out there," he announced. "But if I'm not mistaken, any one could have reached the floor below by way of the fire-escape. Is that right?"

"Undoubtedly," replied Kirk.

"An important discovery," approved Chan. "On the gown of one of the lady guests were iron rust stains, which might have been suffered by—— But who am I to speak thus to keen man like the Captain? You made note of the fact, of course?"

Flannery reddened. "I—I can't say I did. Which lady?"

"That Mrs. Enderby, who witnessed fleeing man. Do not mention it, sir. So happy to be of slightest service."

"Let's go back down-stairs," growled Flannery. On the floor below, he stood for a long moment, looking about. "Well, I got to get busy here."

"I will say farewell," remarked Chan.

"Going, eh?" said Flannery, with marked enthusiasm.

"Going far," smiled Chan. "To-morrow I am directed toward Honolulu. I leave you to the largest problem of your life, Captain. I suffer no envy for you."

"Oh, I'll pull through," replied Flannery.

"Only the witless could doubt it. But you will travel a long road. Consider. Who is great man silent now on couch? A famous detective with a glorious record. The meaning of that? A thousand victories—and a thousand enemies. All over broad world are scattered men who would do him into death with happy hearts. A long road for you, Captain. You have my warmest wishes for bright outcome. May you emerge in the shining garments of success."

"Thanks," said Flannery.

"One last point. You will pardon me if I put in final oar." He took up from the table a little yellow book, and held it out. "Same was at the dead man's elbow when he fell."

Flannery nodded. "I know. The Cosmopolitan Club book. It can't mean a damn thing."

"Maybe. I am stupid Chinese from tiny island. I know nothing. But if this was my case I would think about book, Captain Flannery. I would arouse in the night to think about it. Good-by, and all good wishes already mentioned."

He made a deep bow, and went through the reception-room into the hall. Kirk and the girl followed swiftly. The latter put her hand on Chan's arm.

"Sergeant—you mustn't," she cried despairingly. "You can't desert me now. I need you."

"You rip my heart to fragments," he replied. "However, plans are set."

"But poor Captain Flannery—all this is far beyond him. You know more about the case than he does. Stay, and I'll see that you're given every facility——"

"That's what I say," put in Barry Kirk. "Surely you can't go now. Good lord, man, have you no curiosity?"

"The bluest hills are those farthest away," Chan said. "Bluest of all is Punchbowl Hill, where my little family is gathered, waiting for me——"

"But I was depending on you," pleaded the girl. "I must succeed—I simply must. If you would stay——"

Chan drew away from her. "I am so sorry. Postman on his holiday, they tell me, takes long walk. I have taken same, and I am weary. So very sorry—but I return to Honolulu to-morrow." The elevator door was open. Chan bowed low. "The happiest pleasure to know you both. May we meet again. Good-by."

Like a grim, relentless Buddha he disappeared below. Kirk and the girl reentered the office, where Captain Flannery was eagerly on the hunt.

Chan walked briskly through the fog to the Stewart Hotel. At the desk the clerk handed him a cable, which he read with beaming face. He was still smiling when, in his room, the telephone rang. It was Kirk.

"Look here," Kirk said. "We made the most astonishing discovery in the office after you left."

"Pleased to hear it," Chan replied.

"Under the desk—a pearl from Gloria Garland's necklace!"

"Opening up," said Chan, "a new field of wonderment. Hearty congratulations."

"But see here," Kirk cried, "aren't you interested? Won't you stay and help us get at the bottom of this?"

Again that stubborn look in Charlie's eyes. "Not possible. Only a few minutes back I have a cable that calls me home with unbearable force. Nothing holds me on the mainland now."

"A cable? From whom?"

"From my wife. Glorious news. We are now in receipt of our eleventh child—a boy."

5

The Voice in the Next Room

Charlie Chan rose at eight the next morning, and as he scraped the stubble of black beard from his cheeks, he grinned happily at his reflection in the glass. He was thinking of the small, helpless boy-child who no doubt at this moment lay in the battered old crib on Punchbowl Hill. In a few days, the detective promised himself, he would stand beside that crib, and the latest Chan would look up to see, at last, his father's welcoming smile.

He watched a beetle-browed porter wheel his inexpensive little trunk off on the first leg of its journey to the Matson docks, and then neatly placed his toilet articles in his suitcase. With jaunty step he went down to breakfast.

The first page of the morning paper carried the tragic tale of Sir Frederic's passing, and for a moment Chan's eyes narrowed. A complicated mystery, to be sure. Interesting to go to the bottom of it—but that was the difficult task of others. Had it been his duty, he would have approached it gallantly, but, from his point of view, the thing did not concern him. Home—that alone concerned him now.

He laid the paper down, and his thoughts flew back to the little boy in Honolulu. An American citizen, a future boy scout under the American flag, he should have an American name. Chan had felt himself greatly attracted to his genial host of the night before. Barry Chan—what was the matter with that?

As he was finishing his tea, he saw in the dining-room door the thing, nervous figure of Bill Rankin, the reporter. He signed his check, left a generous tip, and joined Rankin in the lobby.

"Hello," said the reporter. "Well, that was some little affair up at the Kirk Building last night."

"Most distressing," Chan replied. They sat down on a broad sofa, and Rankin lighted a cigarette.

"I've got a bit of information I believe you should have," the newspaper man continued.

"Begging pardon, I think you labor under natural delusion," Chan said.

"Why—what do you mean?"

"I am not concerned with case," Chan calmly informed him.

"You don't mean to say——"

"In three hours I exit through Golden Gate."

Rankin gasped. "Good lord. I knew you'd planned to go, of course, but I supposed—— Why, man alive, this is the biggest thing that's broke round here since the fire. Sir Frederic Bruce—its' an international catastrophe. I should think you'd leap at it."

"I am not," smiled Charlie, "a leaping kind of man. Personal affairs call me to Hawaii. The postman refuses to take another walk. Very interesting case, but as I have heard my slanging cousin Willie say, I am not taking any of it."

"I know," said Rankin. "The calm, cool Oriental. Never been excited in your life, I suppose?"

"What could I have gained by that? I have watched the American citizen. His temples throb. His heart pounds. The fibers of his body vibrate. With what result? A year subtracted from his life."

"Well, you're beyond me," said Rankin, leaning back and seeking to relax a bit himself. "I hope I won't be boring you if I go on talking about Sir Frederic. I've been all over our luncheon at the St. Francis in my mind, and do you know what I think?"

"I should be pleased to learn," returned Chan.

"Fifteen years make a very heavy curtain on the Indian frontier, Sir Frederic said. If you ask me, I'd say that in order to solve the mystery of his murder last night, we must look behind that curtain."

"Easy said, but hard to do," suggested Chan.

"Very hard, and that's why you—— Oh, well, go on and take your boat ride. But the disappearance of Eve Durand is mixed up in this somehow. So, perhaps, is the murder of Hilary Galt."

"You have reason for thinking this?"

"I certainly have. Just as I was about to sit down and write a nice feature story about that luncheon, Sir Frederic rushed into the *Globe* office and demanded I hush it all up. Why should he do that? I ask you."

"And I pause for your reply."

"You'll get it. Sir Frederic was still working on one, or maybe both, of those cases. More than that, he was getting somewhere. That visit to Peshawar may not have been as lacking in results as he made out. Eve Durand may be in San Francisco now. Some one connected with one of those cases is certainly here—some one who pulled that trigger last night. For myself, I would *cherchez la femme.* That's French——"

"I know," nodded Chan. "You would hunt the woman. Excellent plan. So would I."

"Aha—I knew it. And that's why this information I have is vital. The other night I went up to the Kirk Building to see Sir Frederic. Paradise told me he was in the office. Just as I was approaching the office door, it opened, and a young woman——"

"One moment," Chan cut in. "Begging pardon to interrupt, you should go at once with your story to Miss June Morrow. I am not connected."

Rankin stood up. "All right. But you're certainly beyond me. The man of stone. I wish you a pleasant journey. And if this case is ever solved, I hope you never hear about it."

Chan grinned broadly. "Your kind wishes greatly appreciated. Good-by, and all luck possible."

He watched the reporter as he dashed from the lobby into the street, then going above, he completed his packing. A glance at his watch told him he had plenty of time, so he went to say good-by to his relative in Chinatown. When he returned to the hotel to get his bags, Miss Morrow was waiting for him.

"What happy luck," he said. "Once again I am rewarded by a sight of your most interesting face."

"You certainly are," she replied. "I simply had to see you again. The district attorney has put this whole affair in my hands, and it's my big chance. You are still determined to go home?"

"More than usual." He led her to a sofa. "Last night I have joyous cable——"

"I know. I was there when Mr. Kirk telephoned you. A boy, I think he said."

"Heaven's finest gift," nodded Chan.

Miss Morrow sighed. "If it had only been a girl," she said.

"Good luck," Chan told her, "dogs me in such matters. Of eleven opportunities, I am disappointed but three times."

"You're to be congratulated. However, girls are a necessary evil."

"You are unduly harsh. Necessary, of course. In your case, no evil whatever."

Barry Kirk came into the lobby and joined them. "Good morning, father," he smiled. "Well, we're all here to speed the parting guest."

Chan consulted his watch. Miss Morrow smiled. "You've quite a lot of time," she said. "At least give me the benefit of your advice before you leave."

"Happy to do so," agreed Chan. "It is worthless, but you are welcome."

"Captain Flannery is completely stumped, though of course he won't admit it. I told him all about Hilary Galt and Eve Durand, and he just opened his mouth and forgot to close it."

"Better men than the Captain might also pause in yawning doubt."

"Yes—I admit that." Miss Morrow's white forehead wrinkled in perplexity. "It's all so scattered—San Francisco and London and Peshawar—it almost looks as though whoever solved it must make a trip around the world."

Chan shook his head. "Many strings reach back, but solution will lie in San Francisco. Accept my advice, and take heart bravely."

The girl still puzzled. "We know that Hilary Galt was killed sixteen years ago. A long time, but Sir Frederic was the sort who would never abandon a trail. We also know that Sir Frederic was keenly interested in the disappearance of Eve Durand from Peshawar. That might have been a natural curiosity—but if it was, why should he rush to the newspaper office and demand that nothing be printed about it? No—it was more than curiosity. He was on the trail of something."

"And near the end of it," put in Kirk. "He told me that much."

Miss Morrow nodded. "Near the end—what did that mean? Had he found Eve Durand? Was he on the point of exposing her identity? And was there some one—Eve Durand or some one else—who was determined he should never do so? So determined, in fact, that he—or she—would not stop short of murder to silence him?"

"All expressed most clearly," approved Chan.

"Oh—but it isn't clear at all. Was Hilary Galt's murder connected somehow with the disappearance of that young girl from Peshawar? The velvet slippers—where are they now? Did the murderer of Sir Frederic take them? And if so—why?"

"Many questions arise," admitted Chan. "All in good time you get the answers."

"We'll never get them," sighed the girl, "without your help."

Chan smiled. "How sweet your flattery sounds." He considered. "I made no search of the office last night. But Captain Flannery did. What was found? Records? A case-book?"

"Nothing," said Kirk, "that had any bearing on the matter. Nothing that mentioned Hilary Galt or Eve Durand."

Chan frowned. "Yet without question of doubt, Sir Frederic kept records. Were those records the prize for which the killer made frantic search? Doubtless so. Did he—or she—then, find them? That would seem to be true, unless——"

"Unless what?" asked the girl quickly.

"Unless Sir Frederic had removed same to safe and distant place. On face of things, he expected marauder. He may have baited trap with pointless paper. You have hunted his personal effects, in bedroom?"

"Everything," Kirk assured him. "Nothing was found. In the desk downstairs were some newspaper clippings—accounts of the disappearance of other women who walked off into the night. Sir Frederic evidently made such cases his hobby."

"Other women?" Chan was thoughtful.

"Yes. But Flannery thought those clippings meant nothing, and I believe he was right."

"And the cutting about Eve Durand remained in Sir Frederic's purse?" continued Chan.

"By gad!" Kirk looked at the girl. "I never thought of that. The clipping was gone!"

Miss Morrow's dark eyes were filled with dismay. "Oh—how stupid," she cried. "It was gone, and the fact made no impression on me at all. I'm afraid I'm just a poor, weak woman."

"Calm your distress," said Chan soothingly. "It is a matter to note, that is all. It proves that the quest of Eve Durand held important place in murderer's mind. You must then, *cherchez la femme*. You understand?"

"Hunt the woman," said Miss Morrow.

"You have it. And in such an event, a huntress will be far better than a hunter. Let us think of guests at party. Mr. Kirk, you have said a portion of these people are there because Sir Frederic requested their presence. Which?"

"The Enderbys," replied Kirk promptly. "I didn't know them. But Sir Frederic wanted them to come."

"That has deep interest. The Enderbys. Mrs. Enderby approached state of hysteria all evening. Fear of dark might mean fear of something else. Is it beyond belief that Eve Durand, with new name, marries again into bigamy?"

"But Eve Durand was a blonde," Miss Morrow reminded him.

"Ah, yes. And Eileen Enderby has hair like night. It is, I am told, a matter that is easily arranged. Color of hair may be altered, but color of eyes—that is different. And Mrs. Enderby's eyes are blue, matching oddly raven locks."

"Never miss a trick, do you?" smiled Kirk.

"Mrs. Enderby goes to garden, sees man on fire-escape. So she informs us. But does she? Or does she know her husband, smoking cigarette on stairs, has not been so idly occupied? Is man on fire-escape a myth of her invention, to protect her husband? Why are stains on her gown? From leaning with too much hot excitement against garden rail, damp with the fog of night? Or from climbing herself on to fire-escape—you apprehend my drift? What other guests did Sir Frederic request?"

Kirk thought. "He asked me to invite Gloria Garland," the young man announced.

Chan nodded. "I expected it. Gloria Garland—such is not a name likely to fall to human lot. Sounds like a manufacture. And Australia is so placed on map it might be appropriate end of journey from Peshawar. Blonde, blue-eyed, she breaks necklace on the stair. Yet you discover a pearl beneath the office desk."

Miss Morrow nodded. "Yes—Miss Garland certainly is a possibility."

"There remains," continued Chan, "Mrs. Tupper-Brock. A somewhat dark lady—but who knows? Sir Frederic did not ask her presence?"

"No—I don't think he knew she existed," said Kirk.

"Yes? But it is wise in our work, Miss Morrow, that even the smallest improbabilities be studied. Men stumble over pebbles, never over mountains. Tell me, Mr. Kirk—was Colonel John Beetham the idea of Sir Frederic, too?"

"Not at all. And now that I remember, Sir Frederic seemed a bit taken aback when he heard Beetham was coming. But he said nothing."

"We have now traversed the ground. You have, Miss Morrow, three ladies to receive your most attentive study—Mrs. Enderby, Miss Garland, Mrs. Tupper-Brock. All of proper age, so near as a humble man can guess it in this day of beauty rooms with their appalling tricks. These only of the dinner party——"

"And one outside the dinner party," added the girl, to Chan's surprise.

"Ah—on that point I have only ignorance," he said blankly.

"You remember the elevator operator spoke of a girl employed by the Calcutta Importers, on the twentieth floor? A Miss Lila Barr. She was at work in her office there last night."

"Ah, yes," nodded Chan.

"Well, a newspaper man, Rankin of the *Globe*, came to see me a few minutes ago. He said that the other evening—night before last—he went to call on Sir Frederic in Mr. Kirk's office, rather late. Just as he approached the door, a girl came out. She was crying. Rankin saw her dab at her eyes and disappear into the room of the Calcutta Importers. A blonde girl, he said."

Chan's face was grave. "A fourth lady to require your kind attention. The matter broadens. So much to be done—and you in the midst of it all, like a pearl in a muddy pool." He stood up. "I am sorry. But the *Maui* must even now be straining at her moorings—"

"One other thing," put in the girl. "You made quite a point of that Cosmopolitan Club year-book lying beside Sir Frederic. You thought it important?"

Chan shrugged. "I fear I was in teasing mood. I believed it hardest puzzle of the lot. Therefore I am mean enough to press it on Captain Flannery's mind. What it meant, I can not guess. Poor Captain Flannery will never do so."

He looked at his watch. The girl rose. "I won't keep you longer," she sighed. "I'm very busy, but somehow I can't let you go. I'm trailing along to the dock with you, if you don't mind. Perhaps I'll think of something else on the way."

"Who am I," smiled Chan, "to win such overwhelming honor? You behold me speechless with delight. Mr. Kirk——"

"Oh, I'm going along," said Kirk. "Always like to see a boat pull out. The Lord meant me for a traveling salesman."

Chan got his bag, paid his bill, and the three of them entered Kirk's car, parked round the corner.

"Now that the moment arrives," said Chan, "I withdrew from this teeming mainland with some regret. Fates have been in smiling mood with me here."

"Why go?" suggested Kirk.

"Long experience," replied Chan, "whispers not to strain fates too far. Their smile might fade."

"Want to stop anywhere on the way?" Kirk asked. "You've got thirty minutes until sailing time."

"I am grateful, but all my farewells are said. Only this morning I have visited Chinatown——" He stopped. "So fortunate you still hang on," he added to the girl. "I was forgetting most important information for you. Still another path down which you must travel."

"Oh, dear," she sighed. "I'm dizzy now. What next?"

"You must at once inflict this information on Captain Flannery. He is to find a Chinese, a stranger here, stopping with relatives on Jackson Street. The name, Li Gung."

"Who is Li Gung?" asked Miss Morrow.

"Yesterday, when delicious lunch was ended, I hear of Li Gung from Sir Frederic." He repeated his conversation with the great man. "Li Gung had information much wanted by Sir Frederic. That alone I can say. Captain Flannery must extract this information from Li."

"He'll never get it," replied the girl pessimistically. "Now you, Sergeant——"

Chan drew a deep breath. "I am quite overcome," he remarked, "by the bright loveliness of this morning on which I say farewell to the mainland."

They rode on in silence, while the girl thought hard. If only she could find some way of reaching this stolid man by her side, some appeal that would not roll off like water from a duck's back. She hastily went over in her mind all she had ever read of the Chinese character.

Kirk drove his smart roadster on to the pier, a few feet from the *Maui's* gang-plank. The big white ship was gay with the color of women's hats and frocks. Taxis were sweeping up, travelers were alighting, white-jacketed stewards stood in a bored line ready for another sailing. Good-bys and final admonitions filled the air.

A steward stepped forward and took Chan's bag. "Hello, Sergeant," he said. "Going home, eh? What room, please?"

Chan told him, then turned to the young people at his side. "At thought of your kindness," he remarked, "I am choking. Words escape me. I can only say—good-by."

"Give my regards to the youngest Chan," said Kirk. "Perhaps I'll see him some day."

"Reminding me," returned Chan, "that only this morning I scour my brain to name him. With your kind permission, I will denote him Barry Chan."

"I'm very much flattered," Kirk answered gravely. "Wish to heaven I had something to send him—er—a mug—or a what-you-may-call-it. You'll hear from me later."

"I only trust," Chan said, "he grows up worthy of his name. Miss Morrow—I am leaving on this dock my heartiest good wishes——"

She looked at him oddly. "Thank you," she remarked in a cool voice. "I wish you could have stayed, Mr. Chan. But of course I realize your point of view. The case was too difficult. For once, Charlie Chan is running away. I'm afraid the famous Sergeant of the Honolulu police has lost face to-day."

A startled expression crossed that usually bland countenance. For a long moment Chan looked at her with serious eyes, then he bowed, very stiffly. "I wish you good-by," he said, and walked with offended dignity up the gang-plank.

Kirk was staring at the girl in amazement. "Don't look at me like that," she cried ruefully. "It was cruel, but it was my last chance. I'd tried everything else. Well, it didn't work. Shall we go?"

"Oh—let's wait," pleaded Kirk. "They're sailing in a minute. I always get a thrill out of it. Look—up there on the top deck." He nodded toward a pretty girl in gray, with a cluster of orchids pinned to her shoulder. "A bride, if you ask me. And I suppose that vacant-faced idiot at her side is the lucky man."

Miss Morrow looked, without interest.

"A great place for a honeymoon, Hawaii," went on Kirk. "I've often thought—I hope I'm not boring you?"

"Not much," she said.

"I know. Brides leave you cold. I suppose divorce is more in your line. You and Blackstone. Well, you shan't blast my romantic young nature." He took out a handkerchief and waved it toward the girl on the top deck. "So long, my dear," he called. "All the luck in the world."

"I don't see Mr. Chan," said the young woman from the district attorney's office.

Mr. Chan was sitting thoughtfully on the edge of the berth in his stateroom, far below. The great happiness of his long anticipated departure for home had received a rude jolt. Running away—was that it? Afraid of a difficult case? Did Miss Morrow really think that? If she did, then he had lost face indeed.

His gloomy reflections were interrupted by a voice in the next stateroom—a voice he had heard before. His heart stood still as he listened.

"I fancy that's all, Li," said the familiar voice. "You have your passport, your money. You are simply to wait for me in Honolulu. Better lie low there."

"I will do so," replied a high-pitched, singsong voice.

"And if any one asks any questions, you know nothing. Understand?"

"Yes-s-s. I am silent. I understand."

"Very good. You're a wonderful servant, Li Gung. I don't like to flatter you, you grinning beggar, but I couldn't do without you. Good-by—and a pleasant journey."

Chan was on his feet now, peering out into the dim passageway along which opened the rooms on the lowest deck. In that faint light he saw a familiar figure emerge from the room next door, and disappear in the distance.

The detective stood for a moment, undecided. Of all the guests at Barry Kirk's party one had interested him beyond all others—almost to the exlusion of the others. The tall, grim, silent man who had made his camps throughout the wastelands of the world, who had left a trail of the dead but who had always moved on, relentlessly, toward his goal. Colonel John Beetham, whom he had just seen emerging from the stateroom next to his with a last word of farewell to Li Gung.

Chan looked at his watch. It was never his habit to hurry, but he must hurry now. He sighed a great sigh that rattled the glasses in their rings, and snatched up his bag. On the saloon deck he met the purser.

"Homeward bound, Charlie?" inquired that gentleman breezily.

"So I thought," replied Chan, "but it seems I was mistaken. At the last moment, I am rudely wrenched ashore. Yet I have ticket good only on this boat."

"Oh, they'll fix that up for you at the office. They all know you, Charlie."

"Thanks for the suggestion. My trunk is already loaded. Will you kindly deliver same to my oldest son, who will call for it when you have docked at Honolulu?"

"Sure." The "visitors ashore" call was sounding for the last time. "Don't you linger too long on this wicked mainland, Charlie," the purser admonished.

"One week only," called Chan, over his shoulder. "Until the next boat. I swear it."

On the dock, Miss Morrow seized Kirk's arm. "Look. Coming down the gang-plank. Colonel Beetham. What's he doing here?"

"Beetham—sure enough," said Kirk. "Shall I offer him a lift? No—he's got a taxi. Let him go. He's a cold proposition—I like him not." He watched the Colonel enter a cab and ride off.

When he turned back to the *Maui*, two husky sailors were about to draw up the plank. Suddenly between them appeared a chubby little figure, one hand clutching a suitcase. Miss Morrow gave a cry of delight.

"It's Chan," Kirk said. "He's coming ashore."

And ashore Charlie came, while they lifted the plank at his heels. He stood before the two young people, ill at ease.

"Moment of gentle embarrassment for me," he said. "The traveler who said good-by is back before he goes."

"Mr. Chan," the girl cried, "you dear! You're going to help us, after all."

Chan nodded. "To the extent of my very slight ability, I am with you to finish, bitter or sweet."

On the top deck of the *Maui* the band began to play—*Aloha,* that most touching of farewells. Long streamers of bright-colored paper filled the air. The last good-bys, the final admonitions—a loud voice calling "Don't forget to write." Charlie Chan watched, a mist before his eyes. Slowly the boat drew away from the pier. The crowd ran along beside it, waving frantically. Charlie's frame shook with another ponderous sigh.

"Poor little Barry Chan," he said. "He would have been happy to see me.

Captain Flannery will not be so happy. Let us ride away into the face of our problems."

6

The Guest Detective

Barry Kirk tossed Chan's suitcase into the luggage compartment of his roadster, and the trio crowded again on to its single seat. The car swung about in the pier shed and emerged into the bright sunlight of the Embarcadero.

"You are partially consumed with wonder at my return?" suggested Chan. The girl shrugged. "You're back. That's enough for me."

"All the same, I will confess my shame. It seems I have circulated so long with mainland Americans I have now, by contagion, acquired one of their worst faults. I too suffer curiosity. Event comes off on boat which reveals, like heavenly flash, my hidden weakness."

"Something happened on the boat?" Miss Morrow inquired.

"You may believe it did. On my supposed farewell ride through city, I inform you of Li Gung. I tell you he must be questioned. He can not be questioned now."

"No? Why not?"

"Because he is on *Maui* churning away. It is not unprobable that shortly he will experience a feeling of acute disfavor in that seat of all wisdom, the stomach."

"Li Gung on the *Maui?*" repeated the girl. Her eyes were wide. "What can that mean?"

"A question," admitted Chan, "which causes the mind to itch. Not only is Li Gung on *Maui,* but he was warmly encouraged away from here by a friend of ours." He repeated the brief conversation he had overheard in the adjoining cabin.

Barry Kirk was the first to speak. "Colonel Beetham, eh?" he said. "Well, I'm not surprised."

"Nonsense," cried Miss Morrow warmly. "Surely he isn't involved? A fine man like that——"

"A fine man," Chan conceded, "and a hard one. Look in his eyes and behold; they are cold and gleaming, like the tiger's. Nothing stands in the way when such eyes are fixed on the goal of large success—stands there long—alive."

The girl did not seem to be convinced. "I won't believe it. But shouldn't we have taken Li Gung off the boat?"

Chan shrugged. "Too late. The opportunity wore rapid wings."

"Then we'll have him questioned in Honolulu," Miss Morrow said.

Chan shook his head. "Pardon me if I say, not that. Chinese character too well known to me. Questioning would yield no result—save one. It would serve to advise Colonel Beetham that we look on him with icy eye. I shudder at the thought—this Colonel clever man. Difficult enough to shadow if he does not suspect. Impossible if he leaps on guard."

"Then what do you suggest?" asked the girl.

"Let Li Gung, unknowing, be watched. If he seeks to proceed beyond

Honolulu, rough hands will restrain him. Otherwise we permit him to lie, like winter overcoat in closet during heated term." Chan turned to Barry Kirk. "You are taking me back to hotel?"

"I am not," smiled Kirk. "No more hotel for you. If you're going to look into this little puzzle, the place for you is the Kirk Building, where the matter originated. Don't you say so, Miss Morrow?"

"That's awfully kind of you," said the girl.

"Not at all. It's painfully lonesome up where the fog begins without at least one guest. I'm all out of visitors at the moment—er—ah—I mean Mr. Chan will be doing me a real favor." He turned to Charlie. "You shall have Sir Frederic's room," he added.

Chan shrugged. "I can never repay such goodness. Why attempt it?"

"Let's go to my office, first of all," Miss Morrow said. "I want the district attorney to meet Mr. Chan. We must all be friends—at the start, anyhow."

"Anywhere you say," Kirk agreed, and headed the car up Market Street, to Kearny. He remained in the roadster, while the girl and Charlie went up to the district attorney's offices. When they entered that gentleman's private room, they found Captain Flannery already on the scene.

"Mr. Trant—I've good news for you," the girl began. "Oh—good morning, Captain."

Flannery's Irish eyes were not precisely smiling at they rested on Charlie Chan. "What's this, Sergeant?" he growled. "I thought you were off for Honolulu at twelve?"

Chan grinned. "You will be delighted to learn that my plans are changed. Miss Morrow has persuaded me to remain here and add my minute brain power to your famous capacity in same line."

"Is that so?" mumbled Flannery.

"Yes—isn't it splendid?" cried the girl. "Mr. Chan is going to help us." She turned to her chief. "You must give him a temporary appointment as a sort of guest detective connected with this office."

Trant smiled. "Wouldn't that be a bit irregular?" he asked.

"Impossible," said Flannery firmly.

"Not at all," persisted the girl. "It's a very difficult case, and we shall need all the help we can get. Sergeant Chan will not interfere with you, Captain——"

"I'll say he won't," Flannery replied warmly.

"He can act in a sort of advisory capacity. You're a big enough man to take advice, I know."

"When it's any good," the Captain added. The girl looked appealingly at Trant.

"You are on leave of absence from the Honolulu force, Sergeant?" inquired the district attorney.

"One which stretches out like an elastic," nodded Chan.

"Very well. Since Miss Morrow wishes it, I see no reason why you shouldn't lend her your no doubt very useful aid. Remembering, of course, that neither one of you is to interfere with Captain Flannery in any way."

"Better say that again," Flannery told him. He turned to Chan. "That means you're not to butt in and spoil things."

Chan shrugged. "It was the wise K'ung-fu-tsze who said, 'He who is out of office should not meddle with the government.' The labor is all yours. I will merely haunt the background, thinking tensely."

"That suits me," Flannery agreed. "I'll make all the inquiries." He turned to the district attorney. "I'm going to get after that Garland woman right away. The pearl she dropped under Sir Frederic's desk—I want to know all about it."

"Please don't think I'm interfering," Miss Morrow said sweetly. "But as regards the women involved in this case, I feel that perhaps I can get more out of them than you can. Being a woman myself, you know. Will you let me have Miss Garland, please?"

"I can't see it," said Flannery stubbornly.

"I can," remarked Trant, decisively. "Miss Morrow is a clever girl, Captain. Leave the women to her. You take the men."

"What men?" protested Flannery. "It's all women, in this affair."

"Thank you so much," smiled Miss Morrow, assuming his unproffered consent. "I will look up Miss Garland, then. There's another woman who must be questioned at once—a Miss Lila Barr. I shall have a talk with her at the first possible moment. Of course, I'll keep you advised of all I do."

Flannery threw up his hands. "All right—tell me about it—after it's over. I'm nobody."

"Quite incorrect," said Chan soothingly. "You are everybody. When the moment of triumph comes, who will snatch all credit? And rightly so. Captain Flannery, in charge of the case. Others will fade like fog in local sun."

The girl stood up. "We must go along. I'll be in to see you later, Captain. Come, Sergeant Chan——"

Chan rose. He seemed a bit uncomfortable. "The Captain must pardon me. I fear I afflict him like sore thumb. Natural, too. I would feel the same."

"That's all right," returned Flannery. "You're going to stick in the background, thinking tensely. You've promised. Think all you like—I can't stop that." His face brightened. "Think about that Cosmopolitan Club book. I'll turn the heavy thinking on that over to you. Me, I'll be busy elsewhere. One thing I insist on—you're not to question any of these people under suspicion."

Chan bowed. "I am disciple of famous philosopher, Captain," he remarked. "Old man in China who said, 'The fool questions others, the wise man questions himself.' We shall meet again. Good-by." He followed the girl out.

Flannery, his face brick red, turned to the district attorney. "Fine business," he cried. "The toughest case I ever had, and what sort of help do I draw? A doll-faced girl and a Chinaman! Bah—I—I——" He trailed off into profanity.

Trant was smiling. "Who knows?" he replied. "You may get more help from them than you expect."

"If I get any at all, I'll be surprised." Flannery stood up. "A woman and a Chinaman. Hell, I'll be the joke of the force."

The two whom Captain Flannery was disparaging found Barry Kirk waiting impatiently in his car. "An inner craving," he announced, "tells me it's lunch-time. You're both lunching with me at the bungalow. Step lively, please."

Atop the Kirk Building, Paradise was ordered to lay two more places, and Kirk showed Chan to his room. He left the detective there to unpack, and returned to Miss Morrow.

"You seem the perpetual host," she smiled, as he joined her.

"Oh, I'm going to get a lot of fun out of Charlie," he answered. "He's a good scout, and I like him. But, by way of confession, I had other reasons for inviting him here. You and he are going to work together, and that means—what?"

"It means, I hope, that I'm going to learn a lot."

"From associating with Chan?"

"Precisely."

"And if you associate with my guest, you'll be bound to stumble over me occasionally. I'm a wise lad. I saw it coming."

"I don't understand. Why should you want me to stumble over you?"

"Because every time you do I'll leap up and look at you, and that will be another red-letter day in my life."

She shook her head. "I'm afraid you're terribly frivolous. If I see much of you, you'll drag me down and down until I lose my job."

"Look on the other side, lady," he pleaded. "You might drag me up and up. It could be done, you know."

"I doubt it," she told him.

Chan came into the room, and Paradise, unperturbed by the impromptu guests, served a noble luncheon. Toward its close, Kirk spoke seriously.

"I've been thinking about this Barr girl downstairs," he said. "I don't know that I've told you the circumstances under which Sir Frederic came to stay with me. His son happens to be an acquaintance of mine—not a friend, I know him only slightly—and he wrote me his father was to be in San Francisco. I called on Sir Frederic at his hotel. From the start he appeared keenly interested in the Kirk Building. I couldn't quite figure it out. He asked me a lot of questions, and when he learned that I lived on the roof, I must say he practically invited himself to stop with me. Not that I wasn't delighted to have him, you understand—but somehow there was an undercurrent in the talk—well, I just sensed his eagerness. It was odd, wasn't it?"

"Very," said the girl.

"Well, after he'd been here a couple of days he began to ask questions about the Calcutta Importers, and finally these all seemed to center on Miss Lila Barr. I knew nothing about the firm or about Miss Barr—I'd never even heard of her. Later he found that my secretary, Kinsey, knew the girl, and the questions were all turned in that direction—though I fancied they grew more discreet. One day in the office I heard Kinsey ask Sir Frederic if he'd like to meet Miss Barr, and I also heard Sir Frederic's answer."

"What did he say?" Miss Morrow inquired.

"He said simply, 'Later, perhaps,' with what I thought an assumed carelessness. I don't know whether all this is important or not?"

"In view of the fact that Miss Lila Barr once left Sir Frederic's presence in tears, I should say it is very important," Miss Morrow returned. "Don't you agree, Mr. Chan?"

Chan nodded. "Miss Barr has fiercely interesting sound," he agreed. "I long with deep fervor to hear you question her."

The girl rose from the table. "I'll call the office of the Calcutta Importers and ask her to step up here," she announced, and went to the telephone.

Five minutes later Miss Lila Barr entered the living-room under the impeccable chaperonage of Paradise. She stood for a second regarding the three people who awaited her. They noted that she was an extremely pretty girl slightly under middle height, an authentic blonde, with a sort of startled innocence in her blue eyes.

"Thank you for coming." The deputy district attorney rose and smiled at the girl in kindly fashion. "I am Miss Morrow, and this is Mr. Charles Chan. And Mr. Barry Kirk."

"How do you do," said the girl, in a low voice.

"I wanted to talk with you—I'm from the district attorney's office," Miss Morrow added.

The girl stared at her, an even more startled expression in her eyes. "Ye—es," she said uncertainly.

"Sit down, please." Kirk drew up a chair.

"You know, of course, of the murder that took place on your floor of the building last night?" Miss Morrow went on.

"Of course," replied the girl, her voice barely audible.

"You were working last night in your office?"

"Yes—it's the first of the month, you know. I always have extra work at this time."

"At what hour did you leave the building?"

"I think it was about ten fifteen. I'm not sure. But I went away without knowing anything of—of this—terrible affair."

"Yes. Did you see any strangers about the building last night?"

"No one. No one at all." Her voice was suddenly louder.

"Tell me"—Miss Morrow looked at her keenly—"had you ever met Sir Frederic Bruce?"

"No—I had never met him."

"You had never met him. Please think what you are saying. You didn't meet him night before last—when you visited him in his office?"

The girl started. "Oh—I saw him then, of course. I thought you meant—had I been introduced to him."

"Then you did go into his office night before last?"

"I went into Mr. Kirk's office. There was a big man, with a mustache, sitting in the second room. I presume it was Sir Frederic Bruce."

"You presume?"

"Well—of course I know now it was. I saw his picture in this morning's paper."

"He was alone in the office when you went in?"

"Yes."

"Was he the person you went there to see?"

"No, he was not."

"When you left the office, you burst into tears." Again the girl started, and her face flushed. "Was it seeing Sir Frederic made you do that?"

"Oh, no," cried Miss Barr, with more spirit.

"Then what was it made you cry?"

"It was—a purely personal matter. Surely I needn't go into it?"

"I'm afraid you must," Miss Morrow told her. "This is a serious affair, you know."

The girl hesitated. "Well—I——"

"Tell me all that happened night before last."

"Well—it wasn't seeing Sir Frederic made me cry," the girl began. "It was—not seeing some one else."

"Not seeing some one else? Please explain that."

"Very well." The girl moved impulsively toward Miss Morrow. "I can tell you. I'm sure you will understand. Mr. Kinsey, Mr. Kirk's secretary, and I—we are—well—sort of engaged. Every night Mr. Kinsey waits for me, and we have dinner. Then he takes me home. Day before yesterday we had a little quarrel—just over some silly thing—you know how it is——"

"I can imagine," said Miss Morrow solemnly.

"It was about nothing, really. I waited a long time that evening, and he didn't come for me. So I thought maybe I had been in the wrong. I swallowed my pride and went to look for him. I opened the door of Mr. Kirk's office and went in. Of course I thought Mr. Kinsey would be there. Sir Frederic was alone in the office—Mr. Kinsey had gone. I muttered some apology—Sir Frederic didn't say anything, he just looked at me. I hurried out again and—perhaps you know the feeling, Miss Morrow——"

"You burst into tears, because Mr. Kinsey hadn't waited?"

"I'm afraid I did. It was silly of me, wasn't it?"

"Well, that doesn't matter." Miss Morrow was silent for a moment. "The company you work for—it imports from India, I believe?"

"Yes—silk and cotton, mostly."

"Have you ever been in India, Miss Barr?"

The girl hesitated. "When I was quite young—I lived there for some years—with my mother and father."

"Where in India?"

"Calcutta, mostly."

"Other places, too?" The girl nodded. "In Peshawar, perhaps?"

"No," answered Miss Barr. "I was never in Peshawar."

Chan coughed rather loudly, and, catching his eye, Miss Morrow dropped the matter of India. "You had never heard of Sir Frederic before he came here?" she asked.

"Oh, no, indeed."

"And you saw him just that once, when he said nothing at all?"

"Only that once."

Miss Morrow rose. "Thank you very much. That is all for the present. I trust Mr. Kinsey has apologized?"

The girl smiled. "Oh, yes—that's all right now. Thank you for asking." She went out quickly.

Barry Kirk had disappeared from the room, and now he returned. "Kinsey's on his way up," he announced. "Grab him quick before they can compare notes—that was my idea. Getting to be some little detective myself."

"Excellent," nodded Miss Morrow approvingly. A tall, dark young man, very well dressed, came in.

"You wanted to see me, Mr. Kirk?" he inquired.

"Yes. Sorry to butt into your private affairs, Kinsey, but I hear you are sort of engaged to a Miss Lila Barr, who works in one of the offices. Did you know about it?"

Kinsey smiled. "Of course, Mr. Kirk. I have been meaning to mention the matter to you, but the opportunity wasn't offered."

"Day before yesterday you had a bit of a quarrel with her?"

"Oh, it was nothing, sir." Kinsey's dark face clouded. "It's all fixed up now."

"That's good. But on that evening, contrary to your custom, you didn't wait to take her home? You walked out on her?"

"I—I'm afraid I did. I was somewhat annoyed——"

"And you wanted to teach her a lesson. What I call the proper spirit. That's all—and please pardon these personal questions."

"Quite all right, sir." Kinsey turned to go, but hesitated. "Mr. Kirk——"

"Yes, Kinsey?"

"Nothing, sir," said Kinsey, and disappeared.

Kirk turned to Miss Morrow. "There you are. The story of Miss Lila Barr, duly authenticated."

"Such a reasonable story, too," sighed the girl. "But it gets us nowhere. I must say I'm disappointed. Mr. Chan—you thought I went too far—on India?"

Chan shrugged. "In this game, better if the opponent does not know what we are thinking. Assume great innocence is always my aim. Sometimes what I assume is exactly what I've got. Others—I am flying at a lowaltitude."

"I'm afraid I should have flown at a lower altitude than I did," the girl reflected, frowning. "Her story was perfectly plausible, and yet—I don't know——"

"Well, one thing's certain," remarked Kirk. "She's not Eve Durand."

"How do you know that?" asked Miss Morrow.

"Why,—her age. She's a mere kid."

Miss Morrow laughed. "Lucky a woman is in on this," she said. "You men are so painfully blind where a blonde is concerned."

"What do you mean?"

"I mean there are certain artifices which fool a man, but never fool a woman. Miss Barr is thirty—at the very least."

Kirk whistled. "I must be more careful," he said. "I thought her sweet and twenty."

He turned to find Paradise at his elbow. The butler had entered noiselessly, and was holding out a silver tray in the manner of one offering rich treasure.

"What shall I do with these, sir?" he inquired.

"Do with what?" Kirk asked.

"Letters addressed to Sir Frederic Bruce, sir. They have just been delivered by the local office of Thomas Cook and Sons."

Miss Morrow came eagerly forward. "I'll take charge of them," she said. Paradise bowed, and went out. The girl's eyes sparkled. "We never thought of this, Sergeant. Sir Frederic's mail—it may prove a gold mine." She held up a letter. "Here—the first thing—one from London. The Metropolitan Police, Scotland Yard——"

Quickly she ripped open the envelope and withdrawing a single sheet of paper, spread it out. She gave a little cry of dismay.

Kirk and Charlie Chan came nearer. They stared at the sheet of paper that had arrived in the envelope from Scotland Yard. It was just that—a sheet of paper—completely blank.

7
Muddy Water

Miss Morrow stood, her brows contracted in bewilderment, looking down at the unexpected enclosure she had found in the envelope with the London postmark.

"Oh, dear," she sighed. "There's just one trouble with this detective business. It's so full of mystery."

Chan smiled. "Humbly begging pardon to mention it, I would suggest you iron out countenance. Wrinkles might grow there, which would be a heart-breaking pity. Occasional amazing occurrence keeps life spicy. Accept that opinion from one who knows it."

"But what in the world does this mean?" she asked.

"One thing I am certain it does not mean," Chan replied. "Scotland Yard in sudden playful mood does not post empty paper over six thousand miles of land and water. No, some queer business has blossomed up near at hand, which it is our duty to unveil." The girl began to smooth the blank sheet.

Chan stretched out a warning hand. Despite his girth, the hand was thin and narrow, with long, tapering fingers. "I beg of you, do not touch further," he cried. "A great mistake. For although we can not see, there is something on that paper."

"What?" she inquired.

"Finger-prints," he answered. Gingerly by one corner he removed the paper from her hand. "The finger-prints, dainty and firm, you have made. The finger-prints, also, perhaps not so dainty, of the person who folded it and put it in envelope."

"Oh, of course," said Miss Morrow.

"I am no vast admirer of science in this work," Chan went on. "But finger-prints tell pretty much truth. Happy to say I have made half-hearted study of the art. In Honolulu, where I am faced by little competition, I rejoice in mouth-filling title of fingerprint expert. Mr. Kirk, have you a drawer with heavy lock, to which you alone hold key?"

"Surely," replied Kirk. He unlocked a compartment in a handsome Spanish desk, and Chan deposited the paper inside. Kirk turned the key, and removing it from the ring, handed it to Charlie.

"Later," remarked Chan, "with lamp black and camel's hair brush, I perform like the expert I have been pronounced. Maybe we discover who has been opening Sir Frederic's mail." He picked up the empty envelope. "Behold—steam has been applied. The marks unquestionable."

"Steam," cried Barry Kirk. "But who in the world—oh, I say. Sir Frederic's mail came through the local office of Thomas Cook and Sons."

"Precisely," grinned Chan.

"And Mr. Carrick Enderby is employed there."

Chan shrugged. "You are bright young man. It is not beyond possibility that the mark of Mr. Enderby's large thumb is on that paper. However, speculation is idle thing. Facts must be unearthed. Miss Morrow—may I rudely suggest—the remainder of Sir Frederic's mail?"

"Yes, of course," said the girl. "I feel rather guilty about this, but when duty calls, you know——"

She sat down and went through the other letters. Obviously her search was without any interesting result.

"Well," she said finally, "that's that. I leave the matter of the blank sheet of paper to you, Sergeant. For myself, I am going to turn my attention to Miss Gloria Garland. What was that pearl from her necklace doing under the desk beside which Sir Frederic was killed?"

"A wise question," nodded Chan. "Miss Garland should now be invited to converse. May she prove more pointed talker than Miss Lila Barr."

"Let me call her up and ask her over here," suggested Kirk. "I'll tell her I want to have a talk with her in my office about last night's affair. She may arrive a bit less prepared with an explanation than if she knows it's the police who want to see her."

"Splendid," approved Miss Morrow. "But I'm afraid we're cutting in most frightfully on your business, Mr. Kirk. You must say so if we are."

"What business?" he inquired airily. "Like Sergeant Chan, I am now attached to your office. And I'm likely to grow more attached all the time. If you'll pardon me for a moment——"

He went to the telephone and reached Miss Garland at her apartment. The actress agreed to come at once.

As Kirk came away from the telephone, the doorbell rang and Paradise admitted a visitor. Captain Flannery strode into the room.

"Hello," he said. "You're all here, ain't you? I'd like to look round a bit—if I'm not butting in."

"Surely no one could be more warmly welcome," Chan told him.

"Thanks, Sergeant. You solved this problem yet?"

"Not up to date of present speaking," grinned Chan.

"Well, you're a little slow, ain't you?" Captain Flannery was worried, and not in the best of humor. "I thought from what I've read about you, you'd have the guilty man locked up in a closet for me, by this time."

Chan's eyes narrowed. "Challenge is accepted," he answered with spirit. "I have already obliged mainland policemen by filling a few closets with guilty men they could not catch. From my reading in newspapers, there still remains vast amount of work to do in same line."

"Is that so?" Flannery responded. He turned to Miss Morrow. "Did you talk with the Barr woman?"

"I did," said the girl. She repeated Lila Barr's story. Flannery heard her out in silence.

"Well," he remarked when she had finished, "you didn't get much, did you?"

"I'll have to admit I didn't," she replied.

"Maybe not as much as I could have got—and me not a woman, either. I'm going down now and have a talk with her myself. She don't look good to me. Cried because her fellow went and left her? Perhaps. But if you ask me, it takes more than that to make a woman cry nowadays."

"You may be right," Miss Morrow agreed.

"I know I'm right. And let me tell you something else—I'm going to be on hand when you talk with Gloria Garland. Make up your mind to that right now."

"I shall be glad to have you. Miss Garland is on her way here to meet us in the office down-stairs."

"Fine. I'll go and take a look at this weepy dame. If the Garland woman comes before I'm back, you let me know. I've been in this game thirty years, young woman, and no district attorney's office can freeze me out. When I conduct an investigation, I conduct it."

He strode from the room. Chan looked after him without enthusiasm. "How loud is the thunder, how little it rains," he murmured beneath his breath.

"We'd better go to the office," suggested Kirk. "Miss Garland is likely to arrive at any moment."

They went below. The sun was blazing brightly in the middle room; the events of the foggy night now passed seemed like a bad dream. Kirk sat down at his desk, opened a drawer, and handed Chan a couple of press clippings.

"Want to look at those?" he inquired. "As I told you this morning, it appears that Sir Frederic was interested, not only in Eve Durand, but in other missing women as well."

Chan read the clippings thoughtfully, and laid them on the desk. He sighed ponderously. "A far-reaching case," he remarked, and was silent for a long time.

"A puzzler, even to you," Kirk said at length.

Chan came to himself with a start. "Pardon, please? What did you say?"

"I said that even the famous Sergeant Chan is up against it this time."

"Oh, yes. Yes, indeed. But I was not thinking of Sir Frederic. A smaller, less important person occupied my mind. Without fail I must go to little Barry Chan on next Wednesday's boat."

"I hope you can," smiled Miss Morrow. "Not many men are as devoted to their families nowadays as you are."

"Ah—you do not understand," said Chan. "You mainland people—I observe what home is to you. An unprivate apartment, a pigeonhole to dive into when the dance or the automobile ride is ended. We Chinese are different. Love, marriage, home, still we cling to unfashionable things like that. Home is a sanctuary into which we retire, the father is high priest, the altar fires burn bright."

"Sounds rather pleasant," remarked Barry Kirk. "Especially that about the father. By the way, I must send my namesake a cablegram and wish him luck."

Miss Gloria Garland appeared in the outer office, and Kinsey escorted her into the middle room. She was not quite so effective in the revealing light of day as she had been at a candle-lighted dinner table. There were lines about her eyes, and age was peering from beneath the heavy make-up.

"Well, here I am, Mr. Kirk," she said. "Oh—Miss Morrow—and Mr. Chan. I'm a wreck, I know. That thing last night upset me terribly—such a charming man, Sir Frederic. Has—has anything been unearthed—any clue?"

"Nothing much," replied Kirk, "as yet. Please sit down."

"Just a moment," said Miss Morrow. "I must get Captain Flannery."

"I will go, please," Chan told her, and hurried out.

He pushed open the door of the office occupied by the Calcutta Importers. Captain Flannery was standing, red-faced and angry, and before him sat Lila Barr, again in tears. The Captain swung about. "Yes?" he snapped.

"You are wanted, Captain," Chan said. "Miss Garland is here."

"All right." He turned to the weeping girl. "I'll see you again, young woman." She did not reply. He followed Chan to the hall.

"You too have some success as a tear-starter," suggested Chan.

"Yeah—she's the easiest crier I've met this year. I wasn't any too gentle with her. It don't pay."

"Your methods, of course, had amazing success?"

"Oh—she stuck to her story. But you take it from me, she knows more than she's telling. Too many tears for an innocent bystander. I'll bet you a hundred dollars right now that she's Eve Durand."

Chan shrugged. "My race," he said, "possesses great fondness for gambling. Not to go astray into ruin, I am compelled to overlook even easy methods of gain in that line."

Captain Flannery was driven back to his favorite phrase. "Is that so?" he replied, and they entered Kirk's office.

When they were all in the middle room, Barry Kirk shut the door on the interested Mr. Kinsey. Captain Flannery faced Gloria Garland.

"I want to see you. You know who I am. I was up-stairs last night. So your name's Gloria Garland, is it?"

She looked up at him a bit apprehensively. "Yes, of course."

"Are you telling your real name, lady?"

"Well, it's the name I have used for many years. I——"

"Oh? So it isn't the real one?"

"Not exactly. It's a name I took——"

"I see. You took a name that didn't belong to you." The Captain's tone implied a state's prison offense. "You had reasons, I suppose?"

"I certainly had." The woman looked at him with growing anger. "My name was Ida Pingle, and I didn't think that would go well in the theater. So I called myself Gloria Garland."

"All right. You admit you travel under an assumed name?"

"I don't care for the way you put it. A great many people on the stage have taken more attractive names than their own. I have nothing done to justify your rudeness——"

"I can quite understand your feeling," said Miss Morrow, with a disapproving glance at the Captain. "From this point I will take up the inquiry."

"I wish you would," remarked Miss Garland warmly.

"Had you ever met Sir Frederic Bruce before you came to Mr. Kirk's dinner party last night?" the girl inquired.

"No, I had not."

"He was, then, a complete stranger to you?"

"He certainly was. Why should you ask me that?"

"You had no private interview with him last night?"

"No. None."

Captain Flannery stepped forward, his mouth open, about to speak. Miss Morrow raised her hand. "Just a moment, Captain. Miss Garland, I warn you this is a serious business. You should tell the truth."

"Well——" Her manner became uncertain. "What makes you think I'm——"

"Lying? We know it," exploded Flannery.

"You broke the string of your necklace last night on your way to the bungalow," Miss Morrow continued. "Where did that accident happen?"

"On the stairs—the stairs leading up from the twentieth floor to the roof."

"Did you recover all the pearls?"

"Yes—I think so. I wasn't quite sure of the number. Of course, I needn't tell you they're only imitation. I couldn't afford the real thing."

Miss Morrow opened her hand-bag, and laid a solitary pearl on the desk. "Do you recognize that, Miss Garland?"

"Why—why, yes. It belongs to me, of course. Thank you so much. Where—er—where did you find it?"

"We found it," said Miss Morrow slowly, "under the desk in this room." The woman flushed, and made no reply. There was a moment's strained silence. "Miss Garland," the girl went on, "I think you had better change your tactics. The truth, if you please."

The actress shrugged. "I fancy you're right. I was only trying to keep out of this. It's not the sort of publicity I want. And as a matter of fact, I'm not in it very deep."

"But you really broke the string in this office, where you had come for a talk with Sir Frederic?"

"Yes, that's true. I caught the necklace on a corner of the desk, when I got up to go."

"Please don't start with the moment when you got up to go. Take it from the beginning, if you will."

"Very good. When I said I had never seen Sir Frederic before last night, I was telling the truth. I had left the elevator and was crossing the hallway to the stairs, when the door of these offices opened and a man stood on the threshold. He said: 'You are Miss Garland, I believe?' I told him that was my name, and he said he was Sir Frederic Bruce, Mr. Kirk's guest, and that he wanted to have a talk with me, alone, before we met up-stairs."

"Yes—go on."

"Well, it seemed odd, but he was such a distinguished-looking man I felt it must be all right, so I followed him in here. We sat down, and he started in to tell me who he was—Scotland Yard, and all that. I'm English, of course, and I have the greatest respect for any one from the Yard. He talked around for a minute, and then he went to the point."

"Ah, yes," smiled Miss Morrow. "That's what we are waiting for. What was the point?"

"He—he wanted to ask me something."

"Yes? What?"

"He wanted to ask me if I could identify a woman who disappeared a great many years ago. A woman who just stepped off into the night, and was never heard of again."

A tense silence followed these words. Quietly Chan moved a little closer. Barry Kirk's eyes were fixed with interest on Gloria Garland's face. Even Captain Flannery stood eagerly at attention.

"Yes," said Miss Morrow calmly. "And why did Sir Frederic think you could identify this woman?"

"Because I was her best friend. I was the last person who saw her on the night she disappeared."

Miss Morrow nodded. "Then you were present at a picnic party in the hills near Peshawar on a certain night fifteen years ago?"

The woman's eyes opened wide. "Peshawar? That's in India, isn't it? I have never been in India in my life."

Another moment of startled silence. Then Flannery roared at her. "Look here—you promised to tell the truth——"

"I am telling the truth," she protested.

"You are not. That woman he asked you about was Eve Durand, who disappeared from a party one night outside Peshawar——"

Chan cut in on him. "Humbly asking pardon, Captain," he said, "you shouldn't be so agile in jumping upon the lady's story." He picked up a couple of clippings from the desk. "Will you be so kind," he added to Miss Garland, "as to mention name of place from which your friend disappeared?"

"Certainly. She disappeared from Nice."

"Nice? Where the hell's that?" Flannery asked.

"Nice is a resort city on the French Riviera," replied Miss Garland, sweetly. "I am afraid your duties keep you too much at home, Captain."

"Nice," repeated Chan slowly. "Then the name of your friend was perhaps Marie Lantelme?"

"That was her name," the actress replied.

Chan selected a clipping, and handed it to Miss Morrow. "Will you condescend to read words out loud?" he inquired. "Most interesting, to be sure."

Again, as in the dining-room of the St. Francis the day before, Miss Morrow read one of Sir Frederic's treasured clippings.

"What became of Marie Lantelme? It is now eleven years since that moonlit June night when a company under English management played *The Dollar Princess* on the stage of the Theatre de la Jetée-Promenade, in the city of Nice. It was a memorable evening for all concerned. The house was sold out, packed with soldiers on leave, and the manager was frantic. At the last moment word had come that his leading lady was seriously ill and with many misgivings he sent for the understudy, a pretty, inconspicuous little chorus girl named Marie Lantelme. It was her big chance at last. She stepped out on the blazing stage and became a woman transformed. The performance she gave will never be forgotten by any one who was in that audience—an audience that went wild, that was on its feet cheering for her when the curtain fell.

"After the performance the manager rushed in high glee to Marie Lantelme's dressing-room. She was a discovery, and she was his. He would star her in London, in New York. She listened to him in silence. Then she put on her simple little frock and stepped from the stage door out upon the jetty. Fame and riches were waiting for her, if she chose to take them. Whether she chose or not will never be known. All that is known is that when she left the theater she walked off into nothingness. Eleven years have passed, and from that day to this no one has ever heard from Marie Lantelme."

Miss Morrow stopped reading, her countenance again in great need of ironing out. Captain Flannery stood with open mouth. Only Chan seemed to have retained his cheerful composure.

"Marie Lantelme was your friend?" he said to Miss Garland.

"She was," replied the actress, "and somehow Sir Frederic knew it. I was appearing in that same company. I must say the clipping exaggerates a bit—I suppose they have to do it to make things interesting. It was an adequate performance—that's what I would have called it. I don't remember any cheering. But there isn't any doubt about her making good. She could have had other parts—better ones than she had ever had before. Yet it's true enough—she left the theater, and that was the last of her."

"You had final view of her?" Chan suggested.

"Yes. On my way home, I saw her standing talking to some man on the Promenade des Anglais, at the entrance to the jetty. I went on, thinking nothing of it at the time. Afterward, of course——"

"And it was this girl Sir Frederic asked you about?" Miss Morrow inquired.

"It was. He showed me that clipping, and asked me if I wasn't in the same company. I said I was. He wanted to know if I thought I could identify Marie Lantelme if I met her again, and I said I was quite sure I could. 'Very good,' he said. 'I may call upon you for that service before the evening is over. Please do not leave to-night until we have had another talk.' I told him I wouldn't, but of course, at the end—well, he wasn't talking to any one any more."

They sat for a moment in silence. Then Miss Morrow spoke.

"I think that is all," she said. "Unless Captain Flannery——"

She glanced at the Captain. An expression of complete bewilderment decorated that great red face. "Me? No—no, I guess not. Nothing more from me, now," he stammered.

"Thank you very much, Miss Garland," the girl continued. "You are going to be in the city for some time?"

"Yes. I've been promised a part at the Alcazar."

"Well, don't leave town without letting me know. You may go now. So good of you to come."

Miss Garland nodded toward the desk. "May I have the pearl?"

"Oh—certainly."

"Thanks. When an actress has been out of a shop for some time, even the imitation jewels are precious. You understand?"

Miss Morrow let her out, and returned to the silent little group in the inner room. "Well?" she remarked.

"It's incredible," cried Barry Kirk. "Another lost lady. Good lord, Eve

Durand and Marie Lantelme can't both be hanging out around here. Unless this is the Port of Missing Women. What do you say, Sergeant?"

Chan shrugged. "All time we get in deeper," he admitted. "Free to announce I find myself sunk in bafflement."

"I'll get to the bottom of it," Flannery cried. "You leave it to me. I'll stir things up."

Chan's eyes narrowed. "My race has old saying, Captain," he remarked gently. " 'Muddy water, unwisely stirred, grows darker still. Left alone, it clears itself.' "

Flannery glared at him and without a word strode from the room, slamming the outer door behind him.

8

Willie Li's Good Turn

Thoughtfully Charlie Chan picked up Sir Frederic's clippings from the desk and taking out a huge wallet, stowed them away inside. Barry Kirk's eyes were on the door through which Flannery had taken his unceremonious departure.

"I'm very much afraid," he said, "that the policeman's lot is not a happy one. The dear old Captain seemed a bit—what's a good word for it? Nettled? Ah yes, nettled is a very good word."

Miss Morrow smiled. "He's frightfully puzzled, and that always makes a policeman cross."

"I hope it doesn't have that effect on you."

"If it did, I'd be so cross right at this moment you'd order me out of your life for ever."

"A trifle baffled, eh?"

"Can you wonder? Was there ever a case like this?" She picked up her coat, which she had brought with her from the bungalow. "All that about Marie Lantelme——"

"Humbly making suggestion," remarked Chan, "do not think too much about Marie Lantelme. She is—what you say—an issue from the side. Remember always one big fact—Sir Frederic Bruce dead on this very floor, the velvet shoes absent from his feet. Wandering too far from that, we are lost. Think of Eve Durand, think of Hilary Galt, but think most of all regarding Sir Frederic and last night. Bestow Marie Lantelme in distant pigeonhole of mind. That way alone, we progress, we advance."

The girl sighed. "Shall we ever advance? I doubt it."

"Take cheer," advised Chan. "A wise man said, 'The dark clouds pass, the blue heavens abide.' " He bowed low and disappeared toward the stairs leading up to the bungalow.

Barry Kirk held the girl's coat. As he placed it about her shoulders the words of a familiar advertisement flashed into his mind. "Obey that impulse." But one couldn't go through life obeying every chance impulse.

" 'All time we get in deeper,' " he quoted. "It begins to look like a long and very involved case."

"I'm afraid it does," Miss Morrow replied.

"What do you mean, afraid? You and I are very brainy people—thanks for including me—and we should welcome a good stiff test of our powers. Let's get together for a conference very soon."

"Do you think that's necessary?"

"I'm sure of it."

"Then it's all settled," she smiled. "Thanks for the lunch—and good-by."

When Kirk reached the bungalow, Charlie called to him from the room formerly occupied by the man from Scotland Yard. Going in, he found the detective standing thoughtfully before Sir Frederic's luggage, now piled neatly in a corner.

"You have investigated these properties of Sir Frederic?" Chan asked.

Kirk shook his head. "No, I haven't. That's hardly in my line. Flannery went through them last night, and evidently found nothing. He told me to turn them over to the British consul."

"Flannery travels with too much haste," protested Chan. "You have the keys, perhaps? If so, I experience a yearning of my own to look inside."

Kirk handed him the keys, and left him alone. For a long time Chan proceeded with his search. Finally he appeared in the living-room with a great collection of books under his arm.

"Find anything?" Kirk asked.

"Nothing at all," Chan returned, "with these somewhat heavy exceptions. Deign to come closer, if you will be kind enough."

Kirk rose and casually examined the books. His offhand manner vanished, and he cried excitedly: "Great Scott!"

"The same from me," Chan smiled. "You have noted the name of the author of these volumes." He read off the titles. *"Across China and Back. Wanderings in Persia. A Year in the Gobi Desert. Tibet, the Top of the World. My Life as an Explorer."* His eyes narrowed as he looked at Kirk. "All the work of our good friend, Colonel Beetham. No other books amid Sir Frederic's luggage. Does it not strike you as strange, his keen interest in one solitary author?"

"It certainly does," agreed Kirk. "I wonder——"

"I have never ceased to wonder. When I look into deep eyes of the lonely explorer last night, I ask myself, what make of man is this? No sooner is Sir Frederic low on the floor than my thoughts fly back to that mysterious face. So cold, so calm, but who knows with what hot fires beneath." He selected one enormous volume, the *Life.* "I feel called upon to do some browsing amid Sir Frederic's modest library. I will advance first on this, which will grant me bird's-eye look over an adventurous career."

"A good idea," Kirk nodded.

Before Chan could settle to his reading, the bell rang and Paradise admitted Mrs. Dawson Kirk. She came in as blithely as a girl.

"Hello, Barry. Mr. Chan, I rather thought I'd find you here. Didn't sail after all, did you?"

Chan sighed. "I have encountered some difficulty in bringing vacation to proper stop. History is a grand repeater."

"Well, I'm glad of it," said Mrs. Kirk. "They'll need you here. Frightful thing, this is. And to think, Barry, it happened in your building. The Kirks are not accustomed to scandal, I never slept a wink all night."

"I'm sorry to hear it," her grandson said.

"Oh, you needn't be. Not sleeping much anyhow, of late. Seems I got all my sleeping done years ago. Well, what's happened? Have they made any progress?"

"Not much," Kirk admitted.

"How could they? That stupid police captain—he annoyed me. No subtlety. Sally Jordan's boy here will show him up."

"Humbly accept the flattery," Chan bowed.

"Flattery—rot. The truth, nothing else. Don't you disappoint me. All my hopes are pinned on you."

"By the way," said Kirk, "I'm glad you came alone. How long as that woman—Mrs. Tupper-Brock—been with you?"

"About a year. What's she got to do with it?"

"Well—what do you know about her?"

"Don't be a fool, Barry. I know everything. She's all right."

"You mean all her past is an open book to you?"

"Nothing of the sort. I never asked about it. I didn't have to. I'm a judge of people. One look—that's enough for me."

Kirk laughed. "What a smart lady. As a matter of fact, you don't know a thing about her, do you?"

"Oh, yes I do. She's English—born in Devonshire."

"Devonshire, eh?"

"Yes. Her husband was a clergyman—you'd know that by her starved look. He's dead now."

"And that's the extent of your knowledge?"

"You're barking up the wrong tree—but you would. A nice boy, but never very clever. However, I didn't come here to discuss Helen Tupper-Brock. It has just occurred to me that I didn't tell all I knew last night."

"Concealing evidence, eh?" smiled Kirk.

"I don't know—it may be evidence—probably not. Tell me—have they dug up any connection between Sir Frederic and that little Mrs. Enderby?"

"No, they haven't. Have you?"

"Well—it was just after the pictures started. I went out into the kitchen——"

"You would."

"My throat was dry. I didn't see any water in the living-room. But what could I expect in a man-run house? In the passageway I came upon Sir Frederic and Mrs. Enderby engaged in what appeared to be a quite serious talk."

"What were they saying?"

"I'm no eavesdropper. Besides, they stopped suddenly when I appeared, and remained silent until I had gone by. When I returned a few moments later, both were gone."

"Well, that may be important," Kirk admitted. "Perhaps not. Odd, though—Sir Frederic told me he had never met Mrs. Enderby when he suggested I invite the pair to dinner. I'll turn your information over to Miss Morrow."

"What's Miss Morrow go to do with it?" snapped the old lady.

"She's handling the case for the district attorney's office."

"What! You mean to say they've put an important case like this in the hands of——"

"Calm yourself. Miss Morrow is a very intelligent young woman."

"She couldn't be. She's too good-looking."

"Miracles happen," laughed Kirk.

His grandmother regarded him keenly. "You look out for yourself, my boy."

"What are you talking about?"

"The Kirk men always did have a weakness for clever women—the attraction of opposites, I presume. That's how I came to marry into the family."

"You don't happen to have an inferiority complex about you, do you?"

"No, sir. That's one thing the new generation will never be able to pin on me. Well, go ahead and tell Miss Morrow about Eileen Enderby. But I fancy the important member of the investigating committee has heard it already. I'm speaking of Mr. Chan." She rose. "I wrote Sally Jordan this morning that I'd met you," she went on, to the detective. "I said I thought the mainland couldn't spare you just yet."

Chan shrugged. "Mainland enjoys spectacle of weary postman plodding on his holiday walk," he replied. "No offense is carried, but I am longing for Hawaii."

"Well, that's up to you," remarked Mrs. Kirk bluntly. "Solve this case quickly and run before the next one breaks. I must go along. I've a club meeting. That's what my life's come to—club meetings. Barry, keep me posted on this thing. First excitement in my neighborhood in twenty years. I don't want to miss any of it."

Kirk let her out, and returned to the living-room. The quick winter dusk was falling, and he switched on the lights.

"All of which," he said, "brings little Eileen into it again. She did seem a bit on edge last night—even before she saw that man on the fire-escape. If she really did see him. I'll put Miss Morrow on her trail, eh?"

Chan looked up from his big book, and nodded without interest. "All you can do."

"She doesn't intrigue you much, does she?" Kirk smiled.

"This Colonel Beetham," responded Chan. "What a man!"

Kirk looked at his watch. "I'm sorry, but I'm dining to-night at the Cosmopolitan Club, with a friend. I made the engagement several days ago."

"Greatly pained," said Chan, "if I interfered with your plans in any way. Tell me—our Colonel Beetham—you have seen him at Cosmopolitan Club?"

"Yes. Somebody's given him a card. I meet him around there occasionally. I must take you over to the club one of these days."

"The honor will be immense," Chan said gravely.

"Paradise will give you dinner," Kirk told him.

"Not to be considered," Chan protested. "Your staff in kitchen deserves holiday after last night's outburst. I am doing too much eating at your gracious board. I too will dine elsewhere—there are little matters into which I would peer inquiringly."

"As you wish," nodded Kirk. He went into his bedroom, leaving Chan to the book.

At six thirty, after Kirk had left, Chan also descended to the street. He had dinner at an inexpensive little place and when it was finished, strolled with what looked like an aimless step in the direction of Chinatown.

The Chinese are a nocturnal people; Grant Avenue's shops were alight and thronged with customers; its sidewalk crowded with idlers who seemed at a loose end for the evening. The younger men were garbed like their white contemporaries; the older, in the black satin blouse and trousers of China, shuffled along on felt shod feet. Here and there walked with ponderous dignity a Chinese matron who had all too obviously never sought to reduce. A sprinkling of bright-eyed flappers lightened the picture.

Chan turned up Washington Street, then off into the gloomy stretch of Waverly Place. He climbed dimly lighted stairs and knocked at a familiar door.

Surprise is not in the lexicon of the Chinese people, and Chan Kee Lim admitted him with stolid face. Though they had said farewell only that morning, the detective's call was accepted calmly by his cousin.

"I am here again," Chan said in Cantonese. "It was my thought that I was leaving the mainland, but the fates have decreed otherwise."

"Enter," his cousin said. "Here in my poor house the welcome never cools. Deign to sit on this atrociously ugly stool."

"You are too kind," Charlie returned. "I am, as you must surmise, the victim of my despicable calling. If you will so far condescend, I require information."

Kee Lim's eyes narrowed, and he stroked his thin gray beard. He did not approve of that calling, as Charlie well knew.

"You are involved," he said coldly, "with the white devil police?"

Chan shrugged. "Unfortunately, yes. But I ask no betrayal of confidence from you. A harmless question, only. Perhaps you could tell me of a stranger, a tourist, who has been guest of relatives in Jackson Street? The name Li Gung."

Kee Lim nodded. "I have not met him, but I have heard talk at the Tong House. He is one who has traveled much in foreign lands. For some time he has been domiciled with his cousin Henry Li, the basket importer, who lives American style in the big apartment-house on Jackson Street. The Oriental Apartments, I believe. I have not been inside, but I understand there are bathrooms and other strange developments of what the white devil is pleased to call his civilization."

"You are an acquaintance of Henry Li?" Charlie asked.

Kee Lim's eyes hardened. "I have not the honor," he replied.

Charlie understood. His cousin would have no part in whatever he proposed. He rose from his ebony stool.

"You are extremely kind," he said. "That was the extent of my desire. Duty says I must walk my way."

Kee Lim also rose. "The briefness of your stop makes it essential you come again. There is always a welcome here."

"Only too well do I know it," nodded Charlie. "I am busy man, but we will meet again. I am saying good-by."

His cousin followed to the door. "I hope you have a safe walk," he remarked, and there was, it seemed, something more in his mind than the conventional farewell wish.

Chan set out at once for Jackson Street. Half-way up the hill he encountered the gaudy front of the Oriental Apartments. Here the more prosperous members of the Chinese colony lived in the manner of their adopted country.

He entered the lobby and studied the letter boxes. Henry Li, he discovered, lived on the second floor. Ignoring the push buttons, he tried the door. It was unlocked, and he went inside. He climbed to the third floor, walking softly as he passed the apartment occupied by Henry Li. For a moment he stood at the head of the stairs, then started down. He had proceeded about half-way to the floor below, when suddenly he appeared to lose his footing, and descended with a terrific clatter to the second-floor landing. The door of Henry Li's apartment opened, and a fat little Chinese in a business suit peered out.

"You are concerned in an accident?" he inquired solicitously.

"*Haie!*" cried Chan, picking himself up, "the evil spirits pursue me. I have lost my footing on these slippery stairs." He tried to walk, but limped painfully. "I fear I have given my ankle a bad turn. If I could sit quietly for a moment——"

The little man threw wide his door. "Condescend to enter my contempt-ible house. My chairs are plain and uncomfortable, but you must try one."

Profuse in thanks, Chan followed him into an astonishing living-room. Hang-chau silk hangings and a few pieces of teak-wood mingled with bla-tant plush furniture from some department store. A small boy, about thir-teen, was seated at a radio, which ground out dance music. He wore the khaki uniform of a boy scout, with a bright yellow handkerchief about his throat.

"Please sit here," invited Henry Li, indicating a huge chair of green plush. "I trust the pain is not very acute."

"It begins to subside," Chan told him. "You are most kind."

The boy had shut off the radio, and was standing before Charlie Chan with keen interest in his bright eyes.

"A most regrettable thing," explained his father. "The gentleman has turned his ankle on our detestable stairs."

"So sorry," the boy announced. His eyes grew even brighter. "All boy scouts know how to make bandages. I will get my first-aid kit——"

"No, no," protested Chan hastily. "Do not trouble yourself. The injury is not serious."

"It would be no trouble at all," the boy assured him. With some difficulty Charlie dissuaded him, and to the detective's great relief, the boy disap-peared.

"I will sit and rest for a moment," Chan said to Henry Li. "I trust I am no great obstacle here. The accident overwhelmed me when I was on the search for an old friend of mine—Li Gung by name."

Henry Li's little eyes rested for a moment on the picture of a middle-aged Chinese in a silver frame on the mantel. "You are a friend of Li Gung?" he inquired.

The moment had been enough for Chan. "I am—and I see his photo-graph above there, tastefully framed. Is it true, then, that he is stopping here? Has my search ended so fortunately after all?"

"He was here," Li replied, "but only this morning he walked his way."

"Gone!" Chan's face fell. "Alas, then I am too late. Would you be so kind as to tell me where he went?"

Henry Li became discreet. "He disappeared on business of his own, with which I have no concern."

"Of course. But it is a great pity. A friend of mine, an American gentle-man who goes on a long, hazardous journey, required his services. The recompense would have been of generous amount."

Li shook his head. "The matter would have held no interest for Gung. He is otherwise occupied."

"Ah, yes. He still remains in the employ of Colonel John Beetham?"

"No doubt he does."

"Still, the reward in this other matter would have been great. But it may be that he is very loyal to Colonel Beetham. A loyalty cemented through many years. I am trying to figure, but I can not. How long is it your honorable cousin is in Colonel Beetham's service?"

"Long enough to cement loyalty as you say," returned Li, non-comitally.

"Fifteen years, perhaps?" hazarded Chan.

"It might be."

"Or even longer?"

"As to that, I do not know."

Chan nodded. "When you know, to know that you know, and when you do not know, to know that you do not know—that is true knowledge, as the master said." He moved his foot, and a spasm of pain spread over his fat face. "A great man, Colonel Beetham. A most remarkable man. Li Gung has been fortunate. With Colonel Beetham he has seen Tibet, Persia—even India. He has told you, perhaps, of his visits to India with Colonel Beetham?"

In the slanting eyes of the host a stubborn expression was evident. "He says little, my cousin," Henry Li remarked.

"Which point of character no doubt increases his value to a man like the Colonel," suggested Chan. "I am very sorry he has gone. While I would no doubt have failed, owing to his feeling of loyalty for his present employer, I would nevertheless have liked to try. I promised my friend——"

The outer door opened, and the active little boy scout burst into the room. After him came a serious, prematurely bearded young American with a small black case.

"I have brought a physician," cried Willie Li triumphantly.

Chan gave the ambitious boy a savage look.

"An accident, eh?" said the doctor briskly. "Well—which one of you——"

Henry Li nodded toward Chan. "This gentleman's ankle," he said.

The white man went at once to Chan's side. "Let's have a look at it."

"It is nothing," Chan protested. "Nothing at all."

He held out his foot, and the doctor ripped off shoe and stocking. He made a quick examination with his fingers, turned the foot this way and that, and studied it thoughtfully for a moment. Then he stood up.

"What are you trying to do—kid me?" he said with disgust. "Nothing wrong there."

"I remarked the injury was of the slightest," Chan said.

He looked at Henry Li. An expression of complete understanding lighted the basket merchant's face.

"Five dollars, please," said the doctor sternly.

Chan produced his purse, and counted out the money. With an effort he refrained from looking in the boy's direction.

The white man left abruptly. Chan drew on his stocking, slipped into his shoe, and stood up. His dignity requiring that he still maintain the fiction, he limped elaborately.

"These white devil doctors," he remarked glumly. "All they know is five dollars, please."

Henry Li was looking at him keenly. "I recall," he said, "there was one other who came to ask questions about Li Gung. An Englishman—a large man. They are clever and cool, the English, like a thief amid the fire. Was it not his death I read about in the morning paper?"

"I know nothing of the matter," responded Chan stiffly.

"Of course." Henry Li followed to the door. "If you will accept advice offered in humble spirit," he added, "you will walk softly. What a pity if you encountered a really serious accident."

Mumbling a good-by, Chan went out. By the door he passed young Willie Li, who was grinning broadly. The event had come to an unexpected ending, but none the less the lad was happy. He was a boy scout, and he had done his good turn for the day.

Chan returned to the street, thoroughly upset. Rarely had any of his little deceptions ended so disastrously. His usefulness on the trail of Li Gung was no doubt over for all time. He consigned all boy scouts to limbo with one muttered imprecation.

Entering a drug store, he purchased a quantity of lamp black and a camel's hair brush. Then he went on to the Kirk Building. The night watchman took him up to the bungalow, and he let himself in with a key Kirk had given him. The place was dark and silent. He switched on the lights, and made a round of the rooms. No one seemed to be about.

He unlocked the compartment in Kirk's desk, and carefully removed the sheet of paper that had arrived in the envelope from Scotland Yard. With satisfaction he noted the paper was of a cheap variety, highly glazed. Along the lines where it had been folded, some one's fingers must have pressed hard.

Seated at the desk, with a floor lamp glowing brightly at his side, he cautiously sprinkled the black powder in the most likely place. Then he carefully dusted it with his brush. He was rewarded by the outline of a massive thumb—the thumb of a big man. He considered. Carrick Enderby was a big man. He was employed at Cook's. In some way he must procure impressions of Enderby's thumb.

He returned the paper to the compartment, and with it the tools of his investigation. Turning over ways and means in his mind, he sat down in a comfortable chair, took up Colonel John Beetham's story of his life, and began to read.

About an hour later Paradise came in from outside. He was absent for a moment in the pantry. Then, entering the living-room with his inevitable silver platter, he removed a few letters and laid them on Kirk's desk.

"The last mail is in, sir," he announced. "There is, I believe a picture post-card for you."

He carried card and tray negligently at his side, as though to express his contempt for picture post-cards. Chan looked up in surprise; he had telephoned the hotel to forward any mail to him here, and this was quick work. Paradise offered the tray, and Chan daintily took up the card.

It was from his youngest girl, designed to catch him just before he left. "Hurry home, honorable father," she wrote. "We miss you all the time. There is Kona weather here now, and we have ninety degrees of climate every day. Wishing to see you soon. Your loving daughter, Anna."

Chan turned over the card. He saw a picture of Waikiki, the surf boards riding the waves, Diamond Head beyond. He sighed with homesickness, and sat for a long moment immobile in his chair.

But as Paradise left the room, the little detective leaped nimbly to his feet and returned to the desk. For Paradise had glued the post-card to his tray with one large, moist thumb, a thumb which had fortunately rested on the light blue of Hawaii's lovely sky.

Quickly Chan applied lamp black and brush. Then he removed the blank paper from the compartment and with the aid of a reading glass, studied the impressions.

He leaned back in his chair with a puzzled frown. He knew now that he need not investigate the fingerprints of Carrick Enderby. The thumb print of Paradise was on the post-card, and the same print was on the blank sheet of paper that had arrived in the envelope from Scotland Yard. It was Paradise, then, who had tampered with Sir Frederic's mail.

9

The Port of Missing Women

Thursday morning dawned bright and fair. Stepping briskly from his bed to the window, Chan saw the sunlight sparkling cheerily on the waters of the harbor. It was a clear, cool world he looked upon, and the sight was invigorating. Nor for ever would he wander amid his present dark doubts and perplexities; one of these days he would see the murderer of Sir Frederic as plainly as he now saw the distant towers of Oakland. After that—the Pacific, the lighthouse on Makapuu Point, Diamond Head and a palm-fringed shore, and finally his beloved town of Honolulu nestling in the emerald cup of the hills.

Calm and unhurried, he prepared himself for another day, and left his bedroom. Barry Kirk, himself immaculate and unperturbed, was seated at the breakfast table reading the morning paper. Chan smiled at thought of the bomb he was about to toss at his gracious host. For he had not seen Kirk the previous night after his discovery. Though he had waited until midnight, the young man had not returned, and Chan had gone sleepily to bed.

"Good morning," Kirk said. "How's the famous sleuth to-day?"

"Doing as well as could be predicted," Chan replied. "You are tip-top yourself. I see it without the formal inquiring."

"True enough," Kirk answered. "I am full of vim, vigor and ambition, and ready for a new day's discoveries. By the way, I called Miss Morrow last night and gave her my grandmother's story about Eileen Enderby. She's going to arrange an interview with the lady, and you're invited. I hope I won't be left out of the party, either. If I am, it won't be my fault."

Chan nodded. "Interview is certainly indicated," he agreed.

Paradise entered, haughty and dignified as always, and after he had bestowed on each a suave good morning, placed orange juice before them. Kirk lifted his glass.

"Your very good health," he said, "in the wine of the country. California orange juice—of course you read our advertisements. Cures anything from insomnia to a broken heart. How did you spend last evening?"

"Me?" Chan shrugged. "I made slight sally into Chinatown."

"On Li Gung's trail, eh? What luck?"

"The poorest," returned Chan, grimacing at the memory. "I encounter Chinese boy scout panting to do good turn, and he does me one of the worst I ever suffered." He recounted his adventure, to Kirk's amusement.

"Tough luck," laughed the young man. "However, you probably got all you could, at that."

"Later," continued Chan, "the luck betters itself." Paradise came in with the cereal, and Chan watched him in silence. When the butler had gone, he added: "Last night in living-room out there I make astonishing discovery."

"You did? What was that?"

"How much you know about this perfect servant of yours?"

Kirk started. "Paradise? Good lord! You don't mean——"

"He came with references?"

"King George couldn't have brought better. Dukes and earls spoke of him in glowing terms. And why not? He's the best servant in the world."

"Too bad," commented Chan.

"What do you mean, too bad?"

"Too bad best servant in world has weakness for steaming open letters——" He stopped suddenly, for Paradise was entering with bacon and eggs. When he had gone out, Kirk leaned over and spoke in a low tense voice.

"Paradise opened that letter from Scotland Yard? How do you know?"

Briefly Charlie told him, and Kirk's face grew gloomy at the tale.

"I suppose I should have been prepared," he sighed. "The butler is always mixed up in a thing like this. But Paradise! My paragon of all the virtues. Oh well—'twas ever thus. 'I never loved a young gazelle——' What's the rest of it? What shall I do? Fire him?"

"Oh, no," protested Chan. "For the present, silence only. He must not know we are aware of his weakness. Just watchfully waiting."

"Suits me," agreed Kirk. "I'll hang on to him until you produce the handcuffs. What a pity it will seem to lock up such competent hands as his."

"May not happen," Chan suggested.

"I hope not," Kirk answered fervently.

After breakfast Chan called the *Globe* office, and got Bill Rankin's home address. He routed the reporter from a well-earned sleep, and asked him to come at once to the bungalow.

An hour later Rankin, brisk and full of enthusiasm, arrived on the scene. He grinned broadly as he shook hands.

"Couldn't quite pull it off, eh?" he chided. "The cool, calm Oriental turned back at the dock."

Chan nodded. "Cool, calm Oriental gets too much like mainland Americans from circling in such lowering society. I have remained to assist Captain Flannery, much to his well-concealed delight."

Rankin laughed. "Yes—I talked with him last night. He's tickled pink but he won't admit it, even to himself. Well, what's the dope? Who killed Sir Frederic?"

"A difficult matter to determine," Chan replied. "We must go into the past, unearthing here and there. Just at present I am faced by small problem with which you can assist. So I have ventured to annoy you."

"No annoyance whatever. I'm happy to have you call on me. What are your orders?"

"For the present, keep everything shaded by darkness. No publicity. You understand it?"

"All right—for the present. But when the big moment comes, I'm the fair-haired boy. You understand it?"

Chan smiled. "Yes—you are the chosen one. That will happen. Just now, a little covered investigation. You recall the story of Eve Durand?"

"Will I ever forget it? I don't know when anything has made such an impression on me. Peshawar—the dark hills—the game of hide-and-seek—the little blonde, who never came back from the ride. If that isn't what the flappers used to call intriguing, I don't know what is."

"You speak true. Fifteen years ago, Sir Frederic said. But from neither Sir Frederic nor the clipping did I obtain the exact date, and for it I am yearning. On what day of what month, presumably in the year 1913, did Eve Durand wander off into unlimitable darkness of India? Could you supply the fact?"

Rankin nodded. "A story like that must have been in the newspapers all over the world. I'll have a look at our files for 1913 and see what I can find."

"Good enough," said Chan. "Note one other matter, if your please. Suppose you find accounts. Is the name of Colonel John Beetham anywhere mentioned?"

"What! Beetham! That bird? Is he in it?"

"You know him?"

"Sure—I interviewed him. A mysterious sort of guy. If he's in it, the story's even better than I thought."

"He may not be," warned Chan. "I am curious, that is all. You will then explore in files?"

"I certainly will. You'll hear from me *pronto*. I'm on my way now."

The reporter hurried off, leaving Chan to his ponderous book. For a long time he wandered with Colonel Beetham through lonely places, over blazing sands at one moment, at another over wastelands of snow. Men and camels and mules lay dead on the trail, but Beetham pushed on. Nothing stopped him.

During lunch the telephone rang, and Kirk answered. "Hello—oh, Miss Morrow. Of course. Good—he'll be there. So will I——I beg your pardon? . . . No trouble at all. Mr. Chan's a stranger here, and I don't want him to get lost. . . . Yes . . . Yes, I'm coming, so get resigned, lady, get resigned."

He hung up. "Well, we're invited to Miss Morrow's office at two o'clock to meet the Enderbys. That is, you're invited, and I'm going anyhow."

At two precisely Chan and his host entered the girl's office, a dusty, ill-lighted room piled high with law books. The deputy district attorney rose from behind an orderly desk and greeted them smilingly.

Kirk stood looking about the room. "Great Scott—is this where you spend your days?" He walked to the window. "Charming view of the alley, isn't it? I must take you out in the country some time and show you the grass and the trees. You'd be surprised."

"Oh, this room isn't so bad," the girl answered. "I'm not like some people. I keep my mind on my work."

Flannery came in. "Well, here we are again," he said. "All set for another tall story. Mrs. Enderby this time, eh? More women in this case than in the League of Women Voters."

"You still appear in baffled stage," Chan suggested.

"Sure I do," admitted the Captain. "I am. And how about you? I don't hear any very illuminating deductions from you."

"At any moment now," grinned Chan, "I may dazzle you with great light."

"Well, don't hurry on my account," advised Flannery. "We've got all year on this, of course. It's only Sir Frederic Bruce of Scotland Yard who was murdered. Nobody cares—except the whole British Empire."

"You have made progress?" Chan inquired.

"How could I? Every time I get all set to go at the thing in a reasonable way, I have to stop and hunt for a missing woman. I tell you, I'm getting fed up on that end of it. If there's any more nonsense about——"

The door opened, and a clerk admitted Carrick Enderby and his wife. Eileen Enderby, even before she spoke, seemed flustered and nervous. Miss Morrow rose.

"How do you do," she said. "Sit down, please. It was good of you to come."

"Of course we came," Eileen Enderby replied. "Though what it is you want, I for one can't imagine."

"We must let Miss Morrow tell us what is wanted, Eileen," drawled her husband.

"Oh, naturally," Mrs. Enderby's blue eyes turned from one to the other and rested at last on the solid bulk of Captain Flannery.

"We're going to ask a few questions, Mrs. Enderby," began Miss Morrow. "Questions that I know you'll be glad to answer. Tell me—had you ever met Sir Frederic Bruce before Mr. Kirk's dinner party the other night?"

"I'd never even heard of him," replied the woman firmly.

"Ah, yes. Yet just after Colonel Beetham began to show his pictures, Sir Frederic called you out into a passageway. He wanted to speak to you alone."

Eileen Enderby looked at her husband, who nodded. "Yes," she admitted. "He did. I was never so surprised in my life."

"What did Sir Frederic want to speak to you about?"

"It was a most amazing thing. He mentioned a girl—a girl I once knew very well."

"What about the girl?"

"Well—it was quite a mystery. This girl Sir Frederic spoke of—she disappeared one night. Just walked off into the dark and was never heard of again."

There was a moment's silence. "Did she disappear at Peshawar, in India?" Miss Morrow inquired.

"India? Why, no—not at all," replied Eileen Enderby.

"Oh, I see. Then he was speaking of Marie Lantelme, who disappeared from Nice?"

"Nice? Marie Lantelme? I don't know what you're talking about." Mrs. Enderby's pretty forehead wrinkled in amazement.

For the first time, Chan spoke. "It is now how many years," he asked, "since your friend was last seen?"

"Why—it must be—let me think. Seven—yes—seven years."

"She disappeared from New York, perhaps?"

"From New York—yes."

"Her name was Jennie Jerome?"

"Yes. Jennie Jerome."

Chan took out his wallet and removed a clipping. He handed it to Miss Morrow. "Once more, and I am hoping for the last time," he remarked, "I would humbly request that you read aloud a scrap of paper from Sir Frederic's effects."

Miss Morrow took the paper, her eyes wide. Captain Flannery's face was a study in scarlet. The girl began to read:

"What happened to Jennie Jerome? A famous New York modiste and an even more famous New York illustrator are among those who have been asking themselves that question for the past seven years.

"Jennie Jerome was what the French call a mannequin, a model employed by the fashionable house of DuFour et Cie, on Fifth Avenue, in New York. She was something more than a model, a rack for pretty clothes; she was a girl of charming and marked personality and a beauty that will not be forgot in seven times seven years. Though employed but a brief time by DuFour she was the most popular of all their models among the distinguished patrons of the house. A celebrated New York illustrator saw her picture in a newspaper and at once sought her out, offering her a large sum of money to pose for him.

"Jennie Jerome seemed delighted at the opportunity. She invited a number of her friends to a little dinner party at her apartment, to celebrate the event. When these friends arrived, the door of her apartment stood open. They entered. The table was set, the candles lighted, preparations for the dinner apparent. But the hostess was nowhere about.

"The boy at the telephone switchboard in the hall below reported that, a few minutes before, he had seen her run down the stairs and vanish into the night. He was the last person who saw Jennie Jerome. Her employer, Madame DuFour, and the illustrator who had been struck by her beauty, made every possible effort to trace her. These efforts came to nothing. Jennie Jerome had vanished into thin air. Eloped? But no man's name was ever linked with hers. Murdered? Perhaps. No one knows. At any rate, Jennie Jerome had gone without leaving a trace, and there the matter has rested for seven years."

"Another one of 'em," cried Flannery, as Miss Morrow stopped reading. "Great Scott—what are we up against?"

"A puzzle," suggested Chan calmly. He restored the clipping to his pocketbook.

"I'll say so," Flannery growled.

"You knew Jennie Jerome?" Miss Morrow said to Eileen Enderby.

Mrs. Enderby nodded. "Yes. I was employed by the same firm—DuFour. One of the models, too. I was working there when I met Mr. Enderby, who was in Cook's New York office at the time. I knew Jennie well. If I may say so, that story you just read has been touched up a bit. Jennie Jerome was just an ordinarily pretty girl—nothing to rave about. I believe some illustrator did want her to pose for him. We all got offers like that."

"Leaving her beauty out of it," smiled Miss Morrow, "she did disappear?"

"Oh, yes. I was one of the guests invited to her dinner. That part of it is true enough. She just walked off into the night."

"And it was this girl whom Sir Frederic questioned you about?"

"Yes. Somehow, he knew I was one of her friends—how he knew it, I can't imagine. At any rate, he asked me if I would know Jennie Jerome if I saw her again. I said I thought I would. He said: 'Have you seen her in the Kirk Building this evening?' "

"And you told him——"

"I told him I hadn't. He said to stop and think a minute. I couldn't see the need of that. I hadn't seen her—I was sure of it."

"And you still haven't seen her?"

"No—I haven't."

Miss Morrow rose. "We are greatly obliged to you, Mrs. Enderby. That is all, I believe. Captain Flannery——"

"That's all from me," said Flannery.

"Well, if there's any more I can tell you——" Mrs. Enderby rose, with evident relief.

Her husband spoke. "Come along, Eileen," he said sternly. They went out. The four left behind in the office stared at one another in wonder.

"There you are," exploded Flannery, rising. "Another missing woman. Eve Durand, Marie Lantelme and Jennie Jerome. Three—count 'em—three—and if you believe your ears, every damn one of 'em was in the Kirk Building night before last. I don't know how it sounds to you, but to me it's all wrong."

"It does sound fishy," Barry Kirk admitted. "The Port of Missing Women—and I thought I was running just an ordinary office building."

"All wrong, I tell you," Flannery went on loudly. "It never happened, that's all. Somebody's kidding us to a fare-ye-well. This last story is one too many——" He stopped, and stared at Charlie Chan. "Well, Sergeant—what's on your mind?" he inquired.

"Plenty," grinned Chan. "On one side of our puzzle, at least, light is beginning to break. This last story illuminates darkness. You follow after me, of course."

"I do not. What are you talking about?"

"You do not? A great pity. In good time, I show you."

"All right—all right," cried Flannery. "I leave these missing women to you and Miss Morrow here. I don't want to hear any more about 'em—I'll go dippy if I do. I'll stick to the main facts. Night before last Sir Frederic Bruce was murdered in an office on the twentieth floor of the Kirk Building. Somebody slipped away from that party, or somebody got in from outside, and did for him. There was a book beside him, and there were marks on the fire-escape—I didn't tell you that, but there were—and the murderer nabbed a pair of velvet shoes off his feet. That's my case, my job, and by heaven I'm going after it, and if anybody comes to me with any more missing women stories——"

He stopped. The outer door had opened, and Eileen Enderby was coming in. At her heels came her husband, stern and grim. The woman appeared very much upset.

"We—we've come back," she said. She sank into a chair. "My husband thinks—he has made me see——"

"I have insisted," said Carrick Enderby, "that my wife tell you the entire story. She has omitted a very important point."

"I'm in a terrible position," the woman protested. "I do hope I'm doing the right thing. Carry—are you sure——"

"I am sure," cut in her husband, "that in a serious matter of this sort, truth is the only sane course."

"But she begged me not to tell," Eileen Enderby reminded him. "She pleaded so hard. I don't want to make trouble for her——"

"You gave no promise," her husband said. "And if the woman's done nothing wrong, I don't see——"

"Look here," broke in Flannery. "You came back to tell us something. What is it?"

"You came back to tell us that you have seen Jennie Jerome?" suggested Miss Morrow.

Mrs. Enderby nodded, and began to speak with obvious reluctance.

"Yes—I did see her— but not before I talked with Sir Frederic. I told him the truth. I hadn't seen her then—that is, I had seen her, but I didn't notice—one doesn't, you know——"

"But you noticed later."

"Yes—on our way home. Going down in the elevator. I got a good look at her then, and that was when I realized it. The elevator girl in the Kirk Building night before last was Jennie Jerome."

10

The Letter from London

Captain Flannery got up and took a turn about the room. He was a simple man and the look on his face suggested that the complexities of his calling were growing irksome. He stopped in front of Eileen Enderby.

"So—the elevator girl in the Kirk Building was Jennie Jerome? Then you lied a few minutes ago when you told Miss Morrow you hadn't seen her?"

"You can't hold that against her," Enderby protested. "She's come back of her own free will to tell you the truth."

"But why didn't she tell it in the first place?"

"One doesn't care to become involved in a matter of this sort. That's only natural."

"All right, all right." Flannery turned back to Mrs. Enderby. "You say you recognized this girl when you were going down in the elevator, on your way home after the dinner? And you let her see that you recognized her?"

"Oh, yes. I cried out in surprise: 'Jennie! Jennie Jerome! What are you doing here?'"

"You saw what she was doing, didn't you?"

"It was just one of those questions—it didn't mean anything."

"Yeah. And what did she say?"

"She just smiled quietly and said: 'Hello, Eileen. I was wondering if you'd know me.'"

"Then what?"

"There were a thousand questions I wanted to ask of course. Why she ran away that time—where she had been——But she wouldn't answer, she just shook her head, still smiling, and said maybe some other time she'd tell me everything. And then she asked me if I'd do this—this favor for her."

"You mean, keep still about the fact that you'd seen her?"

"Yes. She said she'd done nothing wrong, but that if the story about how she left New York came out it might create a lot of suspicion——"

"According to your husband, you made no promise?" Flannery said.

"No, I didn't. Under ordinary conditions, of course, I'd have promised at once. But I thought of Sir Frederic's murder, and it seemed to me a very serious thing she was asking. So I just said I'd think it over and let her know when I saw her again."

"And have you seen her again?"

"No, I haven't. It was all so strange. I hardly knew what to do."

"Well, you'd better keep away from her," Flannery suggested.

"I'll keep away from her all right. I feel as though I'd betrayed her." Eileen Enderby glanced accusingly at her husband.

"You were not in her debt," said Enderby. "Lying's a dangerous business in a matter of this kind."

"You're lucky, Mrs. Enderby," said the Captain. "You've got a sensible husband. Just listen to him, and you'll be O.K. I guess that's all now. You can go. Only keep this to yourself."

"I'll certainly do that," the woman assured him. She rose.

"If I want you again, I'll let you know," Flannery added.

Chan opened the door for her. "May I be permitted respectful inquiry," he ventured. "The beautiful garment marked by iron rust stains—it was not ruined beyond reclaim?"

"Oh, not at all," she answered. She paused, as though she felt that the matter called for an explanation. "When I saw that man on the fire-escape I became so excited I leaned against the garden railing. It was dripping with fog. Careless of me, wasn't it?"

"In moment of stress, how easy to slip into careless act," returned Chan. Bowing low, he closed the door after the Enderbys.

"Well," said Flannery, "I guess we're getting somewhere at last. Though if you ask me where, I can't tell you. Anyhow, we know that Sir Frederic was looking for Jennie Jerome the night he was killed, and that Jennie Jerome was running an elevator just outside his door. By heaven, I've a notion to lock her up right now."

"But you haven't anything against her," Miss Morrow objected. "You know that."

"No, I haven't. However, the newspapers are howling for an arrest. They always are. I could give 'em Jennie Jerome—a pretty girl—they'd eat it up. Then, if nothing else breaks against her, I could let her off, sort of quiet."

"Such tactics are beneath you, Captain," Miss Morrow said. "I trust that when we make an arrest, it will be based on something more tangible than any evidence we've got so far. Are you with me, Mr. Chan?"

"Undubitably," Chan replied. He glanced up at the frowning face of the Captain. "If I may make humble suggestion——"

"Of course," agreed Miss Morrow.

But Chan, it seemed, changed his mind. He kept his humble suggestion to himself. "Patience," he finished lamely, "always brightest plan in these matters. Acting as champion of that lovely virtue, I have fought many fierce battles. American has always the urge to leap too quick. How well it was said, retire a step and you have the advantage."

"But these newspaper men——" protested the Captain.

"I do not wish to infest the picture," Chan smiled, "but I would like to refer to my own habit in similar situation. When newspapers rage, I put nice roll of cotton in the ears. Simmered down to truth, I am responsible party, not newspaper reporter. I tell him with exquisite politeness to fade off and hush down."

"A good plan," laughed Miss Morrow. She turned to Barry Kirk. "By the way, do you know anything about this elevator girl? Grace Lane was, I believe, the name she gave the other night."

Kirk shook his head. "Not a thing. Except that she's the prettiest girl we've ever employed in the building. I'd noticed that, of course."

"I rather thought you had," Miss Morrow said.

"Lady, I'm not blind," he assured her. "I notice beauty anywhere—in elevators, in cable cars—even in a lawyer's office. I tried to talk to this girl once or twice, but I didn't get very far. If you like, I'll try it again."

"No, thanks. You'd probably be away off the subject."

"Well, it all sounds mighty mysterious to me," he admitted. "We thought Sir Frederic was on the trail of Eve Durand, and now it seems it must have been a couple of other women. The poor chap is gone, but he's left a most appalling puzzle on my doorstep. You're all such nice detectives—I don't want to hurt your feelings—but will you kindly tell me whither we are drifting? Where are we getting? Nowhere, if you ask me."

"I'm afraid you're right," Miss Morrow sighed.

"Maybe if I locked this woman up——" began Flannery, attached to the idea.

"No, no," Miss Morrow told him. "We can't do that. But we can shadow her. And since she is one who has some talent for walking off into the night. I suggest that you arrange the matter without delay."

Flannery nodded. "I'll put the boys on her trail. I guess you're right—we might get on to something that way. But Mr. Kirk has said it—we're not progressing very fast. If there was only some clue I could get my teeth into——"

Chan cut in. "Thanks for recalling my wandering ideas," he said. "So much has happened the matter was obscure in my mind. I have something here that might furnish excellent teeth-hold." He removed an envelope from his pocket and carefully extracted a folded sheet of paper and a picture post-card. "No doubt, Captain, you have more cleverness with fingerprints than stupid man like me. Could you say—are these thumb prints identically the same?"

Flannery studied the two items. "They look the same to me. I could put our expert on them—but say, what's this all about?"

"Blank sheet of paper," Chan explained, "arrive in envelope marked Scotland Yard. Without question Miss Morrow has told you?"

"Oh, yes—she mentioned that. Somebody tampering with the mail, eh? And this thumb print on the post-card?"

"Bestowed there last night by digit of Paradise, Mr. Kirk's butler," Chan informed him.

Flannery jumped up. "Well, why didn't you say so? Now we're getting on. You've got the makings of a detective after all, Sergeant. Paradise, eh—fooling with Uncle Sam's mail. That's good enough for me—I'll have him behind the bars in an hour."

Chan lifted a protesting hand. "Oh, no—my humblest apologies. Again you leap too sudden. We must watch and wait——"

"The hell you say," Flannery cried. "That's not my system. I'll nab him. I'll make him talk——"

"And I," sighed Barry Kirk, "will lose my perfect butler. Shall I write him a reference—or won't they care, at the jail?"

"Captain, pause and listen," pleaded Chan. "We have nothing here to prove Paradise fired fatal bullet into Sir Frederic. Yet somehow he is involved. We watch his every move. Much may be revealed by the unsuspecting. We hunt through his effects. To-day, I believe, he enjoys weekly holiday. Is that not so?" He looked at Kirk.

"Yes, it's Black Thursday—the servants' day off," Kirk said. "Paradise is probably at the movies—he adores them. Melodrama—that's his meat."

"Fortunate event," continued Chan. "Cook too is out. We return to bungalow and do some despicable prying into private life of Paradise. Is that not better Captain, than searching through crowded atmosphere of movie theaters to make foolish arrest?"

Flannery considered. "Well, I guess it is, at that."

"Back to the bungalow," said Kirk, rising. "If Miss Morrow will lend a hand, I'll give you tea."

"Count me out," said Flannery.

"And other liquids," amended Kirk.

"Count me in again," added Flannery. "You got your car?" Kirk nodded. "You take Miss Morrow then, and the Sergeant and I will follow in mine."

In the roadster on their way to the Kirk Building, Barry Kirk glanced at Miss Morrow and smiled.

"Yes?" she inquired.

"I was just thinking. I do, at times."

"Is it necessary?"

"Perhaps not. But I find it exhilarating. I was thinking at that moment about you."

"Oh, please don't trouble."

"No trouble at all. I was wondering. There are so many mysterious women hovering about this case. And no one is asking you any questions."

"Why should they?"

"Why shouldn't they? Who are you? Where did you come from? Since you're not very likely to investigate yourself, perhaps I should take over the job."

"You're very kind."

"I hope you won't object. Of course, you look young and innocent, but I have your word for it that men are easily fooled." He steered round a lumbering truck, then turned to her sternly. "Just what were you doing on the night Eve Durand slipped from sight at Peshawar?"

"I was probably worrying over my home work," the girl replied. "I was always very conscientious, even in the lowest grades."

"I'll bet you were. And where was this great mental effort taking place? Not in San Francisco?"

"No, in Baltimore. That was my home before I came west to law school."

"Yes? Peering further into your dark past—why, in heaven's name, the law school? Disappointed in love, or something?"

She smiled. "Not at all. Father was a judge, and it broke his heart that I wasn't a boy."

"I've noticed how unreasonable judges are. Times when they've talked to me about my automobile driving. So the judge wanted a boy? He didn't know his luck."

"Oh, he gradually discovered I wasn't a total loss. He asked me to study law, and I did."

"What an obedient child," Kirk said.

"I didn't mind—in fact, I rather liked it. You see, frivolous things never have appealed to me."

"I'm afraid that's true. And it worries me."

"Why should it?"

"Because, as it happens, I'm one of those frivolous things."

"But surely you have your serious side?"

"No—I'm afraid that side was just sketched in—never finished. However, I'm working on it. Before I get through you'll be calling me deacon."

"Really? I'm afraid I've never cared much for deacons, either."

"Well, not exactly deacon, then. I'll try to strike a happy medium."

"I'll help you," smiled the girl.

Kirk parked his car in a side street, and they went round the corner to the Kirk Building. It was Grace Lane who took them aloft. Kirk studied her with a new interest. Strands of dark red hair crept out from beneath her cap; her face was pale, but unlined and young. Age uncertain, Kirk thought, but beauty unmistakable. What was the secret of her past? Why had Sir Frederic brought to the Kirk Building that clipping about Jennie Jerome?

"I'll be along in a minute," Miss Morrow said, when the elevator stopped at the twentieth floor. Kirk nodded and preceded her to the roof. She followed almost immediately. "I wanted to ask a question or two," she explained. "You see, I gave Grace Lane very little attention on the night Sir Frederic was killed."

"What do you think of her—now that you've looked again?"

"She's a lady—if you don't mind an overworked word. This job she has now is beneath her."

"Think so?" Kirk took Miss Morrow's coat. "I should have said that most of the time, it's over her head."

The girl shrugged. "That from you, deacon," she said, reproachfully.

Chan and Captain Flannery were at the door, and Kirk let them in. The Captain was all business.

"Hello," he said. "Now if you'll show us that butler's room, Mr. Kirk, we'll get busy right away. I've brought a few skeleton keys. We'll go over the place like a vacuum cleaner." Kirk led them into the corridor.

"How about the cook's room?" Flannery added. "We might take a look at that."

"My cook's a Frenchman," Kirk explained. "He sleeps out."

"Humph. He was here the other night at the time of the murder?"

"Yes, of course."

"Well, I'd better have a talk with him some time."

"He speaks very little English," Kirk smiled. "You'll enjoy him." He left the two in the butler's bedroom, and returned to Miss Morrow.

"I suppose you hate the sight of a kitchen," he suggested.

"Why should I?"

"Well—a big lawyer like you——"

"But I've studied cook-books, too. You'd be surprised. I can cook the most delicious——"

"Rarebit," he finished. "I know. And your chocolate fudge was famous at the sorority house. I've heard it before."

"Please let me finish. I was going to say, pot roast. And my lemon pie is not so bad, either."

He stood solemnly regarding her. "Lady," he announced, "you improve on acquaintance. And if that isn't gilding the lily, I don't know what is. Come with me and we'll dig up the tea things."

She followed him to the kitchen. "I've got a little apartment," she said. "And when I'm not too tired, I get my own dinner."

"How are you on Thursday nights?" he asked. "Pretty tired?"

"That depends. Why?"

"Servants' night out. Need I say more?"

Miss Morrow laughed. "I'll remember," she promised. With deft hands she set the water to boiling, and began to arrange the tea tray. "How neat everything is," she remarked. "Paradise is a wonder."

"Tell that to my grandmother," Kirk suggested. "She believes that a man who lives alone wallows in grime and waste. Every home needs a woman's touch, according to her story."

"Absurd," cried the girl.

"Oh, well—grandmother dates back a few years. In her day women were housekeepers. Now they're movie fans, club members, lawyers—what have you? Must have been a rather comfortable age at that."

"For the men, yes."

"And men don't count any more."

"I wouldn't say that. I guess we're ready now."

Kirk carried the tray to the living-room, and placed it on a low table before the fire. Miss Morrow sat down behind it. He threw a couple of logs on to the glowing embers, then, visiting the dining-room, returned with a bottle, a siphon and glasses.

"Mustn't forget that Captain Flannery doesn't approve of tea," he said.

Miss Morrow looked toward the passageway. "They'd better hurry, or they'll be late for the party," she remarked.

But Chan and Flannery did not appear. Outside the March dusk was falling; a sharp wind swept through the little garden and rattled insistently at the casements. Kirk drew the curtains. On the hearth the fresh logs flamed, filling the room with a warm, satisfying glow. He took from Miss Morrow's hand his cup of tea, selected a small cake, and dropped into a chair.

"Cozy—that would be my word for this," he smiled. "To look at you now, no one would ever suspect that old affair between you and Blackstone."

"I'm versatile, anyhow," she said.

"I wonder," he replied.

"Wonder what?"

"I wonder just how versatile you are. It's a matter I intend to investigate further. I may add that I am regarded throughout the world as the greatest living judge of a lemon pie."

"You frighten me," Miss Morrow said.

"If your testimony has been the truth, so help you," he answered, "what is there to be frightened about?"

At that moment Chan and Flannery appeared in the doorway. The Captain seemed very pleased with himself.

"What luck?" Kirk inquired.

"The best," beamed Flannery. He carried a piece of paper in his hand. "Ah—shall I help myself?"

"By all means," Kirk told him. "A congratulatory potion. Mr. Chan—what's yours?"

"Tea, if Miss Morrow will be so kind. Three lumps of sugar and the breath of the lemon in passing."

The girl prepared his cup. Flannery dropped into a chair.

"I see you've found something," Kirk suggested.

"I certainly have," the Captain replied. "I've found the letter from Scotland Yard that Paradise nabbed from the mail."

"Good enough," cried Kirk.

"A slick bird, this Paradise," Flannery went on. "Where do you think he had it? All folded up in a little wad and tucked into the toe of a shoe."

"How clever of you to look there," Miss Morrow approved.

Flannery hesitated. "Well—er—come to think of it, I didn't. It was Sergeant Chan here dug it up. Yes, sir—the Sergeant's getting to be a real sleuth."

"Under your brilliant instruction," smiled Chan.

"Well, we can all learn from each other," conceded the Captain. "Anyhow, he found it, and turned it right over to me. The letter that came in the Scotland Yard envelope—no question about it. See—at the top—the Metropolitan Police——"

"If it's not asking too much," said Kirk, "what's in the letter?"

Flannery's face fell. "Not a whole lot. We'll have to admit that. But little by little——"

"With brief steps we advance," put in Chan. "Humbly suggest you read the epistle."

"Well, it's addressed to Sir Frederic, care of Cook's, San Franciso," said Flannery. He read:

> "Dear Sir Frederic:
> "I was very glad to get your letter from Shanghai and to
> know that you are near the end of a long trail. It is indeed

surprising news to me that the murder of Hilary Galt and the disappearance of Eve Durand from Peshawar are, in your final analysis, linked together. I know you always contended they were, but much as I admire your talents, I felt sure you were mistaken. I can only apologize most humbly. It is a matter of regret to me that you did not tell me more; what you wrote roused my interest to a high pitch. Believe me, I shall be eager to hear the end of this strange case.

"By the way, Inspector Rupert Duff will be in the States on another matter at about the time you reach San Francisco. You know Duff, of course. A good man. If you should require his help, you have only to wire him at the Hotel Waldorf, New York.

"With all good wishes for a happy outcome to your investigation, I am, sir, always, your obedient servant, Martin Benfield, Deputy-Commissioner."

Flannery stopped reading and looked at the others. "Well, there you are," he said. "The Galt affair and Eve Durand are mixed up together. Of course that ain't exactly news—I've known it right along. What I want to find out now is, why did Paradise try to keep this information from us? What's his stake in the affair? I could arrest him at once, but I'm afraid that if I do, he'll shut up like a clam and that will end it. He doesn't know we're wise to him, so I'm going to put this letter back where we found it and give him a little more rope. The sergeant here has agreed to keep an eye on him, and I rely on you, too, Mr. Kirk, to see that he doesn't get away."

"Don't worry," said Kirk. "I don't want to lose him."

Flannery rose. "Sir Frederic's mail isn't coming here any more?" he inquired of Miss Morrow.

"No, of course not. I arranged to have it sent to my office. There's been nothing of interest—purely personal matters."

"I must put this letter back, and then I'll have to run along," the Captain said. He went into the passageway.

"Well," remarked Kirk, "Paradise hangs on a little longer. I see your handiwork there, Sergeant, and you have my warmest thanks."

"For a brief time, at least," Chan said. "You will perceive I am no person's fool. I do not arrange arrest of butler in house where I am guest. I protect him, and I would do same for the cook."

Flannery returned. "I got to get back to the station," he announced. "Mr. Kirk, thanks for your—er—hospitality."

Miss Morrow looked up at him. "You are going to wire to New York for Inspector Duff?" she asked.

"I am not," the Captain said.

"But he might be of great help——"

"Nix," cut in Flannery stubbornly. "I got about all the help I can stand on this case now. Get him here and have him under foot? No, sir—I'm going to find out first who killed Sir Frederic. After that, they can all come. Don't you say so, Sergeant?"

Chan nodded. "You are wise man. The ship with too many steersmen never reaches port."

11

The Muddy Water Clears

Flannery departed, and Miss Morrow picked up her coat. Reluctantly Kirk held it for her. "Must you go?" he protested.

"Back to the office—yes," she said. "I've oceans of work. The district attorney keeps asking me for results in this investigation, and so far all I have been able to report is further mysteries. I wonder if I'll ever have anything else."

"It was my hope," remarked Chan, "that to-day we take a seven-league step forward. But it is fated otherwise. Not before Monday now."

"Monday," repeated the girl. "What do you mean, Mr. Chan?"

"I mean I experience great yearning to bring Miss Gloria Garland to this building again. I have what my cousin Willie Chan, a vulgar speaker, calls a hunch. But this morning when I call Miss Garland on the telephone I learn that she is absent in Del Monte, and will not return until Sunday night."

"Miss Garland? What has she to do with it?"

"Remains to be observed. She may have much, or nothing. Depends on the authentic value of my hunch. Monday will tell."

"But Monday," sighed Miss Morrow. "This is only Thursday."

Chan also sighed. "I too resent that with bitter feelings. Do not forget that I have sworn to be on boat departing Wednesday. My little son demands me."

"Patience," laughed Barry Kirk. "The doctor must take his own medicine."

"I know," shrugged Chan. "I am taking same in plenty large doses. Mostly when I talk of patience, I am forcing it on others. Speaking for myself in this event, I do not much enjoy the flavor."

"You said nothing about your hunch to Captain Flannery," Miss Morrow remarked.

Chan smiled. "Can you speak of the ocean to a well frog, or of ice to a summer insect? The good Captain would sneer—until I prove to him I am exceedingly correct. I am praying to do that on Monday."

"In the meantime, we watch and wait," said Miss Morrow.

"You wait, and I will watch," suggested Chan.

Kirk accompanied Miss Morrow to the door. *"Au revoir,"* he said. "And whatever you do, don't lose that lemon pie recipe."

"You needn't keep hinting," she replied. "I won't forget."

Upon Kirk's return, Charlie regarded him keenly. "A most attracting young woman," he remarked.

"Charming," agreed Kirk.

"What a deep pity," Chan continued, "that she squanders glowing youth in a man's pursuit. She should be at mothering work."

Kirk laughed. "You tell her," he suggested.

On Friday, Bill Rankin called Chan on the telephone. He had been through the *Globe's* files for the year 1913, he said—a long, arduous job. His search had been without result; he could find no story about Eve Durand. Evidently cable news had not greatly interested the *Globe's* staff in those days.

"I'm going to the public library for another try," he announced. "No doubt some of the New York papers carried the story. They seem our best bet now. I'm terribly busy, but I'll speed all I can."

"Thanks for your feverish activity," Chan replied. "You are valuable man."

"Just a real good wagon," laughed Rankin. "Here's hoping I don't break down. I'll let you know the minute I find something."

Saturday came; the life at the bungalow was moving forward with unbroken calm. Through it Paradise walked with his accustomed dignity and poise, little dreaming of the dark cloud of suspicion that hovered over his head. Chan was busy with the books of Colonel John Beetham; he had finished the *Life* and was now going methodically through the others as though in search of a clue.

On Saturday night Kirk was dining out, and after his own dinner Chan again went down into Chinatown. There was little he could do there, he knew, but the place drew him none the less. This time he did not visit his cousin, but loitered on the crowded sidewalk of Grant Avenue.

Catching sight of the lights outside the Mandarin Theater, he idly turned his footsteps toward the doorway. The Chinese have been a civilized race for many centuries; they do not care greatly for moving-pictures, preferring the spoken drama. A huge throng was milling about the door of the theater, and Chan paused. There was usually enough drama in real life to satisfy him, but to-night he felt the need of the painted players.

Suddenly in the mob he caught sight of Willie Li, the boy scout whose good deed had thwarted his best laid plans on the previous Wednesday evening. Willie was gazing wistfully at the little frame of actors' pictures in the lobby. Chan went up to him with a friendly smile.

"Ah, we meet again," he said in Cantonese. "How fortunate, since the other night I walked my way churlishly, without offering my thanks for the great kindness you did me in bringing a physician."

The boy's face brightened in recognition. "May I be permitted to hope that the injury is improved?" he said.

"You have a kind heart," Chan replied. "I now walk on the foot with the best of health. Be good enough to tell me, have you performed your kind act for today?"

The boy frowned. "Not yet. Opportunities are so seldom."

"Ah, yes—how true. But if you will deign to come into the theater as my guest, opportunities may increase. Each of the actors, as you know, receives in addition to his salary a bonus of twenty-five cents for every round of applause that is showered upon him. Come, and by frequent applauding you may pile up enough kind acts to spread over several days."

The boy was only too willing, and buying a couple of tickets, Chan led him inside. The horrible din that greeted them they did not find disconcerting. It was, in fact, music to their ears. Even at this early hour the house was crowded. On the stage, with the casual, offhand manner they affected, the Chinese company was enacting a famous historical play. Chan and the boy were fortunate enough to find seats.

Looking about, the detective from Hawaii saw that he was in a gathering of his own race exclusively. The women members of the audience were arrayed in their finest silks; in a stage box sat a slave girl famous in the colony. Little, slant-eyed children played in the aisles; occasionally a mother sent out to the refreshment booth in the lobby a bottle of milk, to be heated for the baby in her arms.

The clatter of the six-piece orchestra never ceased; it played more softly at dramatic moments, but comedy lines were spoken to the accompaniment of a terrific fusillade. Chan became engrossed in the play, for the actors were finished artists, the women players particularly graceful and accomplished. At eleven o'clock he suggested that they had better go, lest the boy's family be troubled about him.

"My father will not worry," said Willie Li. "He knows a boy scout is trustworthy."

Nevertheless Chan led him to the lobby, and there stood treat to a hot dog and a cup of coffee—for the refreshment booth alone was Americanized. As they climbed the empty street to the Oriental Apartments, Charlie looked inquiringly at the boy.

"Tell me," he said, still speaking in Cantonese, "of your plans for the future. You are ambitious. What profession calls you?"

"I would be an explorer, like my cousin Li Gung," the boy answered in the same rather stilted tongue.

"Ah, yes—he who is attached to Colonel John Beetham," nodded Chan. "You have heard from your cousin stories of Colonel Beetham?"

"Many exciting ones," the boy replied.

"You admire the Colonel? You think him very great character?"

"Why not? He is man of iron, stern but just. Discipline is with him important thing, and all boy scouts know that is right thinking. Many examples of this our cousin told us. Sometimes, Li Gung said, the caravan would revolt. Then the Colonel would snatch out gun, facing them with his bravery, alone. The caravan would tremble and proceed."

"They knew, perhaps, that the Colonel would not hesitate to fire?"

"They had seen him do it. One event Li Gung spoke about I can never forget." The boy's voice rose in excitement. "It was on the desert, and the Colonel had told them what they must do, and what they must not do. A dirty keeper of camels, a man of low character, he did a thing which the Colonel had forbidden. In an instant he lay on the sand, with a bullet in his heart."

"Ah, yes," said Chan, "I would expect that. However, it is an incident I have not encountered in any of the Colonel's books."

They were at the door of the apartment-house. "Accept my thanks, please," Willie Li said. "You have done a very kind deed to me."

Chan smiled. "Your company was a real pleasure. I hope we meet again."

"I hope it, too," answered Willie Li warmly. "Good night."

Chan walked slowly back to the Kirk Building. He was thinking of Colonel Beetham. A hard man, a man who did not hesitate to kill those who opposed their will to his. Here was food for thought.

On Sunday Barry Kirk called up Miss Morrow and suggested a ride into the country and dinner at a distant inn. "Just to clear the cobwebs from your brain," he put it.

"Thanks for the ad," she answered. "So that's how my brain strikes you? Cobwebby."

"You know what I mean," he protested. "I want you to keep keen and alert. Nothing must happen to that pie."

They spent a happy, care-free day on roads far from the rush of city traffic. When Kirk helped the girl out of the car before her door that night, he said: "Well, to-morrow morning Charlie springs his hunch."

"What do you imagine he has up his sleeve?"

"I haven't an idea. The more I see of him, the less I know him. But let's hope it's something good."

"And illuminating," added Miss Morrow. "I feel the need of a little light."

She held out her hand. "You've been lovely to me to-day."

"Give me another chance," he said. "Give me lots of 'em. I'll get lovelier and lovelier as time goes on."

"Is that a threat?" she laughed.

"A promise. I hope you don't mind."

"Why should I? Good night." She entered the lobby of her apartment-house.

On Monday morning Chan was brisk and businesslike. He called Gloria Garland and was much relieved to hear her answering voice. She agreed to come to the bungalow at ten o'clock, and Charlie at once got in touch with Miss Morrow and asked her to come at the same hour, bringing Captain Flannery. Then he turned to Kirk.

"Making humble suggestion," he said, "would you be so kind as to dispatch Paradise on lengthy errand just as ten o'clock approaches? I do not fancy him in bungalow this morning."

"Surely," agreed Kirk. "I'll send him out for some fishing tackle. I never get time to fish, but a man can't have too much tackle."

At fifteen minutes of ten Chan rose and got his hat. He would, he said, himself escort Miss Garland to the bungalow. Going below, he took up his stand in the doorway of the Kirk Building.

He saw Miss Morrow and Flannery enter, but gave them only a cool nod as they passed. Mystified, they went on up-stairs. Kirk met them at the door.

"Here we are," growled Flannery. "I wonder what the Sergeant's up to. If he's got me here on a wild goose chase, I'll deport him to Hawaii. I'm too busy to-day to feel playful."

"Oh, Chan will make good," Kirk assured him. "By the way, I suppose you've got that elevator girl—Jennie Jerome, or Grace Lane, or whatever her name is—under your eagle eye?"

"Yes. The boys have been shadowing her."

"Find out anything?"

"Not a thing. She's got a room on Powell Street. Stays in nights and minds her own business, as far as I can learn."

Down at the door, Chan was greeting Gloria Garland. "You are promptly on the minute," he approved. "A delectable virtue."

"I'm here, but I don't know what you want," she replied. "I told you everything the other day——"

"Yes, of course. Will you be kind enough to walk after me? We rise aloft."

He took her up in a car run by a black-haired Irish girl, and they entered the living-room of the bungalow.

"Ah, Captain—Miss Morrow—we are all here. That is correct," Charlie said. "Miss Garland, will you kindly recline on chair."

The woman sat down, obviously puzzled. Her eyes sought Flannery's. "What do you want with me now?" she asked.

The Captain shrugged his broad shoulders. "Me—I don't want you. It's Sergeant Chan here. He's had a mysterious hunch."

Chan smiled. "Yes, I am guilty party, Miss Garland. I hope I have not rudely unconvenienced you?"

"Not a bit," she answered.

"One day you told us of the girl Marie Lantelme, who disappeared so oddly out of Nice," Chan continued. "Will you kindly state—you have still not encountered her?"

"No, of course not," the woman replied.

"You are quite sure you would recognize her if you met her?"

"Of course. I knew her well."

Chan's eyes narrowed. "There would be no reason why you would conceal act of recognition from us? I might humbly remind you, this is serious affair."

"No—why should I do that? I'll tell you if I see her—but I'm sure I haven't——"

"Very good. Will you remain in present posture until my return?" Chan went rapidly out to the stairway leading to the floor below.

They looked at one another in wonder, but no one spoke. In a moment, Chan returned. With him came Grace Lane, the elevator girl whom Mrs. Enderby had identified as Jennie Jerome.

She came serenely into the room, and stood there. The sunlight fell full upon her, outlining clearly her delicately modeled face. Gloria Garland started, and half rose from her chair.

"Marie!" she cried. "Marie Lantelme! What are you doing here?"

They gasped. A look of triumph shone in Chan's narrow eyes.

The girl's poise did not desert her. "Hello, Gloria," she said softly. "We meet again."

"But where have you been, my dear?" Miss Garland wanted to know. "Where did you go—and why——"

The girl stopped her. "Some other time——" she said.

In a daze, Flannery rose to his feet. "Look here," he began. "Let me get this straight." He moved forward accusingly, "You are Marie Lantelme?"

"I was—once," she nodded.

"You were singing in the same troupe as Miss Garland here—eleven years ago, at Nice? You disappeared?"

"I did."

"Why?"

"I was tired of it. I found I didn't like the stage. If I had stayed, they would have forced me to go on. So I ran away."

"Yeah. And seven years ago you were in New York—a model for a dressmaker. Your name then was Jennie Jerome. You disappeared again?"

"For the same reason. I didn't care for the work. I—I'm restless, I guess——"

"I'll say you're restless. You kept changing names?"

"I wanted to start all over. A new person."

Flannery glared at her. "There's something queer about you, my girl. You know who I am, don't you?"

"You appear to be a policeman."

"Well, that's right. I am."

"I have never done anything wrong. I am not afraid."

"Maybe not. But tell me this—what do you know about Sir Frederic Bruce?"

"I know that he was a famous man from Scotland Yard, who was killed in Mr. Kirk's office last Tuesday night."

"Ever see him before he came here?"

"No, sir—I never had."

"Ever hear of him?"

"I don't believe so."

Her even, gentle answers put Flannery at a loss. He stood, considering. His course was far from clear.

"You were running the elevator here last Tuesday night?" he continued.

"Yes, sir, I was."

"Have you any idea why Sir Frederic was hunting for you? For Marie

Lantelme, or Jennie Jerome, or whoever you really are?"

She frowned. "Was he hunting for me? How strange. No, sir,—I have no idea at all."

"Well," said Flannery, "let me tell you this. You're a pretty important witness in the matter of Sir Frederic's murder, and I don't intend you shall get away."

The girl smiled. "So I judge. I seem to have been followed rather closely the past few days."

"Well, you'll be followed even more closely from now on. One false move, and I lock you up. You understand that?"

"Perfectly, sir."

"All right. Just tend to your work, and when I want you, I'll tell you so. You can go now."

"Thank you, sir," the girl replied, and went out.

Flannery turned to Miss Garland. "You recognized her the other night, didn't you?" he demanded.

"Oh, but I assure you, I didn't. I recognized her to-day for the first time."

"Which is plenty time enough," said Chan. "Miss Garland, we are sunk deep in your debt. I permit you now to depart——"

"Yeah—you can go," added Flannery. "Take some other car and keep away from your old friend until this thing's cleared up."

"I'll do that," Miss Garland assured him. "I'm afraid she didn't want me to identify her. I do hope I haven't got her into trouble."

"That depends," answered Flannery, and Kirk showed the actress out.

Chan was beaming. "Hunch plenty good, after all," he chuckled.

"Well, where are we?" Flannery said. "The elevator girl is Jennie Jerome. Then she's Marie Lantelme. What does that mean?"

"It means only one thing," said Miss Morrow softly.

"The Captain is pretending to be dense," suggested Chan. "He could not really be so thick."

"What are you talking about?" Flannery demanded.

"My hunch, which has come so nicely true," Chan told him. "The elevator girl is Jennie Jerome. Next, she is Marie Lantelme. What does it mean, you ask? It means one thing only. She is also Eve Durand."

"By heaven!" Flannery cried.

"Consider how the muddy water clears," Chan went on. "Eve Durand flees from India one dark night fifteen years ago. Four years later she is found in Nice, playing in theater. Something happens—maybe she is seen and recognized—again she runs away. Another four years elapse and we encounter her in New York, walking in model gowns. Again something happens, again she disappears. Where does she go? Eventually, to San Francisco. Here opportunities are not so good, she must take more lowly position. And here Sir Frederic comes, always seeking for Eve Durand."

"It's beautifully clear," approved Miss Morrow.

"Like lake at evening," nodded Chan. "Sir Frederic, though he has looked long for this woman, has never seen her. He can upearth here no one who can identify Eve Durand, but he remembers once she was Marie Lantelme, once Jennie Jerome. In this great city, he learns, are two people who have known her when she was wearing these other names. He asks that they be invited to dinner, hoping that one or both will point out to him the woman he has trailed so long."

Flannery was walking the floor. "Well—I don't know. It's almost too good to be true. But if it is—if she's Eve Durand—then I can't let her wander around loose. I'll have to lock her up this morning, if I could only be sure——"

"I am telling you," persisted Chan.

"I know, but you are guessing. You've identified her as those other two, but as for Eve Durand——"

The telephone rang. Kirk answered, and handed it to Flannery, "For you, Captain," he said.

Flannery took the telephone. "Oh—hello, Chief," he said. "Yeah—yeah. What's that? Oh—oh, he is? Good enough. Thank you, Chief. I sure will."

He hung up the receiver and turned to the others. A broad smile was on his face.

"We're going to find out, Sergeant, just how good a guesser you are," he said. "I'll put a couple of extra men to following this dame, but I won't do anything more until to-morrow. Yes, sir—by to-morrow evening I'll know whether she's Eve Durand or not."

"Your words have obscure sound," Chan told him.

"The Chief of Police has just had a wire," Flannery explained. "Inspector Duff of Scotland Yard is getting in to-morrow afternoon at two thirty. And he's bringing with him the one man in all the world who's sure to know Eve Durand when he sees her. He's bringing the woman's husband, Major Eric Durand."

12

A Misty Evening

When Chan and Kirk were left alone, the little detective sat staring thoughtfully into space. "Now Tuesday becomes the big day for keen anticipation," he remarked. "What will it reveal? Much, I hope, for my time on the mainland becomes a brief space indeed."

Kirk looked at him in wonder. "Surely you won't go on Wednesday, if this thing isn't solved?"

Chan nodded stubbornly. "I have made unspoken promise to Barry Chan. Now I put it into words. Tomorrow Eve Durand's husband arrives. In all the world we could have selected no more opportune person. He will identify this elevator woman as his wife, or he will not. If he does, perhaps case is finished. If he does not"—Charlie shrugged—"then I have done all possible. Let Captain Flannery flounder alone after that."

"Well, we won't cross our oceans until we get to them," Kirk suggested. "A lot may happen before Wednesday. By the way, I've been meaning to take you over to the Cosmopolitan Club. How about lunching there this noon?"

Chan brightened. "I have long nursed desire to see that famous interior. You are most kind."

"All set, then," replied his host. "I have some business in the office. Come down-stairs for me at twelve thirty. And when Paradise returns, please tell him we're lunching out."

He took his hat and coat and went below. Chan strolled aimlessly to the window and stood looking down on the glittering city. His eyes strayed to the Matson dock, the pier shed and, beyond, the red funnels of a familiar ship. A ship that was sailing, day after to-morrow, for Honolulu harbor. Would he be on it? He had sworn, yes—and yet—— He sighed deeply. The door-bell rang, and he admitted Bill Rankin, the reporter.

"Hello," said Rankin. "Glad to find you in. I spent all day yesterday at the public library, and say, I'll bet I stirred up more dust than the chariot in *Ben Hur.*"

"With any luck?" Chan inquired.

"Yes. I finally found the story in the files of the *New York Sun.* A great newspaper in those days—but I won't talk shop. It was just a brief item with the Peshawar date line—I copied it down. Here it is."

Charlie took the sheet of yellow paper, and read a short cable story that told him nothing he did not already know. Eve Durand, the young wife of a certain Captain Eric Durand, had disappeared under mysterious circumstances two nights previously, while on a picnic party in the hills outside Peshawar. The authorities were greatly alarmed, and parties of British soldiers were scouring the wild countryside.

"Item has date, May fifth," remarked Chan. "Then Eve Durand was lost on night on May third, the year 1913. You found nothing else?"

"There were no follow-up stories," Rankin replied. "And no mention of Beetham, as you hoped. Say—what in Sam Hill could he have to do with this?"

"Nothing," said Chan promptly. "It was one of my small mistakes. Even great detective sometimes steps off on wrong foot. My wrong foot often weary from too much use."

"Well, what's going on, anyhow?" Rankin wanted to know. "I've hounded Flannery, and I've tried Miss Morrow, and not a thing do I learn. My city editor is waxing very sarcastic. Can't you give me a tip to help me out?"

Chan shook his head. "It would be plenty poor ethics for me to talk about the case. I am in no authority here, and already Captain Flannery regards me with the same warm feeling he would show pick-pocket from Los Angeles. Pursuing the truth further, there is nothing to tell you, anyhow. We are not as yet close to anything that might indicate happy success."

"I'm sorry to hear it," Rankin said.

"Situation will not continue," Chan assured him. "Light will break. For the present we swim with one foot on the ground, but in good time we will plunge into center of the stream. Should I be on scene when success is looming, I will be happy to give you little secret hint."

"If you're on the scene? What are you talking about?"

"Personal affairs call me home with a loud megaphone. On Wednesday I go whether case is solved or not."

"Yes—like you did last Wednesday," Rankin laughed. "You can't kid me. The patient Oriental isn't going to get impatient at the wrong minute. Well, I must run. Remember your promise about the hint."

"I have lengthy memory," Chan replied. "And already I owe you much. Good-by."

When the reporter had gone, Charlie stood staring at the copy of that cable story. "May third, nineteen hundred thirteen," he said aloud. With a surprisingly quick step he went to a table and took from it the *Life* of Colonel John Beetham. He ran hastily through the pages until he found the thing he sought. Then for a long moment he sat in a chair with the book open on his knee, staring into space.

At precisely twelve thirty he entered Kirk's office. The young man rose and, accepting some papers from his secretary, put them into a leather brief-case. "Got to see a lawyer after lunch," he explained. "Not a nice lawyer, either—a man this time." They went to the Cosmopolitan Club.

When they had checked their hats and coats and returned to the lobby in that imposing building, Chan looked about him with deep interest. The

Cosmopolitan's fame was wide-spread; it was the resort of men active in the arts, in finance and in journalism. Kirk's popularity there was proved by many jovial greetings. He introduced Chan to a number of his friends, and the detective was presently the center of a pleasant group. With difficulty they got away to lunch in one corner of the big dining-room.

It was toward the close of the lunch that Chan, looking up, saw approaching the man who interested him most at the moment. Colonel John Beetham's hard-bitten face was more grim than ever, seen in broad daylight. He paused at their table.

"How are you, Kirk?" he said. "And Mr. Chan. I'll sit down a moment, if I may."

"By all means," Kirk agreed cordially. "How about lunch? What can I order for you?"

"Thanks, I've just finished," Beetham replied.

"A cigarette, then." Kirk held out his case.

"Good of you." The Colonel took one and lighted it. "I haven't seen you since that beastly dinner. Oh—I beg your pardon—you get my meaning? . . . What a horrible thing that was—a man like Sir Frederic—by the way, have they any idea who did it?"

Kirk shrugged. "If they have, they're not telling me."

"Sergeant Chan—perhaps you are working on the case?" Beetham suggested.

Chan's eyes narrowed. "The affair concerns mainland police. I am stranger here, like yourself."

"Ah, yes, of course," responded Beetham. "I just happened to recall that you were on the point of leaving, and I thought, seeing you had stayed over——"

"If I can help, I will do so," Chan told him. He was thinking deeply. A man like Colonel Beetham did not note the comings and goings of a Charlie Chan without good reason.

"How's the new expedition shaping up?" Kirk inquired.

"Slowly—rather slowly," Beetham frowned. "Speaking of that, I have wanted a chat with you on the subject. Your grandmother has offered to help with the financing, but I have hesitated—it's a stiff sum."

"How much?"

"I have part of the money. I still need about fifty thousand dollars."

Kirk's eyebrows went up. "Ah, yes—quite a nest-egg. But if grandmother wants to do it—well, it's her own money."

"Glad you feel that way about it," said Beetham. "I was fearful the other members of the family might think I was using undue influence. The whole idea was hers—I give you my word."

"Naturally," Kirk answered. "I'm sure she would enjoy it, at that."

"The results will be most important from a scientific point of view," Beetham continued. "Your grandmother's name would be highly honored. I would see that she had full credit."

"Just what sort of expedition is it?" Kirk asked.

The tired eyes lighted for the first time. "Well, I had a bit of luck when I was last on the Gobi Desert. I stumbled on to the ruins of a city that must have been flourishing early in the first century. Only had time to take a brief look—but I turned up coins that bore the date of 7 A.D. I unearthed the oldest papers in existence—papers that bore the scrawl of little children—arithmetic—seven times seven and the like. Letters written by the military governor of the city, scraps of old garments, jewelry—amazing mementoes of the past. I am keen to go back and make a thorough investigation. Of course, the trouble in China will interfere, rather—but there is always trouble in China. I have waited long enough. I shall get through somehow. I always have."

"Well, I don't envy you," Kirk smiled. "The way I've always felt, when you've seen one desert, you've seen 'em all. But you have my best wishes."

"Thanks. You're frightfully kind," Beetham rose. "I hope to settle the matter in a few days. I am hoping, also, that before I leave, the murderer of Sir Frederic will be found. Struck me as a good chap, Sir Frederic."

Chan looked up quickly. "A great admirer of yours, Colonel Beetham," he said.

"Admirer of mine? Sir Frederic? Was he really?" The Colonel's tone was cool and even.

"Undubitable fact. Among his effects we find many books written by you."

Beetham threw down his cigarette. "That was good of him. I am quite flattered. If by chance you are concerned in the hunt for the person who killed him, Sergeant Chan, I wish you the best of luck."

He strolled away from the table, while Chan looked after him thoughtfully.

"Reminds me of the snows of Tibet," Kirk said. "Just as warm and human. Except when he spoke of his dead city. That seemed to rouse him. An odd fish, isn't he, Charlie?"

"An odd fish from icy waters," Chan agreed. "I am wondering——"

"Yes?"

"He regrets Sir Frederic's passing. But might it not happen that beneath his weeping eyes are laughing teeth?"

They went to the check-room, where they retrieved their hats and coats and Kirk's brief-case. As they walked down the street, Kirk looked at Chan.

"Just remembered the Cosmopolitan Club year-book," he said. "You don't imagine it meant anything, do you?"

Chan shrugged. "Imagination does not seem to thrive on mainland climate," he replied.

Kirk went off to his lawyer's and Charlie returned home to await a more promising to-morrow.

On Tuesday afternoon Miss Morrow was the first to arrive at the bungalow. She came in about three thirty. The day was dark, with gusts of wind and rain, but the girl was glowing.

Kirk helped her off with her rain-coat. "You seem to be filled with vim and vigor," he said.

"Walked all the way," she told him. "I was too excited to sit calmly in a taxi. Just think—in a few minutes we may see the meeting between Major Durand and his long lost wife."

"The Major has arrived?" Chan inquired.

"Yes—he and Inspector Duff came half an hour ago. Their train was a trifle late. Captain Flannery went to the station to meet them. He telephoned me they'd be along shortly. It seems that, like a true Englishman, the Major didn't care to talk with anybody until he'd gone to a hotel and had his tub."

"Don't blame him, after that trip from Chicago," Kirk said. "I believe little Jennie Jerome Marie Lantelme is on the elevator."

Miss Morrow nodded. "She is. I saw her when I came up. I wonder if she is really Eve Durand? Won't it be thrilling if she is!"

"She's got to be. She's Charlie's hunch."

"Do not be too certain," Chan objected. "In the past it has often happened

I was hoarsely barking up incorrect tree."

Kirk stirred the fire, and drew up a wide chair for the girl. "Here you are—a trifle large for you, but you may grow. I'll give you a tea later. These Englishmen probably can't do a thing until they've had their Oolong."

The girl sat down, and, dropping into a chair at her side, Kirk began to talk airily of nothing in particular. He was conscious that at his back Chan was nervously walking the floor.

"Better sit down, Charlie," he suggested. "You act like a man in a dentist's waiting-room."

"Feel that way," Chan told him. "Much is at stake now for me. If I have taken wrong turning, I shall have to endure some Flannery sneers."

It was four o'clock, and the dusk was falling outside the lofty windows, when the bell rang. Kirk himself went to the door. He admitted Flannery and a thick-set young Englishman. Two men only—Kirk peered past them down the stairs, but the third man was not in evidence.

"Hello," Flannery said, striding in. "Major Durand not here yet, eh?"

"He is not," Kirk replied. "Don't tell me you've mislaid him."

"Oh, no," Flannery answered. "I'll explain in a minute. Miss Morrow, meet Inspector Duff, of Scotland Yard."

The girl came forward, smiling. "I'm so glad," she said.

"Charmed," remarked Duff, in a hearty, roast-beef-of-Old-England voice. He was surprisingly young, with rosy cheeks, and the look of a farmer about him. And indeed it had been from a farm in Yorkshire that he had come to London and the Metropolitan police.

"The Inspector and I went from the train to my office," Flannery explained. "I wanted to go over the records of our case with him. The Major stopped at the hotel to brush up—he'll be along in a minute. Oh, yes—Mr. Kirk, Inspector Duff. And this, Inspector, is Sergeant Charlie Chan, of the Honolulu police."

Chan bowed low. "A moment that will live for ever in my memory," he said.

"Oh—er—really?" Duff replied. "The Captain's told me of you, Sergeant. We're in the same line—some miles apart."

"Many miles apart," conceded Charlie gravely.

"Look here," said Flannery, "it will be just as well if the Major doesn't meet that girl in the elevator until we're all set for it. Somebody should go below and steer him into a different car."

"I will be happy to perform that service," Chan offered.

"No—I know him by sight—I'll do it," Flannery replied. "I want to have a word with the men I've got watching her. I saw one of them in front of the building when I came in. Inspector—I'll leave you here. You're in good hands." He went out.

Kirk drew up a chair for the English detective. "Give you tea when the Major comes," he said.

"You're very kind, I'm sure," Duff answered.

"You have been all over the case with Captain Flannery?" Miss Morrow inquired.

"I have—from the beginning," Duff replied. "It's a shocking affair—shocking. Sir Frederic was deeply respected—I might even say loved—by all of us. It appears that he was killed in the line of duty, though he had retired and was, supposedly, out of all that. I can assure you that the murder of one of its men is not taken lightly by Scotland Yard. We shall not rest until we have found the guilty person—and in that task, Sergeant, we shall welcome help from every possible source."

Chan bowed. "My abilities are of the slightest, but they are lined up beside your very great ones."

"I had hoped, Inspector," Miss Morrow said, "that you would be able to throw considerable light on this affair."

Duff shook his head. "I'm frightfully sorry. There are so many other men—older men—on our force who would have been of much greater service. Unfortunately I am the only Scotland Yard man in the States at the moment. You see—I'm a bit young——"

"I'd noticed that," smiled the girl.

"All these events that appear to be linked up with Sir Frederic's murder happened before my day. I shall do my best—but——"

"Will you have a cigarette?" Kirk suggested.

"No, thanks. My pipe, if the young lady doesn't object."

"Not at all," said Miss Morrow. "It's quite in the Sherlock Holmes tradition."

Duff smiled. "But the only point of similarity, I fear. As I say, I have been with the Metropolitan police a comparatively brief time—a mere matter of seven years. Of course I have heard of the Hilary Galt murder, though it happened many years ago. As a young policeman I was shown, in the Black Museum, the famous velvet slippers they found Galt wearing that disastrous night. Coming to Eve Durand, I am familiar, in a casual way, with the story of her disappearance. In fact, I had, once, a very slight connection with the case. Five years ago there was a rumor that she had been seen in Paris, and Sir Frederic sent me across the Channel to look into it. It was merely another false alarm, but while making the investigation I chanced to encounter Major Durand, who was also on the ground. Poor chap—that was one of a long series of disappointments for him. I hope he is not to suffer another here to-night."

"How did the Major happen to come to America at this time?" Miss Morrow inquired.

"He came in answer to a cable from Sir Frederic," Duff explained. "Sir Frederic asked his help, and of course he hastened to comply, landing in New York a week ago. When I got off the Twentieth Century in Chicago I discovered Durand had been on the same train. We joined forces and hurried on to San Francisco together."

"Well, he, at least, can help us," Miss Morrow suggested.

"I fancy he can. I repeat, I have been over the case carefully, but I have had no inspiration as yet. One angle of it interests me tremendously—those velvet slippers. Why were they taken? Where are they now? They appear to be again the essential clue. What do you say, Sergeant?"

Chan shrugged. "Slippers were exactly that long time ago," he said. "On which occasion they led positively no place."

"I know," smiled Duff. "But I'm not superstitious. I shall follow them again. By the way, there is one point on which I may be able to offer some help." He turned suddenly to Kirk. "You have a butler named Paradise?" he inquired.

Kirk's heart sank. "Yes—and a very good one," he answered.

"I have been interested in Paradise," said Duff. "And Paradise, I understand, has been interested in Sir Frederic's mail. Where is he now?"

"He's in the kitchen, or his room," Kirk replied. "Do you want to see him?"

"Before I go—yes," Duff said.

Flannery came through the hall, followed by a big, blond man in a dripping Burberry coat. Major Eric Durand, retired, looked to be the sportsman type of Englishman; his cheeks were tanned and weatherbeaten, as though from much riding in the open, his blue eyes alert. Indoors, one would picture him sitting in a club with a cigar, a whiskey and soda, and a copy of the *Field*.

"Come in, Major," Flannery said. He introduced the Britisher to the company, and Kirk hurried forward to take the Burberry coat. There followed a moment of awkward silence.

"Major," Flannery began, "we haven't told you why we got you here. You have come to San Francisco in response to a cablegram from Sir Frederic Bruce?"

"I have," said Durand quietly.

"Did he give you any idea of why he wanted you to come?"

"He intimated that he was on the point of finding—my wife."

"I see. Your wife disappeared under unusual circumstances some fifteen years ago, in India?"

"Precisely."

"Did you ever hear of her after that?"

"Never. There were many false reports, of course. We followed them all up, but none of them came to anything in the end."

"You never heard of her at Nice? Or in New York?"

"No—I don't think those were among the places. I'm sure they weren't."

"You would, of course, know her if you saw her now?"

Durand looked up with sudden interest. "I fancy I would. She was only eighteen when she was—lost." Miss Morrow felt a quick twinge of pity for the man. "But one doesn't forget, you know."

"Major," said Flannery slowly, "we have every reason to believe that your wife is in this building tonight."

Durand took a startled step backward. Then he sadly shook his head. "I wish it were true. You've no idea—fifteen years' anxiety—it rather takes it out of a chap. One stops hoping, after a time. Ah, yes—I wish it were true—but there have been so many disappointments. I can not hope any more."

"Please wait just a minute," Flannery said, and went out.

A strained silence followed his exit. The ticking of a tall clock in a corner became suddenly like the strokes of a hammer. Durand began to pace the floor.

"It can't be," he cried to Duff. "No—it can't be Eve. After all these years—in San Francisco—no, no—I can't believe it."

"We shall know in a moment, old chap," Duff said gently.

The moments lengthened horribly. Chan began to wonder. Durand continued to pace back and forth, silently, over the rug. Still the hammer strokes of the clock. Five minutes—ten——

The outer door was flung open and Flannery burst into the room. His face was crimson, his gray hair disheveled.

"She's gone!" he cried. "Her elevator's standing at the seventh floor, with the door open. She's gone, and no one saw her go!"

Durand gave a little cry and sinking into a chair, buried his face in his hands.

13

Old Friends Meet Again

Major Durand was not the only one to whom Flannery's news came as a shock and a disappointment. On the faces of the four other people in that room dismay was clearly written.

"Gone, and no one saw her go," Chan repeated. He looked reprovingly at the Captain. "Yet she was under watchful eye of clever mainland police."

Flannery snorted. "She was, but we're not supermen. That woman's as slippery as an eel. There were two of my boys on the job—both keen lads—well, no use crying over spilt milk. I'll get her. She can't——"

The door opened and a plain clothes man entered, bringing with him a little old cleaning woman with straggling gray hair.

"Hello, Petersen—what is it?" Flannery asked.

"Listen to this, Chief," said Petersen. "This woman was working in an office on the seventh floor." He turned to her. "Tell the Captain what you told me."

The woman twisted her apron nervously. "In 709 I was, sir. They go home early, and I was alone there at my work. The door opens and this red-headed elevator girls runs in. She's got on a rain-coat, and a hat. 'What's the matter?' I says, but she just runs on into the back room, and sort of wondering, I follow her. I'm just in time to see her climb on to the fire-escape. Never a word she said, sir—she just disappeared in the night."

"The fire-escape," repeated Flannery. "I thought so. Have you looked at it, Petersen?"

"Yes, sir. It's one of those—you know—a person's weight lets down the last flight of steps to the ground. A simple matter to go like that."

"All right," Flannery answered. "Some one must have seen her when she came out of the alley. We'll go down and have a look round." He turned to the cleaning woman. "That's all. You can go."

The woman passed a second plain clothes man in the hall. He came quickly into the living-room.

"I've got a lead, Captain," he said. "Boy in the cigar store on the corner. He says a girl with a Kirk Building uniform under her coat rushed in a few minutes ago and used his telephone."

"Did he hear the call?"

"No, sir. It's a booth phone. She was there only a few minutes, and then she hurried out again."

"Well, that's something," Flannery said. "You boys wait for me—I've got a car. First of all, I'll send out the alarm. I'll have men at the ferries and the railroad stations—she's a marked woman with that uniform. I'll pick her up before midnight——"

"On what charge?" asked Miss Morrow gently.

"Oh—oh, well—as a witness. I'll take her as a witness. Still that will mean a lot of publicity I don't want at this time. I have it. I'll take her on a charge of stealing. The uniform is your property, Mr. Kirk?"

"Yes—but I don't like that," protested Kirk.

"Oh, it's just a fake. We won't press it. I've got to get her on some pretext. Now—if I can use your phone——"

Flannery talked to some purpose to the station house, and the hue and cry after that elusive woman was once more under way. He rose full of energy.

"I'll get her," he promised. "It's a bad set-back to our plans, but it's only for a minute. She can't get away——"

"She is one who has had some success at getting away in the past," Chan reminded him.

"Yeah—but not this time," answered the Captain. "She's never had me on her trail before." He blustered out, followed by his two men.

Major Durand slumped dejectedly in his chair. Inspector Duff was puffing calmly on his well-seasoned pipe.

"It's a bit of hard luck," he remarked. "But patience—that's what counts in this work, eh, Sergeant Chan?"

Charlie beamed. "At last I meet fellow detective who talks same language with me."

Barry Kirk rose and rang the bell. "How about a cup of tea?" he said. He stepped to the window and looked out. Swords of light marking the streets floated dimly in the mist, far below. The wind howled, rain spattered on the panes, the city was shrouded and lost. "It's one of those nights—a little something to warm us up——" He was silent. What a night it was—made to order for the man or woman who sought to slip away and never be seen again.

Paradise entered with calm dignity and stood in the brightly lighted room, his shock of snow-white hair lending him an air of stern respectability.

"You rang, sir?" he said.

"Yes," Kirk replied. "We'll have tea, Paradise. Five of us here——" He stopped. The butler's eyes were on Inspector Duff, and his face was suddenly as white as his hair.

There was a moment of silence. "Hello, Paradise," Duff said quietly.

The butler muttered something, and turned as though to go out.

"Just a moment!" The Inspector's voice was steely cold. "This is a surprise, my man. A surprise for both of us, I fancy. When I last saw you, you were standing in the dock at Old Bailey." Paradise bowed his head. "Perhaps I shouldn't have been inclined to give you away, Paradise, if you had behaved yourself. But you've been opening mail—haven't you? You've been tampering with a letter addressed to Sir Frederic Bruce?"

"Yes, sir, I have." The servant's voice was very low.

"So I understand," Duff continued. He turned to Barry Kirk. "I'm sorry to distress you, Mr. Kirk. I believe Paradise has been a good servant?"

"The best I ever had," Kirk told him.

"He was always a good servant," went on Duff. "As I recall, that fact was brought out clearly at the trial. A competent, faithful man—he had many references to prove it. But unfortunately a few years ago, in England, there was some suspicion that he had put hydrocyanic acid in a lady's tea."

"What an odd place for hydrocyanic acid," said Kirk. "But then, of course, I speak without knowing the lady."

"The lady was his wife," Duff explained. "It seemed to some of us that he had rather overstepped a husband's privileges. He was brought to trial——"

Paradise raised his head. "Nothing was ever proved," he said firmly. "I was acquitted."

"Yes, our case collapsed," admitted Inspector Duff. "That doesn't often happen, Mr. Kirk, but it did in this instance. Technically, at least, Paradise can not be adjudged guilty. In the eyes of the law, I mean. And for that reason I might have been inclined to keep all this to myself, if I had not heard of his queer work with that letter. Tell me, Paradise—do you know anything about Eve Durand?"

"I have never heard the name before, sir."

"Have you any information in the matter of an old murder in Ely Place—the murder of Hilary Galt?"

"None whatever, sir."

"But you opened an envelope addressed to Sir Frederic Bruce and substituted a blank sheet for the letter you found inside. I think you had better explain, my man."

"Yes, sir. I will do so." The servant turned to Barry Kirk. "This is very painful for me, Mr. Kirk. In the two years I have been with you I have done nothing dishonorable before—before this act. The gentleman has said that I poisoned my wife. I may call attention to the fact that he has some animus in the matter, as he conducted the investigation and was bitterly disappointed when a jury acquitted me. A natural feeling——"

"Never mind that," said Duff sharply.

"At any rate, sir," the butler continued to Kirk, "I was acquitted, for the very good reason that I was an innocent man. But I knew that, innocent or not, the fact of my having been tried would not be—er—pleasant news for you."

"Anything but," agreed Kirk.

"I thought it would be best if the matter remained in its former oblivion. I have been happy here—it is an excellent post—the very fact of its height above the ground has inspired me. I was always fond of high places. So I was in a bit of a funk, sir, when you told me Sir Frederic Bruce was coming. I had never had the pleasure of his acquaintance, but I'd had my brief moment in the public eye and I feared he might do me the honor to remember me. Well, he arrived and—unfortunately—he recognized me at once. We had a long talk here in this room. I assured him that I had been unjustly accused, that I had never done anything wrong, and that I was living a model life. I begged him to keep my secret. He was a just man. He said he would look into the matter—I presumed he wanted to hear Scotland Yard's opinion of the evidence—and would let me know his decision later. And there the matter stood, sir, on the night Sir Frederic met his unhappy end."

"Ah, yes," said Kirk. "I begin to see."

"What I did later was done from a misguided wish to retain your respect and confidence, sir. A messenger from Cook's put into my hand that packet of letters, and I saw on the top what I thought was the dreaded missive from Scotland Yard. If I may be allowed to say so, I went a bit balmy then. I believed that Sir Frederic had cabled about me to the Yard, and that this was the answer. It would no doubt fall into the hands of the police——"

"It was too early for any answer yet," Kirk told him.

"How could I be sure, sir? In this day of the air-mail and other time-saving devices. I determined to have a look at that letter, and if it did not concern me, to put it back in place——"

"But it didn't concern you, Paradise," said Kirk.

"Not directly, sir. However, it mentioned that Inspector Duff was in New York. I had enjoyed the honor of Inspector Duff's personal attention in my—er—my ordeal, and I was panic-stricken. The local police, reading the letter, might send for him, with results that are all too apparent now. So in my madness I slipped a blank sheet of paper into the envelope and resealed it. It was a clumsy subterfuge, sir, and one I deeply regret. Not the clumsiness, but the deceit, sir—that pains me. Everything has always been above the table with us, sir."

"I should hope it had," said Kirk.

"I am perhaps going too far when I ask you to overlook my defection, Mr. Kirk. I assure you, however, that it was my fondness for you, my keen desire to remain in your service, that prompted my rash act. If we could only go back to the old basis, sir—of mutual confidence and esteem——"

Kirk laughed. "I don't know. I shall have to think this over. Are you sure you're fond of me, Paradise?"

"Very, sir."

"Have you analyzed your emotions carefully? No little hidden trace of resentment, or disapproval?"

"None whatever, sir. I give you my word."

Kirk shrugged. "Very well. Then you might go and prepare the— er—the tea. In the usual manner, please."

"Thank you, sir," answered Paradise, and departed.

"The poor old dear," said Miss Morrow. "I'm sure he never did it. He was the victim of circumstances."

"Perhaps," admitted Duff. "Personally, however, I thought the evidence very strong. But I was new to the work at that time, and I may have been mistaken. At any rate, I am happy to have been able to eliminate Paradise from our case. It clears the air a bit."

"He may be eliminated from the case," Barry Kirk remarked. "But I'm free to admit that to me he is more important than ever."

"You don't believe he had anything to do with killing Sir Frederic?" Miss Morrow inquired.

"No—but I'm afraid he may have something to do with killing me. I'm faced by a private and personal problem—and a very pretty one, too. I'd hate to lose Paradise, but I'd hate to lose myself even more. Imagine taking the glass of good old orange juice every morning from a hand that has been up to tricks with hydrocyanic acid. Not so good. Charlie, as a guest here, you're interested. What do you say?"

Chan shrugged. "It may be he disliked his wife," he suggested.

"I should hate to think he was fond of her," Kirk replied. "But at that, he's a good old soul. And some wives, no doubt, drive a man too far. I think I'll let him stay a while. However"—he looked at Miss Morrow—"something tells me I'll do an awful lot of eating out."

"Sergeant Chan," Duff said, "you have not been idle. What discoveries have you made in our case so far?"

"None but the slightest," Chan told him. "I am very bright in tracking down Paradise here, and we have just seen the value of that. Alas, there are sprouting crops that never ripen into grain."

"True enough," agreed the Inspector. "But you must have had ideas along other lines, too. I should be interested to hear them."

"Some time we have little talk," Charlie promised. "For the present—I hesitate to speak of it. I am not without tender feeling to my heart, and I know only too well the topic must be one of deep pain to Major Durand. He must pardon my rudeness if I have keen desire to hear something of that far-away night when Eve Durand was lost."

Durand came out of a deep reverie. "Ah, yes—what's that? The night when Eve—of course, it was all so long ago."

"Yet a moment you are not likely to forget," suggested Chan.

Durand smiled ruefully. "I'm afraid not. I have tried to forget—it seemed the best way. But I have never succeeded."

"The date was the third of May, in the year 1913," Chan prompted.

"Precisely. We had been living in Peshawar just six months—I was assigned to a regiment there only a month after our marriage, in England. A God-forsaken place, Peshawar—an outpost of empire, with a vengeance. No place to bring a woman like Eve, who had known nothing save the civilized life of the English countryside."

He paused, deep in thought. "Yet we were very happy. We were young—Eve was eighteen, I was twenty-four—young and tremendously in love. The discomforts of that far garrison meant nothing—we had each other."

"And on this night under question," Chan persisted.

"There was a gay social life at the garrison, and Eve took an important part in it, as was natural. On the evening you ask about, we had arranged a picnic party in the hills. We were to ride our ponies out of the town and up a narrow dirt road to a small plateau from which we could watch the moon rise over the roofs of Peshawar. The plan was rather foolhardy—the hills were full of bandits—I was a bit fearful at the time. But the ladies—they insisted—you know how women are. And there were five men in the party, all fully armed. There seemed no real danger."

Again he paused. "Eve wore her jewels—a pearl necklace her uncle had given her—I remember protesting against it before we set out. She only laughed at me. Sometimes I have thought—— But no, I do not like to think that. Was she killed for her necklace, her rings? I have had to face it.

"At any rate, we packed our supper and rode out of the town. Everything went well until the hour arrived to go home. Then some one suggested a game of hide-and-seek——"

"You recall who suggested that?" asked Chan.

"Yes—it was Eve. I objected, but—well, one doesn't like to be a spoil sport, and the party was in a gay humor. The women scattered among the tamarisks—disappeared into the shadows, laughing and chatting. Within the half-hour we had found them all—save one. We have not found her yet."

"How terrible," Miss Morrow cried.

"You can scarcely realize the true horror of it," Durand returned. "Those black hills filled with innumerable dangers—oh, it was a foolish thing, that game. It should never have happened. Of the night that followed—and the long, hot dreadful days after that—I need not go on, I'm sure." He bowed his head.

"There were five men," said Chan. "Yourself already counted."

"Five men, yes," Durand replied. "And five charming girls."

"Five men—the other four officers, like yourself?" Charlie continued.

"Three of them were officers. One was not."

Chan's face lighted. "One was not?"

"No. The party was given in his honor, in a way. You see, he was a famous man—every one was eager to pay tribute to him. He had just been a guest at the Viceregal Lodge, he'd spoken in the throne-room, and they'd pinned medals and things on him. All India was ringing with his praises. He'd recently come back from a beastly perilous journey through Tibet——"

Chan's eyes narrowed. "He was an explorer?"

"One of the best. A brave man."

"You are referring to Colonel John Beetham?"

"Yes, of course. Then you knew?"

Kirk and Miss Morrow sat up with sudden interest. Chan nodded. "I had guessed," he said. He was silent for a moment. "Colonel Beetham is at this moment in San Francisco," he added.

"Really?" answered the Major. "An odd coincidence. I should like to meet him again. He was most sympathetic."

"The party was in his honor, you have said?" Charlie went on.

"Yes—a sort of farewell. You see, he was leaving the next day. Leaving for home, but not by the conventional route—not Beetham. He was going by caravan through the wilds of Afghanistan and across the great salt desert of Persia to Teheran."

"Through Khyber Pass?" Chan asked.

"Oh, yes—through the Khyber. A dangerous business, but he had a big retinue of servants who had been with him on other expeditions—and the Emir of Afghanistan had invited him. He left early the next morning and I have never seen him since."

"Early the next morning," Chan repeated slowly. "Going home." He stared for a moment at the misty window. "I had hoped to go home in the morning myself. But always something rises up making me break my word to my little son. What a despicable father he will think me. However"—he shrugged—"what is to be, will be."

Paradise came into the room, pompously wheeling a tea-wagon. There was a moment of uncomfortable silence.

"Tea, sir," said the butler.

"I hope so, I'm sure," replied Kirk.

Paradise served Miss Morrow, and then turned to Inspector Duff. "What will you have in yours, sir?" he inquired.

The Inspector looked him firmly in the eye. "One lump of sugar," he said. "And—nothing else."

14

Dinner for Two

With a grave face Paradise served the tea, passed sandwiches and cakes, and then silently withdrew. Barry Kirk paused with his cup at his lips, an inquiring look in his eyes. Inspector Duff saw it and smiled.

"I may tell you," he said, "that hydrocyanic acid has a quite distinctive odor. A pungent odor of peach blossoms."

"That's very good of you," answered Kirk. "I shall remember what you say. And you, Charlie—you'd better do the same. At the first intimation that we are in a peach orchard, we call up the employment agency and engage a new butler."

"I have made a note," Chan told him.

"At any rate," Kirk continued, "life's going to be rather a sporting proposition from now on. 'To be, or not to be: that is the question.' "

"We must treat Paradise with kindly consideration," Chan suggested. "We must bear in mind that a good word has heat enough for three winters, while a hard one wounds like six months of cold. It is going to improve our characters."

"I'll say it is," agreed Kirk. He looked at Major Durand and reflected that perhaps the conversation was a bit flippant in view of that gentleman's mission in San Francisco. Poor devil—what a life he must have led. Seeking about to include him in the talk, Kirk was able to hit upon nothing save the aged and obvious bromide. "Tell us, Major," he said. "What do you think of the States?"

"Ah, yes," replied Durand. "My impressions. Well, really, I'm afraid I can't be very original. My sole impression so far is one of—er—bigness. Size, you know. My word—your country is tremendous."

Duff nodded. "We could talk of little else on the train coming out. You can scarcely imagine the effect of America on the minds of men who hail from a country like England. There, a ride of a few miles in any direction and you are on the coast. But here—day after day we looked from the car windows incredulous, amazed. We thought we should never come to the end of our journey."

"No doubt about it," Kirk returned, "there's plenty of the United States. Too much, some people think."

"We haven't said that," Durand reminded him, smiling faintly. "However, the possibilities of such a country seem endless. I may add"—he looked at Miss Morrow—"that I find your young women charming."

"How very polite of you," she smiled.

"Oh, not at all. I really mean it. If you will pardon me—I did not quite catch your connection with this affair?"

"I am in the district attorney's office," she told him.

"Like our crown prosecutor, the district attorney," Duff explained. "This young woman is, I believe, a student of the law."

"My word," said Durand. "Just fancy. Then it surprises me there is not more respect for law in the States."

"Thank you," Miss Morrow answered. "That's flattering to me, if not to the States."

Durand rose. "You must forgive me if I run along," he said. "I have found the long journey somewhat fatiguing—and added to that is the disappointment I suffered a few moments ago. I pretended, of course, that I had no hope, but it wasn't quite true. As a matter of fact, despite all the false rumors in the past, I still go on hoping. And this time, with the word of a man like Sir Frederic Bruce involved—well, my mind will never be at rest until I have seen the woman who left so suddenly to-night."

"She may yet be found," Duff suggested.

"I hope so, I'm sure. Are you coming, old chap?"

"Of course," Duff replied, rising.

"You and I must have that talk soon, Inspector," Chan said.

Duff stopped. "Well, I've always thought there's no time like the present. You go ahead, Major, and I'll follow."

"Very good," Durand answered. "I have engaged a room for you at the St. Francis Hotel. I trust you'll approve of my choice."

"That was thoughtful of you," Duff told him. "I'll see you shortly."

Durand turned to Barry Kirk. "You've been very hospitable to a stranger."

"Not at all," Kirk said. "You must drop in often. I hope you won't be lonely here. I'll send you a card for a club or two, and if you like, we'll have a little party occasionally."

"Frightfully kind, I'm sure," Durand replied warmly. "A thousand thanks." He added his farewells and went out.

"Poor man," Miss Morrow said.

"A nice chap," Duff remarked. He turned briskly to Charlie. "But this isn't getting us forward, Sergeant. Where shall we begin? I learned from Captain Flannery that no records of any case were found among Sir Frederic's effects?"

"None whatsoever," Chan corroborated.

"Then it looks like theft as well as murder, for unquestionably such records were kept. Somewhere—unless they have been destroyed by the same hand that killed Sir Frederic—there must be in existence detailed accounts of the Hilary Galt case, as well as the disappearance of Eve Durand——"

"You have heard that, in Sir Frederic's thinking, these two matters boast some obscure connection?" Chan asked.

Duff nodded. "Yes, I saw the copy of the letter from my Chief at the Yard. I should say from the sound of it that he's as much in the dark as we are. But I have already cabled him for any information he may have."

"You act with beautiful speed," Chan approved. "One thing this Major Durand has told us puts new face on whole matter. Up to now, it was entirely unknown round here that Colonel John Beetham attended picnic that unforgotten night at Peshawar."

"What about Beetham? He's in San Francisco, you say?"

"Very much so. He was present at dinner. A strange, silent, mind-beguiling man."

Miss Morrow spoke suddenly. "Why, of course," she cried. "Colonel Beetham at the picnic—that means he knew Eve Durand. On the night he came here to dinner, he must have been brought up in the elevator by little Jennie Jerome Marie Lantelme. If she was Eve Durand, he probably recognized her."

"Undubitably," Chan agreed.

"Why, that makes it all very simple," Miss Morrow continued. "I'll get hold of him at once, and ask him——"

Chan raised his hand. "Humbly begging pardon to cut in—would you ask a blind man the road?"

"Why—I—what do you mean?"

"I have known for some days that the Colonel was in neighborhood of Peshawar that early May, 1913. Until to-night I did not dream he was member of picnic party. Even so, the last act I would consider would be to make inquiries."

"Surely you don't think——"

"I have not decided what to think. A member of that party—the fact may mean much, or it may mean nothing at all. On chance that it means much, let us say nothing to the Colonel just yet. To do so might defeat our own ends. There was once a man who pinched the baby while rocking the cradle. His work was not regarded a very large success."

Miss Morrow smiled. "I shall take your advice, of course."

"Thank you. Before we act, permit that I dig about some more amid events of past." Chan turned to the Inspector. "Dropping the Colonel for the moment, I mention those velvet slippers."

"Yes," said Duff. "The velvet slippers. A bit of a mystery, they are. Carried off by the murderer, it seems. But why? And what did he—or she—do with them? It's not unreasonable to suppose they were hurriedly chucked away somewhere. In England, we have a system in such a case—we advertise and offer a reward."

"Splendid idea," agreed Chan.

"Surely Captain Flannery has thought of it?"

Chan shrugged. "Captain acts much like little child caught in cross-woven net. He can only struggle, always getting deeper. But I must restrain my criticism. Free to admit the plan had not occurred even to me."

Duff laughed. "Well, I'll look the Captain up after dinner and suggest that he try it. By the way, I'm quite at a loss—the city is new to me. Could I prevail on you, Sergeant, to dine with me? We can talk things over, and afterward you can show me about, and direct me to Flannery's office."

"Deeply pleased at the invitation," Chan beamed. "I have much to learn. Where better could I study than in your distinguished company?"

"Well—er—that's a bit strong," returned Duff. "However, we'll have a jolly little dinner. Any time you're ready——"

"I procure hat and coat with instant action," Chan replied.

Duff turned to Kirk and the girl. "Great pleasure to meet you both," he said. "Miss Morrow, to work with a charming young woman on a case will be a new experience for me—and a delightful one."

"You must think it an utterly ridiculous situation," she remarked.

"I haven't said so," he smiled.

Chan returned, and he and Duff went out together. Miss Morrow took up her coat.

"Just a minute," Kirk protested. "Where are you going?"

"Home," she told him.

"To a lonely dinner," he suggested.

"You needn't hint. I can't invite you to-night. I shall need loads of time to prepare that pie——"

"Of course. I was hinting. But oddly enough, I've gone sort of cold on the idea of dining here in my cozy little nest. I propose to go where there are lights, laughter, and a waiter I can trust. And unless you prove more cruel than you look, I'm not dining alone."

"But I really should go home—and freshen up."

"Nonsense—you're blooming now. Like a peach tree covered with blossoms—I wonder how I came to think of that? No matter—will you join me?"

"If you want me to."

Kirk rang the bell, and Paradise appeared at once. "Ah—er—I'm dining out to-night," the young man explained.

Paradise looked distressed. "Very good, sir. But if I may make so bold——"

"Yes—what is it?"

"I trust this is not a sign of waning confidence in me, sir? I have been hoping for the old relations between us——"

"Nonsense. I often dine out. You know that."

"Certainly, sir." The butler made a gloomy exit.

"Good lord," sighed Kirk, "I'm afraid he's going sensitive on my hands. I suppose that just to show I trust him, I'll have to give a large dinner and invite all the people of whom I'm especially fond."

"A large dinner?"

"Well—fairly large. My grandmother, and Charlie Chan, and a few old friends from the club. And—er—would you come?"

"If I didn't, it wouldn't be because I was afraid of Paradise."

They descended to the street. It was a night of mist, with occasional fierce rain. Kirk found his car and helping the girl in, drove from the deserted business district to Union Square, where bright lights were gleaming on the wet pavements. The cable-car bells rang cheerily, a flotilla of umbrellas bobbed jauntily along the sidewalk; the spirits of the people of San Francisco, habitually high, are not to be damped by a little rain. "How about Marchetti's?" Kirk inquired.

"Sounds good to me," Miss Morrow answered.

They entered the little restaurant. On the dance floor the first of the cabaret acts was under way; a young, good-looking chorus pranced about to the strains of a popular air. Barry Kirk was known there, and the result was a good table and an obsequious head waiter. They gave their order.

"I like this place," said Kirk. "They never confuse noise with merriment." A pretty little blonde awarded him a sweet smile in passing. "Awfully cute girls, don't you think?"

"Yes, aren't they?" Miss Morrow answered. "Do you like cute girls?"

"Like to see 'em going by—on the other side. Never cared much for their conversation. It has no weight. Now, you take a lawyer, for instance——"

"Please," she said. "Don't make fun of me. I'm not in the mood for it to-night. I'm tired—and discouraged."

"Tired—that's all right," he replied. "But discouraged—what about? As I understand it, you've been a big success in your work."

"Oh, no I haven't. I've got on—a little way—but am I going any farther? Have you forgotten—this is an anniversary. A week ago to-night——"

"You dined with me for the first time. I hope——"

"A week ago to-night Sir Frederic was killed, and I embarked on my first big case. Up to this minute I haven't contributed a thing to its solution——"

"Oh, yes, you have. Of course, you haven't solved the puzzle, but there's plenty of time——"

"Oh, no, there isn't. At any moment the district attorney may tell me I'm out. I've got to make good quickly—and how can I? Look back—what have we accomplished to date?"

"Well, you've found Eve Durand."

"And lost her. That is—if the little elevator girl was Eve Durand."

"She must be. Charlie says so."

Miss Morrow shook her head. "Charlie's clever, but he's been wrong. He admits it freely. You know, something happened to-night while we were waiting for Captain Flannery to lead that girl into the room. Something inside me. Just a hunch—a woman's intuition—I suddenly felt quite sure that she wasn't Eve Durand after all."

"You don't say. And what basis did you have for that hunch?"

"None whatever. But I felt we were on the wrong trail altogether. She might very well be Jennie Jerome, and Marie Lantelme too, and still not be Durand's lost wife. Don't forget there are many other possibilities for that role."

"For example?"

"How about Lila Barr—the girl in the office of the Calcutta Importers? You remember what you told us—how interested Sir Frederic was in her? Just what did that mean?"

"I'd be happy to tell you—if I knew."

"But you don't. Then there's Eileen Enderby and Gloria Garland. In spite of their stories about why Sir Frederic wanted to see them—are they out of it? And Mrs. Tupper-Brock. No—we can't be sure that the elevator girl was Eve Durand. We've just been guessing—Chan's been guessing. And we'll never know now."

"Why not? Flannery will find her."

"You don't really believe that? If you do, you've more faith in the poor old Captain than I have. Suppose he does find her, and she is Eve Durand—what of it? She'll simply refuse to talk, and we'll be no nearer knowing who killed Sir Frederic than we ever were."

"I brought you here for an evening of gaiety," Kirk said sternly, "and you sit there thinking black thoughts."

"Just a minute—let me go on. It's such a comfort to talk things over. Who killed Sir Frederic—that's my problem. The identity of Eve Durand may not have as much to do with the matter as we think. It may even prove to have nothing to do with it at all. Who pulled that trigger in your office last Tuesday night? Carrick Enderby? It's quite possible. Eileen Enderby? There were those stains on her frock—did she climb down the fire-escape on some sinister errand? Dismissing the Enderby family, there are others. How about Gloria Garland? Mrs. Tupper-Brock?"

"Each of whom, of course, arrived at my dinner with a pistol hidden under her gown?" smiled Kirk.

"Each of whom knew she was to meet Sir Frederic that night. The pistol could have been arranged. To go on with the list—there's Paradise. I like him, but I can't see that his story of this afternoon puts him completely beyond suspicion. On the contrary. Outside the bungalow, there was that pale young man from the accountants' office."

"Oh yes—name of Smith," said Kirk. "I'd forgotten all about him."

"I haven't," Miss Morrow replied. "Then, there's Li Gung, the Chinese who fled to Honolulu next day. What was his hurry? Isn't it possible that he climbed up the fire-escape—— Oh, what's the use? The list seems endless." Miss Morrow sighed.

"And incomplete, as you give it," added Kirk.

"You mean——"

"I mean the man who accompanied Li Gung to the dock. Colonel John Beetham."

"Absurd! A man like Colonel Beetham—famous throughout the world—a man who has won all the medals and distinctions there are for gallant conduct—as though he could do anything base, anything despicable."

"Just there," said Kirk, "your sex betrays you. Not one of you women can resist a handsome, distinguished-looking Englishman. Speaking as a less romantic male, I must say that the Colonel doesn't strike me quite so favorably. He has courage, yes—and he has a will that gets him where he wants to go, and damn the consequences. I shouldn't care to be one of his party on the top floor of Tibet and too weak to go on. He'd give me one disgusted look, and leave me. But wait a minute—I believe he'd do me one last kindness before he left."

"What's that?"

"I think he'd pull out a gun and shoot me. Yes, I'm certain he would, and he'd go on his way happy to know there was one weakling who would never trouble him again."

"Yes, he's a hard, determined man," Miss Morrow admitted. "Nevertheless, he wouldn't kill Sir Frederic. Poor Sir Frederic wasn't interfering with his plans in any way."

"Oh, wasn't he? How do you know he wasn't?"

"Well—I can't see——"

"Let's leave Beetham to Chan," Kirk suggested. "The little man has an air about him—I believe he knows what he's doing. And now will you drop all this and dance with me—or must I dance alone?"

"I don't know. In my position, I have to give an impression of being serious—the public——"

"Oh, forget your public. He wouldn't venture out on a night like this. Come along."

Miss Morrow laughed, and they danced together on the tiny floor. For the rest of the evening she permitted Kirk to lead the conversation into more frivolous channels—a task at which he excelled. The change seemed to do her good.

"Well," said Kirk, as he signed the check, "you can be gay, after all. And I must say it becomes you."

"I've forgot all my worries," replied the girl, her eyes sparkling. "I feel as though I should never think of them again."

"That's the talk," Kirk approved.

But before they got out of the room, Miss Morrow's worries were suddenly brought back to her. Along one wall was a series of booths, beside which they walked on their way to the door. Opposite the final booth the girl half stopped, and glanced back over her shoulder at Barry Kirk. In passing he too looked into the compartment, and then hastily moved on. He need not have effaced himself so hurriedly, for the two people who were dining together in the booth were so deep in serious conversation they were oblivious to everything.

In the street Miss Morrow turned to Kirk. "What did I tell you?" she cried. "There are other women involved in this affair besides that poor little elevator girl."

"And what did I tell you," Kirk answered, "about your handsome British hero?"

Miss Morrow nodded. "To-morrow," she said, "I shall look into this. Just what, I wonder, is the connection between Colonel Beetham and Mrs. Helen Tupper-Brock?"

15

The Discreet Mr. Cuttle

When Charlie Chan rose on Wednesday morning, the rain was over and the fog was lifting. Bravely struggling through remnants of mist, the sun fell on a sparkling town, washed clean for a new day. Chan stood for a long time looking out at the magnificent panorama over bay and harbor, at the green of Goat Island and the prison fortress of Alcatraz. Along the water-front stretched a line of great ships as though awaiting a signal that should send them scurrying off to distant treaty ports and coral islands.

Chan's heart was heavy despite the bright morning. At twelve noon would sail the ship on which he had sworn to depart, the ship that would come finally to rest under the tower that bore the word "Aloha." There would be keen disappointment in the little house beneath the algaroba trees on Punchbowl Hill, as there was disappointment in the detective's heart now. He sighed. Would this holiday never end? This holiday so filled with work and baffling problems? This holiday that was no holiday at all?

When he entered the dining-room Barry Kirk was already at the table, but his glass of orange juice stood before him, untouched.

"Hello," said the host. "I waited for you."

"You grow increasingly kind with every dawn," Chan grinned.

"Oh, I don't know. It isn't exactly kindness. Somehow, I don't seem in any hurry to quaff California's favorite beverage this morning. Take a look at it. Does it strike you as being—er—the real thing?"

As Chan sat down, Paradise appeared in the doorway. Without a moment's hesitation, Chan lifted his glass. "Your very good health," he remarked.

Kirk glanced at the butler, and raised his own glass. "I sincerely trust you're right," he murmured, and drank heartily.

Paradise gravely said his good mornings and, setting down two bowls of oatmeal, departed. "Well," Barry Kirk smiled, "we seem to be O.K. so far."

"Suspicion," Chan told him, "is a wicked thing. That is written in many places."

"Yes—and where would you be in your work without it?" Kirk inquired. "By the way, did you get anything out of Duff last night?"

"Nothing that demands heavy thought. One point he elucidated carried slight interest."

"What was that?"

"Begging respectful pardon, for the present I will ponder same with my customary silence. You dined here?"

"No. Miss Morrow and I went to a restaurant."

"Ah—a moment's pleasant recreation," said Chan approvingly.

"That was the idea."

"You enjoy society of this young woman?"

"I do not precisely pine in her presence. You know, she's not so serious as she pretends to be."

"That is good. Women were not invented for heavy thinking. They should decorate scene, like blossom of the plum."

"Yes, but they can't all be movie actresses. I don't mind a girl's having a brain if she doesn't act up-stage about it—and Miss Morrow never does. We had a very light-hearted evening, but we weren't blind. As we left the restaurant, we made a little discovery."

"Good, what was it?"

Kirk shrugged. "Shall I ponder same with my customary silence? No, I won't be as mean as you are, Charlie. We saw your old friend Colonel John Beetham relaxing from the stern realities of life. We saw him dining with a lady."

"Ah, yes. Which lady?"

"A lady we have rather overlooked so far. Mrs. Helen Tupper-Brock."

"That has interest. Miss Morrow will investigate?"

"Yes. I'm going to pick up Mrs. Tupper-Brock this morning and take her down to the district attorney's office. I don't look for any brilliant results, however. She's cold and distant, like the winter stars. Good lord—I'm getting poetic. You don't suppose it could be something I've had for breakfast?"

"More likely memories of last night," Chan answered.

When the meal was finished, Kirk announced that he was going down to the office to attend to a few letters. Chan rose quickly.

"I will accompany, if I may," he said. "I must produce letter of explanation for my wife, hoping it will yet catch out-going boat. It will be substitute for me—a smaller substitute." He sighed.

"That's right," Kirk remembered. "You were going out on the tide today, weren't you? It's a shame you can't."

"What will little Barry think of me?"

"Oh, he's probably sensible, like his namesake. He'll want you to stay where duty lies. And how proud he'll be—in the future—over your success in running down the murderer of Sir Frederic Bruce."

"Still have some running to do," Chan admitted. "One more week—I give myself that. Then, whatever has happened, I shift mainland dust off my shoes and go. I swear it, and this time I am firm like well-known Gibraltar rock."

"A week," repeated Kirk. "Oh, that will be ample. You'll be sitting pretty then."

"On deck of boat bound for Honolulu," Chan said firmly. "Quoting local conversation, you bet I will."

They went below, and Kirk seated himself at the big desk. Kinsey was out; "collecting rents," Kirk explained. Chan accepted paper and an envelope and took his place at the stenographer's desk by the wall.

But his mind did not seem to be on the letter he was writing. Out of the corner of his eye he watched Kirk's movements carefully. In a moment he rose and came over to Kirk's desk. "Pen enjoys stubborn spasm," he explained. "The ink will not gush. Who calls it fountain pen?"

"There are pens in here," Kirk said, leaning over to open a lower drawer. Chan's keen eyes were on the papers atop the desk. Noted for his courtesy, his actions were odd. He appeared to be spying on his host.

Charlie accepted a pen and returned to his writing. Still he watched Kirk from the corner of his eye.

The young man finished his letter and started another. When he had completed the second, he stamped them both. Simultaneously Chan sealed his own letter, stamped it, and rose quickly to his feet. He held out his long, thin hand.

"Permit me," he said, "that I deposit our mail in the hallway chute."

"Why—thank you," Kirk replied, giving him the letters.

When Charlie returned, Kirk was on his feet, consulting his watch. "Want to hear Mrs. Tupper-Brock's life story?" he inquired.

The detective shook his head. "Thank you all the same, I will not interpolate myself. Miss Morrow is competent for work. Already, I have several times squirmed about in the position of fifth, unnecessary wheel. This once I will loiter elsewhere."

"Suit yourself," Kirk answered carelessly. He took up his hat and coat and disappeared.

When Chan went up-stairs by the inner route, he found Bill Rankin waiting for him in the living-room of the bungalow. The reporter looked at him with amusement.

"Good morning," he said. "I presume you're sailing this noon?"

Chan frowned. "Missing boats is now a regular habit for me," he replied. "I can not go. Too many dark clouds shade the scene."

"I knew it," smiled Rankin. "Before you go you've got to give me a story that will thrill the town. I was sure I could depend on you. A great little people, the Chinese."

"Thanks for advertising my unassuming race," Chan said.

"Now, to get down to business," Rankin continued. "I've brought you a little present this bright morning."

"You are pretty good."

"I'm a clever boy," Rankin admitted. "You know, your rather foggy remarks about Colonel John Beetham have set me thinking. And when I think—get out from under. I have read the Colonel's *Life*, from cover to cover. I imagine I need not tell you that on May fourth, nineteen hundred and thirteen, Beetham set out on an eight months' journey from Peshawar to Teheran, by way of Afghanistan and the Kevir desert of Persia?"

"I too have unearthed that," nodded Chan.

"I thought you had. But did you know that he had written a book—a separate book—about that little jaunt? A bit of a holiday, he called it. Not real exploring, but just his way of going home."

Chan was interested. "I have been unaware of that volume," he replied.

"It isn't as well known as his other books," went on Rankin. "Out of print now. *The Land Beyond the Khyber,* he called it. I tried every book store in town, and finally picked up a copy over in Berkeley."

He produced a volume bound in deep purple. "It's the little present I mentioned," he added.

Chan took it eagerly. "Who shall say? This may be of some value. I am in your debt and sinking all the time."

"Well, I don't know about its value. Maybe you can find something I have overlooked. I've been through it carefully, but I haven't found a thing."

Chan opened the book. "Interesting item flashes up immediately," he said. "Unlike Colonel Beetham's other books, this has dedication." Slowly he read the inscription on the dedicatory page: "To one who will remember, and understand."

"I noticed that," Rankin told him. "It begins to look as though the Colonel has his tender moments, doesn't it? To one who will remember and understand. A boyhood sweetheart, probably. One who will remember the time he kissed her under the lilacs at the gate, and understand that he goes on his daring trips with her image in his heart."

Chan was deep in thought. "Possibly," he muttered.

"You know, these Englishmen aren't as hard-boiled as they seem," Rankin continued. "I knew a British aviator in the war—a tough baby, he ate nails for breakfast. Yet he always carried a sprig of heather on his plane—the memento of an old love-affair. A sentimentalist at heart. Perhaps Colonel Beetham is the same type."

"May very well be," Charlie agreed.

Rankin got up. "Well, I suppose my dear old Chief is crying his eyes out because I haven't shown up. He loves me, even though he does threaten to cast me off because I haven't solved the mystery of Sir Frederic's murder."

"You are not alone in that fault," Chan told him.

"I—I don't suppose you could give me any little morsel for our million panting readers?"

"Nothing of note may yet be revealed."

"Well, it does seem high time we were getting a glimpse behind that curtain," Rankin remarked.

Charlie shook his head. "The matter is difficult. If I were in Peshawar—but I am not. I am in San Francisco fifteen years after the event, and I can only guess. I may add, guessing is poor business that often leads to lengthy saunters down the positively wrong path."

"You hang on," advised Rankin. "You'll win yet and when you do, just let me be there, with a direct line to the office at my elbow."

"We will hope that happy picture eventuates," Chan replied.

Rankin went out, leaving Charlie to the book. He sat down before the fire and began to read eagerly. This was better than interviewing Mrs. Tupper-Brock.

At about the same time, Barry Kirk was going blithely up the steps of his grandmother's handsome house on Pacific Heights. The old lady greeted him in the drawing-room.

"Hello," she said. "How do you happen to be up and about so early? And wide awake, if I can believe my failing eyesight."

"Detective work," he laughed.

"Good. What can I do for you? I seem to have been left entirely out of things, and it annoys me."

"Well, you're still out, so don't get up any false hopes," he returned. "I'm not here to consult with you, wise as I know you to be. I'm looking for Mrs. Tupper-Brock. Where is she?"

"She's up-stairs. What do you want with her?"

"I want to take her for a little ride—down to see Miss Morrow."

"Oh, so that young woman is still asking questions? She seems a bit lacking in results, so far."

"Is that so? Well, give her time."

"I rather fancy she'll need a lot of it. Mixing up in affairs that should be left to the men——"

"You're a traitor to your sex. I think it's mighty fine of her to be where she is. Give this little girl a great big hand."

"Oh, I imagine she doesn't lack for applause when you are about. You seem very much taken with her."

"I am, and don't forget it. Now, how about calling Mrs. Tupper-Brock? Please tell her to come, and bring her hyphen."

Mrs. Kirk gave him a scornful look, and departed. In a few minutes the secretary appeared in the room. Poised and cool, as always, she greeted Barry Kirk without enthusiasm.

"Good morning," he said. "I'm sorry to disturb you, but Miss Morrow—you met her at my dinner—would like to see you. If you can come now, I'll drive you down in my car."

"Why, of course," returned the woman calmly. "I'll be just a moment."

She went out, and Mrs. Kirk reappeared. "What's the matter with that boy of Sally Jordan's?" she demanded. "I thought he'd have this thing solved long ago. I've been watching the papers like a bargain hunter."

"Oh, Charlie's all right," Kirk said. "He's slow, but sure."

"He's slow enough," admitted the old lady. "You might tell him that I'm growing impatient."

"That'll speed him up," Kirk smiled.

"I wish something would," his grandmother snapped. "What's all this about Helen? Surely she's not entangled in the case?"

"I'm not free to say, one way or another. Tell me, have you given Colonel Beetham that money yet?"

"No—but I believe I will."

"Take my advice and hold off for a few days."

"What? He isn't in it, is he? Why—he's a gentleman."

"Just take my advice——" began Kirk. Mrs. Tupper-Brock was in the hall, waiting for him.

"Now you've got me all excited," complained Mrs. Kirk.

"That's bad, at your age," Kirk said. "Calm down."

"What do you mean—my age? I read of a woman the other day who is a hundred and two."

"Well, there's a mark to shoot at," Kirk told her. "So long. See you later."

Mrs. Tupper-Brock sat at his side in the roadster, stiff and obviously not inclined to talk. A few remarks on the weather yielding no great flood of conversation, Kirk abandoned the effort. They rode on in silence, and finally he ushered her into Miss Morrow's office.

The deputy district attorney made a charming picture against that

gloomy background. Such was not, however, her aim at the moment. Alert
and businesslike, she greeted Mrs. Tupper-Brock and indicated a chair
beside her desk.

"Sit down, please. So good of you to come. I hope I haven't inconveni-
enced you?"

"Not in the least," the woman replied, seating herself. There was a moment's silence.

"You know, of course, that we are hunting the murderer of Sir Frederic
Bruce," Miss Morrow began.

"Naturally," Mrs. Tupper-Brock's tone was cool. "Why did you wish to
see me?"

"I wondered whether you have any information that might help us."

"That's hardly likely," responded Mrs. Tupper-Brock. She took out a
lace-edged handkerchief and began to turn it slowly in her hands.

"No, perhaps not," Miss Morrow smiled. "Still, we are not justified in
ignoring any one in this terrible affair. Sir Frederic was a complete stranger
to you?"

"Yes, quite. I met him for the first time on that Tuesday night."

"Did you also meet Colonel Beetham for the first time that night?"

The handkerchief was suddenly a tiny ball in her hand. "No—I did not."

"You had met him before?"

"Yes. At Mrs. Dawson Kirk's. He had been to the house frequently."

"Of course. You and the Colonel are quite good friends, I hear. Perhaps
you knew him before he came to San Francisco?"

"No, I did not."

"While the Colonel was showing his pictures, you remained on the davenport with Miss Garland. You saw nothing of a suspicious nature?"

"Nothing whatever." The handkerchief lay in a crumbled heap in her
lap. She took it up and once more began to smooth it.

"Have you ever lived in India?"

"No—I have never been there."

"Did you ever hear of a tragic event that happened in India—at
Peshawar? The disappearance of a young woman named Eve Durand?"

Mrs. Tupper-Brock considered. "I may have read about it in the newspapers," she admitted. "It has a dimly familiar sound."

"Tell me—did you by any chance notice the elevator girl who took you
up to the bungalow the night of Mr. Kirk's dinner?"

Again the handkerchief was crushed in the woman's hand. "I did not.
Why should I?"

"She was, then, quite unknown to you?"

"I fancy she was. Of course, one doesn't study—er—that sort of person."

"Ah, yes." Miss Morrow sought an inconsequential ending for the interview. "You are English, Mrs. Tupper-Brock?"

"English, yes."

"A Londoner?"

"No—I was born in Devonshire. I stayed there until my—my marriage.
Then my husband took me to York, where he had a living. He was a
clergyman, you know."

"Thank you so much."

"I'm afraid I have been of very little help."

"Oh, but I hardly looked for anything else," Miss Morrow smiled. "These
questions are a mere formality. Every one at the dinner—you understand.

It was good of you to come." She rose.

Mrs. Tupper-Brock restored the handkerchief to her bag, and also stood up. "That is all, I take it?"

"Oh, quite. It's a lovely day after the rain."

"Beautiful," murmured the woman, and moved toward the door. Kirk came from the corner where he had been lolling.

"Any other little service I can do?" he asked.

"Not at present, thanks. You're immensely valuable."

Mrs. Tupper-Brock had reached the outer room. Kirk spoke in a low voice. "No word of the elevator girl?"

"Not a trace," Miss Morrow sighed. "The same old story. But just what I expected."

Kirk looked toward the other room. "And the lady who has just left," he whispered. "A complete dud, wasn't she? I'm awfully sorry. She told you nothing."

The girl came very close, fragrant, young, smiling. Kirk felt a bit dizzy. "You are wrong," she said softly. "The lady who has just left told me a great deal."

"You mean?"

"I mean she's a liar, if I ever met one. A liar, and a poor one. I'm going to prove it, too."

"Bright girl," Kirk smiled, and, hurrying out, caught up with Mrs. Tupper-Brock in the hall.

The return ride to Mrs. Dawson Kirk's house was another strained, silent affair, and Kirk parted from the dark, mysterious lady with a distinct feeling of relief. He drove back to the Kirk Building and ascended to the twentieth floor. As he got out of the elevator he saw Mr. Cuttle trying his office door. Cuttle was not only the night-watchman, but was also assistant superintendent of the building, a title in which he took great pride.

"Hello, Cuttle," Kirk said. "Want to see me?"

"I do, sir," Cuttle answered. "Something that may be important." Kirk unlocked the office and they went in.

"It's about that girl, Grace Lane, sir," Cuttle explained, when they reached the inner room. "The one who disappeared last night."

"Oh, yes." Kirk looked at him with sudden interest. "What about her?"

"The police asked me a lot of questions. Where did I get her, and all that. There was one point on which I was silent. I thought I had better speak to you first, Mr. Kirk."

"Well, I don't know, Cuttle. It isn't wise to try to conceal things from the police."

"But on this point, sir——"

"What point?"

"The matter of how I came to hire her. The letter she brought to me from a certain person——"

"From what person?"

"From your grandmother, sir. From Mrs. Dawson Kirk."

"Good lord! Grace Lane came to you with a letter from my grandmother?"

"She did. I still have the letter. Perhaps you would like to see it?"

Cuttle produced a gray, expensive-looking envelope. Kirk took out the enclosure and saw that the message was written in his grandmother's cramped, old-fashioned hand. He read:

"My dear Mr. Cuttle:
    The young woman who presents this letter is a good
friend of mine, Miss Grace Lane. I should be very pleased
if you could find some employment for her in the building—I have thought of the work on the elevators. Miss
Lane is far above such work, but she has had a bad time
of it, and is eager to take anything that offers. I am sure
you will find her willing and competent. I will vouch for
her in every way.

Sincerely yours,
MARY WINTHROP KIRK."

Kirk finished, a puzzled frown on his face. "I'll keep this, Cuttle," he
remarked, putting the letter in his pocket. "And—I guess it was just as well
you said nothing to the police."

"I thought so, sir," replied Cuttle with deep satisfaction, and retired.

16

Long Life and Happiness

Kirk hurried up to the bungalow. He found Charlie Chan seated in a chair
by the window, completely engrossed in Colonel John Beetham's description of *The Land Beyond the Khyber.*

"Well," said Kirk, "here's news for you. I've just got on the trail of another
suspect in our little case."

"The more the increased merriment," Chan assured him. "Kindly deign
to name the newest person who has been performing queer antics."

"Just my grandmother," Kirk returned. "That's all."

Charlie allowed himself the luxury of a moment's surprise. "You overwhelm me with amazement. That dear old lady. What misendeavor has she
been up to?"

"It was she who got Grace Lane—or whatever her confounded name
is—a job in the Kirk Building." The young man repeated his talk with
Cuttle and showed Chan the letter.

Charlie read Mrs. Dawson Kirk's warm endorsement with interest. He
handed it back, smiling. "Grandmother now becomes a lady to be investigated. Humbly suggest you place Miss Morrow on her track."

Kirk laughed. "I'll do it. The resulting display of fireworks ought to
prove a very pretty sight." He called Miss Morrow and, having heard his
story, she suggested an interview with Mrs. Kirk at the bungalow at two
o'clock.

The young man got his grandmother on the wire. "Hello," he said, "this
is Barry. Did I understand you to say this morning you'd like to be mixed
up in the Bruce murder?"

"Well—in a nice way—I wouldn't mind. In fact, I'd rather enjoy it."

"You've got your wish. Just at present the police are after you."

"Mercy—what have I done?"

"I leave that to you. Think over your sins, and report here at two o'clock."

Miss Morrow wants to question you."

"She does, eh? Well, I'm not afraid of her."

"All right. Only come."

"I shall have to leave early. I promised to go to a lecture——"

"Never mind. You'll leave when the law has finished with you. I suggest that you come prepared to tell the truth. If you do, I may yet be able to keep you out of jail."

"You can't frighten me. I'll come—but only from curiosity. I should like to see that young woman in action. I haven't a doubt in the world but what I can hold my own."

"I heard different," replied Kirk. "Remember—two o'clock. Sharp!"

He hung up the receiver and waited impatiently for the hour of the conflict. At a quarter before two Miss Morrow arrived on the scene.

"This is a strange turn," she said, when Kirk had taken her coat. "So your grandmother knows Jennie Jerome Marie Lantelme?"

"Knows her!" replied Kirk. "They're great friends." He handed over the letter. "Read that. Vouches for her in every way. Good old grandmother!"

Miss Morrow smiled. "I must handle her gently," she remarked. "Somehow, I don't believe she approves of me."

"She's reached the age where she doesn't approve of anybody," Kirk explained. "Not even of me. A fine noble character, as you well know. Yet she discovers flaws. Can you imagine!"

"Absurd," cried Miss Morrow.

"Don't be too nice to her," Kirk suggested. "She'll like you better if you walk all over her. Some people are made that way."

Charlie entered from his room. "Ah, Miss Morrow. Again you add decoration to the scene. Am I wrong in presuming that Captain Flannery has apprehended Eve Durand?"

"If you mean the elevator girl, you are quite wrong. Not a trace of her. You still think she was Eve Durand?"

"If she wasn't, then I must bow my head in sackcloth and ashes," Chan replied.

"Well, that's no place for anybody's head," Kirk remarked.

"None the less, mine has been there," Chan grinned.

Mrs. Dawson Kirk bustled in. "Here I am, on time to the minute. Please make a note of that."

"Hello," Kirk greeted her. "You remember Miss Morrow, of course."

"Oh, yes—the lawyer. How do you do. And Mr. Chan—look here, why haven't you solved this case?"

"A little more patience," grinned Chan. "We are getting warm now. You are under hovering cloud of suspicion at last."

"So I hear," snapped the old lady. She turned to Miss Morrow. "Well, my dear, Barry said you wanted to cross-question me."

"Nothing cross about it," Miss Morrow said, with a smile. "Just a few polite questions."

"Oh, really. Don't be too polite. I'm always suspicious of too polite people. You don't think I killed poor Sir Frederic, I hope?"

"Not precisely. But you've written a letter——"

"I suppose so. Have a habit of writing indiscreet letters. And old habits are hard to break. But I always put 'burn this' at the bottom. Somebody has failed to follow my instructions, eh?"

Miss Morrow shook her head. "I believe you omitted that admonition in this case." She handed the letter to Mrs. Kirk. "You wrote that, didn't you?"

Mrs. Kirk glanced it through. "Certainly I wrote it. What of it?"

"This Grace Lane was a good friend of yours?"

"In a way, yes. Of course, I scarcely knew the girl——"

"Oho," cried Barry Kirk. "You vouched for her in every way, yet you scarcely knew her."

"Keep out of this, Barry," advised the old lady. "You're not a lawyer. You haven't the brains."

"Then you knew Grace Lane only slightly, Mrs. Kirk?" the girl continued.

"That's what I said."

"Yet you recommended her without reservation? Why did you do that?"

Mrs. Kirk hesitated. "If you'll pardon me, I regard it as my own affair."

"I'm sorry," Miss Morrow replied quickly, "but you will have to answer. Please do not be deceived by the setting of this interview. It is not a social function. I am acting for the district attorney's office, and I mean business."

Mrs. Kirk's eyes flashed. "I understand. But now, if you don't mind, I'd like to ask a few questions."

"You may do so. And when you have finished, I will resume."

"What has this girl, Grace Lane, to do with the murder of Sir Frederic Bruce?"

"That is what we are trying to determine."

"You mean she had something to do with it?"

"We believe she had. And that is why your recommendation of her is no longer your own affair, Mrs. Kirk."

The old lady sat firmly on the edge of her chair. "I shan't say a word until I know where all this is leading us."

"It'll lead you to jail if you don't stop being stubborn," suggested Barry Kirk.

"Indeed? Well, I have friends among the lawyers, too. Miss Morrow, I want to know Grace Lane's connection with Sir Frederic."

"I have no objection to telling you—if you will keep the matter to yourself."

"She's the most indiscreet woman on the west coast," Kirk warned.

"Hush up, Barry. I can keep still if I have to. Miss Morrow——?"

"When Sir Frederic came here," Miss Morrow explained, "he was seeking a woman named Eve Durand, who disappeared from India fifteen years ago. We suspect Grace Lane was that woman."

"Well, why don't you ask her?"

"We'd be glad to, but we can't. You see, she's disappeared again."

"What! She's gone?"

"Yes. Now I have answered your questions, and I expect you to do as much for me." Miss Morrow became again very businesslike. "Grace Lane was undoubtedly brought to you by a third person—a person you trusted. Who was it?"

Mrs. Kirk shook her head. "I'm sorry. I can't tell you."

"You realize, of course, the seriousness of your refusal?"

"I—well, I—good heavens, what have I got mixed up in, anyhow? A respectable woman like me——"

"Precisely," said Miss Morrow sternly. "A woman honored throughout the city, a woman prominent in every forward-looking movement—I must say I am surprised, Mrs. Kirk, to find you obstructing the course of justice. And all because this person who brought Grace Lane to you is now asking you to keep the matter secret——"

"I didn't say that."

"But I did. It's true, isn't it?"

"Well—yes—it is. And I must say I think she's asking a good deal of me——"

"She? Then Grace Lane was brought to you by a woman?"

"What? Oh—oh, yes. Of course. I'll admit that."

"You have admitted it," chuckled Barry Kirk.

"Tell me this," Miss Morrow went on, "before you left to come down here, did you let Mrs. Tupper-Brock know where you were going?"

"I did."

"Did you tell her you expected to be questioned by me when you got here?"

"Y-yes."

"And was it then that she asked you not to reveal the fact that she was the person who brought Grace Lane to you, with a request that you help the girl?" Mrs. Kirk was silent. "You needn't answer," Miss Morrow smiled. "As a matter of fact, you have answered. Your face, you know."

Mrs. Kirk shrugged. "You're a clever young woman," she complained.

"Since that is settled, and I now know that it was Mrs. Tupper-Brock who introduced the Lane girl to you," Miss Morrow continued, "there is no real reason why you shouldn't give me the details. How long ago did it happen?"

Mrs. Kirk hesitated, and then surrendered. "Several months ago," she said. "Helen brought the girl to the house. She told me she had met her on a ferry—that they were old friends—had known each other in Devonshire, a great many years back."

"In Devonshire. Please go on."

"Helen said this girl had been through a lot——"

"What?"

"I didn't ask. I have some delicacy. Also, that she was destitute and in desperate need of work. She was such a pretty, modest, feminine little thing, I took an immediate fancy to her. So I got her the job in this building."

"Without consulting me," Kirk suggested.

"Why should I? It was a matter requiring instant action. You were off somewhere as usual."

"And that's all you know about Grace Lane?" inquired Miss Morrow.

"Yes. I made inquiries, and found she was doing well and was, apparently, happy. When we came up here the other night, we spoke to her. She thanked me, very nicely. I'm sorry she's been hounded out of town."

Miss Morrow smiled. "One thing more. Have you noticed any signs of a close friendship between Mrs. Tupper-Brock and Colonel Beetham?"

"I believe they've gone out together occasionally. I don't spy on them."

"Naturally not. I think that is all, Mrs. Kirk."

Mrs. Kirk stood up. She appeared to be in a rather chastened mood. "Thanks. Fortunately, I can still get to my lecture on time."

"Just one point," added the girl. "I'd rather you didn't repeat this conversation to Mrs. Tupper-Brock."

"Me—I won't repeat it to anybody." The old lady smiled grimly. "Somehow I don't seem to have come out of it as well as I expected." She said good-by and made a hasty exit.

"Bully for you," cried Kirk, with an admiring look at Miss Morrow.

She stood, frowning. "What did I tell you this morning? Mrs. Tupper-Brock was lying, but I didn't expect confirmation so soon."

"Going to have her on the carpet again?" Kirk asked.

"I am not. What's the good of more lies? Grace Lane was an old friend—which may mean that Grace Lane will write to Mrs. Tupper-Brock from wherever she is hiding. I am going to make immediate arrangements with the postal authorities. Mrs. Tupper-Brock's mail will reach her through my office from now on."

"Excellent," approved Chan. "You have wise head on pretty shoulders. What an unexpected combination! May I inquire, what is our good friend Flannery doing?"

"The Captain has taken a sudden fancy to Miss Lila Barr. I believe he has ordered her to his office at five this afternoon, for what he calls a grilling. I can't be there, but if I were you, I'd drop in on it."

Chan shrugged. "I fear I will look in vain for welcome inscribed in glowing characters on the mat. However, I will appear with offhand air."

Miss Morrow turned to Barry Kirk. "I do hope your grandmother won't hold my inquisition against me."

"Nonsense. You were splendid, and she's crazy about you. I saw it in her eyes when she went out."

"I didn't," smiled the girl.

"You didn't look carefully. That's where you make a mistake. Examine the eyes about you. You'll find a lot more approval than you suspect."

"Really? I'm afraid I'm too busy—I must leave that sort of thing to the old-fashioned girls. Now, I must run along. There's just a chance I can find Grace Lane for Captain Flannery. Some one must."

"And it might as well be you," quoted Kirk. "I'll hope to see you again soon." He showed her out.

At four thirty Charlie Chan strolled to the Hall of Justice and walked in on Captain Flannery. The Captain appeared to be in rare good humor.

"How are you, Sergeant," he said. "What's new with you?"

"With me, everything has aged look," Chan replied.

"Not getting on as fast as you expected, are you?" Flannery inquired. "Well, this should be a lesson to you. Every frog ought to stick to his own pond. You may be a world-beater in a village like Honolulu, but you're on the big time over here. You're in over your depth."

"How true," Charlie agreed. "I am often dismayed, but I think of you and know you will not permit me to drown. Something has happened to elevate your spirit?"

"It sure has. I've just pulled off a neat little stunt. You see, I had a grand idea. I put an ad in the morning paper for those velvet slippers——"

"Ah, yes," Chan grinned. "Inspector Duff warned me you were about to be hit by that idea."

"Oh, he did, did he? Well, I'm not taking orders from Duff. I was on the point of doing it some days ago, but it slipped my mind. Duff recalled it to me, that's all. I put a very cagy advertisement in the paper, and——"

"Results are already apparent?" Chan finished.

"Are they? I'll say so." Flannery took up something wrapped in a soiled newspaper. The string had already been loosened, and casting it aside, he revealed the contents of the bundle. Before Chan's eyes lay the red velvet slippers from the Chinese Legation, the slippers found on the feet of Hilary Galt that tragic night in London, the slippers in which Sir Frederic Bruce had walked to his death little more than a week ago.

"What happy luck," Charlie said.

"Ain't it?" agreed Flannery. "A soldier from out at the Presidio brought them in less than an hour ago. It seems he was crossing to Oakland to visit his girl last Wednesday noon, and he picked this package up from one of the benches on the ferry-boat. There was nobody about to claim it, so he took it along. Of course, he should have turned it over to the ferry people—but he didn't. I told him that was all right with me."

"On ferry-boat to Oakland," Chan repeated.

"Yes. This guy'd been wondering what to do with his find, and he was mighty pleased when I slipped him a five spot."

Charlie turned the slippers slowly about in his hands. Again he was interested by the Chinese character which promised long life and happiness. A lying promise, that. The slippers had not brought long life and happiness to Hilary Galt. Nor to Sir Frederic Bruce.

"Just where," Chan mused, "do we arrive at now?"

"Well, I'll have to admit that we're still a long ways from home," Flannery replied. "But we're getting on. Last Wednesday, the day after the murder, somebody left these slippers on an Oakland ferry-boat. Left them intentionally, I'll bet—glad enough to be rid of 'em."

"In same identical paper," Charlie inquired, "they were always wrapped?"

"Yes— that's the paper this fellow found them in. An evening paper dated last Wednesday night. A first edition, issued about ten in the morning."

Chan spread out the newspaper and studied it. "You have been carefully over this journal, I suspect?"

"Why—er—I haven't had time," Flannery told him.

"Nothing of note catches the eye," Chan remarked. "Except—ah, yes—here on margin of first page. A few figures, carelessly inscribed in pencil. Paper is torn in that locality, and they are almost obliterated."

Flannery came closer, and Charlie pointed. A small sum in addition had evidently been worked out.

$$\begin{array}{r} \$79. \\ 23. \\ \hline 103. \end{array}$$

"A hundred three," Flannery read. "That's wrong. Seventy-nine and twenty-three don't add up to a hundred three."

"Then we must seek one who is poor scholar of arithmetic," Chan replied. "If you have no inclination for objecting, I will jot figures down."

"Go ahead. Put your big brain on it. But don't forget—I produced the slippers."

"And the newspaper," Charlie added. "The brightest act you have performed to date."

The door opened, and a man in uniform entered. "That dame's outside, Captain," he announced. "She's brought her fellow with her. Shall I fetch 'em in?"

"Sure," Flannery nodded. "It's Miss Lila Barr," he explained to Chan. "I got to thinking about her, and she don't sound so good to me. I'm going to have another talk with her. You can stay, if you want to."

"Overwhelmed by your courtesy," Chan responded.

Miss Lila Barr came timidly through the door. After her came Kinsey, Kirk's secretary. The girl seemed very much worried.

"You wanted me, Captain Flannery?"

"Yeah. Come in. Sit down." He looked at Kinsey. "Who's this?"

"Mr. Kinsey—a friend of mine," the girl explained. "I thought you wouldn't mind——"

"Your fellow, eh?"

"Well,—I suppose——"

"The guy you was crying about that night you came out of the office where you saw Sir Frederic?"

"Yes."

"Well, I'm glad to meet him. I'm glad you can prove you've got a fellow, anyhow. But even so—that story of yours sounds pretty fishy to me."

"I can't help how it sounds," returned the girl with spirit. "It's the truth."

"All right. Let it go. It's the next night I want to talk about now. The night Sir Frederic was killed. You were working in your office that night?"

"Yes, sir. Though I must have left before—the thing—happened."

"How do you know you left before it happened?"

"I don't. I was just supposing——"

"Don't suppose with me," bullied Flannery.

"She has good reason for thinking she left before the murder," Kinsey put in. "She heard no shot fired."

Flannery swung on him. "Say—when I want any answers from you, I'll ask for 'em." He turned back to the girl. "You didn't hear any shot?"

"No, sir."

"And you didn't see anybody in the hall when you went home?"

"Well—I—I——"

"Yes? Out with it."

"I'd like to change my testimony on that point."

"Oh, you would, would you?"

"Yes. I have talked it over with Mr. Kinsey, and he thinks I was wrong to—to—say what I did——"

"To lie, you mean?"

"But I didn't want to be entangled in it," pleaded the girl. "I saw myself testifying in court—and I didn't think—it just seemed I couldn't——"

"You couldn't help us, eh? Young woman, this is serious business. I could lock you up——"

"Oh, but if I change my testimony? If I tell you the truth now?"

"Well, we'll see. But make sure of one thing—that it's the truth at last. Then there was somebody in the hall?"

"Yes. I started to leave the office, but just as I opened the door, I remembered my umbrella. So I went back. But in that moment at the door, I saw two men standing near the elevators."

"You saw two men. What did they look like?"

"One—one was a Chinese."

Flannery was startled. "A Chinese. Say—it wasn't Mr. Chan here?" Charlie smiled.

"Oh, no," the girl continued. "It was an older Chinese. He was talking with a tall, thin man. A man whose picture I have seen in the newspapers."

"Oh, you've seen his picture in the papers? What's his name?"

"His name is Colonel John Beetham, and I believe he is—an explorer."

"I see," Flannery got up and paced the floor. "You saw Beetham talking with a Chinese in the hall just before Sir Frederic was killed. Then you went back to get your umbrella?"

"Yes—and when I came out again they were gone."

"Anything else?"

"No—I guess not."

"Think hard. You've juggled the truth once."

"She was not under oath," protested Kinsey.

"Well, what if she wasn't? She obstructed our work, and that's no joking matter. However, I'll overlook it, now that she's finally come across. You can go. I may want you again."

The girl and Kinsey went out. Flannery walked the floor in high glee.

"Now I'm getting somewhere," he cried. "Beetham! I haven't paid much attention to him, but I'll make up for lost time from here on. Beetham was

in the hall talking with a Chinaman a few minutes before the murder. And
he was supposed to be up-stairs running his magic lantern. A Chinaman—do
you get it? Those slippers came from the Chinese Legation. By heaven, it's
beginning to tie up at last."

"If I might presume," said Chan, "you now propose to——"

"I propose to get after Colonel Beetham. He told Miss Morrow he didn't
leave the room up-stairs. Another liar—and a distinguished one this time."

"Humbly asking pardon," Chan ventured, "Colonel Beetham very clever
man. Have a care he does not outwit you."

"I'm not afraid of him. He can't fool me. I'm too old at this game."

"Magnificent confidence," Charlie smiled. "Let us hope it is justified by
the finish."

"It will be, all right. You just leave Colonel Beetham to me."

"With utmost gladness," agreed Chan. "If you will allot something else
to me."

"What's that?" Flannery demanded.

"I refer to faint little figures on newspaper margin."

"Poor arithmetic," snorted Flannery. "And a poor clue."

"Time will reveal," said Chan gently.

17

The Woman from Peshawar

Barry Kirk answered the ring of the telephone the next morning at ten,
and was greeted by a voice that, even over the wire, seemed to afford him
pleasure.

"Good morning," he said. "I'm glad to hear from you. This is what I call
starting the day right."

"Thanks ever so much," Miss Morrow replied. "Now that your day has
begun auspiciously, would you mind fading away into the background and
giving Mr. Chan your place at the telephone?"

"What—you don't want to talk to me?"

"I'm sorry—no. I'm rather busy to-day."

"Well, I can take a hint as quickly as the next man. I know when I'm not
wanted. That's what you meant to convey, isn't it——"

"Please, Mr. Kirk."

"Here's Charlie now. I'm not angry, but I'm terribly, terribly hurt——"
He handed the telephone to Chan.

"Oh, Mr. Chan," the girl said. "Captain Flannery is going to interview
Colonel Beetham at eleven o'clock. He's all Beetham to-day. He's asked me
to be on hand to remind the Colonel about his testimony the night of the
murder, and I suggest you come, too."

"The Captain demands me?" Chan inquired.

"I demand you. Isn't that enough?"

"To me it is delicious plenty," Charlie replied. "I will be there—at Captain
Flannery's office, I presume?"

"Yes. Don't fail me," Miss Morrow said, and rang off.

"Something doing?" Kirk asked.

Chan shrugged. "Captain Flannery has hot spasm about Colonel Beetham. He interrogates him at eleven, and I am invited."

"How about me?"

"I am stricken by regret, but you are not mentioned."

"Then I hardly think I'll go," Kirk said.

At a little before eleven, Charlie went to the Hall of Justice. In Flannery's dark office he found Miss Morrow, brightening the dreary corner where she was.

"Good morning," she said. "The Captain is showing Inspector Duff about the building. I'm glad you're here. Somehow I've got the impression Captain Flannery doesn't care much for me this morning."

"Mainland police have stupid sinking spells," Chan informed her.

Flannery came in, followed by Inspector Duff. He stood for a minute glaring at Charlie and the girl.

"Well, a fine pair you are," he roared. "What's the idea, anyhow?"

"What *is* the idea, Captain?" asked Miss Morrow sweetly.

"The idea seems to be to keep me in the dark," Flannery went on. "What do you think I am? A mind-reader? I've just been talking with Inspector Duff about Colonel Beetham, and I discover you two know a lot more about the Colonel than you've ever told me."

"Please understand—I haven't been tale-bearing," smiled Duff. "I mentioned these things thinking of course the Captain knew them."

"Of course you thought I knew them," Flannery exploded. "Why shouldn't I know them? I'm supposed to be in charge of this case, ain't I? Yet you two have been digging up stuff right along and keeping it to yourselves. I tell you, it makes me sore——"

"Oh, I'm so sorry," cried Miss Morrow.

"That helps a lot. What's all this about a servant of the Colonel's—a Chinaman named Li Gung? Are you willing to talk now, Sergeant Chan, or are you still playing button, button, who's got the——"

"I'm the guilty one," the girl cut in. "I should have told you myself. Naturally, Mr. Chan must have thought I had."

"Oh, no," Chan protested. "Please shift all guilt from those pretty shoulders to my extensive ones. I have made mistake. It is true I have pondered certain facts in silence, but I was hoping some great light would break——"

"All right, all right," Flannery interrupted. "But will you talk now, that's what I want to know? When did you first hear about Li Gung?"

"At noon of the day Sir Frederic was killed, I have great honor to lunch with them. After lunch he takes me apart and talks of this Li Gung, a stranger visiting relatives in Jackson Street. He suggests I might make cunning inquiries of the man, but I am forced to refuse the task. On morning after murder I am in stateroom of *Maui* boat, foolishly believing I am going to Honolulu, when I hear Colonel Beetham in next cabin saying farewell to one he calls Li Gung. The Colonel directs that Gung lie low in Honolulu, and answer no questions."

"And all that was so unimportant I never heard of it," stormed Flannery. "How about the fact that Beetham was one of the guests at the picnic near Peshawar?"

"We did not learn that until Tuesday night," Miss Morrow informed him.

"Only had about thirty-six hours to tell me, eh? On May fourth, nineteen hundred and thirteen, Colonel Beetham left Peshawar by way of the—er—the Khyber Pass to go to—to—to make a trip——"

"To Teheran by way of Afghanistan and the Kevir Desert of northern Persia," Duff helped him out.

"Yes. You told the Inspector that, Sergeant. But you never told me."

Charlie shrugged. "Why should I trouble you? The matter appears to mean nothing. True enough, I might make a surmise—a most picturesque surmise. But I see you, Captain, floundering about in difficult murder case. Should I ask such a man to come with me and gaze upon the bright tapestry of romance?"

"Whatever that means," Flannery returned. "If I hadn't got that Barr girl in, I'd still be in the dark. I was too smart for you—I hit on Beetham's trail myself—but that doesn't excuse you. I'm disappointed in the pair of you."

"Overwhelmed with painful regret," Chan bowed.

"Oh, forget it." A man in uniform ushered Colonel Beetham into the room.

The Colonel knew a good tailor, a tailor who no doubt rejoiced in the trim, lithe figure of his client. He was faultlessly attired, with a flower in his button-hole, a stick in his gloved hand. For a moment he stood, those tired eyes that had looked on so many lonely corners of the world unusually alert and keen.

"Good morning," he said. He bowed to Miss Morrow and Chan. "Ah—this, I believe, is Captain Flannery——"

"Morning," replied Flannery. "Meet Inspector Duff of Scotland Yard."

"Delighted," Beetham answered. "I am very happy to see a man from the Yard. No doubt the search for Sir Frederic's murderer will get forward now."

"I guess it will," growled Flannery, "if you answer a few questions for us—and tell the truth——"

The Colonel raised his eyebrows very slightly. "The truth, of course," he remarked, with a wan smile. "I shall do my best. May I sit down?"

"Sure," replied Flannery, indicating a dusty chair. "On the night Sir Frederic was killed, you were giving a magic lantern show on the floor above——"

"I should hardly have called it that. Motion pictures, you know, of Tibet——"

"Yes, yes. You did a lecture with these lantern slides, but toward the end you dropped out and let the performance run itself. Later Miss Morrow here asked you—what was it you asked him, Miss Morrow?"

"I referred to that moment when he left the machine," the girl said. "He assured me that he had not been absent from the room during the interval."

The Captain looked at Beetham. "Is that right, Colonel?"

"Yes—I fancy that is what I told her."

"Why?"

"Why? What do you mean?"

"Why did you tell her that when you knew damn well you had been down on the twentieth floor talking with a Chinaman?"

Beetham laughed softly. "Have you never done anything that you later regretted, Captain? The matter struck me as of no importance—I had seen nothing of note on my brief jaunt below. I had a sort of inborn diffidence about being involved in the scandal. So I very foolishly made a slight—er—misstatement."

"Then you did go down to the twentieth floor?"

"Only for a second. You see, a motion-picture projector and seven reels of film make a rather heavy load. My old boy, Li Gung, had assisted me in bringing the outfit to Mr. Kirk's apartment. I thought I should be finished by ten, and I told him to be back then. When I left the machine at fifteen minutes past ten, I realized that I still had another reel to show. I ran down-stairs, found Gung waiting on the lower floor, and told him to go home. I said I would carry the machine away myself."

"Ah, yes—and he left?"

"He went at once, in the lift. The lift girl can verify my statement—if—"

"If what?"

"If she will."

"You were going to say—if we can find her?"

"Why should I say that? Isn't she about?"

"She is not. In her absence, maybe Li Gung can back up your story?"

"I'm sure he can—if you care to cable him. He is in Honolulu at the moment."

"He left the next noon, on the *Maui?*"

"Yes, he did."

"You saw him off?"

"Naturally. He has been with me more than twenty years. A faithful chap."

"When you said good-by, you told him to lie low over in Hawaii."

"Yes, I—yes, I did. You see, there was some trouble about his passport. I was fearful he might get into difficulties."

"You also told him to answer no questions."

"For the same reason, of course."

"You knew he would have to show his passport on landing. If it wasn't O.K. did you suppose lying low after that would do any good?"

"Show his passport at another American port? Really, you know, I'm frightfully ignorant of your many rules and regulations. Quite confusing, I find them."

"You must—a man who's traveled as little as you have, Colonel."

"Ah, yes. Now you're being sarcastic."

"Oh, don't mind me," Flannery said. "We'll drop Li Gung. But I'm not through yet. I understand you were at Peshawar, in India, on the night of May third, nineteen hundred and thirteen."

Beetham nodded slowly. "That is a matter of record."

"And can't very well be denied, eh? You went out into the hills on a picnic. One of the party was a woman named Eve Durand." Beetham stirred slightly. "That night Eve Durand disappeared and has never been seen since. Have you any idea how she got out of India?"

"If she has never been seen since, how do you know she did get out of India?"

"Never mind. I'm asking you questions. You remember the incident?"

"Naturally. A shocking affair."

Flannery studied him for a moment. "Tell me, Colonel—had you ever met Sir Frederic before the other night at Barry Kirk's bungalow?"

"Never. Stop a bit. I believe he said he had been at a dinner of the Royal Geographical Society in London, and had seen me there. But I did not recall the meeting."

"You didn't know that he had come to San Francisco to find Eve Durand?"

"Had he really? How extraordinary."

"You didn't know it?"

"Of course not."

"Could you have given him any help if you had?"

"I could not," replied Beetham firmly.

"All right, Colonel. You're not thinking of leaving San Francisco soon?"

"In a few days—when I have completed arrangements for my next long expedition."

"You're not leaving until we find out who killed Sir Frederic. Is that understood?"

"But, my dear fellow—surely you don't think——"

"I think your testimony may prove valuable. I'm asking you—is it understood?"

"Perfectly. I shall hope, however, for your early success."

"We all hope for it."

"Of course." Beetham turned to Inspector Duff. "A frightful thing. Sir Frederic was a charming fellow——"

"And much beloved," said Duff evenly. "Please don't worry. Everything possible is being done, Colonel Beetham."

"I am happy to hear that." Beetham rose. "Now—if there's nothing more——"

"Not at present," said Flannery.

"Thank you so much," replied the Colonel, and went debonairly out.

Flannery stared after him. "He lies like a gentleman, don't he?" he remarked.

"Beautifully," sighed Miss Morrow, her eyes on the door through which the explorer had gone.

"Well, he don't fool me," Flannery continued. "He knows more about this than he's telling. If he was anybody but the famous Colonel Beetham, I'd take a chance and lock him up this morning."

"Oh, but you couldn't," the girl cried.

"I suppose not. I'd be mobbed by all the club women in the Bay District. However, I don't need to. He's too well known to make a getaway. But I'd better keep him shadowed at that. Now, let's get to business. If only Li Gung was here, I'd sweat something out of him. What was that Sir Frederic told you, Sergeant? About Li Gung's relatives in Jackson Street? I might look them up."

"No use," Chan answered. "I have already done so."

"Oh, you have? Without a word to me, of course——"

"Words of no avail. I made most pitiful failure. I am admitted to house, but plans are foiled by kind act of boy scout——"

"A boy scout in the family, eh?"

"Yes—name of Willie Li. The family of Henry Li, Oriental Apartment House."

Flannery considered. "Well, the young generation will talk, if the old one won't. Willie ought to have a chance."

"He has obtained it. He tells me little—save that once on a hard journey Colonel Beetham kills a man."

"He told you that? Then he knows something about Beetham's journeys?"

"Undubitably he does. He has overheard talk——"

Flannery jumped up. "That's enough for me. I'll have Manley of the Chinatown Squad bring the kid here to-night. They're all crazy about Manley, these Chink kids. We'll get something."

The telephone rang. Flannery answered, and then relinquished it to Miss Morrow. As she listened to the news coming over the wire, her eyes brightened with excitement. She hung up the receiver and turned to the others.

"That was the district attorney," she announced. "We've got hold of a letter mailed to Mrs. Tupper-Brock from Santa Barbara. It was written by Grace Lane, and it gives her present address."

"Fine business," Flannery cried. "I told you she couldn't get away from me. I'll get a couple of men off in a car right away." He looked at Miss Morrow. "They can stop at your office for the address."

She nodded. "I'm going right back. I'll give it to them."

Flannery rubbed his hands. "Things are looking up at last! Make it seven to-night—I'll have the kid here then. Sergeant—you're coming. I may want your help. And you can look in if you like, Inspector."

"Thanks," Duff said.

"How about me?" asked Miss Morrow.

He frowned at her. "I'm not so pleased with you. All those secrets——"

"But I'm so sorry." She smiled at him. "And I was a little help to you in finding Grace Lane, you know."

"I guess you were, at that. Sure—come along, if you want to."

The party scattered, and Charlie Chan went back to the bungalow, where he found Barry Kirk eagerly awaiting news. When he heard the plan for the evening, Kirk insisted on taking Miss Morrow and Chan to dinner. At six thirty they left the obscure little restaurant he had selected because of its capable chef, and strolled toward the Hall of Justice.

The night was clear and cool, without fog, and the stars were bright as torches overhead. They skirted the fringe of Chinatown and passed on through Portsmouth Square, the old Plaza of romantic history. It was emptied now of its usual derelicts and adventurers; the memorial to R. L. S. stood lonely and serene in the starlight.

Flannery and Duff were waiting in the former's office. The Captain regarded Barry Kirk without enthusiasm.

"We're all here, ain't we?" he inquired.

"I thought you wouldn't mind," smiled Kirk.

"Oh, well—it's all right. I guess it's pretty late now to bar you out." He turned to Miss Morrow. "You saw Petersen, didn't you?"

"Yes. I gave him the address."

"He had Myers with him. Good men, both of them. They'll be in Santa Barbara this evening, and can start back at sunrise. Barring accidents, they'll bring Grace Lane into this office late to-morrow afternoon. And if she gets away from me again, she'll be going some."

They sat down. Presently a huge police officer in plain clothes, with a khaki shirt, came in. He was kindly and smiling, but he had the keen eye of a man who is prepared for any emergency. Flannery introduced him.

"Sergeant Manley," he explained. "Head of the Chinatown Squad for seven years—which is a good many years longer than any one else has lived to hold that job."

Manley's manner was cordial. "Glad to meet you," he said. "I've got the kid outside, Captain. I picked him up and brought him along without giving him a chance to run home for instructions."

"Good idea," Flannery nodded. "Will he talk?"

"Oh, he'll talk all right. He and I are old friends. I'll bring him in."

He disappeared into the outer office and returned with Willie Li. The boy scout was in civilian clothes, and looked as though he would have welcomed the moral support of his uniform.

"Here you are, Willie," Manley said. "This is Captain Flannery. He's going to ask you to do him a big favor."

"Sure," grinned Willie Li.

"All boy scouts," Manley went on, "are American citizens, and they stand for law and order. That's right, ain't it, Willie?"

"In the oath," replied Willie gravely.

"I've explained to him," Manley continued, "that none of his family is mixed up in this in any way. They won't be harmed by anything he tells you."

"That's right," said Flannery. "You can take my word for it, son."

"Sure," agreed the boy readily.

"Your cousin, Li Gung," Flannery began, "has been a servant of Colonel Beetham's for a long time. He's been all over the world with the Colonel?"

Willie nodded. "Gobi Desert. Kevir Desert. Tibet, India, Afghanistan."

"You've heard Li Gung tell about his adventures with the Colonel?"

"Yes."

"Remember 'em?"

"Never going to forget," replied Willie, his little black eyes shining.

"You told your friend Mr. Chan here that the Colonel once shot a man for some reason or other?"

The boy's eyes narrowed. "Because it was necessary. There was no crime there."

"Of course—of course it was necessary," rejoined Flannery heartily. "We wouldn't do anything to the Colonel because of that. We have no authority over things that happen outside of San Francisco. We're just curious, that's all. Do you remember what trip it was during which the Colonel shot this man?"

"Sure. It was the journey from Peshawar through Khyber Pass over Afghanistan."

"It happened in Afghanistan?"

"Yes. A very bad man. Muhamed Ashref Khan, keeper of the camels. He was trying to steal——"

"To steal what?"

"A pearl necklace. Colonel Beetham saw him go into the tent—the tent which no man must enter at cost of his life——"

"What tent what that?"

"The woman's tent."

There was a moment's tense silence. "The woman's tent?" Flannery repeated. "What woman?"

"The woman who was traveling with them to Teheran. The woman from Peshawar."

"Did your cousin describe her?"

"She was beautiful, with golden hair, and eyes like the blue sky. Very beautiful, my cousin said."

"And she was traveling with them from Peshawar to Teheran?"

"Yes. Only Li Gung and the Colonel knew it when they went through the pass, for she was hidden in a cart. Then she came out, and she had her own tent, which Colonel Beetham said no man must enter or he would kill him."

"But this camel man—he disobeyed? And he was shot?"

"Justly so," observed Willie Li.

"Of course," agreed Flannery. "Well, son—that's all. I'm very much obliged to you. Now run along. If I had anything to say in the scouts, you'd get a merit badge for this."

"I have twenty-two already," grinned Willie Li. "I am Eagle Scout." He and Manley went out.

Flannery got up and paced the floor. "Well, what do you know?" he cried. "This is too good to be true. Eve Durand disappears in the night—her poor husband is frantic with grief—the whole of India is turned upside down in the search for her. And all the time she's moving on through Afghanistan in the caravan of Colonel John Beetham—the great explorer every one is crazy about, the brave, fine man no one would dream of suspecting." Flannery turned to Chan. "I see now what you meant. Romance, you called it. Well, I've got a different name for it. I call it running away with another man's wife. A pretty scandal in the Colonel's past—a lovely blot on his record—by heaven—wonderful! Do you see what it means?"

Chan shrugged. "I see you are flying high tonight."

"I certainly am—high, wide, and handsome. I've got my man, and I've got the motive, too. Sir Frederic comes to San Francisco hunting Eve Durand. And here is Colonel John Beetham, honored and respected by all—riding the top of the wave. Beetham learns why Sir Frederic has come—and he wonders. He hears the detective has been in India—has he found out how Eve Durand left that country? If he has, and springs it, the career of John Beetham is smashed. He'll be done for—finished—he won't collect any more money for his big expeditions. Is he the sort to stand by and watch that happen? He is not. What does he do?"

"The question is for mere effect," suggested Chan.

"First of all, he wants to learn how much Sir Frederic really knows. At dinner he hears that about the safe being open. He's crazy to get down there and look around. At the first opportunity he creeps downstairs, enters Mr. Kirk's office——"

"Through a locked door?" inquired Chan.

"The elevator girl could get him a key. She's Eve Durand—don't forget that. Or else there's Li Gung—he's on the scene—maybe that's just by accident. But he could be used—the fire-escape——Anyhow, Beetham gets into the office. He hunts like mad, gets hold of the records, sees at a glance that Sir Frederic has discovered everything. At that moment Sir Frederic comes in. The one man in the world who knows how Eve Durand got out of India—and will tell. The man who can wreck Beetham for ever. Beetham sees red. He pulls a gun. It's a simple matter for him—he's done it before. Sir Frederic lies dead on the floor, Beetham escapes with the records—the secret of that old scandal is safe. By the Lord Harry—who'd want a better motive than that!"

"Not to mention," said Chan gently, "the velvet slippers. The slippers of Hilary Galt."

"Oh, hell," cried Flannery. "Be reasonable, man! One thing at a time."

18
Flannery's Big Scene

Greatly pleased with himself, Captain Flannery sat down behind his desk. His summing up of the case against Beetham seemed, to his way of thinking, without a flaw. He beamed at the assembled company.

"Everything is going to work out fine," he continued. "To-morrow evening in this room I stage my big scene, and if we don't get something out of it, then I'm no judge of human nature. First, I bring in Major Durand. I tell him Eve Durand has been found and is on her way here, and while we're waiting I go back to the question of how she got out of India. I plant in his mind a suspicion of Beetham. Then I bring the woman into the room—after fifteen years' suffering and anxiety, he sees his wife at last. What's he going to think? What'll he ask himself—and her? Where's she been? Why did she leave? How did she escape from India? At that moment I produce Colonel Beetham, confront him with the husband he wronged, the woman he carried off in his caravan. I tell Durand I have certain knowledge that his wife left with Beetham. Then I sit back and watch the fireworks. How does that strike you, Sergeant Chan?"

"You would chop down the tree to catch the blackbird," Chan said.

"Well, sometimes we have to do that. It's round-about, but it ought to work. What do you think, Inspector?"

"Sounds rather good, as drama," Duff drawled. "But do you really think it will reveal the murderer of Sir Frederic?"

"It may. Somebody—the woman, or Beetham—will break. Make a damaging admission. They always do. I'll gamble on it, this time. Yes, sir—we're going to take a big stride forward to-morrow night."

Leaving Captain Flannery to an enthusiastic contemplation of his own cleverness, they departed. At the door Chan went off with Inspector Duff. Kirk and the girl strolled up the hill together.

"Want a taxi?" Kirk asked.

"Thanks. I'd rather walk—and think."

"We have something to think of, haven't we? How does it strike you? Beetham?"

She shrugged her shoulders. "Nonsense. I'll never believe it. Not if he makes a full confession himself."

"Oh, I know. He's the hero of your dreams. But just the same, my lady, he's not incapable of it. If Sir Frederic was in his way—threatening his plans—and it begins to look as though he was. Unless you don't believe that Eve Durand was in the caravan?"

"I believe that," she replied.

"Because you want to," he smiled. "It's too romantic for words, isn't it? By George, the very thought of it makes me feel young and giddy. The gay picnic party in the hills—the game of hide-and-seek—one breathless moment of meeting behind the tamarisks. 'I'm yours—take me with you when you go.' Everything forgotten—the world well lost for love. The wagon jolting out through the pass, with all that beauty hidden beneath a worn bit of canvas. Then—the old caravan road—the golden road to Samarkand—the merchants from the north crowding by—camels and swarthy men—and mingled with the dust of the trail the iron nails lost from thousands of shoes that have passed that way since time began."

"I didn't know you were so romantic."

"Ah—you've never given me a chance. You and your law books. Eight months along that famous road—nights with the white stars close overhead, dawns hazy with desert mist. Hot sun at times, and then snow, flurries of snow. The man and the woman together——"

"And the poor husband searching frantically throughout India."

"Yes, they rather forgot Durand, didn't they? But they were in love. You know, it looks to me as though we had stumbled on to a great love story. Do you think——"

"I wonder."

"You wonder what?"

"I wonder if it's all true—and if it is, does it bring us any closer to a solution of the puzzle? After all, the question remains—who killed Sir Frederic? Captain Flannery hadn't an iota of proof for any of his wild surmises involving Beetham."

"Oh, forget your worries. Let's pretend. This deserted street is the camel road to Teheran—the old silk road from China to Persia. You and I——"

"You and I have no time for silk roads now. We must find the road that leads to a solution of our mystery."

Kirk sighed. "All right. To make a headline of it, Attorney Morrow Slams Door on Romance Probe. But some day I'll catch you off your guard, and then—look out!"

"I'm never off my guard," she laughed.

On Friday morning, after breakfast, Chan hesitated a moment, and then followed Barry Kirk into his bedroom. "If you will pardon the imposition, I have bold request to make."

"Certainly, Charlie. What is it?"

"I wish you to take me to Cosmopolitan Club, and introduce me past eagle-eyed door man. After that, I have unlimited yearning to meet old employee of club."

"An old employee? Well, there's Peter Lee. He's been in charge of the check-room for thirty years. Would he do?"

"An excellent choice. I would have you suggest to this Lee that he show me about club-house, roof to cellar. Is that possible?"

"Of course." Kirk looked at him keenly. "You're still thinking about that club year-book we found beside Sir Frederic?"

"I have never ceased to think of it," Chan returned. "Whenever you are ready, please."

Deeply mystified, Kirk took him to the Cosmopolitan and turned him over to Peter Lee.

"It is not necessary that you loiter on the scene," Chan remarked, grinning with pleasure. "I will do some investigating and return to the bungalow later."

"All right," Kirk replied. "Just as you wish."

It was close to the luncheon hour when Chan showed up, his little eyes gleaming.

"What luck?" Kirk inquired.

"Time will reveal," said Chan. "I find this mainland climate bracing to an extremity. Very much fear I shall depopulate your kitchen at lunch."

"Well, don't drink too heartily of the hydrocyanic acid," Kirk smiled. "Something tells me it would be a real calamity if we lost you just at present."

After luncheon Miss Morrow telephoned to say that Grace Lane, accompanied by the two policemen, would reach Flannery's office at four o'clock. She added that they were both invited—on her own initiative.

"Let us go," Chan remarked. "Captain Flannery's big scene should have crowded house."

"What do you think will come of it?" Kirk asked.

"I am curious to learn. If it has big success, then my work here is finished. If not——"

"Yes? Then what?"

"Then I may suddenly act like pompous stager of shows myself," Chan suggested.

Flannery, Duff and Miss Morrow were in the Captain's office when Chan and Barry Kirk walked in. "Hello," said the Captain. "Want to be in at the finish, eh?"

"Pleasure would be impossible to deny ourselves," Chan told him.

"Well, I'm all set," Flannery went on. "All my plans made."

Chan nodded. "The wise man digs his well before he is thirsty," he remarked.

"You haven't been doing any too much digging," Flannery chided. "I got to admit, Sergeant, you've kept your word. You've let me solve this case without offering very much help. However, I've been equal to it. I haven't needed you, as it turned out. You might as well have been on that boat ten days ago."

"A sad reflection for me," said Chan. "But I am not of mean nature. My hearty congratulations will be ready when desired."

Colonel Beetham was ushered into the room. His manner was nonchalant, and, as always, rather condescending.

"Ah, Captain," he remarked, "I'm here again. According to instructions——"

"I'm very glad to see you," Flannery broke in.

"And just what can I do for you to-day?" inquired Beetham, dropping into a chair.

"I'm anxious to have you meet—a certain lady."

The Colonel opened a cigarette case, took out a cigarette, and tapped it on the silver side of the case. "Ah, yes. I'm not precisely a lady's man, but——"

"I think you'll be interested to meet this one," Flannery told him.

"Really?" He lighted a match.

"You see," Flannery went on, "it happens to be a lady who once took a very long journey in your company."

Beetham's brown, lean hand paused with the lighted match. The flame held steady. "I do not understand you," he said.

"An eight months' journey, I believe," the Captain persisted. "Through Khyber Pass and across Afghanistan and eastern Persia to the neighborhood of Teheran."

Beetham lighted his cigarette and tossed away the match. "My dear fellow—what are you talking about?"

"You know what I'm talking about. Eve Durand—the lady you helped out of India fifteen years ago. No one suspected you, did they, Colonel? Too big a man—above suspicion—all those medals on your chest. However, I know you did it—I know you ran away with Durand's wife—and I'll prove it, too. But perhaps I needn't prove it—perhaps you'll admit it——" He stopped.

Beetham unconcernedly blew a ring of smoke toward the ceiling, and for a moment watched it dissolve. "All that," he remarked, "is so absolutely silly I refuse to answer."

"Suit yourself," replied Flannery. "At any rate, Eve Durand will be here in a few minutes, and I want you to see her again. The sight may refresh your memory. I want you to see her—standing at her husband's side."

Beetham nodded. "I shall be most happy. I knew them both, long ago. Yes, I shall be a very pleased witness of the touching reunion you picture."

A policeman appeared at the door. "Major Durand is outside," he announced.

"Good," said Flannery. "Pat—this is Colonel Beetham. I want you to take him into the back room—the second one—and stay with him until I send for the both of you."

Beetham rose. "I say, am I under arrest?" he inquired.

"You're not under arrest," returned Flannery. "But you're going with Pat. Is that clear?"

"Absolutely. Pat—I am at your service." The two disappeared. Flannery rose and, going to the door leading into the anteroom, admitted Major Durand.

The Major entered and stood there, somewhat at a loss. Flannery proffered a chair. "Sit down, sir. You know everybody here. I've great news for you. We've located the woman we think is your wife, and she'll be along in a few minutes."

Durand stared at him. "You've found—Eve? Can that possibly be true?"

"We'll know in a minute," Flannery said. "I may tell you I'm certain of it—but we'll let you see for yourself. Before she comes—one or two things I want to ask you about. Among the members of that picnic party was Colonel John Beetham, the explorer?"

"Yes, of course."

"He left the next morning on a long journey through the Khyber Pass?"

"Yes. I didn't see him go, but they told me he had gone."

"Has any one ever suggested that he may have taken your wife with him when he left?"

The question struck Durand with the force of a bullet. He paled. "No one has ever made that suggestion," he replied, almost inaudibly.

"All the same, I'm here to tell you that is exactly what happened."

Durand got up and began to pace the floor. "Beetham," he muttered. "Beetham. No, no—he wouldn't have done it. A fine chap, Beetham—one of the best. A gentleman. He wouldn't have done that to me."

"He was just in here, and I accused him of it."

"But he denied it, of course?"

"Yes—he did. But my evidence——"

"Damn your evidence," cried Durand. "He's not that kind of man, I tell you. Not Beetham. And my wife—Eve—why, what you are saying is an insult to her. She loved me. I'm sure of it—she loved me. I won't believe—I can't——"

"Ask her when she comes," suggested Flannery. Durand sank back into the chair and buried his face in his hands.

For a long moment they waited in silence. Miss Morrow's cheeks were flushed with excitement; Duff was puffing quietly on his inevitable pipe; Charlie Chan sat immobile as an idol of stone. Kirk nervously took out a cigarette and then put it back in the case.

The man named Petersen appeared in the door. He was dusty and travel-stained.

"Hello, Jim," Flannery cried. "Have you got her?"

"I've got her this time," Petersen answered, and stood aside. The woman of so many names entered the room and halted, her eyes anxious and tired. Another long silence.

"Major Durand," said Flannery. "Unless I am much mistaken——"

Durand got slowly to his feet, and took a step forward. He studied the woman intently for a moment, and then he made a little gesture of despair.

"It's the old story," he said brokenly. "The old story over again. Captain Flannery, you *are* mistaken. This woman is not my wife."

19

A Vigil in the Dark

For a moment no one spoke. Captain Flannery was gradually deflating like a bright red balloon that had received a fatal puncture. Suddenly his eyes blazed with anger. He turned hotly on Charlie Chan.

"You!" he shouted. "You got me into this! You and your small-time hunch. The lady is Jennie Jerome. She is also Marie Lantelme. What does that mean? It means she is Eve Durand. A guess—a fat-headed guess—and I listened to you. I believed you. Good lord, what a fool I've been!"

Profound contrition shone in Charlie's eyes. "I am so sorry. I have made stupid error. Captain—is it possible you will ever forgive me?"

Flannery snorted. "Will I ever forgive myself? Listening to a Chinaman—me, Tom Flannery. With my experience—my record—bah! I've been crazy—plumb crazy—but that's all over now." He rose. "Major Durand, a thousand apologies. I wouldn't have disappointed you again for worlds."

Durand shrugged his shoulders wearily. "Why, that doesn't matter. You meant it kindly, I know. For a moment, in spite of all that has happened, I did allow myself to hope—I did think that it might really be Eve. Silly of me—I should have learned my lesson long ago. Well, there is nothing more to be said." He moved toward the door. "If that is all, Captain——"

"Yes, that's all. I'm sorry, Major."

Durand bowed. "I'm sorry, too. No doubt I shall see you again. Goodby."

Near the door, as he went out, he passed the girl who called herself Grace Lane. She had been standing there drooping with fatigue; now she took a step nearer the desk. Her face was pale, her eyes dull with the strain of a long, hard day. "What are you going to do with me?" she asked.

"Wait a minute," growled Flannery.

Miss Morrow rose, and placed a chair for the other woman. She was rewarded by a grateful look.

"I just remembered Beetham," said Flannery. Again he scowled at Chan. "I've tipped off my hand to him—for nothing. I can thank you for that, too."

"My guilty feeling grows by jumps and bounds," sighed Charlie.

"It ought to," the Captain replied. He went to the inner door and called loudly: "Pat!" Pat appeared at once, followed by the Colonel. For an instant Beetham stood staring curiously about the room.

"But where," he remarked, "is the touching reunion? I don't see Durand. No more do I see his wife."

Flannery's face grew even redder than usual. "There's been a mistake," he admitted.

"There have been a number of mistakes, I fancy," said Beetham carelessly. "A dangerous habit, that of making mistakes, Captain. You should seek to overcome it."

"When I want your advice, I'll ask for it," responded the harassed Flannery. "You can go along. But I still regard you as an important witness in this case, and I warn you not to strike out for any more deserts until I give you the word."

"I shall remember what you say," Beetham nodded, and went out.

"What are you going to do with me?" Grace Lane persisted.

"Well, I guess you've had a pretty rough deal," Flannery said. "I apologize to you. You see, I got foolish and listened to a Chinaman, and that's how I came to make a mistake about your identity. I brought you back on a charge of stealing a uniform, but probably Mr. Kirk won't want to go ahead with that."

"I should say not," cried Barry Kirk. He turned to the woman. "I hope you won't think it was my idea. You can have a bale of my uniforms, if you like."

"You've very kind," she answered.

"Not at all. What is more, your old position is yours if you want it. You know, I'm eager to beautify the Kirk Building, and I lost ground when you left."

She smiled, without replying. "I may go then?" she said, rising.

"Sure," agreed Flannery. "Run along."

Miss Morrow looked at her keenly. "Where are you going?"

"I don't know. I——"

"I do," said the deputy district attorney. "You're going home with me. I've got an apartment—there's loads of room. You shall stay with me for this one night, at least."

"You—you are really too good to me," replied Grace Lane, and her voice broke slightly.

"Nonsense. We've all been far too unkind to you. Come along."

The two women went out. Flannery sank down behind his desk. "Now I'm going at this thing in my own way for a change," he announced. "This has been an awful upset, but I had it coming to me. Listening to a Chinaman! If Grace Lane isn't Eve Durand, who is? What do you say, Inspector Duff?"

"I might also warn you," smiled Duff, "against the dangers of listening to an Englishman."

"Oh, but you're from Scotland Yard. I got respect for your opinion. Let's see—Eve Durand is about somewhere—I'm sure of that. Sir Frederic was the kind of man who knows what he's talking about. There's that Lila Barr. She fits the description pretty well. There's Gloria Garland. An assumed name—Australia—might be. There's Eileen Enderby. Rust stains on her dress that night. But I didn't see them. May have been there—probably not. Another guess on Sergeant Chan's part, perhaps."

"There is also," added Charlie, "Mrs. Tupper-Brock. I offer the hint with reluctance."

"And well you may," sneered Flannery. "No—if you fancy Mrs. Tupper-Brock, then right there she's out with me. Which of these women—I'll have to start all over again."

"I feel humble and contrite," said Chan. "In spite of which, suggestions keep crowding to my tongue. Have you heard old Chinese saying, Captain—'It is always darkest underneath the lamp'?"

"I'm fed up on Chinese sayings," replied the Captain.

"The one I have named means what? That just above our heads the light is blazing. Such is the fact, Captain Flannery. Take my advice, and worry no more about Eve Durand."

"Why not?" asked Flannery, in spite of himself.

"Because you are poised on extreme verge of the great triumph of your life. In a few hours at the most your head will be ringing with your own praises."

"How's that?"

"In a few hours you will arrest the murderer of Sir Frederic Bruce," Chan told him calmly.

"Say—how do you get that way?" queried Flannery.

"There is one condition. It may be hard one for you," Chan continued. "For your own sake, I beseech you to comply with same."

"One condition? What's that?"

"You must listen once more—and for the last time—to what you call a Chinaman."

Flannery stirred uneasily. A hot denial rose to his lips, but something in the little man's confident manner disturbed him.

"Listen to you again, eh? As though I'd do that."

Inspector Duff stood up, and relighted his pipe. "If it is true that you respect my opinion, Captain—then, quoting our friend, I would make humble suggestion. Do as he asks."

Flannery did not reply for a moment. "Well," he said finally, "what have you got up your sleeve now? Another hunch?"

Chan shook his head. "A certainty. I am stupid man from small island, and I am often wrong. This time I am quite correct. Follow me—and I prove it."

"I wish I knew what you're talking about," Flannery said.

"An arrest—in a few hours—if you will stoop so far as to do what I require," Chan told him. "In Scotland Yard, which Inspector Duff honors by his association, there is in every case of murder what they call essential clue. There was essential clue in this case."

"The slippers?" asked Flannery.

"No," Charlie replied. "The slippers were valuable, but not essential. The essential clue was placed on scene by hand now dead. Hand of a man clever far beyond his fellows—how sad that such a man has passed. When Sir Frederic saw death looking him boldly in the face, he reached to a bookcase and took down—what? The essential clue, which fell from his dying hand to lie at his side on the dusty floor. The year-book of the Cosmopolitan Club."

A moment of silence followed. There was a ring of conviction in the detective's voice.

"Well—what do you want?" inquired Flannery.

"I want that you must come to the Cosmopolitan Club in one-half hour. Inspector Duff will of course accompany. You must then display unaccustomed patience and wait like man of stone. Exactly how long I can not predict now. But in due time I will point out to you the killer of Sir Frederic—and I will produce proof of what I say."

Flannery rose. "Well, it's your last chance. You make a monkey of me again and I'll deport you as an undesirable alien. At the Cosmopolitan Club in half an hour. We'll be there."

"Undesirable alien will greet you at the door," smiled Charlie, "hoping to become desirable at any moment. Mr. Kirk—will you be so good as to join my company?" He and Barry Kirk went out.

"Well, Charlie, you're certainly in bad with the Captain," said Kirk, as they stood in the street waiting for a taxi.

Chan nodded. "Will be in even worse presently," he replied.

Kirk stared at him. "How's that?"

"I shall point him the way to success. He will claim all credit, but sight of me will make him uncomfortable. No man loves the person who has guided his faltering footsteps to high-up rung of the ladder."

They entered a taxi. "The Cosmopolitan Club," Chan ordered. He turned to Kirk. "And now I must bow low in dust with many humble apologies to you. I have grieviously betrayed a trust."

"How so?" asked Kirk, surprised.

Chan took a letter from his pocket. It was somewhat worn and the handwriting on the envelope was a trifle blurred. "The other morning you wrote letters in office, giving same to me to mail. I made gesture toward mail chute, but I extracted this missive."

"Great Scott!" cried Kirk. "Hasn't that been mailed?"

"It has not. What could be more disgusting? My gracious host, at whose hands I have received every kindness. I have besmirched his confidence."

"But you had a reason?" suggested Kirk.

"A very good reason, which time will uncurtain. Am I stepping over the bounds when I seek to dig up your forgiveness?"

"Not at all," Kirk smiled.

"You are most affable man it has yet been my fate to encounter." The taxi had reached Union Square. Chan called to the driver to halt. "I alight here to correct my crime," he explained. "The long-delayed letter now goes to its destination by special, fleet-footed messenger."

"I say—you don't mean——" Kirk cried in amazement.

"What I mean comes gradually into the light," Chan told him. He got out of the taxi. "Be so kind as to await my coming at the club door. The guardian angel beyond the threshold is jealous as to who has honor of entering Cosmpolitan Club. It has been just as well for my purpose, but please make sure that I am not left rejected outside the portal."

"I'll watch for you," Kirk promised.

He rode on to the club, his head whirling with new speculations and questions. No—no—this couldn't be. But Charlie had an air——

Shortly after he had reached the building Charlie appeared, and Kirk steered him past the gold-laced door man. Presently Flannery and Duff arrived. The Captain's manner suggested that he was acting against his better judgment.

"I suppose this is another wild-goose chase," he fretted.

"One during which the goose is apprehended, I think," Chan assured him. "But there will be need of Oriental calm. Have you good supply? We may loiter here until midnight hour."

"That's pleasant," Flannery replied. "Well, I'll wait a while. But this is your last chance—remember."

"Also your great chance," Chan shrugged. "You must likewise remember. We do wrong to hang here in spotlight of publicity. Mr. Kirk, I have made selection of nook where we may crouch unobserved, but always observing. I refer to little room behind office, opening at the side on check-room."

"All right—I know where you mean," Kirk told him. He spoke to the manager, and the four of them were ushered into a little back room, unused at the moment and in semi-darkness. Chairs were brought, and all save Charlie sat down. The little detective bustled about. He arranged that his three companions should have an unobstructed view of the check-room, where his friend of the morning, old Peter Lee, sat behind his barrier engrossed in a bright pink newspaper.

"Only one moment," said Chan. He went out through the door which led behind the counter of the check-room. For a brief time he talked in low tones with Lee. Then the three men sitting in the dusk saw him give a quick look toward the club lobby, and dodge abruptly into his hiding-place beside them.

Colonel John Beetham, debonair as usual, appeared at the counter and checked his hat and coat. Kirk, Flannery and Duff leaned forward eagerly and watched him as he accepted the brass check and turned away. But Chan made no move.

Time passed. Other members came into the club for dinner and checked their belongings, unconscious of the praying eyes in the little room. Flannery began to stir restlessly on his uncomfortable chair.

"What the devil is all this?" he demanded.

"Patience," Charlie admonished. "As the Chinese say, 'In time the grass becomes milk.' "

"Yeah—but I'd rather hunt up a cow," Flannery growled.

"Patient waiting," Chan went on, "is first requisite of good detective. Is that not correct, Inspector Duff?"

"Sometimes it seems the only requisite," Duff agreed. "I fancy I may smoke here?"

"Oh, of course," Kirk told him. He sighed with relief and took out his pipe.

The minutes dragged on. They heard the shuffle of feet on the tiled floor of the lobby, the voices of members calling greetings, making dinner dates. Flannery was like a fly on a hot griddle.

"If you're making a fool of me again——" he began.

His recent humiliation had been recalled to his mind by the sight of Major Eric Durand, checking his Burberry and his felt hat with Peter Lee. The Major's manner was one of deep depression.

"Poor devil," said Flannery softly. "We handed him a hard jolt to-day. It wasn't necessary, either——" His accusing eyes sought Chan. The detective was huddled up on his chair like some fat, oblivious Buddha.

A half-hour passed. Flannery was in constant touch with the figures on the face of his watch. "Missing my dinner," he complained. "And this chair—it's like a barrel top."

"There was no time to procure a velvet couch," Chan suggested gently. "Compose yourself, I beg. The happy man is the calm man. We have only begun to vigil."

At the end of another half-hour, Flannery was fuming. "Give us a tip," he demanded. "What are we waiting for? I'll know, or by heaven, I'll get out of here so quick——"

"Please," whispered Charlie. "We are waiting for the murderer of Sir Frederic Bruce. Is that not enough?"

"No, it isn't," the Captain snapped. "I'm sick of you and your confounded mystery. Put your cards on the table like a white man. This chair is killing me, I tell you——"

"Hush!" said Chan. He was leaning forward now, staring through the door into the check-room. The others followed his gaze.

Major Eric Durand stood before the counter. He threw down the brass check for his coat and hat. It rang metallically in the silence. Peter Lee brought them for him. He leaned across the barrier and helped Durand on with his coat. The Major was fumbling in his pockets. He produced a small bit of cardboard, which he gave to Peter Lee. The old man studied his treasures for a moment, and then handed over a black leather briefcase.

Chan had seized Flannery's arm, and was dragging the astonished Captain toward the club lobby. Kirk and Duff followed. They lined up before the huge front door. Durand appeared, walking briskly. He stopped as he saw the group barring his way.

"Ah, we meet again," he said. "Mr. Kirk, it was thoughtful of you to send me that guest card to your club. I deeply appreciate it. It arrived only a short time ago. I shall enjoy dropping in here frequently——"

Charlie Chan's fat face was shining with joy. He raised his arm with the gesture of a Booth or a Salvini.

"Captain Flannery," he cried. "Arrest this man."

"Why—I—er—I don't——" sputtered Flannery.

"Arrest this man Durand," Chan went on. "Arrest him at same moment while he holds beneath his arm a brief-case containing much useful information. The brief-case Sir Frederic Bruce checked in this club on the afternoon of the day he died."

20

The Truth Arrives

All color had drained from Durand's face. It was gray as fog as he stood there confronted by the triumphant little Chinese. Flannery reached out and seized the leather case. The Major made no move to resist.

"Sir Frederic's brief-case," Flannery cried. His air of uncertainty had vanished; he was alert and confident. "By heaven, if that's true, then our man hunt is over." He sought to open the case. "The thing's locked," he added. "I don't like to break it open. It will be a mighty important piece of evidence."

"Mr. Kirk still holds in possession Sir Frederic's keys," suggested Charlie. "I would have brought them with me but I did not know where they reposed."

"They are in my desk," Kirk told him.

A curious group was gathering about them. Chan turned to Flannery. "Our standing here has only one result. We offer ourselves as nucleus for a crowd. Humbly state we should go at once to bungalow. There the matter may be threshed out like winter wheat."

"Good idea," replied Flannery.

"I also ask that Mr. Kirk visit telephone booth and request Miss Morrow to speed to bungalow with all haste. It would be amazing unkindness to drop her out of events at this junction."

"Sure," agreed Flannery. "Do that, Mr. Kirk."

"Likewise," added Charlie, laying a hand on Kirk's arm, "advise her to bring with her the elevator operator, Grace Lane."

"What for?" demanded Flannery.

"Time will reveal," Chan shrugged. As Kirk sped away, Colonel John Beetham came up. For a moment the explorer stood, taking in the scene before him. His inscrutable expression did not change.

"Colonel Beetham," Charlie explained, "we have here the man who killed Sir Frederic Bruce."

"Really?" returned Beetham calmly.

"Undubitably. It is a matter that concerns you, I think. Will you be so good as to join our little party?"

"Of course," Beetham replied. He went for his hat and coat. Chan followed him, and retrieved from Peter Lee the pasteboard check on receipt of which the old man had relinquished Sir Frederic's property.

Kirk, Beetham and Chan returned to the group by the door. "All set," announced Flannery. "Come along, Major Durand."

Durand hesitated. "I am not familiar with your law. But shouldn't there be some sort of warrant——"

"You needn't worry about that. I'm taking you on suspicion. I can get a warrant when I want it. Don't be a fool—come on."

Outside a gentle rain had begun to fall, and the town was wrapped in mist. Duff, Flannery and Durand got into one taxi, and Chan followed with Kirk and the explorer in another. As Charlie was stepping into the car, a breathless figure shot out of the dark.

"Who was that with Flannery?" panted Bill Rankin.

"It has happened as I telephoned from the hotel," Charlie answered. "We have our man."

"Major Durand?"

"The same."

"Good enough. I'll have a flash on the street in twenty minutes. You certainly kept your promise."

"Old habit with me," Chan told him.

"And how about Beetham?"

Chan glanced into the dark cab. "Nothing to do with the matter. We were on wrong trail there."

"Too bad," Rankin said. "Well, I'm off. I'll be back later for details. Thanks a thousand times."

Chan inserted his broad bulk into the taxi, and they started for the Kirk Building.

"May I express humble hope," remarked the little detective to Kirk, "that I am forgiven for my crime. I refer to my delay in mailing to Major Durand your letter containing guest card for Cosmopolitan Club."

"Oh, surely," Kirk told him.

"It chanced I was not yet ready he should walk inside the club," Chan added.

"Well, I'm knocked cold," Kirk said. "You must have had your eye on him for some time."

"I will explain with all my eloquence later. Just now I content myself with admitting this—Major Durand was one person in all the world who did not want Eve Durand discovered."

"But in heaven's name—why not?" Kirk asked.

"Alas, I am no miracle man. It is a matter I hope will be apparent later. Perhaps Colonel Beetham can enlighten us."

The Colonel's voice was cool and even in the darkness. "I'm a bit weary of lying," he remarked. "I could enlighten you. But I won't. You see, I have made a promise. And like yourself, Sergeant, I prefer to keep my promises."

"We have many commendable points in common."

Beetham laughed. "By the way—that was extremely decent of you—telling the reporter I wasn't concerned in this affair."

"Only hope," responded Chan, "that events will justify my very magnanimous act."

They alighted before the Kirk Building and rode up to the bungalow. Paradise had admitted Flannery and Duff with their prisoner.

"Here you are," said Flannery briskly. "Now, Mr. Kirk—let's have that key."

Kirk stepped to his desk and produced Sir Frederic's keys. The Captain, with Duff close at his side, hastened to open the case. Charlie dropped down on the edge of a chair, his intent little eyes on Major Durand. The Major was seated in a corner of the room, his head bowed, his gaze fixed on the rug.

"By George," cried Duff. "It's Sir Frederic's case, right enough. And here—yes—here is what we have been looking for." He took out a typewritten sheaf of paper. "Here are his records in the matter of Eve Durand."

The Inspector began to read eagerly. Flannery turned to Durand.

"Well, Major—this settles your hash. Where did you get the check for this brief-case?"

Durand made no reply. "I will answer for him," Charlie said. "He extracted same from the purse of Sir Frederic the night he killed that splendid gentleman."

"Then you visited San Francisco once before, Major?" Flannery persisted. Still Durand did not so much as raise his eyes.

"Naturally he did," Chan grinned. "Captain Flannery, at any moment reporters will burst upon you desiring to learn how you captured this dangerous man. Would it not be better if I told you so you will be able to make intelligent reply?" Flannery glared at him. "The matter will demand your close attention. I search about, wondering where to begin."

Duff looked up. "I suggest you start with the moment when you first suspected Durand," he said, and returned to his perusal of the records.

Chan nodded. "It was here in this room, same night when Durand arrived. Have you ever heard, Captain,—do not fear, it is not old saying this time. Have you ever heard Chinese are psychic people? It is true. A look, a gesture, a tone of voice—something goes click inside. I hear Mr. Kirk say to the Major he will send guest card for club or two. And from the sudden warmth of the Major's reply, I obtain my psychic spasm of warning. At once I ask myself, has the Major special interest in San Francisco clubs? It would seem so. Is he, then, the man we seek? No, he can not be. Not if he came entire distance from New York with good Inspector Duff.

"But—I advise myself—pause here and ponder. What has Inspector Duff said on this point? He has said that when he got off Twentieth Century in Chicago, he discovered Major had been on same train. I put an inquiry to myself. Has this clever man, Duff, for once in his life been hoodwinked? Inspector does me high honor to invite to dinner. During the feast, I probe about. I politely inquire, did he with his own eyes see Major Durand on board Twentieth Century while train was yet speeding between New York and Chicago? No, he did not. He saw him first in Chicago station. Durand assures him he was on identical train Inspector has just left. He announces he, too, is on way to San Francisco. They take, that same night, train bound for coast.

"The matter, then, is possible. Men have been known to double back on own tracks. Study of time elapsed since murder reveals Major may have been doing this very thing. I begin to think deep about Durand. I recall that at luncheon when Sir Frederic tells us of Eve Durand case, he makes curious omission which I noted at the time. He says that when he is planning to go to Peshawar to look into Eve Durand matter, he calls on Sir George Mannering, the woman's uncle. Yet husband is living in England, and he would know much more about the affair than uncle would. Why, then, did not Sir Frederic interrogate the husband? I find there food for thought.

"All time I am wondering about Cosmopolitan Club year-book, which hand of Sir Frederic drops on floor at dying moment. Mr. Kirk kindly takes me to lunch at club, and checks a brief-case. I note check for coat is of metal, but brief-case check is of cardboard, with name of article deposited written on surface by trembling hand of Peter Lee. A bright light flashes in my mind. I will suppose that Sir Frederic checked a brief-case containing records we so hotly seek, and check for same was in pocket when he died. This the killer extracts; he is clever man and knows at last he has located papers he wants so fiercely. But alas for him, club-house door is guarded, only members and guests may enter. In despair, he flees, but that check he carries with him spells his doom unless he can return and obtain object it represents. He longs to do so, but danger is great.

"Then fine evidence arrives. The velvet slippers come back to us on tide of events, wrapped in newspaper. On margin of paper, partially torn, are figures—a money addition—$79 plus $23 equals $103. This refers to dollars only. Cents have been torn off. I visit railroad office. I decide what must have been on that paper before its tearing. Simply this, $79.84 plus $23.63 equals $103.47. What is that? The cost of railroad fare to Chicago with lower berth. Then the person who discarded those slippers was on Oakland ferry Wednesday morning after murder, bound to take train from Oakland terminal to Chicago. Who of all my suspects might have done that? No one but Major Durand.

"I think deep, I cogitate, I weave in and out through my not very brilliant mind. I study time-tables. Presume Major Durand was on that train out of Oakland Wednesday noon. He arrives in Chicago Saturday morning at nine. He is still distressed about check for brief-case, but his best plan seems to be to proceed eastward, and he hastens to LaSalle Street station to obtain train for New York. He arrives in time to see Inspector Duff, whom he met once in Paris, disembarking from Twentieth Century. He is smart man, a big idea assails him. First he will give impression he is alighting from same train, and then he will return to California in company of Scotland Yard Inspector. Who would suspect him then? So the innocent Inspector Duff himself escorts the killer back to the scene of the crime.

"All this seems to possess good logic. But it hangs on one thing—has brief-case been checked by Sir Frederic? This morning I visit with Peter Lee, keeper of Cosmopolitan Club check-room. I can scarce restrain my joy to learn Sir Frederic did indeed leave such an object the day he died. His dying gesture, then, was to call our attention to the fact. He sought to present us with essential clue—what a man he was! I fondle the case lovingly, observing dust. Inside is no doubt very important information. But I do not desire to open it yet. I desire to set a trap. I have unlimited yearning to show Captain Flannery the man we have sought, standing by the check-room counter with his brief-case under his arm. Such evidence will be unanswerable.

"So I leave club, very happy. The affair has now pretty well unveiled itself. I have not yet discovered motives, but I am certain it was Major Durand who objected so murderously to the finding of his lost wife. He has not come to this country in answer to a cable from Sir Frederic. This is a lie. Sir Frederic did not want him. But he has learned, probably from the woman's uncle, that Sir Frederic is on point of revealing wife. For a reason still clouded in dark, he determines this must not happen. He arrives in San Francisco same time as Sir Frederic. He locates great detective, learns of the office, watches his chance. To prevent detective from revealing wife, two things are necessary. He must destroy the records, and he must kill Sir Frederic. He decides to begin with records, and so on night of dinner party he forces his way into office, unseen by anybody. He is searching when Sir Frederic creeps in on the velvet slippers and surprises him. His opportunity has come, Sir Frederic is unarmed, he shoots him dead. But his task is only half completed, he hunts frantically for records. He does not find them. But he finds the check for the briefcase. He abstracts same, casts longing thought toward club, but does not dare. On the next train out he flees, the check burning in his pocket. If only he could return. In Chicago his great chance arrives.

"Building on all this, I set to-night my trap. And into it walks the man who killed Sir Frederic Bruce."

Inspector Duff looked up. He appeared to have been reading and listening at the same time. "Intelligence, hard work and luck," he remarked. "These three things contribute to the solution of a criminal case. And I may add that in my opinion, in this instance, the greatest of the trinity was intelligence."

Chan bowed. "A remark I shall treasure with jealous pride all my life."

"Yes, it's pretty good," admitted Flannery grudgingly. "Very good. But it ain't complete. What about the velvet slippers? What about Hilary Galt? How is Galt's murder mixed up in all this?"

Chan grinned. "I am not so hoggish. I leave a few points for Captain Flannery's keen mind."

Flannery turned to Duff. "Maybe it's in those records?"

"I've got only about half-way through," Duff answered. "There has been one mention of Hilary Galt. It says here that among the people who called at Galt's office on the day the solicitor was murdered was Eric Durand. Captain Eric Durand—that was his rank at the time. To discover the meaning of that, I shall have to read further."

"Have you learned," Chan inquired, "this thing? Did Sir Frederic know which of the ladies we have suspicioned was Eve Durand?"

"Evidently he didn't. All he knew was that she was in the Kirk Building. He seemed to favor Miss Lila Barr."

"Ah, yes. Was he aware how Eve Durand escaped from India?"

"He was, beyond question."

"He knew she went by the caravan?"

"By the caravan, through Khyber Pass. In the company of Colonel John Beetham," Duff nodded.

They all looked toward the Colonel, sitting silent and aloof in the background. "Is that true, Colonel Beetham?" Flannery asked.

The explorer bowed. "I will not deny it longer. It is true."

"Perhaps you know——"

"Whatever I know, I am not at liberty to tell."

"If I make you——" Flannery exploded.

"You can, of course, try. You will not succeed."

The door opened, and Miss Morrow came quickly through the hall. With her came the elevator girl. Jennie Jerome? Marie Lantelme? Grace Lane? Whatever her name, she entered, and stood staring at Eric Durand.

"Eric!" she cried. "What have you done? Oh—how could you——"

Durand raised his head and looked at her with bloodshot eyes. "Go away from me," he said dully. "Go away. You've brought me nothing but trouble—always. Go away. I hate you."

The woman backed off, frightened by the venom in his tone. Chan approached her.

"Pardon," he said gently. "Perhaps the news has already reached you? It was this man Durand who killed Sir Frederic. Your husband—is that not true, Madam?"

She dropped into a chair and covered her face. "Yes," she sobbed. "My husband."

"You are indeed Eve Durand?"

"Y—yes."

Charlie looked grimly at Flannery. "Now the truth arrives," he said. "That you once listened to a Chinaman is, after all, no lasting disgrace."

21

What Happened to Eve Durand

Flannery turned fiercely on Eve Durand. "Then you've known all along?" he cried. "You knew the Major had been here before—you saw him that night he did for Sir Frederic——"

"No, no," she protested. "I didn't see him—I never dreamed of such a thing. And if he knew I was in the building that night, he took good care to keep out of my way. For if I had seen him—if I had known—it would have been the final straw. I'd have told. I'd have told the whole story at once."

Flannery grew calmer. "Well, let's go back. You're Eve Durand—you admit it at last. Fifteen years ago you ran away from your husband in Peshawar. You went with the caravan of Colonel Beetham here——"

The woman looked up, startled, and for the first time saw the explorer. "That's all true," she said softly, "I went with Colonel Beetham."

"Ran away with another man—deserted your husband? Why? In love with the Colonel——"

"No!" Her eyes flashed. "You mustn't think that. Colonel Beetham did a very kind act—an indiscreet act—and he shall not suffer for it. Long ago, I made up my mind to that."

"Please, Eve," said the Colonel. "I shan't suffer. Don't tell your story on my account."

"That's like you," she answered. "But I insist. I said if I was ever found, I'd tell everything. And after what Eric has done now—it doesn't matter any longer. Oh, I shall be so relieved to tell the whole terrible thing at last."

She turned to Flannery. "I shall have to go back. I was brought up in Devonshire by my uncle and aunt—my parents had died. I wasn't very happy. My uncle had old-fashioned ideas. He meant well, he was kind, but somehow we just didn't get along. Then I met Eric—he was a romantic figure—I adored him. I was only seventeen. On my eighteenth birthday we were married. He was assigned to a regiment stationed in Peshawar, and I went with him.

"Even before we reached India, I began to regret what I had done. I was sorry I hadn't listened to my uncle—he never approved of the match. Under his dashing manner I found that Eric was mean and cheap. He was a gambler, he drank too much. His real character appalled me—he was coarse and brutal, and a cheat.

"Soon after our arrival at Peshawar, letters began to come from London—letters in dirty envelopes, the address written in an uncultivated hand. They seemed to enrage my husband; he wasn't fit to associate with after their appearance. I was puzzled and alarmed. On a certain day—the day of the picnic, it was—one of those letters was put in my hand during Eric's absence. By that time I was desperate. I knew only too well the outburst that would come when he saw it. I hesitated for a while. Finally I tore it open and read it.

"What I read wrecked my life for ever. It was from a porter in an office building in London. It said he must have more money—at once. It didn't hint—it spoke openly. Everything was all too plain. Eric—my husband—was being blackmailed by the porter. He was paying money to keep the man quiet. If he didn't, the porter threatened to reveal the fact that he had seen Eric leaving a London office one night a year previously. Leaving an office on the floor of which lay Hilary Galt, the solicitor, with a bullet in his head."

Eve Durand paused, and continued with an effort. "My husband, then, was being blackmailed for the murder of Hilary Galt. He came home presently, in rather a genial mood—for him. I said: 'I am leaving you at once.' He wanted to know why, and I gave him the opened letter.

His face went gray, and he collapsed. Presently he was on his knees, groveling at my feet, pleading with me. Without my asking for it, he gave me the whole terrible story. Hilary Galt and my uncle, Sir George Mannering, were old friends. On the morning of that awful day, the solicitor had sent for Eric and told him that if he persisted in his intention of marrying me, he—Mr. Galt, I mean—would go to my uncle with the story of certain unsavory happenings in Eric's past. Eric had listened, and left the office. That night he had gone back and killed Hilary Galt, and the porter had seen him coming away.

"He did it for love of me, he said. Because he must have me—because he was determined nothing should stand in his way. I must forgive him——"

"Pardon," put in Chan. "Did he, in that unhappy moment, mention a pair of velvet slippers?"

"He did. After—after he had killed Mr. Galt, he saw the slippers lying on a chair. He knew that Scotland Yard always looks for an essential clue, and he resolved to furnish one. One that meant nothing, one that would point away from him. So he tore off Hilary Galt's shoes and substituted the slippers. He was rather proud of it, I think. Oh, he was always clever, in that mean way of his. He boasted of what he had done, of how he had thrown Scotland Yard off the scent. Then he was pleading again—he had done it for me—I must not tell. I couldn't tell. I was his wife—no one could make me tell. Heaven knows, I had no desire to tell, all I wanted was to get away from him. I said again that I was going. 'I'll kill you first,' he answered, and he meant it.

"So I went on that picnic, with my life all in pieces, frantic, insane with grief and fear. Colonel Beetham was there—I had met him once before—a fine man, a gentleman, all that Eric was not. He was leaving in the morning—it came to me in a flash. He must take me with him. I suggested the game of hide-and-seek—I had already asked the Colonel to meet me in a certain spot. He came—I made him promise never to tell—and I explained to him the horrible position I was in. If I tried to leave openly I was afraid—I was sure—Eric would carry out his threat. Colonel Beetham was wonderful. He arranged everything. I hid in the hills all night. He came with Li Gung in the wagon at dawn—he had added it to his caravan, intending to abandon it when we got through the pass. I rode out hidden in that, and beyond the Khyber there began for me the most wonderful adventure a woman ever had. Eight months through that wild country on a camel—the stars at night, the dust storms, the desert stretching empty but mysterious as far as the eye could see. Outside Teheran I left the caravan and got to Baku alone. From there I went to Italy. Eight months had passed, as I say, and the hue and cry had died down.

"But now I realized what I had done. Colonel Beetham was a hero, he was honored everywhere. What if it became known how I had left India? No journey could ever have been more innocent, but this is a cynical world. Doing a kind act, a gallant act, Colonel Beetham had put himself in the position, in the world's eyes, of running away with another man's wife. If it became known, the Colonel's splendid career would be wrecked. It must never become known. I made up my mind I would see to that."

"And you have," remarked Beetham softly. "Gentlemen, you have just heard what I did referred to as a gallant act. But it was as nothing compared with Eve Durand's gallantry ever since."

"First of all," the woman went on, "I wrote a letter to Eric. I told him he must never try to find me—for his own sake. I said that if I was found, if the story came out of how I had left India, I would not hesitate a moment. I would clear Colonel Beetham's name at once by a clear account of why I had gone. I would say I left because I discovered my husband was a murderer. Eric didn't answer, but he must have received the letter. He never tried to find me after that. He did not want any one else to find me—as he has recently proved to you."

She paused. "That is about all. I—I have had rather a hard struggle of it. I sold my jewelry and lived on the proceeds for a time. Then I went to Nice, and under the name of Marie Lantelme, I got a place in the opera company. There, for the first time, I realized that another man was on my trail—a man who would never give up. Sir Frederic Bruce of Scotland Yard, in charge of the Hilary Galt case. He knew that Eric had visited Galt's office the day of the murder, and when he read of my disappearance in India, he must have sensed a connection. One night when I came from the theater in Nice, an Inspector from Scotland Yard stopped me on the Promenade des Anglais. 'You are Eve Durand,' he said. I denied it, got away from him, managed to reach Marseilles. From there I went to New York. I changed my appearance as much as I could—the color of my hair—and under the name of Jennie Jerome, secured a position as a model. Again Scotland Yard was on my track. I had to disappear in the night. Eventually I arrived in San Francisco, desperate, penniless. On a ferry I met Helen Tupper-Brock, who had lived near us in Devonshire. She has been so kind—she got me my position here. I was happy again, until Sir Frederic Bruce came, still following that old trail."

Durand got slowly to his feet. "I hope you're satisfied," he said thickly. "Oh, Eric——"

"You've done for me. You ought to be satisfied now." His eyes flamed red. "You've saved the spotless reputation of your damned Sir Galahad——"

"You're going to confess?" cried Flannery.

Durand shrugged his shoulders hopelessly. "Why not? What else is left?" He turned his glazing eyes on Charlie Chan. "Everything this devil said was true. I admire him for it. I thought I was clever. But he's beat me——" His voice rose hysterically. "I killed Sir Frederic. Why shouldn't I? It was the only way. He stood there grinning at me. My God—what a man! He wouldn't give up. He wouldn't call quits. Sixteen years, and he was still at my heels. Sixteen years, and he wouldn't forget. Yes, I killed him——"

"And the velvet slippers?" Chan inquired softly.

"On his feet. The same old velvet slippers I'd left in that office, long ago. I saw them just after I fired, and then my nerve went. It was like a judgment—my trade-mark—on the feet of Sir Frederic—pointing to me. I snatched them off—took them with me. I—I didn't know what to do with them. My nerve was gone—but I'd killed him first. Yes—I killed him. And

I'm ready to pay. But not in the way you think."

Suddenly he wheeled about and crashed through the French window into the garden of the bungalow.

"The fire-escape," Flannery shouted. "Head him off——"

The Captain, Duff and Chan were close behind. Charlie ran to the fire-escape at the left. But it was not that for which Eric Durand was headed to-night. He leaped to the rail that enclosed the garden; for an instant his big figure poised, a dark silhouette against the misty sky. Then silently it disappeared.

They ran to the rail and looked down. Far below, in the dim light of a street lamp, they saw a black, huddled heap. A crowd was gathering around it.

22

Hawaii Bound

Their pursuit so tragically ended, the three men came slowly back into the living-room of the bungalow.

"Well," said Flannery, "that's the end of him."

"Escaped?" Miss Morrow cried.

"From this world," nodded the Captain. Eve Durand gave a little cry. Miss Morrow put an arm about her. "There's work for me below," added Flannery, and went quickly out.

"We'd better go home, my dear," said Miss Morrow gently. She and Eve Durand went to the hall. Kirk followed and opened the door for them. There was much he wanted to say, but under the circumstances silence seemed the only possible course.

"I can get my car," he suggested.

"No, thanks," answered Miss Morrow. "We'll find a taxi."

"Good night," he said gravely. "I shall hope to see you soon."

When he returned to the living-room, Colonel Beetham was speaking. "Nothing in his life became him like the leaving it. What a washout that life was! Poor Major."

Duff was calmly filling his pipe, unperturbed. "By the way," he drawled, "I had a cable about him this morning. He was dishonorably discharged from the British Army ten years ago. So his right to the title may be questioned. But no doubt you knew that, Colonel Beetham?"

"I did," Beetham replied.

"You knew so much," Duff continued. "So much you weren't telling. What were you doing on the floor below that Tuesday night?"

"Precisely what I told Flannery I was doing. I ran down to inform Li Gung that he needn't wait."

"I didn't know but what you'd gone down for a chat with Eve Durand?"

The Colonel shook his head. "No—I'd had my chat with Eve. You see, I'd located her several days before the dinner party. After losing track of her for ten years, I came to San Francisco on a rumor she was here. My errand on the floor below was with Li Gung, as I said it was."

"And the next day you shipped him off to Honolulu?"

"I did, yes. At Eve's request. I'd arranged that two days before. She heard

Sir Frederic was interested in him, and she was afraid something might happen to wreck my next expedition. The thing was unnecessary, Li Gung would never have told, but to set her mind at rest, I did as she asked."

Duff looked at him with open disapproval. "You knew that Durand had committed one murder. Yet you said nothing to the police. Was that playing the game, Colonel Beetham?"

Beetham shrugged. "Yes, I think it was. I'm sure of it. I did not dream that Durand had been in San Francisco the night of Sir Frederic's murder. Even if I had known he was here—well—you see——"

"I'm afraid I don't," snapped Duff.

"There is really no reason why I need explain to you," Beetham went on. "However, I will. Something happened on that long trek across Afghanistan and the Kevir Desert. Eve was so brave, so uncomplaining. I—I fell in love. For the first and last time. What she has done since—for me—damn it, man, I worship her. But I have never told her so—I do not know whether she cares for me or not. While Durand lived, he was my rival, in a way. If I had given him up—what would my motive have been? I couldn't have been quite sure myself. I did suggest that Eve tell her story, but I didn't press the point. I couldn't, you see. I had to leave the decision to her. When she escaped that night from Flannery's men, I helped her. If that was what she wanted, I was forced to agree. Yes, Inspector—I was playing the game, according to my lights."

Duff shrugged. "A nice sense of honor," he remarked. "However, I will go so far as to wish you luck."

"Thanks," returned Beetham. He took up his coat. "I may say that, no doubt from selfish motives, I was keen to have you get him. And Sergeant Chan here saw to it that I was not disappointed. Sergeant, my hearty congratulations. But I know your people—and I am not surprised."

Chan bowed. "For ever with me your words will remain, lasting and beautiful as flowers of jade."

"I will go along," said Beetham, and departed.

Duff took up Sir Frederic's brief-case. "Perhaps you would like to look at these records, Sergeant," he remarked.

Chan came to with a start. "Pardon my stupidity."

"I said—maybe you want to glance at Sir Frederic's records?"

Charlie shook his head. "Curiosity is all quenched, like fire in pouring rain. We have looked at last behind that curtain Sir Frederic pictured, and I am content. At the moment I was indulging in bitter thought. There is no boat to Honolulu until next Wednesday. Five terrible days."

Duff laughed. "Well, I've been through the records hastily," he went on. "Sir Frederic had talked with certain friends of that porter in London. But the man himself had died before the Yard heard about him, and the evidence of his associates was hazy—hardly the sort to stand up in the courts. It needed the corroboration of Eve Durand, and that was what Sir Frederic was determined to get at any cost."

"How did Sir Frederic know that Eve Durand was in San Francisco?" Barry Kirk inquired.

"He got that information from a letter written by Mrs. Tupper-Brock to an aunt in Shanghai. There is a copy of the letter here. In it Mrs. Tupper-Brock mentioned that Eve Durand was in this city, employed in the Kirk Building. All of which explains his eagerness to make his headquarters with you, Mr. Kirk. But he hadn't located her—he died without that satisfaction, poor chap. His choice was Miss Lila Barr. He didn't dare say anything to Mrs. Tupper-Brock, for fear Eve Durand would slip through his fingers again. On the night of the dinner he was setting a trap—the desk unlocked, the safe open. He rather hoped some one would creep in for a look around. That and the chance of identifying Jennie Jerome, or Marie Lantelme—on these things he placed his reliance."

"He would have won, if he had lived," Chan remarked.

"No doubt in it. In Peshawar he established to his own satisfaction the manner in which Eve had left India. When he found her he would have told her what he knew, and she would have related her story, just as she did here to-night. His long search for the murderer of Hilary Galt would have ended then and there. Poor Sir Frederic." Duff picked up his coat, and Kirk helped him. "I'll take the brief-case," the Inspector continued. "It will be useful at the Yard." He held out his hand. "Sergeant Chan, meeting you would alone have repaid me for my long journey. Come to London some day. I'll show you how we work over there."

Chan smiled. "You are too kind. But the postman on his holiday has walked until feet are aching. Free to remark that if he ever takes another vacation, same will be forced on him at point of plenty big gun."

"I don't wonder," replied Duff. "Mr. Kirk—a pleasure to know you, too. Good-by and good luck to you both."

Kirk let him out. When he returned, Charlie was standing at the window, staring down on the roofs of the city. He swung about. "Now I go and pack."

"But you've five days for that," Kirk protested.

Charlie shook his head. "The guest who lingers too long deteriorates like unused fish. You have been so good—more would make me uncomfortable. I remove my presence at once."

"Oh, no," Kirk cried. "Good old Paradise will serve dinner in a few minutes."

"Please," Chan said, "permit me the luxury of at last beginning to mean what I say."

He went into his bedroom and in a surprisingly brief time returned. "Luggage was pretty much ready," he explained. He glanced toward the window. "Bright moon shines to-night in Honolulu. I am thinking of those home nights—long ones with long talks, long sipping of tea, long sleep and long peaceful dreams." He went to the hall, where he had left his coat and hat. "I am wondering how to make words of the deep thanks I feel," he said, returning. "Faced with kindness such as yours——"

The door-bell rang, a sharp, insistent peal. Charlie stepped into the bedroom. Kirk opened the door, and Bill Rankin, the reporter, rushed in.

"Where's Charlie Chan?" he demanded breathlessly.

"He's gone into his room," Kirk answered. "He'll be out in a minute."

"I want to thank him," Rankin continued loudly. "He sure treated me like a prince. I beat the town. And I've news for him—a woman has just been murdered over in Oakland under the most peculiar circumstances. There are all sorts of bully clues—and since he can't leave until next week——"

Kirk laughed. "You tell him," he suggested.

They waited a moment, then Kirk went into the bedroom. He cried out in surprise. The room was empty. A door leading to the passageway stood open. He stepped through it, and discovered that the door at the top of the stairs leading to the offices was also ajar.

"Rankin," he called. "Come here, please."

Rankin came. "Why—where is he——"

Kirk preceded the reporter down-stairs. The offices were in darkness.

In the middle room, Kirk switched on the light. After a hurried glance around, he pointed to the window that opened on to the fire-escape. It had been pushed up as far as it would go.

"The postman," Kirk remarked, "absolutely refuses to take another walk."

"Done an Eve Durand on us!" Rankin cried. "Well, I'll be dog-goned."

Kirk laughed. "It's all right," he said. "I'll know where to find him—next Wednesday noon."

Intent on verifying this prediction, Barry Kirk appeared in Miss Morrow's dusty office the following Wednesday morning at eleven. He had stopped at a florist's and bought an extravagant cluster of orchids. These he handed to the deputy district attorney.

"What's the idea?" she asked.

"Come on," he said. "The morning's as bright as a new gold piece, and down at the docks there's a ship about to set out for the loveliest fleet of islands in any ocean. The flowers are my bon voyage offering to you."

"But I'm not sailing," she protested.

"We'll pretend you are. You're going as far as the pier, anyhow. Get your hat."

"Of course." She got it, and they went down the dark stairs.

"Have you heard anything from Charlie Chan?" she asked.

"Not a word," Kirk told her. "Charlie isn't taking any chances. But we'll find him aboard the boat. I'd gamble all I've got on that."

They entered his car, and Kirk stepped on the gas. "What a morning," he remarked. "Cooped up in that dark office of yours, you've no idea the things that are going on outside. Lady—spring is here!"

"So it seems. By the way—you know that Colonel Beetham sailed last night for China?"

"Yes. What about Eve Durand?"

"She's starting to-morrow for England. Her uncle has cabled her to come and stop with him. The Colonel is to be in the Gobi Desert for a year, and then he's going to England too. It will be spring in Devonshire when he arrives. A very lovely spring, they seem to think."

Kirk nodded. "But a year away. Too bad—so long to wait. Enjoy the spring you've got. That would be my advice."

He steered his car on to the pier. Another sailing day—excitement and farewells. Tourists and traveling salesmen, bored stewards waiting patiently in line.

Miss Morrow and Kirk ran up the gang-plank on to the deck of the big white ship. "Just stand here by the rail, please," said Kirk. "With the orchids——"

"What in the world for?"

"I want to see how you'll look in the role. Back in a minute."

When he returned, Charlie Chan was walking lightly at his side. The detective's face was beaming with a satisfaction he could not conceal.

"Overwhelmed by your attention," he said to the girl.

"Where have you been?" she cried. "We've missed you terribly."

He grinned. "Hiding from temptation," he explained.

"But Captain Flannery has taken all the credit for your wonderful success. It isn't fair."

Chan shrugged. "From the first, I knew my work on this case was like bowing in the dark. Why should I care? May I add that you present charming picture of loveliness this morning?"

"What does she look like to you, Charlie?" Kirk inquired. "Standing there by the rail with those flowers?"

"A bride," answered Chan promptly, as one who had been coached. "A bride who sails for honeymoon in pleasant company of newly-captured husband."

"Precisely," Kirk agreed. "She's rehearsing the part, you know."

"The first I've heard of it," objected Miss Morrow.

"Wise man has said, 'The beautiful bird gets caged,' " Chan told her. "You could not hope to escape."

The girl handed him a little package. "This is for—the other Barry—with my love."

"My warmest thanks. He will be proud boy. But you will not give him all your love. You will not overlook original of same name. Chinese are psychic people, and I have sensed it. Am I right? My precious reputation hangs shaking on your answer."

Miss Morrow smiled. "I'm very much afraid—you're always right."

"Now this is truly my happiest day," Chan told her.

"Mine too," cried Kirk. He took an envelope from his pocket. "That being arranged, I also have something for little Barry. Give it to him with my warm regards."

Chan accepted the envelope, heavy with gold pieces. "My heart flows over," he said. "Small son will express thanks in person when you arrive in Honolulu thrilled with the high delight of honeymoon."

"Then he'll have to learn to talk mighty soon," Kirk answered. "But with a father like you——"

The final call of "visitors ashore" was sounding. They shook hands with Charlie and ran. At the top of the gang-plank they were engulfed in a very frenzy of farewell. Mad embraces, hasty kisses, final promises and admonitions. Kirk leaned quickly over and kissed Miss Morrow.

"Oh—how could you!" she cried.

"Pardon me. I was still pretending you were going too."

"But I'm not. Neither are you."

"No one will notice in this mêlée. Come on."

They descended to the pier, and ran along it until they stood opposite Charlie Chan. The detective had procured a roll of bright pink paper, and holding fast to one end, he tossed it to the girl.

Kirk smiled happily. "If any one had told me two weeks ago I was going to kiss a lawyer—and like it——" He was interrupted by the hoarse cry of the ship's siren.

Slowly the vessel drew away from the pier. The pink streamer broke, its ends trailing in the water. Charlie leaned far over the rail.

"Aloha," he called. "Until we meet again." His fat face shone with joy. The big ship paused, trembled, and set out for Hawaii.

The Black Camel

1

Morning at the Crossroads

The Pacific is the loneliest of oceans, and travelers across that rolling desert begin to feel that their ship is lost in an eternity of sky and water. But if they are journeying from the atolls of the South Seas to the California coast, they come quite suddenly upon a half-way house. So those aboard the *Oceanic* had come upon it shortly after dawn this silent July morning. Brown misty peaks rose from the ocean floor, incredible, unreal. But they grew more probable with each moment of approach, until finally the watchers at the rail were thrilled to distinguish the bright green island of Oahu, streaked with darker folds where lurk the valley rains.

The *Oceanic* swung about to the channel entrance. There stood Diamond Head, like a great lion—if you want the time-worn simile—crouched to spring. A crouching lion, yes; the figure is plausible up to that point; but as for springing—well, there has never been the slightest chance of that. Diamond Head is a *kamaaina* of the islands, and has long ago sensed the futility of acting on impulse—of acting, as a matter of fact, at all.

A woman traveler stood by the starboard rail on the boat deck, gazing at the curved beach of Waikiki and, up ahead, the white walls of Honolulu half hidden in the foliage behind the Aloha Tower. A handsome woman in her early thirties, she had been a source of unending interest to her fellow passengers throughout that hot monotonous voyage from Tahiti. No matter in what remote corner of the world you have been hiding, you would have recognized her at once, for she was Shelah Fane of the pictures, and hers was a fame equal to that of any president or king.

"A great piece of property" film salesmen had called her for eight years or more, but now they had begun to shake their heads. "Not so good. She's slipping." Golden lads and lasses must, like chimney-sweepers, come to dust, which is something the film stars think about when they can not sleep at nights. Shelah had not been sleeping well of late, and her eyes, as they rested on peaceful Tantalus with its halo of fleecy cloud, were sad and a little wistful.

She heard a familiar step on the deck behind her and turned. A broad, powerful, keen-looking man was smiling down at her.

"Oh—Alan," she said. "How are you this morning?"

"A bit anxious," he replied. He joined her at the rail. His was a face that had never known Klieg lights and make-up; it was deeply lined and bronzed by tropic suns. "Journey's end, Shelah—for you at least," he added, laying his hand over hers. "Are you sorry?"

She hesitated a moment. "Rather sorry—yes. I shouldn't have cared if we had just sailed on and on."

"Nor I." He stared at Honolulu with the bright look of interest that comes naturally to British eyes at sight of a new port, a new anchorage. The ship had come to a stop at the channel entrance, and a launch bearing the customs men and the doctor was speeding toward it.

"You haven't forgotten?" The Britisher turned back to Shelah Fane. "This isn't journey's end for me. You know I'm leaving you behind here to-night. Sailing out at midnight on this same ship—and I must have your answer before I go."

She nodded. "You shall have it before you go. I promise."

For a brief moment he studied her face. A marked change had crept over her at the sight of land. She had come back from the little world of the ship to the great world whose adoration she expected and thrived on. No longer calm, languorous, at peace, her eyes were alight with a restless flame, her small foot tapped nervously on the deck. A sudden fear overwhelmed him, a fear that the woman he had known and worshiped these past few weeks was slipping from him for ever.

"Why must you wait?" he cried. "Give me your answer now."

"No, no," she protested. "Not now. Later to-day." She glanced over her shoulder. "Were there reporters on the launch, I wonder?"

A tall, handsome, hatless youth with a mop of blond hair waving in the breeze rushed up to her. His energy was a challenge to the climate.

"Hello, Miss Fane. Remember me? Met you when you went through here on your way south. Jim Bradshaw, of the Tourist Bureau, press-agent of beauty, contact man for Paradise. Our best aloha—and here's a lei to prove it." He hung a fragrant garland about her neck, while the man she had called Alan moved quietly away.

"You're awfully kind," Shelah Fane told him. "Of course I remember you. You seemed so glad to see me. You do now."

He grinned. "I am—and besides, that's my job. I'm the door-mat on the threshold of Hawaii, with 'welcome' written all over me. Island hospitality—I have to make sure that my advertisements all come true. But in your case, I—well, believe me, it isn't any strain." He saw that she looked expectantly beyond him. "Say, I'm sorry, but all the newspaper men seem to be lingering in the arms of Morpheus. However, you can't blame them. Lulled as they are by the whisper of the soft invigorating trade-winds in the coco-palms—I'll finish that later. Just tell me what's doing, and I'll see that it gets into the papers. Did you complete the big South Sea picture down in Tahiti?"

"Not quite," she answered. "We left a few sequences to be shot in Honolulu. We can live here so much more comfortably, and the backgrounds, you know, are every bit as beautiful——"

"Do I know it?" the boy cried. "Ask me. Exotic flowers, blossoming trees, verdant green hills, blue sunny skies with billowy white clouds—the whole a dream of the unchanging tropics with the feel of spring. How's that? I wrote it yesterday."

"Sounds pretty good to me," Shelah laughed.

"You'll be some time in Honolulu, Miss Fane?"

She nodded. "I've sent for my servants," she told him. "They've taken a house for me on the beach. I stifle in hotels—and then, too, people are always staring at me. I hope it's a large house——"

"It is," Bradshaw cut in. "I was out there yesterday. They're all set and waiting for you. I saw your butler—and your secretary, Julie O'Neill. Speaking of that, some day I'd like to ask you where you find secretaries like her."

Shelah smiled. "Oh, Julie's much more than a secretary. Sort of a daughter—almost. Though of course that's absurd to say, for we're nearly the same age."

"Is that so?" said the boy—to himself.

"Julie's mother was a dear friend of mine, and when she died four years ago, I took the child in. One must do a good deed occasionally," she added, modestly looking down at the deck.

"Sure," agreed Bradshaw. "If we don't we'll never be tapped for the Boy Scouts. Julie was telling me how kind you've been——"

"I've been amply repaid," the star assured him. "Julie is a darling."

"Isn't she?" replied the boy heartily. "If I had my rhyming dictionary along, I'd give you a good description of the girl right here and now."

Shelah Fane looked at him suddenly. "But Julie got in only two days ago——"

"Yes—and so did I. Made a flying trip to Los Angeles, and came back on the same boat with her. The best crossing I ever had. You know—moonlight, silver seas, a pretty girl——"

"I must look into this," said Shelah Fane.

Two of the passengers joined them: a weary, disillusioned-looking man whose costume suggested Hollywood Boulevard, and a dashing girl of twenty. Shelah yielded to the inevitable. "Mr. Bradshaw, of the Tourist Bureau," she explained. "This is Miss Diana Dixon, who is in my new picture, and Huntley Van Horn, my leading man."

Miss Dixon lost no time. She sparkled instantly. "Honolulu is an adorable place. I'm always so thrilled to come here—such beauty——"

"Never mind," cut in the star. "Mr. Bradshaw knows all that. None better."

"Always happy to have my ideas confirmed," bowed the boy. "Especially from such a charming source." He turned to the man. "Mr. Van Horn—I've seen you in the films."

Van Horn smiled cynically. "So, I believe, have the natives of Borneo. Has Shelah told you anything about our latest epic?"

"Very little," Bradshaw replied. "Got a good part?"

"It always has been a good part," Van Horn said. "I trust my rendering of the rôle will not impair its future usefulness. If it does, many of our leading studios will have to close. I'm a beach-comber, you see, and I've sunk lower and lower——"

"You would," nodded the star.

"I'm wallowing in the depths, and quite comfortable, thank you," went on Van Horn, "when—if you can believe it—I'm saved. Absolutely rehabilitated, you know, through the love of this primitive, brown-skinned child."

"Which child?" asked Bradshaw blankly. "Oh, you mean Miss Fane. Well, it sounds like a great plot—but don't tell me, don't tell me." He turned to the star. "I'm glad you're going to take a few shots in Honolulu. That sort of thing makes us very happy at the Tourist Bureau. I must run along—one or two other celebrities on the ship. Fellow named Alan Jaynes—very wealthy——"

"I was talking with him when you came up," Shelah said.

"Thanks. I'll go after him. Diamond mines—South Africa—he sounds good. We're strong for the arts in Hawaii, you know, but as for money—well, when that appears in the harbor, then we really get out the flags. See you all later."

He disappeared down the deck, and the three picture people moved over to the rail.

"Here comes Val," said Huntley Van Horn, "looking like the man who wrote the tropics."

He referred to Val Martino, director of Shelah's latest picture, who was rapidly approaching along the deck. He was a short, stocky, gray-haired man, dressed in a suit of immaculate white silk. Above a flaming red tie loomed his broad heavy face. It was almost the same shade as the tie, suggesting that Mr. Martino had never concerned himself with such trivial matters as blood pressure and diet.

"Hello," he said. "Well, here we are. Thank heaven, Tahiti has been attended to. From this on, I'll take my tropics after they've been ruined by American plumbing. Was that a newspaper man you were talking with, Shelah?"

"Not precisely. A boy from the Tourist Bureau."

"I hope you laid it on thick about the new picture," he continued. "You know, we'll need all the publicity we can get."

"Oh, let's forget the picture," returned the star a bit wearily.

The *Oceanic* was drawing slowly up to the peer, on which a surprisingly meager crowd was waiting. Shelah Fane gazed at the group with interest and some disappointment. She had rather hoped for a vast throng of schoolgirls in white, bearing triumphal leis. But this had happened when she went through before; she could not expect history to repeat itself—and it was, too, only seven in the morning.

"There's Julie," she cried suddenly. "There—near the end of the pier. See—she's waving." She returned Julie's signal.

"Who's that beside her?" Van Horn inquired. "Good lord—it looks like Tarneverro."

"It is Tarneverro," Miss Dixon said.

"What's he doing here?" the leading man wondered.

"Perhaps he's here because I sent for him," said Shelah Fane.

A quiet black-garbed maid stood at her side. "What is it, Anna?"

"The customs men, madam. They're going through everything. You'd better come. They want talking to, it seems."

"I'll talk to them," said the star firmly, and followed the maid into her suite.

"Well, what do you know about that?" Van Horn remarked. "She's sent for that phony fortune-teller to come all the way from Hollywood——"

"What do you mean, phony?" cut in Miss Dixon. "Tarneverro is simply wonderful. He's told me the most amazing things about my past—and about my future, too. I never take a step without consulting him—and neither does Shelah."

Martino shook his great head impatiently. "It's a rotten scandal," he cried, "the way most of you Hollywood women have gone mad over voodoo men. Telling them all your secrets—some day one of them will publish his memoirs, and then where will you be? A few of us try to lift the industry to a dignified plane—but, oh, lord—what's the use?"

"No use," my dear fellow," said Van Horn. He looked across the intervening stretch of water at the tall lean figure of the fortune-teller. "Poor Shelah—there's something rather touching in such faith as this. I presume she wants to ask Tarneverro whether or not she shall marry Alan Jaynes."

"Of course she does," Miss Dixon nodded. "She wants to know if she'll be happy with him. She cabled Tarneverro the day after Jaynes proposed. Why not? Marriage is a serious step."

Martino shrugged. "If she'd only ask me, I'd read her future quick enough. She's nearly through in pictures, and she ought to know it. Her contract expires in six months, and I happen to know—in strict confidence, you understand—it won't be renewed. I can see her taking a long journey by water then—going abroad to make a picture—the beginning of the end. She'd better grab this diamond king quick before he changes his mind. But no—she's fooling around with a back-parlor crystal-gazer. However, that's like you people. You won't grow up." He walked away.

The formalities of the port were quickly ended, and the *Oceanic* docked. Shelah Fane was the first down the plank, to be received by the eager arms of her secretary. Julie was young, impetuous, unspoiled; her joy was genuine.

"The house is all ready, Shelah. It's a knockout. Jessop is there, and we've found a Chinese cook who's a magician. The car's waiting."

"Really, dear?"

The star looked up into the dark deep-set eyes of the man at Julie's side. "Tarneverro—what a relief to see you here. But I knew I could depend on you."

"Always," said the fortune-teller gravely.

What the crowd lacked in numbers, it made up in noise and confusion. Anna, the maid, was overwhelmed with boxes and bags, and seeing this, Tarneverro went to help her. There was no condescension in his manner; he treated her with the same courtly grace he would have shown the star.

Alan Jaynes and Bradshaw appeared on the scene. The latter went over to greet Julie with as much warmth as though he had just arrived after a long hard voyage from some distant port. Jaynes stepped quickly to Shelah's side.

"I shall be damnably anxious," he said. "This afternoon—may I come then?"

"Of course," she nodded. "Oh—this is Julie—you've heard about her. Julie, please tell him the number of our house. We're just beyond the Grand Hotel, on Kalakaua Avenue."

Julie told him, and he turned back to Shelah. "I shan't keep you——" he began.

"Just a moment," said the star. "I want to introduce an old friend from Hollywood. Tarneverro—will you come here, please?"

The fortune-teller handed a couple of bags to Shelah's chauffeur, and came at once. Jaynes looked at him with some surprise.

"Tarneverro—I want you to meet Alan Jaynes," the star said.

They shook hands. "Glad to know you," remarked the Britisher. As he gazed into the other man's face, he experienced a sudden sensation of deep dislike. Here was power; not the power of muscle, which he had himself and could understand; but something more subtle, something uncanny, inexplicable and oddly disturbing. "Sorry, but I must dash along now," he added.

He disappeared into the crowd, and Julie led them to the waiting car. Tarneverro, it appeared, was stopping at the Grand, and Shelah offered to drop him there.

Presently they were bowling along through Honolulu's streets, under a flaming blue sky. The town was waking to another leisurely day. Men of many races languidly bestirred themselves; at the corner of King Street a boy offered the morning paper, and a fat brown-skinned policeman lazily turned a stop-go sign to let them pass. Shelah Fane, like all passengers newly descended from a ship at this port, felt rather dazzled by the brightness and the color.

"Oh, I shall enjoy this," she cried. "I've never stayed here longer than one day before. What a relief to be out of the South Seas."

"But they're romantic, aren't they?" Julie asked.

"The illusions of youth," the star shrugged. "I shan't destroy them. Only don't mention Tahiti to me again as long as I live."

"Not quite like the books," Tarneverro nodded. He sat, mysterious even in that bright world, at Shelah's side. "I discovered that for myself, long ago. You're staying here for some time, I take it?"

"A month, I hope," the star answered. "A couple of weeks still to go on the picture, and then, I trust, a fortnight's rest. I want it badly, Tarneverro. I'm tired—tired."

"You need not tell me that," he said. "I have eyes."

He had, indeed, eyes; eyes that were cold and piercing and rather disquieting. The car sped on past the old royal palace and the judiciary building, and turned off into Kalakaua Avenue.

"It was so good of you to come over here," Shelah told him.

"Not at all," he replied evenly. "I started the day after I got your cable. I was due for a vacation—my work, you know, is not precisely restful. Then, too, you said you needed me. That was enough. That will always be—enough."

Julie began to chatter about the islands: she mentioned the warm caressing waters of Waikiki, the thrill of haunting native music in the purple night, the foreign pageant of the streets.

"All of which," smiled Shelah, "sounds very much to me like James Bradshaw in one of his more lyric moods."

Julie laughed. "Yes, I guess I was quoting Jimmy. Did you meet him, Shelah?"

"I met him," the star nodded.

"He's really very nice," Julie assured her. "Especially when he isn't talking shop."

The pink walls of the Grand Hotel appeared at that moment through a network of majestic palms, and Shelah directed the chauffeur to turn in at the gates.

"I must talk with you very soon," she said to Tarneverro. "I have so much to ask you. You see——"

He raised a slim white hand. "Don't tell me, please," he smiled. "Let me tell you."

She glanced at him, a little startled. "Oh—of course. I need your advice, Tarneverro. You must help me again, as you have helped me so often in the past."

He nodded gravely. "I shall try. With what success—who knows? Come to my apartment at eleven o'clock—it is number nineteen, on the first floor. There is a short flight of stairs leading to my corridor just at the left of the hotel desk as you enter. I shall expect you."

"Yes, yes." Her voice was trembling. "I must settle this thing to-day. I'll be there."

Tarneverro bowed from the hotel steps, and as the car drove off Shelah was conscious of Julie's frank young eyes fixed on her with a disapproval that was almost contempt.

The head bell-man touched Tarneverro's sleeve. "Excuse. There is a man who waits to see you. This one."

The fortune-teller turned to perceive a bulky Chinese who approached him with an amazingly light step. The ivory face was wearing a somewhat stupid expression; the black eyes were veiled and sleepy-looking. Not a very intelligent Chinese, Tarneverro thought, wondering vaguely what this visit presaged.

The Oriental placed one hand on his broad chest, and achieved a grand bow despite his waist-line.

"A thousand pardons," he remarked. "Have I the undisputable honor to address Tarneverro the Great?"

"I am Tarneverro," answered the other bruskly. "What can I do for you?"

"Permit that I introduce myself," continued the Chinese, "unworthy of your notice though I am. The name is Harry Wing, and I am humble business man of this island. Do I extend my remarks too far when I say I wish to see you alone?"

Tarneverro shrugged. "What for?"

"The matter is of pressing urgency. If I might suggest—your room——"

The fortune-teller gazed for a moment into that placid mask of a face, behind which life seemed nonexistent. He capitulated. "Come along," he said. Obtaining his key at the desk, he led the way.

Once inside the door of number nineteen, he turned to confront his odd visitor, who had followed on noiseless feet. The curtains of the sitting-room were drawn back as far as they would go, and the place was flooded with light. With his customary forethought, Tarneverro had selected an apartment on the mountain side of the hotel, and a restless cool wind from the Koolau Range swept in at the window and stirred the papers lying on a desk.

The countenance of the Chinese was still without expression, even under the piercing scrutiny the fortune-teller now gave it.

"Well?" said Tarneverro.

"You are the famous Tarneverro," began Harry Wing in a respectful singsong. "Among Hollywood people you have vast reputation as one who lifts dark veils and peers into uncertain future. Black as lacquer that future may be to ordinary eyes, but to yours, they say, it is clear as glass. Permit me to add this reputation pursues you even to Hawaii, dogging like shadow at your heels. The rumor of your mystic skill floods the street."

"Yes?" put in Tarneverro shortly. "What of it?"

"I am, as I say, business man of small importance to everybody but myself. Now I begin to speak to you frankly that opportunity arouses itself in my path. I can amalgamate my business up together with that of my cousin from a north province. Future looks bright, but qualms assail me. Will the merge have success? Is my cousin honorable as cousin of mine should naturally be? Can I trust him? In fewer words, I desire dark veil lifted, and you are man to do the business. I stand ready to make generous payment for this lifting."

Tarneverro's eyes narrowed, and for a long time he stood staring at this unexpected customer for his wares. The Chinese waited motionless as a Buddha, with his hands in his trousers pockets, his coat thrown back. The fortune-teller's glance rested for a moment at a point just below the fountain-pen pocket on his visitor's waistcoat.

"Impossible," he said, with sudden decision. "I am here on a vacation, not to practise my profession."

"But rumor remarks," objected the other, "that you have already done work with crystal——"

"For one or two of the hotel managers—as a friendly gesture," Tarneverro cut in. "I received no fee of any sort. I will not do this kind of thing for the general public."

Harry Wing shrugged. "The matter then becomes sad disappointment for me," he answered.

A grim smile spread over the seer's dark face. "Sit down," he said. "I have spent some time in China, and I understand how great is the interest of your people in fortune-tellers. So for a moment, while you were telling me why you came, I thought you were speaking the truth."

The visitor frowned. "I am now rapidly failing to understand you."

Still smiling, Tarneverro dropped into a chair facing the Oriental. "Yes, Mr.—ah—er—Wing, I believe you said—momentarily I was deceived. And then a certain little gift of mine came to my aid. You have been kind enough to speak of my success. I have succeeded—why? Because I happen to be psychic, Mr. Wing——"

"Chinese people are psychic, too."

"Just a moment. As I stood there listening to you, a psychic wave swept over me. I had a feeling—a feeling of—what? Of stern men who sit in police stations and are sworn to enforce the laws. Of detectives pursuing evil-doers, landing them at last—and then, a court of justice, so-called, a learned judge. That, my friend, is the feeling I had. Rather amazing, don't you think?"

His visitor's expression had lost suddenly all its stupidity. The little black eyes snapped with admiration.

"Amazing smart act on your part, yes. But as for me, I do not think it was psychic feeling. A moment ago I beheld your eyes resting with fierce understanding on locality of my own waistcoat from which detective badge was recently removed. The pin has left indelible marks. You are number one detective yourself, and I congratulate you."

Tarneverro threw back his head and laughed. "*Touché!*" he cried. "So you are a detective, Mr.—er——"

"The name is Chan," said the bulky Chinese, grinning broadly. "Inspector Chan, of the Honolulu police—former times Sergeant, but there has been upheaval in local police department, and I am rewarded far beyond my humble merits. Trap which has just failed so flatly, I add in justice to me personally, was not my idea. I informed Chief it would not work unless you happened to be extreme dull-wit. Since you turn out clever beyond expectation, it did not. No bitter feelings. I pause only to call attention to local ordinance which says men like you must not practise dark arts in this town without obtaining permission. A word being spoken to the wise, I rise to accomplish my exit."

Tarneverro also stood up. "I am not going to practise among your towns-people," he announced. He had dropped the tense air of mystery which he evoked for the benefit of film stars, and seemed quite human and not unlikable. "It has been a pleasure to meet you, Inspector. As for my own detective prowess, I may say in confidence that it is rather useful in my work."

"Must be so," returned Chan. "But such skill as yours should be at service of public. Frequently in Los Angeles murder mystery leaps into print and never gets solved. I study them all with fiery interest. The Taylor case—what an amazing happening was there—*haie,* it is still mystery. And case of Denny Mayo, famous actor of handsome countenance, dead in his home at night. How many years—three and more—and Denny Mayo is still unavenged by Los Angeles police."

"And never will be," added the fortune-teller. "No, Inspector, that is not in my line. I find it safer to dwell on the future and soft-pedal Hollywood's past."

"In such course, wisdom may abide," agreed Chan. "None the less, how happily I would welcome your aid if some such worrisome puzzle stared into my face. I will say good-by, Mr. Tarneverro. Memory of your cleverness will linger in my poor mind for long time to come."

He slipped quietly out, and Tarneverro glanced at his watch. With a leisurely air, he placed a small table in the middle of the room, and taking from a bureau drawer a gleaming crystal, stood it thereon. Then he stepped to the window and drew the curtains part way across, shutting out a goodly portion of the bright light outside. Glancing about the darkened room, he shrugged his shoulders. Not such an impressive stage-setting as his studio in Los Angeles, but it would have to serve. Sitting down by the window, he took out of his pocket a bulky letter and, slitting the flap of the envelope, began to read. The curtains, caught in the fierce grip of the trade-wind, swirled about his head.

At eleven o'clock Shelah Fane knocked on the door, and he ushered her into his sitting-room. She was gowned in white and appeared younger than she had at the dock, but her eyes were clouded with worry. Tarneverro's manner was professional now; he was cold, remote, unsympathetic. He seated her at the table behind the crystal; then, drawing the curtains all the way, plunged the room into almost complete darkness.

"Tarneverro—you must tell me what to do," she began. He sat down opposite her.

"Wait," he commanded. He looked fixedly into the crystal. "I see you standing at the rail on the boat deck of a steamer, under a brilliant moon. You are wearing a dinner gown—it is gold and matches your hair. There is a scarf of the same color about your shoulders. A man is standing at your side; he points, and offers you a pair of glasses. You raise them to your eyes—you catch the last faint glimmer of the lights along the front at Papeete, the port from which you sailed a few brief hours ago."

"Yes, yes," murmured Shelah Fane. "Oh, Tarneverro—how do you know——"

"The man turns. I can see him only dimly, but I recognize him. To-day, on the pier—Alan Jaynes—was that his name? He has asked you a question—marriage, perhaps—but you shake your head. Reluctantly. You want to say yes—yet you don't. You put him off. Why? I feel you love this man."

"I do," the star cried. "Oh, Tarneverro—I really do. I knew him first at Papeete—only a week—but in a place like that——The first night out—it was just as you say—he proposed to me. I haven't given him my answer yet. I want to say yes—to have a little happiness now—I've earned it, I think. But I—I'm afraid——"

He lifted his piercing eyes from the crystal. "You're afraid. Something in your past—you fear it will return to haunt you——"

'No, no," the woman cried.

"Something that happened long ago."

"No, no—it isn't true."

"You can not deceive me. How long ago? I can not quite determine, and it is necessary that I know."

The trade-wind mumbled at the curtains. Shelah Fane's eyes wandered helplessly about the darkened room, then came back to Tarneverro's.

"How long ago?" the man demanded again.

She sighed. "Three years ago last month," she said in a voice so low he had to strain to hear.

He was silent for a moment, his mind racing like an engine. June—three years ago. He gazed fixedly into the crystal; his lips moved. "Denny Mayo," he said softly. "Something about Denny Mayo. Ah, yes—I see it now."

The wind tore the curtains apart, and a wide strip of dazzling light fell across Shelah Fane's face. Her eyes were staring, frightened.

"I shouldn't have come," she moaned.

"What about Denny Mayo?" Tarneverro went on relentlessly. "Shall I tell you—or will you tell me?"

She pointed to the window. "A balcony. There's a balcony out there."

As one who humors a child, he rose and looked outside. He came back to the table. "Yes, there's a balcony—but no one is on it."

He sat down again, and his bold commanding eyes sought hers. She was trapped, and helpless.

"Now!" said Tarneverro the Great.

2

The House on the Beach

After a brief twilight, the dark sweeps over Waikiki Beach like Old Man Mystery himself. In the hours before the moon, like a climbing torch, ascends the purple sky, the sense of hearing comes into its own. Blackness covers the coco-palms, yet they may be heard rustling at the trade-wind's touch; the white line of the breakers is blotted out, yet they continue to crash on that unseen shore with what seems an added vigor. This is night in the real sense of the word, intriguing, awe-inspiring, but all too short, for the moon is waiting an early cue.

A solitary floor lamp was burning in the huge living-room of the house Shelah Fane had rented at Waikiki. The paneled walls, the furniture and the floor, all fashioned of rare native woods, gleamed faintly in the half-light; the green of exotic plants was everywhere. The French windows that faced the street were closed, but those on the ocean side, leading on to a great screened lanai, stood wide, and through them at regular intervals came the roar of the surf, which was running high.

Shelah Fane came into the room. She walked with a quick nervous step, and in her eyes was a look of apprehension—almost of terror. It was a look that had been there ever since her return from that interview with Tarneverro in his apartment at the Grand Hotel. What had she done? She asked this of herself over and over. What had she done? What was the secret of this dark man's power that he had so easily dragged from the inner recesses of her mind a story she had thought safely buried for ever? Once away from the strange influence of his presence she had been appalled at her own indiscretion. But it was too late then for anything save regret.

With her unerring instinct for the spotlight, she sat down under the single lamp. Many cameras had clicked in Hollywood since that distant time when, like a rocket, she had flashed into the picture sky, and nowadays the spotlight was none too kind to her. Kind to her hair, yes, which seemed to spring into flame, but not so considerate of the lines of worry about her eyes, about her small tense mouth. Did she know? Longer than most rockets she had hung blazing in the sky; now she must endure the swift lonely drop in the dark.

Her butler, Jessop, came in, a spare elderly Englishman who had also found in Hollywood the promised land. He carried a florist's box. Shelah looked up.

"Oh, Jessop," she said. "Did Miss Julie tell you? The dinner hour is eight-thirty."

"I understand, madam," he answered gravely.

"A few of the young people are going for a dip before we dine. Mr. Bradshaw for one. You might show him to the blue bedroom to dress. The bath-houses are dark and need cleaning. Miss Julie and Miss Diana will dress in their rooms."

Jessop nodded, as Julie came in. The girl wore an afternoon gown, and her face was innocent of make-up. She was enthusiastic, happy, young—a touch of envy darkened the star's fine eyes.

"Don't you worry, Shelah," Julie said. "Jessop and I have planned everything. It will be like all your parties—a knockout. What's that, Jessop? Flowers?"

"For Miss Fane," explained the butler, and handing the box to the girl, left the room.

Shelah Fane was looking about her, a frown on her face. "I've been wondering, Julie. How in the world can I arrange a good entrance on the party, in a place like this? If only there were a balcony, or at least a broad flight of stairs."

Julie laughed. "You might come suddenly through the lanai, strumming a ukulele and singing a Hawaiian song."

The star took her seriously. "No good, my dear. I'd be entering on the same level with the guests, and that is never effective. To make the proper impression, one must appear suddenly from above—always remember that, darling. Now, in Hollywood——"

The girl shrugged. "Oh, just come in naturally for once, Shelah. There's a lot in novelty, you know." She had torn the cord from the box of flowers, and now she lifted the lid. "Lovely," she cried. "Orchids, Shelah."

The star turned, without interest. Orchids were nothing new in her life. "Nice of Alan," she said languidly.

But Julie shook her head. "No," she announced, "they're not from Mr. Jaynes, evidently." She read the card aloud. " 'With love from one you have forgotten.' Who could that be, Shelah?"

"Who couldn't it be?" smiled the star a bit wistfully. She rose with sudden interest. "I wonder—let me see the card." She glanced at it. " 'With love from one——' " Her eyes lighted with quick understanding. "Why, it's Bob's writing. Dear old Bob! Just fancy—with love—after all these years."

"Bob?" inquired the girl.

Shelah nodded. "Bob Fyfe—my first and only husband, dear. You never knew him—it was long ago. I was just a kid, in the chorus of a musical show in New York, and Bob was an actor, a legitimate actor—such a good one, too. I adored him then, but along came Hollywood, and our divorce. And now—with love—I wonder? Can it be true?"

"What's he doing in Honolulu?" Julie asked.

"Playing in stock," Shelah replied. "Leading man at some theater here. Rita Ballou told me all about him, this morning when I called her up." She took the orchids. "I shall wear these to-night," she announced. "I never dreamed he would even speak to me. I—I'm touched. I'd like to see Bob again." A thoughtful look crossed her face. "I'd like to see him at once. He was always so kind, so clever. What time is it—oh, yes——" She glanced at a watch on her wrist. "Seven-twenty. What was the name of that theater? Rita told me. The Royal, I think she said——"

The door-bell rang briskly, there ensued a snappy bit of dialogue in the hall and Jimmy Bradshaw burst through the curtains. He was, it seemed, in a light-hearted mood.

"Here we all are," he cried. "Everybody who really matters. Well, Miss Fane, how does it feel to be foot-loose and care-free on a palm-fringed shore—way down in the warm southern seas?"

"It's really very restful," Shelah smiled. She nodded at Julie. "I'll be back in a moment. I want a pin for these flowers."

She disappeared into the hall, and Bradshaw turned quickly to the girl.

"You're looking great," he cried. "It's the climate. Not that you didn't look fairly good at the start——"

"Tell me," she cut in. "What do you think of Shelah?"

"Shelah?" He paused. "Oh, she's all right. Nice and friendly but—a bit artificial—a good actress, on and off. In the past two years I've met enough screen stars to start a Hollywood of my own, and what I always say is—doffing my hat to southern California—you can have 'em."

"You don't really know Shelah," protested the girl.

"No, I guess not. She's been kind to you, and that makes her aces up with me. But my own preference in women—and I've looked very carefully over the field——"

"Oh, you have, have you?"

"My ideal—since you've asked me, and I'm glad you have—is a rather different sort. Lovely, of course, young, innocent, ingenuous—and pretty crazy about yours truly. That—and you may quote me freely—is the girl for me."

Diana came suddenly through the curtains. She, too, still wore an afternoon gown.

"Hello, big boy," she said. "You ready for that swim with me?"

"Sure," replied Bardshaw. "With you—and anybody else who wants to come along." He looked at Julie. "Let's go. Before the moon rises is my idea. It's the best time. Any one else going—or is it just—the three of us?"

Julie shook her head. "No one else, I guess. The others are afraid of spoiling their make-up."

"Which is one advantage of youth over doddering age," the boy returned. "Well, come along——"

Shelah appeared, wearing the orchids on her shoulder.

"Just about to dip into the world-famed waters of Waikiki," Jimmy informed her. "Won't you join us?"

"Some other evening," she told him. "You know, I'm hostess to-night."

"You are missing," said Bradshaw impressively, "one of the thrills of a lifetime. The silken surf beating on coral sand, the dark, star-strewn sky above, perhaps the pastel loveliness of a lunar rainbow—boats run from Los Angeles and San Francisco once a week, and the fare is within the reach of all——"

The door-bell rang again. Accompanied by Shelah, the young people went out into the hall.

"Get your suit," Julie said to the boy. "I'll show you where to change. Let's make it a race. The first one into the water gets a prize."

"I'll win it," answered Bradshaw. "I'll name it too." They clattered up the polished stairs.

Again the bell sounded. Shelah was just beside the door, but she did not open it; she considered such an act beneath the dignity of a star. Instead she returned to the living-room and waited for Jessop to do his duty. After a brief delay, he did it, and two new guests appeared in the living-room. Shelah advanced to meet them—a dark, rather faded woman of thirty, followed by a big blond man who had an air of nonchalant authority.

"Rita Ballou," the star cried. "Why—it's ages! And Wilkie—I'm so glad."

"Hello, darling," said the woman she called Rita.

The man came forward. "Look here, Shelah. What time did you say dinner was to be?"

"Eight-thirty—but it doesn't matter——"

Ballou turned to his wife. "Good lord—can't you ever get anything straight?"

"What's the difference?" the woman replied. "We can have a chat with Shelah before the others come." She turned to the star. "So sorry we missed you when you went through before. We were on the mainland."

"Haven't missed you this time, thank heaven," added Wilkie Ballou. "By gad, you're as blooming as ever."

"How *do* you do it?" inquired Rita sweetly. Her cold eyes flashed green with envy as she looked at Shelah.

"She's found the fountain of youth," suggested Wilkie admiringly.

"I've always heard that was in Hawaii," smiled the star. She looked hard at Rita. "But it isn't," the look added.

Rita understood. "Not at all," she said grimly. "It's in the beauty shops of Hollywood, and you know it. Over here, women fade quickly——"

"Nonsense," protested Shelah.

"Yes, they do. Oh—I've learned my lesson—too late. I should have stayed in Hollywood and gone on with my career."

"But, my dear,—surely you're happy with Wilkie?"

"Of course. The way I would be with the toothache."

Wilkie shrugged. "Overlook it, Shelah," he said. "We've been rowing all the way out here. Rita's nerves, you know."

"Is that so?" remarked his wife. "I guess any one would have nerves with a husband like you. Honestly, Shelah, he's got a better imagination than what's his name—Shakespeare. If he'd only drop sugar planting and go in for writing scenarios—but never mind us. Tell me all about Hollywood. I'd love to be back."

"I'm making a long stop here—we'll have lots of time to chat later," Shelah explained. "Some of the crowd are going for a swim before dinner. Care to go along?"

Rita put one hand to her perfect coiffure, and shrugged "Not for me," she cried. "I'm so sick of swimming I gag at the sight of my tub. You've no idea, my dear—three years married and living in Honolulu—these people over here are like fish. They suffocate when you bring 'em ashore."

They heard the noise of a new arrival in the hall, and Alan Jaynes came into the room, handsome and upstanding in his dinner clothes. Shelah's heart sank suddenly at sight of him. While she was introducing him to the Ballous, Julie and Jimmy Bradshaw rushed in, wearing gay beach robes over their bathing-suits. They paused, with obvious reluctance, for further introductions.

"Where's Miss Dixon?" Bradshaw inquired. "She hasn't gone out, has she?"

"Nonsense," cried Julie. "Diana will take ages. She always does."

"Then the race is between us two," said the boy, and dashed through the open window on to the lanai, with Julie at his heels.

"What a good-looking boy," Rita remarked. "Who is he?"

Shelah explained Mr. Bradshaw's place in the world's work. Rita stood up.

"Let's all go down to the beach," she said.

"The beach—in high-heeled slippers?" protested Wilkie.

"I can take them off, can't I?" Rita demanded. She was moving toward the window.

"Go along," the star said. "We'll follow later."

Rita went out.

Without enthusiasm, Wilkie lifted his great bulk from the chair. "That means I go, too," he explained, and did so.

Shelah turned to Alan Jaynes with a nervous little laugh. "Poor Wilkie—he's so jealous. And with reason, I'm afraid—at least, he had reason in the old days."

Jaynes came quickly to her side. "So sorry I couldn't see you this afternoon. Your headache—it's better, I trust?"

She nodded. "Much better."

"I've brought you a bit of an offering. It's hardly worthy of you, of course." He handed her a corsage bouquet wrapped in tissue-paper.

She unwrapped it. "Lovely," she said.

" But too late," remarked Jaynes. "I see you're wearing some one's orchids."

Shelah laid his gift on a table. "Yes, Alan."

"I hope that doesn't mean——" he began, frowning. "Shelah—it can't mean that. I—I couldn't go on without you."

She faced him. "You'll have to, Alan. I'm so sorry. But I—I can't marry you."

His expression clouded. "It's true, then," he said.

"What's true?"

"The thing Van Horn told me this afternoon. I refused to believe it of you—it's too childish—too ignorant. You send for that damned fortune-telling charlatan, and he decided it for you. He advised you not to take me." She turned away, without speaking. The man's face flushed with anger. "If you had any sane reason," he continued, controlling himself with an effort, "I'd take my medicine quietly. But this—this is too much. To let a fakir—a crystal-gazer—a cheap fraud, come between us—by the lord, I won't stand for it. I thought on the boat you loved me——"

"Maybe I did," she answered sadly.

"Then nothing in this world shall stop me——"

"Wait, Alan, wait, please," she cried. "It's for you—I'm doing this for you. You must believe that. There could be no happiness for us——"

"So that's what he told you, eh?"

"That's what he told me, but he was only repeating what was in my heart. The past, Alan—the past won't die——"

"I've told you I don't give a hang about what's past."

"Oh, but you don't know, Alan—and I can't tell you. I'm trying to do the decent thing—you're so fine and straight—I couldn't bear it if I ended by dragging you through the dust. Please, Alan, please——"

"I don't want to understand," Jaynes cried. "I only want you—to love and take care of—see here, my time is brief, so pitifully brief. I must leave at midnight—you know that. Forget this fool of a fortune-teller. I can't understand your faith in him. I can't approve it, but I'm willing to overlook it. You aren't to blame, I fancy. Your temperament, your way of life. Forget him, my dear, and give me your word before I go——"

She shook her head. "I can't," she said brokenly. "I can't."

For a long moment Jaynes looked at her. Then, with great dignity, he turned on his heel.

"Where are you going?" Shelah cried.

"I don't know," he answered. "I must think this thing out."

"But you're dining here——"

"I don't know," the man repeated. "I couldn't talk to your friends just now. I want to be alone for a few minutes. I may return later." He seemed dazed, uncertain of himself.

Shelah was at his side, her hand on his sleeve. "Alan, I'm so sorry—so unhappy."

He turned, and took her in his arms. "By heaven—you loved me on the ship. I won't give you up. I can't." His glance fell on the orchids, fastened to the shoulder-strap of her gown by a small diamond pin. "No one shall take you from me," he cried and, releasing her, went quickly out.

Shelah Fane walked slowly to a chair, and drooped into it. Pain and a desperate unhappiness were in her face, and she was not acting now. For a few moments she sat there, then gradually came back to her surroundings. She glanced at her watch—a quarter of eight. Quickly she rose and went to the French windows at the rear.

The moon was still in hiding, and the broad lawn that lay between the house and the pounding surf was shrouded in darkness. She heard, far away, the exultant cry of Julie battling with a breaker, and then the answering call of Jimmy Bradshaw. There was an odd air of expectancy about her as she stepped out on the lanai. She crossed it to the screen door that opened on to the lawn and stood there, peering out. Under a near-by hau tree she thought she saw, in the blackness, an even blacker shadow. Suddenly it moved. With a little cry of recognition, she flung open the door and ran swiftly across the grass.

Meanwhile, Alan Jaynes was striding grimly along Kalakaua Avenue in the direction of the Grand Hotel. Five minutes brought him to the cool lofty lobby of that famous hostelry. He passed the head bell-man, whose smile of welcome froze suddenly on his face as he caught the look in the Britisher's eyes.

Jaynes turned to the left, moving past shop windows filled with jade and Oriental silks, then past the flower booth where, earlier in the evening, he had purchased the bouquet which now lay unappreciated on Shelah Fane's table. In another moment he reached the entrance to the big lounge of the hotel, and stood there at the top of a short flight of steps.

It was a beautiful room, with those three great arches opposite the entrance like triple paintings of the tropic sky. But Jaynes had no eye for beauty to-night. Most of the guests were at dinner, and the lounge had a deserted air. Seated not far away, however, talking pleasantly with an elderly couple who had the look of tourists, the Britisher saw the man he wanted.

He descended the steps, and crossed to this man's chair. "Stand up," he ordered in a husky voice.

Tarneverro the Great looked at him with an expressionless face. "I should have expected a bit more courtesy," he said evenly. "But then—I scarcely know you."

"Stand up," Jaynes repeated, "and come with me. I want a talk with you."

For a moment the fortune-teller sat, quietly measuring the man who towered above him. Then he rose, and making his apologies to the two old people, he walked at Jaynes' side down the long room.

"What is all this——" he began.

They stopped at an archway near the far end. Outside a series of brilliant lights bathed the hotel lawn in white, making an ideal stage-setting for some drama of the tropics. But the stage was empty; the drama was all inside the lounge.

"I want an explanation," said Jaynes roughly.

"An explanation of what?"

"I have done myself the honor of asking Miss Shelah Fane to marry me.

I had every reason to believe she intended to do so—but to-day she consulted you about the matter—a matter that concerns you not at all. You advised her against a marriage with me."

Tarneverro shrugged. "I do not discuss with outsiders what goes on at my readings."

"You're going to discuss it with me. Make up your mind to that!"

"Suppose I did—what could I say? I tell my clients only what I see in the crystal——"

"Rot!" cried Jaynes. "You tell them whatever happens to suit your fancy. What was your reason for this advice to Shelah?" He came closer and stared into the seer's face. "Are you, by any chance, in love with her yourself?"

The fortune-teller smiled. "Miss Fane is most charming——"

"We don't need your evidence on that point——"

"Most charming, but I do not permit myself the unwise luxury of a sentimental attachment for my clients. I advised her as I did because I saw no happiness possible in this proposed marriage." His tone grew serious. "Incidentally, whether you appreciate it or not, I did you a favor to-day."

"Really?" said Jaynes. "But I'm not asking favors of a mountebank like you."

A dark flush spread over Tarneverro's face. "There can be no point in prolonging this interview," he remarked, and turned away.

Jaynes seized him quickly by the arm. "We'll prolong it this far. You are going to Miss Fane at once and tell her you're a fraud, a fake, and that you wish to retract all you said to her to-day."

Tarneverro shook off the other's grasp. "And if I refuse?" he said.

"If you refuse," Jaynes answered, "I propose to give you a thrashing you won't forget for many a day."

"I do refuse," said Tarneverro quietly.

Jaynes' arm shot back, only to find itself in a surprisingly firm grip. He turned. Val Martino, the director, was at his side; his was the grip on the Britisher's arm. Beyond Martino, Huntley Van Horn, resplendent in Hollywood evening garb, looked on with an air of amused interest.

"Now, now," bellowed Martino, his face even redder than usual. "Cut this out, please. Too much of it in the pictures already. We can't have it, Jaynes, we can't have it."

For a moment the four stood motionless. A new figure strolled upon the scene, a broad bulky Chinese in a dinner coat. Tarneverro hailed him. "Ah, Inspector Chan. Just a moment, please."

Charlie came closer. "It is Mr. Tarneverro," he remarked. "The lifter of the veil."

"Inspector," the fortune-teller said, "may I present Mr. Van Horn, and Mr. Martino? And this is Mr. Alan Jaynes. Inspector Chan, of the Honolulu police."

Chan bowed gracefully. "The honor is immense. Distinguished company, as a blind man could see."

Jaynes glared at Tarneverro. "Very good," he sneered. "Hide behind the skirts of the police. It's what I would expect of you."

"Now, now," Martino interposed. "A slight misunderstanding, Inspector. There will be no trouble—I am sure the good name of the industry is too precious to all of us. It is certainly very precious to me."

Van Horn looked at his watch. "Eight o'clock," he announced. "I believe I'll roll along down to Shelah's. Anybody coming?"

The director shook his head. "Not yet. I'll be down presently." The actor walked slowly away. Martino, his grip still firm on the Britisher's arm, sought to lead him off. "Come out on the terrace," he pleaded. "We'll talk this matter over."

Jaynes turned to the fortune-teller. "I'm not sailing until twelve," he said. "In the meantime, we may meet again." He permitted Martino to lead him down the room.

"I trust that last prediction falls short of truth," Chan said to Tarneverro. "I do not have much liking for light I observe in gentleman's eye."

Tarneverro laughed. "Oh, he'll come around. I have offended him, quite unintentionally." He looked thoughtfully at Charlie. "By the way, Inspector, this is a happy meeting. I was thinking of calling you up. Just how do you plan to spend the evening?"

"I attend Rotary Club banquet in this hotel," Chan explained.

"Good. You'll be here some time?"

Chan nodded. "I fear so. It happens very few after-dinner speeches are equipped with self-stopper."

"Until eleven, perhaps?"

"It seems terribly possible."

"I am dining at a friend's house down the beach," Tarneverro said. "At the house of Miss Shelah Fane, in fact. Some time between now and eleven o'clock I may have a very important message for you, Inspector."

Chan's eyes opened slowly. "A message? Of what nature?"

Tarneverro hesitated. "This morning you happened to speak of certain murder cases in Los Angeles that remain unsolved. I told you then that I preferred to keep out of that sort of thing. We are not always able to follow our preferences, Inspector." He moved away.

"One moment," said Chan. "You have sought to quench the fire of my curiosity by tossing upon it a handful of straw. May I repeat my question—what sort of message?"

The fortune-teller gave him a long look. "A message calling upon you to arrest the murderer of—but there, I mustn't say too much. There's many a slip, as you have no doubt learned from your own experience. I shall be happy to have you so near—until eleven, at least. After that I presume I can reach you at your home?"

"With ease," Charlie told him.

"Let us hope for success," smiled Tarneverro cryptically, and went to rejoin his elderly acquaintances in the center of the lounge. For a second Chan looked after him. Then, shrugging his broad shoulders, he turned to find the banquet room.

3

Flowers for Shelah Fane

Huntley Van Horn strolled down Kalakaua Avenue in the direction of Shelah Fane's house. On this tiny island in the midst of the rolling Pacific, few outward signs of a romantic past survived. He might have been on Hollywood Boulevard: the parade of automobiles along that stretch of American asphalt was constant, a trolley clattered by, he walked on a concrete sidewalk under the soft yellow glow of modern street-lamps. Yet, beyond the range of those lamps, he was conscious of the black velvet of a tropic night. He caught the odor of ginger blossoms and plumeria, a croton hedge gave way to one of hibiscus, topped with pale pink flowers that were doomed to die at midnight.

He came to the number Shelah had impressed on his memory and turned in through the gates on to a broad drive that curved before a wide front door. Passing beneath a prolific banyan tree, two centuries older than the motion pictures, he rang the bell. Jessop admitted him.

"Oh, Mr. Van Horn," the butler said. "I'm happy to see you again."

"How have you been?" the actor inquired.

"In splendid health, sir. I trust you enjoyed your little jaunt to Tahiti?"

Van Horn tossed down the straw hat he had substituted for the silk topper in which he had won the approval of several million women. "A primitive country, Tahiti," he smiled. "It would have reminded you of Hollywood, Jessop."

The butler permitted himself a discreet smile. Van Horn pushed on into the living-room, and Jessop followed.

"No one here?" the actor cried. "Lord—am I as early as all that?"

"Oh, no, Mr. Van Horn. Some of the guests are enjoying the bathing, which I understand is rather famous in certain quarters. A few, I believe, are on the beach. Would you care to join the—er—the other young people in the water, sir?"

Van Horn grinned. "The diplomatic service lost a good man in you. No—much as I am tempted to classify myself with youth, the matter involves too damn' much dressing and undressing. I shall remain, high and dry, on the shore."

"Just as well, sir," nodded Jessop. "It is already eight-fifteen, and the dinner hour is rapidly approaching. I shall be forced to summon them in shortly."

Van Horn stared about the room. "What—no cocktails?"

"There has been a slight delay, sir. The gentleman who was to supply us with the raw material—the very raw material, between you and me, sir—has only just come. I was busy with the shaker when you rang." He went over and stood by the French window opening on to the lanai. "You will find the ocean just out here, sir," he explained.

Van Horn laughed, and stepped on to the lanai. The butler followed him to the screen door, and held it open.

"Ah, yes," said the actor. "I hear the roar of surf. No doubt I shall find the sea in that same general neighborhood." He paused in the doorway, and indicated a light gleaming through the trees some distance to the right. "What's over there?"

"It's a sort of summer-house, or pavilion, sir," Jessop explained. "At least, it would be a summer-house in England, where we have summers. It may be a few of the guests are in there."

Van Horn went out on the lawn, and started across it in the direction of the light. Suddenly he heard, above the pounding of the breakers, voices on the beach. He stood for a moment, undecided which way to go.

Jessop, meanwhile, returned to the living-room. An old bent Chinese came shuffling in.

"My dear Wu Kno-ching," the butler protested, "in a well-run house, the cook's place is in the kitchen."

The old man blandly ignored the rebuke. "What time dinnah?" he asked.

"As I have told you, the dinner is set for eight-thirty," replied Jessop. "It may, however, be somewhat delayed."

Wu Kno-ching shrugged. "Wha' kin' house this is? Dinnah mebbe sometime plitty soon aftah while. I get dinnah leady boss say wait dinnah goes to hell." He departed, murmuring further reproof.

The screen door slammed behind Wilkie Ballou; he crossed the lanai aimlessly and entered the living-room.

"I fear this idea of a swim is going to delay dinner, sir," Jessop said to him.

"What? Oh, yes—I suppose so. Have you any cigarettes here? My case is empty."

Jessop proffered a box containing cigarettes, and taking one, Ballou dropped into a chair. The butler officiated with a match, then retired to the kitchen.

Returning fifteen minutes later, he found the Honolulu man sitting just as he had left him.

"Things are getting rather serious, sir," Jessop remarked. He carried a large dinner gong. "I had always supposed, from my reading, that the Chinese are a notably patient race."

"They have that reputation, yes," nodded Ballou.

"Their representative in our kitchen, sir, is doing nothing to sustain it," Jessop sighed. "He informs me with great passion that dinner is waiting. I'll just go down to the shore and see what this will do." He nodded toward the gong and disappeared. Presently he could be heard in the distance, beating a not unmusical tattoo.

Ballou lighted a fresh cigarette. Jessop returned, and at his heels came Rita Ballou and Van Horn.

"You should have stayed, Wilkie," Rita said. "I've just been getting all the latest Hollywood gossip."

"I'm not interested," Ballou growled.

"Poor Wilkie," his wife smiled. "It's close to his bedtime, and he hasn't even had his dinner. Cheer up. It won't be long now."

Diana Dixon arrived, quite out of breath. "I suppose we're late," she cried. "You should have been in with us. It was glorious—but not half long enough. I could have stayed for hours. Cocktails—that's an idea."

She took one from the tray which Jessop held before her. The other guests likewise needed no urging. Huntley Van Horn lifted his glass.

"To our hostess, if any," he remarked.

"That's right—what's become of Shelah?" Rita Ballou said. "We saw her for a moment when we came——"

"Shelah," said Van Horn, with a cynical smile, "is no doubt lurking in the background waiting to make a grand and impressive entrance. She will ride in on a white charger, or descend on us from a balloon. You know, she goes in for that sort of thing——"

Julie and Jimmy Bradshaw rushed in, glowing and in high spirits. "Hello, Mr. Van Horn," the girl cried. "Are you all that's come?"

"To think," he groaned, "that you could be so rude to me."

"Oh, you know what I mean," she laughed. "Where are all our other guests? Val Martino, Mr. Jaynes, Tarneverro——"

"Tarneverro coming?" Van Horn lifted his eyebrows. "In that case, I will have a second cocktail. Thanks so much."

Quite unexpectedly there was the sound of steel guitars at the front door, and of many fresh young voices singing a Hawaiian song. Julie cried out with delight.

"A serenade from Shelah's admirers," she said. "Isn't that sweet? She will be pleased." Her beach robe streaming behind her, she ran to the door and threw it open. She stood gazing out at a vast throng of high-school girls, laden with flowers. They stopped their song, and a young Japanese girl stepped forward. "We would like to see Shelah Fane, please."

"Of course," said Julie. "Just wait, and I'll get her. While you're waiting, if you don't mind—will you sing *The Song of the Islands?* It's Miss Fane's favorite, you know."

She left the door open and returned to the living-room. "Come on, Jimmy—we'll find Shelah. I think she's in the pavilion."

"Sure," said Jimmy. They went out on the lawn.

"Couldn't be better," Julie cried. "For Shelah's entrance on the party, I mean. That crowd outside serenading her as she comes in—she'll love it."

"Good lord," said Bradshaw, disapproval in his voice.

"Oh, I know," the girl answered. "It's silly, but poor Shelah's what she is. Her life has made her so, and she can't change." They went on across the soft lawn under the hau trees and the algarobas. The sweet haunting strains of *The Song of the Islands* came to them on the evening breeze. "Hurry," Julie said, "Shelah must get in there before that song ends."

She ran up the steps of the pavilion, with Bradshaw close behind. He pushed open the door of the single room. For a second he stood there, then he turned swiftly and caught the girl in his arms.

"No, no," he cried. "Don't go any farther."

His tone frightened her. "What do you mean?"

"Turn around and go back," he pleaded, but she tore away from him and ran inside.

"You'll be sorry," he warned.

And she was sorry, it seemed, for above the voices of the serenaders and the distant whine of steel guitars, her own voice rose in a sharp cry of fright and terror.

Shelah Fane lay on the floor beside a small straight-backed chair. She had been stabbed through the heart; her priceless ivory gown was stained with crimson. Outside, that little group of her admirers continued to sing fervently their serenade.

Julie knelt by the star's side, and Bradshaw looked away. In a moment he went over and lifted the girl to her feet. "We'd better go," he said gently. "There's nothing we can do."

He led her to the door. She looked up at him through her tears. "But who—who——" she murmured.

"Ah, yes——" he answered. "That, I'm afraid, is the big question now."

He found, on the inside of the pavilion door, an unexpected key. They went outside, and the boy locked the door, putting the key in his pocket. Slowly they walked back to the house. Huntley Van Horn greeted them.

"Did you tell Shelah?" he said. "The stage is all set. Her guests are gathered in the living-room, her great public is singing lustily at the door—it's a grand entrance——" He stopped at sight of Julie's face.

"What's happened?" cried Rita Ballou shrilly.

Bradshaw stood looking about the little group. Jessop came in and, picking up the silver tray on which he had served the cocktails, prepared to collect the empty glasses. Outside the door, *The Song of the Islands* trailed off into silence.

"Shelah Fane has been murdered in the pavilion," said the boy in a low voice.

There was a sudden crash. Jessop had been guilty of his first error in forty years of service. He had dropped the silver tray.

"I beg pardon," he said to no one in particular.

Outside, Shelah Fane's admirers began another song. Bradshaw dashed through the curtains to the front door.

"Please," he cried. "Please—no more to-night. You must go away now. Miss Fane can't see you. She is—she is ill."

"We are so sorry," said the girl who seemed to be the leader. "Will you give her the flowers, please?"

They began to load him down with fragrant blossoms. Presently he staggered back into the hallway, his arms filled with a riot of color. Julie was standing there, her eyes wide, her face deathly pale.

"Flowers," said Bradshaw. "Flowers for Shelah Fane."

With a choking cry, Julie fell in a heap at his feet.

4

The Camel at the Gate

Down at the Grand Hotel, Charlie Chan was well started on what he perceived was going to be an excellent dinner. The hour of Rotarian oratory was not near enough to worry him, the food was good and he felt at peace with the world. He did not know the name of the small fish that lay on the plate before him, but one taste had led him to approve most heartily of its quality. He was leaning forward to apply himself with increased diligence to the task at hand, when a bell-boy touched him on the shoulder.

"You are wanted on telephone very quick," said the boy.

A sense of vague unrest troubled him as he walked down the long lobby to the telephone booth. He would have preferred a life of quiet meditation, but a ruthless fate was always breaking in upon him with some new problem that must be solved. What now, he wondered, as he entered the booth and pulled the door to behind him.

He was greeted by an excited young voice. "Say, Charlie,—this is Jim Bradshaw of the Tourist Bureau. Huntley Van Horn told me I could find you at the hotel."

"Yes—and now you have found me. What is it that has brought you to this state of high disturbance?"

In jumbled phrases Bradshaw poured out his story. Charlie listened calmly.

"Shelah Fane," the boy was saying. "You know what that means, Charlie. This news of mine will be cabled all over the world to-night. You're going to be in the limelight as you never were before. Better get down here as fast as you can."

"I will arrive at once," Charlie answered. Was that a sigh, Bradshaw wondered, that came over the wire? "Let nothing be touched until I touch it," the detective added.

He hung up, then called the police station and gave certain directions. At last he came from the booth, mopping his perspiring brow with his handkerchief. For a moment he stood motionless, as though gathering his strength for the task that lay before him. Another case, another murder, and he knew that what the boy had said was true: this time he would work in a bright spotlight indeed. Shelah Fane! Not for nothing did he have numerous children who, as he often said, were movie crazed. He knew only too well the interest that had always centered about the woman who now lay dead a short distance down the beach.

"A thousand-mile journey begins with one step," he sighed, and took it—in the direction of his hat.

When he returned to the door of the hotel, he encountered Tarneverro. The fortune-teller also carried a hat, and seemed on the point of going out. "Hello, Inspector," he said. "You haven't finished your dinner already?"

"I have not," Charlie answered. "I am rudely wrenched away by important business. The most important I have encountered for some time."

"Yes?" returned Tarneverro lightly.

Charlie's small eyes were fixed upon the other's face with a fierce intensity. Not too soon to collect impressions, to weigh, to measure, to study.

"Miss Shelah Fane," he said slowly, "is just now found murdered at her home."

For hours afterward he was to speculate upon the look that crossed that dark mysterious face.

"Shelah!" Tarneverro cried. "Good God!"

"You were on your way there, perhaps?" Charlie continued.

"I—I—yes—of course——"

"Do me the honor to ride with me. I desire to ask questions."

Val Martino hurried up. "I say, Tarneverro—are you going down the beach?"

Tarneverro told him the news. The director heard it with surprising calmness.

"Too bad," he said evenly. He was thoughtful. "Well, there goes six months' hard work. That picture's ruined. I'll never find anybody to double for her—I've tried it——"

"Good lord, man!" cried Tarneverro angrily. "Shelah is dead, and you babble about your picture."

"Sorry," said Martino. "Sorry for poor Shelah. But even in the movies, the show must go on."

"What became of that fellow Jaynes?" Tarneverro asked suddenly.

"Right after we left you, he shook me off and strolled down the beach. He was in a state of mind—well, you saw that. Wasn't coming to the dinner—but I fancy I'd better find him and bring him down, eh?"

"Yes, yes," Chan said hurriedly. "I must see him. Come, Mr. Tarneverro. Speed is necessary." He led the fortune-teller out to the drive, where his battered flivver was waiting. "The vehicle is none too grand," he apologized, "but it moves. Will you kindly leap inside?"

Silently Tarneverro climbed into the little two-seater. Charlie started the car.

"This is a terrible thing," the fortune-teller said. "Poor Shelah—I can scarcely realize it."

Charlie shrugged. "Time to be philosophical," he suggested. "You have perhaps heard old Eastern saying. 'Death is the black camel that kneels unbid at every gate.' Sooner or later—does it matter which?"

"I know, I know," Tarneverro continued. "But, in a way, I'm afraid I'm responsible for this. Oh, lord, the more I think about it, the clearer it becomes. Poor Shelah's blood is on my head."

"Your remarks have interesting sound," Charlie remarked, as the car moved through the hotel gates on to the avenue. "Explain, if you will be so kind."

"This evening," the fortune-teller went on, "I told you I might call on you to make an arrest in a very important murder case. I fully expected to do so. I'll tell you what I meant by that, as briefly as possible.

"Shelah Fane had cabled me from the ship, asking me to meet her here. It seems that this fellow Jaynes had proposed to her, and she wanted my advice. For some time past she had been in the habit of coming to me with all her problems. She loved Jaynes, she wanted to marry him—but she was afraid of what the future might hold in store. She feared that at any moment the world might discover that for three years or more she had gone about burdened with a terrible secret."

"What secret?" Charlie inquired.

"This morning," Tarneverro continued, "you spoke of Denny Mayo, who was found dead in his home in Los Angeles some three years ago. The police have been at sea on the case from the start. But Shelah Fane—she knew who murdered Denny Mayo. She was in Mayo's house, paying a harmless call, on the night of the murder. The door-bell rang, and she foolishly hid in another room. She saw the thing done. All this she confessed to me this morning. What is more, she told me that Denny Mayo's murderer is at this moment in Honolulu."

Charlie's eyes gleamed in the dark. "She told you the name?"

Tarneverro shook his head. "I'm sorry. She didn't want to, and I made no effort to press her. Her reason, of course, for not revealing her connection with this affair at the time, was that to do so would ruin her career. She had kept silent all these years, but she hesitated to marry a man of whom she was really fond and perhaps drag him through some very unpleasant publicity later on."

"A natural hesitation," Chan approved. "You encouraged it?" He had stopped the car in the drive of Shelah's house, but he made no move to alight.

"I did, of course," Tarneverro said. "More than that, I strongly advised her to lift this burden from her mind and find peace at last. I assured her that if she revealed the name of the guilty person of her own accord, no police in the world would be inclined to punish her for her long silence. I trust I was right in that?"

"Speaking for myself only, yes," nodded Charlie.

"I suggested she refuse Jaynes for the present, and go through with this unpleasant duty which I felt she owed to society. I said I thought it would be extremely foolish for her to marry any man with such a threat hanging over her happiness. If he really cared for her, I pointed out, Jaynes would marry her in the end. If he didn't care that much, then it was better to discover it now."

They alighted and stood under the banyan tree. Charlie peered into the fortune-teller's face. "And if Jaynes did not marry her——" he suggested.

Tarneverro shrugged. "You are on the wrong track there," he said. "I had no sentimental interest in Shelah Fane. But I didn't fancy my rôle—the secret she confided in me was a bit more than I'd bargained for. I felt, too, that for the sake of her own happiness she ought to get rid of this burden at last. So, I pleaded with her to make public the name of the guilty person in the Mayo case."

"And she agreed?" Charlie asked.

"Not precisely. The idea rather frightened her. She said she would think it over, and give me her decision to-night. 'Write me a brief statement, with that name included,' I told her, 'give it to me at dinner this evening, and I will make everything as easy for you as possible.' I was confident of gaining my point, or I would never have spoken to you about it. Yes, I would have gained it—but now—now——"

"Now," Chan said, "the killer of Denny Mayo has silenced this woman for ever."

"Precisely."

"But in what manner did this person discover she was hovering on a point of revealment?"

"I can't tell you," Tarneverro replied. "There is a balcony outside my room. That's a possibility, but not a likely one, I fear. Or it may be that Shelah consulted the killer, told him—or her—that she could no longer remain silent. It would have been like her. She was indiscreet, impulsive." They moved toward the steps. "I hope that what I have told you will prove helpful, Inspector. It gives you the motive, at least, and it narrows your search. Believe me, I shall be at your side through this investigation. You are going to have all the help I can possibly give you. I want, even more than you, the name of Shelah's murderer."

"Your help will be valuable indeed," Chan told him. "What did I say to you this morning—you are number one detective yourself. I did not dream that so soon we would be working side by side."

Jessop admitted them, and they went into the living-room where the two Ballous and Van Horn sat in gloomy silence. Charlie stood gazing at this small group with thoughtful deliberation. Jimmy Bradshaw entered behind him, his bathing-suit abandoned for dinner clothes.

"Hello, Charlie," he said in a low voice. "You're needed here, all right. In the pavilion—clear over to the right on the lawn. I locked the door as soon as we found what had happened. Here's the key."

"You are bright boy," said Charlie, pleased. "That fact has long been apparent as the morning sun." He turned to the others. "It will naturally be understood that no one leaves this house until I grant permission. Mr. Tarneverro, will you kindly accompany me?"

He walked with the fortune-teller in silence across the lawn, white now under the rising moon. Chan went up the steps first, and unlocked the door. With marked reluctance, Tarneverro followed.

Charlie went over and dropped down on one knee beside Shelah Fane. Slowly he looked from her to the fortune-teller. "Long time I have been in present business," he said softly, "but rough blunt feelings do not come natural to me yet. I am sorry for this lady. Never before this moment have I seen her—yet I am so very sorry." He stood up. "The black camel has knelt at plenty famous gate to-night," he added.

Tarneverro remained some distance from the body. He seemed to control himself with an effort. "Poor Shelah!" he muttered. "Life was very sweet to her."

"It is sweet to all of us," Charlie nodded. "Even the beggar hesitates to cross a rotting bridge."

"I can never forgive myself," the other continued. "What you see here began this morning in my apartment."

"What is to be, will be," Chan comforted. "We will not move unfortunate one until arrival of coroner. I have already telephoned the station. But we will look about, Mr. Tarneverro. Do not forget—you are to help." He knelt again, and lifted Shelah Fane's left arm. "Here is already some evidence. There has been a struggle, and wrist-watch was smashed in process. Crystal is broken, and"—he placed the watch to his ear—"the working of the time-piece immediately ceased to function. The hands remain stationary at two minutes past eight. So soon, without an effort, we know exact moment of tragedy. That is indeed something."

"Two minutes after eight," Tarneverro said. "At that moment, Jaynes,

Martino, Van Horn, you and I were in the lounge of the hotel. Remember—Van Horn looked at his watch, remarked it was eight o'clock, and said he was starting down here."

"Of course," Chan nodded. "The alibis arrive in one huge flock." He pointed to the orchids, crushed on the floor. "Further evidence of the struggle. Bouquet was torn off, trampled under foot."

"All of which looks a bit like jealousy," responded Tarneverro, frowning. "Can we be wrong about the motive, after all? No—it might be anger, too."

Charlie was crawling about the rug. "Peculiar thing," he remarked. "Flowers were fastened by pin—you may note the shoulder-strap is torn—but no pin is here now." He examined the orchids, and made a thorough search of the floor, while Tarneverro watched him. "It is true," he added, standing up, "the pin which fastened flowers is strangely missing."

He stepped to an old mahogany dressing-table, a handsome piece in its day, but now banished to the beach house. The table had a glass top, and leaning over, he studied this with a microscope he had taken from his pocket. "One more point," he said. "This corner here has lately received fierce nick. What can that mean?"

Tarneverro had picked up an expensive gold mesh bag that was lying on the table, and was studying the contents. "No use," he said. "The usual compact, and a few dollars. For a moment I had a crazy thought that perhaps Shelah had already written down for me that name we want. It would have been a very happy chance. The case would have been over before it started."

"Cases do not permit themselves the luxury of such easy solution," sighed Chan. "If letter such as you warmly desire had been in this room, murderer would have it now. No—fate is never so kind. We must take long way round. Come—we have finished here for the present. Much more to be done later."

They went out, and Charlie locked the door. As they moved across the lawn, he enumerated the clues. "A watch stopped at two minutes past eight in fierce struggle. A bouquet of orchids crushed in same, the pin that held them in place oddly lost. A fresh nick on glass corner of dressing-table. Enough for the moment, maybe."

As they entered the living-room, Jessop was ushering in Martino and Alan Jaynes. The latter's face was pale beneath its bronze, and he was obviously much upset.

"We will all acquire chairs," Chan suggested. "Many questions must now be asked."

Jessop came forward and faced Tarneverro. "I'm sorry, sir," he said. "With all the excitement, I quite forgot it."

"Forgot what?" asked Tarneverro, surprised.

"This letter, sir." He took a large elaborate envelope from his pocket. "Miss Fane requested me to give it to you the moment you arrived."

Tarneverro stretched forth his hand, but Charlie stepped quickly between them. He took the envelope. "So sorry. But the police are in charge here now."

"Naturally, sir," Jessop bowed, and backed away.

Chan stood there, a rather helpless-looking figure, holding the letter in his hand. Could it be true? Was the answer to this puzzle so soon within his grasp? A long understanding look passed between him and Tarneverro. The room seemed filled with people, milling about, seeking chairs. Charlie lifted his right hand to slit the envelope.

The floor lamp furnished the only illumination in the room. Chan took a step nearer it; he had the envelope open now, and was about to remove the contents. Suddenly the lamp went out, and the room was plunged into darkness. There followed the sound of a blow, then another, a cry and the fall of a rather solid body.

The place was in an uproar. Out of the blackness came an insistent demand for lights. The lamps in the wall brackets flashed on, revealing Jessop at the switch.

Charlie was slowly rising from the floor. He rubbed his right cheek, which was bleeding slightly.

"Overwhelmed with regret," he said, glancing at Tarneverro. "Famous god Jove, I hear, nodded on occasion. For myself, I fear I have just taken most unfortunate nap." He held out his left hand, in which was a tiny fragment of envelope. "Vital portion of letter," he added, "seems to have traveled elsewhere."

5

The Man in the Overcoat

For a long moment Chan stood with that fragment of letter in his hand. His expression was calm and unruffled, a very inaccurate indication of what was going on in his heart. Before a room filled with people some person had tricked and therefore disgraced the famous detective of the Honolulu police.

Charlie Chan had lost face in the presence of seven witnesses. Though he had lived many years in Hawaii, he was still Oriental enough to feel a hot bitter anger that startled even himself.

He sought to conquer that feeling immediately. Anger, he had been taught, is a poison that destroys the mind, and he would have need of all his faculties in the ordeal that impended. In this affair he was face to face with an adversary who was not only in a desperate mood, but who was also clever and quick to act. Well, so much the better, Charlie told himself; he would find all the more satisfaction in defeating such an opponent in the end. For he would win out; on that he was fiercely determined. The unknown person who had killed, first Denny Mayo, and then, to protect that secret, Shelah Fane, would be brought to justice at last, or Inspector Chan could never find peace again.

Tarneverro was glaring at him with ill-concealed indignation. "So sorry," he remarked coldly, "but the police are in charge here now."

Chan nodded. "You are eminently correct in that sneer. Never before in my life has such a happening aroused itself in my path. But I give you my word"—he looked slowly around the little group—"the person who struck that blow will pay. I am in no mood that turns the other cheek tonight."

He took out his handkerchief and applied it to the cheek that had, unfortunately, been already turned. It did not need the trace of red on the white linen to tell him that the hand that had hit him wore a ring. His right cheek—then the blow had probably come from some one's left hand. On the left hand of Van Horn, he noted a large seal ring; he turned to Wilkie Ballou, and on that gentleman's left hand he caught the glint of a diamond.

Covertly he pursued his study; Bradshaw, Martino, Tarneverro and Jaynes were all innocent of jewelry.

Tarneverro held his arms aloft. "You may start with me," he said. "You are, of course, going to search every one in this room."

Charlie smiled. "I am not quite such fool as that. Person who favored me with vigorous blow is not likely to hold incriminating letter in guilty possession. Besides," he added casually, as he walked away, "the matter is of small importance anyhow."

Tarneverro lowered his arms. It was quite evident from his expression that he heartily disapproved Charlie's omission of what he considered an essential move. But Chan ignored him. The detective was making a swift examination of the cord which stretched from the lamp to an electrical socket a few inches above the floor. The plug, wrenched from its place, lay before him, its two protruding prongs mute evidence that its removal had been a simple matter. It had only been necessary to step on the cord anywhere along its length, move the foot a short distance away from the wall, and the thing was done. Simple, yes, but a bit of quick thinking on some one's part. Charlie restored the plug, and the lamp flashed on again.

He came back to the center of the room. "We waste no time in fruitless search for letter now," he remarked. "I propose instead to fix in my mind our little group of characters, and perhaps learn from their lips just what they were engaged in doing at two minutes past eight to-night." He stood gazing at them thoughtfully. "I have some hesitation where to begin. Mr. Ballou, yours is familiar face, so I will start in your vicinity. Will you kindly state position in this house of yourself and Mrs. Ballou?"

The millionaire looked at him with all the arrogance of the white man who has lived for a long time among what he considers inferior races. "Why should I do that?" he inquired carelessly.

"Murder has been committed," replied Charlie sternly. "I recognize your high position on this island, but you are not above question. Will you deign to reply, please?"

"We came here as dinner guests," Ballou said. "We are—we were—old friends of Miss Fane."

"You knew her in Hollywood?"

"Yes."

"Mrs. Ballou was, before her marriage to you, herself actress on famous silver screen?"

"What if she was?" flared Ballou.

"Why not be polite, Wilkie?" rebuked his wife. "Yes, Inspector, I was in the pictures, under the name of Rita Montaine. And if I do say it, I was rather well known."

Chan bowed. "Could one of your charm be otherwise? May I inquire, please, how long you have been married?"

"Three years this month," she told him amiably.

"You resided, perhaps, in Hollywood up to moment of your marriage?"

"Oh, yes."

"Do you recall—was Mr. Ballou in Hollywood for some time previous to that marriage?"

"Yes—he hung around for several months, pleading with me to give up my career and take him." Her husband snorted. "You may not recall it now, Wilkie, but you did."

"What the devil," cried Ballou irritably, "has all that got to do with the murder of Shelah Fane? I believe, Inspector, that you are exceeding your authority. You'd better be careful—I'm not without influence——"

"So sorry," said Chan soothingly. "I will come at once to the present. You arrived here to-night at what hour?"

"At seven-thirty, but Mrs. Ballou got the invitation over the telephone, and as usual"—he glared at his wife—"she balled things up."

"At seven-thirty," put in Chan hastily, cutting off Rita's reply. "Describe actions down to present moment, please."

"What are you getting at?" objected Ballou roughly. You don't think I killed Shelah Fane, do you? By gad, I'll speak to some one down at the station about this. Do you know who I am——"

"Oh, who are you, anyhow, Wilkie?" his wife put in wearily. "Why not tell the Inspector what he wants to know and have done with it?" She turned to Chan. "We arrived about seven-thirty, and after a little chat with Miss Fane, stepped out on the beach to watch the bathers. It was about a quarter to eight when we went out there, I imagine."

"You were engaged in this manner how long?"

"Answering for myself, I was on the beach until Jessop came out at eight-thirty. About ten minutes before that, Mr. Van Horn joined us and my husband got up and strolled toward the house."

"At two minutes past eight, then, yourself and husband were seated side by side on sand. You heard no cry or other indication of disturbance?"

"None at all. The two girls in the water were doing more or less screaming—you know how people will. But that's not the sort of thing you mean?"

"Not precisely," replied Chan. "Thank you so much. We drop you for the present."

Julie O'Neill came slowly into the room. The new pink evening gown she had looked forward to wearing at the party was back on its hanger, and she had donned a simple little dress of gray chiffon. Her face was still decidedly pale, but she seemed calm and collected now. Chan turned to her.

"Good evening. I am so sorry to be here. Not until this moment have I encountered the pleasant thrill of seeing you. Would you mind informing me just who you are?"

Bradshaw came forward. He introduced Julie to Chan, and went on to explain the girl's place in the household.

"My heart's deepest sympathy," Charlie remarked. "As mere matter of form, I must ask about your actions during this most tragic evening."

"I can tell you all about that," Bradshaw informed him, "and kill two birds—oh, sorry—I mean to say, give you my own story at the same time. I arrived at the house early for a swim with Miss O'Neill. The last time we saw Miss Fane was in this room when we came down dressed for the water—that was about seven-forty. She was here with Mr. and Mrs. Ballou, and Mr. Jaynes."

"You went immediately to the beach?"

"We did—and on into the water. It was marvelous—pardon me if I put in a small advertisement for the local bathing beach. What I mean to say is, Miss O'Neill and I were together from the time we saw Miss Fane until about eighty-thirty, when Jessop rang the gong calling us in. It was soon after that we made our unhappy discovery."

"You remained in water at all times?"

"Oh, no—we came back to the beach now and then. Mrs. Ballou was there from the start, as she says. Mr. Ballow disappeared toward the last and Mr. Van Horn showed up."

"At two minutes past eight, then, you and Miss Julie were either in water or making brief excursion to shore?"

"One or the other—we had no means of knowing the time, of course. It went very quickly. We were surprised when Jessop called us in."

Chan turned to the girl. "Miss Fane was wearing tonight pretty nice bouquet of orchids on shoulder?"

Julie nodded. "Yes."

"Fastened with pin, no doubt?"

"Of course."

"Did you by any chance note the pin?"

"No, I didn't. But I remember her saying she was going to her room to get one. Perhaps her maid can tell you about that."

"Are you in position to know who it was sent those orchids?"

"I am," Julie replied. "There was no name, but Miss Fane recognized the writing on the card. She said they came from her ex-husband, Bob somebody—he's an actor playing with a stock company in Honolulu."

"Bob Fyfe," explained Rita Ballou. "He's in the company down at the Royal. They were married when Shelah was quite young, and I believe she was always very fond of him, even after the divorce."

Alan Jaynes rose and, taking a small cigar from a case, lighted it, then walked nervously about the room, seeking a place to throw the match.

"A discarded husband," mused Charlie. "Ah, yes, I would expect at least one of those. This man should be notified at once, and arrive here with all speed possible."

"I'll attend to it, Charlie," offered Jimmy Bradshaw.

"Warmest thanks," Chan remarked. As the boy left the room, he turned to the others. "We now resume somewhat rude questioning. Mr. Van Horn, you are actor, perhaps?"

"Perhaps?" laughed Van Horn. "Well, that's flattering. The reward of ten years' hard work."

"You have, then, been in Hollywood for the past ten years?"

"Ten years and a half—lost in what the amiable Mr. Mencken calls the sewers of Hollywood."

"And before that?"

"Oh, before that I led a most romantic life—ask my press-agent."

"I seek to determine facts," Charlie said.

"In that case I shall have to tell you that I came there, wide-eyed and innocent, from an engineering school. I planned to build bridges, but my fatal beauty intervened."

"You have appeared with Miss Shelah Fane in other pictures before this one?"

"No." Van Horn grew more serious. "I scarcely knew her until I was engaged for this part."

"I do not need to ask where you were at two minutes past eight to-night?" Chan continued.

"No, you don't," the actor agreed. "I was in the same room with you. You'll remember I looked at my watch and remarked that it was eight o'clock, and that I was toddling along down here. At two minutes past the hour I was still where you could see me—if you cared to avail yourself of the privilege."

"You came to this house immediately?"

"Yes—I walked. Exercise—that's how I keep in trim. I got here about eight-fifteen—I didn't hurry. Jessop let me in. We had a little chat, and at about eight-twenty I joined Mrs. Ballou on the beach, as you've already heard."

Jimmy Bradshaw returned. "I got that man Fyfe at the theater," he announced. "My news just about bowled the poor fellow over. He said he would be through after the second act, and would come right along."

"Thank you most warmly," Chan nodded. "You have most helpful nature." He turned to Martino. "You are what they call a director, I think."

"Yes, they call me that," replied Martino grimly. "Among other things."

"You have been engaged in this work a long time?"

"Not very long. I was formerly an actor, on the English stage. Got interested in the pictures, you know, and eventually went to Hollywood."

"Could you mention date of arrival?"

"Surely. I landed there two years ago last March."

"At that date, you saw the place for the first time?"

"Yes—of course."

Charlie nodded. "With regard to this evening, I can also omit to ask from you your exact location at two minutes past eight."

"Naturally. I was with you and these other chaps at the hotel. As I believe I told you, when I left you just after eight o'clock, I went with Mr. Jaynes on to the terrace. I tried to calm him a bit, but he broke away and wandered down the beach. I sat there on the beach walk for some twenty-five minutes, admiring the set. When I saw you again, I had just been upstairs to get my hat, intending to come down here."

Charlie looked over at Alan Jaynes, nervously smoking his small cigar in a distant corner. "Mr. Jaynes," he said.

The Britisher rose and approached him, consulting his watch as he did so. "Yes?" he remarked.

Charlie regarded him gravely. "You are, I believe, one of the people who suffer most from this death to-night?"

"What do you mean by that?"

"It is reported that you loved Shelah Fane."

"Reported—by whom?" The man looked angrily at Tarneverro.

"No matter," said Chan. "You had asked her to marry you?"

"I had."

"Then you loved her?"

"Look here—must you make a public inquisition of this?"

"So sorry. It is, I perceive, somewhat indiscreet on my part. Mr. Bradshaw has told me you were in this room at seven-forty to-night."

"I was. I had come to dinner."

"And to have, first of all, a private conversation with Miss Fane?"

"Yes. But the nature of that conversation is none of your business."

Charlie smiled. "Alas! I know so much that is none of my business. You ask for her final decision in the matter of marriage. She rejects you, and you suspect Mr. Tarneverro here is responsible for the action. You tramp angrily back to hotel, seeking to make quarrel with this same Tarneverro. So, at two minutes past eight, you stand in hotel lounge, glowering. Which, dear sir, is fortunate affair for you."

"I take it," Jaynes said, "that you have fixed the moment of this—this murder, at two minutes after eight?"

"I have," Chan replied.

Jaynes tossed his cigar into an ash-tray with a gesture of deep relief. "Thank God for that. Have you any more questions?"

"You saw Miss Fane for final time when you left this room at about fifteen minutes before eight?"

"That was the last time I saw her—yes."

"Then you did not return here between eight-five and eight-thirty-five?"

"I did not."

"Have you ever been in Hollywood, Mr. Jaynes?"

The Britisher laughed bitterly. "I have not—and I'm not likely to go there."

"That is all, sir," Chan nodded.

"Thank you. I'll say good-by. I happen to be sailing on the *Oceanic* at midnight."

Charlie looked at him in sudden surprise. "You are leaving Hawaii to-night?"

"I am."

The detective shrugged. "I am so sorry to disappoint you. The matter is impossible."

"Why should it be?" Jaynes demanded.

"You are somewhat deeply involved in this affair."

"But you say you've fixed the moment of the murder—and at that moment I was standing in your presence. It's a perfect alibi."

"Perfect alibis have way of turning imperfect without warning," Charlie informed him. "I regret that I can not allow you to sail. The *Oceanic* will be carefully watched, and no one connected with this affair will be permitted to leave the island aboard her. Or on any other ship, for the present."

An angry flush spread over the Britisher's face. "On what grounds do you keep me here?"

"As an important witness in present case," Chan replied. "I will go to extreme length of swearing out warrant, if necessary."

"I can at least go back to the hotel," Jaynes suggested.

"When I permit it," Charlie said gently. "Meanwhile, I hope you will find for yourself a comfortable chair."

"Jaynes glared at him, then receded into the background. The door-bell rang, and Jessop admitted two men. One was a tall angular American with a deputy sheriff's badge, the other a small anxious-looking Japanese.

"Ah, Mr. Coroner," Chan greeted the deputy, who doubled in that rôle. "And Kashimo. As usual, Kashimo, you are demon for speed to get on job. Is it too much to assume that you arrive here with horse and carriage?"

The deputy spoke. "They sent him to fetch me, and he finally managed it. Where did this thing happen, Charlie?"

"In a moment I lead you to the place," Charlie said.

"Maybe I search house," suggested Kashimo.

Chan regarded him sadly. "It would appear that there was great shortage of detectives at station house to-night," he said. "No, Mr. Kashimo, please do not search house—at least, not until somebody tells you what you are searching for." He turned to the deputy. "If you will follow me——"

Diana Dixon came into the room. She wore a white evening gown, and her elaborate make-up was sufficient explanation of the long delay in her appearance. Chan looked at her with interest.

"Here is some one about whom I have not heard before," he said.

"Who in the world——" began Diana, staring at him.

"Do not be alarmed," smiled Charlie. "I am Inspector Chan, of Honolulu police. You are in Hawaii now."

"Oh, I see," she answered.

"Your name, please?"

She gave it.

"You are guest in house, perhaps?"

"I am. Miss Fane as kind enough to take me in. You know, I've just come up from the South Seas with her—I acted in her last picture."

"An actress," nodded Chan. "I find myself dazzled by so much fame and beauty. All the same, I collect myself to inquire—what have you been engaged in doing this evening?"

"Why, I've been in swimming," she told him.

"When did you last see Miss Fane?"

"When I went up-stairs to put on my bathing-suit—I don't know what time that was. Mr. Bradshaw had just come, and Miss Julie and he and I went up to change. We left Miss Fane standing here in the hall. Some one was ringing the door-bell."

"You came down and entered the water with these young people?"

"Oh, no—it took me a lot longer to change. It was eight o'clock when I was finally ready—I noticed the clock on my dressing-table just before I left my room. I'd no idea it was so late—so I hurried down——"

"You did not see Miss Fane?"

"No, I didn't. This room was empty when I came through it. I crossed the lanai and stepped out on the lawn——"

"At a little time past eight?"

"Yes—it must have been three or four minutes past the hour. As I ran over the lawn, I saw a man come hurriedly away from the pavilion——"

"You saw a man leaving the pavilion? Who was he?"

"I don't know. I couldn't see his face. I thought he was one of the guests, and I shouted hello. But he didn't answer."

"You are able to describe him?" Chan asked.

"Not his face—that was in shadow, as I told you. But he was wearing a coat—an overcoat—I thought it odd on a night like this. The coat was open, and a streak of light from the kitchen window fell on his shirt-front. He was dressed in evening clothes, you see, and across his white shirt——" Suddenly she turned pale and sat down weakly in the nearest chair. "Oh, my God," she cried, "I never thought of it before."

"You never thought of what before?" Charlie prompted.

"That stain on his shirt—that long, narrow, bright red stain," she gasped. "It—it must have been blood."

6

Fireworks in the Rain

For a moment, stunned by the picture Miss Dixon's words presented, the assemblage was silent. Then a low murmur, a buzz of amazed comment, filled the room. Charlie Chan stood looking at his newest witness speculatively, as though he asked himself whether her statement could possibly be true.

"Most interesting," he said at last. "There has been, then, on these grounds to-night, a gentleman whose presence was up to this moment unsuspected by me. Whether or not he carried blood-soaked shirt bosom——"

"But I tell you I saw it," the girl protested.

Chan shrugged. "Perhaps. Oh, most humble pardon—I do not question your truth. I merely mention overwrought nerves, or maybe optic illusion. You must excuse if I say I might admit murderer would be so clumsy at his work as to inundate himself, but reason totters on pedestal to add that such a man would rush from scene of crime with coat flapping open on his error. Rather I would picture him with garment wrapped close to hide away this crimson evidence. But what does it matter? We must at any rate pursue thought of man with overcoat. The idea in itself presents portrait of queer human being. Overcoat in smiling tropics, even over evening dress, is unaccustomed garb." He turned to Julie. "And what, please, is name of man servant in this house?"

"You mean Jessop?" she inquired.

"I mean the butler. Will you summon him—if I am not getting too obnoxious?"

Julie went into the hall, and Charlie turned to the deputy sheriff. "I find it impossible to accompany you to scene of crime just yet. Same took place in small beach house at right of lawn—please accept this key. You may begin examination, and I will join you when I have interrogated servants here."

"Did you find the weapon, Charlie?" asked the coroner.

"I did not. That was, I think, carried off by the assailant. He was person, you will find, who had wits in good control." Charlie turned to the Japanese. "Kashimo, you may enjoy yourself by keen observation of the neighborhood. But if you repeat one former performance and spoil any footprints for me, I will at once arrange for you to return to former position as janitor of fish market."

The coroner and the little Japanese went out. At the same moment Jessop held open the curtains and followed Julie into the room. The butler was pale and agitated.

"The name is Jessop?" Charlie inquired.

"Yes—ah—sir."

"You understand who it is that I am?"

"I take it you represent the local constabulary, sir."

Chan grinned. "If it will help you to endure society of person like me, Jessop, I offer statement that my humble efforts on one occasion met with the complete approval of a gentleman from Scotland Yard."

"Really, sir?" answered Jessop. "The memory must be most gratifying to you."

"It is, indeed. How long is it now that you have been Miss Fane's butler?"

"Two years, sir."

"You were in Hollywood before that, maybe?"

"For about eighteen months, I was."

"A butler, always?"

"Always a butler, sir. I had a number of berths before I went with Miss Fane. I am bound to say that I was unhappy in all of them."

"The work was, perhaps, too difficult?"

"Not at all, sir. I objected to the familiarity of my employers. There is a certain reserve that should exist between servant and master. I found that lacking. The ladies I worked for would often weep in my presence and tell me stories of unrequited love. The gentlemen who engaged me were inclined to treat me like some long-lost brother. One in particular was accustomed to address me as 'old pal,' and when a bit under the influence, would embrace me in the presence of guests. A man has his dignity, sir."

"It has been well said, without dignity there can be no stature," Charlie assured him. "You found Miss Fane of a different type?"

"I did indeed, sir. A lady who knew her place as I knew mine. There was never any undue informality in her treatment of me."

"Relations were, then, of the happiest?"

"That they were. I should like to add that I am quite heart-broken by this evening's business, sir."

"Ah, yes—coming to this evening—did any of the gentlemen whom you admitted here to-night wear an overcoat, Jessop?"

"An overcoat, sir?" Jessop's white eyebrows went up.

"Yes. With dinner costume, you understand."

"No, sir," replied Jessop firmly. "No such gaucherie of dress was evident, Constable."

Chan smiled. "Kindly look about the room. Do you recall admitting any visitor with exception of those now visible to your view?"

"No, sir," returned Jessop, surveying the party.

"Thank you. When did you last see Miss Fane?"

"It was in this room, at about twenty minutes after seven, when I brought her a box of flowers. I heard her voice after that, but I did not see her."

"Please detail your activities from hour of twenty minutes past seven onward," Chan requested.

"I was engaged with my duties, sir, in the dining-room and the kitchen. I may add that it has been a rather trying evening, in my department. The Chinese cook has exhibited all the worst qualities of a heathen race—I'm sure I beg your pardon."

"A heathen race," repeated Charlie gravely, "that was busy inventing the art of printing at moment when gentlemen in Great Britain were still beating one another over head with spiked clubs. Pray excuse this brief reference to history. The cook has been in uproar?"

"Yes, Constable. He has proved himself sorely deficient in that patience for which his people have long been noted. Then, too, the—er—the bootlegger, to use one of your—or their—American phrases, has been unforgivably late."

"Ah—you already possess bootlegger?"

"Yes, sir. Miss Fane was a temperate woman herself, but she knew her duties as a hostess. So Wu Kno-ching, the cook, arranged with a friend to deliver a bit of liquor just out of the laboratory, and a wine of the most recent vintage."

"I am deeply shocked," Chan replied. "Wu's friend was late?"

"He was indeed, sir. As I say, I was busy with my duties from the moment I gave Miss Fane the flowers. At two minutes past eight——"

"Why do you make selection of two minutes past eight?"

"I could not help but overhear your questions to these others, sir. At that moment I was in the kitchen——"

"Alone?"

"No, sir. Wu was there, of course. And Anna, the maid, had dropped in for a cup of tea to sustain her until dinner. I called Wu's attention to the fact that it was already past eight o'clock, and we had a few words about the bootlegger's tardiness. The three of us remained there together until ten after eight, when Wu's friend made a rather sheepish appearance, and I immediately set about to do what I could with the ingredients he brought. At fifteen past eight, I came out to admit Mr. Van Horn. From that point on I was in and out of this room, sir, but I did not leave the house until I went to the beach and sounded the dinner gong."

"I am obliged to you for a most complete account," Charlie nodded. "That is all, Jessop."

The butler hesitated. "There is one other matter, Constable."

"Ah, yes. What is that?"

"I do not know whether or not it has any significance, sir, but it came back to me when I heard this terrible news. There is a small library up-stairs, and to-day, when I had cleared away the luncheon things, I went in there to secure a book, planning to take it to my room as a recreation during my siesta. I came suddenly upon Miss Fane. She was looking at a photograph and weeping most bitterly, sir."

"A photograph of whom?"

"That I couldn't say, sir, save that it was of some gentleman. She held it so I could not obtain a better view of the face, and hurriedly left the room. All I can tell you is that it was a rather large photograph, and was mounted on a mat that was Nile green in color."

Chan nodded. "Thank you so much. Will you be kind enough to dispatch heathen cook into my presence, Jessop?"

"I will indeed, sir," replied Jessop, and withdrew.

Charlie looked about the circle. "The matter lengthens itself out," he remarked kindly. "I observe beyond windows a cool lanai crowded with nice Hongkong chairs. Any who wish to do so may stroll to more airy perch. One thing only I ask—please do not leave these grounds."

There followed a general movement, and amid a low buzz of comment all save Bradshaw, Julie, Tarneverro and Chan went out on the dim lanai. The fortune-teller looked keenly at Charlie.

"What have you accomplished?" he wanted to know.

Charlie shrugged. "Up to the present moment, I seem to have been setting off fireworks in the rain."

"That's precisely what I thought," Tarneverro said impatiently.

"Do not lose heart," Chan advised. "Changing the figure, I might add that to dig up the tree, we must start with the root. All this digging is routine matter that does not fascinate, but at any moment we may strike a root of vital importance."

"I sincerely hope so," Tarneverro remarked.

"Oh, you trust Charlie," Bradshaw said. "One of Honolulu's first citizens, he is. He'll get his man."

Wu Kno-ching came in, mumbling to himself, and Charlie addressed him sharply in Cantonese. Looking at him with sleepy eyes, Wu replied at some length.

The high-pitched, singsong exchange of words between these two representatives of the oldest civilized nation in the world grew faster and louder, and on Wu's part, seemingly more impassioned. The three outsiders stood there deeply interested; it was like a play in some dead language; they could not understand the lines but they were conscious of a strong current of drama underneath. Once Chan, who had up to that point been seemingly uninterested, lifted his head like a bird-dog on the scent. He went closer to the old man, and seized his arm. One recognizable word in Wu's conversation occurred again and again. He mentioned the "bootleg-gah."

Finally, with a shrug, Chan turned away.

"What's he say, Charlie?" asked Bradshaw eagerly.

"He knows nothing," Chan answered.

"What was all that about the bootlegger?"

Charlie gave the boy a keen look. "The tongue of age speaks with accumulated wisdom, and is heard gladly, but the tongue of youth should save its strength," he remarked.

"Yours received and contents noted," smiled the boy.

Chan turned to Julie. "You have been spoken of Miss Fane's maid. She alone remains to be interviewed. Will you be so good as to produce her?"

Julie nodded and went out. Wu Kno-ching still lingered at the door, and now he burst into a tirade, with appropriate gestures. Charlie listened for a moment, and then shooed the old man from the room.

"Wu complains that no one eats his dinner," he smiled. "He is great artist who lacks appreciation, and his ancient heart cracks with rage."

"Well," remarked Jimmy Bradshaw, "I suppose it's an unfeeling thing to say, but I could put away a little of his handiwork."

Chan nodded. "I have thought of that. Later, perhaps. Why not? Do the dead gain if the living starve?"

Julie returned, followed by Anna, the maid. The latter was a dark thin woman who moved gracefully.

"The name, please?" Chan inquired.

"Anna Rodderick," she answered. There was just a trace of defiance in her tone.

"You have been with Miss Shelah Fane how long?"

"Something like a year and a half, sir."

"I see. Before that you were perhaps employed elsewhere in Hollywood?"

"No, sir, I was not. I went with Miss Fane the day after my arrival there, and I have never been employed by any one else in the picture colony."

"How did you happen to go to California, please?"

"I was in service in England, and a friend wrote me of the higher wages that prevailed in the States."

"Your relations with Miss Fane—they were pleasant?"

"Naturally, sir, or I wouldn't have remained with her. There were many other positions available."

"Did she ever admit you into her confidence regarding personal affairs?"

"No, sir, she did not. It was one of the things I liked about her."

"When did you last see your mistress?"

"At a bit before seven-thirty. I was about to go down to the kitchen for a cup of tea, for I saw that my dinner was likely to be long delayed. Miss Fane came to her room—I was in the one adjoining. She called to me and said she wanted a pin for some orchids she had in her hand. I went and got it for her."

"Kindly describe the pin."

"It was a rather delicate affair, set with diamonds. About two inches long, I should say. I fastened the flowers to the shoulder-strap of her gown."

"Did she remark about those flowers?" Charlie inquired.

"She said they were sent to her by some one of whom she was once very fond. She seemed a bit excited."

"What happened next?"

"She sat down at the telephone," Anna told him. "There is an extension in her room. She looked up a number in the telephone book and then busied herself with the dial, sir."

"Maybe you heard subsequent conversation?" Chan suggested.

"I am not accustomed to spying, sir. I left her at once and went down to the kitchen."

"You were in the kitchen at two minutes past eight?"

"Yes, sir. I recall the hour because there was a great deal of talk between Jessop and the cook about the bootlegger."

"You were still in the kitchen when this bootlegger came, at ten minutes past eight?"

"I was, sir. A little later I went back to my room."

"You did not see your mistress again?"

"No, sir, I did not."

"One other thing." Chan looked at her thoughtfully. "Kindly speak of her manner during the day. Was it same as always?"

"I noticed nothing unusual."

"You did not note that she was seen with a portrait—the portrait of a gentleman—during the afternoon?"

"I was not here this afternoon. It was our first day ashore, and Miss Fane kindly gave me a few hours off."

"Have you ever seen, among Miss Fane's possessions, portrait of gentleman mounted on Nile-green mat?"

"Miss Fane always carried with her a large portfolio, containing many pictures of her friends. It may be such a one is among them."

"But you never saw it?"

"I have never opened the portfolio. That would seem too much like prying—if I may say so, sir."

"Do you know where portfolio is now?" Charlie asked.

"I believe it is lying on a table in her room. Shall I fetch it for you?"

"A little later, perhaps. Just now I would inquire—you are familiar with jewelry usually worn by Miss Fane on occasion of evening party? Aside from diamond pin fastening orchids, I mean?"

"I think so, sir."

"Will you come with me, please?"

Leaving the others in the drawing-room, he led the maid across the moonlit lawn in the direction of the pavilion. They went in, and Anna lost her composure for a moment at sight of Shelah Fane. She gave a strangled little cry.

"Kindly conduct thorough search," Chan said to her, "and inform me if all jewelry is at present time in place."

Anna nodded without speaking. The coroner came over to greet Chan.

"I've made my examination," he said. "This is a pretty big thing, Charlie. I'd better send somebody to help you out."

Chan smiled. "I have Kashimo," he answered. "What more could any man ask? Tell Chief I will report entire matter to him at earliest convenience." They stepped out on the lanai of the pavilion, and at the same moment Kashimo crept like a correspondence-school sleuth from a cluster of bushes at the corner of the building.

"Charlie—come quick," he whispered hoarsely.

"Kashimo has discovered essential clue," Charlie said. "Please join us, Mr. Coroner."

They followed the Japanese through the bushes and out upon a public beach that bounded the property on the right. On that side of the pavilion, which stood flush with the dividing line, was a single window. Kashimo led them to this, and swept a flash-light over the sand.

"Footprints-s-s!" he hissed dramatically.

Charlie seized the light and knelt on the sand. "True enough, Kashimo," he remarked. "These are footprints, and peculiar ones, too. Shoes were old and battered, the heels are worn down unevenly, and in sole of one shoe was most unfashionable hole." He stood up. "I fear that fortune has not been smiling on owner of that footwear," he added.

"I am one to find things," remarked Kashimo proudly.

"You are," smiled Charlie, "and for once you do not destroy clue the moment you come upon it. You are learning, Kashimo. Warm congratulations."

They returned to the lawn of Shelah Fane's house. "Well, Charlie, this is up to you," the deputy said. "I'll see you early in the morning—unless you want me to stay."

"Your duty is accomplished," Chan answered, "or will be when you have made proper arrangements in city. Body will of course be taken at once to mortuary."

"Certainly," the deputy replied. "Well, good-by—and good luck."

Chan turned to Kashimo. "Now great opportunity arises for you to perform your specialty," he said.

"Yes-s-s," Kashimo answered eagerly.

"Go to house, inquire for bedroom of Miss Shelah Fane, and search——"

"I go now," cried Kashimo, leaping away.

"Stop!" commanded Charlie. "You are one grand apprentice detective, Kashimo, but you never pause to inquire what it is you sleuth for. On table of that room you will find large portfolio of photographs. I very much desire to see portrait of gentleman mounted on mat that is colored Nile green——"

"Nile is new word to me," the Japanese complained.

"Yes—and I have no time for geography lesson now," sighed Chan. "Bring me all photographs in room mounted on cardboard colored green. If none such is in portfolio, search elsewhere. Now be off. The portrait of a gentleman, remember. If you return with pretty picture of Fujiyama I will personally escort you back to private life."

Kashimo sped across the lawn, and Charlie again entered the pavilion. Anna was standing in the center of ths room.

"You made investigation?" he inquired.

"I did," she said. "The pin that fastened the flowers is nowhere about."

"A matter already known to me," he nodded. "Otherwise the ornamental equipment is complete?"

"No," she replied. "It isn't."

He regarded her with sudden interest. "Something is missing?"

"Yes—an emerald ring—a large emerald that Miss Fane usually wore on her right hand. She told me once that it represented quite a bit of money. And—it has disappeared."

7

The Alibi of the Watch

Charlie sent the maid back to the house, and then sat down in the straight-backed chair before the dressing-table. The sole illumination in the little room came from two pink-shaded lamps, one on either side of the mirror. Thoughtfully he stared into the glass where, dimly reflected, he caught occasional glimpses of an ivory satin gown. Shelah Fane now lay on the couch where the coroner had placed her. All the loves and the hates, the jealousies, the glittering triumphs of this tempestuous career were ended to-night. A woman of flame, they had called her. The flame had flickered and died like a candle in the wind—in the restless trade-wind blowing from the Koolau Range.

Chan's small eyes narrowed in an intense effort at concentration. In one of her more indiscreet moments, Shelah Fane had seen Denny Mayo murdered. For three years she had carried the secret about with her until—and this moment was even more indiscreet—she poured it into the willing ears of Tarneverro the Great, a crystal-gazer—a charlatan, no doubt. That same night, the black camel had knelt before her gate.

Carefully in his mind, the detective began to go over the points his investigation had so far revealed. He was not one to carry a note-book, but he took an envelope from his pocket, and with a pencil began to write a list of names on the back. He was thus engaged when he heard a step behind him. Looking over his shoulder, he saw the lean mysterious figure of Tarneverro.

The fortune-teller came forward and dropped into a chair at Chan's side. He stared at the detective, and there was disapproval in that stare.

"Since you have asked me to work with you in this affair," he began, "you will perhaps pardon me if I say I think you have been extremely careless."

Charlie's eyes opened wide. "Yes?" he said.

"I refer to Miss Fane's letter," continued Tarneverro. "It may have been the answer to all our questions. In it the poor girl may have written the name we so eagerly seek. Yet you made no move to search the people in that room—you even pooh-poohed the idea when I offered it. Why?"

Chan shrugged. "You think, then, we have to deal with a fool? A miscreant who would take pretty complete pains to obtain the epistle, and then place it on his own person where a search would instantly reveal it? You are wrong, my friend. I had no taste for revealing how wrong you were, at the expense of further embarrassment for myself. No, the letter is hidden in that room, and sooner or later it will be found. If not—what of it? I have strong feeling that it contains nothing of the least importance."

"On what do you base that feeling?" Tarneverro inquired.

"I have plenty as a base. Would Shelah Fane have written big secret down and then given it to servant who must pass it along to you? No, she would have awaited her opportunity and then delivered it to you with her own hand. I do not reprove you, but I believe you attach undue importance to that probably innocent epistle."

"Well, the murderer certainly thought it important. You can't deny that."

"Murderer was in state of high excitement and took unnecessary risk. If he takes few more like that, we are at trail's end."

Tarneverro, with a gesture, dismissed the matter. "Well, and what have you discovered from all your questions?" He glanced at Chan's notes.

"Not much. You perceived that I was curious to learn who was in Hollywood three years ago last month. Assuming that the story is true—the story you say Shelah Fane told you this morning——"

"Why shouldn't it be true? Does a woman make a confession like that as a joke?"

"Never," answered Chan, somewhat sharply for him. "And for that reason I am remarking I assume it to be true. It is, then, important to locate our many suspects in June three years ago. I have written here the names of all who were in Hollywood at that time, and consequently may have slain Denny Mayo. They are Wilkie Ballou, Rita his wife, Huntley Van Horn. And—ah, yes—Jessop, the butler. I regret that, overwhelmed by account of bloody shirt, I neglected to make inquiries of Miss Dixon."

"She has been in Hollywood six years," the fortune-teller informed him. "I know from what she has told me during the readings I have given her."

"One more." Charlie wrote down the name. "I may, I presume, add Miss Julie—though very young at the time. Of these, for the hour of two minutes past eight to-night, two have been accounted for. Jessop presents plenty good alibi and Huntley Van Horn has perfect one, to which I myself can swear. Other things I learned—not very important—but it struck my mind, as it must have struck yours, that Mr. Alan Jaynes was breathless with anxiety to leave Hawaii to-night. Do not forget—it is within grounds of possibility that Denny Mayo murder had nothing to do with death of Shelah Fane. This Jaynes was in overwrought state; his may be fiercely jealous nature; he may have looked at those orchids, the gift of another, on the lady's shoulder, and——"

"But he, too, has the alibi of the watch," Tarneverro suggested.

"Alas! yes," Chan nodded.

For a moment they sat in silence. Then Tarneverro rose, and walked slowly toward the couch. "By the way," he said casually, "have you made a thorough examination of this watch?"

"So sorry." Chan rose and followed him. "You now call my attention to fact that I have neglected most obvious duty." Tarneverro was bending over, but Chan stopped him. "I will remove it at once and have careful look at it—though I am so dense I do not quite grasp your meaning."

Taking a linen handkerchief from his pocket, he spread it over his left hand. With his other hand he unfastened the narrow black ribbon from Shelah Fane's wrist, and lifting the costly little watch, laid it on the handkerchief. He went back and stood directly under one of the lights, staring down at the timepiece.

"*Haie*, I seem in stupid mood to-night," he sighed. "I am still at sea. Crystal is broken, watch has ceased to function at precisely two minutes past eight——"

"Permit me," said Tarneverro. "I will be more explicit." He took both handkerchief and watch, and with the linen always between his fingers and the metal, turned the stem of the fragile timepiece. At his touch, the minute hand moved instantly.

A flash of triumph shone in the fortune-teller's eyes. "That," he cried, "is more than I dared to hope for. The murderer had been guilty of a small error—it was very kind of him. He adjusted the stem so that the time shown on the face of the watch could be altered at will—and in his haste he forgot to readjust it. Surely I needn't tell you what that means."

Charlie gave him a look of enthusiastic approval. "You are detective of the first class yourself—give me credit that I noted same this morning. I can never cease to be grateful to you. Of course I grasp meaning now."

Tarneverro laid the watch down on the glass top of the dressing-table. "I think we may be sure of one thing, Inspector," he remarked. "At whatever hour the murder took place, it was certainly not at two minutes past eight. We are dealing with a clever man. After he had killed Shelah Fane he removed her watch, set the time back—or perhaps forward—to two minutes past eight, and then smashed the thing as though to indicate a struggle." The fortune-teller's eyes lighted; he pointed to the corner of the dressing-table. "That's the explanation of the nick in the glass. He banged the watch against that corner until he had stopped its running."

Chan was instantly on the floor. "There is no glass beneath," he said.

"No, no," Tarneverro continued. "There wouldn't be. The broken glass was naturally found where Miss Fane fell. And why? Because this unknown person removed the watch with a handkerchief, as you have done; he swung it against the table in that handkerchief to catch the bits of crystal, and carried the wrecked remains intact to the spot where he wanted them. A bright boy, Inspector."

Charlie nodded. Obvious chagrin was in his manner. "But you are brighter boy. Almost I am on verge of resigning in disgust at my own stupidity.

You should take my badge, Mr. Tarneverro, for you are the smart detective on this case."

Tarneverro gave him an odd look. "You think so, do you? I'm afraid you exaggerate—the matter was really simple enough. It came into my mind that too many of us had alibis in this affair. I thought how easy it would be to change the time on the face of a watch. That is what happened here. The murderer set it at a moment then past, for which he had already established an alibi—or at a future time for which he proposed to get an alibi forthwith. However, when a man is excited he is likely to slip up somewhere—and this chap stumbled when he forgot to push down that little stem before he left."

Chan sighed. "I am, as I remarked, bubbling with gratitude toward you, and yet I am appalled. Whole flock of alibis is now quite ruined, and the field broadens like some boundless prairie. Van Horn's alibi is gone, the alibis of Martino and of Jaynes, they are gone too, and—begging humble pardon, Mr. Tarneverro—you have likewise destroyed the alibi you yourself possessed."

The fortune-teller threw back his head and laughed. "Do I need an alibi?" he cried.

"Perhaps not," Charlie grinned. "But when a tree falls, the shade is gone. Who knows? Even you might regret the loss of that shade in time."

"It may happen that I have another tree," suggested Tarneverro.

"If that is true, I congratulate you." Charlie glanced around the room. "I must have poor unfortunate lady removed now to house, then lock this place until finger-print expert can do work early in morning. You will observe we do not move with vast speed here in Hawaii. It is our lovely climate." He put the watch in the dressing-table drawer, and he and Tarneverro went out, Chan again locking the door. "We will now continue to living-room, which we will seek to obtain to ourselves. Perhaps there you will deign to keep on with remarkable research. I travel in luck to-night. What could I do without you?"

A little group of chairs on the lawn indicated the whereabouts of most of the guests. In the living-room they came upon Julie and Jimmy Bradshaw, seated close together. The girl had evidently been crying, and Mr. Bradshaw's manner suggested that he played the rôle of comforter. Chan gave Julie the key to the pavilion, and told her gently what must be done. She and the boy went out to seek the aid of the servants.

When they had gone, Charlie walked throughtfully up and down the big room. He peered into receptacles that held flowers and plants, opened the few books he came upon and ruffled the pages.

"By the way," Tarneverro remarked, "have you made an inspection of Miss Fane's bedroom?"

"Not yet," Chan answered. "So much to do, and only you and I to do it. I have sent Kashimo, our Japanese sleuth hound, on an errand, from which he will doubtless return in course of week or two. As for myself——" He was walking across a rug, and paused. "As for myself——" he repeated. He rubbed his thin-soled shoe back and forth over a spot in the rug. "As for myself," he added a third time, "I have plenty good business here."

He stooped and threw back the rug. There on the polished floor lay the big envelope that had been snatched from his hand earlier in the evening. One corner was missing, but otherwise the letter was intact.

"Fortunate that Miss Fane preferred such thick note-paper," Charlie said. He picked up the envelope. "I fear I can not offer my unknown friend warm congratulations on his originality this time. But he was very hurried gentleman when this matter engaged his attention—I must remember that."

Tarneverro came close, his dark eyes gleaming. "By gad—Shelah's letter. And addressed to me, I believe?"

"I remind you again that the police are in charge," Chan said.

"They were in charge before," Tarneverro answered.

"Ah, yes. But history will not repeat just yet." Charlie removed the note from the envelope, and read. He shrugged his shoulders, and passed the missive to the fortune-teller. "Once I was right," he remarked.

Tarneverro looked down at the huge sprawling handwriting of one who was generous of note-paper as of all things. He frowned at what he saw.

> Dear Tarneverro:
>   Please forget what I told you this morning. I must have been mad—mad. I intend to forget it—and so must you—oh, Tarneverro, promise me you will. Pretend that I never said it. I shall refuse poor Alan to-night—it will break my heart—but I'll do it. I am going on alone—perhaps in the end I may even find a little happiness I want it so much.
>
>   Yours ever
>   SHELAH FANE.

"Poor Shelah!" The fortune-teller stood for a moment, staring at the letter. "She hadn't the courage to go through with it—I might have known. A pitiful letter—I don't be-believe I would have insisted, after all." He crushed the paper in his hand fiercely. "The murderer of Denny Mayo was safe—she wasn't going to tell on him—he killed her for nothing. She's gone, and she might be here. By heaven—I'll get him if it's the last act of my life!"

Chan smiled. "I have a similar ambition, though I trust the accomplishment will not finish off my existence." His Japanese assistant came stealthily into the room. "Ah, Kashimo, have you enjoyed pleasant week-end upstair?"

"Pretty hard job, but I got him," Kashimo announced proudly. "Found in jar under potted plant."

Chan reached out his hand. To his surprise Kashimo proffered, not the photograph Charlie expected, but a handful of torn bits of glazed paper and of heavy green cardboard. Some one had ripped the portrait on the green mat to bits, and then attempted to conceal the wreckage.

"What have we now?" Chan said. He stood looking in wonder at the handful of scraps that he held. His eyes sought Tarneverro's. "Here is a matter worthy of consideration. Person unknown does not wish me to look upon the photograph over which Shelah Fane wept this afternoon. Why? It is then portrait of the man you had asked her to betray?"

"It may have been," Tarneverro agreed.

"Course now becomes clear," Charlie announced. "I must view this photograph, so with all patience at my command, I propose to fit these scraps together again." He pulled a small table up before the windows that faced the street.

"I investigate outside the house," Kashimo remarked.

"Much the safest place to have you," Chan returned. "By all means investigate very hard."

The Japanese went out.

Charlie removed the table cover, and sat down. On the smooth top he began carefully to lay together the pieces of the photograph. The task, he saw, was going to be long and arduous. "I never was bright man with jigsaw puzzle," he complained. "My daughter Rose was pride of family at that work. I would enjoy to have her at my side."

He had made scant progress when the door of the lanai opened, and a group of the guests entered the living-room. Wilkie Ballou walked at the head, and after him came Van Horn, Martino, Jaynes and Rita Ballou. Diana Dixon followed; she seemed detached from the crowd, which had the air of a delegation.

A delegation it was, evidently. Ballou began to speak, in his most commanding tone.

"See here, Inspector—we've talked it over and there's no earthly reason why you should keep us here any longer. We've all been questioned, we've told you what we know, and now we propose to leave."

Charlie tossed down the as yet unplaced bits of the photograph and rose. He bowed politely.

"I recognize you are impatient with good reason," he said.

"Then you're willing for us to go along?" inquired Ballou.

"I am—and I say it with extreme pain—quite unwilling," Chan replied. "Unfortunately, new developments keep popping off like firecrackers on New Year holiday, and I have something still to talk about with you."

"An outrage!" Ballou cried. "I'll have your badge for this."

Charlie rewarded him with a maddening smile. "That may happen—tomorrow. But looking only at to-night, I am placed in charge of this case, and I say—you will remain here until I tell you to depart."

Jaynes pushed forward. "I have important business on the mainland, and I intend to sail at midnight. It is now long past ten. I warn you that you must call out your entire force if you propose to keep me here——"

"That also can be done," answered Charlie amiably.

"Good lord!" The Britisher looked helplessly at Wilkie Ballou. "What kind of place is this? Why don't they send a white man out here?"

A rare light flared suddenly in Charlie's eyes. "The man who is about to cross a stream should not revile the crocodile's mother," he said in icy tones.

"What do you mean by that?" Jaynes asked.

"I mean you are not yet safely on the farther bank."

"You know damn' well I've got an alibi," cried the Britisher angrily.

Chan's little eyes surveyed him from head to foot. "I am not so sure I do," he remarked calmly.

"You said yourself you had fixed the time of this affair——"

"How sad," cut in Charlie, "that we pass through this life, making so many errors as we go. Me, I am stupid blunderer. Your alibi, Mr. Jaynes, has been punctured like bubble with a pin."

"What!" cried Jaynes.

Van Horn and Martino stirred with sudden interest.

"Back off and cool down," Chan continued. "And accepting my advice, speak no more of alibis. You have already said too much."

Like a man dazed, Jaynes almost literally obeyed Chan's orders. Charlie turned to Rita Ballou.

"Madam, my humblest apologies and regrets. I hold you here with the utmost grief. It has occurred to me that there is a dinner long prepared—I fear the passage of time has wrecked most of it now. But if I might suggest——"

"Oh, I couldn't eat a thing," Rita told him.

"No, of course, the very thought is horrifying," Chan nodded. "Such heartlessness would be quite out of place." Julie and Bradshaw came in. "Nevertheless I urge that you all go out to your positions at the table and at least partake of one cup of coffee. The event will shatter strain, and make easier the period of waiting. Coffee, as you know, stimulates and fortifies the mind."

"Not a bad idea," said Huntley Van Horn.

"Miss Julie——" Chan suggested.

The girl smiled wanly. "Yes, of course. I'll tell Jessop to get things ready. You must forgive me. I'd quite forgotten we had guests to-night."

She turned and went out. Charlie walked back to the small table where his task lay uncompleted. At that instant a French window facing the street was thrust suddenly open, and the trade-wind swept into the room like a miniature hurricane. Instantly the air was filled with torn bits of photograph, swirling about like snow in a Minnesota blizzard.

Kashimo stuck his head into the room. "S-s-s," he hissed. "Charlie!"

"Splendid work, Kashimo," said Chan through his teeth. "What is it now?"

"I find window unlocked," announced the Japanese triumphantly, and withdrew, closing the aperture behind him.

Concealing his disgust, Charlie moved around the room, retrieving the bits of photograph from most unlikely places. Tarneverro and some of the others came promptly to his aid. In a few moments, he again held a little packet of scraps in his hand. He walked about still seeking, but no more were in sight.

He resumed his place at the table, and for a few moments he worked hard. Then he shrugged his shoulders, and stood up.

"What's the trouble?" Tarneverro asked.

Charlie looked at him. "No use. I have now little more than half the pieces I had before." For a moment he stood staring about that innocent-appearing little group. It was in his mind to search every one of them, but a glance at Ballou reminded him that such action would mean a hot battle, and he was ever a man of peace. No, he must reach his goal by some other path. He sighed, and placed what he had left of the photograph in his pocket, as Kashimo dashed in. More in sorrow than in anger Charlie regarded his ambitious confrére.

"Detectives were practically extinct at station house when they sent you out to-night," he said.

The door-bell rang, a loud, insistent peal. Jessop being in the distant kitchen, Jimmy Bradshaw went to the door. Those in the living-room heard a few sharp quick words in the hall, and a man strode into their midst. He was a handsome fellow of forty, gray at the temples, with great poise of manner and a keen eye. The grease-paint of the theater was still on his face. He stood, looking about him.

"Good evening," he said. "I am Robert Fyfe—at one time the husband of Miss Shelah Fane. This is terrible news some one telephoned me a short time ago. I came the instant my part in the piece was finished—without stopping to remove my make-up or change my costume. Most unprofessional—but I must ask you to overlook it."

"Shall I take your overcoat?" Jimmy Bradshaw asked.

"Thank you so much." He stepped to the curtains and handed Jimmy the coat. As he turned back toward the room, Diana Dixon's scream rang out, shrill and unexpected. She was pointing at Robert Fyfe's shirtfront.

Diagonally across that white expanse lay the bright red ribbon of the

Legion of Honor. Startled, Fyfe looked down at it.

"Ah, yes," he said. "I came in my stage costume, as I told you. This week, you see, I happen to be playing the rôle of a French ambassador."

8

The Beach-comber's Shoes

During the long silence that followed, Charlie stood gravely regarding this handsome actor who had, all unknowing, made the best entrance of his career. The actor looked back at him with a cool level stare. Still no one spoke, and Fyfe began to realize that the gaze of every one in the room was upon him. Accustomed though he was to the scrutiny of crowds, he found something a bit disconcerting in this situation. He stirred uneasily, and sought for words to break the spell.

"What is all this about Shelah? I came at the earliest possible moment, as I say. Though I had not seen her for many years——"

"How many years?" cried Chan quickly.

Fyfe looked him over casually. "You must pardon me," he said, "if I do not at once grasp your position here——"

Nonchalantly Charlie pushed back the left side of his coat, revealing his badge of office. It was a gesture of which an actor could approve—business, not words.

"I am in charge," Chan said. "You were, you say, at one time husband of Miss Shelah Fane. You have not seen her for many years How many?"

Fyfe considered. "It was nine years ago, in April, when we parted. We were both playing in New York—Miss Fane in a Ziegfeld revue at the New Amsterdam, and I was doing a mystery play at the Astor. She came home one night and told me she had a splendid offer to go to Hollywood for a picture—she was so excited, so keen for the idea, that I hadn't the heart to oppose her. A week later, on an April evening, I said good-by to her at the Grand Central Station, wondering how long I could hold her love. Not very long, as it turned out. Within a year she went to Reno, and it was all quite painless—for her, I fancy. Not quite so painless for me—although I had felt it coming, that night at the station. Something had told me then that I was seeing her for the last time."

"You no doubt appeared in Los Angeles in later years," Chan suggested, "at moments when Miss Fane was in Hollywood?"

"Oh, yes—of course. But we never met."

"Do you happen to recall—were you playing in Los Angeles three years ago, in June?"

Charlie was struck by the look that came into the actor's eyes. Was it, perhaps, a look of understanding? "No," said Fyfe firmly. "I was not."

"You are plenty positive," Chan commented.

"I happen to be—yes," Fyfe replied. "Three years ago I was touring with a company that did not reach the coast."

"It is a matter that can easily be verified," the detective reminded him slowly.

"Certainly," agreed Fyfe. "Go ahead and verify it."

"Then you assert," Chan continued, "that you have not seen Shelah Fane since that moment in New York station, nine years ago?"

"I do."

"You did not see her in Honolulu to-day?"

"No."

"Or to-night?"

A pause. "No."

Julie entered. "The coffee is ready," she announced. "Please, all come into the dining-room."

"I make haste to endorse that suggestion," Chan put in.

Reluctantly they filed out, assuring one another that they could eat nothing, that the idea was unthinkable, but that perhaps a cup of coffee——Their voices trailed away beyond the curtains. Of the dinner guests, only the fortune-teller lingered.

"Please go, Mr. Tarneverro," Chan said. "Small stimulant will increase action of that fine brain on which I lean so heavily."

Tarneverro bowed. "For a moment only," he replied, and left the room.

Charlie turned to Kashimo. "As for you, I suggest you travel out to lanai, sit upon a chair and think about your sins. When you appeared a moment ago like Jack of the box, you scattered precious evidence to the winds."

"So sorry," Kashimo hissed.

"Please be sorry on the lanai," Charlie advised, and hurrying him out, closed the windows after him. Turning, he came back to Robert Fyfe. "I am happy to be alone with you," he began. "Though you may not have guessed, you are most interesting figure who has yet popped into this affair."

"Really?" The actor dropped into a chair and sat there, a striking figure in his ambassadorial costume. His manner was calm, unperturbed, and seemingly he was in the frankest of moods.

"Very interesting indeed," Charlie continued. "I gaze at you, and I ask myself—why is he lying to me?"

Fyfe half rose from his chair. "Look here. What do you mean?"

Chan shrugged. "My dear sir—what is the use? When you visit lawn pavilions to call on ex-wives, how careless to flaunt distinctive red ribbon on chest. It might even be mistaken by excitable young women for—blood. Matter of fact—it was."

"Oh," said Fyfe grimly. "I see."

"The truth—for a change," went on Chan gently.

The actor sat for a moment with his head in his hands. Finally he looked up.

"Gladly," he answered. "Though the truth is a bit—unusual. I hadn't seen Shelah Fane since that night in the station—until to-night. This morning I heard she was in town. It was quite startling—what the news did to me. You did not know Miss Fane, Mr.—er—Mr.——"

"Inspector Chan," Charlie informed him. "No, I had not the pleasure."

"It was really that—a pleasure." Fyfe half smiled. "She was a remarkable girl, aflame with life. I'd once been very fond of her and—I never got over it. No other woman ever meant anything to me after Shelah left. I couldn't hold her—I don't blame her for that—no man could hold her long. She wanted romance, excitement. Well, as I say, I learned this morning she was in town, and the news thrilled me—it was as though I heard her voice again after nine years' silence. I sent her flowers, with a message—love from some one you have forgotten. Have I said she was impetuous? Wild, unreasoning, sudden—and irresistible. My flowers had barely reached this house when she called me on the telephone. She caught me at the theater, made up, ready to go on. 'Bob,' she said, 'you must come at once. You must. I want so much to see you. I am waiting.' "

He glanced at Chan, and shrugged. "Any other woman, and I would have answered: 'After the show.' Somehow, that was never the way one replied to Shelah. 'Coming'—that was always the answer when Shelah spoke.

"It was a rather mad idea, but possible. I had arrived at the theater early, I needn't go on for forty-five minutes. I had a car and could drive out here, if I rushed it a bit, in fifteen minutes each way. So, at seven-thirty, I went into my dressing-room on the ground floor of the building, locked the door on the inside, and stepped through a window into the alley that runs along beside the theater.

"Shelah had told me about the pavilion, she said she was giving a dinner party, but that I needn't meet any of the guests—my make-up, you know, and all that. She wanted to see me alone, anyhow. I reached here about seven-forty-five. Shelah met me on the lawn, and we went to the pavilion. She looked at me in a strange way—I wondered if she still cared for me. I was shocked at the change in her—when I knew her she was fresh and lovely and so very gay. Hollywood had altered her greatly. Oh, well—none of us grows younger, I suppose. We wasted precious time in reminiscences, living over the past—somehow, it seemed to make her happy, just to remember. I was nervous about the time—I kept looking at my watch. Finally I said that I must go."

He was silent. "And then——" Chan prompted.

"Well, it was odd," Fyfe continued. "I'd got the impression over the telephone, and even more so after I saw her, that she wanted my advice about some terribly pressing matter. But when I told her I was going, she only stared at me in a sort of pitiful way. 'Bob,' she said, 'you still care for me a little, don't you?' She was standing close to me, and I took her in my arms. 'I adore you,' I cried, and—but I needn't go into that. I had that moment—no one can take it from me. Thoughts of the happy past came back—I was torn between my love for Shelah and that damn' watch ticking in my very brain. I told her hurriedly that I would return after the play, that I would see her daily during her stay here, that we would swim together—I had a wild idea that perhaps I could win her all over again. And perhaps I could have done it—but now—now——" His voice broke. "Poor Shelah! Poor girl!"

Chan nodded gravely. "It has been well said, those who live too conspicuously tempt the notice of Fate."

"And I suppose no one ever lived more conspicuously than Shelah," Fyfe added. He gave Charlie a quick penetrating glance. "Look here, Inspector—you mustn't fail me. You must find out who has done this awful thing."

"Such is my aim," Chan assured him. "You departed at once?"

"Yes. I left her standing there—standing there smiling, alive and well. Smiling, and crying too. I dashed out of the pavilion——"

"It was now what time?"

"I know only too well—it was four minutes past eight. I rushed down the drive, found my car where I'd left it before the house, and motored back to town as quickly as I could. When I stepped through the window of my dressingroom, they were hammering like wild men on my door. I opened it, said I'd been having a nap, and went out with the stage manager to the wings. I was five minute late—the stage manager showed me his watch—eight-twenty. But that wasn't serious—I went on and played my rôle—and I was just coming off after the first act when some young man telephoned me the terrible news."

He stood up. "That, Inspector Chan, is my story. My visit out here to-night may prove embarrassing for me, but I don't regret it. I saw Shelah again—I held her in my arms—and for that privilege I stand ready to pay any price you can name. Is there anything more I can tell you?"

Chan shook his head. "For the present, no. I ask that you remain on scene a brief time. Other matters may arise later."

"Of course," nodded Fyfe.

The bell rang, and Charlie himself went to the door. Peering into the night, he beheld a burly dark-skinned man in the khaki uniform of the Honolulu police.

"Ah, it is Spencer," he said, "I am very glad to have you here."

The officer came into the hall, dragging after him a figure that, anywhere save on a tropic beach, would have been quite unbelievable.

"I picked this up on Kalakaua Avenue," the policeman explained. "I thought you might like to see him. He's a little mixed on what he's been doing to-night."

The man to whome he referred shook off the officer's grip and stepped toward Charlie. "I trust we're not too late for dinner," he remarked. He stood for a moment looking about the hall and then, as though prompted by old memories, removed from his head a limp and tattered hat of straw. "My chauffeur is really rather stupid. He lost his way."

His manner was jaunty and debonair, no mean triumph considering his costume. Aside from the hat, which he now clutched in a thin freckled hand, that costume consisted of a badly soiled pair of white duck trousers, a blue shirt open at the throat, a disreputable velvet coat that had once been the color of Burgundy and the remnants of a pair of shoes, through the holes of which peered the white of his naked feet.

The buzz of conversation from the dining-room had died, the group in there appeared to be listening, and Charlie hastily held open the curtains to the living-room. "Come in here, please," he said, and they entered to find Fyfe waiting there alone. For a moment the man in the velvet coat stared at the actor, and under the yellow ragged beard that had not known barber's scissors for a month, a slow smile appeared.

"Now," Chan said. "Who are you? Where do you live?"

The man shrugged. "The name," he replied, "might be Smith."

"It might also be Jones," Charlie suggested.

"A mere matter of taste. Personally, I prefer Smith."

"And you live——"

Mr. Smith hesitated. "To put it crudely, Officer, I'm afraid I'm on the beach."

Charlie smiled. "Ah, you uphold noble tradition. What would Waikiki be without beach-comber?" He went to the window that led to the lanai and summoned Kashimo. "Kindly search this gentleman," he directed.

"By all means," the beach-comber agreed. "And if you find anything that looks like money, in heaven's name let me know about it at once."

Kashimo's search revealed little—a piece of string, a comb, a rusty pocket-knife, and an object which at first glance looked like a coin, but which turned out to be a medal. Charlie took this and studied it.

"Temple bronze medal, Third Prize, Landscapes in Oils," he read. "The Pennsylvania Academy of Fine Arts." He looked inquiringly at Smith.

The beach-comber shrugged. "Yes," he said. "I see I shall have to confess it all now—I'm a painter. Not much of a one at that—the third prize only, you will observe. The first medal was of gold—it might have come in handy of late, if I'd won it. But I didn't." He came a bit nearer. "If it's not asking too much—just what is the reason for this unwarranted intrusion into my affairs? Can't a gentleman go about his business in this town without being pawed by a fat policeman, and searched by a thin one?"

"We are sorry to inconvenience you, Mr. Smith," Charlie replied politely. "But tell me—have you been on the beach to-night?"

"I have not. I've been in town. I walked out—for reasons which we needn't take up now. I was going along Kalakaua when this cop——"

"Where down-town have you been?"

"In Aala Park."

"You talked with some one there?"

"I did. The company was not select, but I made it do."

"Not on the beach to-night." Chan was staring at the man's feet. "Kashimo, you and Spencer will kindly escort this gentleman out to spot below window where you discovered footprints, and make careful comparison."

"I know," cried the Japanese eagerly. He went out with the other policeman and the beach-comber.

Chan turned to Fyfe. "Long arduous task," he commented. "But man, without work, becomes—what? A Mr. Smith. Will you be seated at your ease?"

The others entered from the dining-room, and to them also Charlie offered chairs, which most of them accepted with poor grace. Alan Jaynes was consulting his watch. Eleven o'clock—he sought Chan's eyes. But the detective looked innocently the other way.

Tarneverro came close to Charlie. "Anything new?" he inquired, under his breath.

"The inquiry widens," Chan answered.

"I'd rather it narrowed down," replied the fortune-teller.

The two policemen and the beach-comber returned through the lanai. Spencer again had the latter firmly in his grip.

"O.K., Charlie," said the uniformed man. "The footprints under the window could have been made by only one pair of shoes in Honolulu." He pointed at the beach-comber's battered footwear. "Those shoes," he added.

Smith looked down, smiling whimsically. "They are a shocking bad pair, aren't they?" He inquired. "But Hawaii, you know, seems to have no appreciation of art. If you've noticed the paintings they buy to hang in their parlors—the wooden waves put on canvas by the local Rembrandts—I may be a third-rater, but I couldn't bring myself to do stuff like that. Not even for a new pair of——"

"Come here!" cut in Charlie sharply. "You lied to me."

Smith shrugged. "You put things bluntly for one of your race, Officer. It may be that I distorted the situation slightly in the interests of——"

"The interests of what?"

"The interests of Smith. I observe that there is something wrong here, and I much prefer to keep out of it——"

"You are in it now. Tell me—did you enter that beach house to-night?"

"I did not I'll swear to that. True, I stood beneath the window for a few minutes."

"What were you doing there?"

"I was planning to make the sand in the shelter of the pavilion my lodging for the night. It's a favorite place of mine——"

"Go back to beginning," cut in Chan. "The truth this time."

"I hadn't been out to the beach for three days and nights," the man told him. "I got a little money, and I've been stopping down-town. When I was out here last, this house was unoccupied. To-day my money was gone—I'm expecting a check—it hasn't come." He paused. "Rotten mail service out here. If I could only get back to the mainland——"

"Your money was gone," Charlie interrupted.

"Yes—so I was forced back to my old couch under the palm trees. I walked out from town, and got to the beach——"

"At what time?"

"My dear sir,—you embarrass me. If you will take a stroll along Hotel Street, you will see my watch hanging in a certain window. I often go and look at it myself."

"No matter. You got to the beach."

"I did. It's public, you know—this one out here. It belongs to everybody. I was surprised to see a light in the pavilion. Somebody's rented the house, I thought. The curtain of that window was down, but it was flapping in the wind. I heard voices inside—a man's and a woman's—I wondered whether it was such a good place to sleep, after all."

He paused. Charlie's eyes were on Robert Fyfe. The actor was leaning forward with a fierce intensity, staring at the beach-comber, his hands clenched until the knuckles showed white.

"I just stood there," Smith continued. "The curtain flopped about—and I got a good look at the man."

"Ah, yes," Charlie nodded. "What man?"

"Why, that fellow there," Smith said. He pointed at Fyfe. "The chap with the red ribbon across his shirt-front. I haven't seen one of those ribbons since the time when I was studying at Julien's, in Paris, and our ambassador invited me round for dinner. It's a fact. He came from my town—an old friend of my father——"

"No matter," Charlie cut in. "You stood there, peeping beneath the curtain——"

"What do you mean?" cried the beach-comber. "Don't judge a man by his clothes, please. I wasn't spying. If I caught a glimpse, as I did, it was unavoidable. They were talking fast, those two—this man, and the woman."

"Yes. And perhaps—equally unavoidable, do not misunderstand me—you heard what they said?"

Smith hesitated. "Well—as a matter of fact—I did. I heard her tell him——"

With a little cry, Robert Fyfe leaped forward. He pushed the beach-comber aside and stood before Charlie. His face was deathly pale, but his eyes did not falter.

"Drop it," he said hoarsely. "I can put an end to your investigation here and now. I killed Shelah Fane, and I'm willing to pay for it."

A shocked silence greeted his words. Calm, unmoved, and quite motionless, Chan stared into the man's face.

"You killed Miss Fane?"

"I did."

"For what reason?"

"I wanted her to come back to me. I couldn't live without her. I pleaded and begged—and she wouldn't listen. She laughed at me—she said there wasn't a chance. She drove me to it—I killed her. I had to do it."

"You killed her—with what?"

"With a knife I carried as one of the props in the play."

"Where is it now?"

"I threw it into a swamp on my way to town."

"You can lead me to the spot?"

"I can try."

Chan turned away.

Alan Jaynes was on his feet. "Eleven-ten," he cried. "I can just make the boat if I hurry, Inspector. Of course, you're not going to hold me now."

"But I do hold you," Charlie answered. "Spencer, if this man makes another move, kindly place him beneath arrest."

"Are you mad?" Jaynes cried. "You have your confession, haven't you——"

"With regard to that," said Charlie, "wait just a moment, please." He turned back to Fyfe, who was standing quietly beside him. "You left the pavilion, Mr. Fyfe, at four minutes past eight?"

"I did."

"You had already killed Shelah Fane?"

"I had."

"You drove to the theater and were in the wings of same at twenty minutes past eight?"

"Yes—I told you all that."

"The stage manager will swear that you were there at twenty minutes past eight?"

"Of course—of course."

Chan stared at him. "Yet at twelve minutes past eight," he said, "Shelah Fane was seen alive and well."

"What's that!" Tarneverro cried.

"Pardon—I am speaking with this other gentleman. At twelve minutes past eight, Mr. Fyfe, Shelah Fane was seen alive and well. How do you account for that?"

Fyfe dropped into a chair and covered his face with his hands.

"I do not understand you," Charlie said gently. "You wish me to believe you killed Shelah Fane. Yet, of all the people in this room, you alone have unshakable alibi."

9

Eighteen Important Minutes

No one spoke. Outside what Jimmy Bradshaw had called the silken surf broke once again on the coral sand. The crash died away, and inside that crowded room there was no sound save the ticking of a small clock on a mantel beneath which fires were rarely lighted. With a gesture of despair, Alan Jaynes stepped to a table and, striking a match, applied it to one of his small cigars. Charlie crossed over and laid his hand on Fyfe's shoulder.

"Why have you confessed to a deed you did not perform?" he asked. "That is something I warmly desire to know."

The actor made no answer, nor did he so much as look up. Charlie turned to face Tarneverro.

"So Shelah Fane was seen alive at twelve minutes past eight?" the fortune-teller remarked suavely. "Would you mind telling me how long you have known that?"

Charlie smiled. "If only it happened you understood Chinese language," he replied. "I would not find it necessary to elucidate." He went to the door, and called Jessop. When the butler appeared, Chan asked that he send in Wu Kno-ching at once. "I am doing something now for your benefit alone, Mr. Tarneverro," he added.

"You are a considerate man, Inspector," the fortune-teller answered.

The old Chinese shuffled into the room; he was, evidently, in a rather peevish frame of mind. His carefully prepared dinner had been ruined by the events of this tragic evening, and he was in no mood to accept the philosophy of the patient K'ung-fu-tsze.

Chan talked with him for a moment, again in Cantonese, and then turned to Tarneverro. "I request that he verify story he told me in native language when I interrogated him in this room some while ago," he explained. "Wu, you have said you lingered in kitchen with Jessop and Anna when clock was speaking the hour of eight. You fretted because dinner was seemingly movable feast, and also because bootlegger of your choice had not shown up and was causing you to lose much face. Am I correct so far?"

"Bootleggah velly late," nodded Wu.

"But at ten minutes past hour, erring friend of yours makes panting appearance with hotly desired liquids. While Jessop begins task of making this poison palatable, you wander away in search of mistress." Chan glanced at the fortune-teller. "Wu informal type servant who pops up anywhere on place with great bland look. Characteristic of the race." He resumed his remarks to the Chinese. "You discover Miss Shelah Fane alone in pavilion. Vindicating your honor, you announce bootlegger friend has finally appeared. What did Missie say?"

"Missie look-see watch, say twelve minutes aftah eight plitty muchee time bootleggah come. I say plitty muchee time dinnah gets on table. Mebbe that can happen now if not new cook needed heah *wikiwiki*."

"Yes. Then she ordered you to get out and not annoy her with your bothers. So you went back to kitchen. That's what you told me before, isn't it?"

"Yes, boss."

"All same true, eh, Wu?"

"Yes, boss. Wha' foah my tell lie to you?"

"All right. You can go now."

"My go, boss."

As the old man moved silently away on his velvet slippers, Charlie turned to meet the penetrating gaze of Tarneverro. "All of which is very interesting," the fortune-teller said coldly. "I perceive that when I pointed out to you the matter of the watch, I was merely wasting my breath. You already knew that Shelah Fane had not been murdered at two minutes past eight."

Charlie laid a conciliatory hand on Tarneverro's arm. "Pray do not take offense. I knew Miss Fane had been seen at that later hour, yes; but I was still uncertain of how watch had been manipulated. I listened, curious and then entranced, to your logical explanation. Could I, at its finish, rudely cry thanks for nothing? A gentleman is always courteous. Much better I shower you with well-deserved words of praise, so you go forward with vigorous and triumphant mood of heart."

"Is that so?" remarked Tarneverro, moving off.

Charlie stepped up to the beach-comber. "Mr. Smith," he said.

"Right here, Officer," Smith answered. "I was afraid you were going to forget me. What can I do for you now?"

"A moment ago you began interesting recital of conversation overheard between this gentleman with ribbon-bedecked shirt-front and lady he met in pavilion to-night. At crucial point you suffered very blunt interruption.

I am most eager that you return to subject at once."

Fyfe rose to his feet, and stared hard at the derelict in the velvet coat. Smith looked back at him, and a speculative, cunning look flashed into his pale gray eyes.

"Oh, yes," he said slowly. "I was interrupted, wasn't I? But I'm used to that. Sure—sure, I was telling you that I heard them talking together. Well, there's no need to go on with it now. I've nothing to add to what the gentleman has already told you." Fyfe turned away. "He was pleading with her to come back to him—said he loved her, and all that. And she wouldn't listen to him. I felt rather sorry for him—I've been in that position myself. I heard her say: 'Oh, Bob—what's the use?' He went on insisting. Every now and then he looked at his watch. 'My time's up,' he said at last. 'I've got to go. We'll thrash this out later.' I heard the slam of the door——"

"And the woman was alone in the room—alive and well. You are sure of that?"

"Yes—the curtain was flapping—I saw her after he left. She was there alone—moving about."

With a puzzled frown, Charlie glanced at Robert Fyfe. "You are not content with one alibi. You have now a second. I do not understand you, Mr. Fyfe."

The actor shrugged. "I find it hard to understand myself, Inspector. A fit of temperament, perhaps. We stage people are inclined to be overly dramatic."

"Then you withdraw your confession?"

"What else can I do?" Chan did not overlook the glance that passed between the immaculate actor and the battered beach-comber. "Others have withdrawn it for me. I did not kill Shelah—that's quite true. But I thought it would be better if——"

"If what?"

"Nothing."

"You thought it would be better if my investigation went no further."

"Oh, not at all."

"Something came out in that conversation with your ex-wife which you feared this man had overheard. Something you want suppressed."

"You have a keen imagination, Inspector."

"Also, I have a custom to discover facts which some people want to hide. Your move has been to this moment successful—but you and I have not finished with each other, Mr. Fyfe."

"I am at your service at any time, sir."

"Thank you so much, but I hope the next time we meet your service will be of more value to my humble self." He looked at Smith. "As for you, though I am desolated by acute pain to make so rude a remark, I believe you mix plenty falsehood with your truth."

The beach-comber shrugged. "There you go—judging a man by his clothes again."

"Not by your clothes, which are silent, but by your tongue, which speaks," Charlie told him. "Mr. Spencer, will you kindly take this man to station house and make record of his finger-prints."

"So many attentions," Smith put in. "I only hope they don't turn my head."

"After which," Chan continued, "you may release him—for time being."

"All right, Charlie," Spencer said.

"One other thing. Pause a moment while I introduce to you all people in this room." Gravely he went through that somewhat lengthy ceremony.

"You have also seen butler and cook. There is in addition a maid, whom I ask that you pause and make note of on your way out. You will speed from station without delay to Pier Seven, from which the boat *Oceanic* sails for coast at midnight. No person you have seen in this house is to sail on that boat. You understand?"

"Sure, Charlie—I'll attend to it," Spencer nodded.

Jaynes stepped forward. "I'd like to remind you that my luggage is aboard that ship—some of it in the hold——"

Charlie nodded. "How fortunate you spoke of that. Mr. Spencer, kindly see that all effects in stateroom belonging to Mr. Jaynes are put ashore in your care. Arrange for such as lie in hold to be guarded for the gentleman at San Francisco dock. Explain he is detained by important business and may be in Honolulu for some time. Is that satisfactory, Mr. Jaynes?"

"It's damned unsatisfactory," the Britisher growled, "but I presume I shall have to make the best of it."

"All you can do," nodded Charlie. "Kashimo, you will accompany Mr. Spencer down-town. Your passionate labors in this house are ended for the night. You retire in glory—and if you come back through unexpected window, you retire for ever. Keep same in mind."

The apprentice detective nodded, and went out after Spencer and the beach-comber. Robert Fyfe stepped forward.

"Is there any necessity for my staying any longer?" he inquired.

Charlie studied him thoughtfully. "I think not. You may go along. You and I will talk together when I have more leisure."

"Any time, Inspector." Fyfe went to the curtains, and held them open. "I am stopping at the Waioli Hotel, on Fort Street," he added. "Drop in at your convenience, won't you? Good night." He went into the hall, where Spencer could be heard talking with the maid. The door slammed behind him, and a second later, the two policemen and Smith also departed.

Charlie stood regarding the tired group in the living-room. "Accept my advice and take heart," he said. "We give Mr. Spencer generous handicap on journey to pier, and then I find great joy releasing this company at last. While we are waiting, there are one or two matters. Since first I spoke with you, it has been found necessary to alter views. Then hour of tragedy was thought certain at two minutes past eight. Now we must advance and say, dreadful event happened some time between twelve minutes past eight and the half-hour. Eighteen minutes there—eighteen important minutes. Each of us must ask himself: What was I doing in those eighteen minutes?"

He paused. His eyes were bright, his manner quite keen and alive—for him. The Chinese are at their best at night; it is their favorite time. But he was alone in his vigor, the others were exhausted and drooping, the make-up of the women stood out, unnatural and far from pleasing, against the pallor of their weariness.

"Eighteen important minutes," Chan repeated. "Miss Dixon, Miss Julie and Mr. Bradshaw disported gaily in breakers, visiting beach occasionally. On that beach Mrs. Ballou sat and idly passed time until dinner. For final ten of those minutes, Mr. Ballou wandered about, no one can say where——"

"I can say where," Ballou cut in. "I came into this room—the butler will verify that. I strolled in here and smoked a cigarette he gave me."

"He remained with you while you smoked it?"

"No—he didn't. He lighted it for me, and went out. When he returned, I was sitting in the same chair——"

"You wish me to note that, eh?" Charlie smiled.

"I don't care whether you note it or not."

Charlie took out a handkerchief and wiped the perspiration from his brow. The tropic night was beginning to live up to its reputation.

"I turn now to the four gentlemen whose alibis have been so rudely shattered. I know where they were at two minutes past eight, but after that——"

"Take me first," said Tarneverro. "You saw me go to join those two people in the lounge of the hotel—they are old friends of mine from Australia. We remained there for a few minutes after you left, and then I suggested that we go out on the lanai that faces the palm court. We did so, and for a time sat and chatted. When I finally looked at my watch, it was precisely eight-thirty. I remarked on the hour and said I was sorry, but I had to go along. We all went inside, I ran up to get my hat, and when I came back to the lobby, I happened on you near the door."

Charlie studied his face. "Your old friends will be willing to swear to all this?"

"I can see no reason why they shouldn't. They know it's true."

Chan smiled. "I congratulate you, Mr. Tarneverro."

"I congratulate myself, Inspector. You may recall that I told you I had another tree."

"Mr. Jaynes," said Chan, turning to the Britisher.

Jaynes shrugged hopelessly. "I have no alibi," he said. "During those eighteen minutes, I was wandering along the beach alone. Make what you wish of it. I didn't come down here."

"Mr. Van Horn—you did come down here?" Charlie addressed the picture actor.

"I did, worse luck," shrugged Van Horn. "The first time in a long and honorable career that I ever got to a party ahead of the hour set. It will be a lesson to me—I can tell you that."

"It was, I believe, eight-fifteen when Jessop admitted you?"

"About that time—yes. He told me that the party—or what there was of it—had moved to the beach. I went out on the lawn. I saw a light in a building which Jessop told me was a summer-house, and I thought of going there. I wish to heaven I had. But I heard voices down by the water, so I went there instead. I sat down by Rita Ballou—but you know all that."

Chan nodded. "Only one remains. Mr. Martino?"

The director frowned. "Like Huntley and Mr. Jaynes," he said, "I have no alibi worth mentioning. You wrecked me along with them when you smashed that eight-two theory." He took a handkerchief from a side pocket and mopped his forehead. "After Jaynes left me and started down the beach, I sat in one of the hotel swings near the water. I should have been busy getting myself a good alibi, I suppose, but I'm not so clever as Mr. Tarneverro here." He gave the fortune-teller an unfriendly look. "So I just sat alone—the scene looked rather good to me. I wished I could get it into a picture—the purple starry sky, the yellow lamps along the water-front, the black hulk of Diamond Head. A picture in color—we'll have 'em that way before long. I amused myself thinking up a possible story—you can't depend on authors for anything. Presently I looked at my watch. It was eighty-twenty-five, so I went to my room to brush up and get my hat. When I came down I met you and Tarneverro here, and heard the news of Miss Fane's murder."

Charlie stood looking thoughtfully at the director. Suddenly he was pushed aside as Tarneverro strode forward.

"That's a nasty scratch on your forehead, Martino," the fortune-teller cried.

Startled, the director put his hand to his brow, and on one finger, as he took it away, he noted a trace of red.

"By jove," he said, "that's odd——"

"You'd better turn over to Inspector Chan the handkerchief you just replaced in your pocket."

"What handkerchief?" Martino produced the one which he had recently passed across his forehead. "Oh, this!"

"I will take it, please," said Charlie. He spread the white square of silk on the table and brought out his magnifying-glass. For a moment he studied the center of the square, then ran his fingers lightly across it. He looked up.

"A queer thing, Mr. Martino," he remarked. "There exist, caught in mesh of this cloth, a few thin splinters of glass. How would you explain that?"

Martino rose quickly, and with a serious face bent over the table. "I can't explain it," he said. "I can't even explain how that handkerchief came to be in my pocket."

Chan regarded him intently. "It is not your property?" he inquired.

"It certainly isn't," the director replied. "I carry two handkerchiefs with my evening clothes. One here"—he indicated his breast pocket above which the ends of a handkerchief were showing—"and another in my hip pocket." He produced a second. "Certainly I'd have no use for a third. I just happened to reach into my side pocket, my hand touched this, and I used it. But I never put it there, and it isn't mine."

"A likely story," Tarneverro sneered.

"My dear Tarneverro," the director said, "when you've made as many pictures as I have, you'll realize that the truth often sounds less probable than fiction." He picked up the little square of silk and handed it to Charlie. "By the way, there's a laundry mark in one corner of that."

"I know," Chan nodded. He stood for a moment, looking at the tiny letter *B* done with black ink on the silk border. He glanced over at Wilkie Ballou. The planter stared back at him, and taking a handkerchief from his own pocket, casually mopped his brow.

10

"Shelah from Denny"

Shrugging his broad shoulders, Charlie turned back to Martino. The director's face was even more crimson than usual, and he was breathing hard.

"Do you wish to make statement," Chan asked, "as to moment when you think this object was placed on your person?"

Martino considered. "When we were leaving the dining room a while back," he said, "we were all crowded together round the door. I thought then that I felt a little tug at my pocket."

"Just who was near you at that instant?"

"It's hard to say. Everybody was there together. The matter is serious, and I don't like to guess." He paused, and glanced at the fortune-teller. "I do recall that Mr. Tarneverro wasn't far away."

"Is that an accusation?" asked Tarneverro coldly.

"Not precisely. I can't be sure——"

"You'd like nothing better than to be sure," the fortune-teller suggested.

Martino laughed. "You've hit it there, my friend. I haven't much love for you, and you know it. If I'd had my way, you'd have been run out of Hollywood long ago."

"Failing that, you've gone about secretly warning the women against me."

"What do you mean, secretly? I've done it openly, and you know it. I've told them to keep away from you——"

"Why?"

"I don't like the look in your eyes, my friend. What was it you told poor Shelah this morning? What did she tell you?"

"That is something I'd not be likely to discuss with you. So you sat on the beach by the water, did you?"

"Oh, don't get too cocky over that alibi of yours," Martino cried. "How did you happen to have it so pat and ready? Reading the future again, eh?"

"Gentlemen, gentlemen," Charlie protested. "We are arriving precisely nowhere by this. I perceive that nerves are very much up on edge, and I am glad to push open doors and put quick end to investigation. You are all free to depart."

There was an instant dash for the hall. Chan followed.

"Just one word to add," he said, "though I am certain that by now the buzz of my voice in your ears must be most tiresome sound. But please remember—you rest on small island in the midst of broad Pacific Ocean. Attempt by any one of you to go aboard ship will be instantly known to us, and regarded with dark suspicious eye. Stay on, I beg of you, and enjoy beauties of spot, on which subject Mr. Bradshaw will be happy to make oration for you any time, any place."

"That's right," the boy nodded. "Loaf on a palm-fringed shore and forget your troubles. Somewhere winter is raging——"

"In July?' Van Horn inquired.

"Sure—at the South Pole, for example. Put Hollywood out of your thoughts. Remember—Hawaii has the climate California thinks it has."

The door closed behind Ballou and his wife. Van Horn, Martino and Jaynes followed promptly. Bradshaw returned to the living-room, where Julie and Diana had remained, leaving the fortune-teller and Charlie in the hall. Tarneverro picked up his hat.

"Inspector," he remarked, "you have my sympathy. You are up against a puzzling case."

"Also I have your help," Chan reminded him. "The thought consoles me."

Tarneverro shook his head. "I'm afraid you over-estimate my powers. But whatever they are, they are arranged on your side. When am I to see you again?"

"I will call on you to-morrow morning," Chan answered. "We will have good long talk. Perhaps, thinking deeply into matter over night, each of us will have new ideas to offer."

"I shall try to supply my share," nodded Tarneverro, and went out. For a moment Charlie stood looking at the door through which he had gone, then turning, he went into the living-room.

"Miss Dixon," he said, "may I make further request of you? Will you ascend stairs with me and point out various rooms, naming the persons to whom they have been assigned? I still have a little searching to do before repose."

"Of course," nodded the actress, "and speaking of repose, I hope you'll search my room first. I feel all in after this dreadful evening."

She and Charlie disappeared. With a forlorn gesture, Julie sank into a chair.

"Poor kid!" said Mr. Bradshaw.

"Oh, Jimmy—it *has* been a dreadful evening, hasn't it?"

"It surely has. Think, Julie, think. You were closer to Shelah Fane than any one else. Have you no idea who did—this terrible thing?"

She shook her head. "I can't imagine. Of course, Shelah had enemies—all successful people have—she was envied, perhaps even hated. But I never dreamed any one hated her as much as this. It's just unbelievable, that's all."

The boy sat down beside her. "Let's forget it for a while. How about you? What are you going to do now?"

"Oh—I suppose I'll go back where I came from."

"Where did you come from? You haven't told me."

"From a theatrical boarding-house in Chicago—I was traveling with my mother when she—she left me. Stage people, you see, all my folks—father too. Mother called San Francisco home, though she seldom saw it. But she was born there—so many good actors were, you know. And she——"

"She was one of the best, I guess," said Jimmy Bradshaw.

"I thought so. I've got a grandmother there now—seventy-two, but she goes trouping occasionally—she's such a darling, Jimmy. I think I'll go to her, and get some sort of job—I could make good in an office, I believe. Grandmother would be glad to have me; we're all that's left of—us."

Bradshaw pulled himself together. "If no one else wants to speak, may I say a few words about Hawaii? Everywhere we have poetry and glamour. The climate breeds happiness and laughter, a natural reflection of the sunlight, the rainbows and the purple hills. Here there are no sunstrokes and no snow. Honolulu has its message of beauty for every heart. As for——"

"Jimmy, what in the world——"

"As for the people, where nature is kind man can not help but be. You will find——"

"I don't get you, Jimmy."

"It's simple enough. I've sold this place to fifty thousand tourists, and now I want to sell it to you. As a substitute for grandmother, you see. No doubt she's a darling, as you say. Maybe I'm not, but I'm young yet. For of course it isn't just Honolulu I'm selling. I'm thrown in, you know. How about it, Julie? A little bungalow nestling under two mortgages and a bougainvillea vine——"

"You—you mean you love me, Jimmy?" the girl asked.

"Oh, lord—did I omit that line? I shall have to rewrite the whole darn piece. Naturally, I love you. Who wouldn't? It may not be the most fitting time for me to say all this, but I don't want you to think that I've fallen into the habit of putting things off, just because I live in the lazy latitudes. I'm crazy about you, and before you write grandmother to come down and meet your boat—she might be away trouping anyhow—I want you to give a thought to Hawaii—and to me. Will you do it, Julie?"

She nodded. "I will, Jimmy."

"That's good enough for me," he smiled.

Chan came silently into the room, and the boy stood up. "Well, Charlie, you ready to go along? I let my brother have my car to-night, so I'm honoring you with my presence in that famous flivver of yours."

"You will be remarkably welcome," Chan told him. "Yes—I travel townward almost at once. There remains one little matter——"

Anna, the maid, came hurriedly into the room. "Miss Dixon said you wanted to see me," she remarked to Chan.

He nodded. "A trifling affair. You told me earlier this evening that a certain ring was missing from Miss Fane's finger after the homicide. An emerald ring."

"I did, sir."

Julie O'Neill was leaning forward, breathless, her eyes wide.

"Is this the ring?" Chan suddenly produced a platinum band decorated with a surprising stone that flashed green in the brightly lighted room.

"That is it, sir," Anna nodded.

Chan turned to Julie. "So sorry to drag you in. But will you kindly tell me—how does it happen I find this bauble in the drawer of your dressing-table?" The girl gasped, and Jimmy Bradshaw looked at her in amazement. "I am very sorry this question comes out, which disappoints me sadly," Charlie continued. "But I should say, things need explanation."

"It's very simple," answered Julie in a low voice.

"Naturally," bowed Chan. "Just how simple, according to your story?"

"Well." She hesitated. "There are only a few of us here—I can speak frankly. Shelah was always hard up. Somehow money meant nothing to her, it slipped through her fingers, it was gone a moment after she got it. She came back from the South Seas in her usual state—more or less broke. Every one was always cheating her, stealing from her——"

"Every one?" Chan repeated. "You mean her servants, perhaps?"

"Some of them, yes—when they had a chance. But that doesn't matter. Shelah arrived here in need of money, as always. She'd drawn all the advance she could get from the company—they haven't been as generous of late as they used to be. To-day, just after she reached the house, she sent for me and said she must have ready money at once. She gave me this ring and told me to sell it for her, if I could. I was to make a round of the jewelers immediately—this afternoon. But I put it off. I wasn't keen for the job. However, I fully intended to go in the morning—if this thing hadn't happened to-night. That's how I chanced to have the ring."

Chan considered. "She gave it to you just after she reached house. At what time, precisely?"

"At eight o'clock this morning."

"You have had it ever since?"

"Yes, of course. I put it in that drawer—I thought it would be safe there."

"That is all you wish to tell me?"

"That is all." The girl seemed on the point of tears.

Charlie turned to the maid. "You may go, Anna," he said.

"Very good, sir." Anna glanced at the girl, and then went out.

Charlie sighed heavily. Even though he came of a nocturnal race, the night was beginning to wear on him. He took the ring beneath a light and examined it with his magnifying-glass. There was, he noted, an inscription inside. "Shelah from Denny." So Denny Mayo came back into the case? Chan shrugged.

When he turned about, he perceived that Julie was weeping silently. Bradshaw had put his arm about her shoulder. "That's all right, honey," the boy said. "Charlie believes you. Don't you, Charlie?"

Chan bowed from the waist. "In the presence of so much charm, could

I have brutal doubts? Miss Julie, I am sorrowed to perceive your over-wrought state. Mr. Bradshaw and I depart at once, leaving to you the solace of slumber. You have youth, and sleep will come. I bid you most sympathetic good night."

He disappeared through the curtains, and with a few whispered words to the girl, Bradshaw followed. Jessop, restraining a yawn but firmly polite as always, saw them out. On the steps Charlie stood for a moment, staring at the sky and drawing in a deep breath of the open air.

"It is something to recall," he said, "that during long painful ordeal in that house, stars were still shining and soft tropic night progressed as usual. What have I not been through? A brief respite will be lovely as soft music in the rain."

They got into his car, waiting alone and lonely in the drive.

"Pretty much up against it, eh, Charlie?" the boy suggested.

Chan nodded. "Dizzy feeling causes my head to circulate. I have upearthed so much, and yet I have upearthed nothing." They bowled along, past the Moana Hotel, in unaccustomed darkness now. The pink walls of the Grand glowed with a new splendor in the moonlight. "When you telephoned me," Chan added, "I was about to begin serious operation on a small fish. One taste I had was excellent. Alas! little fish and I will never meet again."

"A shame to spoil your dinner," Bradshaw replied.

"I will be content if your news does not also spoil my reputation," Charlie told him. "How am I going to emerge from the affair? In shining garments of success, or in sackcloth with ashes?"

"I called up the morning paper," the boy told him. "Used to work there, you know. They were short of men at the moment, and I landed the job of covering the story so far. Got to go back now and write it. I'll say that the police haven't a notion just at present—is that correct?"

Charlie barely avoided a collision with the curb. "Have you no better understanding of your task than that? Say nothing of the sort. Police have many clues and expect early arrest."

"But that's the same old bunk, Charlie. And judging from your talk, it isn't true in this case."

"Seldom true in any case," Chan reminded him. "You should know that."

"Well, I'll say it—to please you, Charlie. By the way, did I hear Tarneverro intimate he was working with you?"

"Yes—he fancies himself as bright assistant."

"He may be bright all right—but are you keen for his help?"

Charlie shrugged. "The bird chooses the tree, not the tree the bird," he remarked.

"Well, Tarneverro's a queer bird, all right. He gives me a funny sensation when I look at him." They rode on in silence for a time. "Anyhow, one thing's certain," the boy said at last.

"Is that really so?" Chan inquired. "Name it, please. I seem to have overlooked it in my haste."

"I mean—Julie had nothing to do with this affair."

Charlie grinned in the dark. "I have recollections myself," he said.

"Of what?"

"Being young—and muddled by love. Since I am now the father of eleven children, it is necessarily some time since I went about with head in clouds and warmly beating heart. But memories remain."

"Oh, nonsense," protested Bradshaw. "I'm looking at this thing coldly—as a rank outsider."

"Then I humbly suggest you have old Hawaii moon overhauled at once," commented Chan. "For it must be losing magic power you write about so glowingly.".

He drew up before the newspaper office, the sound of his brakes grating noisily in the deserted street. On the lower floor of the building one lonely light burned dimly, but the up-stairs windows were bright yellow with activity. There men sat sorting the cable news that was flowing in from the far corners of the world, from Europe, Asia, the mainland—brief bits of information thought worthy of transmission to this small island dreaming in the midst of the great Pacific.

Jimmy Bradshaw moved as though to alight, then paused. Out of the corner of his eye he glanced at Charlie. "I don't suppose I can have it now, can I?" he inquired.

"You can not," Chan replied firmly.

"What are you talking about?" asked the boy innocently.

"Same thing you are," Charlie grinned.

"I was referring to that handkerchief you took away from the picture director."

"So was I," answered Charlie blandly.

"Then you knew it was mine?"

"I gathered that, yes. Small initial *B* was on it. Also I perceived you perspiring with no means to quench it. I was greatly moved to admiration by your restraint—not once did you make use of coat sleeve. You are going to tell me that it was taken from your pocket?"

"It must have been—yes."

"At what moment?"

"I don't know, but I suppose some one took it when I was in swimming."

"You are sure of that?"

"Well, it seems the only possible explanation. But I didn't notice it was gone until a long time afterward."

"And a still longer time after that—you mention the affair to me."

"It's my confounded modesty again, Charlie," the boy laughed. "I just couldn't stand the limelight. Let me look at the thing, anyhow."

Charlie handed it over, and Bradshaw examined it carefully in the dashboard light. "Mine all right." He pointed at the mark. "That's my alias at the laundry. This is pretty sinister, if you ask me."

Charlie took back the handkerchief. "I have very good notion to put you in jail," he remarked.

"And trifle with the power of the press?" the boy reminded him. "Think twice, Charlie. I didn't do away with our distinguished visitor. That's not the sort of Hawaiian hospitality I go in for." He hesitated. "I could use that handkerchief to-night."

"So could I," Chan answered.

"Oh, well, then I'll just have to drip perspiration on this immortal story I'm about to write. So long, Inspector."

"So long," Chan returned. "And please keep handkerchief out of that same story, and out of your conversation, or you will hear from me."

"O.K., Charlie. It stays a big secret. Nobody in on it but you and me—and the laundry."

11

Midnight in Honolulu

Chan drove slowly on to Halekaua Hale, at the foot of Bethel Street, the home of the police. Parking his car, he ascended the worn stone steps. A light was burning in the detectives' room, and going in, he encountered his Chief.

"Hello, Charlie," that gentleman said. "I've been waiting for you. Drove over to Kalaua to-night, or I'd have been with you down the beach. This is a pretty mix-up, isn't it? Got anything yet?"

Sadly Chan shook his head. He glanced at his watch. "The story has length," he suggested.

"Guess I'd better hear it, anyhow," replied the Chief. In him, there was no lack of vigor. The ride in the moonlight to Kalaua had been restful and refreshing.

Charlie sat down and began to talk, while his Chief listened intently. He took up first the scene of the murder, the absence of any weapon, the unsuccessful attempt of the murderer to fix the moment of the crime at two minutes past eight. Coming to the question of clues, he mentioned the loss of the diamond pin which had held the orchids.

"That's something," nodded the Chief, lighting a cigar.

Chan shrugged. "Something we do not possess," he pointed out. He went on to repeat Shelah Fane's story of her presence at the murder of Denny Mayo—the tale she had told Tarneverro, according to the fortune-teller, that morning.

"Fine—fine," cried the Chief. "That gives you the motive, Charlie. Now if she had only written down the name, as this Tarneverro wanted her to——"

With acute distaste, Charlie added the incident of the letter's loss. His Chief looked at him with surprise and a marked disapproval.

"Never knew anything like that to happen to you before. Lose your grip, Charlie?"

"For a moment, I certainly lost grip and letter too," Chan replied ruefully. "As the matter turned out, it did not have much importance." His face brightened as he added the later discovery of the letter under the rug, proving that it was of no value save as a corroboration of Tarneverro's story. He went on to the destruction of the portrait over which Shelah Fane had been seen weeping bitterly in the afternoon.

"Some one didn't want you to see it," frowned the Chief.

"I arrived at the same deduction myself," Charlie admitted. He pictured the arrival of Robert Fyfe on what was obviously his second visit to Waikiki within a few hours, and then turned to the subject of the beach-comber.

"We took his finger-prints and let him go," put in the Chief. "He hasn't nerve enough to kill a fly."

Chan nodded. "You are no doubt correct in such surmise." His report of Fyfe's subsequent, easily punctured confession, evidently puzzled his superior. He mentioned the handkerchief with the telltale slivers of glass found in Martino's pocket, and Jimmy Bradshaw's somewhat belated claim to its ownership. He was by this time rather out of breath. "So matter stands at present," he finished.

His Chief was looking at him with an amused smile. "Well, Charlie, sometimes I've thought you weren't entirely satisfied here since your return from the mainland," he said. "Pretty quiet, you thought it. No big cases like over there. Just chasing a few scared gamblers down an alley—not very thrilling, was it? Honolulu didn't seem to be big enough for you any more. I guess it's big enough to-night."

"I experienced uncomfortable feeling maybe it is too big," Chan admitted. "How will I come out of this? Considerable puzzle, if inquiry is made of me."

"We mustn't let it stump us," replied the Chief briskly. He was an intelligent man, and he knew where to lean. He foresaw that he was going to do some heavy leaning in the next few days. With an appraising glance, he surveyed his assistant. Charlie looked sleepy and somewhat worn—nothing alert, nothing clever in his appearance now. The Chief consoled himself with memories. Chan, he reflected, was ever keener than he looked.

He considered. "This Tarneverro, Charlie,—what sort of fellow is he?"

Chan brightened. "Ah, perhaps you go to heart of the matter. Tarneverro appears dark as rainy night, but it is his business to act so. He owns a quick mind. And he seems fiercely eager to assist poor policeman like me."

"A bit too eager, maybe?"

Charlie nodded. "I have thought of that. But consider—he offers to produce testimony of old couple with whom he sat until moment murder was discovered. Truth of that will be examined to-morrow, but I do not doubt it. No—I am plenty certain he did not visit house of Shelah Fane until I took him there. Other points absolve him."

"What, for example?"

"I have told you he spoke to me before murder was done, hinting we would to-night make arrest in famous case. That would have been strangely foolish move if he contemplated murder himself. And Tarneverro is not foolish—he goes far the other way. Then, too, indicating he has earnest desire to assist he points out the matter of the watch. It was bright act—not very necessary since I already knew facts from Wu Kno-ching—but all same plenty good proof he sincerely aims to help. No, I do not believe him guilty killer, and yet——"

"Yet what, Charlie?"

"I prefer to hold that safe in mind for the present. It may mean much, and it may mean nothing."

"You've got something on Tarneverro?" asked the Chief, looking at him keenly.

"With regard to killing—not one solitary thing. At moment when that took place, I believe he was most decidedly elsewhere. Gazing in another direction—kindly permit that I gaze that way a few hours longer before I divulge my thoughts." The plump detective put one hand to his head. "*Haie*, just now I wander, lost in maze of doubts and questionings."

"You'll have to cut that out, Charlie," his Chief told him in a kindly but somewhat worried tone. "The honor of the force is at stake. If these people are going to come over here to our quiet little city and murder each other at Waikiki, we've got to prove to them that they can't get away with it. I rely on you."

Chan bowed. "I'm afraid you do. Appreciate the distinction, and will do all my humble talents permit. Now I will wish you good night. The evening has worn on me like some prolonged dispute."

He went out into the battered old hall, just as Spencer entered from the street. Chan looked at his watch.

"The *Oceanic* has sailed?" he inquired.

"Yeah—she's out."

"With none of our friends aboard, I trust?" Chan said.

"None that I saw goin' aboard—and I guess I was there first. One of 'em showed up, though."

"Which one?"

"That Alan Jaynes. He came in a car from the Grand Hotel, an' collected his baggage. I heard him swearin' under his breath when the ship backed away from the pier. I helped him load up, an' he went back to the beach. He give me a message for you."

"What was that?"

"He said he was sailing on the next ship, and all hell couldn't stop him."

Charlie smiled. "None the less, I shall see that the province he mentions breaks loose at the dock if he tries it."

He went down the flight of steps to the street. Through the moonlight he saw approaching him the jaunty figure of Smith, the beach-comber.

"This is a pretty idea, Officer," that gentleman said. "You give me a nice ride down to the station, and then you kick me out. How am I going to get back to my bedroom? I've walked it once to-night."

Charlie reached into his pocket and held out one hand in which lay a small coin. "You may make the distance by trolley," he suggested.

Smith looked down at the coin. "A dime," he remarked. "Ten cents. I can't get on a street-car and offer the conductor a dime. A gentleman has to have the prestige of a dollar."

Tired as he was, Chan laughed. "So sorry," he answered. "There may be much in what you say. But I believe it wiser at this time to proffer you the ride and no more. The hour is late, and you should be able to maintain your dignity on very little prestige tonight."

Stubbornly Smith shook his head. "I've got to have the prestige of a dollar," he insisted.

"You mean you've got to have a drink," shrugged Chan. "If the coin is unsatisfactory, I regretfully withdraw it." He moved toward his car. "So sorry that I travel in opposite direction from your couch beneath the palm."

Smith followed him. "Oh, well," he said, "perhaps I'm a bit too sensitive. I'll take the dime." Charlie gave it to him. "Just a loan, Inspector. I'll make a note of it."

He hurried away down Bethel Street in the direction of King. With one foot on the running-board of his little car, Charlie stared after him. Finally he abandoned the flivver and followed. The empty streets were as bright as day, the risk was great, but Chan was an old hand at the game. Smith's battered shoes flopped noisily on the deserted sidewalk, but the detective moved as though on velvet slippers.

The beach-comber turned to the right on King Street and, dodging in and out of doorways, Chan followed. As his quarry neared the corner of Fort, Charlie waited anxiously in a shadowed nook. Would Smith pause at that corner for a Waikiki car? If he did, this pursuit came to nothing.

But Smith did not stop. Instead he crossed over and hastened down Fort Street. The moon shone brightly on his enormous flapping hat, on the shoulders of his absurd velvet coat. Charlie's interest revived at once. On what errand did the beach-comber set forth at this hour of the night?

Selecting the opposite side of the thoroughfare from that which Smith traveled—it was darker and better suited to his purpose—Chan trailed his man down Fort. Past the principal shops of Honolulu, in each of which a dim light burned, they moved along. Smith came to the entrance of the Waioli Hotel, and stopped there. Hiding in a dark doorway across the street, Chan saw him peer into the hotel lobby. The place was deserted save for a watchman who dozed in a chair behind the great glass window. For a moment the beach-comber hesitated and then, as though changing his mind, turned and retraced his steps. Charlie squeezed his great bulk against the door behind him, in a panic lest he be discovered.

But he was safe. All unsuspecting, Smith hurried back to the corner of King, there to await the Waikiki car. Charlie remained in hiding until the car arrived. He saw the beach-comber mount to a seat and ride away—without the prestige of a dollar.

Slowly Chan walked back to the station house. What did this mean? Evidently when Robert Fyfe announced his address to the detective, he was also proclaiming it to the battered Mr. Smith. And Smith desired to see the actor at once, on urgent business.

Charlie was getting into his flivver when the Chief came down the steps of Halekaua Hale.

"Thought you'd gone home," Charlie," he said.

"I was for a moment delayed," Chan explained.

His superior came up eagerly. "Anything new?"

"I remain just where I always have been," the detective sighed.

"You're not really as much in the dark on this case as you say you are?" asked the Chief anxiously.

Chan nodded. "The man who sits in a well, sees little of the sky."

"Well, climb out, Charlie, climb out."

"I am planning swift ascent," the detective answered, and starting his engine, sped off at last in the direction of his house on Punchbowl Hill.

12

Nobody's Fool

The night was breaking, and a gray mist lay over Waikiki. Smith, the beach-comber, shivered slightly and stirred on his bed of sand. He put out his hand, as though to draw up over his thin ill-clad body a blanket that was not there. Turning over, he muttered in his sleep, then lay motionless again.

The gray mist turned to pink. Above the mountains to the east a small segment of sky became a deep gold in color, against which a few scattered clouds stood out, black as the recent night. Smith opened his eyes, and gradually came back to a recognition of his surroundings. He did not choose to sleep on the beach, but for some reason the usual bitterness with which he awoke to the realization that he was broke again was missing to-day. Something pleasant had happened—or was about to happen. Ah, yes. He smiled at the hau tree above him, and the tree showered him with mahogany-red blossoms that had been yellow when he retired for the night. He would have preferred grapefruit and coffee, but flowers were more in keeping with the scene.

He sat up. The gold in the eastern sky was spreading, and now the rim of the sun appeared. The snow-white beach was lapped by water that had in it a glint of gold to match the sky. At his left stood Diamond Head, that extinct volcano. He had always a sort of fellow feeling for Diamond Head, being a bit on the extinct side himself. His mind went back to the events of the preceding night. Good fortune had taken him by the hand and led him to that pavilion window. Too often in these last years he had been blind to opportunity. He was resolved that he would not be blind now.

He got to his feet and, removing his scanty clothing, revealed underneath a frayed pair of bathing trunks. Gathering all his courage, he ran down to the water and plunged in. The shock revivified him. He struck out boldly; one thing at least he had learned on tropic beaches, and that was the art of the swimmer. As he cut through the water the wasted years fell away from him, old ambitions returned, he made plans for the future. He would win back to his former self, he would leave this languorous spot where he had never intended to stay anyhow, he would be a man again. The money that would put his feet back on the highroad was finally within his grasp.

The sun, warm and friendly, crept up the eastern sky. Smith plunged far under the waves, swam there, felt more energetic with every exploit. Finally he returned to shallow water, and walking carefully to avoid the coral, came from his bath back to his bedroom. For a time he sat, leaning against the abandoned hulk of a boat in the shelter of which he had spent the night. The hot sun served as his towel, and he rested, at peace with the world. A delicious feeling of laziness spread over him. But no, no—this wouldn't do.

He donned his clothes, took a broken piece of comb from his pocket, and applied it to his yellow beard and hair. His toilet was completed, and breakfast was now the order of the day. Above him hung clusters of coconuts; often these had been forced to serve. But not this morning, he told himself with a smile. Through a scene of brightness and beauty, he walked slowly toward the Moana Hotel. It was a scene that had, in its way, contributed to Mr. Smith's downfall, for every time he sought to paint it, he threw down his brush in disgust and bemoaned the inadequacy of his talent.

On the sand outside the hotel, an early beach-boy lay strumming a steel guitar and singing a gentle song. Smith went promptly to join him.

"Good morning, Frank," he said.

Frank turned his head. "Hello," he answered dreamily. The beach-comber sat down beside him. Suddenly Frank looked at him, his dark eyes wide and earnest. "I'm not going to sing for tourists to-day," the beach-boy announced. "I'm just going to sing for the blue sky."

Smith nodded. Coming from any other race, this would have been a stilted and theatrical remark, but the beach-comber knew his Hawaiians better than that. He had watched them arrive each morning on their beloved beach, staring at it as though its beauty were brought to their attention for the first time, diving into its familiar waters with cries of delight that betokened a happiness rare in this modern world.

"That's the ticket, Frank," Smith nodded approvingly. He suddenly introduced a more practical note. "Got any money?" he inquired.

The boy frowned. What was this money all the *haoles* seemed so interested in, so vocal about? It meant nothing to him, and never would.

"I guess so," he replied casually. "Dollar in my coat, I think."

Smith's eyes glittered. "Lend it to me. I'll pay it back before night. All the rest I owe you, too. How much do I owe you, anyhow?"

"Can't remember," Frank answered, and sang again.

"I'll have lots of money before the day's out," Smith continued, a note of excitement in his voice.

Frank sang softly. A queer thing to get excited about, money, when the sky was so blue, the water so warm, and there was such a deep satisfaction just in lying on the white beach and humming a song.

"In your coat, you say?" Smith persisted.

Frank nodded. "Go and get it. The locker door's open."

Smith went at once. When he returned he held a dollar bill in one hand, and in the other a small canvas.

"I'm taking that picture I left with you, Frank," he explained. "Something tells me there's a market for my work at last." He stared at the painting critically. A dark-skinned, black-eyed girl stood against a background of cool green. She held a crimson flower between her lips, and she had the look of the tropics, of lazy islands lost in southern seas. "You know," the beach-comber added with almost reluctant admiration, "that's not half bad."

"Yeah," said Frank.

"Not bad at all," Smith continued. "But then, they told me I had talent, Frank. I heard it in New York—and in Paris too. Talent—maybe a touch of genius—but not much else. No backbone—no character—nothing to back it up. You've got to have character, my boy."

"Yeah," repeated Frank idly.

"You know, Frank, painters without half my skill—oh, hell, what's the use? Why should I complain? Look at Corot, Frank. Not one of his pictures was sold during his lifetime. Look at Manet. You know what the critics did to Manet? They laughed at him."

"Yeah," continued Frank. He threw down his guitar, leaped to his feet and, running across the sand, dove like a fish into two feet of water. Smith looked after him. He shook his head.

"No interest in painting," he muttered. "Just music. Well, that's something." He put the bill in his pocket, tucked the canvas under his arm, and went out to the street.

A trolley was approaching, bound for the city, and Smith swung aboard. He offered the dollar proudly—after this, perhaps, the conductor would not judge every one by his clothes. Once or twice, on the way into town, he looked again at his painting. His opinion of it grew even better.

At a lunch room in town he treated himself to a breakfast such as he had not known in several days, then moved on to the Waioli Hotel. His entrance there evoked no great enthusiasm. The clerk stared at him with open disapproval. "What do you want?" he inquired coldly.

"Mr. Fyfe stopping here?" the beach-comber asked.

"He is—but he sleeps late. I can't disturb him."

"You'd better disturb him." There was a sudden note of authority in Smith's voice. "I've an appointment—very important. Mr. Fyfe wants to see me more than I want to see him."

The clerk hesitated, and then took up a telephone. In a moment he turned to the beach-comber. "Be down right away," he announced.

Boldly Smith dropped into a chair and waited. Fyfe appeared almost at once; evidently he had not slept late to-day. There was a worried look in his eyes. He came over to the beach-comber. "You wanted to see me?" he said. "I'm on my way to the theater. Come along."

He left his key at the desk and strode toward the door, Smith struggling to keep up with him. They walked in silence. Finally the actor turned.

"Why be so indiscreet?" he inquired. "You could have telephoned me and I'd have met you."

Smith shrugged. "Telephoning costs money," he replied. "And I haven't much money—yet."

There was a world of meaning in that last word. Fyfe led the way from the more modern quarter of the city into the Oriental district. They moved on past shops crammed with silks, linens, embroideries, jade and porcelains. Bales and baskets filled with the foodstuffs of the Orient encroached upon the sidewalk.

"I take it you expect to have money soon?" Fyfe said at last.

Smith smiled. "Why not? Last night I did you a favor. Oh—I'm nobody's fool. I know why you made that fake confession. You were afraid I was going to repeat what I heard when I was standing outside that window. Weren't you?"

"Just what did you overhear?"

"Enough, believe me. I heard that woman—the woman somebody killed later on—I heard her tell you that she——"

"Never mind!" The actor looked nervously about. Nothing but flat expressionless faces, dark eyes that avoided his.

"I think I fell in with your plan very neatly," Smith reminded him. "When that Chinese detective, after he'd punctured your confession, asked me again what I'd heard—well, I said what you wanted me to, didn't I? I backed up what you'd been saying. I could have exploded a bomb right then and there—but I didn't. Please remember that."

"I do remember it. And I rather expected you'd be around this morning to blackmail me——"

"My dear sir"—Smith raised a thin freckled hand—"you might have spared me that. I have some shreds of respectability left, and—er—what you said is scarcely in my line. It just occurred to me that as an intelligent man, a practitioner of one of the allied arts, you might possibly be interested in my work." He indicated the canvas. "I happen to have a sample with me," he added brightly.

Fyfe laughed. "You're a rather subtle person, Mr. Smith. Suppose I did buy one of your paintings—what would you do with the money?"

Smith licked his lips. "I'd get out of this place for ever. I'm fed up here. For the past year I've been thinking about going home—to my folks in Cleveland. I don't know whether they'd be glad to see me—if I had decent clothes and a bit of money in my pocket—that might help."

"How did you get here in the first place?" the actor inquired.

"I went down to the South Seas to paint. Might be a good place for some people—but for me—well, the first thing I knew I was on the beach. After a long time, my people sent me money to come home. I managed to get aboard a boat, but unfortunately it stopped for a day at this port. And—have you tried any of the *okolehau* they call a drink in this paradise?"

Fyfe smiled. "I understand. You forgot to go back to your ship."

"My dear sir," Smith shrugged, "I forgot the world. When I woke up, my boat was two days out. Oddly enough, my father seemed annoyed. A rather impatient man."

They reached the river and, crossing a narrow stone bridge, entered Aala Park where, because of its convenient location, the dregs of the town congregate. Fyfe indicated a bench. They sat down together, and Smith handed over his canvas.

The actor glanced at it, and a look of surprise crossed his face. "By jove," he cried, "that's damned good."

"Glad to hear you say so," beamed Smith. "A bit unexpected, too, eh? I'm not what you'd call a born salesman, but I can't help pointing out that the thing might be valuable some day. There's just a chance. Think of the pride you could take in saying to your friends: 'Ah, yes—but I recognized his talent long ago. I was his first patron.' "

"Is this your real name—down here in the corner?"

The beach-comber hung his head. "My real name—yes," he replied.
Fyfe laid the canvas on his knee. "Just—what is the price?" he inquired.
"What am I offered?" Smith countered.

"If you're really sincere about wanting to go home," said the actor, "I'll be happy to arrange it for you. Not now, of course—the police wouldn't let you go at present. But when this has blown over a bit, I'll buy you a ticket—and give you something besides. In return for this canvas, you know."

"How much besides?"

"Two hundred dollars."

"Well, I don't know——"

"Make it two fifty. Look here, you're not dealing with a millionaire. I'm an actor on a salary, and it's none too big. I've had a long engagement in Honolulu, and I've saved a bit. I'm offering you about all I've got. If it's not enough, I'm sorry."

"It's enough," said the beach-comber slowly. "I don't mean to be hard on you. I'm not very proud of this, you know. But it's my chance—my chance to get away—lord, I've got to take it. We'll call it a bargain—a ticket to the mainland as soon as they'll let me go, and two fifty in my jeans. But say—how about meantime—I need a small advance now."

"For *okolehau*, eh?"

Smith hesitated. "I don't know," he said frankly. "I hope not. I don't want to touch it. I might talk, and spoil everything. I'm not thinking so much of you—spoil everything for myself, I mean." He stood up. "I won't touch it," he cried suddenly. "I'll fight and I'll win. I give you my word of honor as a gentleman."

Fyfe looked him over, wondering what that was worth. He took out his wallet.

"I'll have to trust you, I suppose. I'll give you fifty now." Smith's eyes gleamed. "It's all I've got on me. Wait a minute!" He pushed away the beach-comber's eager hand. "Remember—you must be careful. If the police find that you've suddenly got money, they're bound to look into it."

"I was thinking of some new clothes," returned Smith wistfully.

"Not now," Fyfe warned. "Before you sail, yes—we'll attend to that. But now—just as you are for a while—and lie low." The actor was standing too, and he stared hard into the other's face. "I'm depending on you. A man who can paint as you can—don't be a fool. Go straight."

"By heaven, I will!" Smith cried, and hurried off across the park. For a moment Fyfe looked after him, then, with his recent purchase under his arm, walked slowly in the direction of the theater.

Smith went on to Beretania Street, and entered a small low-ceilinged room through a doorway that bore above it the faint sign: "Nippon Hotel." Behind the narrow desk stood a polite little Japanese. On the wall at his back hung the picture of a great liner cleaving the waves, under the words: "*Nippon Yusen Kaisha.*"

"Hello, Nada," Smith said jauntily. "My old room vacant?"

"So sorry," hissed the Jap.

Smith threw a bill on to the counter. "Here's ten in advance," he remarked.

"So sorry you stay away such long time," hastily amended the clerk. "Room all ready—yes-s."

"I'll go and brush up a bit," Smith told him. "My baggage will be along later."

"You have money from home, I think," Nada smiled.

"Money from home, nothing," Smith responded airily. "I've sold a picture, Nada. You know, that's more than Corot ever did." He leaned across the counter confidentially. "Poor old Corot, Nada, never got on to himself. It's all in being outside the right window at the right time."

"Mebbe so," agreed Nada. "Much better you go along now. Room numba seven, like always."

"It's great to be home," Smith answered, and went out, whistling a merry tune.

13

Breakfast with the Chans

An hour after Smith took his morning swim, Charlie Chan rose, and stepping to his bedroom window, looked down on the bright panorama of town and sea. From Punchbowl Hill the view was one to stir the heart with beauty: green valleys and gleaming water, at this season the crimson umbrellas of the poinciana, golden shower trees blooming in generous profusion, here and there a brick-red bougainvillea vine. Charlie's lot was cast in a pleasant setting, and he loved to stand thus of a morning and reflect on his good fortune.

To-day, however, he preferred to reflect on the problem that lay before him. Insoluble it had appeared when he went to bed, but he had slept soundly in the knowledge that what is to be will be, and now he felt a new energy stirring within him. Was he, then, a mainland policeman to be stumped and helpless in the face of a question that had, no doubt, some simple answer? It was a matter, however, that called for prompt and intelligent action on his part. He thought of the crane who, waiting for the sea to disappear and leave him dry fish to eat, died of starvation. Chan had no intention of emulating that stupid bird.

It was a far from silent house that lay about him. Eleven children in one family make of early morning something of a bedlam. He heard their voices here, there and all about, shouting, expostulating, laughing and, in one case at least, weeping bitterly. With a comfortable feeling that the day had begun as usual, he prepared himself for his tasks.

In the dining-room he found that his three eldest children were lingering about the table, and as he entered, he saw them regarding him with a keen interest he had not aroused in that quarter for a long time. They all spoke at once, and he realized the cause of their interest. One of their heroines, according to the morning paper, was murdered, and they were going to see the miscreant punished or know the reason why.

"Quiet!" Charlie cried. "Can a man think beneath a tree filled with myna birds?" He turned to his oldest son, Henry, dapper in college-cut clothes and engaged in lighting a cigarette. "You should be at the store."

"Going right along, Dad," Henry replied. "But say—what's all this about Shelah Fane?"

"You have read it in the paper Some one most unkindly stabbed her. Now, get on to your work."

"Who did it?" said Rose, the oldest girl. "That's what we want to know."

"A few others languish in same fix," her father admitted.

"You're on the case, aren't you, Dad?" Henry inquired.

Charlie looked at him. "In Honolulu, who else would be summoned?" he asked blandly.

"Well, what's the dope?" went on Henry, who had been Americanized to a rather painful extent. "When do you grab the guilty party, and what's his name?"

Charlie again looked at him, and sighed. These children were his link with the future—what sort of future, he often wondered.

"As I have frequent reason to point out, your language is sadly lacking in dignity," he reproved. "I have not yet apprehended the wrong-doer, and as a consequence, I do not know his name."

"But you will, won't you, Dad?" Rose put in. "You're not going to fall down on it, are you?"

"When have I ever so much as stumbled?" he wanted to know.

She was smiling at him mischievously. "Now, Dad——"

"When I was youthful," Chan broke in hastily, "it was regarded deadly sin to question all-pervading wisdom of father. He was honored and respected by children. Such a hint of failure as you have just offered would have been impossible."

She got up and came round to him, still smiling. "Times have changed. You're not going to fail, of course. We all know that. But this is one case your family is really interested in. So move fast, won't you? Don't take too much time out for Oriental meditation."

"Should I pause to think deeply," he replied, "I would be plenty lonesome man in this new world."

Rose kissed him and went out on her way to the bank where she was employed during the summer vacation. Henry stood up languidly.

"Will you be wanting the car to-night, Dad?" he inquired.

"If I ever wanted it, to-night will be the time," his father answered.

Henry frowned. "I guess I'll have to buy one," he said. "I can get a good second-hand bus on the installment plan——"

Charlie shook his head. "Work—and pay your way as you go," he advised. "Then you need fear no midnight knock upon the door."

"Old stuff," replied Henry, and made a leisurely exit.

Chan shrugged, and attacked his breakfast. Evelyn, aged fifteen, was addressing him. "Gee—I thought Shelah Fane was swell. I saw her in some swell parts."

"Enough!" cried Charlie. "Vast English language is spread out before you, and you select for your use the lowliest words. I am discouraged."

His wife appeared with his oatmeal and the tea. She was a jolly-looking woman, nearly as broad as Chan, with a placid smiling face. If her children and her husband had far outdistanced her in the matter of adjustment to a new land, she was, judging from her calm eyes, not at all distressed. "Heah about Shelah Fane," she remarked. "Plitty tellible thing."

"What do you know about Shelah Fane?" Charlie asked, surprised.

"All time chillun make talk, Shelah Fane, Shelah Fane," his wife said. "I think mus' be velly fine woman. I want you catch bad man plenty quick."

Chan choked on his hot tea. "If I do not, I perceive I am expelled from my own household. May I respectfully ask that you give me time. Much work to be done on this case."

"Mebbe you have moah tea," his wife suggested.

He drank a second cup, and then rose from the table. Evelyn brought his hat; they all seemed eager to speed him on his way. At the door he barely avoided falling over a round-faced little boy with keen black eyes that recalled those of his father. "Ah—the small Barry." He lifted the child and gave him an affectionate kiss. "Every day you grow more handsome, like fine namesake, Mr. Barry Kirk. Be good boy, now, and do not eat the plaster."

He went out and got his car, and as he drove down the hill he thought about his children. He had always been proud of the fact that they were all American citizens. But, perhaps because of this very fact, they seemed to be growing away from him—the gulf widened daily. They made no effort to remember the precepts and the odes; they spoke the English language in a manner that grated on Charlie's sensitive ear.

He passed the Chinese cemetery, with its odd headstones scattered down the sloping hillside. There lay his mother, whom he had brought from China to spend her last years in the house on Punchbowl Hill. What would she think if she could see her descendants now: see Henry in his dapper clothes; see Rose, brisk and efficient, planning to go to a university on the mainland in the autumn; hear Evelyn speaking that shabby, out-moded slang she picked up on the school grounds? His mother would not have approved, Charlie knew. She would have mourned for the old ways, the old customs. He mourned for them himself—but there was nothing he could do about it.

Reaching the business district of the city, he turned his attention to the tasks that lay before him. These were many, and he planned in what order he should attack them. Robert Fyfe was uppermost in his thoughts, so he drove at once to the Waioli Hotel.

Mr. Fyfe, the clerk said, had gone out with a man. What man? The description left no doubt as to the identity of Fyfe's caller, and Charlie frowned. What did Smith want of the actor? What had he overheard when he stood outside that pavilion window? Why had Fyfe confessed to a crime he had not committed? He couldn't have committed it, obviously. Not if his story of his actions on the previous night was correct—ah, yes, Charlie reflected, he must look into that.

"I think I heard Mr. Fyfe say he was going to the theater," the clerk remarked.

Chan was not up on the drama. "What theater, please?" he inquired.

"The Royal," the clerk told him, and Charlie went there.

He entered from the street, passing from a tiled lobby into the dark auditorium. On the stage the members of the stock company were rehearsing next week's piece. A few old kitchen chairs represented exits and entrances, and the players stood about, waiting for their cues. At the moment Fyfe was delivering a long speech; he gave it languidly, as though it were something with which he had no personal concern.

Charlie walked down the dim aisle. A man with a green velour hat pulled low over his eyes, who sat at a small table on the stage with the play script in his hand, looked down at the detective with evident annoyance. "What do you want?" he barked.

"Just one word, please, with Mr. Fyfe," Chan replied.

The actor stepped forward and, shading his eyes from the glare of the footlights, peered into the auditorium.

"Oh, yes—Inspector Chan," he said. "Won't you come up, please?"

Panting from the effort, Charlie boosted his heavy bulk on to the stage.

Fyfe was smiling and cordial. "What can I do for you this morning, Inspector?" he inquired.

Charlie regarded him through half-shut eyes. "Not much, I fear, unless maybe mood has altered overnight. You will recall I arranged for you, somewhat against your wish, a very nice alibi. I am here now to verify myself. A mere matter of form."

"Surely," nodded Fyfe. "Oh, Wayne," he called. Reluctantly the man in the green hat got up and came over to them. "This is Mr. Wayne, our stage manager—Inspector Chan, of the Honolulu police. The Inspector is here regarding that affair last night. Wayne—what time was it when you rang up last evening?"

"Eight-twenty," growled Wayne. "Five minutes late."

"I was standing beside you when you rang up?"

"Yes—you were. Though where you were when we were hammering on your door, I'm damned if I know."

"The Inspector, however, does," Fyfe returned. "Was that all you wanted, Mr. Chan?"

"One other thing." Chan addressed the stage manager. "In play which you perform this present week, does Mr. Fyfe in actor capacity indulge in use of knife?"

"A knife?" repeated Wayne. "Why, no—there's no knife in this play. It's a polite drawing-room comedy."

"Thank you so much," Charlie said, bowing. "That is all." He turned on Robert Fyfe a speculative eye. "Will you come with me, please?"

He led the way down into the auditorium, thinking deeply as he did so. Shelah Fane was seen alive at eight-twelve. Robert Fyfe was in the wings of the theater, ready to go on, at eight-twenty. Just eight minutes—no one could possibly travel the distance from Waikiki to town in that time. Fyfe's alibi was perfect. And yet——

In the darkened foyer back of the last row Charlie paused, and the two leaned on the rail.

"I am still wondering, Mr. Fyfe," the detective remarked, "why you made false confession that you killed Shelah Fane."

"I'm inclined to wonder a bit myself, Inspector."

"Obviously you did not kill her."

"I'm afraid you must think me a fool," Fyfe said.

"Other way about, I think you very smart man."

"Do you really? That's flattering, I'm sure."

"There was reason for that confession, Mr. Fyfe."

"If there was, it has quite escaped my memory at this time, Inspector."

"Much better you tell me. Otherwise you place obstacle in path of justice."

"I must be the judge of that, Mr. Chan. I do not wish to hinder you. On the contrary I am eager for your success."

"Under such a circumstance, I find that difficult to believe." Chan was silent for a moment. "You have seen our friend the beach-comber this morning?"

Fyfe hesitated. He regretted more than ever the public nature of his meeting with Smith. Then he threw back his head and laughed—a laugh too long delayed, as Charlie noted.

"I certainly have," the actor admitted. "He called on me almost before I was up."

"For what purpose?"

"To get money, of course. I imagine he is making the rounds of the people he met last night. He seemed to think that the mere meeting gave him a sort of claim on us all."

"You are too busy with plural words," Chan protested. "His claim, I think, was on you alone." The actor said nothing. "You gave him money?" Charlie persisted.

"Why—yes—a few dollars. I was rather sorry for him. He is not a bad painter——" Fyfe stopped suddenly.

"How do you know he is not a bad painter?" Chan was quick to ask.

"Well—he—he left a canvas with me——"

"This canvas?" Charlie stepped down the aisle, and picked up something from a vacant seat. "I noted it as we came back here together," he explained. "If you do not mind, I will take it to light and examine it."

"By all means," the actor agreed.

Charlie walked to the door, and pushing it open, gazed for a moment at the painting. The eyes of that girl, posed against green shrubbery, seemed strangely alive. He came back to Fyfe's side.

"You are correct," he remarked, dropping the canvas into one of the chairs. "The man has talent. Pity such a one must resort to—blackmail."

"Who said it was blackmail?" demanded Fyfe.

"I say so. Mr. Fyfe, I could place you beneath arrest—"

"Isn't my alibi satisfactory?"

"Quite. But you hamper my work. For the last time—what was it Smith, the beach-comber, heard your ex-wife say to you?"

The stage manager came to the footlights, and called.

"I'm so sorry," said Fyfe, "but I'm keeping the company. I really must go along——"

Chan shrugged. "The inquiry is young, as yet. Before I am through, I will know, Mr. Fyfe."

"Drop in any time," said Fyfe blandly, holding out his hand. "Too bad I must leave you now, but an actor's life, you know——"

Chan gravely shook hands, and the actor hurried up the aisle. As he returned to the bright street, Charlie wore a puzzled frown. He knew that behind Fyfe's suave manner there lurked something of vital importance —something that might, indeed, solve his problem. Yet he would never get it from Fyfe. The beach-comber—ah, perhaps. He made a mental note of the beach-comber.

Climbing back into his flivver, Chan drove over to King Street and turned in the direction of Waikiki. As he passed the public library, set well back from the street amid great trees, he was tempted to stop. It occurred to him that he ought to read, in a Los Angeles paper, the story of Denny Mayo's murder. Buried in the yellowed columns describing that spectacular moment in the movie colony's history, he might discover a line that would at once put him on the true scent in his search for Shelah Fane's assailant.

With quick decision he swung about and returned to the library. In another moment, he was addressing the woman at the library desk.

"Is it possible that I obtain at once Los Angeles paper for June, three years ago?" he inquired.

"Certainly, Mr. Chan," she answered. "Just fill out the card."

He filled it hastily, and saw it passed to a young assistant. The girl started to move toward the files, glancing at the card as she did so. She turned and came back.

"I'm sorry," she said. "I just happened to remember. That volume of the *Los Angeles Times* is in use just now."

"In use?" Chan was surprised.

"Yes. A gentleman took it out half an hour ago."

"Can you describe this gentleman?"

The girl nodded toward the reading-room. "He's still there. By that farther window."

Chan went over and peered round the corner of a bookcase. Seated bent over a huge gray-bound volume, he saw Huntley Van Horn. The picture actor did not look up; he seemed grimly intent on what he was doing. With a gesture toward the desk, meant to convey the fact that he dropped the whole matter, Chan walked softly out of the building.

14

The Pavilion Window

Charlie went to the street, got into his flivver, and in another moment was traveling rapidly toward Waikiki. It was good to feel the faithful little car shuddering under him again; so often in the past it had carried him along on the trail of innumerable clues. Many of these clues had led him, as he put it, "into presence of immovable stone wall." Thereupon he had swung the car about, seeking a new road. And the road that ended in victory had, in most cases, stretched before him at last.

As he sped through the brilliant morning, he thought of Huntley Van Horn. He pictured the cinema actor on the night before, walking across the lawn at the very moment when the black camel must have been kneeling at Shelah Fane's gate. No one was with the actor, no one saw him; he could easily have stepped into the pavilion, silenced the woman for ever and then calmly joined the two people on the beach.

What sort of man was Van Horn? Charlie wished he had read a few of the movie gossip magazines his children were always bringing into the house. Not the sleek, pretty boy type of film favorite, that was evident. Cynical, aloof, well-poised, he was the type who could keep his own counsel and turn an expressionless face on any one who sought to pry into his affairs. Ah, yes—Mr. Van Horn would bear thinking about. Such thinking might yield a rich reward.

But it was not with Van Horn that Chan was immediately concerned. He was on Kalakaua Avenue now, and though the sun was still shining above him, he had entered a zone where rain was falling. He saw, as he approached the hotels, tourists who wore rain-coats and carried umbrellas; evidently they took this liquid sunshine with a seriousness that amused a *kamaaina* like Charlie. He turned sharply to the right and, moving on past the lovely gardens of the Grand Hotel, parked his car in the drive at the rear. Walking unconcerned through the drizzle, he went over and ascended the hotel steps.

The head bell-man, a Chinese boy with a winning smile, greeted him in Cantonese. Chan paused to chat for a moment. No, he explained, he was not looking for any one in particular; he would, with kind permission, stroll about a bit. He crossed the high cool lobby, returning the jovial greeting of a young assistant manager.

He walked down the long corridor, toward the lounge. Unlike many of his fellow citizens of Honolulu, he had no feeling of somewhat resentful awe in this impressive interior. Having been to the mainland he regarded himself as a traveled man, a judge of hotels, and he approved heartily of this recent addition to the charms of Waikiki. He nodded affably at the flower girl, and stood for a moment in the entrance to the lounge. This room always inspired him. Through the great archways opening on the terrace he caught the shimmer of the sea, breath-taking fragments of a scene no coast in the world can surpass.

The huge room was empty of guests, but a few silent Oriental servants were busy arranging the floral decorations for the day. On tiny slivers of bamboo stuck in bowls of sand, they mounted innumerable hibiscus flowers, beautiful and fragile blossoms that would fade when evening came. Chan passed through to the terrace facing the ocean, and luck was with him. The only occupants of the place at that moment were the two old people with whom he had seen Tarneverro talking the previous evening. He stepped over to the Hongkong chairs where they sat, and stood looking down at them. The man put aside his morning paper; the woman glanced up from her book.

Chan bowed low. "May I wish you good morning," he said.

"Good morning, sir," the old man replied courteously. There was a pleasant Scotch burr to his words, and his face, lined by hard work under a hot sun, was as honest as any Charlie had ever seen.

Chan pushed back his coat. "I am Inspector Chan of the Honolulu police. You have, I think, perused in the morning paper story of quick finish of noted actress. I am sorry to intrude my inspeakable presence between you and this charming view, but gentleman you know was friend of the departed lady. It therefore becomes inevitable that I speak to you for short moment."

"Happy to meet you," said the old gentleman. He rose, and pulled up a chair. "Be seated, Inspector. I am Thomas MacMaster, of Queensland, Australia, and this is Mrs. MacMaster."

Chan achieved a notable bow, and the old lady gave him a quick kindly smile. A bit of idle chatter seemed in order.

"You are enjoying nice holiday?" the detective inquired.

"That we are," returned MacMaster. "And we've earned it, eh, Mother? Aye, after long years on a sheep ranch, we're off to revisit old Scotland at last. A very leisurely journey, Inspector; we mean to miss nothing along the way. And delighted we are"—he waved toward the beach—"that we did not miss this bonny spot."

His wife nodded. "Aye, bonny it is. We're very much afraid we'll no have the strength of character to move on."

"Speak for yourself, Mother," MacMaster said. "When the moment comes, I'm sure I'll have strength for two. Do not forget that Aberdeen is waiting."

"In behalf of Honolulu," beamed Chan, "my warmest thanks for all these treasured compliments. I recognize they come from honest lips, and my heart feels itself deeply touched. But reluctantly I must approach subject of last night's homocide. May I open my remarks by pointing out that some *malihini*—some stranger—must be responsible for this cruel event? Here people are kind, like climate. We seldom murder," he added feelingly.

"Of course," murmured the old lady.

Looking up, Charlie saw Tarneverro in the doorway. The fortune-teller's dark face lighted with satisfaction when he saw the group on the terrace, and he came rapidly down the steps. Chan sighed. He would have preferred to do this thing himself.

"Ah, good morning, Inspector," Tarneverro said. "Good morning, Mrs. MacMaster. And how are you, sir?"

"A wee bit lost," answered the old man. "I can not feel just right and not be at my work. But Mother tells me I must learn to rest."

"You certainly must—you have it coming to you," Tarneverro smiled. "Inspector, I am happy to see you on the job this early hour. You are no doubt here to verify my alibi, and that is quite fitting and proper. Have you asked these two friends of mine the important question?"

"I was approaching it with suitable preparation."

"Ah, yes," the fortune-teller continued. "Mr. MacMaster, in the matter of that unfortunate affair last night—I happen to have been one of the few people in the Islands acquainted with the poor girl, and it is important that I establish to the Inspector's satisfaction the fact that I was elsewhere at the moment of her death. Luckily I can establish it—with your help." He turned to Charlie. "After I left you in the lounge last night, you saw me return to my conversation with Mr. and Mrs. MacMaster. Mr. Mac-Master will tell you what happened after that."

The old man frowned thoughtfully. "Mr.—er—Tarneverro suggested that we go out on the veranda—I believe you call it a lanai—that looks across the palm court. We did so, and for the matter of a half-hour sat talking about the old days in Queensland. Finally Mr. Tarneverro had a look at his watch. He said it was thirty minutes after eight and that he must leave us, as he had a dinner engagement down the beach. We stood up——"

"Begging humblest pardon," Chan cut in, "did you by any chance consult own timepiece?"

"Aye, that I did," returned the old man. His manner was very earnest and there was an unmistakable ring of truth to his words. "I took out my watch—" He removed an old-fashioned timepiece from his pocket. " 'I'm a wee bit fast,' I said. 'Eight-thirty-five, I make it. Mother, it's time old folks like us went up-stairs.' You see, on the ranch we were always early abed, and well-established habits are hard to break. So we came into the hotel. Mother and I stopped at the elevators, and Mr. Tarneverro went round the corner to his own room on the first floor. While we waited for the lift, I stepped to the desk to set my watch the correct time. Eight-thirty-two it was then, and I made the change. Those are the facts, Inspector, and Mother and I will swear to them."

Chan nodded. "The speech of some is like wind in empty space," he said. "But blind man could see your word is good."

"Aye, it always has been. From Aberdeen to Queensland no one has ever questioned it, Inspector."

"You have known Mr. Tarneverro long time?" Charlie asked.

Tarneverro answered. "Ten years ago," he remarked, "I was playing in a Melbourne theater. I was an actor in those days, you know. Our company stranded, and I went out to Mr. MacMaster's ranch, a few miles from Brisbane, to work for him. I stayed a year—the happiest year of my life. For as you may see by looking at them, these two are the kindest people in the world, and they were like father and mother to me——"

"We did nothing," the old lady protested. "It was a joy to have you and——"

"Alone and lonely as I was," Tarneverro interrupted, "it was great luck to come upon people like these. You can imagine my delight when I ran across them again at this hotel the other day." He rose. "I take it that is all you wanted to know, Mr. Chan. I'd like to have a talk with you."

"That is all," remarked Chan, rising too. "Lady,—sir,—may vacation continue as happy as it is this bright morning on undescribably lovely beach. I am so pleased that our paths met here at famous crossroads."

"We share that pleasure, sir," MacMaster replied. His wife nodded and smiled. "We'll be thinking of ye as we travel on to Aberdeen. Our very best wishes for success."

Charlie and the fortune-teller went inside, and sat down on a sofa. "You are favorite of the gods," Chan remarked. "If I needed alibi I would ask nothing better than word from honest people such as those."

Tarneverro smiled. "Yes—they're a grand pair. Simple and wholesome and addicted to all the old virtues." He paused. "Well, Inspector, you know where I was during those vital eighteen minutes. How about the others?"

"I know also where Robert Fyfe was," Charlie replied, "though much about his actions puzzles me. Speaking of the rest, they have no such luck. Not one has offered alibi."

Tarneverro nodded. "Yes—and one among them may need an alibi badly before this affair is ended. You had, I take it, no flash if inspiration in the night?"

Chan sadly shook his head. "I had nothing but plenty good sleep. And you?"

The other smiled. "I'm afraid I weakly fell into a dreamless slumber too. No—I have thought hard, but I'm afraid I can't help you much. There are so many possibilities. Shall we go over them? Rita and Wilkie Ballou. Both in Hollywood at the time of Denny Mayo's death. Mayo was said to be a bit careless with the ladies—and it is clear that Ballou is a notably jealous man."

"I think about Ballou," remarked Chan slowly.

"It might pay," Tarneverro agreed. "He was wandering about—came into the living-room to get a cigarette—claims he stayed there. Turning from him for the time being, there's Alan Jaynes. His state of mind was rather emotional last night. Who knows anything about him? Suppose that like that of Ballou, his is a wildly jealous nature. He saw those flowers—not his—on the shoulder of the woman he loved. We found them trampled under foot, as though in rage. The Mayo affair, as I believe you pointed out, may have had nothing to do with Miss Fane's murder, after all. Perhaps it was just a case of mad unreasoning jealousy——"

"Perhaps," answered Chan calmly. "There is also Martino."

"Yes—Martino," repeated the fortune-teller. A black look swept across his handsome face. "It would give me great pleasure to help you pin this thing on him. He has made some very rude remarks about me——"

"What sort of man you call him?" Charlie asked.

"Oh, he seems to have brains," Tarneverro admitted. "And a kind of rude strength—a queer combination, the esthete and the brute in one package. He wasn't in Hollywood when Mayo was killed, but once again—perhaps we are on the wrong trail there. Martino's been a bit of a ladies' man—there may have been some unsuspected relationship between him and Shelah Fane. Certainly that handkerchief in his pocket had a fishy look to me. Of course he denied he owned it—who wouldn't? But if any one placed it on Martino's person, he was taking a tremendous and unnecessary risk. Why not throw it into the bushes—drop it on the lawn? Why attempt the difficult, the dangerous? The handkerchief, Inspector, may have been Martino's own property. He may have gone on carrying it after the murder, quite innocent of the fact that it contained those splinters of glass. Unless"—the fortune-teller paused—"unless you have evidence that it belonged to some one else?"

Chan regarded him with sleepy eyes. "I have so little evidence," he sighed. "Languishing in such a state, how gladly I hear you talk. Continue, please, to dispense logic and eloquence, those twin blossoms of speech. I now bring up the name of Huntley Van Horn."

Tarneverro regarded him keenly. "Have you anything on Van Horn?"

"I regret to note that he has no alibi. Also, he was at proper place at proper time to do the deed." Chan paused, and decided he would keep some matters to himself. "Aside from that, I have nothing of importance. Deign to state your opinion of the man."

"Well," said Tarneverro, "I haven't thought much about Van Horn. He's an odd, rather bitter sort of chap—a notorious bachelor—the despair of all the women. No breath of scandal has ever touched him. I have always admired the fellow, though heaven knows he has never been any too friendly to me. He's an intelligent chap, with excellent taste—a bit conceited, perhaps, but no man could receive the adulation he does, and escape that." He considered a moment. "No, Inspector," he added with sudden decision, "in spite of the fact that his opportunities were excellent, as you point out, I can not see Huntley Van Horn as our quarry in this affair."

Charlie rose. "Thank you for this little conversation." He glanced at his watch. "Now I must haste to home of Shelah Fane. You will accompany me?"

"I'm sorry," Tarneverro replied, "but I am not at liberty to do so just at present. You'll let me know of any new developments, won't you? It isn't mere curiosity on my part. If we are to work together I must, of course, know what you are doing."

"We will encounter from time to time," Chan assured him. They walked to the hotel door.

The head bell-man said something to Tarneverro in Cantonese, and the fortune-teller regarded him with a blank uncomprehending look. "What does he say?" he inquired of Charlie.

"He makes most respectful inquiry after your health this splendid morning," Chan translated.

"Oh, I'm fine, Sam," Tarneverro smiled. There was a puzzled expression on Sam's broad face. "So long, Inspector," the fortune-teller continued. "Ring me up if you strike anything new. I'll be hunting about myself—anything I can do—well, I'm with you to the finish, as I told you."

"You are so extremely kind," bowed Chan, and returned to his car.

The front lawn of Shelah Fane's house, when Charlie arrived there, lay peaceful and serene in the shade of its ancient banyan tree. Jessop answered the door, perfect in manner and attire, as always.

"How are you, Constable?" he said. "The morning is rather on the gorgeous side, is it not?"

"Presume so," agreed Chan. "It is matter we do not notice here. All mornings much the same."

"Which must, if I may say so, sir, grow a trifle monotonous in time." The butler followed Chan into the living-room. "Now in England, Constable, drawing back the curtains of a morning is something of a sporting proposition."

Charlie stood looking about the great room, where so much had happened the night before. It was calm, quiet and sunny now.

"Miss Julie and Mr. Bradshaw are in the neighborhood of the beach, sir," Jessop remarked. "One of your officers—a Mr. Hettick, I believe—is busily engaged in the pavilion."

"Ah, yes—Hettick is our finger-print expert," Charlie explained. "I will go outside at once." On the lawn he encountered the two young people, who greeted him warmly. "So sorry to develop into pest," he said to Julie. "But path of duty is often rocky one."

"Why, you could never be that," she smiled. "We've been expecting you."

He glanced at her, so fresh and lovely, her blue eyes wide and innocent. He thought of the emerald ring.

"Well, how did you like my story in the paper this morning?" Bradshaw wanted to know.

"My perusal was of necessity hurried," Chan replied. "Imagine it covered the ground."

"Is that the best you can say for it?" the boy complained.

Charlie shrugged. "Always think twice before you scatter tributes," he answered. "If no one had praised the donkey's song, he would not still be singing." He grinned. "The comparison is, of course, unhappy one. I take it you enjoy a pleasant morning?"

"Oh, I just ran out to help Julie," the boy told him. "I've been acting as a shock-absorber between her and the reporters. The fellows on the evening paper weren't very polite. They seem a bit miffed the story didn't break right for them."

"A natural feeling," Chan replied.

"What are you going to do now?" asked Bradshaw.

"Propose to look about in bright light of day," Charlie answered.

"I'll help you," Bradshaw said. "Julie you just sit down and relax. Close your eyes and try not to think. Nobody ever has at Waikiki and you can't tell—it might be dangerous."

The girl smiled at him and dropped on to a beach chair.

"Want to keep the poor kid cheered up," Badshaw explained, as he and Chan walked toward the pavilion. "This has been a pretty tough shock for her. But in time I think I can convince her that all her troubles are over. That is—if she'll marry me."

"You possess excellent opinion of yourself," Charlie smiled.

"Why shouldn't I? I know myself so well."

As they reached the pavilion, Hettick came out. He had been brought over from the mainland at the time of the reorganization to strengthen the force, and he had never been very cordial to Charlie, whom he had replaced in the rôle of finger-print expert.

"Good morning, Mr. Hettick," Chan said politely. "Have you had successful time of it?"

"Not very," the man replied. "Plenty of prints, but mostly those of the murdered woman. All the others can be accounted for, I guess. Come inside, and I'll show you——"

"One little moment," interrupted Charlie. "First I take careless stroll about outside of place."

Followed by Bradshaw, he made his way through some bushes at the side of the cottage, and came out on the public beach that bounded the grounds on the west. Beneath the single pavilion window which opened on that beach—the one under which Smith had stood the previous night—he paused.

A great many footprints were there now, and those of the beach-comber barely distinguishable. Charlie stooped down and carefully sifted the sand. With a little cry of satisfaction, he stood erect again.

"Important discovery," he announced.

Bradshaw came nearer. He saw in Charlie's palm the remains of a small cigar, the size of a cigarette.

"Trampled into the sand," Charlie added. "I would never have expected to find this here."

"Why—I know only one man who smokes these," the boy cried. "I saw him—last night——"

"You are quite correct," Chan beamed. "One man, and who would believe he could act so careless? I am consumed with wonder. When did Mr. Alan Jaynes stand outside this window—and why?"

15

"Two Juices of the Orange"

Charlie took an empty envelope from his pocket and carefully placed his latest discovery inside it. He and the boy again penetrated the bushes and entered the pavilion. Hettick was sitting idly by the dressing-table, with the paraphernalia of his calling spread out before him.

Dropping down on a wicker chair, Chan glanced around the room where, only the night before, he had encountered tragedy. The detective's face was placid and serene; he might have been awaiting the luncheon bell untroubled by any problem. Through an enormous plateglass window he watched a liner from the coast move slowly into port.

"You have enjoyed no luck here, Mr. Hettick?" he inquired.

"Not much," replied Hettick. "The things on the table are covered with prints—all those of the murdered woman herself. I got her record at the mortuary this morning. By the way, the coroner asked me to tell you he had postponed the inquest until to-morrow. He expects you to have something by then."

Chan shrugged. "Thank him for the compliment. Also inform him I will exchange places with him at any moment." His gaze returned to the room; the woodwork, he noted, had recently been painted white. Suddenly he rose and stepped to the small window opening on the beach. "You have not tested this sill, I believe," he remarked.

"No—as a matter of fact, I haven't," Hettick answered. "I meant to, but it slipped my mind."

Chan grinned. "Mind gets so slippery in warm climate. May I humbly suggest you do so now?"

Hettick came over and covered the sill with his lamp black. With practised hand he applied the camel's-hair brush.

Charlie and the boy crowded close. "Ah!" cried Chan. On the smooth white surface of the sill were the marks of some one's fingers and thumb.

"These were not made by Shelah Fane?" Charlie inquired.

"No," answered Hettick. "Those were left by a man's hand."

Chan stood, deep in thought. "Recent, too. We achieve some progress now. A man's hand. A man opened that screen, climbed up on sill. Why? To enter room, of course. When? Last night, when murder was in atmosphere. Yes, we move, we advance." He paused. "What man?" In his coat pocket, his fingers touched the envelope containing the cigar stub. He turned with sudden decision. "One thing is certain. I must without delay obtain thumb prints of Alan Jaynes." Smiling at Jimmy Bradshaw, he added: "Police have fine clue and promise early arrest. But if you publish one word of this, I recall matter of your laundry and put you in jail at once."

"I won't use it, Charlie," promised the boy. "What are you going to do now?"

"I propose to leave you with nobody for company—except Miss Julie. And who is she?"

"Wait a minute, and I'll tell you. She's the most——"

"Later," cut in Chan. "Much later. Mr. Hettick, I request that you remain here until my return. Your keen eye will be required. I am off for session at Grand Hotel."

He left the pavilion, and the boy followed. As Charlie passed out of sight around the corner of the house, Bradshaw went over to where Julie sat. He dropped down beside her.

"Has that funny policeman gone?" she asked eagerly.

"For a few minutes. He'll be back before he's missed." Looking up at her, the boy thought he saw an expression of fear cross her delicate face. He wondered. "Charlie has just made an important discovery outside the pavilion window," he added.

"W-what?" she inquired.

"I don't believe he'd like to have me tell you," Bradshaw answered. Not just yet, at any rate. But—what about this Alan Jaynes? You don't know him very well, do you?"

"Scarcely at all," the girl replied. "I never saw him until yesterday morning, Shelah met him in Tahiti—I believe she was very fond of him. But Shelah was fond of—so many people. She was even—fond of me." Without warning Julie turned away her head and burst into tears.

Bradshaw got up and laid a hand on her heaving shoulder. "Now—now," he said uncomfortably. "You mustn't do that. You're ruining all my press stuff. Waikiki, the abode of peace, the crescent beach where happiness rules supreme. Suppose one of these tourists who took me at my word should see you."

"I-I'm sorry," she sobbed. "I'm not happy; I can't be."

"No, of course you can't—not at this moment, I mean. But why not look ahead to all the happiness that's coming, and draw a little advance on that?"

"I'll—I'll never be happy again," she told him.

"Nonsense. I'm going to make the world as glamorous for you as I've made this town in the Tourist Bureau ads. When we're married——"

She pushed him away. "We'll never be married. Oh, it's terrible. I'm horrid, really—and you don't suspect. You'll hate me—when you know."

"Do tell! Look at me." He leaned over and kissed her.

"You mustn't," she cried.

"I've got to," he smiled. "It's my duty. I've advertised this place for its romance, and romance there must be if I have to attend to it myself. Now listen to me—inside a week or less all this will be over, and you can begin to forget. Charlie Chan is going to solve the puzzle at any minute——"

"Oh—do you think so?"

"He's sure to. You can't keep anything from Charlie."

"I wonder," said the girl.

"I know," Bradshaw replied firmly.

Scarcely sharing Bradshaw's confidence, Chan was at that moment entering the lobby of the Grand Hotel. He waved a hand toward the bellman, and went at once to the desk.

"I arrive again," he remarked to the clerk. "For a nonpaying guest, I am plenty much in evidence around this place. Will you give me number of room occupied by Mr. Alan Jaynes, if you will be so good?"

The clerk smilingly gave it to him, and pointed out the house telephones at the right of the desk. Charlie was relieved to hear the Britisher's answering voice. He politely requested a moment's conversation, and Jaynes replied that he would come down immediately.

Charlie walked with unaccustomed speed to the lounge. A small Filipino bell-boy was there alone, and the detective summoned him.

"I wish to be served with two of your delicious orange-juice drinks," he announced.

"Yes, sir," replied the boy.

"I will also accompany you while you secure same." The boy appeared taken back, but it was not his rôle to argue. From out of the jungle he had come to learn that the guest is always right.

Charlie followed his small guide to the serving pantry, where they encountered a man in a white apron.

"Inspector Chan, of the Honolulu police," Charlie explained briefly. "I have just engaged to purchase two juices of the orange. Will you hand me the glasses in which you propose to place same, please?"

The servant was too weary to be surprised. The climate, as he often explained to his wife, had got him. He produced the glasses and Charlie, removing an immaculate handkerchief from his pocket, began to polish them briskly.

"This action, I hasten to say, involves no criticism of you," he remarked. "But I am reading lately about germs." He grinned. "A very dangerous form of animal life." It could be noted, however, that it was only the outside of the tumblers that concerned him. He completed the task, set the objects of his attention carefully down on the tray the boy had brought, and reaching into his pocket, handed a quarter to the serving man. "You will do me great favor if you will fill these receptacles without placing fingers on same." He turned to the boy. "That also applies to you. Do you understand? You are not to touch those glasses. Set tray on table as it is. Otherwise, when moment arrives for your tip, I develop far-away look in eye and can not see you."

Returning to the lounge, Charlie found the Britisher already there. "Ah—Mr. Jaynes," he said. "I am happy to see you again. You had good night's rest, I hope?"

Jaynes stared at him. "No," he replied, "I didn't; but what of it?"

"So sorry," Chan cried. "Waikiki is famous sleeping place, and being old resident of Honolulu, I experience deep pain when it fails to live up to reputation. Will you do me the honor to join me on this sofa?"

He dropped down on the seat, which creaked protestingly beneath him.

"Harsh voice of furniture proclaims to world my excessive avoirdupois," he continued affably. "I diet and I fast, but to no avail. What is to be, will be. Man—who is he to fix own weight upon the scales? All that is determined elsewhere."

Jaynes sat down beside him. "What can I do for you this morning, Inspector?" he inquired.

"You can accept, if you will be so kind, renewed apologies for detaining you on this island. Some people pronounce it Paradise, but even Paradise, I can appreciate, looks not so good when one is panting to travel elsewhere. Again my warm regrets. I assure you I apply myself with all possible speed to task of clearing up mystery, so that you may make quick exit."

"I'm glad to hear that," nodded Jaynes. He took out a case and offered Charlie one of his little black cigars. "No?" He lighted one himself. "You are making progress, I hope?"

"I encounter difficulties," Charlie admitted. "Those who know, don't talk; those who talk, don't know. But that is always to be expected in my work. Within last hour I think I see faint glimmer of light ahead. Ah——"

The Filipino boy had arrived with the tray; he set it down on a small table before them. "I should have said, Mr. Jaynes, that I am on orange-juice diet, and the hour of drink is here I have ventured to order same for you."

"Oh, no, thanks," replied the Britisher. "I don't believe——"

"Same is all prepared," Charlie protested, and a note of imminent offense crept into his voice. "The beverage is harmless. You are not going to refuse?"

"Well—thank you," said Jaynes. At the moment he wanted nothing less, but he knew how easily the feelings of a Chinese may be hurt, and he could not risk any further offense to this particular representative of the race. "You are very good." He reached for a glass.

Beaming, Charlie lifted his own. "We will drink to my quick success, since you desire it equally with me." He imbibed heartily, and set the glass down. "Presume mild nature of the liquid gives you hearty pain. I have noted how bitterly men from your country resent this prohibition."

"What prohibition?" Jaynes inquired.

"Ah, you mock and jeer. Well, it is noble expermient, but it is not new, as many think. The Emperor Yü, who came to the throne of China in year 2205 B.C., said when he tasted liquor for the first time, this will do my people much harm, and forbade its use. His edict had good effect for a while, but later got lost in dim pages of history. China," added Chan, drinking again, "like the purse of a generous man, has endured much. But it still survives."

Jaynes was looking at him with a deep curiosity. Had this odd policeman dropped in merely to discuss prohibition? Charlie noted the look.

"But to return to our mutton broth," he said. "I desire to make inquiries of you regarding last night. You are most unfortunate man not to possess nice alibi for motions during time of homicide. You were, as I understand things, wandering about plenty mad at fatal hour?"

"I'm afraid I was," Jaynes admitted.

"From the moment when you left Martino on beach until he went out and found you with announcement of murder, you exist quite alone?"

"Yes."

"Making your walk, how far down beach did you penetrate?"

"Only as far as the Moana Hotel. I sat there under the banyan tree and tried to think what I had better do."

"You did not—will you join me in another quaffing—ah, yes—you did not travel on to property of Shelah Fane?"

"I've just told you," replied Jaynes, "that I went only as far as the Moana. As I say, I sat down there to try to figure things out. When I had grown a bit calmer, it occurred to me that perhaps I was making a big row about nothing. A woman who could be so easily influenced by a silly fortune-teller—I asked myself whether she would, after all, make a satisfactory wife. Her life was far removed from mine—I began to feel that the whole affair might turn out to have been a mere passing infatuation with both of us. I resolved to take the boat at midnight and, if possible, forget the entire business. After that was decided, I felt better. I came back here, past the Outrigger Club, and just outside the hotel Martino met me with the appalling news of the poor girl's murder."

"No one noted you at Moana under banyan tree?"

"I fancy not. I sat in a dark corner."

"Were you ever in pavilion where Shelah Fane encountered finish?"

"No—I never saw the place."

"Then you could not have been in the neighborhood at any time? Hovering about window, for example?"

"Well, hardly." Without prompting, Jaynes took up his glass and drained it. Suddenly he stared at Charlie. "I say—why do you ask me that?"

"I seek only to narrow search," Chan explained. "That will be all, thank you. Can you name hour of next boat to mainland?"

"I certainly can," answered the Britisher. "There's one to-morrow at noon. I hope to heaven—"

"I will extend myself to the utmost," smiled Chan. "Though, to look at me, many might remark that I had already done so."

Jaynes laughed. "Don't let that thought deter you," he said. "You'll do your best, I know. By the way, I'm afraid I was a bit rude to you last night—but I was very anxious to get away. For many reasons—not only my business in the States—but this whole terrible affair—I wanted to be out of it. I still do. You understand?"

"I understand," nodded Chan gravely. His left hand, in the side pocket of his coat, touched a certain envelope. "I will say good morning," he added.

He stood watching the Britisher cross the terrace and stroll toward the sea. Sensing some one at his back, he turned just in time. An old bent Chinese who continually paraded the lounge in his native costume, armed with a brush and dust-pan, was reaching for the glasses.

"*Haie!*" Chan seized the withered hand. "Do not touch, or the wrath of the seven watchful gods descends upon you." He took out his handkerchief and tenderly wrapped it round the glass from which Jaynes had drunk. "I am removing this, and the affair does not concern you."

But evidently the old man thought it did concern him, for he followed Charlie to the desk. There Chan encountered one of the managers. "I should like to purchase this object," he said, revealing what the handkerchief held. "Kindly name price."

"The manager laughed. "Oh, that's all right Take it along. What are you doing, Charlie? Collecting finger-prints from our harmless guests?"

"You are close to truth," nodded Chan. "Save perhaps with that word harmless. Thank you so much. And now will you kindly call off this aged gentleman who thinks he has captured one of the forty thieves?"

The manager said something to the servant, who moved away, muttering to himself. His comments, Chan knew, were not complimentary, but he gave no heed. He hurried through the door to his car.

Deep in thought, he drove back to Shelah Fane's house. Were the finger-prints on this glass identical with those on the window-sill in the pavilion? If they were, then he was approaching journey's end.

Hettick was waiting, and to him Charlie entrusted his precious cargo, still redolent of orange juice. The expert set quickly to work. Presently he stood by the window, the tumbler in one hand, a magnifying-glass in the other. Chan came close, awaiting the verdict.

Hettick shook his head. "Nothing like it," he announced. "You've been on the wrong trail this time, Inspector."

Keenly disappointed, Chan sat down in a chair. So it had not been Alan Jaynes who entered this room last night? It had all seemed to fit in so neatly that up to this minute he had not had a doubt of it. On the wrong trail, eh? He hadn't cared for the way in which Hettick had said that. The men at the station had been in a rather unfriendly mood since Charlie's return from the mainland. They had expected to find him in a haughty and triumphant state of mind since his exploits there, and the fact that he had shown no trace whatever of such an attitude, had done nothing to lessen their envy. He had been forced to endure many joking remarks that held an undercurrent of hostility.

On the wrong trail, eh? Well, who didn't take the wrong path occasionally in this business? Where was the superman so good that he never erred?

On the wrong trail. Chan sat deep in thought Jaynes had been outside that window—the stub of the small cigar, which he had evidently forgotten, was proof enough. But it was not he who had pushed up the screen and entered, leaving the imprint of fingers on the white sill. Some one else had done that. Who? Who else had been—

Suddenly Charlie smote his forehead a resounding blow. "*Haie*—I have been complete and utter idiot. I move too fast, without proper thought. Everybody seeks to hurry me—even my own family. And I was not built for hurry. Hurry is the wind that destroys the scaffolding." He turned to Hettick. "What has become of finger-print record of beach-comber, taken at station last night?"

"Oh," replied Hettick. "I've got that here." He produced a manila envelope from his pocket and removed a glass plate. "Do you think——"

"I think, yes—a little late, but still I think," said Charlie. He took the plate from the unresisting hand of his brother officer and hurried to the window. "Come quickly," he called. "Your glass—look! What is your decision?"

"They are the same," Hettick announced.

Triumph shone brightly in Charlie's little eyes. "At last I arrive somewhere," he cried. "Smith, the beach-comber, was in this room last night! Am I forever on wrong trail or do I have my lucific moments?"

16

A Word of Warning

Chan's air of calm detachment had vanished for the moment, and he walked the floor as though inspired by his latest discovery.

"Smith, the beach-comber," he said once more. "Dreary bit of human wreckage cast up on shore of splendid island. Ragged remnant of a man—how busy he was around this building last night. A big evening, I think, in the life of Smith."

Hettick was gathering up the tools of his trade. "Well, I believe I'll go back to the station now," he remarked. "I've given you boys something to work on. Go out and make the most of it."

"Ah, you are clever detective," Chan grinned. "Things slip from mind sometimes, but when humble fellow worker recalls them, then you move on like avenging demon. You have given us material indeed. Yes, please return to station at once. I will arrive later, and in meantime I respectfully suggest that you send out alarm call for Smith. Tell Chief beach-comber must be pulled into station with no delay. Let all low dives be explored. Put Kashimo on it. He is our most passioned searcher, and what is better, he knows all cracks and crannies of modest little underworld."

Hettick promised he would deliver the message, and departed. Charlie followed at his heels. He saw Julie and Bradshaw on the lawn, and paused beside them. "You wish ride to town?" he inquired of the latter.

"No, thanks," Bradshaw replied. "I've got my car today. Besides Julie has just persuaded me to stay for lunch."

"May life hold for her no sterner task than such persuasion," smiled Chan. "I do not wish to cloud your future, Miss Julie, but must warn you that I return here soon."

He was skirting the house when Jessop appeared at the lanai door. "Ah—er—Constable," he said. "May I ask you to step inside just a moment?"

Struck by the seriousness of the butler's manner, Charlie passed through the door which the servant held open. "You have something to say to me?" he asked.

"I have, sir. Kindly come with me." Jessop led the way into a small reception-room near the front of the house. He entered it first—evidence of unusual abstraction on his part. "Oh—I beg your pardon, sir. I'll just close this door, so we may have an undisturbed tête-à-tête."

"Time is none too plentiful with me—" Chan began, somewhat surprised by these elaborate preparations.

"I know that, Constable, I will—er—plunge in at once." In spite of this promise, he hesitated. "My old father, who was for more than forty years the trusted employee of a rather exacting duke, remarked to me in my youth: 'A good servant, Cedric, sees all, knows all, but tells nothing.' It is only after prolonged and mature consideration, Constable, that I have determined to ignore that excellent counsel."

Chan nodded. "Circumstances," he remarked, "upset cases."

"Precisely, sir. I have always been a law-abiding man, and what is more, I am eager to see you get to the bottom of this matter without—if I may say so—further delay. Last evening I chanced to be busy in the hall at the moment when you were engaged in interviewing Miss Julie regarding the emerald ring. This may suggest to you that I was eavesdropping, but I can assure you that such duplicity was farthest from my thoughts. I heard the young lady tell you that Miss Fane had given her that ring early in the morning, and that she—Miss Julie, I mean—had held it in her possession from that moment on, until you discovered it in her room."

"Such was Miss Julie's story," Charlie agreed.

"I am at a complete loss to understand it, sir. I don't know what she meant by her testimony—but I do know this. At about seven last night, Miss Fane called me to her room and gave me the letter which I was to deliver to Mr. Tarneverro immediately on his arrival at the house. As she passed over the missive, I distinctly saw, gleaming on her right hand, the ring in question. I am positive on that point, Constable, and prepared to offer a sworn statement along those lines."

Chan was silent for a moment. He thought of Julie O'Neill, so young, so innocent-looking. "Thank you very much," he said at last. "What you say seems of vast importance."

"I only hope it may not be so important as it appears," Jessop replied. "I tell you this, Constable, with considerable reluctance. I have nothing against Miss Julie—a charming young woman—indeed she is, sir. I was tempted for a long time to remain silent, but it struck me that my duty lay, most decidedly, in the opposite direction. Like yourself, I desire to see the miscreant in this affair adequately punished. Miss Fane was always extremely kind to me."

Chan moved toward the door. "I shall act upon your information at once," he announced.

Jessop looked uncomfortable. "If my name could only be kept out of it, sir——"

"Same may not be possible," Charlie told him.

Jessop sighed. "I recognize that, Constable. I can only say again that I am quite positive I saw the ring. My eyesight is excellent, which, to a man of my age, is a matter of deep satisfaction."

They went out into the hall. Anna, the maid, was slowly coming down the stairs. Chan turned to Jessop.

"Thank you again," he said. "You may go now."

The butler disappeared toward the kitchen, and Charlie waited for Anna at the foot of the stairs.

"Good morning," he remarked pleasantly. "I desire one word with you, please."

"Of course," replied Anna, and followed him into the living-room.

"You recall story of Miss Julie regarding the ring?"

"Naturally, sir."

"Same was given her by Miss Fane in early morning and remained in her possession. Have you anything to say regarding that?"

"Why—why what do you mean, sir?" the maid returned.

"You did not yourself see the ring on Miss Fane's finger during the day? Or when she came to you to procure pin for orchids?"

"If I did, it made no impression on me, sir."

"You see things, yet they make no impression?"

"You know how it is, sir. Things become familiar and you don't really notice. What I mean is—the ring may or may not have been there. I'm afraid I can't say, sir."

"You wish the matter to stand at that?"

"I fear it must, as far as I am concerned."

Chan bowed. "Thank you—that is all."

He stepped through a French window, and walked slowly across the lanai. He had no heart for the task that faced him now, but many such tasks had confronted him in the past, and he had never faltered. Stepping out on the lawn, he went over to a beach swing where Bradshaw and the girl were sitting.

"Miss Julie," he began. The girl looked up at him, and at sight of his grave face, her own paled.

"Yes, Mr. Chan," she said in a low voice.

"Miss Julie, you have told me Miss Fane gave you that emerald ring soon after her arrival yesterday morning. Why did you tell me that?"

"Because it's the truth," Julie answered bravely.

"Then how do you account for fact that ring was seen on her finger last evening at seven?"

"Who says it was?" the girl cried.

"Is that important?"

"It is very important. Who says it was?"

"I learn it from what I think reliable source."

"You have no means of knowing how reliable, Mr. Chan. Who made that statement? Not Miss Dixon—she isn't up yet. It must have been one of the servants. Jessop, perhaps. Was it Jessop, Mr. Chan?"

"What does it matter—"

"But I assure you it matters very much. Because, you see, I don't stand very well with Jessop. There's an old grudge between us—on his part, at least."

"You will, please, explain what you mean by that?"

"Of course. As I told you last night, Miss Fane's servants were always cheating her. When I first became her secretary I shut my eyes to it, because I'm no tale-bearer. But about a year ago, her finances became terribly involved, and I began an investigation. I discovered that Jessop had a most shameless arrangement with the tradespeople—all the bills were padded outrageously and Jessop was getting a share of the profits.

"I said nothing to Miss Fane—I knew what that would mean—a temperamental outburst, tears and recriminations, and probably a grand scene of forgiveness in the end. She was always so kind-hearted. Instead I went to Jessop, told him I know what he was doing and that the thing must stop. He was most indignant. All the other servants in Hollywood, he told me, were doing the same, and he seemed to consider it a sort of royal prerogative. But when I threatened to tell Miss Fane, he backed down and agreed to put an end to the practice. I fancy he did, too, but since that time he has always been very cool to me, and I know that I have never been forgiven. So you see why I asked you if it was Jessop who told that—falsehood about the ring."

"Just where do you stand—as you say it—with Anna?"

"Oh, Anna and I have always been on the most friendly terms," Julie answered. "A good steady girl who saves her money and buys bonds with it. It's money honestly come by—I'm sure of that because"—Julie smiled faintly—"the poor thing has never had a chance to pad bills. None of them passes through her hands."

Chan looked at Julie's flushed face for a long moment. "Then you desire to repeat that Miss Fane herself gave you the ring yesterday morning?"

"I certainly do. It's the truth, Mr. Chan."

Charlie bowed. "I can only accept your word, Miss Julie. It is quite possible—the person who told me of seeing the ring last night may have been moved by ancient grudge—I thought of it at the time. Miss Julie, I say to myself, too fine and sweet for underhand work. You will note, Jimmy, that you and I have tastes in common."

"Which does you credit," smiled Bradshaw.

"Which credits us both," amended Chan. "I will no longer hang about, a blot on this lovely scene. My kindest good-by—until we meet again."

He walked thoughtfully to his car, and drove away through the hot noon sunshine. "So many roads that wind and wind——" He had read that somewhere. He sighed. So many roads—would the little car finally leap down the right one?

As he approached the Grand Hotel, Huntley Van Horn was again in his thoughts. He was reluctant to reappear so soon at the hotel's main entrance so, parking his car in the street, he entered the grounds and walked toward the palm court. A group of excited tourists was gathered beneath the tallest of the coco-palms, and looking aloft, Charlie saw one of the beach-boys, in a red bathing-suit, climbing the tree with the agility of a monkey. He stood for a moment, admiring the boy's skill.

"The kid's clever, eh, Inspector?" remarked a voice at his elbow.

He turned and looked into the smiling gray eyes of Van Horn. They were standing a little apart from the others, and the picture actor was the recipient of many awed, adoring glances from young women who were ostensibly there to watch the beach-boy.

"Ah, Mr. Van Horn," Chan said. "This meeting is indeed most fortunate. I am calling here for the sole purpose of seeing you."

"Really?" The actor looked up at the tree. "Well, he seems to have traveled as far as he can on that one. Shall we go on the veranda—pardon me, the lanai—and have a chat?"

"The idea is most suitable," Charlie agreed. He followed Van Horn and they sat down in a secluded corner. The boy had descended the coco-palm

and stood now the center of an admiring group, hugely enjoying the limelight. Chan watched him.

"Sometimes in my heart," he remarked, "arouses hot envy of the beach-
boys. To exist so happily—to have no cares and troubles, no worries—ah,
that must be what men mean by Paradise. All they ask of life is one bathing-
suit, slightly worn."

Van Horn laughed. "You have worries, I take it, Inspector?"

Charlie turned to him; he had decided to be frank. "I have." He paused.
"You are one of them," he added suddenly.

The picture actor was unperturbed. "You flatter me," he answered. "Just
how am I worrying you, Inspector?"

"You worry me because in this matter of Miss Shelah Fane's murder you
are quite defenseless. Not only do you possess no alibi, but of all those
concerned, you were nearest to the scene of her death. You walked across
lawn at very important moment, Mr. Van Horn. I could not worry about
you more if you were own son."

Van Horn grinned. "That's kind of you, Inspector. I appreciate it. Yes—I
am rather badly cast in the story of the crime. But I rely on you. As an
intelligent man, you must realize that I could have had absolutely no motive
for killing the poor girl. Until I joined her company to make this picture,
I scarcely knew her, and all through our journey and the work together,
we were on the friendliest terms."

"Ah, yes," Chan watched the actor's face eagerly. "Were you likewise on
friendly terms with Denny Mayo?" he inquired.

"Just what has Denny Mayo to do with all this?" Van Horn asked. Despite
his best efforts, his expression was not quite so casual as he wanted it to
be.

"May have much to do with it," Charlie told him. "I seek to upearth facts.
Maybe you assist me. I repeat—were you on friendly terms with Denny
Mayo?"

"I knew him fairly well," Van Horn admitted. "A most attractive chap—a
wild Irishman—you never could tell what he was going to do next. Every
one was very fond of him. His death was a great shock."

"Who killed him?" Charlie asked blandly.

"I wish I knew," Van horn replied. "Last night, when I heard you asking
everybody about three years ago last June, in Hollywood, I sensed that you
thought his death involved in this somehow. I'm curious to know the connection."

"That, no doubt," said Charlie, "is why you haste to library early this
morning to do hot reading about Mayo case?"

Van Horn smiled. "Oh—so you found me among my books, eh? Well,
Inspector, as my press-agent will tell you, I'm of rather a studious type.
There's nothing I like better than to curl up in a corner with a good
book—real literature, mind you——"

Charlie raised a protesting hand. "The wise man, knowing he is under
suspicion," he remarked, "does not stoop to tie his shoe in a melon patch."

Van Horn nodded. "An old Chinese saw, eh? Not bad either."

"You will," said Chan sternly, "before we leave these chairs, tell me the
reason for your visit to library this morning."

Van Horn did not reply. He sat for a moment with a frown on his
handsome face. Then he turned with sudden decision.

"You've been frank with me, Inspector. I'll be the same with you. Though
when you've heard my reason for that visit, I fear you'll be more puzzled
than ever." He took from his pocket an envelope bearing the crest of the

Grand Hotel, and drew out a single sheet of note-paper. "Will you please read that?"

Chan took the paper. It bore a brief note, type-written and unsigned. He read:

> Just a word of warning from a friend. You should go at once to the Honolulu Police Library and remove from the bound volumes of all Los Angeles papers carrying the Denny Mayo murder story, certain rather damaging references to your own part in that affair.

Charlie looked up. "Where did you get this?"

"I found it under my door when I awoke this morning," the actor told him.

"You went to library at once?"

"Directly after breakfast. Who wouldn't? I couldn't recall that I'd ever been mentioned in connection with the case—there was no reason why I should have been. But naturally—my curiosity was aroused. I went down and read every word I could find regarding Mayo's murder in the *Los Angeles Times*—the only paper they had. And oddly enough——"

"Yes?" Chan prompted.

"It was just as I thought. My name wasn't mentioned anywhere. I've had a rather puzzled morning, Inspector."

"Natural you should," nodded Charlie. "A queer circumstance, indeed. Have you any idea who wrote this note?"

"None whatever," returned Van Horn. "But the purpose of it seems to be clear. Somebody has sought to cast suspicion in my direction. It's a delicate little attention, and I appreciate it. He—or possibly she—figured that I would go to the library and sign for that volume, and that of course you would soon find it out. After that, you would fancy me deeply involved in this affair, and would spend precious time sleuthing in the wrong direction. Fortunately, you took the unusual course of coming to me at once with your suspicion. I'm glad you did. And I'm damned glad I kept the letter."

"Which, after all, you may have written to yourself," Chan suggested.

Van Horn laughed. "Oh, no—I'm not so deep as all that, Mr. Chan. The letter was under my door when I rose. Find out who wrote it, and you may find the murderer of Shelah Fane."

"True enough," agreed Charlie. "I will keep it now, of course." He stood up. "We have had a good talk, Mr. Van Horn, and I am grateful for your confidence. I go my way with one more puzzle burning in my pocket. Add a few more, and I collapse from mental strain. I trust I have not held you away from luncheon."

"Not at all," the actor replied. "This has been a very lucky interview for me. Good-by, and all my best wishes for success."

Chan hastened through the palm court, and at last set his flivver on the road to the city. As he moved along, he thought deeply about Huntley Van Horn. Despite his airy manner, the actor had seemed to be open and sincere. But could he, Charlie wondered, be sure of that? Could he ever be sure in this world? Deceit sprouted everywhere and thrived like a weed.

Suppose Van Horn was sincere? Who put that note under his bedroom door while he slept? Chan began to realize that he was engaged in a duel—a duel to the death. His opponent was quick and wary, cleverer than any person he had yet encountered in a long career. How many of these clues were false, dropped but to befuddle him? How many real?

An inner craving told him that lunch would be a pleasant diversion; he was never one to put such promptings aside. But as he approached the public library an even greater craving assailed him—a keen desire to read for himself the story of Denny Mayo's murder. With a sigh for the business man's lunch that must languish without him a little longer, he stopped the car and went inside.

The desk was deserted for the moment, and he turned into the reading-room at his right. There was just a chance that the big volume taken out by Van Horn early that morning was not yet restored to its place on the shelves. Yes—there it lay, on the table at which he had seen the picture actor sitting. Save for one or two children, the place was deserted. Charlie rapidly crossed the room and opened the book.

It happened that he knew the date of the Mayo tragedy, and he sought immediately the issue of the subsequent morning. His eyes opened wide. Under an eight-column head, "Movie Actor Found Murdered in Home," a great torn gap stared at him.

Quickly he examined the pages, and then sat back, dazed and unbelieving. Every picture of Denny Mayo had been ruthlessly cut from the book.

17

How Denny Mayo Died

Chan sat motionless for a long time, deep in thought. Some desperate person was determined that he should not look upon the likeness of Denny Mayo. The captions to the pictures were for the most part intact. "Denny Mayo When He First Came to Hollywood." And here again: "Denny Mayo as He Appeared in *The Unknown Sin.*" But in every instance the reproduction of the actor's face was destroyed.

Who had done this thing? Huntley Van Horn? Perhaps. Yet if that were so, Van Horn's methods were crude and raw for so suave a gentleman. To go boldly to the library, ask for this volume, sign his name to the slip as he claimed to have done, and then mutilate the yellowed page, would be unbelievably naive. It invited swift and inevitable detection. It certainly did not sound like Van Horn.

With a ponderous sigh, Charlie applied himself to the story that had surrounded Denny Mayo's pictures. The actor had come to Hollywood from the English stage, and had won immediate success. He had lived with one servant in a detached house on one of the best Los Angeles streets. On the night of the murder the servant, after completing his usual duties, took the evening off. He went out at eight o'clock, leaving Mayo in excellent spirits.

Returning at midnight, the man let himself in through the kitchen door. Seeing a light in the living-room, he went there to ask if anything further was required of him before he went to bed. On the floor of the room he discovered the actor, dead some two hours. Mayo had been shot at close range with his own revolver, a delicate weapon which he was accustomed to keeping in the drawer of his desk. The revolver was lying at his side, and there were no finger-prints on it—neither his own nor those of any unknown person. No one had been seen entering or leaving the house which occupied a dark position under its many trees.

Unfortunately, the following morning—and Charlie's eyebrows rose at this—the police had permitted the general public to swarm through the house. Actors, actresses, directors, producers—all friends, they claimed, of the dead man—had paraded through the rooms, and if any vital clue was still lying about it could easily have been destroyed. In any case, no vital clue was ever found. Those the police discovered led nowhere.

Little was known about Mayo's past; he had come from far away, and no member of his family stepped forward during the investigation. It was rumored that he had a wife in England, but he had not seen her for several years, never mentioned her to his friends—might, possibly, have been divorced. His life in Hollywood had not been spectacular; women admired him, but if he returned this admiration in any instance, he had been most discreet about it. If any one had a grudge against him——

Further along in the story, a name caught Charlie's eye, and he sat up with sudden interest. Hastily he read on until he came to it. Mayo had been working in a picture, and as his leading woman he had had an actress named Rita Montaine. Miss Montaine was engaged to marry a certain Wilkie Ballou, a prominent figure in Honolulu, scion of an old family there. Some obscure person testified that he had overheard a quarrel between Mayo and Ballou—it concerned a party to which Mayo had taken Miss Montaine. But the witness had heard Ballou make no threats against the actor.

Nevertheless, Ballou had been questioned. His alibi was complete, sworn to by Miss Montaine herself. On the night of Mayo's death the actress said that she and Ballou had been together from six o'clock until after midnight. They had taken a long ride in Ballou's car and danced together at a roadhouse far from the scene of the crime. She admitted that she was engaged to Ballou and intended to marry him soon.

These two faded from the limelight. Charlie read on, through the helpless meanderings of a completely baffled police. He turned page after page, no new developments arose, and amid a frantic sputtering on the part of the reporters, the story gradually died out.

How about that alibi of Ballou's? Sworn to by the woman who was going to marry him. Was she also ready to lie for him?

Chan picked up the heavy volume and returned to the main room of the library. He laid his burden down on the desk, behind which stood a bright young woman. Without speaking, he opened the book and indicated the mutilated pages.

If his aim had been to annoy the young woman, he could have found no better means. Her cry of dismay was immediate and heartfelt. "Who did this, Mr. Chan?" she demanded.

Charlie smiled. "Thanks for touching faith in my ability," he remarked. "But I can not tell you."

"It was taken out by Mr. Van Horn, the actor. This sort of thing is prohibited by law, you know. You must arrest him at once."

Chan shrugged. "It was also lying on table from time Mr. Van Horn left it, early to-day, until well past noon. What proof have we that Van Horn mutilated it? I know him well, and I do not think him complete fool."

"But—but——"

"I will, with your kind permission, speak to him over wire. He may be able to cast little light."

The young woman led him to the telephone, and Chan got Van Horn at the hotel. He explained at once the condition in which he had found the book.

"What do you know about that!" Van Horn remarked.

"Alas! very little," Charlie returned. "The volume was in the intact state when you saw it?"

"Absolutely. Perfectly O.K. I left it on the table about nine-thirty and went out."

"Did you see any one known to you about place?"

"Not a soul. But I say, Inspector, this throws new light on that note I got this morning. Perhaps the intention of my unknown friend was not so much to involve me, as to get that volume out of the files. He—if it was a he—may have hoped that the thing would happen just as it has happened—that I would take it out and leave it where he could find it without himself signing a slip. Have you thought of that?"

"So much to think of," Chan sighed. "Thank you for the idea." He went back to the desk. "Mr. Van Horn left the volume in original state. He is certain of that. Was it noted that any one else examined it this morning?"

"I don't know," the young woman replied. "The librarian in charge of that room is out to lunch. Look here, Mr. Chan, you've got to find who did this."

"Plenty busy with murder just now," Charlie explained.

"Never mind your murder," she answered grimly. "This is serious."

Chan smiled, but the young woman was in no mood to join him. He promised to do his best and departed.

A glance at his watch told him that he had not time for his usual leisurely lunch. He had instead a sandwich and a glass of milk, then went to the station. The Chief was pacing the floor of the detectives' room.

"Hello, Charlie," he cried. "I've been wondering where you were. Pretty busy this morning, I take it?"

"Like fly on hot griddle," Chan answered. "And just as eager to get off."

"Haven't got anything yet, eh?"

"Have so much I am worn out," Charlie told him. "But no idea who killed Shelah Fane."

"That's what we want," the Chief insisted. "The name—the name. Good lord, we ought to get somewhere pretty soon."

"Maybe we will," replied Chan, with just the slightest inflection on the "we." He sat down. "Now I will relate morning's adventures, and it can happen that your keen brain will function where mine wanders lonely in the dark."

He began at the beginning: his visit to the theater, Robert Fyfe's cast-iron alibi, his admission that he had given the beach-comber money in exchange for a painting. He mentioned his call at the library and his discovery there of Huntley Van Horn, then went on to the two old people on the terrace of the hotel, who had accounted so readily for Tarneverro's actions on the previous night.

"They may be lying," said the Chief.

Charlie shook his head. "You would not say that if you saw them. Honestly gleams like unceasing beacon from their eyes."

"I'll judge of that for myself," remarked his superior. "What was their name? MacMaster? I'll talk with them later. Go on."

Charlie continued. He told of finding the stub of the small cigar of a sort smoked only by Alan Jaynes, beneath the pavilion window.

"Oh, lord," sighed the Chief. "They can't all be in it. Somebody's kidding you, Charlie."

"You go back to singular pronoun," smiled Chan. "A moment ago it was we. But that was only in regard to approaching moment of success, I think."

"Well, somebody's kidding us, then. Have it your own way. You got Jaynes' finger-prints?"

"I slyly obtained same. But it was print of Smith, the beach-comber, we discover on window-sill."

"Yes—that was something we can really act on. I sent out the word to pick him up right away. They'll bring him in any minute now. What have you been doing since then?"

Charlie repeated Jessop's story about the ring, which, he pointed out, might mean merely the repayment of an old grudge. He showed his Chief the letter which Van Horn had offered in explanation of his visit to the library. Finally he told of the mutilation of the bound volume of the newspaper, and ended with the mention of Ballou and his wife in the story of the Denny Mayo murder case.

For a long time, when he had finished, his Chief sat in silence. "Well," he said at length, "according to your investigation, they're all in it, I guess. Good heavens, can't you draw any deductions from all this?"

"Kindly state what are your deductions," answered Chan with gentle malice.

"Me? I don't know. I am stumped. But you—the pride of the force——"

"Kindly recall—I have never been demon for speed. While I stumble about this way, I am fiercely thinking. Large bodies arrive late. Grant me time."

"What do you propose to do now?"

"I consider a little social visit with Mrs. Ballou."

"Great Scott, Charlie—watch your step. Ballou's an important man in this town, and he's never been very friendly to me."

"I plan to use all possible diplomacy."

"You'll need it, and then some. Don't offend him, whatever you do. You know—these old families——"

Charlie shrugged. "I have not lived in Honolulu all these years in state of blindness. Do not worry. I move now on feet shod with velvet, and my voice drips oil and honey."

Kashimo came in. He walked with dragging step and had a discouraged air.

"Well, where's this fellow Smith," demanded the Chief.

"No place, sir," said Kashimo. "Melted like ice."

"Melted, hell! You go out again, and don't come back without him."

"Look everywhere," Kashimo complained. "All funny joints, up-stair, in cellar. Comb town. No Smith."

Charlie went over and patted him on the back. "If at first you have drawn blank, resume the job," he advised. He took a slip of paper from a desk and began to write. "I give you a list of unsavory places," he explained. "Maybe you overlook some. Perhaps, after all, I have better knowledge of city's wickedness than honored member of Young Men's Buddhist Association like yourself."

He handed his list to the Japanese, who took it and left, followed by Charlie's kindly encouragement.

"Poor Kashimo," Chan remarked. "When there is no oil in the lamp, the wick is wasted. In dealing with such a one, friendly words bring best results. Now I go forth to wallow some more in bafflement."

"I'll be waiting to hear from you," his Chief called after him.

Charlie set out for the Manoa Valley home of the Ballous. The business district disappeared behind him, and he traveled a street lined with great houses set on rolling lawns. Above his head flamed flowering trees, now in the last weeks of their splendor. He sped past Paunahou Academy, and as he penetrated farther into the valley, he left the zone of sunshine for one of darkness. Black clouds hung over the mountains ahead and suddenly, borne on the wind, came a wild gust of rain. It beat fiercely on the top of the little car and blurred the windshield. Yet a mile away, at Charlie's back, Honolulu sparkled in the midday sun.

He reached the handsome house of Wilkie Ballou, and Rita received him in the dark drawing-room. Her husband, she explained, was up-stairs dressing for his afternoon golf. In Honolulu a real golfer pays no attention to rain; it may be pouring on his street, but bright and sunny round the corner. Rita's manner was cordial, and Chan took heart.

"I am so sorry to obtrude my obnoxious presence," he apologized. "If you never saw me again, I feel sure you would like it well enough. But—mere matter of form—I must inflict little talk on every one present at sad affair last night."

Rita nodded. "Poor Shelah! How are you getting on, Inspector?"

"I make splendid progress," he informed her blithely. There was, he felt, no occasion to go into that. "Would you speak with me little while about days when you were famous Hollywood figure?"

With bored eyes, Rita looked out at the rain lashing against the window. "I certainly will," she said.

"May I add that you broke heart of my eldest daughter, who is great film fan, when you retired from silvery sheet? No one, she moans, is ever so good as you were."

Rita's face brightened. "She remembers me? That's sweet of her."

"Your fine skill will never be forgotten anywhere," Chan assured her, and knew that he had made a friend for life.

"How can I help you?" she inquired.

Chan considered. "You knew Miss Fane in Hollywood?"

"Oh, yes, quite well."

"It is wisely forbidden to speak ill of those who have ascended the dragon, but sometimes we must let old rules go down the board. Was there at any time scandal in the lady's life?"

"Oh, no, none whatever. She wasn't that sort, you know."

"But she had what you call love-affairs?"

"Yes, frequently. She was emotional and impulsive—never without a love-affair. But they were all harmless, I'm sure."

"Did you hear that once she loved a man named—Denny Mayo?" Charlie watched Rita's face closely, and he thought she looked a little startled.

"Why, yes—Shelah was rather wild about Denny at one time, I believe. She took it rather hard when he was—killed. You knew about that, perhaps?"

"I know all about that," answered Chan slowly. But to his disappointment, the words seemed to leave the woman quite calm. "You had acquaintance with this Denny Mayo yourself, I think?"

"Yes—I was in his last picture."

Chan had an inspiration. "It may be you have photograph of Mayo somewhere among possessions?"

She shook her head. "No—I did have some old stills, but Mr. Ballou made me burn them. He said he wouldn't have me mooning about over the dear, dead past when I was——" She stopped, her eyes on the door.

Charlie looked up. Wilkie Ballou, in a golf suit, was in the doorway. He strode grimly into the room.

"What's all this about Denny Mayo?" he demanded.

"Mr. Chan was simply asking me if I knew him," Rita explained.

"Mr. Chan should mind his own business," her husband growled. He walked over and faced Charlie. "Denny Mayo," he said, "is dead and buried."

Chan shrugged. "I am so sorry, but he does not stay buried."

"He stays that way as far as my wife and I are concerned," Ballou answered, and there was a certain dignity about him as he said it.

For a moment Chan looked sleepily into the hostile eyes of the millionaire. "Your alibi for the night of Mayo's murder," he ventured, "seems to have enjoyed a fine success."

Ballou flushed. "Why not? It was the truth."

"So naturally, it prevailed." Chan moved toward the door. "I am sorry if I have disturbed you——"

"You haven't disturbed me in the least," Ballou snapped. "Just what did you expect to find here, anyhow?"

"I thought I might chance upon photograph of Denny Mayo."

"And why should you want his photograph?"

"Some unknown person objects to my looking at it."

"Is that so?" said Ballou. "Well, you won't find Mayo's picture here. Or anything else that will interest you, for that matter. Good day, Inspector; and I must ask you not to call again."

Charlie shrugged. "I travel where duty takes me. Would much prefer to loll in station house—but can you study swimming on a carpet? No—you must go where waters are deep. Good day, Mr. Ballou."

Rita followed him into the hall. "I'm afraid we haven't been able to help you," she remarked.

"Thanks all same," bowed Chan.

"I'm so sorry," the woman said. "I want to see you succeed. If there was only something I could do——"

Chan's eyes caught the flash of rings on her fingers. "There might be," he remarked suddenly.

"Anything," she replied.

"Last night you saw Miss Shelah Fane after long separation. Quick glance of women catches points men despise to notice. You recall all she was wearing, no doubt?"

"Why, of course. She had on a stunning gown—ivory satin, it was——"

"I speak mostly of jewels," Chan told her. "What woman is so blind she fails to note other woman's jewelry?"

Rita smiled. "Not I. She had on a gorgeous string of pearls, and a diamond bracelet——"

"And her rings?"

"Only one. A huge emerald I remember seeing in Hollywood. It was on her right hand."

"This was when you last encountered her? The young people were already in the water enjoying warm swim?"

"Julie and that boy were—yes."

Charlie bowed low. "My gratitude has no bounds. Now I must go on with my work. Good-by."

He went out into the perpetual valley rain, and turned his car toward the sunlit beach.

18

The Bell-man's Story

Julie and Jimmy Bradshaw sat on the white sand of Waikiki and gazed at an ocean that stretched, apparently empty of life, from this curving shore all the way to the atolls of the South Seas.

"Well, I suppose I'd better be getting along downtown," remarked the boy. He yawned, and dropping on his back, watched the white clouds drift lazily across a cobalt sky.

"Picture of a young man filled with pep and energy," Julie smiled.

He shuddered. "Very poor taste, my girl, introducing words like that into a conversation at Waikiki beach. It must be that, after all, I have given you a very imperfect idea of the spirit of this place. Here we loaf, we dream——"

"But you'll never get anywhere," Julie reproved.

"I'm there already," he answered. "Why should I bestir myself? When you're in Hawaii you've no place to go—you've reached heaven, and a change couldn't possibly be an improvement. So you just sit down and wait for eternity to end."

Julie shrugged. "Is that so? Well, I'm afraid I'm not built that way. Great for a vacation, yes—this place is all you say of it. But as a permanent residence—well——"

He sat up suddenly. "Good lord, you mean I haven't sold you on it? Me—the greatest descriptive writer in history—and I've failed to put over the big deal of my life. James J. Bradshaw strikes a snag—meets failure face to face—it seems incredible. Where have I slipped up, Julie? Haven't I made you feel the beauty of this island——"

"Beauty's all right," the girl replied. "But how about its effect on character? It seems to me that when you've stopped moving, you're going back."

"Yeah," he smiled. "I went to a Rotary Club luncheon once myself—over on the mainland. Boys, we gotta progress or perish. Last year we turned out ten million gaskets, this year let's turn out fifteen. Make America gasket-conscious. Take it from me——"

"What were you saying about getting back to the office?"

He shook his head. "I thought I'd cast you for the rôle of Eve in this paradise, and what a serpent you turn out to be. Getting back to the office is something we never do over here. We don't want to wake the poor fellows who didn't go out."

"That's just what I've been saying, Jimmy."

"But dear Mrs. Legree, you don't need to be chained to an office desk in order to accomplish things. You can work just as well lying down. For instance, a minute ago I was well started on a new appeal to tourists. 'Come—let the laughing lei girl twine her garlands of flowers about your shoulders. Try your skill at riding Waikiki's surf, or just rest in lazy luxury——' "

"Ah, yes—that's what you prefer to do——"

" 'Under the nodding coco-palms.' Don't you like our coco-palms, Julie?"

"They're interesting, but I think I prefer the redwoods. You draw a deep breath in a redwood forest, Jimmy, and you feel like going out and licking the world. Can't you see what I mean? This place may be all right for people who belong here—but you—how long have you been in Hawaii?"

"A little over two years."

"Did you intend to stay here when you came?"

"Well, now—let's not go into that."

"You didn't, of course. You just took the line of least resistance. Don't you ever want to go back to the mainland and make something of yourself?"

"Oh—at first——" He was silent for a moment. "Well, I've failed to make the sale on Hawaii, I guess. That will always leave a scar on my heart, but there's something more important. Have I sold myself? I'm keen about you, Julie. If you'll say the word——"

She shook her head. "Don't let's go into that, either, Jimmy. I'm not what you think me—I'm horrid, really—I—oh, Jimmy, you wouldn't want to marry a—a liar, would you?"

Hs shrugged. "Not a professional one—no. But a clumsy amateur like you—why, you do it as though you'd had no experience at all."

She was startled. "What do you mean?"

"All that about the ring. Why, in heaven's name, do you go on with it? I've been wise ever since this morning, and as for Charlie Chan—say, I admire the polite way he's treated you. I don't believe you've fooled him for a minute."

"Oh, dear—I thought I was rather good."

"What's it all about, Julie?" the boy inquired.

Tears were in her eyes. "It's about—poor Shelah. She took me in when I was broke and without a friend—she ws always so good to me. I'd—I'd have done anything in the world for her—let alone tell a little lie."

"I won't ask you to continue," Bradshaw remareked. "I don't have to. Don't look around. Inspector Chan of the Honolulu police is approaching rapidly, and something in his walk tells me that this is the zero hour for you. Brace up. I'm with you, kid."

Charlie joined them, amiable and smiling. "Not too welcome, I think. But anyhow I attach myself to this little group." He sat down, facing the girl. "What is your opinion of our beach, Miss Julie? Here you are deep in the languid zone. How do you like languor, as far as you have got with it?"

Julie stared at him. "Mr. Chan, you have not come here to talk to me about the beach."

"Not precisely," he admitted. "But I am firm believer in leading up. Suitable preparation removes the sting of rudeness. Making an example, it would have been undecently abrupt for me to stride up and cry: 'Miss Julie, why do you lie to me about that emerald ring?' "

Her cheeks flushed. "You think I have been—lying?"

"More than think, Miss Julie. I know. Other eyes than Jessop's saw the ring on Miss Fane's finger long after you immersed in waters of Waikiki last night."

She did not reply. "Better own up, Julie," Bradshaw advised. "It's the best way. Charlie will be your friend then—won't you, Charlie?"

"Must admit feeling of friendship would suffer a notable increase," Chan nodded. "Miss Julie, it is not true that Miss Fane gave you that ring yesterday to obtain cash for it?"

"Oh, yes, it is," the girl insisted. "That much is true."

"Then she took it back later?"

"Yes—just after she returned from her interview with Tarneverro, about noon."

"Took it back, and wore it when she died?"

"Yes."

"After the tragedy, you again obtained possession?"

"I did. When Jimmy and I found her, I went in and knelt beside her. It was then I took the ring."

"Why?"

"I—I can't tell you."

"You mean you won't."

"I can't, and I won't. I'm sorry, Mr. Chan."

"I also get deep pain from this." Charlie was silent for a moment. "Can it happen you removed the ring because name of 'Denny' was engraved inside?"

"Wh—what do you know about Denny?"

Chan sat up with sudden interest. "I will tell you, and perhaps you will grow frank. I have learned that Shelah Fane was in Los Angeles house the very night Denny Mayo was murdered there. Consequently, she knew name of killer. It was scandal in her past she was eager to conceal. Perhaps, to aid that concealment, you yourself wished name of Denny Mayo kept out of all discussions. A natural desire to shield your friend's reputation. But as you see, your actions have not availed. Now you may speak, with no injury to your dear benefactor."

The girl was weeping softly. "Yes, I guess I might as well tell you. I'm so sorry you know all that. I'd have given anything to keep Denny Mayo out of this."

"You were aware, then, of that scandal in Miss Fane's past?"

"I suspected that something was terribly wrong, but I didn't know what. I was quite young—I had just come to Shelah—at the time of Denny's—accident. On the night it happened, Shelah arrived home in a state of hysteria, and I was there alone with her. I took care of her the best I could. For weeks she wasn't herself. I knew that in some way she was connected with Mayo's murder, but until this moment, I never learned the facts. I was young, as I say, but I knew better than to ask questions."

"Coming to yesterday——" Chan prompted.

"It was just as I told you—yesterday morning she said she must get hold of money at once, and she gave me the ring to sell. Then she went down to the Grand Hotel to see Tarneverro, and when she came back she was sort of hysterical again. She sent for me to come to her room—she was walking the floor. I couldn't imagine what had happened. 'He's a devil, Julie,' she cried. 'That Tarneverro's a devil—I wish I had never sent for him. He told me things about Tahiti and on the boat—how could he know—he frightened me. And I've done something terribly foolish, Julie—I must have been mad.' She became rather incoherent then. I asked her what it was all about. 'Get the emeralds' She told me. 'We mustn't sell it, Julie. Denny's name is inside it, and I don't want any mention of that name now.' "

"She was hysteric, you say?"

"Yes. She was often that way, but this was worse, somehow. 'Denny Mayo won't die, Julie,' she said. 'He'll come back to disgrace me yet.' Then she urged me to get the ring, and of course I did. She told me we'd find something else to sell later. Just then she was too upset to discuss it. In the afternoon, I saw her crying over Denny Mayo's picture."

"Ah," cried Chan, "that was portrait of Denny Mayo mounted on green mat?"

"It was."

"Continue, please."

"Last night," Julie went on, "when Jimmy and I made our terrible discovery in the pavilion, I thought at once of what Shelah had said. Denny would come back to disgrace her yet. Somehow, I thought, his death must be connected with Shelah's. If only his name could be kept out of it—otherwise I didn't know what scandal might be revealed. So I slipped Denny's ring from her finger. Later, when I heard mention of the photograph, I ran up-stairs and tore it into bits, hiding them under a potted plant."

Chan's eyes opened wide. "So it was you who performed that act? And later—when pieces of photograph scattered into wind—was it you who concealed large number of them?"

"Oh, no—you've forgotten—I wasn't in the room when that happened. And even if I'd been there, I wouldn't have been clever enough to think of that. Some one came to my aid at a critical moment. Who? I haven't the least idea, but I was grateful when I heard about it."

Chan sighed. "You have made everything a delay," he remarked, "and cause me to waste much precious time. I can admire your loyalty to this dead woman——" He paused. "*Haie*, I would enjoy to know such a woman. What loyalty she inspired. An innocent girl obstructs the police in defense of her memory, a man who could not have been guilty pleads to be arrested as her murderer, doubtless from same motive."

"Do you think Robert Fyfe took those lost bits of the photograph?" Bradshaw inquired.

Charlie shook his head. "Impossible. He had not yet arrived on scene. Alas! It is not so simple as that. It is not simple at all." He sighed. "I fear I will be worn to human skeleton before I disentangle this web. And you"—he looked at the girl—"you alone have melted off at least seven pounds."

"I'm so sorry," Julie said.

"Do not fret. Always my daughters tell me I am too enormous for beauty. And beauty is, of course, my only aim." He stood up. "Well, that is that. Jimmy, do not let this young woman escape you. She has proved herself faithful one. Also, she is most unexpert deceiver I have ever met. What a wife she will make for somebody."

"Me, I hope," Bradshaw grinned.

"I hope so, too." Charlie turned to the girl. "Accept him, and all is forgiven between you and me. The seven pounds is gladly donated."

She smiled. "That *is* an offer. Oh, Mr. Chan, I'm so happy that everything is settled between us. I didn't like to deceive you—you're so nice."

He bowed. "Even the aged heart can leap at talk like that. You give me new courage to go on. On to what? Alas! the future lies hidden behind a veil—and I am no Tarneverro."

He left them standing together beneath a hau tree, and walked slowly to his car. Emerging from the drive, he narrowly escaped collision with a trolley. "Wake up, there!" shouted the motorman in rage, and then, recognizing a member of the Honolulu police force, sought to pretend he'd never said it. Charlie waved to him and drove on.

The detective was lost in a maze of doubt and uncertainty. The matter of the emerald ring was clear at last—but still he was far from his goal. One point in Julie's story interested him deeply. It had been Denny Mayo's picture that he had sought to put together the previous night.

Up to now he had thought himself balked in that purpose by some one who did not wish him to know the identity of the man over whose portrait

Shelah had wept so bitterly. But might the motive not have been the same that prompted the destruction of the pictures at the library? The same person, undoubtedly, had been busy in both instances, and that person was bitterly determined that Inspector Chan should not look upon the likeness of Denny Mayo. Why?

Charlie resolved to go back and relive this case from the beginning. But in a moment he stopped. Too much of a task for this drowsy afternoon. "Much better I do not think at all," he muttered. "I will cease all activity and put tired brain in receptive state. Maybe subconscious mind sees chance and leaps on job during my own absence."

In such a state of suspended mental effort he turned his car into the drive of the Grand Hotel and, parking it, walked idly toward the entrance. A stiff breeze was blowing through the lobby, which was practically deserted at this hour of the day.

Sam, the young Chinese who rejoiced in the title of head bell-man, was alert and smiling. Charlie paused. There was a little matter about which he wished to question Sam.

"I hope you are well," he said. "You enjoy your duties here, no doubt?" Leading up, he would have called it.

"Plenty fine job," beamed Sam. "All time good tips."

"You know man they call Tarneverro the Great?"

"Plenty fine man. Good flend to me."

Charlie regarded the boy keenly. "This morning you spoke to him in Cantonese. Why did you do that?"

"Day he come, he say long time ago he live in China, knows Chinese talk plitty well. So he and I have talk in Cantonese. He not so good speaking, but he knows what I say allight."

"He didn't seem to understand you this morning."

Sam shrugged. "I don't know. This moahning I speak all the same any othah day he has funny look an' say don' unnahstand."

"They are peculiar, these tourists," Chan smiled.

"Plenty funny," admitted Sam. "All same give nice tips."

Charlie strode on to the lounge, and through that to the terrace. He sat down there.

His vacation from thinking had been brief indeed, for now he was hard at it again. So Tarneverro understood the Cantonese dialect. But he did not wish Charlie Chan, whom he was so eager to assist in the search for Shelah Fane's murderer, to know that he understood it. Why was that?

A smile spread slowly over Charlie's broad face. Here at last was a fairly simple question. Tarneverro's initial act in helping to solve the murder had been the pointing out of the fact that the watch had been set back, and that the alibis for two minutes past eight were consequently worthless.

But would he have done that if he had not first overheard and understood Charlie's conversation with the cook—if he had not known that Wu Kno-ching had seen Shelah Fane at twelve minutes past eight and that the gesture with the watch was, accordingly, useless? His prompt display of detective skill had seemed, at the time, to prove his sincerity. But if he understood Cantonese, then he was simply making a virtue of necessity and was not sincere at all.

Charlie sat for a long time turning the matter over in his mind. Was his eager assistant, Tarneverro the Great, quite so eager as he appeared to be?

19
Tarneverro's Helping Hand

Val Martino, the director, came down the steps from the hotel lounge, a dashing figure in his white silk suit and flaming tie. He might have been the man on the cover of some steamship folder designed to lure hesitating travelers to the tropics. His gaze fell on Charlie, lolling at ease in a comfortable chair and looking at though he had not a care in the world. The director came over immediately.

"Well, Inspector," he remarked, "I scarcely expected to see you in such a placid mood just now. Unless you have already solved last night's affair?"

Chan shook his head. "Luck is not so good as that. Mystery still remains mystery, but do not be deceived. My brain moves, though my feet are still."

"I'm glad of that," Martino replied. "And I hope it gets somewhere soon." He dropped into a chair at Charlie's side. "You know that thing last night just plain wrecked two hundred thousand dollars' worth of picture for me, and I ought to hurry to Hollywood on the next boat and see what's to be done about it. Whoever killed Shelah certainly didn't have the best interests of our company at heart, or he'd have waited until I finished my job. Oh, well—it can't be helped now. But I must get away as soon as possible, and that's why I'm plugging for you to solve the problem at once."

Chan sighed. "Everybody seems to suffer from hurry complex. An unaccustomed situation in Hawaii. I am panting to keep in step. May I ask —what is your own idea on this case?"

Martino lighted a cigarette. "I hardly know. What's yours?" He tossed the match on the floor, and the old Chinese with the dust-pan and brush came at once, casting a look at Charlie which seemed to say: "This is exactly the sort of person I would expect to find in your company."

"My ideas do not yet achieve definite form," Chan remarked. "One thing I do know—I am opposed in this matter by some person of extreme cleverness."

The director nodded. "It looks that way. Well, there were several clever people at Shelah Fane's house last night."

"Yourself included," Charlie ventured.

"Thanks. Naturally, that had to come from you. But it's true enough." He smiled. "I am speaking, of course, in confidence when I say there was another man present of whose cleverness I have never had the slightest doubt. I don't like him, but I've always thought him pretty smooth. I refer to Tarneverro the Great."

Chan nodded. "Yes, he is plenty quick. One word with him, and I had gathered that."

The director flicked the ash from his cigarette on to the floor. The old Chinese brought an ash-tray and set it close beside him on the small table.

"There are all kinds of seers and crystal-gazers fattening on the credulity of Hollywood," Martino continued. "But this man is the ace of the lot. The women go to him; and he tells them things about themselves they thought only God knew. As a result——"

"How does he discover these things?" Charlie asked.

"Spies;" the director answered. "I can't prove it, but I'm certain he has spies working for him night and day. They pick up interesting bits of news about the celebrities, and pass them along to him. The poor little movie girls think he's in league with the powers of darkness, and as result they tell all. That man knows enough secrets to blow up the colony if he wants to do it. We've tried to run him out of town, but he's too smart for us. You know, I'm rather sorry I stopped Jaynes last night when he wanted to beat Tarneverro up. I believe it would have been a grand idea. But on the other hand, Shelah's name would have been dragged into it, and remembering that, I broke up the row. The pictures are my profession, there are lots of fine people in the colony, and I don't like to see them suffer from harmful publicity. Unfortunately the decent ones must share the disgrace when the riffraff on the fringe misbehaves."

"Was it your intention," Chan inquired, "to hint that Tarneverro the Great may have killed Shelah Fane?"

"Not at all," responded Martino hastily. "Don't get me wrong. I was only trying to point out that is you sense a clever opponent in this affair, you should remember that there are few men cleverer than the fortune-teller. Further than that, I say nothing. I don't know whether he did it or not."

"For the time between eight and eight-thirty last night," Chan informed him, "Tarneverro has most unshakable alibi."

Martino stood up. "He would have. As I told you, he's as slick as they come. Well, so long. Good luck to you—and I mean that with all my heart."

He strolled off toward the glittering sea and left Chan to his thoughts. In a few moments the detective arose with sudden decision and went to the telephone booth in the lobby. He got his Chief on the wire.

"You very much busy now?" he asked.

"Not especially, Charlie. I've got a date with Mr. and Mrs. MacMaster here at five-thirty, but that's an hour away. Is anything doing?"

"Might be," Chan answered. "I can not tell. But I will shortly require backing of your firm authority for little investigation at Grand Hotel. Pretty good idea if you leaped into car and rode out here at once."

"I'll be right with you, Charlie," the Chief promised.

Going to the house phone, Charlie called the room of Alan Jaynes. The Britisher answered in a sleepy tone. The detective informed him that he was coming up immediately to talk with him and then stepped to the hotel desk.

"Without calling room, can you ascertain if Mr. Tarneverro is in residence?" he asked.

The clerk glanced at the letter box. "Well, his key isn't here," he said. "I guess that means he's in."

"Ah, yes," nodded Chan. "If you will be so kind, do this big favor for me. Secure Mr. Tarneverro on wire, and say that Inspector Chan passed through here in too great rush to bother himself. But add that I desire to see Mr. Tarneverro soon as can be in lobby of Young Hotel downtown. Say it is of fierce importance and he must arrive at once."

The clerk stared. "Down-town?" he repeated.

Chan nodded. "The idea is to remove him from this hotel for a brief space of time," he explained.

"Oh, yes," smiled the clerk. "I see. Well, I suppose it's all right. I'll call him."

Charlie went up to the room occupied by Alan Jaynes. The Britisher admitted him, yawning as he did so. He was in dressing-gown and slippers, and his bed was somewhat disheveled.

"Come in, Inspector. I've just been having forty winks. Good lord—what a sleepy country this is!"

"For the *malihini*—the newcomer—yes," Chan smiled. "We old-timers learn to disregard the summons. Otherwise we would get nowhere."

"You are getting somewhere, then?" Jaynes asked eagerly.

"Would not want to say that, but we are traveling at good pace—for Hawaii," responded Charlie. "Mr. Jaynes, I have come to you in spirit of most open frankness. I am about to toss cards down flat on table."

"Good," Jaynes said heartily.

"This morning you told me you had never been in pavilion, never even loitered in neighborhood of place?"

"Certainly I did. It's the truth."

Charlie took out an envelope, and emptied on to a table the stub of a small cigar. "How, then, would you explain the fact that this is found just outside window of room in which Shelah Fane met sudden death?"

Jaynes looked for a long moment at this shabby bit of evidence. "Well, I'll be damned," he remarked. He turned to Chan, an angry light in his eyes. "Sit down," he said. "I can explain it, and I will."

"Happy to hear you say that," Chan told him.

"This morning, when I was in my bath," the Britisher began, "about eight o'clock, it must have been, some one knocked on my door. I thought it was the house-boy, and I called to him to come in. I heard the door open, and then the sound of footsteps. I asked who it was, and—why the devil didn't I break his neck last night?" he finished savagely.

"You have reference to the neck of Tarneverro the Great?" Charlie inquired with interest.

"I have. He was here in this room, and said he wanted to see me. I was rather taken aback, but I told him to wait. I stood up in the tub and began a brisk rub-down—will you come with me to the bathroom, Mr. Chan?"

Surprised, Chan rose and followed.

"You will observe, Inspector, that there is a full-length mirror affixed to the bathroom door. With the door slightly ajar—like this—a person standing in the bath has a view of a portion of the bedroom—the portion which includes the desk. I was busy with my rub-down when I suddenly saw something that interested me keenly. A box of those small cigars was lying on the desk, with a few gone. I saw, in the mirror, Mr. Tarneverro walk over and help himself to a couple of them. He put them in his pocket."

"Good," remarked Chan calmly. "I am much obliged to the mirror."

"At first I thought it was merely a case of petty pilfering. Nevertheless, I was deeply annoyed, and I planned to go out and order him from my room. But as I finished drying myself and got into my dressing-gown, it occurred to me that something must be in the air. I decided to say nothing, lie low, and try to find out, if possible, what the beggar was up to. I didn't guess—I'm a bit dense, I'm afraid—it never popped into my mind that he wanted to involve me in Shelah's murder. I knew he had no love for me, but somehow—that's not the sort of thing——

"Well, I came out and asked him what he wanted. He looked me boldly in the eye and said he had just dropped in to urge that I let bygones be bygones, and shake hands on it. No reason why we shouldn't be friends, he thought. Felt that Miss Fane would wish it. Of course, I was aching to throw him from the window, but I controlled myself. Out of curiosity, I invited him to have one of my cigars. 'Oh, no, thanks,' he said. 'I never use them.'

"He ran on about Miss Fane, and how it would be best if we dropped our enmity of last night. I was cool but polite—I even shook hands with him. When he had gone, I sat down to think the thing out. What could have been his purpose in taking those cigars? As I say, I couldn't figure it. Now, of course, the matter is only too clear. He proposed to scatter a few false clues. By gad, Inspector—why should he take the trouble to do that? There's just one answer, isn't there? He murdered Miss Fane himself."

Chan shrugged. "I would be happy to join you in thinking that, but first several matters must be wiped away. Among others—an air-tight alibi."

"Oh, hell—what's that?" Jaynes cried. "A clever man always has an alibi." His heavy jaws snapped shut. "I appreciate what Mr. Tarneverro tried to do for me—I do, indeed. When I see him again——"

"When you see him again, you will make no noise," Charlie cut in. "That is, if you wish to be of help."

Jaynes hesitated. "Oh—very good. But it won't be easy. However, I'll hold my tongue if you say so. Was there anything else you wanted?"

"No, thanks. You have supplied me with plenty. I go on my way with renewed energy."

Waiting for the elevator, Chan thought about Jaynes' story. Was it true? Perhaps. It seemed a rather glib explanation, but was the Britisher clever enough to concoct such a tale on the spot? He appeared to be a stolid, slow-thinking man—always going somewhere to be by himself and figure things out. Could such a man—Charlie sighed. So many problems!

He stepped cautiously from the elevator and peered round the corner. The coast seemed to be clear and he went to the desk. "Has Mr. Tarneverro departed?" he inquired.

The clerk nodded. "Yes—he went out a moment ago, in a great hurry."

"My warmest thanks," Charlie said.

His Chief was coming up the hotel steps, and he went to greet him. Together they sought out a secluded corner.

"What's up?" the Chief wanted to know.

"Number of things," Chan replied. "Mr. Tarneverro bursts into investigation and demands our strict attention."

"Tarneverro?" the Chief nodded. "That fellow never has sounded good to me. What about him?"

"For one point," Charlie answered, "he understands Cantonese." He told of making that discovery, which had served to turn his thoughts toward the fortune-teller. "But since I called you, even more important evidence leaps up," he added. Briefly he repeated Jaynes' story about the cigars.

The Chief whistled. "We're getting there, Charlie," he cried.

Chan shrugged. "You overlook Tarneverro's alibi——"

"No, I don't. I'll attend to that later. By the way, if you see that old couple from Australia about, keep out of their way. I've arranged for them to come to my office, as I told you, and I don't want to talk with them here. We can handle them better amid the proper surroundings. Now, what is it you want to do?"

"I desire," Chan answered, "to make complete search of Tarneverro's apartment."

The Chief frowned. "That's not quite according to Hoyle, Charlie. I don't know. We have no warrant——"

"Which is why I asked you to come. Big man such as you are can arrange it. We leave everything as we found it, and Tarneverro will not know."

"Where is he?"

Charlie explained the fortune-teller's present whereabouts. The Chief nodded. "That was a good idea. Wait here, and I'll have a talk with the management."

He returned presently, accompanied by a tall lean man with sandy hair. "It's all fixed," the Chief announced. "You know Jack Murdock, don't you, Charlie? He's going with us."

"Mr. Murdock old friend," Chan said.

"Well, Charlie, how you been?" Murdock remarked. He as an ex-police-man, now one of the house detectives for the hotel.

"I enjoy the usual good health," Charlie replied, and with the Chief, followed Murdock.

After the house detective had unlocked the door and admitted them to Tarneverro's sitting-room, he stood looking at Chan with a speculative eye.

"Not going to rob us of one of our most distinguished guests, are you, Charlie?" he inquired.

Chan smiled. "That is a matter yet to be determined."

"Quite a little affair down the beach last night," Murdock continued. "And you're in the limelight, as usual. Some people have all the luck."

"Which they pay for by having also all the worry," Chan reminded him. "You are in soft berth here. Fish course last night was excellent. Did you taste it?"

"I did."

"So did I—and that was as far as I got," sighed Chan. "Limelight has many terrible penalties." He glanced about the room. "Our object is to search thoroughly and leave no trace. Fortune favors, however, for we have plenty time."

He and the Chief went to work systematically, while the house detective lolled in a comfortable chair with a cigar. The closets, the bureau drawers and the desk were all gone over carefully. Finally Charlie stood before a trunk. "Locked," he remarked.

Murdock got up. "That's nothing. I've a skeleton key that will fix it." He opened the trunk, which was of the wardrobe variety, and swung it wide. Chan lifted out one drawer, and gave a little cry of satisfaction.

"Here is one thing we seek, Chief," he cried, and produced a portable typewriter. Placing it on the desk, he inserted a sheet of note-paper and struck off a few sentences. "Just a word of warning from a friend. You should go at once to the Honolulu Public Library and——" He finished the note, and taking another from his pocket, compared the two. With a pleased smile he carried them to his Chief.

"Will you kindly regard these missive and tell me what they suggest to you?" he said.

The Chief studied them for a moment. "Simple enough," he remarked. "Both were written on the same machine. The top of the letter *e* is clogged with ink, and the letter *t* is slightly out of alignment."

Chan grinned and took them back. "Long time confinement in station house does not cause you to grow rusty. Yes—it is just as you say. Two notes are identical, both being written on this faithful little machine. Happy to say our visit here is not without fruit. I must now put typewriter in place so our call will go unsuspected. Or would go that way, if it was not for lingering odor of good friend Murdock's cigar."

The house detective looked guilty. "Say, Charlie—I never thought of that."

"Finish your weed. Damage is now done. but take care luxury of present job does not cause brain to stagnate."

Murdock did not smoke again, but let the cigar go out in his hand. Charlie continued to explore the trunk. He had about completed his search without further good fortune when, in the most remote corner of the lowest compartment. he came upon something which seemed to claim his interest.

He walked up to his Chief. In the palm of his hand lay a man's ring, a large diamond in a heavy setting of gold. His superior stared at it. "Take good look," Chan advised, "and fix same in your mind."

"More jewelry, Charlie?"

Chan nodded. "Seeking to solve this case, it seems we wander lost in jewel store. Natural, perhaps, since we deal with Hollywood people." He restored the ring to its place, closed the trunk and locked it. "Mr. Murdock, that will end business here."

They returned to the lobby, where the house detective left them. Chan accompanied the Chief out to the drive.

"What did you mean about the ring, Charlie," asked the latter.

"Little story which I have been perhaps too reluctant to repeat," smiled Chan. "Why? Perhaps because it concerns most distasteful moment of my long career. You will recall that last night, in house down the beach, I stood in middle of floor with letter written by Shelah Fane held firmly in my hand. Suddenly light goes out. I am most rudely struck in the face—struck and cut on the cheek, proving the assailant wore a ring. Lights go on, and the letter is gone."

"Yes, yes," cried the Chief impatiently.

"Immediately I make a survey—of the men in the room, who wears ring? Ballou and Van Horn—yes. Others do not. Mr. Tarneverro, for example, does not. Yet yesterday morning, when I visited him in room, I noted that ring I have called to your attention, on his finger. What is more, when we rode down to Shelah Fane's house after news of murder, I perceived the diamond gleaming in the dark. I saw it again when he helps me make investigation in pavilion. Yet when lights flash on after theft of letter, ring is no longer in evidence. What would be your reaction to that, Mr. Chief?"

"I should say," the Chief returned, "that Tarneverro struck that blow in the dark."

Charlie was thoughtfully rubbing his cheek. "Oddly enough," he remarked, "such was my own reaction."

20

One Corner of the Veil

They went over and stood by Charlie's car. A puzzled frown wrinkled the Chief's brow. "I don't get this, Charlie."

"On which point," returned Chan placidly, "we are like as two reeds bending beside stream."

"Tarneverro hit you. Why?"

"Why not? Maybe he feels athletic."

"He'd just been telling you about that letter—hoping that the two of you would run across it somewhere—and when you got it he knocked you down and took it away from you."

"No doubt he wished to examine it in private."

The Chief shook his head. "Beyond me—way beyond me. He stole a cigar from Jaynes, hurried down and dropped the butt outside the pavilion window. He wrote a note to Van Horn, sending him off to the library on a fool's errand. He—he—what else has he done?"

"Perhaps he has murdered Shelah Fane," Charlie suggested.

"I'm sure he did."

"Yet he owns fine alibi."

The Chief looked at his watch. "Yes—I'll attend to that alibi at five-thirty, if those old people show up as they promised. What are you going to do now?"

"I follow you to join in that interview, but first I make stop at public library."

"Oh, yes, of course. Come as soon as you can. I—I think we're getting somewhere now."

"Where?" inquired Chan blandly.

"Lord knows—I don't," replied the Chief, and hurried to his own car. He got away first, and Charlie followed him through the big gates to Kalakaua Avenue.

It was nearly five o'clock, the bathing hour at Waikiki was on, and along the sidewalk passed a perpetual parade of pretty girls in gay beach robes and stalwart tanned men in vivid dressing-gowns. Other people had time to enjoy life, Charlie reflected, but not he. The further discoveries of the afternoon baffled him completely, and he had need of all his Oriental calm to keep him firmly on the pathway of his investigation. Tarneverro, who had sworn that his dearest wish was to assist in finding the murderer of Shelah Fane, had been impeding the search from the start. The fortune-teller's dark face, with its deep mysterious eyes, haunted Chan's thoughts as he flivvered on to town.

Stopping at the public library, he again appeared at the desk.

"Would you kindly tell me if the young woman in charge of reading-room is now on scene?" he asked.

The girl appeared, upset and indignant over the morning's events. She would never again leave a newspaper file idle on a table, but the Japanese boy whose work it was to return such items to the shelves was taking the day off. She remembered Van Horn, of course; she had seen him in the films.

"Were other striking personalities present in reading-room during the morning?" Charlie inquired.

The girl thought. Yes—she remembered one. A rather peculiar-looking man—she recalled especially his eyes. Chan urged her to a further description, and was left in no doubt as to whom she referred.

"Did you perceive him examining newspaper file left by actor?"

"No, I didn't. He came in soon after Mr. Van Horn left, and stayed all morning, reading various papers and magazines. He seemed to be trying to pass the time."

"When did he leave?"

"I don't know. He was still here when I went out to lunch."

"Ah, yes," Chan nodded. "He would be."

"You think he cut the book?"

"I have no proof, and never will have, I fear. But I am sure he mutilated the volume."

"I'd like to see him in jail," said the girl warmly.

Charlie shrugged. "We have tastes in common. Thank you so much for significant information."

He drove quickly to the police station. The Chief, alone in his room, was gruffly talking over the telephone. "No—no—nothing yet." He slammed the receiver on to its hook. "Good lord, Charlie, they're hounding me to death. The whole world wants to know who killed Shelah Fane. The morning paper's had over a hundred cables. Well, what about the library?—Wait a minute."

The telephone was ringing again. The Chief's replies were none too gentle.

"That was Spencer," he announced, hanging up. "I don't know what's got into the boys—they seem to be helpless. They can't find a trace of that confounded beach-comber anywhere. He's of vital importance, Charlie; he was in that room last night——"

Charlie nodded. "He must assuredly be found. I am plenty busy man, but it seems I must go on his trail myself. As soon as interview with old people is ended——"

"Good! That's the ticket. You go out the first chance you get. What was I saying?—Oh, yes—the library. What did you find there?"

"No question about it," Charlie replied. "Tarneverro is man who destroyed pictures of Denny Mayo."

"He is, eh? Well, I thought so. Doesn't want you to know what this Mayo looked like. Why? I'll go mad if this keeps up. But there's one thing sure, and I'm clinging to it. Tarneverro's our man. He killed Shelah Fane, and we've got to pin it on him." Chan started to speak. "Oh, yes—I know—his alibi. Well, you watch me. I'll smash that alibi if it's the last act of my life."

"I was going to name one other objection," Chan told him gently.

"What's that?"

"If he contemplated killing of Shelah Fane, why did he announce first to me that we are about to arrest killer of Denny Mayo? Why, as my boy Henry would say, bring that up?"

The Chief put his head in his hands. "Lord, I don't know. It's a difficult case, isn't it, Charlie?" A plain-clothes man appeared at the door, announcing Mr. Thomas MacMaster and wife. "Show them in," cried the Chief, leaping to his feet. "We can do one thing, anyhow, Charlie," he said. "We can smash that alibi, and when we've done that, maybe things will clear up a bit."

The old Scotch couple entered, and at the guileless and innocent look of them, the Chief received a severe shock. The old man approached Chan with outstretched hand.

"Ah, good evening, Mr. Chan. We meet again."

Charlie got up. "Would you kindly shake hands with the Chief of Detectives. Mrs. MacMaster, I would also present my superior officer to you. Chief desires to ask a few polite questions." He stressed the polite ever so slightly, but his superior got the hint.

"How do you do, madam," he said cordially. "Mr. MacMaster—I am sorry to trouble you."

"No trouble at all, sir," replied the old man, with the rolled *r* of Aberdeen. "Mother and I have never had much to do wi' the police, but we're law-abiding citizens and glad to help."

"Fine," returned the Chief. "Now, sir, according to what you told Inspector Chan here, you are both old friends of the man who calls himself Tarneverro the Great?"

"Aye—that we are. It was in his younger days we knew him, and a splendid lad he was. We're deeply fond of him, sir."

The Chief nodded. "Last night you say you sat with him on one of the lanais of the Grand Hotel from a few minutes after eight until half past the hour."

"That is what we said, sir," MacMaster returned, "and we will swear to it in any court you put us in. It is the truth."

The Chief looked him firmly in the eye. "It can't be the truth," he announced.

"Why—why, what do you mean, sir?"

"I mean there's a mistake somewhere. We have indisputable evidence that Mr. Tarneverro was elsewhere during that time."

The old man drew himself up proudly. "I do not like your tone, sir. The word of Thomas MacMaster has never been questioned before, and I have not come here to be insulted——"

"I don't question your word. You've made a mistake, that's all. Tarneverro left you at eight-thirty, you claim. Did you verify that by your own watch?"

"I did."

"The watch might have been wrong."

"It was wrong."

"What!"

"It was a wee bit fast—a matter of three minutes. I compared it with the hotel clock, which stood at eight-thirty-two."

"You're not—pardon me—a young man, Mr. MacMaster?"

"Is that also forbidden by law in the States, sir?"

"What I mean is—your eyes——"

"My eyes, sir, are as good as yours, and better. Mr. Tarneverro left us at eight-thirty—the correct time. He had been with us since we came out from our dinner, save for a brief period when he talked with a gentleman at the far end of the lounge. And during that time he did not leave our sight. That I say—and that I'll stand by"—he banged a great fist on the desk—"until hell freezes over!"

"Father—don't get excited," put in the old lady.

"Who's excited?" cried MacMaster. "You have to be emphatic wi' a policeman, Mother. You have to talk his language."

The Chief considered. In spite of himself, he was impressed by the obvious honesty of the old man. He had planned to bully him out of his testimony, but something told him such tactics would be useless. Hang it all, he reflected, Tarneverro did have an alibi, and a good one.

"You second what your husband says, madam?" he inquired.

"Every word of it," the old lady nodded.

The Chief made a helpless gesture, and turned toward MacMaster. "All right," he remarked. "You win."

Charlie stepped forward. "May I have honor to address few remarks to these good friends of mine?" he inquired.

"Sure. Go ahead, Charlie," replied the Chief wearily.

"I make simple inquiry," Chan continued gently. "Mr. Tarneverro was young man starting career when he visited your ranch, I believe?"

"He was that," agreed MacMaster.

"An actor on theatrical stage?"

"Aye—and not a very successful one. He was glad of the work wi' us."

"Tarneverro very odd name. Was that what he called himself when he worked with you?"

The old man glanced quickly at his wife. "No, it was not," he said.

"What name did he offer at that time?"

MacMaster's jaw shut hard, and he said nothing.

"I repeat—what name did he offer when he worked with you?"

"I'm sorry, Inspector," the old man replied. "But he has asked us not to refer to the matter."

Chan's eyes flashed with sudden interest. "He requests that you do not mention his real name?"

"Yes. He said he had done wi' it, and asked us to think of him as Mr. Tarneverro."

Charlie felt his way carefully. "Mr. MacMaster, a serious situation looks us hard in the face. Murder was done last night. Tarneverro is not guilty man. You prove same yourself by offer of alibi, which is accepted by us in sincere spirit, because we know it is spoken same way. You have performed that favor for him. You do it gladly because you love truth. But more even dear friend has no right to ask of you. You have said you are law-abiding, and no one exists who is stupid enough to doubt that. I wish to know Mr. Tarneverro's name when he was with you in Australia."

The old man turned uncertainly to his wife. "I—I don't know. This is a difficult position, Mother."

"You will not prove him murderer by giving it," Charlie continued. "Already you have saved him from that, but you will impede our work if you withhold same—and I am plenty certain you are not kind of man to do that."

"I don't understand," the Scotchman muttered. "Mother, what do you think?"

"I think Mr. Chan is right." She beamed upon Charlie. "We have done enough when we swear to his alibi. If you won't tell, Father, I will. Why should a man be ashamed of his real name?—And it was he real name, I'm sure."

"Madam," said Chan. "You have proper view of things. Deign to mention the name."

"When we knew Tarneverro on the ranch," continued the old lady, "his name was Arthur Mayo."

"Mayo!" cried Chan. He and the Chief exchanged a triumphant glance.

"Yes. He told you this morning he was alone when he came to work for us. I can't think why he said that—it wasn't true. You see, he and his brother came to us together."

"His brother?"

"Yes, of course—his brother, Denny Mayo."

21
The King of Mystery

Chan's breath came a little faster as he listened to this unexpected bit of news. Tarneverro was Denny Mayo's brother! No wonder, then, that the fortune-teller had been so eager to learn from Shelah Fane the name of Mayo's murderer. No wonder he had offered to help Chan to the limit of his ability in the task of finding out who had silenced Shelah just as she was, supposedly, on the point of telling.

And yet—had he carried out that promise to asisst? On the contrary, he had evidently been placing in Chan's way every obstacle possible. Puzzles, puzzles—Charlie put his hand to his head. This man Tarneverro was the king of mystery.

"Madam, what you say is very interesting," the detective remarked. His eyes brightened. On one point, at least, light was breaking. "Will you be kind enough to tell me—was there resemblance in features between those two men?"

She nodded. "Aye, there was, though many people might not have noticed, because of the difference in age and coloring. Denny was blond, and Arthur very dark. But the first time I saw them, standing side by side in my kitchen, I knew they were brothers."

Chan smiled. "You have contributed something to our solution, madam, though up to moment of present speaking, only the gods know what. I think that is all we now require of you. Do I speak correctly, Chief?"

"Yes, that's right, Charlie. Mr. MacMaster, I'm obliged to your wife and you for this visit."

"Not at all, sir," the old man answered. "Come, Mother. I—I'm not quite comfortable about this. Perhaps you've talked a wee bit too much."

"Nonsense," Thomas. No honest man is ashamed of his name—and I'm sure Arthur Mayo is honest. If he's not, he's sore changed from what he was when we knew him." The old lady rose.

"As for the alibi," her husband said stubbornly, "we stick to that—through thick and thin. Tarneverro was with us from eight to eight-thirty, and if the murder was done in that half-hour, he didn't do it. To that I'll swear, gentlemen."

"Yes, yes—I suppose you will," the Chief replied. "Good evening, sir. Madam—a great pleasure to meet you."

The old couple went out, and the Chief looked at Charlie. "Well, where are we now?" he inquired.

"Tangled in endless net, as always," Chan answered. "One thing I know—Tarneverro waits for me at Young Hotel. I will call him at once and request his presence here."

When he had done so, he came back and sat down beside his superior. His brows were contracted in thought.

"The case spreads itself," he remarked. "Tarneverro was Denny's brother. That ought to give us big boost toward our solution, but other way about, it only increases our worry. Why did he not tell me that? Why has he, as matter of fact, fiercely struggled to keep it from me? You heard what lady said about resemblance. That explains at once why all pictures of Mayo were torn to bits. Tarneverro was willing to travel long length to make sure we do not discover this fact just related to us." He sighed. "Anyhow, we have learned why portraits were destroyed."

"Yes, but that doesn't get us anywhere," the Chief replied. "If it was his brother who was killed, and he was on the point of asking you to arrest the murderer as soon as Shelah Fane revealed the name, I'd think that he would naturally tell you of his connection with Mayo—especially after the news of Miss Fane's death. It would have been a logical explanation of his interest in the case. Instead of telling you, he tries desperately to keep the relationship hidden." The Chief paused. "Strange none of these Hollywood folks ever noticed a resemblance between Mayo and the fortune-teller."

Chan shook his head. "Not likely they would. The two visit town at widely separated times, and were not seen together there. Many people, Mrs. MacMaster said, would not note the resemblance, but Tarneverro flatters me by assuming I am one who would. As for others, he knows well it is the kind of likeness almost no one sees until it is pointed out. Then everybody sees it. Human nature is like that."

"Human nature is getting to be too much for me," growled the Chief.

"What course do you propose to take with this fortune-teller when he gets here?"

"I plan to walk softly. We will say nothing about his many misendeavors, but we will speak of this thing we have just learned. What reasons will he give for his silence? They may have vast significance."

"Well, I don't know, Charlie. It might be better to keep him in the dark even on that point."

"Not if we pretend we hold no suspicion whatever. We will assume instead a keen delight. Now we know he has every reason to help us, and the skies brighten above our weary heads."

"Well, you handle him, Charlie."

A few moments later Tarneverro strode debonairly into the room. His manner was aloof and a bit condescending, as though he found himself in quaint company but was man of the world enough to be at home anywhere. He nodded at Charlie.

"Ah, Inspector, I waited for you a long time. I'd about given you up."

"A thousand of my humblest apologies," Chan returned. "I was detained by heavy weight of business. May I present my honored Chief?"

The fortune-teller bowed. "A great pleasure. How are you getting on, Inspector? I've been very eager to know."

"Natural you should be. Only a moment ago did we upearth fact which makes us realize how deep your interest is."

Tarneverro glanced at him keenly. "What do you mean by that?"

"I mean we discover that Denny Mayo was your brother."

Tarneverro stepped over and laid his walking-stick on a desk. The act, it seemed, gave him a moment for thought.

"It's true, Inspector," he remarked, facing Chan again. "I don't know how you found it out——"

Charlie permitted himself a quiet smile of satisfaction. "Not many things remain buried through investigation such as we are making," he remarked gently.

"Evidently not." Tarneverro hesitated. "I presume you are wondering why I didn't tell you this myself?"

Chan shrugged. "Undoubtedly you possessed good reason."

"Several reasons," the fortune-teller assured him. "For one thing, I didn't believe that such knowledge would help you in any way in solving the case."

"Which is sound thinking," Chan agreed readily. "Still—I must confess slight hurt in my heart. Frankness between friends is like warm sun after rain. The friendship grows."

Tarneverro nodded and sat down. "I suppose there's a great deal in what you say. I'm rather sorry I kept the relationship to myself, and I apologize most humbly. If it's not too late, Inspector, I will give you the whole story now——"

"Not at all too late," Chan beamed.

"Denny Mayo *was* my brother, Inspector, my youngest brother. The relationship between us was more like that of father and son. I was intensely fond of him. I watched over him, helped his career, took pride in it. When he was brutally murdered, the shock was a terrible one for me. So you can easily understand why I say"—his voice trembled with sudden passion—"that to avenge his death has been for three years my chief aim—indeed my only aim. If the person who killed Shelah Fane is the same man or woman who murdered Denny—then, by heaven, I can not rest until justice is done."

He rose and began to pace the floor.

"When I heard the news of Denny's murder, I was playing in a London production. There was nothing I could do about it at the moment—I was too far away. But at my earliest opportunity I went to Hollywood, determined to solve the mystery of his death. I thought that the chances of my doing so would be better if I did not arrive in the picture colony as Denny's brother, but under an assumed name. At first I called myself Henry Smallwood—it was the name of a character I had lately played.

"I looked around. The police, it was evident, were completely at sea on the case. Gradually I became impressed by the number of seers and fortune-tellers of various sorts in Hollywood. They all seemed to be prospering, and it was rumored that they were the recipients of amazing confidences and secrets from the lips of the screen people.

"A big idea struck me. In my younger days I had been an assistant to Maskelyne the Great, one of a long line of famous magicians, and a man of really remarkable powers. I had some talent in a psychic way, had told fortunes as an amateur and had the nerve to carry the thing through. Why not, I thought, take an impressive name, set myself up as a crystal-gazer, and by prying into Hollywood's secrets, seek to solve the mystery of poor Denny's death? The whole thing looked absurdly simple and easy."

He sat down again.

"So for two years, gentlemen, I have been Tarneverro the Great. I have listened to stories of unrequited love, of overwhelming ambition, of hate and intrigue, hope and despair. It has been interesting, many secrets have been whispered in my ear, but until recently the one big secret I longed to hear was not among them. Then, out of a blue sky, yesterday morning at the Grand Hotel, my moment came. I finally got on the trail of Denny's murderer. It took all my will power to control myself when I realized what was happening. Shelah Fane told me she was in Denny's house that night—she saw him murdered. I had difficulty restraining myself—I wanted to leap upon her then and there and wring the name of his killer from her reluctant lips. Three years ago I would have done it—but time—well, we grow calmer with the passage of time.

"However, once I discovered she knew, I would never have left her until she told. When you saw me last night, Inspector, my hopes were running high. I proposed to take you with me to her home after the party, and between us I felt certain we could drag out that name at last. I intended to hand the guilty person over to you immediately, for"—he looked at the Chief—"I need hardly tell you that I have never thought of avenging the crime in any other manner. From the first, I proposed to let the courts deal with Denny's killer. That was, of course, the only sane way."

The Chief nodded gravely. "The only way, of course."

Tarneverro turned toward Chan. "You know what happened. Somehow this person discovered that Shelah was on the verge of telling, and silenced her for ever. On the very threshold of triumph, I was defeated. Unless you find out who killed poor Shelah, my years of exile in Hollywood will very likely go for nothing. That's why I'm with you—that's why I want"—his voice trembled again—"the murderer of Shelah Fane more than I've ever wanted anything in all my life before."

Charlie looked at him with a sort of awe. Was this the man who had been scattering all those false clues about the place?

"I am glad of this frankness, lately as it arrives," the detective said, with an odd smile.

"I should have told you at once, I presume," Tarneverro continued. "I was, as a matter of fact, on the point of explaining my relationship to Denny as we rode down to Shelah's house. But, I reflected, the information would not help you in the least. And I did not want it to become known why I was telling fortunes in Hollywood. If it did, of course my career there would be ended. Suppose, I said to myself, Inspector Chan fails to find Shelah Fane's murderer. In that case I must go back to Hollywood and resume my quest. They are still coming to me with their secrets. Diana Dixon consulted me to-day. That is why, until Denny's murderer is found, I do not want my real name made public. I rely on you gentlemen to be discreet."

"You may do so," Chan nodded. "Matter remains buried as though beneath Great Wall of China. Knowing how firmly you are with us in this hunt adds on new hope. We will find Shelah Fane's murderer, Mr. Tarneverro—and your brother's all same time."

"You are making progress?" asked the fortune-teller eagerly.

Charlie regarded him fixedly. "Every moment we are approaching nearer. One or two little matters—and we are at journey's end."

"Good," said Tarneverro heartily. "You know now my stake in the affair. I hope you will forgive me that I didn't reveal it fully at the start."

"Explanation has been most reasonable," smiled Chan. "All is forgiven. I think you may now be excused."

"Thank you." Tarneverro glanced at his watch. "It is getting on toward the dinner hour, isn't it? I'm sorry that what I have told you is of no vital importance in your search. If there were only some really valuable contribution that I could make——"

Chan nodded. "Understand your feeling plenty well. Who knows? Your opportunity may yet arise." He escorted Tarneverro from the room, and out the front door of the station house.

When he returned, the Chief was slumped down in his chair. He looked up with a wry smile. "Well," he remarked, "what was wrong with that picture?"

Charlie grinned. "Pretty much everything," he responded. "Tarneverro plenty queer man. He wants to help—so he robs cigar from Mr. Jaynes and drops same outside pavilion window. He thirsts for my success—so he writes note that causes me to waste time on innocent Mr. Van Horn. He has mild little reason, of no importance, for not telling me he is Denny Mayo's brother—but he rages about destroying pictures of Denny as though he would keep matter from me or die in the attempt. He beholds letter in which may be written name of Denny's killer, and when I am about to open it, he kicks out light and smashes me in face." Chan rubbed his cheek thoughtfully. "Yes, this Tarneverro plenty peculiar man."

"Well, where do we go from here?" the Chief inquired. "It begins to look like one of your stone walls, Charlie."

Chan shrugged. "In which case, we circle about, seeking new path. Me, I get renewed interest in beach-comber. Why was he in pavilion room last night? More important yet, what was conversation he overheard between Shelah Fane and Robert Fyfe, for suppression of which Fyfe pays handsome sum?" He moved toward the door. "Kashimo has now played his game of hide-and-seek long time enough. I go to bestow inside small quantity of provisions, and after that I myself will do a little scouring of this town."

"That's the talk," his Chief cried. "You go after that beach-comber yourself. I'll eat down-town too, and come back here as soon as I've finished. You'll find me here any time after seven."

Charlie went to the telephone and called his house, getting his daughter Rose on the wire. He announced that he would not be home for dinner. A sharp cry of protest answered him.

"But, Dad,—you must come home. We all want to see you."

"Ah—at last you begin to feel keen affection for poor old father."

"Sure. And we're dying to hear the news."

"Remain alive a small time longer," he advised. "There are no news as yet."

"Well, what have you been doing all day?" Rose wanted to know.

Chan sighed. "Maybe I should put my eleven children on this case."

"Maybe you should," she laughed. "A little American pep might work wonders."

"That is true. I am only stupid old Oriental—"

"Who says you are? I never did. But Dad, if you love me, please hurry."

"I will speed," he answered. "If I do not, I perceive I can not come home to-night."

He hung up the receiver and went to a near-by restaurant, where he ate a generous dinner.

Refreshed and fortified, he was presently strolling down King Street toward Aala Park. Dusk was falling over that littered stretch of ground, the campus of the undergraduates in the hard school of experience. They lolled about on the benches, some of them glancing up at Charlie with hostile eyes under discreetly lowered lids. There was muttering as he passed, an occasional curse from the lips of some one who had met the detective under circumstances none too pleasant. He paid no attention to any of them—he was seeking a man in a velvet coat and duck trousers that had once been white.

The Park yielded nothing. He crossed to a street of mean shops and shabby business. Above his head, on a fragile balcony, an enormous Filipino woman in a faded kimono puffed on an after-dinner cigar. Charlie moved along into a section of Honolulu quite unknown to tourists who breathed the pure air of the beach and raved about the beauty of these islands. There was no beauty in the River District, only squalor and poverty; seven races jumbled together in an international slum. He heard voices raised in bitter argument, the weeping of children, the clatter of sandals, and, even here, the soft whine of Hawaiian music. *The Song of the Islands* floated lazily on the fetid air. Over a doorway that led to a dark and dirty stair, he saw the sign: "Oriental Cabaret."

He paused for amoment in the glare of the lights that formed this sign. A girl was approaching, dark-skinned, slender, graceful. He stood aside to let her pass, and saw her face. The tropics, lonely islands lost in vast southern seas—a lovely head against a background of cool green. Quickly he followed her up the stairs.

He came into a bare room with a sagging roof. There were many tables with blue and white checkered cloths; painted girls were eating at the rear. A suave little proprietor came forward, rubbing his hands with outward calm, but somewhat disturbed inside.

"What you want, Inspector?"

Charlie pushed him aside and followed the girl he had seen below. She had taken off her hat and hung it on a nail; evidently she worked here.

"Begging your pardon," Chan began.

She looked at him, fear and defiance mingling in her smoldering eyes. "What you want?"

"You are acquainted with *haole*—white man—Smith, the beach-comber?"

"Maybe."

"He painted your portrait—I have seen it. A beautiful thing."

The girl shrugged. "Yes, he come here, sometimes. I let him make the picture. What of it?"

"Have you seen Mr. Smith lately?"

"Not for long time—no."

"Where does he live?"

"On the beach, I think."

"But when he has money—where then?"

The girl did not reply. The proprietor came forward. "You tell him, Leonora. Tell Inspector what he asks you to."

"Oh, well. Sometimes he live at Nippon Hotel, on Beretania Street."

Chan bowed. "Thank you so much." He wasted no time in that odorous cluttered room, but hastened down the dark stair. In a few moments he entered the Nippon Hotel. The sleek little Japanese behind the desk greeted him with a cordiality Chan knew was rankly insincere.

"Inspector, you honor my house."

"Such is not my purpose. *Haole* named Smith—he stops here?"

The clerk took a register from beneath the desk. "I look see——"

Charlie reached out and took the book from his slightly resisting hands. "I will see. Your eyes are notably bad. Archie Smith, room seven. Lead me there."

"Mr. Smith out, I think."

"We will discover if he is. Please make haste."

Reluctantly the Japanese led him across an open courtyard, filled with a neglected tangle of plants and flowers. The Nippon Hotel was a cluster of shabby sheds, antiquated outbuildings. They stepped on to a lanai; a Japanese woman porter, bent low under a heavy tin trunk, staggered by. The clerk moved on into a musty hallway, and pointed to a door. The numeral seven—or what was left of it—hung by one nail on the panel.

"In there," said the Jap, and with a hostile look, disappeared.

Chan opened the door of number seven, and entered a dim low-ceilinged room. One dirty bulb was burning over a pine table, and at table sat Smith, the beach-comber, with a canvas on his knees. He looked up, startled.

"Oh," he said. "So it's you?"

Chan regarded him sleepily. "Where you been all day?"

Smith indicated the canvas. "The evidence is right here, Inspector. I've been sitting in my palatial studio painting that courtyard outside. Glad you dropped in—it's been a bit dull since I finished." He leaned back in his chair and critically surveyed his work. "Come and look at this, Inspector. Do you know, I believe I've got something into it—a certain miasmic quality. Did you ever realize before that flowers can look mean and sinister? Well, they can—in the courtyard of the Nippon Hotel."

Chan glanced at the painting and nodded. "Yes, plenty good, but I have no time to be critic now. Get your hat and come with me."

"Where are we going—to dinner? I know a place on the Boulevard St.-Germain——"

"We go to the station house," Charlie replied.

"Wherever you say," nodded Smith, and putting aside the canvas, picked up his hat.

They crossed Aala Park to King Street. Chan regarded the derelict with an almost affectionate gaze. Before he and Smith parted company again, the beach-comber was going to tell him much—enough, perhaps, to solve his problem and put an end to all his worries.

The Chief was alone in the detectives' room. At sight of Charlie's companion, he brightened visibly. "Ah, you got him. I thought you would."

"What's it all about?" Smith asked jauntily. "I'm flattered, of course, by all these attentions, but——"

"Sit down," said the Chief. "Take off that hat." Thank heaven, here was some one who needn't be handled any too gently. "Look at me. A woman was killed last night at Waikiki, in a separate building on the grounds of her home. What were you doing in the room where she was killed?"

Beneath the yellow beard, Smith's face paled. He wet his lips with his tongue. "I was never in that room, Chief."

"You lie! We found your finger-prints on the windowsill. Look at me. What were you doing in that room?"

"I—I——"

"Come on, brace up. You're in a tight place. Tell the truth, or you'll swing for this. What were you doing——"

"All right," said Smith in a low voice. "I'll tell you about it. Give me a chance. I didn't kill anybody. It's true, I was in that room—in a way——."

"In a way?"

"Yes. I opened the window and climbed up on the sill. You see——"

"Kindly start at beginning," Chan cut in. "We know you arrived at window of pavilion to hear man and woman talking inside. What was said we pass over for the minute. You heard the man leaving the room——"

"Yes—and I went after him. I wanted to see him—but he got into a car and drove away down the avenue. I couldn't catch him. So I ambled back and sat down on the beach. Pretty soon I heard a cry—a woman's cry—from that pavilion. I didn't know what to do. I waited a while, and then I went over and looked through the window. The curtain was down, but it flapped about. Everything was quiet—I thought the place was empty. And then—well, really—I'm a little embarrassed about this. I'd never done such a thing before. But I was desperate—strapped—and when you're that way you get the feeling, somehow, that the world owes you a living——"

"Get on with it," barked the Chief.

"Well, just inside the window I caught a glimpse of—of a diamond pin. I thought there was no one inside, so I pushed up the screen and climbed on to the sill. I stooped over and picked up the pin—and then I saw her—the woman—lying over there by the table—stabbed, dead. Well, of course I realized at once that was no place for me. I lowered the screen, hid the pin in a little secret safety-deposit box of mine on the beach, and strolled as casually as I could to the avenue. I was still moving when that cop picked me up, an hour later."

"Is pin still on beach?" Chan inquired.

"No—I got it this morning." Smith reached into his trousers pocket and produced it. "Take it quick—I don't want it—don't let me ever see it again. I must have been crazy, I guess. But as I say—when you're down and out——"

Charlie was studying the pin. It was a delicate affair, a row of fine diamonds set in platinum. He turned it over. The pin itself was broken midway, and the end of it was lost.

The Chief was looking sternly at the beach-comber. "Well," he said, "you know what this means. We'll have to lock you up——"

"One moment, please," broke in Charlie. "Finding of pretty pin is good enough, but it is not vital to us. Vital matter is, what did this man hear Shelah Fane and Robert Fyfe saying to each other while he lingered outside pavilion window? Something of great importance—something Mr. Fyfe made false confession to quiet—something he has paid Mr. Smith nice sum to conceal. But now Mr. Smith changes mind. He will not conceal it any longer."

"Oh, yes, I will," cried Smith. "I mean—it was nothing—nothing——"

"We hold you for theft," cut in Charlie. "Do you enjoy prisons? I think not. Neither does territory enjoy supporting you there. Under a certain circumstance, memory of theft might fade from our minds for ever. Am I speaking correctly, Chief?"

The Chief was dubious. "You think it's as important as that, Charlie?"

"It is of vast importance," Chan replied.

"All right." He turned to the beach-comber. "Tell us the truth of what you heard last night, and you can go. I won't press the charge. But—it's got to be the truth, this time."

Smith hesitated. His rosy dream of the mainland, decent clothes, respectability, was dying hard. But he shuddered at the thought of Oahu Prison.

"All right," he said at last. "I'll tell you. I hate to do it, but—oh, well —there's Cleveland. My father—a punctilious man. Easily annoyed—growing old, you know. I've got to get out of this jam for his sake, if not for my own. When I came up to that window, Inspector——"

Chan raised his hand. "A moment, please, I have keen desire to see Robert Fyfe in this room when you tell the story." He looked at his watch. "I can reach him at hotel, I think. Excuse me." He took up the telephone and summoned Fyfe. Then he went over and sat down in a chair at the beach-comber's side. "Now we will rest as comfortable as may be. You, Smith, explore your mind and arrange story in advance. Kindly remember—the truth."

The beach-comber nodded. "You're on, Inspector. The truth this time." He looked down at his battered shoes. "I knew it was too good to last. Got a cigarette? No? Neither have I. Oh, well, life's like that."

22

What the Beach-comber Heard

They sat in silence, and the minutes dragged by. Smith's pale gray eyes stared hopelessly into the future, a future where he walked for ever, broke and forlorn, along a curving beach. Lighting a big cigar, the Chief picked up the evening paper. Charlie Chan took the diamond bar pin from his pocket and studied it, deep in thought.

Ten minutes passed, and then Robert Fyfe entered the room. He came in as though he were stepping on to a stage: suave, smiling, sure of himself. But as his gaze fell upon Smith the smile faded suddenly, and a frown replaced it.

"Good evening," the actor said. "I can give you about twenty minutes, Mr. Chan, and then I must run. It wouldn't do to be late at the theater again to-night."

"Twenty minutes will be ample plenty," nodded Charlie. "Mr. Smith and yourself have met before. Over here sits my Chief."

Fyfe bowed. "Ah, yes. I take it you have called me here for some important reason, Inspector?"

"Seems important to us," Chan answered. "I will squander no words. Last night you hold famous conversation with ex-wife in beach pavilion. The true contents of that talk have not yet been revealed. First when matter is discussed, you confess to crime you did not do, in order to change subject.

Then, this morning, you discover yourself sudden lover of art, and buy picture from Smith, hoping to keep him quiet." He looked fixedly at the actor. "I rejoice you got nice painting, Mr. Fyfe. Because that will be all you get. Smith can not longer keep quiet. Smith is about to speak."

A look of distress crossed the actor's face, and was succeeded by one of anger. He wheeled about and faced the beach-comber. "You contemptible——"

Smith raised a protesting hand. "I know—I know. What a broken reed I've turned out to be. I'm as sorry about this as you are, old man. But these keen lads here have got something on me—something rather serious—it means prison unless I ditch you. And I've slept in the pure open air so much—somehow a prison cot doesn't appeal to me. Frightfully sorry, as I said, but I'm going to throw you over. By the way, have you got a cigarette?"

Fyfe glared at him for a moment, and then, shrugging his shoulders, opened a silver case and held it out. Smith helped himself.

"Thanks. It's a wretched affair, Mr. Fyfe, and—no, that's all right, I've got a match—the sooner we get it over with, the better." He lighted the cigarette, and took a long pull at it. "To return to our favorite subject—last night on the beach—I went up to that pavilion window and they were in there together—this man and Shelah Fane. She was doing most of the talking—got a look at her—lovely, even more so than in the films. I'd rather like to have painted her—wearing that cream-colored gown——"

"Come, come," cried the Chief. "Get on with it."

"That's what I'm trying to do. I just wanted to point out how beautiful she was—a woman like that ought to be allowed at least one—shot."

Chan stood up. "What is your meaning now?"

"I mean she'd taken it, anyhow. She was telling Mr. Fyfe all about it—how three years ago, in Hollywood, she killed a man——"

With a groan Fyfe sank into a chair, and covered his face with his hands. "Killed what man?" the Chief demanded.

"Ah, yes—the name." Smith hesitated. "Denny, I think she called him. Yes, that was it—Denny Mayo."

There was a moment's tense silence, and then Fyfe leaped to his feet. "Let me tell this," he cried. "It will sound dreadful, if he tells it. Let me explain about Shelah—she was emotional, impetuous. I'll try to make you understand——"

"I don't care who tells it," said the Chief. "But I want it told, and quick."

Fyfe turned to Chan. "You heard, Inspector, how she called me at the theater—a distracted, pitiful call—and said she must see me at once. I answered that I'd come after the show, but she said no, that might be too late. If I'd ever loved her, I must come at once. She had something to tell me, she wanted my advice, she was desperate. So—I went.

"I met her on the lawn; she seemed overwhelmed with anxiety and fear. We went to the pavilion and she burst at once into her story. Some years after our divorce, she told me, she met this Denny Mayo—she fell madly in love with him—I could picture it. I knew how Shelah loved. Wildly, unreasonably. Mayo seemed to care for her; he had a wife in London, a dancer in musical comedies, but he promised to divorce her and marry Shelah. For a time Shelah was happy—and then one night Mayo asked her to come to his house.

"That was three years ago—a night in June. She went to his place at the hour he had suggested. He told her that he was through; that his wife had had an accident and was unable to work any longer; that he believed he owed a duty to this woman—at any rate he was going to write her to join him in Hollywood. Poor Shelah went a little mad then. Quite out of her senses. There was a revolver in the drawer of Mayo's desk, she got it, pointed it at him, threatened to kill him and herself. I have seen her in such moments; she was not responsible, I know. They struggled over the weapon, it went off in her hand. She stood looking down at Mayo, dead at her feet.

"She came to her senses then, I fancy. At any rate, she took her handkerchief and removed her fingerprints from the gun. She stole out of the house and went home unobserved. She was safe. Not once did the investigation point to her. Safe—but never happy again. From that day she lived in torment.

"A few weeks ago, in Tahiti, she met Alan Jaynes. She wanted to marry him, but she was haunted by that memory of the past. She'd fallen into the habit of consulting this fellow Tarneverro about everything; he had impressed her deeply with his cleverness. She sent for him to meet her here, and yesterday morning she went to his apartment.

"When she went there, she had no intention of telling him anything about Denny Mayo. She merely wanted him to read her future, to advise her as to whether a marraige with Jaynes would turn out happily. But he—he seemed to exert some mysterious power over her. Perhaps he hypnotized her. In any case, the first thing she knew, she found herself confessing the whole terrible story to the fortune-teller——"

"Stop!" cried Chan, with unaccustomed bruskness. "Ah, pardon me—one moment, please. You mean to say she told Tarneverro that she herself killed Denny Mayo?"

"Of course she did. I——"

"But Tarneverro relates different story."

"Then he lies. Shelah confessed to him that she had killed Denny—don't you understand—that's why she was so frightened, why she sent for me. I was the only one she could turn to, she said. She hadn't liked the light she saw in Tarneverro's eyes when she made her confession. She was deathly afraid of the man. She was sure he planned to use that confession in some way that would do her infinite harm. She clung to me, pleaded for my help. But what could I do? What was there to be done?"

Fyfe sat down as though exhausted by his story. "I tried to reassure her, promised to help her all I could—but I pointed out to her that I must get back to the theater at once. She begged me to stand by, stay with her—but you know, gentlemen, the show must go on. I had never disappointed an audience in my life—I refused to do it then. I left her and returned to town."

Again Fyfe buried his face in his hands. "If I had only stayed with her—but I didn't. The next thing I heard, poor Shelah was—murdered. I intended to tell the police the whole story at once, but somehow—when it came right down to it—I couldn't. Shelah, who had always been so straight and fine, such a good pal, so generous and kind. I pictured that blot on her past, that wild thing she had done in one irresponsible moment, cabled to the ends of the earth. She was gone. To find her murderer would never bring her back. No, I thought, keep Shelah's name unsullied. That's your job now.

"Then this accursed beach-comber came in and started his story. I went a little mad myself. I'd always loved Shelah—I loved her still—more than ever when I saw her last night. So I made my melodramatic confession to shut off the investigation. I don't know whether I'd have gone through with it or not—this morning when I woke up it seemed that I had carried chivalry a bit too far. Fortunately for me, I didn't have to go through with it—Mr. Chan disproved my confession on the spot. But I had succeeded in my purpose, I had given Smith here a tip, and when he came to me to day I was ready and willing to pay all I had to keep him quiet. I couldn't bear the thought of Shelah disgraced before the world that had so greatly admired her."

Charlie got up and laid his hand on the actor's shoulder. "You have caused me much trouble but I forgive freely, for you are gallant gentleman. Pardon me if I grow tiresome with much pounding on one point, but it is of vast importance. You are quige sure that Miss Fane told her story to Tarneverro exactly as she told it to you?"

"Absolutely," Fyfe replied. "And if you can find any connection between Tarneverro and Denny Mayo, then the fortune-teller killed her. That's certain."

Charlie exchanged a long look with his Chief. The latter turned to Smith. "You can go along," he said. "And don't let me see you here again."

The beach-comber rose quickly. "You won't—not if it's left to me," he remarked. "Of course, if you keep dragging me in——" He walked over to Fyfe. "I really am sorry, old man. I want you to know—in one respect at least I kept my word—I haven't had a drink all day. I sat in my room—money in my pocket—sat there and painted a lot of wicked-looking flowers, with my throat as dry as the Sahara. It was a tough assignment, but I came through it. Who knows—maybe I've got a chance yet. Here"—he took a roll of bills from his pocket—"this is yours."

"Why, what is it?" Fyfe asked.

"Thirty-two bucks—all I've got left of the fifty. Sorry it isn't more, but I bought a bit of canvas and some brushes—a chap can't just sit in a room, you know."

Fyfe stood up, and pushed the money away. "Oh, that's all right. It was a rather good painting—that's how I feel about it. Keep the money and get yourself some decent clothes."

Smith's pale gray eyes shone with gratitude. "By heaven—you're a gentleman. It does a fellow good to meet you. I feel something stirring within me—can it be a great resolve? They tell me there's a scarcity of stewards on the boats. To-morrow morning I'll buy myself some new things, and sign on for the trip to the coast. San Francisco—it's only a short walk from there to Cleveland. Yes—by the lord—I'll do it."

"Good luck to you, Fyfe answered.

"Thanks. May I trouble you—one more cigarette? You're very kind." He moved to the door, stopped and came back. "Somehow, Chief, I don't like to leave you. Will you do me a favor?"

The Chief laughed. "I might," he said.

"Lock me up until morning," the beach-comber went on. "Don't let me go into the street with all this money on me. I might be held up, or possibly—possibly——What I mean is, put me in a safe place overnight, and the chances of getting rid of me tomorrow will be a lot better than they look right now."

"With pleasure," nodded the Chief. "Come with me."

Smith waved a hand at Charlie Chan. "Remind me in the morning, Inspector, I owe you a dime—ten cents." He followed the Chief from the room.

Charlie turned to Fyfe. "You are now in demand at playhouse. I am deeply grateful for all you have told."

"Mr. Chan—if you could only keep this thing about Shelah from reaching the public—"

Charlie shook his head. "I am so sorry, but I fear same can not be done. The matter has vital connection with her murder."

"I suppose it has," Fyfe sighed. "Well, anyhow, you've been mighty decent to me, and I appreciate it."

Chan bowed him out.

Left alone, the detective stared thoughtfully into space. He was standing thus when the Chief strode again into the room. For a moment they regarded each other.

"Well," the Chief said, "so Tarneverro's story was a lie. And you've based your whole investigation on it. It's not like you, Charlie, to be tricked like that."

Chan nodded. "If I had time to do so, I would droop my head in shame. However, I choose now to forget the past. From this point on, my investigation takes new turn——"

"What do you mean—from this point on?" his Chief demanded. "The case is ended—don't you know that?"

"You think so?"

"I'm sure of it. In the morning Shelah Fane tells Tarneverro she killed Denny Mayo. Mayo was his brother. In the evening, she's found murdered. What could be simpler than that? I'm going to arrest the fortune-teller at once."

Charlie raised his hand. "No, no—I advise against that. You forget his alibi, solid as stone wall, not to be shaken."

"We'll have to shake it. It's evidently false. It must be. Either those old people are lying to save him, or else he tricked them as he tricked you——"

"I do not think so," Chan said stubbornly.

"What's the matter with you, Charlie? Losing your grip? We never had a clearer case than this. The little matter of the alibi——"

"Something else, too," Chan reminded him. "Why did Tarneverro say he would call me down the beach to arrest a murderer? His words stick in my mind and will not be unlodged. I tell you firmly, this problem not yet solved."

"I can't understand you, Charlie."

"Only one thing made clear by Mr. Fyfe's interesting story. I know now why Mr. Tarneverro did not wish me to open letter written by Shelah Fane. He feared I would learn at once his tale of seance with the lady was false in details, and house of cards would tumble about his ears. Fortunate for him, letter when finally opened was so worded as to add strength to his lie. 'Please forget what I told you this morning. I must have been mad—mad.' Then he knew that blow struck in the dark was not needed, after all. Must have wished to give himself a few resounding kicks." Chan paused. "Yes, Mr. Tarneverro has muddled me with his deceit from very start. Still, I do not believe him guilty of murder."

"Well, what do you propose to do?" the Chief demanded. "Just sit here and twiddle your thumbs, with me to help you?"

"I am no thumb-twiddler," replied Chan with spirit. "I propose to act."

"On what? We have no more clues."

Charlie took the diamond pin from his pocket. "We have this." He handed it over. "Will you kindly oblige by making study of same?"

The Chief examined it. "The pin itself is broken in the middle, isn't it? Half of it seems to be gone."

Chan nodded. "Undubitably gone. And when we find that missing end, our case is solved."

The Chief looked puzzled. "What do you mean?"

"How was pin broken? When watch was smashed, murderer wished to provide further evidence of struggle that might make smashing of watch more probable. So he tore off orchid flowers and trampled them beneath foot. When he ripped off flowers, pin unfastened and came with them. No doubt it lay on floor, point uppermost. Perhaps that point drove deep into heel of murderer's shoe, and broke off there. Did this happen, and did it go unnoticed by killer? It might. If so, there may be tell-tale scratches on polished floors of house at Waikiki. I speed there at once to look for same."

The Chief pondered. "Well, there might be something in it, at that. I'll give you a chance to find out. Go along, and I'll wait here for news."

In the doorway, Charlie encountered Kashimo. The little Japanese was worn and dispirited. "Have combed town twenty, maybe fifty, times. Mr. Smith no longer exists."

"A fine detective you are," growled the Chief. "Smith is out there in a cell now. Charlie found him."

Disappointment and distress showed in the eyes of the Japanese. Charlie paused at the door and came back. He patted the little man's shoulder.

"Cheer yourself up," he said kindly. "Be good boy, attend all meetings of Y. M. B. A., and you will yet win success. Nobody is perfect. Take look at me. Twenty-seven years on force, and I am nowhere near so clever as I thought I was."

He walked slowly from the room.

23

The Fateful Chair

Charlie rode out to the beach for what he hoped would be his final call at Shelah Fane's house. The moon had not yet risen, the sky was purple velvet pierced by ineffectual stars, the flowering trees hid their beauty somewhere in the calm breathless dark. Twenty-four hours ago, in this same period of impenetrable light before the coming of the moon, the black camel had knelt at Shelah Fane's gate.

Though he knew now the secret in the woman's past, knew that she had done a grievous wrong, he still thought of her with the deepest sympathy. She had never stood in court to answer for her crime, but she had suffered none the less. What torture those three years must have been! "Perhaps in the end I may find a little happiness. I want it so much"—thus she had written in her last pitiful note. Instead she had found—what? The black camel waiting to carry her away into the unknown.

Whatever the motive behind her murder may have been, Chan reflected, the act itself was heartless and cruel. He was firmly resolved that the person who had killed her should be found and made to pay. Found—but how? Would the little pin resting in his pocket come nobly to his aid? He hoped desperately that it would, for it was his sole reliance now.

The banyan tree's shade was like ink on the front lawn of the huge rambling building that had been the famous star's last home. Chan parked his car, switched off its lights, and leaped nimbly to the ground.

Jessop, serene and dignified as ever, let him in, "Ah, Constable, I was rather expecting you. What a pleasant evening to be abroad. Mild and fragrant, I should call it, sir."

Chan smiled. "I am too busy man, Jessop, to have concern with perfumes of the night."

"Ah, yes, I presume your time is fairly well occupied, Constable. Is there—if I may make bold to inquire—any news regarding the homicide?"

Chan shook his head. "Not up to present moment."

"I regret to hear that, sir. The young people are on the beach—Miss Julie and Mr. Bradshaw, I mean. Whom did you wish to interrogate?"

"I wish to interrogate the floors of this house," Chan told him.

Jessop raised his white eyebrows. "Indeed, sir. My old father used to say that walls have ears——"

"Floors, also, may repeat a story," Charlie returned. "If you have no inclination for objecting, I will begin in living-room."

He pushed through the heavy curtains. Diana Dixon was sitting at the piano, softly playing. She got up.

"Oh, hello," she said. "You want somebody?"

"I want somebody very much," Chan nodded. "At end of trail I hope to find him—or her."

"Then you haven't yet discovered who killed poor Shelah?"

"I have not. But subject is unhappy one. Why are you not on beach? That is place for youth at this hour?"

Diana shrugged. "What's the beach without a man? And there aren't enough to go round, evidently."

"A situation rare in your neighborhood, I will wager," Charlie smiled.

"Oh, a change does us all good." She watched him as he stood there, looking impatiently about the room. "What are you going to do now? I'm so thrilled by all this——"

"Now, I am going to be unbearably rude," he replied. "I find myself in uncredible position of wanting to dispense with your company. Will you kindly wait on the lanai?"

She pouted. "I hoped you were going to ask me to help you."

"In such charming company as yours, I fear I could not keep mind on work." He held open the French window. "As a very great favor, please——"

With obvious reluctance she went out, and he closed the window after her. He did not wish to appear undignified in the presence of a witness, and it was his intention now to be undignified indeed. He turned on all the lights in the room and with some difficulty, got down on his knees. Taking a magnifying-glass from his pocket, he began a close scrutiny of the highly polished floor wherever it was uncovered by rugs.

For a long time he crept about, until his knees ached. But he did not mind that, for his efforts were richly rewarded. Here and there he encountered numerous little scratches which had been, without doubt, recently made. He breathed hard, and his black eyes shone with satisfaction.

Suddenly a brighter idea struck him. He scrambled to his feet and hurried to the dining-room. The table, he was happy to note, was the same size it had been on the previous evening. Jessop was putting away silver in the sideboard. He turned.

"I observe," Chan remarked, "that you have not yet reduced size of dining table."

"I couldn't, sir," replied the butler. "All the leaves are already out. The former occupants of this house, it would appear, were of a most hospitable temperament."

"Just as well," nodded Chan. He was pleased to see that the big table stood on the bare floor; the room was without rugs save for a small one that lay in the doorway. "Do me a great favor, if you will, Mr. Jessop. Kindly place ten chairs about this board, in identical positions they occupied last night."

Puzzled, Jessop obeyed. When he had finished, Charlie stood for a moment in deep speculation.

"They now stand just as they did when you served dinner guests with coffee, some twenty-two hours ago?"

"Precisely," the butler assured him.

Without a word, Charlie pulled back a chair and disappeared beneath the table. One by one, mute evidence of his activity there, the chairs were pushed away, while Jessop stared with an amazement rarely seen on his imperturbable face. With a flash-light added to his equipment, Chan made the long circuit. Finally he came up as though for air.

"Were place-cards used for last night's dinner?" he inquired.

"No, sir. It was a rather informal affair, and Miss Fane told me she would seat the guests herself."

"Then when they came in here for coffee, they sat in no prearranged order?"

"Oh, no, sir. They just sat anywhere their fancy dictated."

"Is there chance you happen to remember who sat in which place?"

Jessop shook his head. "I'm sorry, Constable. It was a somewhat disturbing evening. I was a bit—unnerved, I fear."

Charlie laid his hand on the chair at the right of the one the hostess would no doubt have occupied. "You can not, then, tell me who it was who reclined here?"

"I'm afraid not, Mr. Chan. One of the gentleman. I fancy. But—I—I really don't know."

Charlie studied a moment. "Thank you so much. The telephone is in the hall closet, I believe?"

"Yes, sir. I will show you——"

"No need to trouble," Chan told him. "I will find it."

He went out to the hall and shutting himself in the hot cubby-hole under the stairs, made numerous calls. Finally he rang up his Chief.

"Inspector Chan speaking," he said. "May I humbly suggest that you bring one other good man with you, and come immediately to house of Shelah Fane?"

"Something doing, Charlie?" asked the Chief.

Chan pulled the door shut as far as it would go. Little beads of perspiration began to pop out on his forehead.

"Pin is about to lead us to success," he replied in a low voice. "On floor of living-room repose plenty fresh scratches. What is more, during time of investigation last night, guests who expected to enjoy dinner sat down round dining table for abbreviated repast. Floor is bare beneath table, and in front of one chair—and only one—more scratches are in evidence."

"Who sat in that chair?" the Chief demanded.

"The murderer of Shelah Fane," Chan answered. "The name I do not yet know. But I have just now summoned to house six guests, who, with three already here, make up complete list. When all are assembled we lead them to dining-room and ask them, please; to sit where they did last night. Chair of dead hostess was at head of table, facing door to hall. Note who sits down in chair at right of hostess. Same will be person we so hotly seek."

The Chief laughed. "Going to make a big drama out of it, eh, Charlie?

Well, that's all right with me, so long as it means success. I'll be with you pronto."

Chan returned to the hall, mopping his brow. He caught a glimpse of the coat-tails of Jessop, hastily disappearing through the curtains of the dining-room door. With an idle step he moved along, and came finally to the lanai, where he encountered Miss Dixon.

"Living-room is again at your disposal," he bowed.

She rose and came toward him. "Did you find what you were looking for?" she asked eagerly.

He shrugged. "Who in this world finds what he looks for? Success—what is it? A bubble that explodes when touched by human hand." And he strolled off toward the beach.

At his right, as he crossed the lawn, lay the pavilion, dark and empty to-night. Close by the sea, seated together in a beach chair intended for one person only, he came upon Julie and Jimmy Bradshaw. The boy rose.

"Why, it's good old Charlie," he cried. "Honolulu's noted sleuth. How are you, and what's the news?"

"News seems to be that spell of Waikiki Beach is still intact," Chan answered. "I am so sorry to interrupt this touching scene."

Bradshaw held out his hand. "Shake, Charlie. You're the first to hear about it. I'm going to be married. And oh, yes,—Julie is too."

"Plenty good news," returned Chan heartily. "May you have half the happiness I wish you—the full amount would be impossible."

"Oh, thank you, Mr. Chan," Julie said.

"You're a great old scout," Bradshaw remarked. "I'll miss you. I'll miss this beach, too——"

"What is that? You leave Honolulu?"

"Oh—sure."

"You depart from this lovely spot, about which you have written one million words——"

"I've got to, Charlie. Have you ever stopped to think about the effect of all this languid beauty on a young man's character? Devastating, that's what it is. On this crescent beach, fanned by the warm breath of the south, and so on—what happens to him? He droops, he stagnates, he crumbles. No more coco-palms for me. Redwoods, Charlie. Do you know about the redwoods? They brace you up. They're my trees hereafter. A big lumber and sap man from the West—that's going to me my rôle."

Chan grinned. "You have failed to win Miss Julie to your views on Hawaii?"

"It looks that way. Sold it to fifty thousand tourists, but not to the girl I love. That's life, I suppose."

"When you go from here, you will leave much beauty behind," Charlie said. "But you will also take much beauty with you, since Miss Julie goes along."

"Which remark, Mr. Bradshaw," Julie laughed, "should have come from you."

"It would have, presently," he answered.

Chan stood staring at the rising moon, the curve of lights along the whispering shore. The sad music of Hawaii came drifting up from the Moana courtyard. "To be young, in love, and on this beach," he said. "What greater happiness than that? Taste it to the full. It happens once, then time moves on. Moment comes when gold and pearls can not buy back the raven locks of youth."

"Why, Charlie,—you're getting sentimental," Bradshaw cried.

Chan nodded. "I think of my own courtship on this shore—so long ago. How long, you wonder? I am now father of eleven children—judge for yourself."

"You must be very proud of them," Julie ventured.

"As proud as they will permit," Chan answered. "At least, I have done my part to link past with future. When I move on, leaving eleven offspring, can any man say I have not been here? I think not."

"You're certainly right on that," Bradshaw assured him.

"May I speak with you in private for a moment?" Charlie said. He walked with the boy back toward the lights of the house.

"What's doing?" Bradshaw wanted to know.

"Plenty will be doing at any moment now. Within the hour I tell you who killed Shelah Fane."

"Good lord!" the boy gasped.

"First, I suggest a task for you. Miss Julie was Shelah Fane's dear friend. Go back and break news gently to her that it was Miss Fane who shot Denny Mayo. Same is now established beyond all doubt."

"You don't mean it?"

"I do. Impart news gently, as I request. Then blow will not hit her with such cruel force as in crowd of people. It will be unhappy shock for her, but she will soon forget. She has your love."

"All I've got, Charlie. Say—this is pretty considerate of you. But then —you think of everything."

"Within my limitations, I try to do so. When news is broken, both of you are to come at once to living-room."

"We'll do that, Charlie. Thanks."

As Chan entered the great room, Diana Dixon was greeting Martino, Van Horn and Jaynes, who had come down from the hotel together. The detective noted with satisfaction that all three were in dinner clothes—was it too much to hope they wore the same shoes as on the previous evening?

"Hello, Inspector," Martino said. "We came as soon as we could make it. What's in the air?"

"A little experiment," Chan answered. "Perhaps our case is *pau* to-night."

Jaynes was lighting a small cigar. "*Pau*—you mean finished? By jove, I hope so. They're holding a cabin for me on to-morrow's boat. I rely on you, Inspector."

"We all do," added the director. "I want to get off myself. Huntley—you and I might take that boat too."

Van Horn shrugged. "Oh—I don't care if I never leave. I was looking at that beach-comber last night. Shouldn't be surprised if he were the happiest man among us."

"Going primitive, eh?" Martino smiled. "I suppose it's the influence of that part you played down in Tahiti."

"It's the thought of Hollywood," responded Van Horn. "Of all the artificial places I've seen, that town wins the embossed medallion."

"Spoken like a true Californian," remarked Jimmy Bradshaw, entering with Julie. "Would you mind if I quoted you on that? Famous picture actor prefers Honolulu's simple ways to the fevered swank of the film colony."

"You do," returned Van Horn grimly, "and I'll deny I ever said it."

"Alas!" grinned Bradshaw. "All the movie actors' best lines have to be left out of their interviews."

Wilkie Ballou and his wife came in. The former wore a linen suit, with white shoes, and Charlie was troubled. If Ballou took the chair that was waiting for some one in the dining-room, then his case might be far from proof even now.

"What's it all about?" Ballou demanded. "I was going to bed early to-night."

"Poor old Wilkie can't stand excitement," Rita remarked. "As for me, I love it. Hello, Diana,—what have you been doing to-day?"

The curtain parted, and Tarneverro stepped noiselessly into the room. He stood for a moment, staring about, a rather worried look in his dark eyes.

"Ah, yes," he said. "We're all here, aren't we?"

Jaynes got slowly to his feet, walked over and proffered a case. "Good evening," he remarked. "Will you have one of my cigars?"

"No, thank you," Tarneverro answered blandly "I don't use them."

"So sorry," replied the Britisher. "I rather thought you did."

Charlie stepped hastily between them. "Will you be seated, please? We are all here, yes—except my Chief. We wait few minutes for him."

They sat down. Rita, Diana and Julie chatted together in low tones. The men were silent, staring into space.

Presently there was a clatter in the hall, and the Chief strode in. After him came Spencer, big and competent-looking. Chan leaped up.

"Ah, Chief,—now we may go forward. I have explained that we desire to make small experiment. You know some of these people——"

Wilkie Ballou shook the Chief's hand. "I'm glad to see you here," he remarked, with a glance toward Charlie.

"Mr. Tarneverro is also known to you," Chan continued, oblivous. He introduced the others. "Now we will all proceed to dining-room," he finished.

"What! Another dinner party?" cried Rita Ballou.

"A peculiar dinner party," Chan told her, "at which no food will be served. Come this way, please."

They filed out, solemn and ill-at-ease now. The presence of the Chief and the burly policeman in uniform had served to impress them with the seriousness of the situation. Not unnaturally, they were asking themselves what all this meant? Was it a trap?

Jessop was on duty in the dining-room, grave and dignified. He waited, ready to seat them at the barren table with the same poise as though it had gleamed with silver, been snowy with linen.

"We are now about to make request," Chan said slowly. "I would remind you that this is important moment and you must think deep before acting. No mistake must be made. Will you kindly sit down at same places you occupied at this table last night?"

A little chorus of dismay greeted his words."But I was so excited, I don't remember," cried Diana, and the others echoed her. For a moment they milled about, puzzled and uncertain. Then Jimmy Bradshaw dropped down at the foot of the table, opposite the empty chair of the hostess.

"I sat here," he announced. "I recall it perfectly. Julie, you were at my right. Mr. Van Horn, you sat at my left."

Julie and the picture actor, with Jessop officiating, took their places.

"Mr. Ballou, you were here beside me," Julie said, and Chan heaved a sigh of relief as the Honolulu man sank into his chair.

"So I was," Ballou remarked. "Thank you for remembering, my dear. Diana, you were at my right."

"True enough," Miss Dixon agreed, and Jessop held her chair. "And,

Val, you were at my right."

"Of course," the director nodded, and sat down.

One side of the table was now completely filled—but it was not the side that interested Charlie.

"You were across from me, Rita," said Diana.

Mrs. Ballou took her place.

Two chairs, aside from the one at the head of the table, remained vacant, with Jaynes and Tarneverro, left to occupy them.

"I believe, Mrs. Ballou, that I had the honor of sitting beside you," remarked Tarneverro, and took the chair at her right.

"So you did," Rita agreed. "And Mr. Jaynes was on the other side." She indicated the chair at her left—the portentous chair before which were tiny scratches such as might have been made by a broken pin protruding slightly from the heel of a shoe.

"I fancy we have it now," smiled Jaynes innocently and sat down.

There was a moment's silence. "You are seated just as you were last night?" Chan inquired slowly.

"We are not," said Huntley Van Horn suddenly.

"Something is wrong?" Charlie asked.

"It is. Mr. Tarneverro is at my left now, but last night Mr. Jaynes was in that position."

"Why, of course," Rita Ballou cried. She turned to Tarneverro. "You and Mr. Jaynes have exchanged places."

"Perhaps we have," the fortune-teller answered amiably. He rose. Jaynes also got up, and took the chair at Rita's right. After a moment's hesitation, Tarneverro dropped into the fateful chair. "I fancy we're all set now," he remarked calmly. "Jessop, you may serve the soup."

Charlie and the Chief exchanged a look, and moved away from the neighborhood of the table. They went into the hall.

"Tarneverro," said the Chief softly. "I knew it. Take a look at his shoes ——"

But Chan stubbornly shook his head. "Something is very wrong here," he insisted.

"Wrong, nonsense! What's got into you, anyhow, Charlie?"

"Extremely wrong," Chan continued. "You can not convict a man with an alibi such as his. All broken pins in world would not avail."

"Then the whole thing's a flop, according to you?"

"So far—yes. But I do not despair. Permit me that I think a moment. There is some explanation of this. Ah, yes—come with me."

They returned to the dining-room. The group about that barren table looked at them expectantly.

"Kindly hold positions just as at present," Chan said. "I come back before I am missed."

He stepped through a swinging door into the kitchen, and they heard his voice in low converse with Wu Kno-ching, the cook. They waited in silence; even the obviously innocent appeared anxious and uneasy. Presently Charlie returned, walking with unwonted briskness and with a grim look on his face.

"Jessop," he said.

The butler stepped forward with a rather startled air.

"Yes, Constable?"

"Jessop, after these people departed last night, others sat at this table?"

The butler had a guilty look. "I'm extremely sorry, sir. It was not quite in order—I would not ordinarily countenance it in a well-run house, but things were rather at sixes and sevens—and we had had no dinner—so we just sat down for a bit of coffee; we needed it badly——"

"Who sat down?"

"Anna and I, sir."

"You and Anna sat down at this table, after the guests had gone? Where did you sit?"

"Over there—where Mr. Martino is now seated, sir."

"And Anna—where did Anna sit?"

"She sat here, sir." And Jessop laid his land on the back of Tarneverro's chair.

For a moment Chan was silent, staring at the butler with unseeing eyes. He sighed heavily, as one who after a long journey sights the end of the trail at last.

"Where is Anna now?" he asked.

"She is in her room, I fancy, sir. Up-stairs."

Charlie nodded at Spencer. "Bring this woman at once," he ordered, and the policeman disappeared. Chan turned to the table. "Our little experiment is ended. Please step back to living-room."

They got up and filed silently across the hall. Charlie and the Chief waited at the foot of the stairway. The Chief said nothing, and Charlie also seemed disinclined to speak. Presently Spencer appeared at the head of the stairs, accompanied by Anna. They descended slowly. His eyes like black buttons in the half-light, Chan faced the woman. With cool unconcern, she returned his stare.

"Come with me," he said. He led her into the living-room, and stood for a moment looking at her feet. She wore high, black shoes, in keeping with her sober uniform. The right one, Charlie noted, seemed somewhat thick about the ankle.

"Anna, I must make very odd request of you," he said. "Will you be good enough to remove right shoe?"

She sat down, and began slowly to unlace it. Tarneverro came forward and stood at Chan's side. The detective ignored him.

He took the heavy shoe from Anna's hand, turned it over, and with his penknife slit the rubber heel. A little half-inch length of gold pin lay exposed, and with a gesture of triumph he lifted it out and held it up.

"You are all witnesses," he reminded them. He turned to Anna. "As for you, I fear you have been grossly careless. When you stamped those orchids under foot, you failed to note this telltale evidence of your act. Ah, well—but for such brief moments of neglect, we would get nowhere in this business." He gave his attention to the shoe. "I note braces built along the sides," he continued. "Meant to protect weak ankle, I think. You have had an accident, madam?"

"My—my ankle was broken—long ago," she replied, in a voice barely audible.

"Broken?" cried Charlie quickly. "When? How? Was it dancing on the stage you broke that ankle? Ah, yes—it was. Madam—I think you were once the wife of Denny Mayo."

The woman took a little step toward him. Her eyes were hard and defiant, but her usually dark face was white as Waikiki's sands.

24

The Veil Is Lifted

Charlie turned to Tarneverro. In the deep-set eyes of the fortune-teller he saw a reluctant admiration. He smiled.

"I have been plenty dense," he said. "This woman is on the scene by no coincidence. When you set up as lifter of the veil in Hollywood, you needed—what? Spies—spies to scatter about the place, and bring you morsels of gossip regarding film people. Your brother's wife had suffered accident, she was no longer able to work at profession, she was penniless and alone. You sent for her. What more natural than that action? You helped her to position, that she might help you."

Tarneverro shrugged. "You have a remarkable imagination, Mr. Chan."

"No, no—you flatter me," Charlie cried. "It has just been proved I have not imagination enough. Only one claim I make for myself—when light at last begins to stream in, I do not close the shutters. Light is streaming in now. Anna's task was not alone to bring you trivial information—she was also to assist you in solving matter of Denny Mayo's murder. Was that why you placed her with Shelah Fane? Had you already some suspicion of Miss Fane? I think so. Yesterday morning in your apartment, actress confessed her misdeed to you. At once you inform Anna that victory has come. You are in high spirits. Your own intention is honest one, you plan to hand Miss Fane to police. Otherwise you would not say to me what you did in Grand Hotel lounge last night. Then—what happened?"

"You tell me, Inspector."

"Such is my purpose. You learn that Shelah Fane is murdered. Without being told, you know who did the deed. The position is hard one for you, but mind works fast as usual. You invent false story about your seance with Shelah Fane, and boost me off on wrong trail at once. You talk about mythical letter Miss Fane was to write for you. Then, to your surprise and dismay, you find real letter was written. It may wreck plans at once, so you strike me down and obtain epistle. Needless act, as it turns out. You rage about, destroying photographs of Mayo to conceal relationship with him. You seek to befuddle me by involving innocent parties. Oh, you have been busy man, Mr. Tarneverro. I might forgive you, but I find it difficult to forgive myself. Why have I been so stupid?"

"Who says you've been stupid, Charlie?" the Chief asked.

"I do, and I remark same with bitter force," Chan answered. "My little duel with this fortune-teller should have been finished long hours ago. Matter was clear enough. I knew he employed spies. I gathered—though I paid not enough attention to fact—that some one had been spying on Miss Fane in Tahiti and on returning boat. I learned that Anna here bought bonds—matter which might indicate more income than simple wage as maid. I listen to Tarneverro's alibi and feel certain he did not do murder himself. What, then, explains his actions? Natural inference for good detective would have been that he protects some one else. Who? I read in newspaper that Denny Mayo had wife. I discover Mayo was Tarneverro's brother, and I hear that Mayo was slain by hand of Shelah Fane. Later —crowning touch—I am told Mayo's wife encountered accident and can no longer follow profession. Do I put two and two together? Do I add up simple sum and get result? No—I fumble around—I flounder like decrepit fish—finally I slide into happy harbor of success." He turned suddenly on Anna, standing pale and silent before him. "For I am in that harbor. It is true, is it not, madam? You killed Shelah Fane!"

"I did," the woman answered.

"Don't be a fool, Anna," Tarneverro cried. "Fight it out."

She gestured hopelessly. "What's the use? I don't care. I've nothing to live for—it doesn't matter what becomes of me. Yes, I killed her. Why not? She——"

"Just a moment," the Chief broke in. "Anything you say, you know, may be used against you."

"You're a little late with that, Chief," Tarneverro said. "She should have a lawyer——"

"I don't want one," Anna went on sullenly. "I don't want any help. I killed her—she robbed me of my husband—she wasn't content to take his love—she ended by taking his life. I've had my revenge, and I'm willing to pay for it. I intend to plead guilty, and get it over with at once."

"Fine," approved the Chief. He saw the territory saved the expense of a long trial.

"You're mad, Anna," cried the fortune-teller.

She shrugged. "Don't mind me. I wrecked all your plans, I fancy. I spoiled everything for you. Forget me and go your way alone."

Her tone was bitter and cold, and Tarneverro, rebuffed, turned away from her. Charlie offered her a chair. "Sit down, madam. I desire to make brief interrogation. It is true that Tarneverro brought you to Hollywood?"

"Yes." She accepted the chair. "I'll take it from the beginning, if you like. While Denny was acting in the pictures, I continued to dance in London music-halls. I was doing well, when I had that accident—I broke my ankle—I couldn't dance any more. I wrote to Denny about it, and asked if I could come to him. I didn't receive any answer—and then I heard he had been killed.

"Arthur—Denny's brother here—was also playing in London at that time. He was kind to me—loaned me money—and then he told me he was going out to the States to learn who had killed poor Denny, if he could. After a time he wrote that he had set up in Hollywood as a fortune-teller, calling himself Tarneverro. He said he needed—help—that he could use me if I was willing to go into service. I had taken a position as wardrobe mistress with a manager for whom I used to dance. It was hard work—and the memories—I longed to get away from it all."

"So you went to Hollywood," prompted the Chief.

"I did, and I met Tarneverro secretly. He said he would place me with Miss Fane. He advised her to get rid of the maid she had, and sent me round the same day to apply for the position. He had discovered that Miss Fane and Denny were once—very close friends—and he thought I might be able to get on the trail of something in her house. He suggested that I change my appearance as much as possible—my way of doing my hair—he feared that Denny might have shown her pictures of me. I followed his instructions, but it was an unnecessary precaution. Denny—he must have lost my pictures—lost them or thrown them away. Miss Fane engaged me, and I was successful in the post. You see—I'd had maids myself. For a year and a half I was with her—helping Tarneverro. But I could discover nothing. Nothing about Denny, I mean.

"Yesterday afternoon Tarneverro and I met on the beach. He told me

Shelah Fane had confessed to killing Denny—confessed it in his apartment that morning. He wanted to get a repetition of that confession with a witness to overhear—he planned it for last night in the pavilion. He would talk with her there alone, and I was to be hiding somewhere about. Then he proposed to send for an officer.

"I returned to this house, almost beside myself with hatred for the woman who had wrecked Denny's life—and mine. I got to thinking—sitting alone in my room. Tarneverro's plan began to look so very foolish to me. The police? I knew what one of your American juries would do with a woman like Shelah Fane—a beautiful, famous woman. They would never convict her—never. There were better ways than the police. I—I kept on thinking. I'm rather sorry I did."

Her eyes flashed. "No—I'm not. I'm glad. I planned it all out. Last night—during the party—that was the time. Plenty of people about—plenty of people who might have done it. I planned the alibi of the watch—I remembered it from a play in which Denny once acted. I was in the kitchen from twenty minutes before eight until ten after the hour. Jessop and the cook were there too. At eight-fifteen I located Shelah Fane in the pavilion—she was waiting there—waiting to make a good entrance on her party—as she always did. She was like that.

"I went to her room and got a knife—one she had bought in Tahiti. I wanted something to wrap it in—a handkerchief—a big one. The door of the blue room was open—I saw a man's clothes. I went in and took the handkerchief from the pocket of the coat—Mr. Bradshaw's coat, I think."

"Ah, yes," remarked Jimmy Bradshaw grimly. "Thanks for the ad."

"I went to the pavilion," Anna continued. "She didn't suspect. I came close to her——" The woman buried her face in her hands. "You won't make me tell that part. Afterward I broke the watch in the handkerchief, put it back on her wrist. But there was no other evidence of a struggle, so I tore off the orchids and trampled them under foot. I went out and buried the knife deep in the sand—I heard voices on the beach—I was frightened. I ran to the house, and went up to my room by way of the back stairs."

"And the handkerchief?" Charlie inquired. "You gave that to Mr. Tarneverro when he arrived?"

"Just a moment," said the fortune-teller. "Anna—when did you and I last talk together alone?"

"On the beach, yesterday afternoon."

"Have we communicated with each other since that moment?"

She shook her head. "No."

"Have I heard you say before that you killed Shelah Fane?"

"No, you have not."

The fortune-teller looked at the Chief. "A little matter," he remarked, "that I am rather keen to bring out."

"But the handkerchief——?" The Chief turned to Anna.

"I dropped it on the lawn. I—I wanted it to be found there." She glanced at Bradshaw. "It wasn't mine, you know."

"Very thoughtful of you," bowed the boy.

"On the lawn, precisely," said Tarneverro, "where I picked it up."

"And put it in my pocket," remarked Martino. "By the way, I haven't thanked you for that."

"Do not trouble," Chan advised him. "You were not the only one Mr. Tarneverro honored with his attentions."

The Chief went over to the woman's side. "Go upstairs," he said sternly. "And get ready. You'll have to go down-town with us. You can tell that story again—at the station." He nodded to Spencer to accompany her.

The woman rose, her manner sullen and defiant, and went from the room, with the policeman at her side.

"Well," said Ballou, "I guess we can all go now."

The Chief gave a sign of acquiescence. Wilkie and Rita left first, followed by Martino, Van Horn and Jaynes. The latter stopped to shake Charlie's hand.

"Thanks," he remarked in a low voice. "I shall make my boat. And on this boat—and all others in the future—I shall try to keep my head."

Diana went quietly up to her room. Chan turned to Julie.

"Go back to beach," he said gently. "Look up at stars, breathe clean fresh air and think of future happiness."

The girl gazed at him, wide-eyed. "Poor Shelah," she whispered.

"Shelah Fane's troubles over now," Chan reminded her. "Do poor lady great kindness, and forget. Jimmy here will help you."

Bradshaw nodded. "I certainly will." He put his arm about the girl. "Come on, Julie. One more look at the coco-palms, and then we're off for the coast, where trees are trees." They moved toward the French window. Bradshaw smiled at Chan over his shoulder. "So long, Charlie. I've got to go now and tone down my adjectives so they'll fit California."

They went out, and Chan turned back into the room to find his Chief staring speculatively at Tarneverro. "Well, Charlie," he remarked. "What are we going to do with our friend here?"

Chan did not answer, but thoughtfully rubbed his cheek. Tarneverro, seeing the gesture, smiled.

"I'm so sorry," he said. "I've made you a lot of trouble, Inspector. But I was in a horrible position—you can realize that. Should I have handed Anna over to you at once? Perhaps; but as I told you last night, I saw immediately that I was responsible for the whole affair. Innocently so, of course, but none the less responsible. I ought never to have told her—but I wanted a witness. If only I had kept my discovery to myself."

"The man who looks back sees his mistakes piled up behind," Chan nodded.

"But I never dreamed Anna would lose her head like that. These women, Inspector."

"They are primitive creatures, these women."

"So it would seem. Anna has always been a strange, silent, unfriendly person. But there was one bond between us—we both loved Denny. When she proved last night how desperately she loved him—well, I couldn't betray her. Instead I fought my duel with you. Fought to the limit of my ability—and lost." He held out his hand.

Chan took it. "Only the churlish are mean-spirited in victory," he remarked.

The policeman in uniform looked through the curtains.

"Right with you, Spencer," said the Chief. "Mr. Tarneverro, you'd better come along. I'll talk to the Prosecutor about you. But you needn't be alarmed. We're not inclined to spend much money over here on chance visitors from the mainland."

Tarneverro bowed. "You're very encouraging."

"You got your car, Charlie?" the Chief asked.

"I have it," Chan told him.

The Chief and Tarneverro went into the hall, and presently Charlie heard the front door slam.

He stood for a moment looking about him at the bright room where his work was *pau* at last. Then, sighing ponderously, he stepped through the curtains and picked up his hat from a table in the hallway. Wu Kno-ching appeared suddenly from the dining-room.

Charlie gazed into the beady eyes, the withered yellow face of his compatriot.

"Tell me something, Wu," he said. "How was it I came upon this road? Why should one of our race concern himself with the hatreds and the misdeeds of the *haoles?*"

"Wha's mallah you?" Wu inquired.

"I am weary," sighed Chan. "I want peace now. A very trying case, good Wu Kno-ching. But"—he nodded, and a smile spread over his fat face—"as you know, my friend, a gem is not polished without rubbing nor a man perfected without trials."

The door closed gently behind him.

Keeper of the Keys

To my son Bob
As quietly as possible
Since he dislikes publicity

1

Snow on the Mountains

The train had left Sacramento some distance behind, and was now bravely beginning the long climb that led to the high Sierras and the town of Truckee. Little patches of snow sparkled in the late afternoon sun along the way, and far ahead snow-capped peaks suddenly stood out against the pale sky of a reluctant spring.

Two conductors, traveling together as though for safety, came down the aisle and paused at section seven. "Tickets on at Sacramento," demanded the leader. The occupant of the section, a pretty blonde girl who seemed no more than twenty, handed him the small green slips. He glanced at them, then passed one to his companion. "Seat in Seven," he said loudly. "Reno."

"Reno," echoed the Pullman conductor, in an even louder tone.

They passed on, leaving the blonde girl staring about the car with an air that was a mixture of timidity and defiance. This was the first time, since she had left home the day before, that she had been so openly tagged with the name of her destination. All up and down the car, strange faces turned and looked at her with casual curiosity. Some smiled knowingly; others were merely cold and aloof. The general public in one of its ruder moments.

One passenger only showed no interest. Across the aisle, in section eight, the girl noted the broad shoulders and back of a man in a dark suit. He was sitting close to the window, staring out, and even from this rear view it was apparent that he was deeply engrossed with his own affairs. The young woman who was bound for Reno felt somehow rather grateful toward him.

Presently he turned, and the girl understood, for she saw that he was a Chinese. A race that minds its own business. An admirable race. This member of it was plump and middle-aged. His little black eyes were shining as from some inner excitement; his lips were parted in a smile that seemed to indicate a sudden immense delight. Without so much as a glance toward number seven, he rose and walked rapidly down the car.

Arrived on the front platform of the Pullman, he stood for a moment deeply inhaling the chilly air. Then again, as though irresistibly, he was drawn to the window. The train was climbing more slowly now; the landscape, wherever he looked, was white. Presently he was conscious of some one standing behind him, and turned. The train maid, a Chinese girl of whose guarded glances he had been conscious at intervals all afternoon, was gazing solemnly up at him.

"How do you do," the man remarked, "and thank you so much. You have arrived at most opportune moment. The need to speak words assails me with unbearable force. I must release flood of enthusiasm or burst. For at this moment I am seeing snow for the first time!"

"Oh—I am so glad!" answered the girl. It was an odd reply, but the plump Chinese was evidently too excited to notice that.

"You see, it is this way," he continued eagerly. "All my life I can remember only nodding palm-trees, the trade winds of the tropics, surf tumbling on coral beach—"

"Honolulu," suggested the girl.

He paused, and stared at her. "Perhaps you have seen Hawaii too?" he inquired.

She shook her head. "No. Me—I am born in San Francisco. But I read advertisements in magazines—and besides—"

"You are bright girl," the man cut in, "and your deduction is eminently correct. Honolulu has been my home for many years. Once, it is true, I saw California before, and from flat floor of desert I beheld, far in distance, mountain snow. But that was all same dream. Now I am moving on into veritable snow country, the substance lies on ground all about, soon I shall plunge unaccustomed feet into its delicious cold. I shall intake great breaths of frigidair." He sighed. "Life is plenty good," he added.

"Some people," said the girl, "find the snow boresome."

"And some, no doubt, consider the stars a blemish on the sky. But you and I, we are not so insensible to the beauties of the world. We delight to travel—to find novelty and change. Is it not so?"

"I certainly do."

"Ah—you should visit my islands. Do not think that in my ecstasy of raving I forget the charm of my own land. I have daughter same age as sou—how happy she would be to act as your guide. She would show you Honolulu, the flowering trees, the—"

"The new police station, perhaps," cried the girl suddenly.

The big man started slightly and stared at her. "I perceive that I am known," he remarked.

"Naturally," the girl smiled. "For many years you have been newspaper hero for me. I was small child at the time, but I read with panting interest when you carried Phillimore pearls on flat floor of desert. Again, when you captured killer of famous Scotland Yard man in San Francisco, I perused daily accounts breathlessly. And only three weeks ago you arrived in San Francisco with one more cruel murderer in your firm grasp."

"But even so," he shrugged.

"Your pictures were in all the papers. Have you forgot?"

"I seek to do so," he answered ruefully. "Were those my pictures?"

"More than that, I have seen you in person. Two weeks ago when the Chan Family Society gave big banquet for you in San Francisco. My mother was a Chan, and we were all present. I stood only a few feet away when you entered the building. True, I was seated so far distant I could not hear your speech, but I was told by others it was brilliant talk."

He shrugged. "The Chan family should have more respect for truth," he objected.

"I am Violet Lee," she went on, holding out a tiny hand. "And you—may I speak the name—"

"Why not?" he replied, taking her hand. "You have me trapped. I am inspector Charlie Chan, of the Honolulu Police."

"My husband and I recognized you when you came aboard at Oakland," the girl went on. "He is Henry Lee, steward of club car," she added proudly. "But he tells me sternly I must not speak to you—that is why I cried 'I am so glad!' when you spoke first to me. Perhaps, said my husband, inspector is now on new murder case, and does not want identity known. He is often right, my husband."

"As husbands must be," Chan nodded. "But this time he is wrong."

A shadow of disappointment crossed the girl's face. "You are not, then, on trail of some wrong-doer?"

"I am on no trail but my own."

"We thought there might have been some recent murder—"

Charlie laughed. "This is the mainland," he remarked, "so of course there have been many recent murders. But I am happy to say, none of them concerns me. No—I am involved only in contemplation of snow-capped peaks."

"Then—may I tell my husband that he is free to address you? The honor will overwhelm him with joy."

Chan laid his hand on the girl's arm. "I will tell him myself," he announced. "And I will see you again before I leave the train. In the meantime, your friendly words have been as food to the famished, rest to the jaded. Aloha."

He stepped through the door of the car ahead, leaving his small compatriot flushed and breathing fast on the chilly platform.

When he reached the club car, the white-jacketed steward was bending solicitously over the solitary passenger there. Receiving the latter's order, he stood erect and cast one look in the direction of Charlie Chan. He was a small thin Chinese, and only another member of his race would have caught the brief flame of interest that flared under his heavy eyelids.

Charlie dropped into a chair and, for lack of anything better to do, studied his fellow traveler, some distance down the aisle. The man was a lean, rather distinguished-looking foreigner of some sort—probably a Latin, Chan thought. His hair was as black and sleek as the detective's, save where it was touched with gray over the ears. His eyes were quick and roving, his thin hands moved nervously about, he sat on the edge of his chair, as though his stay on the train was but a brief interlude in an exciting life.

When the steward returned with a package of cigarettes on a silver tray and got his money and tip from the other passenger, Chan beckoned to him. The boy was at his side in an instant.

"One juice of the orange, if you will be so good," Charlie ordered.

"Delighted to serve," replied the steward, and was off like a greyhound. With surprising speed he returned, and placed the drink on the arm of Charlie's chair. He was moving reluctantly away, when the detective spoke.

"An excellent concoction," he said, holding the glass aloft.

"Yes, sir," replied the steward, and looked at Chan much as the Chinese girl on the platform had done.

"Helpful in reducing the girth," Chan went on. "A question which, I perceive, does not concern you. But as for myself—you will note how snugly I repose in this broad chair."

The eyes of the other narrowed. "The man-hunting tiger is sometimes over-plump," he remarked. "Still he pounces with admirable precision."

Charlie smiled. "He who is cautious by nature is a safe companion in crossing a bridge."

The Steward nodded. "When you travel abroad, speak as the people of the country are speaking."

"I commend your discretion," Charlie told him. "But as I have just said to your wife, it is happily unnecessary at this time. The man-hunting tiger is at present unemployed. You may safely call him by his name."

"Ah, thank you, Inspector. It is under any conditions a great honor to meet you. My wife and I are both long-time admirers of your work. At this moment you seem to stand at very pinnacle of fame."

Charlie sighed, and drained his glass. "He who stands on pinnacle," he ventured, "has no place to step but off."

"The need for moving," suggested the steward, "may not be imminent."

"Very true." The Detective nodded approvingly. "Such wisdom and such efficiency. When I met your wife, I congratulated you. Now I meet you, I felicitate her."

A delighted smile spread over the younger man's face. "A remark," he answered, "that will find place in our family archive. The subjects are unworthy, but the source is notable. Will you deign to drink again?"

"No, thank you." Chan glanced at his watch. "The town of Truckee, I believe, is but twenty-five minutes distant."

"Twenty-four and one-half," replied Henry Lee, who was a railroad man. The flicker of surprise in his black eyes was scarcely noticeable. "You alight at Truckee, Inspector?"

"I do," nodded Charlie, his gaze on the other passenger, who had evinced sudden interest.

"You travel for pleasure, I believe you intimated," the steward continued.

Chan smiled. "In part," he said softly.

"Ah, yes—in part," Henry Lee repeated. He saw Chan's hand go to his trousers pocket. "The charge, I regret to state, is one half-dollar."

Nodding, Charlie hesitated a moment. Then he laid the precise sum on the silver tray. He was not unaware of the institution of tipping. He was also not unaware of the sensitive Chinese nature. They would part now as friends, not as master and menial. He saw from the light in Henry Lee's eyes that the young man appreciated his delicacy.

"Thank you so much," said the steward, bowing low. "It has been great honor and privilege to serve Inspector Charlie Chan."

It chanced that at the moment the detective's eyes were on the foreign-looking passenger at the other end of the car. The man had been about to light a cigarette, but when he overheard the name he paused, and stared until the match burned down to his finger-tips. He tossed it aside, lighted another and then came down the car and dropped into the seat at Charlie's side.

"Pardon," he said. "Me—I have no wish to intrude. But I overhear you say you leave the train at Truckee. So also must I."

"Yes?" Chan said politely.

"Alas, yes. A desolate place, they tell me, at this time of year."

"The snow is very beautiful," suggested Charlie.

"Bah!" The other shrugged disgustedly. "Me, I have had sufficient snow. I fought for two winters with the Italian Army in the North."

"Distasteful work," commented Chan, "for you."

"What do you mean?"

"Pardon—no offense. But one of your temperament. A musician."

"You know me, then?"

"I have not the pleasure. But I note flattened, calloused finger-tips. You have played violin."

"I have done more than play the violin. I am Luis Romano, conductor of the opera. Ah—I perceive that means nothing to you. But in my own country—at La Scala in Milan, at Naples. And also in Paris, in London, even in New York. However, that is all finished now."

"I am so sorry."

"Finished—by a woman. A woman who—but what of this? We both alight at Truckee. And after that—"

"Ah, yes—after that."

"We travel together, Signor Chan. I could not help it—I heard the name. But that was lucky. I was told to look out for you. You do not believe? Read this."

He handed Charlie a somewhat soiled and crumpled telegram. The detective read:

"MR. LUIS ROMANO, KILARNEY HOTEL, SAN FRANCISCO: DELIGHTED YOU ARE COMING TO TAHOE TO VISIT ME. OWING TO VERY LATE SPRING, ROAD AROUND LAKE IN POOR CONDITION. LEAVE TRAIN TRUCKEE, I WILL TELEPHONE LOCAL GARAGE HAVE CAR WAITING, YOU WILL BE DRIVEN TO TAHOE TAVERN, AT TAVERN PIER MY MAN WILL WAIT FOR YOU WITH MOTOR-LAUNCH, BRING YOU DOWN TO MY PLACE, PINEVIEW. OTHER GUESTS MAY JOIN YOU IN CAR AT TRUCKEE, AMONG THEM MR. CHARLIE CHAN, OF HONOLULU. THANKS FOR COMING.

"DUDLEY WARD."

Chan returned the missive to the eager hand of the Italian. "Now I understand," he remarked.

Mr. Romano made a gesture of despair. "You are more fortunate than I. I understand to the door of this place Pineview—but no further. You, however—it may be you are old friend of Mr. Dudley Ward? The whole affair may be clear to you."

Charlie's face was bland, expressionless. "You are, then, in the dark yourself?" he inquired.

"Absolutely," the Italian admitted.

"Mr. Dudley Ward is no friend of yours?"

"Not at all. I have yet to see him. I know, of course, he is a member of a famous San Francisco family, very wealthy. He spends the summers at his place on this high lake, to which he goes very early in the season. A few days ago I had a most surprising letter from him, asking me to visit him up here. There was, he said, a certain matter he wished to discuss, and he promised to pay me well for my trouble. I was—I am, Signor, financially embarrassed—owing to a circumstance quite unforeseen and abominable. So I agreed to come."

"You have no trace of idea what subject Mr. Ward desires to discuss?"

"I have an inkling—yes. You see—Mr. Ward was once the husband of—my wife." Chan nodded hazily. "The relationship, however, is not very close. There were two other husbands in between us. He was the first—I am the fourth."

Charlie sought to keep a look of surprise from his face. What would his wife, on Punchbowl Hill, think of this? But he was now on the mainland, with Reno only a few miles away.

"It will be perhaps easier for you to understand," the Italian went on, "if I tell you who is my wife. A name, Signor, known even to you—pardon—to the whole world. Landini, the opera singer, Ellen Landini." He sat excitedly on the edge of his chair. "What a talent—magnificent. What an organ—superb. And what a heart—cold as those snow-covered stones." He waved at the passing landscape.

"So sorry," Chan said. "You are not, then, happy with your wife?"

"Happy with her, Signor? Happy with her!" He stood up, the better to declaim. "Can I be happy with a woman who is at this very moment in Reno seeking to divorce me and marry her latest fancy—a silly boy with a face like putty? After all I have done for her—the loving care I have lavished upon her—and now she does not send me even the first payment of the settlement that was agreed on—she leaves me to—"

He sank into the chair again. "But why not? What could I expect from her? Always she was like that. The husband she had was never the right one."

Chan nodded. "Ginger grown in one's own garden is not so pungent," he remarked.

Mr. Romano wakened to new excitement. "That is it. That expressed it. It was always so with her. Look at her record—married to Dudley Ward as a girl. Everything she wanted—except a new husband. And she got him in time. John Ryder, his name was. But he didn't last long. Then—another. He was—what does it matter? I forget. Then me. I, who devoted every waking hour to her voice, to coaching her. It was I, Signor, who taught her the old Italian system of breathing, without which a singer is nothing—nothing. If you will credit it—she did not know it when I met her."

He buried his head emotionally in his hands. Charlie respected the moment.

"And now," went on Mr. Romano, "this boy, this singer—this what's his name. Will he command her not to eat pastries—seeking to save that figure once so glorious? Will he prepare her gargle, remind her to use it? Now I recall the name of the third husband—he was Dr. Frederic Swan, a throat specialist. He has lived in Reno since the divorce—no doubt she flirts with him again. She will flirt with me, once she has hooked this boy. Always like that. But now—now she can not even send me the agreed settlement—"

Henry Lee approached. "Pardon, Inspector," he announced. "Truckee three minutes."

Mr. Romano dashed her the door, evidently bound for the Pullman and his baggage. Charlie turned to his compatriot.

"So happy to know you," he said.

"Same for you," replied Henry Lee. "Also, I hope you gain much pleasure from your journey. In part," he added, with a grin. "I am going to watch newspapers."

"Nothing about this in newspapers," Charlie assured him.

"If you will pardon my saying it," replied Henry Lee, "I watch newspapers just the same."

Charlie went on back to his Pullman. Swift dark had fallen outside the windows, the snow was blotted from view. He gathered up his bags, turned them over to the porter and proceeded to don the heavy overcoat he had purchased for this journey—the first such garment he had owned in his life.

When he reached the car platform, Mrs. Lee was awaiting him. "My husband has told me of his happy moment with you," she cried. "This is notable day in our lives. I shall have much to tell my small man-child, who is now well past his eleventh moon."

"Pray give him my kind regards," said Charlie. He staggered slightly as his legs were struck from behind by some heavy object. Turning, he saw a tall man with a blond beard, who had just snatched up a bag from the platform—the object, evidently, which had struck Chan so sharp a blow.

Expectantly Charlie waited for the inevitable apology. But the stranger gave him one cold look, pushed him ruthlessly aside and crowded past him to the car steps.

In another moment the train had stopped, and Charlie was out on the snowy platform. He tipped his porter, waved good-by to the Lees and took a few steps along the brightly lighted space in front of the station. For the first time in his life he heard the creak of frost under his shoes, saw his own breath materialized before his eyes.

Romano came swiftly up. "I have located our motor," he announced. "Come quickly, if you will. I secured a view of the town, and it is not even a one-night stand."

As they came up to the automobile waiting beside the station, they beheld the driver of it conversing with a man who had evidently just left the train. Charlie looked closer—the man with the blond beard. The latter turned to them.

"Good evening," he said. "Are you Dudley Ward's other guests? My name is John Ryder."

Without waiting for their response, he slipped into the preferred front seat by the driver's side. "John Ryder." Charlie looked at Romano, and saw an expression of vast surprise on the Italian's mobile face. They got into the rear seat without speaking, and the driver started the car.

They emerged into the main street of a town that was, in the dim light of a wintry evening, reminiscent of a moving picture of the Old West. A row of brick buildings that spoke of being clubs, but behind the frosted windows of which no gaiety seemed to be afoot to-night. Restaurants with signs that advertised only the softer drinks, a bank, a post-office. Here and there a dusky figure hurrying through the gloom.

The car crossed a railroad spur and turned off into the white nothingness of the country. Now for the first time Charlie was close to the pines, tall and stern, rooted deep in the soil, their aroma pungent and invigorating. Across his vision flitted a picture of distant palms, unbelievable relatives of these proud and lofty giants.

The chains on the tires flopped unceasingly, down the open path between the snow-banks, and Charlie wondered at the sound. On their right now was a tremendous cliff, on their left a half-frozen river.

The man on the front seat beside the driver did not turn. He said no word. The two on the rear seat followed his example.

In about an hour they came upon the lights of a few scattered houses; a little later they turned off into the Tavern grounds. A vast shingled building stood lonely in the winter night, with but a few lights burning on its ground floor.

Close to the pier entrance the driver stopped his car. A man with a boatman's cap came forward.

"Got 'em, Bill?" he inquired.

"Three—that's right, ain't it?" the garage man inquired.

"O. K. I'll take them bags."

Bill said good night and departed, strangely eager to get back to town. The boatman led them on to the pier. For a moment Chan paused, struck by the beauty of the scene. Here lay a lake like a great dark sapphire, six thousand feet above the sea, surrounded by snow-covered mountains. On and on they moved down the dim pier.

"But," cried Romano—"the lake—it does not freeze."

"Tahoe never freezes," the guide explained scornfully. "Too deep. Well, here's the launch." They paused beside a handsome boat. "I'll put your stuff aboard, but we'll have to wait a minute. They's one more coming."

Even as he spoke, a man came hurrying along the pier. He joined them, a bit breathless.

"Sorry," he said. "Hope I haven't kept you waiting, gentlemen. I stopped at the Tavern for a minute. Guess we might as well get acquainted. My name is Swan," he added. "Dr. Frederic Swan."

One by one he shook hands with each of them, learning from each his name. As this newcomer and the man with the blond beard climbed aboard, Romano turned to Charlie and said softly:

"What is it? What is it you call it when you reach a town and all the hotel rooms are filled?"

"So sorry," Chan said blankly.

"All right—I will get it. It has happened to me so often. A—a convention. That is it. A convention. My friend, we are about to attend one of those. We are going to attend a convention of the lost loves of Landini."

He and Chan followed the others aboard, and in another moment they were skimming lightly over the icy waters in the direction of Emerald Bay.

2

Dinner at Pineview

The mountains were breathlessly still under the black sky, the wind blew chill from their snowy slopes and as the spray occasionally stung Charlie Chan's broad face, he reflected with deep inner joy upon the new setting to which fate had now transplanted him. Too long, he decided, had he known only the semi-tropics; his blood had grown thin—he drew his great coat closer: his energy had run low. Yes—no doubt about it—he was becoming soft. This was the medicine that would revive him; new life was coursing in his veins; new ambitions seethed within him; he longed for a chance to show what he could really do. He began to regret the obviously simple nature of the matter that had brought him to Tahoe; the affair was, on the face of it, so easy and uncomplicated that, as his son Henry might have phrased it, he had come just for the ride.

Though the moon had not yet risen, he could discern the nature of the lake shore on their starboard side. The dim outlines of one huge summer home after another glided by; each without a light, without a sign of life. Presently, in the distance, he saw a lamp burning by the water's edge; a little later and it multiplied into a string of them, stretched along a pier. The boat was swinging in-shore now; they fought their way along against the wind. As they reached the wharf, the passengers in the launch looked up and saw a man of about fifty standing, hatless and without an overcoat, above them. He waved, then hurried to help the boatman with the mooring ropes.

Evidently this was their host, Dudley Ward, debonair and gracious even in a stiff wind. He greeted them as they came ashore. "John, old boy," he said to Ryder, "it was good of you to come. Doctor Swan, I appreciate your kindness. And this, no doubt, is Mr. Romano—a great pleasure to welcome you to Pineview. The view is a bit obscured, but I can assure you the pines are there."

The boat was rocking violently as Charlie, always politely last, made a notable leap for the pier. Ward received him, literally, in his arms.

"Inspector Chan," he cried. "For years I have wanted to meet you."

"Desire has been mutual," Chan answered, panting a bit.

"Your native courtesy," Ward smiled. "I am sorry to remind you that you heard of me only—er—recently. Gentlemen—if you will follow me—"

He led the way along a broad walk from which the snow had been cleared toward a great house set amid the eternal pines. As their feet sounded on the wide veranda, an old Chinese servant swung open the door. They caught the odor of burning wood, saw lights and good cheer awaiting them, and crossed the threshold into the big living-room of Pineview.

"Sing, take the gentlemen's coats." The host was alert and cordial. Charlie looked at him with interest; a man of fifty, perhaps more, with gray hair and ruddy pleasant face. The cut of his clothes, and the material of which they were made, placed him at once; only a gentleman, it seemed, knew the names of tailors like that. He led the way to the tremendous fireplace at the far end of the room.

"A bit chilly on Tahoe to-night," he remarked. "For myself, I like it—come up here earlier every year. However—the fire won't go so badly—nor will those." He waved a hand toward a tray of cocktails. "I had Sing pour them when we sighted you, so there would be no delay."

He himself passed the tray. Ryder, Romano and Swan accepted with evident pleasure. Charlie shook his head and smiled, and Ward did not press him. There was a moment of awkward silence, and then the irrepressible Romano, posing with feet far apart in front of the blaze, raised his glass.

"Gentlemen," he announced, "I am about to propose a toast. No other, I believe, could be more appropriate at this time. However little she may mean to you now, whatever you may think of her at this late day—"

"One moment," Ryder spoke, with his accustomed cool rudeness. "I suggest you withdraw your toast. Because, as it happens, I want this drink."

Romano was taken aback. "Why, of course. I am so sorry. Me—I am too impetuous. No one, I am sure, has more to forgive than myself."

"Beside the point," said Ryder, and drained his glass.

Swan also drank, then laughed softly. "We have all much to forgive, I fancy," he remarked. "And to forget. Yes, it was always herself Landini thought of first. Her own wishes—her own happiness. But that, of course, is genius. We ordinary mortals should be charitable. I myself have supposed for many years that I hated the very name of Ellen Landini—and yet when I saw her a few moments ago—"

Dudley Ward paused in his task of refilling the glasses. "A few moments ago?" he repeated.

"Yes. I drove up from Reno to the Tavern, and dropped in there for a chat with my friend, Jim Dinsdale, the manager. When I came into the lobby I thought it was deserted, but presently I saw a woman's green scarf lying on a table. Then I looked over to the fire and saw her—the woman—sitting there. I went closer—the light was poor—but even before my eyes told me. I knew that it was Ellen. I had known she was in Reno, of course, but I hadn't wanted particularly to see her. When we parted years ago—well, I needn't go into that. Anyhow, I've been avoiding her. Yet now we were meeting again—the stage all set, as though she'd arranged it, alone together in the dim-lighted lobby of a practically deserted hotel. She jumped up. 'Fred,' she cried—"

Romano came close, his face glowing with excitement. "How was she

looking, Signor? Not too much flesh? Her voice—how did her voice seem
to you—"

Swan laughed. "Why—why, she seemed all right to me. In fact—and this
is the point of what I started out to say—after all she'd done to me, I felt
in that moment the old spell, the old enchantment. She seemed charming,
as always. She held out both her hands—"

"She would," snarled Ryder. "May I have another drink?"

"She was lovely," Swan went on. "Just at that moment Dinsdale came in,
and with him a young fellow named Beaton—"

"Hugh Beaton," Romano cried. "The infant she has snatched from the
cradle. The callow child she would exchange for me across the counters
of Reno. Bah! I, too, must drink again."

"Yes, it turned out that way," Swan admitted. "He was her latest flame.
She introduced him as such, with all her old arrogance. Also his sister,
quite a pretty girl. The romance was rather gone from our meeting."

"What was Landini doing at the Tavern?" Ward inquired.

"I gathered she was a friend of Dinsdale, and had just driven over for
dinner. She's not stopping there, of course—she's served four weeks of her
cure at Reno, and she's not staying out of the state more than a few hours.
Naturally, I didn't linger. I hurried away." He looked about the group.
"But pardon me. I didn't mean to monopolize the conversation."

"It was Ellen who was doing that," smiled Dudley Ward, "not you. Up
to her old tricks again. Dinner, gentlemen, is at seven. In the meantime,
Sing will show you to your various rooms, though I'm afraid you'll have
to sort out your own baggage in the upper hall. Doctor Swan, I've assigned
you a room, even though, to my regret, you're not staying the night. Ah
Sing—where is the old rascal?"

The servant appeared, and led the procession above.

Ward laid a hand on Charlie Chan's arm. "At a quarter to seven, in my
study up-stairs at the front of the house," he said softly. "For just a few
minutes."

Chan nodded.

"One more thing, gentlemen," Ward called. "No one need dress. This
is strictly stag, of course."

He stood and watched them disappear, an ironical smile on his face.

Presently Charlie entered a warm and pleasant bedroom, meekly following Ah Sing. The old man turned on the lights, set down Chan's bags, then
looked up at his compatriot from Honolulu. His face was lean and the
color of a lemon that has withered, his shoulders were hunched and bent.
His eyes alone betrayed his race; and in them Chan detected an authentic
gleam of humor.

"P'liceman?" said Ah Sing.

Charlie admitted it, with a smile.

"Some people say plitty wise man?" continued Sing. "Maybe."

"Maybe," agreed Charlie.

Sing nodded sagely, and went out.

Charlie stepped to the window, and looked down an aisle of tall pines
at snow-covered hills and a bit of wintry sky. The novelty of this scene so
engrossed him that he was three minutes late for his appointment with his
host in the study.

"That's all right," Dudley Ward said, when Chan apologized. "I'm not
going over the whole business here—I'll have to do it anyhow at the table.
I just want to say I'm glad you've come, and I hope you'll be able to help
me."

"I shall extend myself to utmost," Charlie assured him.

"It's rather a small matter for a man of your talents," Ward went on. He was sitting behind a broad desk, over which an alabaster lamp cast its glow. "But I can assure you it's important to me. I got you in here just to make sure you know why I invited these three men up here tonight—but now I've done it, I realize I must be insulting your intelligence."

Chan smiled. "On second thoughts, you changed original plan?"

"Yes. I thought when I wrote you, I'd just get in touch with them by letter. But that's a terribly unsatisfactory way of dealing with things—at least, I've always thought so. I like to see a man's face when I'm asking him questions. Then I heard this Romano was in San Francisco, and broke—I knew money would bring him here. Swan was already in Reno, and Ryder—well, he and I've been friends from boyhood, and the fact that he was Ellen's second husband never made any difference between us. So I resolved to bring them all together here to-night."

Charlie nodded. "A bright plan," he agreed.

"I'll ask all the questions," Ward continued. "What sort of replies I'll get, I don't know. None of them loves Landini any too much, I imagine, but because of one reason or another—perhaps in view of promises made long ago—the information we are after may be difficult to get. I rely on you to watch each one carefully, and to sense it if any one of them fails to tell the truth. You've had plenty of experience along that line, I fancy."

"I fear you over-estimate my poor ability," Charlie protested.

"Nonsense," cried Ward. "We're bound to get a clue somewhere. We may even get all we're after. But whether we do or not, I want you to feel that you are here not just as an investigator, but as my guest, and an honored one." Before him on the desk stood twin boxes; one of bright yellow, the other a deep crimson. He opened the nearer one, and pushed it toward Chan. "Will you have a cigarette before dinner?" he invited. Charlie declined, and taking one himself, Ward rose and lighted it. "Cozy little room, this," he suggested.

"The reply is obvious," Chan nodded. He glanced about, reflecting that some woman must have had a hand here. Gay cretonnes hung at the windows; the shades of the several lamps about the room were of delicate silk; the rug was deep and soft.

"Please use it as your own," his host said. "Any work you have to do—letters and the like—come in here. We'll be getting on down-stairs now, eh?" Charlie noted for the first time that the man's hands trembled, and that a faint perspiration shone on his forehead. "A damned important dinner for me," Ward added, and his voice broke suddenly in the middle of the sentence.

But when they reached the group down-stairs before the fire, the host was again his debonair self, assured and smiling. He led his four guests through a brief passageway to the dining-room, and assigned them to their places.

That great oak-paneled room, that table gleaming with silver, spoke eloquently of the prestige of the family of Ward. Ever since the days of Virginia City and the Comstock Lode, the name had been known and honored in this western country. No boat around the Horn for the first Dudley Ward; he had trekked in with the gold rush, a member of that gallant band of whom it has been well said: "The cowards never started, and the weaklings died on the way." Now this famous family had dwindled to the polished, gray-haired gentleman at the head of the table, and Charlie, thinking of his own eleven children at home in Honolulu, glanced around the board and sighed over the futility of such a situation.

In its earlier stages, the dinner seemed a trifle strained, despite the urbane chatter of the host. Charlie alone knew why he was there; the others seemed inclined to silent speculation. Evidently Ward was not yet ready to enlighten them. As Ah Sing moved along with the main course, Charlie said a few words to him in Cantonese, and got a brief answer in the same dialect.

"Pardon, please," Chan bowed to his host. "I take the liberty of asking Ah Sing his age. His reply is not altogether clear."

Ward smiled. "I don't suppose the old boy really knows. In the late seventies, I fancy—a long life, and most of it spent in our service. I know it's not the thing to talk about one's servants—but Ah Sing years ago passed out of that category. He's been one of the family for as long as I can remember."

"I have heard, my heart bursting with pride," Chan said, "of the loyalty and devotion of old Chinese servants in this state."

Ryder spoke suddenly. "Everything you have heard is true," he said. He turned to Ward. "I remember when we were kids, Dudley. Great Scott, how good Sing was to us in those days. The stuff he used to cook for us—grumbling all the time. Huge bowls of rice with meat gravy—I dream of them yet. He'd been with you ages then, hadn't he?"

"My grandfather picked him up in Nevada," Ward replied. "He came to our house when I was just three years old. I remember, because I had a birthday party that day on the lawn, and Sing was serving—his first day. There were a lot of bees down in the meadow: and I imagine they were attracted by Sing's cooking, just as we kids were. Anyhow, I remember Sing—a young man then—marching toward us proudly bearing the cake, when a bee suddenly stung him on the leg. He dropped the cake, let out a yell and looked at my mother accusingly. 'Melican buttahfly too damn hot,' he complained. If I were to write my memoirs, I think I should have to begin with that—my first conscious recollection."

"I guess I missed that party," Ryder said. "It came a couple of years too soon for me. But I remember many a later one, in Sing's kitchen. Always a friend in need to us boys, Sing was."

Ward's face was serious. "They're dying out," he remarked. "The ones like Sing. Somebody ought to put up a statue in Golden Gate Park—or at least a tablet somewhere on one of the famous trails—to the best friends Californians ever had."

Sing came in at that moment, and the subject was dropped. A long silence ensued. Romano and Swan seemed to be getting rather impatient over the long delay in reaching the real business of the evening. Since the discussion that had broken out on their first entrance, Ellen Landini had not been so much as mentioned. Romano's cheeks were flushed, his white hands fluttered nervously over his plate, he fidgeted in his chair. Swan also showed various signs of restlessness.

Coffee was finally brought, and then a tray of cut-glass decanters were set before Dudley Ward.

"I have here, gentlemen," he remarked, "some Benedictine, crème de menthe, peach brandy. Also, some port wine. All pre-prohibition—you break no law in my house. What will you have? Just a moment—Sing! Where the devil is that boy?" He rang the bell, and the old Chinese hurriedly returned. "Sing—take the gentlemen's orders—and fill them. And now—"

He paused, and they all looked at him expectantly. "Now, gentlemen, you are wondering why you are here. You are wondering why Inspector

Chan, of the Honolulu Police, is here. I have kept you waiting an intolerably long time. I know, but the truth is, I am loath to bring this matter up. To introduce it properly I shall have to go into a subject that I had hoped was for ever dead and forgotten—my life with Ellen Landini."

He pushed his chair back from the table, and crossed his legs. "Sing—you haven't overlooked the cigars? Ah, yes—gentlemen, help yourselves. I—I married Ellen Landini nearly twenty years ago, in San Francisco. She had just come to town from the islands, a young girl of eighteen, with a voice—even then it was magical. But she had more than the voice, she had a freshness, a vivacity, a beauty—however, I needn't go into her charm, surely not in this company. She gave a little concert, I saw her, heard her sing. The courtship was brief. We were married, and went to Paris on our honeymoon.

"That year in Paris—I shall never forget it. I want to be fair. She was wonderful—then. She studied with the best teacher in Europe, and what he told her about her voice made her supremely happy. It made me happy, too—for a time.

"Only gradually did I come to see that this wonderful year had wrecked my dreams—my hopes for a home, for children. Domestic life was now impossible for us. She was determined to become a professional singer. I saw myself, the prima donna's husband, carrying a dog about Europe, waiting at stage doors, enduring for ever an artistic temperament. The career did not appeal to me. I said so.

"Perhaps I was unreasonable. I want, as I have said, to be fair to her. Men were not so complacent about careers for their wives in those days. At any rate, there began a series of endless quarrels. I brought her home from Paris, to San Francisco, and thence, since it was spring, up to this house. I could see she would never be reconciled to the life I wanted."

He was silent for a moment. "I apologize humbly," he went on, "for dragging you into affairs that should be private. I must add, however, that our quarrels became daily more bitter, that we began to say unforgivable things, to hate each other. I could see her hate in her eyes when she looked at me. One June day—in this very room—matters came to a climax and she left the house. She never returned.

"I refused to divorce her, but when, nearly a year later, she applied for a divorce in some middle-western state, on a false charge of desertion, I did not contest the suit. I still loved her—or rather, the girl I thought I had married—but I realized she was lost to me for ever. I balanced the account and closed the books."

He turned to the doctor. "Doctor Swan—won't you try that brandy again? Just help yourself, please. So far, gentlemen, you can see no reason for my story. But there is something more—and only within the past ten days have I come upon the trail of it.

"I have been told, by some one who ought to know, that when Ellen Landini left my house she carried with her a secret which she had not seen fit to divulge to me. I have heard, from a source I believe reliable, that less than seven months after she left this place, she gave birth to a child, in a New York hospital. A son. Her son—and mine."

He did not go on for a moment. All the men about the table were looking at him, some with pity, some with amazement.

"I have said," Ward went on, "that Ellen hated me. Perhaps with reason—oh, I want to be just. She hated me so much, evidently, that she was determined I must never have the satisfaction of knowing about—my boy. Perhaps she feared it would start the old argument all over again. Perhaps it was just—hate. I—I think it was rather cruel."

"She was always cruel," said Ryder harshly. He laid a sympathetic hand on Dudley Ward's arm.

"At any rate," Ward went on, "she gave this child for adoption to some wealthy friends of hers. It wasn't legal adoption, of course. But she agreed to give him up for ever, to let him be known by another name, never to try to see him. She could do that. Her career was everything.

"That, gentlemen, ends my story. You can see my position. I am not—not so young as I was. My brother and sister are both dead, childless. Somewhere in this world, if the story is true, and the boy lived, I have a son, now nearly eighteen. All this—is his. I intend to find him." His voice grew louder. "By heaven, I will find him. As far as Landini is concerned, bygones are bygones. I have no more hatred. But I want my boy.

"That is why," he continued in a lower tone, "I have sent for Inspector Chan. I shall back him to the limit in this search. I've had only ten days—I've only started—"

"Who told you all this?" Ryder inquired.

"Ah—that's rather interesting," Ward replied. "It was Ellen's return to this part of the world that, indirectly, brought it out. It seems that about eight years ago, when Ellen came to Nevada to divorce—er—Doctor Swan, she was, at the moment, interested in—you will pardon me, Doctor—"

Swan smiled. "Oh, that's perfectly all right. We've all been victims—we can speak freely here. She wanted to divorce me because she had fallen in love—or thought she had—with her chauffeur, a handsome boy named Michael Ireland. I came out to fight the divorce—but she got it anyhow. She didn't, however, get Michael. It was one of her few defeats in that line. The day before her divorce, young Michael eloped with Ellen's maid, a French girl named Cecile. The maid just took him away from her. It was rather amusing. Michael and his wife are still living in Reno, and the former is a pilot for a passenger airplane company over there."

"Precisely," nodded Ward. "When I first came up here two weeks ago I sent to Reno for a couple of servants—a cook and an up-stairs maid—and the latter happened to be Michael's wife. It seems they're not very prosperous, and she'd decided to go into service temporarily. She knew, of course, my connection with Ellen Landini when she came here, but for a time she said nothing. Naturally, I had never seen or heard of the woman before. But it appears that Ellen is doing a great deal of flying during her stay in Reno, and her favorite pilot is Michael Ireland. Cecile is wildly jealous, and that is no doubt what led her to come to me with the story about my son. She claims she went with Ellen as personal maid shortly before the baby was born, and that she had been sworn to eternal secrecy in the matter."

Ryder shook his head. "The story of a jealous woman," he remarked. "I'm sorry, Dudley, but aren't you building a bit too much on that? Not the best evidence, you know."

Ward nodded. "I know. Still, I can't well ignore a thing as important as this. And as the woman told it, I must admit it had the ring of truth. Also, I recalled certain little things that had happened, things that Ellen had said during her last mad weeks in this house—it is quite possible the story is true. And I mean to find out whether it's true or not."

"Have you questioned Landini?" asked Doctor Swan.

"I have not," replied Ward. "In the first excitement of the moment, I called her hotel in Reno, but before I got the connection, I had sense enough to ring off. Inspector Chan may have an interview with her later, if he sees fit, but I would expect nothing to come of it. I know her of old.

"No, gentlemen, it is to you three that, at the beginning of this hunt, I have seen fit to pin my hopes. You have all, like myself, been married to Landini. I do not believe that she would ever have deliberately told any of you about this child, but even so—these things sometimes come out. A telegram opened by mistake, a telephone call in some strange city, a chance meeting—by one or another of these methods, one of you may have come upon her secret. I am not asking you to be disloyal in any way. But I do contend that if Ellen deceived me in this matter, it was a piece of unwarranted cruelty, and as man to man, I ask you, if you can, to relieve me of this horrible suspense. Nothing shall happen to Landini, or to the boy, save to this advantage. But—you can see—I am in hell over this—and I must know—I must know."

His voice rose to an almost hysterical pitch as he looked appealingly about the table. John Ryder spoke first.

"Dudley," he said, "no one would be happier to help you now than I would be—if I could. God knows I have no wish to spare the feelings of Ellen Landini. But as you know, my life with her was of the briefest—and that was the only lucky break I ever got where she was concerned. So brief and so hectic that I never heard of this matter you have brought up to-night—never dreamed of it. I—I'm sorry."

Ward nodded. "I was afraid of that." He looked toward Swan and Romano, and his expression changed. "Before we go any further, I may add that I am willing to pay handsomely—and I mean no offense—for any information that may be of help. Doctor Swan—you were married to Landini for several years—"

Swan's eyelids narrowed. He toyed with his coffee cup, took out his eyeglasses, put them on, restored them to his pocket.

"Don't misunderstand me," he said slowly. "Landini means nothing to me, despite what I said earlier about her charm when I saw her again at the Tavern. It isn't very pleasant to be thrown over for a chauffeur." Across his usually pleasant face shot a look of malevolence that was startling and unexpected. "No," he added harshly. "I have no wish to protect the woman—but I'm sorry to say that this is—well, it's all news to me."

Ward's face was gray and tired as he turned to Romano. The opera conductor shot his cuffs and spoke.

"The figures—er—the figures of the amount you wish to pay, Mr. Ward—I leave them entirely to you. I rely on your reputation as a gentleman."

"I think you may safely do so," replied Ward grimly.

"Landini—she is still my wife—but what does she mean to me? In New York were drawn up terms of settlement by which I was to release her for this new divorce. Has she made the initial payment? She has not. I must live—is it not so? Once I had a career of my own—I was aimed high for success—all gone now. She has done that to me. She has wrecked my life—and now she casts me off." He clenched his fist that lay on the table, and a sudden fire gleamed in his dark eyes.

"You were going to tell me—" suggested Ward.

"There was, sir, a telegram opened by mistake. I opened it. It held some news of that son of hers. She told me little, but enough. There was a son. That much I can say. I have, of course, no recollection of the signature on the telegram."

"But—the town from which it was sent?" Ward cried.

Romano looked at him—the sly anxious look of a man who needs money—needs it badly enough to lie for it, perhaps.

"The town I do not now remember," Romano said. "But I will think—I will think hard—and it will come to me, I am sure."

Ward looked hopelessly at Charlie Chan. He sighed. At that instant, from the big room beyond the passage came the slamming of a door, and then, sharp and clear, the bark of a dog.

The four guests of Dudley Ward looked up in amazement, as though they found something sinister and disquieting in that bark. Sing came shuffling in and, leaning over the chair of the host, spoke in a low tone. Ward nodded, and gave a direction. Then, an ironical smile on his face, he rose to his feet.

"Gentlemen," he said, "I hope you will not be too much annoyed by my peculiar sense of humor. I have acted on impulse—and I may have been wrong. But it came to me when Doctor Swan spoke of his encounter at the Tavern—there was just one person lacking to make our party complete. And since she was so near—"

"Landini," cried Ryder. "You have invited Landini here?"

"For a very brief call—I have."

"I won't see her," Ryder protested. "I swore years ago I'd never see her again—"

"Oh, come on, John," Ward said. "Be modern. Landini will regard it as a lark—I didn't tell her you were all here, but I know she won't care. Doctor Swan has already seen her. Mr. Romano has no objections—"

"Me?" cried Romano. "I *want* to talk to her!"

"Precisely. I am willing to forget the past. Come on, John."

Ryder's eyes were on the table. "All right," he agreed.

Dudley Ward smiled. "Gentlemen," he said, "shall we join the lady?"

3

The Fallen Flower

But when they stepped through the passage into the living-room the lady was not there. Two men were warming themselves before the fire: one, a round, cheery, red-faced little man, the other a pale youth with black curly hair and a weak but handsome face. The older of the two stepped forward.

"Hello, Dudley," he said. "This is like old times, isn't it? Ellen back at the old house again and—er—ah—and all that."

"Hello, Jim," Ward replied. He introduced his guests to Jim, who was, it appeared, Mr. Dinsdale, manager of the Tavern. When he had finished, the hotel man turned to the boy who accompanied him.

"This is Mr. Hugh Beaton," he announced. "Ellen and Mr. Beaton's sister have gone up-stairs to leave their wraps, and—"

Mr. Romano had leaped to the boy's side and was shaking his hand. "Ah, Mr. Beaton," he cried, "I have wanted to see you. There is so much I must say."

"Y-yes," replied the boy with a startled air.

"Indeed—yes. You are taking over a very great responsibility. You, a musician, need not be told that. The talent—the genius—of Ellen Landini—it is something to guard, to watch over, to encourage. That is your duty in the name of Art. How does she behave with the pastries?"

"The—the what?" stammered the boy.

"The pastries? She has a wild passion for them. And it must be curbed. It is no easy matter, but she must be held back with a strong hand. Otherwise she will—she will expand—she will grow gross. And cigarettes. How many cigarettes do you permit her each day?" "I permit her?" Beaton stared at Romano as at a madman. "Why—that's no affair of mine."

Romano looked toward high heaven.

"Ah—it is as I feared, You are too young to understand. Too young for this huge task. No affair of yours? My dear sir, in that case she is lost. She will smoke her voice into eternal silence. She will wreck her great career for ever—"

He was interrupted by a commotion at the head of the stairs, and Ellen Landini began to descend. The long stairway against one side of the room afforded her an excellent entrance. Of this she was not unaware; indeed, she had just sent her companion back on a trivial errand in order that she might have the stage to herself. Which of itself was a good description of Ellen Landini, once young and lovely and innocent, but now a bit too plump, a bit too blonde, and a bit too wise in the tricks of the trade.

She had decided on a dramatic entrance, and such was the one she made, holding in her arms a small Boston terrier who looked world-weary and old. Dudley Ward awaited her at the foot of the stairs; she saw him and him alone.

"Welcome home, Ellen," he said.

"Dudley," she cried. "Dear old Dudley, afer all these years. But"—she held aloft the dog—"but poor Trouble—"

"Trouble?" repeated Ward, puzzled.

"Yes—that's his name—but you don't know. You wouldn't. From the baby in *Madame Butterfly*. My baby—my sweet poor baby—he's having a chill. I knew I shouldn't bring him—it's bitter cold on the lake—it always was on this lake. Where's Sing? Call Sing at once." The old man appeared on the stairs behind her. "Oh, Sing—take Trouble to the kitchen and give him some hot milk. Make him drink it."

"My take 'um," replied Sing with a bored look.

Landini followed him with many admonitions. A young girl in a smart dinner gown had come unostentatiously down the stairs, and Ward was greeting her. He turned to the others.

"This is Miss Leslie Beaton," he said. "I'm sure we're all happy to have her here—"

But Landini was back in the room, overflowing personality and energy and charm. "Darling old Sing," she cried. "The same as ever. I've thought of him so often. He was always—" She stopped suddenly as her eyes moved unbelievingly about the little group.

Dudley Ward permitted himself a delighted smile. "I think, Ellen," he said, "you already know these gentlemen."

She wanted a moment, obviously, to get her breath and she found it when her glance fell on Charlie Chan. "Not—not all of them," she said.

"Oh, yes—pardon me," Ward answered. "May I present Inspector Charlie Chan, of the Honolulu Police? On vacation, I should add."

Charlie stepped forward and bowed low over her hand. "Overcome," he murmured.

"Inspector Chan," she said. "I've heard of you."

"It would be tarnishing the lily with gilt," Charlie assured her, "to remark

I have heard of you. Speaking further on the subject, I once, with great difficulty, heard you sing."

"With—great difficulty?"

"Yes—you may recall. The night you stopped over for a concert in your home city, Honolulu. At the Royal Hawaiian Opera House—and they had but recently applied to it the new tin roof—"

The great Landini clapped her hands and laughed. "And it rained!" she cried. "I should say I do remember! It was my only night—the boat was leaving at twelve—and so I sang—and sang. There in that boiler-factory—or so it seemed—with the downpour on the tin above. What a concert! But that was—some years—ago."

"I was impressed at the time by your extreme youthfulness," Charlie remarked.

She gave him a ravishing smile. "I shall sing again for you some day," she said. "And it will not be raining then."

Her poise regained, sure of herself now, she turned to the odd party into which Dudley Ward had brought her. "What fun," she cried. "What wonderful fun! All my dear ones gathered together. John—looking as stern as ever—Frederic—I miss the reflector on your forehead. I always think of you wearing that. And Luis—you here—of all people—"

Mr. Romano stepped forward with his usual promptness. "Yes, you may bet I am here," he replied, his eyes flashing. "I, of all people, and of all people I will be present at a good many places to which you travel in the future—unless your memory speedily improves. Must I recall to you an arrangement made in New York—"

"Luis—not here!" She stamped her foot.

"No, perhaps not here. But somewhere—soon—depend on that. Look at your shoes!"

"What is wrong with my shoes?"

"Wet! Soaking wet!" He turned hotly on young Beaton. "Are there, then, no rubbers in the world? Is the supply of arctics exhausted? I told you—you do not understand your job. You let her walk about in the snow in her evening slippers. What sort of husband is that for Ellen Landini—"

"Oh, do be quiet, Luis," Landini cried. "You were always so tiresome—a nurse. Do you think I want a nurse? I do not—and that is what I like about Hugh." She stepped toward the boy, who appeared to draw back a bit. "Hugh is more interested in romance than in arctics—aren't you, my dear?"

She ran her fingers affectionately through the young man's black hair, a theatrical gesture that was a bit upsetting to all who saw it. Dudley Ward, looking hastily away, caught on the face of Hugh Beaton's sister an expression of such bitter disgust that he sought to divert the girl's attention.

"Your first visit west, Miss Beaton?" he inquired.

"My very first," she answered. "I love it, too. All except—"

"Reno."

"Naturally—I don't like that. The place sort of puts a blight on one's outlook—don't you think? What price romance—after seeing Reno?"

"Pity you feel that way," Ward said. He looked at her admiringly. Hugh Beaton's sister was even prettier than he was. But there was a worried look about her brown eyes; the lips that should be always laughing were drawn and tired.

"Dudley—it's marvelous to be back here." Landini was drawing him again into the general conversaion. "It's just as well you invited me, because I was coming anyway. Several times I've been on the point of descending on you."

"I should have been charmed," Ward replied.

"And surprised," she laughed, "because I mean that literally—descending on you. You see, I've flown over you often, and seen that flying field you've had cleared behind the house."

"Oh, yes," Ward nodded. "So many of my friends have planes—and I like to fly a bit myself."

"My pilot told me he'd land any time," Landini continued. "But some-how—the hour never seemed right—too late—too early—or we had to hurry back."

"You enjoy flying, I hear?" It was Doctor Swan who spoke, and there was an expression on his face that mingled malice and contempt.

"Oh—I adore it! It's the biggest thrill in the world. It's living—at last. Especially here, above the snow-capped mountains, and these marvelous lakes. And I've found such a wonder of a pilot—"

"So I've been told," Swan answered. "But as I recall, you found him some years ago—"

Landini walked quickly to where John Ryder was standing, as far apart from the others as he could get.

"John," she said, "I'm so happy to see you again. You're looking well."

"Unfortunately," Ryder said, "I'm looking better than I feel. Dudley, I'm afraid I shall have to be excused. Good night." He bowed to the room in general, and went hastily up the stairs.

Ellen Landini shrugged her generous shoulders and laughed. "Poor John," she said. "Always he took life so seriously. What is to be gained by that? But we are what we are—we can not change—"

"Ellen," said Dudley Ward, "you enjoy seeing the old place again?"

"I adore it," she sparkled. "I'm simply wild with joy."

He looked at her in amazement—still sparkling, after all these years. Not since she came in had she let down for a minute. He thought back to the days of their marriage. It had been one of the things that had driven him mad. "Every day is Christmas with Landini," he had once complained to himself.

"Then perhaps you'd like to take a tour about," Ward continued. "There are a few changes—I'd like to show them to you. If my guests will be so very good as to excuse me."

There was a polite murmur, and Dinsdale raised his glass. "These high-balls of yours, Dudley, excuse anything," he laughed.

"Good," smiled Ward. "Ellen, I want you to see the old study, I've just had it done over by a decorator. Probably all wrong. And as we can't afford any scandal, I'm taking along a chaperon. Inspector Chan—will you join us?"

"With great pleasure," smiled Charlie. "Everybody knows policeman al-ways on hand when least needed."

Ellen Landini laughed with the others, but there was a deeply puzzled look in her blue eyes. Dinsdale came forward, looking at his watch.

"Just to remind you, Ellen," he said. "You'll have to be starting soon if you're to be back in Reno by midnight."

"What time is it, Jim?"

"It's twenty-five minutes to ten."

"I'm starting at ten, and I'll be back in Reno before eleven."

He shook his head. "Not to-night—over these roads," he said.

"To-night," she laughed. "But not over these roads. Not for little Ellen."

Hugh Beaton looked up. "Ellen—what are you talking about?" he asked.

She gave him a loving glance. "Now, be a good boy. You and Leslie go back by car from the Tavern. It's a nasty old car, and you're liable to have a few blowouts just as we did coming over, but that won't matter to you. However, I must make better time. I had an inspiration when Dudley here called up and invited me to drop in on him. I telephoned to Reno for my favorite plane and pilot, and they'll be here at ten. Won't it be glorious? There's a gorgeous moon—I'm simply thrilled to death." She turned to Ward. "Michael told me you have lights on the field?"

Ward nodded. "Yes. I'll turn them on presently. Everything's in order—that's a grand idea of yours. But then—your ideas always were."

Romano, who had been talking violently with Hugh Beaton in a corner, rose quickly. "I will go to my room," he announced, "and I will make you a list. The things she must do, and the things she must not do. It will be useful—"

"Oh, please don't trouble," Beaton protested.

"It is my duty," Romano said sternly.

Ward stood aside, and let his guests precede him up the stairs. Romano walked close to Landini's side, and as they came into the upper hall, he swung on her. "Where is my money?" he demanded.

"Luis—I don't know—oh, hasn't it been sent?"

"You know very well it has not been sent. How am I to live—"

"But, Luis—there has been trouble—my investments—oh, please, please don't bother me now."

"I suggest, Mr. Romano," Ward said, "that you comply with Madame Landini's wishes. This, I believe, is the door of your room."

"As you say," shrugged Romano. "But, Ellen, I have not finished. There must be an understanding before we part."

He disappeared, and the three others went into the study in front. Ward flashed on the floor lamps, and Landini dropped into the chair beside the desk. Both men saw that her face was suddenly drawn and haggard, all the vivacity gone. Then she *did* let down at times. It was not always Christmas, it was sometimes the morning after.

"Oh, the little beast," she cried. "I hate him. Dudley, you can see what my life has been—lived in a whirlwind, excitement, madness, filled all the time with noisy nothings. I'm so tired—so deathly tired. If only I could find peace—"

Charlie Chan saw that Ward's face was filled with genuine tenderness and pity. "I know, my dear," said the host, as he closed the door. "But peace was never for you—we knew that in the old days. It had to be the limelit highway—the bright parade. Come—pull yourself together." He offered her one of the colored boxes on the desk. "Have a cigarette. Or perhaps you prefer this other brand." He reached for the companion box.

She took one from the latter, and lighted it. "Dudley," she said, "coming here has taken me back to my girlhood. It has touched me deeply—" She looked toward Charlie Chan.

A sudden harshness came into Ward's eyes. "Sorry," he said. "Mr. Chan stays. I was wondering why you accepted my invitation to-night. I see now—it was to pull this airplane stunt. The spectacular thing—the thing you would do. Has it occurred to you to wonder—why I invited you?"

"Why—I thought, of course—after all, you did love me once. I thought you would like to see me again. But when I saw John, and Frederic, and Luis—I was puzzled—"

"Naturally. I invited you, Ellen, because I wanted you to realize that I am in touch with your various husbands. I wanted you, also, to meet Inspector Charlie Chan who, as you know, is a detective. Inspector Chan and

I have begun tonight an investigation which may take us many weeks—or which may end here and now. You have it in your power to end it. Ellen, I have no bitterness, no ill will for you at this late date. I have thought it over so long—perhaps I was wrong from the first. But I have brought you to Pineview to ask you, simply—where is my son?"

Charlie Chan, watching, reflected that here was either a great actress or a much maligned woman. Her expression did not change. "What son?" she asked.

Ward shrugged his shoulders. "Very well," he said. "We won't go any further with it."

"Oh, yes, we will," said Ellen Landini. "Dudley—don't be a fool. Some one has told you a lie, evidently. Don't you know they've been lying about me for years? I've got so I don't mind—but if you've heard something that's made you unhappy—that's sending you off on a wild-goose chase—well, I'd like to stop that, if I can. If you'll only tell me—"

"No matter," said Ward. "What's the use?"

"If you take that tone," she replied, "it's hopeless." She was surprisingly cool and calm. "By the way—hadn't you better turn on the lights on the field? And I should like a small blanket for Trouble—he'll need it, in addition to the robes in the plane. I'll send it back to you. He'll go with me, of course. He loves it."

"Very well," nodded Ward. "I'll see about it, and then I'll get down to those lights." He went to the door. "Cecile," he called. "Oh, Sing—send Cecile to me, please."

He stepped back into the room. "Cecile?" said Ellen Landini.

"Yes," Ward said. "An old servant of yours, I believe. The wife of your wonder pilot. You didn't know she was here?"

Landini lighted another cigarette. "I did not. But I might have guessed it these last few minutes. A liar, Dudley, always, with a temper like the devil. She stole from me, too, but naturally, one expects that. But the truth was not in her. I don't know what cock-and-bull story she has told you, but whatever it is—"

"What makes you think it was she who told me?"

"I have discovered that a lie has been told in this house, Dudley, and now I discover Cecile is here. It's effect and cause, my dear."

"You wanted me, sir?" The Frenchwoman at the door was about thirty, with lovely eyes, but an unhappy and discontented face. For a long moment she stared at Landini. "Ah, Madame," she murmured.

"How are you, Cecile?" the singer asked.

"I am well, thank you." She turned to Ward, inquiringly.

"Cecile," said her employer, "please go and get Madame Landini a small blanket of some sort—something suitable to wrap about a dog."

"A dog?" The eyes of the Frenchwoman narrowed. There was a moment's silence, and in the quiet they all heard, suddenly, a far-off but unmistakable sound—the droning of an airplane. Ward flung open the French windows that led on to a balcony, which was in reality the roof of the front veranda. The others crowded about him, and in the moonlit sky, far out over the lake, they saw the approaching plane.

"Ah, yes," cried Cecile, "I understand. Madame returns to Reno by air."

"Is that any affair of yours?" Landini asked coldly.

"It happens to be, Madame," the woman answered.

"Will you get that blanket?" Ward demanded.

Without a word, the Frenchwoman went out. Ward looked at his watch. "Your pilot's ahead of time," he said. "I must hurry out to those lights—"

"Dudley—would you do something—" Landini cried.

"Too late. When the plane has landed—"

He hastened out. The singer turned to Charlie.

"Tell me," she said. "Do you know which is Mr. Ryder's room?"

Charlie bowed. "I think I do."

"Then please go to him. Send him here at once. Tell him I must see him—he must come—don't take no for an answer! Tell him—it's life and death!"

She fairly pushed the detective from the room. He hurried down the hall and knocked on the door of the room into which he had seen Ryder ushered before dinner. Without awaiting an answer, he opened it and entered. Ryder was seated reading a book beside a floor lamp.

"So sorry," Charlie remarked. "The intrusion is objectionable, I realize. But Madame Landini—"

"What about Madame Landini?" asked Ryder grimly.

"She must see you at once—in the study at the front. She demands this wildly. It is, she tells me, life and death."

Ryder shrugged. "Rot! There is nothing to be said between us. She knows that."

"But—"

"Yes—life and death—I know. Don't be fooled by her theatrics. She was always that way. Kindly tell her I refuse to see her."

Chan hesitated. Ryder got up and led him to the door. "Tell her that under no circumstances will I ever see her again."

Charlie found himself in the hall, with Ryder's door closed behind him. When he got back to the study Landini was seated at the desk, writing madly.

"I am so sorry—" the detective began.

She looked up. "He won't see me?" I expected it. No matter, Mr. Chan. I have thought of another way. Thanks."

Chan turned, and went down the hall toward the head of the stairs. As he passed the open door of Romano's room he saw the conductor, walking anxiously up and down. Ryder's door remained closed. The noise of the plane was momentarily growing louder.

In the living-room Dinsdale and Hugh Beaton were alone, evidently vastly uninterested in the spectacular approach of Landini's pilot. Charlie was not so callous and, stepping out the front door, he crossed the porch and walked a short distance down the path to the pier. He was staring up at the lights of the plane, when some one approached from the direction of the water. It was Doctor Swan.

"Went out on the pier to see it better," Swan said. "A beautiful sight, on a night like this. Wish I could go back in it myself." The aviator was turning in toward the house.

"Shall we find the landing field?" Charlie suggested.

"Not for me," Swan shivered. "It's somewhere at the back, God knows where. I'm going to get my things—I want to start for the Tavern as soon as Ellen has made her grand exit." He ran up the steps to the house.

Michael Ireland, it appeared, was planning a few stunts. Despite the tallness of the pines, he swept down on the house, dangerously near. Hurrying through the snow to the rear, Charlie was conscious that the plane was circling about above the roof of Pineview. Aviators never could resist the spectacular. Presently Chan came upon a cleared place, flooded with lights, and there, when the pilot had completed his exhibition, he finally brought the plane down, in a skillful landing.

"Pretty work," cried a voice at Chan's elbow. It was Dudley Ward. "By gad, that lad knows how to drive his old two-seater."

He hurried out to meet Ireland on the field, and led him back to where Charlie stood. All three went up the narrow path to the back door, and entered a long passage that led to the front of the house. As they passed the open door of the kitchen Chan saw a large woman, evidently the cook. With her was Landini's dog, whining and still shivering from its chill. Ward led on to the living-room.

"Nice night for it," he was saying to Ireland, a husky red-cheeked man of thirty or so. "I envy you—the way you brought her down." Dinsdale and Beaton rose to greet them, and the aviator, pulling off a huge glove, shook hands all round. "Sit down a minute," Ward continued. "You'll want a drink before you start back."

"Thank you, sir," Ireland replied. "And maybe I'd better be havin' a word with my wife—"

Ward nodded. "I fancy you had," he smiled. "I'll arrange that. But first of all—what will it be? A highball?"

"Sounds good to me," Ireland answered. He looked a bit apprehensive and ill at ease. "Not too much, Mr. Ward, please—"

Ryder appeared on the stairs, lighting a cigarette. Half-way down, he paused. "Has Landini gone?" he inquired.

"Come along, John," Ward said genially. "Just in time for another little drink. Is that right for you, Ireland?"

"Just, thank you," the aviator replied.

From somewhere up-stairs came a sharp report that sounded unpleasantly like the firing of a pistol.

"What was that?" asked Ryder, now at the foot of the stairs.

Ward set down the bottle he was holding and looked toward Charlie Chan. "I wonder," he said.

Charlie did not pause to wonder. Pushing Ryder aside, he ran up the stairs. He was conscious of figures in the upper hall as he passed, figures he did not pause to identify. Chinese, he had always contended, were psychic people, but he did not have to be particularly psychic on this occasion to know which door to seek. It was closed. He pushed it open.

The lights in the study were out, but for a first glance the moonlight sufficed. Landini was lying just inside the French windows that led on to the balcony. Charlie leaped across her and peered out the open window. He saw no one.

Black shapes crowded the doorway. "Turn on the lights," Charlie said. "And do not come too close, please."

The lights flashed on, and Dudley Ward pushed forward. "Ellen!" he cried. "What's happened here—"

Chan intercepted him and laid his hand on the host's arm. Beyond Ward he saw frightened faces—Romano, Swan, Beaton, Dinsdale, Ireland, Cecile. "You are psychic, Mr. Ward," Charlie said gravely. "All same Chinese race. Three days before the crime, you summon detective."

"Crime!" repeated Ward. He sought to kneel beside the singer, but again Chan restrained him.

"Permit me, please," the Chinese continued. "For you, it means pain. For me, alas, a customary duty." With some difficulty, he knelt upon the floor, and placed his fingers gently on Landini's wrist.

"Doctor Swan is here," Ward said. "Perhaps—can nothing be done?"

Chan struggled back to his feet. "Can the fallen flower return to the branch again?" he asked softly.

Ward turned quickly away, and there was silence in the room. Charlie stood for a moment, staring down at the body. Landini lay on her back; those evening shoes whose dampness had so distressed Romano were but a few inches away from the threshold of the open windows. In her dead hands was loosely held a chiffon scarf, bright pink in color, contrasting oddly with her green gown. And just inside the windows, close to her feet, lay a dainty, snub-nosed revolver.

Charlie removed his handkerchief from his pocket and stooping over, picked up the weapon. It was still warm, he noted through the handkerchief. One cartridge had been fired. He carried it over and deposited it on the desk.

There for a long moment he stood staring, behind him the murmur of many voices. He appeared to be lost in thought, and indeed he was. For an odd thing had suddenly occurred to him. When he had last seen Landini sitting at this desk, the two boxes containing cigarettes had been close at her elbow, both open. Now they had been restored to their places, farther back on the desk. But on the crimson box rested the yellow lid—and on the yellow box, the crimson.

4

Upward No Road

As Charlie stood, silently regarding those boxes whose lids had become so strangely confused, he was conscious that some newcomer had pushed his way into the room. He swung around and beheld the shrunken figure of Ah Sing. The old Chinese held a blue bundle under his arm, which he now proffered to the room at large.

"Blanket," he announced, his high shrill voice sounding oddly out of place at that moment. "Blanket fo' lil dog."

Chan watched him closely as his beady eyes fell on the silent figure by the window. "Wha's mallah heah?" the old man inquired. His expression did not change.

"You can see what's the matter," Charlie replied sharply. "Madame Landini has been murdered."

The dim old eyes turned to Chan with what was almost a look of insolence. "P'liceman him come," he muttered complainingly. "Then woik fo' p'liceman him come plitty soon too." He glanced at Ward accusingly. "What my tell you, Boss? You clazy invite p'liceman heah. Mebbe some day you lissen to Ah Sing."

Somewhat nettled, Chan pointed to the blanket. "What are you doing with that? Who asked you to bring it?"

"Missie ask me," the old man nodded toward the figure on the floor. "Missie say she send Cecile fo' blanket, no catch 'um. She say, Sing, you catch 'um like goo' boy."

"When was this?"

"Mebbe half past nine, between ten."

"Where was the airplane at that time? Over the house?"

"Not ovah house no moah. Mebbe on field."

"I see," Chan nodded. "The blanket is no longer required. Take it away."

"Allight, p'liceman," nodded the old man, and did so.

Charlie turned back and addressed Dinsdale. "I have really no authority in this place," he remarked. "Those who are out of office should not meddle with the government. There is, I presume, a sheriff?"

"Bygad, yes," Dinsdale said. "Young Don Holt—this will be a whale of a job for him. He was elected less than a year ago. His dad, old Sam Holt, has been sheriff of this county for fifty years but he went blind a while back, and as a sort of tribute to him, they put up young Don. He'll be a puzzled kid over this. Horses are his specialty."

"Does it chance that he lives near by?" Charlie inquired.

"He lives down at the county-seat," Dinsdale answered, "but he has charge of the riding stables at the Tavern during the summer, and it happens he's over there to-night. I'll get him on the telephone, and he can reach here inside of twenty minutes by boat."

"If you will be so good," Charlie said, and Dinsdale went quickly out.

For a moment Charlie stared at the varied group gathered in that little room. How unfortunate, he reflected, that he could not have announced this killing to them suddenly, and watched their faces at the news. But alas, they had come upon him in the dark, they had known of the tragedy almost as soon as he, and whatever their reception of this knowledge, he was never to learn it now.

Nevertheless, their faces were an interesting study. That of Romano, the emotional, was pale and drawn, and there were tears in his brown eyes. Doctor Swan's was taut and excited. Dudley Ward had dropped into a chair beside the fire, and was shading his eyes with his hand. Beaton and his sister stood as far from the body as possible, the girl was crying, and the young man comforted her. The look on the face of Cecile was a mixture of fright and sullenness, while Michael's expression was dazed and puzzled, bespeaking an honest but somewhat stupid simplicity. As for John Ryder, his blue eyes were cold as usual, and they looked at the woman who had once been his wife and no sign of pity or regret.

"I think it much better," Chan said, "if you all returned to the living-room below. You understand, naturally, sad state of affairs which makes it necessary you do not take departure now."

"But I've got to get back to Reno," Swan cried.

Charlie shrugged. "You must not place blame on me. Place it on guilty shoulders of one who fired this recent shot."

Dinsdale returned. "I got hold of the sheriff," he announced. "He's on his way."

"Thank you so much," Charlie said. "Mr. Dinsdale, you will remain here with Mr. Ward and myself, but I am inviting the others down-stairs. Before you go," he added, as they started to file out, "I must inquire—though there is no stern necessity to answer, for I am stranger here myself—has any one of you seen this before?" He lifted the snub-nosed revolver from the desk, and held it high in the handkerchief.

"I have," said Dinsdale promptly. "I saw it once before, only to-night."

"Where was that?" Charlie asked.

"At the Tavern," the hotel man continued. "Ellen Landini and I were engaged in a small financial transaction, and that revolver fell from her bag when she opened it. I picked it up, and handed it back—"

"Quite true," nodded Luis Romano, coming close and staring at the weapon. "It is Ellen's property. Some years ago there was an attempt to hold her up in a hotel room, and always since she has insisted on carrying that with her. I pleaded with her—I did not approve—and now she has been killed with her own revolver.”

“Others, then, must have known she carried it,” mused Chan. “Mr. Beaton?”

The young man nodded. “Yes—I’ve seen it many times. It’s hers, all right.”

Suddenly, Charlie swung on the girl at Beaton’s side. “And you, Miss Beaton?”

She shrank away from him as he held the weapon close. “Yes—yes—I’ve seen it too.”

“You have known it was always in Madame Landini’s bag?”

“I have known it—yes.”

“For how long?”

“Ever since I met her—a week ago.”

Chan’s voice softened to its customary tone. “What a pity,” he said. “You are trembling. It is too cold for you here, with these windows open.” He restored the revolver to the desk. “You should have a scarf,” he continued. “A pretty pink scarf to match that gown of yours.”

“I—I have,” she said. She was on her way toward the door.

“This one, perhaps,” Charlie cried. He stepped to the side of the dead woman and lifted one corner of the chiffon scarf that lay in her lifeless hands. “This, perhaps, belongs to you,” he continued. The girl’s eyes had followed him, fascinated, and now her scream rang out sharply in the room. Her brother put his arm about her.

“My scarf,” she cried. “What is it doing—there?”

Chan’s eyebrows rose. “You had not noticed it before?”

“No—no, I hadn’t. It was dark when I came in here—and after the lights went on—I never really looked in this direction.”

“You never really looked,” Chan went on thoughtfully. He dropped the corner of the scarf and rose. His eyes strayed to the boxes on the table. “I am so sorry—I can not return your property just at this moment. Later, perhaps—when the sheriff of the county has beheld it—in a dead woman’s hands. You will all go now—thank you so much.”

When the last one had left, he closed the door and turned to Dinsdale and Ward. The latter had risen, and was anxiously pacing the floor.

“Confound it, Inspector,” he cried. “That young woman is my guest. You don’t for a moment think—” He paused.

“I think,” said Chan slowly, “that one of your guests has to-night stooped to murder.”

“Evidently. But a woman—a charming girl—”

Chan shrugged. “There is no such poison in the green snake’s mouth as in a woman’s heart.”

“I don’t know who said that first,” Ward replied, “but I don’t agree with him. No—not even after all that has—that I’ve been through.” He stood for a moment, staring down at the dead woman on the floor. “Poor Ellen—she deserved better than this. I’ll never forgive myself for inviting her over here. But I thought we might induce her to tell—” He stopped. “By heaven—I hadn’t thought of it until now. Shall we ever find the truth about my boy—after this? Ellen was our best chance—perhaps, in the final analysis, our only one.” He stared hopelessly at Charlie.

“Do not despair.” Charlie patted his shoulder pityingly. “We will persevere—and we will succeed, I am sure. This event may really speed our search—for among the papers and effects of this lady we may find our answer. However, matter of even fiercer importance now intrudes itself. Who killed Ellen Landini?”

"What's your guess, Mr. Chan?" Dinsdale inquired.

Charlie smiled. "Guessing is cheap, but wrong guess expensive. I cannot afford it, myself."

"Well, I'm a spendthrift. Sleuth all you like, but I can tell you now Romano killed her."

"You have evidence, perhaps—"

"The evidence of my eyes—I noticed he was sore at her about something. Money, I imagine. He's Latin, excitable—"

Charlie shook his head. "Ah, yes. But Latins do not become so excitable they forget where financial advantage lies. Landini alive was worth money to him, but with Landini dead—unless—unless—"

"Unless what?"

"No matter. We will look into that later. There is long tortuous path to climb, and the wise man starts slowly, conserving his strength for a swift finish. By the way, you spoke of moment at Tavern to-night when Landini opened bag to pay you money?"

"Yes, so I did," Dinsdale replied. "I meant to explain it. Last week I called on Ellen in Reno to invite her over to the Tavern for dinner. While I was there, a C. O. D. package arrived—there was the usual wild hunt for cash, which ended in her borrowing twenty dollars from me. To-night she insisted on repaying it—and that was when the revolver dropped out of her bag."

"She did repay it?"

"Yes, with a brand-new bill which she peeled from a great roll of them in her purse."

"Odd," Charlie said. "There are no bills in her purse now."

"Good lord," cried Ward. "Not only a murderer but a petty thief. I'm afraid I've carried hospitality too far."

"What did I tell you?" the hotel man said. "Romano."

Charlie rose. "When I came to mainland," he remarked, "I was engaged deep in puzzling case. Remnant of that effort, I have in my baggage lamp-black and camel's-hair brush. Same are useful in matter of finger-prints, and while we await the sheriff, I may as well obtain them."

He went to his room. While he searched his luggage for the tools of his trade, he heard the sound of footsteps ascending the stairs. Presently he found what he was looking for, and returned to the study. A tall, black-haired young westerner in riding boots, breeches and leather coat was standing in the center of the room.

"Inspector Chan," said Dinsdale, "meet Don Holt."

"Hello, Inspector," the young man cried, and seized the hand of the Chinese in a grip that almost lifted him from the floor. "Pleased to meet you—and I'm telling you I never meant that so heartfelt before in all my born days."

"You have grasped situation?" inquired Charlie. He set down his burden and caressed his right hand with his left, seeking to restore the circulation.

"Well—in a way—at least I've gathered there is a situation. Coroner lives over to the county-seat, so he won't be able to see this lady till to-morrow. But I got a Tahoe doctor on the way to make a preliminary examination, and after that I guess we can move her down to town—what town there is. So far—am I right?"

"So far you appear to act with most commendable speed," Chan assured him.

"I know, but this is my first case of this—this sort of thing, and I can assure you, Inspector, I'm trembling all over like a roped yearling. Mr.

Ward was just telling me you was here, on a visit to him. He says he's got a little job for you, but it can wait while you give the county and me a helping hand. How's that sound to you?"

Charlie looked at Ward. "We are, of course, very lucky to be able to enlist the inspector's services," his host remarked. "My affair can wait."

"In which case," Charlie said, "my very slight talents are yours to command, Mr. Holt."

"Fine," Holt answered. "I could speak a couple of volumes on the way that makes me feel, but action, not words, is my specialty. Let's get down to brass tacks. What happened here to-night, anyhow? Who was all them people down-stairs? Where do we start, and how soon?"

They all looked at Charlie, and patiently he went over the events of the evening, up to the firing of the shot and the discovery of Landini's dead body. The young man nodded.

"I get you. At the time the shot was fired, who was unaccounted for?"

"Quite a number," Charlie told him. "Of the guests, Miss Leslie Beaton, whose scarf, oddly enough, is clutched in dead woman's hands. Also, Dr. Frederic Swan and Mr. Luis Romano. Of the servants, Cecile and—er—Ah Sing."

"Five of 'em," commented the sheriff. "Well, it could have been worse. It really is only four, because I've known Ah Sing since I was ten inches tall, and he wouldn't—"

"Pardon," said Chan.

Mr. Holt laughed. "I know," he said. "That's no way for a sheriff to act. Getting ideas all set in advance—anything can happen, at that. Well, that's lesson number one. Just deal 'em out to me as we go. And now, Inspector, you just go ahead and solve this case, and don't pay any attention to me."

"Ah, but I must pay attention to you. You are constituted authority in this place, and everything I do must be done with your approval and permission."

"Granted in advance," nodded Holt. "What I want is results, and I guess you can get 'em. You see, I got a sort of family reputation to uphold—"

Chan nodded. "Yes—I have heard of your honorable father. Maybe we also call him in. It has well been said—in time of severe illness summon three doctors. One might be good."

"Dad *was* good," the young man replied softly. "But he's blind now."

"A terrible pity," Charlie said. "But even a blind man, if he has been over the road before, may point out the way. Just now, however, you and I are in charge. You have spoken of lesson number one. May I, with all humility, now proffer the second lesson?"

"Shoot," said Holt.

"It has been my good fortune to know famous detectives, some from Scotland Yard. All these say, in case of homicide, first duty of detective is to examine position of body as it fell. What does that examination suggest to you?"

The boy considered. "I should say—well, she may have been shot from the balcony. Or at least by some one standing in the window."

"Precisely. The body is well arranged to present that effect. Let us now examine the room. Kindly come and view this desk. You observe upon it fine particles of—what?"

"Tobacco," Holt answered.

"Correct. Very fine tobacco, such as is contained in cigarettes. Observe these two boxes, in which cigarettes of two brands are kept. What strikes you?"

"Somebody got twisted and put the wrong lids on them."

"So it would seem," Chan nodded. "Somebody was in very great hurry, no doubt. The time for escape was brief, for the shot was heard instantly below. We will open boxes." He did so, using his handkerchief, which he pulled from under the weapon. "Behold. Cigarettes are not piled in neat order, but are in unsettled state. They were tossed back hurriedly. What shall we say to that? Was there a struggle at this desk? When last I saw Madame Landini she was seated here. Was the struggle here, and was she then dragged to window in hope to make it appear killing was done from balcony? Why else should there be this frantic effort to tidy desk? The time was brief, but there was just enough, perhaps—though great haste was needed, so great that wrong lids got on to boxes. The killer could have so performed, then fled through open window and escaped into another room that opens on balcony. I should have examined those rooms at once—it may be killer lurked there until all were crowded into this study, then moved away—perhaps crowded into study himself. You will perceive that your new assistant has sinking spells of stupidity."

"Ain't we all?" grinned Holt. "What you say's mighty interesting. I take it you think, then, that the lady was shot by some one who was with her in this room, and not from the balcony?"

Chan shrugged. "I am merely putting facts on parade. I find it wise not to draw conclusion too rapidly. We get answer too quick, we may be wrong, like my children who labor with algebra. I leave it open for present. Lady may, in spite of all I say, have been shot from balcony. She may even have been shot on balcony, and taken step back into room before falling. Perhaps doctor can tell us that. We will now travel to balcony, if you please."

All four stepped through the windows, past the dead Landini, and came into the bracing night air. The lake lay calm and chill under the full moon; the stars here were dim and remote, Chan noted, lacking the friendliness of those in the Hawaiian sky. Charlie took a deep breath.

"I regret there is no snow here," he said to Ward.

"Unfortunately, no," his host replied. "I had this balcony cleared off when we first came, and Sing has kept it swept and garnished ever since. Otherwise the snow piles against the windows and chills the rooms."

Charlie shrugged. "After many years I encounter snow, and the clue of the footstep is denied me. Such, I presume, is life." He examined the scene. "Two other rooms, I perceive, open on this veranda. This one is—"

"That," said Ward slowly, "is the room Landini used to have as a sitting-room. I have kept it—just as she left it."

Charlie tried the window. "Locked from the inside, of course. Naturally, if killer went that way, he—or she—would attend to that. We will study threshold in the morning." He led the way to the windows on the opposite side of the study. "And this room?" he inquired.

"It's my bedroom," Ward told him. "I believe Sing showed the ladies here with their wraps." He peered through the window into the room, where a dim light was burning. "Yes—there are coats on the bed—"

"And a woman's scarf," added Chan, at his side. "A green scarf. The one Landini should have been clutching in her hands. Her own."

Ward nodded. "I suppose so." Chan tried this window with the same result as before, and they returned to the study.

"Next step," said Chan to the sheriff, "finger-prints. Matter about which we hear so much, and from which we get so little."

"Oh, lord, I suppose so," the young man answered. "I've got a homicide squad, but he's sick in bed. Finger-prints are in his department—I wonder if he knows it. My Dad never took a finger-print in his life."

"Ah, but we are more unfortunate—we live in age of science," Charlie smiled. "Great marvels happen all times, and world gets less human by minute. Sorry to say I possess utensils to get scientific here and now. I will proceed to examine fatal pistol and discover not a print on it. The suspense will be terrible. Humbly suggest you ease your mind by careful study of room."

He sat down at the desk and busied himself with his lampblack and brush. Don Holt began a careful survey of the room, as suggested. Dudley Ward picked up a log, and was about to place it on the fire, when a cry from Chan startled him.

"Please," Charlie called, "just a moment, if you will be so good."

"Why—er—what—" Ward was puzzled.

"The log, pardon me. Not just now," Chan explained.

Ward nodded and put the log back in the basket. Presently Charlie stood up.

"Suspense now over," he announced. "No print on pistol anywhere. Gloves, held in handkerchief, wiped clean—take your honorable choice. Something more suggestive, though—there are also no marks on lids of pretty colored boxes. I think we may go below—"

Holt approached him, holding out his great hand. In it Chan beheld a cheap little gold pin, with semi-precious stones.

"Ah—you make discovery," Charlie said.

"Bedded deep in the carpet," the sheriff explained. "Somebody stepped on it, I guess."

"Plenty ladies around here," Charlie remarked. "That was not Landini's—we know that much. It has not the rich look of prima-donna jewelry. Let us carry it below—and I suggest that you now remove pink scarf, so we may take that also. But one thing remains to be done here. Gentlemen—if you will do me the favor to await me one moment—"

He went briskly out, and walked part way down the stairs to a point where he had a clear view of the room below. The silent little party seated there looked up at him with interest. The detective's eye lighted on one who sat far from the others. "Mr. Ryder," he said.

For a moment there was no reply. "Yes?" said Ryder finally.

"If you please—will you be so good as to return to the study?"

With annoying slowness, Ryder got to his feet. Chan waited patiently. When finally the bearded man reached him on the stairs, the Chinese bowed low. "You are quite right," he said. "He who hurries can not walk with a stately step. Precede me, I beg of you."

They came again into the room where Landini lay. "I don't quite know," Ryder said, "why I should have the honor of a separate inquisition."

"You will yet learn," Chan assured him. "Have you met Mr. Don Holt, sheriff of this county?"

"I've not had the pleasure," Ryder replied, shaking hands.

"Mr. Ryder," Charlie began, "it is not my purpose to keep you here for long time. Before tragic passing of this lady, I visited your room with urgent message from her to you. A message which you belittled. You hurried me out, closing door almost against my back. And then—"

"Then—what?"

"Kindly detail your acts from that moment until lady's murder."

"A simple matter," Ryder said easily. "I sat down and resumed my reading. Shortly afterward I heard the airplane approaching. I went on reading. Then I heard it over the house."

"You went on reading?"

"Precisely. After a time, I thought the airplane must have landed. Ellen Landini, I decided, was leaving by plane. So—I went on reading."

"An interesting book," Charlie nodded. "But sooner or later—you put it down."

"Yes—I went to the door, opened it and listened. Everything was rather quiet—I couldn't hear Landini's voice—so I decided she must have gone out on the field. I went to the stairs—"

"One moment, please. From the time I left you, until I saw you again on the stairs, you did not visit any other part of house? This room, for example?"

"I did not."

"You are certain on that point?"

"Of course I am."

"Mr. Holt," said Chan, stepping to the fireplace, "will you come here, please?" The sheriff did so. "Permit that I point out to you certain matters," Charlie continued. "We have here"—he took up the poker—"the completely consumed ashes of a letter, written, I may tell you, on paper similar to that on desk. And over here, in far corner, we have partly consumed envelope, burned but slightly at top. Will you be so kind as to rescue same?" Holt took it up in his fingers. "What would be address on envelope, Mr. Sheriff?"

The young man examined it. "Why—it says: 'Mr. John Ryder. Urgent. Private.' In a big bold hand—but it doesn't look like a man's writing, at that."

"Mr. Ryder will tell you whose writing it is," Chan suggested.

Ryder glanced at it. "It is the writing," he said, "of Ellen Landini."

"Correct," cried Chan. "It was addressed to you as private and urgent. It was sealed. It was torn open, and the letter removed. Who would do that, Mr. Ryder?"

"I'm sure I don't know," Ryder answered.

"Not many in this house," Chan continued. "No gentleman, surely—no lady. Such would not tear open the letter of another, marked private. No, it appears to me, Mr. Ryder, there is only one person who could have opened that letter. Yourself."

Ryder stared at him coldly. "A natural inference, Mr. Chan," he replied. "However, even if you were correct—and I can tell you at once that you're not—what of it? Surely you haven't forgotten that at the moment Landini was killed, I was standing at the foot of the stairs, in the living-room below."

Charlie turned to the sheriff. "You and I—we have long journey to take together," he remarked. "Often it will seem matter of upward, no road, downward, no door. But the man with a tongue in his head can always find the way. Let us go down-stairs and exercise our tongues."

5

Downward No Door

The five men descended to the living-room at once. A glance at the formidable company that awaited them there caused Charlie's heart to sink. He looked toward the sheriff. The young man nervously cleared his throat. "This is sure too bad," he began. "It's going to be pretty unpleasant for all of us, I guess. I'm Don Holt, sheriff of the county, and I don't aim to cause no innocent person any unnecessary trouble. But I got to get to the bottom of this business, and the shorter the route, the better for all of us—well, most of us, anyhow. I've asked Inspector Chan, who's had more experience in this line than I have, to give me a hand here, an' I want to say right now, that when he asks, you answer. That's all, I reckon."

A diversion at the door interrupted the proceedings. Sing admitted a small gray-haired man with a black satchel, who proved to be the doctor from Tahoe Holt had mentioned. The young man took him aside for a brief talk, and then called to Sing, who led the newcomer upstairs.

"I guess we can get goin' now," said Holt, looking helplessly at Charlie. Charlie nodded. "We begin with least important of the gathering," he announced. "When fatal shot was fired, terminating brilliant career of one who was much beloved, six men were present in this room. One of these, Mr. Ryder, has already made statement. I would learn from remaining five all actions just before they met here, their conduct and locations, and when they last saw Landini. In this way, some light might be thrown. Since hour of the clock is uncertain, we can perhaps fix times by location of airplane overhead. I myself was one of these five. Answering my questions without asking same, I last saw Landini above in study while airplane was still over lake. She had requested I summon to her side Mr. Ryder, and I reported back to her he refused to accede. She was then writing hurriedly at desk. I left her, came down here, and went outside, where I eventually met Mr. Ward and Mr. Ireland at edge of field." He turned to the aviator. "Mr. Ireland, we can pass over you completely. You can scarcely be involved in this, or have any information of any sort."

The big Irishman nodded. "All I know is, Landini called me up to come and get her. And I came." He looked up, and his eyes met those of his wife. "I had to," he added. "That's my job. I'm workin' for others."

"Exactly," said Charlie. "Mr. Ward—you last saw Landini—"

"You were with me, Inspector," Ward replied. "You remember I left the study to turn on the lights at the field, as soon as we saw the plane over the lake. The lights are worked from a small shed in back of the hangar. We keep it closed and locked. I had to get the keys, and the lock stuck—a bit rusty, I fancy. It was a hurry-up job, but I got them on in time."

Chan turned to Ireland. "When did the lights blaze on?" he asked. "It was while I was circling over the house, I think," the aviator said. "Thanks a lot," he added to Ward. "But it wouldn't have mattered if you hadn't made it—the moon was good enough."

"Leaving two of the five," Charlie persisted. "Mr. Dinsdale and Mr. Beaton. It is my impression that neither left this room during the evening, until after the shot was fired. Am I correct?"

"In my case, yes," Dinsdale said. "A good fire and a good drink—all the airplanes in the world landing in the back yard couldn't rout me out. Yes—I sat here, right from the time I came until we heard the shot and ran upstairs."

"And Mr. Beaton was with you?"

"Well—not all the time—"

"No—no, I wasn't, that's true." Young Beaton stood up, fragile and pale and evidently very nervous. "You see—I went outside. You remember you went through the room, Mr. Chan, and then we heard you talking with some one out there, and in a minute Doctor Swan came in. He said the airplane was a beautiful sight, or something like that, so I said I guessed I'd have a look at it too. I went out—it was just coming in from over the lake then. I stepped down on to the path, and suddenly I heard a voice up above me."

"Ah—you heard a voice," repeated Charlie with sudden interest.

"Yes—it—it was Ellen—I couldn't mistake that, of course. And I heard her say—she was calling to somebody, really—I heard her call: 'Oh, it's you, is it? I'm freezing—get me my scarf. It's on the bed in the next room. The green one.' "

Chan smiled with sudden understanding. "Ah—most interesting. You heard Miss Landini ask for her scarf?"

"Yes, yes," cried the boy eagerly. His manner was almost pathetically ingenuous. "It's true, Mr. Chan. It really is. I know it sounds—"

"Let us not trouble how it sounds. Continue, please."

"I went a little farther along the path, and I saw Landini standing alone on the balcony just over the front door. She was looking up and waving her handkerchief. Then the airplane came down terribly close, and began to circle around the house. I started to cough and realized I didn't have my hat or overcoat—so I hurried inside. Anyhow—the picture sort of sickened me—Ellen standing there and waving like a mad woman—"

"That's O. K., Inspector," Dinsdale said. "He was out there only a few minutes."

"But long enough," shrugged Chan, "to hear Landini demand a scarf. Her green scarf. How much better, Mr. Beaton, if you had not added that last."

The boy's face contorted. "But it's the truth," he cried. "I'm telling it to you just as it happened. Somebody came into that room, and she asked for her scarf. And—and—"

"And the person, intending murder and wishing to incriminate innocent girl, returned with your sister's scarf. You are asking me to believe that?"

"I'm not asking you to believe anything," the boy almost screamed. "I'm just telling you what happened. I'm just trying to help you—and you won't believe me—you won't believe me—"

"Never mine, Hughie." His sister got up and patted him on the back. "Please don't get so upset."

"It happened, I tell you."

"I know. I know."

"Thank you, my boy," Charlie said gently. "I have not said I do not believe you. As a matter of fact—" He paused, his eyes on the sheriff. Mr. Holt was staring at Leslie Beaton with the most unsheriff-like look Chan ever remembered having seen in his long career. He sighed. A new complication, perhaps.

"As a matter of fact," Charlie continued, "this brings you, Mr. Ireland, unexpectedly back into limelight. Though you had not yet arrived on the

place, it must be that you, none the less, were one of the last people to see
Landini alive."

Ireland shifted in his chair. "Maybe I was," he remarked. "It didn't strike
me before. When I turned in over the house, I looked down and seen some
dame waving to me from the balcony. I dropped down to see who it was—"

"You knew well enough who it was," flashed his wife.

"How could I, dearie? I thought maybe it was you. So I got down as near
as I dared, and I seen it was Landini—"

"So then you stunted around, risking your neck to give her a thrill—"

"Now, dearie, I just circled round a few times, to get my bearings and
locate the field—"

"Did you, then, think the field was on the roof?" Cecile sneered.

Her husband shrugged. "I knew where it was, and I knew what I was
doing. I don't need no back-seat drivers—"

"Pardon," Chan said. "How many times did you circle the house?"

"Three times."

"And three times you beheld Landini on that balcony."

"No—only the first. The last two times she'd gone inside."

"And could you see—were the windows open?"

"Well—I couldn't be sure of that."

"Thank you so much." Charlie walked off to a corner of the room with
the sheriff. "Which concludes all those who were in this room when shot
was fired," he said in a low tone. "Now we advance to more important
sector of our attack."

"But say," demanded Holt. "Oughtn't we to be writing all this down in
a book?"

Chan shook his head. "Not my method. Sight of paper and pencil sometimes has deleterious effect on speaker. I keep all this in mind, and at early
opportunity, I make slight notes of it."

"My gosh—can you do that?" Holt answered. "I've forgot it already."

Charlie smiled. "Large empty place makes good storehouse," he remarked, tapping his forehead. "Now we proceed."

"Just a minute," Holt laid his hand on the detective's arm. "Who's that
girl in the pink dress?"

"Owner of the pink scarf," Chan answered. "And I would humbly recall
to you for the next few minutes the stern realities of lesson number one."

They went back to the other end of the room, and Chan again faced the
assembly. "We come now," he said, "to members of this party who were
not in view when death came to unfortunate lady above. One of these has
already made at least partial statement. Sing, here, was probably last person
to see Landini alive, having been dispatched for blanket, he says, after
airplane landed. What you do, Sing, up to that time?"

"My don' know," shrugged Sing.

"You must know," replied Chan sternly.

"Mebbe my min' own business," suggested Sing slyly.

Charlie glared at him. He was finding his own compatriot a bit trying.
"Listen to me," he said. "This is murder case, understand—murder case.
You answer my question, or maybe the sheriff here lock you up in big jail."

Sing stared at the young man. "Who—him?" he asked, incredulous.

"That's right, Sing," Holt said. "You answer. Understand."

"Allight," agreed Sing. "Why you no say so light away? My jes' go aloun'
tendin' to own business."

"What was your business? What did you do?" Chan continued patiently.

"Boss see me in hall, say you catch 'um Cecile. My catch 'um. Then my go down-stair. Go out back step watch landing field. Boss come out, say to me, 'Sing, Landini want something, you catch 'um.' "

"Just a minute." Chan turned to Dudley Ward.

"That's right," Ward said. "I'd just passed Cecile on the back stairs and I gathered she had no intention of getting that blanket. I was in too much of a hurry about the lights to argue, so I just sent Sing to attend to it."

"My go in house," Sing continued when urged. "Heah lil dog bark in kitchen. Stop lissen. Plitty soon go up-stah, membah Missie. Go to room, say, 'What you want, Missie?' She say, 'Sing, you catch 'um blanket like go' boy, covah up dog.' Dog, dog, dog all time when she 'lound. My go out—"

"The airplane had now landed on the field?" Charlie inquired.

"Yes."

"How you know that?"

"Damn noise quiet now. My go my loom—"

"On the third floor?"

"Yes. My catch 'um blanket. Plitty soon heah noise. Mebbe pistol. So my come down with blanket—"

"Very slowly, I judge," remarked Chan.

"Wha's th' mallah?" inquired Sing. "Plenty time. Plitty soon see Missie gits shot. Too bad," he added, without emotion.

"Thank you so much," said Chan, with obvious relief. "That will do, for the present." He glanced at Holt. "Probably the last person to see Landini alive. I'll talk with him later, alone." He turned to the conductor. "Mr. Romano, so sorry to say I have somewhat warm interest in your actions for half-hour preceding this sad event."

"Me?" Romano gazed at him with innocent eyes.

"You, indeed. When I last saw you, airplane was still over lake, and you walked about room with panther tread. What next?"

"Ah, I recall," said the musician slowly. "I was engaged in making a list of rules for this young man—a list which, alas, will not now be required. I was no doubt at that moment seeking to determine whether or not I had fully covered the ground. I saw you pass my door on your way downstairs—"

"And continued with the list, maybe?"

"No," Romano answered, "not at all. It comes to me—now Landini must be alone. I hasten to the study, she is writing letter, she puts it in envelope, seals the flap. Now, I say, is come the time to talk about that settlement. I am—what you say—broke. I am—am I right?—flat. Landini addresses the envelope. 'I am so sorry,' she say, 'but, Luis, I am in financial difficulty too. My investments do not pay proper dividends.'

"Then I say, impassioned, 'Ellen, you can not afford a new husband at this time. Why not cling to the old? I am still fond of you'—but, Mr. Chan"—his old voice broke—"need I discuss that scene?"

"Not at all," Chan answered, "except to tell me her reply."

"It was," Romano bowed his head, "it was not flattering to me. Imagine, if you can—after all I had done for her—cared for her like a bambino.—The airplane was now approaching the house. She leaped to her feet, flung wide the windows. 'Come and see me in Reno,' she cried. 'I will do what I can.' And she ran on to the balcony."

"And you, Mr. Romano?"

"Me—I was broken-hearted. I stared at her there on the balcony—it was to be my last sight of her alive—though of course I did not know that. Then I returned to my room, closed my door. I sat by the window, staring out at the snow, the dark trees, the sad night. Flung off, like an old coat,

I sorrowed. But I was indignant, too. I remembered all I had done—"

"Ah, yes. And you sat there, brooding, until you heard the shot."

"It is true. I heard the shot, and for a time, I wondered. Then, I hear footsteps, voices, and I follow you in here to your sad discovery."

"Tell me this." Chan studied him keenly. "You were still the husband of Ellen Landini—at the least for two weeks more. As such, will you inherit any property she may leave?"

Romano shook his head. "Alas, no. At the time the settlement was drawn up—the one which she so cruelly ignored—she told me she was making a will, leaving everything she had to her future husband—to Mr. Hugh Beaton here."

Surprised, Chan turned to the young man. "Did you know of this, Mr. Beaton?"

Beaton looked up wearily. "Yes—she told me about it. Naturally, I didn't want her to do it."

"Do you know whether the will was made or not?"

"She told me one day it had been drawn up. Signed, too, I suppose. I didn't ask any questions. I hated the whole idea."

Charlie looked at Miss Beaton. "You, too, had heard of the affair?"

"I had," said the girl softly. "But I paid no attention. It didn't matter."

Chan turned back to Romano. "What a sad position for you. Wife, money, everything lost. Do you, may I ask, happen to have that list you drew up for Mr. Beaton?"

"It is in my—" Suddenly he stopped. "It is in my room. I will get it for you."

"So sorry." Chan's eyes narrowed. "You were about to say, I think, that it is in your pocket."

"You are mistaken," Romano said, but his pale face had suddenly grown paler than ever. "What does it matter, at any rate?"

"It matters so much," Chan continued gently, "that unless you empty pockets here and now, I must reluctantly do same for you. Believe me, such a barbarous action would bring me pain."

Romano stood for a moment, considering.

"The story," he said finally, "of my interview with my wife was not quite complete. I—a man does not willingly speak of such things—but—" He reached into a trousers pocket and took out a roll of crisp new twenty-dollar bills, which he handed to Chan. "Just before Ellen rushed on to the balcony she removed these from her bag, flung them on the desk. I—I accepted them. My case—was—desperate." He dropped into a chair and covered his face with his hands. Chan looked down on him with real pity.

"I am so glad," the detective said, "that you saw way clear to amending own story. Unfortunately, these must remain with sheriff at present as evidence. But in meantime—we will see—way will be found—do not worry, Mr. Romano." He turned with sudden grim determination on Doctor Swan. "And now, Doctor, your turn arrives. Where did you go after you left me in path before house?"

"I haven't much to tell," said Swan. "I came in here, had a word or two with Dinsdale and Beaton, and then went up-stairs—to the room that had been assigned me before dinner. I was planning to leave at the earliest possible moment."

"Ah—and you had left something in that room you wished to obtain?"

"No—I had nothing up there. My coat and hat were in the closet down here. I had no luggage—it was not my intention to spend the night."

"You had nothing up there—then why did you go?"

Swan hesitated. "The windows of that room faced the back. I figured I could see the plane land—and—"

Charlie and the sheriff exchanged a look.

"Well, I'll be frank with you," Swan went on. "As a matter of fact, it occurred to me that after Ireland had landed his plane, he'd probably come inside for a moment. I didn't care to meet him. He knows what I think of him."

"And you know what I think of you," said Ireland sneeringly.

"No man," continued Swan, "can look forward to a social meeting with a greasy chauffeur who once made love to his wife behind his back—"

Ireland was on his feet. "Is that so—"

"Sit down," said Don Holt. "Now this is getting to be a case that I can handle. Sit down, Ireland, and shut up."

Big as he was, the aviator was not inclined to argue with the sheriff. He sat down, and Holt looked somewhat disappointed.

"Let us continue," said Chan, "peacefully. You went up-stairs to avoid Mr. Ireland, Doctor Swan?"

"Yes. I went into that room and closed the door. It was not my intention to come out of there until Ellen and the plane had gone. I watched it land, and I was standing by the window waiting to see it depart before returning down-stairs. That is where I was when the shot was fired. It's not much of an alibi, I know, but—"

"I'll say it's not much of an alibi," growled Ireland. "A fat chance you've got putting that over. Especially when they find out you've been black-mailing poor Landini for seven years—"

"That's a lie," cried Swan, trembling with fury.

"Blackmailing," remarked Chan. He looked at Dudley Ward.

"Yeah—blackmailing," Ireland repeated. "She told me all about it. Two hundred and fifty a month for seven years, and the other day she told me she couldn't pay any more. I advised her to order this buzzard to scram. Did she tell you, Doctor? I guess she did—from the looks of to-night."

"You'd better be careful," said Swan through his teeth. "You're not out of the woods yet yourself."

"Me?" Ireland said. "Why—I was flying around in the sky, innocent as a bird. I had nothing to do with this—"

"But—your wife?" cried Swan. "How about your wife—or don't you care what happens to her? Poor Cecile—wandering about up-stairs almost insane with jealousy—and with good reason, too, I imagine. Where was Cecile when that shot was fired—that's what I want to know."

"The proper authorities," Chan put in, "will resume the inquiry into this case—if you have no objection, Doctor Swan. Cecile—pardon, Mrs. Ire-land—we come now, with the doctor's kind assistance, to you. Courtesy has not ruled us, you will observe. It appears to be a matter of ladies last."

"I—I know nothing," the woman said.

"As I feared. But let us push questions, none the less. When last I saw you, you had been sent to obtain blanket for dog. You did not busy yourself with such task?"

Her eyes flashed. "I did not. I had no intention of doing so."

"Hot anger was in your heart?"

"Why not? I had just seen Michael's plane—I knew that woman had sent for him to take her home in the moonlight. And he, like a fool—"

"It was my job, I tell you," Ireland persisted sullenly.

"And how you hated it, eh? No matter. I thought, 'Let her find her own blanket for that accursed dog.' I was on my way down the back stairs, when

Mr. Ward hurried down after me. He asked about the blanket—I told him frankly I would not get it. 'I wonder where Sing is,' he said, and hastened past."

"And you—"

"Me—I went to the kitchen, where the cook was. I heard Michael risking his life above the house. I waited—I would have a word with him, I thought. The plane landed—and Michael came into the passageway, as I expected. But he was not alone—Mr. Ward and Mr. Chan were with him. I was too unhappy—'I will have no scene here,' I said, so I let him pass. Then I started up the back stairs again—my place was above—and I figured how I would send Sing to bring Michael to me there. But on the stairs—"

"Ah, yes—on the stairs," nodded Charlie.

"I—I paused to weep, Monsieur. I was so very unhappy. I had known from the sound how close Michael had come to the house—reckless, a fool—to impress that woman, with whom he was always infatuated—"

"Bologny," interrupted her husband.

"You were—you know it. But I will say no more of the dead. I wept quietly for a moment, then I dried my eyes and started again up the stairs. It was then I heard the shot—loud, unexpected, clear. That—that is all."

Chan turned to Holt. "The little object, please, which you found embedded in study carpet."

"Oh—oh, yes." The sheriff found it and turned it over. Charlie held it out to the woman. "Have you, by any chance, ever seen this pin before?" he inquired.

She glanced at it. "Never, Monsieur."

Chan showed it to her husband, closely studying his face as he did so. "You—Mr. Ireland. Have you seen it before?"

"Me? No. Why should I?"

Charlie put it in his pocket. "Long routine business," he remarked. "But it comes shortly now to a finish. One person alone remains—"

"I know." Leslie Beaton got up and stood, facing him. Tall, slender and appealing, she seemed at first glance quite helpless and lost. But—thought Chan—a competent look in those deep eyes of hers. Not for nothing had she cared for a spineless, artistic brother; she had learned, meanwhile, to take care of herself.

"I'm awful sorry about this," Don Holt said. And looked it.

"Don't worry," the girl replied. She flashed him a friendly smile. "These things will happen, I imagine, even to the kindest-looking of sheriffs. You will want to know of my actions here to-night, Mr. Chan. I'll be as brief as I can—"

"But you needn't stand," Holt protested. He picked up a large chair in one hand, and tossed it casually into position for her.

"Thank you," she remarked. "Well, Mr. Chan—when we heard the airplane over the lake, I was the first out of this room. I got my brother's overcoat, put it on and ran out to the pier. I went to the end and watched the plane approaching. It was a lovely thing—if I hadn't been—well, like Cecile—a bit unhappy, I could have been terribly thrilled. Doctor Swan appeared presently, and we watched it together. We had—a little chat, and then he went back to the house. I believe he met you just outside. I—I stayed where I was."

"Ah, yes," Chan nodded. "For how long?"

"I watched the airplane circle over the house—"

"You saw Landini on the balcony, perhaps?"

"No—the trees came together there—I couldn't see the study windows.

But I saw Mr. Ireland circling, and then I saw him come down somewhere in the rear. By that time I was thoroughly chilled, so I ran back to the living-room. Hugh and Mr. Dinsdale were here together. I imagined we would be starting back to the Tavern as soon as Ellen had gone, so I ran up the stairs to the bedroom where our wraps were."

"One of the rooms next to the study where Landini died?" Chan suggested.

She shivered slightly, but went on. "Yes—of course. I sat down at the dressing-table to powder my nose—rearrange my hair—when suddenly, in that next room, I heard a shot—"

"One moment," Chan cut in, "pardon so much. But you heard first—what? A struggle?"

"No—nothing."

"But voices, perhaps?"

"Nothing at all, Mr. Chan. You see, there is no door connecting the rooms."

"Ah, I see," Chan replied. "Continue, please."

"Well—I just heard this shot. And—I sat there. I couldn't quite comprehend what had happened. Then I heard people running along the hall, crowding into the study. And I followed them. That's—that's all."

"Alas," Charlie answered. "I wish very much that it were. But—Mr. Holt—that pink scarf—one end of which I see hanging from your pocket—"

"Say—I'm sorry," Holt said. "I'm afraid I've mussed this up something terrible. You know—when I tucked it in there—I hadn't seen you—"

"It's all right, I'm sure," the girl replied.

"It is not all right—pardon me," cried Chan sternly, taking the scarf. "Excuse that I call attention to the fact, but we are not enjoying social hour of tea. This is your scarf, Miss Beaton?"

"As I told you, up-stairs."

"It was found in dead hands of Ellen Landini? How do you account for same?"

"I can not account for it, Mr. Chan."

He took the pin from his pocket. "Have you seen this before?"

"It is mine."

"It is yours. It was found by the dead woman's side."

"It's a little old pin I used to fasten my scarf. When I left the scarf on that bed up-stairs, I just carelessly stuck the pin it it. That's all."

"You are alone in room next to one in which murder occurs. Your scarf and your pin are in dead person's presence. And you can not explain—"

"Perhaps, as my brother said—"

"Your brother made gallant effort to think up explanation. It is not enough, Miss Beaton. I have long experience in these matters, and never before have I encountered evidence so damaging—"

"But—" Suddenly the girl's face was stricken with fear. "Surely you don't think that I—that I could—kill Landini? What motive—"

"What motive?" cried Doctor Swan. "What motive, indeed?"

With one accord, they turned and looked at the doctor.

"I'm sorry, Miss Beaton," he said. "It's rather painful—such a charming girl, too. But under the circumstances, I should be shirking my duty shamefully if I did not recall our little conversation on the pier—what you said—"

"Very well," said the girl in a low voice. "What did I say?"

"Our little conversation about Landini," the doctor continued suavely. "Your last words to me, as I recall, were: 'I hate her! I hate her! I wish she were dead!'"

6
Three O'clock in the Morning

A tense silence followed in that big bright room, broken at last by the collapse of a burning log, which fell into a hundred pieces, sending sparks and embers in all directions. Sing moved forward to attend to it, and at that moment young Hugh Beaton faced Doctor Swan. He was livid with rage; an utterly unexpected transformation seemed to have taken place in the boy.

"You contemptible liar!" he cried hoarsely.

"Just a minute," Swan replied coolly. "It so happens I am telling the truth. Am I not, Miss Beaton?"

The girl's eyes were on the handkerchief which she twisted nervously in her hands. "You are," she said softly.

"So sorry," Charlie began. "But, Miss Beaton, it now becomes necessary for us to know—"

"Yeah—I suppose it does," said the sheriff. "But look here, there's no need of any more of this inquisition in front of everybody. Mr. Ward—is there another room—"

Ward rose. "Yes," he answered. "You may use the dining-room, if you wish. If you'll come with me—"

"That's the idea," Holt approved. "The rest of you stick right here—understand? Now, Miss Beaton—yes, your brother too—and Doctor Swan—you come along with me and the inspector." As they followed Ward, he added to the girl: "I don't aim to make any public show of you. Some things is private."

"You're very kind to me," the girl said.

Ward ushered them into the dining-room, closed the door and disappeared. Doctor Swan was looking rather sheepish.

"Miss Beaton, believe me—I am very sorry that I was faced with such an unpleasant duty," he remarked. "Still—you understand my position—"

"Oh, we understand it, all right," her brother cried hotly. "Try to pin this terrible thing on some one else if you can. Your own situation is pretty shaky. Looking out the window when the shot was fired—enjoying the beautiful snow! Did you carry my sister's scarf into the study? Was it you Landini asked to—"

"Hughie," interrupted his sister, "please be quiet."

"Most admirable suggestion," Chan smiled. "It is Miss Beaton who should be talking now. So sorry, my dear young lady—but why did you cry out that you wished Landini dead?"

The girl sat down in the chair which Don Holt had placed for her near the fire.

"It's quite true," she began. "I did say that. I said I hated too. I did hate her. To explain I have to go back—a long way back—and even then—I doubt if you will quite understand. You don't know what it is to be poor—horribly poor—and to have some one in the family with a great gift, a gift you believe in—to slave and struggle and fight for that person's training and education. That's—that's what happened to us."

"Must you tell all this?" her brother protested.

"I have to, Hughie. You see, we knew very early that Hugh had a voice—and from then on, everything went for that. My father wearing the same old overcoat year after year—my mother going without, scrimping, saving—neither having any fun, any joy in life—just to pay for Hugh's education. New York—and then, Paris—and finally, after years of that sort of thing—Hugh giving a concert here and there, making a little money at last—seemingly on the threshold of a great career. The moment we'd always dreamed about. And then this woman, pouncing on him, threatening to ruin everything—"

"You're wronging her, my dear," said the boy.

"Wronging her! She was fifteen years older than you. Had she any interest in your career? Would she have helped you to success—of course not. We all knew that. You knew it yourself. You said, only the other day—"

"Never mind. She's dead now."

"I know," the girl nodded. "I don't want to say anything—I just want to make clear my feeling about her." She turned to Chan and the sheriff. "It just seemed I couldn't let this marriage happen," she explained. "I mustn't. I came out here to try to stop it if I could. I talked with her—she laughed at me. I became desperate—I wanted to save Hugh from this terrible mistake. He was just a passing fancy with her, I felt. I was furious when she began going around with this Ireland person—"

"Stop it," put in the boy. "There was nothing in that. It was—Ellen's way." He was very white.

"It was not much of a way," the girl replied. "It sickened me. To-night when she called him up, and left us to go home alone—I was furious. Hughie might weakly stand for that sort of thing—"

"Go on," the boy said. "Tell 'em I'm weak—no good—spineless. Tell 'em I always have been. That you've always had to care for me—mother me—"

"Have I said so?" the girl answered gently. "Don't be angry, Hughie. I'm only trying to explain the mood I was in when I went out on that pier. Soon Doctor Swan came out. I'd met him before in Reno. We got to talking about Landini, and I—I went a little wild, I guess. I told him what I thought about her marrying my brother—and as the plane came nearer, I burst into tears, and I—I said I hated her and I wished she was dead. And I did—I did—but I didn't kill her." She was weeping now. "I—I know it looks terrible," she went on. "I was in the next room. My scarf was in her hands, and my pin beside her. Why—how? I don't understand. I can't explain it. Some one—put them there. Some one who must have known how I felt toward her. For what other reason?"

She stopped suddenly, staring at Doctor Swan. Charlie and the sheriff were also looking at the doctor. Landini's third husband felt of his collar nervously, and his face flushed slightly.

"Yeah," nodded Don Holt. "Might be something in that theory, Miss Beaton. Well, we won't detain you in here any longer. I want to say right now, I understand exactly how—"

"Quite true, quite true," Charlie put in. "Yes, Miss Beaton, you may return to other room. But I would falsify facts if I hid from you you are for present moment in dangerous position. Later discoveries may clear same up. With deep sincerity I may say, I hope so." He smiled. "You see, I like the sheriff."

Holt stared at him. "What's that got to do with it?" he wanted to know.

"Another mystery which time, I trust, will solve," Charlie said. "Mr. Sheriff, will you be good enough to remain in this room with me for one moment?"

After the others had gone, Charlie sat down and motioned Holt to a chair near by.

"Well?" said Holt rather gloomily.

"Feel somewhat same way myself," nodded Chan. "Well! A moment's summing up in order now. By this time we have questioned all those who were not present in my vision when the shot was heard. What have we got?"

"Not much, if you ask me," sighed Holt. "Swan and Romano were shut up in their rooms, looking out the windows. Oh, yeah? Cecile was climbing the back stairs, Sing was foraging for a blanket in his room, and Miss Beaton was right next door to the study, powdering her nose. Dog-gone it, I wish she'd been somewhere else. But anyhow, she was there when the shot was fired. And that accounts for the five. What's the answer?"

"Somebody is lying," Chan remarked.

"Sure—somebody is certainly lying. But which one? Romano?"

Charlie considered. "Romano had the money from her purse. Did she, then, give it to him? Or did he slip in to protest matter of settlement, lose temper, kill her, and himself remove money? Possible. No alibi."

"That fellow Swan," mused Holt. "I don't like him."

Charlie shook his head. "Again—please maintain neutral attitude. But—Swan—I can not say I admire his looks myself. Did he kill the lady? Possible. No alibi."

"Cecile had a mighty good motive," the sheriff reflected.

"So far—absolutely nothing connects Cecile with murder," Charlie reminded him. "And yet, she is quite possible selection. She has no—" He paused, and a slow smile spread over his face. "Note the peculiar situation," he added. "Perhaps not so strange to you, but to me, with my experience, up to this minute unheard of. Five people not accounted for at time of shooting, and of the five not one has even offered alibi. I wonder—"

"What?" inquired Holt eagerly.

Chan shrugged. "No matter. It lightens work—we have no alibis to investigate. But it also adds heaviness—we have, alas, five healthy suspects. I have kept you here to remind you of one thing—we are near state line. It is your duty to see that no one of five departs across that line to-night."

"I know. I suppose there'll be an argument. Perhaps we could put some of them up at the Tavern."

"It is very late," Chan replied. "Romano, Cecile and Sing remain here naturally. You must persuade the good doctor and Miss Beaton to do the same—for to-night at least. There are plenty rooms. I will be responsible."

"Suppose one of them slips out in the night," suggested Holt.

"Only the thief oils his wheelbarrow," Chan said, as they rose. "And only the guilty flee. It would be a happy solution. I shall be sitting just inside my door all night. I shall try not to take nap—but I can not guarantee. For I now realize suddenly that I have been napping all evening."

"How so?" Holt inquired.

"There were six, not five, unaccounted for at time of shot."

"Six?" Holt cried. "Good lord—another one. Who?"

"I forgot the cook," Chan explained. "Most impolite of me—for she is very good cook. Perhaps very good witness, too. If you will arrange matter of overnight stay, I will visit kitchen. You might join me there, when able."

"Sure," said Holt. He paused. "I suppose I may as well let Ireland go back to Reno?"

"Why not?" Chan shrugged. "He could have had nothing to do with killing. Yes, Ireland, Dinsdale and young Beaton, if he wishes—these may go."

Separating from Holt, he followed the passageway toward the rear until he came to the kitchen door. Looking in, a homey scene greeted him. Beside an old-fashioned kitchen range, in a large easy chair, sat the ample figure of the cook, sound asleep. At her feet, on a bit of old carpet, lay Trouble, the dog, also mercifully slumbering. Chan smiled and moved on to the back steps.

For a time he walked about outside, using a flashlight he had obtained from his luggage when he went for the finger-print paraphernalia. He studied the path which led to the hangar, but the snow on that was packed hard, and no clear footprints were discernible. The lights on the field were still blazing, and Michael Ireland's plane stood like an actor in a spotlight.

The examination yielded him nothing, and he paused for a moment, staring at the clear beauty of the distant mountains, then went inside. Holt was standing beside the kitchen door.

"Sleeping, eh?" he said, nodding toward the cook.

"The slumber of innocence," Chan smiled. "Matters are now arranged for the night?"

Holt nodded. "All set. Swan put up a battle—got to get back to Reno—lot of appointments early in the morning. But he's staying all right—that bird's not putting anything over on me. I don't like—oh, yes, lesson number one. Anyhow, I hate the sight of him. Miss Beaton is staying—Cecile's fixing her up with the necessary feminine doodads. Her brother has decided to put up here for the night, too."

"We shall be a large party," Chan answered.

The cook was stirring in her chair, and the two stepped into the kitchen.

"So sorry to disturb you," Charlie apologized.

"Sure, I should be in me bed," the woman answered. "Why am I here—oh, yes—the poor lady. I was afther forgettin'—"

"Let me explain, Mrs.—" Holt began.

"O'Ferrell," she added.

"Mrs. O'Ferrell. I am Don Holt, sheriff of the county."

"God have mercy on us," she cried.

"And this is Inspector Chan, of the Honolulu Police."

"Honolulu, eh? Sure, he got here quick."

Charlie smiled. "Honored, if I may say so. Earlier this evening I had great pleasure to sample your cooking, and I bow to you in humble congratulation."

"You talk very nice," she responded, pleased.

"But sterner topics now engage us," he continued. "You are evidently aware of what happened a short time ago?"

"Murder," she said. "I am. I don't hold with it."

"We none of us hold with it," he assured her. "That is why we seek the murderer. It becomes necessary to ask a few questions, which I know you will answer gladly."

"I will that. I'll not be at peace in this house, with a murderer havin' the run of it. But I'm afraid I can't help ye much. I been busy in this room all evenin', for a dinner like that is no joke, nor is washin' dishes afther a picnic, ayether. I'm supposed to have the help of Sing, but like a will-o'-the wisp he's been this night, now here, now gone."

"He's been in and out occasionally, however?"

"In an' out is right."

"Well, Mrs. O'Ferrell, let us take it from the time you heard the airplane. Where was the plane when you first heard it?"

"I couldn't tell you that exactly, Mr. Chan, but it must have been some distance off, over the lake, ye might say. I heared it buzzin', an' I thinks, now what can that be, an' thin Cecile—no, wait a minute—thin Mr. Ward himself stops in that door, an' asks me have I seen Sing. I says I think Sing is on the back porch, an' Mr. Ward is hardly gone, whin Cecile comes in mad as a hornet, with somethin' about her husband, an' a blanket, an' this opera singer, an' what-not. An' thin the plane comes over th' house, an' from that minute I have me hands full, what with Cecile ravin' and this poor lamb at me feet"—she indicated the dog—"scared near out of his wits be the noise."

"Ah—Trouble was frightened by the plane?"

"He was that, sir, an' no mistake, cryin' an' whinin' an' carryin' on until I had to take him on me lap, an' comfort him, an' him tremblin' all over like gelatine."

"And Cecile—"

"Cecile wint out in th' passage, like she was waitin' f'r some one. I see Mr. Ward an' you an' the leather man come in, but I didn't hear anny talk from Cecile. I was too busy with th' dog to come to th' door. Look at him, th' poor little orphan, sleepin' there so peaceful an' not knowin' his loss."

Chan smiled. "We will leave him in your care for the present, Mrs. O'Ferrell, and I'm sure he could not be in kinder hands. That is all. I suggest you retire for the night."

"Thank ye kindly, sir, but I'll not rest in me bed until this wild murderer is caught. Ye'll move as fast as ye can, I hope."

Charlie shook his head. "We must collect at leisure what we may use in haste," he explained. "The fool in a hurry drinks his tea with a fork." He and Holt went into the passage. At the foot of the back stairs, Holt stopped. "A lot we got out of that," he remarked glumly.

"You think so?" Chan asked.

The sheriff looked at him suddenly. "We didn't get anything, did we?"

Charlie shrugged. "He who fishes in muddy waters can not tell the great catch from the small."

"Yeah. I guess this is the back stairway, isn't it? I told that doctor to wait for me up-stairs—he'll think I've forgot him. Let's go up."

They found the doctor in the study, his work evidently completed, his bag closed on the desk, and himself with professional calm seated by the fire. He rose as they entered.

"Well," he said, when he had been introduced to Chan, "I've made the examination, although the coroner, of course, will want to make another in the morning. Poor Landini—I knew her as a young bride in this house, and she comes back to it to die. Um—er—that is, of course, beside the point. Nothing much to be said. The bullet entered about four inches below the shoulder, and pursued, I believe, a downward course. Perhaps the person who fired it was standing over her, and she was on her knees." He looked at Chan.

"Perhaps," Chan said. He seemed very sleepy, and not overly keen. The doctor turned to Holt.

"We can tell more about that to-morrow," he continued. "The caliber of the gun—that must wait until to-morrow, also."

Holt held out the small pearl-handled revolver. "We've found this," he said.

"One thing, Doctor," Charlie remarked. "Was death, in your opinion, instantaneous? Or could the lady have taken a step or two after the wound?"

The doctor considered. "I can tell you better after we have probed for the bullet," he said. "At present, all I can say is—there is a chance that she did move after the shot. But you must understand—"

He was interrupted by the loud whirring of an airplane engine, and then the steady drone of it moving off, evidently away from the house.

"It's Ireland," said the sheriff to Charlie. "I told him he could go."

"Naturally," nodded Chan. He stepped on to the balcony and watched the plane as it moved out over the sapphire lake. Much had happened, he reflected, since that machine had first been sighted in the still night sky.

"I'd like to be getting along," the doctor was saying. "I had a hard night last night."

"Sure," said Holt. "We can take this poor lady with us, I guess. I phoned Gus Elkins to wait up for us. We'll need some blankets, won't we? I hope everybody's out of that room down-stairs—especially the women—"

Charlie took up his lampblack and brush from the desk. "While you busy yourself with unhappy task," he said, "I will make superficial investigation of room next door—that old sitting room of Ellen Landini's—through which her slayer must have left the scene. Kindly visit me there before taking departure for the night."

"I'll do that," Holt promised.

Some fifteen minutes later he pushed open the door of the room in question. Chan was standing in the center of it, all the lights, both on the walls and in the ceiling, were blazing. The atmosphere of the place was faintly out-of-date, for the furnishings were those of twenty years before, though probably this made no impression on Holt.

"What luck?" the young man inquired.

"A little," Charlie shrugged.

Holt went over and examined the catch fastening the windows that opened on to the balcony. "Any prints on this?" he asked.

"None whatever," Chan answered. "There are also no prints on door-knob, either side."

"But there should be—shouldn't there?" Holt inquired. "I mean—if everything was O.K.?"

"There should be dozens," Charlie admitted. "But alas—too many people read detective stories now—get finger-print complex. All have been rubbed away."

"Then Landini's murderer did come this way," Holt mused. "And probably went this way to reach her, too. Leaving the window unlocked so he could return through it."

Chan nodded. "You are learning fast. Pretty soon, your instructor must take lessons from you. Yes—the firing of that pistol must have been pre-meditated. Otherwise, the killer could not have come through here without smashing glass in the window."

"Anything else to make you think he—"

"Or she," suggested Chan.

"Or she, escaped through this room?"

Chan pointed. There was a dressing-table against one wall of the room, and overturned on the floor in front of it was a heavy bench.

"Some one came, hurrying in the dark," he said. "Knee met sharp edge of plenty solid bench, which is turned on side. Maybe somebody have pretty sore knee."

Holt nodded. "I hope so. Even if a bad infection sets in, it will be all right with me. This room doesn't connect with any other, does it?"

"No—that is closet door over there," Chan told him.

"Well, I'd better be getting alone," Holt said. "I'll be up early in the morning, of course. Poor Landini is in my launch, and the doctor has already taken his boat and gone. He was a candidate for coroner himself last election, and lost out, so he's not very keen about this job."

They went down-stairs, through the living-room, which was now deserted. Chan stepped outside, and walked toward the pier with his new-found friend.

"I'm certainly glad to have you on this job with me," Holt remarked. "It just looks hopeless. I can't see any light ahead."

"Be cheerful," urged Charlie. "When the melon is ripe, it will fall of itself. I have always found it so."

"Have you got any clue?" asked the boy.

"Clue?" Chan smiled. "I have so many clues, I would sell some very cheaply. Yes," he mused, "if I was complaining man, and were asked for complaint against this case, I would say, bitterly, too many clues. Pointing all ways at once."

"I'll have to take your word for it," Holt sighed.

"But long experience shows," added Chan briskly. "That in time clues fall into place, false ones fade and wither, true ones cluster together in one unerring signboard. I may say I am interested in this case. Unusual event has roused itself and occurred here to-night, and one unusual clue may point our final path.—But I anticipate." They had come to the pier. Charlie held out his hand. "Good night. I enjoy knowing you, if you permit my saying so. I enjoy knowing cool fresh country like this. I am plenty happy."

"Fine," said Holt. "Let's all be happy. See you to-morrow, Mr. Chan."

"Just one matter." Charlie laid a hand on his arm.

"What's that?"

"The bullet for which they probe in the morning—get it, and guard it well. It must on no account be lost."

"I'll hang on to it," Holt promised, and ran down the pier to his launch.

Charlie came back to the living-room to find Dudley Ward waiting there.

"Ah, Mr. Chan," he said. "I fancy you're the last of my guests to retire."

"I will do so at once," Charlie assured him. "So sorry to delay your own rest."

"Not at all," Ward answered. He sank into a chair. "But I am rather weary, at that. Poor Ellen—I shall never forgive myself for inviting her here. However, I was so anxious—about my boy."

"How natural," Chan said.

"I am more anxious than ever, now," Ward continued. "I hope, in the terrible excitement of to-night, you won't forget why you have come here, Inspector. You must, of course, find who killed Landini if you can—but you must also find my boy. He needs me more than ever—with Landini gone."

"I am not forgetting same," Chan nodded.

"You heard what Ireland said about Doctor Swan's having blackmailed poor Ellen," Ward went on. "Did it occur to you that he might have known about the boy, and been threatening to tell me of him?"

"It did," Chan nodded gravely.

"Of course, he denied at dinner that he had ever heard of the child—"

"He was lying," Charlie said firmly.

"You thought so?" Ward inquired.

"I was certain of it. Just as I was sure Romano was lying when he said he had."

"Well, I am glad to have such expert confirmation of my own opinion," Ward went on. "I went to Swan's room a moment ago to loan him some things—and I told him what I thought. I pleaded with him, if he knew anything of the boy, to tell me about him. He still denied any knowledge."

"Still lying," Chan suggested.

"I think so," Ward agreed. "Well, we must look elsewhere, perhaps. But as a last resort, we must not forget Doctor Swan."

"I shall not forget him," Chan promised. "And now—if you don't mind—I will go to my room."

"Ah, yes," said Ward, rising. "You know where it is. I have just remembered that I forgot to turn off the lights on the landing field. I must send Sing to attend to that—then perhaps I can retire for the night myself."

Charlie had been in his room but a few minutes, when Ward knocked on his door. "Just to say you must let Sing or me know if you want anything," he remarked. "Good night, Inspector."

"Good night, Mr. Ward," Chan said.

There was, he noted, plenty of wood in the basket beside his fireplace. That would come in handy, if he was to keep his promise to Don Holt and sit up through the night. A rather silly promise, he reflected, as he began to undress. No one of these people would be so foolish as to attempt escape.

Nevertheless, he changed to pajamas, dressing-gown and slippers, put another log on the fire, opened his door a few inches and sat down in a comfortable chair just inside it. He looked at his wrist-watch. One thirty. All was quiet in the hall outside, save for the sounds that afflict an ancient wooden house on a frosty night. Crackings, creakings, moanings. But the human company, Chan knew, were in their beds.

He settled more deeply into his upholstered chair, to think about this case upon which he was so unexpectedly engaged. Pictures flashed through his mind—the calm lake under the stars—Dudley Ward greeting his fellow-husbands on the pier—Landini lively and vivacious on the stairs, holding aloft the dog, Trouble— Ireland circling the house in his plane—Landini lying on the study carpet—promised to sing for him some day—never would sing for him now—never—

Chan sat up with a start. He looked at his wrist-watch. Ten minutes to three. Too comfortable, that chair. But what had startled him?—ah, now he knew. A groan—a faint groan from somewhere outside his door. Not the groan of an old house in the night, but of a human being in pain.

Charlie slipped out into the hall, which was in utter darkness. Feeling his way along the wall, still somewhat confused by sleep, he approached the head of the stairs. His foot encountered some soft object on the floor.

Then at last he remembered his flash-light, and removed it from the pocket of his dressing-gown. Its glare fell on a supine figure at his feet—then on the face—the lined yellow face of Ah Sing.

The old man groaned again, and raising one thin hand, rubbed his even thinner jaw.

"No can do," he protested feebly. "No can do."

7

The Blind Man's Eyes

For a moment Chan stood looking down at the crumpled figure of Ah Sing, and a wave of pity for this loyal servant who had been with the house of Ward so many years swept through him. He bent over solicitously. "What has happened here?" he asked. Gently he shook the old man. "Who has done this thing to you?"

Sing opened his eyes, sighed and closed them again.

Rising, Charlie found the switch on the wall with his flash, and turned on the light in the upper hall. He surveyed the many doors. With the exception of his own, all were closed; they seemed blind, uninterested, secretive. He walked down the hall and knocked softly on the door of Dudley Ward's room.

Presently it opened and Ward appeared, a weary gray-haired man in pajamas, looking older than Chan had thought him.

"Mr. Chan!" he exclaimed. "Is anything wrong?"

"There has been," Chan explained, "an accident."

"An accident! Good lord! What now!" Ward ran into the hall and, seeing Sing, went with Charlie toward the recumbent figure.

"I find your servant unconscious from blow in face."

"A blow! Who the devil—"

At sound of the familiar voice, the old man sat up. He looked his master over disapprovingly.

"What's mallah you?" he demanded. "You clazy? You walk loun' heah no bathlobe, no slippahs, you catch 'um plenty col'. You mebbe die."

"Never mind that," Ward said. "Who hit you, Sing?"

Sing shrugged. "How my know? Plenty big man, mebbe. Plenty big fist. Jus' hide in dahk an' hit me. Tha's all."

"You didn't see him?"

"How my do that?" He struggled to get to his feet, and Charlie helped him. "No light nowheh." With a groan he pushed Chan aside, and tottered unsteadily into Ward's room. In a moment he returned with bathrobe and slippers. "Heah, Boss—you lissen to Sing. You go loun' like clazy man, you catch 'um all kin' col'."

Ward sighed and submitted meekly to the additions to his costume. "Very well," he said. "But what were you doing down here, anyhow?"

"What my always do?" Sing queried in a complaining voice. "Woik, woik, all time woik. Wake up, take look-see clock, think mebbe moah bettah my go down cellah fix fiah. People all ovah house, too many people, they wake up say too col'." He viewed his master as one who had been meaning to speak of this matter for some time. "Too much woik this house. Nevah no stop. Too much fo' me. No can do. No can do."

"He's been talking like that for fifty years," Ward explained to Chan, "and I have to battle him tooth and nail to get another servant on to the place. God knows I don't want him to get up at three in the morning and fix the furnace. Well"—he turned to Sing—"did you fix it?"

"My fix 'um," nodded the old man. "Put new logs down-steh, too. Then came up heah, fist come out f'om dahk, catch 'um my jaw. Tha's all."

Charlie patted him on the back. "You go to bed now," he suggested. "Too many people in this house—you have spoken truly there. Not very nice people, some of them. Aged men should not consort with ruffians. Eggs should not dance with stones."

"Goo' night," replied Sing, and departed.

Chan turned to his host. "I note you are shivering," he said. "Kindly step into my room for a moment. I have maintained my fire, which you will find welcome, I think." He led the way and indicated a chair. "Who, I would ask, has perpetrated this latest outrage?"

Ward sat down, and stared into the fire. "Don't ask me, please," he said wearily. "I'd like to get my hands on him, whoever he is. A harmless old man like Sing—but good lord—I'm all at sea."

"I am inclined to wonder," Chan mused. "In a way, the sheriff left me in charge here to-night. Can it be that one of my birds has flown? With your permission, I intend to make a brief survey."

"Maybe you'd better," Ward nodded.

"The rooms of Romano, Ryder and Swan I know," Charlie continued. "I will also, I think, investigate that of young Hugh Beaton, if you will acquaint me with his door."

Ward did so, and Chan went out. In less than ten minutes he returned.

"The loss of one night's sleep means ten days of discomfort," he smiled. "Happy to say none of the gentlemen we mentioned faces such a fate. I opened the door of each, flashed light on bed. One and all they appeared to slumber."

"Well—that gets us nowhere," Ward remarked.

"As far as I expected," Charlie replied. "Yes, they slumbered—and not one faced the door. The long arm of coincidence, I believe it is called. Speaking for myself, I was plenty glad to find them here at all, asleep or otherwise."

Ward rose. "I may as well go back to bed, I fancy. It is not easy for me to sleep to-night, Inspector. Ellen dead—in this old house where I had expected to spend a happy life with her. And to-morrow we must go over to Reno and look into her affairs." He laid his hand on Chan's arm. "I'm afraid," he added.

"Afraid?" Chan asked.

"Yes. Suppose—I have a son. A boy who has never heard of me—never seen me. It came to me to-night—after I went to bed. What will I mean to him? Less than nothing. Love—affection—never, under those conditions. Too late, Mr. Chan. Always too late, for me."

"Go back and seek for sleep, at least," Charlie said gently. "As for the future—when you have reached the river, then is the time to take off your shoes."

After Ward had gone, Charlie put fresh logs on the fire and sat down—in front of it this time, but with his door open. He was thoroughly awake now, and four o'clock in the morning is an excellent time to think. What was behind this unprovoked attack on Sing? Or was it unprovoked? Did Sing know who it was that had struck him? If so—why should he hide it? Fear, no doubt, fear of the white man inspired in the old Chinese of mining-camp days by years of rough treatment and oppression.

A clue. Charlie eagerly searched his mind for a clue. "No can do," he old man had muttered, semiconscious on the floor. But that was probably just the refrain that ran through all his days: "Too much woik this house. No can do." The complaint under which he hid his real devotion.

Chan sighed. It was too early, he decided, to place this attack in the scheme of things, too early to come to any real decision regarding the murder of Landini. For the present, the mere marshaling of facts must suffice, and so he sat and marshaled them in that mind which he had called "large, empty place that makes good storehouse." He marshaled them while the chill dawn crept across the lake, and somewhere behind the snow-capped peaks a yellow sun was rising. Doors began to slam, the voice of Mrs. O'Ferrell was heard in the land, and from the distant kitchen came, faintly, the bark of a dog.

While Chan bathed and shaved, His mind was filled with trouble. Trouble, the dog.

When finally Charlie was ready to go down-stairs, the sun was on the lake, and a prospect of breath-taking beauty was spread before him. He opened his window and leaned far out enjoying the cool, fresh, bracing mountain air. In the darkness of the night he had had his doubts, but now he felt he could conquer the world. Problems, puzzles—he welcomed them.

He walked, with his chest well out, through the chilly hall and down the stairs. The delicious odor of bacon and coffee floated about him. He knew he would enjoy his breakfast, even though, at the same table, sat the murderer of Ellen Landini.

Reaching that table, he found Ward, Ryder and Swan already there. They greeted him with varying degrees of cordiality. At Chan's heels came Romano, his sartorial elegance a bit cheapened by the clean light of day. Scarcely had he and Charlie sat down when Leslie Beaton appeared, and all the men rose.

"Ah, Miss Beaton," said Ward, "So happy to have you here. And looking, if I may say so, as fresh and beautiful as the morning."

"I thought I'd have to appear in an evening gown," she smiled. "But Cecile saved the situation. She's really a brick." She turned upon her heel for inspection. "What do you think of it?"

She was referring to the morning frock in which she was garbed. Evidently it met with their approval.

"I think it's cute," the girl went on. "But why shouldn' it be? Cecile is French. Of course, there's not enough of me to fill it, quite. But I'm so hungry, I'm sure there will be—after breakfast." When she was seated, she looked suddenly at Chan. "I'll simply have to go over to Reno today and get my things—"

"That," said Charlie, "depends on the sheriff. Do not, I beg of you, squander such a charming smile on me."

"Oh, I have others," she assured him. "Plenty for the sheriff, too." For the first time, the shadow of the night before crossed her face. "Must—must we really stay here?"

"Come, come," said Ward with forced gaiety. "That's not exactly complimentary to me. And I'm trying so hard to be the perfect host."

"Succeeding, too," the girl replied. "But the conditions—they are unusual. One can't help feeling that underneath you may be—for all your kindness—an unwilling host."

"Never—to you," Ward murmured. And as Sing appeared at his elbow, he added: "What fruit will you have? We have all kinds—of oranges."

"I'll have the nicest kind," said the girl. "Good morning, Sing. Why—the poor man! He's hurt his face."

Chan had already noted that the left jaw of the servant was swollen and discolored. Sing shrugged his shoulders and departed.

"Sh," said Ward. "He's had an accident. We won't say anything about it—he's rather sensitive, you know."

"He's limping, too," the girl went on.

"It was rather a bad accident," Ward explained. "He fell on the stairs, you see."

"Poor Sing's getting old," Ryder remarked. "I was noticing it last night. He doesn't see very well. Shouldn't he have glasses, Dudley?"

Ward grimaced. "Of course he should—and has. Or had, rather. But he broke them about a month ago—and you know how stubborn he is. I've been pleading with him ever since to get them fixed—by George, I'll take them over to Reno with me this morning. An optician over there has his prescription."

Hugh Beaton came in, glum and in the mood of genius at breakfast. The repast continued, to the accompaniment of a conversation that was surprisingly cheerful, all things considered.

But in this Charlie took no part. He had several new facts to marshal in the storehouse of his mind. So Sing was limping this morning? It seemed impossible he could have hurt his leg in the fall that resulted from an encounter with an unknown fist. He had given no indication of such an injury at the time. And—there was the overturned dressing-table bench in the old sitting-room next to the study up-stairs.

And Sing needed glasses. Usually wore them, in fact. Well, that fitted in, too. The confusion of the box lids. For a moment Charlie's appetite lost some of its keenness. But no—too early yet, he decided. Get all the facts in mind. Wait until you reach the river before you start to unlace your shoes.

After breakfast, Charlie visited the kitchen for a brief call on Mrs. O'Ferrell and Trouble. He spoke enthusiastically of the former's coffee—so much so she never dreamed that he greatly preferred tea. The dog romped in a friendly fashion at his feet.

"Look at him—the little darlin'," Mrs. O'Ferrell remarked. "Sure, I've only knowed him a few hours, an' he's like an old friend."

Charlie picked up the dog and stroked it musingly. "I have known him but a brief time myself," he said, "and yet I have for him a deep affection."

"I been thinkin'," the cook continued. "If no wan else wants him, couldn't you leave him here, Mr. Chan? What with the lady gone, an' no wan to take care iv him—"

"As to that," Chan replied, "I can not say. I can only tell you that at least once—Trouble must go back to Reno." He put the dog on the floor, gave it a final pat and moved to the door. "Yes," he repeated firmly. "Trouble must make that journey to Reno. And he must make it—by airplane."

Leaving Mrs. O'Ferrell deeply mystified by this cryptic statement, he returned to the big living-room. Most of the guests were there, and in the center of the room stood Don Holt, the sheriff. Beside him was a man who would have been a figure of distinction in any company, tall, erect, with snow-white hair. Chan's heart was touched as he noted the sightless eyes.

"Morning, Mr. Chan," cried Don Holt. "Great day, ain't it? I brought my Dad along—want you to know him. Father— Inspector Chan, of Honolulu."

Chan took the groping hand in his. "To meet an old-time sheriff of the mining camps," he said. "An honor I have always longed for, but never dreamed should encounter."

"Old-time is right, Inspector," replied Sam Holt, with a grim smile. "And the old times—they don't come back. I sure am glad that you're on hand to give my boy a lift."

"I am plenty happy, too," Chan assured him.

"Well, we're all ready for business, I reckon," Don Holt said. "Miss Beaton here has just been telling me that she's got to go to Reno to get her toothbrush—and—and—I said I guessed we'd better let you decide."

Charlie smiled. "A diplomatic reply. You put all the young lady's disfavor on me."

"Then you don't think—"

"There were, you recall," Chan continued, "five—no, six—people not in view at a certain fatal moment last night. None of the six must cross state line—"

Swan pushed forward. "What about me? I've got a dozen appointments to-day. And not so much as a clean collar on this side of the line."

"What a pity," Chan shrugged. "Give us a list of what you desire from your residence—and the location of same. Also—if you so desire—the key." Swan hesitated. "We go there in any case," Chan added meaningly.

"Oh, very well," Swan agreed.

"Say—that's an idea," young Holt said. "Miss Beaton—if you'll give me a list—"

"Not quite the same," she smiled.

"Well—ah—er—maybe not, come to think of it," he admitted, suddenly embarrassed.

"We will take Miss Beaton's brother with us," Chan suggested. "He may be given the list."

"That's a fine idea," Holt cried. The girl shrugged and turned away. "Now"—the young sheriff turned to Chan—"before we go, I guess we better have a talk. Up-stairs—what do you say?"

Ah Sing suddenly appeared from the dining-room. He stood for a moment, staring at Sam Holt, then hurried over and grasped the old man's hand.

"Hello, Shef," he cried. "Haply see you."

"Hello, Sing," Sam Holt answered. "I'm happy to—er—to see you, too. But I ain't sheriff no more. Things change, boy. We're old men now."

"You go on being shef fo' me," Sing insisted. "Always shef fo' me."

On the handsome face of Sam Holt appeared an expression that was a mixture of regret and resignation. He patted his ancient friend on the back affectionately, then put his arm about the other's shoulder.

"Take me up-stairs, boy," he said. "I want to see that there study. Used to know my way about this house so well—I could travel it in—in the dark. But now—I sort of forgit. Lead the way, Sing."

With loving solicitude the servant helped him up the stairs, and his son and Charlie followed. When they all reached the study, Sam Holt turned to Sing.

"More better you run along now," he remarked. "I see you later. Wait a minute. You catch 'um Dudley Ward—tell him Sam Holt's up here."

Sing departed, and the old man began to move slowly, feeling his way about the room. His son stepped forward to assist him. "This is the desk, Dad," he said. "Where we found the loose tobacco—and the boxes with the jumbled cigarettes." He added aside to Chan: "I've been all over the case with him this morning."

"An excellent course," nodded Charlie heartily.

"And here," the boy went on, "these are the windows, Dad."

"There used to be a balcony out there."

"There still is. That was one of the last places Landini was seen alive. By the aviator, you know."

"Oh, yes—by the aviator. But Sing—Sing saw her last?"

"Yes—when she sent him to bring the blanket."

"Needn't go all over it again," his father objected. "My memory's as good as yours, I reckon. Give me a chair, son." He sat down in a velvet-covered chair before the fire. "Poor Ellen Landini. Mighty curious, Mr. Chan, that she had to come way back to this house to hand in her chips. Knew her, long ago. Beautiful. Beautiful girl. Somebody's comin' down the hall."

Dudley Ward appeared in the doorway and greeted the old sheriff cordially.

"Jes' wanted to pay my respects, Dudley," Sam Holt said. "Tell you I'm sorry about—all this. Poor Ellen—I was jes' sayin'. Kyards always seemed stacked against her, somehow. You too, boy, you too." He lowered his voice. "Don was tellin' me that story—mebbe a son—a kid somewhere—"

"Maybe," Ward said.

"Who knew about that, Dudley?" the old man continued. "Of course, Mr. Chan—and that other three—Swan, Romano, Ryder? And Sing, I reckon. Of course, you'd tell Sing. But who else?"

"Why—nobody, Sam. Just this woman—this Cecile. The woman who told me the story first."

"Nobody else, boy?"

"Not that I know of."

"Well—'taint important. Don tells me you're all goin' off to Reno—you run along an' git ready. Don't let me keep you."

When Ward had gone, Don Holt got up and shut the door. "Anything happen last night?" he inquired of Charlie.

Quickly Chan reported the assault on Sing. Both men received the account with rising indignation. Charlie ended with the information that Sing was limping this morning.

"Oh, yes—that bench in the next room," Don Holt said. "Still— maybe that's not the tie-up. Might have cracked it when this guy hit him and he fell. No—Sing's got nothing to do with this—we can bank on that. I ain't going to waste any time on Sing."

Sam Holt was idly plucking with his thin old hand at the arm of his chair. "Ain't it about time Cash Shannon showed up, son?" he inquired.

"Ought to be," the boy agreed. "Cash is a cowboy down at the stables," he explained to Charlie, "and a deputy of mine. I'm havin' him up here to-day to keep an eye on things while we're all away. I'll go down an' see if he's got here yet."

"Shet the door when you go out," Sam Holt suggested. When he heard it close, he said: "Mr. Chan, I'm sure glad you're with us on this case. I reckon, from what Don tells me about ye, you an' me would sort of think along the same lines. I ain't never had no use for science—the world was gittin' along a whole lot better before science was discovered."

Charlie smiled. "You mean finger-prints, laboratory tests, blood analysis—all that. I agree, Mr. Holt. In my investigations of murder I have thought, always, of the human heart. What passions have been at work—hate, greed, envy, jealousy? I study always —people."

"Always people—you said it, Mr. Chan. The human heart."

"Yes—though even there, one meets difficulties. As a philosopher of my race has said: 'The fishes, though deep in the water, may be hooked; the birds, though high in the air, may be shot; but man's heart only is out of our reach.'"

Sam Holt shook his head. "Mighty purty language, that is, but man's heart ain't always out of our reach. If it was, you an' me wouldn't of made no record on our jobs, Mr. Chan."

"Your statement has truth," Chan nodded.

For a long time the former sheriff of the mining camps did not speak. His sightless eyes were turned toward the fire, but his hands were busy. He seemed to be gathering some invisible substance from the arm of his chair with his right hand, and depositing it in his left.

"Mr. Chan," he said suddenly, "how close kin you git to the heart of Ah Sing?"

"It overwhelms me with sadness to admit it," Charlie answered, "for he is of my own origin, my own race, as you know. But when I look into his eyes I discover that a gulf like the heaving Pacific lies between us. Why? Because he, though among Caucasians many more years than I, still remains Chinese. As Chinese to-day as in the first moon of his existence. While I—I bear the brand—the label—Americanized."

Holt nodded. "You've stated the case. These old Chinese in this stretch of the state ain't never been anything else. Maybe they didn't admire the ways of the stranger—I dunno. Which I wouldn't of blamed 'em. But they was born Chinese, an' they stayed that way."

Chan bowed his head. "I traveled with the current," he said softly. "I was ambitious. I sought success. For what I have won, I paid the price. Am I an American? No. Am I, then, a Chinese? Not in the eyes of Ah Sing." He paused for a moment, then continued: "But I have chosen my path, and I must follow it. You are sitting there as one about to tell me something."

"I'm sitting here wondering," Sam Holt replied. "Can I make you understand what Ah Sing's been to me—a friend fer fifty years? I used to take the Ward boys an' him camping, up where it's really high. We used to lay out under the stars—why, I'd ruther cut out my tongue—than say a word—but duty's duty—an' this is my boy's first big case—" He stopped, and held something out to Chan. "Mr. Chan—what is this I been pulling from the arm of my chair?"

"It is light, airy fuzz," Chan told him. "Sort of fuzz readily yielded by wool blanket in contact with velvet."

"And the color, man—the color?"

"It—it appears to be blue."

"Blue. Landini sent Sing fer a blanket. He came back with it after you found the body. Came back with—a blue blanket. You sent him away with it. Yes, Don was tellin' me. He took it and went out—he never laid it down?"

"That is quite true," said Chan gravely.

"He never laid it down—that time," the old sheriff continued, his voice trembling, "but—God help me—that blanket had been in this room before."

Neither spoke. Chan regarded the old man with silent admiration.

Sam Holt rose, and began to stumble about the room. He found an unobstructed path, and started to pace it.

"It's all clear. Mr. Chan. He was sent fer that blanket—he came back with it—Landini was here alone—he threw the blanket over that chair—he shot Landini with her own revolver. Then he snatched up the blanket, tidied up that desk, went through the room next door—open because he'd planned it all—and when the stage was clear, walked calm-like on to the scene with the blanket he'd been sent fer. As simple as that. And do I have to tell you why he killed her, Mr. Chan?"

Charlie had listened to this with growing conviction. Now his eyes narrowed. "I was wondering why you asked Dudley Ward whether or not Sing knew about the child. You did it most adroitly."

"The kid," said old Sam Holt. "The kid—there's our answer." He offered Charlie the collection of fuzz. "Put it in an envelope, please. We'll compare it with that blanket later—but it ain't really necessary. Yes, Mr. Chan—that lost boy of Dudley Ward's was the first thing I thought of when Don told me the story of the murder." He stumbled back to his chair and dropped into it.

"You see, sir, I knew the way of these old Chinese servants with the boys of the family. They love 'em. Year after year I seen old Sing cookin' an' slavin' fer Dudley Ward an' his brother—takin' care of 'em since they left the cradle—lovin' an' scoldin' 'm an' treatin' 'em always like babies. An' I knew what it must have meant to Sing that they was no little boys in this house, or in the big house down in 'Frisco. Jes' loneliness in the kitchen, no kids beggin' fer rice an' gravy. An' then he hears that there was a kid—only Landini kept it dark—never let its father know—never brought it out here where it belonged. He hears that, Mr. Chan, an' what happens? He sees red. He hates. He hates Ellen Landini—an' I kain't say I blame him.

"Even Dudley Ward doesn't suspect what's in the old man's heart. He invites Landini over here. An' Sing gits his chance. Yes, Mr. Chan—it was Sing who came into this room last night an' killed Landini—an' I would ruther be hung myself than say it."

"I have somewhat similar feeling," Charlie admitted.

"But you reckon I'm right."

Chan glanced toward the envelope into which he had put the wool from the blue blanket. "I very much fear you are."

The door opened, and Don Holt entered. "Come along," he said. "Cash is here, an' we're off to Reno. Why—what you two looking so solemn about?"

"Shet the door, son," said Sam Holt. He rose and moved toward his boy. "You know what I said to you this morning—about Sing?"

"Oh, but you're all wrong, Dad," the boy assured him.

"Jest a minute. You know how Sing appeared in this room right after the murder, with a blue blanket under his arm?"

"Sure I do."

"Well—if I was to tell you I found blue fuzz from a blanket on the arm of that thar chair over there—what would you say? You'd say the blanket had been in this room before Sing appeared with it, wouldn't you?"

Don Holt considered. "I might," he admitted. "And then again—I might say that it had come back here later—after the murder."

"What do you mean by that?" his father asked.

"Why, when we carried Landini out of the house last night, we wrapped her in blankets. Sing brought them to us here. Blue blankets they were, too. And while I don't exactly recall, we may have laid 'em across that chair before we used 'em."

A delighted smile spread over Sam Holt's face. "Boy," he said, "I ain't never been so proud of you before. Mr. Chan, I reckon I've gone and wandered into the wrong pew. What do you think?"

"The wrong pew, perhaps," Charlie replied politely, "but maybe correct church. Who can say?"

8

The Streets of Reno

When they came down-stairs, Doctor Swan was waiting for them beside the fire. He handed the sheriff an envelope and also a folded sheet of paper. "A letter to my landlady," he explained. "And a list of things I'll need—you'll find a bag in the closet to put them in. I hope to heaven I'll be able to get home pretty quickly—what do you think?"

"I hope so, too, Doctor," the sheriff replied.

"You—have no clue, I suppose?"

"None at all," responded the young man. "Except that some one, who knew all about how Miss Beaton felt toward Landini, planted that pink scarf and the pin. We're investigatin' that."

The doctor gave him an unpleasant look and turned away.

Romano came up, looking rather forlorn. "Pleasant journey," he remarked.

"Sorry you ain't goin' anywhere," smiled Don Holt.

Romano shrugged. "Me—I have no place to go—and no money to take me there, if I had."

"Does it chance," Chan inquired, "that there exists some errand we could perform for you in Reno?"

"None," Romano answered. "But"—he came closer, and lowered his voice—"would you be kind enough to inquire of Miss Meecher as to whether or not poor Ellen ever signed that new will?"

"Miss Meecher?"

"Yes—an estimable woman—Ellen's secretary. Estimable, but alas—so—what you call—close-mouthed."

Charlie nodded. "Do not fret, I beg of you. That is one of the things we visit Reno to discover."

"Good," cried Romano. "Splendid news. Excellent."

Leslie Beaton and her brother appeared, the latter going at once for his hat and coat. Don Holt had stepped to the door leading to the kitchen, and he now returned with a youth whose costume suggested that a rodeo was impending. Bright blue corduroys were tucked into high-heeled boots, his shirt was yellow silk embroidered with pink roses, around his neck was a crimson scarf, and he carried a two-gallon hat in his hand.

"Folks," said Holt, "this here is Cash Shannon, my deputy. You'll be seein' more of him—if your eyes can stand it."

"Pleased to meet you," remarked Mr. Shannon cordially.

"Miss Beaton—I hope you won't mind him—much," Holt went on.

"Not at all," the girl smiled. "He's to keep an eye on me, I presume?"

"Lady," said Cash in a deep emotional voice, "the softest snap of my life. Easy to look at—that's what you are."

Holt laughed. "Don't pay any attention to him. He's such a fast worker he gets all tangled up. A lady's man—jes' born that way."

"Better that than a woman-hater, like you," Cash averred.

"A woman-hater," cried the girl. "You mean Mr. Holt?"

"Lady—you said it. These divorcees we git round here has jes' naturally soured him on the sex. Takes a herd of 'em out on a picnic, an' comes back ravin' about their war-paint an' their cigarettes, an' how women ain't what they used to be—an' probably never was."

"Some women," Holt corrected. "I never said all."

"I ain't deaf," Cash returned. "All women, you always said." He squinted his eyes. "Ain't never heard you make no exception—until now."

"Well, let's get going," said Holt hastily.

Dudley Ward appeared, ready for the journey. Miss Beaton went with them to the veranda, pronounced the moving gorgeous and moved on with the little group to the pier. Chan and Don Holt walked with the old sheriff, but he seemed perfectly able to keep a straight course down the path. Cash Shannon came up behind them.

"Say, listen, Don," he remarked in a lous whisper, "you're crazy. If that dame done murder, I'm Al Capone."

"Get the girl off your mind," Holt smiled. "Remember, you're here to watch a lot of people. Sing, and the doctor, and Romano—that little Italian guy. Cecile, too. How do you know they ain't all goin' out the back door right now?"

"I get you," nodded Cash. "Mebbe I better go back."

"Mebbe you had. An' when it comes to this girl, jes' keep one thing in mind. You ain't the sheriff. You're jes' the deputy."

"Yes, sir," responded Cash, and returned reluctantly to the house.

As they were about to step into the sheriff's launch, the front door banged, and Sing ran like a rabbit down the path. He was waving wildly.

"Hey, Boss," he panted when he reached them. "Heah—you catch 'um umbrella."

"Umbrella," Ward protested. "The sun's shining."

"Sun him shine now." Sing announced, portentously. "Plitty soon lain him fall. Sing know. You lissen to Sing."

"Oh, all right," Ward grinned. "Give it to me." Sing handed it to him, and retired up the path. "Let's get off quick," Ward continued. "He's forgot to make me put on my arctics. Poor chap—I'm afraid he is getting old, after all."

They guided Sam Holt into the launch, then Ward, Beaton and Chan followed. Don Holt turned to the girl. "Look out for that Cash," he warned. "He's got a Romeo complex. I'll be back on the job myself by sundown."

"Fine," she smiled. "I'll feel much safer then."

The launch put-putted and they swept off over the sunlit lake. As they turned toward Tahoe, they could see the girl waving to them from the pier. A shrill cry from the house caused them to look back. Sing was standing on the steps, waving an arctic in each hand.

They all laughed, and Dudley Ward said, above the noise of the motor, "Great! Two victories over Sing in one morning. I slipped into his room and got his broken glasses." He held up a spectacles case. "Mr. Chan—please don't let me forget them while we're in town."

Charlie nodded, but did not reply. The loveliness of the scene, so foreign to anything he had ever encountered before, enchanted him. The vista of snow-clad mountains, of deep blue water, of dark green pines, might indeed have thrilled one far less sensitive to beauty. And the air—he pitied all those who could not breathe such air this morning. Those of the cities, who awoke to the same old scent of gasoline—even those of his own Honolulu, who awoke to an air likely to send them, mentally at least, back to slumber. He was grateful to the fate that had brought him to this spot.

All too soon they reached the Tavern pier. As he walked with Sam Holt along the unsteady planks, solicitous lest the old sheriff's cane become caught in one of the many cracks, he sought to express some of his admiration for the Sierra Nevada country.

"Yes—it's a good place, I reckon," Holt said. "I was born here seventy-eight years ago, and I've stuck close. Read about them Alps in Switzerland. Used to think I'd like to see 'em. Kain't see my own mountains—no more. Are we alone, Mr. Chan?"

"We are," said Charlie. "The others are now far in advance."

"I reckon you an' me—we're goin' to accept Don's explanation about the fuzz on that chair?"

"With the greatest of pleasure," smiled Chan. "On the part of both."

Sam Holt smiled, too. "I reckon so. But that don't mean we don't have to push ahead an' solve this case, Inspector."

"I am keenly aware of the fact," Charlie assured him.

"Nothing else against Sing—except that bench which got kicked over. You kain't prove anything by that. Ain't nothin' else, is they?"

"Not—not much," Chan answered. "Be very careful, please. The next plank is of a faulty nature."

"I remember it," Sam Holt replied. "What was Dudley Ward sayin' about Sing's glasses? They got broke? When was that?"

"A long time ago—so I understand."

"He wasn't wearin' 'em when you come last evenin'?"

"No—his sight was his own."

Holt hesitated. "Mr. Chan—the person who mixed them box lids last night wasn't seein' any too well."

"I am forced to agree," Charlie replied.

"Has it jes' happened to occur to you that the story told by that Beaton boy may have been correct? That Ellen Landini may have sent some person for her green scarf?"

"It has occurred to me," Chan admitted.

"And the person came back with a pink one. Mr. Chan—that person wasn't seein' any too well, either."

"I understand," Chan replied.

Holt shook his head. "If that boy Sing don't stop poppin' back into this thing like he was the killer, he'll jes' plumb break my heart," he said.

"Cease to worry," Charlie replied sympathetically. "Maybe pretty quick we eliminate him."

"Or else—"

"In any case, Mr. Holt," Chan continued, "please be so good as to accept my advice, so humbly offered. Cease to worry."

Don Holt was waiting for them at the pier's end. "Mr. Chan—the car's ready for us up in the drive. Dad, what are you going to do to-day?"

"Never mind, son. I kin take care of myself. I'm havin' lunch with Jim Dinsdale, an' other times I'll jes' loll round an' mebbe do a little thinkin'."

"Well, you be careful," the young sheriff said. "Better keep inside—you don't want any cold—at your age. And whatever you do, watch your step—"

"Run along," cut in Sam Holt. "My God—anybody would think I was a baby in the cradle to hear you. Mr. Chan—you got sons, I suppose?"

"Abundantly," Charlie answered.

"They treat you this way?"

Chan took his hand. "Princes have censors," he remarked, "and fathers have sons. A happy day to you—and once again—so proud to meet you."

On the way to the drive in front of the garage, Chan encountered Dudley Ward. "Now we are on our way," the detective said, "to important discoveries, I hope. May I venture the wish that such stirring morning does not find you—as you said last night—"

"Afraid?" Ward finished. "No, Mr. Chan. A man is likely to feel a little low at four in the morning. If I have a boy somewhere, it will be happy news for me. I'm starting late, but by heaven, I'll win his respect and affection if it's the last act of my life. It will give me what I've lacked and needed for many years—an incentive—something to live for."

Hugh Beaton joined them from behind. A silent young man, Charlie reflected. He had scarcely spoken all morning; his face was pale and drawn. No doubt the events of the night before were a bit hard on the artistic temperament.

Don Holt herded them into a big closed car, which he said belonged to Dinsdale, and they were off. Down through the scattered village, then on to Truckee, a bit more cheery in the bright morning. There they came on to the main highway, almost clear of snow, and the sheriff stepped on the gas.

They entered Reno through quiet pleasant streets that in no way suggested anything but the average western town. Charlie looked eagerly about him; here was no hint of night clubs, fargo games, bars and merry prospective widows. The main street, Virginia, seemed the usual one, save for a preponderance of lawyers' offices and beauty parlors.

"Just a moment, Sheriff," Ward said. "Here's that optician's. I'll drop these glasses now—it will take some time to fix them. If you don't mind."

"Sure, I don't," returned Holt amiably. He waited while a car slipped out of a parking place, and then moved in. Ward left them.

"Well, Mr. Chan," Holt remarked, "what do you think of the biggest little city in the world?"

"So far," Charlie told him, "it refuses to sustain its reputation."

"You got to get it gradually," the sheriff explained. "For instance—them black chiffon nightgowns in that window. Not for the western trade, Mr. Chan. An' all these beauty parlors—women have gone dippy over war-paint, but the local girls couldn't support so many. And that nurse in the funny dress—with them cute kids—goin' to have a brand-new papa, the poor little devils. Gradually, it soaks in. The best people from the East come here—and raise hell with the West."

But at this end of the street, Chan reflected, the West still ruled. Cowboys whose costumes were a faded imitation of the Cash Shannon splendor, cattle men and ranchers—and here an Indian woman with a papoose strapped to her back. It was not until Ward returned and they crossed the bridge over the yellow, tumbling Truckee River, that they began to mingle with the best people from the East. Holt parked in front of the new hotel, sliding in beside a long, low, foreign car, over which a glowering chauffeur, also foreign, stood guard. At the left was the dignified white court-house, the heart of the community. They entered the busy lobby of the hotel, and although Charlie never guessed it, he beheld a Patou hat and a Chanel ensemble for the first time in his life.

"I wonder," Hugh Beaton said timidly, "may I go up to my—to our—rooms now?"

He looked so pale and helpless that the sheriff gave him a kindly pat. "You gather up all the stuff you and your sister will need, and—"

"Need—for how long?" Beaton asked.

"How the heck should I know? Jes' gather up some stuff, an' meet us here in this lobby—say, at three o'clock. Run along, kid—an' cheer up." He turned to Charlie. "Why are you lookin' at me like that, Inspector?"

Chan smiled. "Ah—I am just thinking. Is that the method of a good detective? Such a one would enter those rooms simultaneously—he would search—he would investigate correspondence."

Holt shrugged his broad shoulders. "I ain't no detective, good or otherwise. Thank the lord. I'm only a sheriff."

The sleek young man at the desk looked at them suspiciously when Holt asked to be shown to Landini's apartment. "Miss Meecher is up there alone," he said. "She's had a frightful morning. The reporters have been so rude."

"Well, we're not reporters," said Holt. He flashed his badge. "I'm the sheriff from over the line, this is Mr. Dudley Ward, of Tahoe and San Francisco, and this is Mr. Charlie Chan, of Honolulu."

Don Holt had a carrying voice, and it was not surprising that three young men at once leaped forward from behind near-by potted palms. They represented various press associations and the local paper, it appeared. The passing of Landini was news all over the world. The method of her passing was better still. After a struggle which reached major proportions, the sheriff and his companions got away, and started up-stairs, where Miss Meecher awaited them. As the elevator ascended, Chan thought of Henry Lee, the steward, with a wry smile. "I shall watch newspapers," Mr. Lee had said.

Miss Meecher greeted them at the door, a repressed, middle-aged woman dressed in black. Very proper-looking, rather grim, but breathing efficiency.

"Come in, gentlemen," she said. She met even Chan without a change of expression—a remarkable woman indeed, he thought. "A terrible thing, this is. No one, evidently, thought to telephone me the news."

"So sorry," Chan remarked, "but up to this morning, no one in authority knew of your existence. The others—Miss Beaton and her brother—were perhaps too overcome."

"Perhaps," she answered. Her voice was as crisp and cool as the mountain air. She added: "I am glad you are here, Mr. Ward. Some one will have to attend to—to the services."

Ward bowed his head. "I'd already thought of it. I shall take full charge—it seems to be my duty. No one else appears to be interested—outside, of course, yourself."

She nodded. "Thank you. Then that is settled." Efficient. No time for emotion. Just—what's the next thing to be done? Well—do it—and move on.

"Might I ask?" Ward continued, "how long you have been with Madame Landini?"

"Over seven years," Miss Meecher replied. "I came first as secretary—lately I have more or less combined that post with the one of—maid. Times have not been so good—with any of us."

Dudley Ward leaned suddenly forward. "I'm sorry," he said, and his voice trembled. "I do not wish to seem abrupt. But there is one question I must ask you—and I can not hold it back—I can not wait. I have heard it rumored—that my wife had a son—my son—about whom she never told me. You can understand my feeling in this matter, I'm sure. I want to ask you—I want you to tell me—was there any truth in this rumor?"

Miss Meecher stared at him. The same expressionless face. "I can not tell you," she said. "I do not know. Madame never mentioned the matter to me."

Ward turned away, and sat looking out the window at his right, across an open space toward the white courthouse which had figured so largely in the life of Ellen Landini. Finally Chan broke the silence.

"Miss Meecher—the sheriff here will tell you that he authorizes me to speak for him—"

"That's right," Holt nodded.

"Had you heard any word from Madame Landini, Miss Meecher, at any time, that might lead you to believe she considered her life in danger?"

"None at all. Of course, she carried a pistol, but that was from a fear of thugs, robbers. I'm sure she was not afraid of any of her intimates. She had no reason to be."

"There are three or four men, Miss Meecher, about whose relations with Landini I wish to make inquiries." The woman's expression finally changed—a little. "Oh, most pleasant inquiries," Chan assured her. "Nothing of scandalous nature. I would mention John Ryder. Her second husband, you know."

"I know."

"She never heard from him? Had correspondence with him?"

"I don't imagine she thought of him, any more."

"Have you the slightest idea why she separated from him? After many years, it would seem he still bears wound."

"I can give you a notion," Miss Meecher said. "Madame's scrap-books of clippings from all over the world always traveled with us. In an early one, when I first came to her, I once read a certain item. Just a moment." She rose briskly, went into the other room and reappeared with a worn old-fashioned book. Opening it, she handed it to Chan, and pointed.

Chan read slowly and carefully a newspaper clipping, now yellow with age:

ELLEN LANDINI SNOWED IN
Recently Divorced San Francisco Singer
in a Cabin "Up the Ravine."

SAN FRANCISCO, Feb. 9—Ellen Landini, the singer, formerly the wife of Dudley Ward, of this city, but who was recently married to John Ryder, a mining man, is snowed in for the winter at Calico mine, in Plumas County. After their marriage Mrs. Ryder gave up her career and took the trail with her husband over the Sierra Nevada Mountains to the Calico claim, of which he is manager. Heavy snow fell soon after the couple had established themselves in the superintendent's cabin up the ravine.

Some mining men who have come down from that country say snow is twenty-five feet deep on the level, and that it is one of the hardest winters northern California has known in many years. Twenty-five feet of snow means candle-light all day in the cabin and no fresh grub and little if any mail; snow on the ground until June and no chance to get out with comfort before summer.

Chan handed the book to the sheriff, and looked at Miss Meecher. "It has aspect of romantic situation," he remarked, "rather than grounds for divorce."

"That," the woman replied, "is what I remarked to Madame when I read it. I—I was somewhat younger at the time. Madame burst into loud laughter 'Romantic, Mary,' she cried. 'Ah, but life is not like that. Romantic to find yourself shut up in one room for eternity with the most colossal bore since the world began! A sullen egotist, with the conversational powers of a mummy. In a week I loathed him, in another I despised him, in a month I could have killed him. I was the first person out of that camp in the spring, and I thanked God it was only a few miles to Reno.' I am quoting Madame, you understand, Mr. Chan."

Charlie smiled. "Ah, yes—that would, I have no doubt, happen. It begins to explain Mr. Ryder. If you do not incline to object, I would remove this clipping."

Miss Meecher looked startled at the idea, but then remembered. "Oh, of course," she said. "It won't matter particularly now."

Chan took the book from the sheriff, and carefully cut out the tale of Landini's second marriage. Meanwhile, Dudley Ward sat, still silent, by the window, apparently hearing none of this.

"We proceed," Chan continued. "And in the course of our proceedings we now arrive at Mr. Luis Romano."

Miss Meecher so far forgot her stern aloofness as to permit herself a shrug of disgust.

"Romano," she said, "we haven't seen him in months. You don't mean to say that he is in this neighborhood?"

"He was at Mr. Ward's home last evening. I gathered his attitude toward Madame Landini. What, if you please, was her attitude toward him?"

"Oh, she tolerated him. He was a harmless little idiot. Why she ever married him I'm sure I don't know—and I'm sure that Madame didn't either. She liked to be petted, pampered, looked after. But there is no real romance in that—and she finally sent him on his way."

"Making a settlement—which she later ignored."

"I'm afraid she did. She couldn't help herself. She owns a great deal of real estate—but ready cash has been very scarce."

"Speaking of real estate—she drew up a will, leaving her property to her new attraction—Mr. Hugh Beaton. I am eager to know—was that will ever signed?"

Miss Meecher suddenly put her hand to her cheek. "Good heavens—I never thought of that. It was—it was never signed."

Even Dudley Ward looked up. "Never signed, eh?" cried Don Holt.

"No. It came from her lawyers three weeks ago. There was something in it that wasn't quite right. She was going to have it fixed here—but she kept putting it off. She was always—putting things off."

"Then Luis Romano inherits her estate?" Chan said thoughtfully.

"I'm afraid he does."

"Do you think he knew this?"

"If he didn't, it wasn't his fault. He kept writing, trying to find out whether or not the will had been signed. He wrote to me, privately. But of course I didn't tell him. Perhaps—perhaps he wrote to her lawyers, in New York."

Chan sat for a moment quietly, considering this startling possibility.

"We drop that for the present," he said finally. "I turn now to Michael Ireland, the aviator. Would you talk about him, please?"

"There's nothing to say," Miss Meecher answered. "I believe there was once a sort of love-affair between him and Madame. It was before my time. Since she came here, she's enjoyed riding about in his plane. But the affair was over—on her side, at least. I'm sure of that."

"And on his side?"

"Well—I suppose I must tell everything. I did overhear him making love to her here one evening. But she only laughed at him."

"So—she laughed at him, eh?" Again Chan considered.

"Yes—she told him to stick to his wife. She reminded him that when she first saw him, he had just come home from the war, and was in uniform. 'It was the uniform, Michael,' I heard her say. 'I loved every man who wore one!'"

Chan's eyes narrowed. "So Ireland served in the war? A steady hand. A clear eye. An expert—" He saw Don Holt looking at him with amazement. "What of it?" he added hastily. "Miss Meecher, there is one I have saved to the last. I refer to Doctor Swan."

"Contemptible," spoke Miss Meecher, and her thin lips closed tightly.

"So I have gathered," Charlie replied. "Since you have come to Reno, he has visited Madame?"

"He has."

"Ah, yes—he lied to us about that. But visits were necessary if he was to follow his trade."

"You mean—as doctor?"

"Alas, no. I mean as blackmailer, Miss Meecher."

The woman started. "Who told you that?"

"No matter. We know it. We know that Madame had long paid him two hundred and fifty dollars a month. Why did she pay him this money?"

"I—I don't know," the secretary said.

"Ah—I am so sorry to contradict a lady," Charlie went on sadly. "But you do know, Miss Meecher. You know quite well Landini paid him this money because he had somehow become aware of the birth of her child. She paid it to him because he threatened that, if she did not, he would acquaint Mr. Dudley Ward, the child's father, with the facts. Come—Miss Meecher—this is not the time for double dealing. I want the truth."

Dudley Ward was on his feet. Perspiration gleamed on his forehead as he faced the woman. "I—I want it too," he cried.

Miss Meecher looked up at him. "I'm sorry," she said. "When you first came in—I wasn't sure—I wanted a moment to think. I—I have thought. It doesn't really matter now, I suppose. You may as well know. Yes—Madame had a son. A lovely boy. I saw him once. Dudley—she called him. He would have been eighteen next January—if—"

"If—what?" Ward cried hoarsely.

"If he—had lived. He was killed in an automobile accident over three years ago. I'm so sorry, Mr. Ward."

Ward had put his hands out, feebly, as though to fend off a blow. "And I never saw him," he said brokenly. "I never saw him." He turned, and walking to the window, leaned heavily against it.

9

Trouble Takes Wing

The three other people in Landini's small sitting-room looked at one another, but did not speak. For a time Ward continued to stare out the window. At length he turned; he was pale, but self-controlled and calm. Blood, the young Sheriff thought to himself, will tell. The cowards never started on that rush of '49, and the weaklings died on the way, but Dudley Ward was descended from a man who had reached journey's end. His voice was steady as he said: "Thank you so much for telling me."

"I knew, of course, the child was dead," Chan remarked, "when you told us Romano was Landini's only heir. You have, perhaps, Miss Meecher, some documents regarding the boy's death?"

She rose. "Yes. I have the telegram that was our first news of it, and the letter that followed from his foster-mother. Madame always kept them close to her."

She opened a desk drawer, and producing these, handed them to Dudley Ward. They waited while he read them. "That is finished," he said finally, and returned them.

"Madame read that letter over and over," Miss Meecher told him. "I want you to know, Mr. Ward, that she adored this boy. Though she rarely saw him, though he regarded himself as the son of—of others—he was always in her thoughts. You must—believe this."

"Yes," Ward said dully, and again turned to the window.

"Then it is true," Charlie said to the woman in a subdued voice, "that Doctor Swan was blackmailing her about this matter?"

"Yes—he was. She did not want Mr. Ward to hear about the boy—even after—the accident."

"Recently she stopped the payments, and Doctor Swan—perhaps he threatened her?"

"He was very violent and abusive about it. I don't believe he had a successful practise, and it appeared that this money meant a lot to him. I don't know that he actually threatened her life, however. But he was a man capable of almost anything."

Chan nodded toward the desk. "I note there long strips of paper with printing. Am I correct in calling them proofs of book?"

Miss Meecher nodded. "They are galley proofs of Madame's autobiography, which I have been helping her to write for the past few years. The book is to be published very soon."

"Ah," returned Charlie, a sudden eagerness in his voice, "would you, perhaps, object if I took same with me and perused them? Some little detail, some chance remark—"

"By all means," Miss Meecher replied. "If you'll be kind enough to return them. As a matter of fact—I'd like to have you read them. I'm afraid you've got rather a—well, a mistaken idea of Madame. If you had really known her as I knew her—" She stopped, and a terrible dry sob shook her thin shoulders. It passed in a moment. "She was really the kindest person—the victim of a wrong impression fostered by her many marriages. She was just restless, unhappy, always seeking romance—and never finding it."

"No doubt she has been misjudged," Chan returned politely. "Public opinion is often an envious dog barking at the heels of greatness. Ah, thank you—you needn't wrap the proofs. This large elastic will suffice. You shall have them back at very earliest moment. Now, I think, Mr. Ward, if you are willing, we will trouble this lady no longer."

"Of course," Ward answered. He looked at Miss Meecher. "There were—photographs—I suppose?"

"Many. They belong to you now." She started on her efficient way, but he laid a hand on her arm.

"Please," he said, "a little later. I—I couldn't bring myself—If you will be so kind, you might gather them up for me."

"I will," she promised.

"You have been so good, Miss Meecher," Chan remarked, bowing low. "Always I shall remember your frankness. It is of such great help."

"There's just one thing," the secretary returned, "that you might do for me."

"You have only to name it."

"Trouble," said the woman. "Trouble, the dog. He and I had much in common—we both loved Madame. I should like to have him, if I might. I am certain Madame would wish it."

"I will despatch him to you with the greatest speed," Chan promised. "Perhaps—by airplane."

"Thank you so much. He—he will be company for me here." And Charlie saw, as he took his leave, that at last there were tears in the eyes of the aloof Miss Meecher.

The three men rode down in the elevator, Chan and the sheriff both slightly uncomfortable at the feeling that there was something they should say to Ward and neither being able to put it into words.

"There are a number of things I must attend to," Ward remarked, when they reached the lobby. "I fancy I'm not concerned in your further investigation here. I'll meet you again on this spot at three."

"That'll be fine," the sheriff said, and Chan nodded. Ward disappeared, and Holt added: "Dog-gone it, I wanted to say something about the kid, but I jes' plumb couldn't."

"There are times," Charlie told him, "when words, though meant in kindness, are but salt in the wound."

"There sure are. Well, what do you say? I had breakfast at six, and it's nearly one. Let's eat, Inspector."

Into the rather effete dining-room Don Holt brought a breath of the West. Women in smart Paris costumes looked up admiringly as he passed, and registered a startled interest at sight of the broad figure which followed meekly at his heels. Ignoring them all, the sheriff sat down and with difficulty selected a man-size lunch from the French items on the menu. When the waiter had departed—a friendly waiter who treated them like old pals—Charlie ventured a question.

"You propose to visit local police?"

Holt grinned. "No—reckon I'll give them a bitter disappointment by passing them up. Nothing to gain, that I can see. Say, won't they be sore! All this lovely publicity, an' they on the outside, lookin' in. But you're going to be all the help I'll need, Mr. Chan. I can see that, right now."

"Sincerely trust you are not too optimistic," Charlie answered. "Can it be you glimpse light of solution ahead?"

"Me?" cried Holt. "I ain't got the slightest idea what's goin' on. But some men—well, you jes' look at 'em, and you get confidence. You're one like that."

Charlie smiled. "I should gaze more often in mirror," he replied. "Myself, I am not so sure. This is hard case. However, Miss Meecher was mine of information."

"Yeah—you got plenty out of her, didn't you?"

"Our success was gratifying. We learn—what? The background of Landini's second marriage—that to John Ryder. Snowed in with him up the ravine—the poor lady has, even at late day like this, my sincere condolences. We learn what may prove vastly important clue—new will was left unsigned, and Romano is happy heir. Did he know this? If he did, then case may end a very simple one. We learn that Swan's blackmail concerned the dead son of Landini, hear of the doctor's anger when payment at last was ended. Also, that Michael Ireland made love, and was repulsed. Is our motive hidden somewhere among these?"

"Also—though I can't see that it means anything—we hear that Ireland was in the war," Holt remarked. "I must say, Mr. Chan—you acted mighty mysterious right there. Last night you said some pretty queer things, too—but I want to assure you here an' now—I ain't going to ask any questions."

"Thank you so much," Charlie said. "But as clues pop up in this case, I promise I will draw them to your attention. We work on the matter together."

"Yeah—but with different brains," grinned Holt. "Well, here's once I guessed right. Filet mignon does mean steak—but not much of it."

After lunch they visited Swan's lodgings. The landlady, who appeared to be waging a battle against age with the assistance of various drug-store preparations, was suspicious at first, but soon succumbed to Don Holt's charm. From then on, she was almost too solicitous. However, they managed a search of the rooms, with absolutely no result, and then proceeded to gather up the articles the doctor had listed.

"Well, I reckon we're jes' errand boys, after all," remarked Holt, as he tossed an armful of gaudy shirts into the suitcase. "And I wanted to get something on this bird, the worst way."

"Ah," nodded Chan, "you still hold him responsible for awkward situation regarding Miss Beaton's scarf."

"He put it there, of course. That's plain enough."

"If he did," Chan continued, "then he also persuaded Landini to grasp it before he killed her. I am plenty sure of that."

"Well, maybe he did," said the sheriff.

They returned presently to the hotel. Ward and Beaton were sitting in the lobby, the latter with two large bags at his feet. A little later they were on their way down Virginia Street. Dudley Ward sat silent, and as they passed the optician's, Chan turned to him.

"You recalled the spectacles of Sing, Mr. Ward?"

Ward came to himself with a start. "No—by George—I forgot all about them—"

"Permit that I go," Charlie suggested. "I need not climb out over luggage, you will perceive."

"That's very kind of you," Ward answered. "Just charge them to me. I have an account there."

Holt parked some distance down the street, and Chan got out. He walked back to the optician's, through a colorful western throng, and going in, made clear his errand. The optician remarked that Sing should have come himself—the frame should have been adjusted on him.

"Sing has but little interest in the affair," Chan remarked. "Which is a great pity, since his eyes are so very bad."

"Who says his eyes are bad?" the man wanted to know.

"Why—I have always understood that he could see very little without these spectacles," Chan returned.

The optician laughed. "He's kidding you," he said. "He can see about as well without them as with them. Except when it comes to reading—and I don't guess Sing does a great deal of that."

"Thank you so much," Charlie responded. "The charge is to be made on Mr. Dudley Ward, of Tahoe."

He returned and handed the glasses to Ward. Holt started the car and in a few moments they were again out on the main road west, rolling along between the snowy hills.

Charlie was turning over in his mind this latest news. Sing was really not deprived of much when he broke his glasses. It was amusing how fate was constantly exonerating the old man. It had probably not been Sing who mixed the box lids.

No one seemed inclined to conversation, so Chan settled in his seat to meditate on the puzzle of those lids. They went over a bump. "Excuse me, folks," Don Holt said. The galley proofs of Ellen Landini's autobiography fell from Chan's lap to the floor of the car. He picked them up and carefully dusted them off. If he had been as psychic as he sometimes pretended to be, he would have known that the answer to this particular puzzle was at that moment in his hands.

Something more than an hour later, they drove up before the Tavern garage. As they alighted, all rather stiff from the ride, Don Holt looked up at the sky.

"Clouding a bit," he commented. "Sort of a dampness in the air, too. Perhaps Sing was right, Mr. Ward. Shouldn't be surprised if we had rain—or maybe snow."

"Sing's always right," Ward answered. "That's why I took the umbrella. And I felt a little uncomfortable about the arctics, too."

They stopped for a moment in the big lounge of the hotel, where a welcome fire was blazing. Charlie took Sam Holt by the arm, and led him to a far corner of the room.

"How was the fishin' down to Reno?" asked the former sheriff.

"A few minnows," Chan answered. "But as you and I know, Mr. Holt, in our business, most innocent-looking minnow may suddenly enlarge to a whale."

"True enough," the old man answered.

"Being somewhat pressed for time," Charlie continued, "I will leave to your son the pleasure of detailed account. Suffice to say, once more our good friend Sing is clear of suspicion." He related his conversation with the optician.

Holt slapped his leg with keen delight. "By cricky, I ain't had so much fun bein' wrong since I played roulette on a crooked wheel, an' run the owner out of Angel's Flats. I sure got off on the wrong foot with this case. Which it served me right—fer I didn't have no business suspectin' that boy—the years I've knowed him. Well, that's out. He didn't mix them lids, nor bungle that scarf business. Who did?"

"At present," Chan returned, "only echo is on hand to answer."

"You'll be answerin' fer yourself soon enough," Holt nodded. "I git more confidence in you every time I hear you speak."

"It will remain one of the triumphs of my life," Chan replied, "that I stood in such high favor with honorable family of Holt. Should events not justify your esteem, I leave this lovely country in the night."

Don Holt joined them. "Hello, Dad," he said. "How about the coroner?"

"Jes' got here an hour ago," his father answered. "Slow, as usual. Down at the mortuary now."

"Reckon we'll have to get his report later, Mr. Chan," the young man said. "By the way, I was talking to Dinsdale this mornin', an' he agreed to take a few of the suspects off Dudley Ward's hands. It'll be a load off your shoulders, too. Cash and me is both down here, an' between us we can handle 'em, I reckon. I thought maybe Swan, an' Romano, an' Hugh Beaton, an'—er—"

"Hugh Beaton would not come over here without his sister," Charlie smiled.

The sheriff blushed. "Well, we could fix her up, too," he said. "It ain't fair to Ward, all the trouble he's had, to load these strangers on him. And it's so near you could go on investigatin' as usual. Dinsdale's all tied up with painters an' decorators now, an' he tells me there's only one room ready to-night. It ain't a very good one—so I thought I'd bring Swan back with me an' put him in it."

Charlie nodded. "I yield him with great pleasure. It will, as you say, narrow my watching."

"Well, we may as well get goin'," Don Holt remarked. "It's comin' on dusk."

Chan shook hands with Sam Holt. "Until we meet again," he said. "Aloha."

"Same fer you," Holt replied. "An' thanks fer that news about Sing. I'll sleep better to-night."

Ward and Beaton joined them, and they went down to the sheriff's launch. The afterglow was fading on tall distant peaks as they swept over the darkening lake. Presently they tied up at Ward's pier. Dudley Ward and Beaton went on ahead. Charlie waited, and helped with the mooring ropes.

"I'll just leave Swan's bag in the boat," Holt said. "I needn't have brought it, in the first place. Not much of a thinker, I reckon."

They were walking up the path. Suddenly Chan put his hand on the young man's arm. "As resident of semitropic country," he remarked, "mostly sprinkled with palms, I have vast interest in these lofty pines. Could you give me name of variety?"

"Why—they're just pines," said Holt. He sought to move on, but Chan still held him.

"We have a tree resembling the pine on our island of Oahu," the detective went on. "It is called the ironwood. At one time I knew the Latin name, but—a busy life—those things escape. It was—it was—no use, I can not recall."

"Too bad," Holt answered, squirming.

"Fine examples of the ironwood border the road to the Pali," Charlie continued. "The bark is much less sturdy, less thick, than that of your trees. Do not go, please." He ran across the snow to pick up a large segment of bark that lay at the foot of a near-by tree. "You behold how thick the bark of your trees is," he added, and handed the piece of the sheriff. "Shall we continue now to the house?"

At the foot of the steps, Holt suddenly stopped and stared at Chan. "What'll I do with this?" he asked, indicating the bark.

Charlie grinned. "Toss it away," he said. "It does not matter."

Sing admitted them, and they found Leslie Beaton and the resplendent Cash seated before the fire. "Back already?" Cash inquired. "Well, this day sure has gone fast."

"Not for Miss Beaton, I reckon," Holt said.

"Oh, indeed it has," the girl cried. "Mr. Shannon has been telling me the most amazing things—"

"Yeah," nodded Holt, "I can imagine. He ought to write for the magazines, old Cash."

"Never do that," said Cash. "I want my audience where I kin see it. I sure had one nice audience to-day."

"Yeah," agreed Holt. "An' how about the rest of these people? Any of 'em still around the place?"

"Sure—they're all here—far as I know."

"Anything happen?"

"Not a thing. That aviator—Ireland, I guess his name is—dropped in on us a while ago. I reckon he's in the kitchen now."

Holt turned to Sing, who was fumbling about the fire. "Look here—Sing—go catch Doctor Swan. Tell him I want to see him." The old man went out. "Well, Cash—much obliged. I guess I can carry on from this point."

Cash frowned. "Don't you think you ought to leave me right here, Chief?" he inquired. "I'd keep my eyes open—"

"Yeah—I know you would," Holt grinned, "but Mr. Chan will do that—an' he'll look in the right direction. Say good night to this kind patient lady that must be nearly dead from the sound of your voice, an' go out to the boat. I'll be with you in a minute."

As Cash reluctantly departed, Doctor Swan came down-stairs. "Ah, Sheriff," he said, "back safely, eh? Did you get my bag?"

"I got it. It's waiting for you out in the launch."

"Waiting for me?" Swan looked slightly startled.

"Yes—we're moving a few people down to the Tavern, and you're the first to push off."

"Of course—that's quite all right. I'll just get my hat and coat, and say good-by to my host."

Sing had appeared on the stairs. "Boss—he sleep. Say, keep evahbody out. My tell 'um you say goo'-by. Hat an' coat light heah." He removed the latter from a closet. "Goo'-by, Doctah."

With a somewhat dazed air, Swan got into his coat. Holt led him outside and, calling to Cash, turned the doctor over to him. When the sheriff returned to the living-room, he found Leslie Beaton alone.

"Why—where's Mr. Chan?" he asked.

"He just ran out the back way," the girl explained. "He told me to tell you to be sure to wait. And he asked me—as a favor to him—to keep you company."

"Always thinking of others. Fine fellow," the sheriff said.

Silence fell. "Nice day," said the sheriff.

"Lovely."

"Not so nice to-night."

"No?"

"Looks like rain."

"Really?"

"Sure does."

More silence.

"Wish I could talk like Cash," the sheriff remarked.

"It's a gift," smiled the girl.

"I know. I wasn't there when they passed it."

"Don't you care."

"I—I never did. Before."

"Are you moving the rest of us to the Tavern?"

"Yes. There'll be a nice room for you to-morrow. Do you mind?"

"I think it's a grand idea."

"Yeah. Cash'll be there."

"Where will you be?"

"Oh—I'll be around, too."

"I still think it's a grand idea."

"That's—that's great," said the sheriff.

In the meantime, Charlie Chan had hurried to the kitchen. Cecile was alone there, with Trouble. "Your husband?" Charlie cried.

"He's just gone," Cecile answered. "Did you wish to see him?"

"I wanted him to do an errand for me," Chan explained. "I desired that he convey Trouble back to Miss Meecher, in Reno."

"You can catch him, I think," Cecile answered. She snatched up the startled dog, and thrust it into Chan's arms, "Michael will be glad to do it, I'm sure."

"Thank you so much," Chan cried and rushed out the door. As he approached the field, the hum of a motor rose on the still evening air. At the first sound of the engine Trouble leaped to life. He trembled with excitement, threw back his head, and time after time he barked a short happy bark. He was almost overcome with joyous anticipation.

As Charlie ran on to the field, he saw that the aviator was about to take off. Near the whirring propeller stood Dudley Ward's boatman. Chan shouted as loudly as he could and hastening to the side of the plane, he held up the dog and explained what he wanted.

"Sure, I'll take him," Ireland answered. "We're buddies, ain't we, Trouble? Crazy about flyin', this dog is."

The detective handed over the excited little terrier, and fell back to a safe distance. He stood and watched the machine taxi across the snowy field, then rise against the green splendor of the pines, and finally melt away into the fast-darkening sky. Deep in thought, he turned and walked back to the house.

When Charlie entered the living-room, the sheriff looked up with an expression that was almost one of relief. "Oh, there you are," he cried, rising hastily. "I was waitin' for you."

"The wait, I trust, was not unpleasant," Chan smiled.

"No—but, of course—I got to get back now. Well, Miss Beaton, I'll be seein' you. I hope your brother got all the things you wanted."

"If he got half of them," smiled the girl, "I'll be in luck. Poor Hugh—he's so artistic." She said good-by and ascended the stairs.

"I also will say good-by," remarked Charlie, and walked with the sheriff out the door and across the veranda. When they reached the path, he added: "Also, I desire to tell you that I just turned Trouble over to Michael Ireland. He is taking the little fellow back to Reno by plane."

"A great idea," said Holt heartily. "Saves time."

Chan lowered his voice. "It was not to save time that I did it."

"No?"

"No. I would like to call to your attention the fact that Trouble was wild with joy at sound of the motor. He was not afraid of the plane to-night."

"Does that mean anything?" asked Don Holt.

"It might. I incline to think it does. In fact, I believe that in this case Trouble is what my old friend, Inspector Duff of Scotland Yard, would call the essential clue."

10

Romano's Lucky Break

The young sheriff stood for a moment, staring across the lake at the last flickering of white on Genoa Peak. He removed his two-gallon hat, as though to give his mind a better chance.

"Trouble," he said, "a clue? I ain't gettin' it, Inspector."

Charlie shrugged. "Nevertheless," he replied, "such statement is based on facts equally well known to you."

Don Holt restored his hat. "Ain't any use, I reckon," he remarked. "You jes' go your way, an' I'll go mine, an' when you get to the top of the hill, drop a rope for me. By the way, when the coroner finishes, maybe you'd like to have a talk with him?"

"Very much indeed."

"Can you run a motor-boat?"

"Sometimes I have been permitted to drive the one belonging to my son, Henry—as a generous recognition of the fact that I paid for same."

"Good. I may give you a ring to-night. I'll send Cash up to spell you here." The sheriff paused. "I wish I had a good sensible deputy in this neighborhood," he added sadly. "A married man."

Chan smiled. "I could bring Miss Beaton to the Tavern with me. Pleasant spin over lake would do her vast good."

"A great idea," agreed the sheriff heartily. "Keep it in mind. Well, good luck. I'm sorry I ain't any use to you."

"Nonsense—you must not be discouraged. I remember well the first important case which came to me. Could I make distinguished progress? Can an ant shake a tree?"

"That's about the way I feel—like an ant."

"But you are indispensable. These are, as my cousin Willie Chan, baseball player, would say, your home grounds. I am only stranger, passing through, and it has been well said, the traveling dragon can not crush the local snake." They walked together toward the pier. "Do not believe, however," Chan continued, "that I consider myself dragon. I lack, I fear, the figure."

"And you don't breathe much fire," Holt laughed. "But I guess you'll get there, jes' the same."

Cash and Doctor Swan were standing near the launch. The latter held out his hand to Charlie.

"Inspector," he remarked, "I fear we must separate for a time. But we shall meet again, no doubt."

"Such is my hope," the detective answered politely.

"I—I don't wish to seem overly curious—but was your visit to Reno successful?"

"In many ways—amazingly so."

"Splendid! I realize it's none of my affair, but Romano has been speculating on the matter all day, so I am moved to ask—does it happen that Landini signed the will—the one leaving her property to Beaton?"

Charlie hesitated but a second. "She did not sign it."

"Ah," nodded Swan. "A lucky break for Romano. Good night, Inspector. I shall see you, no doubt, at the Tavern."

"Good night," Chan answered thoughtfully.

Cash was already in the launch, Swan followed, and Don Holt took his place at the wheel. In a moment they were off.

Charlie stood watching the little boat as it sped along the brief three miles of shore-line that separated Pineview from the Tavern. Swan, he reflected, would not be far away if he wanted him, and Swan was the sort of man who might be wanted at any moment.

Walking slowly up the path, Chan paused at the foot of the steps. There he stood for a moment, staring up into the branches of the lofty pines. His glance moved thoughtfully from the lowest branch of the tree nearest the house to the balcony outside the study. He retreated a few steps to obtain a better view of the study window. Suddenly a light flashed on inside. Sing appeared and drew the curtains.

Deep in meditation, Chan proceeded, not up the steps, but around to the rear of the house. There were various sheds and a good-sized garage between him and the hangar. From one of the sheds, a man emerged.

"Good evening," said Chan. "It was you, I believe, who brought us down in the launch last night?"

The man came closer. "Oh—good evenin'. Yes—I'm Mr. Ward's boatman."

"You do not live on the place?"

"No, not now. I'm here jes' July an' August. Other times, when Mr. Ward wants me, he telephones my home down t' Tahoe."

"Ah, yes. You just now assisted Mr. Ireland in the starting of his plane. Did you by any chance do the same here last night?"

"Lord, no, mister. I wasn't here last night. Soon's I landed you all at the pier, I scurried back home. Mr. Ward said I wouldn't be needed no more, an' we was havin' the weekly meetin' of the contract bridge club at our house."

Charlie smiled. "Thank you. I will not detain you further."

"Terrible thing, this murder," the boatman ventured. "Ain't had one o' them round here in years."

"Terrible, indeed," Chan nodded.

"Well—I guess I better be hurryin' back to supper. The wife ain't none too pleased with me to-day, anyhow. Say, mister—you don't happen to know anything about a psychic bid, do you?"

"Psychic?" Chan frowned. "Ah, you refer to bridge. I don't play it."

"Well, maybe you're right," replied the boatman, and hastened round the house, evidently bound for the pier.

The door of the garage was open, and Chan stepped inside. Only a flivver there at present, he noted—perhaps a larger car could not as yet make its way up the road from the Tavern. For a while the detective explored the place as well as he could in that dim light. He had just come upon a long ladder lying at the rear, when one of the doors banged shut, and he had to hurry to make the opening in time. Sing stood just outside, about to adjust a padlock.

"Hallo," cried the old man, startled. "Wha's mallah you? You no b'long this place."

"Merely taking look-see," Chan explained.

"You look-see too much," grumbled Sing. "Some day, some place, you get in, no can get out. Why you no min' own business, hey?"

"So sorry," Chan replied humbly. "I go now and buy a fan to hide my face."

"Allight. Plenty time you do," Sing nodded.

Feeling decidedly embarrassed, Charlie walked toward the house. Always, he reflected, he seemed to be coming off second-best in encounters with Sing. He stamped the snow from his shoes, entered the rear door and heard at once the voice of Mrs. O'Ferrell.

"Take that out iv here," she was saying in a loud voice. "I won't have it in me kitchen."

"It will not injure you." It was Cecile who answered.

"That's as may be," replied Mrs. O'Ferrell, "but I've cooked f'r thirty year without—ah, Mr. Chan—is it you?" she added, as Charlie appeared in the doorway.

"Indubitably," replied Charlie, "and deeply sorry to interrupt."

"Sure, 'tis nothing," Mrs. O'Ferrell replied. "I was just tellin' this Frinch girl that I've cooked f'r thirty year without guns in me kitchen, an' I ain't goin' to start now."

Cecile produced a small revolver from the folds of her skirt. "I am so nervous," she explained to Chan. "All the time, since last night, I am so jumpy and nervous. So I ask Michael to bring me this—from Reno."

"An' now we can all be nervous, an' with good reason, too," the cook added.

"There is no cause for alarm," Cecile assured her, "Michael has taught me—" she paused.

"Mr. Ireland taught you to use it," Chan finished for her.

"Yes. He—he was in the war, you understand."

"An avaitor, it may be."

"Ah—he wished so much to be an aviator. But no—that did not happen. He was sergeant of infantry." Cecile started for the door. "Do not fret, Mrs. O'Ferrell. I will take this to my room."

"An' look which way ye point it, even there," admonished Mrs. O'Ferrell. "Thim walls on the third floor is none too thick." She turned to Chan, as Cecile went out. "I don't hold with guns," she said. "The way I see it, the fewer guns they is, the fewer people gets killed."

"You are exponent of disarmament," smiled Chan.

"I am that," she replied firmly. "An' it's a lonely thing to be—among the Irish."

"Among any people, I fear," Chan replied gravely. "I have paused here, Mrs. O'Ferrell, to offer most humble apologies. It was not possible to retain the little dog at Pineview. It was not even possible, under the circumstances, that you should bid him farewell."

The woman nodded. "I know. Cecile was tellin' me. It's sorry I am to lose him—but if there was thim had a better claim—"

"There was one who had such claim," Chan assured her. "I am so very sorry. I trust I am forgiven."

"Don't mention it," said Mrs. O'Ferrell.

Charlie bowed. "He who keeps the friendship of a prince," he said, "wins honors. But he who keeps that of a cook, wins food. My preference runs to the latter—when the cooking is as superlative as yours."

"Ye have a nice way of talking, Mr. Chan. Thank ye so much."

As he spoke with Mrs. O'Ferrell, Charlie had been conscious of music in the distant living-room. Walking down the passageway and pushing open the door, he saw that Romano was seated at the piano, and that Hugh Beaton stood beside him. Only a few lights were on in the big room, the reflection of firelight was on the paneled walls, the scene was one of peace and harmony. Romano played well, and Beaton's voice was surprisingly good as he sang, not very loudly, words in a language Chan did not recognize. The detective tiptoed toward the fire and dropped into a chair.

Presently the music stopped and Romano, leaping to his feet, began to pace the floor excitedly.

"Excellent," he cried. "You have a really excellent voice."

"Do you think so?" Beaton asked eagerly.

"Ah—you lack confidence—you lack courage. You need the proper push—the proper management. Who has arranged your concerts?"

"Why—the Adolfi Musical Bureau—mostly."

"Paugh! Adolfi—what does he know! A business man—with the heart of a plumber! I—Luis Romano—I could manage you. I could make of you a huge success. Do I know the game? Signor—I invented it. From one end of the country to the other I would make you famous—in Europe, too. For a salary, of course—"

"I have no money," the boy said.

"Ah—but you forget. You have Landini's money—and there is plenty believe me. I know. Plenty—though mostly now in real estate. Times will change—the real estate will sell. A house in Washington Square—an apartment building on Park Avenue—a summer place at Magnolia—"

"I don't want them," Hugh Beaton said.

"But you should leap at the chance. I tell you, you need confidence. A voice like yours—all this money to exploit it—I will assist, gladly."

"I gave a concert in New York," the boy told him. "The reviews weren't very good."

"The reviews! Bah! Critics are sheep—they never lead. They follow. The path must be pointed out to them. I could arrange it. But first—you must believe in yourself. I tell you—you can sing." Suddenly Romano walked over to the chair where Charlie was seated. "Mr. Chan, will you kindly give this foolish boy your opinion of his voice?"

"To me," Charlie answered, "it sounded most beautiful."

"You see!" Romano turned to Beaton, gesturing violently. "What have I told you? A layman—an outsider—one who knows little of music—even he says so. Then will you believe me—Luis Romano—born with music in the very soul? I tell you that with Landini's money—"

"But I won't take Landini's money," the boy repeated stubbornly.

Charlie rose. "Do not worry," he said. "You will not be called upon to take it. It was not left to you."

Romano leaped forward, his dark eyes glowing. "Then the will was never signed?" he almost shouted.

"It was not signed," Chan told him.

Romano turned to Beaton. "I am sorry," he said. "I will not be able to accept the position you have so kindly offered me. I will be otherwise engaged. But I repeat—you have a wonderful organ. You must believe. Confidence, my boy, confidence. Mr. Chan, if Landini died intestate, her property is left—"

"To her son, perhaps," Chan answered, keenly regarding the Italian.

Romano paled suddenly. "You mean—she had a son?"

"You yourself said so, last night."

"No, no—I had no real knowledge on that point. I was—"

"Lying?"

"I was desperate—I explained that. Any chance that offered—have you ever been hungry, Mr. Chan?"

"You were telling the truth, unconsciously, Mr. Romano. Landini had a son—but he died three years ago."

"Ah—poor Landini! That was just before our marriage. I would not know."

"So I fancy her property is yours, Mr. Romano."

"Thank heaven for that," remarked Hugh Beaton, and started up the stairs.

Romano sat, staring into the fire. "Ah, Landini," he said softly, "she would never listen to me. Time after time, I tell her—you must cease to procrastinate. You must not for ever put things off. You say, I will do this, I would tell her, and you never do it. Where will it finish? It has finished in fortune for me. She never took to heart what I said—and now that means fortune for me."

For a time Charlie stood gazing down at this temperamental man whose sudden changes from one mood to another presented him with one of the greatest puzzles of his life.

"Yes," he said slowly, "the murder of Landini means fortune for you."

Romano looked up suddenly. "You will think I killed her," he cried. "For the love of God, don't think that! Landini—she was dear to me—I worshiped her—I adored her marvelous voice—do not think I would silence that—"

Chan shrugged. "For the present, I do not think at all," he answered, and turning, went up-stairs to his room.

His last words to Romano were not quite accurate. Seated in a chair before his fire, he thought very hard indeed. Could Romano have known that the will was unsigned? In that case, would he have made the determined effort to become the manager of Hugh Beaton? To acquire some portion of Landini's estate, by way of Beaton's pocket? No—hardly. And yet—ah, yes—his suggestion of the managership had been made with Charlie in the room, listening.

Might that not have been, then, a sly trick—for the man was undoubtedly sly. To make Chan think that he expected nothing, that he had resigned himself to the idea of Landini's money going to Beaton. When all the time, he knew only too well—

Charlie sighed ponderously. A problem, that was. And Cecile? Sending for a pistol—would a guilty person, who had already fired one pistol in that house, openly parade another? Probably not. But—might that not be a gesture of innocence, staged for his special benefit? Cecile was another sly one—her eyes betrayed her.

Leaning back in his chair, Chan considered the situation. About time, he reflected, that something definite, something a little less hazy and preposterous in the line of a clue, offered itself. Suddenly remembering, he rose and took the galley proofs of Landini's autobiography from the table where he had laid them a moment ago. Adjusting a floor lamp, he read the first three chapters of the woman's story. They were well written, he thought, with a touch of wistful nostalgia for the days of her youth that rather touched him. Especially since the scene of those days was his own beloved Honolulu.

A glance at the wrist-watch which his daughter Rose had given him on his latest birthday told him it was time to prepare for dinner. As he left his room, at a few minutes before seven, he saw Dudley Ward in the study at the front of the house. He went there at once.

"Ah, Mr. Ward," he said as he entered. "We are to have your company at dinner. You are brave man."

"Sit down, Mr. Chan," Ward answered. "Yes—I'm coming to dinner. I have had many sorrows in my life, but I have never yet tried to share them with my guests."

Chan bowed. "A true definition of hospitality," he replied. "Mr. Ward—if

I could find proper words—but such, alas, evade me."

"I understand," Ward said gently. "You're very kind."

"And speaking of kindness," Charlie went on, "I am telling myself that I must not impose upon yours. I was brought here for a certain task. That task, I am sorry to say, is now accomplished."

"And you should have your check," said Ward, reaching toward a drawer of his desk.

"Please," cried Chan. "That idea had not occurred to me. What I meant was that I should no longer impose upon you in the rôle of guest—"

"*That* idea," Ward interrupted, "had not occurred to me. My dear sir, the sheriff has asked you to stay. I demand that you stay—at least as long as you see a chance of solving this unhappy puzzle."

"I had no doubt of your feeling. But have you thought of this—embarrassment might arise."

Ward shook his head. "How so?"

Charlie got up and closed the door. "At moment of murder," he remarked, "five persons were wandering alone in house. In Swan, Romano, Miss Beaton and Cecile I presume you have no great personal interest. There was one other."

"One other? Pardon me—but I have been so terribly upset."

"The last person to see Landini alive."

"Sing! You can't mean Sing?"

"Who else?"

For a long moment Ward was silent. On his face was an expression that Charlie had seen before. Where? Ah, yes, on the face of Sam Holt whenever the matter of Sing's possible guilt came up. The old Chinese, Chan thought, was a man who was much beloved.

"Surely you haven't found anything—" Ward said at last.

"So far, nothing," Charlie answered. "We have been combing the hair of an iron donkey."

"Just as I thought," Ward nodded. "Mr. Chan, I have known Sing since I was a child, and no kinder soul ever lived. I appreciate your speaking to me about the matter—but I'll take a chance on Sing." He rose. "Perhaps we'd better go down to dinner. I don't like to keep Mrs. O'Ferrell waiting—" He stopped suddenly. "Five persons, you said, unaccounted for."

"I said five," Charlie admitted.

"Six, Mr. Chan. Haven't you forgot Mrs. O'Ferrell?"

"Indubitably. But what interest could that lady have had in Landini?"

"None whatever, that I know of," Ward replied. "But accuracy, Mr. Chan—accuracy. I should have thought you would be a stickler for that."

"It is true, I always have been," Chan assured him. "We will, in the future, call it six."

He opened the door into the hall. Sing was standing very close to it.

"You hully up, Boss," the old man cried, "or mebbe bimeby you no catch 'um dinnah."

"Coming right along," Ward said. He insisted on Charlie's going first and they stepped into the hall. Sing went limping ahead of them and, still limping, disappeared in the direction of the back stairs.

11

A Balcony in Stresa

The rest of the party awaited them in the living-room: Leslie Beaton, a charming picture in a blue gown by the fire, her silent brother, Romano, looking undeniably cheerful, and Ryder, grim and dour as always.

"Are we all here?" Ward asked. "I don't see Doctor Swan."

Evidently Sing had not kept his promise to pass on Swan's farewell. Chan explained the matter.

"Indeed," Ward answered. "Miss Beaton—may I have the honor? I trust I am not to lose any more of my guests."

As they moved into the dining-room, the girl said something about leaving on the morrow, and Ward murmured his regrets. When they were all seated, their host remarked: "Some one was singing down here this evening. Rather well, too."

"I hope I didn't disturb you," Hugh Beaton said.

"Disturb me? I enjoyed it. You have a remarkably fine voice."

"What did I say to you, Mr. Beaton?" Romano cried. "You would not believe me. Yet my opinion is highly regarded in some quarters. Even Mr. Chan agreed—"

"Ah, yes," Charlie said. "But I am glad to have the corroboration of Mr. Ward and yourself. For I am no expert. The croaking raven thinks the owl can sing. However, in this case, it was no owl I heard."

Beaton smiled at last. "Thanks, Mr. Chan," he remarked.

"What is wrong with this brother of yours?" Romano demanded of the girl. "He has a great gift, and does not trust himself."

"The artistic temperament, I'm afraid," Leslie Beaton remarked. "Of late, Hugh has lost faith in himself. One of his reviews in New York was bad, and he can't seem to recover."

"One of them!" Roman shrugged. "Ah, he knows nothing of life. He needs a manager—a man of intelligence and musical taste—"

"Yourself," smiled the girl.

"I would be ideal," Romano admitted.

"You could at least teach him self-confidence."

"That—yes. A bold front—it is vital to success in the modern world. And I could teach him more. At present, I do not believe I am available. But I would be glad to find a substitute."

"That's good of you," the Beaton girl replied.

Her brother stared morosely at his plate. A silence fell.

"I am so sorry you're leaving Pineview," Ward said presently to the girl. "But then, I realize there is little entertainment here."

"It's a charming place," she murmured, and in the silence that again fell upon the company, Charlie realized the strain it must be on the host to keep up the conversation. Modestly, he sought to help.

"There is vast entertainment here," he said. "Particularly for me. At home, I am amateur student of trees. I know the palms—the cocoanut, the royal, all of them. But I must confess myself shamefully ignorant of the coniferous trees."

"The what?" asked Leslie Beaton.

"The coniferous trees. Those bearing cones, you understand."
She smiled. "I've learned something to-day."
"That is good," he told her. "Learning which does not daily advance,
daily decreases. Myself, I am fond admirer of study. He who listens to the
chatter outside the window, and neglects his books, is but a donkey in
clothes."
"That sounds very sensible," she assured him.
"I believe so. For that reason, I shall, if I can find leisure, study the pines,
the firs and the cedars. I am slightly familiar—in books—with the Scottish,
the Corsican, the umbrella pine. The Austrian, too. Mr. Romano, when
you fought so bravely on the northern front, you must have come in contact
with Austrian pines."
"With many things I came in contact," Romano told him. "Maybe an
Austrian pine. Who shall say?"
"No doubt. I am at a loss to classify the local variety. Perhaps, Mr. Ryder,
you can help me?"
"What should I know about it?" Ryder demanded.
"But you have been mining man in these parts. You have been snowed
in among these very trees." Ryder gave him a startled look. "Is it too much
to hope that you are interested in this subject?"
"It certainly is," the other told him.
"Ah," Chan shrugged, "then perhaps I must pursue my studies alone.
In a certain family of pine, the bark grows much thicker near the ground,
and becomes more fragile as one ascends. Are these pines of that family?
I must investigate. Alas—I have not much of the figure for tree climbing."
He gazed blandly about the table. "I envy you all your delectable slender-
ness."
Sing appeared at that moment with the main course, and as the conversation again lagged after his departure, Charlie deserted the pines, a subject
which did not seem to interest his hearers to any extent, and launched into
a little talk on the flora of the Hawaiian islands. Miss Beaton, at least,
became an ardent listener. She asked many questions, and the dinner hour
slipped by.
"I've always wanted to go to Hawaii," she told him.
"Save it," he advised, "for honeymoon. Any husband seems possible
under Waikiki sky. And the kind you will achieve—he will appear Greek
god."
The dinner presently ended, and they returned to the living-room, where
Sing served coffee, and cordials from Dudley Ward's precious stock. For
a time they sat and smoked, but before very long, Charlie arose.
"If you will pardon me," he said, "I go to my room."
"More study?" asked the girl.
"Yes, Miss Beaton." His eyes narrowed. "I am reading very interesting
work."
"Would I enjoy it?"
"Not, perhaps, so much as I. Some day, we will allow you to decide." He
paused for a moment beside John Ryder's chair. "Excuse, sir, that I intrude
my business on this pleasant scene, but I would be greatly obliged if you
would grant me an interview above."
Ryder looked out from the cloud of cigar smoke that enveloped him—an
unfriendly look, "What about?"
"Need I tell you that?"
"If you wish me to come."
Chan's usually kind face hardened. "He who acts for the emperor, is the

emperor," he remarked. "And he who acts for the sheriff—is the sheriff."

"Even if he's a Chinaman?" sneered Ryder, but rose to go.

As Chan followed him up the stairs, hot anger burned in his heart. Many men had called him a Chinaman, but he had realized they did so from ignorance, and good-naturedly forgave them. With Ryder, however, he knew the case was otherwise, the man was a native of the West coast, he lived in San Francisco, and he understood only too well that this term applied to a Chinese gentleman was an insult. So, no doubt, he had intended it.

It was, therefore, in a mood far less amiable than was his wont, that the plump Chinese followed the long lean figure of Ryder into the latter's room. The door, as he closed it after him, might have almost been said to slam.

Ryder turned on him at once. "So," he remarked, "judging from the conversation at dinner, you have been prying into my private affairs."

"I have been asked by the sheriff of this county to assist in important case," Charlie retorted. "For that reason I must examine the past of Madame Landini. It is with no glow of self-congratulation, my dear sir, that I find you lurking there."

"I lurked there, as you put it, very briefly."

"One winter only?"

"Just about that long."

"In a cabin—up the ravine." Charlie removed a bit of paper from his pocket, and passed it to Ryder. "I found this among Landini's clippings," he explained.

Ryder took it and read it. "Ah, yes—she would save that—among her souvenirs. To her, I suppose, it was a mere passing incident. To me, it was much more." He handed back the clipping and Chan took it, staring silently at the mining man. "What else do you want to know? Everything, I fancy. Good Lord—what a profession yours is! You may as well sit down."

Charlie accepted this grudging invitation, and Ryder took a chair on the opposite side of the fire.

"I'd always admired Landini," the latter began, "and when she split up with Dudley I followed her, after a decent interval, to New York. I found her in a rather discouraged mood. She said she'd marry me—give up her career—it was a case of whither thou goest—you know. A grand overpowering love. And it lasted—nearly a month.

"You see, I was bound for the mine, and she came along—a great lark, she thought it. Then it started to snow—and she couldn't get out. So she began to think. Night after night, with only the candles burning, she talked of Paris, New York, Berlin—what she'd given up for me. After a time, I talked of what I'd given up for her—my peace of mind, my freedom. And our hatred for each other grew.

"Toward the end of the winter, I fell ill—desperately ill—but she scarcely looked at me. She left me there in my bunk, at the mercy of a stupid old man who worked for us. When the first sled went out in the spring, she was on it, with scarcely a good-by to me. I told her to go—and be damned. She got a divorce in Reno—incompatibility—God knows I couldn't argue that."

He was silent for a moment—staring into the fire. "That's the whole story—a winter of hate—what a winter! There is no hate in the world such as comes to two people who are shut up together in a prison like that. Can you wonder that I have never forgotten—that I never wanted to see her again—that I did not want to see her last night, when Dudley foolishly invited her here? Can you wonder that I loathed the very mention of her name?"

"Mr. Ryder," Chan said slowly, "what was in that letter Landini wrote to you just before she died? The letter you tore open, read and then burned in the study fireplace?"

"I have told you," the man replied, "that I did not receive the letter. I couldn't, therefore, have opened it, read it or burned it."

"That is your final statement?" Charlie asked gently.

"My only statement—and the truth. I did not go to the study. I remained in this room from the time you left me until you saw me again on the stairs."

Chan got slowly to his feet, walked to one of the windows and stared out toward the empty flying field. "One more question, only," he continued. "This morning, at breakfast, you remark to Mr. Ward that you have noticed Sing's eyes are bad—that he requires glasses. When did you notice that?"

"Last night, just after I came," Ryder answered. "You see, years ago, when I was a kid, I used to spend a lot of time at this house. One summer I taught Sing to read. English, I mean. I asked him, when we came in here last night, if he'd kept it up. I couldn't quite gather whether he had, or hadn't, so I picked up a book from the table and told him to read me the first paragraph. He held it very close to his eyes—couldn't seem to see very well. I made up my mind I'd mention the matter to Dudley."

Chan bowed. "It was most kind of you—to teach him the art of reading. But then—you are very fond of him?"

"Why shouldn't I be? A grand character, Sing. One of the real Chinese."

The implication was not lost on Charlie, but he ignored it. "I, too, have great admiration for Sing," he replied amiably. He moved to the door. "Thank you so much. You have been very helpful."

Slowly he walked back along the hall to his own room, passing as he did so the spot where, only a few hours before, he had found Sing unconscious from a brutal blow to the face. So much had happened since, he had almost forgotten that incident. Among his many puzzles, he reflected, the assault on Sing was one of the most perplexing.

He entered his room, closed the door and took up again the galley proofs of Ellen Landini's story. Seated in the chair beside the floor lamp, he read two more chapters. The spell of the woman's personality, as it crept from these inanimate sheets, began to take hold of his imagination. Warm, glowing, alive, she wrote gaily and with increasing charm. Her earliest marriage, those glorious days in Paris when first she was told that she was one of the gifted, would walk among the great. Her enthusiasm was contagious.

Chapter Six. As he stared at this caption, it came to him to wonder how many chapters there were in all. He turned to the final galley, and worked back from there to the beginning of the final chapter. Twenty-eight, it was. Well, in twenty-eight chapters, perhaps he could find something that would help him.

His eyes fell casually on the beginning of that last chapter. The names of foreign far-off places—always they intrigued and held him. Almost unconsciously he began to read:

> "After my marvelously successful season in Berlin, I came
> for a rest to Stresa, on lovely Lago Maggiore. It is here, on
> a balcony of the Grand Hotel et des Iles Borromées that
> I write the concluding chapters of my book. Where could
> I have found a more beautiful setting? I gaze in turn at the

aquamarine waters, the fierce blue sky, the snow-capped Alps. Not far away, I am enraptured by Isola Bella, with its fantastic palace, its green terraces of orange and lemon trees rising a hundred feet above the lake. The thing that has always made life worth while for me—"

Charlie's small black eyes opened wide as he read on. His breath came faster; he uttered a little cry of satisfaction.

Twice he read the opening paragraph from start to finish, then rose and paced the floor, overwhelmed with an excitement he could not suppress. Finally he came back and lifted that particular galley from the company of its fellows. Galley one hundred and ten, he noticed. He folded it carefully, placed it safely in the inner pocket of his coat, and patted affectionately the spot where it reposed.

He must show this to the young sheriff. That was the fair thing to do—no clues should be concealed. And he had now, he thought exultantly, the clue he had been looking for, the clue that would ultimately lead them to success.

12

So You're Going to Truckee?

Charlie had sat down again and was plunging with renewed hope into the sixth chapter of Landini's story, when Sing knocked on his door. Cash Shannon, the old Chinese announced, was below, and desired to speak with the detective at once. Recalling his conversation with the sheriff, Chan went immediately down-stairs. Ryder and Ward were smoking by the fire, Miss Beaton and her brother had evidently been reading, and Romano sat at the piano, his playing suspended for the moment. The resplendent Cash stood in the center of the room, smiling his confident smile.

"Hello, Mr. Chan," he remarked. "Don wants you to run down to the Tavern fer a while. He says to take his boat. I come up in her, an' she's out there now, rarin' to go."

"Thank you so much," Charlie answered. "Miss Beaton, would you perhaps enjoy brief spin on lake?"

She leaped to her feet. "I'd love it."

"Air ain't so good to-night," suggested Cash, his smile vanishing. "Kinda damp. Rain or snow, mebbe."

"I'd love that, too," Leslie Deaton added.

"Things is pretty dull down to the Tavern," Mr. Shannon persisted. "Couldn't recommend it as no gay party."

"I'll be ready in a moment," the girl called to Chan from the stairs.

Cash continued to stand, gazing sadly at his hat. "Sit down, Shannon," Dudley Ward suggested. "You're to stay here until they return, I take it."

"Seems to have worked out that way," Cash admitted. He looked at Charlie. "What ideas you do git," he added.

Chan laughed. "Sheriff's orders," he remarked.

"Oh—I begin to see it now," Cash replied. "An' I broke a date with a blonde to come down here."

Leslie Beaton reappeared, her face flushed and eager above the collar of a fur coat. "Hope you won't be long," Cash said to her.

"There's no telling," she smiled. "You mustn't worry, Mr. Shannon. I'll be in the best possible company. Are you ready, Mr. Chan?" Out on the path, she looked aloft. "What—no moon?" she cried. "And not even a star. But plenty of sky. And such a joy to get a breath of fresh air."

"I fear our friend Cash does not approve our plans," Chan ventured.

She laughed. "Oh, one afternoon of Cash is sufficient unto the day. You know, I think there's a lot to be said for the strong silent men."

She got into the launch, and Chan took his place at her side. "Trust my avoirdupois is not too obnoxious," he remarked.

"Plenty of room," she assured him. He started the motor, and swung in a wide circle out on to the lake. "It *is* a bit damp and chilly, isn't it?" the girl said.

"Some day," he replied, "I should enjoy privilege of escorting you along Honolulu water-front, accompanied perhaps by lunar rainbow."

"It sounds gorgeous," she sighed. "But I'll never make it. Too poor. Always too poor."

"Poverty has its advantages," Chan smiled. "The rats avoid the rice boiler of the lowly man."

"And so does the rice," nodded the girl. "Don't forget that."

They sped along the shore, great black houses, bleak and uninhabited, at their left. "You have learned, I take it, that your brother is not to inherit the estate of Langini," Charlie said.

"Yes—and it's the best news I've had in years. Money that came that way wouldn't have done Hugh any good. In fact, it would probably have ruined his career."

Chan nodded. "But now—his precious career is safe. You must not be offended, but Landini's death is, I suspect, a great relief to you."

"I try not to think of it as such. It was, of course, a terrible thing. And yet—we're frank in these days, aren't we, Mr. Chan?—it has released my brother. Even he, I believe, feels that."

"You have talked with him about it?"

"Oh, no. But I knew, without being told, that he was heart-sick over his predicament. He never really intended to become engaged to her. She sort of—well, jollied him into it. She had a way with her, you know."

"I know," Chan agreed.

"Somehow, I couldn't help feeling sorry for her at times, in spite of everything. She was still seeking romance—she needed it, you might say, in her business. And she was thirty-eight years old!"

"Incredible!" cried Chan, with a secret smile at he young girl beside him. "Poor foolish Landini." The lights of the Tavern popped up ahead. "One question I would like to ask, if I may," he continued. "You said last night you had met Doctor Swan before. Could you tell me the circumstances?"

"Surely. It was over in Reno. Some people had taken me to a gambling place—just for a lark, you know. Doctor Swan was there, playing roulette."

"Did he have aspect of confirmed gambler, please?"

"He seemed pretty excited, if that's what you mean. One of our party knew him, and introduced us. Later, he joined us at supper. He sat beside me, and I talked to him about Landini. I wish now I hadn't."

"You still believe he placed your scarf in Landini's hands?"

"He must have."

Chan nodded. "He may have. I can not say. But should you meet him to-night, please do me one vast favor. Assume that he did not try to involve you, and be cordial to him."

"Cordial to him? Why, of course—if you ask it."

"That is so good of you. It happens that I have small plan forming in rear of my mind, and I shall require your help. This much alone I need tell you now—I am eager to watch Doctor Swan while he gambles."

"I don't know what it's all about," the girl smiled. "But rely on me."

They were now beside the pier. Chan tied up the launch, and walked with the girl up the steps of the terrace to the Tavern. The lights were blazing in the big lounge; Charlie pushed open the door and followed the girl inside.

Don Holt at once came forward and took charge of Leslie Beaton, with that shy manner of his which was at the same time full of authority. Moving on to the fireplace, Chan encountered Dinsdale, the manager, Doctor Swan, Sam Holt and a small nervous man in a black suit.

"I don't know as this is any picnic for you," the young sheriff was saying to the girl. "Jes' thought maybe you'd like to come for the boat ride."

"That part of it was fine," she assured him.

"But this don't look so gay, does it?" he said, his eager look fading.

"Oh, I don't know. Who's the little man in black?"

"Well—he's the coroner."

"Good. I've never met a coroner. Having new experiences al the time. Up to last night, I'd never met a sheriff. And I got through that all right."

"You sure did, as far as the sheriff's concerned," Don Holt said. "Now—er—Mr. Chan an' I got a little business, an' then I guess I'll be free for—the rest of the evening. I'm afraid that's about all that's goin' to happen—jes' the rest of the evening."

"That sounds exciting enough for me," she smiled.

He left her with Dinsdale and Swan before the fire and walked down to the far end of the big room, whither Charlie had already led Sam Holt and the coroner. "Well, Inspector," he said, "I reckon you've already met Doctor Price?"

"I have had that pleasure," Chan returned. "He assures me that Landini was murdered by person or persons unknown. He has, you will observe, caught up with us in our search."

"The usual verdict, of course," the physician remarked. "Unless you gentlemen have some evidence of which I am not aware." He waited for an answer.

Chan shook his head. "It is now less than twenty-four hours since the killing," he remarked, looking at his watch. "Our researches in that time have been amazingly extensive, but lack definite results. It is the same old story. Like pumpkins in a tub of water, we push one suspect down, and another pops up. However, we do not despair. Tell me, Doctor—what of the course of the bullet?"

Doctor price cleared his throat. "Ah—er—the bullet, which was of thirty-eight caliber and obviously from the revolver of the deceased, entered the person of the deceased four inches below the left shoulder, and after that pursued a downward course—"

"Then it was fired from above?"

"Undoubtedly. The deceased may have been struggling with her assailant, she may have fallen to her knees, and the assailant, standing above her, fired—"

"How close was weapon held?"

"I can not say. Not very, I believe. At least, there were no powder marks."

"Ah, yes," Chan nodded. "One thing more interests me. Could the dec—I mean, the lady, have taken any step after the wound was received?"

"Which I asked him myself," put in Sam Holt. "He don't know."

"There might be two schools of thought on that problem," the doctor said. "You see, the human heart is a hollow muscular organ, more or less conical in shape, situated in the thorax between the two lungs. It is enclosed in a strong membranous sac, called the pericardium—"

"He jes' runs on like that," Sam Holt explained. "The sum of it all is, he don't know."

Charlie smiled. "At least, you have the bullet?" he inquired of the sheriff.

"Yes—Doc gave it to me. I got it over there in Jim Dinsdale's safe, along with Landini's revolver."

"Excellent," Chan nodded. "And who would have the combination to this safe?"

"Why—nobody but Dinsdale and his bookkeeper."

"Ah, yes. Dinsdale and his bookkeeper. Presently we may give more thought to the safe. Mr. Coroner, I thank you so much."

"Don't mention it," returned Doctor Price briskly. "I am staying here with Jim overnight—anything more I can tell you, you have only to ask. Glad to have met you. I'm turning in now—want to get an early start in the morning."

He went down the room, said something to Dinsdale and disappeared toward a distant corridor. Charlie and the two Holts joined the little group by the fire.

"Draw up and sit down, gentlemen," Dinsdale remarked. "I was just telling Miss Beaton how glad we'll be to have her come down here to-morrow. Of course, the Tavern isn't officially open, and things are a bit dull, but we can show her a little excitement, I reckon. There's a few newspaper reporters coming up from San Francisco on the morning train, and they'll stir things up. They usually do."

"Newspaper reporters," cried Don Holt in dismay.

"Yes—and that Reno bunch will be back here to-morrow. They've been prowling round the neighborhood all day. Claimed they wanted to find Mr. Chan."

"Well, I hope it's Mr. Chan they find," Holt said. "Lord, I wouldn't know what to say to 'em."

"The secret," Charlie told him, "is to talk much, but say nothing. Not your specialty, I fear. Leave them to me—I will act as buffer. I have the figure."

"To-morrow sounds interesting," Leslie Beaton remarked, "but how about to-night? Where's the night life around here?"

Dinsdale laughed. "Night life? I'm afraid you'll have to come back later in the summer."

"Oh—but I've heard the gambling wasn't all on the other side of the state line," the girl continued, and Charlie gave her a grateful smile. "There must be a few places—"

"There ain't any in my county," Don Holt said firmly.

"Well, let's get out of your old county, then. I feel like going places and doing things. Surely there must be a city, or a town, or at least a village, nearer than Reno."

"Well, there's Truckee," Dinsdale ventured dubiously. "Summers we sometimes run over there in the evening. Not much doing now, I'm afraid. But there's two or three restaurants, and a movie—and you might dig up a game."

"Not if it's in Sheriff Holt's county," the girl said mockingly.

"But it ain't," replied the sheriff. "It's over the county-line, so you can't tell—it might turn out to be the modern Babylon you're longing for. Get your coat, an' we'll have a look at it." His manner was gay enough, but there was a note of disappointment in his voice.

"That'll be grand," the girl cried. She went over to Sam Holt's chair, and bent above him. "You're coming with us, you know," she said.

"Shouldn't do it," he answered. "But say—I like your voice. Sounds lively. Full o' spirit, which young folks' voices is generally too tired nowadays to suit me. Sure, I'm coming. Fresh air never hurt nobody."

Leslie Beaton turned to Swan. "Doctor—you don't mind a little game, as I recall."

"Well, really—I think I'd better stay here," Swan replied. But his eyes had brightened.

"Nonsense—we won't go without you," the girl said, while Don Holt stared at her in amazement.

"Oh—in that case—" Swan stood up at once.

Dinsdale felt he should stay at the Tavern—a guest is a sort of responsibility, he explained, and there was no one about to take his place in the office. He offered his car for the trip, along with certain vague suggestions of the "So you're going to Truckee" order.

But Truckee, when they had covered fifteen miles of snowy road and rolled on to its startled main thoroughfare, responded with the gloomiest welcome imaginable. Even the spirits of Leslie Beaton dropped at the prospect. Tired old store-fronts listing, it seemed, with the wind, a half-darkened drug store, the lighted windows of a few restaurants dripping with steam. Don Holt drew up to the curb.

"Here you are, folks," he smiled. "Night life in these parts. I don't know what you're looking for, but it ain't here."

"Isn't that a light in the Exchange Club, over the Little Gem Restaurant?" Doctor Swan inquired.

"It might be, at that. I'm afraid you have the gambler's instinct, Doctor. Maybe we are in Babylon, after all. Anyhow, it won't hurt to inquire."

Holt led them into the Little Gem. An odor of fried fish and other delicacies of the lake country nearly bowled them over. The proprietor of the establishment, a swarthy Greek known locally as "Lucky Pete," was shaking dice with a customer.

"Hello, Pete," Holt said. "What's the big excitement in these parts tonight?"

"Dunno," returned Pete, stifling a yawn. "Is there any?"

"Jes' dropped in to find out," Holt said. "A few friends of mine—from Reno."

Pete nodded. "Pleased to meet them. The slot machines are over in the corner."

"Nothing doing up-stairs?" Holt asked.

"Not these days—no. Tables all covered—times is bad. A few members of the Club—prominent gentlemen of the city—they play poker."

Chan stepped forward. "Is this a private game—or can anybody enter?"

Pete surveyed him critically. "You can go up an' ask," he suggested.

"Doctor Swan—what do you say? Shall we purchase small supply of chips?" Charlie inquired.

"We'll take a look, first," Swan replied cautiously.

It appeared there was an inner stairway, which identified Lucky Pete as the real steward of the Exchange Club. The five, led by Don Holt, ascended. Charlie and old Sam Holt brought up the rear.

"Watch what you do in this place, Inspector," Holt said. "A Greek! How did a Greek find Truckee—unless they closed all the other towns to him?"

"Greek people," Charlie answered, "appear to be born with geography of the world in one hand."

In the big bare room above, half hidden in darkness, were numerous gambling tables, covered with brown canvas. Under the solitary light, five men played poker with soiled cards.

"Evening, gentlemen," said Don Holt. "Things don't seem to be prospering around here right now."

"Not much doing," one of the players responded. "Unless you'd like to sit in on this game."

Holt looked around the faces at the table and shook his head. "I hardly think so. We've got jes' a few minutes—"

"Small contributions gratefully received," said another player, who had the pale face and artificial-looking hair of a croupier.

"We might take a brief turn to try luck," remarked Charlie. "Doctor Swan—what is your reply? Ten dollars spent in chips by each—and leave in one half-hour, win or lose?"

Swan's eyes glittered, his cheeks were flushed. "I'm with you," he replied.

"Good," Charlie replied. "It is now nine-thirty. Gentlemen—we drop out at ten precisely. May we squeeze in?"

Don Holt gave Chan a dazed look. "All right," he agreed. "Miss Beaton and I will wait down-stairs. Father—"

"Git me a chair, son," the old man said. "I sure do like to hear the sound of them chips again. What is it, boys—straight, whisky or draw?"

"Draw," answered one of the boys. "How about you, Dad? Oh—excuse me."

"I'll jes' listen in," explained Sam Holt. "That's all I'm doin', nowadays."

"Would you be so good, gentlemen," remarked Chan, "as to explain to me the value of these chips? I am, you understand, a novice."

"Yeah," returned the man with the pale face. "I've met them novices before."

Don Holt and the girl returned to the aggressive odors of the room below.

"Like something to eat?" the sheriff inquired.

"Never wanted anything less in my life," she smiled.

"Well, I guess we better order something anyhow. It'd look better. You can't go huntin' night life, an' not spend any money. A table, or the counter?"

She walked past several tables, studying the cloths. "The counter, I believe," she told him.

He laughed. "That's pickin' 'em," he nodded. They sat up to the counter. "Now, what would you like? Wait a minute—I meant to say, what will you take?"

"How about a sandwich and a glass of milk?"

"Well—you're fifty per cent right, anyhow. Stick to the sandwich—that was an inspiration. But as for the milk—"

"No?"

He shook his head. "No. It don't do to pioneer in the West anymore. Jes' play safe an' make it what's known in these parts as a 'cup cawfee.' "

"I'm in your hands," she told him.

Pete appeared, and Don Holt ordered two ham sandwiches and two cups of coffee. As the man departed, the sheriff glanced toward the stairs. "Well, Inspector Chan is sure havin' fun to-night," he remarked. "Some people, you jes' can't keep 'em away from a gamblin' table."

The girl smiled. "Is that what you think?"

"Why shouldn't I think it? Say, I hope he's good—those boys up there invented the game. At ten o'clock we leave—if I have to draw a gun. Your big fling at night life ends then, so make the most of it while you can."

She gave him a quick look. "You're not so very pleased with me this evening, are you?" she inquired.

"Who—me? Why—why sure I am. Maybe I'm a little disappointed—you see, I been tellin' myself perhaps you *would* like the county-seat, after all. It's quite a busy little town, but of course—"

"Of course—what."

"I don't mean that you're to blame. It ain't your fault. You're jes' like all the other girls, that's all. Restless, always wantin' excitement. I see it on the parties I take out from the Tavern. What's got into the women nowadays? The men are O.K. They'd like to relax, an' take a look at the mountains. But the girls won't let 'em. Come on, boys, is their slogan. What'll we do now? I want to go places, an' do things."

"Don't you?"

"Don't I what?"

"Want to go places, and do things?"

"Sure—when there's somewhere to go, an' something to do. But when there ain't, I can sit all the way back in my chair, an' not have any nervous breakdown."

"Everything you say is pretty true," the girl replied. "Women are a bit restless—and I'm as bad as any of them, perhaps. But I've got too much spirit to sit here on this very unsteady stool and be unjustly accused. It wasn't my idea—coming out to find a gambling house to-night."

"But—but you suggested it."

"Of course I did. However, it was only to please Mr. Chan. He told me he was eager to watch Doctor Swan while the doctor was busily engaged in gambling."

A look of perplexity clouded Don Holt's fine eyes. "He did? Well, then—say, I reckon there's a pretty humble apology due from yours truly."

"Nothing of the sort," the girl protested.

Pete appeared with the repast, and she smiled at the thickness of the sandwich that stood before her. "I wonder if I could really open my mouth that wide," she went on. "It's worth trying, don't you think?"

The young sheriff was still puzzling over her news. "So Mr. Chan wanted to watch Swan gamble," he mused. "It's too much for me. I wonder what the inspector's got on his mind."

In the room above the inspector appeared to have much on his mind, including a rapid, tense and deadly game of poker. Scarcely once since it started had he taken his eyes from Doctor Swan. Every move of the latter's hands as he made his ante, pushed out his bet, lost or raked in the chips and sorted them, he watched with extreme care. Either because of this absorption or due to inexperience, Chan played badly, and his stack of chips was close to the vanishing point.

"Ah," he murmured, "how true it is that dollars going into a gambling house are like criminals led to execution. Doctor, might I trouble you—would you exchange ten white chips for a blue?"

"Gladly," nodded Swan, "but—pardon me—you are offering me a red chip, Mr. Chan."

"Forgive the error," smiled Charlie, correcting it. "Not for worlds would I cheat you, my dear Doctor."

When Don Holt came to get them at ten o'clock, Charlie held up one white chip. "Behold," he said, "my stack has melted like snow under stream of hot water. I use my last chip to ante." He took his five cards, glanced at them, and threw them down. "No cards," he said. "The situation is hopeless. I withdraw."

Swan remained in for the hand, lost it and also stood up. "I'm about even," he remarked. "A lot of hard work for nothing." He counted his stack, and pushed it toward the banker. "Seven dollars and twenty-five cents," he added.

"Better stick a little longer, gentlemen," the banker said in a hard voice.

"No," Charlie said firmly. "We go along now—with the sheriff." The five hard-boiled gamblers looked up with sudden interest. "Ten o'clock—is that not correct, Sheriff?"

"Jes' ten," Don Holt returned. "Time to get goin'."

There was no further protest against their doing so from the gamblers, who appeared to have lost all interest in the noble sport themselves. Presently the little group from Tahoe was out in the car, and the sleeping town receded rapidly behind them.

"I think it was lots of fun," Leslie Beaton cried. "So quaint and unusual."

"But not very profitable," muttered Doctor Swan. "Eh, Mr. Chan?"

"Profit and pleasure so seldom found on same street," Charlie answered.

When they reached the Tavern, Swan said good night and retired to his room down the same corridor as that into which the coroner had disappeared. Dinsdale suggested that Miss Beaton come and look at the suite he was preparing for her. "There's a small sitting-room, with a fireplace—" he was saying, as they moved away.

Chan turned quickly to the Holts. "Humbly suggest you owe me ten dollars," he said. "The amount of money invested in poker game just now. Place it on your expense account for county to pay."

"Hold on a minute," Don Holt replied. "I ain't getting this. I'm glad to pay the ten, of course—but what did we get for it?"

Chan smiled. "We eliminated Doctor Swan from list of our suspects."

"What!"

"I am, perhaps, getting a few paces ahead of myself," Charlie conceded. He took galley one hundred and ten from his pocket, and gently unfolded it. "Tonight, I am perusing the autobiography of Landini, and happy luck smiles upon me. Will you be so good as to read aloud to your honorable father, the first paragraph of Chapter Twenty-Eight?"

The young sheriff cleared his throat. " 'After my marvelously successful season in Berlin, I came for a rest to—to Stresa, on lovely Lago'—Lago—say, what language is this, anyhow?"

"It is Italian," Chan told him. "Lago Maggiore—the second largest of the Italian lakes, I believe."

" '—Lago Maggiore,' " continued Holt uncertainly. " 'It is here, on a balcony of the Grand Hotel et des—des—more Italian—that I write the concluding chapters of my book. Where could I have found a more beautiful setting? I gaze in turn at the aquamarine waters, the fierce blue sky, the snow-capped Alps. Not far away, I am enraptured by Isola Bella, with its fantastic palace, its green terraces of orange and lemon trees rising a hundred feet above the lake. The thing that has always made life worth while for me is color—plenty of color, in personality, in music, in scenery. I have pitied many people in my life, but none more so than one I knew who was color-blind—' "

"By the Lord Harry!" cried old Sam Holt.

" '—color-blind,' " repeated his son doggedly, " 'a poor luckless soul to whom all this gorgeous beauty would seem as a mere monotonous prospect of dull gray; lake, mountains, trees, sky—all the same. What a tragedy!' "

"Color-blind," Don Holt said again, as he laid down the galley.

"Precisely," nodded Chan. "A person, who, sent for a green scarf, comes back with a pink one. A poor luckless soul who, having murdered Landini and desiring to give semblance of order to desk, places on the yellow box the crimson lid, and on the crimson box, the yellow."

"Mr. Chan," old Sam Holt said, "you've sure struck the right lead now."

"Who was this person?" Chan went on. "That remains to be discovered. One thing I know—it was not Doctor Swan, who for one half-hour to-night sorted so carefully the chips, blue, red and white. He is eliminated, but we proceed with high heart now, for we may be pretty sure that the person Ellen Landini pitied—the one who would not have enjoyed to sit with her on the balcony of the Grand Hotel et des Iles Borromées—that is the person who murdered her."

"So you think," Don Holt said slowly, "that she was killed near the desk? By someone who was in the room with her at the time?"

"I am certain of it."

"Then why all that talk about pine trees, and pieces of bark lying on the ground?"

Chan shrugged. "Might it not be that I am truly amateur student of trees? But what is the use? Can you make public believe that policeman is something more than dumb brute thinking only of man-hunt? Can you convince it that he may have outside interests of gentler nature? Alas—can you borrow a comb in a Buddhist monastery?"

13

Footsteps in the Dark

Dinsdale and the girl returned at that moment, and Charlie hastily restored galley one hundred and ten to his pocket.

"Sorry I can't put you higher up," the hotel man was saying. "The view would be better, of course. But I'm using only the ground floor at present, and just the one wing, at that."

"It's awfully good of you to take us at all," Leslie Beaton assured him. "Now, Mr. Chan, hadn't we better be going? I just remembered poor Cash."

"For whom, perhaps, time does not travel so rapidly as it did this afternoon," Chan replied. "You are quite right, we must hasten." Don Holt and the girl went outside, and Dinsdale followed. Charlie turned to the old sheriff. "Good night, sir. We have something to work on now. As I recall—you once enjoyed camping journeys with Sing—"

"Funny," said Sam Holt, "the way you an' me—we always come back to Sing. I was jes' thinkin' of him myself. Yes, I camped with him, but I don't recollect he was color-blind. Leastways, he never showed it ef he was."

"You are quite sure? An unusual number of Chinese are."

"Dog-gone it, Mr. Chan," cried the old man, "let's try not to think about Sing. Why should we? Fine character, he's always been. Model of all the virtues."

"Ah, yes," nodded Chan, "the real virtues. But was murder any great vice in era from which Sing dates? I think not—if the motive was good. The motive—that was what counted then. And would count to-day, with Sing, I think."

"I ain't listenin'," Sam Holt replied grimly.

Charlie smiled. "I can not find it in my heart to blame you. It will, you may well believe, pain me deeply if I have traveled all this distance to put an ornament of my own race in hangman's noose. But let us not anticipate."

"Good advice, that is," the old man agreed. "But hard to follow, at my age. I said this afternoon I'd sleep better to-night—but—I dunno. Don't seem to need much of it at my age—an' it ain't so easy to sleep when you kain't tell the daylight from the dark. Somethin' tells me this case is goin' to change the world—fer a few of us. My boy—"

"One of finest young men I have had the honor to meet," Chan put in.

"I know. I wouldn't tell him, Mr. Chan, but I know. Ain't never paid much attention to girls, Don ain't. But I heard somethin' in his voice to-night when he was talkin' to the Beaton girl—"

Chan laid his hand gently on the old man's shoulder. "A splendid young woman. Most of her life so far has been devoted to her brother. She knows the meaning of loyalty."

Sam Holt sighed with relief. "Then that's all right. Ain't nobody's opinion I'd take before yours, Mr. Chan. Yes, that's all right—but that boy Sing! By the lord, Inspector, I'll be a happy man when we git out o' the woods on this case—even ef I kain't see the mountaintops myself." He held out his hand. "Good night."

There were deep understanding and sympathy in their hand-clasp. Chan left the old man standing by the fire, his sightless eyes turned toward the open door.

Dinsdale spoke his farewell on the terrace, where flakes of snow were beginning to sift gently down. "More of it," the hotel man grumbled. "Is spring never coming? Seems to me the weather's all haywire these last few years."

Miss Beaton and the sheriff were waiting beside the launch. "Water's churning pretty lively," the latter remarked. "I'll take you back."

"Ah, yes," nodded Chan. "But I am sorry to remind you that, though we walk a thousand miles along the way with a friend, moment of good-by is still inevitable."

"For which remark," Don Holt replied, "you draw the back seat, an' the snow that goes with it. Hop in."

The pier lights faded suddenly behind them as they nosed into impenetrable dark. From out the soft blackness of the night came the drifting snow, thicker now, cool and refreshing. Chan lifted his face, delighting in the touch of the whirling flakes, so different from the liquid sunshine of steamy Honolulu days. Again a feeling of renewed energy swept over him.

Unerringly Don Holt found the lights of Dudley Ward's pier, and they moored the boat. Sing let them in, muttering vaguely on the ways of people who never knew when to come home, and the steadily multiplying labors in this house. Romano and Cash were alone in the living-room, the latter in the midst of a rather conspicuous yawn.

"Here we are—back already," remarked Don Holt.

"Thought you'd all been drowned," said Cash. "Maybe we might as well stay on fer breakfast now."

"Wait till you've been asked," suggested Holt. "All serene, I take it?"

"Sure—everybody in bed hours ago—except me an' the perfessor, here.

He's been tellin' me all about music. I reckon I'll be a wow on my ukulele from this on."

"Most exciting to meet you, Mr. Shannon," Romano remarked. "Always I have deep interest in Wild West cinemas."

"I don't know what you're calling me, Mister," returned Cash. "Don't sound very complimentary, but I'm too sleepy to care. Well, Don, do we hit the down trail now?"

It appeared that they did, and the two departed. Miss Beaton said good night and hastened up-stairs. Chan was hanging his hat and coat in the closet at the rear, when Romano approached him. "If possible, I would enjoy word with you," he said.

"The enjoyment would be mutual," Charlie returned. "Shall we sit here by the fire? No. Sing, I perceive, is annoyned—we will retreat to my room." He led the way up-stairs, and politely proffered a chair before the fireplace. "What, my dear Mr. Romano, is hovering in your mind?"

"Many things," Romano replied. "Mr. Chan, this news I have heard to-day—this fortune that has dropped into my lap—it works a vast difference in my life."

"A pleasant one, no doubt," Chan replied, also taking a chair.

"Naturally. From a pauper I ascend suddenly to the position of a man of property. What is my first reaction? To get away from this spot, lovely as it may be—to hasten to New York—to realize on my inheritance, and then to move on to the continent, where alone I feel at home. I shall sit in the twilight while the band plays in the Piazza at Venice, and I shall be grateful to Landini. I shall climb the stairs of the Opera in Vienna—but I perhaps move too quickly. What I am asking, Mr. Chan, is—how far has this matter of Landini's murder traveled to solution?"

"So far," Charlie told him, "we have been ringing wooden bell."

"Which, if I interpret correctly, means you are nowhere?"

"In that neighborhood," Chan replied.

"Alas, it is unfortunate," Romano sighed. "And we unlucky ones who are unable to give satisfactory account of ourselves—how long must we languish here, waiting?"

"You must languish until guilty person is found."

"Then we may go?" asked Romano, brightening.

"All those of you who are not concerned—yes. All those who will not be required to give evidence at trial."

For a long moment Romano stared into the fire. "But one who had such evidence—one who had, perhaps, assisted in the arrest of the guilty—such a one would be forced to linger here?"

"For a time. And he would undoubtedly be commanded to return for the trial."

"That would be most unfortunate for him," replied Romano suavely. "But long ago I find there is no justice in this American law. Ah, well—I must be patient. Paris will be waiting, Vienna will still be the same, and I shall sit again in the Opera at Milan. Perhaps direct once more—who knows? Yes—I must—what you call it?—bide my time." He leaned forward and whispered. "Did you, also, hear a noise outside that door?"

Chan rose, went softly over and flung it open. No one was there.

"I think you are unduly nervous, Mr. Romano," he said.

"And who, I pray, would not be nervous?" Romano replied. "All the time, I feel I am watched. Everywhere I go—every corner I turn—prying eyes are on me."

"And do you know why that should be?" Chan said.

"I know nothing," Romano answered loudly. "I have no part in this affair. When Landini was murdered, I was in my room, the door closed. I have testified to that. It is the truth."

"You had nothing else to say to me?" Chan inquired.

"Nothing whatever," Romano said, rising. He was calm again. "I merely wished to tell you I am very eager to go to New York. It means nothing to you, of course, but I am praying for your sudden success, Mr. Chan."

Charlie's eyes narrowed. "Sometimes success comes like that. Suddenly. Who knows? In this case it may happen."

"I hope with all my heart it will," bowed Romano. His eyes were on a table by the fire. "Is it that you have written a book, Inspector?"

Charlie shook his head. "Landini has written book," he replied. "I have been perusing galley proofs of same."

"Ah, yes. I knew of Landini's book. As a matter of fact, I assisted occasionally in the writing."

"Were you, by any chance, present when last chapter was written? Same was composed, I believe, at Stresa, on Lago Maggiore."

"Alas, no," Romano answered. "I was detained in Paris at the time."

"But you know Stresa? I understand it is beautiful spot."

Romano raised his hands. "Beautiful, Signor? Ah, the word is not enough. Oh, bella, bella—Stresa is heavenly, it is divine. Such coloring in the lake, the sky, the hills. Beloved Stresa—I must not forget—it is one of the places to which dear Ellen's money shall take me. I really believe I shall have to make a list. There are so many lovely places." He moved toward the door. "I hope I have not troubled you, Signor," he said. "Good night."

But he had troubled Charlie slightly. What did this interview mean? Was Romano concealing important evidence? Was his door, after all, not quite so tightly closed as he pretended at that moment when Ellen Landini was shot?

Or was he merely seeking to divert suspicion to others? Always he gave the impression of slyness; what could be slyer than for a guilty man to hint that perhaps he could tell something if he chose? And that play-acting about a noise at the door—rather hollow, rather unconvincing.

Charlie stepped quietly into the hall. All was silent below, and cautiously he crept down-stairs. No one seemed to be about, so with only the flickering fire to show him the way, he went to the closet and removed his hat, his overcoat, and those strange arctics which had come into his life when he decided to take this simple little trip to Tahoe. Returning to his room, he placed all these articles within easy reach, got out his flash-light and inspected it, and then—settled down to read the autobiography of Ellen Landini.

At one o'clock Charlie stopped reading, put down the galleys and stepped to his window. Pines, lake, sky, all had disappeared; the world seemed to end three feet away in a mixture of white and black. The outlook appeared to give him immense satisfaction; he was smiling as, with some difficulty, he got into the arctics and fastened them. He donned the unaccustomed overcoat, put his black felt hat securely on his head and took up his flash-light with a steady hand. Extinguishing all but one of his lights, he went into the hall and closed the door silently behind him.

It was the back stairs he chose to-night, and all down their length and along the passageway to the back door, he half expected to encounter the ubiquitous figure of the aged Sing. But no Sing loomed in his path. He let himself out on to the snowy back porch, and started toward the garage where only a few hours before he had come upon a ladder. The amateur student of trees was again immersed in thoughts of his favorite line of research.

But fate intervened, and Charlie did not visit the garage that night. For, flashing his light cautiously along the path, he suddenly perceived that there were fresh footprints ahead of him. Some one else had left Pineview by the back way to-night—and not so long ago.

To one who had hitherto known footprints only as something to be found in sand along a sunlit beach, the idea was fascinating. Almost unconsciously he followed the trail, up the flight of outdoor stairs that led to the road, which was some distance above the house. There he paused, and considered.

Who had left this house since eleven o'clock, which was about the time the snow had begun to fall? Had one of his charges escaped from his care? The falling snow was rapidly covering these tracks, but they seemed fresh ones, none the less. The quickest answer appeared to lie ahead.

He began to travel, as rapidly as his girth permitted, down the road that led in the direction of the Tavern. The wind howled through the long fragrant aisles of the pines, the storm wrapped him in a damp embrace. But he made speed, for his energy was great, and the languor of the semi-tropics was far-off and forgotten.

About half a mile down the road he came to the house of Dudley Ward's nearest neighbor. He remembered having seen it from the water—a great rambling barracks built of wood. Its windows were closed and shuttered for the winter, no sign of life was anywhere about it. And yet—the footprints which Charlie followed unmistakably turned off at this point. Turned off, and went unerringly down the path to the rear door.

A bit skeptical now, Charlie did the same. Perhaps, he reflected, he was merely on the trail of a watchman, or some equally harmless person. For a moment he stood on the rear porch. Then he reached out and tried the back door of the deserted house. A little thrill ran down his spine—for it opened at his touch.

At any rate, this was not housebreaking, he thought as he went inside. He found himself in a passageway, similar to the one in Ward's house, and again he stopped, alert for some sound of human habitation. The wind rattled the windows and sighed around the eaves, but nothing moved or seemed to live in these empty rooms. Yet at his feet, Chan's flash-light showed him, was a trail of loose snow leading off into the dark.

He followed this trail, out of the passage into a front hall. Great shadows danced about him on the walls; in distant rooms he saw ghostly chairs and sofas swathed in white. Undaunted, he pushed on, up the carpeted stairs where the fresh snow lay. It led him to a closed door at the rear of the second-floor hall, and there it stopped. He tried the door, quietly, and found it locked.

A brief examination of the sill decided him, and he had raised his hand to knock, when he thought he heard the closing of a distant door. He waited. Undoubtedly stealthy footsteps were crossing the polished floor of the down-stairs hall. Charlie was thinking very fast.

He had been in somewhat similar situations before, and had learned that all the advantage lies with the side which attacks suddenly and unexpectedly. Putting his flash-light in his pocket, he moved softly and swiftly to the stairs and began to descend. Half-way down he stopped and so, almost, did his heart. For the person in the hall below had lighted a match.

Charlie crouched close to the wall, the shadows flickered about him, but the life of a match is brief, and evidently he was still safe when the flame expired. Safe—in a way—except for the fact that the unknown intruder was coming rapidly up the stairs.

He had the top position, and there was nothing else for it—Charlie gathered all his strength and leaped, straight into the surprise of his life. For it was obviously a giant upon whom he fell; a giant who kept his footing and took Chan, avoirdupois and all, into his arms. In another second the plump detective from the islands was engaged in a struggle he would long remember. They staggered together down the stairs; their swaying forms hit the newel post, and an old-fashioned lamp that had been established there for thirty years crashed down in a million pieces. Next they were rolling on the floor, Charlie grimly determined to keep in so close an embrace that this terrible stranger would have no chance to square off for a blow. One blow from that source, he felt, would ruin him for ever.

Not in such good condition as he used to be, Chan reflected, as the fight went doggedly on. Getting on in years, easily winded—ah, youth, youth. No use pretending, it left one day, never to return. About this struggle now—he was losing it. Unmistakably. He was on his back, the stranger's hands were at his throat; he sought, vainly, to tear them away. A flash of the little house on Punchbowl Hill, the bougainvillea vine hanging over the veranda—then the dark, slowly enveloping his senses.

Then the stranger, sitting down violently on Charlie's generous stomach, and the voice of Don Holt, crying, "Good Lord—is that you, Mr. Chan?"

"Alas," said Chan. "At night all cats are black."

Holt was helping him to his feet, deeply solicitous. "Say—I sure am sorry about this, Inspector. Of course—I never suspected. I hope I haven't hurt you much. How do you feel?"

"How does sparrow feel when hit by cannon-ball?" Charlie returned. "A little disturbed. However, I expect to survive. And I am delighted we have met, though I must disparage the details of our meeting. For there is something strange afoot in this house to-night."

"I reckon there is," Holt answered. "I was sound asleep when the coroner came to my room—"

"One moment, please," Chan interrupted. "I will hear that later. Just now I think it important that we investigate a certain door up-stairs. Without delay." He got out his flash-light and, to his surprise, found it still working. "Will you be kind enough to follow me?"

Quickly he led the sheriff to the locked door on the second floor. "Track of snow brought me here," he explained. "And behold." He pointed. On the doorsill was more snow, a portion of a heel-print where a foot had recently trod.

"Then somebody's inside," said Holt, in a hushed voice.

"Somebody," nodded Chan. "Or something," he added.

The sheriff raised a great fist, and the sound of his blow against the panel echoed loudly through the house. "Open up here!" he shouted.

In the dead silence that followed there was something sinister and disturbing. Holt rattled the knob, and then moved back a few feet.

"Well," he said, "we already owe for that lamp downstairs. Might as well add a little damage here. Will you turn the light this way, Inspector?"

Charlie illuminated the scene, and the sheriff lunged forward. There came the sound of splintering wood as the lock gave way and the door swung open. Chan's flash swept the room inside. An ordinary bedroom, it seemed to be, as one after another the articles of furniture emerged from the shadows. An ordinary bedroom—and on the floor beside the bed, the motionless figure of a man.

As they stood for a moment in the doorway, Chan thought suddenly of Romano. Romano sitting nervously in that other bedroom, asking what would happen to one who—perhaps—assisted in the arrest of the guilty. Had there been real fear in the Italian's eyes when he whispered: "Did you, also, hear a noise outside that door?"

Kneeling, the sheriff turned the figure on the floor face up. Chan joined him with the lamp—and they were looking into the dead eyes of Doctor Swan.

14

Thought is a Lady

For a moment, while the yellow glare of Chan's flash-light rested idly on the face of the dead doctor, there was no sound save that of the storm roaring about the old house.

"Exit Doctor Swan," said the sheriff grimly. "I wonder what this means?"

"I believe," Chan answered, "it means that blackmailer has met with obvious finish. Was Doctor Swan enclosed safely in room last night when fatal shot was fired at Landini? It never did seem probable. Suppose he hovered about in hall, desiring one final word with his former wife. Suppose he learned who killed her. Would such a man report at once to police? Or would he, instead, see new delightful path for blackmail opening up before his dazzled eyes?"

"Sounds reasonable," Holt agreed.

"I think it happened. Suppose he is summoned down here to-night to receive first instalment of his wickedly earned money. And receives instead the bullet of a desperate person who can not pay—or, knowing that the demand will be endless, will not pay. Ah, yes, from murderer's standpoint, this would be wiser course. I can not truthfully say I disagree. But you were about to tell me how you chance to be here?"

"The coroner had the room next to Swan's at the Tavern," Holt replied. "He was waked up about twelve-thirty by the banging of a shutter. The noise seemed to come from Swan's room. The coroner stood it as long as he could, and then he rapped on Swan's door. Well, to cut it short, nobody answered—an' that was how I come into it.

"We saw right away that Swan had left by the window. I followed his footprints to the road, where they turned in this direction. It looked like the doctor was staging a getaway. Say, I didn't stop for anything—I jes' hurried along on his trail. Didn't even have a flash-light—not so strong on preparedness as you are. But I did have a full box of matches—jes' used my last down-stairs."

"You walked the two miles or more from the Tavern?"

"Sure—when I wasn't running. When I got to the point behind this house where Swan had turned off, I looked up and got the glimmer of a flash-light back of the hall shutters on the second floor—yours, I reckon. So I pushed open the back door, and came in."

"The back door was still unlocked?" Chan asked thoughtfully.

"Sure."

Charlie considered. "The killer of Doctor Swan must have intended this house as temporary hiding-place for victim," he reflected. "Would he then have departed, leaving door unlocked for any passer-by to enter? I think not. The answer is, of course, he was still in house when we arrived. He may even be here now. Come—we waste valuable time."

Hastily he led Don Holt down-stairs and through the passageway to the rear door. He turned the knob. But now the rear door was locked, and there was no key in sight.

"Haie!" Chan cried. "Our friend has made his escape—perhaps while we were tumbling in mortal conflict in the hall. Where was he hiding when we entered?" He made an investigation of the plentiful snow along the passage. "Ah, yes." Pushing open the door into a butler's pantry, he sadly pointed out to Hold more snow on the linoleum inside. "Let us place order for ample supply of sackcloth and ashes," he remarked gloomily. "You and I, my boy, both walked to-night within three feet of the murderer we so hotly seek. Alas, this winter climate is not so invigorating to the mental processes as I had hoped it would be."

The sheriff returned to the back door and fiercely rattled the knob. "He's got a fine start on us, too," he said.

"Man inclined to exercise would not need to look farther for nice pair of dumb-bells," Chan answered. "Pardon vile slang, which I acquire from my children, now being beautifully educated in American schools. Come, we must seek new footprints leading away from this rear door. They are our only hope."

They ran to the big front door, where somewhat rusted bolts again delayed them. After a struggle, however, they got it open, and hastened around to the back of the house. The snow was very damp now. "Turning to rain," Holt announced, looking up at the sky. "This'll have to be a quick job."

There were, indeed, new footprints in the snow at the back. They led away, not to the road, but around the house, on the opposite side from that which Chan and the sheriff had traveled. Breathlessly the two representatives of the law followed them—straight to the pier. At the edge of the restless water beneath the pier, the footprints stopped abruptly.

"That ends that," sighed Holt. "This guy had a row-boat, I reckon." He stared at the wild waters. "Wouldn't care to be traveling out there to-night," he added.

Charlie was bending eagerly with his flash-light above the last visible prints just before they entered the water. "No use," he said, sighing ponderously. "Fresh snow obscures any identifying marks. Snow, I fear, has been a little too highly spoken of as aid to detectives in hour of need."

They returned to the front veranda of the house. Holt continued to study the lake. "With this rain coming on," he remarked, "I don't believe a rowboat could keep afloat out there."

"If man who killed Swan, and then escaped after we entered house, brought boat," Chan said, "then who was person whose tracks I followed down from Pineview by the road? Did he perhaps carry boat on back?"

"Oh—you followed somebody down here, too?"

"I assuredly did, and I believe he was the man we seek."

"Perhaps he took a boat from this place."

"No—I observed boat-house intact. Might I make another suggestion?"

"By all means. I'm through."

"Might he not have stepped into water and run along shore for some distance? Beach is flat here."

"By golly, that's right," agreed the sheriff. "He could travel by that method for a mile in either direction. Of course, he'd probably leave the water as soon as he thought himself safe. There's an idea—we could follow the shore—"

"In which direction?"

"Why—you take one way, and I'll take the other."

Charlie shook his head. "No use," he said. "Already this gentleman has had twelve minutes' start. As for me, my avoirdupois precludes success—and even your thin legs, I think, would fail."

Holt sighed. "It seemed the only chance," he said.

Charlie smiled. "There will be other chances," he replied. "Do not despair. Our quarry will be caught—but by subtler means than running along-shore in the rain. For I perceive we now have rain."

"Yes, spring has come," Holt answered. "And here I am, too tangled up in murder to enjoy the thought."

"From the black sky, white water falls," smiled Chan, looking aloft. "This may yet prove very pleasant spring for you."

"Oh, yeah?" the sheriff replied. "Well, in the meantime, what next? Here we are, stuck down here, in a deserted house with a dead man—no telephone, and nothing but our feet to get away on. Here's my suggestion. I'll go back to the Tavern and get the coroner, while you go and see what's doing at Pineview."

"So sorry to disagree," Chan said. "Everything would no doubt be quiet at Pineview—every one in bed and asleep by the time I reached there. No change—save that I might possibly find back door, which I left unfastened, now locked. In such case, I must raise row, or stand in rain until morning. Besides, is it wise to leave this place unguarded? We might return to find our dead man gone. Suppose the killer still lurks among the trees, sees us both depart, and proceeds to follow out hastily the plan I am sure he intended to pursue at leisure—to drop body of Swan far out in lake, to hide it in hills, to dispose of it in some manner. No. Plan for yourself is excellent, but I shall linger here, awaiting return of the honorable sheriff, the coroner and light of another day."

"Well." Holt looked back into the dim empty house. "It's no job I would rise in meeting to ask for, but if you want it, it's yours. But what in Sam Hill will you do with yourself? I'll be gone quite some while."

"There is no need of hurry on your part. First, I shall open front door very wide, seeking to exchange stale air of long-closed house for fresher breath of first spring night. Then, I shall find comfortable chair in parlor, repose in it and think."

"Think?"

"Precisely. Thought is a lady, beautiful as jade, so do not fear I shall be lonely. Events of to-night make me certain I must not neglect the lady's company longer."

"Well, look out for yourself, if you stay here," Holt remarked. "That's not a pretty picture you painted—the killer creeping back. I haven't got my gun with me, or I'd loan it to you."

Charlie shrugged. "I hold with Mrs. O'Ferrell—the less guns, the fewer gets killed. However, have no anxiety. The chair I sit in will be like seat for guest of honor at Chinese dinner. It will face the door, so I may note enemy's approach."

"Then I'll be going—" Holt began.

Charlie laid a hand on his arm. "Already that lady inspires me—I see Doctor Swan, standing on pier to-night, just before you took him to the Tavern in your launch. What was it he desire so eagerly to know?"

"That's right," Holt said. "About Romano and the will. Did Romano get Landini's property?"

"And was he, consequently, a good blackmail prospect?" Chan's eyes narrowed. "It would seem to me, Sheriff, that Swan came here to-night to meet a man of whom, physically, he had no fear. A small man—like Romano."

Don Holt scowled. "But Romano. If he had done either of these killings wouldn't he have been more likely to use a knife?"

"Ah—excellent reasoning," Charlie cried. "I am proud of you. However, you forget—or perhaps you do not know—that Romano, like Ireland, served in the war. An Italian officer—he must have known well the use of the revolver. But no matter—I merely continue to marshal facts for the storehouse of my mind. A pleasant journey to you."

"Yeah—in the rain, on foot," smiled Holt. "Well, good-by—and good luck."

He ran down off the porch and disappeared toward the road in the rear. Chan retired inside, leaving the door open, and moved on into a large living-room. A pleasant place this must be, he thought, on summer nights, with its splendid view of the lake. He removed a sheet from a large chair and placing the latter in what seemed the safest corner, dropped into it. Then he shut off his light, and put it in his pocket.

The rain beat against the house, the wind roared, and Charlie thought back over this wintry case upon which he, detective of the semi-tropics, was now so unexpectedly engaged. First of all he thought of people: of Sing, whose beady little eyes even Chan could not read; of Cecile, jealous and angry last night when she heard the airplane over the lake; of Ireland, clumsy and uneasy when out of his plane, but so expert when in it. He considered Romano, broke and according to his own confession, desperate—but now come into money through Landini's sudden passing. Hugh Beaton, sick of the bargain he had made; his sister, jealous as Cecile, but in a different way—a high-strung, impetuous girl. Dinsdale—since he was including them all—evidently so aloof from all this—but an old friend of the singer, none the less. Ward, who had started it all and encountered two tragedies. Ryder, with the scornful blue eyes above the blond beard, and Swan—dead now in that room above. Had it been, after all, attempted blackmail that led to Swan's death? How young Hugh Beaton had raged at the doctor last night after the murder—and how Michael Ireland and Swan had snarled at each other.

The rain outside seemed to increase in fury, and Charlie decided he had had enough of the open door. He crossed over, closed it and returned to his chair. Once more, he decided, he would take things from the beginning—the sudden shot upstairs, Landini on the floor, the boxes with the mixed lids—ah, he had been over all this a hundred times. But—and he started up suddenly in his chair—there was one thing he had forgotten. Not yet had he carefully considered the events before the murder.

He was back, then, on the train, repeating from memory his talk with Romano; he was riding up from Truckee to the Tavern; again the icy spray of the lake stung his cheeks, he was going ashore at Pineview, the ex-husbands of Landini were drinking before the fire. Then followed dinner—his excellent memory recalled vividly every incident at the table, nearly every word that had been spoken. He heard again the bark of the dog announcing the arrival of the singer—felt again the vibrant, colorful personality of Landini—ah, what a pity her brilliant career was so soon to end.

But beyond the shot that ended it, Chan did not trouble now to explore. He gazed around this strange room, listened for a moment to the spatter of rain at the windows, and then, oblivious to any killer who might return, he curled up comfortably in his chair, drew his overcoat closer and fell into a deep and peaceful sleep. After all, a man must sleep.

He awoke with a start to find the sheriff bending over him. A semblance of dawn seemed to be floating through the house, but the rain still beat against the window-panes.

Beyond Don Holt stood the coroner.

"Sorry to disturb you," Holt said. "We just dropped in."

Charlie yawned, sat up and was about to step to the window for a look at his beloved Honolulu. Then he remembered.

"Anything exciting happen?" Holt wanted to know.

"I—I think not," Chan said. "No—as I recall now—nothing happened. Ah, yes—the coroner. He will want to go up-stairs."

He leaped briskly to his feet, and led the way to the room above. The others followed, not so briskly. They could all see, in the semi-darkness, the body of Swan, lying as it had been left by Charlie and the sheriff the night before.

"We need more light here, I think," Chan said. "I will admit some, such as it is." He went to the window, opened it and threw back the blinds. For a moment he stood leaning over the window-sill, then Don Holt was surprised to see him climbing through the window.

"What are you doing?" the sheriff inquired.

"Small polar expedition of my own," Chan replied. He had dropped to a balcony some two feet below the window. It was covered by about twelve inches of snow, now melting rapidly. At one side of the window, close to the house wall, was a spot which had melted more rapidly than the rest, leaving a small hole. Charlie bared one arm to the elbow, and plunged it deep into the crevice. With an expression of triumph on his face, he held up an automatic pistol so those inside the room could see.

"Man who buries his treasure in the snow," he said, "forgets that summer is coming."

15

Another Man's Earth

Chan handed the revolver to the sheriff and began a rather cumbersome climb back into the room.

"Guard weapon well," he suggested. "It may prove valuable—who knows? How many cartridges exploded, please?"

"Why, one, of course," the sheriff replied.

"Ah, yes—the bullet from which, now reposing in poor Doctor Swan, the coroner will later obtain for us. You may handle pistol freely, Sheriff. The killer we deal with does not leave finger-prints—even with his footprints he is careful man. In spite of his care, however, his discarded weapons may yet tell us much."

"You think so?" inquired Holt.

"I hope so." For a time Charlie stood studying the revolver as it lay in the sheriff's hand. "This one has somewhat old-fashioned look," he suggested.

"Sure does," Don Holt agreed.

"You are, of course, too young to have fought in the war?"

"Too young by six years—I tried it," smiled the sheriff.

Charlie shrugged. "No matter. All sorts of weapons were issued in the war—on many fronts. We must seek other path."

Doctor Price stood up. "All right," he said, "that's all I can do now. We may as well take this man down to the village."

"What would you deduce?" Chan inquired.

"I believe he was shot at close range, and without a struggle," the coroner replied. "Certainly there was no struggle here—though he may have been killed elsewhere, and carried to this room."

"Very probable," Chan nodded. "For that reason, I make no extended examination of the place."

"I don't believe the poor devil had any inkling of what was about to happen to him," Doctor Price continued. "That's just a guess, of course. The bullet entered his side—it may have been fired by some one who was walking close to him—or slightly behind him. All things that we'll never know, I reckon." There came the honk of a horn behind the house. "That's Gus Elkins. I told him to follow us with his ambulance." He yawned. "Gosh—I expected to be on my way back to the county-seat before this."

While Doctor Price and Mr. Elkins attended to the removal of Swan's body, the sheriff and Charlie made a tour of the house, restoring it to order, in so far as they could.

"You an' me—I reckon we'll take my old flivver and get over to Pineview," the sheriff said. "We come up by road—lake looked pretty choppy. But say—wait till you hit the road." He kicked aside some broken glass in the lower hall. "Hope you ain't feelin' any ill effects from our friendly tussle."

"He who goes out on the hills to meet the tiger must pay the price," returned Charlie.

Holt laughed. "Sure was a mix-up. I was wonderin' when I walked back to the Tavern what we ought to do next. Somebody had a key to the back door of that house, I said. So I sent a wire down to the owner in San Francisco an' asked him who that would be."

"Excellent," Charlie returned. "It was what I was about to suggest. But now you are moving a little ahead of me on our rocky path."

"I ain't so sure about that," Holt said. "How did you get on with your home work while I was away? Going to do a lot of heavy thinkin', I believe you told me."

Charlie's eyes narrowed. "Alas," he answered, "I fear that, like my little son Barry, I toppled in sleep on to my books."

"Oh, yeah?" Don Holt answered.

In a few moments the ambulance had gone, and Chan climbed into the flivver beside the sheriff. "Feel at home in such seat," he commented. They started with a jerk. "But not on such road. Not much melting snow on Punchbowl Hill."

Daylight had come, but a sullen counterfeit daylight. The rain beat down on the top of the car, and on Don Holt's two-gallon hat as he leaned far out to follow the road—the windshield wiper, he explained, was not working. The wind had died, the pines were silent and dripping; they plowed on through slush a foot deep.

"Wonder how we'll find all the folks at Pineview," the sheriff said presently. "Including the murderer. I guess there ain't much doubt he'll be there, waiting for us."

"He may be," Charlie agreed.

"Well—let's have a check-up. Who's there now? Romano, Ryder and Ward. Hugh Beaton—and his sister."

"A charming lady, Miss Beaton," Chan suggested.

"Yeah—she's all right. But don't get me off the track—I'm countin'. Let's see—well, that's about all—except Sing and Cecile—I sort of had that French dame on my mind, but after this, she don't look so good. That's the list."

"And Mrs. O'Ferrell," Chan added.

"Yeah—I can see her plowin' down through the snow to put a bullet in Swan. Say—I never been able to figure out what you meant—about Trouble bein' a clue."

"So sorry," Chan replied. "But we all have our little mysteries to sting us, as summer flies pester the horse. For example, in own mind I am convinced blow received by Sing in defenseless face on night of murder was vastly important clue. But—I can not figure it. However, we must be patient. You and I—we will both learn in time."

They left the car on the road above and descended the steps to the back door of Pineview. Sing was shaking a duster on the porch. He gave Charlie a slightly startled look.

"Wha's mallah you?" he demanded. "My think you up-stah in bed, you come home back step, plenty wet."

"I was called away on business," Charlie explained.

"Hello, Sing," the sheriff said. "Don't worry about Mr. Chan. I've been taking care of him. Anybody up yet?"

"Nobody only me," Sing replied. "My get up sunlise, woik, woik, woik. Too much woik this house. No can do."

Inside, they found Sing's statements somewhat inaccurate. Mrs. O'Ferrell was busy in the kitchen, and gave hem a cheery greeting. Proceeding to the living-room, they found Leslie Beaton, reading a book.

"Hello—you're up early," Holt remarked.

"The same for you," she replied, "and as for Mr. Chan—I don't believe he ever sleeps. Was that he—or should I say him—I saw in the road behind the house in the night?"

"It may have been," Charlie said quickly. "Again, it may not. Elaborate the statement, if you will be so good."

"I couldn't sleep very well," the girl went on. "Can any one—in this house? My room is in an ell in the rear, close to the road. I went to the window and looked out. I saw a shadowy figure, hurrying up the steps, and fairly running along the road."

"Sounds pretty active for the inspector," smiled Holt. "Do you know what time this was?"

"Yes—it was precisely ten minutes after twelve. I looked at my watch."

Chan leaned toward her eagerly. "Describe this person," he urged.

"Impossible," she answered. "It was snowing hard. It might have been anybody—even a woman, for that matter. I was somewhat worried. I went into my brother's room—he's right next door—and wakened him. But he told me to go back to bed, and forget it."

Hugh Beaton at that momen appeared on the stairs. His face seemed paler than usual; here were dark circles about his eyes, and his manner was extremely nervous. He saw Charlie and the sheriff.

"What's happened now?" he cried. "For God's sake—what is it now?"

"It is nothing," Charlie replied soothingly. "You arise early."

"Why shouldn't I? my nerves are all shot to pieces, in this God-forsaken place. When are you going to let us out of this prison? What right have you—"

"Please, Hughie," his sister cut in. "Mr. Ward might hear sou—and he's been so kind to us."

"I don't care if he does hear me," the boy retorted. "He knows I don't want to stay here. When do we go o the Tavern? You promised to-day—"

"And it will be to-day," Holt said, looking at him with a trace of contempt. Temperamental artists were not in the sheriff's line. "Brace up."

"Tell me," Chan said. "When your sister came in to wake you last night—"

"When she—oh yes. I remember now. What was that all about?"

"You remember, Hughie," said the girl, "I told you I'd seen somebody leaving the house."

"Oh, yes. Well, did somebody leave? Is some one missing?"

"Somebody did leave," Charlie explained. "We think he returned, however. But not until, in an empty house down the road, he had shot and killed Doctor Swan."

There was silence for a moment. "Doctor Swan," gasped the girl. Her face was as white as her brother's. "Oh, that's too terrible."

"It's no more terrible than the killing of Ellen," her brother said, and his voice sounded hysterical. "We've got to get out of here, I tell you. To-day. This minute." He rose and stared wildly about.

"A little later," Holt remarked calmly.

"But I tell you—my sister—she's in danger here. So are we all—but I have to look after her—"

"A natural feeling," Chan said. "Your sister will be taken care of—and so will you. I presume you heard nothing in the night—save, of course, your sister's entrance. You can throw no light on this?"

"None. None whatever," the boy answered.

"Most unfortunate." Charlie rose. "I go to my room to freshen up drooping appearance. I return soon," he added to the sheriff.

He went up, leaving the three young people in the living-room. Cecile was standing just inside his door.

"Ah, Monsieur," she cried. "Your bed is untouched."

"I know," he replied. "I did not sleep last night. Just a moment, if you will be so kind. Do not go."

"Yes, Monsieur." She regarded him with troubled eyes.

"Your husband, Madame? When did you see him last?"

"When he left here just before dinner. Surely you recall? He took the little dog in his plane."

"He did not return to this neighborhood last night?"

"How could he? Such a night. He could not fly in such weather."

"But he is not an expert chauffeur? He could return in automobile."

"If he returned, I did not know it. I do not understand of what you speak, Monsieur."

"He and Doctor Swan—they were not the best of friends?"

"Michael hates him, as you saw yourself. He despises him, and with many good reasons. But why do you ask?"

"Because"—Charlie keenly watched her face—"because, Madame, Doctor Swan was murdered in this vicinity last night." Still he watched her. "Ah, that is all. You may go now."

She left without a word, and after hastily washing his hands and his as yet unshaven face, Charlie went out and knocked on Romano's door. The conductor let him in; he was partly dressed, his face was covered with lather, and he held a razor in his hand.

"Enter, Inspector," he invited. "You will pardon my condition. The hour—it is an early one."

"Events conspire to give me no rest," Chan told him. "Continue, please, to shave. I will repose here, on edge of bathtub. There is a word or two—"

"What do you wish, Signor?"

"You heard no one about this house last night? You saw no one leave by the rear door?"

"I am a sound sleeper, Inspector."

Quickly Chan told him what had occurred. He wished the Italian had removed more of that lather before hearing the news. But—wasn't the swarthy forehead now somewhat more in harmony with the white lather?

"Swan, eh?" said Romano slowly. "Ah, yes—he knew too much, that one, Inspector. Him, he could not hold his tongue. Only yesterday, when we were having long day together, he spoke indiscreetly to me."

"He said—what?"

"Nothing definite, you understand. I could not give you words. But already I thought his greedy fingers counted fresh bank-notes. That is dangerous business—blackmail."

Chan studied the Italian's face. From the first, this man had baffled him.

"And in my room last night," he said, "you, yourself, hinted at knowing something, too."

An expression of vast surprise crossed Romano's face.

"I, Signor? The day is young—you are still dreaming."

"Nonsense. You spoke of—"

"Ah, my English—it is not good. You do not understand me when I speak it."

"You asked if any one who could give information in this case would have to remain here after giving it."

"Did I say that? I must have been thinking of Doctor Swan."

"Unusual, if you were," Chan answered. "I should not say you devoted much thought to others. Of yourself, you think. Then consider this—if you have information which you withhold, it will go hard with you when mater is discovered."

"I have no information," Romano answered suavely. "All I can say is, I trust this new murder will speed your search, for speed is what I most desire. In the meantime, you are permitting Miss Beaton and her brother the privilege of changing their residence to the Tavern to-day. Can you deny the same to me? You can not. I will not stay in this house another day."

"Ah—you begin to remember, now," Chan smiled. "You are afraid here. You do know something, after all."

"Signor," cried Romano passionately, "you insult my honor. Ellen Landini was dear to me—her memory is dearer still—would I conceal the name of her assassin? No! A million times, no! Anyhow," he added more calmly, "I do not know the name. Must I tell you again?"

"For the present—no," bowed Chan, and left the room.

Down-stairs, he found Hugh Beaton nervously pacing the floor, while his sister and the sheriff sat before the fire. The latter's conversational powers seemed to be ebbing fast, and Charlie was happy to help him out. In a few moments John Ryder came down the stairs, carefully groomed as always, remote and aloof.

"Beastly day, isn't it?" he remarked. He glanced at the sheriff. "Hello,

Mr. Holt. Anything new?"

"Nothing unusual," Holt said. "Another murder, that's all."

"Another what?" It was Dudley Ward who spoke, from the stairs.

Charlie Chan explained, watching both men alternately as he did so. Ryder's expression never altered; Ward looked only a little older, a little more worn, as he listened.

"A nasty bounder, Swan," Ryder said coldly. "But, of course—murder is a bit extreme."

"None too kind to Ellen," Ward remarked thoughtfully. "But then—I guess none of us were, for that matter."

"Speak for yourself, Dudley," answered Ryder warmly. "Don't begin to idealize the woman, just because she's dead."

"I'm not idealizing her, John," Ward returned. "I'm just trying to keep in mind her virtues—and they were many. And it has occurred to me these last few days, that she was not too lucky in her choice of husbands." His eyes were on Romano, sleek and dapper, who was now coming down the stairs.

"Bleakfast leady now," announced Sing, from the rear.

"Come on, Don," Ward said. "You're eating with us."

"That's—that's mighty good of you," replied the sheriff.

"Nonsense. Sing—set another place!"

Sing muttered something about the amount of work in this house, and retired. But when they reached the dining-room, the old Chinese was there ahead of them, briskly and efficiently making a place for Holt.

The meal was eaten for the most part in silence. When it was ended, and they were back in the living-room, Holt informed Leslie Beaton and her brother that he would send his launch for them at nine-thirty, and that they should be packed and ready for the move to the hotel.

"You bet I'll be ready," young Beaton cried. Seeing his sister's eyes on him, he added: "Of course, Mr. Ward, I appreciate your hospitality. And the way Leslie's looking at me, I suppose I ought to add, I had a nice time." His tone was childish and disagreeable.

"Hardly that," Ward replied amiably. "But I shall miss your sister and you very much, and I hope you may some day return for a stay under happier conditions."

"You've been wonderful," Leslie Beaton told him. "I shall never forget you. The perfect host—at the most imperfect moment."

Ward bowed. "I shan't forget you," he said.

Romano popped to the front. "There will be a place in your launch for me?" he asked.

"What do you mean?" inquired Holt.

"I mean I also—with deep regret, Signor Ward—am leaving here to-day for the Tavern. Inspector Chan has agreed."

Holt glanced at Charlie, who nodded. "All right," the sheriff said. "You can have Swan's room. You've heard what happened to him."

Romano shrugged. "Ah—he wandered too far away. Me—I stick close to the hotel."

"Well, see that you do," Holt replied.

Charlie followed the sheriff into the passage at the rear. "Pardon me," he inquired. "You have revolver we discovered in snow?"

"Sure. You want it?" Holt produced the weapon.

"I will take it brief while. When our friends come down to Tavern, I will be with them. Tell me, is there train to Oakland this morning?"

"Yes—there's one about ten-thirty. Say"—an expression of dismay spread over the sheriff's face—"you ain't leaving, are you?"

"No. Not at this date."

"Who is?"

"We will discuss the matter later."

"So long, then." Holt lowered his voice. "Well, we had a nice breakfast, didn't we? But that's about all we got, eh?"

"Not quite." Chan's eyes narrowed. "We received also, from Miss Beaton, very pretty alibi for her brother at twelve-ten last night."

"My gosh," the sheriff said. "I never thought of that."

"I did not think you would," smiled Charlie.

He went at once to his room where, for a time, he experimented with lampblack and brush on the automatic pistol. Then, leaving the weapon on his desk, he hurried at last to the refreshing solace of his morning bath. He had just finished shaving when Sing appeared in his room with a supply of wood. Chan came out from the bath to find the old man staring at the pistol.

"Hello, Sing," he remarked, "you see that before, maybe?"

"I no see him."

"You are quite sure?"

"I no see him—tha's no lie, Boss."

Charlie's eyebrows went up at this unexpected tribute of respect. "Mebbe you catch 'um killer—hey, Boss?" the old man added.

Chan shrugged. "I am stupid policeman—my mind is like the Yellow River." He paused. "But—who was it said—even the Yellow River has its clear days?"

"No savvy," responded Sing, and started out.

Charlie laid a hand on the thin old arm.

"Delay one moment, if you will be so good," he said in Cantonese. "You and I, honorable Sing, are of the same race, the same people. Why, then, should a thousand hills rise between us when we talk?"

"They are hills you place there with your white devil ways," Sing suggested.

"I am so sorry. They are imaginary. Let us sweep them away. How many years did you have when you came to this alien land?"

"I had eighteen," the old man replied. "Now I have seventy-eight."

"Then for sixty years you have carried another man's heaven on your head, and your feet have trod upon another man's earth. Do you not long to return to China, ancient one?"

"Some day—" the old man's eyes glittered.

"Some day—yes. But a man takes off his shoes to-night. How does he know he will put them on again in the morning? Death comes, Ah Sing."

"My bones return," Sing told him.

"Yes—that is much. But to see again the village where you were born—to walk again on the soil where your bones are to rest—"

The old man shook his head sadly. "Too much woik this house," he said, lasping into English. "No can go. No can go."

"Do not despair," Charlie returned, dropping his somewhat rusty Cantonese. "Fate settles all things, and all things arrive at their appointed time." He took a clean white shirt from his bag and proceeded to put it on. "A very dull day, indeed," he added, stepping to the window and gazing out at the dripping pines. "On such an occasion, the attire of man should compensate. You understand what I mean—I should wear gay clothes, happy clothes. My brightest necktie, perhaps."

"Tha's light," nodded Sing.

"I have a very red necktie—my daughter Evelyn gave it to me on Christmas, and she herself put it in my bag when I left. It is, my dear Sing, the reddest necktie the eyes of man have seen. And this, I believe, is the fitting day for it." He went to his closet, removed a tie and drew it around his neck. For a moment he faced the mirror, and while he tied the knot, he watched the expression on the old man's withered countenance. He turned about, to give Sing the full effect.

"There," he beamed, "that will brighten this bloomy day. Eh, Sing?"

"Velly good," agreed Sing, and walked slowly from the room. Charlie stood looking after him, his eyes narrowed, his face very thoughtful.

16

That Boy Ah Sing

At half past nine, Cash Shannon appeared with the sheriff's launch. When it came to brightening the day and atoning for the weather, Cash took second place to no man. Indeed, at the mere sight of his colorful costume, the weather seemed to be giving up the struggle; the rain had stopped, and the clouds raced madly through the sky as though seeking to give the sun an opening. There was no doubt that the storm was over, nature would soon be smiling but not, probably, as brightly as Cash at the sight of Leslie Beaton.

He appeared slightly surprised at the number of passengers he was to carry, for Romano added himself and his luggage to the group on the pier, and Charlie made it known that his not inconsiderable person was also to be included. However, once they were started, Cash paid no attention to any one save the girl.

"Well, I guess you might call this the opening day at the Tavern," he remarked to her. "If I was the management—which I ain't—there'd be tea on the terrace, music in the casino, an' flags hanging all over the place."

"What *are* you talking about?" she inquired.

"Any time a girl like you comes to a hotel, ought to be some sort of celebration. That's the way I figure it. Say—how do you get on with a horse?"

"I ride a little."

"Well, we'll change all that. You'll ride a lot, the next few days. Some of the trails are open now an' say—the plans I got—"

"If you will be so kind," called Chan, from behind him. "Please make utmost speed."

"What for?" inquired Cash.

"I have some plans myself," smiled Charlie.

The instant the launch had landed, he leaped ashore and hurried to the hotel. Old Sam Holt was seated by the fire, and greeted Chan with every evidence of pleasure.

"Been waiting to talk to you," he said. "Sorry I wasn't with you last night up the road."

"We have much to discuss," Charlie answered. "But first there is a matter that requires great haste. Where is your son, please?"

"I reckon he's out to the stables. I'll send one of the boys." The old man made his way to the desk, gave the order and returned. "What's on your mind now, Inspector Chan?"

"You will denounce me bitterly when I tell you," Chan replied.

" 'Tain't easy to picture that," the old man said. "You mean—"

"I mean I propose to call into this case some one we both agree is absolutely worthless. A scientist."

Sam Holt laughed. "Wal—gener'ly speakin', Mr. Chan. Gener'ly speakin'. O' course, mebbe I'm a leetle unreasonable. An' if you cave in on th' point, I reckon I kin cave in with you."

"A gentleman I met in San Francisco a few weeks ago," Charlie explained. "An instructor of physics at the University of California, in Berkeley. I had a serious talk with him, and I thought—" Don Holt approached and Chan leaped to his feet. "Mr. Sheriff, tell me—have you bullet from body of the recent Doctor Swan?"

"Sure—I got it," Holt replied, producing it. "Another thirty-eight. The coroner—"

"Haste is required," Chan cut in. "Pardon the abrupt manner. But inform me—can we place some one on the ten-thirty train at Truckee—and if so, whom?"

Cash had just entered with Leslie Beaton and her brother. The deputy was loaded with bags, and eternal adoration of the fair sex gleamed in his eyes. Holt laughed.

"I'll say we've got some one we can put on that train," he chortled. "And good riddance, too. Hey—Cash."

Cash dropped the luggage and came over. "What is it, Chief?"

"Get a bag packed, kid. You got to catch the Oakland train at Truckee, an' you got to step."

"Me?" cried Cash in dismay. "But say, I just made a date with Miss Beaton to exercise a couple horses at three o'clock—"

"Thanks a lot," smiled Holt. "I'll be glad to take care of that for you. Get a move on, boy. I'm tellin' you." Cash hurried out toward the stables, "Now, Mr. Chan—that's the best idea you've ever had in your life. Where's he goin', and why?"

"To begin operations," Charlie said, "kindly bring me from safe of Mr. Dinsdale, Landini's revolver, and along with it bullet from same which killed her. Also, please obtain for me one very large and strong Manila envelope." He sat down at a writing-desk, and took the pistol which had slain Swan from his pocket, This he laid on the desk. The bullet he had just received from the sheriff, he put in an envelope and marked. Then he took a sheet of notepaper and hasily began to write.

He had finished the letter when Young Holt returned and placed before him the pearl-handled pistol that had been Landini's property, and the other bullet. The latter was put into a second small envelope and marked, and Charlie then proceeded to insert a marked piece of paper in the barrel of each gun. He took the big envelope Holt handed him, wrote a hasty name and address on the outside, and put into it the two weapons and the two small envelopes. He then sealed the flap, and handed the big envelope to he sheriff.

"It bears, you will note, an address in Berkeley. Tell the good Cash to alight at Oakland and visit this man at once. He is to obtain answer to question in my letter—to-night if possible—and wire same to you instantly. Impress upon him great need of speed."

"Fine," answered Holt, looking at his watch. "I'll let him take my car, and he can just about make it. He can leave the car in a garage near the station in Truckee."

He hurried out. Sam Holt, who had been listening, came up. "And this perfessor at Berkeley, Mr. Chan," he said, "what does he claim he kin do?"

"He claims," Charlie replied, "that if he has both pistol and bullet, he can tell how far latter has traveled."

"He's a liar," said Holt promptly.

"Perhaps," smiled Chan. "But the wonders of science—who are we to question them? And I have some curiosity to know how far these bullets traveled—especially that one found in poor unhappy Landini. My friend also claims that many times, from portion of thumb-print found on head of shell, he can reconstruct full print of person who had pushed same into carriage. That would be useful in other instance."

"He's a colossal liar," insisted the old sheriff.

"We shall see," Chan old him. "If you will pardon me for one moment, I have telephone call to make."

He went into a booth, and in a few minutes he was greeting Miss Meecher in her Reno hotel.

"So sorry to disturb you," he said.

"That is quite all right," she answered. "Is there any news?"

"None save that of Doctor Swan's unexpected passing, about which you have no doubt heard."

"Yes—a bell-boy just told me. It seems rather terrible."

"Entire case is terrible. Miss Meecher, you are in receipt of Trouble?"

"Oh—you mean the dog? Yes, Mr. Ireland brought him in last night. Poor little fellow—he just roams about the apartment, looking for his mistress."

"That is very sad. However, he is in kind hands, I know. There is a question, Miss Meecher, which I must ask you."

"I'll tell you anything I can."

"Naturally. You have told me that you and Madame Landini worked on her biography together. Do you recall beginning of last chapter, written on balcony of hotel at Stresa, where she spoke of knowing color-blind person?"

"Why, yes, I do," Miss Meecher replied.

"Did it chance that she mentioned to you the name of this person?"

"No, she didn't. I remember she wrote that herself, and when I came to type it I was slightly curious. But she wasn't about at the moment, and though I meant to ask her later, it slipped my mind. It didn't seem imporant, anyhow." There was a brief pause. "Is it important, Mr. Chan?"

"Not even slightly," replied Chan heartily. "I was, like you, somewhat curious. But it does not matter. My real intention in calling up—I would ask has anything developed you think I should note?"

"I believe not. There's a wire from Madame's attorneys in New York asking me if it is true she never signed the will. It seems Romano is already in touch with them."

"Ah, he is no wastrel of time, this Romano."

"Shall I wire them the truth?"

"By all means. And kindly give my best regards to the anxious little dog. I have great likeness for him."

"Thank you so much," Miss Meecher replied.

As Charlie emerged from the booth, two young men entered the hotel lounge from the terrace. One of them—tall, lean, a bit graying at the temples—rushed forward eagerly.

"As I live and breathe," he cried. "My old friend. Charlie Chan. You remember me—Bill Rankin, of the *San Francisco Globe*?"

"With a pleasant glow," Chan replied. "You were my very good ally when Sir Frederic Bruce was killed."

"And here I am, all ready to be an ally once again. Oh—this is Gleason of the *Herald*. He thinks he's a newspaper reporter, too. What ideas these youngsters get!"

"Hello, Mr. Chan," Gleason said. "We just missed you down at Pineview. But we had a nice ride on the lake."

"Let's get down to cases," said Rankin. "This sheriff up here, Inspector, is a swell guy, but he won't talk. That was never your trouble, as I recall."

"Talk was my weakness," grinned Chan.

"Of course, you never said anything, but it made copy. Now, what's the dope? Who bumped off Landini?"

"Surely you do not think I have solved such a problem already?"

"Why not? You've had over twenty-four hours. Not slowing up on us, are you? Getting old—no, I can tell you're not by looking at you."

"The case," said Chan, "has many angles. We labor hard, but it will not be brought to solution in a day. No tree in the forest bears cooked rice."

"Yeah," smiled Rankin, "I'll remind my managing editor. Might make a head-line. 'Inspector Chan Says No Tree in Forest Bears Cooked Rice.'"

"Look here, Mr. Chan," Gleason said solemnly, "surely you have some results to report to our readers. That's what they want. Results."

"Ah, this American passion for results," Charlie sighed. "Yet the apple-blossom is so much more beautiful than the dumpling."

"And can we send back an armful of apple-blossoms?" laughed Rankin. "You met my editor once. He wants a pan of dumplings, warm from the oven."

"So sorry," Chan apologized. "I suggest first of all, you get lay of land."

"We got it," Gleason replied. "Say, what was in that big envelope you just sent the drug-store cowboy flivvering off with? We asked him—but of all the nasty tempers—"

"Ah," nodded Chan, "perhaps it was Landini's will."

"Carried it with her wherever she went, eh?" Rankin grinned.

"Just a suggestion," Chan told him. "Who inherits her property? Merely one of the angles."

"By gad—we never thought of that," Gleason cried. "How about it, Bill?"

"What was the name of her lawyers in Reno?" Rankin inquired. "Thanks, Inspector. There might be a story in that. I think I'll take a run over there for lunch—"

"I'm right with you," Gleason assured him. "We'll see you later, Mr. Chan. Thanks for the tip."

"It was nothing," Charlie smiled. As the two went out, he walked over and sat down beside Sam Holt. "Ah, the reporters—they are upon us," he murmured.

"Like the pest of the locust," the old man said. "I could hear what he told 'em. Gave 'em somethin' to think about, eh?"

"I did," Charlie replied. "While we think of something else. Your son has told you all concerning last night, I presume?"

"He did—in a terrible hurry. You think this Swan knew too much about who killed Landini?"

"I'm certain of it. I also, Mr. Holt, think there is one other who knows something concerning the matter."

"Yes, Mr. Chan?"

"Romano, the Italian, fourth and final husband of great singer—he hinted to me that his door was not too tightly closed on night of murder. Vast numbers were about on that second floor when Landini died. This morning, Romano's courage fails him. He will say no more. We should get together, sir, and put bolster under that courage."

"He's up a Pineview, ain't he?"

"No—he came down with us, and took Swan's room. Your son is approaching—the three of us will descend on this man. We may conquer by numbers."

Five minutes later the representatives of the law were facing Romano in his small bedroom. The conductor, frightened and nervous, sat on the edge of his bed and protested.

"I tell you I know nothing, gentlemen. Mr. Chan, he mistakes what I say. *If*—I told him. *If* a person knew, I said. Observe that if, please."

"Look here," said Don Holt, "you know something—don't deny it. You don't want to tell because you're afraid it will delay you in getting back to the bright lights an' spending Landini's money. Well, it might—I can't promise. If I can fix things so it don't, I will. But one way or the other, Mister, you're tellin'. Or I lock you up. Get that, an' get it quick."

"I am—I am so upset," wailed Romano. "This American law—it is confusing. What I saw—it was nothing, really. But I will tell. You understand, I am in my room, looking upon snow of flying field, I see plane alight, and for a time I watch it. Then—it comes to me—Landini will be going now. Have I accomplished my purpose? No. A few bills, thrown to me like I am a beggar—I, who have every right to demand. Am I not the husband? I go to my door. I will demand from Landini a definite appointment in Reno.

"I open that door, you understand. I am on point of moving into the hall. Opposite is the study door, now closed. Before I can move, it opens, and—a man—he steps into my view. I watch him. With stealthy look around he slips silently into the room beside the study—the one at my left as I stand."

"Landini's old sitting-room," Chan nodded.

"Something in that man's manner—it gives me pause," continued Romano. "Me—I am not easily suppressed, but for the moment I am just that. And then, suddenly—from the study rings out—what? A shot, gentlemen. The shot that means Landini's death."

"All right," said Don Holt. "But who was the man?"

"The man I saw," replied Romano, with drama. "The man who slips so slyly from one room to another. That man was Sing."

In the silence that followed, Charlie heard Sam Holt sigh wearily.

"Fine," remarked Don Holt. "You keep that to yourself now, an' you'll be all right."

"Me—I will keep it," Romano cried. "And I hope—so much—I will be all right."

Charlie and the old sheriff walked together down the corridor. "It keeps comin' back to Sing," Sam Holt said. "Fer all we kin do, Mr. Chan—it keeps comin' back to him."

"Quite true," Chan replied, "but consider. Romano is the man who profits most by Landini's death. A man who may well have killed her. And a sly one, like a thief amid the fire. One of the slyest I have ever encountered. Suppose he sought to turn attention from himself? His eye lights on—"

"Poor old Sing," finished Holt, slapping his thigh. "Which is the first it would light on, I reckon. Sing, that looks helpless, an' not so quick on the come-back." He stopped. "Still—I ain't so sure, Inspector."

"No?" inquired Chan.

"No. If Romano was cookin' up a story about Sing, would he ha' done it so dog-gone well? Wouldn't he say he seen Sing creepin' into the study, an' then heard the shot? Would he say he seen him creepin' out o' the study, an' then the explosion came? No, Inspector—I got a sort o' sick feelin' Romano's story sounds like the facts. Sing brings th' blanket, an' finds Landini alone. He goes out, into her old room, opens the windows fer a way of escape, runs back to the study by way of the balcony, kills her an' then gits out the way he came. If he killed her, that's the way he done it, an' Romano is too close to it fer comfort, the way I feel."

"Romano is sly and clever," repeated Charlie. "He studied situation, maybe."

The old man laid his hand on Charlie's arm. "Don't it beat all," he said, "the way that boy Sing keeps poppin' back, an' the way you an' me, we jest go on makin' excuses fer him? What I want to know is—how long kin we keep it up?"

Don Holt was waiting for them in the lounge. "Well," what do you think of that story?" he inquired. "Something behind it, if you ask me. Why, I've knowed old Sing since I was a baby. Reckon I'd better keep a sharp eye on that Romano, after this."

"There ye are, Inspector," Sam Holt said. "One more vote for Sing."

"Won't you stay here for lunch?" Don Holt invited.

"You are very kind," Charlie replied. "But I fear we leave Pineview too much alone. I believe it wiser to return."

"Maybe you're right," agreed the sheriff. "Tell that boatman on the pier I said to run you up to the house. I—"

A young woman summoned him into Dinsdale's office. Chan said good-by to Sam Holt and hurried toward the pier. He was stepping into a launch when Don Holt ran across the terrace and called to him.

"Just took a wire from San Francisco," the sheriff said as he reached Chan's side. "From the owner of the house where we found Swan. He says there's just one person up here has a key to that rear door. He leaves it here in case of an emergency."

"Ah, yes. And he leaves it with—"

"He leaves it with Sing," Holt answered. "You'd better look into the matter when you get to Pineview."

Charlie sighed. "The man who would avoid suspicion should not adjust his hat under a plum tree. He is always adjusting his hat—that Sing."

17

The Net Closes In

Chan found the living-room at Pineview deserted and walked rapidly through it to the kitchen. There conditions appeared to be somewhat chaotic. Sing and Mrs. O'Ferrell seemed to be jointly preparing lunch, and the latter was red of face and evidently quite flustered.

"Sing," said Chan sternly from the doorway, "I must speak with you immediately."

"Wha's mallah you?" Sing replied. "My velly busy. You go 'way, Boss."

"I'll say he's busy," cried Mrs. O'Ferrell indignantly. "It was understood whin I come to this house I was to do the cookin', an' no wan else. An' here he's been all mornin', stirrin' up hivin knows what. Sure, an' it's me notice they get afther this—"

"Sing," Charlie repeated, and his voice was firm, "come here!"

The old man inspected a pot at the rear of the stove, dropped the lid hastily and come to the door.

"Wha's mallah, Boss? This velly bad time fo' talk—"

"This plenty good time. Sing—you got key to big house down the road?"

"Sure, my got key. All time got key. Plumber come, light man come—they want key. My got 'um."

"Where you got 'um?"

"Hang on hook, in hall, outside."

"What hook? Show me."

"My velly busy now. All time woik this house. No can do—"

"Show me, and be quick!"

"All light, Boss. Keep collah on. My show you." He came into the passage and pointed to a hook beside the rear door. It was empty. "Key all gone now," he commented, without interest.

"Gone—where?"

"No savvy, Boss."

"When did you see it last?"

"No savvy. Yeste'day, day befo'—mebbe las' week. My got to go now."

"Wait a minute. You mean somebody has stolen the key?"

Sing shrugged. "What you think, Boss?"

"Do you know that Doctor Swan was murdered in that house last night? And the person who did it had your key?"

Mrs. O'Ferrell gave a startled cry.

"Too bad, Boss," Sing answered. "Solly—got to get back to kitchen now."

Charlie sighed and let him go. "Does it chance you had noticed that key, Mrs. O'Ferrell?" he inquired.

"Sing showed it to me whin I first come," she answered. "There was a tag on it, tellin' what it was for. Sure, I niver give it a thought from that day to this."

"You wouldn't know, then, when it disappeared or who probably took it?"

"I would not, Mr. Chan. It's sorry I am I can't help you." There was a clatter from the kitchen. "Excuse me, please, sir. Sure, I don't know whether it's me or Sing that's gettin' lunch."

Charlie went to his room to freshen up. When he returned down-stairs, Ward and Ryder were in the living-room.

"Our ranks are somewhat depleted," the host said. "It's going to seem a little lonely from now on."

"I'll have to be getting back on the job myself very soon," Ryder told him. "If there's nothing I can do for you, old man. I—I don't believe the sheriff can hold me here. Do you think so, Mr. Chan?"

"Seems nothing against you," Chan admitted.

"I hear your business is even more prosperous than usual, John," Ward remarked.

Ryder brushed an imaginary bit of lint from the lapel of his beautifully tailored coat. "I can't complain," he admitted. "If I've got nothing else from life, I've at least got money. More than enough."

At the luncheon table, Sing appeared to be in a state of great excitement.

He served Charlie and Ward first with chops and vegetables, meanwhile assuring Ryder that the latter was not forgotten. "You wait, You see," he said repeatedly. Presently he appeared, triumphantly bearing aloft an enormous bowl, which he set before the mining man.

"Rice," cried Ryder. "Sing—you old rascal!"

"Like ol' time," chuckled Sing, patting him on the back. "You wait now. You see."

He fairly ran to the kitchen, reappearing almost at once with another bowl. "Chicken glavy. You smell 'um, hey? Like ol' time—when you lil boy."

"Sing—this is wonderful," Ryder remarked, evidently touched. "I've been dreaming of your rice and gravy for nearly thirty years. Nothing has ever tasted so good since those old days in your kitchen."

"Sing goo' cook, hey?"

"The best in the world. Thank you a million times." Charlie thought Ryder had never seemed so human before.

"Ah—er—" Ward looked slightly embarrassed. "It seems that you and I are rather out of things, Mr. Chan. You must forgive Sing's peculiar ideas of hospitality."

"Not at all," Chan replied. "You and I will have plenty lunch. And I believe Sing's ideas of hospitality are excellent. With him, old friends are best friends. Who could place blame on him for that?"

"This is a real bowl of rice," Ryder was saying. "Not one of those little bowls. A real, big bowl. And the gravy—come to think about it, I don't know that I'll ever go home."

After lunch, Chan retired to his room to finish the last few galleys of Landini's story. Nothing more of interest has cropped up, but the personality of the writer had steadily grown upon him, and now, as he finished, he was one of the singer's friends, he felt. More than ever, he was determined to find her slayer—wherever the trail might lead.

He went down-stairs again. Pineview was deserted. He put on his arctics, for though the spring sun was now warm in the sky, things were a bit damp underfoot. Going outside, for a time he wandered about among the sheds at the rear, trying various doors. All, save those of the garage, were tightly padlocked. At the latter spot he looked longingly for a moment at the ladder. Evidently the pine trees again intrigued him.

He moved around to the front of the house. Much of the snow on the lawn had melted, leaving only a thin coating of slush. Now and again he stopped, to pick up a cone or a fallen branch; idly, aimlessly, the student of the pines seemed to be gathering data on a favorite subject. Murders, the stern realities of his trade, policemen and sheriffs, appeared to be far from his thoughts.

And at that moment, Charlie was surprisingly far from the thoughts of the sheriff. Don Holt was seated in the saddle on his favorite mount, and beside him along the narrow trail under the pines, rode Leslie Beaton. The magic air of Tahoe had brought into her cheeks a color that was not for sale in the beauty parlors of Reno, and her eyes were shining with a new enthusiasm for life.

"It sure was a grand idea Cash had," the sheriff remarked. "Inviting you to go on this ride."

"Poor Cash! What a pity he was called away."

"He's the kind that's likely to get called away," Holt responded grimly.

"He never even said good-by to me."

"They wasn't time. You see, Cash's good-bys is likely to be long an' lingering—like that guy Romeo's. I reckon you're missin' old Cash."

"Cash is a fluent talker."

"I'll say he is. By this time, he'd have told you all about—how—pretty you look."

"Do you think so?"

"I know he would."

"I mean—do you think I look—all right?"

"Fine. But I ain't got the words, somehow."

"Too bad. Cash's absence begins to look like a great calamity."

"I was afraid you'd feel that way. Always been cooped up in cities, ain't you?"

"Always."

"This air is doin' you a lot of good. It would do you more good—if you stayed."

"Oh—but I must go back East. I have to work for a living, you see."

The sheriff frowned. "Cash would explain to you—that you needn't go. He's pretty convincin', that boy." They came into a clearing, and turned their horses about. Far below lay the lake, reflecting snow-capped peaks beyond. "Mighty nice view, ain't it?" said the sheriff.

"It sort of takes my breath away," the girl answered.

"Makes you a little dizzy, eh? This is where old Cash would have staged a big emotional scene. About how you was the loveliest girl he'd ever met—how he couldn't live without you—"

"Don't, please," smiled the girl. "I seem to be missing so much."

"Oh, you ain't missing a lot. Cash got engaged to three girls on this very spot last summer."

"You mean he's fickle?"

"Well—you know—these fellows that talk a lot—"

"I know. But the strong silent men ought to strike a happy medium now and then—don't you think?"

"I reckon that's right, too." The sheriff took off his hat, as though to cool a fevered brow. "You—you think you could like this country?"

"The summers must be lovely."

"That's jest it. The winters—I don't know. I wish you could come down an' look at the county-seat—before you go away. It ain't a very big town. I reckon you wouldn't like it."

"No—perhaps not. Can we see Pineview from here?"

"It's over there—in that bunch of trees. Gosh—I'd plumb forgot. Pretty big job we got on our hands, at Pineview."

"Does it mean a lot to you—to succeed?"

"I'll say it does. I got to live up to Dad's reputation. He kind of expects it, I guess. But I don't know. Even with Mr. Chan's help—we don't seem to be going very strong."

For a moment the girl did not speak. "I'm afraid I haven't been quite fair with you," she said at last. "I wonder if you'll ever forgive me?"

"I reckon so. But what do you mean?"

"About the night of Landini's murder. I can't imagine why I was so silly—but it seemed quite terrible. Involving some one who might perhaps be innocent—getting involved myself—I—I just couldn't."

"You couldn't what?"

"I wanted to think it over—I've done that—and I see I've been a fool. All the time I really wanted to help you—I do now. You know—I was in the bedroom next door when I heard the shot that killed Landini."

"I know."

"Well, somehow, the shot seemed to be on the balcony. So—I didn't just sit there dumbly. I ran to the balcony window, opened it and looked out. And I saw a man leave the study, run along the balcony and disappear through the window of the room beyond—a man with a blanket under his arm."

"Sing."

"Yes—it was poor Sing. It seemed incredible—I couldn't believe it. But Sing ran out of the study just after that shot was fired. I'm so sorry I didn't tell you before."

"You've told me now," Holt replied gloomily. "Gosh—I'd rather be hung myself. But there's nothing to it—duty is duty, an' I took the oath. I reckon we'd better be goin' back."

They started down the trail along which they had come. Again on that homeward trek Holt was the strong silent man—oppressively silent, now. When they parted before the Tavern stables, the girl laid her hand on his arm. "You forgive me for not telling sooner, don't you?"

He looked at her solemnly in the dusk. "Sure I do," he answered. "I reckon, when I come to think of it, I'd forgive you for almost anything."

As he led the horses into the stable, he saw his father sitting alone in the office, near the door. Presently he went inside and sat down.

"Ain't no more doubt, I reckon," he said. "Sing killed Landini. I got it straight from a reliable party this time." He repeated Leslie Beaton's story. "Mebbe I'd better go up an' get him now," he finished.

"Hold yer horses," Sam Holt replied. "We got to consult Mr. Chan. Yes—I guess there ain't much doubt—but it don't do to jump too soon. We want to git all the evidence we kin, first. Wasn't the coroner goin' to hold an inquest on Doctor Swan about this time?"

The young man looked at his watch. "Yes—that's right."

"You go over there, son," Sam Holt said. "Pick up anything you kin. There's plenty o' time fer Sing."

As soon as the sheriff had gone, Sam Holt's groping hands sought for the telephone on the desk. In another moment he was talking to Charlie Chan at Pineview.

"Yes," he was saying, "it's Sing, Inspector. The net is closin' in. Matter o' fact, it's about closed."

"As I expected," Chan replied softly. "What do you suggest?"

"Git down here as quick as ye kin, Mr. Chan—an' fetch Sing with ye. Don't say nothin' to nobody—but have him bring his bag. Jest a little bag—about what a man would need—in jail."

"Ah, yes—in jail," Chan repeated thoughtfully.

"Ye'll find me in the office o' the stables," Sam Holt went on. "Them reporters drove me out o' the Tavern."

"I understand," Charlie replied. "There is an old flivver here. We shall arrive most speedily in that."

And they did. Twenty minutes later, Charlie pushed open the door of the over-heated little office.

"Hello, Mr. Chan," Sam Holt said. "Somebody with ye, ain't they? Well, tell him to wait in th' stable. You an' me needs a little talk."

There was an air of tense expectancy about Charlie as he came in alone and took a battered old chair beside the roll-top desk at which Holt sat. "New evidence has leaped to view?" he inquired.

"It sure has," Holt answered. "After we heard from Romano, Inspector, I got to thinkin'. Sentiment is sentiment, but duty is duty. So I got that doctor over here the Tahoe doctor that helped Don bring Landini's body down to town the night o' the murder. I says to him, 'Sing brought you blankets,' I says, 'to wrap about Landini. Blue blankets. Do you remember,' I says, 'was they ever laid on a velvet chair in that room?' " Holt paused.

"And the doctor's answer?" inquired Charlie.

"Seems I was a better detective than I wanted to be. Mr. Chan," Holt went on grimly. "That doctor took them blankets from Sing at the door, an' laid 'em on the floor beside the body. They never touched a chair. He was dead certain about that. Yes, sir—that blue blanket was in the room before the murder—they ain't no doubt about it."

"I congratulate you on keen deduction you performed that morning in the study," Charlie said.

"Kick me, Mr. Chan, an' I'll be more obliged," Holt replied. "Yes, sir—jest as I thought—Sing fired that shot. We got the blanket evidence, the hurt knee from that dressing-table bench. We got Romano, that seen him slip through that room next door, jest before the shot. An' we got some one else—some one who seen him leave the study jest after it."

"That is news to me," Chan remarked. Sam Holt told him of Leslie Beaton's story. Charlie shook his head. "Too many people on that floor at time," he remarked sadly.

"Too many fer poor ol' Sing," agreed Holt. "Got him comin' an' goin', we have. Don wants to lock him up."

"A natural course," Chan nodded.

"I wonder," said Sam Holt. Charlie looked at him keenly. "I wonder," went on the old sheriff. "I've been thinkin', Mr. Chan. A blind man gits a lot o' time to think, an' I been at it this afternoon, at it hard."

"You have been thinking of all the clues in this case, perhaps?" Chan suggested gently.

"I have. What you said to Don about the dog. An' all this interest of yours in the pine trees, Mr. Chan."

Charlie smiled. "Mr. Holt—the best clue of all, you do not know. I did not recall it myself until last night, while I waited alone in creaking house of death. I propose to make a slight narration. I intend to tell you, from start to finish, every event that occurred, every word that was spoken, at dinner my first night at Pineview. Before the murder, you understand."

He moved close to the old man, and in a low confidential voice, he spoke for some ten minutes. When he had finished, he leaned back in his chair and studied Sam Holt's face.

Holt was silent for a moment, playing with a paper-knife on the desk. At last he spoke. "Mr. Chan—I am seventy-eight years old."

"An honorable age," said Charlie.

"A happy one, too, because I am here, among my own people, in the country I've always known. But now—jes' supposin'—I was in some foreign country—what would I want more than anything—"

"You would wish to see again your native village—to walk upon the soil wherein your bones were some day to rest."

"You're a smart man, Mr. Chan. You git me right away. Inspector—Don ain't never even made ye a deputy. You ain't got no real authority here."

"I am well aware of the fact," nodded Charlie.

Sam Holt rose and stood there, a distinguished figure, a figure of honor, of integrity. "And I—I am blind," he said.

Chinese do not easily weep, but suddenly Charlie Chan felt a stinging in his eyes. "Thank you," he said. "I speak for entire race when I say it. You will pardon me now, I know. I have little errand to perform."

"Of course ye have," said Holt. "Good-by, Mr. Chan. An' if it should so happen that I don't ever meet a certain friend o' mine ag'in—give him my love an' say I'm proud I knowed him."

Chan stepped through the door and closed it after him. In the dim shadows several feet away, he saw the bent figure of old Sing. He went over to him. "Come on, Sing," he remarked. "You and I got journey to make." Suddenly he saw looming in the doorway the powerful figure of Don Holt. He seized the old Chinese and drew him back into the shadows.

Don Holt opened the office door. "Hello, Dad," he said. "You know, I been thinkin' some. I reckon I ought to go down to Pineview now—"

"Step in, son," came the voice of the old sheriff. "Step in, an' we'll talk it over."

The door of the office closed behind the young man, and Charlie hurried Sing out to the car in which they had come down together from Pineview. He motioned to the old man to get in beside him, and they set off along the Tavern drive. When they came to the main entrance, Chan turned toward Truckee.

"Wha's mallah now?" ventured Sing. "Mebbe I catch 'um jail, hey?"

"You're a wicked man," Chan replied sternly. "You have caused us much worry and suffering. Jail is what you richly deserve."

"I catch 'um jail, hey, Boss?"

"On the contrary," Chan replied, "you catch 'um boat for China."

18

Rankin Drops a Bomb

A boat for China! Charlie could not see the face of the old man who sat at his side in the car that sped along the road to Truckee, but he heard a tremendous sigh. Of relief?

"All light, Boss," Sing said.

"All right?" repeated Chan with some bitterness. "Is that the extent of your remarks? We are doing you a great favor, a tremendous kindness, and you reply, all right. The courteous man, Ah Sing, would not permit his tongue to stop at that."

"My velly much obliged."

"That is better. It still appears inadequate, but it is slightly better."

They traveled along the wet road in silence. Chan's face was grim and determined. This next hour, he reflected, was not to be the happiest of his career. All those years on the Honolulu force, beset with temptations, but always honest, always irreproachable. And now—to come to the mainland, to do what he was doing—would his conscience ever be clear again? Ah—thank the gods—the lights of Truckee were twinkling just ahead.

Chan drove at once to the station. "Train for San Francisco arrives in twenty minutes," he announced. "I have consulted time table." They entered the waiting-room, Sing carrying his small bag. "You got money, Ah Sing?" Charlie asked.

"My got 'um," the old man answered.

"Then purchase for yourself a ticket," Chan ordered. "I am sorry, but we do not also furnish fare."

As Sing returned from the ticket window, the detective noted that he was limping.

"Your knee still troubles you?" Chan inquired.

"Velly bad knock," Sing admitted. He put his foot on a bench, and rolling up his wide trousers, exhibited a considerable expanse of black and blue.

"Ah, yes," Chan said. "The wound you acquired when you bumped into dressing-table bench in Landini's old sitting-room?"

"Tha's when. Aftah my shoot—"

"Enough!" Charlie cried. He glanced uneasily around at the other people in the room, and spoke in Cantonese. "Do not poke your finger through your own paper lantern. The luck is running high for you to-night, ancient one. Be cautious, lest the heart of the law yet harden against you."

Sing appeared to be properly impressed. They sat down side by side on the narrow bench, and for a time, neither spoke.

"The government has fallen upon evil times," Chan said at last. "You understand, it can not even afford to squander small piece of rope on man like you. Old man who will die soon, in any case. So it says—return to China—"

"I will go," Sing remarked in his native tongue.

"I envy you. You will walk again the streets of the village where you were born. You will supervise the selection of your own burial place. I myself will see that your trunk is prepared and sent to you while you await the boat. Where shall I send it?"

"To the establishment of my brother, Sing Gow, in Jackson Street. The Fish Shop of the Delicious Odors."

"It shall be done. For you, the past died this afternoon. The future is born to-night. You understand?"

"I understand."

"I am the bearer of an affectionate message for you, ancient one. Mr. Sam Holt has sent it. He is proud to have known you."

Sing's face softened. "An honorable man. May the four nails of his coffin be of purest gold."

"To match his heart," Chan agreed. His own heart stirred with relief as he heard the approach of the train. "Come," he said, rising. "Your vehicle draws near."

They stepped on to the platform. In another moment the train thundered up to the station. Charlie held out his hand.

"I am saying good-by," he shouted in Sing's ear. "May your entire journey be on the sunny side of the road."

"Goo'-by," Sing answered. He took a few steps toward the train, but turned and came back. Removing something from his pocket, he handed it to Chan. "You give 'em Boss," he directed. "My fo'get. Tell 'um Boss too much woik that house. Sing go away."

"I will tell him," Charlie agreed. He led Sing back to the steps of a day coach and helped him aboard.

Retiring to the shadows close to the station, Chan stood watching. He saw the old man drop into a seat and remove his hat. In the dim gas-light the wizened face was stolid, emotionless. The train gathered momentum, and Ah Sing was swept quickly from view. Still Chan hesitated, deep in thought. For the first time in his life—but this was the mainland, strange things happened here. And after all, Inspector Chan had no real authority.

When he got back to Tahoe, Chan again turned in at the Tavern gate. The stables were dark and deserted, and leaving the Pineview flivver parked in the drive, Charlie entered the hotel. Dinsdale was alone beside the office desk.

"Good evening, Mr. Chan," he said. "Warming up a bit after the rain, isn't it?"

"That may be," Charlie replied. "I fear I had not noticed."

"No—I suppose you're a pretty busy man," Dinsdale returned. "By the way—of course it's none of my business, but—er—are you getting anywhere?"

"So sorry. There is nothing yet able to be announced."

"Well, of course, I didn't mean to butt in."

"Ah, but you are naturally interested. You were old-time friend of poor Madame Landini, I believe?"

"Yes. I knew her even before her first marriage. A beautiful girl—and a fine woman. I hope you haven't been judging her entirely from the viewpoint of her discarded husbands."

"For a time, I made that error," Chan replied. "Then I read Madame's own life-story, and my opinion changed. I agree with you—a splendid woman."

"Good!" cried Dinsdale with unexpected vehemence. "I'm glad you feel that way. Because if you do, you'll be almost as eager to see her murderer hang as I am. By the way, we'll be having dinner in half an hour. Please stay, as my guest."

"I will be only too happy," Chan bowed. He indicated a youth who had just come in and taken his place behind the desk. "Would you be so kind as to have this young man call Pineview, and inform whoever answers that I will not dine there to-night?"

"With pleasure," Dinsdale answered.

"And now—if you can tell me the number of Mr. Sam Holt's room?"

"It's number nineteen—at the end of that corridor over there."

At Charlie's knock, Sam Holt called for him to come in. He entered to find the old sheriff standing in the middle of the room, adjusting his necktie.

"Hello, Mr. Chan," he said, as he reached unerringly for his coat, which lay on the bed.

"Ah, you know my step," Charlie remarked. "It indicates, I fear, the heaviness of my person."

"Nothin' of the sort," Holt replied. "It's the lightest step in the whole shebang, except mebbe that Miss Beaton's."

"But my weight—" Chan protested.

"I don't keer about yer weight. You step like the tiger, Inspector Chan."

"Yes?" sighed Charlie. "But a tiger who lets his prey escape."

"Then I take it ye've gone an' done that errand?"

"I have done it—yes."

"Ye ain't regrettin' it, are ye?"

"Not unless you are, Mr. Holt."

"Which I reckon I'm never goin' to do, Mr. Chan. Howsomever, I'm glad to see ye first—before ye've talked to Don. I ain't told Don anything yit."

"The wisest course, no doubt," Charlie agreed.

"It sure is. Ye know, Don really is in authority here. 'Taint with him like it was with you an' me. He's took the oath, an' he's honest, the boy is. Reckon he'd feel he'd jest have to go after a certain party, an' bring him back. An' ye kain't depend on juries no more, Inspector."

"I fear you are right."

"In the old days—wa'al, it would ha' been different. But—they's women on the juries now, Mr. Chan. An' women ain't got no sentiment. They're hard, women are—since they took to runnin' the world."

"I have noticed that myself," Charlie nodded.

"Yes, I jes' figured we better give that certain party all the start we could,"

The door of the room beyond the bath opened, then slammed. "It's Don," Sam Holt whispered.

"I will await you both in the lobby," Chan whispered back. "It happens I am dining here to-night."

He made a guilty sort of exit, aided by old Sam Holt, who was looking rather guilty himself. Reaching the lounge, he selected a chair and sat down by the fire. In a few moments, a door from the terrace opened and Leslie Beaton entered.

"Hello, Mr. Chan," she cried. "Glad to see you again. I've been out admiring the view. It's marvelous."

"You like this mountain country?" Chan asked.

"I love it." She urged him back to his chair, and took the one beside it. "You know—sometimes I believe I'll stay here. Would that be a good idea, do you think?"

"Happiness," Charlie told her, "is not a matter of geography."

"I suppose not."

"Wherever we are, life is the same. The sweet, the sour, the pungent and the bitter—we must taste them all. To the contented, even the cabbage roots are fragrant."

"I know," she nodded. "Would I be contented here?"

Chan shrugged. "I seek to win reputation as philosopher, not as fortune-teller," he reminded her. "If I were assaying latter role, I would say it would depend on whether you have a companion or not. You can not applaud with one hand."

"Oh, well—I'm sorry I brought the matter up," laughed the girl. "Let's change the subject—shall we? Looking around for a new topic my eye lights—inevitably—on your necktie, Mr. Chan. I'm not accustomed to making personal remarks, but somehow that's the sort of necktie one just can't ignore."

"Ah—one might call it red," he replied.

"One couldn't very well call it anything else," she admitted.

"It was present from my young daughter, Evelyn, on recent Christmas," he told her. "I had forgot I was so brilliantly adorned. But I remember now—I put it on this morning. For a purpose."

Young Hugh Beaton came up at that moment, in a rather cheerful mood for him. Even one day at the Tavern seemed to have proved good medicine. He greeted Charlie in friendly fashion, and led his sister off to the dining-room. Presently Romano appeared, arrayed in evening clothes as though he were about to conduct an opera.

"Mr. Romano—how do you do," Charlie remarked. "You quite confound me by your formal attire. When I—I must disgrace dining-room with necktie such as this."

"What is wrong with the necktie?" Romano responded. "Me, I dress not for others, but for myself. You should do the same. Attired as I am now, I feel I am already back in some metropolitan center, such as New York. The thought—it gives me great happiness. The reality—it will be sublime."

"Patience," Chan counseled. "In time, the mulberry leaf becomes silk."

Romano frowned. "Not so comforting, that. The process sounds complicated. But in the meantime, one may still eat." He moved away.

Don Holt and his father appeared. "Hear you're staying for dinner," the former said. "Fine! You'll sit with us, of course."

"But I am Mr. Dinsdale's guest," Charlie protested.

"That's all right—we'll take a table for four," Dinsdale said briskly, coming up just then. He led them into the dining-room. Don Holt looked a bit disappointed, for he knew discussion of the case must now be postponed until later. Chan, however, was deeply relieved. He had no desire for such a discussion with the sheriff of the county at the moment. Indeed, he did not look forward to it at any moment.

Toward the close of the dinner, Dinsdale was called away. Don Holt lost no time.

"I reckon Dad's told you about my talk with Miss Beaton this afternoon," he began. "The way I see it, that puts the murder of Landini right in old Sing's lap. It's like I told you at the first—I've knowed Sing ever since I was a kid. Always been fond of him, too. But when I took the oath of office, there wasn't anything in it about protecting my friends. I got my job to do, and—"

He was interrupted by the arrival of the amiable Bill Rankin, who leaned suddenly above the table. Chan sighed with relief.

"Hello," cried the reporter. "All the forces of the law, breaking bread together. Gosh—think of the poor criminals on a night like this. Well, what's the good word to send down to the yawning presses?"

"You must find your own words," Charlie told him. "Has your day disclosed nothing?"

Rankin dropped into Dinsdale's empty chair. "We had a nice time in Reno. Called on Miss Meecher. I suppose you know this sleek boy named Romano stands in line for all Landini's property?"

"We do," said Don shortly.

"Well, Romano was at Pineview the night of the murder," Rankin went on cheerily. "Sort of puts the lad in the running, doesn't it? He knew the singer—and the money—was slipping away from him in a couple of weeks. He knew Landini had a pistol in her hand-bag. Need I say more?"

"Thank you so much," grinned Chan. "Gentlemen, our case is solved. Odd we did not think of this ourselves."

"Oh, you thought of it all right," Rankin laughed. "But what I'm getting at is—wouldn't you like to think of it all over again, just for to-morrow morning's paper?"

"Has libel law been repealed?" Charlie asked blandly.

"Libel? Innuendo, Mr. Chan. A game at which I am probably the most expert player west of the Rockies. Well, if that little point doesn't interest you, maybe you'll answer me a question."

"I must hear it before I can answer it," Charlie replied.

"You'll hear it, all right. Why did you take that old Chinese servant, Sing, over to Truckee this evening in a flivver, and put him on a train for San Francisco?"

Charlie Chan had known a long and active career, but never before had he encountered such an embarrassing moment as this. In the dead silence that followed the innocent dropping of Rankin's bomb, Chan looked across and saw the fine eyes of Don Holt ablaze with sudden anger. Old Sam Holt's hand trembled as he hastily set down his water glass. Charlie did not speak.

"You can't keep that dark," Rankin went on. "Gleason ran over to file a couple of stories with the telegrapher at the station, and he saw you. What was the big idea?"

The reporter looked directly at Chan, and was amazed at the answering look he received from one who had, a few moments ago, appeared so glad to see him.

"I took Sing to Truckee as a favor—from one Chinese to another," Charlie said slowly. He rose to his feet. "Sing desired to make a visit to San

Francisco, and as there were several points I wanted investigated down there, I decided to permit that he go. The matter means little, one way or the other, but I prefer that for the present you write nothing about it."

"Why, sure—if you say so," Rankin returned pleasantly. "It just seemed rather queer, that's all."

But Charlie was already walking rapidly away from the table. Don Holt and the old sheriff followed closely at his heels. He moved on, straight through the lobby and into Dinsdale's small private office. As he expected, the others did the same.

Don Holt came in last and slammed the door shut behind him. His face was white, his eyes dangerously narrowed.

"So," he said, through his teeth, "you took him there as a favor—from one Chinese to another? Some favor—if you're asking me!"

"Hold yer horses, Don," his father cried.

"I've been double-crossed," the boy went on. "I've been made a fool of—"

"Wa-al, ef ye have, son—I done it. I told Mr. Chan to take Sing to Truckee. I told him to help him git away—to China."

"You!" cried Holt. "To China! An' all the time ye knew he was guilty as hell. You knew he went into that room—you knew he fired that shot—"

"I knew all that, son."

"Then how could you let me down like this? Get out o' my way!"

"Where you goin'?"

"Goin'? I'm goin' after him, of course. Am I sheriff of this county, or ain't I? You two sure have took a lot on yourselves—"

Dinsdale opened the door. "Telegram for you, Don," he said. "They're phoning it from Truckee. I've switched it in here." He looked in a puzzled way at the young sheriff's face, then withdrew and closed the door.

Don Holt sat down at the desk and took up the receiver. Chan looked at his watch and smiled.

"Hello! Hello! This is Don Holt. What! What! Say that again. All right. Thanks. Mail it up to me here, if you will."

Slowly the young man swung around in the swivel chair, and his eyes met Charlie's. "What was it you asked that bird down in Berkeley about them pistols?" he inquired.

"It was a simple question concerning the bullets," Chan replied calmly. "What does he say?"

"He—he says both them bullets came from the gun that killed Swan," Don Holt answered perplexedly. "He says neither one of 'em came from Landini's Gun."

"Wa-al," drawled Sam Holt, "them scientists kain't always be wrong. Now an' then one of 'em's bound to strike the right lead."

Don Holt stood up, and gradually the puzzled look faded from his face. He smiled suddenly at Charlie.

"By the Lord Harry!" he said. "Now I know why you was always talkin' about the pine trees."

19
Chan Climbs a Ladder

Don Holt walked up and down the small room excitedly. "It's beginning to straighten out," he continued. "The dog—I'm gettin' that, too."

Charlie nodded. "Good little Trouble. It was he who set me on correct trail that very first night. Already I had experienced my first doubts. Of the five unaccounted for at time of killing, not one offered alibi. You will recall I commented to you on that. Strange, I thought. The guilty, at least, usually has alibi ready and waiting. I wondered. Could it be that the guilty was not among those five? Could it be he was among those standing in my sight when supposedly fatal shot was fired?"

"Then we went out and talked with Mrs. O'Ferrell," the young sheriff said.

"Correct. Landini had remarked she would take dog with her in the plane. 'He loves it,' she had said. But according to story of Mrs. O'Ferrell, Trouble had wailed and cried most pitifully when plane arrived over house. No happy barks of anticipation such as I reported to you when, on subsequent evening, he heard sound of plane. Instead, every evidence of grief. Why did he grieve? I considered. As all those who know me have learned to their distress, Chinese have proverb to fit every possible situation. There is one—I recalled it as I talked to Mrs. O'Ferrell."

"What is it?" Don Holt asked.

"The dog, wherever he is, knows his master's mood," Charlie quoted. "Poor little Trouble—did he know that, at moment plane was over house, Landini was dying? Yes, I cried inwardly, that was it. Why not? In terrific din made by airplane, a dozen shots might have been fired and gone unheard. But by some sixth sense which we can not explain, the dog was aware. He knew that when the airplane had landed, and we all stood with the aviator in the living-room and Ryder strolled down the stairs, Ellen Landini was already dead. She was dead some time before the firing of that shot which brought us all to her side.

"The shot we heard, then, had been merely to mislead. Who had fired it? Sing, probably. From the first I suspected him—last night I was sure. For I recalled the dinner on the evening of my arrival at Pineview—before I had even seen Ellen Landini. I recalled what Ryder had said: 'Always a friend in need, Sing was.' "

Holt nodded. "So Ryder said that, did he?"

"He did, and his statement was quite correct. A friend in need. All the way from chicken gravy and rice, to the firing of a deceiving bullet from the study window into the pines."

"Do you know what was in that letter Landini wrote to Ryder?" Holt asked.

"Alas, no. There are several things which I must yet accomplish at Pineview. The message from professor at Berkeley is important, but our evidence is not complete. I propose to go now and complete it. But first, I must ask a thousand pardons. When I set Sing on road to China, I was, I fear, law-breaker myself."

"That's all right," Sam Holt remarked. "Don't you apologize, Mr. Chan.

I ain't goin' to. We saved this young hot-head here from a mighty embarrassin' situation."

"I reckon you did," Don Holt agreed. "I'm sorry for anything I said."

Charlie patted the boy on the arm. "You were remarkably restrained. And you will note, I did not answer back. I recalled our conflict last night in hall of empty house. With most complimentary intention, I add that the man who has once been bitten by a snake, fears every rope in the roadway."

The sheriff laughed. "Well, I'll take it as a compliment, anyhow. And I'm glad you got Sing out of the way. I don't suppose he thought he was doin' anything wrong, but if he was around here now, I'd sure have to arrest him as an accessory. By the time I'm through with this business, I probably won't know where he is."

"You certainly will not," Chan smiled, "if you are depending on your honorable father for help. Or on my humble self. I go now to Pineview to investigate those matters which I mentioned. After brief talk with your father, you will know precisely how to act." He glanced at his watch. "Give me, however, one hour."

Holt nodded. "One hour, exactly," he agreed.

The moon was shining and a warm breeze was blowing through the pines as Charlie traveled the lonely road back to the house where he had been a guest for several days. Now his moment of triumph was drawing close, but he was not in a mood to gloat. As in so many other cases, he found it impossible to view things from the standpoint of a scientific machine. Always he thought of people—of the human heart. For that reason, his own heart was never to know elation in moments such as this.

But by the time he had driven into the Pineview garage, he had put aside his regrets. He was brisk and businesslike. Now at last he lifted that ladder at which he had only this afternoon cast longing eyes, and boosting it to his shoulder, he cautiously carried it around the house to the front lawn. A light streaming from the dining-room windows indicated that Ryder and his host were still lingering over dinner.

Placing the ladder against the tall tree from which, Chan was sure, that piece of bark had fallen, he climbed aloft, his plump figure finally disappearing among the thick branches. There, for a time, his flash-light played like a will-o'-the-wisp. Finally he found what he was seeking—what he sought in vain that afternoon on the ground—the bullet Sing had fired from the open window of the study, in order to provide an alibi for a friend. This bullet would complete the story told by the two pistols down at Berkeley: he took out his pen-knife and began to dig it from its resting-place.

With the slug securely in his pocket, he lowered himself from among the branches and found the ladder. He had gone half-way down it when he was aware of a tall, able-bodied man waiting for him in the darkness below.

"Oh—is it you, Mr. Chan?" said Michael Ireland. "Cecile seen somebody from the window, and she sent me out to get him—whoever he was. Her nerves ain't none too good, you know."

"So sorry I have disturbed her," Charlie replied, stepping on to the ground. "Assure her, please, that there is no cause for alarm. I merely pursue my harmless investigations."

"Sure," remarked Ireland. "Can I give you a hand with that ladder? Kinda heavy, ain't it?" They carried the ladder back to the garage.

"I was not aware that you were with us to-night," Charlie said. "Did you make the journey by plane?"

"Yes. An' I was wantin' to talk to you, Mr. Chan."

"I am a great believer in the here and now."

"Well—it's Cecile. Always kinda nervous an' flighty—you know women. Since this Swan business she's all on edge ag'in—an' she telephoned me to come over n' take her home. I says, I ain't so sure the sheriff will let you leave—but she just set off the fireworks—you know how it is. So I said I'd ask."

"I know how it is," nodded Charlie. "But you are now asking the wrong person."

Ireland shook his head. "No, I ain't, Mr. Chan. I called up the sheriff a little while ago, an' he said everything down here was in your hands. He said you would tell me when Cecile could go."

Charlie considered. He glanced at his watch. "Ask me again in half an hour—if you will be so kind."

"O.K.," Ireland answered. "In half an hour." He started away, but suddenly stopped. "Say—what's going to happen in half an hour?" he demanded.

Chan shrugged. "Who shall say? If you will pardon me now, I remain in open for few more minutes."

He waited while Ireland went reluctantly up the back steps and reentered the house. Then he removed from his pocket an enormous bunch of keys. With this in his hands, he disappeared among the sheds at the rear of the garage.

Some ten minutes later, Chan went into the house by the rear door. Mrs. O'Ferrell, Cecile and Ireland were in the kitchen, and they regarded him with anxious eyes as he passed. He went on up the back stairs, walking as quietly as the tiger to whom Sam Holt had compared him. Reaching the hall above he leaned over the stair-rail and listened; far in the distance, in the dining-room, he heard voices. He went into his room and locked the door behind him.

For a short time he was busy at his desk, and it was obvious that fingerprints concerned him. Then hastily he began to pack his suitcase. When everything was accounted for, he stood the case in the hall, placed with it his overcoat and hat, and again listened. The sound of voices still came from the dining-room. After a brief visit to the study, he returned to the hall, gathered up his things and went down-stairs.

The firelight flickered in friendly peaceful fashion on the walls of the great living-room. Chan set down his luggage and stood for a moment, looking musingly about him. He was reliving a scene; the scene in that room at the moment, two nights ago, when Michael Ireland came in for a drink. He pictured Beaton and Dinsdale beside the fire, Ward preparing the highball, Ireland waiting expectantly in that big easy chair, Ryder strolling nonchalantly down the stairs. Five men in all; six if you included Chan himself.

The picture faded from his mind. He walked slowly through the passage that led to the dining-room, and stood there in the doorway.

Ward and Ryder were seated at the table, coffee cups before them. Impelled by his innate sense of hospitality, the former leaped to his feet.

"Hello, Mr. Chan," he cried. "We missed you at dinner. Won't you have something now? Sing!" He stopped. "Damn it, I keep forgetting. Sing, Mr. Chan, has disappeared."

"No matter," Charlie answered. "I have eaten a sufficiency, Mr. Ward. But I appreciate your kindness, none the less."

Ryder spoke. "Perhaps Mr. Chan can throw some light on the disappearance of Sing?" he suggested.

Charlie drew a chair up to the table. "I can," he nodded. They waited in silence. "I am grieved to tell you, Mr. Ward, that all evidence uncovered has pointed with painful certainty to Sing as the person who fired that shot at Landini—the shot that took us up to the study to find her dead body on the floor."

"I don't believe it," Ward cried hotly. "I don't care where the evidence points. Sing never did it—"

"But if Sing himself admits he did—"

Ward stood up. "Where is he? I'll go to him at once."

"That, I fear, is impossible," Charlie replied. "The sheriff was about to arrest him when—he dropped from sight."

"He got away?" Ryder cried.

"For the time being," Chan answered. "He may yet be apprehended." He turned to Ward. "I am so sorry, Mr. Ward. This must be a great shock for you, I know. I have paused for brief moment only to inform you that with deep regret, and with warm glow of thanks for your hospitality, I leave this house at once. There is nothing more I can do."

"I suppose not," Ward replied. "But you must not go until one thing is settled. I promised you a thousand dollars to undertake the search for my boy—"

"But the search was so brief," Chan protested.

"No matter. There was nothing about that in our agreement. Wait here just a moment, please. I shall write you a check."

He left the room. Charlie turned to see an unaccustomed smile on the face of John Ryder.

"You find only pleasure in the escape of Sing," the detective remarked.

"Need I conceal that, Mr. Chan?"

"Sing was a very good friend of yours."

"One of the best I ever had."

"Ah, yes—chicken gravy and rice," nodded Charlie.

Ryder made no answer. In another moment Ward returned, and handed Charlie a check.

"I accept this with crimson cheeks," Chan said, and having placed it in his pocketbook, he looked at his watch. "It is time I am going," he added, and rose to his feet.

"Won't you have a farewell drink?" Dudley Ward suggested. "But you don't drink, do you? It's just as well because, come to think of it, there's nothing to drink. Poor John and I have been sitting here with parched throats all evening—you see, Sing had the keys to the sideboard, and the cellar, too."

"Thank you so much for reminding me," Chan cried. "I was on the point of forgetting." He took from his pocket a great key-ring, on which hung more than a score of keys. "This was entrusted to me by your servant—just before his escape."

"That's a bit of luck," Ward answered. He took the keys and stepped to the sideboard. "What will it be, John? A cordial with your coffee?"

"I don't mind," Ryder said.

From the sideboard Ward took four cut-glass decanters, and set them on a tray. He placed the tray before his friend. "Help yourself," he suggested. He secured a larger and heavier decanter, and put it at his own place. "Mr. Chan—you won't change your mind?"

"I am great believer in proper ceremony," Charlie answered. "In old days, in China, refusal to drink parting libation would be slur on hospitality of the host. A small taste—if you will be so good."

"Fine," Ward cried. He placed another glass before Ryder. "John—give the inspector—which do you prefer, Mr. Chan?"

"A little of the port wine, please." Suddenly Chan's voice grew louder. "One thing more. In China, in the old days, refusal of the host to pour the parting libation himself might well have been regarded as a slur on the guest."

There was a sudden silence in the room. Charlie saw Ryder hesitate, and look inquiringly at Ward. "But I do not press the point," Charlie continued, with an amiable smile. "You understand, I recall my first dinner at this table. I recall how courteous you were, Mr. Ward—how you served the cocktails yourself—how nothing was too much trouble—until that tray of decanters was put before you. And then—how you shouted for Sing—how Sing had to return from the kitchen before the cordials could be served. Ah—these little things—they register in the mind of a detective. Many hours later I remembered, and I said to myself—can it be that Mr. Ward is color-blind?"

He paused, and another tense silence filled the room.

"It was an interesting question," Charlie continued. "Only to-night I answered it once and for all. There were two varieties of ink on your study desk up-stairs, Mr. Ward. Black on the right, and red on the left. A moment ago I slipped in and took the very great liberty of changing the position of the inkwells. You will forgive me I hope." He tapped the pocket into which he had put his purse. "The check you just gave me was written in red ink, Mr. Ward. So you are color-blind after all."

"And what if I am?" Ward asked.

Charlie leaned back at ease in his chair. "The person who killed Landini was first sent by her for a green scarf. He returned to her bringing a pink one. Later, in vague impulse to straighten the desk and alter the look of affairs, he put a crimson lid on a yellow box, and a yellow lid on a crimson one. No, thank you, Mr. Ryder." He waved aside the glass Ryder was holding out. "I could not quite bring myself to drink with a man I am about to arrest for murder."

"Murder!" cried Ward. "Are you mad, Inspector?"

"No—it was you who went mad—night before last in the study."

"I was in the living-room when the shot was fired. You saw me there."

"Sing's shot into the pine trees—yes. But alas, Landini was actually killed in noise and confusion of the moment when airplane was roaring over the house."

"At which moment I was turning on the lights of the landing field. You heard what the aviator said—"

"That those lights flashed on while he was above the house. And he was correct—they did. But you, Mr. Ward, did not turn them on." Charlie took an envelope from his pocket and held up, very carefully, the wooden handle of an electric light switch. "Short time ago, aided by a bunch of keys from Sing, I entered shed at rear of hangar from which light was managed. I removed this article from its place. On it are two sets of finger-prints. Each set is from the fingers of your faithful servant, Ah Sing." He dropped the switch back into its envelope. "Two very good alibis," he added. "Sing's shot into the trees—your claim of having turned on the lights. Both gone. Both useless now."

Looking up, he saw that a terrible change had come over the usually genial Ward. He was trembling with rage, his face was purple, his mouth twitching. "Damn you!" he screamed. He snatched up the heavy decanter from the table, and his muscular arm drew back to strike. Then his eyes strayed to the door at Charlie's back, his purpose faltered, and, as suddenly as it had come, his fury passed.

"Cool off, Dudley," said the voice of old Sam Holt from the doorway. "I told you when you was a kid that temper of yours would finish you some day."

Dudley Ward slumped into his chair, and covered his face with his hands.

"I guess you were right, Sam," he muttered. "I guess you were right, at that."

20

After the Typhoon

The old sheriff stepped into the room, and Don Holt followed. Charlie looked at his watch.

"One hour, to the minute," he remarked to the younger Holt. "Fortunate you are man of your word. I feared I was about to lose a most important piece of evidence."

"Then you got what you came after?" Don Holt inquired.

"I got it." Chan handed an envelope to the sheriff. "Handle of light switch from shed at rear of hangar," he explained. "On it, finger-prints of Sing who turned off lights on landing field when unhappy evening had ended. Also, more finger-prints of Sing, who evidently turned them on in first place."

"So Dudley Ward never went near them lights," nodded Holt.

"Such is the inference we must naturally draw," Chan agreed. "I am handing precious cargo over to you. Also, in this other envelope, bullet from Landini's gun, which I have recently dug from pine tree."

Ryder pushed forward, his expression unpleasant and contemptuous as usual. "And you expect to convict my friend on evidence like that?" he cried.

"It will all help," shrugged Chan. "We will in addition trace the owner of a revolver which now reposes in Berkeley."

"That may not be so easy," sneered Ryder.

"Perhaps not." Charlie turned and looked At Ward. "If difficulties arise, we can still bring back to this scene the accessory to the crime, Ah Sing. Of course, in such case, he also would suffer punishment—"

Ward leapt to his feet.

"Oh, stop it," he cried passionately. "What's the use? Let Sing alone. Let him go. I killed Landini, and I killed Swan, too."

"But look here, Dudley—" Ryder protested.

"What's the use, I say?" Ward went on. "Forget it, John. I've nothing to live for—nothing to fight for. Let's get on with it. Let's get it finished. That's all I want now." He sank back into his chair.

"I am so sorry, Mr. Ward," Chan said gently, "that visit to your home must finish in such manner. Let us, as you say, get on with it. I will detail a few happenings in this house night before last, and perhaps if I am wrong, you will correct me. You and I went with Madame Landini to the study. You accused her of hiding from you knowledge of your son. She denied it, but you were not satisfied. The airplane appeared, you left presumably to turn on the lights of landing field. When you left, Landini was wildly seeking to communicate with John Ryder.

"You could not turn on lights until you located Sing, who had keys of everything about this house. You found him on rear porch, on his way to manage lights himself. You sent him along, telling him that later he must bring blanket to study for Landini's dog.

"With more questions for Landini, you returned to study. She, meanwhile, has written letter to Ryder, who has refused to see her. When you enter, she is on balcony waving to aviator. 'Oh, it is you, is it?' she says. 'I'm freezing—get me my scarf. It's on the bed in the next room. The green one.' The great Landini, giving orders as of old. You go into next room, return with pink scarf. She snatched it from you. Did she chide you then? Did she say, I had forgot you were color-blind? No—the questions are only rhetorical. They do not matter. She decides Miss Beaton's scarf will do. And then—your eye lights on the desk—on the letter she has written and addressed to John Ryder."

Charlie paused. "I wonder what was in that letter?" he said slowly.

"You seem to know everything," Ward answered. "What do you think was in it?"

"I believe that news of your son's death was in it," Chan replied.

Ward did not speak for a moment. He sighed wearily. "You *do* know everything," he said at last.

"You were curious about that letter," Charlie continued. "Always a little jealous of Ryder, perhaps. You asked Landini what it meant. Your unhappy temper grew hot. You snatched up the envelope, ripped it open, and read. Landini was asking Ryder, your best friend in the house, to break to you gently the news that your boy had died.

"Died—and you'd never seen him. Your temper was terrible then. Murder was in your heart. From the drawer of your desk you removed a revolver—an automatic—and turned on the woman. She screamed, struggled with you above the desk, the boxes of cigarettes were upset. The aviator was once more just overhead, the din was terrific. You cast Landini from you, she fell, you fired at her from above. And the roar of the plane died away in the distance. Just as the roar of your frightful anger was dying away in your brain.

"You were dazed, weak, unsteady. A neat man, always, you unconsciously sought to straighten things on the disordered desk. It came to you that perhaps it might help to pretend Landini had been shot from the balcony. You dragged her to the window—and from her hand-bag, opened in the struggle, her own revolver fell. You examined it—the same caliber as yours. At that moment, Sing entered the room, beneath his arm, a small blue blanket.

"What happened then? Whatever it was, it happened quickly. Whose idea was it—the alibi of the shot to be fired by Sing? Yours or his—that does not matter. He was your loyal servant. You knew that he would protect you as he had protected you from your childhood. He was your keeper of the keys."

"That says it," old Sam Holt cried. "Keeper of the keys. For sixty years Ah Sing had been slammin' the doors on the Ward family skeletons, an' turnin' the keys on them. I know all about it—don't I, Dudley? An' he'd a' done it this time—only Inspector Chan had his foot in the door."

"I'm afraid he did," Ward admitted.

"So you left it all to Sing," Charlie went on, "and hurried down to the landing field to greet a new guest. Ah, your manners, Mr. Ward—they were always so perfect. But a golden bed can not cure the sick, and good manners can not produce a good man. You made the aviator welcome, and we came inside. While up above, Sing kept the faith. As my friend, Inspector Duff of Scotland Yard, would say—he carried on."

Charlie rose. "We need no longer shade the scene with dark pictures of the past. I do not dwell on murder of Swan. It is not for his death that you will be tried."

"I'm sorry I won't," Ward answered grimly. "Because I rather imagine I did the world a service there. A dirty blackmailer—he was at the door of the study when I—when Landini died. When I went to him later on to take him things for the night, he threatened me, demanded money. I told him I would get him some the next day in Reno, and I did. Last night I telephoned to him he could get it if he'd meet Sing at the house down the road. Then I got to thinking—he would suck at me, like a leech, for ever. So I didn't send Sing—I went myself. And when Swan came, eager for his first drop of blood—I finished him. Yes—I'm rather proud of what I did to Swan."

"And I am very grateful," Chan said. "We needed that revolver of yours, Mr. Ward—as cherry trees need the sun. I wondered at first why you did not toss weapon into lake, but remembering the famous clarity of Tahoe waters near the shore, I applauded your wisdom. You planned to come back later with boat, and carry both Doctor Swan and the pistol far out—but ah, the best-laid plans—how often they explode into disaster." Charlie nodded at Don Holt. "Sheriff—I am turning this man over to you. With only one question in my mind—who, on the night of Landini's murder, struck the loyal and faithful Sing that cruel blow in the face?"

Ward confronted the detective, and a red dangerous light was gleaming in his bloodshot eyes. "What's that got to do with it?" he cried. "My God—don't you know enough now? Are you never satisfied? What's that got to do with it?"

"Nothing, Dudley," old Sam Holt put in soothingly. "Not a thing in the world. Mr. Chan, I reckon we won't insist on knowin' the answer to that."

"Of course not," answered Charlie promptly. "My connection with the case is now completely finished. I go to procure my things."

Ten minutes later the two Holts, Chan and the now silent Ward, stepped into the sheriff's launch. Ryder had been left in charge at Pineview, and Don Holt had also persuaded Ireland to remain overnight. The little boat cut its way through the silvery water; on distant peaks gleamed the snow that was still a nine days' wonder in the eyes of the detective from Hawaii.

They walked up the Tavern pier toward the hotel. "I asked the coroner to be ready," Don Holt remarked to Chan. "We're driving down to the county-seat right off, an' takin' Ward with us. By the way, I'd like to stop at the Tavern for just a minute. I wish you and Dad would take Ward around to the drive. That is—if you think I can trust you."

"We have enjoyed brief lapse," Charlie replied, "However, I believe we are now quite safe custodians."

"Yes—I reckon you are. An' that lapse—I'm grateful for it. Sixty years of loyalty an' love—say, jail would have been a fine reward for that."

As young Holt entered the Tavern lounge, the two newspaper men from San Francisco leaped upon him. It appeared that the coroner had been a trifle indiscreet, and a torrent of questions was the result.

"Nothin' to say," the sheriff replied. "Only this. I just arrested Dudley Ward, an' he's confessed. Nothin' more—only—give all the credit to Charlie Chan."

Rankin turned to his companion. "Did you hear what I heard? A mainland policeman giving the credit to Charlie Chan!"

"They grow 'em different up here in these mountains," Gleason answered. "Come on—the phone's in the office. I'll match you for the first call."

As they disappeared, Holt saw that Leslie Beaton was seated near by.

"Fine," he cried, as she rose and approached him. "You're the very person I wanted to see."

"Dudley Ward," she remarked, her eyes wide. "Why—that's incredible."

"I know—but I can't discuss it now. I'm in an awful rush. I want to say—Cash will probably turn up here early in the morning."

"You mean—he'll be company for me while you're away?"

"Yeah—I'm afraid he will. I wired him to take a little vacation in San Francisco, but he's the sort who will see through that. Yes—he'll pull in here at dawn. And the first thing he'll do—he'll want you to take a ride up to that clearing where we was this afternoon."

"Will he really?"

"Sure. An' I wish—as a sort o' favor to me—I wish you wouldn't go."

"But what shall I tell poor Cash?"

"Well, you might tell him you been there already."

"Oh! But Cash isn't the sort to be put off with an excuse like that."

"No, I guess he ain't." The sheriff turned his hat about in his hands, staring at it as though it were something that caused him much embarrassment. "Well, then—you might—just as a favor, too—tell him you're going to—to marry me."

"But would that be the truth?"

"Well—I know you ain't seen the county-seat yet—"

"I haven't—no. But I've seen the sheriff."

He looked at her, his fine eyes glowing. "By golly. Do you mean that?"

"I guess—that is, I reckon I do."

"You'll marry me?" She nodded. "Say," cried Don Holt, "that's great. I'll have to run now. But I'll be seein' you."

He started off. "Just a minute," said the girl. "Let me get this straight. Is it you I'm going to marry—or Cash?"

He came back, smiling. "Yeah—I don't wonder you're sort o' mixed." He took her in his arms and kissed her. "I reckon that might help you to remember," he added, and disappeared.

Charlie and Sam Holt were waiting beside the car, in which the coroner was already at the wheel. A dim figure huddled in the rear seat. "Mr. Sheriff," Chan said. "Your prisoner informs me he will plead guilty." He took out his pocketbook and removed a narrow slip of paper. "So I imagine you will not require this check for evidence at the trial."

"What is it?" Holt inquired.

Chan explained.

"No, we won't need it," said Holt, handing it back. "You jes' keep it—an' use it."

But already Charlie was tearing it slowly across and across. He tossed the pieces into the air. Dudley Ward leaned suddenly forward from his place in the rear of the car.

"You shouldn't have done that," he protested.

"So sorry," Chan bowed. "But I could not enjoy spending the money of one whose association with me ended in disaster for him."

Ward slumped back in the car. "And I always thought," he murmured, "that Don Quixote was a Spaniard."

The sheriff had seized Chan's hand. "You're a grand guy, Charlie," he said. "Will you be here when I come back to-morrow?"

"If you come early—yes."

"Don't go till I see you. By that time, maybe I'll be able to think up some words that'll tell you what your help has meant to me."

"Not worth mentioning," Chan replied. "In this world, all sorts of men could help one another—if they would. The boat can ride on the wagon, and the wagon on the boat. Good night—and my best wishes for—for ever."

Charlie and the old sheriff watched the car start, then walked around the Tavern and out upon the pier. Near the end of this stood a sheltered group of benches, and on one of these they sat down together.

"Kinda hard case," remarked old Holt.

"In many ways," Chan agreed. He contemplated the snow-capped mountains, gorgeous in the moonlight. "From the moment I made up my mind that shot we heard was but empty gesture, I was appalled at possibilities. Did Hugh Beaton climb to balcony and kill Landini, and did his sister fire shot to protect him, as she had protected him all her life? I wondered. Or did Michael Ireland shoot Landini from plane, and did Cecile fire again to save her husband? It was intriguing thought, and for a time I played with it. But no—I told myself sadly that jealous wives are not so obliging. Then I recalled the serving of the cordials that first night at dinner—and at last my eyes turned toward the guilty one."

"He never was no good, Dudley wasn't," mused Sam Holt. "I knowed it from the days he was a kid. Terrible temper, an' a born drunkard. Yes—even the giant redwoods—they got rotten branches. The family of Ward had theirs, an' Dudley was the last—an' rottenest. If his name had come up sooner—I could ha' told ye. That time long ago Landini run away from him—he was tryin' to beat her. Sing stepped in—good ol' Sing—locked him in his room—helped Landini git away. I tell you, Mr. Chan, when Landini hid the news of that baby from Dudley Ward, she knew what she was doin'. She knew he wasn't fit to care fer it."

"Poor Landini," Charlie remarked. "What unlucky fate she had when matter of husbands comes up. Romano—grasping as he was—I imagine he was the best—and the kindest."

"I reckon he was," nodded Holt.

"I presume it was Ward who struck Sing that night of the murder?"

"Sure it was. I didn't think we needed to humiliate him no more—but sure, he struck Sing. An' why? Because Sing had the keys to the sideboard, an' Ward wanted booze. He wanted to git drunk an' fergit what he done, but Sing had sense enough to know how dangerous that would be. So he refused to give up them keys, an' Ward knocked him down. I used to see him in them tempers as a boy. He's no good, Mr. Chan. We don't need to waste no sympathy on Dudley Ward."

"Yet Sing would have died for him. Would never have left him, if he hadn't seen Ward's pistol on my desk this morning, and thought his master was in danger. When, as he thought, we blundered and selected him as the murderer, he was delighted to go away. I believe he would have gone to the gallows just as cheerfully."

"Of course he would. But Sing never saw Dudley Ward growed up. He saw him allus as a little boy, beggin' fer rice an' gravy in the kitchen."

They rose and walked back along the pier, the waters lapping peacefully beside them.

"After a typhoon there are pears to gather," Charlie mused. "From this place I take away golden memories of two men. One was loyal and true beyond all understanding. Of my own race—I shall recall him with unseemly pride. The other—yourself, Mr. Holt."

"Me? Oh, hell, Mr. Chan, I ain't nobody. Never was. Jes' been goin' along fer seventy-eight years, doin' the best I kin."

"The greatest of Chinese emperors, being asked to suggest his own epitaph, replied in much the same vein," smiled Charlie.

In the Tavern lounge, he bade the old man good night. As he turned, he saw Leslie Beaton approaching.

"Ah," Chan remarked, "I perceive my necktie now has serious competition. I refer to your cheeks, Miss Beaton."

"Excitement," she explained. "You see, I'm engaged. At least—I think I am."

"I know you are," Charlie told her. "I also knew you were going to be, from the moment I saw the young sheriff's eye light upon you."

"You really are a great detective, aren't you?" she replied.

Chan bowed. "Three things the wise man does not do. He does not plow the sky. He does not paint pictures on the water. And he does not argue with a woman."